SABRE SECURITY

THE COMPLETE TRILOGY

J ROSE

WILTED ROSE PUBLISHING LTD

Published by Wilted Rose Publishing Ltd
Edited by Nice Girl Naughty Edits
Proofreading by Kim BookJunkie
Cover Design by Books & Moods

ISBN (eBook): 978-1-915987-16-7
ISBN (Paperback): 978-1-915987-17-4

www.jroseauthor.com

J ROSE SHARED UNIVERSE

All of J Rose's contemporary dark romance books are set in the same shared universe. From the walls of Blackwood Institute, to Sabre Security's HQ, and the small town of Briar Valley, all of the characters inhabit the same world and feature in Easter egg cameos in each other's books.

You can read these books in any order, dipping in and out of different series and stories, but here is the recommended order for the full effect of the shared universe and the ties between the books.

For more information: www.jroseauthor.com/readingorder

CORPSE ROADS

SABRE SECURITY #1

TRIGGER WARNING

Corpse Roads is a contemporary reverse harem romance, so the main character will have multiple love interests that she will not have to choose between.

This book is very dark and contains scenes that may be triggering for some readers. This includes physical and psychological abuse, torture, sexual assault and abuse, imprisonment, graphic violence, serial murder, PTSD and Trichotillomania.

If you are triggered by any of this content, please do not read this book.

This is a slow burn romance, so the relationships will develop over time, and the spice level will build up with each book.

"Beware that, when fighting monsters, you yourself do not become a monster… For when you gaze long into the abyss, the abyss gazes also into you."

- Friedrich Nietzsche

PROLOGUE

WHITE NOISE - BADFLOWER

HARLOW

IF WE CONFESS OUR SINS, *he is faithful and just to forgive us, and to cleanse us from all unrighteousness.*

Whispering the words in my hoarse voice, I link my shaking hands and squeeze my eyes shut. In these dark, desperate moments, I often feel like God is watching my suffering—laughing and thoroughly amused.

My prayers have never been answered.

No one is coming to save me.

Tipping my head upwards, I stick my tongue out and catch the falling water droplets leaking from the basement ceiling. It's rare that I'm brought food or water.

Good behaviour is rewarded in this paradise of darkness, but even after years of learned obedience, hunger is my constant companion. The devil whispers to me sometimes, telling me to fight back.

It never lasts. They beat the defiance from my bones with violent malice, breaking skin and bruising organs. I've been shattered a thousand times, then glued back together in a haphazard jigsaw puzzle just as many.

If I scream when told to and kneel as Pastor Michaels unlocks my cage, I'm awarded brief slivers of life. Enough to keep me alive. I fantasise about being bad most nights, certain it's the only way to escape this life of misery.

"P-Please... I w-want to go home," her broken voice whimpers.

"Shhhh," I hush.

Peering through the half-light, I find the curled-up ball of despair in the cramped cage adjacent to mine. Laura was so bright and full of life when she was dragged down here, unconscious and bleeding.

She's told me stories about her family and friends, tales of a world that I've never seen. Her dreams and hopes, regrets and wishes. She promised that we'd see it together one day. It was a pinkie promise agreed upon between our cages, borne of desperation and grief.

There's a heavy clank that sends dread spiking through my veins. Light floods into the dank basement, illuminating the steep, rotting staircase and a shining pair of boots. It's time for nightly prayers.

"No... p-please... let me go!" Laura shouts, backing into a tight corner for protection. "I want to go home!"

"Be quiet." I kneel before the cage door.

"I won't just lay there and play dead!"

"Stop talking, Laura! You'll get us both in trouble."

Lowering my head, I fix my gaze on my filthy hands. The right index finger is swollen and hot to the touch with a steady throb from my missing nail. Blood is still crusted around the infected digit.

Pastor Michaels ripped it out a few days ago when I dared to ask for a drink of water. On the rare occasions that I grow weak enough to beg for sustenance, my courage is swiftly punished.

In the dead of winter, my left arm still hurts. I asked to be freed once, too young and stupid to know better. The bone was shattered in two places with a steel-capped boot.

"Evenin', folks. Ain't this a fine day, eh?"

Pastor Michaels' greeting feels like razor blades slicing me into blood-slick ribbons. My entire body trembles, and my heart explodes in my chest. I bite my lip, trying to breathe through it.

It's worse if I pass out.

Far, far worse.

He draws to a halt outside my rusted cage, rapping on the bars until I lift my chin. Meeting Pastor Michaels' clear, green gaze, I swallow the vomit burning my throat.

"Done your nighttime prayers, sinner?"

I nod once.

"If I can't hear you, then the Lord Almighty certainly can't."

"Yes, s-sir," I murmur, barely above a whisper.

"Good little girl. Again."

Turning his broad back to me, I watch him approach Laura's cage next. My eyes fall shut as he unlocks the door with an ornate skeleton key. The words come to me without thinking.

"Lord have mercy on me, a sinner."

"Louder," he barks.

"Please Lord, have mercy. Free me from my sins and grant me your almighty forgiveness."

Laura's cries soon turn into agonised screams. The sound reverberates around me, deafening my empty prayers. Some of the girls before her screamed when Pastor Michaels knelt between their legs, unclipping his belt buckle. Others didn't.

I think I hear Laura trying to scramble away, followed by the crunch of her body being thrown into the metal bars. Peeking one eye open, I watch her crumple to the concrete, boneless and barely conscious.

"What happens to sinners, Harlow?" Pastor Michaels shouts.

"They burn in eternal damnation."

"You hear that, Laura? It's your fault that you're here. Selling your body is an unforgivable sin. *Unforgivable*."

Pastor Michaels likes to punish prostitutes the most. At least, I think that's what they're called. Mrs Michaels calls them that, or *sluts*. I don't know what that word means, but it sounds bad.

Her voice gets all low and hissy when she talks about some of the girls brought down here for their final judgement. She says they bring the devil out in Pastor Michaels.

The devil isn't inside of him though.

He *really is* the devil.

Grabbing Laura by the throat, he smashes his lips against her mouth, trapped open in a scream. My stomach threatens to revolt. I can't afford to throw up the meagre crust of bread I was rewarded with for being a good girl.

Laura jerks and wails as Pastor Michaels' hands roam over her naked body. When he pushes a thick finger inside of her, she screeches like she's being dipped in acid.

"I am a messenger of God, you filthy whore. You will submit to my will or burn for an eternity in hell."

"Get your fucking hands off me!"

Striking Laura across the face, Pastor Michaels' gold ring leaves a deep, oozing cut. He pins her against the bars, raising the heavy silver cross from his chest. The chanting begins.

I cower in the corner of my cage, my arms covering my head. It does nothing to eliminate the sound of sobbing and Pastor Michaels' pleasured grunts. He doesn't even remove his ceremonial robes to do it, though he always takes care to pull a little foil packet from his pocket.

This part always makes the girls beg for death. When he has growled out his release, the final steps of the ritual proceed. I keep my eyes tightly shut until it's all over. Pastor Michaels whispers a final, fervent prayer before leaving the basement.

Laura's blood seeps into my cage from the deep, vicious carvings in her skin. The Holy Trinity. Beautiful symbols that are desecrated as they're engraved with serrated steel.

Most girls die quickly. The ritual cleanses them of their sins, but they aren't forgiven. Not by this cruel God. They're freed into the punishing arms of the devil to escort them down to hell.

Pastor Michaels usually slashes the girls' throats or chokes them to death when he's had his fill, but not Laura. She's been trouble since the beginning, according to Mrs Michaels.

He leaves Laura barely clinging to life. It's a brutal game, and the final punishment for her relentless defiance is a slow, agonising death, with no choice but to bleed out until her last breath.

"H-Harlow…"

"No," I sob, clamping my hands over my ears.

Laura whispers into the dark, begging for relief. She tells me that it's going to be okay, and I'm strong enough to find my own way out of here without her. I don't believe a word of it. I'm nothing.

"Please… don't make me… d-die like this."

"You're the one that's leaving me. Like everyone else."

"Not… this… help me," she gurgles.

"I won't do it. No."

"P-Please… friend. My s-s-sister."

Peering through the gloom, I stare at her broken form. She's splayed out on the floor of her cage, unable to move as the slashes carved into her body slowly kill her.

Once bright, platinum-blonde hair is now a deep shade of crimson. I can't see her eyes, usually full of mischief. I'm glad.

"Help… me…"

"Don't make me do this," I plead.

"H-Harlow… it hurts… p-please…"

Covering my face with my hands, I feel my heart splinter into jagged shards of despair. It never gets easier, watching my friends die. No matter how hard I try to shut myself off from it.

"I d-don't want you to go… I'll be alone again."

Laura lets out a wet cough. "Never… a-alone. I'm h-here."

I won't tell you what happens next. God is listening to us, even now. If he hears, I'll be in even more trouble. In the silent aftermath, I curl back into a ball.

She's at peace now.

My torment, however, is just beginning.

Laura's fresh blood has flooded my cage, coating me in her warmth. I have no choice but to sleep in what's left of my friend. Her spirit has departed this world at my hand.

"Goodbye," I whisper to the dead silence.

Laura doesn't respond.

Now, I'm alone until the next girl arrives.

The cycle begins again.

This is my life. It has been for as long as I can remember. My parents—angry, terrifying Pastor Michaels and cruel, cold Mrs Michaels—tell me this is all I deserve.

This existence.

This pain.

This suffering.

I've learned to close off all thoughts of a world beyond these bars. The stories I'm told are just that—flights of fantasy, a taunting glimpse of a world I'll never be allowed to see.

Lord, please forgive me.
All I wanted was to give her some peace.
Forgive me for what I've done.
Of course, there is no reply.

CHAPTER 1
HARLOW

HOLDING OUT FOR A HERO - NOTHING BUT THIEVES

"NO FUNNY BUSINESS," Mrs Michaels instructs.

Fighting off the shiver wracking my thin frame, I bite back a sob. She throws a scrap of bread across the stained concrete floor. Her lip is curled in a sneer beneath tangled grey hair and pronounced wrinkles.

I'm too weak and feverish to accept the gift, unable to even lift a finger. I should be kneeling in the prayer position, my hands clasped and head lowered.

"Take it or you won't eat for another week."

"I c-can't," I whisper, too dehydrated to cry.

"I said *take it,* devil child!"

Her foot connects with my ribs—once, twice, three times. I bite down hard on my tongue until blood floods my mouth. It silences my screams as the bones in my ribcage shatter spectacularly.

Mrs Michaels grabs me by the hair and drags my limp body across the cage. I can't stop her. This latest bout of sickness has stolen any remaining strength I possessed. I've barely moved for days.

"Do you know why God has made you sick?"

For what I did to Laura.

"Answer the question, whore!"

I'm smashed into the bars face first. Agony melts my flesh like unholy flames, igniting every shredded nerve within me. Hellfire is raining down on my unworthy soul.

"Because you're a filthy little bitch. You think I don't see the way you look at your father? He's saving your corrupted soul, yet all you can think about is spreading your fucking legs."

If he heard her use that word, he'd take the belt to her. I've seen it happen. Only once. Pastor Michaels whipped his wife until the milky flesh of her behind was dripping red. She could barely walk for days.

"Say thank you for the food," Mrs Michaels demands.

Swallowing hot, coppery blood, I let out a gargle. She drops me back down onto the floor with a final curse, then exits my cage. Lying on my back, I dip in and out of consciousness for what seems like forever.

The throaty growl of a car engine startles me awake sometime later. Terror and relief wash over me. My parents have left to find their next sinner, ready for punishment. Another girl.

They're gone again.

If I die down here in their absence, no one would notice.

Feeling around blindly, my fingertips scrape against the hunk of stale bread. For the first few days of this latest torment, I was starving. Enough to dominate my every thought.

But now... the thought of eating repulses me. The fever hit yesterday and there's nothing left in me to fight it off. I'm so tired of the constant cycle. Death is beckoning me.

"This is my punishment for what I did," I state, addressing the adjoining cage.

The pile of bones doesn't answer me, swimming in unidentifiable bodily matter and scraps of clothing. I don't know how long ago Laura was—her death, that is.

I've blocked it out of my memory, like so many other things. I still talk to her. She's alive somewhere in this room, a spirit lingering in the place between here and the afterlife, like layered sheets of wallpaper.

Her ghost is my only source of comfort. As her skin turned black and peeled away from her bones, revealing organs that soon liquified, Pastor Michaels grew apocalyptically angry.

His last voyage out to stalk his prey was unsuccessful, and he cursed Laura's remains for tempting him, just like the others. I still remember her wails of pain as he hurt her repeatedly in the weeks before her death.

He *touched* her. That always made Mrs Michaels mad. She would beat me afterwards to vent her hatred while Pastor Michaels' victims watched and bled from between their legs, helpless.

After forcing the bread down, I lie back and try to sleep. It doesn't come. Despite everything, I'm terrified of being alone here. What if they don't come back?

The unknown scares me so badly. My world spans the size of this basement, and my entire existence is dependent on the Michaels. I'll starve to death if they don't come back. Maybe that would be a good thing.

"Please... let me die," I sob.

You're so weak, Harlow.

Giving up so easily?

Ignoring my scathing inner voice, I scrub my aching eyes that refuse to cry any more tears. I haven't had a drink of water in far too long, my lips are cracked and dried out.

I want to scream and shatter into pieces that are sharp enough to rip a hole in the fabric of this world and escape into heaven's light. Surely, I've atoned enough. The price has been paid in my blood, time and time again.

They'll be gone for the rest of the night.

Why aren't you running?

"I can't run. The cage is locked," I scream uselessly.

Pull yourself together.

You are the darkness now.

Don't be afraid of it.

Time ticks by as my sanity spirals. The fever and dehydration are doing something to me. I'm hearing things that aren't here, taunting whispers and invisible voices.

I think about Laura. Abbie before her. Tia. Freya. Adelaide. Lucy. Countless others who, despite my best efforts, I can't remember anymore. Their faces are blank in my mind.

There have been so many lives lost in this dark place. I was so glad when the girls started to arrive after spending so long in the basement alone, my solitude only broken by daily beatings.

Then the violence began. The killings. Rituals. Prayers and slashed throats. Bloated corpses and blackened skin. Relief turned to horror, then numbness took over. It became a new normal to watch torture on a daily basis.

You're alive. They aren't.

Don't be ungrateful.

You still have a chance.

"Leave me alone. I can't do this anymore."

Get the hell up, Harlow.

Wrapping my shaking hands around the bars, I grit my teeth through the pain and drag myself up. The stubborn little voice inside of me refuses to give up, even as my body fails me.

Searching the basement, nothing has changed. It's still dank and empty, freezing cold and dark as night. The rusty, age-spotted cage door is still locked. There's nothing.

Laura didn't die for nothing.

Her blood is on your hands.

Make it count.

Acid rises from my empty stomach, but nothing comes out. I dry heave while clutching my aching midsection. When I'm done, I limp across the cage to reach between the bars, straining until I find the next cage.

You want to get out of here?

God isn't going to do it for you.

A fire burns beneath my skin. It's not the fever, but something else. A delicate, damaged butterfly of hope that has finally had enough. My fingers search through cold goo, wrapping around something hard.

It's a bone.

Laura's… arm.

I drag the prize back to my cage, silently crying as chunks of matted hair and rotting flesh smear across my palm.

"What now?"

This cage is rusted to hell.

Jam it in the door.

Use your strength.

"What strength? This is so stupid. He's going to kill me."

Jesus, Harlow.

You're arguing with yourself here.

Shaking my fuzzy head, I search the door's mechanism with my fingers and find the hinges. They're strong but old, corroded by the damp air.

Working with nothing but intuition, I jam Laura's brittle bone between the slices of metal, working it back and forth. I'm praying. Begging. Pleading for salvation.

The bone snaps.

Shards fall through my fingertips.

I scream in frustration, smashing my fists against the bars hard enough to jolt my broken ribs. Pain ripples through me so intensely, it blurs my vision. I fight to remain upright.

When the wave of agony dissipates enough for me to take a breath, I reach out for another bone. My fingers connect with something hard and textured in the dark.

I think it's her leg bone this time. Long and curved, it's crusted with dried blood. Returning to the cage door, the bone snaps again, too weak to withstand the lock.

Do you want to die here?

"No!" I shout back.

Then keep working.

Dripping with ice-cold sweat, I begin to lose energy. This will never work. I'm destined to die here, among the ghostly screams of the girls I failed to protect.

In many ways, I see the darkness into which I was born as a comforting absence of light. In these shadows, I learned to swallow my screams and play the obedient good girl.

A few desperate tears manage to escape my eyes, despite my dehydration. I lick the salty liquid away as it stings my sore lips. It isn't enough. If I don't get out, I'm going to die.

One more try. If this doesn't work, I'll accept my death. With a frantic scramble, I manage to seize Laura's other leg. Slotting the joint into place, I go slower this time, coaxing the groaning metal.

This cage has never changed. The hinges are old, weakened by rust. A loud, metallic groan fills my ears. Then, *snap*. There's a frightening thunderclap of noise.

The door... *cracks open.*

It worked.

I'm paralysed, staring at the open doorway like a deer in headlights. I can't step through it. I haven't set foot outside this cage before, and even the rest of the shadowy basement feels terrifying.

Clutching my shirt tight to my emaciated body, I cuddle Laura's damaged leg bone even closer. She will never walk free, just like the others didn't. But… I could take her with me. If I can find the strength to do it.

"Move, Harlow," I order shakily. "Just move."

Each footstep outside the cage echoes like a gunshot going off. The floor is wet and slippery, laced with putrefied scents. Laura's body has long since melted into festering lumps of matter.

I'm glad I can no longer smell my own stench. Blood and dirt are crusted to me like a disgusting second skin. Crossing the basement, all I can hear is my pounding heartbeat.

The boards of the narrow staircase creak beneath my meagre weight as I dare to take a step upwards. I freeze, too scared to even blink. Pastor Michaels will break every last bone in my body.

But they aren't here.

Move, Harlow!

Reaching the top of the ancient staircase, I find the basement door unlocked. Why would Pastor Michaels lock it when his little pet is safely secured in her cage? He clearly never thought I'd try to run.

Feeling my way through the darkness, I emerge into a tight cupboard. Another door leads me into a wider space, the scent of mothballs and mildew heavy in the air.

It has a high ceiling, arched and adorned with empty candle holders. Dirty stone floors are occupied by an audience of destroyed chairs. This place looks like… a chapel. I'm not sure how I know that.

There are no personal effects or ties to the monsters that inhabit this place. It's abandoned, the perfect killing field for their crimes. Silence wraps around me, deep and unnerving.

I am utterly, terrifyingly alone.

This is a mausoleum of my childhood.

Dragging my hand along the wall for guidance, I reach a wooden door. There are more empty rooms on the left, with the remains of a broken bed crumbling into ruin.

Past and present are superimposed over each other as I look around. Damp stone walls are replaced by peeling, rotten wallpaper, and empty candle holders rest within bronze chandeliers.

I know this place.

I've seen it before.

The cage is all I've ever known but that certainty is stripped away as I feel my scalp burning with the memory of being dragged through these rooms by my hair.

I shake the dark thoughts aside.

There isn't time for this.

Facing the door, it's littered with various locks and bolts. There's no way I will get out of here. No matter how many times I slam myself into the slab of wood, screaming as my broken ribs twist and splinter, it doesn't budge.

Sliding down the wall, I hug my knees to my chest, ready to succumb to death. It won't take long. If I'm still alive when my parents return, they'll reopen the healed scars on my body and let me bleed.

No, Harlow!

This isn't what Laura wanted.

"Laura isn't here!"

Yes, she is.

I look down at the bone in my arms. She's still with me, her essence distilled into blood-stained calcium. Laura died believing that I'd get out one day. I can't let her down.

Frantic, I search the chapel again. The stained-glass windows are high, and I'd certainly hurt myself trying to get through. If it buys my freedom, though, I'll walk through fire and offer my soul for the devil's fury.

I will do anything to feel the wind in my hair and finally see what the sun looks like. I've always wanted to know. Laura and the other girls told me such beautiful stories. I cried as they described the daylight.

Do something about it.

Let's get out of here.

Heaving the last unbroken chair nearly kills me. I have no strength. Throwing it with a furious scream, the flimsy structure hits a wall beneath the window and smashes into useless pieces.

Yanking handfuls of my brown, ragged hair, I scream again. I'm not strong enough to throw another. Grabbing an old candle holder instead, I tuck Laura's bone under my arm for safe keeping.

The altar is the last piece of furniture to remain standing. It barely registers my weight as I climb up, agonised tears soaking my cheeks. I can just reach the nearby arched window.

Smash it.

What have you got to lose?

"Everything," I reply to myself.

Or nothing.

Hit it, Harlow.

Crashing the candle holder into the window with everything I have left, satisfying cracks spread like cobwebs in the glass. Over and over, I scream and smash, letting the glass slice my exposed skin.

The pain doesn't stop me.

Fresh air does, though.

The freezing blast hits me straight in the face. I almost stumble backwards from the weight of it... pure, fresh air. So clean, it physically burns my lungs.

Dark, oppressive woodland stretches out in all directions I can see. The church is buried in trees, thick vines of ivy and dense shrubbery. Moonlight barely pierces the smothering sarcophagus.

Only someone who knows exactly where this is could find it. We're in the middle of no man's land. I could be the last human alive out here; reality is so removed.

Run, Harlow.

Run and don't look back.

"I… c-can't," I stutter.

This is your only chance.

"What if they catch me?"

What if you stay?

They will punish you for this.

Biting my lip, I excavate the truth. "I'm scared."

That's why you have to run.

You've survived much worse.

I tighten my grip on Laura and manoeuvre myself into the window frame. More shards of glass rip into my skin, but the splash of warm blood doesn't slow me down.

Taking a final deep breath, I launch myself into the dark. I'm airless for a brief, beautiful moment before my body smacks into the ground so hard, something inside me snaps. I scream myself hoarse.

Just a broken bone.

Run, Harlow.

I ignore the worsening pain that's flooding every inch of me, using Laura's leg to push myself up. My bare feet sink into the grass. It's wet, earthy, and feels like absolute heaven.

This is it.

With no time to waste, I begin limping away from the church. I'm so unsteady, I have to use the bone for balance. Sheer adrenaline pushes me forward.

I'm numb in the face of what lies ahead. Into the dark. Into the unknown. Into... the future. A world that scares me to death, but it can't be any worse than the life I'm leaving behind.

CHAPTER 2
HUNTER

NATURAL BORN KILLER - HIGHLY SUSPECT

CRUNCHING the disposable coffee cup in my hand, I toss it into the bin and settle back in the leather chair. A steady thump behind my eyes threatens to distract me from filing this stupid incident report.

"That bad, huh?" Enzo chuckles.

"You could always file your own damn report."

"You're the bossman, not my area."

I stack the papers and crack my neck. "I seem to remember all of us raiding that warehouse, dickhead. Would it kill you guys to do some paperwork?"

"If we had some new leads, we could be doing more important things than filing paperwork."

I spread my hands, indicating to the walls of my office that are plastered with crime scene photographs, maps and reports.

"You know something I don't? We've been at a dead end for weeks. Until another victim turns up, we're screwed."

"Since when do we wait for the bodies to pile up?" Enzo frowns.

"Since we've been three steps behind Britain's most notorious serial killer for the last six months, and there is still no end in sight."

Abandoning my seat, I pace beside the lengthy conference table to expel some of my frustration. Enzo is my best friend and second in command, but he sure as hell knows how to get under my skin, even after a decade of working together.

"We have other clients to get on with."

"None more pressing than this," he points out, his boots propped up on the table. "The SCU is clueless, Hunter. They can't solve this without us."

"They can't solve this with us, dammit."

Joining me, Enzo lays a heavy hand on my shoulder. "We have a better shot at it together. Plus, the retainer fee is too good to give up. Let's go back to the evidence. Take another look."

I turn back to the master board we have set up on the back wall of my office, spiralling into organised chaos. Each victim in the last five years has their own place on the board with all of their information and autopsy reports spread out. Tiny red cord connects anything relevant.

"Eighteen girls in five years." Enzo runs a hand over the dark scruff on his chin.

At well over six foot six and two hundred pounds of pure muscle, he's the enforcer to my stratagem and planning. Enzo is a scary motherfucker to all but those who know him best—my team.

We're proudly known as the finest investigators and most prestigious private security firm in England. Sabre Security is a multi-million-pound success story, borne of determination and hard work.

After a tumultuous twelve years in the business and several high-profile cases in recent years, we've reached new heights. Everything changed after we took down Blackwood Institute and its parent company, Incendia Corporation.

Expanding into new premises was necessary as our team doubled in size with the influx of attention and new funding. While we run the main divisions, our trusted subordinates are working to build new areas of the firm.

"Too many lives," I agree, an unbearable weight on my shoulders.

We were drafted in last year by the Serious Crimes Unit. Despite undergoing a full reconstruction and new in-house regulations to protect against corruption, they're seriously slacking with this case.

Even after our work whipping them into shape, the fumbling fools took one look and swiftly surrendered all responsibility. That's where we stepped in.

The SCU prefers to sign extortionate cheques rather than continue wrestling with this impossible case. We take on government contracts regularly, but this has proven to be beyond anything we imagined.

The victims are all the same—young girls from working-class backgrounds, many of them living in poverty and forced into sex work as a result. All brutally murdered, raped and carved with religious iconography.

"You hear from Theo about those traffic reports?" Enzo muses.

"He's still working on it. The last girl went missing nearly two months ago and there's no body yet. Perhaps she's still alive."

"You really believe that?"

Meeting his intelligent amber eyes, I shake my head. This man knows my thought processes better than I do at times. We've worked together for so long, our minds and bodies are completely in tune.

Building Sabre up to the reputable firm that it is today has taken absolutely everything from us. Even loved ones. We sacrificed it all, but we never lost our love for each other.

"She's dead. But why is there no body?"

He tugs a photograph down from the wall to examine it closer.

"Something's changed. Maybe the killer was spooked? Or they're dragging it out this time. Who knows?"

"She'll turn up eventually. They all do."

My blasé attitude when discussing death should disturb me, but honestly, it's self-preservation at this point. We've handled many messy cases since dismantling Incendia five years ago, though none quite on this scale.

I've seen things that I'll never forget and suffered for it, but I still go to sleep every night knowing we've done our best to make the world a safer place.

"Perhaps we should revisit the last victim. Maybe we missed something," Enzo suggests, replacing the photograph of the missing woman.

"We picked that crime scene apart, along with the SCU. There was nothing to report, clean as a fucking whistle. We're not dealing with an amateur here."

We lapse back into tense silence, studying various reports and brainstorming for new ideas. It isn't until the door to my office slams open that we startle back to the real world. We're both far too accustomed to losing ourselves in death and destruction.

The blur of blonde curls and bright-blue flannel reveals our techie and third team member, Theodore Young. He drops his laptop on the table and straightens his usual graphic t-shirt, this one depicting some complex mathematical symbol that worsens my headache. It's rare that he makes an appearance outside of his computer lab these days.

"It's a miracle." Enzo smirks.

"Are we sure he's real and not a mirage?"

"Throw something at him to check."

Frowning at us both, Theo slides his phone from his pocket and hands it over to me while mouthing the word *Sanderson*. Great, that's the last thing I need. The SCU is breathing down our necks for results they can't find themselves.

"Rodriguez," I greet.

"You're a hard man to track down, Hunter."

"Apologies. We were in a meeting."

Sanderson snorts like the annoying bastard he is. This man is the definition of a middle-aged pencil pusher, happy to dole out the dirty work while he keeps his hands clean.

"I got somethin' for ya."

Pinching the bridge of my nose, I force some patience. "Be more specific."

"Next victim has turned up. Meet me at the hospital, half an hour."

"Same MO? Body dumped and carved up?"

"Nah," Sanderson answers grimly. "She's alive."

The line goes dead. I toss Theo's phone back to him, my mind spinning with possibilities. Relaying the information to the others, they both look equally stunned. I refasten my tie and grab my car keys from the desk, already racing against the clock.

My desperation to get this fucking case behind us overrules any misgivings

I may have about working with a man like Sanderson. We need results. I'm done facing victims' families with zero answers.

Enzo grabs his leather jacket as Theo's eyes bounce around the room, like he expects me to drag him along too. Field work is not his forte.

"Keep working on those camera feeds for the upcoming raid. We'll take care of the SCU."

"Call me if you need backup," he offers.

"We'll be fine. See you at home?"

He mumbles, refusing to agree with me. The bedroom we set up for him when we bought the luxurious townhouse in outer London remains untouched, even five years later.

Though, that wasn't when our problems started. Theo pulled away from our group the day he lost his reason for existing.

Meeting Enzo in the garage, we greet a handful of employees on the way to our blacked-out SUV. Everyone defers to us, their heads lowered with respect.

After dismissing them, we climb in and set the navigation for the hospital. It won't take long to get there from Sabre's HQ.

"We'll catch this sick bastard," Enzo states, mostly to himself.

"I hope you're right. This case is starting to get to me."

Both smoothing professional masks into place, we leave no room for weakness. It's a necessity in our line of work, something we aren't always the best at. Emotion comes with caring about what we do.

Enzo is far worse than me, a complete sucker for a sob story. He's adopted many strays into Sabre's ranks over the years.

Heading out, we prepare to face our first living victim.

Only this time, I hope it will be the last.

Sanderson doles out handshakes before leading us into a private meeting room. It's a small space down the corridor from the intensive care unit in London's biggest hospital.

I glare at his back, cloaked in an ill-fitting shirt that's stained with sweat marks. He loves to lord his authority over us, even though Sabre could reduce the SCU to rubble in a matter of hours.

"Take a seat, gentlemen."

Folding myself into one of the hospital chairs, Enzo lingers behind me. He always plays the watchful bodyguard. Even among government employees, he trusts no one but our team.

People always have hidden agendas in this business. Caution is necessary. We've learned to keep our cards very close to our chests or risk imminent death.

"Cut the shit. What happened?" I ask bluntly.

Sanderson looks between us. "One week ago, a stray kid was reported by a delivery driver. They found her holed up in the back of the truck, half frozen to death. She was admitted to intensive care."

Fiddling with my Armani watch beneath my shirt sleeve, I stifle an eye roll. He's grasping at straws, looking for his moment in the spotlight.

This doesn't fit our MO. We're looking for bodies, not teen runaways. Our killer would never leave one of his victims still breathing.

"This is a waste of time," Enzo grumbles.

"Just listen," Sanderson snaps. "It wasn't brought to my attention until the medics had her stabilised. She was a mess. They called the police first, so it took a while for us to catch wind of this. Trust me, you need to see this shit."

Snapping open a brown, battered briefcase, he pulls out a stack of glossy, full-page photographs. I take the bundle and quickly lose my train of thought as I spot the awaiting horror.

Despite months of working on this case, nothing could prepare me for this. The victim bears identical markings to every single female known to our investigation. Old, vicious scars that disfigure over half of her entire body.

I feel Enzo's breath on my neck as he leans in to inspect the gruesome evidence, growling out a curse. He's right to be alarmed. If the woman survived this, she's a seriously tough son of a bitch. And possibly our first real lead.

"Where is she?" I demand.

"Sedated and under our protection."

His protection means jack shit; we both know that. I'll have a full unit of our agents down here in under half an hour. Reading my mind without a word, Enzo steps outside to make the call.

"How bad is she?"

Sanderson sighs. "You want the short version?"

"I want everything."

"Sepsis nearly killed her. It was left untreated for a long time while she fled. Two broken ribs, shattered radius in her left arm, and severe dehydration. Plus years' worth of badly healed injuries that indicate a long history of abuse."

He gulps, oddly emotional.

"What else?" I prod.

"She's tiny and weak from malnourishment. Dunno how the fuck she made it out alive. Looks early to mid-twenties, I'd say."

I unclench my fists and glance back down at the photographs. The ugly scars cover her torso in harrowing detail. She should have died from these injuries alone. All the other victims did.

The religious symbolism of the Holy Trinity has tied every murder together, if nothing else. All of the women were carved up prior to death. Some were butchered like pieces of meat, the slices cutting down to the bone in places.

"These are old marks."

Sanderson shrugs. "Looks like she's been held captive."

"We weren't aware of any other victims, let alone hostages. Any idea how long she was held for?"

"She's being eased off sedation as we speak. I'll interrogate the victim and get us some answers."

I don't think so, dickhead.

This is a very delicate situation that could alter the course of our entire case. The girl doesn't need this wanker interrogating her.

"Our team is on the way. We'll take her into protective custody and handle questioning from there."

"You don't have the authority to do that," Sanderson blusters. "She's mine, Rodriguez."

"Your authority means fuck all to me. Back off or I'll give your boss a call. You'll be on your way to retirement in no time."

Sanderson's face turns purple with rage. "You wouldn't dare."

"Try me. I've worked closely with the superintendent over the years. She'll be happy to do me a favour."

Cursing me out, Sanderson takes a step back. "What exactly gives you the right to take jurisdiction here?"

"We have to assume the killer will come looking for the girl. Sabre is best equipped to deal with that eventuality. This is our case."

"I hope you know what you're doing, asshole."

"Stay out of my way or I'll bury you. Have a great afternoon."

Stacking the photographs to take with me, I exit into the corridor. Enzo is wrapping up a phone call, and his eyes connect with mine. I can spot the riot of tension and anger a mile off.

It takes a lot to rattle the big guy. He's used to wrapping himself in barbed wire to get through the hard cases, but those goddamn slashes are harrowing on a corpse, let alone a living person.

"The Anaconda team is coming."

"Keep this quiet until we know more. I'll deal with the SCU and get them to sign the girl over to us. We'll need to get forensics in there immediately."

"If she's been here for a week, a lot of the evidence will already be gone," Enzo points out.

"Just do it, for fuck's sake." I grab my phone to call the superintendent. "Sabre has a new client."

CHAPTER 3
HARLOW

THE RAGING SEA - BROADSIDE

ADELAIDE'S TEAR-STAINED *face stares back at me from her cage. Blood is gushing from between her legs, creating a crimson tidal wave.*

"You stupid little whore!"

Pastor Michaels' malicious scream cracks through the basement. He's staring at the mess inside the opposite cage, the keys dangling from his fist.

"You'll never have my baby," Adelaide says with a blood-stained smile. "My life isn't yours to take."

He shouts obscenities, fumbling to get the key into the cage door. I watch through my tears as Adelaide raises her hand, reaching for some invisible light that we can't see.

"No!" Pastor Michaels bellows. "You cannot die!"

Her hand drops, landing on the swell of her pregnant belly. I watch her mouth slacken as her soul departs from this mortal plane.

Adelaide is dead.

Pastor Michaels turns to me, his eyes dark with accusation. "You did this. I was going to save that baby from damnation! You'll pay for this, Harlow!"

With a scream lodged in my throat, I startle awake. For several disorientating seconds, I can still see Pastor Michaels striding towards me, removing his belt with threatening grace.

A frenetic beeping sound cuts through my terror, slamming me back into the painful husk of my body. Bright lights burn my retinas. I blink hard, my cheeks wet with streaming tears.

As my vision settles, I'm certain I've died. Everything around me is so clean. Light floods the white-dipped room, more than I've ever seen. The shadows that clung to my childhood are nonexistent.

Where am I?

Is this… heaven?

I search for the long-sought-after angels that blessed so many of Pastor Michaels' sermons. Every violent act he committed was supposed to bring him closer to his reward.

But he isn't here, and I was never destined to see God's light. How did I escape the basement? Is this real? It can't be.

Tendrils of truth seep beneath my skin, offering disjointed snippets. It's like staring into the bleak depths of a frozen lake, and the answers are trapped beneath the surface.

Trees. Stars. Biting wind. Exhaustion. Agony. Did I… run somewhere? I can feel the pain of sharp rocks slicing my bare feet to shreds. Knives tearing into my ribcage as broken bones were jolted around. The rest is a blur.

"Miss? Can you hear me?"

Someone is gently touching my arm. A woman, her smile wide and encouraging. I try to flinch back, but the layers of wires and needles wrapped around me are like a prison.

"Take a deep breath for me. I'll go and get the doctor."

She disappears from the room. I grab the line that's feeding air into my nostrils and yank it out. This isn't my home. I have no idea where I am. I need to leave, before he finds me.

More memories come as I fight to escape the bed. Towering trees. Soft, spongy moss beneath my bleeding feet. Icy water. Concrete. Old bricks. Lights. Engines. Cardboard and whistling wind.

"Hello?"

I'm slammed back to reality again. Someone else is staring down at me beneath a headful of greasy hair, with a rounded face that's lined with wrinkles.

"You got a name? I'm Sanderson."

Licking my dry lips, not a single sound escapes.

"You're in the hospital. We found you last week. You were pretty banged up. Care to explain what happened?"

He scans over me, cataloguing everything on display. My left arm is encased in thick plaster while the other is bandaged in places. Every inch of my skin is bruised and marked with deep scratches.

Sinners don't ask questions, Harlow.

They submit or pay the price.

Pastor Michaels' voice is so loud in my head, I jerk upright. The machine next to me explodes with a loud beeping as I pull at the wires across my chest. It sounds like a heartbeat, wild and out of control.

"Calm down or we will be forced to sedate you!"

My lungs stop functioning. It's like the devil is sitting on my chest, resolving to claim the pitiful remains of my life. The room is fading fast with each second that I can't breathe.

I'm too overwhelmed by the light, the voices, the sheer presence of real, living people. I can't trust them. Pastor Michaels is coming for me. He will torture me to the very last second of my life for running.

"What the *hell* is going on in here?"

This voice is harsh, barked, terrifying. A tall, muscled mountain slams through the door with an ominous crash. His broad shoulders brush the door frame as his two furious eyes eat up the room.

Everyone takes a collective step away from him. The giant's fearsome scowl sweeps over them all, condemning each person with a hate-filled glance.

"This is none of your concern," Sanderson says with a visible gulp. "I'm just doing my job."

"She's our client. You're out of bounds. The superintendent signed off on the order ten minutes ago."

"This is my jurisdiction!"

He takes a threatening step towards Sanderson. "I have the authority to toss you out and break your legs while doing it. This is your final chance to leave."

The deep, throaty boom of his voice fills the room with dread. With each person that's thrown out, the vice-like grip on my lungs eases. I take my first breath as the door slams shut on Sanderson's glare.

Smoothing a huge hand over his mop of glossy, black hair, the giant turns to meet my eyes from across the room. Brilliant orbs of raw amber stare back at me with curiosity.

The violent threat that hardened his voice isn't present in his gaze. I don't find evil or malice there. Beneath the obvious hardness, there's something... inexplicably soft.

"Hey there. Sorry about that. You should put the oxygen back in, it'll help with your breathing."

With trembling hands, I surrender. The wires won't let me out; there are too many of them. I grab the one I tore out and slot the two nozzles back into my nose.

I'm met by a flow of pure, clean air, and I force myself to take a breath. The giant inches even closer, stopping at the end of my bed. He's huge, an immovable boulder blocking my only exit.

"It's okay," he offers in a remarkably gentle voice. "No one is going to hurt you. Sanderson won't be back."

Nostrils flaring, he demonstrates breathing in, then blowing the air back out through his wide, chiselled lips. I follow his direction with well-practised obedience.

A small smile tugs at his mouth, but he doesn't allow himself to become distracted from instructing me until the beeping machine quietens. My heart stops hammering my painful ribs so hard.

"There you go. Better?"

I manage a small, timid nod.

"My name is Enzo Montpellier. I work for a private security firm, and we'll be keeping you safe from now on." He glances around the room. "Do you know where you are?"

All I can do is nod again.

"You've been in the hospital for over a week. Lucky to be alive, I hear. So, are you going to tell me your name?"

Pain is still screaming through me, despite the steady *drip, drip, drip* of fluids being fed into my body. My voice comes out in a raw gasp.

"H-H-Harlow."

"It's nice to meet you, Harlow. I'd like to help you, but I need you to answer a few questions."

Laura's face flashes into my mind. Spit bubbles escaping her slack mouth, joining the trails of blood as she slowly turned blue with my hands at her throat. Her tears falling in silent rivers, leading her into the arms of death.

"Can you tell me how you got here?" Enzo asks, his thick brows furrowed in a frown.

He's going to find out what I did and drag me back to Pastor Michaels' basement from hell. My parents will systematically break every last bone in my body until nothing but crumbs remain.

They'll slice the remaining unmarked places on my skin to remind me of the Lord Almighty and all he has done for me. Only when I've been thoroughly desecrated will my carcass be allowed to die.

"Breathe, Harlow. I'm losing you again."

My eyes are screwed tightly shut. All I can see is the walls of my cage closing in, inch by suffocating inch. As my surroundings melt away, the warmth of someone's hand on mine is like a punch to the chest.

Sometimes, the other girls would hold my hand, late at night. I fumble with my fingertips, snagging on a loose shirt sleeve. Is it Laura? Is she back? Have my sins been cleansed?

With the fabric bunched in my grip, I refocus on my breathing. In and out. The warmth is strangely comforting, like the softness of an invisible blanket draped over me.

"That's it, good girl."

The rough growl of a voice breaks my hazy dream. Laura isn't holding me. A stranger is. A man. He's going to kill me. Break me. Beat me. I have to start running.

"Deep breaths. Come on, like I showed you."

Silent minutes trickle by as I wrestle with myself. The giant's weight settling on my bed causes the springs to groan in protest. Rather than shuffling away, I grip his sleeve even tighter.

My legs curl closer to his body, seeking shelter from the biting chill of the basement in my head. It doesn't go unnoticed. Gentle fingers prise my hand from his sleeve, taking it in his calloused palm instead.

Maybe he isn't here to kill me.

Maybe… he's a friend.

"I'm here with you. Focus on my voice, nothing else."

"The l-l-light," I stutter out.

"Too bright?"

His weight disappears from the bed. The sharp pressure on my eyes vanishes as the fluorescent lighting winks out, draping the room in early evening shadows.

I manage to open my eyes, breathing evenly again. Enzo has settled back on the edge of the hospital bed, watching me closely.

"Thank you."

"Welcome back, little one."

His midnight-black hair is buzzed short on the sides and left long on top, adding to his edgy, aloof vibe. He wears a plain black t-shirt and worn leather jacket over some strange, dark-green trousers.

It's nothing like Pastor Michaels' processional robes or his wife's demure, floral frocks. The girls were always naked when brought down to join me, covered only by blood splatters.

"Where?" I manage to ask.

My throat aches with the single word. I'll soon lose my voice. It doesn't last long after so many years spent screaming into darkness.

"London," Enzo answers crisply. "The authorities transferred you to the intensive care unit. You were found in the back of a construction truck, looked like you'd been travelling for days"

"D-Days?"

"At least. Where did you come from? Did you hitchhike?"

I lose my breathing for a third time, spiralling back into panic. It's all too much. I'm glad I can only remember bits of how I got here. My bruised and beaten brain is keeping me safe.

"Listen to my voice, Harlow. I promise you that you're safe. Whoever is out there... they won't find you. I won't allow it."

"No… not safe. He's coming."

"Who's coming?"

I try to sit up and fail, pain lancing back through me as I slump against the pillows. "I need to pray. I'm dirty… bad, bad Harlow… he's coming…"

"Who? Tell me."

The warmth and tenderness drains from Enzo's voice. Staring up at him, his face transforms into someone else's. Strong angles and handsome smile lines dissolve into cold, righteous fury.

Grey hair supersedes his glossy, black locks. Enzo's tender, amber eyes dissipate, infected by ribbons of dark blue. So dark, it's like I'm looking into the void. I'm staring at my father.

"I'm s-so sorry," I whimper.

Pastor Michaels' lips remain tightly sealed. He doesn't need to speak. The sermons he espoused are forever scored into my brain.

Slamming my hands over my ears, I start screaming at full volume. Anything to get him away from me. The machines go crazy, adding to the chaos as I writhe and buck in the bed.

Loud voices sneak past the tight grip I hold on my imploding head, feeding into my sense of panic. Two hands grab my shoulders, pinning me down on the bed. The sharp scratch of a needle pierces my skin.

You evil little girl.

I'm going to find you, Harlow.

You'll regret ever running from me.

I fall back into my memories. Deeper and deeper, lost to the ravages of years spent in captivity. This was a mistake. I never should've left. Pastor Michaels will kill me when he finds me, far more brutally than any of the others.

Whatever they injected me with begins to kick in. My hands slacken and fall to my sides while my head crashes against the soft pillow. Pain is fading back into numbness.

I try to keep my heavy eyelids open, but an almighty force is weighing them down. The last thing I see is Enzo, trapped behind a sea of frantic nurses, watching me with determination.

CHAPTER 4
HARLOW

DEAD LETTER & THE INFINITE YES - WINTERSLEEP

"RECOVERY FROM SEPSIS CAN TAKE A WHILE," Doctor David explains. "We caught it just in time. It's a miracle that you travelled alone with such a severe infection."

"I was… h-hearing things," I admit, studying my nail-less index finger. "This voice was telling me to keep going, no matter what."

His blue eyes meet mine. "You were very brave, Harlow."

"No. I'm not brave."

"I wouldn't be so sure. You've survived something horrific. Give yourself some credit for getting this far."

He resumes taking notes of the latest readings on the array of machines surrounding my hospital bed. The other nurse hasn't returned after she forcibly sedated me.

I have a feeling that Enzo has something to do with her disappearance. The last thing I remember is the incandescent rage on his face as they pinned me down and slipped a needle in my arm.

"All looking good," Doctor David concludes.

He looks a few years younger than Pastor Michaels. I think I like him, but my trust is nonexistent. Monsters can wear many masks, and the kindest smiles often hide the sickest of souls.

"We need to discuss your recovery," he says, placing the clipboard down. "You're lucky to be alive with these injuries."

"Lucky," I repeat, the word alien on my tongue.

"The sepsis infection has been brought under control. You have two broken ribs, which will take time to heal. Keep them strapped with compression wraps, and I'd recommend lots of hot baths. You'll be given pain medication to take home."

"Home?"

"I understand arrangements are being made for you as we speak."

Worry settles over me. Pastor Michaels will be out there right now, burning the world to ash as he searches for me. There's a reason I was kept alive for all this time while others were murdered.

I'm his daughter. The beginning and end of the sick ritual that he's perfected over time, fine-tuning the art of brutalisation with each fresh kill. My body bears the same marks that killed each girl he stole.

"We performed surgery to set your broken arm," Doctor David continues, startling me back to the room. "You'll be in the cast for several weeks while it heals. Physiotherapy may be required."

Nodding, I pick at the sore flaps of skin around my missing nail. The sharp bite of pain grants me some clarity. Enzo said I was safe. Pastor Michaels can't get to me here, surely?

"Harlow?"

I startle as he rests a hand on my shoulder, quickly removing it when he spots the look on my face.

"We need to talk about your diet now that you're off the feeding tube. I understand the idea of eating may seem impossible, given all that's happened. Extended periods of malnourishment do that."

"I… f-feel sick just thinking about food," I concede, my voice strained. "They didn't feed me often… where I was held."

His gaze softens with sympathy. I hate the way that look makes me feel, my skin crawling with self-hatred. I don't want to be the broken person my parents made me.

"You need to stick to a strict, high-calorie diet to gain some weight. I'm concerned about your immune system. The infection nearly killed you, and in your current state, a common cold could wipe you out."

"Put some weight on." I clear the lump in my throat. "Got it. I'll try my best, Doctor David."

"Our nutritionist will write up a meal plan for you to take away. Lots of protein shakes for meal replacement, some light foods to try. You will need to take it slow, avoid anything rich or heavy."

A dull ache starts behind my eyes. Between the bright sunlight pulsing through the window and the doctor's information dump, I'm feeling overwhelmed. It's all so much.

"Do you have any questions for me, Harlow? I'm sure this all sounds like a lot. You'll return to me for regular checkups to keep your recovery on track in the coming months."

"How old am I?" I blurt out.

"You don't know?"

I avoid the concerned look on his face. Admitting it out loud makes me feel sick with vulnerability. My life before the confines of this clinical room feels so far away now. Like an endless nightmare from which I've finally awoken.

Part of me doesn't believe it. Everything I've grown up believing is being systematically dismantled with each passing second. The world isn't a fiery wasteland of sinners and angels, battling to reach the welcoming relief of God's light.

Running a hand over his face, Doctor David takes the empty seat at my bedside. "We're having difficulty tracking down your medical records. You're a ghost, Harlow. All I have are best guesses."

"Why can't you find them?"

"Your case is being treated as classified. There are some powerful people outside, arguing about what to do with you. We've tried to identify you based on our records… but there's nothing."

"You're saying… I'm n-not real?"

"That's not what I'm saying," he assures me. "I'm sure there's an explanation. I'll be discharging you into protective custody, and the right people are working on your case. They will get you answers."

Strands of dark-blonde hair cover his eyes as he writes some more notes. I stare down at my fingers, peeking out through the thick plaster encasing my broken arm.

They don't look like my fingers. This doesn't look like my body. Everything about this is wrong. Any moment now, I'll startle awake, trapped in the familiar imprisonment of my cage.

"Doctor?"

His head snaps up. "Yes, Harlow?"

"I d-don't… uh, feel real. Is that normal?"

Brows furrowing, he places his pen down. "What do you mean, exactly?"

Raising my hand, I touch the tender skin of my face. I caught a glimpse earlier when a different nurse gave me a sponge bath. There are two vertical stripes staining my skin in mottled shades of purple and green.

The marks perfectly match the bars that Mrs Michaels smashed me into on my last night. Her personal brand of evil has left an indelible mark on me, and in a twisted way, I'm relieved. I have proof.

"How old do you think I am?" I ask instead.

Doctor David sighs at my obvious topic change. "Early twenties. May I ask when you got your first period?"

My mouth falls open. I know what that word means. Adelaide usually haunts my bad dreams, more than the others do. Her story is the most horrifying of all.

The other girls bled between their legs every now and then. I learned about periods from them. But Adelaide never did. Her belly was swollen when she arrived, begging for mercy.

Not for her own life—but for her baby's. Pastor Michaels broke her nose and called her a slut. He was determined to save the child's unborn soul. In his mind, she didn't deserve to be a mother because she survived by selling her body.

Adelaide died in excruciating pain.

I can still hear her screeching wails.

"I've n-n-nev…" I stammer. "Never… h-had it."

Doctor David's jaw hardens. I look away as anger flashes in his eyes. I'm not worthy of their care and attention, not after what I've done to get here. They should've let me die instead.

"Lunch time," he declares suddenly. "I'll send the nurse in with something suitable. Time to get better, eh?"

Patting my hand, he disappears with his note-clustered paperwork. I'm left staring up at the ceiling, blinking away tears.

The nurse bustles in shortly after, disconnecting the empty bag of medication flowing through the port in my arm.

"I'll get your protein shake," she offers, leaving the IV line unhooked. "How about some jelly, hmm? It'll be nice and light on your stomach."

"Okay… thank you."

Left alone again, I push back the bedcovers and attempt to move my legs. Every muscle screams in protest, and it takes several minutes to place my bandaged feet on the floor.

I blink away the rush of dizziness and manoeuvre myself up. The pain isn't so bad; I feel weak more than anything. How I made it here, I can't even begin to imagine.

I've heard the nurses gossiping outside my room, trading theories. If I ran, it must've been for miles. Beaten, broken and starved. The level of desperation that takes is unthinkable.

Limping over to the window, I take in the hospital grounds. Loud vehicles come and go beneath me, flashing with blue lights. I'm not sure where we are. London sounds vaguely familiar.

"Look who's up!"

The nurse walks back in, placing a plastic tray on the table over my bed. I quickly take her outstretched hand before my legs fold. She tucks me back into bed and bustles away.

The tray in front of me holds a cup of gloopy, sludge-like liquid. One sniff and nausea rushes over me. Instead, I pick up the clear pot filled with wiggling red stuff.

After managing two tiny spoonfuls, I feel painfully full. My stomach aches, threatening to revolt. Abandoning the food, I turn and stare out of the window again.

The day has slipped by. On the horizon, a fiery ball of light and heat is being swallowed by darkness. The colours fascinate me, like paint strokes brought to life on a giant canvas.

"You were right," I whisper to Laura's memory in my head. "The sunset is so beautiful. I wish you were here too."

There's a gentle knock at the door before it cracks open. Enzo peeks inside, his raven hair floppy and slightly damp, like he's freshly showered. It shows off his glowing, animal-like amber eyes.

Wearing a tight, short-sleeved black t-shirt, his rippling forearms and toned shoulders stretch the bounds of the fabric. There's a buttery leather harness strapped across his muscular back. My heart stutters at the gun tucked inside.

"Hey, Harlow. Can I come in?"

I pull the covers closer to my chest. "Um, sure."

His thick-soled army boots thud like thunderclaps as he stomps into the room. The ceiling almost brushes his head, he's so tall. Like the branches of a powerful, ancient oak tree.

Anxiety slithers down my spine, but it's tempered by the inexplicable sense of warmth that radiates from his gentle smile. It looks foreign on his face, softening features a little too hard and rough to be classically handsome.

"You're looking better," he comments softly.

"I guess."

"Have you been up long?"

"I slept most of the day, before I saw Doctor David." My eyes stray back to the window. "I wanted to go outside, but they wouldn't let me out alone."

"It's for your own protection," Enzo answers, a shoulder propped against the wall. "It's not much of a view, anyway. I'm not a huge fan of London myself."

"Do you live here?"

"On the outskirts, about an hour away." His intense gaze doesn't waver. "Our base of operations is more central. It's not far from here. We take contracts across the country though."

His phone buzzes, breaking our staring match. Enzo fishes it out of his pocket, and I watch his face darken as he notes the caller ID before answering.

I recognise the device—Mrs Michaels had one. She would play gospel songs on it as she cleaned blood and dead bodies in her husband's lair of death.

"Yeah, she's awake. Alright, understood." Enzo flashes me an apologetic smile as he ends the call. "Sorry, that was my... co-worker. He's coming to say hello."

I shuffle backwards on the bed, wincing as my ribs protest. What if this person wants to hurt me? What if they're all lying? What if I wake up back in my cage? These men could all work for Pastor Michaels.

"You can trust Hunter. We've known each other for our whole lives," Enzo states calmly. "I promised you that everything would be okay, and I meant it."

"Why?"

"Because we're good men, Harlow. You've been through a lot, and it's our job to make things easier for you from here on out. We're the best in the business."

"Do you help people?"

His gaze softens again. "Yeah, little one. We help people."

Creeping across the room like a stealthy jungle cat, Enzo outstretches a meaty palm. It's twice the size of my hands. I should be running as far away from this menacing giant as possible.

But when I look into his eyes, there's nothing but a soft concern that doesn't match his burly exterior. He moves slowly, giving me time to adjust to his presence, before taking the empty seat next to me.

"What h-happens n-now?" I whisper.

"We will take you somewhere safe. It's called protective custody. You'll be comfortable and we'll make sure you're looked after."

"You don't h-have questions? About where I was?"

His lips twist in another small smile. "You catch on quick. Our priority is making sure you're okay. We never expected to find you…"

"Alive?"

"Truthfully, we didn't even know about you. Another girl is missing, and we believe she's connected to your story too."

Pain crashes into me with the realisation that I am inarguably alone. Nobody was even trying to find me. It's a heavy blow.

"We're glad you're alive," Enzo adds with a meaningful look. "Our firm has been working on this case for over a year now. We're hoping you will be able to help us."

His words finally catch up to me, and I frantically look around the room, searching and finding nothing. Not even the threadbare shirt that I escaped in. How did I not notice before? She isn't here.

"What is it? What's wrong?" Enzo demands, reaching for his gun.

"I h-had... I'm looking…"

Tugging my long, brown hair until my eyes burn with tears, I realise how broken I am. Those endless miles of starlight and blood-stained footsteps were not travelled alone. The memories are becoming clearer with each breath I take.

"Harlow?" Enzo urges, still on high alert.

"Was I found with anything?"

Relaxing infinitesimally, he braces his elbows on his knees. "Not that I'm aware of. I can get someone to check, though, if you want. In the truck?"

Nodding, I want to thank him, but no words will come out. My throat is thick with bitter regret. I promised to myself that I'd get Laura out... the parts of her that remained anyway.

The thought of her remains being left behind to rot alone is unbearable. Tears start to stream down my cheeks, thick and fast. I can't hold them back any longer. I've failed her.

"What is it?" he asks.

"I… I shouldn't be here," I choke out.

Enzo reaches out, his thumb stroking over my cheek to catch my tears. I flinch at his touch, expecting pain instead of comfort. He freezes, horror filling his expression.

"I'm so sorry," Enzo rushes to apologise. "I didn't mean to scare you."

"You don't scare me," I answer quickly. "I just... I'm not used to… well, people."

"That's fine. I apologise again."

We lapse into awkward silence. Enzo stares at his feet, wearing a pained frown. I can tell that he's beating himself up. For such an imposing guy, he wears his heart fully on his sleeve.

There's a sharp rap on the door and he moves to answer it, exchanging hushed words with whoever's on the other side. When both men enter the room, I sit up ramrod straight.

"Easy, Harlow." Enzo raises his hands in a placating manner as he spots my panic. "This is the co-worker I mentioned."

Standing next to Enzo, an imposing figure drinks me in with his molten-chocolate eyes, framed by thick lashes. He's almost as tall as Enzo, but much trimmer, his body sculpted with lean muscle instead of bulk.

Wearing a pristine charcoal suit, his long, chestnut-brown hair is tied at the nape of his neck, highlighting his trimmed beard that covers the symmetrical lines of his picture-perfect looks.

He's very handsome, attractive in a model-like way that Enzo could never achieve with his terrifying exterior. Despite that, there's a veneer of coldness that seems to cloak his posture.

As he comes closer, I can see a sleek panel of black metal attached to his left ear. It's a hearing aid, partially covered by flyaway hair. There's an old scar bisecting his eyebrow too, the only blemish on his spotless appearance.

"It's a pleasure to meet you," he greets, his voice smooth like honey. "My name is Hunter Rodriguez."

"You too. I'm Harlow."

"Any last name?"

My mouth dries up. "Uh, no. Just Harlow."

Hunter nods, lacing his hands behind his back as he paces the room. "As Enzo has explained, we own a private security firm that has been put in charge of your care."

Leaning in the corner of the room, Enzo watches his friend closely. There's a weird tension between them that fuels my anxiety.

"We perform large-scale criminal investigations, among other things," Hunter continues brusquely. "You are a person of interest to one of our current cases."

"A p-person of interest?"

His cold eyes land on me. "We're investigating a spate of serial killings spanning the last five years. They appear to be motivated by religious ideology. Bodies carved with holy symbols and dumped."

"Hunt!" Enzo hisses.

He ignores Enzo completely. This slick businessman has an acid tongue. My cheeks burn hotter than hell as I stare down at the hospital gown I'm wearing.

Holy symbols.

I can see them; they're burned onto my retinas. The scars twist my flesh into ugly disfigurations. If they've seen the other bodies, they know what Pastor Michaels does.

"We're going to move you to a secure location and ensure you get the help you need to recover." Hunter halts, casting me an emotionless look. "You're going to help us with our investigation."

Enzo curses under his breath. He looks ready to use the gun strapped to his body with each harsh word that Hunter wields.

"Do you understand?" Hunter demands.

I nod, fear binding my tongue.

"Good. I have two agents stationed outside of your room for protection. We intend to move you in a couple of days when your consultant signs off on the discharge."

I plaster a neutral expression into place. People lie, I know that. Like when Pastor Michaels stroked my sweaty hair and told me he loved me after beating me to a pulp with his belt.

It didn't stop him from breaking skin and bone. Like Hunter, he wielded his words as a weapon, only using his fists to deliver the final, back-breaking blows.

Hunter clears his throat. "You were found in the back of a construction truck heading south from Cambridge. My team has traced it back to a depot. It appears you hopped on from a lorry."

"Hunt," Enzo warns in a low voice.

"That lorry was traced back to a warehouse in Nottingham." Hunter ignores his friend's thunderous expression. "How far did you hitchhike? Were you being held nearby?"

Enzo marches up to him. "Enough! Jesus."

"It's a simple question."

"She is in no position to answer your fucking questions. Have some goddamn empathy."

They're almost nose to nose, the lash of anger slicing into me like a whip. I hate confrontation. Enzo glances at me and blanches, taking several steps back from Hunter with another curse.

The names and places he's thrown at me mean nothing. All I can remember are the jagged shards of broken memories. My mind checked out as I ran for my life.

"Fine," Hunter growls, flashing me a look. "We'll talk more in a couple of days. Be ready to leave then."

Turning on the heel of his luxurious leather shoe, Hunter storms from the room without another word. Enzo watches him go with a biting glare.

"He seems… um, nice," I say awkwardly.

Enzo's chest rumbles with a laugh. "No need to bullshit me. He's a miserable son of a bitch. Are you going to be okay?"

"I'll be fine."

"If you need anything, ask one of the men stationed outside. Becket and Ethan are both good agents. They'll protect you."

He stares at me from across the room, looking like he wants to say more. I'm hit by a wave of exhaustion that pulls at my already heavy eyelids. It's been an intense day.

"Rest, Harlow. We'll be back soon."

With a final, unhappy nod, Enzo sweeps from the room. The moment the door shuts, my throat aches with the force of emotion ramming into me. I feel like I've been deserted on an island.

The niggling voice of fear sneaks back in as the shadows in the room seem to grow without Enzo here to ward them off. He was the first warmth and real human contact I've experienced for a long time.

I survived the basement alone, but in this unknown place, I feel more afraid than ever before. All I want is for Enzo to come back and stand guard, his intimidating size scaring everyone else off.

Lord, I truly must be broken.

Pastor Michaels succeeded.

CHAPTER 5
ENZO

EVEN IN THE DARK - JXDN

MY FEET SMACK against the pavement in a rhythmic beat. I focus on the road ahead and crank my classic rock music up even louder. I like it high enough to hurt my eardrums when I'm feeling like this.

I've circled the suburbs of rural London twice, in all its luxurious, middle-class charm. The miles passed by quickly as I lost myself in the simple act of exercise.

It takes a lot to exhaust me. Years of suffering from insomnia have given me a superhuman ability to run on absolutely nothing. After tossing and turning in bed for an hour, I called it quits and pulled my running gear on.

I can't stop thinking about Harlow. Her wide, frightened blue eyes, bird-like features and gently curling brown hair have filled my mind since I left the hospital last night.

Finishing my tenth mile, I circle back home. Countless red-brick townhouses, fashionable apartments and closed cocktail bars frequented by the filthy rich pass me by.

After twelve years of running Sabre Security, we could afford to buy property somewhere more upmarket. This was supposed to be our family home when we bought it several years back.

In reality, the house is as empty as our lives. The family we once were shattered a long time ago. Hunter comes home just to pass out. Theo's room is untouched. I can't catch a single night's sleep without being haunted by the past.

The brick wall that encloses the property comes into view, topped with lacquered black spikes and concealed CCTV cameras. We live amongst normal society, but our home is a fortress of solitude.

With a generous garden and tall birch trees for privacy, you can just spot the painted pillars marking the entrance to our Victorian-style mansion. Red bricks are broken by generous windows, fitted with specially made bulletproof glass. We went all out.

I let myself through the electric gate, cursing the complicated security system that Theo had one of his techies install. Leaning in for a retinal scan when it's pitch-black is a feat, but it would take an army to break in.

Inside the house, I toe off my trainers and rest against the wall. My body is exhausted, but my mind still won't quiet. There's a thump of feet on wooden floors as Lucky comes padding over.

She licks my legs in greeting, and I bend down to scratch behind her ears. Her pearly-blonde fur practically gleams in the moonlight leaking through the window panes.

She's a golden Labrador retriever, and weighs a hell of a lot when she insists on climbing into bed for a cuddle. I'm the only one that lets her do it. We got her not long after we moved in.

"Good girl," I murmur.

We head into the kitchen together. The under-counter lights are on, revealing Hunter sitting with his back to me at the kitchen island. He's shirtless, showing years of scars and the tattoos that cover everywhere from his throat down.

As usual, he's nursing a cup of tea, his dark-green sweatpants hanging low on his hips. I approach slowly, noting his hearing aid on the marble countertop. I'd like to avoid a broken nose if I startle him.

He's been known to take it out, preferring the silence his permanently damaged eardrums provide while deep in thought. Hunter's completely deaf in his right ear.

An explosion caused his hearing to decline over time. Only his left ear retains some functioning, so he relies on the hearing aid to live a somewhat normal life. It affects him a lot more than he lets on.

Offering him a wave, I grab a bottle of water from the fridge, draining it in three quick gulps. Hunter reattaches his hearing aid, switching it on so we can talk.

"Couldn't sleep?" he guesses.

"Something like that."

"Me neither. This case is fucked up, man."

I splash my face in the kitchen sink. "You're telling me. I'm ready to never look at a mutilated body again."

"Like anything is ever that easy."

"What about the girl?"

"She's been given medical clearance to leave in the morning. I'm sending Doctor Richards in for a full psych eval before we take her to the safe house. We can't have a messy suicide on our hands too."

Cringing at his words, my hands clench into tight fists. "She wouldn't. Harlow's a fighter. How else did she escape in such a state?"

Hunter studies me closely. I fucking hate it when he does that. I'm not a client, and he always sees far more than I'd like. He's fiercely intelligent and, sometimes, far too ruthless.

I'm the brawn to his brains, but my emotions get the better of me more than his do. I feel enough for both of us. It's why I stick to the physical side of the business—training recruits, running active operations, beating on the bad guys on occasion.

I couldn't do what Hunter does. My fists speak more than his fancy words ever could, but we need him to keep us afloat. He has the tongue of a politician and the stratagem of a military commander.

Hunter's intelligence does make him vulnerable. While his ability to get inside the heads of our perpetrators makes him so brilliant, it's also his greatest threat. He feels more than he lets on and bottles it up, ruling with an iron fist instead.

"Don't get attached, Enzo. She's a client."

"I'm aware," I growl back.

"Are you?" He drains the rest of his tea. "We will have to grill her hard to get the information we need to hunt this motherfucker down. There isn't time to be gentle."

"You said that more questions could wait. She's traumatised, Hunt. We have to give her time."

"As soon as she's in our custody, we need to get to work. This sick son of a bitch has evaded us for too long. I'm done playing games."

Fighting the urge to break his fucking face, I drag my sweaty shirt over my head while storming from the room. I need a shower and a few hours of sleep, but I know the latter won't come.

Hunter's warning infuriates me because it's true. Even if I don't want to admit it. I can't afford to get attached. Not after last time.

Love is a weakness.

In our world, love gets you killed.

The next morning, grumpy and sleep deprived, I camp out in the intensive care waiting area. Hunter is in the small meeting room down the corridor, ironing out the final details with Sanderson and another SCU representative.

We have a safe house lined up for Harlow in East London. It's a grey, faceless apartment, more of a prison than her first taste of freedom. Once she enters that place, she won't leave.

Not until this is all over and it's safe to do so. The thought of her—alone and scared with nobody to hold her close—is pushing me over the edge. I promised we'd keep her safe.

This is internment, not protection.

She will suffer for it.

The door to the meeting room opens. Hunter strides out, smoothing his designer, three-piece grey suit. Sanderson follows, his face red and eyes lowered as he quickly makes an excuse to leave.

The spineless worm has been making our lives difficult for months, angered by his department's decision to hire external help. It effectively removed this case from his control.

"All done?"

Hunter closes his briefcase, depositing it on the coffee table. "We're good. Is the doc out yet? I'd like to wrap this up fast."

"Not yet."

Sighing, Hunter takes a seat, scrubbing a hand over his beard. I don't think either of us slept last night. We lapse into silence and wait for the shrink to finish his assessment.

It takes another two hours before Doctor Richards emerges from the intensive care unit, pulling on an expensive wool coat to protect against the winter chill.

"Afternoon, gents."

Surging to his feet, Hunter offers a hand for him to shake. "Thanks for coming in, doc. We appreciate it."

We've worked with Lionel Richards for several years now, and he's assisted on many of our high-profile cases. The fame granted to us after Blackwood sent his career into the stratosphere too.

"So?" Hunter prompts.

"You do like to give me a challenge." Richards sighs, smoothing his wild bush of silver hair. "I'm not sure what to make of this one."

"What the hell does that mean?" I snap tiredly.

He spares me an assessing glance. "When was the last time you got some sleep, Enzo? You look dead on your feet."

"You're not here to assess me, doc. Just fucking spit it out already. We have places to be."

Raising his hands in surrender, he takes the seat opposite us. Richards is used to my attitude. He supported the entire team when we were on the verge of selling up.

We felt unable to go on after everything that happened back then, but with his help, we made our way through and rebuilt. Family and friends convinced us to keep working, despite our grief.

"Harlow is suffering from severe PTSD as a result of her imprisonment, extensive abuse and brutalisation." Richards adjusts his spectacles. "She will need to see me every week for the foreseeable future."

"How long was she held captive?" Hunter fires off.

"To her account, she has never seen the outside world. I am inclined to believe she is experiencing dissociative amnesia."

"What does that mean?" I ask next.

"It's a common response to very extreme cases of trauma. She can't recall a lot of her time spent in imprisonment, only flashes here and there."

Hunter swears under his breath. Harlow's memories are our best shot at tracking down the killer. Our case now lives and dies by the testimony she will provide.

"Oddly enough, she presents with a reasonable level of understanding and social development for her age." Richards shakes his head. "Only so much can be learned from others."

"You don't think she was held captive for her whole life?" Hunter guesses.

"I'd hesitate to speculate at this stage," he replies. "We need to take this very slow. Push too soon, and she will close down. Her mind is a puzzle that needs to be pieced back together."

"We don't have time, doc."

"Then interrogate her and watch that poor girl spiral. I don't need to tell you how trauma can affect a person. Her risk of suicide is already significant."

I shiver at his angered words. We've had enough experience with traumatised clients. Hunter deflates, taking a moment to reconsider.

"Is it the same perp?" I ask uneasily.

"I can't answer that," Richards responds. "She has been subjected to extreme psychological and physical torture, complete isolation, and emotional abuse."

"So?"

"Your killer rapes and butchers young women. It's not exactly the same kettle of fish. Serial killers don't tend to hold their victims for long."

"You've seen the marks," Hunter points out. "She bears the same scars that every dumped body had. Only they're old, healed. Why didn't he kill her as well?"

None of us has an answer. We've all suffered through studying the photographs of Harlow's body in further detail. The harrowing scars on her body match our morgue of dead bodies perfectly.

We had further analysis performed by forensics. Down to the symbolism of the Holy Trinity carved into Harlow, the knife patterns matched to a high degree. It was likely the same blade used.

"I'm not here to draw conclusions." Richards stares at Hunter. "I shall leave that to your team. Harlow is my patient now. I am more concerned for her mental stability."

"Should we be worried?" I frown at him. "Are we safe to move her?"

"I believe there is some cause for concern. Re-introducing Harlow to society needs to be handled with the utmost delicacy. That's why I'm not recommending an inpatient stay."

I breathe a sigh of relief.

"She needs to feel safe, supported," Richards outlines. "Isolating her in a hospital could exacerbate her symptoms and lead to further dissociation."

I cut Hunter a sharp look. He still won't admit that I'm right, despite the heated argument we had on the drive over. This safe house is a terrible fucking idea.

Ignoring me, he stares down at his phone. "She'll have a full team for security. I'll see to it that regular visits with yourself are arranged. We have questions that need answering, doc. I would appreciate your help."

"Harlow's been through something horrific," Richards says emphatically. "This needs to be handled with extreme care. That doesn't involve sticking her in some faceless apartment with a team of spooks."

I knew he'd be on my side. Richards is the best in the business. This is exactly why we pay him the big bucks to consult for us.

"So, what do we do with her then?" Hunter snaps.

Pulling a colourful scarf on, Richards inclines his head. "I trust you to think of the right thing. Set up a regular therapy slot for her with my secretary. I'll await your updates on her living arrangement."

Once Richards has breezed from the ward, Hunter's head falls into his hands. His long hair is in a bun today, exposing the thick muscles of his neck and the beginnings of his chest tattoo peeking under his shirt collar. I give him a moment to gather himself.

The distance between myself and Harlow's room feels like a whole goddamn ocean. I want nothing more than to stand between her and the rest of the world, whatever it takes to keep her safe.

Christ, this is bad.

We're in seriously hot water.

"This is turning into a clusterfuck." Hunter reads my mind with a sigh. "Clearly, the safe house isn't a good idea."

"Let's take her back to HQ. We can go from there."

Hunter nods. "Go get her."

Heading for Harlow's hospital room, I slide my best emotionless mask into place. I need to get my shields up before she worms her way any further under my skin.

She's our responsibility, but not one of us. The sooner I realise that, the better. Rapping on the door, I peek inside and find her bed deserted.

Reaching for my gun holster, I'm ready to tear the hospital apart to find her when the sound of running water draws my attention. Entering the room, I remain poised, ready to pounce.

A familiar pair of slender legs stands stiff before a mirror in the corner. Breathing hard, I force myself to relax. She's here.

"Harlow?"

She slowly turns around and her wide, cerulean eyes meet mine. Her right hand is tugging a nest of impossibly long hair over her shoulder, while her broken left arm is strapped to her chest.

"What are you up to?" I ask suspiciously.

Her teeth sink into her bottom lip. "Considering a haircut."

Inching into the room, I stop behind her. I can feel her body heat in the tiny gap between us. Another step, and her small, pert ass would be pressed right up against me.

Fucking dammit, Enzo. I can't be thinking shit like that around her. She's vulnerable and innocent. I'm supposed to be protecting her, not slavering over her like a fucking dog.

"The doc thought it would be a good idea."

"We can arrange a haircut. But for the record, I like your hair."

Limping past me, Harlow returns to her hospital bed and grabs the light-blue hoodie left for her to wear. She unclips the sling holding her broken arm, attempting to wrestle it over her head.

"Come here." I walk over, grabbing handfuls of fabric. "Let me help. Put your head through here, like this."

When her head pops through the hole, there's a ghost of a smile on her lips. She lets me pull it over her small body and I grab the sling, slipping it back over her head.

"Thank you," she says quietly, sliding her broken arm into place. "Guess I'm going to need a hand for a while."

"Nothing wrong with asking for help. Are you ready?"

"I… I think so."

Even in borrowed sweats that swamp her legs, she looks better for getting out of a hospital gown. The loose, V-necked shirt beneath her hoodie shows off her collarbones and a hint of scar tissue on her chest.

I don't point it out. The last thing I want is to embarrass her, and she doesn't need to know about the photographs. We've taken something from her, something irreplaceable. Her choice. If I could unsee those scars, I would.

Harlow sits down on the bed, staring at her feet. I realise that she's silently crying. Her shoulders are shaking with each sob. A pair of unlaced black Converse wait for her on the linoleum.

"What is it?"

"I don't know how to do it," she whispers.

Realisation dawns. I fight the urge to take her in my arms and hold her tight. There's a certain fire in her gaze, and I can't wait for her to realise that.

"Here, let me."

Sinking to one knee in front of her, I ease the Converse over the light bandages still on her feet and loosely tie the laces.

She watches with curiosity, her bright eyes analysing each movement. I have to force myself to look away as her teeth bite into her pink bottom lip.

"Thanks, Enzo. Could you show me again sometime? If that's not too much trouble."

Her soft request sends tingles down my spine. I nod, rising to my full height. Hesitating for a moment, her tiny palm slides into my outstretched hand.

"Got everything? You ready?"

Harlow quickly nods. "I have nothing to bring."

"Then let's move. Stick with me and don't speak to anyone apart from myself and Hunter. Got that?"

She gulps before nodding. Her fear hurts me on a bone-deep level. Unable to stop myself, I find my calloused fingers tilting her chin up so that her aquamarine eyes meet mine.

Wide, afraid, the endless blue depths of the ocean stare back at me. Her irises are flecked with the faintest shades of pale green, but it's the flames of courage that astound me.

"You're going to be okay."

"I don't think... I mean… I'm not sure what that means." Harlow chews her lip again. "To be okay or safe."

"Then allow me to show you."

Cursing myself, I can't take the words back. I really don't want to as the most beautiful smile twists her lips, all lit up with fragile hope just for me.

Her hand squeezes mine. "Lead the way."

Jesus fuck, I'm an idiot. Hunter is telling me not to get attached. Little does he know, it's already too late. She's under my skin.

That can only mean one thing.

Trouble.

CHAPTER 6
HARLOW

NEW EYES - ECHOS

KEEPING my hand tucked in Enzo's paw-like grip, I'm given a huge paper bag full of medications and instructions. The nurse's words wash over me, but Enzo nods, listening to it all and taking the bag for me.

I'm glad one of us is able to pay attention.

All I can focus on is my shallow breathing.

Out in the waiting area, I find a familiar face carved in frustrated lines as he peers down at his phone. Hunter's dressed smartly in another suit, his hair slicked into a neat bun and beard freshly trimmed.

He looks up as we enter, his eyes narrowing on my hand still clutched tight in Enzo's. Panicking, I try to let go. My cheeks are flaming, and I have no idea why.

These men are so confusing. Enzo tightens his grip, casting me a warning look that ends my futile attempts to escape his grasp.

"I really hate hospitals," Hunter declares darkly. "Let's get the hell out of here and never come back."

Enzo nods. "The car is parked downstairs."

I'm guided to an odd metal door in the wall. Hunter presses something and I gape in shock as the wall splits into two with a ding.

The slices of metal part to reveal a small room, built straight into the wall. It looks a lot like another cell to me. My eyes sink shut as I begin to panic all over again.

"Harlow? You good?"

I'm surprised to find Hunter peering down at me when my eyes peek open a fraction. There's a flash of concern on his face before it's wiped away.

"I'm not getting in there," I force out.

"The elevator? It won't hurt you."

"I'm not getting in."

His nostrils flare and he strides away, opening another door off to the side.

It reveals a metal staircase leading down. We begin to descend the stairs in frigid silence.

When Hunter's phone rings, he answers it with a barked greeting. I feel sorry for whoever is on the end of the line. He suddenly raises a hand for Enzo to halt behind him.

I crash straight into Enzo's back, nearly losing my balance on the stairs. His strong, trunk-like arm wraps around my waist before I can fall, placing me back on my feet.

"Careful," he quips with a smile.

Before I can thank him, Hunter curses colourfully.

"Fucking hell. You've got to be kidding me."

"What is it?" Enzo immediately asks.

Listening to the urgent voice on the end of the phone, I find myself spiralling out of control. The simple curse word triggers something inside of me that I can't suppress.

It's another forgotten memory, wrapped in pain and misery. The darkness of the basement washes over me like a storm cloud, chilling me to the bone with the familiar scent of blood.

We don't use that word here, Christie.

Lay still or I'll slice your throat instead.

There's a good girl.

My mind is filled with the visual of Pastor Michaels pinning Christie's naked body to the floor of her cage. He carved the holy marks into her stomach while she sobbed uncontrollably.

I'd forgotten the sheer intensity of her wailing. She was younger than the others, less able to handle the torture. Her screams overwhelm me as I sink against the stairwell's wall.

"Shit!" Enzo swears, his hands landing on my shoulders. "Come on, Harlow. Stay with me."

I shove his hands away with a silent cry, unable to cope with the feel of someone touching me.

"What's happening?" Hunter barks.

"What does it look like, idiot?"

"Sort her out. We have a situation downstairs."

Hunter's words ignite something within me. The flare of anger catches alight and burns through my mind. Seizing the powerful emotion, I use it to pull myself out of the darkness.

Sweet, glorious air enters my lungs as I fight to retake control. When I manage to open my eyes, Hunter's watching me with mild astonishment.

"She can sort herself out," I reply shakily.

"So I can see."

It's my turn to be astonished as Hunter offers me a hand. Enzo watches us, open-mouthed. As I'm pulled up, my tightly wrapped ribs burn with pain. I bite down on my tongue to hold it in.

"What's the situation?" Enzo speaks up.

Hunter offers him a grim look. "The press are camped outside. They've caught wind of something and reckon we've found another body. They're fishing for an update."

"Goddammit. We can't let them see her."

"Why?" I ask cluelessly.

"The last thing we need is your face plastered all over the news when we're trying to keep you safe." Hunter runs a hand over his man bun. "Enzo, I need you to field questions. Tell them nothing."

He nods. "Get Harlow past while they're not looking. I'll meet you in the garage when the coast is clear."

Sparing me a final look, Enzo jogs ahead down the staircase. We follow behind him at a much slower pace. Hugging my broken arm to my chest, I feel a bit lost without his hand in mine.

"What happens if they see me?"

Hunter shrugs off his suit jacket at the bottom of the stairs. "The people we're keeping you from will know exactly where you are."

Short of breath, I press the still-sore wound where Pastor Michaels ripped the nail out. The burst of pain is immediate, slicing through my fear like a flash of lightning.

From outside, I can hear the greedy roar of voices. Shouting, heckling, demanding attention. The odd flash of light accompanies the chaos, even as Enzo's voice booms over them all.

"Put this over your head." Hunter pulls his jacket over me and wraps an arm around my shoulders. "Hold on to me and don't let go."

Fisting my hand in his pressed shirt, I shut my eyes, letting him guide me. Warmth radiates from Hunter's skin, seeping through the material of his shirt. It feels weirdly intimate to cling to it.

He smells peppery, like spices and exotic adventures. Pastor Michaels only ever smelled like blood. I want to bathe in this new, exciting scent. Let it wash over me, washing all the bad stuff away.

"You smell really good," I blurt without thinking.

Hunter stumbles before righting himself. "Huh?"

"Uh, n-nothing."

The shouting fades as we march ahead. His suit jacket is soon removed from my head, and I blink, looking around what seems to be a parking garage. There are cars everywhere.

Hunter's still holding me close as we walk up to a huge, blacked-out beast. The wheels are almost as big as me, and it's painted in a sleek, matte-black colour.

"Get in," Hunter orders, opening the back door.

Staring inside, I doubt my ability to climb in. My starved, tiny body betrays me. With a mutter, a pair of strong hands land on my hips. My breath catches in my throat.

Hunter doesn't apologise as he hoists me into the back of the car and slams the door in my face. I can still feel the burning heat where his hands squeezed my hips.

Impure sinner.

God does not condone pleasures of the flesh.

I will beat the devil from your bones.

Mrs Michaels always said that sinners make men stupid, steering them away from the path of God. My father never touched me as he touched the other girls. That did nothing to lessen her fury, though.

Hunter slides into the driver's seat and fires up the engine. It vibrates with a throaty, powerful purr, breaking the uncomfortable silence. The minutes trickle by until Enzo suddenly appears and clambers inside.

"How bad?" Hunter snaps impatiently.

"Someone from the hospital must have leaked the story. They know we have information that we're withholding. With our reputation, they've rolled out the live cameras."

"Goddammit," Hunter curses, throwing the car into reverse. "We'll be splashed over the fucking newspapers by morning."

"HQ is compromised. We can't take her there now that they've put the dots together. We need to give this time to blow over."

They share an intense conversation with lingering looks and frowns. It's fascinating to observe. They're almost like two halves of one person.

"You win." Hunter slides a dark pair of sunglasses into place. "This is a temporary measure. Don't make me regret this."

"Regret what?" I dare to ask.

Enzo's eyes meet mine in the rear-view mirror.

"You're coming home with us."

I'm woken up by someone shaking me. Hunter's familiar spicy scent hits my nostrils. After spending so long starved of all contact, it seems I've become sensitive to the slightest smells and tastes.

"Wake up, Harlow. We're here."

Blinking sleep from my eyes, I find his grumpy face softened with exhaustion. He offers me a hand, stepping back to give me space to stretch my limbs.

I accept the offer of help, but my entire body is throbbing with pain. My last pill was several hours ago. Hunter must read something on my face, and he leans in to scoop me out of the car.

I'm placed back on my feet in the middle of a circular driveway. Two other cars are parked nearby—a smaller, sportier model, and one with a soft-top roof painted a beautiful shade of red.

"Where are we?" I say around a yawn.

"Home."

Hunter helps me over to the massive house waiting for us. The open doorway is flanked by two stone pillars, stretching upwards into a brightly lit monster of a building.

It looks old, not that I know much about the real world, let alone buildings.

I like the way these tiny vines seem to creep over the bricks. Dark, glossy leaves contrast against the rich-red brick.

"Your home?"

Hunter gestures inside. "Like I said, this is only a temporary measure while the vampires are chasing us for a story."

"What are vampires?"

Hunter sighs for the hundredth time. "Never mind."

We step into a large entrance painted in a crisp shade of grey. Sparkles reflect off the shining wooden floors from a jewelled light hanging high above us. The effect is mesmerising.

Easing my shoes off, I wince at the pain across the soles of my bandaged feet. I've barely taken a breath before the sound of footsteps against wood races towards us.

A blur of golden fur launches across the room with an excited yip. The toned body of an animal collides with my legs, and I nearly fall over from the sheer size and weight of my attacker.

"Down, Lucky!" Hunter shouts. "Fucking dog."

The creature doesn't listen to her owner. She wraps herself around me, preening as I bury my fingers in her velvet fur. She's a huge dog, reaching almost to my waist with strong, muscular limbs.

"Sorry." Hunter takes off his navy coat and hangs it up, his suit now rumpled. "She gets lonely when we work late."

"It's okay."

"Just push her away if you want."

Lucky seems to sense her owner's bad attitude. She snorts and disappears through a large archway where Enzo's voice greets her. I follow the sound, emerging into a kitchen.

The marble countertops are accentuated with stainless steel and several intimidating appliances. Modern amenities meet classic, expensive charm in a perfect blend of old and new.

Enzo waits for us, leaning against the vast oven top. "Are you thirsty? Hungry? We have some of that crappy protein powder from the hospital."

"Sounds delicious," Hunter mutters sarcastically. "I'd rather pluck out my eyeballs instead of drinking that, but thanks."

"Not for you, jackass. Harlow?"

Shifting my weight, I bite my lip. Will he strike me if I ask for a drink? Tell me that sinners don't deserve to be sated, and instead I must beg for God to forgive me if I want to live?

Enzo's gaze is scorching as he watches me deliberate. He loses patience before I summon the courage to speak. Opening the giant, gleaming fridge, he offers me a bottle of water.

I'm almost afraid to take it. My feet are rooted to the spot as new sights and smells overwhelm me. I recognise all of these objects, and I have no idea how.

"For you," Enzo prompts.

I reluctantly pull the bottle from his grasp. He gives me an encouraging nod and returns to the fridge, pulling two dark-brown bottles out and passing one to Hunter.

The pair of them settle against the kitchen island, taking long pulls from their drinks. Lucky is loudly scarfing her dinner in the corner of the room, her tail wagging happily.

It breaks the tense silence as I stare down at my bandaged feet. I'm searching for something to say and coming up empty. Unanswered questions lay heavy in the air between us.

Enzo clears his throat. "I'll get the guest room set up. We should have some clean sheets and towels after your folks stayed last month."

"Round up Leighton too," Hunter adds. "If he's in."

"Doubt it. Friday night; he'll be out until dawn."

Hunter tosses his empty bottle before loosening his tie. "One less thing to worry about. You hear from Theo?"

"He called to say the reporters have dissipated from the hospital. Probably returned home to write more shitty articles about us."

"Nothing new there."

Hunter absently fiddles with his hearing aid. It seems to be a nervous tick, his impenetrable mask showing a tiny crack of weakness. Enzo disappears upstairs with a tired smile.

"Tomorrow... we need to talk," Hunter finally says. "You should rest for tonight. It's been a long day."

"Talk?"

"We need to discuss what happened to you and where we go from here. I'm offering you our protection, Harlow. It isn't free."

Embarrassment stains my cheeks pink. I can feel the shame burning my insides. I would never take what they've done for me for granted, but the threat is clear, even unspoken.

Hunter is in charge.

I have to do what he says.

They could easily kick me out onto the street to fend for myself. I don't even know where we are, let alone how to function in the world alone. I don't trust them, but I trust the unknown even less.

"I'll tell you what I can. My memory is patchy. Doctor Richards says more of it will come back over time."

Hunter's hand brushes against my arm, startling me back to silence. An unnamed emotion dances in his dark eyes, showing another precious glimpse beneath his armour.

"We'll get them," he promises in a gruff whisper. "The people who hurt you. It's what we do."

His words strangle me to death.

"You c-can't. They're dangerous."

"So are we, Harlow."

I'm overcome by the image of their corpses splayed across the basement's floor, bloated with rot and their skin slowly sloughing off.

Perhaps Pastor Michaels will repeat Abbie's cruel death. He fancied an experiment one day and peeled the skin from her bones with his knife. She died before he got very far.

"This is what we do, what we're trained to do," Hunter reassures calmly. "You don't need to worry about us. Okay?"

"Who else will worry about you?"

My question takes him aback. Hunter stares at me for a moment longer, his lips parted, before he strides away without answering me. I'm left alone in their sparkling kitchen, feeling filthy and out of place.

Lucky returns, her wet nose nudging my belly for attention. While stroking her, I briefly consider grabbing my shoes and hightailing it out of here.

I don't belong somewhere like this, bruised and trembling amongst their expensive possessions. Truthfully... I don't know where I belong. At least in the basement, I knew the status quo.

"Harlow!" Enzo shouts down the stairs.

Shuddering, I fight the instinct to duck and hide. His raised voice tangles with Pastor Michaels' in my mind, and my skin breaks out in terrified gooseflesh.

"Come on up," he adds.

Steeling my spine, I make myself walk out of the kitchen. The curved staircase leading upwards is a challenge, and I'm panting by the time I finally reach the top.

On the second floor, carpets are lit by soft lamps, casting shadows against the cream walls. Everything about their space is masculine, but it still manages to be comfortable, albeit sparse.

"Enzo?" I ask uncertainly.

"I'm in here, little one."

I creep across the hallway towards the last door on the left, passing several others. The room beyond is cloaked in colourful light that beckons me inside with open arms.

Pale-blue walls meet grey carpets, contrasting the lines of dark, polished wood. The room is dominated by a large bed with two bright, multi-coloured lamps on either side.

They remind me of the stained-glass windows in the chapel, dappling coloured shadows across the walls. Huge windows have been cut into the ceiling, revealing the gleam of starlight.

I peek in the attached bathroom, finding even more luxury. Just the idea of running water and a real toilet makes my eyes burn with tears. I've gotten used to the degradation of a bucket.

"We don't have guests often," Enzo says as he finishes fluffing the pillows. "Hunter's parents come and visit sometimes."

Running a hand over the fluffy, grey bedspread, I feel even worse for disgracing this beautiful room. The sheets are crisp and smell like summer nights, full of floral blooms. It was a luxury when that rare scent filtered into the basement.

"I don't know what to say," I reply in a tiny voice.

"You don't need to say anything." He watches me take in the room, wearing another reluctant smile. "Make yourself at home."

I run my fingers over the smooth wood of the bedside table, marvelling at the softness of everything. There's no dripping water, mould or piles of bones. Nothing but clean lines and luxury.

Enzo ducks out, returning with my paper bag of medications and another bottle of water. I accept the pills he drops into my palm without question. I'm hurting too much to care.

"Do you need anything else? I'm no good at sponge baths, but I can show you how to use the shower."

The thought of anything else today makes me want to run and scream. It's all too much. My eyes are drooping with fatigue.

"I'm good, Nurse Enzo," I joke, pulling back the covers on the bed. "Do you mind if I go to sleep?"

"Of course not. My room is across the hall. If you need anything in the night, just shout. I don't sleep much, so I'll hear."

Enzo backtracks, flicking off lights on the way out. Before he disappears, I call his name, mustering a small smile.

"Yeah?"

"Thank you for… well, everything." I unclip my sling to avoid meeting his eyes. "I don't know what I would've done if you guys didn't find me."

"You don't need to thank me."

"Yes, I do. No one's ever looked out for me before."

Enzo rubs the back of his neck, his stubble-strewn cheeks heating up. The sight makes my toes curl in the most extraordinary way. I have no idea what this weird feeling in my belly means.

"You're welcome, Harlow. Get some sleep, alright?"

The door clicks shut behind him. I tentatively climb into the bed, keeping my borrowed clothes in place. The idea of being naked in an unknown place is not appealing.

Everything about this room is so wrong. Laying down, the bed cradles my battered body, and the pillows are softer than air. I'd be more comfortable sleeping in someone else's blood.

Sinners don't deserve clothes or food.

Stop your whining or I'll give you something to cry about.

I stare up at the ceiling. I'm too exhausted to even sleep, my senses on high alert despite my safe surroundings. It's all so new and unknown. I can't handle it.

Leaving the comfort of the bed, I curl up on the carpet in the furthermost corner, keeping a direct view of the door. My broken ribs hate the position, but the pain is a familiar comfort. It reminds me of home.

As sleepless hours pass, I let my flimsy pretence crumble into ruin. My sobs grow louder, more frantic, forcing me to bite down on my fist to remain silent. I don't want anyone to hear me.

I cry until nothing remains in me but broken pieces that I can never fix. I cry for the girl I used to be. I cry for the girl I am now. I cry for all those who lost their lives while I remained alive.

But most of all, I cry because I have no idea what lies ahead. For the first time in my life, I have a potential future. Hope. Maybe a fresh start. That's more terrifying than any punishment I've endured.

CHAPTER 7
LEIGHTON

CONVERSATIONS - JUICE WRLD

THE BOUNCER GIVES me a rough shove. I sprawl across the pavement outside the nightclub, spitting blood. With an exasperated sneer, he leaves me to stumble to my feet.

My jeans are ripped from the fall. In my drunken haze, I can't feel the pain of my busted nose. Some dickhead clocked me right in the face for running my stupid mouth, like usual.

"Fighting again, stretch?"

Diablo smokes a cigarette, standing on the street corner. I stagger over, attempting to remain upright. The whole world is spinning with the litres of alcohol in my veins.

"You seem surprised," I drawl.

"You wanna watch yourself. They'll throw you back in the slammer for that shit." Diablo claps me on the shoulder. "You've only been out for a couple of months."

"Still doesn't feel like returning home."

"Never will again. You come to see those bars as more than brick and mortar," he says, blowing a smoke ring. "I did, anyway. Family means more on the inside than out. You feel me?"

"I have family out here. They don't give a damn whether I'm in or out of prison. Nobody wants to help the family fuck-up."

"Now that ain't true, is it?"

Diablo shouts a taxi down and shoves me in the back, handing off a stack of notes to the driver. He knows my address from previous drunken nights.

Hunter would hang, draw, and fucking quarter my delinquent ass if he knew that. Me and Diablo have become friends after we both got out of prison recently. He understands me a little too well.

I dip in and out as the miles race by. The imposing shadow of my new home welcomes me when the taxi pulls up on the curb. He keeps all of Diablo's money, shoving my drunken ass out with a curse.

By some miracle, I make it to the front gate without falling over and lean in for a retinal scan to allow me inside. Hunter has a stick up his pompous rear end about security.

The rising dawn offers some light as I scratch around, finally unlocking the front door. I have to abandon my beer-stained shoes before clambering upstairs. Everyone must be fast asleep.

Blindly heading for my bedroom, I undo my belt and rip my sweaty shirt over my head. I could sleep for a thousand years after far too many vodka shots and drunken dares. The last girl's lipstick is still smeared on my neck.

Fuck me, she was hot.

Almost worth the right hook.

Eyes already shut, I collapse on the bed with a groan. My head hurts something fierce. Rather than blissful silence, there's a strange squeak before the light slams on.

It quickly escalates into a full-blown, blood-curdling scream. The sound lances through my head like a fucking bayonet.

"ENZO!"

Rolling over, I faceplant on the floor with a grunt. The screaming gets louder and louder, reverberating around the room with soul-sucking terror.

"Harlow!"

There's a thud as the bedroom door slams back open and a bare-chested Enzo arrives like a bat out of hell. Lucky is hot on his heels, her teeth drawn back in a threatening grimace.

"Leighton!" he yells, spotting me on the floor. "What the fuck are you doing in here?"

"Trying to find my goddamn bed," I shout back.

"This isn't your room!"

He approaches the bed, his hands outstretched in a soothing manner. The screaming has died down into a gasping whimper that stabs me in the heart.

Managing to pull myself up, I realise what a mistake I've made. This is the spare room, and there's a shaking wreck in the bed I just tried to climb into. A fucking girl.

Her hazelnut-coloured hair stands up in all directions, like she was deep asleep before I stumbled in here. Beneath a sheet of tears, her sweetheart-shaped face is scrunched up, almost in pain.

Enzo approaches like he's stalking a deer, ready to pounce at any second. He sinks onto the bed, gently wrapping his arms around the sobbing woman.

"It's me, Harlow. Open those pretty eyes."

"Please... d-don't hurt me... I'm sorry for r-running," she stutters through her tears. "I'll pray, I will. Don't hurt me…"

"Come on, little one. Take a nice deep breath."

"I'm s-s-sorry, I'll pray harder…"

"Enzo? A little context would be nice," I complain, managing to find my feet. "Who the hell is this chick?"

"Shut up, Leigh. You're a fucking idiot."

The girl curls into Enzo's side without opening her eyes. Holding her in an intimate embrace, Enzo murmurs quiet instructions to ease her panic attack.

She looks to be in seriously rough shape. I've seen some shit in prison, and this girl's been beaten to within an inch of her damn life. She's covered in bruises, including two stripes down her face.

I've seen enough guys getting their skulls broken against bars to know what causes those marks.

Eventually, she falls silent. Tears cease to streak down her cheeks. Lucky jumps up on the bed, settling by her side. The girl's fingers bury in her fur before she passes out again.

"She's exhausted," Enzo comments. "I found her sleeping on the floor a few hours ago. She barely stirred as I put her back to bed."

Carefully extricating himself, he settles her tiny body back on the bed and pulls the sheets up to her chin. I frown at the alien creature in my friend's body.

Enzo is many things. Brutal. Violent. Unshakeable. Tender is not a word I'd use to describe this tough son of a bitch. I have no idea who's standing in front of me, but it isn't the man I know.

"As sweet as this is, an explanation would be awesome. Who is she, and why was she sleeping on the floor?"

"Call me sweet again and I will crush your skull with my fucking pinkie finger," Enzo warns, grabbing me in a headlock. "Get out."

I'm escorted downstairs, his arm wrapped around my throat like a steel noose. The kitchen lights are now on, sealing my death sentence. I never should've come home.

Hunter's fixing a cup of tea, dressed in a pair of sweats. He spares me an exasperated look as Enzo finally releases me.

"What time do you call this, Leigh?" Hunter's eyes narrow on me. "What happened to you?"

I briefly touch my face, feeling the tender skin around my nose and flecks of dried blood.

"I call this early, Hunt. Some asshole tried to steal my hookup, so I punched him. Turns out, she was his girlfriend. Whoopsie me."

"You're drunk," he deadpans.

"I sure as hell hope so after what I just saw. You seen Enzo around? Someone's hijacked his body and made him go fucking soft."

I'm delivered a smack on the head that makes my ears ring. Enzo's face is downright unnerving. He looks ready to serve my carved-out organs for breakfast.

Hunter takes a sip of tea as he considers me. "You know the rules. Stick to curfew. Keep your nose clean and out of trouble. You should not be stumbling in at five o'clock in the morning."

"Drunk and attacking our house guest," Enzo adds.

"I'm a grown man of twenty-four. I don't need a curfew." I give them my best shit-eating grin. "Since when do we have guests? Let alone hot, screaming ones."

Enzo tries to hit me again, but I dance back, easily dodging his next swing. He's big and strong, but that makes him slow. I'm quick on my feet and well accustomed to defending myself.

"You live under my roof, so you follow the rules," Hunter reminds me.

"Alright, *Dad.* If I mow the lawn, can I get my allowance?"

"Don't be a smartass," Enzo growls.

"You're not my father!"

Slamming his cup down, Hunter faces me with obvious weariness. He looks far older than his thirty-four years. There are ten years between us, but he's always shouldered the burden for us both.

The person I remembered before I was convicted wasn't here when I came out, three years later. A lot of shit went down in my absence. I lost more than just my freedom.

"I'm trying to help you," he spells out. "Giving you a job and a place to stay. Nowhere else would employ a convict. The least you can do is act like you give a damn and respect the house rules."

"You act like I'm some hardened criminal."

"You served time."

"And you love to remind me of that fact!" I shout back. "I'm your fucking brother, not some stranger!"

Enzo steps between us before I can wrap my hands around Hunter's throat. He shoots us both placating looks.

"Harlow is asleep upstairs. Let's not wake her, hmm?"

"Is anyone going to tell me why there's a kid sleeping upstairs?" I ask again.

"She's an adult, and a client," Hunter answers at last.

"A client? In the spare bed?"

"We're keeping her out of the spotlight," Enzo reveals.

"And between your sheets."

Stepping closer, Enzo pins me with an ice-cold glower. "You want to try that again, Leigh? Between what?"

Fearing the integrity of my skull if I push him again, I raise my hands and take a step back. I don't fancy getting squashed by the ogre anytime soon.

"Harlow is part of a case we're working on." Hunter doesn't lift his eyes from his phone. "If you bothered to turn up for work, you'd know all about it. Sleep it off, Leigh. We'll talk when you're sober."

"Yeah, I'll pass on the heart to heart. Thanks for the invite though, bro. Great catching up with you."

Flipping Hunter the bird, I storm from the kitchen, leaving them to bitch about me in peace. The frame rattles as I slam my bedroom door shut like a petulant child.

Fuck being an adult.

Those assholes aren't worth it.

CHAPTER 8
HARLOW

HEART-SHAPED BOX - ASHTON IRWIN

MY ENTIRE BODY feels heavy as I creep downstairs without making a sound. It's getting light outside. After almost two days in bed, I feel slightly more ready to face the world.

I drank the protein shake left on my bedside table and swallowed another handful of meds before going back to sleep yesterday. Nobody disturbed me, but the food and medication had replaced itself when I woke up to pee.

It felt good to sleep, knowing I was safe at last. As soon as I surrendered to exhaustion, that was it. I couldn't move again, barely able to limp to the bathroom before getting back into bed.

The kitchen is blessedly empty. I tip my mouth under the tap and take several frenzied gulps of water. Dribbles run down my chin as I fill my belly, wiping off my mouth when I'm done.

Water on tap. It's a crazy thought to me. I often had to lick droplets from the walls of the basement, relying on leaks and the occasional mercy of my tormentors.

These people have everything.

It reminds me of all I've lived without.

It's raining outside—slanted, silvery bullets that pelt the ground in a rhythmic shower. I trail over to the sliding door that leads to luscious greenery as far as the eye can see. The garden is beautiful.

Lucky trots to my side, her breath fogging up the glass. Petting her head, I twist the lock and step out into the cold air. She breaks into a run, bounding across the lawn with a yip.

My feet carry me into the falling rain. With my head tilted upwards, I can catch the droplets on my tongue. They taste sweet, unlike the putrid water that sustained me for so long.

Lucky finds me in the middle of the lawn, a ball locked between her drooling fangs. She drops it right at my feet.

"You're a real softie, you know that?"

Bending over with gritted teeth, I manage to pick up the ball and toss it across the grass. She chases, her satisfied barking disturbing a cluster of birds. I watch them take flight with awe.

Instead of returning inside, I ease myself down onto the wet grass to watch the world wake up. My bandages are already soaked through, but I tuck my plastered arm inside my hoodie for protection.

The rain is coming down thick and fast, hammering into me like the beat of fists on flesh. It feels exactly as I imagined. My skin is being sloughed off, stripped down layer by layer. I'm being cleansed.

There's this weird smell in the air that comes with a fresh rainfall. I can't get enough of the heady scent. If I could, I'd bottle it and keep it close so it can't be stolen from me again.

That's where Enzo finds me, what feels like hours later, drenched and shivering violently, but more content than I've ever felt. Even Lucky has abandoned me and gone back inside to get warm.

"Harlow? What on earth are you doing?"

His voice startles me from the meditative state I've slipped into. Looking up, I find his angry amber eyes staring down at me.

"Hey," I reply with a smile.

Enzo scans my sopping wet clothes and the tremor of my cold body. He's wearing a pair of loose pyjama bottoms and a tight tank top that exposes the chiselled expanse of his chest, covered in a smattering of dark hair.

"Hey," he echoes. "You're soaking wet."

"So?"

"I don't want you to get sick again. Come inside and warm up before I lose my mind."

"I'm fine out here. It's nice."

"Harlow, it's raining."

Sighing, I wiggle my toes in the wet grass. "I never saw the sky. Raining or not, it's beautiful. The wind makes me feel less alone."

"Why?" Enzo asks with interest.

"It's like the world is screaming along with me."

Sealing his lips, he crouches down and slides his hands underneath my arms. I'm too cold to protest as I'm cradled against his chest, our bodies pressed tightly together. He turns to head back inside.

"Are you hungry?"

I nuzzle his tank top, loving the blanket of warmth his skin provides. "No. I've been drinking the shakes you left for me."

"How do you know it was me?"

"Because Hunter would have woken me up and asked those questions he promised to hit me with."

"Damn, Harlow. You've got him nailed already."

His chest rumbles, vibrating against my cheek. I should be embarrassed, snuggling up to him like a baby bear. Now that we're inside, I can feel just how cold I am. He feels like a furnace.

"Shower," Enzo decides, carrying me upstairs. "You need to warm up. What the hell were you thinking?"

My teeth chatter against each other, silencing my answer. The shower looked so intimidating when I arrived; I don't know if I'll be able to work it. I'm afraid of breaking something.

"I like the cold."

"It isn't good for you though," he argues.

Carrying me back to the bedroom, Enzo shoves open the bathroom door with his shoulder. Inside, the slick, modern en-suite awaits. Dark-slate tiles are matched with silver finishings, the space revolving around a walk-in shower.

He places me down on the counter space next to the sink basin. Protests are lodged in my throat as Enzo begins to unwind the muddied bandages covering my feet, his jaw clenched tight.

The brush of his fingertips against my inner ankles causes a zip of electricity to race down my spine. I almost gasp out loud at the foreign sensation. It's like he's hitting me with tiny, delicious bolts of lightning.

"Your feet are healing well," he mumbles, inspecting the soles of my feet. "The water might sting some of the deeper cuts."

Tossing the dirty bandages, his eyes coast back up to meet mine. There's a hint of nervousness there, a perplexing contrast to the sheer gravity of his physical presence. I manage a shrug.

"The pain doesn't bother me."

"It bothers me." Enzo's hand skates up my leg before he realises and pulls it back.

At the last second, I grab his wrist. Enzo looks startled by my initiation of more contact. I feel comfortable around him in a way that I've never experienced before.

Subconsciously, I'm craving the closeness, desperate to avoid the crushing emptiness of being alone again. That's when the bad thoughts creep back in. I'll do anything to keep them at bay.

"I've survived much worse," I whisper, my thumb resting over the steady pulse of his heartbeat.

"That isn't the comfort you think it is, little one. Surviving is one thing. This is the start of your time to actually live."

Pulling his hand from mine, he clears his throat and moves to turn the shower on. Water cascades from a silver disc in the ceiling, the hot spray creating billowing clouds of steam in the bathroom.

"How do I work it?"

Enzo spares me a glance. "Pull this lever to adjust the temperature, and this one to turn it off. Don't burn yourself."

I'm mesmerised by the waterfall imprisoned in slices of frosted glass. It's like my very own rainstorm. I'd be quite happy to spend all day here.

"I'll find some fresh clothes." Enzo retreats to the doorway. "Leighton's should fit you until we go shopping."

"I'll be fine wearing whatever. No shopping required."

"You need clothes, toiletries, the works."

"I don't need anything," I try again.

"Why are you fighting me on this?"

"You've given me enough."

When I think Enzo is going to give in and return to the gentle giant I know, he closes the space between us again. His expression is stormy as he slowly, deliberately, trails his eyes over my entire trembling body.

"That was then, this is now. You need everything. I'll damn well get it for you, and you'll damn well wear it. Got that?"

I refuse to break eye contact.

"And if I don't?"

"I'm not accustomed to that word, Harlow. You'll learn soon enough. We take care of our own in this house."

With a final pointed look, he leaves me in peace. My heart threatens to break through my ribcage as I stare after his retreating back. Being bossed around by Enzo feels different from the orders I was forced to abide by before.

The ingrained need to obey is there, but without the all-consuming pull of fear. I know he won't hurt me. There's no darkness within him, spitting and writhing in its bid to escape. I've gotten good at sensing it.

Now Hunter, he's a whole other puzzle entirely. I'm fairly certain he hates my guts, even after the limited time we've spent together. I'm only good for one thing to him—information.

What happens when I give it to him?

When does their protection end?

These thoughts plague me as I hide in the shower, holding my plastered arm outside the door at an awkward angle to keep it dry. There are all kinds of bottles lined up, begging to be smelled.

I wash myself over and over again, testing each fragrance and savouring the scented steam. Washing shampoo from my hair is a challenge with only one hand. It brushes my lower back in snarled knots.

After spraining my arm trying to reach the ends, I give up. Washing my hair with bottled water was easier than this. Pastor Michaels would occasionally offer me the luxury of bathing, usually when he was disgusted by the scent emanating from my cage.

Avoiding the fogged-up mirror as I step out, I find a pair of dark-red sweatpants left on the bed. They're too long, bunching around my ankles as I slip on the oversized white t-shirt next.

My feet are sore, but well into the healing process, so I don't bother re-wrapping them. There's no hope for my bird's nest of hair. I try to untangle it with my fingers while trailing back downstairs.

It's still raining outside, obscuring the winter's day in fog and gloom through the large bay windows. After a tentative descent down the stairs, I'm hit by the sound of someone yelping.

"Shit, that's hot."

"You think? The toaster doesn't make it cold, genius."

"Fucking thanks, Hunt. Wanker."

"You're so welcome. Call me that again and I'll tell your parole officer you've been out drinking until sunrise most nights."

"Don't you dare. I'm not above murdering you in your sleep."

With his shirt-covered back to me, Hunter sits at the breakfast bar. For the first time, I notice dark swirls of ink peeking out around his neck. I didn't realise he had tattoos.

The intricate-looking designs are obscured through the blue fabric. His chestnut hair is hanging loose today in glossy waves, complementing his slate-coloured suit.

"Hi," I say awkwardly.

He startles as I limp in, surveying me with a lingering glance. There's a complicated sheet of paper in his hands. It takes a moment for the word to click into place. Newspaper. I know that one.

"Jesus Christ. Cereal it is."

Spinning on the spot, the newbie's eyes flare with surprise. He's dressed in tight sweatpants and a muscle t-shirt that shows off his tanned, lean body. He's shorter than the other two, but stocky and well-built.

I take note of the thick scarring across his knuckles, contrasting the child-like grin on his lips. His hair is shaggy and very overgrown, covering his ears with slight curls in the exact same shade as Hunter's waves.

Propping his elbow on the breakfast bar, he faces me with amusement dancing in his forest-green eyes.

"Well, if it isn't Goldilocks. Risen from the dead!"

Hunter snorts as he returns his attention to the newspaper, dismissing us both.

"I don't know what that means."

"She speaks!" He unleashes a megawatt smile. "I'm Leighton, Hunter's better-looking brother. Sorry for, erm… you know. The other night."

"Trying to get into bed with me?"

His easy grin widens. "Yeah, that."

"You're lucky Enzo didn't knock you out," Hunter comments. "Or worse. He was well within his right to shoot you."

Leighton proudly flexes his biceps. "I reckon I could take him. What say you, Harlow? I think I prefer Goldilocks. You know, the girl that breaks in and sleeps in the bears' beds?"

I choke on thin air. I've got no idea what he's ranting about. Leighton spares me a cheeky wink, returning to prepping his breakfast while humming under his breath.

Seeing no other option, I take the empty bar stool next to Hunter. I can tell he's studying me over his newspaper as I wince while sitting down. The meds I swallowed upstairs haven't kicked in yet.

"Breakfast, Goldilocks?"

Leighton plops a bowl down in front of me, tipping some golden clusters into it from a bright-yellow box.

"What… ah, what is this?"

Leighton's smile falters. "Huh? Cereal?"

"She's on a strict diet from the hospital," Hunter chips in sternly. "Protein shakes for weight gain and light foods only. Not your sugary crap."

Leighton rolls his eyes. "Nobody wants to drink that tasteless shit. Let the girl live a bit."

Staring down into the depths of the bowl, I watch him pour milk in and add a silver spoon. Mrs Michaels brought me milk once, when I helped clean up after a particularly messy night.

It was the only time she was remotely kind towards me. I think she was relieved to have some company in the dark hours after the ritual was complete. When I slipped on a puddle of urine, she soon lost her temper again.

"What are your plans today, Leigh?" Hunter fastens his collar, adding a silk tie. "I'm leaving for the office if you'd care to show your face at work."

Leighton wrinkles his nose in distaste. "It's far too early for the 'w' word. I'll be resuming my *Greys Anatomy* marathon."

"Great. Sounds real productive."

"Someone's gotta make the most of that fancy subscription you pay for. It's a hardship, but I'll shoulder the burden."

Hunter catches me staring as he stands and smooths his trousers, offering me a tiny frown. Panicking, I take a mouthful as a distraction.

My eyes almost roll back in my head. This stuff is insane. I've never tasted anything like it.

"Good?" Leighton smirks.

"It's so… so…"

I shrug, unable to explain the taste of something other than the most basic food to sustain life. Leighton's attention is firmly fixed on my mouth as I take another spoonful.

"Note to self. The girl likes sugar puffs. Very interesting."

I can't help but smile at Leighton's antics.

"I'm off," Hunter interrupts us. "I have an intelligence briefing in an hour." He casts me a look that kills my appetite. "We'll be having that talk later on."

I hug my aching arm to my chest, nodding silently. Leighton casts Hunter a sour look before filling his own bowl with cereal.

"You're killing the fun. Go play scary secret agent. I'll take good care of Harlow." Leighton's voice is light and teasing. "I'm sure we can find some trouble to get up to."

I can't hold in my squeak of shock as Hunter flashes across the kitchen. He grabs hold of Leighton's shirt and pins him against the fridge with a low hiss of fury.

"Keep your hands to yourself or find another place to live. Harlow's under my protection. She doesn't need you messing up what little life she has left."

Leighton shoves him back with significant strength. "Don't touch me. I'm not a child. I know how to conduct myself."

"Do you? Could've fooled me"

"Fuck you, Hunt."

Locked in a bubble of rage, they look ready to kill each other. I want to duck underneath the nearby table and hide from the confrontation.

As Hunter's words sink in, anger replaces my anxiety. Somehow, somewhere, I find the strength to squeeze out a furious sentence.

"My life isn't little."

Hunter gives me a side-look.

"Of course it isn't." Leighton breaks free, brushing his rumpled clothes off with a glower.

"Is that what you think of me?" I ask tearfully.

Looking between us both, Hunter looks lost for words. It's the first time I've seen him unsure of himself. Leaving him spluttering, I clamber down from the stool and walk out without looking back.

Neither of them follows me.

Shame weighs me down like lead.

If that's what Hunter thinks of me, I don't want to be around him. I'd crawl back into my cage if I could at this moment. In that hellish wasteland, I know the rules and expectations.

I can play the game, and play it well.

This place… it's too much.

I want my life to be big. Bigger than the whole world and every last monstrous person in it. The killer blow, though? Hunter's right.

I'll never be more than the pathetic person my parents made me. A broken doll, destined for little more than hell's final taste of oblivion.

He who be worthy shall find redemption.

Get on your knees and pray, Harlow.

Pray for the Lord to forgive you.

Running without seeing, I collapse in a darkened corner. The prayers are already rolling off my tongue on instinct. My fingers slot together as I struggle to kneel despite my injuries.

I recite my prayers for forgiveness four times. Just as I was taught, a lesson forged in the devil's punishing fires. The words are scorched on to the very fabric of my splintered mind.

It still isn't enough.

Nothing will ever be enough.

CHAPTER 9
ENZO

COME UNDONE - MY DARKEST DAYS

AFTER ANOTHER GRUELLING RUN, I pass Hunter leaving in the driveway. His expression is steely as he speeds away in the convertible Mercedes. My exhausted wave is unreturned. Charming.

He doesn't tend to use that car in the winter. We have the company SUV for cooler weather, and the convertible is more of a toy to satisfy his inner adrenaline junkie. Speed limits don't usually stop him.

My phone vibrates in my pocket as I step inside the house.

Brooklyn: Saw you running just now. Talk to me, big guy.

I quickly tap out a response.

Enzo: Stuff on my mind. Call you later.

Her response comes immediately.

Brooklyn: You better. Don't make me come over there.

Tucking my phone away, I bypass the kitchen, needing to shower before dealing with Leighton's attitude. Under the spray, I set the temperature to cold.

It's a trick I've learned over the years. I've barely slept since Harlow came home with us. Her presence has me on high alert for any potential threats, even when I should be asleep.

In the privacy of my shower, she floats back into my mind. That tiny spitfire is never far from my thoughts at the moment. Her crystal-clear, innocent eyes, and the small curves that round her body.

I should be fucking ashamed as I wrap my hand around my cock. Head lowered beneath the spray, I work my shaft in fast pumps. All I can think about is the feel of her gripping my wrist earlier.

She's so small and delicate, even for a twenty-odd year old. I'd break her if I touched her. But that doesn't stop me from fantasising about a world where I could cross the professional boundary between us.

When I've grunted my release, I wash off and step out of the shower. Guilt twists in my gut. The last thing Harlow needs is me fucking up her life. She's facing enough shit as it is.

Scraping a hand through my wet hair, I bypass my work clothes and throw on a pair of ripped, black jeans with a plain tee. Hunter can take care of Sabre alone today; I've had enough of his foul mood.

My priority is Harlow. I won't leave her alone in a world that she has no knowledge of. Fuck the rules. Someone has to look after her. Why shouldn't that be me? I can keep things professional.

Lightly knocking on her bedroom door, I peek inside. Her bed has been neatly made and lies empty. She was still in the shower when I left to go running.

Heading downstairs, I find Leighton bustling around the kitchen. He's washing up empty bowls while cursing to himself, the ceramics clattering as they're tossed about.

"Are you cleaning?" I watch in disbelief.

He casts me a glare. "I'm not some uncivilised caveman."

"Isn't that what people go to prison to become?"

"Ha ha, fucking hilarious. Hunter upset your girlfriend."

"She's a client, not my girlfriend."

"Whatever, man. She's refusing to come out or speak to me, so I'm trying to do something useful here instead."

"Why didn't you call me?"

Leighton tosses the tea towel down with exasperation. "Not everything is my fault, you know? Fuck this. I'll be upstairs."

Leaving him to continue pouting, I tear through the house. Hunter's book-lined office is deserted, along with the formal dining room that we don't use, and the downstairs gym.

When I attempt to open the sliding door that leads into the den at the back of the house, it refuses to budge. Something's barricading it.

"Harlow? It's me. Can you let me in?"

"Go away, Enzo," her timid voice replies.

"Not a chance. You have ten seconds to open this door before I break it down."

After five seconds, my very limited patience expires. The chair she had propped under the handle splinters as I use my shoulder to smash the door open by force. It falls off its hinges with a pained groan.

Shoving the destroyed door aside, I squint to see into the pitch-black room. The navy-blue curtains are drawn against the rainy day, adding to the darkness. This room is where we spend most of our time together, limited as that may be these days.

It's a generous family space, lined with stained black flooring and light, panelled walls. There's a huge log burner in the centre of the room, surrounded by perfectly cut wooden logs packed into the sides of the fireplace.

Above it, we have a top-of-the-line flat screen television and sound system Hunter insisted on when movie nights used to be a common occurrence. Two dark-green, velvet sectionals fill the floor, with cosy cushions and blankets.

The thick, woven rug beneath my bare feet adds a final layer of warmth. Hunter and Leighton's mum used to work as an interior designer. She took one look at our sparse, lifeless house and insisted on making it a home.

"Harlow? I can't see a damn thing. Where are you?"

"Leave m-m-me alone," she hiccups.

I flick on a lamp and follow the sound of quiet sobbing until I find her. She's curled up in the furthermost corner, half hidden by a towering bookshelf that fills the back wall.

I'm afraid to even go near her for fear she'll splinter into a thousand pieces. I'm no shrink like Doctor Richards. Hell, I can hardly understand my own bloody head. This is all new territory for me, but I can't stand helpless as another person dies.

Not again.

"You want some company?"

Harlow stares blankly over my shoulder, tears running down her cheeks in thick rivulets. Crouching down, I join her on the floor, folding my body into the uncomfortable corner.

The little ballbreaker has staked a claim on me already. Each second I spend around her only cements that bond even more. Despite the past, I always help people in need. It's hardwired into my DNA to look after the vulnerable.

"Enzo... am I broken?"

Taking a leap of faith, I prise her hands away from her face, revealing devastating doe eyes that resemble the lightest tropical ocean.

"Broken? No. Perhaps a little damaged, but it's nothing we can't fix."

"You don't know me. I c-can't... be fixed."

Engulfing her hands in mine, I squeeze lightly. "You're still here, aren't you? That's one hell of an achievement."

"Is it, though?"

"Yes," I assure her. "You're doing better than you think."

She nods to herself. "Can we get out of here or something?"

I weigh up the risks, daggered by the desperate look in her eyes. She looks like she's going insane, trapped in this house with us.

"Please?"

Her final plea breaks my resolve.

"Hunter's going to fucking fire me for this." I offer her a hand. "Let's go. We can go somewhere out of the city to avoid the press."

Harlow lets me help her up, brushing off her oversized, borrowed clothes. I ignore the fact they belong to Leighton, and how much that annoys me. My possessive asshole is clearly in overdrive.

Throwing on my leather jacket in the entrance hall, I watch as Harlow shrugs on her hospital hoodie. She cringes at the sight of her unlaced Chucks on the shoe stand.

Grabbing the shoes, I gesture for her to take a seat on the stairs. Her mobility is still limited, but she seems to be moving with slightly less pain than when she first arrived.

"Foot," I demand.

"I can give it a go."

"Watch one more time, alright?"

Easing the shoe on her left foot, I take my time tying the laces, giving her a moment to observe. She reaches for the second shoe and awkwardly ties a bow, favouring her unbroken arm.

"Quick learner?"

Harlow stares at her feet. "Apparently."

"Sure you haven't done this before?"

"At this point? I don't know."

I plaster on a neutral expression to conceal my worry. The disturbing gaps in her memory are on the long list of issues we need to discuss now that she's awake.

Rifling in the cupboard under the stairs, I come up with a worn denim jacket that should fit over her hoodie. It smells like Leighton—the bitter tinge of cigarettes with a citrus undertone.

"Put this on, it's cold out."

Harlow accepts the jacket and slides one arm in, folding the other over her cast. "Thanks."

"That looks good on you!" a smug voice calls out.

Bounding down the staircase like an excited puppy, Leighton is dressed in faded blue jeans and an old band t-shirt, his shaggy hair still wet from the shower. He's an unashamed Aerosmith fan, courtesy of his obsession with nineties movies. He's made us watch *Armageddon* at least ten times.

The motherfucker must have overheard us talking in the den. He shoots me a bright grin, then offers Harlow a hand up before I can.

"Mind if I tag along?"

She looks uncertain. "Why are you asking me?"

"Because your voice is heavenly, kitten."

I choke on a barked laugh. Fuck me gently. Even Harlow cracks a smile. Rolling with the punches, Leighton mock-sighs as he steers her outside into the rain.

Kicking him out of the shotgun seat so Harlow can ride up front, I boost her into the SUV. The feel of her hips in my palms nearly breaks my resolve. I can't seem to keep my hands off her.

I have to grit my teeth as I slam her door and head for the driver's seat. Leighton has slipped into the back, his feet propped up as he scrolls on his phone with a half smile.

"Alright, rules." I pin him with a stare. "No funny business. Harlow shouldn't even be leaving the house. Don't make me regret letting you come along."

"What do you take me for?" He frowns.

"I mean it, Leigh."

"Yeah, I got it. Loud and clear. So, what are we doing?"

Stopping for a retinal scan to unlock the gate, I take a right towards the main road out of London. "Harlow needs some stuff."

"I don't," she replies shortly.

"You do. Don't argue with me, Harlow."

Lips pursed, she looks out of the window. "Someone's got to."

Leighton smirks at me. "Hah. Is this your first lovers' quarrel? That's cute. We should commemorate the occasion."

"Shut the fuck up before I leave you on the side of the road."

We head through the rainy suburbs, merging into the morning traffic. The city is the last place we should take Harlow. Anonymous or not, her safety is paramount.

"What kind of stuff are we getting?" Leighton breaks the silence.

"She has nothing."

"At all? How is that possible?"

Harlow's face empties of all emotion as she slips back into blank numbness. Leighton knows a little of our work from the first few weeks he bothered to turn up to HQ, before he got bored.

Prison changed him. He isn't the carefree kid I once knew. He was always troubled, growing up in Hunter's impressive shadow, but that place stole the last of his youthful innocence.

"Is this something to do with... *that* case?"

I glower at him in the mirror. "Yes."

"You mean the serial k—"

"Yes."

Leighton averts his eyes with a nod. The bright-red tinge that spreads over Harlow's cheeks is simultaneously adorable and infuriating. I hate that she feels ashamed.

"Could've told me," Leighton says under his breath.

"Could've asked."

"I hate that you guys keep secrets from me."

"Show any amount of interest in the life Hunter is trying to build for you, and you won't feel so left out."

"You're being unfair."

I stare at the road ahead. "Life isn't fair. I think you'll find there's more to the world than the bottom of a liquor bottle."

Leighton sulks until we pull into a quiet shopping centre nearly an hour later. Harlow wakes up from her nap as we park, her eyes lit with excitement at our new surroundings.

Leaving Leighton to retrieve a trolley, I help her down from the car and pull a purple beanie from my pocket. She lets me tug it over her long hair, then I add a spare pair of Hunter's aviators.

"I look ridiculous," she murmurs.

"Better to look ridiculous and stay safe."

"You think the reporters will be here?"

"They'll be camped outside of HQ. The press are looking for the other missing person. Like I said, we didn't know about you."

She seems to cave inwards, her shoulders hunching and chin dipped down. I can't protect her from the truth forever. She's in for a grilling when Hunter returns home anyway.

"How long has she been missing for?" Harlow asks.

"About two months."

"And you think it's the same people that held me?"

I catalogue her nervous twitching. "It fits the same MO. Our killer follows a pattern. We're certain he snatched this victim."

"Does she have a name?"

I decide to take a risk.

"Laura Whitcomb."

Harlow lurches to the side and promptly vomits across the car park. I spur into action, rubbing her back and shouting for Leighton to return. People are watching us with concern.

"You're okay," I whisper, shielding her from sight.

"Stop saying that! I'm n-not... nothing is... no."

It's the first time I've heard Harlow raise her wispy voice. Wiping her mouth, she pins me with a devastated look. I suddenly regret pushing too soon.

"She's dead. Laura's gone."

"How do you know?"

"I… watched him carve her into pieces. She died a long time ago. You won't ever find her."

Distraught tears are streaming down her cheeks, leaking pain and suffering that I can't take away. It only adds to the simmering anger that's kept me awake since we took on this fucking case.

"Who killed Laura? Tell me."

"I c-c-can't," she stammers.

"Why not?"

"He will k-kill all of you."

Leighton chooses that moment to reappear, plastering on a cheery smile that I'd love to wipe off with my fist. We haul Harlow up, her featherlight body balanced between us.

"Let's go home," I decide, unlocking the car. "This was a bad idea. It's too much for you."

Harlow yanks her hand from mine. "No, I want to do this. My life... it's not little. It can't be little."

I have no idea what she means. Leighton seems to understand and offers her a smile.

"You got it, Goldilocks. Come on, let's get you out of those sweats before you give Enzo an aneurysm. He's the jealous type."

He traps her in place with his arms braced on either side of the trolley. It's another invasion of her personal space, but Harlow doesn't seem to mind the closeness right now.

In fact, I'd argue her body is craving the familiarity of human touch while she's so lost and afraid. Blowing out a breath, she forces herself to calm down. Fuck if it doesn't take my breath away.

Letting them head inside, I retrieve my phone from the pocket of my leather jacket and hit Hunter's name. He answers on the second ring.

"Rodriguez."

"Hey, I've got something."

"Talk to me."

My sigh rattles down the line. "Whitcomb is already dead."

"Where did you get that from?"

"Harlow."

Hunter hollers at someone in the background, ordering them to clear the room. He should be in an intelligence meeting about our upcoming narcotics raid right about now.

We've been playing cat and mouse with a large crime syndicate for several months. The next two weeks will be crucial as we wrap the case up. When he comes back on the line, his voice is bleak.

"Not exactly unexpected. Did she witness it?"

"I think so. Richards needs to be there to take her full statement. I'm worried about how Harlow will react."

"If Whitcomb's dead and Harlow escaped, this son of a bitch will be out there right now, stalking his next victim."

"She's not ready," I reply softly.

"Fuck, Enz. We have the government breathing down our necks and more resources invested in this than I care to admit. I need results."

"Hunter, ease up. We have to do this right."

There's a long, pregnant pause.

"I'll speak to Richards about setting something up. He can be there to supervise. You can't protect her forever though."

"I'm just playing this smart." I rub the ache between my eyes. "She's no good to us rocking in a corner. We can't catch this guy without her help."

Theo's voice filters through from the background. As head of the intelligence department, he works closely with some of our best agents. The legwork behind this raid has kept him busy for months.

"I'm coming," Hunter replies to him. "Theo's traced Harlow hitchhiking on four different vehicles so far. I have samples from forensics to have a DNA test done for her."

"You think she has a family?" I guess, feeling sick at the thought.

"No one's looking for her. She's a ghost, but we have to be thorough. We need new leads to identify the killer."

"What about the raid this week? We've been planning it for months. Everything is in place."

"I need you here to run point," he answers firmly. "This operation requires our full attention. Theo will keep working on Harlow's case."

The line goes dead, and I stare at my phone for a few seconds. My loyalties should lie with my best friend, my company, and the ongoing investigation. Sabre matters above all else.

It's the family I've created for myself, one case at a time. Our ranks are made up of talented individuals, all let down by the world. I've found friends for life, family even, in the bleakness of my profession.

I can't let Harlow threaten our equilibrium. Regardless of the pathetic scrap of hope it offers to my cold heart to be needed by someone again.

CHAPTER 10
HARLOW

SPEAKING OFF THE RECORD - HOTEL MIRA

THE PEN SHAKES in my hand as I'm overcome by trembling. Each word I manage to write is wobbly, like a child's love letter. Just recalling the names I can remember has exhausted me.

Little details come back to me with each word. Hair colours, broken smiles, heart-wrenching stories shared in the dead of night. All of the girls had someone they loved, even from afar.

He took that from them.

Worst of all, I know there are others. Their identities are blurred in my mind, like polaroid photos with the faces scratched out. It's killing me to know that I've forgotten them.

Slamming the pen down, I grab handfuls of my stupidly long hair. My heart is beating too fast. Pumping blood. Keeping my vital organs alive. Suspending me in life, when all I deserve is death.

Tugging on my hair, I gasp as a few strands come away in my hands. The sizzle of pain is a welcome distraction. Breathing deeply, I wrap a thin strand around my fingers.

Pain cleanses us of all our sins.

We suffer for him.

Fire races across my scalp as I pull again, harder this time. The strands rip away from my head with a faint pop. It hurts even more, and I nearly cry from the relief.

"God loves us for our labours," I whisper hoarsely.

Staring down at the list of girls that looked into my eyes before they took their last breath, I feel physically sick. None of them had to die. I scrawl another name at the bottom, biting back a sob.

Harlow Michaels.

I should've joined them on this deathly list. The night he carved his marks into my flesh, I saw the fabled light. It was so close, inches away. I could almost taste it on my tongue.

Why did I survive, when they didn't? For what purpose did God spare my life? There has to be a reason for all this pain and bloodshed. I can't live in a world where the darkness exists for no goddamn reason.

"Goldilocks? You awake?"

I'm still staring at the scrawled list when Leighton trails into my bedroom. He stops at the end of the bed, noting the paper clutched in my hands.

"Harlow?"

My eyes snap up to his. "Yes?"

"Are you… erm, alright?" His brows draw together in a worried frown. "I mean, you don't look alright. Like, at all."

My fist closes around the piece of paper before he can spot the names. Blood is pumping through me so fast, I feel dizzy with the steady, relentless throb. It's an endless taunt.

Alive.

Alive.

Alive.

A hand brushes my shoulder, startling me from my daze. I shoot upright so fast, my knees crumple. Leighton catches me halfway down to the thick carpet.

"Woah, easy."

My hand bunches in the soft material of his blue t-shirt. He wraps his arms around me as we both fall backwards onto the neatly made bed.

"Harlow?" Leighton repeats urgently.

"Sorry," I stumble out. "Lost m-my balance."

He doesn't loosen his grip on my body. "Don't scare me like that, Goldilocks. What's on the piece of paper?"

Forcing myself to relax, I lean into his embrace. He smells like a tantalising cocktail of lemon and lime, the fragrances clinging to his overgrown hair. I love the way it spills over his ears without a care in the world.

"The past," I answer quietly. "Are they back yet?"

"Nope." Leighton shifts, still keeping one arm around me. "Enzo texted to check in on us though."

"It's been days since Hunter left." I bite my lip so hard, blood leaks into my mouth. "What's he waiting for? I thought he wanted to… you know, interrogate me."

"They're snowed under with some urgent operation. I wouldn't worry. The longer Hunter's away, the better for all of us."

I glance up at him. "Why don't you two like each other?"

"It's complicated." He shrugs, his eyes straying away. "Shall we watch a movie or something? I'm bored."

"You're always bored."

Leighton smirks. "I spent all morning setting Hunter's stationary in jelly. The stapler's taking a while to set."

"Wait, what?"

He finally stands, stretching his arms up so high, his t-shirt rides up. My throat suddenly tightens. I can see a flash of his firm, washboard abs, covered by a carpet of soft fuzz.

"You know, like the scene in *The Office*? He's been a dick recently. It's only fair."

I make myself look away from the slither of skin that's setting my pulse rate high. Leighton's been my only company for the last few days as I've rested up, alternating between napping, showering, and choking down protein shakes with pain meds.

He loves physical affection, which took some getting used to. I wasn't prepared when he brought me a grilled cheese the other day and climbed into bed to chat while I ate.

The casual touches and whispers of motiveless affection were unnerving at first, but I'm slowly adjusting to Leighton's constant need for assurance and attention. He's a sweet person.

"I don't know what you're talking about, Leigh."

His nose crinkles with adoration at the offhand nickname. "You're kidding, right? You've never seen it?"

I shake my head.

"What about *Friends*?"

"Like, did I have any friends?"

"No." His expression grows even more horrified. "The show, Harlow. *Friends*? No?"

My cheeks burn. "Not a clue."

Cursing under his breath, Leighton snatches the screwed-up piece of paper from my hand before I can react. Panic rushes over me, but he simply tosses it onto the dresser and offers me his hand.

"We're rectifying this situation immediately. You're not going to sit here and wait for Hunter to come home. We've got catching up to do."

Gently pulling me up, he grabs the discarded mustard cardigan I left hanging on the wardrobe door and tucks it around me. My heart stutters at the thoughtful gesture.

"Enzo needs to buy you some more shit," he complains, taking my hand again. "Those bags we got the other day weren't enough."

I'm dragged out of the room, his skin burning into mine like a cattle brand. All I can smell is his citrusy shower gel, clinging to his skin in a delicious, inviting cloud.

"He bought way too much."

Leighton gives me a side look. "Yeah, that really wasn't a lot."

Making it downstairs with several aching ribs and a lot of controlled breathing, Leighton guides me into the den. I'm steered towards the huge sofa and dumped in a nest of cushions.

"Get comfy," he orders with a stern look. "Doctor's orders."

Taking the other corner, Leighton stretches his toned legs out. He's dressed for a rainy afternoon, his sweats well worn and fitted perfectly to his muscular frame.

Grabbing a knitted blanket, he covers me with it and fusses over me like a mother hen. His half smile is amused as I squirm and evade his touch-feely hands.

"We can't have you catching a cold on my watch," he explains. "Enzo threatened to mount my head on a spike outside the house if I don't keep you safe."

"Safe from what?" I gesture around the room. "This place is a fancy prison. There are even people guarding our cell."

"They're outside for security, apparently." Leighton settles in while flicking through channels. "Ever seen a movie?"

His questions are always subtle, slipped into casual conversation. Bit by bit, my secrets are being unravelled.

I hum a noncommittal response.

"That's a no then. Mystery girl, you're killing me here."

"Your indecision over my nickname is killing me," I reply without thinking.

Leighton barks a laugh. "What can I say? You're impossible to pin down, Goldilocks. I'll figure you out someday."

"Good luck with that."

"Is that a challenge?"

"Not in the slightest."

Settling on a movie, the screen erupts in an explosion of colour. Cars battle each other in the opening scenes, racing at breakneck speed through a flash of gunfire.

"Shit," Leighton curses. "Are you okay with an action movie? I didn't think."

I'm so entranced by the screen, I don't answer him. The scene changes, depicting a rich, vibrant city glittering with lights. I'm tempted to touch the TV, desperate to experience the alternate reality within its glass walls.

It doesn't matter how I know what the magical contraption is. Like most things, I'm learning not to question it. There are a lot of items in this house that are familiar, even if I can't remember why.

"Hunter hates these kinds of movies," Leighton reveals, his foot brushing mine. "He's a closeted rom-com lover."

"Rom-com?"

"Fluffy shit."

I snuggle into the soft blanket. "Hunter doesn't strike me as a… um, fluffy person."

Choking on a laugh, Leighton grins at me. "I love it when you say exactly what you're thinking."

"Is that a bad thing?"

"Hell no. You should do it more."

We refocus on the movie as a fight scene unfolds. I shock myself by watching the whole thing, repressing a shiver when blood sprays against the heavy beat of fists.

By the end of the movie, I'm hanging on to the edge of my seat and ready for more drama. Stories have always fascinated me. My world was so small for so long, I learned to cling to the scraps I received.

Most of the girls spoke to me. Some told me all about the intricate details of their lives. Hopes, dreams, passions. I lived vicariously through them, and it was the most freedom I ever felt.

Humming under his breath, Leighton flicks the TV over to something else. A group of friends are trading jokes over coffee—a black, sludge-like liquid in their cups.

"That looks so gross."

He collapses back into laughter. "Enzo drinks coffee like he's mainlining heroin. You should smell his breath."

"It smelled okay to me."

Rolling onto his side, Leighton ignores the TV and watches me instead. "You're a breath of fresh air."

"Huh?"

"We live in a world where everyone knows everything." His green eyes scour over me. "And in walks this gorgeous creature who can't name cereal brands or recognise a show like *Friends*."

We stare at each other, the show disregarded. There's something in the way that Leighton looks at me—an almost playful challenge, like he's daring me to prove him wrong.

He sees me differently than the others. I'm not treated like broken glass, a second away from implosion. Leighton is sensitive, but he still talks to me like we're two normal friends, hanging out.

"You're an enigma, Harlow."

"Well, I'm not sure I like that nickname."

Still chuckling, he bounces off the sofa in a blur of energy and disappears into the kitchen. When he returns, balancing two plastic bowls, I quickly grab one before he drops it on my head.

"What is this?" I ask quizzically.

Plonking himself down several inches closer to me, he indicates for me to help myself. I take a sniff of the contents, assaulted by sweet and salty scents. My mouth immediately waters.

"Popcorn," Leighton says around a mouthful.

"Pop…corn?"

"Like popped corn, mixed with butter and stuff."

"That makes no sense. Are you just making this up?"

Shaking his head, Leighton grabs a piece of popcorn and holds it in the air. His hand travels closer to my closed mouth. With the food pressing against my lips, he raises an eyebrow in challenge.

"Open up."

"No chance."

"Don't you trust me?" he asks simply.

Unable to resist the draw of his wide, impish smile, I relent and take a bite. Flavours burst across my tongue, causing me to moan before I can stop myself.

"Woah. S'good."

"Told you." Leighton nudges my shoulder playfully. "Have at it. Put some meat on those bones."

We lapse back into comfortable silence as the show plays. He's so relaxing to be around, more so than the others. Their intensity is a lot for me to handle, but Leighton's like a cool, welcome breeze on a blistering summer's day.

Stretching his legs back out, he sneaks underneath my blanket. With his knee brushing mine, I have to work on breathing through the automatic brush of anxiety. While he does make me feel at ease, the implicit trust I feel around him is even scarier.

"Harlow? Do you mind if I ask you a question?"

Leighton's voice is gentle and coaxing, tuned to melodic perfection. I'm unable to fight his siren's call.

"I guess so."

"I was wondering if you'd tell me about what happened to you?"

I choke on a mouthful of popcorn, chasing it down with a gulp of bottled water. Leighton looks contrite beneath his haphazard hair, dropping his eyes to our blanketed legs.

"I d-don't… ah, why?" I splutter.

"I'm not spying for Hunter, if that's what you're thinking," he answers sadly. "I just… I like spending time with you."

My voice catches. "I… like being with you too."

"Well, I wanted to know if there's anything I should be doing, or anything I *can* be doing, to help you. No matter how small."

His words make my stomach do this weird flippy thing that's usually reserved for Enzo's soft glances. I stuff the unknown feeling down to the depths of my heathen soul.

The guys said it themselves. This is only temporary. Once they have what they want—the sinister information buried deep in my brain—who knows where I'll be sent.

This little slice of respite is bound to expire. Letting them in will only make it hurt more. When I let the girls get close to me, it killed another fractured piece of my heart to watch them die.

"My, ah, the people that, erm… they are very religious. Where I came from, that is," I explain awkwardly.

"How so?"

I take a deep breath for courage. "Pastor Michaels' job is to punish the sinners. He calls it redemption, but it's not."

"Pastor Michaels? That's his name?"

Exhaustion has loosened my tongue. Despite getting more rest than I ever achieved in the freezing cold darkness, I feel more drained than ever. Lying is too hard.

"Yeah."

"And does he help many of these… sinners?"

Our eyes meet—cerulean on viridian, confidence on terror. His inner light is calling to my darkness, demanding the truth. I'm powerless to hide my internal torment.

"Yes, many," I choke out. "Too many."

"I'm so sorry, Goldilocks."

Leighton's scarred hand reaches out and takes mine. His skin is rough, calloused, contrasting with his endearing exterior. I'd love to know how he got his scars, and what anguish lies beyond his facade.

"But you know, you're free now," he adds.

"To do what?"

Leighton's sparkling smile isn't cocky or full of his usual swaggering confidence. It's simple, sweet. Like he's genuinely interested in helping me rebuild from the ruins of my life.

"Whatever you want. I can help you."

"For what possible reason?" Tears sear the backs of my eyes. "You don't know me. Hunter made it clear; I'm just another job."

"That isn't true."

"Yeah, it is. Once it's over, I'll be gone."

"What makes you think that?" Leighton snaps, his voice turning dark and dangerous.

It takes a moment for me to find the right words. I'm enraptured by the anger twisting in his irises, rising to the surface. The truth slips free.

"Because people don't like to look at broken things. Look at me, Leigh. Take a long, hard look. Nobody wants this weak, stupid person around forever."

His hand is still in mine, tightening like a noose. I don't pull away. His gaze is cutting into me, sharp and painful, burning with defiance.

"I'm looking, Harlow. I see you."

Warmth cradles my heart, beginning to thaw the icy edges. He sees me. Somebody actually sees me.

"You do?" I whisper back.

Leighton's lips twist in a tiny smile. "I do."

Giving my fingers one last squeeze, he releases my hand and looks back at the screen, his throat working up and down. What is he feeling? Thinking? Does he feel the same way I do? I can't decipher the emotion on his face.

I stare at him for a moment, contemplating. My fingertips still tingle from where they were wrapped around his, mourning the loss of touch. I decide to take a leap into the unknown.

"Leighton?"

"Yeah?" He spares me a hopeful glance.

Licking my dry lips, I try to find a smile just for him.

"Thank you for being here."

He reciprocates without a beat of hesitation, his smile far brighter and happier than mine. I'm dazzled by it, caught in the sun's devastating rays of pure light.

"Anytime, Goldilocks. I'll always be here."

CHAPTER 11
HARLOW

WITHOUT YOU - PLTS

AFTER MORE RESTING, recuperating and learning all about Gotham's eccentric conveyor belt of villains, Leighton is snoring his head off next to me. There's popcorn stuck to his face while three-day stubble is smattered across the strong line of his jaw.

Grabbing a blanket, I tuck him in and take the time to pick the kernels from his cheek. He shudders a little at my gentle touch, seeming to go on high alert.

I slow my movements, letting my fingers stroke against his skin. We've spent a lot of time together in the past week, our solitude broken by regular text messages from Enzo and his men patrolling outside the front gate.

A tiny, almost imperceptible whimper escapes Leighton's lips. His eyes are moving behind his shut lids, battling an invisible enemy. Waiting for him to drop back off, I untangle our entwined limbs.

There's more behind his carefree exterior.

I've seen darkness in him too.

Sneaking my way out of the den, I catch sight of the fading sun outside. Anticipation slips down my spine. Lucky is nipping at my heels as I sneak through the French doors without stopping to grab a coat.

I don't care about the cold. This has become our nightly routine in the last few days, come rain or shine. Once outside, icy air wraps me in its familiar embrace.

I begin the long, peaceful walk around the perimeter of the garden. It's huge, littered with shrubbery and twisted, gnarly trees. Lucky trots by my side, yipping occasionally.

We circle the garden, inspecting the falling leaves that paint the scene in orange and yellow. Autumn is surrendering itself to the harsh reality of winter in a riot of warm, burnished colours.

"Here we go," I whisper, sinking to the wet grass.

Lucky settles by my side, her strong body curled against mine. I stroke every part of her, from her velvet ears to her shimmering, golden coat. She licks my cheek in return.

Laura had a dog when she was a kid. Something called a Staffie. She talked to me a lot. I know she hated her job, using her body to make money. Her brother was the only family she had left.

Every night, she'd walk the streets, convincing herself to keep going in his name. Each penny she earned would free him from a life of poverty that didn't afford her the same opportunities.

Laura was smart and fiery. Unapologetically alive. She loved sunny days and hated snow—cold weather meant less work. Her entire existence revolved around the life she was determined to build for her sibling.

We're going to get out of here, Harlow.

I'll show you the sun.

I promise. Together.

With my eyes on the blazing horizon, I feel my tears flow again. After all these years, I finally see what I've been missing—the unparalleled beauty of the world as it falls asleep.

This is my new favourite time of day. I can almost feel Laura's ghost next to me. In my imagination, her bloodied hand rests on mine as she watches the sunset with me.

When I look to the side, I can see her flowing auburn hair and sweet, gentle gaze. She smiles, piercing the numbness that's wrapped around my bones. Reaching out, I try to cup her cheek, but my fingers pass straight through her, and she vanishes.

My hand hangs in the air, limp and useless. I'm staring at nothing. Laura isn't really here. I'm alone. Every step I've ever taken has been utterly alone. Laura is dead. She begged for the abyss and left me to face the devil without her by my side.

"I'm so scared, Lucky," I admit brokenly.

The dog butts my shoulder in response.

"What happens now? How am I supposed to… live?"

My aching eyes sink shut as the sun disappears, the final rays gone from sight. A sudden shiver rolls over me as feeling returns, but I don't move to return inside.

The numbness comes and goes every day. Sometimes it lasts for hours, and I stare at the TV screen, feeling detached and unreal. It makes me feel so lost and out of control.

Teeth gritted, I take a handful of hair and separate the individual strands. It burns as I pull them, one at a time, letting the hair fall to the grass. Each burst of pain punches through my numb shield.

Pull.

Pull.

Pull.

A small pile gathers. I feel sick with shame just looking at it. I don't need

Doctor Richards to tell me this isn't normal. Sometimes, I catch myself doing it without realising, surrounded by torn-out hair.

It's all about pain.

Control.

Clarity.

This is the only thing that works.

Coming back to my senses, awareness slams into me like an avalanche. The numb sense of detachment slowly abates. Until next time, I'm back in my body.

"Harlow? Are you out here?"

Quickly blowing the hair away, I pull Lucky closer and remain tucked away from sight. There's a string of curses before silence resumes, an empty chorus to my never-ending supply of tears.

No matter how much I pull or make myself hurt, I can't remove the image of Laura's mouth foaming with blood from my memories. Her eyes connected with mine one final time between the bars as I sobbed uncontrollably.

Ignoring Lucky's whines, I painfully position myself on my knees, linking my stiff fingers together. The cast on my arm makes it difficult, but I've been in worse states.

When Mrs Michaels broke my other arm all those years ago, I could barely move. It must have been for months, because at least two girls came and went during that time.

"Please, forgive me of my sins," I recite shakily. "I don't know where I belong in this world. Show me the path of the righteous."

There's shouting from back inside the house, sounding far away with the sprawling gardens hiding me from sight. The bluster of loud, frantic voices threatens to distract me.

An argument is rumbling somewhere. I remain focused, reciting the words scored across my heart. I'm so wrapped up in the ritual, I don't notice the pad of tentative footsteps.

"For fuck's sake. Shouldn't have brought her home."

Startling, I peek open an eye. Hunter inches around the perimeter of the grounds, holding something in his hands. He looks rumpled, his blue shirt wrinkled and collar ripped open, while his loose hair stirs in the wind.

Before I can slink away, Lucky starts barking. *Traitor.* His head cocks, tracking the sound with the ease of a well-trained bloodhound.

"Shut up, damn dog," he curses.

There's a distinct, metallic click. I peer through my curtain of tears long enough to see Hunter tuck a gun back into the leather strap wrapped around his shoulders.

"Harlow?"

"Go away, Hunter," I plead.

"That's not gonna happen. Get your ass up right now."

His furious tone makes me flinch. I bite down on my inner cheeks hard enough to draw blood, bracing myself for the inevitable strike. I knew this was too good to last.

Maybe he'll beat me with his belt or lock me in some evil basement beneath their beautiful home. He has the devil in him. I can see it imprinted across his skin like a mirage.

"What are you doing?" he thunders.

I whimper in response, my eyes flinging open to meet his.

"Fuck, love." He looks mortified, his face paling. "I'm not going to hit you. Alright?"

With a shuffle, the terrifying pillar of power sits down opposite me, crossing his broad legs in the grass. Hunter's face is an open wound of guilt as he intently studies me.

"What are you doing out here?" he asks more gently.

"I l-like… watching the s-sunset."

"You do?"

I manage a timid nod. "It's… peaceful."

Hunter runs a hand over his messy hair. Chestnut flyways are pointing in every direction. He looks so tired, his beard less sculpted and more caveman-like as it grows out.

Part of me wants to take care of him and ensure he's okay. I've seen enough people suffer to build a hatred for the pain of others. He can't have slept much since I last saw him.

"I'm sorry I haven't been around," he offers, keeping his voice low. "There have been some complications back at HQ."

"To do with me?"

"No, we've been planning a raid for the last six months. Last night, we made our move. The case is being wrapped up as we speak."

Hugging myself tight, I wince at the twinge of my broken arm. Hunter notices, the brief flash of gentleness vanishing. He climbs to his feet and offers me a hand.

"Come inside. We should talk properly."

With reluctance, I let him help me back up. The feel of his fingers gripping mine is strangely soothing. I thought he would chew me out or drag me off to some lair to inflict his questioning.

Lucky sprints ahead when she spots Enzo waiting back inside the house. Too busy frowning at me with his huge arms crossed, he's unprepared for Lucky smashing straight into him.

Despite being the size of a mountain, Enzo falls under her weight and loses himself to a storm of excited licking. I can hear him cussing out the beast from here.

Hunter snorts. "Someone should've filmed that."

"I think he would kill you if you did," I murmur back.

"Worth it."

"What were you doing out there alone?" Enzo barks as we approach, climbing back to his feet. "Dammit, Harlow. It isn't safe to wander around."

"Your people have been watching me this entire time." I gesture back outside. "I've been taking a walk every night."

He scrapes a hand through his tangled, raven locks. "We were worried. You weren't here when we got home."

Taking a chance, I reach up and briefly touch his bicep. "I'm sorry, Enzo."

"It's… fine." A heavy breath whooshes out of his nostrils. "Come inside. Get warm."

We pile around the marble breakfast bar as Hunter boils the kettle for several cups of tea. He seems to drink the stuff like water. It must flow in his veins instead of blood.

Enzo retrieves a thick, grey hoodie and drapes it over me. His woodsy scent clings to the material, and it reminds me of fallen leaves draped in the fragrance of pine trees.

"You been okay?" he asks quietly. "Sorry things took longer than we thought."

"Leighton's kept me company." I tighten the hoodie around me. "He's made me watch some terrible TV shows though."

Hunter scoffs while steeping his tea bag. "Sounds about right. Mr Slacker could be a professional couch potato."

"He has looked after me," I reply sharply before backtracking. "I mean… he, well, I don't know. He's nice."

"Nice?" Enzo repeats in confusion. "Our Leighton?"

I avoid both of them looking at me like I'm an alien and adjust my plastered arm for a distraction. The thud of half-awake footsteps approaches the kitchen to disrupt our awkward moment.

"Jesus." Leighton stumbles in, rubbing his eyes. "Are you two real or is this a bad dream?"

"Sit down, Leigh." Hunter sighs.

He tightens the blanket wrapped around him like a cape. "Sorry, who are you again?" His eyes meet mine. "Harlow, I rented us the extended edition of *Batman Begins*. Ready for a rewatch?"

There's still popcorn stuck to his face as he winks at me. The other two look more than a little confused.

I clear my throat. "Leighton made a list of his top-ten favourite movies. We're working through them all."

"Seriously? *Batman* made the top ten?" Enzo deadpans.

Leighton's mouth drops open. "Don't knock it, Enz. You know I'm wet for Christian Bale. What a man."

His eyes blow wide. "You're… wet for him? That's the word you're choosing? Seriously?"

"Dude, did you see him topless?"

Hunter slams several cups of tea down. "Focus, idiots. We're not debating fictional fucking characters right now. Jesus Christ."

Smirking, Leighton helps himself to Hunter's tea. Before he ends up with a broken nose, he retreats to the empty table on the other side of the room. Hunter's glower deepens with each step.

"You were saying?" Leighton slurps the tea. "Dang, bro. This is a mean cuppa. You've been holding out on me."

"Give it back before I come over there and rearrange your face."

"Didn't you know that sharing is caring?" Leighton singsongs.

Sliding his tea over to Hunter before a fight breaks out, Enzo braces his hands on the breakfast bar and turns to me.

"Drink up. Have you taken your pain meds?"

"Not yet," I admit, taking a sip of sweetened goodness.

Enzo makes everyone wait as he thumps back upstairs to retrieve my evening pills. I'm dying of embarrassment while the other two stifle the urge to kill each other.

When Enzo returns, he deposits the brightly coloured tablets in front of me. I shiver under the weight of his sharp gaze. He's seriously going to stand there and watch me swallow them.

"You don't need to watch," I whisper.

"You were outside without a coat again," he answers crisply. "Someone has to make sure you look after yourself."

Washing them down with a warm mouthful of tea, I stick my tongue out for him to inspect.

"Satisfied?" I ask him.

"Not in the slightest," he grumbles under his breath. "Let's get this over with. She needs to rest."

Rolling his eyes, Hunter returns his attention to me. "Harlow, I understand that Laura Whitcomb is deceased."

I manage a nod.

"We were expecting this news after nearly two months, but we still don't have a body. I need to take your statement. The killer is still out there, perhaps searching for his next victim."

All of them are studying me now, tearing apart my defences and stealing my secrets for their own satisfaction.

"What do you need me to do?" I ask wearily.

Hunter drains his cup in one long gulp. "The press have started to join up the dots. We need to release a statement before that happens, announcing that you're cooperating with the investigation."

"Fuck no," Enzo hisses. "We can't tell those assholes that Harlow's alive and helping us. It's too dangerous for her."

"We have to get out in front of this, Enz. We've been contracted by the SCU. That's public money. Transparency is our only option."

Anxiety brushes over me like a phantom's skeletal hand. "You w-want me to… s-speak to those people?"

Hunter shakes his head. "Forget them. We'll handle it. You need to sit down with us and tell us everything you know."

There's no escaping me, sinner.

You thought you could be someone else.

Pathetic, soulless demon.

Shaking Pastor Michaels' voice from my mind, I look into Hunter's chocolatey irises. He's so hard to get a read on—passionate one moment and cold the next—but I think he wants to help.

If I can't trust him, I can at least trust his actions. They've kept me safe, given me clothes and a warm bed. It's more than anyone's ever done for me. I'm safe because of them.

"I'll tell you what you need to know," I finally say. "I can't remember everything. It's all so blurry still."

"Any information will help." Hunter glances up at Enzo. "I'll have Richards meet us at HQ tomorrow to supervise."

"You want to take her in?" Enzo asks in surprise.

Hunter shrugs, pulling his wild hair back. "We can do everything there where it's safe and secure. Theo needs to meet Harlow, and he's got some updates for the team."

Enzo falls quiet again. He's studying me with such intensity, I shift uncomfortably in my seat. There's raging fire and violence in his eyes. I've seen that look before.

It scares the living daylights out of me. Rage can corrupt even the gentlest of souls, and he's teetering on the edge of that dangerous fall.

Leighton claps his hands together. "Well, it looks like I'm returning to the office. Christian and his sexy body will have to wait."

I don't miss the way Hunter narrows his eyes at him.

CHAPTER 12
HARLOW

MANIC MEMORIES - DES ROCS

AS WE WIND into Central London, a dark atmosphere descends. The streets and urban surroundings grow busier, with endless fancy cars and people rushing about.

I watch with my nose pressed against the tinted window. There are so many human beings, wearing different clothes and hairstyles, and no two people look alike.

Some are smiling and some not, some walk while others run. It's dizzying, the sheer variety of it all. I feel intimidated by the size of the world I've been locked away from.

"Why don't you live here?" I ask randomly.

"We like our privacy and quiet," Enzo answers from the passenger seat. "This place is a fucking cesspit."

"I don't mind the city," Hunter chimes in. "We have several spare apartments in HQ. I stay there sometimes."

Leighton is strapped in beside me, his hand wrapped around mine. I don't mind. The way his thumb strokes over my knuckles is reassuring, grounding me in the present.

"I spend more time here than with them and sleep wherever I pass out, princess."

"That's worse than Goldilocks."

"I will pin your nickname down eventually," he vows with a wink.

The buildings grow so high, they touch the dreary, cloud-covered sky. I study the glass monsters in awe and blanch a little at the one we head straight for.

The skyscraper is a towering, black monstrosity, cloaked in darkness and hard steel lines. The windows are tinted extra dark, concealing all activity inside. There's even a helicopter pad on the roof.

I'd imagine it's the closest thing to an evil lair in the real world, like

Batman's cave. We finished the trilogy last night. It's now entered my top three, thanks to Leighton.

Batman reminds me of Enzo a little—a colossal beast, intense and deadly, but with hidden kindness that only certain people are allowed to see. I'm not sure he'd appreciate that comparison.

"Welcome to Sabre," Hunter says grandly.

Leaning out of the window for a retinal and fingerprint scan, he replaces his dark aviators and speeds into a busy parking garage. The city is swallowed by awaiting shadows.

I bite my lip, watching several armed guards press their hands to their foreheads before pushing them into the air. It seems to be a mark of respect that Hunter returns, his emotionless mask in place.

We park up in a bay with his surname printed in indelible ink. The others slide out of the car as Leighton helps me down. Enzo quickly muscles him out of the way and wraps an arm around my shoulders.

"Dickhead," Leighton mutters.

Enzo ignores him as he holds me close. "Everyone here works for us, so there's no need to be afraid. Don't wander off though. This building is massive."

Silently, all three of them move to block me in without a word to each other. Even Leighton is looking more subdued as we stop at a heavily armed entry door. Several guards greet Hunter and Enzo, stepping aside for them.

Escorted through a spotless corridor, we emerge into a glittering glass paradise. I have to suck in a deep breath. So many people are buzzing about, dressed in slick suits and smart dresses, talking on phones or to each other.

The ceiling is impossibly high, further than I can see. Giant lights stretch down in crystal droplets. Every surface is carved in glass or marble, sticking to clean, white lines that give a clinical feel.

Layers of beefed-up security guards line every corner of the cavernous reception. Ahead of me, moving metal teeth carry people upwards like stairs in motion.

"What is that thing?"

"Escalator," Leighton supplies.

I cast him a grateful nod. "Huh."

Several people stop and shake Hunter's hand or incline their heads towards Enzo with clenched jaws. No one dares to step near him. They're both treated with an air of superiority.

"Come on." Hunter sighs, seeming tired with the formalities. "Theo's waiting for us upstairs."

We pack into an elevator that awaits down another slick corridor. Hunter has to scan a special black pass, causing the doors to slide shut with a quiet beep.

I fist my good hand in Enzo's tight, black t-shirt, terrified by the odd sense of inertia in this tight space.

"You're okay," he comforts under his breath.

"I hate these things."

"Breathe. We'll be there soon."

When the elevator opens on a brightly lit floor, I rush out of the enclosed prison as fast as possible. Hunter escorts us into a nearby office, tapping in a code to open the frosted-glass door.

My breathing is shallow as I step inside the space. Light washes over me, blazing through a series of floor-to-ceiling windows. The vast expanse of London awaits in high-definition grandeur.

Trailing over, I rest my palm against the glass, greedily taking in the view. It's like we're in heaven looking down upon the world, safe and secure in our high-rise bubble. I feel invincible up here.

Leighton joins me. "Like the view?"

"It's so high."

"You scared?"

Shaking my head, I smile at the little ant people on the ground. I'm away from the clutches of anyone looking to hurt me. They can't penetrate this glass fortress wrapped in clouds and wealth.

In the corner, there's a glass desk situated before the windows with a stunning, panoramic view. Neat stacks of books sit on every available surface around the room, with framed photographs and odd trinkets.

Hunter drops his suit jacket and keys on the desk, seeming at ease. On the console next to him, I can see several framed photographs of him, Enzo, and even Leighton, smiling and posing.

"Hey, Hunt?" Leighton inspects the room. "Did you feng shui this place with a bloody ruler? This is some obsessive shit."

Hunter glares at him while straightening the stack of papers on his desk so they sit at a perfect right angle. Snorting, Leighton pulls out a chair at a long, dark-wood conference table.

Before I can sit down next to him, I glance around the rest of the spacious office. My heart immediately plummets as my extremities go numb with the wave of shock.

This can't be real.

Every inch of the back wall is plastered in thick layers of paperwork. There are more sheets of paper than I can count, typed lines of ink and endless photographs stuck on top with little pins.

Strands of red cord are wrapped around the pins, connecting different sections. Every inch of wall space is covered in a chaotic contrast to the ruthlessly organised office.

My feet carry me without thinking. I'm numb, helpless, pulled back into the embrace of detachment. Studying the walls, an awful weight curls in the pit of my stomach.

I count every photograph pinned in place. Altogether, there are eighteen girls staring back at me. I'm sickened as I check the various profiles. I recognise every single one of them—some made it on to my list.

Others could be complete strangers, but their faces resonate in the back of my mind. I know that I watched them die, even if I can't remember it.

"This c-can't be h-happening," I stammer.

"Sit back down, little one."

Enzo's hand lands on my arm. I jump so fast, I end up crashing into the wall in my haste to get away from him. Papers rain on my head as my healing arm flares with pain.

Panting hard, I stare up at the towering, black-haired beast above me. I don't recognise him anymore. The numbness has infected every part of me, metastasising, taking over everything.

"Stay away from me!"

"Harlow?" he asks, frowning. "It's me."

"N-No... I c-can't... stay back!"

His next words are drowned out by screaming, echoing on repeat in my head. Countless voices. Different tenors. Soft. Raspy. Feminine. Scratchy. Desperate. Pained. Hopeful. Pleading. Dying. Gone.

I'm drowning in glimpses of memories I'd compartmentalised. Their bloodstained words slide down my throat like swallowing bullets. Voices and faces are disjointed.

Please, just let me go.

I want to go home.

What do you want from me?

Let me out.

Don't touch me!

Scrambling up despite my throbbing body, I touch the nearest photograph. It's Tia. I remember her well. She has a beautiful, confident smile in the picture, with another woman's purple-painted lips sealed on her cheek.

Pastor Michaels had a special word for her, one that I refuse to repeat. Something to do with her kissing other girls. God doesn't like that. I can't imagine being capable of such mindless hatred.

God is supposed to love all of his creations. Why should it matter who kisses who? She talked about Kara, her girlfriend, a lot. The happiness she radiated, even in the basement, was heartwarming.

"I'm so sorry," I whisper, pulling the photograph down.

The strange men around me are deathly silent, watching me unravel while cataloguing every clue I give away. Pressing my lips to Tia's pixelated face, I reattach her to the wall.

Every other girl that I watched die waits for me to acknowledge them, all accusing me with their printed eyes. I wouldn't call them my friends, not in the conventional sense.

These brave human beings were all my sisters. I never had a family, but somehow, I found kindred spirits in the darkness of my captivity. We were bound by tragedy rather than blood.

I'm the only one that knows what happened to them. The weight of responsibility is crushing me to death. I have to remember all of them, even if it kills me.

"Do you know these women?"

I look up, and the world snaps back into focus. I know these people.

Hunter. Enzo. Leighton. My brain stumbles, attempting to reorientate itself. It's excruciating, the way reality punches into me.

"Harlow?" Hunter repeats.

All I can do is nod.

"I'm sorry, but I need you to say it out loud for the record."

I stroke my fingertips over Christie's braid, her photograph pinned a few metres down from Tia's. She didn't like me much, preferring to shiver and weep alone in a curled-up ball.

I kept her company regardless, whispering whatever comfort I could. She died as silently as she lived. I hate myself for admitting that I was glad in some way. It made it easier to watch her violent death.

"Yes."

"How?" he demands.

Turning to face them all again, I gulp hard. "There was a cage next to mine in the basement where I was kept. It was rarely empty."

Hunter looks away, shuffling through papers on his desk with his scruff-covered jaw set in an unyielding line. Conversely, Enzo refuses to look anywhere but straight at me.

His expression is even more murderous than usual, borderline animalistic. He looks ready to tear the entire office apart with his bare hands. Seeming calmer, Leighton smooths his hair in an absent-minded fashion.

"All of them?" Hunter clarifies.

"Yes," I make myself say. "Some of them I recognise, but I don't remember exactly what happened. There were so many."

Hunter and Enzo take seats on the opposite side of the table. There's no sign of the doctor from the hospital or the mysterious Theo. I take my seat, feeling small beneath their brutal gazes.

Hunter places his phone in the middle of the table. It's already recording, but he repeats today's date and all of their names. I'm startled to find that it's nearly November.

"Introduce yourself," he orders firmly.

I clear my throat. "Harlow."

"Surname?"

The name Michaels doesn't fit, even if it's the name my parents used. If I prescribe it to myself, I will be nothing more than their daughter.

Just another cruel, malicious joke from God that inflicts misery on others. I have to be more than that. If I could strip my skin off and burn it to escape them, I would.

"I don't… ah, know. I can't remember."

Hunter nods, his pen poised. "Tell us everything."

CHAPTER 13
THEO

SCAVENGERS (ACOUSTIC) - THRICE

FINGERTIPS FLYING ACROSS MY KEYBOARD, I squint at the breadcrumb trail I've been tracking for the past week. It's painstaking work, using a mixture of CCTV footage, private feeds and traffic cams.

I'm tracking the path of the victim to London—Harlow, I should say. She is a person, after all. I'm not great with those.

Silence and predictability are my companions, the controllable comfort of computers and code that lies within my manipulation. People? Not so easy to control.

I avoid other human beings out of sheer necessity. Even the guys—my teammates and supposed family—are intolerable to me. My social anxiety has always been bad. It's ruining my life now.

The woman in question dominates the huge screen stretched out across the wall of my office, playing a live feed of Hunter's interrogation. Rather than overwhelm her, we opted to play this another way.

Doctor Richards sits by my side, twirling his cufflinks as he listens intently while taking notes. He agreed to watch from here, on standby if needed.

"How long were you held captive?" Hunter asks.

"I don't remember a time when I wasn't held in a cage." Harlow stares past them all. "But I know things… stuff that I shouldn't. So I have no idea."

"Do you remember your childhood?"

She shrugs. "Beatings. Being starved and tormented. The girls didn't start showing up until later, when they got bored with hurting me. I was so happy to have some company."

"Nothing before that?" Hunter presses.

Harlow shakes her head. "Just the cage. When the girls started to come, they spoke to me, taught me things. Reminded me that I was real. It felt so good after being alone for so long."

"Jesus," Richards mutters. "Poor woman."

I press my lips together, glancing back down at my laptop screen. The last known sighting of the latest victim, Laura, was way up north. That's the direction from which Harlow hitchhiked.

I'm still working to pin down her exact route. She hopped across more than eight vehicles over several days, sneaking in undetected. She's damn lucky the journey didn't kill her.

"Still think this is amnesia?" I ask the shrink.

Richards nods, his eyes bleak. "She's disassociating. Fight-or-flight mode kicks in, changing how traumatic experiences are stored in the long-term memory. Unfortunately, memory loss is to be expected."

"Who held you, Harlow?" Hunter draws our attention back. "I want names."

Her fingers worry her hoodie sleeve. "Pastor Michaels and Mrs Michaels aren't good people. They like to hurt others. God sent them to punish the sinners and prepare for the rapture."

I can't help but wince. She's been indoctrinated, a warped reality bruised and beaten into her. The medics placed her age at approximately twenty-two. That's a long fucking time.

"Was it Pastor Michaels who hurt the other women?" Enzo asks gently. "Did he kill them?"

Harlow nods, biting her lip. "Mrs Michaels was in charge of cleanup. Pastor Michaels is God's servant. He does the Lord's bidding."

"Clean up?" Hunter repeats.

"The bodies." Harlow looks a little green. "They left a lot of mess. She'd sometimes make me help. If I refused, something was usually broken."

"And how did he kill these women?"

"You've seen the bodies, haven't you?" she replies numbly.

Hunter stares, demanding her answer. He's being pretty rough with her, despite the doctor's warnings. Anyone can see she is traumatised. I'm surprised by how well she's holding up.

I've witnessed plenty of people break down in Hunter's presence. He isn't one to mince his words or tread carefully through life. That's what Enzo's here for.

"Pastor Michaels punished them for their sins," Harlow whispers hoarsely. "To make them repent."

"How?" Hunter pushes. "Tell us."

"Ease up," Richards whispers.

Harlow stiffens, retreating inwards. "You know how."

"I want to hear it from you," Hunter prods further.

Shaking his head, Richards makes some more notes and shifts, seeming uncomfortable. I know he wanted to do things a different way. Enzo did too.

Neither of them wanted Harlow to be put in this position so soon, but what Hunter wants, Hunter gets. We're all beholden to his rules around here.

"Pastor Michaels beat them until they prayed," Harlow eventually answers. "Sometimes… he'd take his clothes off and… t-touch them. It usually got them to comply."

No one knows quite how to stomach that. I don't believe for a second that she's as naive as she's playing. Years of watching this abuse must have taught her some things.

"Did he… do these things to you?" Hunter asks carefully.

She shakes her head. Enzo relaxes a fraction, still holding himself as tight as a coiled spring, prepared to unleash hell at any moment. He'll be running tonight instead of sleeping, I'm sure of it.

"Before he… killed them, he had a special knife. From God, you see." Harlow grows increasingly pale. "He used it to carve holy symbols into their bodies. It cleansed them of all evil."

Disregarding another of Richards' warnings, Hunter retrieves a sealed folder. He pulls out a single, glossy photograph, then offers it to Harlow.

On it, the discarded body of Tia Jenkins has been captured in painstaking horror. The Holy Trinity is slashed into her skin, blackened and melted off with decay from the dump site.

"Like this?" he questions.

Harlow's hand covers her mouth, shaking badly. "She fought so hard. He strangled her in the end, tired of waiting for her to die."

Tia Jenkins' body was found sprawled out in a forest up north. She'd been there for weeks already, her skin feasted on by maggots and flies. Harlow can barely look at the horrifying picture.

"The bodies were left with me for a while," she reveals. "Sometimes for hours, sometimes days. Eventually, Mrs Michaels took them away."

"What?" Enzo's voice is razor sharp.

Harlow ducks her head, a waterfall of tears flowing freely. "He liked to make me sleep in their blood, to remind me. If I was bad, he left them for longer. Laura… she… he didn't…"

She chokes on a wet sob, like she needs to throw up but can't. Something is begging to be let free, but she's holding it back with all of her strength.

Leighton snarls at Hunter to stop, gathering Harlow in his arms. I've barely seen him since he was released from prison a few months ago. He looks so different.

"We need to stop here," Richards says.

"This has to be done," I remind him.

"Not so damn heavy-handedly."

"Do you want another girl to go missing?"

"I want to see my patient being cared for, Theo!"

He snaps his notepad shut with a frustrated sigh. It takes a lot to get under the shrink's thick skin. He's consulted for Sabre on many occasions, including cases as bloody as this.

But everything about this feels different somehow. We've become invested after months of failure. It's now personal, and hearing firsthand what this monster is capable of only makes it worse.

"You don't have to carry on," Leighton offers.

He's stroking Harlow's long hair. They seem friendly with each other. She's shaking violently in his arms, a bomb primed to explode.

"We can stop," he adds.

"I have to do this." Harlow pushes him away. "Laura… she… they kept her body for much longer, until there was nothing left. The smell was so bad, it made me pass out sometimes."

Hunter deliberately looks up at the camera where he knows I'm watching. I gather my laptop and the waiting evidence bag. Richards watches me go with reluctance.

Walking down the corridor, I let myself into Hunter's office. Several heads snap in my direction.

"Take a seat, Theo."

Following Hunter's order, I place my belongings down next to Enzo. Harlow is looking at me, on the very edge of her seat. I can already tell that she doesn't like strangers, fear is written all over her.

I avoid her eyes, too socially anxious to make my own introduction. This is beyond my remit. I'm more accustomed to working behind the scenes than dealing with victims.

"This is Theo, head of intelligence," Hunter explains. "He has been tracking your route here."

She gives me a tiny nod in greeting. "Hi."

"At Enzo's request, we looked a little deeper into your last transportation and found something… unusual."

There's a flash of panic on Harlow's face. "You did?"

"Show her," Hunter instructs.

Without saying a word, I snap on a pair of latex gloves and reach for the evidence bag. Inside lies a bloodied, dirty lump of calcium—a bone, the femur, to be precise.

"You found her," Harlow keens. "Laura."

I place the item back in the bag. DNA evidence has already confirmed it belonged to the Whitcomb girl, but establishing Harlow's involvement was important. Now, we know she is who she says she is.

"Care to explain why you had this in your possession?" Hunter quips.

"I just wanted to get out… I didn't… I…"

Harlow drops Leighton's hand to fist her hair so tight, I'm worried she'll tear the whole lot from her scalp. Her eyes are blown wide and lit with fear as she rises.

The seat falls back with a bang, and Enzo follows, stalking her like an attentive predator. She's breathing hard through clenched teeth.

"Hold it together, Harlow," he advises.

"I had no other choice… I tried and tried, but the cage was locked. The only thing I could reach was… was… Laura's skeleton."

Stunned silence drapes over the room.

"I used it to break the door," she finishes, trembling all over. "It took so long, but the hinges snapped. I took all I could of her with me and left the rest."

Backing away from us all, Harlow retreats into the furthest corner. Enzo tries to approach, but each step in her direction increases her sobs, until he's forced to fall back. She doesn't respond to her name.

The door to the office slams open with a crash. Richards stalks in, his tweed coat flapping behind him, looking far angrier than I've seen him for a long time.

"I warned you about too much, too soon," he shouts angrily. "This is unprofessional and, frankly, unethical!"

Hunter doesn't flinch. "We have a job to do."

"Not at the expense of those you are supposed to protect. Dammit! I won't stand for this!"

Hunter looks away, rubbing a hand over his slicked-back ponytail. The silence is punctuated by Harlow's cries as she curls into herself. She still won't allow anyone to get close, completely unresponsive.

Leighton is frozen metres away from her, itching to move closer. Enzo looks ready to tear his own hair out at the root as he repeats her name, over and over.

Richards is right—she's lost in her head. I recognise the signs. Guilt gut-punches me at the mess we've made. She isn't a suspect here. Hunter's letting the case cloud his judgement.

Before I know what I'm doing, I've eased past the others with the evidence bag. Harlow's tear-filled eyes latch on to the plastic-wrapped body part in my hands.

"I think this is yours," I whisper shamefully. "I'm sorry for taking her away, Harlow. She was your friend."

"F-For me?" she stammers.

"You can have her back to say goodbye."

"Theo," Hunter warns darkly.

Ignoring him, I sink to my knees and hold out the bone as a peace offering. Harlow tentatively accepts it, her bottom lip wobbling. She studies the remaining piece of the last girl she saw alive.

"I'm so sorry, Laura. I thought… I just wanted to help you," she murmurs, stroking the femur. "I wish I could've taken all of you."

No one utters a single word, watching the devastating sight as Harlow holds her friend close. She spares me a quick look.

"Thank you for giving her back to me."

I sit back on my haunches, nodding. It's been a long time since anyone thanked me for… well, anything. Harlow's eyes are haunted as she holds my gaze for a moment.

"I lied to you all," she says, looking back at the others. "My name is Harlow Michaels. They're my parents."

"What the fuck?" Hunter curses loudly.

But Harlow's already gone, cradling the femur to her chest like it's a teddy bear. Her eyes are open, but empty. Unseeing.

"Hunter," Richards calls sternly. "A word, please."

Retreating to the other side of the office, Leighton stands and storms over to butt into their conversation. I can hear them arguing about suspending the rest of the interrogation.

"Harlow," Enzo begs, lingering behind me. "Why can't she hear me?"

"Careful," I advise. "Don't spook her."

Harlow's body is in our presence, but the essence of her has been scooped out. All we can do is wait for her to come back. Climbing to my feet, I gesture for Enzo to take my place.

He crawls closer to her, an impressive feat at his size. Slowly and carefully, he manages to ease the bone from her hands and pass it back to me. Harlow doesn't even notice, too spaced out.

I take the evidence and carefully repackage it. The Whitcomb family has something to bury now. Enzo takes his time lifting Harlow into his lap, and she soon collapses against his chest.

It triggers a barrage of memories that wash over me before I can clamp them down. Each one hits like a bullet between the eyes.

Bright-pink strands of hair sliding through my fingers. The love of my life's nose buried in Enzo's chest. His eyes squeezed tightly shut as insomnia surrendered its control.

We had someone before, what feels like a lifetime ago. She made us whole. Happy. Complete. I haven't felt that since the day we lost her.

"I'm gonna get Harlow out of here," Enzo rumbles.

I have to look away from them to conceal my grief. "Sure. Go before Hunter stops you."

Holding Harlow's trembling body like she weighs little more than air, Enzo strides from the room without another word. No one would dare stop him with the bone-chilling anger on his face.

"I'll see them out," Richards announces, his face grim.

Hunter watches him go with exasperation. Gathering my stuff, I straighten my plaid shirt, needing a moment to collect myself. It's been a long time since I thought of… *her*. Seeing Harlow has stirred all that shit back up again.

"You need to rush through her DNA profile," Hunter barks as I approach him. "I want dates, relatives, the works. If she had so much as a fucking cold as a kid, I want to know about it."

I clear my throat. "I'll see what I can do."

"No one passes completely under the radar for twenty-two years. I want this done quietly. Enzo and Richards clearly want to continue walking on eggshells."

"Got it, boss."

"We need to inform Whitcomb's family now that we have confirmation," Hunter adds. "Hudson can do it. He questioned the different victims' families earlier in the case."

"Thought you wanted to keep Harlow's presence between us?"

Hunter shakes his head. "We have to do a press announcement anyway. Get Kade to bring the whole team in to be briefed tomorrow. I'll speak to them myself."

With a final nod, I manage to break free from his office. Things are stepping up a gear if we're bringing in the Cobra team. They're our secret assets—ruthless and merciless in perfect measure.

I grab my phone and bring up the contacts with a sigh. I haven't called anyone for a long time.

"I was starting to wonder if you were dead," Hudson answers with a grunt. "Unless you're calling me from the afterlife, in which case, kudos."

"Hilarious," I return dryly. "Is this a bad time?"

"Gimme a sec."

The sound of fists meeting flesh rattles down the line, along with someone's yelping in the background. I hang tight as Hudson shouts at someone, the line muffled before he returns with a low growl.

He's been on clean-up duty all week after our successful narcotics raid. Enzo trained Hudson himself, breeding the perfect henchman to beat, break and bully his way to fast results.

"Free now. What's up, Theo?"

"Need you all to come in tomorrow."

"Got something for us?" he asks excitedly. "I'm tired of these lowlife gang bangers."

"You're not gonna like what we have instead. Hunter will brief you in the morning."

"Gotcha. Theo, why don't you come—"

"I have to go," I interrupt, hanging up.

Returning to my lonely office, I hit the coffee machine and settle in my desk chair. My phone vibrates with a text, but I don't bother checking it. Hudson needs to give up.

I'm not interested in playing happy families like the last five years have changed anything that happened back then.

I don't want their help.

I don't want their company.

All I want is the one fucking person I can't have… because she's dead.

CHAPTER 14
HARLOW

.HAUNTED. - DEAD POET SOCIETY

THE SKITTERING of a pebble hitting my window startles me awake in a split second. The meaty tissue of my heart bruises itself against my rib cage, the fuel of terror pumping through my veins.

I was running through thick woodland in my dream, wracked by pain and desperation. The voices of eighteen ghosts followed my footsteps with wailing cries.

Crack.

Am I dreaming still?

Is someone… here?

A louder crack pierces the silence. It's pitch-black outside—I fell asleep with the blinds wide open, bathing me in moonlight. Falling asleep each night is proving difficult after the interrogation.

It's still playing on repeat in my mind, and has been ever since, no matter how hard I try to forget about it. Telling them everything felt like scooping out the innards from inside my empty carcass.

Crack.

Throwing back the covers, I hug my plastered arm and creep across the room to the source of the noise. From what I can see of the driveway, it's empty. Not a single soul in sight.

Leighton didn't go out drinking, and I heard the others come home from another long day of work several hours ago. It must be my imagination. Lying back down in my huge bed, I fight to go back to sleep, but it's no use.

I'm wide awake, as I have been every night this week. Absent-mindedly, my fingers twine with strands of my hair and begin pulling. I can't resist the compulsion.

It's becoming an addiction, tearing my hair out and revelling in the blissful familiarity of pain. Hiding it is becoming harder as the little voice infects every hour of my day, not just the moments I feel unreal.

Another half an hour of silence and I can't stand it anymore. Throwing on a loose pair of sweats to cover my bare legs, I sneak downstairs after cleaning the hair from my pillow.

Moonlight is dappled across the polished tiles, lighting my path to the fridge. I grab one of the glass bottles of milk that gets delivered to the front gate every day. I swear, the real world is so weird.

As I'm retrieving my warm milk from the microwave, there's another crash from behind me. The mug slips from my hands and shatters on the tiled floor, sending scalding hot liquid over my feet.

I yelp, slipping over and landing amongst the ceramic shards with a thud.

"You stupid, foolish child."

Dread slips beneath my skin and lances through my heart with its icy shards. I'd forgotten how malicious his voice sounds, filled with holy determination.

"I'm asleep," I whisper to myself. "This isn't real."

When I look down at my hands, blood is seeping from the slices that the mug inflicted. I absently smear the red spill, feeling its sticky warmth. It feels real. The pain is tangible. Do people bleed in dreams?

"Harlow. Kneel before your father."

Breath held, I make myself look up. In the doorway, Pastor Michaels is staring at me with a smarmy grin. His processional robes are in place—rich, crushed-red velvet and gold thread that contrasts his silvery coiffe of hair.

I blink repeatedly, hoping he'll vanish. How is he here? No. It can't be. Screwing my eyes shut, I rub them hard before reopening. He's still standing there.

"This isn't real."

His smile takes a violent edge. "I'm as real as you are."

"You're not here," I reassure myself.

"Aren't I? It was easy enough to break in."

As I stare up at my father, fear slamming into me like tumultuous ocean waves, the room goes wonky. Everything is warping and twisting, the air seeming to reform in new visions of horror.

Pastor Michaels inches closer, drawing a long, curved knife from his robes. It's still stained with Laura's blood.

Drip, drip, drip.

"Harlow," he repeats. "Kneel."

Drip, drip, drip.

"Kneel before your father."

Drip, drip, drip.

The blade glints in the moonlight, illuminating crimson stains. His footsteps approach. My heart somersaults, threatening to explode into pieces. Before his fists can meet my flesh, I scramble to my feet.

"I said kneel! Do what the Lord demands of you!"

Searching for something to protect myself with, my fingers wrap around the handle of a knife protruding from the kitchen block. It cuts the air with a metallic swoosh, thrust out in front of me.

Pastor Michaels' face darkens into an ugly shade of red. I can see the enraged fog perfusing his entire being, transforming the appearance of a normal, friendly man into a monster.

"Stay back!" I scream at him. "I won't kneel for you. I won't fucking kneel for anyone!"

"We don't use that kind of language here," he yells back, his spittle spreading across the floor. "Perhaps the time has come for you to move on, heathen child. I will free you from this sinful place."

Darkness oozes across the floor as he lunges towards me, like the devil himself is breaking free from Pastor Michaels' mortal shell. I scream and race across the kitchen, attempting to flee.

When his hand grabs my shoulder, I gather whatever scraps of courage I can find and grip the blade tighter.

"I'll kill you! Get away from me!" I threaten.

"Harlow! Stop!"

The words don't resonate, nor does the different voice throwing them at me. Spinning back around, I take advantage of the momentum and launch at Pastor Michaels.

We both tumble to the tiled floor, the impact jarring my broken arm. I grit my teeth through the pain. I won't die here.

"I hate you!" I shout, out of control. "You're a monster!"

"Harlow, it's me. Stop!"

"No!"

My one good hand sails into his face, and I savour the sharp crack of his nose. Slick blood coats my knuckle, spurring me into a frenzy. Each punch feels like salvation.

I'm breaking free, smashing the prison of my childhood to pieces. My punches rain down, albeit weak and feeble, but I don't stop.

"Harlow… please! Fuck, I can't hear anything."

This voice doesn't sound right. It's high and panicked, but underscored by a warm, honey-like quality. Pastor Michaels doesn't sound like that.

Snatching my knife back up from the floor, I ignore the niggle of anxiety at the back of my mind and press the blade against his throat.

One slash.

That's all it would take.

"I hate you," I repeat, sobbing.

"Harlow," the man beneath me repeats. "Drop the knife. It's okay. I've got you."

This isn't right. Pastor Michaels doesn't have a thick, chestnut beard, or glossy hair that tickles his shoulders. The processional robes on the chest I'm straddling disappear, leaving nothing but bare, tattooed skin behind.

Pastor Michaels' face morphs before my very eyes. Harsh lines and bitter hatred become wide eyes and plush, inviting lips that are stained bright red.

The knife is heavy in my grip, cutting skin to release more blood. The moment I realise who I'm pinning to the floor, I immediately toss it aside, terrified by the blood soaking into me.

"Oh my God," I exclaim in horror. "Hunter!"

His eyes pull me into their chocolate depths as he frantically searches for the hearing aid that fell from his ear during my attack. The longer he can't find it, the more panicked he becomes.

"Fuck," he curses. "Where is it?"

Spotting the tiny black device under a kitchen counter, I quickly pass it over to Hunter. He slots it back into place, and when it connects, the fear on his face dissipates.

"Okay," he says to himself. "Okay."

I want to drown in the molten pools of his eyes and never take another breath. I attacked Hunter. I… cut his throat. I nearly killed him! I'm no better than the monsters that birthed me.

"Harlow," he pleads, cupping my cheek with one hand. "I need you to take a breath for me. Everything is okay. You're safe."

"No! You're bleeding!"

"I'm fine, Harlow. Just startled, that's all."

"You c-couldn't hear… I did that to you."

"Breathe, sweetheart. It was an accident. Not the first time, and it won't be the last."

Despite his oddly gentle words, all I can do is stare at the blood dripping down his clavicle from his gushing nose. I did that. Me. It felt so good to fight back.

I hurt him.

I enjoyed it.

What does that make me?

Climbing off his body, I spiral deeper into despair. My back hits the marble breakfast bar until I can't run any further. Hunter ignores his injuries and pursues me.

He's a pillar of power and intimidation, but in this moment, his expression is broken. He looks indescribably sad. Does my pain entertain him? Am I nothing more than another fractured specimen for him to study?

"He was so real," I say, the words dark and ugly. "I could… f-feel him. His voice. The s-smell of his skin… everything. He was so real!"

"It was a dream," Hunter assures me. "You were sleepwalking or something. None of it was real."

"But I attacked you! I thought you were… my father."

"I'm not. Can you see me now?"

I stare into his coffee-coloured irises. "Yes."

"Do I look like him?"

"N-No."

Tentatively, Hunter reaches for my hand. I'm too stunned to protest. He raises it to his chest, placing it right above his pounding heartbeat. I can feel it hammering away.

His tattooed skin is hot to touch, softened by a patch of brown fuzz across his defined pectorals. His tongue darts out to clean the blood from his lips, still weeping from his nose.

"Look at me," he commands sternly.

I obey without hesitation, trapped in his gaze.

"He isn't here. Look at me, feel me. Know that I'm not him."

His voice is mesmerising, gliding over me like thick treacle. My hand moves of its own volition. I trace the hard planes of his chest, over the dark swirls of ink that mark his tattoo.

It wraps itself around his torso, sneaking up to the ropy muscles of his neck. I can pick out individual elements—an intricate tree, wrapped in beautiful vine leaves that spreads across his stomach.

Birds with vast, powerful wings fly across the slope of his ribcage to escape, blending into the path of shadowy storm clouds and strobes of white ink that paint individual raindrops.

It's a thunderstorm, painted on his body in a real-life canvas. Hunter is exactly that—deadly and mesmerising all at once.

"You're home with me," he murmurs, his voice growing throaty. "Nobody is ever going to touch you again. I won't let them."

A thick lump gathers in my throat. I let Hunter slide his arms under my legs, too numb to protest. He lifts me until I'm pressed against his bloodstained chest.

We head upstairs, where the distinct sound of Leighton's snoring can be heard. I expect Hunter to take me back to my bedroom, but he bypasses it and heads to the other end of the hallway.

I'm carried into a dark room, assaulted by masculine scents. Hunter's spicy aftershave, fresh linens, and the smell of rainfall from the open window. It's intoxicating, the essences that make up his persona.

"How you didn't wake Enzo up, I'll never know," he grumbles. "It's a miracle he didn't come down and shoot us both by accident."

I try for a joke. "Maybe there is a God."

Hunter's chest rumbles with an almost laugh that doesn't quite escape his lips. He steps into an en-suite, keeping the main light off and flicking on the mirror light instead.

It emanates a warm glow that reveals his neat, organised bathroom. It's identical to mine, but every single bottle is stacked in regimented lines, the labels all facing forward.

"Let's get you cleaned up."

"You're the one bleeding," I point out.

Hunter lifts me onto the bathroom counter, next to the sink basin. He cocks a sculpted eyebrow at me.

"Look at your hands, Harlow."

I glance down. The slices I felt from the broken mug were real, blood seeping down my arms in a warm, steady flow. I didn't even notice it amidst the madness.

"Oh."

"Oh," he echoes. "You did a good job there, didn't you?"

The accusation in his voice grates against me.

"It's not like I did this on purpose," I argue back. "It all felt… real. Everything I was seeing and hearing."

Hunter's attention doesn't waver from my face. "I can see that."

Reaching under the sink, he pulls out a small metal box. Inside, there's a basic first aid kit. I reluctantly hold out my hands, letting him clean the blood with a damp cotton pad.

He works in concentrated silence, cleaning and inspecting. My eyes begin to droop as the adrenaline pours out of me.

"Nearly done," Hunter whispers. "Rest on my shoulder if you need to."

I force my eyes back open. "No. I need to clean you up."

"I'm a big boy, Harlow. I can take care of myself."

"But… you shouldn't have to."

He halts, a bloodied cotton pad in hand. The air between us feels weird—almost like it's charged with electricity. I can feel the tension gliding across my sensitised skin.

Hunter's lips are parted, still stained with blood, his breath escaping in a low hiss. Almost in slow motion, his thumb skates along my jawline, up to my cheek, and down to the slope of my bottom lip.

I don't dare move as he traces it with a look of confusion, his eyes flitting up and down in rapid succession.

"I take care of myself," he repeats, his brows furrowed.

"Because there's no one else to do it?"

His head is moving closer, eating up the pitiful distance between us. My legs are parted, his body eased between them as he cleans me up. I can feel the heat of his pelvis against my thighs.

My legs tighten without my permission, squeezing his frame closer. I don't even realise I'm doing it until a low growl emanates from his chest.

"Harlow."

I quickly take control of myself, releasing his waist. "S-Sorry."

"Don't be."

His thumb is still on my bottom lip. With the care of a skilled warrior tracking down his prey to devour, Hunter slips the roughened digit between my lips. I hardly know how to react.

As the very tip of his thumb touches my tongue, a delicious, tingling warmth pools between my legs. I feel my cheeks flush at the sensation. It feels so good. What is he doing to me?

"Hunter," I whimper around his thumb.

He takes a huge step back, staring at me like he can't quite believe what just happened. I immediately feel cold. The distance between us is agonising. I can't breathe with him so far away from me.

"I'm being unprofessional," he curses himself. "Fuck, I'm so sorry. I don't know what I'm doing. This… we… us, it can't happen."

"What can't happen?" I ask cluelessly.

His eyes burn in low embers. "Jesus, Harlow. Never mind. Go back to bed. We can figure things out in the morning."

Snapping the first aid kit shut, he busies himself, shoving it away with a loud clatter. I gulp hard and slide down from the counter, feeling like I've been punched in the chest.

His dismissal hurts more than I thought it would. I leave Hunter washing the blood from his bruised face, still breathing hard as he tries not to look at me again.

"Sorry," I whisper before walking away.

His scent clings to the sheets of his unmade bed as I walk past. The urge to climb in and nestle down is so strong, my feet almost carry me over to it. All I can think about is his arms around me.

I have to make myself leave, escaping the lion's den before he swallows me whole. The walk back to my bedroom is marked by emptiness as tears threaten to spill down my cheeks.

Hunter really must hate me.

He doesn't want me—whatever it means to *be wanted*.

I wonder what that's like.

CHAPTER 15
HUNTER

THE MADNESS - FOREIGN AIR

"SABRE SECURITY HAS CONFIRMED that a living victim has come forward," the newscaster explains. "She is said to be in protective custody and cooperating with the investigation."

Watching the news coverage from behind my desk, I rub my aching temples. We're about to drop an atomic bomb. Our non-disclosure window has run out and we're shit out of luck.

A reporter taps the comms in his ear. "Sorry to interrupt, but we're receiving breaking news that another body has been found."

Chaos ensues as they read through the statement we released to the national news agency. We kept details to a minimum, confirming Whitcomb's death without giving any more information.

Her next of kin, a seventeen-year-old brother, has been informed. He was the one who raised the alarm when his sister and main caregiver didn't return home from work.

Now, he has nothing more than a bone to remember her by. They were dirt poor, living on the poverty line. I've already instructed one of our teams to arrange a funeral, courtesy of Sabre. It's the least we can do.

My phone buzzes on the desk.

"Rodriguez."

"Hunter," Lucas greets with a heavy sigh. "Well, it's going down as well as expected. Interview requests are flooding in already."

"Deny them all."

For a country terrorised by a serial killer that snatches women without leaving a trace and carves them into pretty pieces, this development is big news. My balls are on the line.

"They want a name."

"We're not fucking giving them one," I hiss into the phone. "Harlow has a right to anonymity. It's a matter of safety."

"I know that, but these people don't care. They'll hire private investigators and terrorise her unless we give more information."

"Let them fucking try."

"They know she's under Sabre's protection," he supplies. "With Whitcomb dead and no new leads, your reputation is going to take a battering for keeping this under wraps."

"Christ, I thought I paid you to help me with this shit."

"You do, which is why I'm telling you—be transparent. The SCU lost public confidence early on in this case and never recovered."

Tell me something I don't know. We intervened and helped to clear up their organisation following a corruption scandal, but even after all that, a lack of funding and budget cuts have worsened the situation.

"Levelling with them is your safest bet," Lucas concludes. "Put Harlow out there. Get her to give a statement."

I knock back the last of my tea. "Just deflect any questions about the Whitcomb girl and keep Harlow's name out of it."

Hanging up the call, I slam my phone down on the desk. Chewing out my own employees has never been my style, but this case is doing things to all of us.

I've been firefighting this escalating nightmare all week. We're being hounded for results in every direction possible. Harlow's testimony only created more unanswerable questions for us.

Every time I think about her, my heart squeezes in pain. It took everything in me to kick her out when I wanted nothing more than to take her to my bed and wipe the sadness from her face.

It's driving me insane to be here every day, unable to be close to her as I want to be. We bump into each other around the house in the evenings, and she can barely look at me after what happened.

I often catch myself staring into her hopeless gaze, searching for a glimmer of strength to ease my guilt. She has this powerful effect on me, sparking emotions that I haven't felt in a long time.

I don't want her to be strong. I want to keep her safe, secure and well out of reach until this madness ends. Last time I felt this way, we lost everything. I can't go through that again.

None of us can.

"Hunt?"

Theo's head pokes through my door.

"What's up?" I sigh.

"I need to speak to you. It's urgent."

My stomach somersaults. "Come in."

He steps into the room, his navy-blue flannel shirt rumpled. There's an old coffee stain down the front of his white tee, and his clear, blue eyes look tired behind glasses half covered by tight, blonde ringlets.

I've been pushing him like crazy, determined to get this case wrapped up as quickly as possible. We're throwing all of our resources at it, for better or for worse.

"I've tracked Harlow all the way to a tiny town near Northumberland." He leans against the wall. "She appears on a CCTV camera approaching from the east on foot."

"Where?" I demand excitedly.

"Seems to be a very rural area bordering a huge nature reserve. Remote, unpopulated. It's safe to assume she escaped from somewhere nearby."

My anticipation rises. This is the biggest breakthrough we've had since we took the case on and spent months trawling through evidence.

"Start scouting the area for potential locations," I rattle off. "Check for churches with the local parish. This bastard could be living right under our noses."

"Harlow's description said the chapel appeared to be abandoned in the middle of nowhere. It may not be registered."

"Goddammit. Fine, we can send some drones to scope out the land. Alert the local police department so we don't get shot down."

Theo nods, taking rapid notes. "The Cobra team has wrapped up their other assignments. I'll rope Kade into some reconnaissance."

"Good. Get it done."

Anxiety is still written across Theo's stony expression. He's generally an awkward person, always has been. His computer code and textbooks wrap him in a security blanket. He wasn't always this detached and lifeless, though.

"What is it?" I sit up in my chair. "Theo?"

"We need to talk about Harlow's identity." He opens a folder, rifling through paperwork. "We've confirmed that Pastor and Mrs Michaels do not exist."

"I see. Well, we know that serial killers use pseudonyms," I muse. "It's hardly surprising they lied about their names."

"I've had the whole intelligence department scouring decades of records." Theo hands me a sheet of paper. "That's a list of ordained pastors in the last forty years. No Michaels."

"So he's a whack job who thinks that he's God's fucking gift."

"Something like that." His eyes dart around the room. "But there's more to it. I just got the report back from forensics."

"Harlow's DNA results?"

Theo nods tightly. "It took a while to compile everything against the national database and verify what we found."

"Just spit it out. What's going on?"

"Well… her name isn't Harlow Michaels, as we anticipated. They're not her parents, Hunt. They never were."

I stare up at Theo's apprehensive face. We tossed this theory around after taking her testimony last week. Having it confirmed means a shitstorm is about to blow up in my stupid face.

"Please tell me she doesn't have family," I blurt.

His blonde eyebrows knit together. "Why would you say that?"

I slam my hands down on the desk. "We've been living with her for weeks and if she has a fucking family out there, we're about to get dragged over the coals for not reuniting them sooner."

Theo's cheeks darken. "These tests take time."

"Like they're gonna give a shit about that!"

I straighten the loose stacks of paperwork I disturbed, internally hating myself for being so callous. Someone has to worry about this firm. No one else seems to give a damn right now.

"Her name is Leticia Kensington," Theo grinds out. "She has a real family. And if there's a single scrap of humanity left in you, then you will do the right thing and call them now."

"Just give me the report and get out of my office. I don't need a goddamn lecture about how to look after my client."

"I'm not done."

Stepping closer, Theo slams the remaining folder of paperwork down in front of me. It's thick, with years' worth of records spilling out. More than a simple DNA report.

"She's been missing for the past thirteen years," he reveals. "This isn't just a murder investigation anymore—she was kidnapped. Harlow wasn't born in that cage."

"Thirteen years? Is this a joke?"

Theo visibly gulps. "She went missing at nine years old. There were zero leads, and the investigation went cold. She was never to be seen again."

Fierce pain begins to pound behind my eyes. Every word that has left Harlow's mouth is either a lie, or a traumatised delusion. Either way, my life is about to get a hell of a lot harder.

"We're so fucking screwed," I mutter to myself.

Theo's eyes narrow. "No. You're fucking screwed."

"What exactly is your problem?"

"You're my problem, Hunt."

"Watch your tone," I warn him. "I'm still the boss around here."

"And that's exactly what's wrong with you! Do you even care anymore? Harlow genuinely needs our help, and all you can think about is closing this case."

"Says the man that abandoned his family! Since when do you care about any of us, including Harlow?"

I regret my harsh words almost immediately. His face shutters, moving back to familiar emptiness as he drops my eyes.

"I thought... you understood me," Theo chokes out. "You and Enzo both moved on like nothing happened to Alyssa. I can't live like that."

"If you think we're fine, you don't know us," I reply in a quieter voice.

"You could've fooled me. It was you who has moved Leighton into her old room, like she never existed."

"It's been five fucking years!" I shout again. "How long can I live in a graveyard? She's gone, Theo! We have to move on."

When I think he's finally going to grow some balls, Theo's mouth snaps shut again. He turns on his heel and strides from the room in a cloud of barely restrained anger, leaving the damned report with me.

I stare after him, feeling like the worst person in the entire world. That's the most he's said to me in a very long time. Losing our fourth team member nearly killed us all, in so many ugly and awful ways.

None of us knew how to deal with our grief; stuffing the skeletons into the closet was simpler and far less painful. But after that, Theo never came back to us.

Fuck!

I stare at the sealed report on my desk. What now? I have no choice but to tell Harlow… but this could very well break her. It will tear apart the fragile foundations of the life she's started to rebuild.

Everything she knows. All the progress we've made. It will all be gone. But as fucking usual, I have no choice but to hurt the people I care about. It always comes down to me.

Absently rubbing at the pain in my chest, I snatch up my phone to text Enzo. Harlow should be in her weekly therapy session with Richards right about now.

I'll go and pick her up myself. Before I unleash a new level of madness upon us with this revelation, I need to know if this was all some elaborate lie.

Would she really lie to us?

Is she protecting the monsters that kidnapped her?

Do I know her at all?

Not bothering to wait for Enzo's response, I toss my suit jacket back on and storm from my office. Her appointment is being held back at the hospital. Richards agreed to meet there after Harlow's check-up with her consultant.

After running every red light in a storm of impatience, I camp out in the waiting area upon arrival. I'm in a foul mood. Harlow would be better off with Enzo, but he's been compromised.

I can see it in his eyes, the way he looks at her like she's his goddamn saviour after years of emptiness. One of us has to remain objective and treat Harlow like the client she is.

Someone slides into the empty seat next to me, ignoring the handful of other chairs in favour of invading my personal space. I run a hand over my ponytail and straighten.

The redhead is a familiar nemesis. She wrote a hit piece about my hearing loss after we took down Incendia Corporation, and scored herself a promotion in the process.

They're lucky I was too busy dealing with my entire life falling apart to sue them for being so fucking heartless.

"Care to give me a statement, Mr Rodriguez? Your press release this morning was deliberately vague."

"Sally Moore." I cast her a frown. "Long time no see."

"You're a hard man to find."

"So I've been told. I have nothing further to add. Refer your questions to my PR agent, Lucas. I pay him enough for it."

"I don't want to speak to your spin doctor."

"Then feel free to sit here in silence. See if I care."

Reaching into her designer handbag, she slides a stack of photographs out and tosses them on the coffee table. The unspoken threat hangs in the air.

I clock the long-range shots of the hospital we're sat in, our tinted SUV coming and going. In one of the pictures, Harlow can be seen climbing out of the car, Enzo's arm wrapped around her waist.

"She's been here for a while," Sally reveals with a grin. "I'm looking forward to getting her statement when she comes out."

Snatching up the photographs, I tuck them into my suit jacket. "This really is scraping the barrel now. Are you that desperate for viewers? Is the network threatening to axe your shit gossip show?"

"I'm doing just fine," she defends hotly.

"Then get out of my face before I file an injunction and have you suspended. You're not getting a statement, and this is a gross invasion of my client's privacy."

She places her phone to her ear and pouts her lips at me. "Bring the cameras up, Jerry. We've got a live interview with Sabre's bossman. Yeah, that's right. I want them all."

Silently cursing, I stand and loom over her. I have enough connections in London to ensure she'll never work again, no matter how many favours it fucking costs me.

But right now, my priority is keeping Harlow as far away from this nightmare as possible. I'm not sacrificing her to the heartless media just to get them off our backs.

"Don't test me. We've played this game before."

"People just want the truth." Her shark-like smile makes my skin crawl. "This is the age of information. You can't keep any secrets."

Spitting with fury, I grab the phone from her hand before she can stop me. Sally shouts as I crush the device beneath my shoe, stamping it into useless shards for good measure.

"Hey! You can't do that!"

I kick it back towards her. "Fucking bill me."

She's still swearing up a storm as I stride away, taking the corridor to where Harlow is having her weekly therapy session. Barging in without knocking, I slam the door behind me to block anyone from seeing in.

The ward matron shouldn't let the vultures get past, but we still need to get the hell out of here. Someone's ass is going to be fired for not spotting the cameras hiding outside the hospital.

"Hunter?" Richards protests from his seat by the window. "This is a private session. You can't just walk in whenever you feel like it."

Harlow is huddled in a high-backed armchair, her trembling knees pulled up to her chest. She looks so fucking good, her bright, furtive eyes framed by curling hair that she hasn't cut yet.

I really need to get Enzo to buy her some warmer clothing; the low-cut tank top she's wearing with grey sweats and an oversized cardigan won't hold up against the cold weather coming.

"I understand, doc. Unfortunately, we have a situation outside. I need to get Harlow out of here."

Richards tucks his glasses into the collar of his pinstriped shirt. "It's always a damn situation with you people."

"You can continue this at another time. I apologise for the interruption."

He stands and gestures for Harlow to do the same. She's unsteady on her feet, struggling to straighten with her tightly wrapped ribs. I offer her a helping hand, which she eyes mistrustfully.

"Sorry, Harlow. I didn't mean to interrupt."

Nodding, she purses her lips and takes my hand. Her limbs are still quaking with fear. Whatever they were discussing, it's left her feeling vulnerable and exposed.

I'm not the right person to deal with her fragile state. Hell, I was intending to come over here and lay into her until she broke and gave up the truth. Being her fucking white knight was not on the agenda.

"I'll catch you up later, Richards."

"Please do," he says pointedly.

We exchange a rapid conversation through eye contact. I nod again, silently asking him to back down. Richards is more than my colleague—he's a friend. I don't have time for one of those today.

Harlow still can't look me in the eye as we creep over to the door. In the corridor, the matron and several nurses are dealing with a horde of cameramen flooding the department. Perfect.

"Goddamn reporters," I curse quietly. "We'll have to find another way out. Keep your head low. Don't let them see your face. Got it?"

She flinches at my barked order. I force myself to be calmer, holding my hand out again until she has the bravery to meet my eyes.

"I'm sorry. Take my hand, Harlow. I'll get us out of here, okay?"

She still doesn't budge. I fight the urge to throw her over my shoulder, kicking and screaming. We don't have time for this.

"Have I ever given you a reason not to trust me?"

Hesitantly, she shakes her head. "I guess not."

"Then there's your answer. I promise I'll look after you."

Her fingers hesitantly link with mine and I squeeze her hand tight. I'm an asshole, but I do care, regardless of what Theo thinks of the person I've become to survive.

Together, we slip out into the corridor and take a right, heading deeper into the bustling hospital. There's a chorus of shouts, followed by the sound of pursuing feet.

"Call security!" a nurse shouts.

"You can't go back there!"

"Stop them!"

Throwing an arm around Harlow, I try my best to conceal her face from the flashing cameras. We duck and weave through endless hallways, trying to lose the greedy mob at our heels.

I've got no clue where we're going. Sally and her soul-sucking cameramen are determined to get an exclusive. I refuse to let them humiliate Harlow the same way they did to me.

"Wait," Harlow blurts.

"There's no time. Move it."

"No, stop. In here."

She throws my arm off and opens a door on our left, leading into a maintenance cupboard. I'm dragged into the darkness as she closes the door behind us, keeping the lights off.

Thirty seconds later, we hear the horde of cameras and Sally's near-hysterical shouting pass by. The noise grows quieter as we huddle together in pitch-black darkness.

"Harlow?" I search around with my hands. "I can't see a thing. Where are you?"

The complete darkness, coupled with my one deaf ear, is disorientating. I can't see if she's okay. Her fingertips ghost over my arm in a hesitant caress that causes my pulse to spike.

"I'm here," she whispers back. "Careful, there's a bucket behind you."

"How the hell can you see anything?"

"I'm used to the dark."

Her hand bunches in my jacket, and I can feel the beckoning heat of her body. Grabbing her wrist, I drag her closer, our bodies colliding in the tight space.

"That was a close one."

"Good thinking there." Hesitantly, I slide an arm around her waist to hold her close. "You covered our asses."

Her small, pert breasts press against my torso. "Believe it or not, I can be useful."

"I never said that you aren't useful."

"You didn't have to."

Still clutching my jacket in a death grip, Harlow guides me back to the door. She opens it a crack to listen, allowing a thin sliver of light to illuminate the cramped cupboard.

"I think they're gone. Who were those people?"

"Reporters," I growl out. "Sally Moore's a soulless bitch. I know her editor, and he owes me a favour. She won't have a job by the end of the week."

The thin strip of light illuminates Harlow's face. I'm trapped by her brilliant blue eyes boring into me, nervous and afraid. Lower still, her glistening bottom lip is caught between her teeth.

"I won't let them hurt you," I find myself promising.

Her eye contact doesn't break. The tension is excruciating. She wears the same broken expression as the night I dismissed her, throwing up impenetrable walls between us.

I want to reach out and bite that lip, tasting her sweetness for myself. A second before giving in, the DNA report comes back to me, and all of its messy implications.

"Your session with Richards… was it good?"

Harlow quickly looks away as the moment passes.

"Fine."

"Did you get any more information we can use?"

The angry little spitfire inside of her rises to the surface, her eyes filling with annoyance. Goddamn me to hell, I'm fucking hard watching her expression darken and hands tighten into fists.

She doesn't look like someone who's deliberately misleading us all, lying her ass off while eating our food and abusing our trust. I just don't see it. My judgement is never wrong.

"I told you everything, Hunter."

"There are significant gaps in your memory," I point out. "We need to establish a reliable timeline."

Surprising me, Harlow places a hand on my chest and shoves me backwards. I nearly topple over a brush propped against the wall before righting myself.

"I was locked in a cage, starved, beaten, and neglected by monsters that enjoyed killing other girls. I can't remember shit because I don't *want* to remember. Get off my back."

Her chest rises and falls in a rapid rhythm. She looks like she wants to punch me in the nose again, but on purpose this time.

"I didn't mean it like that," I backtrack.

"Yeah. You did."

Through the slanted light, I can see her lips are twisted into a grimace. It hurts me to see the pain I'm causing. I don't usually give a fuck, but with her, I'm not in control of my feelings.

"Give me a break, Harlow." I attempt to approach her, my hands spread. "I'm trying to fix this mess. It's nothing personal."

"Well, I'm trying to figure out how to be alive in this crazy, confusing place. You're not making it any easier."

My hands hang mid-air as I wrestle with my need to touch, protect, and cherish her. Even if it goes against every last warning bell blaring inside me. Caring only equals heartache.

"You're right," I blurt.

She halts. "Huh?"

Blowing out a breath, I prepare to plunge into the deep end. "I want to chase down every last lead and make them talk. Not being in control is hard for me."

"That's not an apology."

I splutter a laugh. There's a hint of a smile pulling Harlow's mouth taut as she stares up at me, a challenge burning in her irises.

The others think she's just a precious wallflower that has to be protected and nourished, but I see the other side too. There's a caged lion beneath her skin, begging to be set free.

"I'm sorry, sweetheart." I run a hand over the rough scruff of hair covering my chin. "I was wrong to push you."

Despite every reason my obsessive mind has already considered, my fingers still twitch with need as I battle not to drag her closer, pin her against the fucking wall and show her exactly what I'm thinking.

"I never thought I'd hear you say that," she murmurs.

"Enjoy it while it lasts. It's not happening again."

Harlow stares at me with an adorable crease between her brows. Unable to stop myself, I reach out and run the tip of my finger over it.

"I thought you hated me."

Her words crash into me like a five-vehicle pileup.

"What on earth made you think that?"

"You barely speak to me. Not like the others do."

Struggling to find an explanation that won't make me sound like an egotistical asshole, I sigh heavily.

"My priority is to solve this case. It doesn't leave room for emotion. The work comes first, you see? Especially when lives are at stake."

"I understand." She looks down, fighting to keep the pain off her face. "As soon as this is over, I'll leave you in peace."

"Fuck, that's not what I meant."

"Isn't it?"

She inches backwards, anxiously fiddling with her hair. The distance growing between us again is strangling me. I don't want to leave this cupboard and go back to how things were.

"They should be gone by now."

Her voice is detached, robotic. Without waiting for my answer, she opens the door and steps out into the corridor, leaving the shadows of our intimate moment behind.

Cursing myself, I follow behind her, wrestling with the truth. We're not good enough for Harlow. She deserves the world, and I can't give it to her. Theo was right.

I have to call her family and share the good news, even if that means giving her up and breaking my teammates all over again. Another loss may be the final nail in the coffin.

I'm not naive enough to ignore the impact she's had on our family in a matter of weeks. Enzo, Leighton—they've accepted her into our family without hesitating. I knew this would happen.

Losing her may be the end of us.

But like usual, I have no fucking choice.

CHAPTER 16
HARLOW

(IF) YOU ARE THE OCEAN (THEN) I WOULD LIKE TO DROWN - VIOLET NIGHT

"IS EVERYTHING OKAY?" I ask for the third time.

Behind the wheel, Enzo is staring at the country road with a clenched jaw. He's been quiet ever since we left the house, without his usual softness and charm.

The bags beneath his amber eyes are more pronounced than usual, ageing him more than his thirty-two years. I couldn't believe it when I found out his age. Enzo doesn't sleep much anyway, but he looks dead on his feet today.

"Everything's fine, Harlow."

"How many times are you going to say that?"

"How many times are you going to ask?" he replies sharply.

My mouth clicks shut. They've all been acting strange for the last few days. I thought it must be something to do with the reporters that tracked us down in the hospital, but this feels like more.

Leighton barely spared me a glance this morning, preferring to go down to the gym in the basement of their home and blast aggressive music. Not even a wink or bad joke.

"Where are we going?" I try instead.

Taking a right, Enzo releases a sigh. "You need more clothes. We only got the basics last time. Hunter wants you to have a phone too, so we can contact you."

"Am I going somewhere?"

"Of course not." Enzo frowns at the road. "It's just a precaution."

His words don't quite ring true. Anxiety wraps around my windpipe as he speeds through the autumnal gloom.

"I still haven't paid you back for the last shopping trip," I worry aloud. "Maybe I should get a job or something. Start pulling my weight around here. I can't stay cooped up forever."

"You don't need a job."

"I can't keep taking handouts, Enzo."

He curses under his breath. "It isn't safe right now. Working is out of the question. If you want to do something in the future, we can discuss that another time."

"I'm an adult. I can make my own decisions."

"Not if those decisions put your life in danger. That's not happening, Harlow. Not on my watch."

I slump back in my seat. His overprotective nature is endearing, but after weeks of resting, attending therapy and taking medication like a good little prisoner, I'm tired of following orders without question.

Winding through the countryside doused in fallen leaves and golden sunshine, we eventually reach a small village. Traditional cottages with picket fences and painted doors line the winding streets.

Passing through the residential area, small shop fronts start to appear as the houses melt away. Enzo finds a tight parking spot, manoeuvring the SUV into it with wordless ease.

The minute the car is parked, I leap out and slam the door shut. My ribs twinge from the sudden drop, but the pain is manageable. I'm not some invalid, no matter what he thinks.

At first, his possessive need to wrap me in cotton wool was appreciated. It's given me the confidence to face the world a little more each day. But with each step I take, I'm changing.

I want to be treated like everyone else.

I want to actually *live*.

Enzo circles the car, pulling on his usual leather jacket. With his ripped, black jeans and dark-green t-shirt, every inch of corded muscle that carves his monstrous frame is on display.

A shiver runs down my spine, but not from fear. I can't explain the way he makes me feel, even when he's being infuriating and suffocating me to death.

"Why are you looking at me like you want to deck me?" he asks with a hint of his usual tenderness.

I drag my purple beanie over my long hair. "Because I'm seriously thinking about it. Why can't I have more freedom?"

Propping his shoulder against the car, he levels me with a serious stare. "No progress with the case doesn't equate to safety. The threat is still real. Do you want to go back to where you came from?"

"N-No," I stutter, seized by panic.

"I will do everything in my power to keep you safe, Harlow. Even if you hate me for it. I won't see you get hurt."

Closing the space between us, I wrap my un-plastered arm around his waist. He engulfs me in a tight embrace, and I can feel his nose buried in my hair. We stand like that forever.

It's like being crushed against a boulder, but the way he holds me is gentle, reverent. He smells like the garden after it has rained—earthy, fresh, full of new beginnings and hope.

My forehead is pressed against the hard planes of his abdominals, and we don't speak for several moments, holding one another. This has been happening more often, but I don't mind.

Touching Enzo is like coming up for air, coughing and spluttering, but thankful to be alive. He makes me feel safe. Cherished. Wanted. Even with the pain and secrets dancing in his eyes.

"What's going on?" I whisper against his t-shirt.

His muscles tense beneath my touch. "I just need you to be okay, little one. Nothing else matters."

"I'm right here, Enzo." Looking up into his amber eyes, I squeeze his waist tight. "Can't you feel me?"

Enzo cups both of my cheeks in a tight, almost desperate grip. I have to fight not to pull away. It's a vulnerable position for me, utterly trapped by his strength, but I'm not afraid.

"I can feel you," he echoes softly. "Harlow, I…"

Waiting for him to finish, the words never come. I wait, beg, silently plead for more. I want him to touch me. Hold me. Claim every last broken piece of me.

The realisation is terrifying. I don't know what all these confusing feelings mean. They've been building for a while now. From the way he looks at me… I think he feels the same way.

"We should go inside," Enzo finishes.

Disappointment stabs me in the chest. His hands drop from my face, taking my hand instead. I'm towed along as we leave the car park, taking a cobbled street into town.

Enzo is a wall of tension next to me as clouds bubble overhead. The first spots of rain kiss my skin with cool relief, gradually picking up until the shower soaks our clothes.

"Put your sunglasses on," he instructs.

"It's literally raining. I'll look more suspicious wearing them."

"Just do it, Harlow. I'm not risking anyone spotting you, especially with those fucking reporters causing mayhem."

Huffing, I release his hand to slide the borrowed sunglasses into place. With my long hair and beanie, I'm as anonymous as a ghost. It's the only reason I haven't cut it yet.

Enzo folds an arm around my shoulders, pulling me close again. I bathe in his pillar of warmth as we walk quicker to escape the rain.

"This place has the best pancake house," he explains, guiding me down another street. "A friend of mine found it last year."

"You don't seem like a pancake kind of person."

"What's that supposed to mean?"

Raising an eyebrow, I take in his huge shoulders and arms, the rippling muscles pulling his leather jacket tight. It's like walking next to a grizzly bear.

People take one look at Enzo and scurry away, even his employees. They don't see what I do. To the world, his sheer physical power is a threat. No one bothers to see what's underneath it.

"You've got the whole Bruce Banner thing going on."

"How on earth do you know that reference?"

I shrug. "Leighton likes movies. I like learning."

"You should choose your own movies from now on. Leighton will melt your brain with that shit."

"I liked it," I defend.

We pass beneath a thick canopy of trees cloaked in twinkling lights. As the rain eases off, little shop fronts begin to throw open their doors and lay out fresh fruits and vegetables, muttering about the unpredictable winter weather.

"What else do you like?" Enzo asks.

Despite devouring knowledge and new experiences from within my comfortable prison, there's still so much about the world that I don't know. My life, despite my best efforts, is exactly as Hunter said.

Little.

More than anything, I'm beginning to feel suffocated rather than protected. In the basement, I couldn't see what I was missing. It was easier to accept my isolation.

"I don't know. I'd like to find out."

"There must be something," Enzo pushes. "Humour me."

"Well, I like to watch the sun rise and set."

He nods, studying me out of the corner of his eye. "Lucky's never had so much company outside. What else?"

"I like the feel of rain on my face and wet grass beneath my feet." I tighten my jacket around me, feeling exposed. "Boiling hot showers are the best, and sleeping with the window open so I can feel the air on my skin at night."

He listens intently, hanging on to every word.

"I like listening to your voice when you're happy. Leighton's laugh too, it's adorable. And don't tell him, but Hunter makes the best tea."

Clearing my throat, I feel heat rise to my cheeks.

"I like not being alone anymore."

Enzo suddenly draws us to a halt. Two calloused fingers lift my chin as he pulls the sunglasses aside. Our eyes collide. Blue on amber, nervous on certain, our lives couldn't be further apart.

"You never have to be alone ever again," he murmurs, searching my face.

"You guys can't look after me forever." I fight to keep my voice even, hoping to hide the fear that rises at the thought of leaving. "I'm a burden to you."

His hand travels along my jawline, exploring the gaunt lines of my face. I'm still struggling to put on weight, despite moving to solid foods a couple of weeks ago.

I hold my breath, unable to stop myself from leaning into his touch. Enzo musters a sweet, heartbreaking smile.

"You are not a burden, Harlow."

"Then what am I? A client?"

He licks his lips. "How about a friend?"

We remain frozen in the street, despite a trail of people passing us by. Enzo doesn't move his hand, staring deep into my eyes. I realise there are tiny stripes of silver in his irises.

"You want to be my friend?" I whisper nervously.

"If you'll allow me."

My voice comes out raspy. "I'd like a friend."

This time when he smiles, he flashes teeth. I think my heart actually stops for a moment. Seriously, what's with these butterflies in my stomach? I need to find a trustworthy female to ask.

"Come on, I'm hungry," he declares.

We resume our slow walk into town, stopping outside a bright-blue shop front with a striped overhang. The sign proclaims it to have the best pancakes in England inside.

Enzo has to duck low to fit through the door, locating a cracked vinyl booth in shades of bright pink and yellow. He looks ridiculous sliding into it.

"Could this get any smaller," he grumbles.

I stifle a laugh. "Please don't break it."

"If I do, it'll be the booth's fault."

A blonde-haired woman trails over, trying not to laugh when she spots his predicament. I tuck my chin low, averting my face before she can attempt to speak to me. Enzo quickly dismisses her and hands me a menu.

"What's good?"

He shifts, making the booth creak. "Everything."

"Not helpful."

"Want me to order for you?"

I breathe a sigh of relief. "Please."

When the waitress returns, Enzo fires off a huge order. Her eyes bulge with shock as she's forced to flip to another page on her little pad. I'm pretty sure he just ordered half the menu.

Once she scurries away, Enzo stretches his long legs out until they brush mine under the table. He still looks uncomfortable.

"Tell me something." I fiddle with the paper napkins on the table. "I want to know more about you guys. I feel like you know everything about me."

He folds his huge arms. "Not much to tell."

"I opened up. It's your turn."

"Fine," he concedes. "Let's see… well, me and Hunter grew up together. Our parents were neighbours. We've always been best friends. I couldn't have gotten through my parents' deaths without him."

"What happened?"

"They died in a mountaineering accident when I was a teenager. It was during a sponsored climb of Mount Everest for a leukaemia charity. Despite years of training, it all went wrong."

Reaching across the table, I take his clenched hand. Enzo's fingers tighten around mine.

"My sister was diagnosed with cancer as a toddler, so my folks did a lot of fundraising for the expedition. There was an avalanche before they could summit. We never recovered their bodies."

"I'm so sorry," I offer, hating his pain.

His hand squeezes mine. "My dad's sister, Hayley, is a saint. She was looking after us while they were away and ended up taking custody of me and my younger sister. She raised us like her own."

"She sounds pretty amazing."

"Yeah, she really is. When Paula got her terminal diagnosis, Hayley devoted everything to her. We practically lived in the paediatric ward until she died."

Enzo stares down at the tabletop, his throat bobbing. I had no idea he'd lost pretty much his whole family. The pain he has to feel is unimaginable. Abbie lost her brother in a motorcycle accident. She told me about it once.

Grief is an impenetrable, lonely prison.

I hate the thought of Enzo suffering alone.

"After Paula died, I dropped out of school. Hunter was already working as a personal trainer, but he was unhappy. We decided to go backpacking around South America for a year."

"So how did you end up founding Sabre?"

Enzo's thumb strokes over my knuckles. "Hunter's dad is a retired police officer, so he grew up around crime scenes. His parents told us to get our shit together and lent us the start-up cash to create the company."

"How old were you?"

"I was twenty at the time. Hunter's a couple of years older than me. Private security seemed like the most flexible and varied job we could find."

I watch the brief smile dancing across his lips. The sense of pride is obvious, from the light that sparks in his eyes as he recalls his humble roots, to the determined set of his shoulders that reflects the unshakeable faith that got him this far.

"It was just the two of us as we established ourselves," Enzo continues. "For several years, we focused on private security. Once we knew the business, we took on more criminal investigations."

"Like my case?"

"Sometimes. We usually get the hard ones that law enforcement can't crack. We're good at what we do. People started to notice, and an investor helped us expand more. Twelve years later, here we are."

"When did Theo join?"

"Around eight years ago. He was nineteen at the time. We got him off a hacking charge that would've resulted in prison time."

I gape at him. "Theo? Really?"

Enzo chuckles. "He has the least respect for the law out of us all, little one. There isn't a database he won't attempt to hack."

In the small amount of time I've spent with Theo, he was kind and thoughtful. I'm struggling to imagine him getting arrested.

"He built the intelligence department from the ground up and broke into a whole new side of the business. We've been very lucky."

"You're good at what you do, that's not luck."

"We've made our fair share of mistakes," Enzo mutters. "There was this case a few years back. We took on a corrupt medical corporation, running an empire of psychiatric institutes. It nearly destroyed the entire company."

His face changes—growing darker, shadowed by suffering and regret. I watch his throat bob with emotion.

"Hunter lost his hearing the year after, and we were grieving for… well, someone important. Getting through it all felt impossible."

"I'm sorry, Enz."

"It's alright. We figured things out."

The waitress reappears with a tray propped over her shoulder. Enzo's mouth slams shut as he accepts the drinks, taking a black coffee and a water for himself.

I don't miss the way she checks out his muscled chest while he's distracted. The urge to scratch her eyes out overwhelms me.

"These all for you, hun?" she asks with a wan smile.

My mouth hangs open, but no words come out. I just stare at her, silently panicking. Her eyebrow raises as she looks at me like I'm stupid. I want to curl up under the table and hide.

"I'll take those," Enzo interrupts, snatching the tray from her. "That'll be all, thanks."

Dismissed, she leaves with a glare sent my way. I work on uncurling my clenched fist as Enzo drops three drinks in front of me. Why can't I be normal? I had to go and embarrass him.

"I thought you could choose."

"Thank you," I force out. "Sorry, I panicked."

"Stop apologising and drink up."

Sticking a straw in the cloudy juice in front of me, I take a long drag and hum in contentment. It's exotic and fruity, kinda like the smell of Leighton's citrus shampoo, but sweeter.

"This is good. What is it?"

"Pineapple juice."

"I have no idea what that is, but I like it."

His smile is toe-curling. Enzo loves pleasing me as much as Leighton enjoys teaching me new things. I watch him sip his steaming mug of coffee and decide to try my own.

Taking two sugars, I dump them in before having a sip. The richness of coffee beans clings to my tongue, offset by sweetness.

"This is good too. It's kinda strong, though."

"That's the point. It kicks your ass in the morning."

"Then why does Hunter drink tea?"

Enzo chuckles around a mouthful. "Because he's a psychopath, obviously. Who else drinks tea instead of coffee?"

"I really have no idea."

Drinking some more coffee, I wince and swallow it down. I won't tell Enzo, but Hunter's tea is far nicer. I'll join him as a psychopath if it means I can drink that instead of this sludge.

"So, what about Leighton?" I change the topic.

Enzo rests his chin on his laced fingers. "Leighton was a good kid. He idolised Hunter growing up, but they fought a lot too. Their folks adored Hunter. He was academic and scarily smart in school."

"Figures."

"Not much has changed. He still lives a whole fucking level above the rest of us peasants. I can't pretend to understand his nut-job brain."

We share a laugh and Enzo takes another sip, studying the pitch-black liquid.

"Leighton was often overlooked. Their dad's an interesting character. He worked a lot but still piled pressure on his kids to excel. Leighton began to act out and started to get in trouble with the law."

"How so?"

"Getting into fights, smoking at school. Going to older kids' parties and drinking. He's always been a bit of a wild child. It hit Hunter hard when Leighton was sent to prison."

I nearly drop my cup of coffee. "What now?"

"It's still a sensitive situation. Leighton's only been out a few months after serving three years. He's isolated himself from his family since getting out. Even their folks haven't seen him yet. They're devastated."

Blinking hard, I struggle to keep up. Part of me can't believe it. Leighton is the warmest, most carefree spirit I've ever met. He's everything that's good in the world, wrapped up in a soft exterior.

"Have I blown your mind?" Enzo laughs.

"Um, a little bit. Why was he in prison?"

"That's his story to tell, little one. Though I wouldn't recommend asking him about it."

Pushing the coffee aside, I return to the juice. The bitter drink is curdling in my stomach with the realisation that I don't know these people as well as I thought. I feel awful for never asking before.

"What about you?"

His thick eyebrows furrow. "Me?"

"Tell me something no one else knows."

He's clearly stumped as he frowns at his huge hands. The roughened skin over his knuckles is discoloured from layers of scar tissue, painting a violent picture of the gentle giant I know.

"I hate my job," he suddenly blurts.

"You're kidding? Why?"

"Every day… all I see is death and pain. We help a lot of people, but we also can't help just as many of them. Those are the cases that make me want to retire, open up a chop shop or something."

"Chop shop?" I repeat.

"Cars. My pops taught me a lot; I used to go to work with him. He owned a chain of mechanic shops in outer London."

"So what's stopping you?"

Enzo chews his lip as he stares at the table. I sense that I should stop prying about his past, but my curiosity is far stronger than my need to be polite.

I want to know everything about them, all the tiny, intimate details that nobody else is close enough to receive. I want to *be* close enough to know those things.

"This is Hunter's dream," he answers carefully. "Sabre wouldn't be a success without his leadership. My place is by his side."

"But… what about your dream?"

He shrugs again. "When our work is done, I'll have a quiet life. Until then, we have a job to do. That's enough for me."

Several steaming plates arrive from the kitchen, and enough food to feed an army clusters the table. The waitress slides a stack of pancakes over to me, covered in strawberries and syrup.

"How did you know what I like?" I grin at Enzo.

He smiles back. "Leighton told me about the pancake disaster the other morning. You know he can't cook for shit, right?"

"I know now. These actually look edible."

Enzo dives in and clears his plate in under a minute, moving on to the next. I've never seen anyone devour a stack of pancakes so fast. It's a wonder he isn't the size of a house.

"A quiet life?" I break the silence.

He wipes his chin. "Maybe a house in the countryside. Lots of land, trees, fields of corn. Some animals. A workshop and place to fix old cars without listening to sirens or gunshots. I hate London."

"That sounds peaceful."

"I like to think so. What about you?"

I swallow a bite of syrupy goodness, caught off guard by his question. "What about me?"

"You must have stuff that you want to do."

His gaze burrows beneath my skin like a laser pointer, challenging me to answer. The pancakes turn to stone in the pit of my stomach. I place my fork down, taking a long drink of juice.

"I'm just trying to survive from one day to the next."

"There's more to life than that, Harlow. We can figure out what you want to do. I said that I'd help you before, and I meant it."

"Really?"

His nod is firm, decisive. "That's what friends are for, right?"

"I have no clue. I haven't had many."

Enzo's hand takes mine again. "We'll muddle through together. Come on, eat up. We still need to go shopping. I'm not having any complaints this time."

CHAPTER 17
HARLOW

SOMEONE SOMEWHERE SOMEHOW - SUPER WHATEVR

FACING the huge pile of bags, I give myself a little shake. I was too tired to unpack when we got back yesterday. Walking around and trying on clothes for so long exhausted me.

I'm still building up my strength, and until I can keep on the weight that I'm supposed to be gaining, I have to take lots of naps when my energy levels crash.

Enzo totally took advantage of my desire to cheer him up and filled countless baskets with winter clothes, accessories and random things that caught my eye. He was like a man possessed.

I now have a full wardrobe of sweaters, long-sleeved t-shirts, a thicker coat and leather-soled boots that keep my feet warm. In the other bag, there's a huge, back-breaking stack of books.

I've trained myself to focus for longer periods of time and can now read without getting a headache. As a result, I've become insatiable. Enzo let me go wild, picking up every single book I looked at.

There's a glossy, white box in the final bag that holds my new mobile phone. I'm pretty sure this goes beyond the essentials he convinced me we were shopping for.

I almost wanted to ask if they do this for all of their clients, but I bit my tongue to avoid an awkward conversation. Hunter ordered it, so we're bound to obey him.

"Lucky," I chastise as she curls up on my new sweater. "You're getting fur everywhere, girl."

Her big, pleading eyes blink up at me.

"Don't look at me like that. You'll get me in trouble for being in here, let alone on the bed."

Nuzzling into the new, turquoise bed sheets, she gets comfy and falls asleep. Hunter would kill me if he saw her in here. He's a stickler for pointless house rules. Anything that gives him control.

After packing my new clothes away, I stack the books on my bedside table and check the window. It's evening already; I've missed my usual sunset walk in the back garden.

Curling up around Lucky's warm, snoring body, I crack the pages of a new book and lose myself to the tale of magic and mystery. Enzo and Hunter won't be home for a while yet.

"Goldilocks?"

Looking up from the pages, I realise the room is cloaked in shadows. The evening has already slipped away. The book gripped me so hard, I don't think I've blinked at all while reading into the night.

"Yeah, I'm in here."

Leighton pops his head around the door, giving me a wave. He went out last night after an argument with Hunter about paying rent, and his door has been shut all day. I didn't want to disturb him.

Propping himself in the doorway, he pushes back his messy mop of brown hair. My heart leaps into my mouth. There's a huge black bruise marring his right eye, and it's swollen all the way shut.

"Oh my God, Leigh!"

"I'm fine," he rushes to explain. "I got into a stupid fight in the club last night. Some asshole was forcing himself on a girl. Serves me right for getting involved."

"So you hit him?"

He smiles broadly. "Obviously. I don't take shit like that. It was worth getting my ass kicked so she could slip away and get a taxi."

He flops down on the bed, disturbing Lucky, who growls her displeasure. Leighton's head lays across my blanketed legs as he snuggles closer to the dog.

"You shouldn't be out fighting." I fold a page corner in the book and set it down. "I don't like seeing you hurt."

His green eyes meet mine. "I'm alright. Did you just fold a page? Do you want Hunter to crucify you?"

"What?" I exclaim in panic.

"No, no," he splutters, reading my fear. "It was a joke, Harlow. He's just weird about books. Dusts them and everything."

Taking a deep breath, I pin Leighton with a glower. "Don't scare me like that. And don't change the topic. Your eye looks bad."

"Are you worried about me, princess?"

"Didn't we discuss the p-word?" I sigh.

"We discussed how much you love it, sure. Other nickname options include pumpkin, honey bunch, and babelicious."

"Ugh, pass on all three, thanks."

"Spoilsport."

With a wink, Leighton snatches up the white box laying unwrapped on my bedside table. It was far too complicated for me to even contemplate.

"Enzo texted and asked me to get you set up. He's stuck dealing with some work shit. Hunter too, I think."

"This late?"

"Apparently." Leighton avoids my eyes, seeming shifty. "Something at the office. I wouldn't worry."

"To do with the case? Or me?"

"Oh, look!" He opens the box and pulls out a sleek, rose-gold phone. "It's pink and everything. How girlie."

Clearing my throat, I watch him plug it in to charge, still avoiding my question. His fingers fly across the screen so fast, it's almost intimidating.

When he hands the phone over to me ten minutes later, I gingerly accept it. The screen glows with too many icons and different functions to process. I hate this thing already.

"I don't know how to use this."

Leighton snorts. "I'll show you. It's easy once you get the hang of it."

He spends half an hour showing me how to send text messages, call people, and search the internet. Man, that place is wild. There's so much to learn. My mind is already spinning with possibilities.

Clicking the camera icon, I lift the phone to capture Leighton in the frame. He sticks his tongue out like Lucky would do, letting me capture a silly picture.

"All four of us are saved on there," he explains, showing me the contacts. "I texted the guys so they will have your number saved."

"All f-four of y-you?" I stutter.

Leighton's eyes sparkle with amusement. "Why does that surprise you?"

"Even Hunter? Theo?"

He ignores the doubt in my voice. "Even them. Although you'll be lucky to get ahold of Theo in daylight hours. From what I hear, he's nocturnal. Sleeps at his desk and works through the night."

"Doesn't he have a room here?"

"Never uses it."

Filing that information away, I ditch the phone on top of my discarded book. The thought of Theo eating and sleeping alone in an office makes my heart ache. He seems like a good person.

"We could try to make a late dinner for everyone." I stroke Lucky's ears as she huffs in contentment. "I'm sure they'll be hungry."

Leighton grins, all mischief. "Sure, I'm up for that. No promises that we won't give them food poisoning with us working in the kitchen."

"Can't be worse than your pancakes."

"Ouch! You wound me. Alright, shift your ass, mystery girl. You won't like me when I'm hangry and hungover."

Safe to say, dinner is a disaster.

In our defence, Leighton is over-ambitious.

He pulls ingredients at random out of the fridge, covering the spotless kitchen in so much mess, it gives me heart palpitations. Hunter will murder the pair of us when he sees the state of it.

We discover that it is possible to burn pasta and still end up with crunchy strands of spaghetti. Apparently, this is a scientific achievement. Leighton says we should win an award for culinary masterminding.

"You really are a terrible cook," I say between belly-hurting fits of laughter. "We can't eat this."

"Aren't you hungry?" Leighton snickers.

It happens so fast, I can't stop myself from slipping into the past. Richards has been teaching me to breathe through the flashbacks, but when they're so intense, I'm left falling to my death.

Aren't you hungry, sinner?

Come here and kiss daddy's cheek.

Be a good girl and we'll give you some dinner.

The rush of memories lance into me with such intensity, I drop the vegetable knife I was slicing an onion with. The kitchen around me melts away with each stuttered breath I take.

It's too late to pull myself back.

The past swallows me whole.

All I can see is Mrs Michaels, an old belt in her hand, striking me over and over. Christie's blue corpse has been dragged out of the cage, left on a thick, plastic sheet to be dismantled.

You will help me, fucking bitch!

Strike.

You disobedient little swine.

Strike.

The pain is so real, I can feel it searing my shredded skin. My younger voice fills my ears, begging for mercy. I refused to help her saw my friend's limbs apart to get rid of.

"Harlow? Harlow?"

Someone's shaking me, repeating this name over and over again. I don't know why. Who am I? Who is Harlow? All I can see is the dark, cramped cell imprisoning me in hell.

Scents assault me.

Blood. Urine.

Filth. Mould.

Rotting corpses.

I'm back behind those bars, screaming for relief as time loses all meaning. Days, weeks, years. My hair grew and body weakened, but nothing else changed.

"Harlow! Talk to me, dammit."

Tears soak my cheeks. Ice invades my extremities, trapping me in a bubble. I'm drowning. Choking. Sinking further and further out of reach. I need to call for help, but nothing comes out.

Their faces are all there. Plastered on the walls of my mind, connected by the same red cord. Every single one of them that died in that Godless place. I can't escape them.

"I'm sorry," I scream at the ghosts.

It isn't enough. They don't want an apology. My words won't bring them back or undo the evil that stole their lives. These ghosts won't ever leave me. Not until justice is served.

Backing into a corner, I cover my ears and squeeze my head; it feels like it might explode. I can still see them, bleeding and gasping for air, begging me with their eyes.

I can't run.

I can't hide.

I'm alive… and they're not. My life isn't free. It doesn't belong to me anymore. The stolen futures of eighteen women live within me.

Someone grabs my shoulders and shakes so hard, my teeth snap together. It doesn't break the sarcophagus trapping me in my head. I'm being chased, the thud of dead feet hunting me down.

"No!" I shout, thrusting a fist outward.

It connects with something hard, eliciting a grunt. I can't see anything but blood. Everywhere. Coating everything. Dripping. Pooling. Congealing. It covers every inch of me.

"Harlow!"

The voice is warped and garbled. Pastor Michaels screamed my name at me when I made him mad, throwing it like a dagger to illicit my obedience. Hearing it now makes me sick.

All I can think about is hurting. Inflicting the pain that's scarred my skin. Peeling off the hands gripping my shoulders, I shove my captor backwards, throwing another punch.

We crash into each other, both grappling for control. I don't stop. Not yet. My cowardice caused those girls to die alone. I can't be weak anymore; they won't let me forget.

"Harlow, stop! I won't fucking fight you!"

The cast encasing my arm cracks against the tiled floor as we both fall. Pain batters into me, over and over, but it isn't enough. I can still see them—their eyes wide, mouths parted, blood pouring out.

Lifting my head, I slam it back down onto the tiled floor. Excruciating pain explodes through my skull, over and over, my surroundings beginning to fuzz at the edges.

"Stop it!"

Thwack.

Thwack.

Thwack.

"I'm sorry," the person weighing me down growls. "You have to stop."

A pair of hands wrap around my throat in a vice-like grip. I'm being strangled by a viper, the oxygen sucked from my lungs.

"Stop… fighting!"

My nails scratch at his tightening hands, desperate for a sliver of air. But it's working. The harder my lungs battle for control, the faster my body is turning limp. I'm losing energy, fast.

Blood is slick against my fingertips as I scratch and battle, frantically attempting to escape. Just as my vision is threatening to darken into unconsciousness, blissful agony wracks over me.

His hands are gone.

My throat seizes and expands, dragging in the sweet nectar of air. I cough and splutter, clutching my throbbing neck. A crushing weight is still pinning me to the floor.

Emerald eyes the colour of fresh moss peer down at me. His terror is palpable, hanging in the air with such potency, I can taste it on my lips. Reality is a razor-sharp wire around my throat.

"Oh fuck, Harlow," Leighton keens, his gaze frantic. "Are you okay? I didn't know what else to do!"

I can't muster a single word. The adrenaline has rushed out of me in a powerful surge, leaving nothing but emptiness. All I can feel is his weight and the crushing beat of his heart against mine, demanding forgiveness.

"I had to stop you from hurting yourself." His hands hover over me, unsure where to begin. "Please… say something. Shit!"

My mouth hangs open, silent.

"Fucking hell. Please don't hate me for doing this."

Grasping my cheeks so tight, it's almost painful, his mouth crashes onto mine. I don't know how to react. Our lips are locked in a bruising collision, and Leighton's determined to win this war.

He's kissing me.

Over and over again.

Pausing, he pulls back and searches my face. Whatever he finds is enough for his lips to return to mine—softer, more hesitant, moving in a tender rhythm that would rival a well-orchestrated symphony.

My lips part, seeking something I can't fathom. His tongue slides into my mouth without hesitating, deepening the kiss until it feels like he's drinking the oxygen that's dared to enter my lungs.

I can't breathe. Can't think. Can't do anything but lie there, filled with delicious heat, letting Leighton chase away the darkness that's infected my mind. He's leaving no room for the bad thoughts.

Our tongues touch, dancing together like twin flames battling to consume the other's light. Fire is racing over my skin, setting my nerves alight, plunging me into a storm of sensation.

I have no idea what I'm doing. His hands are running over me, stroking down my body to cup my hips. Heat gathers between my thighs, stoked by the pressure of something hard pushing against me.

Breaking apart with a pained gasp, Leighton's forehead meets mine. "Jesus, Harlow. What the hell did we just do?"

"Leigh—"

"Don't say anything. This is my fault."

He stares down at me with such regret, I feel like I've been stamped on. My eyes shutter, recoiling from the sting of rejection.

"No!" He panics, grabbing my chin to pull my eyes back up to his. "I didn't mean it like that. I've wanted to kiss you for weeks."

"You… have?"

Noses brushing, his lips whisper over mine again. "Yeah. That's why I'm apologising. You don't need me fucking things up for you."

Gasping for each pained breath, I feel the tingle of my extremities. I'm back. My brain is determined to drown me, kicking and screaming, but he's brought me back to life.

"Please, Leigh." My voice is a raw rasp. "Kiss me again."

"What?"

I do the only thing I can to remain in control. My lips seek his out, harder and faster. I want to taste him again, feel our souls brush against each other in a passionate waltz.

I've never felt anything like the electrical current running beneath my skin right now. It's powerful, obliterating any doubt or fear in my mind. I don't want distance between us.

I need Leighton to hold me in this world, before I lose myself permanently. He's the only thing that's broken through the icy lake of my isolation. I can't do it alone. The voices are still there.

My cream sweater rides up as his hips press into me, rocking slightly. Each brush feels like a lightning bolt. I'm not naive; my harrowing past taught me the basics.

I know that he wants me, his body tells me enough. The thought of it sends fingertips of anxiety across my scalp, intermingling with the screams of countless bad memories.

But this isn't Pastor Michaels.

It's just… Leighton.

Sweet, loving Leighton. He would never hurt me… would he? There are shadows within him, carefully concealed behind a playful smirk. I've seen them. I want to trust him, but life has taught me to be wiser.

The whispers of doubt are eviscerated when his hand sneaks beneath my sweater, stroking over the slope of my exposed skin. His touch is magnetic, stealing my whole attention.

Teeth nipping my bottom lip, his hand travels higher, grazing over the lighter wrapping that I've recently swapped in to help my healing ribs. When his thumb caresses the underside of my breast, I can't help but whimper.

He's going to touch me there. I can feel my nipples stiffening into hard peaks. His index finger travels lower, down the slope of my stomach, and halts as it reaches a solid ridge.

My scars.

He can't see them.

I push him away, gulping down air as he hovers above me. His eyes are hooded with desire, pupils blown wide.

"Did I go too far?" he murmurs.

I attempt to catch my breath. "No… I just, well, the others will be home soon. We should… um, stop."

Leighton sighs, his head landing on my chest. "You're right. They'll fucking kill me if they knew we were… ahem, doing this."

"This?" I repeat with a tiny smile.

He breathes against my collarbones. "This. I don't have any fancier words right now."

Stupidly, we both burst into laughter. We're surrounded by mess, his hands look like he tried to pet a rabid kitten, and I've been choked half to death. This entire thing is an almighty chaos.

Rolling off me, Leighton offers a hand. I let him ease me up until we're both kneeling, staring at the other with curiosity.

"What does this mean?" I bite my lip.

His eyes are focused on my neck. It will bruise, I'm sure of it. My throat still feels sore. I can't believe he had to resort to that.

"You scared me," Leighton admits in a soft voice.

"I scared myself."

"My cellmate in prison used to have panic attacks. I could hardly reason with him when it happened. Sometimes, he'd lash out and start a fight. It was the only thing that made sense to him."

Leighton startles, seeming to realise what he's revealed. I take his hand and intertwine our fingers.

"Enzo told me about your prison sentence."

The fear on his face increases. "Of course, he did."

"Not the full story, don't worry. Just that you served time and came out recently. You can talk to me, if you want."

Shaking his head, Leighton stands and slides his hands under my arms to pull me up. Neither of us knows how to approach the madness that just unfolded, so we begin to clean up in silence.

I'm rinsing off a chopping board with one hand when he stops behind me, depositing several more dishes to be cleaned next. His breath is hot against my ear.

"Does that happen often?" he asks.

"What?"

"These… attacks. Losing yourself like that."

Gulping, I focus on washing the soapsuds from the board. "More than the others realise. I usually find my own way back."

"How?"

I clamp down on the sudden desire within me that wants to be honest. He deserves that much, but I can't admit it. The growing bald patch beneath my thick mane of hair is a dirty secret.

"I don't know. I just do."

The crash of the front door opening startles us both. Leighton leaps away from me, and I immediately mourn his body heat.

"Anyone home?"

"In here," Leighton calls back.

Striding into the kitchen, Hunter carries his charcoal suit jacket over one shoulder, ripping his blue tie off with his spare hand. My mouth goes dry at the sight.

Whatever Leighton's stirred in me… that hungry, wanton creature is refusing to return to her sinful locker. Hunter's tattoos are peeking out of his shirt, hinting at the beauty beneath.

"What are you two doing?" he asks suspiciously.

Leighton shrugs, his lips sealed tight.

"Ruining dinner," I blurt.

Hunter laughs. It's a deep, throaty sound that scares the living daylights out of me. I can't believe what I'm hearing. Leighton looks equally unnerved as we exchange glances.

"You tried to cook?" Hunter chuckles.

Leighton glares at him. "I was feeling optimistic. I'm not that bad, jeez. You ate enough of my grilled cheese growing up."

"We're lucky the house didn't burn down. And for the record, your grilled cheese sucked. I was usually too hungover to care."

"Sucked?" he repeats in outrage.

Hunter snorts as he deposits his jacket. "Just order takeout. We have enough problems without getting food poisoning."

Leighton claps his hands together and perches at the kitchen island while scrolling on his phone. He gives me a pointed look, trying hard not to smile. I drop his gaze before I embarrass myself.

Hunter definitely doesn't need to know what we were doing. I'm still not certain he isn't going to kick me out soon, and if he knows I've been kissing his brother, we're all in for a battering.

"How was work?" I ask awkwardly.

Fiddling with his hearing aid, Hunter seems apprehensive. When the tension reaches breaking point, he finally stops avoiding me.

"You're going to find out soon enough anyway." He folds his arms while sighing. "We've been passed a missing person's report. Could be nothing, but we're looking into it."

My entire body goes cold. "What? Is it him?"

"We don't know. She's younger than the other victims and comes from an affluent family. It seems a bit out of character."

"Where?"

Hunter studies me for a moment. "A university campus in Leeds. She was walking home from a late lecture and took a shortcut. We can't see past the CCTV blind spot."

"A student on campus?" Leighton chips in. "Doesn't sound like the same MO. This asshole wouldn't risk getting caught like that."

"I agree," Hunter answers, twisting the tie in his hands. "The whole country is on edge. The police could be jumping to conclusions."

Flicking off the tap, I attempt to dry the chopping board with one hand, but end up dropping it. Hunter plucks it from the air with ease, his frown trained on me.

"You don't need to worry about this, Harlow. We're only investigating as a precaution. I still think the suspect is in hiding. Losing you has spooked him for the time being."

Helping himself to a beer from the fridge, Hunter removes the cap with his teeth, taking several large gulps.

"Is Enzo eating?" Leighton hums from his phone.

"He's working late on some stuff. Order enough, we can set it aside for later on."

"Gotcha. Credit card, big bro."

"In my coat," Hunter grumbles under his breath.

Leighton leaves us in tense silence. I can tell Hunter is watching me again, even as I hide behind a curtain of hair.

"We need to go somewhere this weekend," he says abruptly. "It's a… uh, work thing. Need your help with something."

"M-Me?" I double-check.

"It's nothing to worry about. I'll explain more on Saturday."

Without another word, Hunter brushes past Leighton on his way back in and disappears upstairs. I stare after him, unsure what has pissed off our resident hurricane so bad.

One minute he's almost smiling, the next he can hardly look at me as he drops these bombshells. His hot and cold attitude is exhausting.

"Keep thinking so hard and your head will explode," Leighton comments, pocketing his phone. "Ignore Mr Happy. He needs to cool off after work."

"I think that was Hunter's head exploding, actually."

Leighton chokes on a laugh. "Believe it or not, Hunter does give a shit. That was as good as it gets with him. Takeout and a lecture."

We return to the den while we wait for the food to arrive. I can hear Hunter's footsteps as he slips downstairs into the gym before the boom of loud music echoes through the floor. He's clearly got stuff on his mind tonight.

We're halfway through *Friends* and watch several more episodes over cartons of noodles and Chinese chicken that Leighton fetches from outside the gate. Hunter's plate sits untouched.

"They were obviously on a break," he yells around a huge mouthful of food. "This is such bullshit."

I jab an elbow into his ribs. "You're the one that's full of shit, Leighton Rodriguez. That is not an excuse for Ross's behaviour."

"Woah!" He almost chokes on a noodle. "Potty mouth, Goldilocks. You spend too much time with me. I'm corrupting you."

"At least we know who's to blame."

"Go and wash your mouth out already."

Despite his teasing tone, I fall silent, struggling with the intense urge to do exactly as he asks. Pastor Michaels made me swallow soap once. I yelled obscenities at him that Adelaide taught me, the pair of us giggling in the dark.

"Harlow? Am I losing you again?"

Covering my eyes, I try to force the bloody images from my mind. She screamed so loud, sometimes at night I can still hear it. I can hear all of them, every last girl that bled out in that freezing wasteland.

"Open your eyes, beautiful."

"I… n-need a m-minute."

Leighton's fingers wrap around my wrist. "I'm here with you, okay? I'm not going anywhere. You're not alone this time."

His breath tickles me, laced with the scent of the beer he finished and the familiar citrusy scent clinging to his sweats and t-shirt. I drink in the reassurance.

"You're home, Harlow. Not there, home." Leighton tucks a piece of hair behind my ear. "No one here is going to hurt you."

"What if I deserve it?"

"Don't make me call bullshit again."

When I feel calm enough to open my eyes, his signature smile is in place. Leighton settles back, but this time, he beckons for me to join him. I deliberate for a second before crawling across the sofa.

He's grinning from ear to ear as I end up curled against his side, my ear resting over his pounding heartbeat.

"Eat up," he orders, banding an arm around me. "No more yelling at Ross. We all know Rachel will forgive him."

"If she does, she's a moron."

"I'm loving his newfound sharp tongue of yours, mystery girl."

"Well, don't get used to it."

Leighton's chest rumbles with a contented noise. "I think I already am."

He refocuses on the TV screen, scarfing down great mouthfuls of food, but I set mine aside. I'm glad he can't see inside my head. No one else needs to know that we're not alone in here. The ghosts are never far away.

In the corner, spilling blood and decaying skin across the hardwood floors, Laura waits in my traumatised imagination. The blood drains from my face as she raises a single finger.

It's pointed straight at me.

The person who killed her.

CHAPTER 18
ENZO

MIDNIGHT DEMON CLUB - HIGHLY SUSPECT

SPLASHING my face in the bathroom sink, I savour the cool shock of water. My eyes are gritty and sore from another sleepless night. That's three in a row, and I'm paying the price.

No amount of cold showers or triple-shot coffees can compete against the smothering grasp of exhaustion. I tried to run last night to wear myself out, but it did nothing to quell my anxiety.

I've been restless ever since Harlow's DNA results came in. Keeping them from her feels wrong after all she's been through, but we have to play this right. I want to research her family first.

We can't gamble with her safety.

Nobody can be trusted right now.

Scraping back my messy, black hair, I leave the bathroom and return to Hunter's office. Tea and coffee have been set up for our meeting, and Theo's already downing his third cup.

He doesn't bother looking up from his laptop as I help myself to more caffeine. This little ray of sunshine has been my constant company this week as we deal with the aftermath of that damned DNA report.

"Where's Hunter?" I rub my eyes again.

"On his way in, I presume," he answers absently. "I'm not his fucking keeper, Enz."

"You're particularly cheery today."

Theo's ice-cold blue eyes meet mine. His scruff of blonde ringlets hangs across his face, messy and tousled. There's a ramen stain on his chest, and his clothes are heavily slept in. We're a mess.

"I have barely slept for weeks." Theo's gaze hardens. "We've had the whole intelligence team assigned to Harlow's case, and I've got three team members off with the flu. Leave me alone."

Sitting down, I take a swig of coffee. "Have you tried yoga? Meditation?

Bit of Pilates? Gotta work out that frustration somehow, man. I can't have you hulking out on me."

"Fuck you," he mutters darkly.

"Hard pass. Your sparkling company is enough."

Glaring daggers at his laptop screen, Theo ignores me completely. This is the most time we've spent together in years. I wish it was under better circumstances, but there's nothing like a tragedy to bring a team together.

"You should come home and sleep in a real bed," I add more seriously. "Eat a hot meal, take a day off. Your room is still there. Untouched."

"I'm fine," Theo insists, his eyelids drooping.

"How much longer is this going to go on?"

"I'm the only one qualified to operate the drones scouting for abandoned churches. I can't take a day off."

"You know full well that Kade got his licence two years ago. Don't give me that shit."

"He's busy."

"Braiding Brooklyn's fucking hair and playing happy families?" I snort, swigging more coffee. "Give it up already."

"I am home," Theo snaps. "This is it, right here. The house has nothing but bad memories and people I have no interest in seeing."

The truth is a bitter pill to swallow. I stare into the depths of my black coffee, trying to remember a time when Theo last smiled.

"Including me?" I ask pointedly.

The harsh bark of my voice causes him to wince. I'm so sick of being treated like a stranger by someone I once considered my brother. This has gone on for too long.

We've fought together. Lost together. Grieved together. Does our history mean nothing to him? He abandoned the family we spilled blood to protect.

"This isn't what Alyssa would've wanted," I add, too tired to dance around it any longer. "You know that."

"How would I know that?" He slams a hand down. "She's dead, Enz. Alyssa can't give a fuck about us anymore. She's gone."

"You have to let go. We can't live in the past." My voice catches. "It won't bring her back to us."

"I'll do whatever the hell I want."

"And how's that working for you?"

"Better than this crappy act you're all putting on," he lashes out. "It's pathetic. Did you even care about her at all?"

"Enough!"

Hunter's furious growl stops us both as he strides into the office. He looks rested, his clothes clean and ironed. Fucking asshole.

"What are you two doing?" he demands, pouring himself the world's largest cup of tea. "Bickering like children when we have more important matters to discuss. What's gotten into you?"

I jab a finger at him. "Don't act all clueless, Hunt. We've been sat in this office for days, doing all the goddamn legwork."

"Leave it," Theo mumbles. "It's not worth it."

"No, I won't. He needs to take some responsibility for the state you're in, Theo."

"If you have a problem, tell me." Hunter levels me a glare over his cup. "We're all adults here. I can't run a business if the pair of you aren't on point."

Slamming his laptop shut, Theo stands and attempts to leave the room. Hunter grabs his shoulder before he can flee, as he always does.

"Where do you think you're going? We have work to do."

Theo grits his teeth. "I'm leaving."

"This is your department." Hunter gestures around the office. "Look how far we've come. We finally have leads."

"Leads?" Theo scoffs. "Fucking leads? We have nothing! An office full of dead girls and a traumatised witness with no memories. This case has taken everything out of us."

Pausing, Hunter looks at him. Actually looks. Not a cursory glance, or his usual emotionless dismissal. Theo stares back—drained, exhausted and at the end of his tether.

"We can't let Harlow down," Hunter says, shocking the hell out of me. "She needs us to catch these bastards. I won't break my promise."

Theo deflates. "I want to help her, Hunt. I really do. But we need more time, more resources. Hell, more evidence. This dickhead is a ghost. He's too good."

"More evidence? A girl is missing! We have eighteen dead bodies and firsthand fucking testimony. What more do you want?"

"I want my family back!" he explodes.

Grabbing fistfuls of Hunter's shirt, Theo's inches from his face. I don't step in. He needs to work through this, once and for all.

"We never left." Hunter pushes the hands off his shirt. "You're the one that checked out, Theo. Your family has always been here."

Gutted and alone, Theo looks around the room. Months of reconnaissance, gathering evidence, working himself to the bone. Harlow doesn't know it, but Theo has done most of the work here. This case has consumed his life.

He's been obsessed with finding the killer, even before we met her. Harlow doesn't even know this man, not really, but he's been fighting her corner since day one, and he's taken no recognition for all his hard work.

"I can't do this anymore." Theo backtracks, hugging his laptop close. "Tell Harlow I'm sorry."

"What does that mean?" Hunter snarls.

I approach them both. "Talk to us, Theo."

"No more talking. You're right. I'm not part of your family, not anymore. You're better without me."

"You are our family," Hunter insists. "That's not what I meant, and you know it. We're going nowhere."

"My family died along with Alyssa." Theo shakes his head. "It's never coming back. I can't stay here for a second longer, trying to fill that void."

"Don't do this," I plead with him.

He can barely look at me. "You told me to stop pretending like I'm okay. You got your wish. I am not okay."

Hunter's expression turns thunderous as he loses patience. "Walk out that door and we're done. That's it."

"Hunter!" I shout at him. "He's trying to ask for help, for fuck's sake. Don't be such a wanker."

Theo snorts, his eyes red. "He doesn't care about us, Enz. He never did. We've bled for this company. Suffered for it, time and time again. Where's the appreciation?"

"You're the one threatening to walk," Hunter supplies.

"Because I'm sick of being a stranger in my own goddamn life!" Theo yells. "You know what? Have it your way. Good luck with the investigation."

Before storming out, he stops and looks at his work laptop. It's an extension of him at this point, a physical manifestation of his brilliant mind. His tech gives him comfort in a cold, cruel world.

Theo drops it on the console so hard, it rattles several framed photographs that Hunter keeps displayed. One of them holds our last picture together. The people we used to be.

Alyssa is in the middle of us, grinning like a maniac. She was so beautiful, confident and sassy, with an acid tongue that kept us all in line. Everything about her was incredible.

Our relationship wasn't normal, not by a long stretch. We fell into sharing her by accident, swept up in the tornado of desire and first love that sucked us all into its destructive path. We loved her so fucking much.

"No," I croak, as the frame wobbles.

Falling from the console, the sound of glass smashing fills the suffocating silence. Pain rolls over Theo's face, matching the blast of agony tearing me up inside.

That was the last photo we dared to display of her. The others were boxed up along with her stuff, tucked into a quiet corner of the attic where none of us could stumble upon them again.

Leaving us with nothing but our memories and grief, Theo storms from the office without stopping. Both of us stare, open-mouthed. Part of me believes he'll come back.

He doesn't.

Theo is gone.

Striding over to the window, Hunter braces his hands on the glass, his head lowered in defeat. I leave him be and kneel beside the mess that Theo left behind.

The frame is ruined, and I slide the photo from it, making myself look at the memory in my hands. Alyssa's arms are wrapped around Theo's neck, her pink hair stirring in the breeze.

His lips are pressed against her cheek, while Hunter stares down at them with a look of happiness. I'm cuddling her from behind, content to share my soulmate with the people I loved most in the world.

My two brothers.

My best fucking friends.

The four of us were a messy, imperfect family, but we made it work. She brought life out in Hunter's weary soul, forced Theo from his anxious shell and quieted my mind enough for me to sleep.

"I'm sorry, Lys," I whisper to her memory. "We've fucked everything up. You'd kick all of our asses."

Her eyes stare back at me, radiating love and acceptance. She didn't give a damn about our sharp edges, the quirks and flaws that made us ruthless enough to run a company like Sabre.

Alyssa was our partner. The glue that bound us together, making us equals. Without her… we're nothing. Like Theo, I've been filling the void with whatever I could to survive.

"Theo will come back."

"I highly doubt it," Hunter replies from the window.

"He didn't mean what he said."

"Yeah, Enz. He did."

Placing the photograph on the console, I make it to the conference table and collapse into an empty chair. Hunter's gaze is fixed on the heavy rain clouds outside.

"I should go after him," I finally say.

"Don't." His forehead rests against the glass. "I'm not going to force him to stay. This is his decision. We have to respect it."

"This isn't right."

"Nothing is right anymore," he snaps, turning to face me. "Nothing has been right for a very long time. The one good thing in our lives right now… and we have to give her up."

I stare at him, disbelieving. "Wait, Harlow?"

"You know who I'm talking about, alright? I won't say it again."

"Jesus. You need to get over yourself."

Scoffing, he fists his long hair. "You think I don't know that? Goddammit, Enz. We all figured out our own ways to survive."

Sighing, I walk over to him, throwing an arm around his tense shoulders. We face the sprawling expanse of London together.

"We have to do this, Hunt. Harlow has a whole other life that she knows nothing about."

"What if it breaks her?" he asks, biting his lip. "All that time she spent suffering and being tortured… she has no idea that those monsters weren't her real parents."

"We will keep her safe, even from herself."

"Just like that?"

"Just like that." I squeeze his shoulders. "We can win this fight. The answers are there. We just have to find them."

Hunter watches the flash of ambulance lights passing on the busy road below us. Several police cars follow, parting the morning traffic.

"You want to reopen her old case," he guesses.

"Nobody gets kidnapped without someone noticing. It's been thirteen years, things have changed."

Considering, he nods. "We can recall the evidence, maybe get in touch with the old investigators. See what they missed."

"We already have the evidence here."

"What?" Hunter frowns at me.

"Theo told me he got the team to collect it a few weeks ago. The boxes are in storage, waiting for us."

He looks mildly stunned. It would be entertaining if we weren't a man down and left to pick up the pieces he left behind.

"Why?" Hunter wonders aloud.

"Fuck knows what goes on in Theo's mind. Come on." I clap him on the shoulder. "Let's lay it out and see what we've got."

Waving off several offers of help, we retrieve the evidence boxes from the locked storeroom down the corridor and bring them back to the office. They fill almost half the table.

It must've taken Theo countless nights to organise all this paperwork, trawling through old police files and filing the important stuff. We didn't even request this. He's done it all himself. It's further proof of how much he really cares.

"That her?" Hunter asks grimly.

I pick up a photograph and nod. The brown-haired, blue-eyed angel staring back at me doesn't look like the woman I know. There's a lightness to her, shining through a wide, toothy grin.

The person I know is hollow-eyed, empty at times, but a golden thread still runs through Harlow. Defiance steels her spine and sass rolls off her sharp tongue without her realising.

She's changing, growing, becoming more comfortable with challenging us and questioning the world around her. Freedom has given Harlow her life back.

"Leticia Kensington," I read, the name still sounding wrong. "This corresponds with the report from forensics. We pulled her school records too."

"That place was a disgrace. How on earth was she allowed to walk home alone when Giana Kensington was running late?"

"You know how it is." Swapping papers, I scan over an evidence log. "Underfunded state school, disillusioned staff. No one gives a fuck when the bell rings and they get to say goodbye to the little shits."

Hunter shakes his head with a chuckle. "Not feeling paternal, Enz? I figured you'd want your own little shit one day."

"We have a Leighton. That's enough."

"I say we put him up for adoption."

Opening another ring binder, Hunter checks the details we've nailed down so far. Our list of information is sparse at best.

"Leticia's been missing for thirteen years and was presumed dead after a year-long investigation turned up no leads." He drops the file with a sigh. "Classic cold case. No evidence, no witnesses."

"Another CCTV blind spot?"

"They lived in a shitty area. Rural, poverty-stricken. No infrastructure or spots for surveillance footage. Looks like she cut across a farmer's field to get home."

We pour more hot drinks, gulping them down in silence. Being surrounded by fragments of Harlow's life is surreal. It feels wrong to have access to all this information while she sits at home, none the wiser.

"Hang on." Hunter snatches up a printed report. "Harlow's family sued the school and won fifty grand in damages."

"Fifty grand?" I repeat.

"Negligence, open and shut case. The school was shut down by the council."

"That's a lot of money."

Hunter nods. "Looks like Theo got a hit on the prison system. Harlow's father was convicted for identity fraud. He went to prison and Giana got all the money."

"Jesus fuck."

"Funnily enough, she didn't mention it."

"Wait, you've spoken to Giana?" I snarl at him.

"I had to break the news. The media are determined to uncover Harlow's identity. I didn't want her to hear from anyone but us."

"Hunt!" I smash a fist against the table. "We have no idea who the fuck these people are. I don't trust them. You shouldn't have just told her that Harlow's alive."

"She's her mother," Hunter defends.

"I don't give a rat's ass who Giana is. We have to keep Harlow safe, even if that means keeping her family from her until we know more. Goddammit."

His eyes narrow. "If Giana found this out from anyone but us, our reputation would have been shattered. She could sue our stupid asses for keeping her daughter from her."

"Reputation, again? Do you care about anything else?"

"Of course, I do," he snaps angrily. "But someone has to think about the bigger picture. You're incapable of being impartial."

"Yeah, well, fuck you too."

Throwing my handful of papers down, I step outside to take some calming breaths. Hunter is the most infuriating, cold-hearted bastard at times. Even if everything he does is for the good of our family. His constant need for logic and order drives me up the wall.

But we're all under pressure.

I can't afford to break like Theo.

Returning to the office, I sit back down and pour some more coffee. Hunter barely spares me a glance. It's rare he knows when to shut the hell up, but he doesn't break the silence first.

"What did Giana say then?" I sigh.

"She was hysterical when I broke the news. We didn't have much time to compare notes."

"We have some more information here. According to public records, she remarried six years ago."

"What about the ex-husband?"

"Oliver Kensington's location is unknown. He was released from prison after serving a seven-year sentence and dropped off the grid. Hasn't been seen since."

"Motherfucker," Hunter curses.

Unease twists in my gut. Harlow deserves the chance to have a real family, but the idea of letting these strangers anywhere near her makes me want to beat the shit out of someone. Something doesn't sit right with this narrative.

I reach for my coffee. "What now?"

"I have to take Harlow to meet her mother." Hunter crosses his arms. "Giana's been calling every hour, asking when we're coming."

"Has Richards agreed to this?"

"Hardly. You know he wouldn't approve."

"Maybe he has a point," I suggest. "We don't want to push Harlow over the edge. She doesn't remember any of this."

"What else can I do, Enz?" Hunter drops his head into his hands. "Harlow can't get better until she knows the truth."

"Then I want to be there."

"Not this time," he snips back. "I need you here now that Theo's fucked off. We still have a missing girl to find, and the intelligence team needs managing."

"Get Kade to do it."

"He's running point on the reconnaissance op in Northumberland. We have to find that damn chapel."

Frustrated, I fight the urge to bang my head against the table. The distance between here and home where we left Harlow asleep this morning is too much. This trip will be even further, and I fucking hate it.

"I won't release her from protective custody until it's safe," Hunter answers my biggest fear. "Regardless of what Giana wants."

"And if Harlow wants to be with her family?"

I can see his reluctance and conflict, no matter the pointless games he plays. Gone is the man that wanted to pack Harlow off to a safe house and never deal with her again.

He's seen what the rest of us are so desperate to protect. She's a butterfly emerging from its chrysalis, beautiful and fragile in the trauma of rebirth.

I will do anything to watch Harlow spread her wings and become the person I know she is inside. Nobody on this damned earth is going to take that pleasure away from me.

"It's our job to protect her," Hunter decides. "Whether she likes it or not, we're her home until these monsters are caught."

I nod at him from across the table. We live and die by the sword, and our family is what keeps us alive. Harlow belongs with us. She's more than a client now.

Not even Theo can walk away from us without a fight. I'll get him back, no matter what it takes. His place is here, by our side. I'm going to get him back and I know exactly the person to help.

"You good here? I need to make a phone call."

Hunter waves me away, his attention caught by another police report. I slip out of the office and into the quiet corridor, reaching a tinted window concealing London's vast horizon.

We saved a family before. Maybe they can be the ones to fix us this time around. No one is more qualified than them.

Holding the phone to my ear, I call the only person left on the planet that I trust with my innermost thoughts. She earned that privilege in a war zone, and our friendship has only grown in the tumultuous years since.

When she answers with a half-awake groan, I can't help but smile. Her voice is heavy with sleep after the team took a few days to recover from their latest assignment.

"Hey, big guy. I've been waiting for you to call me back."

"Brooke." I breathe out a sigh. "It's been a hell of a month."

"You're telling me. The news has been dragging your asses over the coals for the entire country to see every night."

"You sound like you're enjoying it."

Her laugh is exasperated. "Hardly. Kade won't tell me shit about the case. Kindly remove the stick from his ass so we can talk about work at mealtimes."

"He put that stick up there, he can take it out."

"Dammit," she growls, disturbing someone napping in the background. "I was hoping you'd put a gag order on him."

"Afraid not, wildfire. He's your mess to sort out, last time I checked."

"Fucking great. Tell me something I don't know."

"Speaking of messes… I need your help. Things have gotten a little fucked up here. Well, more than a little."

I can hear the smile in Brooklyn's voice.

"I'll be there in half an hour."

CHAPTER 19
HARLOW

BAD PLACE - THE HUNNA

STARING out of the window at the twisting country lane hugging Hunter's beast of a car, I watch the empty fields melt away. We've been driving all afternoon, only stopping to fuel up and grab some late lunch.

Hunter's being even more tight-lipped than usual. He's barely spoken a word to me since we left Leighton still asleep back home. I'm not stupid. This trip isn't for fun. I have a bad feeling about wherever we're going.

"Nearly there," he mumbles.

"Where are we going?"

"Croyde is up ahead. You'll like Devon. It's nice and quiet compared to London."

"Will we see the sea?" I ask excitedly.

His chocolatey eyes slide over to me. "Yeah. I've booked us a hotel on the coast for the night."

As anxious as I am to find out what on earth we're doing here, the idea of seeing the ocean has my fingers spasming with anticipation. This is exactly the change of scenery I've been craving.

Tia loved the beach; it was her happy place. She grew up in Skegness, amongst slot machines and arcade games. Her stories were the best—summer holidays spent touring the pier's attractions.

Remembering her late-night tales whispered between bars, a muddled, dream-like memory slips into my mind. I can see it so clearly as the hum of the car engine fades into the background.

There's soft, golden sand between my little toes. The summer sun beats down on me, carried by the whip of strong, coastal winds. Saltwater washes over my skin with a slight sting, filling the bright-pink bucket I've dipped into the sea.

Where am I?

Is this place… real?

The car jolts as we hit a pothole, slamming me back down to reality. I have to suppress a gasp. The clinging embrace of my fantasy remains, taunting me with images of a place I've never seen.

I shake the cobwebs from my head. A dream—that's all it was. More and more, these disjointed images appear at random moments. I dream about places I've never seen, conversations I've never had, nonexistent relatives that cuddled me close.

None of it is real.

With Hunter's eyes focused on the road, I can turn towards the door and begin to pull at my hair. Each snapped follicle lances me with relief. More. More. The pain brings me back to the present.

My motto accompanies each sharp tug.

Just a dream.

Just a dream.

Just a dream.

"Here we are," Hunter declares, turning into a tiny town centre. "This is Croyde. It'll be dead in the winter months."

Releasing my hair, I plaster on an award-winning smile. No one would ever know that I'm being eaten alive by doubt. At least, that's what I tell myself each day.

With the winter temperature setting in and thick, swirling clouds covering the skyline, there's nobody on the roads. We pass thatched cottages and slick cobblestone roads that rise and fall with the cliffs.

It's beautiful. Deserted and quaint, like the traditional English villages you see in movies. Hunter navigates the tight roads as we begin to descend, winding through a cluster of closed shop fronts.

"Where is everybody?"

"There's a winter storm blowing in." He glances in the rearview mirror, noting an estate car several yards back. "Not much appeal for tourists, especially this time of year."

"Do you think it will snow?"

"Possibly. It's pretty rare on the coast, but the forecast said to prepare. I'd like to get this wrapped up as fast as possible."

I bite my lip. "Why the urgency? Couldn't it wait until after the storm, whatever this thing is?"

"No." He refocuses on the road, the nerve in his neck twitching. "It couldn't wait."

Leaving the main stretch of the town, we climb a steep hill that leads to a proud, three-story building overlooking the shoreline. Peeling white paint and wide bay windows are battered by the rising wind. It looks alone, isolated on a deserted cliff.

"This is the hotel." Hunter pulls into a half-empty car park, studying the building area. "It's the best I could do."

"I like it."

He's too busy studying the road behind us, where the blue estate car has passed the turn and carried on down to the coast. Hunter seems to deflate a little.

"Everything okay?"

"Yeah," he answers. "It's nothing."

Climbing out of the car together, he grabs our overnight bags and gestures for me to go ahead. We approach the hotel, our bodies swaying in the high winds. It's even colder than it was back home.

"Go sit down." Hunter points to a plush chair in the window, half hidden by potted plants and curtains. "I'll check us in."

My leg jiggles nervously as he approaches the front desk, handing off our overnight bags to the awaiting staff. They seem slightly startled to have a guest at this time of year.

Outside, rain is beginning to fall. It's thicker, mixed with snow to form a blanket of sleet. I don't realise my feet are moving until it's too late. They carry me out into the rising storm, desperate to taste the first winter snow.

It whips my face in ice-cold lashings, cutting through the haze that accompanies every second of my days. I feel like I can breathe easier in the midst of the storm, surrendering to a force bigger than myself.

"Harlow! Get back here!"

I ignore Hunter's yelling and carry on walking towards the sound of roaring waves. I'm being pulled towards the water, dragged by a soundless chorus of whispers. Tia's living inside of me, ready to be reunited with the sea.

"Harlow, wait up." A hand snatches mine, pulling me to a halt. "We're in the middle of a fucking storm."

I push Hunter away. "I'm fine. I have to see it."

"See what?" he shouts above the wind.

My eyes are locked on the dark horizon. "The sea. She wants me to see it."

"Who?"

He curses colourfully as I take off, following the descending path that cuts into the side of the cliff. Rather than turn back, he follows, tightening his pea coat and chequered scarf around him.

"Catch a cold and you'll only have yourself to blame," Hunter smarts, but he doesn't sound angry. "Jesus, Harlow."

"I have to see it," I repeat.

"Why? What's gotten into you?"

The flash of images slices into my brain again. Sand. Water. Giggling. Ice lollies and high-pitched squeals. I need to know what it means, why this place is tugging at something buried inside of me.

"I've never been here before, and even though it's impossible, I feel like I have."

Hunter tries to grab me again, digging his heels in. "We can't do this here, sweetheart. Let's go back inside."

"No. We're so close."

Darkness is descending quickly, but the glow of streetlights marks our path down the hill. The tang of salt in the air increases until I can smell the freshness of water, tantalisingly close.

Ahead of us, the cliffs finally give way to nature's unspeakable violence. Undulating waves of grey and dark blue beat the coastline into submission, roaring so loudly, it almost deafens me.

I stop at the sand's edge, staring into inky blackness. There's no light out here, just God's raw, ephemeral beauty in the crash of waves.

"It's beautiful."

Hunter stops by my side. "And cold."

Ignoring him, I hop down onto the sand before he can protest again. The promise of water calls to me, beckoning through the loud gale. It's like the wind is screaming my name, welcoming me home.

"Harlow!" Hunter shouts.

Stopping to toe off my leather boots and socks, I sprint straight into the sea without a care for the falling snow. Freezing cold water soaks into my cuffs, burning layers of skin until my bones ache.

I'm being cleansed in fire and ice.

The sea is setting me free.

My senses feel alive for the first time in years. Sloshing my bare feet around, I marvel at the touch of stones beneath the water. Their sharp corners cut into me, breaking through the numbness.

Wild wind sears my cheeks, whipping strands of hair out from my beanie. The taste of salt and ozone from the arriving storm are welcome reminders of nature's callous touch.

Splashing marks Hunter's arrival in the water. I spin around to find him sloshing closer towards me, his tailored charcoal trousers getting soaked. He doesn't look mad, somehow.

"Mind if I join you?"

I gesture around the deserted beach. "We have the place to ourselves."

Standing together in the darkness, shoulder to shoulder, we're both shivering all over. The storm clouds roll ever closer, begging to unleash their destructive force.

"Do you recognise this place?" Hunter shuffles closer to take my frozen hand.

It feels so natural to curl our fingers together. He's the single source of gravity in this lawless place. We could drown in the tide, but I know he'd still save me.

Not even God could avoid Hunter's wrath. He wouldn't allow me to die without his signed approval, and even then, I'd be beholden to his rules and regulations.

"Yes," I admit, catching wet snow on my tongue. "I've been here before. I know I have. Why did you bring me?"

His grip tightens. "I have a story to tell you, Harlow. It isn't a pleasant one, but you need to hear it regardless."

It feels like we're the last two people alive out here—trapped in a bubble of cold air and secrets, far from the chaos of criminal investigations and obligations.

And still, the past clings.

"I'm scared," I make myself admit.

Grasping my chin, Hunter raises my eyes to his. They look black in the darkness of the storm, but warmer than ever before. Emotion stares back at me for the first time.

"I know you are, sweetheart." His thumb strokes over my parted lips. "Come inside. Please."

Nodding, I let him tow me back to shore. The cold sinks deep into my core as we hobble back up the sand in sodden clothes. Relentless wind bruises us, angry and out of control, until we reach the hotel.

"You should warm up," Hunter worries, still holding me close. "I think I saw a fire in the bar area."

We pass the reception staff's gaping stares, dripping water through clusters of chairs and tables. Firelight fills the quiet bar, with only a small handful of people sipping wine and talking in low whispers.

"Want a drink?" Hunter asks.

I slide into a plaid armchair next to the open fireplace. "Do I need one to hear this?"

He hesitates. "Yes."

"Then I'll have a drink."

Disappearing and returning with two glasses, he takes the seat next to me. I eye the measure of dark-amber liquid.

"What is it?"

Hunter takes a mouthful, wincing slightly at the burn. "Try it and find out. Go easy, though."

"Am I even allowed to drink?"

"You're an adult. Decide for yourself."

Hunter watches as I take a sip, letting the fiery mouthful slip down my throat and warm my belly. It tastes awful, but I kinda like it.

"I didn't think you'd actually do it."

I cough and manage another mouthful. "People can surprise you. I'm not a kid you have to look after."

"I'm aware."

"So talk to me like an adult."

Sitting back in my armchair, I stare straight into Hunter's perceptive orbs. He holds my gaze without attempting to hide it.

"You have been here before," he reveals.

I take another sip of liquor, despite feeling sick at his words. Deep down, it isn't a surprise. I've felt the impending doom for a while now.

"When?"

The fire dapples light across his symmetrical features. "When you were a child. Your name isn't Harlow Michaels."

The bar falls away until it's just us, stargazers chasing the next meteor shower, now caught in the path of imminent destruction.

"Pastor and Mrs Michaels aren't your parents. They don't actually exist. Those are pseudonyms your kidnappers chose."

My heart shatters against my ribcage. "So, I don't exist?"

"Your name was Leticia Kensington. Who you choose to be now is up to you." His brows are furrowed. "Harlow is the name they gave you when you were taken from your family, thirteen years ago."

All I can do is stare blankly as my entire world burns to ashes around me. I should feel something, anything, but my body is numb. I can't find it in me to shed a single tear.

"It was all a lie," I say in a dead voice.

"I'm sorry, Harlow."

From the pocket of his wet coat, Hunter retrieves a white envelope. He hesitates before pulling out a small stack of photographs and placing them on my trembling leg.

"Leticia loved to draw," he says quietly. "She was a keen reader, well above her age range. Her mum had to ban her from staying up late, hiding under her duvet with a torch and a book."

He turns the first photograph over. Two adults stand on a beach not unlike the one we just found, a wrapped-up toddler swinging between them.

"She enjoyed playing on the beach," he continues, his irises poisoned by emotion. "Her grandma lived nearby. She'd take Leticia to feed the seagulls and get ice cream, even in the winter."

The next photograph shows a wizened, silver-haired woman with a little girl bouncing on her knee. Her loving smile strikes the killer blow.

"I know her." I pick it up and run a finger over her face. "She smelled like gingerbread biscuits and loose-leaf tea."

When I found the courage to look in the mirror a couple of weeks ago, it was hard to face the grief staring back at me in hollow-eyed brutality. The little girl cuddling her grandmother is still me, but younger, healthier.

"Why now?" I choke out.

He clasps my shaking leg. "We've found your real mum. You're not related to those monsters, and you never were."

I swallow my remaining drink in three quick gulps. It doesn't help the rising magma of rage seeping into my veins.

"Did she even look for me?"

Hunter rubs the back of his neck. "The police investigation fizzled out. Not enough evidence or resources."

"So the police gave up. Did she do the same?"

"Harlow, it isn't that simple."

I throw his hand aside. "Isn't it? Where is she, Hunter? What has my mother spent the last thirteen years doing?"

"She remarried," he admits. "Your dad went to prison for identity fraud and Giana met someone new. They have a five-year-old son."

Standing up in a rush, I'm still holding the empty glass. Hunter doesn't even flinch as it smashes into the exposed brick of the fireplace, sending shards flying into the air.

It isn't enough to calm me down. I want to break every single piece of furniture here, over and over again. My knees are knocking together with the strength of emotion pulsing through me.

"Upstairs." Hunter grabs me by the elbow, waving off the startled shouts of outraged bar staff. "Put it on my room bill, alright?"

"Let go of me," I growl, attempting to escape him.

"Not another fucking word," he orders.

Strong-arming me past the gossiping staff, I'm pushed into the awaiting elevator outside the bar. His painful grip on my elbow doesn't relent until we reach the second floor and find our room.

"We need to keep a low profile," he hisses in my ear. "I know you're upset, but it isn't safe to make a scene in front of people."

"Get your hands off me!"

He manages to scan the key card to unlock the door. "I said I'd keep you safe. Let me do my goddamn job."

"Because that's all I am, right? A job."

The insecurity slips out before I can clamp my mouth shut. Hurt spreads across Hunter's face, and it feels so good. I don't want to be the only one suffering. He should feel it too.

Inside the room, our overnight bags await on a double bed. I stare at it, every inch of me shaking with fury.

"Do you often share beds with your clients?"

He storms past me to inspect the mini bar. "It's obviously a mistake. You need to calm down."

"Calm down? I just found out my entire life is a lie, I've forgotten the only family I ever had and my mum wasted no time replacing me. Don't tell me to calm down."

Slamming the tiny fridge shut, Hunter rounds on me. He doesn't even look mad, more like weary with the world.

"You're hurting," he deadpans. "If you need to take it out on me, that's fine. But if you don't lower your voice, someone will come knocking."

Marching up to him, I grab a handful of his still-damp shirt. Deep down, I know that none of this is his fault. He's delivering the news that I'm sure they've long suspected.

I knew something was coming. I've had all these weeks to prepare, knowing that my life was going to be blown up when the pieces fell together, but it's done nothing to lessen the all-consuming pain.

"When Pastor Michaels was angry, he hurt others." I breathe in his familiar spicy scent. "I want to hurt you right now."

"If that's what you need to do, go ahead."

"Why?" I almost sob.

Reaching out to cup my cheek, Hunter closes the small space left between us. His chest is pressed against my breasts, and the tips of our noses touch. I can't move a single inch.

"Because I'm not a good person," he rasps. "I've dedicated my life to helping people, but it doesn't cancel out all the pain I've inflicted."

"I… I don't believe that."

"It's true." His eyes bore into me, intense and relentless. "In twelve years,

I've killed two hundred and fifteen people. Bombings, assassinations, executions. Sabre benefitted from every kill."

I can taste his torment. It wraps around me, a familiar blanket of anguish, matching the festering pit of darkness where my heart used to be.

"I counted them all," Hunter whispers. "Every last one. Names, faces, dates. I won't let myself forget how we got here."

Releasing his shirt, I slip my fingers inside his open collar, stroking the tendrils of dark ink rising from his torso.

"Why do you count them?"

"Because the day I stop caring, I become a monster." He releases a long-held breath. "That's who I save people like you from. And it's exactly who I should've saved Alyssa from."

"Alyssa?" I repeat cluelessly.

His eyes squeeze shut. "The last woman I loved died in my fucking arms. She bled out, and I couldn't do a thing to stop it."

Someone, as Enzo said. She has a name, after all—the one who left such a gaping hole in their hearts.

"Is she why you can't stand to be around me?"

Hunter looks like I've slapped him. "What on earth are you talking about? Harlow, fuck. Why do you think I'm here?"

"To do your job?"

He starts to walk me backwards until my legs hit the bed. Hunter pushes me back onto the mattress and covers my body with his. Any signs of hesitation have evaporated.

"I have wanted to touch you since the moment I laid eyes on you," he says with fire. "Every time Leighton made you smile, or Enzo held your hand, I wanted to put a bullet in their skulls and take their place."

His hips pin me to the bed, pressing into me in a slow, seductive grind. Each movement causes these stupid little whimpers to escape my mouth. I feel like I'm on fire.

"Tell me to stop," he pleads.

Brushing loose hair from his face, I smash my mouth against his instead. Hunter's lips part, moving in a feverish dance. He doesn't run or plaster on a mask like every other time I've imagined this.

I'm trapped in a hurricane of calculation and precision, surrendering to Hunter's will. His lips are like fists beating me black and blue. I can't run from the onslaught, and I don't want to.

My legs slide open without being told, letting him settle between them. The new position causes a throbbing pressure to explode in the slick space between my thighs.

I can feel his hardness pushing against me, hot and demanding. The fear I thought I'd feel isn't there. After all I've learned, and with the terror of what's to come, I want to mean something to someone. Even if it's just for a moment.

"Fuck, Harlow," he breaks the kiss to gasp. "We can't do this right now. You're not ready."

"Please," I moan, writhing on the bed.

"Shhh." He kisses along my jawline, throat, clavicle. "I'll make you feel good. Just not that."

Hovering over me, he unbuttons his shirt and tosses it aside. I drink in the hard planes of his chest—defined pectorals, a fuzz of light-brown hair covering the gorgeous ink I glimpsed before.

"This wasn't how I expected this conversation to go."

"Hunt," I whine. "I don't want to think about that right now. Or ever again. Just… make me forget. Please."

He strips off his trousers, leaving only a skin-tight pair of black boxers. His legs are powerful, tanned, and my eyes bulge at the lump straining to escape its fabric prison between them.

"Eyes up here," he scolds, flexing countless rippling muscles. "If I make you uncomfortable, tell me to stop. Promise?"

Nodding fast, I bite my lip as his hand sneaks beneath my sweater. My breasts are small enough that I don't have to wear a bra, and the moment he realises, his throat bobs.

"Answer me," he demands, his fingers wrapping around a hardened nipple. "I want to hear you say it."

"Promise," I moan in pleasure.

Kneading my breast with one hand, he traces the seam of my jeans, reaching the button. My pulse skips as he unzips them and begins to ease the fabric over my hips.

That's when I freak out.

Bolting upright so fast, I gasp at the pain lancing through my ribs, I shove his hands away from me. Terror is constricting my lungs.

"I can't… I…"

"Shit," Hunter curses, his face pale. "This was a bad idea."

"No!" I rush to explain. "It's not you. I… well, it's hard to explain. I don't want to scare you with what's underneath."

Hunter rolls onto his side and tugs me against his chest. I nuzzle into his neck, revelling in the closeness I've wanted for so long. If he sees my scars, he'll run away screaming. That would kill me.

"Harlow, I know what's underneath."

My head snaps up. "What?"

"The police took pictures while you were unconscious in the hospital. I saw everything before we even met."

Clinging shame settles over me. I feel physically sick. Shuddering, I try to pull away, but his arms band around me.

"Don't you dare hide from me. I won't take that shit. You have nothing at all to be ashamed of."

Stupid, embarrassed tears begin to roll down my cheeks. I can't believe he's seen the real me, and yet, he's still here. Any sane person would've run away screaming by now.

"I look disgusting," I whisper through my tears. "The scars… they're everywhere. I don't want you to see me like that."

Hunter holds me tight and starts kissing the tears away, one at a time. Not a single droplet escapes his attention.

"Let me see," he murmurs.

"You don't want to do that."

"Yeah, I do."

I'm desperate to feel whole again. All I want is a moment, a glimpse. I can settle for being someone else tonight. A person worthy of his care and attention.

Gently unfastening the Velcro sling holding my plastered arm in place, he sets it aside and kisses my fingertips, halting at the edge of my cast. The sweater is pulled off, inch by inch, as I hold my breath. He won't let me cower or hide, holding eye contact the whole time.

My jeans are stripped off next, unveiling every gnarly inch of skin I'm so desperate to hide. I lie there in my plain white panties, wearing a mosaic of bruises across my ribs. The doctor said I could stop using the wrap now.

I know what I look like.

It's an ugly sight.

Intricate scarring covers most of my thin torso. Scars stretch down from the underside of my breasts, over my ribcage, and across the entirety of my stomach.

It begins with a perfect circle above my belly button, sliced deep enough to leave horrendous marks, even now. The knife lines branch out into three curved domes, connected by a central triangle.

The Holy Trinity.

Father, Son, and Holy Spirit.

I should have died that night. It was before Pastor Michaels perfected his ritual. He came at me in a state of animalistic blood lust, tired of coaxing my compliance with scraps of food and beatings.

The knife cuts are so deep, I can't feel anything over some patches of skin. The damage is permanent. He worked in methodical silence, creating a piece of art for the Lord's approval. I came so close to walking into the light.

Something in me refused to let go. I was tired, starved, desperate for a reprieve from the violence. God took one look at his offering and cast me out, back into the darkness of the cage.

I survived.

That was only the beginning.

"Please don't look," I beg him, biting back a sob.

His eyes refuse to look away.

"Harlow, you're beautiful inside and out," Hunter proclaims softly. "These marks are part of you. They tell me how strong, brave and fucking formidable you are. All I see here is proof of that."

His mouth crushes back on mine, cementing his words. Heat pulsates through the grip of anxiety holding me prisoner. Hunter pins my broken arm over my head, exposing my breasts.

Lips trailing down my neck, he sucks and nibbles on the sensitive slope of skin. The light bruises from the incident with Leighton have faded, leaving no evidence of our collision.

Does it matter that I kissed him too?

What would he say if he saw this?

Tiny bites and open-mouthed kisses force me to cast all thoughts of Leighton aside as his brother takes my nipple back in his mouth. Excitement zips down my spine. It feels so good to be touched.

Thumbs stroking over the tender skin of my ribcage, Hunter kisses all the way down to my belly button. I hate that he's seeing my scars up close, but when his tongue flicks around a gruesome lump of skin, I see stars.

"You're so fucking beautiful," he repeats, kissing each violent slash of the knife.

Reaching the edge of my panties, his fingers hook underneath the elastic. That's when I realise how damp the material is. I panic, closing my thighs around his head.

"What is it?" he demands.

"N-Nothing," I stammer.

Pushing my thighs back open, he looks at the wet cotton as his smile turns devilish. I have to cover my mouth as he takes a deep, unapologetic inhale of my panties.

"Little Harlow is so wet," he muses. "You're dripping, sweetheart. I can see your thighs glistening. Is that all for me?"

His beard is so rough against my skin. Back arching, I silently plead for relief. I don't know how to do it myself. Cold air meets my most private area as he tosses the panties aside.

"Hunt," I gasp again. "Please…"

"Please what?"

"I don't… I… ah…"

As he leans in, the rough scruff of his beard brushes over my folds. The combination of sensations almost sets off an explosion inside of me. I've felt around while showering, and I know the basics.

He easily finds the bud of nerves that I haven't dared to touch before. Rolling it between his fingers, Hunter smirks up at me.

"Look at this perfect pussy, untouched and waiting for me. Do you want me to taste you, Harlow?"

Tongue flicking against my sensitive bud, he sets off that internal wave of pleasure again, hitting me harder this time. I moan as my eyes squeeze tightly shut.

The warmth of Hunter's tongue flicks between my folds. He licks and sucks at my core, each stroke reminiscent of an expert violinist playing his favourite instrument.

"I want to see how tight you are," he says.

Gasping loudly, my legs spread further as his finger drags over my entrance. I'm so wet and feverish, I can't stop the tiny trembles that wrack over me at his touch.

"Have you ever fingered yourself?"

"I don't know what that means," I pant.

"Dammit, Harlow. You're really pushing my self-control right now. I'm going to touch you. If it hurts, I'll stop."

A scream of pleasure pours out of me as he begins to push his finger into my slick opening. The pressure is intense at first, causing anxiety to trickle down my spine, but I trust him.

Rubbing his thumb over my bundle of nerves, Hunter slides his finger out, gathering more moisture before he pushes it back inside. He goes deeper this time, reaching a part of me that feels like pure bliss.

Each time he pushes in and out, the feeling overwhelming my entire body intensifies. Something is building up, spiralling higher and higher, a volcano of rapture preparing to explode.

"That's it, beautiful," Hunter encourages. "You look so good, spreadeagled and crying out for me. I want to see you come."

"See me what?"

I scream out a curse as he thrusts a second finger inside me, working them both in perfect synchronisation. It feels like heaven and hell are battling each other beneath my skin.

I open my eyes long enough to meet his gaze—dark and wicked. The Hunter I know has gone. A sinful demon has taken his place, and I'll happily sell my soul to him.

"Like this," Hunter says huskily. "Let go."

His movements speed up, thrusting and teasing, pushing me closer to the edge with each rotation. My body takes over as ecstasy engulfs me. I cry out again, louder, like a wounded animal.

Warmth spreads between my thighs, coating his hand in fluids. I flush with embarrassment. Is that normal? Hunter pulls his fingers out and checks I'm watching as he raises them to his mouth.

I gape, watching him lick the glistening moisture from each digit. When he's finished, he ducks back between my legs. His mouth returns to my pussy, licking every last drop of moisture up.

"Hunter," I say dreamily. "Stop."

"Not a chance. You taste like fucking heaven."

Looking up at me beneath a mop of tousled hair, his eyes are twinkling with satisfaction. There's still stickiness smeared across his lips as he licks them clean.

Lord above, I've never seen the devil so clearly in real life. Not even in the harrowing stare of my supposed parent. This man walks in another sinful realm entirely.

"Are you okay?" he asks worriedly.

"Okay? After that?"

Hunter nods frantically.

"I'm not sure I can form words yet."

His lips spread in a smirk that screams of mischief. It's like I'm staring down at Leighton, dimples and all. Jesus Christ.

I shouldn't be thinking about Hunter's brother after that, but it doesn't stop me from wondering what it would be like to do this with him too. I can't get that kiss off my mind.

"Come here," he commands.

Carefully lifting my arm, I crawl across the mattress until I'm in Hunter's lap. My legs wrap around his waist, pinning us flush together. He's pressed up against my bare pussy, hard and throbbing.

"Should I be doing… erm, something about that?" I stumble out. "I want to make you feel good too."

Hunter nuzzles my throat, his beard scratching my sweat-covered skin. "Not tonight. Let me hold you instead."

Positioning me on his chest like I'm a tiny baby, I curl closer, oddly unafraid of my nakedness. He's seen it all now, and he didn't run.

I'm safe here. No demons can come to claim my soul while Hunter's fending them off. They wouldn't dare challenge him. I'm certain the devil would take one look and run from this man, screaming and promising never to return.

Tomorrow, I must reckon with the past.

But for tonight, I can rest.

Nothing can hurt me here.

CHAPTER 20
LEIGHTON

THE SEARCH - NF

MY FEET THUMP against the treadmill in a steady, brutal rhythm.

Thump, thump, thump.

I picture Harlow—asleep and at peace next to me on the sofa, her thumb wrapped between her lips in a child-like gesture that reveals her vulnerability. But she's so much more than that.

Thump, thump, thump.

I hate her little whimpers of pain as she battles invisible demons, thrashing in her sleep, running from my touch when I try to help. Even unconscious, she doesn't trust the unknown.

Thump, thump, thump.

Fuck, I hope she's okay right now. Hunter's a drill sergeant. He'll keep her safe and secure. This entire trip is a terrible idea, but Giana insisted on meeting her daughter in person.

They've already been gone for two days. Apparently, a storm rolled in, so they've holed up in the hotel to let it pass over. The idea of Hunter and Harlow stuck in close quarters is laughable.

Enzo will riot and tear the country to shreds if this Giana woman even thinks about taking Harlow from us. She belongs right here, far from anyone that would dare hurt her.

I run until I feel like I'm gonna puke. Falling off the treadmill in a sweaty heap, I stare up at the ceiling of the basement gym. Exercise is what kept me alive in prison.

It provided a brief solace from the chaos of living with thousands of angry, trapped men. That place broke something in me that can't be fixed. But since Harlow, I've been feeling more like my old self.

After catching my breath, I rest against the wall and knock back a bottle of water. My workout shorts are drenched with sweat. I've been at it for over an hour, too restless to sit around.

Enzo should be home from the office soon, but fuck knows. He's been a miserable, sleepless bastard since they left. I fucking miss Harlow. She sweetens him up.

Cleaning the equipment in silence, I nearly drop the towel when a deafening crash reverberates down the stairs. The sound of smashed glass and someone shouting is unmistakable.

Fuck!

No one else is home.

Reaching under the weight bench, I grab the gun that Hunter taped into place. Checking the chamber, it's fully loaded. You don't grow up around our old man without learning to shoot.

Creeping upstairs, more crashing sounds echo through the empty house. It sounds like someone is beating the shit out of some china plates. I cock the gun in front of me, ready to shoot.

If that psycho bastard has come looking for Harlow, I'll put a bullet between his eyes, and then in his dick. The others can have what's left of him to finish off.

"Enzo?" I shout. "Is that you, man?"

Someone gasps in pain from inside the kitchen. Keeping the gun positioned, I creep through the hallway and into the dimly lit room.

"Theo? What the fuck?"

Every single glass, bowl and plate we own is smashed into pathetic pieces across the marble floor. Sitting cross-legged amongst the carnage is a sweating, bleeding moron.

"Leigh," he slurs.

Theo's glasses are crooked on his reddened face, and his usually neat curls are sticking up like he's been electrocuted. I can smell the vodka and beer rolling off him from here.

"Damn, buddy." I lower the gun. "This is impressive for you. Did you have to break the whole kitchen?"

"Yes!" Theo shouts drunkenly. "Tell Hunter to fucking f-fuck himself." He picks up a discarded spoon from the floor. "Here, g-give him this to help."

I accept the spoon while smothering a laugh. "You're bleeding. Christ, did you have to pull this shit when I'm home alone? I already get blamed for everything around here."

Picking my way through the debris, I grab a cloth and soak it with water. Theo's staring up at the ceiling with half-open eyes, clutching his sliced left hand.

I sink down next to him, our shoulders brushing. "Come on, give it up. If you need stitches, you're screwed with me here."

Wrapping his hand, I check there's no embedded glass and apply pressure to halt the bleeding. He's lucky it's nothing major.

Hunter really would kill me if I let one of his best friends die on the kitchen floor. They could bury us in matching graves.

"What happened?"

Theo groans in pain. "I found the local pub."

"That good, huh? I'm impressed."

"My head hurts."

"Serves you right." I check his hand and nod. "You're good, drunkard. Doesn't need stitches."

"Awesome," he drawls.

"We wouldn't want to fuck up your perfect office hands, would we? Look, not a single mark or scar."

"Fuck you, Leighton."

Snorting, I grab a brush from under the sink. "Is that any way to speak to your saviour? I should've let you bleed out instead."

He clutches his head as I clean up, getting all the broken crockery hidden in the bin. Enzo will have to make an Ikea trip before Hunter returns. I ain't shouldering the blame this time around.

Hooking my hands underneath Theo's armpits, I haul him into a barstool. "That's it, bud. Let's get you cleaned up."

"Don't need your help," he grumbles.

"Sure you don't. I'll make coffee, but please don't throw up. I draw the line at cleaning your vomit."

"If I do, it'll be on your head."

Flicking Hunter's fancy espresso machine on, I locate some painkillers and dump them in front of Theo with some water. He missed a few glasses and cups in his destructive stupor.

He can't even muster a thank you. By the looks of him, he's had an absolute skinful. The stench of liquor is clinging to his flannel shirt and rumpled jeans.

"I heard you had a fight with the terrible twosome the other day and stormed out. Didn't think we'd see you again."

"Where'd you hear that?" Theo guzzles the water.

"Enzo was beating the shit out of the punching bag downstairs. I managed to get a few words out of him before he went all caveman."

"Yeah, well, he deserves it."

With two coffees made, I fall into the seat next to him. Theo's far from my favourite person, but I can extend enough empathy to help the poor guy.

Dealing with Hunter and Enzo for years on end is bound to drive anyone to drink, let alone with the pressure of this fucked up case on top of that.

"They said you walked out," I push again.

Theo removes his dirty glasses and tosses them aside to rub his temples. "I did. Waste of fucking space."

"Hunter is?"

"No, me," he clarifies. "Things were supposed to get easier with time, you know? This grief stuff. Richards said… time."

Sipping my coffee, I watch the emotions cycle through him. Alyssa's death messed them all up. She was an awesome person. I was behind bars when she passed, but it still hurt. We were friends, but she was their everything.

"It's been years," Theo admits roughly. "Why hasn't it gotten easier, huh? I'm so tired of hurting. I can't do it anymore."

"Do you really want to know what I think?"

"Why not? Nobody else is listening to me."

"Well, I think you're waiting for things to go back to how they were. You know, before."

Theo nods. "Perhaps."

"You're holding out for something that isn't going to happen. How can you be happy, living in the past like that?"

"Fuck, Leigh," he curses. "When you put it like that, I sound dumb as hell. I know she's dead."

I rest a hand on his hunched shoulder. "You're still grieving. You think I didn't spend three years behind bars wanting to go back and make a different choice? It's human instinct."

Gulping the coffee down, Theo replaces his glasses. They're slightly crooked and still dirty, but he looks more like himself when his blue eyes meet mine.

"So how do I turn off human instinct?"

"You don't. Follow it somewhere else instead."

"Somewhere else?" he repeats, nose wrinkled.

"Anywhere's better than the hell you're in, right?"

Theo barks a bitter laugh. "When did you get so smart?"

I knock my cup into his. "Plenty of time to practise my wise buddha skills in the slammer. That and years of drunken conversations with strangers. It's good for the soul."

His head slumps and hits the breakfast bar. "Christ, I've been such a dickhead. I said some shitty stuff to Hunter and Enzo."

"You put up with them for all these years. That's earned you some leeway to be a dickhead, in my opinion."

"Jeez, how comforting."

Headlights suddenly light up the house as the security gate slides shut. A car parks, and we both watch as four figures step out. His monstrous frame betrays Enzo's presence. He disengages the security system before unlocking the front door.

"Leighton!"

"This'll be good," I mutter to Theo's slumped head. "In here, Enz."

Halting in the doorway, Enzo takes one look around the half-destroyed room and spots us both. His face hardens.

"Theo, I have been looking all over the city for you," he shouts. "You couldn't even answer your goddamn phone?"

His head doesn't lift. "Thought you'd take the hint three days ago, Enz. I don't wanna talk."

"We have bigger problems than your temper tantrum."

The front door closes as Enzo's three passengers enter the house. I straighten, pushing the gun underneath a discarded newspaper that Hunter left behind.

"Theodore Young!" a familiar voice yells. "I'm going to kill you in your sleep and piss on your fucking corpse for good measure."

Tall, wiry, and wrapped in a leather jacket, Brooklyn West strides into the room with the confidence of a trained killer. Her ash-white hair brushes her shoulders these days, choppy and wild, highlighting her pierced nose.

Pert lips turned up in a fearsome scowl, she trains her silver-grey eyes right on me. Hell, I didn't need to hide the gun after all. She never leaves the house without one.

"Howdy, Brooke." I wave playfully. "Can you leave my corpse piss free, please? I didn't come home drunk. Well, this time."

Her mouth drops. "Leighton! Son of a bitch."

Behind her, two slabs of authority and power stomp into the room. With hair the colour of midnight, enough dark tattoos to reach his throat and several black eyebrow piercings, Hudson Knight is an unnerving sight.

He's dressed in his usual ripped jeans and black t-shirt, showcasing more tattoos that drench his generous biceps in darkness. Every inch of him is covered. I'd cross the damn road to get away from this motherfucker.

"Baby Rodriguez," he drawls. "Long time no see."

Yanked from my bar stool, he traps me in a painful headlock and scrubs my hair. Fuck me, it's like being body rolled by a crocodile.

"Can't breathe," I croak.

"Don't kill the little asshole yet." Enzo sighs from across the kitchen. "He has his uses."

Hudson snorts as he releases me. "Yet."

Brushing myself off, I'm hit by another tornado as Brooklyn pulls me into a suffocating hug. I swear, my ribs actually creak.

"Leigh," she whispers in my ear. "Fuck, man. Where have you been? We've been calling and texting non-stop."

"Sorry, B. Things have been hectic."

"We live a mile away, you asshole." She shoves me backwards and pins me with a glare. "You could've come over when you got out."

"Yeah… I know."

I brace myself to face the final pillar of intimidation. Hudson's older brother, Kade Knight, is more beefed up and sinewy than I remember him. He doesn't look like a geeky Clark Kent wannabe anymore.

Wearing his usual open-necked dress shirt and pressed trousers, the spotless fabric perfectly matches his slicked-back, golden-blonde hair and sharp hazel eyes.

"Leighton." He nods tightly. "You're looking good."

I stifle an eye roll. "Come here, idiot."

He chuckles and pulls me into a tight embrace. Before I went to prison, I got to know their ragtag group pretty well. They crashed into our lives without warning after Blackwood Institute was shut down.

The other guys—Eli, Phoenix, and Jude—aren't usually far away. This dysfunctional family is joined at the hip. They moved down the road after Hunter bought this place, keeping close relationships with the whole team.

"As charming as this little reunion is," Enzo interrupts, "we have an emergency here."

"What's going on?" I quickly ask. "Harlow?"

"No, she's still safe with Hunter." He jabs a thumb at Theo. "If this one bothered to turn on his phone, he would know what's going on. Our missing girl turned up."

"What?" Theo stiffens.

"The intelligence team has carried on searching," Kade answers grimly. "They spotted a suspicious vehicle leaving the abduction area using false plates."

"You found the bastard's car?" I gape at them.

Enzo braces his hands on the breakfast bar. "I traced it myself using ANPR cameras. Dispatched local police to an industrial site and found the van burnt out, no sight of the perp."

"Girl's body was left inside," Hudson says with a shrug. "No carvings, as far as we can tell. Autopsy will confirm."

"So it's not our killer," Theo surmises.

"Doesn't look like it." Enzo shakes his head. "That's not the reason we've been searching the streets of London for you."

Stepping forward, Kade pulls an iPad from his leather satchel and places it in front of us. I lean closer. There's a photo of a printed note on the screen.

Harlow,

'Let him know that whoever brings back a sinner from his wandering will save his soul from death and will cover a multitude of sins.' James 5:20.

Come home.

With love,

Your father.

I fight the urge to smash Kade's iPad to smithereens. "What the fuck is wrong with this sick son of a bitch?"

"That was delivered to HQ, which as we know, is publicly listed property registered to Sabre."

"Pastor Michaels knows Harlow is with you," Kade highlights.

Enzo's expression is dark. "Exactly. It was posted so we can't trace it. No fingerprints or DNA."

"A dead end then," I grit out.

Enzo replies with a stony nod.

"Why would he break his silence now?" Theo asks.

"He's been laying low, waiting to see if Harlow would lead you straight back to him," Brooklyn guesses with a shrug. "Now, he's ready to play again."

"I should've found him." Theo stands and almost falls over in his drunken state. "Now he's coming for Harlow. It's my fault."

The coffee has done little to sober him up. Before anyone can answer, Brooklyn storms straight up to him and smacks him around the head hard enough to send his glasses flying.

"You are the most frustrating genius I have ever met, and I agreed to marry that work in progress over there." She gestures towards Kade, exchanging grins with his tattooed brother.

"Hey, you're marrying me too." Hudson sticks his hand in the air like a school kid. "I earned the title of favourite fiancé fair and square, blackbird. Don't fucking leave me out like that."

"Hud," she growls at him. "Shut up. One infuriating male bastard at a time, please."

"Jesus Christ," Kade curses as he packs his iPad away. "We're doomed at this rate."

Wading through the thicket of disgruntlement, Enzo turns on Theo. The pair stare at each other for several loaded seconds.

"You've been working this investigation for months, alongside every other job we threw at you." Enzo looks exasperated. "No one has tried harder than you."

"Not hard enough."

"Killing yourself won't catch this killer," he offers, lowering his voice. "And it won't bring her back."

Theo looks away. "I know. I'm sorry for what I said."

"Yeah," Enzo echoes. "Me too."

Brooklyn steps between them with her hands on her hips. "Does that mean you've kissed and made up? We have actual work to do."

I pull her close and kiss her blonde hair. "Damn, I've missed you keeping these morons in line."

She elbows me in the ribs. "You could've enjoyed my charm a long time ago if you bothered to call. When I'm done beating the stupid out of Theo, you're next on my shit list. Better run."

"Nah. I reckon I can take you on."

Hudson cracks his knuckles from behind me. "Try it, pal. Prison or not, I can still turn your skull into a fucking hat."

"Hunter can always find a new brother," Kade chimes in.

I have no doubt they mean it. Murder is a very small price to pay when it comes to their girl. To buy a temporary peace, Enzo hands out a round of beers. We crowd around the breakfast bar, disregarding the mess in the kitchen.

Kade raises an eyebrow when he discovers the gun under the newspaper, but Brooklyn gives me a proud fist bump.

"No beer for you." Enzo makes Theo another coffee instead. "We need you back in the lab."

Theo rubs his bloodshot eyes. "I'll go when I can stop seeing three of you. One Enzo is enough for anybody."

"I'll join you," Kade offers. "I've narrowed down the search zone for the chapel in Northumberland, but the forest is too thick. The drone was damaged."

"Not the P300?" Theo winces.

I fight the urge to facepalm. Those drones are nothing more than hunks of soulless metal, not his prized possessions.

"Has anyone heard from Hunter?" I change the topic.

Draining his beer, Enzo's face is stony. "He's taking Harlow to meet Giana in the morning."

"How did she take the news?"

"He didn't say in his text message."

Rolling the bottle in my hands, I wrestle with the inexplicable sense of unease that's keeping me on edge. The sooner Harlow comes home, the better we'll all feel.

Pastor Michaels is alive and kicking.

That means she's in imminent danger.

CHAPTER 21
HARLOW

FAMILY - BADFLOWER

HE WHO BE *worthy shall reach the kingdom of God.*

That isn't you, sinner.

You will never be worthy of the Lord's love.

Parked up on the curb a stone's throw from a neat row of cottages, Pastor Michaels' voice taunts me. He's louder than usual, rising from the mist of his shallow grave.

I stare at the red door of number thirty-five on Terrence Avenue. It's a small house, basic, entirely unsuspecting.

Almost too normal.

This could have been my life.

Clusters of hibernating blackberry bushes wind around the white picket fence. A tall apple tree dominates the garden, casting shadows as snowflakes continue to fall.

No flowers are blooming at this time of year. The fruit growing has been stripped from its brambles, consumed and tossed aside. It's like the whole garden is trapped in a deathly state of stasis.

I wonder how many times I crossed their minds. Did Giana see my face the day her second child was born? Was I even an afterthought?

"We can go in when you're ready." Hunter fastens his silver-grey tie in the driver's seat. "I'd like to set off this afternoon though."

I lick my cracked lips. "Sure."

His ringtone pierces the tension between us. With a quick glance at the screen, Hunter ignores the third call this morning.

He's been dodging calls all weekend since we stayed for an extra couple of days. I needed time to think and come to terms with my entire life being ripped apart overnight.

It wasn't so bad, sharing a cramped hotel room with Hunter in the dead of winter. Things feel different now. He actually sees me for who I am, and we've talked through the news until I felt able to face Giana myself.

His phone rings again.

"Answer if you need to."

"They're all adults," he says, switching it off. "I run that company all year round. They can cope for another day on their own."

"I really don't mind."

He reaches out to take my hand over the console. "Well, I do mind. You need me more right now."

The feel of his fingers clasping mine makes my pulse skip a beat. I'm still not used to the casual affection he's started to give. I half expect him to throw me out of the car and tell me this whole thing was a dumb mistake.

"Do I look alright?" I ask apprehensively.

"You look fine, sweetheart."

Dressed in plain blue jeans and a loose linen shirt, my parka keeps me warm against the early December chill. I've left my mousy-brown hair loose and natural, spilling down my back.

"What if she doesn't remember me?" I slip a hand into my hair and pull sharply. "What if I don't recognise her?"

"Harlow."

I stare ahead, gripping a strand of hair.

"Harlow, look at me."

Hunter's coffee-coloured eyes stare into mine when I muster the courage to look. He strokes his thumb over my cheek with a smile.

"It's going to be okay. I'm here and we can leave at any time. You don't owe her anything, alright?"

I make myself nod. "Alright."

Exiting the car, he circles around to let me out. I leave my phone and small handbag behind. The only person who needs to know where I am is right here, pulling me into his arms.

Hunter is dressed in his usual battle armour—a blue dress shirt and matching navy pea coat that complements his still-tanned skin. He's cleaned up his beard and pulled his hair into a neat bun, highlighting the old scar that bisects his eyebrow.

"I told her to make sure the kid wasn't home," he explains as we approach the cottage. "Figured that would be too much."

"Thank you."

The red door stands out against the snow-covered garden. It's stark, a violent shade of crimson, spilling blood across the lawn in a curtain of mortality. I'm almost afraid to touch it.

There's a car covered up in the driveway, and Hunter takes a quick glance under the plastic sheet.

"What are you doing?" I hiss at him.

"Checking her story out," he replies with a whistle under his breath. "That's one piece-of-shit old Beamer. Interesting."

"Why?"

He glances at me. "She kept the money when your dad got convicted. What happened to it all?"

"Well… I don't know."

"Maybe we'll find out." Hunter rests a hand on the door. "Ready for this?"

"As I'll ever be."

I shrink into his side as he raps three times. Seconds later, the lock snicks and the door cracks open. Two green eyes run over Hunter, already sparkling with tears.

"Giana?" he prompts.

"Mr Rodriguez," she rushes out.

Holding the door open, Giana Kensington steps out onto the cluttered porch. She's short and slim—not much taller than me—but she wears her miniature-sized look with elegance.

Her silky, off-white blouse is tucked into her skinny jeans while her nutty-brown hair is pulled back in a loose knot that frames her middle-aged features.

Taking a deep breath, I step forward from behind Hunter. The moment she spots me, the tears begin to fall. Her hands clamp over her mouth as she takes thirty seconds to study every inch of me.

"Um, hi," I say awkwardly.

"Leticia?" Giana whimpers from behind her hands. "My God, you're so… so big."

"It's Harlow now. Not… that."

Hand flicking to her throat, she fingers a delicate silver locket as we stare at each other. I desperately try and fail to recognise her. Her hair is lighter than mine, our eyes are different colours.

She could be a stranger.

This person isn't my mum.

That title belongs to another woman, cruel and careless, beating my little body until her fists cracked and bled. Mrs Michaels has stolen the right to a loving parent from me. I can't get that back.

"Come in," Giana blurts, backtracking inside her home. "Gosh, don't stand out in the snow. I'm so sorry."

I let Hunter take the lead. He pulls off his coat and turns to me, an eyebrow raised. When I don't move, he gently pulls me inside and eases the parka from my shoulders. I can't lift a finger.

"Breathe," he whispers.

Pushing me in front of him, I catch the moment Giana sees my broken arm. The colour drains from her face.

"What happened?"

"As I said on the phone, Harlow is still recovering," Hunter answers diplomatically. "She contracted sepsis and underwent surgery for her broken arm around two months ago. She's due to have the cast off next week."

Giana can make all sorts of deductions from those brief slivers of information. I'm not sure I want her to know so much about me.

"How are you feeling, Letty?" she asks with a forced smile.

"Harlow," Hunter reminds her.

"Right." She ducks her head, flushing again. "I'm sorry… shall we make some tea? My husband, Foster, should be home soon with the dog."

We follow her through a narrow hallway into the kitchen out back. Her home is comfortable, albeit cramped, painted in muted tones. I resolutely ignore the kid-sized shoes scattered next to the staircase.

In the farmhouse-style kitchen, I study the spread that Giana's laid out. Sandwiches, biscuits and miniature cakes. She hums nervously while filling two tea pots, casting me looks every other second.

The room is warm, inviting, fit for a family. I can't help but notice the cluster of framed photos on the windowsill. The news still hasn't sunk in, and I'm desperate for proof.

"Can I?"

Giana nearly drops the teapot she's holding. "Oh, well, um… help yourself. Do you… remember her?"

Picking up the first frame, I hug my grandma to my chest. I can't believe she was actually real. Sitting on a picnic blanket, she's building a sandcastle with a miniature shovel and bucket.

"A little," I admit. "She's been popping up in my dreams for a while. I had no idea she was real, let alone family."

Giana remains at a safe distance, but she looks desperate to cross the kitchen. Whether to hug me or hurt me, I don't know. I can't trust her. Not after Mrs Michaels.

"She always took you to the beach when you went to stay. No matter how many times I told her it's illegal to feed those damn seagulls. You were the shining light in her whole world."

My finger traces her silk-spun hair.

She was real.

Maybe, all my dreams are.

"Grandma Sylvie," I whisper.

Placing the frame down before I drop it, I take the empty seat next to Hunter. Giana sits opposite, clocking the way he takes my hand in his. Her eyebrows pull together.

"As I explained on the phone, the current situation is a little delicate," Hunter begins, taking a sip of tea.

The cup shakes in Giana's hand. "I saw the press announcement. I'm glad you kept Let—ah, Harlow's identity private."

"I'm afraid to say that it won't be long before the media connect the dots. Secrets have a way of getting out. We've had some issues with reporters tracking Harlow's movements."

"That cannot be allowed to happen," she gasps.

"We will keep Harlow safe, no matter what. I can also confirm that we have reopened the case into her abduction. You'll need to be interviewed again, by my team this time."

"Oh, of course," Giana agrees uneasily.

"We will continue to dedicate our entire company to this case until all is said and done."

"What if it doesn't work?" I croak. "We can't fight this forever. Other people need your help too."

"Harlow," Hunter snaps. "We're not having this discussion."

When Giana attempts to pat my arm, I shift backwards, out of her reach. She pales even further. Tension is carving her entire frame into a marble statue.

Clearing his throat, Hunter refills his teacup. "I need to ask you about your ex-husband. We have some questions for him."

"I haven't seen him for over a decade," she replies in a sharp voice. "Our marriage ended when he was convicted. I moved here to be closer to my mother before she passed."

"You haven't heard from him since he was released?"

Hesitating, she touches the locket around her neck again. "There was a letter. It arrived on the tenth anniversary of the abduction."

"We'll need to take that into evidence."

"Well, if I can find it… um, we've moved since then."

"What did he say?" I fire at her.

Giana bites her lip. "Harlow… he wasn't a good man. In some ways, I'm glad you can't remember what he put us through."

"You don't get to say that." I hold back the tears threatening to spill. "My memories were stolen. I lost everything."

"And I didn't?" she counters.

Wiping her cheeks, she looks to Hunter for help. He's too busy guzzling his hourly dose of tea to pull her out of the hole she's dug.

"What happens now?" Giana clears her throat.

"Harlow will remain in protective custody until the threat has been dealt with."

She looks crestfallen. I hate that I want to wipe that look off her face with my fist. Violence isn't in my nature, but she doesn't get to sit here and cry for a girl that died a long time ago.

I'm not going to be her happy ending. Giana wants a daughter, a second chance. Like she hasn't been given that privilege already.

"I suppose that makes sense." She looks over to me. "But there is a bed for you here. I know you don't remember me, but I'd like the chance for us to be friends."

"Friends?" I repeat incredulously.

"If you'd like."

"But… I don't understand. You thought I was dead."

"Letty—"

"Stop calling me that! Letty is dead!" I shout, losing my temper. "She was killed a long time ago. You weren't there."

"Harlow," Hunter warns.

"No! She needs to hear what happened to me while she sat here with her new hus—"

My mouth clicks shut as the front door slams. Heavy footsteps thud down the hallway, and Giana scrubs her tears away as a tall, dark-haired man freezes in the doorway.

He's middle-aged, trim and smartly dressed in a quilted jacket over his dark-green sweater. Pale eyes are framed by thick, black glasses.

"Foster." Giana smiles weakly. "Come in, meet our guests. We were just catching up."

Hunter stands, clasping Foster's outstretched hand. "Hunter Rodriguez. Director of Sabre Security."

"Good to meet you," Foster greets, appearing nervous. "My wife has told me about you. Hope I'm not interrupting."

His gaze strays over to me. I can't bring myself to shake his hand. I'm sure he's comparing me to the little girl he's seen pictures of all these years.

"Hey there." He smiles brightly. "I'm Foster. You must be Letty."

"Harlow," Giana says in a panic. "It's Harlow now."

Foster quickly recovers. "Oh right, of course. I apologise. How are you, Harlow?"

"You know," I answer vaguely. "Bearing up."

He takes a seat as Giana busies herself pouring more tea. The tension is suffocating. I still want to shout and rave, throw my pain at these strangers and force them to drink it like poison.

"So," Foster prompts. "What were you talking about?"

Giana's eyes widen. "Well, uh. We… Harlow… I mean, Hunter was just telling us a bit more about himself."

Without hesitating, Hunter fills the awkward silence. Foster enquires about Sabre's expansion plans, seeming a little starstruck. He knows a hell of a lot about the company that's taken me in.

Giana can't tear her eyes away from me. There's something intense in her gaze, a secret message that I can't decipher. I don't know what the hell she expects me to say now.

I'm not her daughter.

That person died.

I wonder how she felt when they discovered I was gone. It's any mother's worst nightmare. Did she run around, screaming and demanding help? Did they put up posters? Knock on doors? I'm not sure she did.

My morbid thoughts take an even darker turn. How did she live with the guilt? Rebuild her life without wanting to end it all? I spent years praying for death. Was she doing the same thing? Part of me wishes she was.

My chair scraping back startles them all.

"I need the bathroom," I rush to explain.

She forces a smile. "Of course, darling. It's down the hall, on the left. Do you need me to show you?"

"I'll be fine."

Their voices pick up the moment I leave the room, urgent and worried. I walk even faster to reach the bathroom. I'm not sure I can trust myself to sit there without flipping out.

While they were getting married, having a baby and tending the damn rose bushes outside, I was being beaten to a pulp, starved and carved up like a hunk of meat for slaughter.

I want to know if they suffered. Grieved. Sobbed and begged God for the slightest glimmer of remorse. Locking the bathroom door behind me, I slump against it.

My breathing is shallow and pained. Hunter won't let me hide for long, but I don't want to see him either. All of them look like one person in my mind—laughing, covered in blood, a belt snapping against his palm.

Come along now, Harlow.

Kneel by the door, there's a good girl.

Ready for your nighttime prayers?

I obeyed Pastor Michaels. For years, I fought. When my strength ran dry, compliance was the only thing that kept me alive. I surrendered so much of myself for one reason.

I actually believed that he was my father. He convinced me it was true, chipping away at my memories with his torture and beatings until I forgot those monsters ever stole me.

Staring into the mirror, soulless eyes look back at me beneath silvery hair and blood-flecked skin. I see him in every part of myself, even my physical appearance. Pastor Michaels is always there.

Even if I wanted a real family, my mind holds no space for them. It's a sinking ship, water spilling in through traumatised holes.

I am your father.

You will obey me or face the consequences.

Don't you want to go to heaven?

"No," I reply to my reflection. "I don't want to go to heaven. I want to go to the depths of hell and see you there."

I'm coming for you, little girl.

Sinners don't get second chances.

You must repent in blood or die trying.

As I stare at the figment of my imagination, it changes. Pastor Michaels' hair grows, becoming white with age and soft like cotton candy. In a second, Grandma Sylvie stares back at me.

"Why did you have to die?" I whisper tearfully. "I don't even know you, but it hurts that I'll never get the chance to."

One blink and she's gone. I'm left staring at an unfamiliar face. Mine. I've managed to put on a few pounds, but my face is still too thin. Pale. Shadowed. Broken. The little girl they remember is dead.

Another thick scar peeks out the collar of my linen shirt. It's fresher than the others, stretching all the way down to my ribcage, twisted and puckered.

When Adelaide and her unborn baby died, the final piece of me broke. That's when I gave up on ever escaping my cage. I stopped fighting, stopped caring, stopped breathing.

All while Giana lived.

It isn't fair.

Unable to suck in a breath, I search for an escape on instinct. I can't go back in there and pretend everything's okay. Opening the small window, I stand on the toilet to climb through it.

You did this, bitch!

It's your fault that baby is dead.

You didn't pray hard enough, you filthy sinner.

My feet hit the lawn and I break into a run without thinking about the people I'm leaving behind. I'm back in that church graveyard, the stretch of desolate woodland ahead of me.

Run, Harlow.

Before it's too late.

Nowhere is safe for you.

Time has rewound. I have to run for my life again. My surroundings pass in a blur, reality drags to a halt and I leave the ruins of Leticia's life behind.

All I've got left is Harlow. The splintered fragments of a person that nobody could ever love. Not even Hunter. They're better off without me here.

CHAPTER 22
THEO

WON'T STAND DOWN - MUSE

FROM THE PRIVATE HELICOPTER, I should have the perfect view of the shoreline that carves the expanse of Devon. Croyde in particular is deserted, whipped by wind and snow, obscuring anything from sight.

If Harlow's down there, she'll be dead from hypothermia by morning. After spending the past two months staying as far away from her as possible, I'm no better than the others.

I've grown close to the idea of her. This case has consumed my whole life for so long, and I've poured more into it than I realised. Harlow has dominated my thoughts every night for months, demanding justice.

"This is a waste of time," Hudson says into his headset. "We can't see shit up here. I doubt she's still in the area."

"What's that supposed to mean?"

His crystal-clear blue eyes meet mine. "She's been gone for twelve hours. We both know the statistics. We're running out of time."

Hudson couldn't mince his words, even if he tried. The guy's a walking offence to civilised society. He's exactly the person we need to cut through the bullshit of organising a wide-scale search party.

"You think he's found her?" he asks gruffly.

I shake my head. "She ran. This is something else. But if we don't find her soon, that sicko may very well take advantage of this opportunity and snatch her again."

"She could be hiding out somewhere. That buys us some time." He scans the misty skyline. "I just have a bad feeling."

"We should have divers looking in the sea."

"Huh?"

"If she jumped… her body will need to be recovered before it's swept away. Or maybe she's out there, waiting for her moment."

Hudson's expression hardens. "Jesus, Theo. You know Hunter won't want to hear that shit."

"His feelings are irrelevant. She ran for a reason."

"You're sure that she's a danger to herself?"

I stare at him, unblinking. "Did you think that Brooke was before she hurt herself? It isn't always obvious."

The vein in his neck throbs. Hudson is an excellent spook—ruthless, violent, an expert manipulator. He's also calm and controlled when a crisis arises.

All except when it comes to his girl. I've seen him butcher men and break necks without blinking for Brooklyn West, usually with a smirk on his face.

"We'll keep looking," he decides. "But doing it from up here is no good. Let's join the others on the ground and regroup."

We ride back down in silence. Hunter has commandeered the hotel they were staying at, paying off the owners as he shipped in a miniature army from Sabre HQ.

The helicopter lands on the hillside, and Hudson offers me a hand as we jump out. Back in the nearby hotel, chaos has broken out. We fight through the rush of people to find the bar.

Inside, the Anaconda team has set up, pouring over ordinance maps and surveillance footage. They've already sent a scouting party out that swept the town centre and surrounding farmers' fields.

"Someone better get me some results, or I'll be mounting your fucking heads outside HQ on a spike."

Commanding over the room, Enzo screams in the faces of everyone shrivelling away from him. Grown men I've worked with for years look petrified in his presence.

"Sir, we swept everywhere in a ten-mile radius," Becket protests, wet blonde hair coated to his neck. "There was nothing. She couldn't have run farther than that on foot."

With a snarl, Enzo grabs a handful of Becket's standard-issue black shirt. He pins him against the wall so high, his feet hang off the floor.

"I'm telling you to go back out there," Enzo shouts at him. "Check dumpsters, old barns, public bathrooms. Fucking libraries! Anywhere she could be hiding."

"We already did," Becket struggles to say, his face turning blue. "She's gone."

"Get back out there or find another goddamn job. Don't come back without the girl! You hear me?"

Hunter usually intervenes and calms his hot-tempered partner. Instead, our team leader inhabits the dark shadows of the room. He's propped up in the corner, an invisible wall of isolation warning everyone off. Desperation leaks off him in tidal waves.

Becket dusts himself off and storms away with a curse that makes my ears burn. His small team follows—a tight-knit group of three men and one woman—heading back out into the falling snow.

They're good operatives, second best behind the Cobra team. If they didn't find her out there, Harlow's already gone. Whether Enzo can admit it or not.

"Well, that was an encouraging pep talk," Hudson quips as he strolls in behind me. "Real calm and inspirational."

Enzo glowers at him. "You're a fine one to talk about being calm."

"When I threaten people, I do it properly. Some knives, a bit of blood, couple of broken bones, perhaps. You've really got to commit."

He's going to get his nose pulverised at this rate. Then Brooklyn will gut Enzo for laying a damn finger on her favourite psychopath.

"Can't see a thing up there." I meet Hunter's frozen gaze. "We need more people on the ground. Any forensic evidence will be deteriorating with each day that she's gone."

"Forensic evidence," Hunter repeats, his voice flat and unyielding. "What are you saying, Theodore?"

Sighing, I take a seat at the cluttered table. "It's just a suggestion."

"And here I was thinking your time at Sabre had come to an end."

"Hunt," Leighton warns from his perch at the table. "Theo came with us as soon as we heard. Lay off him."

I incline my head in thanks. The younger Rodriguez brother is far too loud and dramatic for my social anxiety to tolerate, but I've started to make peace with his place in our lives.

Pacing the room, Hunter dismisses me with a glower. He has ditched his suit jacket in favour of a rumpled shirt and loaded gun holster. Everyone else looks equally dishevelled.

"I never should've brought her here." Hunter fists his loose hair with another curse. "This was a huge mistake."

"You did what you thought was best," I point out.

He scoffs. "How many times can I use that excuse? My best judgement has caused us enough casualties over the years."

Powering up my laptop, I hammer the keys hard. Sabre has extracted a very heavy toll on us all. Casualties have paid for the luxury our team lives in. Luxury I cannot fucking stand.

The hum of an engine outside the hotel causes our remaining staff to scatter, taking handfuls of paperwork and laptops elsewhere. I know who it is without looking up. Hudson's 1967 Mustang GT has a very specific growl.

"Took them long enough," Hudson complains.

Enzo scrubs a hand over his face. "I told Brooklyn to grab the other three. We need all hands on deck for this."

"You dragged them back in from retirement?" Hunter frowns at his teammate. "Why?"

"Because they're the only ones that can think like Harlow," I answer for him. "None of us can begin to understand."

There are worse people to enrol than the infamous inmates that turned our company upside down. Enzo's right. Only Brooklyn and her men can fathom what Harlow's been through.

"Enzo, sit down." Hunter slumps into a chair. "We've got our best people out there."

"Sit down?" Enzo's face darkens. "Sit down?!"

"Lower your damn voice."

"Fuck you, Hunt." He points an accusing finger. "Harlow's out there and it's your fault for not keeping her safe. I will not sit down and wait for that bastard to find our girl."

Snatching up his leather jacket and gun holster, Enzo brushes straight past Brooklyn in the hotel entrance as she yells his name. Hunter's fist crashes against the table.

"Our girl," he mutters. "I warned him. I fucking warned him and now look at us."

"Did you warn yourself too?"

Hunter bares his teeth at me. "You're one to talk. I've seen the whole bloody cupboard of evidence you've collected on Harlow. How long's that collection been going on?"

"It's my job."

"Bullshit. It's bordering on obsessive."

"I'm trying to help her!" I raise my voice.

Leighton's forehead thumps against the table in frustration. Before Hunter can hit back, we're joined by our latest arrivals, sliding the panelled doors shut against the rest of the hotel.

Hudson straightens from his casual lean against the wall. "Who drove then? Keys. Now."

Pouting, Phoenix tosses them through the air. His shaggy, chin-length hair is currently a lurid red colour, compared to the lime green it was when I saw him last.

With impish features, a shining nose ring, and tight black jeans that show off his toned legs, he's the resident wind-up in their team and an all-round pain in our asses.

"Sorry, Hud. I dented the bonnet."

"Not funny." Hudson narrows his eyes. "If there's so much as a scratch on my baby, I'll run over your video games. No more GTA for you."

Phoenix's lips curl into a grin. "Who needs games? That was a sweet as hell ride. I'll steal your baby myself and live out my real-life gangster fantasy."

"Fucking try it," Hudson invites.

"Behave, the pair of you," Kade warns, combing his blonde hair back. "We've got our baby right here. I'm sure she'll take great pleasure in castrating you with a rusty knife."

Ignoring the testosterone-fuelled entourage, Brooklyn rolls her eyes as she strips off her leather jacket, revealing jeans and her usual obscure band t-shirt.

"Too busy for any castrations tonight," she answers. "Put it in my diary for tomorrow. And I'm not your fucking baby, alright?"

Phoenix fist bumps the air. "Score. I'm off the hook."

Growing serious, the three of them take their seats, but not before Hudson drags Brooklyn in for a lip-smacking kiss that leaves her cheeks pink.

Both silent and apprehensive, the other two people to reject a job offer from Hunter step forward. I greet Eli with a nod that he silently returns. His brown ringlets are messy, hanging over vivid-green eyes and sharp cheekbones.

He's the most reserved member of their rowdy bunch. For several years, Eli struggled with selective mutism. When we met almost six years ago, he couldn't speak a single word.

It took long-term speech therapy and a lot of expensive cheques for him to regain his tongue. In the aftermath, he opted to pursue a career in academia rather than join Sabre's ranks.

"Eli," Hunter greets with a sigh. "Thanks for coming."

He takes the seat next to Kade. "Of course."

The last man lingers by the closed doors, observing us all. Jude is still dressed in his work clothes—a smart shirt and black trousers, his lanyard hanging from his neck.

Working with Sabre wasn't on Jude's list of priorities after years of being imprisoned and tortured, but that's a whole other story. He took a few years to recover before returning to his old profession as a psychologist.

Jude now works in a local rebab centre alongside Phoenix, who runs a recovery group for addicts. The latter worked his way up using nothing but determination and repurposed shitty life experiences.

"Theo," he greets, his light-brown hair cropped close to his head. "It's been a while."

"It has. How's the centre?" I ask him.

Jude shrugs, pulling off his lanyard. "I'm still looking for an excuse to get Phoenix locked up to give us some peace and quiet."

"Hey," Phoenix exclaims. "I got you that job, dickhead."

He winks at him. "Sorry, Nix."

With everyone seated, we all look at Hunter. He's staring at a full-page shot of Harlow that's been printed for reference. It's a selfie she took with Leighton during one of their late-night movie marathons. Their grins are wide.

"Hunt?" Kade prompts.

Still, he doesn't move an inch. That damned photograph has him in a grief-stricken trance. When we lost Alyssa, Hunter checked out on us. It got worse when he lost his hearing. We came close to losing him forever.

He carries this entire company on his back, even as it slowly crushes him to death. That man's a bloody martyr if I ever saw one.

Shoving aside my anxiety, I stand up. "Harlow's been gone for over twelve hours. We've combed the surrounding area, as she escaped on foot. No sign of her."

"We also searched the coastline," Hudson adds, an unlit cigarette hanging from his lips. "Our next move would be to bring in divers."

Hunter shakes himself, taking the photograph and turning it over so he can't meet Harlow's blue eyes.

"Why would divers be necessary?" he asks cooly.

Hudson stares straight ahead. "If she's gone in…"

"No," Hunter thunders. "I don't believe that's a scenario we need to explore."

"Why not?" Jude asks while taking a seat.

Out of them all, he knows exactly what Harlow's going through. This man has nerves of steel, borne from the darkest of evils that a human can endure.

"Harlow is recovering," Hunter grinds out.

"From long-term imprisonment, abuse and psychological torture. I know, I'm familiar with it."

"She wouldn't hurt herself."

Jude rests his elbow on the table, unveiling the stump where his left hand should be. "I understand that you care about her. Denial won't help you."

"I am not in denial, Jude."

"Is that why your agents are out there looking for her while you sit here, staring at photographs?"

"Careful." Hunter's tone grows frigid. "You may not work for me, but I will still throw you out of this hotel with my bare hands."

Jude's mouth turns up with amusement. I think he'd shatter Hunter's spine with his pinkie finger and not break a sweat.

"Richards sent me her notes," he continues, unfazed. "Harlow is suffering from dissociative amnesia and severe PTSD. She presents a huge risk to herself."

"I said she's recovering. End of discussion."

"Harlow might not even know that she's lost. Reality can twist and turn in cases of extreme trauma. Accidents happen."

"Jude! Enough!" Hunter yells at him. "You think I don't feel bad enough? Fuck! This happened on my goddamn watch!"

Grabbing his chair, he smashes it to pieces in a silent storm of rage. None of us flinch. With a shout of fury, he braces his hands on the wall and lets his head fall.

"There's something else." Leighton frowns at his laced fingers. "I've spent a lot of time with Harlow. She's been… hurting herself."

"What? Since when?" I cut the silence.

He shrugs. "I don't know when it started, but I've caught her pulling her own hair out several times. She doesn't even know she's doing it half of the time."

Jude raises an eyebrow. "Self-harm can take many forms. We all know that."

Lips pursed, Brooklyn stands up and dares to approach Hunter. I doubt anyone else would have the courage to right now. She bends down to whisper in his ear, somehow coaxing him to come back to the table.

"Do you think this is a cry for help?" he asks with a sigh.

"People don't always want to end their lives." Jude spares his family a quick glance. "They just want the pain to stop."

"To what end?"

"The world's a scary place when you've been kept from it for so long. I think Harlow may be looking for an out."

"Is that your professional opinion?" I ask next.

"It's what I know, Theo. I've been where she is."

Looking back down at my laptop, I churn his words over. Harlow didn't survive thirteen years of sheer hell to go and do something like that. I've seen the determination in her.

"Kade, laptop." I load my TOR browser to access the dark web. "I want to see every surveillance feed in Devon. Domestic and commercial. She has to be somewhere."

"You want to use the new AI program?" He grabs his satchel to start unloading. "We're still awaiting approval from the Ministry of Defence."

"Do I look like I care about the law right now? The Prime Minister can pull his finger out of his ass another time to get us security clearance."

He begins setting up cables and screens. "Alright, then. Let's give this baby a whirl."

CHAPTER 23
HARLOW

PRAY - JXDN

MRS MICHAELS STANDS *in the gloomy shadows of the basement, watching silently. She refuses to take her eyes off her husband. He says that he's my father, but really, he's the monster beneath the bed.*

I've read books I'm not supposed to about bad people before. They always pretend to be angels, but they're the ones that hurt you most. God's worst devils in their perfect disguise.

He invades my cell, a black belt in his hand. The smooth leather thwacks against his palm, over and over. Each strike makes me scoot backwards in the cage I've inhabited for what feels like weeks now.

"Why do you continue to defy me, sinner?"

"I'm not a sinner," I argue back. "Grandma says that I'm a good girl. That's why she gives me ice cream every day. And Mummy gave me a gold star for moving up another reading grade."

"We're trying to save you. Your soul will face damnation without my help. Yet, every day you've spent here, you continue to defy us. Your parents. Why is that?"

Wiping snot from my face, I scream at him. "I want to go home."

"You are home. We're your parents now."

"No! You're bad people."

"The unholy always condemn those who threaten their indecent pleasures."

Pastor Michaels loves to rant about obscure Bible verses that I don't understand. For days, I've covered my ears and blocked him out. When I dared to try to escape, he hit me in the face.

I heard something crunch, and my face is hot and swollen. It hurts when I breathe now. I want my mummy to come and kiss it better.

"It's time. Bend over, there's a good girl."

"No!" I shout, clutching my baggy shirt. "You can't make me."

He stalks towards me, grabbing my child-sized body and pinning me against the metal bars. With his spare hand, he raises the filthy t-shirt I was given to wear, exposing my bare behind. They took my pink panties a while ago.

"Count with me, sinner."

His strength forces my back to bend. I scream as the leather connects with my butt cheeks, the buckle biting into my flesh.

"I said count!"

One.

Two.

Three.

"He who be worthy shall rejoice in the kingdom of paradise," Pastor Michaels chants.

Four.

Five.

Six.

"Pray for forgiveness and the Lord shall be merciful."

Seven.

Eight.

Nine.

"You will obey your parents, or we'll take the shirt away too."

It hurts so bad, I can't hold on to the meagre contents of my stomach. He hits me over and over again until I stop crying and lie empty in my own blood and vomit. Mrs Michaels doesn't say a word, watching from her perch in the corner.

"I am your father now."

I find the strength to look up at him.

"Say it," he warns, holding the belt at the ready. "Say it!"

"You're m-m-my father," I sob blindly. "I'm s-sorry."

"There, there, child. That wasn't so hard now, was it?"

His weathered hand strokes over my hair, sticky with blood and sweat. The tenderness of his touch is petrifying after so many awful beatings.

"I have to hurt you, Harlow," Pastor Michaels whispers. "It's the only way to save you. But don't worry, you're almost there. This next bit will be easy."

I'm too tired to repeat that Harlow isn't my name. I can't remember why. What is my name? Isn't it Harlow? I don't know why that doesn't feel right.

It doesn't matter anymore. I just want the pain to stop. If playing along and calling myself Harlow does that, then I'll be the good girl he's hoping for.

"Lay down," he instructs. "Time to pray."

All I can see is the glinting of the knife in his hands, inching closer to me. I'm too weak to fight back as he slices my t-shirt into dirty ribbons.

Mrs Michaels joins him in my cell, the sleeves of her floral dress rolled up. If she hits me again, I'm not sure I'll survive it. Her anger is raw and brutal.

"We must purge the demons from your soul," Pastor Michaels recites, kneeling over me.

"P-Please… don't hurt m-me."

"Hold her down."

Following orders, Mrs Michaels kneels behind me. She pins my thin wrists above my head, using her knees to weigh me down.

I try to buck my legs, but every part of my body is screaming at me to stop fighting back. They planned it perfectly, wore me down, stole my strength.

Now, I can't stop it.

Evil is coming for me.

"In the name of the Father, the Son, and the Holy Spirit, I purge thee of your sins. You may ascend to the kingdom of the Almighty. Lord, have mercy on Harlow's soul."

I don't feel the knife slicing deep into my torso. I don't feel the blood pouring out of me with each intricate cut, carving some kind of pattern. My mind detaches, letting me roam freely in the darkness.

I'm not Letty anymore.

I'm just... Harlow.

I never meant for any of this to happen.

All I wanted was to be free.

After running from Hunter and a house full of painful secrets, my feet lead me in one direction. Somehow, I knew that she'd be here.

I find her at the back of the deserted graveyard, with her headstone covered in frost-bitten vines. The little girl that haunts the eyes of my long-lost family.

Leticia Kensington.

Beloved Daughter.

Gone, but not forgotten.

They buried me. Wept. Prayed. Mourned an empty, child-sized coffin. My own family gave up on the hope of ever finding me alive. It feels like they never cared at all.

Ignoring the wail of distant police sirens and helicopter rotors beating through the stormy air, I curl into a ball next to my own grave. Six feet lower, the box I belong in lies untouched.

I should dig through the frozen ground and crawl into it. I'm desecrating the earth I lie on, infecting it with the evil sins bursting out of my pores. The world has forsaken me.

"Harlow!" someone shouts.

I cover my head with my arms, hiding from sight. The sunlight is fading, and the graveyard's shadows conceal me from sight, but I know that won't stop them from hunting me down.

"Harlow? There you are."

His booted feet stop a few inches away. My teeth are chattering together, I'm so cold. Exhaustion has set in after hours of lying on the cold, hard ground, letting the snow settle on my body.

Squatting down, he pulls my arms aside to check my face. Hysteria climbs up my throat, begging for an exit, but no scream comes out. I don't recognise him.

"You must be Hunter's whore." The man chortles as he studies me. "Nice of you to slip away from your guard dog. You did my job for me."

"You're n-not one of the guys," I garble out.

His thin lips pull into a grin. "I'm a friend. Come along, we need to get out of here before that helicopter lands."

I wish I could say that I fought. Screamed. Bucked and thrashed. The stranger wraps his strong arms around me and I'm weightless, tossed over his shoulder as a needle slides into my neck.

Perhaps I was always born to be captive, like those animals in the zoo that can't breathe fresh air without having a heart attack. They need four walls of impenetrable bars to survive.

"That's it," he coaxes, stroking my mane of soaking-wet hair. "Go to sleep, Harlow. Sabre can't save you now."

The afterlife beckons me with open arms as I slip unconscious. Ghosts welcome me home. Familiar faces, screams, pleas for help. One heart-shaped face stands out.

Laura.

This is your punishment.

You never deserved to escape.

I'll be seeing you soon.

Far-off shouting and the blare of a ringing phone cuts through the fog engulfing me. Laura smiles, slow and lazy, before she's swallowed whole by the light burning my retinas.

Agony lances through my temples as I lift my head. Shadows fade, and a dimly lit room settles around me. The curved walls are made of bare, roughened stone. Cobwebs. Discarded needles. Ashes and cigarette butts.

This isn't the basement.

Pastor Michaels hasn't found me.

Dragging myself up, my knees knock together as I fight to remain upright without passing back out. I'm dressed in my jeans and the ripped linen shirt, stained with blood and filth.

Gritting my teeth, I search the strangely shaped room. There's a small window that's been boarded over with wood. I can hear the wind whistling through it. We must be near the sea.

The arched door in the corner is locked. I press my ear against the rotting wood, straining to hear something. I'm met with silence. Based on the light streaming through the boarded-up window, it's the next day at least.

How long was I unconscious for? The guys must be out there right now, burning the country to ashes in search of me. I was so stupid to run away like that.

Foolish Harlow.

They don't care about you.

No one is coming to save you this time.

Desperation takes hold. I hammer my fist on the door, screaming for someone to let me out. When that fails, I growl and lift the sling over my shoulder, freeing my plastered arm.

"Hello? Please… let me out!"

Using my hand to beat on the door even louder, a shout of annoyance answers me. Footsteps draw closer on the other side, and I shuffle backwards as the lock clicks.

At the last second, I grab one of the used needles from the floor and hold it behind my back. The needle still looks sharp. Door creaking open, a short, heavily muscled man wearing a blue baseball cap steps inside.

"Who are you?" I scream at him.

Glazed-over eyes study me. Inching back further, I grip the needle tight. I can stab it into his eye if I have to. With a snarl, he flashes across the room, his arms banding around me.

"No! Let me go!"

I'm lifted into the air.

"Shut the fuck up, little bitch," he orders.

"I said let go!"

Growling under his breath, he runs straight at the curved wall. I'm smashed into the stone so hard, I see stars. His arms are the only thing keeping me upright, and I'm forced to drop the needle.

"P-Please…"

"Jesus. Do you ever shut up?" he hisses, the scent of tobacco washing over me. "Let's see if we can silence that tongue of yours, before I cut it out."

Tossed over his shoulder, we wind down a spiral staircase that's carved from more stone. At the bottom there's a circular room, strewn with empty beer bottles and piles of rubbish.

"Where are we?" I gasp.

He jolts me on his shoulder. "Silence, whore. I don't want to hear a damn word out of you."

Ducking into a smaller room, full of broken furniture, I'm dumped into a sagging chair with a thud. His fist slams into my jaw before I can ask any more questions.

My head snaps to the side, ringing with pain. I lick my split lip, a hot dribble of blood running down my chin.

"No funny business," he scolds.

Another figure steps into the empty doorway. "Now now, calm down, Jace. No need to scare our guest of honour."

Boasting scarred knuckles and a fearsome expression, the man that snatched me from the graveyard offers me a sleazy smile. He's older, wrapped in bronze skin that's lined with wrinkles.

"I was wondering when you'd wake up." He saunters into the room, a gun in hand. "That dose of ketamine was a bit excessive, I know."

Dismissing his lackey, he pulls up another chair closer to me. I can smell the stench of alcohol and cigarettes on his dark clothing.

"The name's Diablo. I'm a friend of Leighton's."

The way he's looking at me is sickeningly familiar. Hungry and curious, his lips are lifted upwards with amusement.

"Leighton?" I repeat.

"Who do you think he goes out drinking with? The kid's got some serious shit going on, you know." He taps his temple. "All up here."

"What d-do you w-want with me?"

"I've been getting close to Leighton for months now." His smile takes a sharp, dangerous edge. "He loves to talk after a few drinks. That boy needs to learn how to keep his mouth shut."

Flipping open his jacket, Diablo pulls out a long, sharpened hunting knife. My heart somersaults. The blade is glinting with menace in Diablo's hands as he uses it to clean his nails.

"Sabre's operations have caused some problems for my organisation, Harlow. London is my city. Their jurisdiction means nothing to me."

"Operations?"

Diablo narrows his eyes. "They raided our biggest warehouse and took something that belonged to us. I want it back. This is a trade, plain and simple. I planned to use Leighton, but you'll do nicely."

Fear pounds through me. "You followed us here?"

"It was easy enough once you left the big city. Now, what should we send them? Perhaps one of your fingers?"

I shrivel back into the chair. "I won't help you to lure Sabre in. No way. You'll have to kill me first."

"So eager to die, are we?" He leans closer, licking his lips. "I've heard all about you. Tell me, did daddy touch his baby girl like he did those other women? Did you like it, Harlow?"

My eyes flit around the room, searching for an escape route. I need to get out of here right now. He knows too much.

"The windows are boarded up and the doors are locked," Diablo supplies. "Do I look like an amateur? This place is a dump, I know. You can thank your boyfriend for that."

"You're w-wrong about them," I stutter out. "They don't care about me. I'm nothing to them. Holding me as bait won't work."

He reaches out and strokes his calloused hand along my jawline. Sickness rises up my throat, forcing me to clamp my mouth shut rather than throw up on him.

My fear of touch comes roaring back so fast, it's disorientating. Living with the guys has desensitised me. I don't want this disgusting snake touching me, though.

"Of course, they care," he says simply. "We've seen the helicopters. The town is crawling with assholes in black, tearing the place apart."

Hunter. Enzo.

Leighton. Theo.

Please, come find me.

"Don't worry." He breaks my silent prayers with a wink. "They won't find you until I want them to."

Pulling his phone out, Diablo shows me a grainy camera feed. It's the rugged, snow-swept coastline of rural Devon, but Croyde is nowhere in sight.

"Say hello to Paulo. He's keeping an eye on our perimeter. We sent your friends a nice little video to get them riled up."

Panning the camera to the left, a huge, decrepit lighthouse comes into view. It's high above the craggy cliffs, isolated from the clustered houses and town centre in the distance.

We're inside.

The guys will never find me.

Tucking his phone away, Diablo shifts even closer. His hand strokes over my throat, teasing my pulse point with a single finger.

I fight to keep still as he caresses my collarbones next, gently tracing the edge of the scar peeking out of my shirt. His breath is hot on my skin.

"Hunter, Enzo and Theodore wiped out our business overnight," he utters in a whisper. "They stole two million pounds in cash and butchered my men with machine guns."

"I c-c-can't help you."

"That's where you're wrong. I know what kind of men run Sabre Security. They won't give up their latest prize without a fight."

Tears spill down my cheeks as he cups my left breast through my shirt. Humiliation settles over me in a clinging cloud.

"They have to choose." He snickers. "Their fucked up little freak or two million pounds. I'm leaving with one."

"I told you. I'm nothing to them."

Diablo's hand slides inside my shirt and pushes the cup of my bra aside. I bite down on a whimper as his fingers pinch my nipple.

"You're living with them, eating their food, wearing their clothes. I don't like being lied to, Harlow. You're one of them."

As his hand sneaks lower, touching the scars that wrap around my torso, I lose it. Obeying won't save me. I know that now. The past has taught me something.

Seething, I lunge from my chair and collide with him. Diablo shouts, grabbing me by the hair and smashing my face into the nearby wall. My vision blackens for a stomach-churning second.

"Bad move," he jeers.

Pinned against the wall, his nails dig into my throat. My windpipe is crushed in his strong hand, tightening, wringing, twisting.

"I'll send them your fucking corpse if I have to." Diablo spits in my face. "But not until I've had my fun with you. I want to see those scars for myself."

Leaning close, his tongue flicks across the steady stream of blood soaking my face. I can't even scream. The violation breaks something in me—a flimsy barrier holding my rabid side back.

Managing to lift my knee, I smash it between his slightly spread legs. Diablo curses, his grip on my throat slackening enough for me to draw in a breath and kick his ball sack again.

"Argh!" he bellows.

Swallowing the blood pooling in my mouth, I advance before he can straighten. My plastered arm collides with his face, his nose exploding with a glorious crack.

I don't stop. It isn't enough to satisfy the monster baying for blood inside of me. Diablo's cupping his broken nose, falling onto his back. I leap on him and straddle his waist.

"I'll f-fucking kill you," he garbles.

I hit him again, spraying his blood across my face. "People worse than you have tried and failed."

Reaching for the knife he dropped on his way down, I hold it over his torso. His life is in my hands, ripe for the taking. I don't have to let him walk away from this.

I'm the girl that left the darkness behind. The girl who survived the devil himself. I've got nothing left to lose and no amount of pain will scare me back into the cage I escaped.

"I don't need anyone to come and save me," I spit at him.

"You w-won't do it."

His eyes widen through a curtain of blood. Whatever he sees on my face, it unnerves him. I'm not alone. The ghosts of the girls are here, seething and writhing at the back of my mind.

"I'm done spending my life afraid of men like you."

Time flashes in blinding snapshots. Diablo screams as the knife buries in his stomach, slicing through fat and muscle like butter.

Teeth bared, I twist the blade inside of him, soaking in the spray of blood. His wails of pain are music to my ears.

"Diablo!"

A cigarette hanging from his mouth, Jace steps back inside, paling when he sees the bleeding mess trapped beneath me. He reaches for the gun tucked into his jeans as I wrench the knife out of Diablo.

Plaster shatters above my head as he fires the first shot. I duck and slide through the expanding pool of blood, avoiding the next bullet. As he runs into the room, I dive to the left, letting the knife sail.

The world narrows as it parts the air, slashing into Jace's left arm before hitting the floor. He screeches, dropping the gun in the confusion.

I don't wait to see him fall. The lighthouse blurs around me. They're screaming in my ears—the ghosts fuelling my rage.

Run.

Run.

Run.

Bursting outside, I'm nearly swept off my feet by the wind. The snow has stopped, settling along the cliffs while the raging torrent of the ocean sweeps into shore.

I can't run down the hillside with the path obscured by snow and frozen ice. All around me, there's nothing but sheer drops and a frozen wasteland.

"You fucking cunt! Get back here!"

Limping into the snow, I scan for an escape route. A sudden crack breaks through the air as something whizzes past me. Jace is in the doorway, the gun in his blood-slicked hand.

"There's nowhere to run, bitch!"

Another crack.

I duck again, sliding over a huge patch of ice. The bullet barely misses me. The only way out is straight ahead where the cliff ends, leaving nothing but thin air.

Dark, foreboding waves await nearly a hundred feet down. The drop is huge, but adrenaline is forcing me forward, closer to oblivion.

"You're gonna pay for stabbing him!" Jace yells, attempting to pick his way across the ice field. "There's nowhere to run!"

"Fuck you," I shout back.

Crack.

Fierce pain tears through my thigh, a burning laser point melting flesh and bone. The bullet passes straight through me, tearing a deep, oozing hole.

"Next bullet's going in your head!"

Reaching the edge, I face the sheer drop. The ledge I threw myself off months ago was nothing compared to this suicide mission.

I'd rather die for my freedom.

Drowning isn't a bad way to go.

"Please," I whisper to God. "Please."

Eyes shut, I leave myself to his heavenly mercy. Plummeting hard and fast, wind tears into my hair and clothes, the roar of waves growing closer with each millisecond.

All my pain and fear are obliterated as I surrender to fate. Water rushes up to meet me, pouring into my throat and lungs as I'm swallowed by ocean waves.

CHAPTER 24
HUNTER

KEEPER - REIGNWOLF

I MUST'VE WATCHED the video a thousand times in the hour since it came in. Harlow looks so small, so broken, her unconscious body crumpled on the floor of some shithole.

"I want my money, Rodriguez," the voiceover croons. "You're going to put the cash back where you found it and I'll let the girl go."

Drawing his foot back, he boots Harlow straight in the stomach. Her mouth lolls open, but she doesn't wake up. They've pumped her full of something.

"My men are waiting in London. You have one hour before I start cutting pieces off your pretty girlfriend."

The video feed cuts. I shove the laptop back, twitching with the need to smash it to pieces. We cleaned that damn warehouse out during our latest raid. The cash was turned over to law enforcement.

It's gone, and we're out of time.

I'm going to break every single bone in this asshole's body, grind his organs into a paste and gouge his eyeballs out with my bare fucking hands when I find him. Death would be too bloody kind.

"It's been thirty hours." Enzo blinks, his eyes sagging with exhaustion. "What is she thinking? Has she given up on us?"

"Don't fucking say that. Harlow knows we would never leave her behind. We're going to find her."

"Hunter!" Theo shouts from across the room.

Surrounded by paperwork, wires, and countless computer screens, he signals me and Enzo over. Theo's working almost head-to-head with Kade, taking three laptops each.

"What is it?" I sigh.

"This guy sent the video from a smartphone, using a burner app to anonymise his number. But it doesn't encrypt the file itself."

Kade turns his closest screen. "We've decoded the metadata to triangulate a rough GPS location. Two other phone signals have moved between the cellular towers in the last twenty-four hours."

"Are they traceable?" Enzo demands.

"Already on it."

Theo studies lines of complex computer script, twitching with adrenaline as he jumps over the code. We're going to need a better lawyer. He's hacking into the national prison system before my eyes.

"Jesus, Theo," I curse.

"We don't have time to issue a warrant for information," he mutters, disabling their security software. "These pieces of shit have to be known to law enforcement."

Enzo nods, watching over his shoulder. "Most of the cartel we dismantled was made up of old-timers."

"I'm in." Theo flicks between several screens, plugging the number into the system and searching.

We all lean closer.

"There." I point a finger at the top search result. "Released from prison earlier this year, still open to the parole board."

Theo clicks on the profile. "Diablo Ramirez."

"Son of a bitch," Enzo breathes. "This bastard was on our hit list for the raid. He was mid-level, responsible for funnelling cash up to the big guy."

Loading the prison record, Theo magnifies the attached mugshot. We all study the face of the man that's holding a gun to our heads.

"We found no trace of him last month." I shake my head. "He's a fucking foot soldier. A nobody."

"That nobody is beating the shit out of Harlow." Enzo glowers at me. "Take this seriously, Hunt. We brought this on her."

"You think I don't know that?" I growl at him.

Leighton rises from his seat at the table next to Brooklyn and her men. His face is whiter than the frosting of snow outside.

"I didn't know who he worked for," he whispers, unable to look at us. "I swear, I didn't fucking know."

"What the hell are you talking about?"

When he refuses to look up from the mugshot on Theo's screen, I roughly grab him. He's wearing the same damned expression as the day he got convicted—a stupid, ashamed child, running from the responsibility.

"What did you do?" I bark in his face.

"I had no idea," he mumbles back.

"Goddammit, Leigh. Do you know this scumbag?'

He bites his lip. "We drink together."

Enzo steps up behind him, causing Leighton to startle when he collides with his barrel chest. There's no running away this time.

"We invited you into our home," Enzo says, seizing his shoulders. "Gave you a fucking job. Money. Anything you needed. One rule, that's all we asked."

"No breaking the law," I finish flatly. "What the fuck are you doing fraternising with this asshole?"

Everyone in the room is watching us with laser eyes, but they don't intervene. This is family business.

"Not all criminals are bad people," Leighton tries to argue. "The pair of you have dodged prison a million times."

"We protect people by any means necessary," I spell out. "You broke some poor fucker's vertebrae over a girl and earned yourself a prison sentence!"

"And clearly, Diablo Ramirez is an exception to that rule," Enzo adds in a thunderous tone. "He works for the damn cartel."

Leighton swallows hard. "He was the only one who knew how hard it was to come home. Do you have any idea how lonely I've been? My own family doesn't recognise me."

"So you became friends with a convicted drug dealer to feel less alone?" I shout furiously. "I've never heard such shit in my life."

"Enough! All of you!"

Slamming her hands on the table, Brooklyn sends papers and empty coffee cups flying. Eli visibly recoils. He still hates loud noises.

"You're all idiots!" She points between us. "Stop arguing about who is to blame. It doesn't fucking matter! What's so special about this girl that she has you at each other's throats?"

"Because she belongs with us!" Enzo booms, shoving Leighton so hard, he falls to his knees with a huff.

Lips spreading in a smile, Brooklyn looks pleased with herself. Enzo realises he's fallen straight into her trap and glances away.

"At last," she comments softly. "Took you all long enough to move on. I didn't think you'd admit it though."

Bracing my hands on my hips, I let my head fall. This shouldn't feel like a defeat. I've spent the last five years battling tooth and nail, keeping the company alive… keeping our family alive.

But accepting Harlow is a defeat. The best fucking defeat I've ever conceded. I'm laying down my arms and surrendering to the truth that I care about her. A hell of a lot.

More than I've cared about anyone since Alyssa passed. Harlow hit our home like a lightning bolt. None of us were prepared for the destruction of the suffocating prison we'd built for ourselves.

Her desolate smiles and unbreakable strength have reminded us of the power of living. Even Theo's coming around, bit by bit, no matter how hard he battles against it. We're all changing.

"Plug Diablo Ramirez into your new software," I order them. "If he's appeared on any CCTV feed in Devon, public or private, I want to know."

"You think he'd be stupid enough to stick around?" Hudson asks, smoking a cigarette in the corner despite the hotel signs.

Plucking the cigarette from his fingers, Jude stabs it out on the table. "Ramirez could be anywhere in the country by now."

"What about the exchange?" Leighton asks as he stands up. "He promised to return Harlow, so he must still be here."

Glowering at Jude, Hudson shakes his head. "You'll be lucky if she isn't dead already. He has no intention of trading."

"Hud!" Brooklyn exclaims.

"Just saying it how it is," he mutters.

"Well, keep your fucking opinions to yourself," Enzo yells at him.

Lapsing back into a ticking time bomb of tense silence, we let Theo and Kade go to work with their very much illegal software. They talk in low, urgent whispers.

Within half an hour, we've got a series of hits on private CCTV footage they've extracted from hacked cameras. Facial recognition software catches our perp right in the act.

"There he is." Kade zooms in the footage and sharpens it with a few lines of code. "He caught up with her just outside of Croyde. She zig-zagged through town on foot towards the graveyard."

"How did she get through town without our scouts picking her up?" Enzo seethes.

Theo studies another frame of camera footage, where Harlow's ducked behind a dumpster to hide and catch her breath.

"She's small, fast and determined," he observes. "By the time our helicopters arrived, she was already at the graveyard with him."

"How did he know we were here?" Hunter asks.

Swiftly sliding past the hotel's flimsy security, Theo runs his facial recognition programme on top of their CCTV camera. It dings with a hit almost immediately.

"Motherfucker," I bark angrily.

Diablo walked past our hotel on the day we arrived, pausing to glance up at the camera before shuffling back into the darkness. He's been here this whole time, waiting and biding his time.

"He followed us."

"Looks like it," Theo confirms. "Traffic cams place him half an hour behind you on the road down to Devon."

Enzo looks ready to explode. "Leigh, did you tell this wanker where Hunter and Harlow were going?"

"No!" Leighton blusters. "Of course not."

"Frankly, I don't believe a word that comes out of your mouth anymore." I pin him with an arctic glower. "Diablo has clearly been running surveillance on the team. You put us all in danger."

"Guys," Theo draws our attention back. "Look at this. He walked past Giana Kensington's house after you entered and tailed Harlow when she left. This was unplanned, but it worked perfectly for him."

"Fuck!" Enzo swears, snatching up his gun holster. "Where's the GPS location for that video? I'm going to rip him a new asshole."

"We're all going," I assure him.

Hudson stands up. "I'll fire up the helicopter."

Quickly packing up and grabbing weapons, we begin to file out of the hotel. Eli and Phoenix opt to hang back, running comms with our team as Theo and Kade track our location from here.

Brooklyn checks the gun in place beneath her leather jacket. "Jude, Hudson and I will follow in the car. Take the helicopter."

Pulling her into a side hug, Enzo nods. "We can scout out the rough area of the GPS location from the air."

"Exactly. You'll find her, big guy." She smiles up at her closest friend and confidante. "Have a little faith."

Eyes connecting with mine, I nod in agreement. In many ways, Brooklyn has become the one constant in all of our lives.

She's spent hours listening to us, cooked us dinner, washed our clothes when grief made it too hard to even lift a finger. The broken phantom of a human we first met has transformed into an incredible person.

Piling out of the hotel, the Cobra team plus Jude load into Hudson's Mustang, speeding off in a spray of gravel. We take the helicopter, with Leighton quietly slipping in the back as I rush through pre-flight checks.

Within minutes, we're gliding through the air. The snow clouds are beginning to clear, unveiling Devon's long, rugged coastline.

"We're gonna get slapped with a fine for flying without a permit," Enzo complains into his headset.

"I couldn't care less about a permit right now."

Steering the glossy, black beast through the wind with ease, we follow the GPS location that Theo's transmitted to the built-in computer. It's a coastal location, deserted on a quiet hillside.

"There's nothing here," Leighton says, frustrated. "The town is miles back. I can't see anyone on the beach."

Dropping down a little, we scan the cliff more closely. Still nothing. They could be speeding down the motorway by now, leaving us to embark on a wild goose chase.

"Let's go down," Enzo decides. "We need to search on foot. There's nothing to see up here."

As we touch down on a quiet stretch of the beach, we leap out onto the wet sand. Devon is touristy in the summer, but in the dead of winter, there's nothing but wind and crashing waves.

"Where do we begin?" Leighton asks anxiously.

"You can stay here." I cut him a hateful look. "I don't need your fucking feelings getting in the way of finding Harlow."

"That isn't fair. Let me help."

"You aren't trained for active operations."

"I care about her too, asshole!"

Enzo grabs Leighton and pushes him forward. "You're coming. Call this lesson number one. Make a mess, and it's your responsibility to clear it up."

Storming past them, I jog towards the pavement winding through the clusters of locked-up houses. We haven't got time for this bullshit. Cold sweat drips down my spine as we go door to door, checking for signs of life.

The GPS was a rough estimate. They could be anywhere in this quiet borough. Brooklyn calls in to say they're combing the housing estate for abandoned properties a mile or so further on.

"There's nothing here!" I yell at them.

Enzo taps the comms in his ear. "Theo, we're getting nowhere. Can you give us any more information?"

Nodding, he spins on the spot, scanning our surroundings again. I battle to keep my nerve. Fear and panic aren't emotions I've handled in a very long time. Not since I lost my hearing.

My phone blares, and I almost drop it in my haste to answer.

"Yeah?"

"Hunter!" Brooklyn screeches down the line. "There's an abandoned lighthouse on the cliff. Hudson and Jude are running up, but we heard gunshots."

Sprinting away, the other two battle to keep up as we return to the beach. It's huge, stretching out towards the next town. Craggy cliffs box in the ocean, with dangerous waves battering the rocks.

Crack.

Up the steep cliff, a decrepit lighthouse looks ready to collapse into ruin. I can just make out specks of people at the very top. If Jude and Hudson are running, it's going to take a while to summit that cliff.

"We need to take the helicopter!" Enzo shouts.

Something's happening. There are several more gunshots, and my heart leaps into my mouth as someone stops at the cliff's edge.

"Oh my God," Leighton exclaims.

All I can see is flowing, brown hair and a white, bloodstained shirt. Harlow stares out at the sea as she inches closer to oblivion.

The wind drowns out our yelling. She's teetering on the verge of a hundred-foot drop, her body swaying in the strong breeze.

We won't get there in time. She's being pursued as more gunshots crack through the air. My vision narrows as the seconds crawl by.

Gunshots.

Spraying blood.

Snow drifts.

Dark, thunderous clouds.

Reality ends as the blur of blood and brown hair plummets over the edge. I'm watching a movie, hammering my fists against the glass as characters take wrong turns and fall victim to the writer's brutality.

She's airborne.

I don't think before throwing myself into the sea. When the water gets too high to wade through, I dive beneath the next wave. The current is violent, battering and bruising me with stormy fury.

I don't know if Harlow can swim.

If she even survives the fall.

The world falls utterly silent as my hearing aid fails in the water. It doesn't stop me from frantically slicing through the sea, my arms powered by a pleading mantra.

I can't lose someone else.

I can't lose someone else.

I can't lose someone else.

In the icy darkness of the water, memories are painted in swirls of sediment. Past and present are entangled as that fateful day washes over me.

Alyssa is cradled in my arms, blood spilling from her mouth. Glassy eyes stare up at me. Her fingertips leave a red stain on my cheek as they fall away.

It's happening again.

Coming up for air, I search the water. It's so wild, I can't see anything. The cliff is a few hundred metres ahead, but Harlow jumped far into the air.

She must be here unless she's slipped beneath the water. Diving back in, I push my exhausted body to move. Each metre of progress takes great effort against the current.

More. More. More.

Lungs burning, my legs and arms beg for relief. Popping up for a breath, the silence is disconcerting in such a lawless place. She could be screaming, and I'd never hear it.

"Harlow! Harlow!"

There.

I squint through the burn of salt water. There's a head bobbing in the relentless waves, being pushed underwater over and over again.

With renewed determination, I dive back down and manage to grab hold of her arm. Kicking hard to get above water, we break the surface together.

I cough and splutter, waiting for her lips to move. She's barely clinging to consciousness, her lips blue and head hanging limp.

"Wake up, sweetheart."

Nothing.

"Wake up!"

There are streaks of dissolving blood on her skin, and a necklace of dark bruising circles her throat. All of this blood is coming from somewhere, but I can't find it in the choppy water.

Holding her afloat with all of the energy I have left, I bob in the water. Everything has drained out of me. I can't get us back to shore.

The helicopter is back in the air, silently flying towards us. I can't hear a single thing without my hearing aid. With rescue in sight, despair still swallows me whole.

Harlow is unresponsive, a dead weight in my arms. My vision is blurry from the salt water, morphing her familiar face into one I haven't seen for nearly six years.

Alyssa stares back at me.

Limp. Lifeless. Dead.

CHAPTER 25
LEIGHTON

HOW - MARCUS MUMFORD & BRANDI CARLILE

I'M the first one there when Harlow wakes up. I've been sleeping on her bedroom floor, dodging Sabre medics, IV drips and hired nurses. They pass me in a blur as I stare at her bed, unblinking.

After everything that happened, Hunter wasn't willing to let her out of his sight. The hospital released her for home treatment when he threatened to shut down the department.

Propped up on my elbow, I'm half-heartedly watching my laptop while lost in thought. I've never felt so fucking alone. None of the others will speak to me, and Harlow nearly died.

It's all my fault.

Every bit of it.

My life has been a series of shitty decisions and fatal mistakes. I'm the family screw-up; nobody expects much from me. Even growing up, my father never gave me a second thought.

The night I lost control and broke Thomas Green's back for sleeping with my girlfriend, I lost any chance of ever proving myself. He will never walk again. I did that, accidental or not.

My anger is well concealed, but it's always been there. The indignation of a kid overlooked and pushed aside. I play a good game, but not many people know the real me.

Diablo was the only one that seemed to understand. The world inside prison is a completely warped reality. Coming home was like being set adrift, without a lifeboat, into the Atlantic Ocean.

"Did Rachel s-seriously f-forgive Ross again?"

Her raspy voice scares the shit out of me. Looking up from my uncomfortable nest on the carpet, I find Harlow watching me through half-lidded eyes.

"Goldilocks?"

"Hey, Leigh."

Her thin smile allows breath to enter my lungs for the first time since she was dragged from the sea. It's fucking dizzying.

"You said it first, Rachel's an idiot," I force out.

"You better not have skipped ahead without me."

I scramble to my feet, stretching sore muscles from camping out on the bare carpet. "I wouldn't dream of it."

Harlow lifts her hand and strokes it over Lucky's ears. The dog hasn't left her side, and not even Hunter had the heart to kick Lucky out of bed. She wanted to be with Harlow.

"I missed you," she whispers weakly.

My feet are rooted on the spot. I can't find it in myself to move any closer to her. People get hurt when I grow close to them. They suffer because of me. I can't do that to her.

"I missed you more."

Wincing when she tries to move, Harlow's eyes dart around the bedroom. It's late at night, the others are all downstairs. Hunter was taking another hysterical call from Giana when I last went down.

We've been taking turns watching Harlow, waiting for the moment her eyes would open. Nobody has slept a wink, and after the madness of the search party, we're all ready to crash.

"What happened?" Harlow murmurs.

A lump gathers in my throat. I have to look away from her before I can answer.

"We all flew back here last night. You were shot, princess. You're lucky it went straight through your thigh. No surgery required."

She tests her arm, the wet plaster cut away and replaced with a brace now that the fracture has healed.

"Diablo?"

I stare at the wall, silent.

"Leigh? Please talk to me."

"Enzo dealt with him," I answer emotionlessly. "The rest of his men are being rounded up by another team as we speak."

"He's… dead?"

"Yeah. Look, I should go. You need to rest and get better."

As I turn to leave the room, my heart seizing painfully, her high-pitched voice stops me in my tracks.

"Please," she whimpers. "Don't go."

"Harlow… I can't stay."

The soft, agonising sound of her crying knifes me straight in the gut. She may as well cut my heart from my chest and crush it. That would hurt less.

With every instinct screaming at me to walk away, I turn around and return to her bedside. The moment I'm close enough, she grabs a handful of my t-shirt in a death grip.

"Stay," she insists.

"The others… it should be them here, not me." I dare to meet her tear-logged eyes. "I trusted Diablo, and he hurt you."

Pulling me closer, the needle taped to her pale skin pulls taut. I peel her hand from my t-shirt before she hurts herself.

"None of this would've happened if I didn't let Diablo get close." I stroke her bluish veins. "I allowed him to manipulate me."

"Nobody allows anyone to manipulate them," Harlow whispers. "You wanted a friend. There's no harm in that."

"Well, my desperate fucking need to feel less alone put you in danger. All for what? A drinking buddy?"

"Leigh, stop."

"No. I don't even deserve to be in this room with you."

Gritting her teeth, Harlow wrestles aside wires and IV lines to free up a space next to her on the mattress. She pins me with a fiery look.

"Get in. No more arguments."

My heart threatens to shatter and slice us both to shreds. All I want is to feel her warmth wrapped around me, to be whole and content. She's reminded me of what it means to belong to someone.

Too bone tired to fight for a single second longer, I slide into the empty spot. Harlow burrows closer, her nose nudging against mine.

"I'm so sorry," she whispers, our lips a breath apart. "I never should've run. It was stupid and reckless."

I stroke her matted hair. "You've got nothing to apologise for. Apart from drooling on Hunter while unconscious, I suppose."

"What?"

"You ruined his favourite shirt."

"You're kidding?" Her voice rises.

"Easy, Goldilocks. I'm joking."

She relaxes against my chest with a sigh. We lie in silence, holding each other so close, it's a wonder either of us can breathe.

I memorise every inch of her. The expanse of her bruised and scarred skin, the tiny blemishes and freckles across her slightly crooked nose. Her thick lashes dappled over dark splotches of exhaustion ringing her crystalline eyes.

She's so fucking beautiful.

I need to remember this moment, capture it in mental ink and hang it on the battered walls of my soul. After prison, I vowed to never again give someone access to the most vulnerable part of myself.

No matter how alone that left me.

But with Harlow, I want to try.

"Please… don't run away again," I plead in a soft whisper. "If you need space, that's fine. Tell someone and we'll make it work."

"I'm sorry," she repeats tiredly.

"Stop apologising. Just don't walk out without saying goodbye. It may not seem like it, but I have… feelings. We all do."

"Feelings?" Harlow echoes.

"The world is a better place with you in it, believe it or not. I don't want to be here if you're not with me."

Seeing her bandaged and bruised after so much progress is excruciating, but I know she'll rise again. The frightened girl that arrived here has blossomed into someone else.

"I think... I have feelings too," she whispers back.

"You do?"

"I didn't want to leave, but seeing Giana was too much. I spent my entire life thinking I was someone else. Now, I don't know who I am."

I press a gentle kiss to her temple. "You're my Harlow."

Her head tilts up so she can look at me. She's breathing hard, and I can feel the pounding of the organ behind her ribcage.

Letting my eyes close, I press my lips to hers. No matter how stupid and downright fucking selfish it is. I want her. I need her. I can't spend another second in this house without her.

The kiss is featherlight, a tender, apologetic brush. We drink each other in with nothing but charged air between us. Running the tip of my tongue over her lower lip, she relents and allows me in.

It's the most subdued kiss of my life, and it may well get me burned alive if the others knew what we were doing up here. I can't find it in myself to care. I'll risk the punishment.

Nothing matters but the feel of her breath tangling with mine, infusing the very essences of our beings into one chaotic, destined knot. Kissing her is the biggest mistake of my life.

She's going to create a war within this family. I know it. I'm running into battle, blinded and unafraid. I'll fight the only family I've ever had if that's what it takes to walk away with her.

When we separate, neither one of us speaks for a long time, until the sound of arguing from downstairs breaks the daze.

"I should go and let them know you're awake." I sigh, brushing the hair back from her face. "Rest, Goldilocks."

She's asleep in an instant. Tangling my fingers in her soft, brown locks, I sift through the layers, afraid of what I'll find. There's a significant bald patch spanning the left side of her crown.

It's uneven and sore, the scalp reddened where she's ripped whole clumps of hair out over time. Gulping hard, I smooth her remaining hair back down.

Fuck.

This is such a mess.

She doesn't stir as I sneak out of bed and back downstairs. I can hear the others in Hunter's office, bickering again. We seem to be lurching from one disaster to another.

In the kitchen, the mess from Theo's drunken brawl last week still remains. None of us have stopped to shower or sleep, let alone clean up. I feel like I've been living on a razor's edge.

As I'm putting the finishing touches on a tray of sandwiches for everyone to eat, footsteps join me in the kitchen. Enzo silently steals one and retreats to inhale his food at the breakfast bar.

"Food?" I ask Hunter.

He shakes his head, hitting the kettle to make another extra-large batch of tea. Pulling out a fresh mug, he leans against the countertop and lets his head fall into his hands.

"What is it?"

Enzo drops his sandwich, seeming to lose his appetite. "Another letter was delivered to HQ while we were away."

Stepping into the room, Theo lingers awkwardly. It's only the second time I've seen him in this house since I've been home.

"It was a warning note," he supplies, his glasses tucked into his ringlets. "Delivered along with three dismembered fingers."

"What the fuck?" I exclaim.

Hunter slams the fridge door as he retrieves the milk. "DNA analysis got a match. Felicity Tate. No known address and not reported missing. She's been admitted into the hospital for several drug overdoses over the years."

"What the hell is this sicko thinking?" Enzo scrubs his face. "This doesn't fit his MO. Serial killers don't break their patterns."

"What did the note say?" I glance between them.

Pulling out his phone, Theo hands it over for me to inspect. I feel like I'm going to puke as I scan over the scrawled writing.

The longer you keep her from me, the more death there will be.

Harlow belongs with her family.
Patience is a gift from God.
Mine is running very short.

"What are these?" I frown at the lines of random numbers. "Coordinates?"

"We've sent Hudson and Kade to check it out." Hunter adjusts his new hearing aid. "They left a few hours ago."

"I have a bad feeling about this," Enzo complains as he retrieves some headache pills. "This bastard is taunting us."

"Let him play his stupid games. Harlow is staying right here, and we're going to hang him from a damn noose when we find him."

Grabbing some bottled water, I inch out of the kitchen. All of them are staring into space while eating the sandwiches I made. It's a start. They're not giving me death glares anymore, at least.

"Harlow's awake," I declare.

Their eyes snap to me, filtering between excitement and trepidation.

"Did she say anything?" Hunter demands.

Pushing aside the memory of her sweet lips on mine, I shrug. "Not much. She's gone back to sleep for now."

He strides from the room without another word. Theo watches him go while Enzo hesitates. If he chews his lip any harder, it'll bleed.

"She'll want to see you."

Enzo looks stricken. "I don't… I can't. We did this to her."

"Just get up there, Enz. Worry about everything else tomorrow. I feel the same, but she needs us more than she needs our guilt right now."

With a tight nod, Enzo follows in his best friend's steps. I'm left with the chatterbox staring at his battered Converse as he deliberates.

"Are you coming up?"

"M-Me?" Theo stutters. "Ah, I don't think so."

"Come on, man. You're here, aren't you?"

"I'm not sure why."

"Because… this is your home."

"I should go." Theo glosses over my words. "Kade and Hudson will call to check in soon. Tell Harlow… tell her…" He lets out a heavy sigh. "Forget it."

I place a hand on his slumped shoulder. The ghost that haunts this house is so often unspoken, existing only in the empty space she left behind. No one feels that more acutely than Theo.

"You're allowed to want something *more*," I offer plainly. "No matter the voice inside your head screaming that you shouldn't. Alyssa would want you to find some happiness."

"What if… we don't deserve it?" he worries.

"We don't." I backtrack, gesturing upstairs. "But regardless, we're all she's got. I won't abandon her like the world did."

Shoving several bottles of water into his empty hands, I grab his flannel shirt and drag him upstairs. In Harlow's room, the awaiting puppy pile is laughable.

Enzo is curled up in the crater I left behind, a tree-like arm holding Harlow against his chest. He's... actually snoring.

"Is he asleep?" I laugh quietly.

Hunter's splayed out in the armchair next to the bed, his bare feet propped up on the mattress. He's staring at the IV line.

"Passed out the moment his head hit the pillow."

Placing the bottled water down, I search for a space to squeeze into. Hunter growls as I dislodge his feet and crawl in on Harlow's other side, so she's sandwiched between me and Enzo.

"You could've taken the floor," Hunter grumbles.

"And miss out on cuddles? No way."

"If the bed breaks, you're fixing it."

"Whatever you say."

Theo hasn't moved from the doorway, watching us all with palpable terror, like he's faced with shark-infested waters rather than a sleepover. He tentatively inches into the room.

Hunter's mouth is hanging open slightly, until I nudge him so he looks away. We don't want to scare Theo off now. This is the closest he's been to us in years.

"We should get a TV in here," I observe, snuggling against Harlow's chest.

Hunter's eyes are already shut. "Are you planning to do this often, Leigh?"

"Aren't you?"

Clicking the light off, Theo takes a fortifying breath before curling up at the end of the bed. It's big enough that he has space to sleep, pulling his legs up to his chest so he's tucked into a tight ball.

"Maybe a bigger bed too," Hunter adds sleepily.

I nearly die when Theo chimes in.

"Agreed."

CHAPTER 26
HARLOW

LAST NIGHT I WATCHED MYSELF SLEEP AND SAW THINGS THAT I WISH I COULD FORGET - AURORA VIEW

I STARTLE AWAKE, fisting the oversized black t-shirt I stole from Hunter's wardrobe. My bed is empty for the first time in a whole week. Breathing hard, I force myself to calm down.

I'm home.

I'm safe.

I'm alive.

The sound of someone's snoring penetrates my panicked brain. In the corner, curled into himself like a sleeping baby, Theo is dead to the world. I can't believe he stayed overnight.

The stack of books on my bedside table is a fresh selection from his wealth of literary goodness. I've been going stir-crazy on bedrest, but his daily visits to talk and discuss book theories have kept me sane.

I've seen a new side to him this week. Beneath the palpable anxiety, stone-cold detachment and awkward charm, there's a kind, caring and thoughtful person.

Easing out of bed without moving my bandaged leg too quickly, I pad over to him. The armchair can't be comfortable. Theo moans in his sleep as I brush tangled, blonde curls from his face.

Without his glasses, he looks so young. I can't believe someone so sweet and compassionate has experienced so much pain. You can see it written in every frown line etched around his eyes.

Slipping on a loose pair of sweats and my favourite cardigan, I silently slip downstairs. Snow is falling outside in thick curtains, dousing the world in a blanket of silence.

Lucky perks up from her bed as I walk into the kitchen. Padding over, she butts her head against my belly, her tongue lolling out.

"Hey, girl," I whisper. "You don't have to sleep down here just because Hunter tells you to, you know."

There hasn't been a whole lot of space in my bed. Enzo's taken to crawling in late at night when he's given up working or running for hours on end. He never speaks, just pulls me against his chest and passes out for four or five hours.

Making myself a cup of tea, I blow the steaming liquid while standing at the sink. The snow looks so beautiful, pristine and glistening like miniature diamonds on the front lawn.

"Got some more tea going, by any chance?"

Stifling a scream, I nearly drop my mug. "Hunt!"

Propped in the doorway, he watches me with a lazy half smile. My mouth dries up in an instant. He hasn't bothered to put a shirt on, wearing only a pair of low-slung, grey pyjama bottoms.

His whole chest is on display, every tanned, chiselled inch. The dark swirls of ink that paint his torso are stark in the early morning daylight.

"Sorry." He snickers. "Couldn't resist. You're up early."

"Yeah. I'll make you some tea."

His smile widens. "Sit down, sweetheart. I've got it."

"No, no. Allow me."

Grabbing another mug, I set to making him a cuppa. My heart is still pounding hard. I'm struggling with my anxiety at the moment, with every creaking floorboard and slammed door causing me to spiral.

"Sleep well?" Hunter asks as he takes a seat.

I open the fridge to grab the milk. "Yeah, not bad. I decided to get up before I become one with the furniture and never walk again."

"You've earned the time to rest."

I hand him the cup of tea with an eye roll. "You don't need to coddle me; I'm not going to run away again. No more lazing around doing nothing. It isn't helping."

"Coddling?" He raises a thick eyebrow.

"You heard me."

Walking over to the French doors, I stare out at the crisp snowflakes while finishing my tea. When Hunter's warmth meets my back, I let myself relax into his embrace as his chin rests on my head.

"What are you doing?" I breathe out.

His chest rumbles with a contented noise. "Isn't this okay? I've hated leaving you to go to the office this week."

"Theo's been dropping by to keep me company." My chest aches with sadness. "Although Leighton still won't talk to me. He's been drinking again."

"I know. I'm dealing with it. Enzo's going to take him to HQ today, get him assigned to some work. He'll be alright."

I turn in Hunter's arms. "You're helping him?"

"He's my brother, Harlow."

"I just thought… well, I didn't think you cared about him." I wince at my own words. "Sorry, that sounds crappy."

Sighing, his hands land on my hips as he pulls me flush against his bare chest. "I get it. We have a complicated relationship. But that doesn't mean I'll watch him beat himself up about Diablo."

"He's lucky to have you."

Hunter chuckles. "Not sure he sees it that way. I've always tried to look after him, even when he didn't want it."

His long hair is damp, spilling over his broad shoulders in dark, slightly curling waves. I play with a strand, biting my lip.

"What is it?" he rumbles.

"Do the others know about… us?"

"Us?"

"Don't play games, Hunt. You know what I mean."

He smirks down at me. My lungs seize up as he drags a single finger along my jawline, his thumb tracing my parted lips like usual.

I silently beg for him to keep touching me. Even if I've spent every night wrapped up in Enzo's arms, and the first thing I did when I woke up was lock lips with Leighton, I need Hunter as well.

"Is there something you want?"

"Yes," I mewl.

His lips brush across my forehead in a torturous tickle.

"And what is that?"

My thighs press together. Heat is pooling in between my legs, building in low, tantalising embers. I can still feel his lips against my pussy in that hotel room.

"Please touch me."

His touch vanishes, and I almost cry out in agony. Hunter's staring at me, a ferocious emotion writhing in his irises.

"You're going to be the death of me," he whispers. "And I couldn't care less. I'm done pretending I don't want you."

His lips smash against mine, so hard that our teeth clang together from the sudden movement. My back meets the French doors as he slides a leg between mine to pin me in place.

The delicious hardness pressing against my core sparks my fervent need to be touched and tasted again. He made me feel things I never imagined. Just thinking about it makes me wet down there.

"Come and buy a Christmas tree with me before I fuck you right here, right now, in the middle of the goddamn kitchen where everyone can hear us."

I choke on thin air. "Excuse me?"

"You heard me."

Trying hard not to pant as his hips rock into mine, I fight to straighten my lust-filled thoughts. "A tree? Now?"

Hunter's beard tickles my neck as he kisses his way down, his hot tongue flicking across my collarbones. Every place he touches feels like it's on fire, searing me down to the bare bones of my skeleton.

"Christmas is next weekend, Harlow."

"Seriously?" I gape at him.

"We've been busy with all the craziness."

"Don't you have to work? Enzo's been running himself ragged. He won't tell me what's going on with the investigation. I know something's happened, but—"

"Harlow," he scolds sharply. "I told you not to worry about it right now. You were kidnapped, threatened and shot. We're big boys, and we will take care of the investigation while you recover."

"We agreed you'd be more honest with me."

"You need to rest," he insists.

"I need you to tell me the truth!"

Defeated, Hunter releases his grip on my hips. "Another body turned up this week. We've been receiving… letters."

I stare at him wordlessly for several awful seconds. Part of me is horrified. Another part is surprised it took this long.

"Letters?"

"Threats, mostly," Hunter explains reluctantly. "The latest one had coordinates. We sent two agents, and they found a body waiting."

Stepping out of his embrace, I rest a hand on the door to stop myself from falling over. Everything is spinning all around me.

"How long ago?"

"Sweetheart—"

"How long, Hunter?!"

He sighs again. "Five days ago. We've identified the victim, no family. Nobody reported her missing. He could've had her for weeks."

Hanging my head, I bite back the furious sob that threatens to tear out of me. That woman doesn't need my tears. None of them did. They needed someone to save them.

"What kind of threats?" I ask in a strained voice.

"We're taking care of it."

"Hunter, if you don't tell me right now, I will walk out of that front door and never look back. I deserve to be treated as an adult."

Taking a seat at the empty table that we never use, Hunter shakes his head. "You're right. I just want to keep you safe, and I thought keeping this under wraps for now was the right call."

"It wasn't."

"Yeah, I see that now."

Softening, I wrap my arms around his lowered head. His nose buries in my stomach as he hides there, breathing deeply.

"I don't always get things right," Hunter admits, his voice muffled by my stolen t-shirt. "Especially when it comes to you."

We cling to each other for a moment. It's strange to see Hunter so vulnerable. He never admits to weakness or mistakes, nor does he let anyone close enough to comfort him.

"It's okay," I murmur back. "None of this is easy or straightforward. You're doing the best you can."

His head lifts. "You don't have to forgive me."

"No, but I am."

His smile is far more devastating than any near-death beating or badly placed knife wound. It slashes against my throat and steals the air from my lungs without a single warning.

"Pastor Michaels wants you back," Hunter explains. "He's threatening to kill more girls if we don't release you from protective custody, presumably so he can snatch you up."

"He s-said that?" I stammer.

Hunter grabs my wrist, his thumb stroking against my pulse point. "We're close, sweetheart. I've got drones and scouting parties searching for the chapel where you were held. We'll get him."

"They've been searching for weeks!"

"And that's why we can't give up now. Once we find this place, we'll raze it to the fucking ground. He can't hide forever."

Trying hard not to fall apart, I focus on each stroke of his skin on mine. I don't want to go back. I'd rather die than live a life of captivity, especially now I've tasted what it means to be alive.

"When you find it, I'm coming with you."

"Not a chance in hell," Hunter growls.

I pull his fingers from my wrist. "This isn't up for discussion. You want me to sit here while he's out there, hunting more women. I need to know that when the time comes, I'll be allowed to help."

"It is far too dangerous."

"You asked me to trust you." Staring into his eyes, I let him see the guilt eating me up inside. "I'm asking you to do the same."

Hunter seems to deflate. "Fuck, Harlow."

"Is that a yes?"

"You're not giving me much of a choice."

Standing up, he crushes me against him in a back-breaking hug. I hold him tight, my eyes stinging. It feels good to finally be accepted into the family and be trusted, like an equal.

"Come on," he says gruffly. "Let's go get this fucking tree."

CHAPTER 27
HARLOW

I NEVER LOVED MYSELF LIKE I LOVE YOU - DEAD POET SOCIETY

"WHAT IS THIS PLACE?"

I stare at the sprawling farm with two huge wooden barns and a queue of people marking the entrance. It's busy, despite the steadily falling snow and frigid temperature.

In the distance, several fields of pointy trees stretch as far as the eye can see. Little dots of people duck and weave through the thicket, children squealing with excitement as they find the perfect tree.

"Christmas tree farm." Hunter pulls a scarf and leather gloves on. "I haven't been here in years. It used to be a tradition… before we stopped celebrating."

The shadows are back on his face, and I hate it. Leaning across the console, I press my lips to his stubbly cheek.

"It's beautiful."

The corner of his mouth lifts. "You ready?"

"Hell yeah."

He walks around the car and opens my door for me, offering two large hands to help me down. I'm enveloped in the scent of his spicy aftershave as he reaches for my beanie and tugs it over my hair.

"Perfect."

"I don't think so," I say shakily.

"I wouldn't be so sure. Come on, let's do this."

We queue with the other locals, holding hands in the swirling snow. This place is in the middle of nowhere. We set off after scarfing down breakfast, leaving before the others woke up for work.

With our entry fee paid, Hunter guides me into the first field. I stare open-mouthed at the rolling hills, scattered with different sizes of Christmas trees. Every inch of it is crammed with luscious green pine.

"Oh my God! Look at them all!"

I take off as fast as my stiff leg will allow. The bullet wound is bandaged up and healing well, but it still hurts when I walk. The doctor dropped by for another check-up yesterday.

"Harlow," he yells after me.

I dive into the tightly packed rows of trees. I've never seen anything like this. Fishing out my phone, I snap a picture and send it to Leighton. This will cheer him up.

My phone buzzes with his response.

Leigh: You went without me? :(

Harlow: I'll bring you a Christmas tree back <3

Leigh: You better. Enzo is making me go to the office. If I'm arrested for murder, please bail me out.

I'm still laughing when a red-faced Hunter manages to catch up to me, yelling his head off.

"What have I told you about running off?"

I show him my phone. "Leighton isn't loving office life."

Hunter rolls his eyes. "Enzo's going to enjoy punishing him with stacks of paperwork. I caught him sneaking a red sock into Leighton's washing the other morning."

"What? Why?"

"He's still pissed at him, but I've told him to back off. This is quiet revenge. Half of Leighton's wardrobe is now pink."

"No wonder he's been in a foul mood."

I turn to face the various sized trees. They're all gorgeous. We walk slowly around the whole field, taking it all in as the snow continues to fall. All of the trees are taller than me.

Hunter intervenes when I can't make up my mind and picks the most monstrous tree possible. It's easily twice my size. I doubt it'll fit in his car, let alone the house.

With our tree chopped, wrapped and transported by a friendly man in thermals, Hunter links his hand with mine and takes me to the onsite coffee shop.

We slip into a smaller barn that's been converted, blasted by warmth from the roaring fire in the back corner. Panelled in dark wood and decorated with wreaths of holly, several trees are dotted about.

Their twinkling lights add to the cosy, comforting atmosphere. The scents of baked cookies, fresh coffee and pine needles wash over me in a mouth-watering cloud.

"This is awesome."

Hunter peers down at me. "I like seeing you happy."

His words turn my insides to mush. I look away from his watchful gaze so he can't see me blushing for the thousandth time.

"I like being happy," I reply honestly.

We find two bright-red armchairs next to the fire. I let Hunter order for me, too mesmerised by the open flames dancing against the bricks. Despite the noise of people around us, I don't feel on edge or afraid.

Everything about this place screams of comfort and familiarity. I thought leaving the house after everything that happened in Devon would be hard, but my curiosity to see the world is stronger.

I refuse to be a victim again.

My life is mine to live.

Hunter returns, sliding off his jacket and gloves as he takes the seat next to me. He looks so handsome, dressed down in jeans and a t-shirt. It's a welcome change from his usual office wear.

"So… how does it work? Christmas?"

"We'll celebrate at home." Hunter stares at the fire. "Mine and Leighton's parents will probably come. Enzo's aunt sometimes makes an appearance. We haven't done this for a long time."

"Why did you stop?"

His throat bobs. "When Alyssa died, being together as a family was too painful. We stopped celebrating and never looked back."

"What about your friends? The ones that helped find me?"

"I'm sure they'll come by. Brooklyn's been bugging me all week about meeting you. They were there while you were unconscious, but you deserve a proper introduction."

Our drinks are plonked down by a friendly waitress, breaking the bubble of privacy encapsulating us. I often forget that anyone else exists when I'm in Hunter's magnetic presence.

He slides a reindeer-themed mug over to me, watching closely for my reaction. It's overflowing with whipped cream and giant, fluffy things covered in chocolate sauce.

"What is it?

"A hot chocolate."

I cast him a glare. "I know what that is. But this thing…"

Selecting one of the fluffy things, I place it on my tongue and almost groan. Hunter smothers a grin, looking beyond cute as he sips his drink.

"Marshmallow," he supplies.

"Yum. I think I've found my new favourite thing."

"Even above popcorn?"

"Nothing is above popcorn," I defend hotly. "Leighton always puts extra butter and salt on it for me. Delicious."

"He's determined to fatten you up."

Hunter moves his chair so it's closer to mine. The rest of the coffee shop is blocked out, leaving us in our own little world. We're both facing the fire, sipping our drinks in companionable silence.

"Hunter?"

He hums a response, his eyes nearly shut.

"Why do you think they took me?"

The question startles him from his fire-induced sleepiness.

"What do you mean?" he asks.

"The Michaels. Why me?"

He takes a sip of hot chocolate. "Well… I don't know, sweetheart. He has a pattern, but the victims are randomly selected."

"They could've chosen anyone." I fiddle with the Velcro on my arm brace. "I'm not wishing what I went through on someone else; I just need to know if there was a reason for it all."

"Does it matter?"

"I think… it does. I'm not sure why."

Licking cream from his lips, Hunter looks thoughtful. "Have you spoken to Doctor Richards about this?"

"Every week. He always says I need to focus on the future instead of trying to make sense of it all. That's what drives people crazy, looking for order in the madness."

"Well, he knows what he's talking about."

Hunter's studying me again in the way that I hate. I don't think he even realises he's doing it. I'm not an exhibit for his portfolio, another chip on Sabre's long record of successes.

"I always thought that everything happens for a reason," I try to explain. "I have to know why this happened to me before I can move on. That's what is holding me back."

Hunter shrugs. "Sometimes there isn't a reason for these things. I've seen a lot of shit. Good people that have suffered. I stopped looking for any sense of order in it all a long time ago."

"But… it isn't fair."

"Life never is. Why did Alyssa die? Why did Leighton go off the rails? Why did I lose my hearing? Why isn't the world fair and equal?"

Anger brews within me. I was looking for an answer, but I'm realising that nobody truly knows how the world works. It's an unknown force that washes our lives to shore, some harder than others.

I spent years praying to a God that didn't listen, being beaten to the rhythm of his sermon while countless twisted Bible stories were etched into my skin with blood and sweat.

"Why?" he repeats sadly. "There isn't an answer."

"Maybe we have to make our own answer in this life," I say slowly. "I don't need to make sense of the madness. Living in it… I think that's enough for me."

His eyes meet mine. "Then I'll hold your hand in the madness. Fuck God and his stupid why. This is our path to forge."

"You will?"

Smiling again, Hunter reaches out to clasp my fingers. "Yeah, I fucking will. I meant what I said about us."

I shuffle closer to press my lips to his. Initiating the kiss feels like a bold move, but he reciprocates without hesitating. This powerful, foreboding man is ready to bow before me.

Somehow, I have to tell him that I have feelings. Strong, complicated ones. And not just for him. All of them mean so much to me. I know it's not normal to feel like this for more than one person.

If I tell Hunter, will he make me leave? Will I lose them all? Because I can't fathom a world where I'm not surrounded by all four of these guys—the people that saved my life before they even knew who I was.

I can't give them up.

I don't want to.

I want… to be theirs.

CHAPTER 28
HARLOW

SUNNY SIDE DOWN - SAD HEROES

"HOLY SHIT. That's a fucking Christmas tree."

I smack Leighton's arm. "Language."

"Sorry, Goldilocks. But seriously, you couldn't find a smaller one? I knew I should've gone with you two yesterday."

He flops down on the sofa with a tired huff, leaving me to continue sorting through a dusty box of decorations. Hunter dragged it in before disappearing into his office to make some phone calls.

It doesn't look like anyone has touched the box in a long time. Whoever last packed everything away was methodical. Each package is labelled in neat, feminine handwriting.

I trace the curling script, imagining the woman that once sat in my place. I finally have a name for the ghostly presence that hangs over this family. *Alyssa.* I feel like I know her, somehow.

"When are we decorating?" Leighton breaks my thoughts.

"Just waiting on Enzo and Theo, I think."

"Snacks? I haven't eaten since second lunch."

I cast him a frown. "Second lunch?"

He winks at me. "I'm a growing boy, you know."

"Keep eating for three people and you'll need to go on a diet. I won't have you breaking my bed with that ass, Leigh."

His mouth drops open so fast, I swear his jaw might break. I'm too slow to scurry backwards as he throws himself at me, shoving the box aside to lean over me and start tickling my ribs.

"Apologise, princess. I am not fat!"

Gasping for air, I writhe on the carpet. "I'm sorry! Parlay!"

"We're not fucking pirates. Parlay doesn't count."

The way he's smiling down at me is a huge relief after his silence this week. I know he's still struggling with what happened, no matter how many times I've told him not to blame himself.

I want my buddy back.

He isn't allowed to self-destruct.

Disappearing to find food, Leighton returns with a doughnut crammed in his mouth, and three more stuck on his fingers. He wiggles a finger to offer me one.

"Yeah, I'll pass." I snicker.

"What?" he says around a mouthful.

"That doesn't look particularly appealing."

Snorting, he stuffs a second doughnut down his throat and collapses onto the sofa. Hunter's still wrapped up with his phone call, and Enzo went out for an after-work run to decompress.

Clicking my tongue, I join Leighton on the sofa and beckon for Lucky to follow. She ends up sprawled out across both of our laps, sneaking bites of doughnut Leighton feeds her when I'm not looking.

"We need a cheesy Christmas movie," Leighton suggests as he grabs the remote. "That'll get us in the spirit."

"Why cheesy?"

"Uh, because all Christmas movies are. I dare you to find a single one that doesn't make you cringe."

I shake my head at him. "Then why do you watch them?"

"It's traditional! The cheesier, the better! That's it. We're starting with the best, and we'll work our way down."

An hour later, I'm laughing so hard, I think I'll pee myself. Who knew that a pair of house robbers could almost die so many times, in so many creative ways? Cringy is definitely the right word, but I secretly love it.

"*Home Alone*? Seriously?" Hunter interrupts.

He walks into the den, carrying armfuls of snacks as he frowns at the TV. Leighton whoops in excitement, spreading his arms to receive the food.

"Harlow hadn't seen it."

"So you figured you'd torture her with this shit, huh?" Hunter slumps onto the sofa, opening a bag of peanuts.

"Shut up, you loved it when you were younger," Leighton bickers.

"I was a kid."

"Your point being? We're starting with the best."

"*Home Alone* isn't the best Christmas movie." Hunter stretches his legs out. "It's over-commercialised and pure fantasy. Nobody survives a brick to the head."

"You take that back." Leighton steals the bag of peanuts from his hands and adds it to his pile of food. "*Home Alone* is awesome."

"Want me to hit you in the face with a brick to check? I'm more than willing to perform an experiment. Give me those back."

"Only if I can return the favour, big bro. And no, they're mine now. You'll have to earn them."

While the brothers agree to arm wrestle for the bag of peanuts, the front door slams shut. Enzo's standing in the entrance, breathing hard and sweating. He gives me a wave before disappearing to shower.

Snuggling into Leighton's side, I open my mouth for him to put a chocolate-covered pretzel inside. Hunter munches on his peanuts triumphantly, the pair exchanging sour barbs.

When Enzo comes back, he's dressed down in sweats and a muscle tee, his black hair like spilled ink against his skin. Dislodging Lucky, he sits down next to me and slings an arm over the back of the sofa to ensconce me in his body heat.

"Hey there, little one."

I smile up at him. "Hi, Enz. Good run?"

"Cold. The roads are icy. Nearly broke an ankle a few times."

"You need to be careful out there."

The secret smile he shoots me makes my heart stutter.

"Are you worried about me, Harlow?"

I look back at the TV, stealing another handful of pretzels to busy my hands. "Nope. Not at all."

"Ouch."

We watch the movie, sharing snacks and laughing as the robbers return for round two. They still get their asses handed to them, and some imaginative use of swinging paint cans later, our second movie is done.

"*It's A Wonderful Life* next," Hunter declares, snatching the remote from Leighton. "Now that's a real Christmas movie."

"It's so depressing," Leighton groans.

"I'm counting on you going into a diabetic coma pretty soon, based on how much sugary crap you just ate."

He rubs his belly. "That was just a starter. We should totally order pizza. I'm still hungry."

Before we can start Hunter's movie, the security system in the entrance way beeps before the door clicks open. Excitement prickles across my skin as Theo calls out.

"Am I late?"

Pulling off a snow-dusted denim jacket, he wipes his glasses on the soft fabric of his flannel shirt. Clumps of snow are sticking to his blonde curls, but the smile on his lips is genuine.

"About two hours late," Hunter drones. "What took you so long? I told Fox and Rayna to cover for you tonight."

Theo meanders into the room. "Yeah, they are. Phoenix rocked up to drag the two brothers home for dinner. He stole my laptop and blackmailed me into eating with them."

Leighton chokes on a bite of chocolate as he laughs. Enzo reaches over me to hammer him on the back, also grinning.

"You went over there?" Hunter asks in surprise.

"Brooklyn cooked. Burnt lasagne."

"Nice." Enzo chuckles. "She brought some to the office for us last week and watched as we ate it. I gave an Oscar-worthy performance."

"Brooke brings in lunch now too?" Theo raises an eyebrow. "Huh. I placed bets on them calling the engagement off in the first three months. Dammit."

"You owe me twenty quid," Hunter points out. "I have more faith in them. We'll get her married off to the lot of them yet."

Toeing off his wet shoes, Theo tentatively pads into the living room. When his blue eyes brush over me, his smile brightens.

"Hey, Harlow. How're you feeling?"

"Good, thanks. I finished *The Picture of Dorian Grey* last night, so we need to discuss."

"I'll dig my spare copy out," he says happily. "It's been a few years. Go for *Frankenstein* next. You'll love it."

"Jesus Christ," Leighton curses. "Fucking nerds everywhere. Someone kill me."

"Careful what you wish for," Enzo threatens. "Nice pink t-shirt, by the way. Very masculine."

"I'm fully in touch with my masculinity, thank you very much. Mess with my laundry again and I'll shave your eyebrows while you're asleep."

"Children, now now." Hunter stands up and stretches. "I'm going to get a beer and dig out the pizza menus."

As he vanishes, I wriggle my way out between the arguing pair of idiots and approach Theo. He's standing awkwardly, seemingly too nervous to sit down with us.

"I'll go grab the books I need to give back to you."

"Harlow, wait." Returning to his coat, he slides something out of the pocket. "I found this on my lunch break the other day."

He holds out a slim, leather-bound volume to me. I tentatively take the old book and flip it over, tracing the title with my fingers.

"*The Grimm Tales*?" I exclaim.

Theo's cheeks flush. "I know it's your favourite of the books I lent you. This is an illustrated edition."

Thumbing through the book, the beautiful, hand-drawn pictures take my breath away. It's beautiful.

"Thank you so much."

"It's nothing," he rushes out.

Before he can run away screaming, I gently wrap my arms around his waist. Theo freezes like a pillar of ice, and I can feel the rapid pumping of his chest with each panicked breath.

It takes a full thirty seconds for his arms to band around me, but when they do, he pulls me close against his narrow waist. The scent of spearmint and old books clings to him like a second skin. It's so soothing.

"No, thank you," I repeat.

"You're welcome."

His voice is light and melodic, so far from the lifeless drone he's spoken with in the past. Offering him a smile, he hesitantly returns it, unleashing two perfect dimples.

"We're going to decorate the tree."

His face drains of all colour. "I, uh. I'm not su—"

I drag him over to the space we cleared in the corner of the room before he can run off. The boxes of decorations are still waiting, and the massive tree dominates the entire corner.

Hunter trails back in with a pack of beers, handing them out to everyone. I eagerly accept mine. With drinks opened and snacks spilling everywhere, we face the towering tree.

"Ready?" Hunter smiles at me.

I glance at Theo instead. His eyes are trained on the labelled box of decorations. The tension builds as we all wait for him to speak.

"Let's do this," he eventually says.

"How about some music, then?" Leighton suggests.

Breaking the silence, he turns the TV channel, and some crazy song begins to blast from the speakers. It's all tinkling bells and terrible singing that sets my teeth on edge.

We string the tree with lights first. Hunter meticulously spreads them amongst the branches, but his ruthless attention to detail becomes even more apparent when it's time for the ornaments.

"Just watch, he'll be getting a tape measure out in a moment," Leighton mock-whispers.

Enzo takes a swig of beer. "Remember the year we snuck downstairs and messed the tree up? He didn't speak to us until New Year's Eve."

"I thought his head was going to explode when he saw it." Leighton snorts. "It was worth the sulking though."

Theo smiles as he listens, sitting cross-legged on the floor. He's put himself in charge of the decorations box. With each memory he unwraps, his posture becomes more relaxed.

It's like he's opening himself up to the pain of being around his family again, but something so simple as decorating a tree is making the grief easier to handle. Not even Alyssa's handwriting slows him down.

Hunter glowers at the tree as Leighton deliberately places the ornaments too closely together or at odd angles, intent on pissing his brother off spectacularly.

"For fuck's sake, Leigh! Are you blind?"

"Nope." Leighton grins at him.

"Then stop messing with my organisation!"

Leaving them to it, I search the room for Enzo. He's leaning against the wall, watching them spar while drinking his second beer. They all fit together so perfectly.

He's got his family back.

I'm the one intruding here.

Swallowing hard, I lie about needing a drink and escape. This is exactly what I wanted—getting them all together, seeing the guys back as a family unit for the first time in so long.

I just didn't expect it to hurt, the realisation that I'll never be one of them. They're good people who deserve to be happy. I can never give them that, no matter how much I want to.

Slipping into the empty kitchen, I hop up onto the counter and wait for the kettle to boil. Tears are prickling the backs of my eyes and I feel stupid for letting the feelings overwhelm me.

I should appreciate what I have right now, not waste my time longing for something that will never be mine. It doesn't matter that the woman they loved is gone, and these four men are screaming out for someone to bring them back together.

"Harlow? Everything okay?"

Swiping under my eyes, I plaster a smile on as Enzo trails into the room and shuts the door.

"Are you okay?" I counter instead.

"I'm fine."

"Well, I'm fine too."

Sighing, he places his beer down. "I really hate that word."

"Then don't use it."

"You started it," he says, moving closer. "Look, this is hard. We haven't done Christmas in a long time. I thought I'd forget, but seeing everything laid out brings the memories back."

Making myself some green tea to avoid looking at him, I sense his imposing frame approaching me. Enzo is a physical presence, an unmovable mountain in an ever-changing landscape.

There's nothing impermanent about him, and I love that. He's the certainty I never had growing up. I know he'll always be here, no matter what, picking up the broken pieces of the people he loves.

"I keep getting snippets of memories after Devon," I admit quietly. "Glimpses, here and there. It's coming back quicker now."

"Your childhood?" Enzo guesses.

"Yeah. I remember more about my parents. The memories don't feel real though; it's more like remembering a story someone told me."

Enzo stops in front of me, his huge hands engulfing my legs. Unable to put it off any longer, I look up at his sad, accepting smile.

"We've been trying to find your dad this week," he reveals. "We need to question him now that we've reopened your old case."

"What? Did you find anything?"

"Not yet. The guy doesn't want to be found. He stopped checking in with his parole officer after a couple of months and vanished. Probably abroad."

"Because he doesn't care," I snap angrily. "None of them do. Even Giana moved on and found a new family."

Enzo squeezes my knee. "Or he cares too much. People don't leave their lives for no reason. Either losing you broke your dad so much that he couldn't stay, or there's something we don't know."

"Like what?" I frown.

"That's what I'm going to find out."

Looking back down at the floor, I feel my throat catch. "What if you find him… and he doesn't want to know me? You said it yourself. He doesn't want to be found."

"Harlow, look at me."

I stare down at my sock-covered feet.

"Come on, little one."

When I finally manage to look up, Enzo's face is soft. He takes a strand of my hair, twirling the length around his index finger and absently studying it.

"How could anyone not want to know you? Fuck, Harlow. You're strong. Beautiful. Intelligent. So goddamn kind and giving, it puts the rest of us to shame."

"Just stop."

"Why should I?"

"Because it isn't true." I push his hands away. "I am none of those things. Do you have any idea what I've done? Who I really am?"

When I try to push Enzo backwards to escape, he steps between my spread legs and plants his feet. I can feel the smooth planes of muscle that make up his torso against my thighs, holding me trapped.

"Those girls' deaths were not your fault," he insists fiercely. "Is that what this is about? You can't keep blaming yourself."

"How do you know it wasn't my fault?"

"I know you."

My laugh is bitter. "That isn't enough."

"It is. You did nothing wrong."

His unwavering faith in me is a guilt-inducing knife twisting in my heathen heart. I don't deserve Enzo's trust or admiration. If he knew the truth, he would cast me out to die alone.

Laura's blood is on my hands.

She died because of me.

Despite feeling like the worst person in the world, my legs tense around him. I can't help it; my body won't listen to me. It wants nothing more than to be touched and worshipped in the darkness of sin.

That's the only revenge I can take on Pastor Michaels. I want to do every twisted, dirty thing he accused other people of. He told me I was a sinner, destined for hell. I want to earn that title.

Enzo's eyes narrow on me. My heart is racing so hard, I can hardly see the room around us. Ever so gently, he cups my cheek in his big, scarred hand. I feel so small and helpless in comparison to him.

"I know you," he repeats bluntly.

"You don't."

"Bullshit, Harlow. Say that crap again and we're going to have a problem. I won't hear it."

Burying my fingers in the length of overgrown hair at the top of his head, I stroke the shaved sides that reveal lumps and bumps in his skull, before moving down to his face.

Smile lines and a five o'clock shadow mark his skin, interrupted by the odd, faded scar. Enzo's eyes slide shut, his chest vibrating with a contended purr.

My friendship with him has always been different from the others, but after everything that's happened, he's been touching me more freely. Sharing a bed is so intimate, more than what mere friends do.

"Enzo?"

His eyes flutter open, revealing amber jewels.

"Yeah?"

"I just wanted to say… I'm sorry for leaving you all."

We stare deep into each other's eyes. I can see the imagined boundaries between us melting away like morning mist. It's all there on display—his hope, fear, the crushing loneliness and forever-present exhaustion.

He sees my anxiety and despair, the desperate need to fix the pain I've caused. Both of us are broken in different ways, but those shattered pieces are calling to each other, magnetised by hope.

"Harlow… the things I want to say to you… do to you… well, you're not ready for it. Do you understand what I mean?"

"Who are you to say I'm not ready?"

His eyes flash into dark, black pinpricks of desire. "You're not."

"Tell me what you want to do, and I'll tell you what I'm ready for."

"Are you bargaining with me, little one?"

I offer him an innocent smile. "What if I am?"

The heat from his body is burning through my clothing. I squirm on the countertop, needing some kind of relief from this relentless tension between us.

I want him to kiss me. Touch me. Worship me like Hunter did, claiming me for his entire team to hear. But I can't do this anymore. They have to know what's going on.

"Is this normal?" I breathe.

"What do you mean?"

"The way you make me feel. All of you, at the same time. I should tell you that Leighton has kissed me. And in Croyde, Hunter, um, he… we—"

"Slept together?" Enzo hisses.

"No! We just kissed and… he touched me. I liked it."

"He was the one who told me to stay away from you!" Enzo's face flushes as he takes a big step back. "That son of a bitch. I can't believe it."

"It wasn't like that, Enz. It just happened."

"With him and not me?" he deadpans.

I should fall to my knees before him or pray for forgiveness from the Lord Almighty. Pastor Michaels would beat me black and blue if he heard any of this. I hate how that makes me want to do this even more.

"You're right to be upset with me," I whisper sadly. "This is all my fault. Sins corrupt a holy man's soul. I've been corrupted. I'm evil."

Before my tears can fall, Enzo rushes back to me. I'm swept into his arms and lifted off the countertop. My back crashes into the nearby cupboard as he pins me against it, his lips seeking out mine.

In a moment I've dreamed about for months, our mouths frantically meet. Fireworks explode within me—bursts of heat and excitement, my nervous system becoming awash with pure sensation.

Enzo's lips are like velvet, teasing my compliance as he takes exactly what he wants without coming up for air. It's not like when the others kissed me. This is ravenous, infuriated.

I feel like I'm being punished, but the twisted voice in my head gladly accepts the beating his hungry lips bring. I'll surrender and take my sentence if it means he will spend forever kissing me just like this. I feel like a missing puzzle piece has slipped into place.

"Fuck the pastor," he hisses against my lips. "Fuck him and everything he has taught you. There isn't an evil bone in your body, Harlow Michaels."

Enzo kisses me again—harder, faster, his entire body rocking into me. The pressure is intoxicating. All I want is to crawl inside his body and hide there, curled around his heart like a cancerous parasite he can never escape from.

He shifts back slightly to let his hand skate down the length of my frame until he's teasing the waistband of my soft yoga pants. My heart rate triples with anticipation.

"Do you want this?" he growls out.

"Y-Yes… I want you, Enz."

Giving me time to change my mind, Enzo eases his hand inside. I'm pinned against the cupboard, a willing victim to his exploration. His teeth nip at my bottom lip as he pulls aside the material of my panties.

I can feel the wetness soaking into them from between my legs. It's embarrassing, but having him dominate me like this is heart-pounding. I feel so special under his attention.

"Did Hunter touch you like this?"

"What?" I refocus on him.

Enzo's fingers gently pinch my bundle of nerves, sending tremors through my body. He buries his face in my neck, his voice strained.

"Or was it more like this?"

He pushes a finger deep inside of my slick opening, causing me to moan out loud. I'm so worked up and wet, it didn't even hurt this time. Bliss pulsates through me.

"Answer me, little one. I want to know why my best friend tasted your sweet pussy before me. I've been waiting very patiently."

"I d-don't…"

Squeezing my eyes shut, I see stars behind my lids as his finger moves in and out of me with confident ease. When he thrusts another finger inside, I'm stretched even wider. I feel so full, ready to burst.

I'm not completely clueless. I know there's more than this to being with someone physically. The thought of sleeping with any of them is petrifying. I've seen how painful and awful it is.

All of the girls that Pastor Michaels touched were left broken, empty shells torn apart by the torture. I can't imagine any of the guys hurting me like that, but it's all I know.

"You're tensing up, baby," Enzo murmurs. "Do you want me to stop?"

While my brain is screaming at me to escape, I clamp down on the flow of bad thoughts. This is exactly what Pastor Michaels wants. I refuse to let him dictate my future any longer.

"No… don't stop," I moan loudly.

"Be quiet, then. I don't want those robbing bastards coming in here and seeing what's mine. They've already had their paws all over you, by the sounds of it."

I can't argue as he slams his lips back down on mine, moving in time to each thrust of his fingers. I know what's coming after the night with Hunter. Tension is pooling in my lower belly, churning with heat and excitement.

As my release builds up, I find myself wondering what it would be like to sleep with Enzo. The movies and TV shows have taught me enough. It doesn't have to be all blood and pain.

I want to be that close to someone, to have their entire world narrow until it's just you. It's the highest form of intimacy. I long for the guarantee that you will become someone's whole world. Nobody can take that away.

"There's my pretty girl. Come for me, Harlow."

Clasping Enzo's shoulders, I dig my nails into his shirt as the feeling bubbling inside of me erupts. Each wave of pleasure is melting me into a boneless puddle.

"So perfect," Enzo whispers in awe.

If anyone walked in right now, there would be no denying what just happened between us. That doesn't seem to bother Enzo as he pulls his hand out, raising two glistening fingers to my parted lips.

"Suck."

"M-Me?" I stutter.

"Do you see anyone else here? Your mess, little one. Clean it up."

His demand has heat flooding my body all over again. I wrap my lips around his wet digits, using my tongue to clean them. Salty fluid bursts in my mouth. I don't love it, but it's not disgusting either.

"Does it taste good?" Enzo asks wickedly.

Giving his fingers one last lick, I wipe my mouth. "It doesn't taste bad."

Pulling me close again, I cuddle his barrel chest. It feels so good to have Enzo's arms around me, my nerves still twitching with the aftershocks of him touching me. I wonder what Hunter or Leighton would think if they knew.

"What happens now?" I ask nervously.

Enzo squeezes me tighter. "I won't let you go for their sake. We've shared before, and we can do it again. It might take some convincing, though, after last time."

"Because of Alyssa?"

He flinches. "You know about her?"

"Not much," I admit, flushing. "Just what I've pieced together. Hunter told me some stuff as well. Did you… um, share her?"

His lips purse as pain is scored across his face. I can see it so clearly in his eyes—the gaping black hole that sucks in all hope and light. I've watched enough people die to know what grief feels like.

"Alyssa gave herself to us, and in turn, we did the same. She became more than a co-worker or a friend." Enzo's throat bobs tellingly. "She was our everything. Losing her tore us apart."

Reaching up, I rest a hand on his stubble-strewn jawline. Enzo's eyes flutter shut as he leans into my touch, placing his huge hand over mine.

"I'm not here to replace anyone," I whisper hoarsely. "I'll never be good enough for you guys, no matter what you think. I wish I didn't want you all, but I do."

His eyes open and lock on mine.

"I'm selfish. After losing so much, I want something good."

"That isn't being selfish," he argues.

"Isn't it?"

Enzo's nose brushes against mine. "No, Harlow. You deserve to be happy. I just don't know if we're the right people to give you that."

The truth stings, but I don't disagree. They're not the right people. Everything they think about me is a lie, and my presence in their lives only sentences them to an eternity of damnation.

Peeling Enzo's hand from my skin, I force my feet to move. Each step feels like the crack of fists breaking my bones, blow after blow. Enzo doesn't stop me from walking away, but I can hear his sigh of defeat as I do.

CHAPTER 29
ENZO

VACCINE - HOMETOWN & YOUNG

"ALRIGHT, LISTEN UP."

Staring out at the packed room in HQ, I clock the various teams. After a breakthrough in the past few days, we're closer than ever to ending this. Hunter's throwing every single resource Sabre has into a final push for results.

On the left table, the whole intelligence department has been dragged from their dark, antisocial caves to experience the light of day. Theo is chugging an extra-large coffee while his staff—Liam, Rayna and Fox—are all glued to their open laptops.

Opposite them sits the Cobra team—Brooklyn, Hudson and Kade. The Anaconda team, in charge of backup operations, is spread out in a rowdy group next to them.

Warner and Tara are breaking open the energy drinks already. Becket glares at his number two, Ethan, urging him to stop arm wrestling with Hudson before any bones are broken. I trained both teams myself. They're the best of the best.

Hunter clears his throat. "Let's recap."

Behind me, five full-size whiteboards display every bit of horror. All the photographs of mutilated bodies spill across the surface in violent detail, and a high-definition map of the country marks each dump site.

"Eighteen girls in five years, one who was pregnant at the time of death, and another body dumped last week." Hunter steps up beside me. "All victims are aged between teens to late twenties, with mixed ethnicities and impoverished backgrounds."

I gesture to several of the familiar faces. "Some of these women were sex workers operating across several different cities up north. They were all taken in public, taking care to avoid being spotted on CCTV. Most of them had no families to bother looking for them."

Hunter strolls past each photograph—blue, lifeless, their flesh carved like prime cuts of meat—until he stops at the whole board dedicated to Harlow.

Her younger self, Leticia Kensington, was a bright-eyed, angelic wisp of a child. Her hair was the colour of melted caramel, long and slightly curling at the ends, matching her impish smile.

Next to that, the comparison photo is stark. Only her brilliant-blue eyes and hair colour are the same. Leighton provided the picture, snapped as Harlow decorated the Christmas tree last weekend.

She has some more meat on her bones now after the past few months, but the childlike innocence and curiosity of her younger self is long gone. Pain intermingled with strength stares back at us.

"Harlow Michaels is our only living witness," Hunter explains. "Assisted in his crimes by his wife, the suspect held Harlow captive while indoctrinating and abusing her."

Theo knocks back the rest of his coffee and brushes tight ringlets from his face before coming to the front of the room.

"Harlow fled captivity on foot," he addresses the room. "We tracked her back to Northumberland. She travelled for nearly a week, hopping from one truck to another, contracting sepsis in the process."

Fishing a remote out of his jeans, he clicks the projector on. It splashes a satellite image on the wall, showing a stretch of woodland in rural Northumberland.

He uses the laser pointer to highlight a deep section of forest, far from the nearest town and inaccessible by any vehicle. It spans a good ten-mile radius in all directions.

"Using drones, we have narrowed down the search zone and used public records to find our target. Rayna, would you mind updating everyone on what you've found?"

Standing up, Rayna flicks purple hair over her shoulder. "We've identified the Mary Magdalene Chapel. Decommissioned for public use in 1936. Over time, the woodland grew and swallowed it whole. No one's seen the place in years."

Staring at the tiny region that could represent our first real breakthrough in months, I feel sick. This might be a turning point, the beginning of the end.

I should be relieved, but this case is the only thing keeping Harlow with us. A sick, broken part of me isn't ready for that obstacle to be removed. No matter how many lives it saves.

"Any signs of activity?" Hunter asks crisply.

Theo shakes his head. "No immediate signs of movement or inhabitation, but the drones can't get through the woods. We need to send a full reconnaissance team."

Nodding, Hunter glances around the room. "This is our first lead in months. We can't afford to screw this up. A team will find the church and check all the surrounding land for evidence."

"Are we expecting to find another prisoner?" Kade flicks through his paperwork. "If so, we'll need forensics and a medical team on site. Whitcomb's corpse is also still unaccounted for."

"As far as we're aware, there haven't been any more victims snatched." Theo looks grim. "But as we know, he has a type. These women aren't always on the police's radar when they vanish."

Hunter looks thoughtful for a moment. "We should be prepared for all possibilities. Make the arrangements just in case."

Kade takes notes and sets to work on his laptop. It will take a lot of coordination, but we have the infrastructure to pull it off.

"There's something else." Hunter clears his throat. "I agreed with Harlow that she could come with us for this bit."

"What?" I blurt incredulously.

Levelling us with a stare, Hunter doesn't appear fazed by the nuclear bomb he's dropped. It's preposterous. After years of fighting, he's finally lost his fucking mind.

"Why on earth would we risk Harlow's safety after everything that's happened?" I ask with a scoff. "Was one near-death experience not enough for you?"

"She asked me herself," Hunter explains. "She knows this sick fuck is out there, threatening to rain shit and misery on our heads if we don't release her."

"Even more reason to keep her safe!"

"She'll just leave herself," Theo agrees unhappily. "That's a lot of guilt for one person to bear. This would give her some control back."

"Seriously? You too, Theo?"

Shrugging, he retakes his seat. "She would be surrounded by a team of highly trained agents. Hell, we may even find this place quicker with Harlow there."

"I can't believe I'm hearing this."

"She isn't a kid, Enz."

"So you're ready to watch someone else get hurt?" I snarl at him. "You, of all people, Theo, know we can't take that risk."

"Enough," Hunter interrupts us. "This is our only shot. If we don't produce results soon, the SCU is going to halt funding and find someone else to take over the case."

That sobers everyone up.

"Who would they find to replace Sabre?" Kade frowns from his table. "We're the best around. Nobody else would stand a chance."

"So far, we've got jack shit to show for months of banging our heads against the wall," Hudson inserts. "Hunter's right; this is our only shot to make some progress."

"At the expense of Harlow's safety," I remind them angrily. "That isn't a price I'm willing to pay. She's going nowhere."

Stepping away from them, I retreat to the back of the room to cool off before I hit someone. The whiteboards reflect every second of our failure in taunting detail. So many lives have been taken.

We failed to protect these women. Not just us, but the whole damned world. Law enforcement. Families. Society. They were marginalised, made vulnerable by their social circumstances. Some have no family to visit their graves.

We have to do better than this.

But I won't sacrifice Harlow to do that.

In every single photograph staring back at me, I see her face. This is her legacy. It's a testament to all the excruciating pain and trauma she endured. I hate the thought of nobody being there to protect her.

Now that we've guaranteed her safety, Hunter wants to throw her back into the firing line. Endangering one life to save the potential many more that will end if we don't do this. It's an impossible calculation to make.

"Food for thought?" Brooklyn saunters up to me, leaving the others to continue talking.

"Something like that."

"Hunter has a good point, big guy. Sometimes the way forward is to go back. This is Harlow's past to unravel. She needs to be there."

"She isn't you, Brooke. The things she has suppressed, years of abuse and torture… pulling at those threads could break her. We'd be taking her straight back to her own personal hell."

"Maybe that's necessary," she murmurs, her eyes on a gruesome crime scene photo. "You helped me put myself back together, once upon a time."

"And it nearly killed you in the process. We had no choice but to tear your memories apart. Harlow doesn't need to be there when we hunt this bastard down."

Brooklyn's silver eyes pierce my skin. "She watched every single one of those women be brutally murdered in front of her eyes. This is her decision to make. You can't stop her from coming."

My forehead collides with the nearest whiteboard. "Dammit, wildfire. This is so fucked."

She rests a hand on my arm, causing her sweater sleeve to ride up. Brooklyn's body is more scar tissue than skin, but unlike Harlow's marks, it was entirely self-inflicted. If anyone knows what it's like to drown in their own demons, it's Brooklyn West.

"I can help her," she offers in a low voice. "She doesn't have to be alone when we go into this place. I'll do what I can to help."

"You'd do that?"

Her smile is crooked. "We owe Sabre a debt that can never be repaid. You didn't let me do this shit alone. I want to be there for Harlow now."

Pulling Brooklyn close, I ruffle her platinum hair while hugging her tightly into my side.

"You don't owe us shit. We're family."

"Then let's solve this case together, as a family," she replies. "Harlow is a part of that now. We can help her."

We seal the bargain with a bone-crunching hug. This angry, sarcastic slip of a woman has become an adoptive sister to us all. I know she'll take care of Harlow, in ways that we never could.

"Alright," I grumble into her hair. "I really fucking hate this plan, for the record."

Brooklyn snorts. "You hate any plan that doesn't involve sushi-rolling us in bubble wrap and killing anyone that gives us a second look."

"Is that a bad thing?"

She pats my back before releasing me. "Nah, it's not a bad thing."

Together, we return to the group. Hunter looks ready to declare his early retirement as Kade and Theo argue about the best route into the thick woodland.

Hudson's feet are propped up on the table as he happily smokes a cigarette in the chaos. Without Jude here to keep him in line, he's reverted back to his caveman ways. Typical.

"Harlow will come with us," I declare.

All eyes snap to me.

"What changed your mind?" Hunter asks.

"As much as I hate it, she has the right to choose. If we take that from her, we're no better than the people we're hunting."

He nods, checking with Theo, who also inclines his head in agreement. The three of us are the only family Harlow has right now. Her life is our responsibility.

"We'll bring in extra agents to beef up the perimeter," I add sternly. "I also want a helicopter in the air and drones surveying the surrounding land for any trouble. Nobody gets near her."

"And if the Michaels are in the church?" Theo replies.

I crack my scarred knuckles. "We rip those pieces of shit apart and let them rot in motherfucking hell, where they belong. I'll do it myself and let Harlow watch the damn show."

With the decision made, Theo sets his team to work mapping a suitable route to our location. This will be a huge logistical operation with lots of moving parts, and we're running short on time.

Dragging me into a quiet corner, Hunter yanks his hair tie out with a growl. Chestnut waves spill over his shoulders, and he takes a shuddering breath. If I didn't know him better, I'd say he's nervous.

"What if someone else is dead in there?"

I swallow hard. "We'd be leading Harlow into a bloodbath."

"Whitcomb's skeleton is a problem," Hunter worries. "This place could be the Grim fucking Reaper's lair. Not to mention the perps themselves."

"It's a huge risk."

His gaze is bleak. "We have no choice but to take it. If there's even a single hint of danger, I want you to grab her and get the fuck out of there. Don't worry about the rest of us."

"We have a safe house in Newcastle. That'll be our designated rendezvous if it all goes up shit's creek."

"Let's hope it doesn't come to that."

Hunter agreeing to this plan wouldn't have happened three months ago. Whether he realises it or not, Harlow's changed him. He never gives people the freedom to make their own decisions.

In our world, control and power come from the top. He's our commander-in-chief; we all follow his direction or suffer the consequences. That's exactly what's kept us alive for so long.

"Harlow's in therapy with Richards upstairs," he says, grabbing his phone from the table. "I'll speak to her."

"She'll need to meet everyone." I glance at the Cobra team, bantering amongst themselves. "They made it through, Hunt. It's possible. We can do the same for Harlow."

"I hope you're right. I'm not ready to lose her."

"Did you figure that out while your tongue was down her throat? Or after you took advantage of her on that damned trip?"

Hunter freezes on the spot.

"Yeah, I know all about that."

"She's a grown adult," he replies quietly. "It was fully consensual. I did not take advantage of her in any way."

"You'd just torn apart the basis of her whole existence, then took her to bed to make it all better. That's taking advantage in my books."

"Careful," he warns.

"How about your scoundrel brother? He's been fooling around with her too behind our backs."

Dragging me further out of earshot, Hunter curses up a storm. "All three of us, huh? I guess we should've seen that coming."

"She's admitted to having feelings for us all."

"Goddammit. I'm not looking to share Harlow with either of you stubborn assholes. We tried it before, and it didn't work."

My hands twitch with the urge to punch Hunter so hard, he regains his fucking hearing.

"Our relationship with Alyssa was not a failure," I whisper harshly. "How could you say that about what we had?"

His eyes stab into me. "Wasn't it? She's dead, and it's our fault. That's a failure in my eyes. Harlow deserves a hell of a lot better."

Before I can argue back, he storms off to head upstairs. There's no point following him or attempting to argue more. If he thinks I'm going to give up Harlow for him, he's sorely mistaken.

I know we're a broken family of hot-headed, unworthy idiots, and Harlow deserves to be with someone capable of loving her in a healthy, normal way, but that doesn't change how I feel.

I'm falling for her.

And I'll die to keep her safe.

Even from us.

CHAPTER 30
HARLOW

EYES ON FIRE - BLUE FOUNDATION

SAT opposite me in the comfortable interview room, Doctor Richards is taking meticulous notes. He's sporting another bright scarf, this one in an ugly shade of mustard yellow.

I enjoy his constant revolving door of crazy outfits. It gives me a distraction as he tortures my mind on a weekly basis. Given recent events, our sessions have been moved to HQ for the foreseeable future.

We've been at it for an hour, but he's resolutely ignoring the ticking clock. My throat aches from talking for so long and choking the emotions that want to overwhelm me.

"What happens next in your dream?" he prompts.

I anxiously pick at a loose thread in my sweater. "Mrs Michaels often hummed choir songs while cleaning up the basement. In my dream, I saw her dismantling a woman's body with a hacksaw. She was too heavy to carry out in one piece."

"What are you doing?"

"Nursing a broken wrist for refusing to help her cut apart my friend. I can still hear the sound of the woman's bones splintering. It felt so real, then I woke up."

"Use your senses. Describe it to me."

"Why?" I rub my tired eyes.

Richards places his pen down. "We have to open up all these tightly wrapped boxes, inspect the contents, and repackage them. It's the only way through."

My stomach hurts so much, I want to curl up in the corner of the room. These sessions are always intense. We've been wading through fragments of memories for a while, piecing together odd dreams and flashes of information that paint a harrowing picture.

The dream I had last night made me vomit when it startled me awake. I haven't eaten since. The sound of skin and bone being sliced keeps reverberating through my head like a broken record player.

"I don't want to talk anymore." I fiddle with my hair, battling the urge to pluck strands out in front of him.

"We still have fifteen minutes."

"Then we can sit in silence!" I snap back.

Lips pursed, Richards jots down some notes. I want to steal his notepad and throw it out of the window. He looks pointedly towards my leg. It's still sore, but the doctor said it's healing well. I was lucky to avoid any tissue damage.

"When confronted by your real family, you ran and placed yourself in danger. Does that seem like a healthy coping mechanism?"

"It was that or risk something worse," I say through clenched teeth. "I couldn't sit there for a second longer."

"Which is perfectly understandable," he combats. "But the way you chose to deal with it wasn't safe or constructive. That's why we're here. You can't keep running from what's going on."

"I'm not running."

"Perhaps you'd like to discuss your self-harming instead. Either way, we need to talk about what's going on. I'm not the kind of therapist that will sit here and let you spiral."

I gape at him. "My… s-s-self what?"

Richards removes his glasses to clean them. "Why don't you tell me?"

"I don't know what you're talking about."

"It may feel good in the short-term." He replaces his glasses and smiles reassuringly. "Using pain to cope with overwhelming feelings."

Linking my fingers, I ignore the screaming voice at the back of my mind. I know what he's talking about. The bald patch underneath my hair has grown bigger and more violent in the past week.

How he knows about it, I don't have to guess. One of the guys must've clocked what's going on and ratted me out. Shame slips over me, hot and clinging, until I want to crawl into a quiet corner to hide.

"It's nothing." I drop his gaze.

"Nobody is judging you, Harlow. It's normal to struggle with the trauma of what you've experienced. I want to help you."

"I don't need help."

"Is that why you're not sleeping or eating? And why you have started hurting yourself to cope? That doesn't seem like someone in control to me."

I close my eyes to hold the tears back. "Every time I sleep, I remember more about my past. The memories won't stop coming, and the more I remember, the worse it hurts."

He abandons note-taking and looks straight at me. Richards isn't a bad person. His job can't be easy, and he hasn't given up on me yet.

"I once treated a man that spent years of his life trapped in the mind of another." His smile is wistful. "Jude was forced to become a whole new person. He shut out the memories of his old life to ease the pain of losing himself."

"He couldn't remember? At all?"

Richards shakes his head. "It took a long time to piece those threads back together. We spent years working together."

"And it worked? He got better?"

"In a manner. Some things never leave us, Harlow. The size of our trauma doesn't shrink over time. With therapy, we learn to grow around it. Slowly but surely."

With a defeated sigh, I unclasp my fingers and make myself sit back in the chair. Richards smiles and picks his pen back up.

"I can remember the sound of her voice, and bits of what she looked like," I admit, squeezing my eyes shut. "It's all there, but it still feels out of reach."

"Then let's take a step closer. Listen to her voice, Harlow. Is it high? Soft? Loud? Quiet? Take in the smallest of details."

"She was crying." I wince, peering into the dark crevasses of my mind. "Her voice was kind of gravelly. She was older than the others."

"Zoom in a little further. Can you see her face?"

Taking a steadying breath, I walk myself back into my caged cell. Dank, dirty, the scent of spilled blood hangs in the air like smoke. Mrs Michaels' off-key humming wraps around me, broken by the awful crunching of the saw moving back and forth.

Pushing further, I follow the sound, returning to the sight that made me sick last night. Mrs Michaels lifts a stiff, blue arm to begin hacking it off, causing the corpse's head to slump and face me.

Empty, misted-over eyes meet mine. She's been dead for several hours. Her skin is grey, rubber-like, and purple around her neck where Pastor Michaels strangled her to death.

"Kiera," I breathe. "That's your name."

Her short hair is caked with dried blood, and her cracked lips once spread in warm, comforting smiles from between our cages. I think… she prayed with me, whispering for her personal God to save her.

"I recognise her," I say shakily. "She was maybe the second girl to arrive. One of the ones I'd forgotten until I saw her picture recently."

"Good," Richards encourages. "What else?"

"We prayed together. She was religious."

"She was?" he repeats, surprised.

"No… that doesn't make sense." Screwing my eyes shut, I try to keep my focus. "Why would he punish a woman of faith?"

"Go deeper. Visualise what happened."

"I'm scared," I admit.

"You're not alone, Harlow. I'm here and I promise that you're safe. These are just memories. They can't hurt you now."

My nails dig into my palms as I make myself go further, drinking in the scents and sounds. Rewinding the clock, I shove Mrs Michaels from the basement and return Kiera to her cell.

Dismembered limbs reattach themselves as her blood cascades back into her prone form. Colour returns as she begins to breathe again, her hands wrapped around the bars as we prayed together.

Our Father, who art in heaven.

Hallowed be thy name.

Pray with me, Harlow.

Here, like this. Shut your eyes.

"I can hardly hear her; there's a rainstorm outside. The basement is leaking. She's praying and her voice is shaking with each word."

"What else is she saying?" Richards croons.

Even after years of captivity, I was scared of the unknown. The women were terrifying to me at first, bringing death and violence into the basement.

It was a relief to have company at last and a harrowing sentence all in one. I could take my own beatings. They became routine, mundane even. But watching theirs was unbearable.

That man isn't your father, Harlow.

He's a monster.

I always knew he had the devil in him.

With a gasp, my eyes fly open. The warm lights of the interview room chase away the shadows that had infected my vision. I'm not in the basement. The past can't drag me back, kicking and screaming.

"I think… she knew him," I choke out on a sob. "Kiera told me that he wasn't my real father. I don't think I believed her."

Richards nods to keep going.

"When he killed her… she wouldn't stop screaming, begging him to spare her the Lord's mercy. He was angry, tearing her clothes off like an animal. It was so cruel, so violent."

I search the flimsy memory for anything else. It's like I'm digging around in an open chest cavity. Everything about this feels so wrong.

"She called him a… a… charlatan. What does that mean?"

Richards rubs his chin. "It sounds like she challenged him, and he didn't like it. Narcissists often don't."

"So she knew he wasn't a real pastor?"

"Potentially," he muses. "We know he gave himself a fake position of power to brutalise women under the guise of repentance. Self-deception cemented in violence."

"This makes no sense."

"Just take a deep breath for me, Harlow. You've achieved a lot here. Let's have a moment to close those boxes again."

Making myself relax, I unclench my hands and take a few deep, controlled breaths. My nails leave searing crescent marks in my skin. Even as Richards guides me through the breathing, I still feel like I'm teetering on a cliff's edge.

If Kiera holds a connection to Pastor Michaels that wasn't identified in the initial police investigation, the guys need to know. This could open a whole new field of enquiry.

"I have to go. Hunter needs to hear this."

Pulling my coat and scarf back on, I try to stand on trembling legs. Richards looks concerned as I try and fail to muster a thankful smile.

"Harlow, you need to stick to what we've discussed. Use your coping mechanisms and support system. These memories are traumatic. They will take some getting used to."

I offer a tight nod. "I will."

"Remember, you're growing around your trauma. Not erasing it. If you need to speak to me before our next session, I'm a call away."

"Thank you, doc."

He smiles back. "Go on, then."

Slipping out of the interview room, I head back to the foyer where I left Leighton scrolling on his phone an hour ago. The leather sofa is empty. He must've gone downstairs to the cafeteria to get food.

Waiting for the elevator to arrive so I can hunt him down, the doors slide open with a ding, revealing a frazzled occupant.

"Hunter?"

He looks up from his phone. "Harlow. I was just coming to get you. Leighton's doing something urgent for me."

"Is everything okay?"

Hair framing his face in disorderly waves, Hunter looks more agitated than when he left the house this morning. Everyone was heading into a big meeting when we arrived.

"I need to talk to you."

"Good timing." Grabbing his arm, I pull him towards a nearby office. "Something came up in therapy. You need to hear this."

Inside the office, Hunter extricates himself from my grip and shuts the door. I don't sit when he gestures towards an empty seat, pacing the small space instead.

Fire ants are eating at my skin, infecting me with doubt and worry. What if my mind is playing tricks again? I've unearthed these memories, but I don't know if I can trust them.

"Harlow?" Hunter asks with concern. "Talk to me, sweetheart. Tell me what you're thinking."

I stop pacing and bite my lip. "You know my bad dream last night? The one that made me sick?"

I scared him almost as much as myself when I woke up screaming like a banshee. He was asleep in the armchair as we'd been watching another black-and-white Christmas movie together.

"We unravelled it in therapy. It was about Kiera."

"Kiera James?" he answers grimly. "She was the second victim to be located. Particularly gruesome, if I recall correctly."

"They… um, dismembered her. That's what I was dreaming about. Mrs Michaels broke my wrist when I refused to help."

"Bloody hell, Harlow."

I wave off his sickened expression. "That's not the important bit. I think she knew him. She told me he wasn't my real father."

"You remembered that?"

"Yeah. She was religious too. He didn't like it when she insulted him, so he rushed through the ritual and strangled her instead."

Hunter takes a moment to process. "This doesn't fit his MO. The other victims were randomly selected for punishment."

"Because this wasn't about repentance and punishing her for sinning. It was some kind of revenge. He killed her out of hatred."

He shakes his head. "This is unbelievable. If he knew her, why was it missed in the previous police investigation?"

"You tell me."

With my news delivered, I feel shaken. Hunter approaches tentatively. When I'm pulled into his arms, I deflate. He rubs circles on my back, his beard tickling the top of my head.

"You're okay," he whispers.

"None of this is okay. He knew her and she was torn apart anyway. Why doesn't anyone else know this? Or am I just losing it?"

"I don't think you're losing it, sweetheart. Let me make some calls and check the records from the previous investigation. You did good."

"Too little, too late." I breathe in his spicy scent, even if I don't deserve to be comforted. "I can't bring her back."

Hunter guides my eyes up to his. "But you can stop anyone else from getting hurt. I have some news."

Panic spears me. "What is it?"

"The intelligence department has tracked down a potential location for where you were held."

"Did you find anything?" I rush out.

"Not that simple. It's deep in thick woodland and can only be accessed by foot. We have to go there and scout it out."

My heart pounds harder. "So we're leaving?"

His smile is tight and unhappy. "None of us like the idea of you being in danger. If Enzo had his way, you would never leave the house again."

"I've spent enough years locked away from the world."

"I know. Look, this is your decision to make, and we respect that. You're going to come with us and help track this place down. A deal's a deal."

He clutches my hands to stop them from shaking. The cold air of the basement is slipping beneath my skin, chilling my thawed heart back into an icy, impenetrable lump. I barely survived escaping.

Can I really go back there? Will I be able to cope with seeing it again? I honestly don't know. This seemed like a good idea, but the reality is another thing altogether.

"I have to do this," I say nervously. "You'll be there, right?"

"Of course." Hunter's fingers link with mine. "You'll have us and the Cobra team to support you. We'll triple security to make sure it's safe. I can't control what we may find inside though."

"You think… another prisoner?"

"Perhaps, if he snatched a girl immediately after dumping the last body for us to find. I don't want to rule it out."

Pastor Michaels has an intricate process, weeks of scheduled beatings and recited scripture to take the sinner from evil, soulless scum to a willing vessel for the Lord's divine retribution.

If there's someone else in there, she'll be knee-deep in her own blood. Nausea engulfs me as I realise what else could be waiting if they haven't bothered to move her yet.

"Laura," I whisper in horror.

Hunter's mouth is an uneasy slash. "She hasn't turned up. You need to be prepared. If we find this place, she might still be inside."

Swallowing the bubble of acid stinging the back of my throat, all I can do is nod. If I open my mouth, something else might slip out. A gnarly, twisted secret that could bring my whole world crashing down.

"We will be home for Christmas at the weekend," Hunter outlines. "We'll head out tomorrow on a private plane."

"Got it," I squeak.

Leaning close, his lips lock on to mine and swallow my silent screams of panic. I don't deserve the hidden sweetness behind Hunter's impenetrable façade, but his kiss pulls me back from the edge.

Pecking my lips again, he tucks me into his side. "Everyone's downstairs. We can go over introductions."

"Can you give me a minute? I need to splash my face and grab some painkillers. My head is killing me."

He scans my face with concern. "Go home and rest; it can wait until tomorrow. Leighton will have to drive you. We've got a lot of planning to do tonight."

"You're sure?"

"We need you rested and ready. Can you find your way to my office from here? There are some tablets in the desk drawer. The code is 041022."

"Got it, thanks."

Firing off a text to Leighton, he presses a kiss to my temple before heading back out to the elevator. The minute he disappears, I let my mask crumble.

If he knew how scared I was, I'd never be allowed to go. The thought of returning to Laura, my childhood and all the dark memories I've been pushing back is unthinkable.

I have no choice.

This could be our chance.

Steeling my spine, I make my way upstairs to Hunter's office. Inside, it's a disorganised mess. The last few weeks of chaos have clearly wreaked havoc on his tidy headspace.

Knocking back some pills, I glance over his cluttered desk. There's a smashed photo frame nestled amongst the stacks of paperwork. I dodge shards of broken glass to stroke my thumb over three familiar faces.

I've never seen Enzo, Hunter and Theo look so happy and content.

Nestled between them, a pink-haired beauty grins at the camera. Her smile radiates so much warmth. Instinctively, I know it's Alyssa.

"I'll keep them safe," I whisper to the ghost.

"Hunter? You in here?"

Startled, I drop the frame so hard, it cracks against the desk. More shards of glass spill across the paperwork as someone enters the room.

"Harlow." Theo sounds surprised as he stops behind me. "Sorry, I didn't mean to scare you. Thought Hunter was up here."

"He's just gone back downstairs."

Theo's eyes land on the smashed frame. He visibly swallows before looking back up at me.

"He spoke to you?" he asks in a strained voice.

"I'm coming with you guys."

"You sure that's a good idea?"

"Do you not want me there?" I ask in return.

"I want you to be safe," he answers with a sigh. "But I actually vouched for this idea. I think it's important for you to be there."

I blink in surprise. "You do?"

He moves to lean against the wall, his glasses shielded by a loose curl. "I admire your strength. I'm not sure I'd do the same in your position."

Heat spreads across my cheeks. I have no idea what to say. Our late-night conversations are about books, theories, obscure ideas and observations about a world that scares us both to death.

Theo's very philosophical and painfully intelligent. It's an attractive, if not slightly awkward, quality to have. I've admired him for a while now. I didn't expect it to be returned though.

"Listen," he begins. "The thing is… well, um, it's a little bit complicated, you know?"

"Uh, I have no idea what you're talking about."

Sighing in frustration, he scrubs his eyes beneath his glasses. "I swear, I had it. Now all the words are jumbled up in my head."

Taking a tentative step closer, I rest a hand on his shoulder. "It's just me. You can tell me anything."

His pale-blue eyes scrape over me, assessing and afraid. I'm stunned as he takes my hand from his shoulder and holds it instead.

"I guess I wanted to apologise," he tries again. "The others have looked after you while I stayed away. I feel… shitty about that."

My eyebrows knit together. "Theo… you gave Laura back to me to say goodbye. You've kept the case going, working night after night. More than that, you've been a good friend."

"A friend?" he echoes.

"Well, I don't think strangers donate their entire library to random people or stay until the sun rises to discuss crazy book theories. That's what friends do."

His smile is a gentle evening breeze that warms the shell of my heart.

Despite his awkward nature, Theo is a soothing presence. Quiet, reserved, observant. But beneath it all, fearsome in his own way.

"Are you friends with the others too?"

"What else would I be?" I answer softly.

For once, he doesn't hesitate or doubt himself.

"I've seen the way they all look at you."

His hand is still wrapped around mine, trembling slightly with each word. Anxiety runs over him like a static charge.

"I don't know what you want me to say."

"I… I… hell, me neither," he falters.

There's something in the loaded air that's sealing us in this room, letting everything else fall away. An emotion. I don't know what it is. The others don't look at me like Theo does.

"Can I just hug you?"

His request catches me off guard.

"You don't need to ask." I smile shyly. "But yeah, that'd be nice."

Offering his own tiny smile, he releases my hand and steps closer until his green flannel shirt is pressed up against my nose. His arms are surprisingly strong beneath the loose clothing he wears, wiry and muscular.

I breathe in his peppermint scent, spiked with the familiarity of parchment and antique books. It's like stepping into a library and being welcomed home into its warm, comfortable arms.

Where Leighton makes me laugh until I want to cry, Enzo treats me like I'm a precious artefact to be loved and protected. Hunter excites me, makes me feel beautiful and powerful.

But Theo… with him, I feel at home. Secure. Wrapped in soft blankets and soothing firelight, the pages of a book spread out on my lap. He's the welcoming arms of the family I always wanted.

His breath stirs my hair. "You feel good."

I tighten my arms around his narrow waist. "Do you live in a library or something? You always smell like books."

"Is that a bad thing?" He chuckles.

"Definitely not."

"My office is a bit of a lair." I feel his fingers stroke down the length of my spine. "I like books more than I like people."

"Seems fair."

Lapsing into silence, we hold each other tight. There's no pressure to separate or speak. I focus on the feel of Theo stroking my back, his breathing evening out as his anxiety fades.

When he releases me, it feels like an eternity has passed. The world has ended around us, succumbed to the ravages of time, and we're the last two humans left in this existence.

He looks at me… like I'm his whole world. That terrifies and excites me so much. I want to dive into his blue-eyed gaze and let myself be consumed by the oceanic waves.

"I haven't done that for a long time," he admits with an adorable blush. "Thank you for not being weirded out."

I can't help but laugh.

"Have you met me? I'm not sure weird is a strong enough label for the stuff going on up here." I gesture to my head. "If you need more hugs, you know where I am."

His eyes sparkle. "I may take you up on that. Listen, the others are waiting for me. I should head back down."

"I need to find Leighton. He's taking me home."

Nodding, Theo offers me his hand again, but it isn't shaking this time. There's a certainty to the way his fingers link with mine.

"Let's find him together."

CHAPTER 31
HARLOW

BURNING THE IRON AGE - TRADE WIND

BUSTLED out of the black-tinted SUV, I throw my backpack over my shoulder. Rain is falling in thick curtains, soaking the smooth tarmac beneath my leather boots. The snow didn't last long.

The time has come.

We're going up north.

The sprawling airport is an unnerving sight. Huge aeroplanes are parked in neat rows, towering well above me like great steel beasts. Everything here is huge, from the miles of runway to the glistening glass buildings of the terminals behind us.

Enzo climbs out of the car and steals my backpack from me before I can protest. "Are you doing okay?"

"Yeah," I answer quickly.

"Are you sure?"

I haven't been able to eat or drink anything, including at dinner last night. It all tastes like ashes in my mouth. Sleep was also impossible, so I'm running on empty.

"Harlow?"

"I just need some space."

Enzo clears his throat. "Okay then."

He silently nods to the various agents standing in formation as we approach them. They're all dressed in black uniforms, packing visible gun holsters and schooled expressions.

"It's alright to be scared," he tries again as we cross the tarmac. "We're all here to help you get through the next couple of days."

I don't respond.

For once, I want Enzo to stay as far away from me as possible. He's too good at teasing the truth from me. If I'm going to keep it together, I need to hold every broken, ugly piece of myself inside.

One wrong move and it'll all crumble to ruin. My secrets are dangerously close to devouring me in a greedy, hellish furnace. Keeping them inside is going to take every ounce of control I have.

We're taking Sabre's private plane for the short flight up north. Their logo is even printed on the gleaming wing. Enzo gestures for me to go ahead, and I tentatively head up the narrow steps.

Inside, their wealth and power are spelled out in cream-coloured leather seats, dark-wood panels and a fully stocked bar lined with different liquors. Two rows of seats sandwich a wide, carpeted aisle.

At the back of the aeroplane, a gaggle of people are messing around with raised voices. I feel Enzo's hand on my lower back, gently guiding me towards them as my lungs seize up.

They fall quiet, and various eyes land on me with curiosity. I recognise a couple of the guys immediately. Becket and Ethan guarded my hospital room, and they offer me smiles of greeting.

The other two with them also wave with friendly smiles. They introduce themselves as Tara and Warner, the final members of the Anaconda team.

Enzo drops my backpack into an empty seat. "Harlow, you haven't officially met the Cobra team yet either. They helped in Devon too."

I manage an awkward nod. "Hi, everyone."

Squeezed into a window seat, a smiling, blonde-haired man waves at me. He's smartly dressed, his crisp, white shirt complementing his kind, hazel eyes.

"Hey, Harlow. We met while you were unconscious. I'm Kade." He gestures to the person next to him. "This is my brother, Hudson."

His brother doesn't speak, nodding instead. From the tattoos inked all the way up to his throat and multiple facial piercings beneath his messy, raven-coloured hair, he looks a little intimidating.

"Ignore this one." A female voice snickers. "He's a teddy bear really, beneath the emo exterior."

Standing up from her seat, the platinum-haired woman is looking at me expectantly. She looks around my age, but she's strong and sinewy like a trained marine. Her ripped jeans match the worn leather jacket wrapped around her shoulders.

"I'm Brooklyn." She tries for a smile, but it looks a little foreign on her mouth. "Enzo's told me a lot about you."

"He… did?" I reply anxiously.

"I knew this introduction was a bad idea," Enzo grumbles behind me. "Brooke, keep any embarrassing stories to yourself or find another job."

She smirks at him. "You're no fun. Come sit next to me, Harlow. I've got plenty of juicy stories to tell you about this lump of meat."

"M-Me?" I stutter.

Brooklyn pats the empty seat next to her. Taking a breath, I move my backpack and slide into the empty spot. Kade and Hudson are sitting behind us, leaving Enzo to move further up the plane.

I watch him go with a sigh of relief. Hunter, Leighton and Theo are piling on board with various bags of equipment, preparing for takeoff. They spot me with Brooklyn, and all seem to relax slightly. Clearly, they trust her implicitly.

"I hate flying," she admits quietly. "Although the bar is well stocked, I suppose. That's a bonus."

"I've never flown before."

"This is nicer than a commercial flight, so you're in luck. Better to sit with us than Captain Cockblock over there."

I choke on a breath. "Excuse me?"

"He said not to embarrass him." Kade sticks his head between the seats with a knowing grin.

"So?" she snarks back.

"I'm not standing between you and Enzo when he comes to break your legs for telling that story. I'd like to keep my face intact."

"Dammit," Brooklyn curses. "Why should I marry you if you won't defend me from leg-breaking assholes?"

He ruffles her shoulder-length hair. "Because I'm a catch, love. Don't complain. We'll defend your honour against anyone but him."

Kade disappears back between the seats, and I can't resist a glance. He has a laptop balanced on his lap as he resumes working. Next to him, Hudson is frowning at the men swarming over the tarmac.

Danger seems to cling to him, shrouding his entire stony persona in a threatening cloud. When he catches me staring, I'm knocked off-kilter by the tiny, reassuring smile he gives me.

"You ready for this, Harlow?"

"I, uh… I hope so."

Hudson cocks his head to the side. "None of us are going to let anyone hurt you. Stick by us. You'll be alright."

"He's right," Brooklyn says beside me. "You're not going into those woods alone. You've got every single one of us by your side."

Turning back to face her, I wring my sweaty hands together. These people don't know me, but they're putting their lives at risk to keep me safe. If anything happens to them, it's on me.

"He's dangerous," I squeeze out. "Pastor Michaels will hurt you to get to me. You don't know the things he's done."

"We don't hurt all that easily." Brooklyn's shoulder bumps mine. "This asshat isn't the first monster we've faced."

In her eyes, something dark and sinister shines. I can see the demons pulling the strings behind her strained smile. Somehow, she has control over them.

Everything about her is calm and assured, with an air of self-awareness. But crackling through that, the threat of violence is palpable. In a weird way, I do feel safe by her side.

"Harlow." She sticks out her hand, palm up. "You're doing the right thing by coming. I think it's brave. If we find the suspect, we'll make him pay for everything he's done."

Biting my lip, I put my hand in hers. Her palm is warm and dry, contrasting my clammy skin. She holds me tight before releasing.

"Promise?" I say under my breath.

Her smile is shark like. "Pinkie swear."

As the final equipment is loaded and the doors shut, the hum of the engine begins to rumble beneath us. My throat closes up as I fasten my seatbelt and fight to remain calm.

Brooklyn pulls out her phone and plugs in a pair of headphones. When she offers one to me, I gingerly accept.

"Takeoff isn't so bad," she whispers conspiratorially. "Shut your eyes and focus on the music."

Slipping it into my ear, she cranks the rock music up loud, props her booted feet up and closes her eyes. I copy her every move and let the aeroplane fall away.

"Circle around everyone."

Outside several black support vans, the car park roped off with police tape lit by flashing blue lights, our group gathers. Eight police officers and a well-sized army of Sabre agents stand at the edge of the forest, holding the perimeter and ready to move in if we need them at any time.

There's a helicopter humming in the air above us in case of an emergency, and the buzz of these little black devices, resembling big, metal cicadas, surrounds the perimeter. Theo calls them drones, whatever that means.

Hunter zips the bulletproof vest over his raincoat. "We're going to split into three teams to cover more ground. Myself, Brooklyn, Enzo and Harlow will take the central path with Fox on comms."

Inspecting several wickedly sharp knives before securing them inside his jacket, Hudson gives me a nod. Brooklyn is already armed, her vest bulging with two guns and an array of knives.

"Ethan, Tara, Kade and Theo will take the eastern route," Hunter continues. "You'll be supported by Rayna on comms."

Seeing Theo suited and booted like the others is a strange sight. His usual flannel shirt and faded jeans have gone, replaced with guns and steely determination. He smiles when our eyes connect.

"Last up, the western path. Becket, Hudson, Leighton and Warner, with Liam on comms. Each team has a trained first aider, and the medical team will be on standby with the local police."

Enzo steps forward as everyone shuffles into their teams. He's terrifying in work mode, roaring at various agents to get equipment organised and cordons set up.

"We've got air support keeping infrared surveillance on the whole forest," he adds. "Communicate, keep your eyes open and shoot to kill."

"We want the perps alive," Hunter corrects him with a sharp glare. "They have a hell of a lot to answer for. No lethal force."

Enzo grumbles, but reluctantly agrees. With the rules laid out, maps distributed and earpieces fitted, everyone prepares to set off. There's ten miles to cover and about six hours of daylight left.

We're racing against the clock. The foreboding forest surrounding us is dripping with malice, cloaked in darkness and mist. Nobody wants to be in there when the sun surrenders.

Before we set off, Theo approaches me. He looks startlingly lethal as he tucks a handgun into his covered holster.

"Be safe, alright?" he says quietly. "We still need to discuss *Jane Eyre* tonight. Make sure you come back in one piece."

"You too." I pull him into a fast hug, careful not to disturb his weapons. "Look after each other."

Behind him, Leighton waits his turn. He crushes me against his chest so hard, I squeak in shock. There's no sign of his usual playful smiles or jokes today.

"I hate this," he murmurs against my hair. "Hunter and Enzo will keep you safe. Just... don't take any risks, alright?"

"I've got it, Leigh."

"I mean it."

Releasing me, he ignores everyone and presses his lips against mine. I freeze, panicked, but he keeps it short and sweet.

"Sorry," he says under his breath. "I had to do that."

Sauntering away, Leighton ignores the death glares being sent his way from Hunter and Enzo. Theo looks more startled, and perhaps a little bit intrigued. They quickly rejoin their respective teams.

Clearing my throat, I find the others at the edge of the forest. Brooklyn double-checks my bulletproof vest, making sure the other two aren't looking as she slides a knife into the pocket.

"Just in case." She winks.

"Thank you."

"Know how to use it?"

I return her small smile. "Well enough."

"Well, alrighty then. Let's get this show on the road. Gentlemen?"

Both checking their earpieces are online, Enzo and Hunter sandwich us between them. We set off in synchronisation with the other two teams, plunging into the silent woodland.

The moss beneath our boots swallows every footstep. Tall trees stretch up into the heavens, casting shadows across thick shrubbery, slippery rocks and layers of thicket.

After walking a little way in, I duck down to stroke my fingers over the uneven ground. The phantom pain of rocks slicing my bare feet flashes through my mind with the earthy scent of the forest.

This place is spookily familiar.

I can feel myself sprinting through it.

"Harlow?" Hunter stops by my side. "All good?"

Straightening, I tighten my grip on the backpack of medical supplies I'm carrying. It's the lightest, and the only one that Enzo was willing to let me shoulder while my leg is still tender.

He's further ahead, walking in lockstep with Brooklyn as they talk. She seems to be a lot closer to him than the others.

"Yeah." I swallow hard. "This place feels familiar. I recognise the trees. They're different from the ones back home."

Hunter falls into step beside me. "Sitka spruce. My dad used to take us hiking when we were kids. He knows all the species."

"Do you get on well with your dad?" I ask randomly.

Climbing up a steep incline, he offers me a hand over the wet, moss-covered rocks.

"Sometimes," Hunter answers. "He's always had very exacting standards. I thrive under that kind of pressure, but it was really rough on Leighton. I didn't like that."

"Enzo said he struggled when he was younger."

"Leighton's always found family hard. Our folks haven't seen him since he left prison. It's breaking my mum's heart, but they can't force him to see them."

"Any idea why?" I clamber over a fallen branch.

"He doesn't want to deal with their disappointment. In his mind, they hate him. In reality, my parents just want their son back. Regardless of whatever he's done. It doesn't matter to them."

Enzo shouts from ahead and gestures towards a narrow path on the left. Tucking his map away, they lead the way as we follow.

"Do you think I'm a bad person for refusing to see Giana again?" I blurt out.

Hunter checks behind us before walking some more. "No, Harlow. That's a different situation. You're entitled to take things at your own pace. She'll still be there when you're ready."

"It isn't different, though, is it? Leighton is afraid your parents won't love him anymore. With Giana… I'm afraid of not being the person she once knew. And what that means for my future."

"Your future is yours to decide," he responds. "Regardless of what Giana wants. Leighton has to do the same. I know you'll both be okay though."

Pausing to scrape gelatinous mud off my walking boots, I look up at Hunter's impassive face.

"How?"

He sends me a crooked smile. "Because you've got us. If you think me, Enzo or Theo are letting either of you off the hook, you've got us all wrong. We're a family. We support each other."

Emotion envelops me. Even with the abject terror of our unknown surroundings, I can't help but feel at home in Hunter's presence. He doesn't scare me anymore. I feel whole around him.

"I'm not sure I deserve a family," I say thickly.

He sticks his hand out for me to take. "Everyone deserves a family, Harlow.

Even fucked up people like us. Maybe we deserve it even more for that reason."

Letting his hand engulf mine, I accept his help over another rocky obstacle in the path. Hunter doesn't let me go after. The forest is a green blur around us, but he's the anchor stopping the fear from overcoming me.

A couple of hours into our search, we stop to drink some water and raid the energy bars in Brooklyn's backpack. She checks in with Hudson and Kade through our comms, gnawing her lip until she hears they're safe.

We pour over our map, marking the section we've scoured with a pen. The chapel was abandoned so long ago, nobody knows exactly where it is anymore. The others haven't reported a sighting yet either.

"Let's try further east, in this section here." Hunter points to a different patch of woods. "I read a land survey from the late 1800s that mentioned Mary Magdalene Chapel being further over."

Enzo's frown deepens. "It's off course. Harder for backup to reach us if we need it. They'll need to approach from the other side."

Nodding, Hunter tightens the laces on his boots. "I just have a gut feeling. It's too overgrown where we are. These trees are old, they would've been cleared for building materials to be transported during construction."

"Alright." Enzo sighs. "Brooke?"

She studies the map for a second longer. "Hudson's group is coming at it from another angle. Between us, we can clear that whole section."

They all look to me next. I nod in agreement, itching to set off again. Every second, I'm glancing around me, searching for Pastor Michaels' savage smile. This place is spine chilling.

Plunging deeper into the forest, we climb across a series of small streams. The sound of rushing water slices through my brain, bringing with it more disjointed flashes.

I slipped and slid that day, wading through water and mud, cutting my hands as I fought to escape. The memories are becoming clearer. Hobbling through a forest with broken bones was excruciating.

Another two hours and we're fighting against the sinking sun. Enzo has snarled at the map several times, checking the compass attached to his backpack and shouting down the earpiece at Fox.

As Hunter and Brooklyn stop to dig out their water bottles, I stroke my fingers on the gnarly bark of the closest tree. They seem to be thinning out a little, even though we're miles into the unknown.

Another stream runs parallel to the route we're taking through thorny bushes and tall trees. Jumping down into the stream, I turn and begin to walk down, following the flow of water instead of going inland.

"Harlow!" Enzo barks. "Wait for us."

But I'm enchanted by the fast flow of the water, breaking over rocks and the odd fallen branch. Something about the trees and slightly lighter moss is calling out to me.

I continue walking down the centre of the stream while the others stumble to keep up with me. It's cold and slippery, but I keep wading through, even as it gets deep enough to reach my ankles.

There's a splash as Enzo joins me. "Come out of there, little one. You'll catch hypothermia at this rate."

"No, we need to keep going."

"It'll be dark in an hour. We're going to turn back and regroup on the southern edge of the forest with Theo's team."

He huffs in annoyance as I ignore him completely. My feet are aching from the cold water seeping into my boots, but it's setting off an alarm bell. Something is calling out to me in sinister whispers.

"The basement flooded a lot," I reveal to him. "Whenever it rained really hard, water gradually pooled on the floor. It seemed to seep in from beneath us."

"Nearby water source?" Enzo guesses.

My footsteps begin to quicken. "Late at night, I could hear it. Trickling away, loud enough to reach me. They brought me bowls of water and changed the bucket in my cell a few times a week."

"Which… would require water," he catches on. "Not something you'd find running in an abandoned property."

The other two seem to realise we've hit upon something and jump down into the water to join us. The further we walk, the deeper the stream becomes. It nearly reaches our calves now.

"On your knees, Harlow," I recite as we plunge into darkness. "If I can't hear your prayers, the Lord Almighty certainly can't."

Enzo stares at me with concern. "Huh?"

The temperature drops when the sun disappears. Mist is rising, coating each leaf and bramble in droplets of moisture. Gushing water accompanies my whispered prayers.

When I spot the first stone brick, the last three months vanish in an instant. Every laugh, smile, kiss and cuddle are gone. Stolen away with silent cruelty. God is laughing at me all over again.

I'm back.

Harlow's come home.

"Holy fuck," Brooklyn curses behind us. "Are you guys seeing this too?"

"Yeah," Hunter says grimly.

Grabbing a thick tree root, I yank myself up the steep bank. It takes several rolls through the dirt to clamber to my feet. The healing wound on my leg is screaming with pain. The trees have thinned even more, forming a narrow clearing.

Climbing out, Enzo walks a few metres before crouching to study the ground. "Tyre tracks. They're old."

He hoists Brooklyn out next, setting her back on her feet. Hunter follows, his face paling as he spots the crumbling stone structure ahead of us.

"How did they get a car through here?" Brooklyn wonders aloud.

Hunter points deeper into the clearing. "There. Something small could make it through."

As I begin to walk ahead, drawn closer by an invisible thread wrapped around my pounding heart, Enzo bars an arm across my chest.

"You've done enough," he says roughly. "Let us go in."

I push his arm aside. "This is my home."

His eyes widen, clouded by worry. Walking on, my boots sink into the mud-covered ground with each step. I can still feel it squelching between my bare toes from my escape months ago.

The chapel is exactly as I remember it. An isolated slice of antiquity wrapped in an earthly tomb. The stone bricks are crumbling, falling into ruin, and I can see the smashed stained-glass window on the side of the building.

"There." I point at it, marvelling at the height. "It's no wonder I broke my arm jumping out of there, really."

Enzo's chest rumbles with an enraged roar. "That's where you jumped from?"

"The door was locked and bolted all over. There was no other way out. I wasn't going to sit and wait for them to come back."

Pausing, all three of them draw guns. Enzo taps his comms over and over, but the signal has finally cut out. We're lost in the wilderness and far from the Lord's light in this intimate circle of hell.

"What should we do?" he asks Hunter.

Studying the chapel, Hunter rolls back his shoulders. "Let's check it out. There's no vehicle parked. We can handle whatever's inside."

"Can we?"

"Yes," Brooklyn answers, shifting closer to me. "I've got Harlow. We're going to be fine. Let's move."

With a nod, I extract the knife she stashed in my pocket and hold it tight. Enzo purses his lips and plunges forward, pulling a small torch from his vest pocket.

The closer we inch, the quieter it becomes. Even the sound of the stream drains away. Evil clings to each vine-covered brick. It's an oozing pyroclastic cloud that consumes us all.

Gun raised, Hunter moves to the left, beneath the shattered window high above us. Shards of glass are still buried in the rotten leaves slowly putrefying beneath our feet.

Raw slabs of carved stone mark the entrance. Creeping up the small incline, I almost run into Enzo's back. They've both halted, staring ahead in silent concentration.

"What is it?" Brooklyn hushes.

Hunter cocks his gun. "Door's open."

"So?"

He moves aside so we can see what's painted on the slab of wood. I recognise the Holy Trinity instantly. It's dried and flaked in places over time, but the dark-brown liquid can only be one thing. I know blood when I see it.

Stooping to duck past the macabre welcome sign, Enzo leads the way into Pastor Michaels' hunting grounds. Hunter keeps casting me apprehensive looks, but I ignore him and step inside the chapel.

"Oh," is all I can muster.

It's been methodically and catastrophically trashed. All the remaining furniture and stained-glass windows are destroyed. Not even the altar stands anymore. It looks like a bulldozer passed through here, intent on obliteration.

After sweeping through the empty living quarters and main worship room, Enzo declares the place clear. Hunter and Brooklyn don't lower their guns. It's pitch-black in here. The darkness can hide malevolent intentions.

Pulling my own torch out, I follow the path my bloodstained feet took. Every now and then, a red smear marks the stone floor. I can just make out the print of my own toes.

"Harlow," Hunter calls out. "Not alone. Show us where it is."

I point the light ahead, through an arched doorway with nothing but clinging shadows beyond.

"Follow me."

Sticking in a close formation, I somehow find myself leading the pack. Dread and nausea have melted into numb acceptance. I was always meant to end up back here. This basement and I have unfinished business.

With the narrow staircase in sight, the first waves of a stomach-churning stench hit us. It's ripe, rancid, so thick you can taste the individual notes of death on the tip of your tongue.

"Motherfucker," Enzo swears. "That's a body."

Muscling his way to the front, Hunter steps in front of me. "I know you have to go down there, but I'm going first. No arguments."

I gesture for him to go ahead. Swallowing hard, he takes a final breath of semi-clean air and plunges into the basement. With every inch, the smell grows. Demons are festering down here in the dark.

The steps groan beneath my feet, underscoring Hunter's silence as he reaches the bottom. He doesn't move another inch.

"Hunt?" Enzo calls urgently.

"Yeah," he responds in a flat voice. "It's… um, clear. He's not here."

But something is, the devil whispers.

Hunter steps aside to let the rest of us down. The slanted beam of light from his torch cuts through the bleak nothingness. It takes my eyes a moment to adjust. The outside world has spoiled me with all its freely available light.

"Harlow," Hunter warns. "Don't look."

It's too late. My feet move without being told, guiding me back to the cage where I spent thirteen years of my life. It's smaller than I remember it. This entire basement is. My home has shrunk, or I've grown.

But this cell doesn't belong to me anymore. Its new inhabitant swings from a rough hunk of rope tied into the perfect noose around her skeletal neck.

Skin, fat and muscle have melted into a black, foul-smelling sludge that clings to a soulless skeleton. Standing outside the broken cell door, I spot the gold wedding band that's fallen from her finger and hit the ground.

"Do not be deceived," I whisper into the dead silence. "God is not to be mocked; for whatever one sows, that will he reap."

"Is that Laura?" Hunter asks in a soft whisper.

Shaking my head, I point to the adjacent cage. Its door is still locked tight, holding another decaying skeleton prisoner. Several of the bones are missing, broken by my cage door, while another has been sent home for burial.

Stepping inside my cage, I pick through the blackened goo to reach the hanging remains. Scraps of floral fabric are fossilised in decaying bodily fluids.

Bending down, I extricate the wedding ring and hold it in the centre of my palm. It cut into my skin enough times when Mrs Michaels beat the devil out of me.

My voice comes out devoid, lifeless, drained.

"Hello, Mother."

EPILOGUE

CORPSE ROADS - KEATON HENSON

THEO

SITTING in the light of the twinkling Christmas tree, I watch Harlow fitfully sleep on the sofa opposite. I finally managed to convince her to swallow a couple of sleeping pills an hour or so ago.

She winces, crying out in her sleep and grappling her neck, like someone invisible is choking her. I rush over, giving her a gentle shake to startle her from the dream.

Harlow sucks in a deep breath before dropping back off. Rather than returning to the sofa, I sink down to the carpet in front of her, staying within touching distance for when the next one hits.

My eyes grow heavy after a while, coaxed shut by the crackling flames of the fire, but my phone vibrating soon snaps me back. I step into the corner to answer.

"Hunt?"

"Yeah," he grunts without a greeting. "Listen, we're wrapping things up here. Forensics have extracted the bodies. We'll be flying back with them tomorrow."

"Okay, good." I rest my forehead on the wall. "Harlow finally went to sleep. I'm taking turns to keep watch with Leighton."

"How's she doing?"

"Not good." My voice thickens with emotion. "She was catatonic on the flight down. Wouldn't speak to anyone. Not even Brooklyn could coax her out of it."

He swears colourfully. "This whole thing is a mess. I'll call Richards and get him to make an emergency visit."

"You think it'll help?"

"I don't know what else to suggest."

Harlow lets out a strangled sob behind me and I race back to the sofa, quickly shushing her again. Her hand fists my t-shirt.

"That her?" Hunter asks fearfully.

"Yeah, she's fighting being asleep. The night terrors look pretty bad. Maybe sedating her was a bad idea."

"Stay with her," he orders.

"Obviously," I snap back. "Sorry, I'm exhausted. Brooklyn said she's going to bring Jude around in the morning. He might be able to help Harlow."

"Good call. We should be back by the afternoon. The superintendent has called a meeting. She's demanding an update."

"What did you tell her?"

Hunter scoffs, sounding as exhausted as I feel. "That we have two more dead bodies and no perp. She's going to steamroll us."

I sigh heavily. "Remind her who got her that fucking job in the first place. She owes us. We need more time and funding to see this through."

"What if he can't be found?"

The resignation in Hunter's voice is an unfamiliar gut punch. I haven't heard that defeat in a long time. Not since we waited for the results from his auditory test and got word that he couldn't hear a thing anymore without the aid he despises so much. Even now, he could still go fully deaf.

"We cannot give up, Hunt. Not now, not ever. Harlow needs us to see this through. It's her life we're talking about."

"I know," he replies tersely. "We will always protect her, but this bastard just slaughtered his own wife."

"What?" I gasp.

"The positioning of the noose was all wrong. Too high, and it was knotted from the back. Pastor Michaels hung his own wife."

"Fucking hell."

"Yeah, exactly. He could be in bloody Timbuktu by now."

"Then… we have to hunt his sadistic ass down and drag him back here to face punishment for his crimes. We owe Harlow that much."

Hunter remains silent.

"Do you love her?" I ask him.

"What?"

"Do you love her?"

He hesitates before answering. "So much it scares me."

"What about Enzo? Leighton?"

"I don't fucking know, Theo. We would all do anything to keep her in our lives, no matter what it takes. What about you?"

With the phone pressed to my ear, I stare at Harlow's slack face. Her hair is splayed across the sofa cushions, showing a hint of the growing bald patch beneath the layers.

I gently run a finger over her sore, swollen scalp. She's stopped trying to hide it entirely now. The flight home was heartbreaking, watching the pile of hair in her lap grow.

Powerlessness is an old friend that I never wanted to be re-acquainted with. I couldn't offer her any sliver of comfort that would be more appealing than the pain she was craving.

"I care about her," I answer his question. "More than I thought possible after Alyssa. I want her to be okay. I want to be the one to make her happy, whatever form that takes."

Hunter breathes down the line. "Then I guess it's settled. This isn't a dead end in the investigation. It's only the beginning."

"Well, there's one more thing."

"What is it?"

I clutch the phone tighter. "Harlow was mumbling a bit when we carried her on to the plane. She said that… she killed Laura. Strangled her so she wouldn't suffer and die slowly."

Hunter inhales sharply. "That can't be right."

"That's all I know."

"I'm sure she was just out of it and triggered by going back there. We can figure it out when the rest of us get home. Sounds like a meaningless ramble to me."

"Alright, I'll keep an eye on her anyway. Stay in touch."

We wrap up the phone call quickly. Hunter's dealing with local police and a media circus that have caught wind of our huge presence up north. He'll fly back with Enzo in the morning.

Hearing the shower flick off upstairs, I tighten the blanket around Harlow's shoulders and pad into the kitchen to heat up the lasagne Brooklyn dropped off for us this morning.

As I'm poking in the fridge for condiments, the security system in the entrance hall goes haywire. The glass bottle of salad dressing in my hand smashes against the tiled floor as I sprint for the door.

"Shit, shit, shit."

The emergency alert has been triggered. Someone's tried to punch in the wrong passcode several times and messed up the retinal scan. Leighton's footsteps skip over several stairs as he bounds down.

"What's happening?" he shouts.

"Intruder at the front gate." I quickly unlock the system and check the camera. "Someone's out there. Can't see a face though."

"Shit. What do we do?"

"Stay here. I'll check it out."

"No, Theo!"

"Stay here," I repeat in a raised voice.

Snatching the gun that Hunter keeps stashed in the bottom drawer of the console—one of many around the house—I slip outside into the falling rain. The lights are all on, illuminating the empty driveway.

There's a shadow slumped just outside the gate, shivering after giving up on breaking through. With the gun raised high, I tentatively approach.

"Who the fuck are you?" I call out.

Nothing.

"Get up or I'll shoot. You're trespassing on private property."

If it's a journalist, I'll kneecap them for the damn thrill of it. I wouldn't be surprised if Sally Moore sent one of her bloodless cronies to fish for an update.

The figure finally stirs, using the gate to wrench himself upright. He's staggering, clearly inebriated, and dressed in threadbare clothing that wouldn't look amiss on a homeless person. Every inch of him is shaking with exertion.

"State your business!" I yell at him.

When there's no response, I cock the gun in warning. He takes one look at me and collapses into an unconscious heap. I'm a split second from shooting when hurried footsteps slap through the rain behind me.

"Theo, wait!"

Harlow stumbles down the slick driveway, soaked and wild-eyed as she escapes Leighton's embrace. I grab her around the waist before she can run past me, yanking her off her feet.

"Get back in the fucking house!" I shout at her.

"No, no," she screams back. "You can't shoot him!"

Jamming her elbow into my stomach, she wriggles free from my arms and lands on her feet. I come to my senses quick enough to stop her from stealing the gun in my hands.

"Harlow, stop!"

"Don't shoot!" She turns to look at the collapsed stranger, timid and uncertain. "I think he's my real father."

To be continued in...
Skeletal Hearts (Sabre Security #2)

BONUS SCENE

HARLOW

"Goldilocks. Wake up."

Stirring in bed, I bat away the tickling sensation beneath my nose. It comes again—under my chin this time, breaking me free from the warm embrace of sleep.

"Wakey wakey," a voice sing-songs.

"Go away, Leigh," I mumble.

"No can do. It's Christmas! Wake up."

Fingers digging into my ribcage, he tickles me so ferociously, I'm forced to peel my heavy lids open. Late morning sunshine blazes through the parted curtains and into my bedroom.

"You've slept all morning," he chastises playfully. "We're waiting to open presents, come on."

Grabbing my pillow, I pull it on top of my head. "Please leave me alone."

He quickly lifts it off and plants a kiss on my cheek in apology. "I know things have been rough, princess. But today is a happy day. We can forget about the world for one day, right?"

I wish we could. But all I can think about is Pastor Michaels still out there, roaming free and hurting God knows how many innocent lives. Not to mention my father's sudden reappearance and hospitalisation.

It's too much.

I can't face the world anymore.

"We need to get you out of this bed." Leighton wrinkles his nose. "And maybe a shower, too."

"Leigh!"

"Sorry." He winks at me. "Just being honest. Get washed, and I'll make you a late breakfast."

"You'll cook? Um… I think I'm okay."

His mouth flops open in indignation. "My cooking isn't that bad!"

"Not exactly good either."

"Wow. No breakfast for you then."

Bouncing off the mattress, he grabs hold of my ankle and begins to tug until I'm falling out of the bed. Landing on the soft carpet with a thud, I glower up at him, finding his gaze fixed on my bare thighs.

"Nice t-shirt."

I tug his shirt down lower to cover my panties. "Thanks."

"As much as I'm enjoying this sight, it's go time. I've waited all morning to open presents and I'm boooored. Come on, move it."

He strides out of the room to give me some privacy, and I promptly crawl back into bed. It's where I've been since we returned from up north. Hunter and Enzo are still there, ripping apart the crime scene.

There's nothing to celebrate today. Christmas means nothing to me now, not after what we found in that basement. I've been numb and free falling since discovering Mrs Michaels' body, left like hanging meat.

"Harlow?" There's a tentative knock at the door.

"Go away, Leigh."

"It's Theo."

My heart squeezes in my chest. "Oh."

The door creaks as it opens, and soft footsteps pad into the room. Theo appears, dressed down in a plain blue tee and sweatpants that hug his lithe legs. His usual colourful flannel shirt is nowhere in sight, revealing his muscled forearms.

"Are you coming down? Leighton's sulking."

"I c-can't face it," I admit, the truth slipping free. "Not today."

Theo nods, his eyes darting around the room. "I get that. Celebrating is probably the last thing on your mind right now. He's just trying to help, though."

"I know."

Lingering awkwardly, he shifts on the balls of his feet. "Want me to leave you alone?"

My first instinct is to nod. Being alone is safe. Secure. No one can hurt me if I'm alone, and I'm not sure my shattered heart can take any more pain right now. But something in his small, hopeful smile stops me.

"No," I blurt.

Theo's brows lift in surprise. "Um, okay."

Creeping across the thick carpet, he circles the bed, uncertain and afraid. I grab a handful of the covers and pull them back to invite him into the warmth. He bites his bottom lip, contemplating the space next to me.

With a breath for courage, he climbs in and stretches out. They've all piled into bed with me before, but it's different this time. I'm suddenly aware of the tiny space between us.

Theo stares up at the ceiling, his jaw working overtime. The heat from his body curls around me beneath the duvet and warms the cold, empty shell of my heart just a little. I unconsciously shift closer.

"You can talk to me, you know," he murmurs.

"There's nothing to say."

"You shouldn't have been the one to find her like that. I'm sorry."

Scrunching my eyes shut, I force the image of Mrs Michaels' face from my mind, bloated and waxy, the noose cinched tight around her throat.

"It's not your fault."

Head turning, his eyes scrape over me, searching and incisive. "We're going to find him. I promise."

"He's gone, Theo."

"No one can hide forever. We'll make this right."

His hand lifts, hanging in limbo for a brief second, before nearing my face. The tips of his fingers stroke over my cheek in the briefest of brushes as he pushes a chunk of unwashed hair behind my ear.

"I promise," he adds in a whisper.

With electricity crackling between us and setting my nerve endings alight, his hand drops from my face. I suck in a stuttered breath as Theo shifts back into his original position, leaving me cold in his absence.

"The others should be home in a couple of days." His eyes move back to the ceiling. "We'll hit the ground running with the investigation. There has to be a lead in that place."

I should be worrying about Hunter and Enzo, both stuck up north, searching for evidence in that evil lair, but instead all I can think about is the curve of Theo's lips, framed by the subtlest of dimples.

"How can you be so sure?" I ask in a tiny voice.

He hesitates, his bottom lip caught between his teeth. "Because I have to be. We need hope to survive."

"Maybe I want to do more than survive."

He glances over at me. "I want that for you too. That's why I have to believe we'll catch him."

Caught in a self-contained bubble, sealing us in the intimacy of silence, we stare at each other. That tiny smile is back again—a minuscule lilting of the lips, tempting me with the promise of a full one.

"Thank you, Theo."

"Of course. Will you come down now?"

My heart drops. "I don't think so."

"That's fine," he rushes to say. "We can hide in here from Leighton all day if that's what you want."

"He isn't that bad." I snort.

"Leighton on Christmas Day? Recipe for disaster, trust me. He's like an excited puppy on speed."

Laughing for what feels like the first time in forever, I watch the grin light up Theo's angular features. His deep, rumbling chuckle emanates from his chest, matching mine.

"Hiding it is," he concludes.

"You two can still enjoy the day."

"Without you? I don't think so."

Heat spreads across my cheeks, and I duck my gaze.

"We could read instead," Theo suggests. "What's on your current list?"

Reaching over to the bedside table, I pick up the leather-bound copy of *Moby Dick* that he lent me. Theo nods in appreciation.

"Good choice. Hand it over."

"You're going to read to me?"

"If… you want?" he finishes uncertainly.

I pass him the book. "Sure."

Settling back into the pillows, he flips open to the marked page and begins to read in a low, comforting voice that makes my lids heavy. I unconsciously snuggle closer to him, our legs brushing together.

"Is this okay?" I hook my leg over his.

His Adam's apple bobs. "Yeah."

Returning his attention to the book, he flips to the next page and continues reading. Heat burns into my thigh from his leg pressing into mine. I keep as still as possible so I don't scare him off.

This is the closest I've ever gotten to Theo. He usually holds me at an arm's length, but recently, things have felt different between us. There's tension. Electricity. Intrigue. I don't know why or how I recognise these feelings.

Sometimes, I catch him looking at me. Staring. He watches me with this unfathomable look on his face, and I have no clue what's running through his mind as he studies me.

With my eyes falling shut, his voice lulls me back into a peaceful place I haven't been able to find alone. I'm not quite asleep, but my entire body feels like it's full of treacle, pumping comfort and warmth through my veins.

"Guys?" Leighton's voice calls.

Theo sighs through his nose. "Incoming."

"Mmm," is all I can manage to groan.

The door clicks open again with Leighton's loud, thudding steps interrupting us. He bounds into the room and does a dramatic double take when he finds me curled around Theo like a spider monkey.

"Am I interrupting?" he jokes. "This sure looks cosy."

"Jackass," Theo mutters under his breath.

"Love you too, Theodore. Mind a third?"

Pulling my leg back, we both shuffle over to free up space in the bed. Leighton ducks out of the room and reappears with a laptop to place between us. Then he's shimmying into the space behind me.

I'm caught in a tight, muscle-lined sandwich, trapped between them both in the bed. I forget how to breathe for a moment. Leighton's crotch is pushing right up against my rear, and I'm certain it's on purpose.

"What are we watching?" Leighton asks.

"None of that action crap you love." Theo closes the book and sets it aside. "If I must be subjected to watching a movie, it has to be something decent."

"Weirdo." Leighton laughs. "What kinda person doesn't like movies?"

"The book is always better."

"He's right," I chime in.

"Pair of weirdos," Leighton corrects himself.

I jab an elbow into his ribs, laughing as he harrumphs in mock-pain. It feels good to laugh again. Even for a moment. The darkness can't suffocate me when I'm around them.

"There's one exception to the rule, of course," Theo informs us. "The Great Gatsby. Now that's an incredible movie."

"And one of your favourite books."

He looks down at me, eyes shining with appreciation. "It is."

"Put it on, Leigh."

He sighs in disappointment. "Fine. I know when I'm outvoted."

Selecting the movie, he lies down and positions the laptop on the bed so we can all see it. I lean back into Leighton's body, and his arm slips around my waist to cuddle me close to him.

Under the sheets, a hand moves to rest above my knee. It takes me a moment to realise it can't be Leighton touching me there. Theo doesn't even look at me—his attention gripped by the opening credits.

The place where his hand touches my skin feels like it's on fire. I just wish he'd move his hand higher, and higher still, to the throbbing place where Hunter, Leighton and Enzo have touched me.

As the movie plays, I get more comfortable, relaxing into their shared embrace. It doesn't take long for the cocoon of aftershave and book-scented warmth to lull me back into a drowsy state.

"Sleep," Theo whispers.

Leighton kisses my shoulder. "We'll be here when the nightmares come."

"You'll wake me up?" I ask groggily.

"Always, princess. We're not going anywhere."

Letting my eyes fall shut fully, I surrender back into the arms of sleep, this time safe in the knowledge that no monsters can hurt me. Not while my protectors are here to keep me from harm.

PLAYLIST

LISTEN HERE:
BIT.LY/CORPSEROADS

White Noise – Badflower
Holding Out For A Hero – Nothing But Thieves
Natural Born Killer – Highly Suspect
The Raging Sea - Broadside
Dead Letter & The Infinite Yes – Wintersleep
Even In The Dark – jxdn
New Eyes – Echos
Conversations – Juice WRLD
Heart-Shaped Box – Ashton Irwin
Come Undone – My Darkest Days
Speaking Off The Record – Hotel Mira
Without You – PLTS
Manic Memories – Des Rocs
Scavengers (Acoustic) – Thrice
.haunted. – Dead Poet Society
The Madness – Foreign Air
(if) you are the ocean (then) I would like to drown – VIOLET NIGHT
Someone Somewhere Somehow – Super Whatevr
Midnight Demon Club – Highly Suspect
Bad Place – The Hunna
The Search – NF
Family – Badflower
Won't Stand Down – Muse
Pray – jxdn
Keeper – Reignwolf
How – Marcus Mumford & Brandi Carlile
Last Night I Watched Myself Sleep and I Saw Things That I Wish I Could Forget – Aurora View

I Never Loved Myself Like I Love You – Dead Poet Society
Sunny Side Down – Sad Heroes
Vaccine – hometown & young
Eyes on Fire – Blue Foundation
Burning The Iron Age – Trade Wind
Corpse Roads – Keaton Henson

SKELETAL HEARTS

SABRE SECURITY #2

TRIGGER WARNING

Skeletal Hearts is a contemporary reverse harem romance, so the main character will have multiple love interests that she will not have to choose between.

This book is very dark and contains scenes that may be triggering for some readers. This includes physical and psychological abuse, torture, sexual assault and abuse, imprisonment, graphic violence, serial murder, PTSD, Trichotillomania, suicidal ideation and attempted suicide.

If you are triggered by any of this content, please do not read this book.

This is a slow-burn romance, so the relationships will develop over time, and the spice level will build with each book.

"Tell me every terrible thing you ever did and let me love you anyway."

- Edgar Allen Poe

PROLOGUE

BLACK WATER – THE PEOPLE'S THIEVES

LETICIA

LONDON BRIDGE IS FALLING DOWN.

Falling down, falling down.

Tugging the hood of my bright-red raincoat up to shield my plaited pigtails, I hum the tune of my favourite song while leaving the school gates.

London Bridge is falling down.

My fair lady.

Rain patters against my coat in a soft drizzle. It's cold, probably a little too cold to be walking home.

Build it up with wood and clay.

Wood and clay, wood and clay.

The hum of cars whizzes past me along the quiet street.

Build it up with wood and clay.

My fair lady.

Staring down at my patent leather school shoes, I count each step. One after another. Cross the road. Check for traffic. Stick to the zebra crossing.

Wood and clay will wash away.

Wash away, wash away.

There's a loud rumble from above me. Heart pounding, I speed up, heading for the outcrop of trees that marks my path home over the nearby farmer's field.

Wood and clay will wash away.

My fair lady.

My legs are tired as I squelch through wet mud and rain puddles. The village vanishes, swallowed by high bushes clustered with tiny, ripe blackberries.

I stop to collect handfuls of berries and fill my pockets. The droplets of sour tartness burst on my tongue. Grandma Sylvie bakes the best blackberry crumble. I better take some for her.

When my pockets are overflowing and my hands are stained dark purple with juice, I return to the rough path cutting through the shoulder-high crops.

It's scary out here. I wish Daddy were here to walk me home like he usually does. Mummy took me to school in her big, loud car this morning. She wasn't happy. I don't ever see her smile anymore.

Send a man to watch all night.

Watch all night, watch all night.

My quiet humming fills the bleakness of the field's silence.

Send a man to watch all night.

My fair lady.

Grandma taught me that song. She picks me up sometimes, when Mummy is asleep on the sofa with her favourite book and an empty wine glass. Or when Daddy doesn't come home for a few days and makes everyone mad.

We get ice cream and feed the seagulls, even in winter. It makes me laugh when their beaks tickle my hand. If you stand real still, they'll peck the food right from your palm.

Checking the sparkly, pink *Dora the Explorer* watch around my wrist, I bite my lip. It's getting dark fast, and I still have half an hour to walk. I come this way with Daddy sometimes, when he can walk straight.

But never alone.

That isn't allowed.

Tummy rumbling, I dig into my supply of blackberries. The pops of sugary sourness keep me going as I squelch through thick, glue-like mud. The rain has stopped now, but my uniform is soaking wet.

Movement in the distance slows my footsteps. The tall stalks of corn are swaying. A headful of thick, chocolate-coloured hair appears first. Then, a big smile and a scary, hooked nose, almost like a clown.

The man waves. Still frozen, I wave back with a blackberry-stained hand. He doesn't look too scary, apart from his big nose. Kind of old and wrinkled, though, like the man who lives next door to Grandma.

"Hey there," he calls out.

Clutching the straps of my backpack, I tentatively approach him. "Hello."

"Are you lost, sweetie?"

"No. I'm going home."

He looks around the deserted field. "Through here?"

I nod, my lip jutted out in defiance.

"Hmm. It's getting a bit dark, isn't it?"

"I'm a big girl. I can walk home alone."

His laugh is tinkly. I like it.

"Well, a big girl like you should be just fine. I don't like the dark, though. Can you show me the way in case I get scared?"

I blink up at him. "You get scared?"

"Sometimes," he replies with a wink.

"The dark isn't scary! Come on. I'll show you."

I reach out a sticky, purple hand. The stranger squeezes my little fingers tight, laughing when he sees the juices splashed across them.

"Hungry?"

"I was picking blackberries for my grandma," I reveal in a whisper. "Don't tell Mummy, though. She gets mad when my clothes are dirty."

"It's our little secret. Can I have one?"

Fishing a blackberry from my pocket, I offer it up to him. The stranger pops it in his mouth and rubs his tummy. I laugh at him. He's very silly.

"Yummy," he praises. "You keep those berries safe now."

"I will. Grandma can bake a crumble to eat later on."

We slip through the stalks of corn, avoiding deep puddles that will get me even dirtier. I'm already streaked with filth and rainwater. I'll have to hide my dress from Mummy. I don't want her to shout.

"What's your name, anyhow?" he asks me.

"Letty." I stare up at my new friend. "What's your name?"

The stranger offers me a lopsided smile. "Michael."

"Pleased to meet you, Mr Michael."

"Well, aren't you a well-mannered little thing."

I'm not sure I like being called a *little thing*, but I don't complain. I don't have many friends. I'd like a real one, even if he is a funny old man.

"What's that on your chest?" I ask nosily.

Michael looks down at the silvery chain around his neck. He pulls it over his head, offering the shiny necklace to me. Excited by the present, I slip it over my head instead.

It's a funny shape. There's a triangle in the middle that looks a bit like a flower, surrounded by a circle. The metal is cool against my purple fingertips.

"That's a Holy Trinity," he explains. "It represents the Father, Son and Holy Spirit. Do you go to church, Letty?"

"Not really," I answer, distracted by the necklace. "But sometimes Mummy shouts at Daddy and tells him to go to hell. That's to do with church, right?"

His smile is getting big—almost too big.

"A little bit. You see, that's where the bad people go."

"Are you saying my daddy is bad?"

"Maybe. That's part of my job. I help the bad people get better."

"Like a doctor?"

Michael laughs again. "A little bit."

"So… you can help my daddy? I don't want him to go to hell. It sounds like a scary place."

"Maybe. What about your mummy?"

I pop another blackberry in my mouth, still studying the necklace. "Sometimes she gets angry. I don't think she likes me much."

"Now, I'm sure that isn't true."

"Could you fix her as well?"

Michael takes my hand, tighter this time. It hurts a little bit.

"We could make a deal."

"What kind of deal?" I ask excitedly.

"I have a very important job to do that I want you to help me with. Did you learn about Noah's ark at school?"

"The big boat with all the animals?"

"Yes." He beams at me. "Noah built a big boat to save all the good people. Do you know what happened to the bad ones?"

I shake my head.

"When the flood came, they all got washed away," he answers. "There's another flood coming, Letty. A big one. It's my job to clean everything up in time, you understand?"

"Cleaning?" I wrinkle my nose. "I don't like cleaning."

Emerging from the swaying stalks of corn, we stop at another cluster of blackberry bushes. My legs and feet hurt from walking such a long way. We're almost there now. I can see the gravel road through the leaves.

There's a funny-looking van parked there. The dark-blue paint is peeling off, and the tyres look ready to pop, they're so old. This must be Michael's car.

We shimmy through the bush and escape to the other side. There are no lights down this road. It isn't a proper path for cars. The mud is all sticky and smeared about, and there's no painted lines.

"My home's over that way." I point to the trees leading away from the field. "Good luck with your cleaning, Mr Michael."

The van beeps as he clicks the set of keys in his hands. Weak, yellow light spills over the mud, illuminating the thick shadows of early evening.

He pulls open the sliding door on the side of the van and gestures inside.

"Hop in, sweetie. I'll drop you off at your grandma's so she can bake that crumble. You must be hungry."

My belly rumbles again. Lunchtime was a long time ago. But I already broke two rules tonight—walking home alone and talking to a stranger. I don't want to get into more trouble.

"I'm okay to walk," I decline politely. "Goodnight."

With a final wave, I tug up my backpack and set off towards the trees covered in pinecones. The squelch of boots following me registers too late as something trips me up.

"Owww!" I wail.

Landing hard on my knees, I slip in the mud. My ankle burns from tripping over a big, boot-covered foot, attached to my new friend.

He looms over me, still wearing that smile, but I don't like it now. There's something scary in his shiny, green eyes. Like when Daddy drinks a whole bottle of naughty juice and starts shouting and smashing things.

"Get in the car, Leticia."

Frightened tears well up in my eyes.

"How do you know my name? I said it's Letty."

He jabs a finger into my chest, right above the necklace. I'd forgotten I was still wearing it. Is he mad now? Will he hurt me like other people do? I didn't mean to steal from him.

"I have a job to do," he says in a snarl. "You stole from me. That's a sin. Do you want to go to hell too?"

"No," I cry loudly. "I'm s-sorry! Please."

His hand smacks against my cheek so hard, it rattles my teeth together. I can't see through the tears pouring out of my eyes. My small body is bundled into his arms with a grunt.

"There's a good girl," he whispers in my ear. "Don't worry. The Lord is just and merciful to forgive those who sin. You'll learn soon enough."

Screaming at the top of my lungs doesn't stop him from throwing me into the back of the van. I try to get up and run, but the door slams shut in my face.

Silence.

Darkness.

I'm trapped.

Crying harder as the engine begins to rumble, the van bounces over bumpy ground. Each lurch sends me jolting from side to side. There's nothing to hold on to in here. Flailing around, I realise I dropped my backpack outside.

"Please," I whimper into the dark. "Stop."

He can't hear me.

Nobody can.

The van crashes over a big bump, sending me flying across the cramped space. I hit the wall so hard, my head cracks on the thick, rusted metal. I slump as everything goes blurry.

The last thing I think of is my daddy. He always said never to walk home alone. And I never got a chance to say goodbye this morning.

CHAPTER 1
HARLOW

DROWN – HOMETOWN & YOUNG

MY BREATH FOGS up the lined glass of the hospital window. Clouds of condensation drip over the smooth surface, obscuring the view inside the clinical room.

Wrapped in clusters of wires, drips and a feeding tube slicing through the core of his being, my father lies asleep. It's been weeks since he spoke a single word to me.

Now, a machine is keeping him alive—pumping blood and breath through his failing organs, suspending his corpse between this cruel world and the Lord's divine light.

Beep.

Beep.

Beep.

God has forsaken him, like the rest of us left to fight for the right to breathe. His body, awash with the aftereffects of years of heavy drinking and drug use, can no longer function alone. Most days, he struggles to lift an eyelid.

Taking a fortifying breath, I let myself into his hospital room. The scent of bleach and disappointment oozes over me, clinging with the persistence of aching regret.

"Dad," I croak.

Nothing.

He's too out of it to know I'm here.

The word *dad* feels foreign on my tongue. I couldn't call Giana by the name my birth granted her. But this broken shade of a man… somehow, I can relate to him. His pain is my pain.

He never forgot me.

I wish I remembered him.

Taking his papery hand in mine, I sit down in the cracked vinyl armchair.

His hair is a dark, muddy blonde colour, ragged and hanging over his bushy eyebrows.

With pronounced cheekbones, thin lips, a narrow nose and ghoul-like skin, he looks more like me than my mother does. The skin hangs from his bones in a humanoid costume.

"What happened to you?" I stroke his knuckles. "Why can't I remember our life together? Before… everything?"

Beep.

Beep.

Beep.

The stillness is broken by the reassurance of his breathing. In and out. Chest rising up and caving down. Life beginning. Life ending. Falling into a brief chasm of death in between each breath.

"Miss Kensington?"

I flinch so forcefully, I almost tug out the needle that's taped against my father's white hand. The door clicks shut as his consultant, Doctor Bannon, pads into the room.

"Sorry," he apologies with a smile. "I wasn't sure if we'd see you today."

"I had physiotherapy for my arm downstairs, and I thought I'd come check on him."

He glances over the machines and writes down some measurements. His furrowed frown doesn't abate.

"How is he?" I make myself ask.

Doctor Bannon spares me a glance. "We're doing our best to keep him stable while we search for a donor match."

"You know I can help."

"No, Miss Kensington. We've had this discussion. You are not well enough to be considered for a partial liver donation."

"You've had this discussion with Hunter. Nobody has bothered to ask me how I feel about it."

His expression softens. "Mr Rodriguez has nothing to do with this decision. I'm prioritising your health. We will find someone else; it just takes time."

I stare down at my booted feet, tears tightening my throat. "My father is going to die unless he gets this transplant."

"He's acutely unwell. We're doing the best we can."

"You've been saying that for the last three weeks."

When he reaches out to place a hand on my shoulder, I screech the chair backwards and shoot upright. Doctor Bannon freezes, his lips pursed.

"I'm sorry, Miss K—"

"That isn't my name," I interrupt him.

He sighs in clear frustration. "Your father is suffering from acute liver failure. He overdosed on heroin and fentanyl. This isn't a quick fix. We're fighting to keep him alive."

"Then let me help!"

"I'm sorry, Harlow. It simply isn't an option while you're still recovering. You should go home and get some rest."

"I don't need to rest," I shout back.

A shadow crosses the window, huge and looming. I recognise the threatening set of Enzo's shoulders without looking up at his stony expression. He's tracked me down.

Huffing, I take one last look at my father's slack face and storm from the room. I'm barely out of the door before a beefy hand encircles my bicep.

"We agreed that I would meet you downstairs," Enzo says gruffly. "You can't just run off like that. It isn't safe."

"I don't need an escort."

He almost yanks me off my feet as I'm forced to halt. Enzo stares down at me, his golden-amber eyes lit with heartache through thick lashes that some would kill for.

Haphazard black hair hangs over his face. Unlike the others, his features are a little too harsh and angular to be classically handsome. He's more rugged and raw, attractive in a different sense. Everything about Enzo is roughened around the edges.

"Is that all I am now? An escort?"

Barbed wire wraps around my throat. I can't even choke out an excuse. Enzo's been there for every single day I've spent despondent and shell-shocked. All I've done is run away from him for the past few weeks.

"I don't know what I want anymore," I admit thickly.

His hand falls from my bicep, curling into a white-knuckled fist. "What are you saying?"

"I don't know."

Nodding, he wipes the look of hurt from his face. "Let's get out of here."

Enzo stuffs his hands in the pockets of his leather jacket and takes off towards the ward's exit. Every step away from me is a sizzling bullet to the heart.

I can't keep myself together right now—how am I supposed to hold his broken pieces as well? Nothing has been the same since we stepped inside that chapel last month.

I'm not the same girl who escaped four months ago, and I've changed again since then. There's a revolving door of Harlows sliding their never-ending supply of masks into place.

All I know is that Pastor Michaels is gone. Mrs Michaels is dead. There is no justice in this lawless purgatory—only more death and destruction. Each breath I take guarantees the suffering of more innocent women.

My real father may die.

Maybe, I should go with him.

Reluctantly following Enzo, we dodge nurses with trolleys and a porter bringing the latest victim to their clinical prison.

Stepping inside the elevator that took me from this same hospital, a whole other Harlow ago, I watch the doors close with a thud.

"Enzo," I begin.

He doesn't even look at me.

"Please say something."

The silence is overwhelming.

"Like what?" he eventually replies.

I watch the flickering light tick down as the parking garage approaches. We can't go on like this. It's killing us both.

"I miss my friend," I force out.

He inhales sharply. "I'm right here."

"None of you have looked at me the same since you saw the basement. I hate it so much."

"Harlow," he interrupts.

"Don't try to deny it. You've barely touched me in weeks. Hunter has withdrawn, and Leighton is miserable. I have no idea where Theo even is right now."

When my lowered head refuses to lift, Enzo suddenly grabs me. My back meets the metal wall of the cage imprisoning us, and two calloused fingers lift my chin. His stare is scorching.

"I look at you the same as I always have," he says softly. "With astonishment and respect. You survived that hellhole. I have no idea how."

My eyes burn with tears. "You don't have to say that, Enz. Just talk to me like a normal human being."

"I am. Nothing has changed."

"You're all treating me like I'm made of broken glass."

At my raised voice, his expression darkens. A thunderstorm settles over him, deadly and dangerous.

Grabbing my shoulders, his fingers dig deep into my skin. The instinct to run screams through my mind. He isn't the gentle giant who last escorted me from this hospital.

"I am trying to protect you," he hisses angrily. "Even from yourself. Can't you see how much I care about you?"

I shrug, unable to answer.

"Fuck, Harlow! You're infuriating."

Giving me no opportunity to argue, I startle when his lips slam against mine. He kisses me like the hospital is collapsing around us, shattering and crushing helpless bodies as it falls victim to God's wrath.

My lips part, granting the wet swipe of his tongue access to my mouth. He tastes like bonfire embers and the tantalising promise of a new dawn breaking the cover of night.

He tastes like home.

Enzo gave me a family again.

When his lips disappear, I gasp for air. His forehead is pressed against mine, our souls straining to reach one another. I can almost hear his heart erratically pounding.

"Still don't know what you want?" he rumbles.

"I'm not… I don't know."

"If you're trying to scare me off, it isn't going to work." He drops a kiss to my temple. "I'm not going anywhere. No matter what you do to push me away."

"I don't deserve you," I whisper back.

His fingers slot between mine. "You don't get to decide that. I'm staying right here. I will never abandon you."

The elevator doors *ding* open, cloaking us in the darkness of the parking garage. Enzo tows me out, refusing to release his grip on my hand. I can't lift my gaze from my feet.

His sweet, generous soul gave me the strength to leave this hospital before. But now, this place serves as a reminder of the lies I've told to them all. The deception I've woven to escape their judgement. I want to be loved.

So did Laura.

I took that from her.

Even if death was waiting for her to succumb, her final moments were godless and excruciating. She choked on blood and the pressure of my hands gripping her throat.

I am a murderer.

Enzo deserves so much more.

Silent tears soaking into my cheeks, I let him drag me through parked cars and covered motorcycles. The hospital hums above us, a nest of activity and sickness. I'm glad to see the back of it.

"We should get some food," Enzo decides. "Leighton has been filing paperwork all day. He'll be ready to eat his own arm."

"Why is Hunter making him do that?"

"He's gotta start somewhere. I'm going to train him up, but he needs to learn some work ethic first."

His arm curls around my shoulders, and I lean into the furnace-like warmth of his muscled torso.

"If Leighton's working now, I should get a job too." I peer up at him. "It's overdue."

Enzo shakes his head. "We've discussed this."

"You're the second person to say that to me today. I'm getting really sick of decisions being made for me."

He abruptly halts. "Shit."

I almost lose my balance, so I grab his elbow to stop myself from faceplanting. We're metres from the blacked-out company SUV, but Enzo's feet are rooted to the spot.

"Motherfucker," he curses.

"What is it?"

He shoves me behind him. "Stay back. I need to call for backup."

I manage to peek around his massive frame. Gloopy, bright-red paint stains the concrete floor, dripping in great globules.

The car has been trashed, from the smashed windows to the dented, scratched body paint. On the bonnet, a single word has been written in spilled paint.

SINNER.

CHAPTER 2
HUNTER

EMPTY – LETDOWN

THE FLOOR of my spacious office is worn bare from frantic pacing. It's all I've done as of late. Paced. Pondered. Negotiated. Threatened. Every day, more walls are thrown in my path.

I've beaten myself to a pulp trying to knock those obstacles down. We're hunting a ghost who speaks in riddles, facing a crisis of faith in our weary teams and slowly cracking under the pressure of a country desperate for answers.

So much death.

Countless litres of blood spilled.

Pain. Heartbreak. Grief.

It's all been for nothing. Each lead creates a new dead end. More problems. Unanswered questions. Black holes of missing information and money pouring down the drain.

I'm losing control of this mess.

More than that, I'm losing *her*.

Refastening my striped, blue tie, I leave my office and head down the corridor to Theo's lair. I don't bother knocking. His cave is near pitch black, the blinds cocooning him in darkness and stifling warmth.

In the corner of the room, a lump is huddled beneath a blanket on his sofa. I grab a half-finished cup of coffee from his desk and upend it on top of the snoring, balled-up figure.

"Argh!"

"Wakey wakey, sleeping beauty."

Theo shoots upright, his mass of light-blonde ringlets dripping with stale coffee. He's wearing the same flannel shirt and blue jeans as he was three days ago, rumpled and stained.

"What the fuck, Hunter?"

"I'm not paying you to sleep."

With a groan, he collapses back on the sofa. "You're not paying me to work twenty-four seven, either. Doesn't stop me from doing it, though. I want a raise."

"Don't we all?"

I backtrack before he can swing an exhausted right hook. Theo wipes his face on his green-and-red shirt, replacing his black glasses as his clear, blue eyes squint up at me.

"Have you finished compiling the latest Kiera James report from the intelligence department?"

He heads for his cluttered desk. "I have."

"Harlow has been asking me for an update. I'd like to be able to give her a better answer than last time."

"The answer hasn't changed," he grumbles. "Kiera was a plain Jane, through and through. Devoted Christian, no children or notable relationships. Vanished into thin air."

"If I wanted a regurgitation of the last four reports I already read, I could've spared myself a trip down here."

He shoots me a glower. "I've got nothing, Hunt."

"Come on. Give me something to offer her."

"I can't wrap an empty box in a fucking red bow and call it a result. We've got nothing."

"Gee, and here I was thinking you're Santa Claus."

"Ha bloody ha."

Taking a seat at his desk, Theo reboots his monstrous array of computer screens. Stacks of paperwork, strewn post-it notes and empty ramen containers litter his workspace.

We've been working flat out since locating the chapel in Northumberland. It took almost two weeks to process and ship all the forensic evidence to HQ. The place was scrubbed, but we still found traces of two DNA signatures.

Both unidentified.

The infamous Michaels.

Not to mention, the swinging, strangled corpse. That was a head fuck in and of itself. Using dental records, we identified the fictional Mrs Michaels and matched one of the DNA profiles to her. We also have a name.

Rosetta Stone vanished in the late seventies after a stint at a now-demolished children's home. She was sixteen at the time. From there, Rosetta ceased to exist.

No marriage records, mortgage applications, bank accounts. Nothing. She ran away from that orphanage and disappeared. Mrs Michaels was born from that gaping black hole, adopting a brand-new, false identity to hide her crimes.

We have the body of a missing woman, accused of aiding and abetting the crimes of a serial killer and rapist, and the DNA of a ghost. Yet, we're standing here with our dicks in our hands, clueless and out of ideas.

"Who can we speak to from that children's home?" I muse out loud. "We need someone to verify Rosetta's identity."

Theo takes a sip from a mug and spits the cold coffee straight back out with a wince. He makes a beeline for his coffee machine to make a much-needed fresh cup.

"Files were burned when it shut down. You know the drill. We're still uncovering mass graves from government-funded hellholes running back then. It was clearly corrupt as hell."

"We don't have a single name?"

"It was demolished in the nineties, facing a dozen different lawsuits and accusations of abuse. Management bulldozed it and removed all traces of it ever existing."

Fierce pain pounds behind my eyes with another impending migraine. I'm not coming up with an answer for Harlow anytime soon.

"What about Kiera's sister?" I sigh tiredly.

Theo picks up a folder and waves it in the air. "She's agreed to be interviewed for our investigation to go over everything."

Running a hand over my slicked-back bun, I clap him on the shoulder. The police investigation into Kiera's murder was lacklustre at best. With any luck, they missed something.

"Set it up. I'll interview her myself."

"Already done," he replies absently.

"When?"

"She's flying down to London end of next week."

"Perfect. Good work."

Theo's brows draw together. "Oh, erm… well, thanks."

"You don't have to look like I just suggested you run naked down Oxford Street."

"That would be less surprising than you thanking me."

I turn to walk out, but my feet glue themselves to the carpet before I can skulk back to my office. Guilt spears me in the chest.

"Am I really that awful?"

Theo's forehead collides with his desk. "You seriously need to ask me that?"

"Clearly, I do."

"You've always been a dick, Hunt. But the last five years have proven you're also a cold-hearted son of a bitch."

My hands clench and unclench at my sides. "It was never about you. Everything I've done has been for this company."

"Including sacrificing your family?"

"I haven't sacrificed anyone," I snap at him. "I've kept you all alive. Even when you didn't want to live."

Storming from the office, I don't give Theo the opportunity to answer. He's always been shortsighted. His existence revolves around solving one puzzle after another, day in and day out, to make him feel alive.

Sabre wouldn't be what it is without his tireless work. I appreciate that fact. But the simple truth is, someone has to get their hands bloody from time to time.

That's my job.

It's a shitty role to play.

I make the hard decisions so nobody else has to. If I wasn't prepared to be unpopular, we'd all be dead by now. The burden of responsibility is heavy on my shoulders. It's a weight I bear alone, or at least, I did.

Harlow is the first person to see past the carefully constructed, professional persona I wear. She took one look at my performance and tore it to shreds without uttering a word.

My phone buzzes in my pocket, and I pick up Enzo's incoming call with a tired sigh.

"What's up?"

"Hunt. We have a problem. I need you to send transport and a team of agents to the hospital."

I brace my hand against the wall. "Is Harlow secure?"

"She's safe. Some asshole trashed the car while we were inside and left a stupid message. We need backup."

Quickly storming back into Theo's office, I snap my fingers to get his attention and fire off rapid instructions. He jerks into action, our sharp barbs forgotten.

Becket and the rest of the Anaconda team are running a reconnaissance op in Central London. We've been paid a hefty sum to investigate a well-loved politician suspected of bankrolling a human trafficking ring.

"Hold tight, the team's coming. What message?"

A photo comes through via text message with a *ding*. I curse under my breath. This is some fucked-up shit. Theo looks over my shoulder and blanches.

"What the hell?" he mutters.

"Pull the surveillance footage from that parking garage," I order him. "I want names."

Down the phone line, I can hear breathless panting in the background. Enzo swears and hangs up the call before I can yell at him. I recognise the sound of Harlow freaking out.

Countless nights spent with her asleep in my arms have given me a shitty ability to sense her distress. Enzo usually joins us, even when I tell him to get lost. Her bed is the only place he manages to get any sleep these days.

"Hunt," Theo calls. "I've got the hospital's CCTV feed. The camera doesn't have Enzo's car in range, but we have three people who enter the garage in the time frame."

I lean over him to take a look. He's right, we don't have a clear shot of the car or who did this. Two middle-aged nurses and a short, stout man come and go, but they look like workers, not crazed lunatics capable of doing this.

"You think one of them did it?" he wonders.

"We have no concrete proof."

"I'll run facial recognition and pull their records anyway. No one else enters or exits through the entrance gate."

"It has to be one of them. Call Hudson and send him to pick them up for criminal damage and harassment."

"Don't you think that's a bit rash?" Theo worries.

"Someone has threatened Harlow's life. I don't give a shit if it's rash or not."

"We've already pissed off the superintendent this month," he reasons. "She's ready to pull the plug without us arresting innocent people and aggravating her further."

"I'm not risking them getting away with this. If these people are innocent, then they'll have nothing to hide."

Theo nods, his lips pursed. "Fine."

We sit in tense silence as we await an update from the team. The alarm clock on his desk ticks down. When half an hour has passed, I redial Enzo with an impatient snarl.

Nothing.

I'll kill him myself.

"Motherfucker isn't answering his phone." I punch in another number. "He knows I hate being ignored."

"Don't we all," Theo comments.

"Watch your tone. I want full profiles on all three of those people. Names, addresses and any connection to Michaels or Harlow."

He gives me a weary salute. "Yes, boss."

The line connects, and Becket barks a greeting. I can hear the hum of his car engine, but it's broken by hysterical crying in the background. Harlow.

"He's found me," she hiccups through sobs. "I'm a sinner. He's found me. I'm a sinner."

"Little busy here," Becket interjects.

"Update?"

"We're twenty minutes out from the house. No sign of a tail or any reporters. Think we're in the clear."

"Put me on loudspeaker."

There's a faint click.

"Go ahead."

"Harlow?" I say urgently. "I know you can hear me, sweetheart. You're safe. Becket is taking you home."

It's excruciating, the sound of her terror. I can't do a damn thing from here. She's out of my reach and unresponsive.

"This wasn't him, Harlow. It's just some punks playing a foolish prank. He hasn't found you."

She still doesn't respond, too busy repeating her frenzied mantra over and over again. I drag my hair tie out and fist the long strands, desperate to crawl through the phone.

"Enz? You there?"

"I've got her," he responds sharply. "What's the latest?"

"CCTV is a bust. We've got three perps in range, but no evidence. Hudson's picking them up for questioning."

"Why would anyone do this?"

"That's exactly what I'm going to find out."

Theo shoots me a thumbs up from his desk chair. He's logged in to our secure server, tracking Hudson's precious Mustang as he peels through Central London, making a beeline for the hospital.

That man is far better than a bloodhound and more likely to tear his victims to shreds with his bare teeth. I hope I'm right and one of those workers did this, or we're sending a paid assassin after three innocent people. Not my best move.

"Send Leighton home to watch Harlow," Enzo demands. "Put the perps in the detention block until I get to HQ."

"Take over here," I suggest instead. "I'm coming home."

"You are?"

"Harlow needs me. She comes first."

Her whimpering quietens, replaced by a relieved inhale.

"Hunter," she manages to say.

I almost fall over from the rush of relief. Hearing her crying in fear makes me want to dismember someone, and not in a fun way. I can't stand knowing someone scared her this bad.

"Hold on, love. I'll be there soon."

Disconnecting the call, I catch Theo looking at me strangely before I exit his office again.

"What?"

He lifts an eyebrow. "You're never one to surrender control, even to Enzo."

"My priorities have changed."

"Since when?"

"Since now. Moving forward, it's family first, and that's exactly what Harlow is to us."

CHAPTER 3
HARLOW

ALL I HAVE – NF

THE FIRST THING I feel is the reassuring warmth of a hard, muscular body wrapped around me. Familiar scents intermingle with the residue of last night's fire.

Lemon and lime.

Toasted marshmallows.

Leftover popcorn.

Someone's trapped beneath me, his chest rising and falling with each deep breath. Opening my eyes, I blink the sleep away and peer down at Leighton's snoring frame.

He's fast asleep.

Sunlight streams through the thick curtains that we forgot to draw in the den last night. The television is still paused on an episode of *The Office*. It's our new thing after finishing *Friends* and bawling our eyes out together at the ending.

I'm secretly rooting for Dwight and Angela to end up together. They're my favourite couple. Leighton's a Jim and Pam fan, so we argue a lot about it over fresh popcorn and over-sweetened cups of tea. Our go-to snacks.

"Leigh?" I gently tap his cheek.

"Go away, Hunt," he complains sleepily. "No work."

I suppress a laugh. "I'm not Hunter, and I really hope you don't wake up with him laying on you like this."

He cracks an eye open before huffing and screwing it shut again. "Too early. Go back to sleep."

Placing a hand on the hardwood floor next to the green, velvet sectional sofa that we're splayed out on, I manoeuvre myself off his body without falling over.

"Harlow," he whines. "Come back."

I stretch to my full height. "Go back to sleep."

He doesn't need more encouragement. His rattled snoring resumes, and I pad through to the kitchen to boil the kettle. Lucky is already waiting at the back door, her tail wagging with anticipation.

"You're never late."

She yips excitedly.

I stroke a hand over her golden fur and unlock the French doors. "Go on then. I'll be out in a sec."

Galloping outside, she stretches her powerful limbs before bounding through the early morning mist. January arrived brisk and cold, bringing frost and the occasional snowfall.

I'm not sure where Christmas went. Our plans were ruined by everything that happened up north. By the time Hunter and Enzo returned home, the festivities were over, and I was in no mood to celebrate anything.

Another year ruined.

I can't say I'm surprised.

It was over a week before I was able to face leaving my room. Facing the real world is still a challenge, even now. After what happened at the hospital the other day, I'm seriously considering becoming a full-time hermit.

The security system buzzes with an alert before the front door clicks open, admitting a sweaty, red-faced Enzo dressed in thermal running gear. He braces his hands on his knees.

"Morning, Enz."

His head snaps up. "You're awake."

"Just about."

I fire up Hunter's fancy machine and set about making him a black coffee. He's barely capable of coherent thought without a constant current of caffeine in his veins.

"Good run?"

Enzo drains his water bottle before chucking it in the steel rubbish bin. "Quiet. Anyone else up?"

"Hunter fell asleep at his desk last night. He hasn't emerged yet. Leighton is doing his best grizzly bear impression in the den. Theo isn't here."

He eyes me suspiciously. "You slept downstairs?"

Sliding him the fresh cup of coffee, I finish my own tea with milk and a generous heap of sugar before shrugging.

"We fell asleep watching TV."

"Must be nice," he complains.

Our eyes connect across the marble breakfast bar, scattered with last night's empty pizza boxes and Hunter's newspaper from yesterday morning.

There are violent purple bags beneath his vivid amber eyes. Shame punches me in the chest. Enzo doesn't sleep unless it's next to me. His skin has to be touching mine for him to finally succumb, usually for a handful of hours at best.

"I'm sorry," I rush to apologise.

"Don't worry about it."

"I should have come up and found you. Did you get any sleep at all?"

"Not important."

I quickly grab his arm before he can disappear to shower. Enzo frowns at where my fingers grip his glistening bicep.

"You're not responsible for my sleep schedule, little one. I've been getting by alone for thirty-two years."

Stepping into his embrace, I wrap my arms around his waist. He smells salty beneath a sheen of sweat, but his earthy, pine tree scent still beckons me in. I rest my head on his hard abdominals and let my eyes slide shut.

"You can call dibs on me tonight."

His chest vibrates with a chuckle. "Dibs? Is that the system we're working on now?"

"I'm not sure there is a system."

"Yeah, me neither."

"We haven't really discussed… well, anything."

Enzo lifts my chin so our eyes meet. A shiver runs down my spine. He still makes butterflies explode in my stomach. The months we've spent living together haven't changed that.

It's like staring up into the threatening grimace of a golden-eyed tiger. Instead of fearing his power, though, I'm comforted by the certainty that he'll tear apart any predator that dares to give me a second glance.

"What do you want to talk about?" he croons.

I squirm as his arms band around me. His grip tightens into a vice-like prison, locking me against his chest. I couldn't run away even if I wanted to.

"Well, the others… erm, us. We haven't really talked about… you know, us."

He cocks an eyebrow. "Smooth. Us?"

A blush creeps up my neck. There's an amused twinkle in Enzo's eyes as the corner of his mouth lifts.

"You've been, um… staying in my bed most nights," I scramble to explain. "And Hunter, you know. He does too. Then Leighton… he… ah, hell. I give up."

"You sure?" He laughs throatily.

"Shut up."

"Oh, no. Feel free to keep going. This is hilarious."

"Stop laughing at me!"

Expression growing serious, his gaze softens with tender affection. Two calloused fingers brush across my cheek before he tucks a strand of long, brown hair behind my ear.

"I know things are confusing right now," he offers. "The case is a mess and we're no better. But I can promise you one thing."

"What's that?"

He leans close, his thick, plush lips ghosting over mine. "None of us are going anywhere. We have a lot of shit to sort out between us, but that fact won't ever change."

I press my mouth against his, my teeth playfully nipping his bottom lip before withdrawing. My confidence is blooming with each touch.

"Do you promise?" I ask huskily.

"Want me to cross my fucking heart?"

"If you're offering."

With a crooked grin, Enzo drags his index finger over his heart. "Then I cross my heart and hope to die. That's what it would take for me to let you go."

Rather than comforted, I feel sick.

"Harlow?" he prompts. "What is it?"

Dread seeps over me in a suffocating cloud. I've already gotten enough people killed. Whether by my hand or not, I enabled all of those women's deaths. I watched from behind the rusted bars of my cage and said nothing.

I can't watch Enzo die too.

Not like Laura.

"Did you find who wrecked your car last week?"

Sighing, he leans against the countertop. "It wasn't one of the people we picked up. I interviewed them myself."

"By interviewed, do you mean that you beat them to within an inch of their lives?"

Enzo's grin widens. "Something like that."

"Jesus, seriously?"

"No, I'm kidding."

I blow out a breath. "Don't scare me like that."

"I sat them down and questioned them. They all had alibis and were working at the time it occurred. It wasn't them."

"Who did this then?"

He shrugs casually. "We've been receiving some weird-as-hell emails, so it could easily be one of those nut jobs."

"Wait, what?"

Enzo hesitates before answering. "There are some people who support what Pastor Michaels is doing to these women. Real Charles Manson shit."

"I don't know who that is."

"Serial killers attract the worst kind of attention," he attempts to explain. "We've been getting people threatening us to let Michaels do his work in peace."

"Why? He's killing people!"

"These psychos think he's some kind of messiah. Reckon he's doing God's work, culling the sinners from the earth in preparation for the rapture or some shit like that."

I wish that freaked me out more. Several months ago, that would have sounded normal. In some ways, it still does. My reality is a confusing combination of past and present.

Indoctrinated and liberated.

Captive and free.

Damned and worthy.

"You think he's been ordering these people to attack us? Was Pastor Michaels behind what happened at the hospital?"

Enzo scrubs a hand over his face. "I doubt it. He's an apex predator. They hunt alone and without a pack."

"He wasn't alone. Mrs Michaels helped him."

"Pastor Michaels slaughtered his only accomplice and hung her like a piece of meat," he highlights. "I doubt he's looking for any more help if she wasn't needed."

Head drooping, I focus on my sock-covered feet. Upstairs, hidden beneath my mattress, Mrs Michaels' golden wedding ring awaits its final resting place.

I'm not sure why I couldn't part with it. On some level, it's a sick fascination for the physical proof of what happened in the confusing blur of those thirteen years.

But deeper, on a more instinctual level, that ring represents the only life I've ever known. Part of me feels safer with it close, a twisted slice of home. I can't bear to let it go yet.

"What about Kiera?" I bite my lip. "She still talks to me. Whispers and snippets of memories are coming back every day."

Enzo's frown deepens. "Talks to you?"

"Like in my dreams and stuff."

"I see. Well, Hunter's going to be interviewing her sister in a couple of days. We'll have more information then."

Grabbing my half-finished cup of tea, I tip out the rest of the liquid. Enzo watches me intently, and I can't stand it for a second longer. They're all just waiting for me to break.

"I want a meeting with all of you." I place the cup down with trembling hands. "I'm involved in this case too."

"Why? I said we'd keep you posted with any updates. That's exactly what we're doing."

"Are you?" I scoff.

When Enzo drops my eyes, I know I've caught him out. My instincts were right. There's something else the team isn't telling me.

"I'm protecting you," he reasons.

"Then stop! I don't need you to."

My control snapping, I grab the discarded cup and throw it so hard, it shatters on the marble countertop. It feels good to watch the broken shards rain down, completely destroyed.

"I gave you Kiera James. I found that chapel. I have done more than my fair share, and you still keep me in the dark."

"You know that isn't the case."

"Isn't it?" I round on him. "What about Mrs Michaels? It's been a whole month. You must have identified her body."

Bingo. Enzo shifts on his feet, blowing out a frustrated breath. After all we've been through and the progress I thought we've made, they still don't trust me.

It hurts.

I'm not one of them.

"Well?" I throw my hands up.

Footsteps approach, breaking our furious stare off. Hunter strolls into the kitchen, wearing his usual soft, green sweats and bare, chiselled abdomen, highlighting his defined Adonis belt.

Intricate tattoos cover his entire chest, wrapping around his torso and dipping into the waistband of his sweats. The inked thunderstorm is depicted in painstaking detail, reflecting the controlled but vicious storm brewing within him.

"I heard shouting," he mumbles.

His burnished, chocolate-brown eyes land on me beneath his long, chestnut hair. The only imperfection on his model-like looks is an old scar that bisects his eyebrow.

"What's going on?"

I fold my arms, lifting my chin with indignation. "Who is Mrs Michaels?"

His shoulders slump. "Sit down, Harlow. This doesn't have to be a fight."

"That seems to be the only way to make you idiots tell the truth. I'm not sitting down. Start talking."

Easing past me to brew his morning fix of tea, Hunter takes a seat at the breakfast bar and gingerly pushes old pizza boxes aside. He looks physically offended by the mess.

"It took some time, but our forensic team has identified Mrs Michaels using old dental records."

Enzo shakes his head as he turns away from us. I'd love to thump him around the face right now. He still doesn't get why I need to know what's happening.

"Her real name is Rosetta Stone." Hunter glances up at me. "She's been missing since the late seventies."

"M-Missing?" I stammer.

He fiddles with his black hearing aid. "We linked her to a dodgy children's home that was shut down in 1994. It wasn't uncommon for these kids to disappear."

"We think she ran away to escape the abuse and neglect." Enzo braces his hands on the counter. "She was sixteen."

"Didn't they look for her?"

"It would've been easy to start again under a new name, pretending to be older to avoid being dragged back there."

My heart pounds faster, exploding into delirious butterflies. It's hard to imagine the monstrous pillar of violence and hatred who haunted my childhood as a little girl.

She was scared and running for her life. Just like me. I hate the way that realisation twists my emotions, leaving me feeling completely lost in the wilderness of my confusion.

"This children's home… have you spoken to the staff? Do they remember her? What if we go there and look around?"

"It's gone," Hunter says gently.

"Gone?" I repeat. "How?"

"Bulldozed and wiped from the records as part of the government's clean-up initiative. They were implicated and wanted to cover their tracks. Any staff members have died or been silenced in the decades since."

My balled-up fist crashes against the counter. "This is such bullshit. You're telling me there's nothing?"

Both men stare at me like I'm an alien.

"She's spending far too much time with your potty mouth of a brother," Enzo complains to his best friend.

"He's teaching her bad habits," Hunter concurs.

"Go and wake the little delinquent up. He can get his lazy backside into the office today to do some damn work."

"I am standing right here," I snap in exasperation. "Any other vital information you've kept from me? Also, you guys say *fuck* literally all the time, but I'm the potty mouth?"

They both burst out laughing, doubled over and wiping away tears. Crossing my arms, I attempt to storm past Enzo to escape into the garden to get away from them.

His arms shoot out to capture me. "Where do you think you're going?"

"Away from you two."

"I don't think so. You wanted to talk, so let's talk."

"You don't get to turn this on me," I defend angrily. "Take me seriously, or this conversation is over."

"Look who's calling the shots," Hunter taunts, an eyebrow raised. "You've changed, sweetheart."

I flush hot, my entire body burning. I'm not sure if it's embarrassment or desire, but the way he's staring at me with a weird look of pride is setting a fire low in my belly.

"Is that a bad thing? People are supposed to change."

Curling his arm around my narrow waist, Enzo tugs me against his chest. We collide with a smack and my face presses up against his heavily beating heart.

"It's not a bad thing," he murmurs. "We're happy to see you figuring out what you want."

"Then why do you keep me in the dark?"

"It's our responsibility to keep you safe while you're healing. You shouldn't be worrying. We have the case under control."

Before I can argue back, Hunter's stool scrapes across the tiled floor and a column of warmth meets my spine. His chin rests on top of my head, imprisoning me between them.

I forget how to blink, breathe or form any logical thought. Enzo's muscles are hard beneath my touch, while Hunter's hot breath stirs my hair. They both smell so good.

"If this is just a job, where does that leave us?"

"Just a job?" Hunter repeats. "Pretty sure I proved otherwise the night you came on my tongue, sweetheart."

Enzo's grip on me tightens. "I didn't consider it my job to make you cry out my name in this very kitchen."

"Careful," Hunter warns him.

My heart seizes with fear. I'm caught between them both. There's no space to run away from the truth. I've been playing a dangerous game without even realising it.

"It's fine by me," Enzo croons.

Hunter's growl vibrates against my back. "I warned you to keep your damn hands to yourself, Enz. Not go behind my back to try to fuck our client."

"Like you didn't do the same thing?" he argues. "We've talked about this. All of us care about Harlow a lot."

"That's exactly why we can't do this."

"Do what?" I ask cluelessly.

I can practically feel their glowers above my head. When I wriggle out from between them, drowning in the testosterone, Hunter's hands grab my hips tight.

His thumbs slip beneath the oversized *Aerosmith* t-shirt that I stole from Leighton's wardrobe to relax in yesterday. He's very precious about his extensive collection, but he never complains about me wearing his clothes.

"Did I say you could move?" Hunter traps me back between them. "Stay right where you are."

His left hand coasts higher, over the scarred expanse of my lower stomach. I bite my lip to hold back a sigh as he teases the waistband of my yoga pants.

"This isn't a game," Enzo hisses at him. "Take your hands off her."

"Why? If I want to touch Harlow, I will. If I want to strip her bare, spread her across the table and fuck her while you watch, I bloody well will."

"Touch her when she doesn't want it and we're going to have a serious problem."

Pushing his taunting hand inside my yoga pants, Hunter's fingers coast even lower. I arch my back, silently pleading for more. He cups my mound over the damp material of my panties, sending spikes of anticipation through my core.

"Seems like she wants it to me," he purrs. "I can feel how wet her pussy is just thinking about me fucking her."

"Stop being a dick." Enzo grabs my shoulders and pulls me closer. "Best friend or not, I'll still put a bullet in your face."

Hunter slips his hand from my yoga pants. "You were the one proposing we share her. How's that plan going, Enz?"

Forehead slick with nervous sweat, I almost teeter when Enzo releases me, on the verge of punching Hunter in the face. He immediately grabs me again, his eyebrows knitted together with concern.

"Share me?" I ask, despite my dizziness.

Neither responds.

"Like you did with Alyssa?"

Her whispered name causes Hunter to step away from us both. The rush of cold air is like a slap to the face. He avoids looking at us both as he storms from the room, a hand fisted in his long, tangled hair.

His office door slams shut down the hall with an audible crack. Enzo shakes his head, running his hands up and down my arms as he tries to comfort me.

"I'm sorry about that."

"Not your fault," I reply in a small voice. "He's got a lot on his plate. I never meant to cause so much trouble."

"You have the right to ask for something… if you want it."

A secret message stares back at me in shades of molten amber through his gaze. I can see the truth. His desires. The future he's so desperately reaching for. It terrifies me.

"What do you want?" I counter softly.

His lips part. "You."

My entire body is humming with anticipation. The embattled, fearful slice of submission left inside me wants to fling open the front door, run until my feet bleed and escape all of these complicated emotions.

"The others want you too," Enzo explains with a sad smile. "That's the problem. We all want the impossible."

I rest a hand over his heart. "What's that?"

His throat bobs tellingly. "Another chance."

Stroking a hand over the razor-sharp line of his carved collar bone, I wrestle with the tears threatening to spill down my cheeks. He still doesn't see it. They deserve every shot at happiness. Far more than I do.

That's why I can't have them.

It's too late for me.

"Maybe I should stay somewhere else."

Enzo's face drains of all colour. "Excuse me?"

"This is all my fault. You're fighting over something that can never happen. If I go now, it'll be easier that way."

He takes a small, protective step away from me. It feels like a knife is twisting in my gut.

"Never happen?" he thunders.

The pain swimming in his eyes makes me feel like the absolute worst human on the planet. He sacrificed everything to make me feel at home; giving me safety, love, their devotion and protection. I've thrown it back in his face.

"I should stand on my own two feet," I reason. "The longer I stay here with you, the harder that will be. I don't want anyone to fight over me."

"You seriously want to leave us?"

I swallow the truth like gulping bullets and nod. Even if it's a bold-faced lie. I'd rather crawl back into my cage than leave them, but I won't hurt Enzo's family any longer.

"You're lying."

"Hey," I snap defensively.

"If you mean it… say it again."

Swallowing down the nausea curdling in my stomach, I try to speak in an even, believable voice.

"I'm an adult, and I have the right to choose where I live. Thank you for everything you've done, but I want to leave now."

Stepping back into my personal space, Enzo slides a finger under my chin. When his mouth slants against mine, stealing a pulse-spiking kiss, I want to collapse in his arms and take it all back.

"That's how I know you're lying," he says huskily. "I expected this bullshit from Hunter, but not you."

Dropping his grip on my chin, he brushes past me. I flinch, trying to grab his t-shirt but failing.

"Enzo—"

"I need to get to the office."

"Please, wait."

Enzo glances back, a wounded bonfire smouldering in his eyes. "Try to leave this house and I'll have the agents guarding the gate drag you back, kicking and screaming."

My haze-filled brain screams out in alarm. I know he'd never hurt me, but the threat is clear. It's the same toxic possession that fuelled Pastor Michaels' abuse. I didn't escape that basement to be controlled by another man.

"You can't do that."

"I'm not bluffing, Harlow. You will stay here until it's safe. When Pastor Michaels is rotting in hell, feel free to leave."

Enzo storms out before I can summon a comeback. I'm left in the empty kitchen, trembling all over and feeling like God has slammed the pearly gates shut in my face with a sneer.

A prison is still a prison.

Even when it's an invisible one.

CHAPTER 4
THEO

THE KID I USED TO KNOW – ARRESTED YOUTH

SAT BEHIND MY CLUTTERED, cup-lined desk, I watch the live feed from the interview room several floors beneath my office. My head is pounding with a sleep-deprived headache.

Reagan James, Kiera's younger sister, sits at the plain wooden table. Her trembling hands are wrapped around a cup of coffee as her red hair covers her tear-streaked face.

Hunter hasn't begun yet.

She's already a mess.

On the camera feed, the door to the room opens. Our two hard-faced masters enter with solemn determination. Hunter is dressed to the nines in his usual three-piece suit, while Enzo is sporting his standard, all-black clothing and leather jacket.

"Miss James," Hunter greets as he takes a seat.

"Mr Rodriguez," she replies.

"Thanks for coming in. We appreciate your cooperation."

Reagan tucks hair behind her ear, showing off a glinting engagement ring. "Anything to help get justice for Kiera. Do you have new information?"

Enzo slaps down a thick folder of evidence. "I'm sure you're aware of the recent developments in the case."

"Of course. It's all over the news."

"We have a live witness cooperating with us, and she has shed some light on your sister's death."

"Is she here? I'd like to meet her myself."

Hunter shakes his head. "I'm afraid that isn't possible. We need to ask you some questions about your sister."

She swallows hard. "What do you want to know?"

My office door creaks, and Leighton slips inside, carrying a heavy evidence box from Hunter's office. I gesture for him to put it down next to the fully stocked bookshelf.

He dusts off his hands, appearing bored beyond belief. The past several weeks of him working here have been hilarious to watch. He's suffering Enzo's seemingly endless wrath, and the punishment is going well.

"Enjoying yourself?"

His eyes narrow. "Shut the hell up. I'm only here because Harlow's having her therapy session upstairs. I'm driving her home after."

"I thought you just loved working here, Leigh."

"Not fucking likely," he grumbles.

With a one-fingered salute, Leighton saunters out of the room. He's slacked off in the months since his release from prison, and after the fiasco with Diablo, he has a lot to make up for. Enzo's prepared to train him up once he earns his forgiveness for everything that happened.

Having Leighton around the office so much has been weird. I feel guilty for how I've treated him, but my coldness towards him has never been personal. He simply represents the finality of Alyssa's exit from our lives.

Turning back to the live interview, I watch Enzo rest a hand on Reagan's shoulder. She's silently crying as they run back through the basics of the case to refresh her memory.

The grief is clearly still raw, despite the years that have passed since Kiera's slaughtered body turned up. I know better than most that time doesn't always equal healing.

"From your previous statements, we know you last saw Kiera the day before her disappearance." Hunter scans over the evidence file. "Tell me, how did she seem?"

Reagan blows her nose. "Normal. My sister lived a quiet life. She worked in the local school, attended church, rarely dated or even looked at men. She was happy."

"No boyfriends then?"

"No, never. Her work and religion were her life. The most socialising she ever did was walking her dog."

Reagan's face collapses as she cries harder.

"Miss James?" Enzo prompts.

"Reggie died last year. I know he was just a dog, but he was the last connection I had to her. Now, she's really gone."

"I'm sorry," he offers gently. "I know this must be difficult."

The iron-willed boulder of muscle has a disturbing talent for slipping past the defences of even the most cautious people. Enzo wields his kind-hearted nature as a weapon when it suits him, but he's the first one to snap spinal cords or shatter noses when shit hits the fan.

"I miss her," Reagan admits. "We were close."

Giving her tissues, Enzo sits back down and rifles through the evidence that Hunter hands him. He slides a printed map of woodland across the table. We know that Kiera was snatched somewhere around that location.

"How often did Kiera take this route for her dog walk?"

Reagan picks up the paper and studies it. "Several times a week. She loved to unplug after dealing with kids all day at work. Being in nature was one of her favourite things."

"This was a regular pattern of behaviour for her?" Hunter presses.

Reagan nods. "For sure."

"Who else was aware of your sister's regular walking route? Friends? Neighbours? Colleagues?"

"It's a small town," she answers. "I moved away after university, but Kiera was happy to live in a village where everyone knows everyone."

Looking at the identical file spread out between empty crisp packets and leftover pizza crusts on my desk, I rifle through the next section of evidence. It's a sparse file, even though Kiera's disappearance shocked the local community.

The whole town rallied around Reagan and her family to conduct regular searches and information campaigns. Everything about this victim was different. This was long before the serialised pattern of murder was established.

Only one other woman, a local sex worker, had died before Kiera and in completely different circumstances. She was the odd one out amongst a repertoire of brutality.

Kiera doesn't fit the victim profile at all—she was in full-time employment, living a quiet life as a devout Christian who was loved by her family and church.

Killing her wasn't safe or strategic.

The whole thing screams of rage.

She was ripped from a close-knit community and brutalised despite her faith. Pastor Michaels didn't select her like he did the others, intent on punishing them for what he considered a life of sin. He tore Kiera apart regardless.

"Can you think of anyone who wanted to hurt your sister?" Enzo asks.

Reagan's staring at a photograph of Kiera, smiling with a caramel-coloured puppy cuddled in her arms. She was sweet and attractive, albeit a little older than the other victims, in her early thirties. The crucifix around her neck is prominent.

"She wouldn't hurt a fly," Reagan whispers. "All my sister wanted was to help people. She volunteered at a local homeless shelter and helped teach the younger children in the clergy."

Trailing off, Reagan's eyebrows knit together. Hunter sits up in his chair, dropping his hand from playing with his hearing aid, as he does when deep in thought.

"What is it?"

Reagan frowns at the photograph in her hands. "There was one person she fell out with. Someone in the congregation. I'd forgotten all about it… but she was very angry."

"What did they argue about?" Enzo urges.

"She wouldn't tell me what happened, but she was so upset after attending church. I remember her acting strange during our Sunday night video call that week."

"How long was this before her disappearance?"

"Perhaps a few months?"

Unease brushes down my spine. For a plain, unremarkable woman with little to no social life, fighting with a member of her church had to be for a good reason.

"Did you tell the police about this?" Hunter questions.

"They didn't think it was important."

"Why?"

"You guys don't go to church," Reagan guesses with a thin smile. "Arguments are what keep these places in business. It isn't exactly breaking news for church members to disagree."

"Then why does it feel significant to you?"

She looks surprised by the sharply worded question. Hunter has always had an ability to examine people's darkest thoughts, past the veneer of thinly veiled bullshit.

"My sister was a gentle person," Reagan explains slowly. "She hated conflict. That's why I was so surprised when she was upset. But I just figured it was nothing, you know?"

Flipping through the preliminary report, I search for any mention of a falling out in the written transcript. There's nothing. Police incompetence and lacklustre investigating is half the reason this motherfucker has killed so many people.

The officers presumed that Kiera ran off with a boyfriend. She was old enough to take care of herself and deemed to be sensible, so in their eyes, limited police time and funding were better spent elsewhere.

When her body rocked up six weeks later, they'd already moved on to the next investigation demanding their cash-strapped time. Their failure enabled her death, and all those that followed.

"Who else knew about this?" Hunter asks crisply.

"I think she said something about the argument happening during a church service. Perhaps someone else who was there might have witnessed it. I'm not sure."

Hunter grabs a piece of paper and a pen. "Any names or contact details you have would be greatly appreciated."

Reagan bites her lip. "I might have a name. I wasn't much of a churchgoer, but I know the old pastor fairly well."

"Anything you can give us."

I snap back to reality when someone knocks on my office door. It's light and timid, announcing Harlow's presence before she peeks her head around the corner. Nobody else has the politeness to knock around here.

"Theo?"

My heart leaps into my throat. Fuck. I'd forgotten how gorgeous she is. I've barely seen her since the night when her father turned up, lifeless and half dead. The circles beneath her eyes are even darker now, much like my own.

"Is this a bad time? I have some books to return."

"Oh, erm… sure. Thanks."

She steps into the office, revealing her small, inviting curves and pert breasts accentuated by a long-sleeved white t-shirt and tight blue jeans beneath her parka coat.

In the months since she stumbled into our lives, she's put on some weight, and it's done her so much good. Despite all the shit that's been thrown her way, she's doing her best to stay alive.

Her flowing brown hair brushes her lower back in tumbling waves, highlighting her piercing aquamarine eyes, cute button nose and sharp but dainty cheekbones.

I'm so entranced, my throat tightening with desire, I forget to turn off the live interview feed. She lets me take the box of books from her hands. Balancing them on my shoulder, I use my spare arm to pull her into a tentative hug.

"Oh," she squeaks.

I release her. "Sorry."

"Don't apologise. I missed you."

Goddammit.

"I missed you too," I force out.

"How have you been?"

"I've been snowed under with the investigation. Sorry that I haven't been around much."

"I understand. I miss our late-night book talks."

Her eyes are fixed on the scuffed brown leather of her laced boots, perfectly tied into bows. Dumping the box of books, my fingers spasm with the need to pull her closer.

There are two halves warring within me, both demanding very different things. Despite my growing feelings for Harlow, that voice is still there. *Alyssa.* The memories still talk to me.

Laughing and teasing.

Telling me she loved me.

Promising me forever.

I hate how this feels like I'm betraying her memory. She's dead and gone. I can at least admit that to myself now. Locking Harlow out isn't going to bring Alyssa back.

After months spent trying to do that, it didn't fucking work. I still ended up right here—standing in front of Harlow, desperate to taste her lips, but too scared to make that leap.

"I enjoyed *The Odyssey*," she blurts.

"You did?"

"It was a good story, albeit a little sexist."

I stifle a laugh. "Well, yeah. Most classic books are."

She mock-shivers. "Not quite as bad as *Pride and Prejudice*, though. That was gross."

"Not a fan of classic romance?"

"I prefer reality to stupid pageantry and star-crossed lovers. Frankenstein's monster killing Victor's entire family when he refused to make him a bride was pretty cool."

Barking a laugh, I watch a smirk blossom on her pink lips. Jesus, this girl. It's not every day you find someone who prefers reading about horrifying monsters that are desperate for love over Mr Darcy and his problematic behaviour.

"Got anything else for me?"

I hook a thumb over my shoulder. "Come take a look." Panicking, I glance at my bookshelf. "Um, please don't judge the amount of trashy fantasy novels I have."

She giggles. "Is it that bad?"

"I can't have the world knowing I'm a nerd."

"I think that ship has already sailed."

Harlow walks over to my bookshelf, each footstep bouncing with excitement. I stand back and simply watch her. The way her fingertips trace over the book spines sets my heart pulsing.

She may as well be caressing the fractured pages of my soul, begging the book to open up to her. I want to do exactly that right now. She holds such unspoken power over me.

"You like sad books," she observes.

I wring my hands together. "Why would I want to read about something happy?"

"Most people do."

"Hope is in very limited supply in this world. I don't want to waste it on characters who don't exist. Give me death and tragedy. Like you said… it's more realistic."

Her brilliant blue eyes flick over to me. "What are you saving your hope for then, Theodore?"

My dick hardens at the teasing use of my full name. All I can think about is bending her over that goddamn bookshelf and burying myself deep inside of her. I haven't even thought about sex for a very long time.

"I don't know yet," I admit hoarsely.

Tension crackles in the charged air between us. All of my defences are annihilated with a mere glance. Harlow burns through the layers of numbness I've constructed over the years, and I'm stunned to realise that I'm glad.

"I'm not sure if I have any hope left to save." Her smile is bittersweet. "But if I did, I would keep it close so nobody could ever steal it from me again."

As we stare at each other, both looking for the right words to offer the other, voices filter back into our awareness. My array of monitors is still playing the live interview. Harlow's gaze strays over to the computer screens.

"What is going on?" she asks suspiciously.

"Oh, erm."

"Is that Kiera's sister?"

"Uh, I don't know if I'm supposed to tell you."

She shakes her head, the annoyance clear on her face. "Not you as well."

I feel like a dick as she abandons her small selection of books and heads for my desk. On the screen, Reagan is crying again. Harlow freezes, her fingers clenched over her mouth.

"My sister didn't deserve to die," Reagan sobs. "She should be here to walk down the aisle with me."

I hover a hand over Harlow's shoulder without touching her. "Maybe you shouldn't be watching this."

"Kiera was my friend," she replies. "I have more of a right than anyone to hear this."

Tiny earthquakes are wracking her entire slim frame as she watches Reagan fall apart, overwhelmed by the interview and array of evidence spread out in front of her.

"Miss James," Hunter interrupts, poised in his seat. "We can leave it here. You've been most helpful."

"I want to see her," Reagan demands.

"Excuse me?"

Her tear-logged eyes glance between them. "I want to meet the girl who let my sister die."

Fuck!

I need to turn this shit off.

"Why did she live when all of us have been left to grieve our loved ones? What makes her so special?"

"That's enough." Enzo gathers the evidence into the file. "Interview suspended. Miss James, you may leave now."

"Why won't she speak up?" Reagan's voice raises. "This monster is out there right now, slaughtering innocent women. All for what? She could make him stop."

Enzo grabs Reagan by the wrist, hauling her out of the seat. He wrestles her from the interview room as she shouts and raves, leaving Hunter to glance up at the camera. He looks as weary and bone tired as I feel.

Protecting Harlow is getting harder.

The world is turning against us.

"Is that what everyone's thinking?" Harlow's voice draws my attention. "Does the entire world want me to… to die?"

"Hell no," I hiss back. "She's grieving."

"They're all grieving! I'm the only one who didn't die."

"That doesn't make you culpable. You were a victim of this son of a bitch. Nobody could ever blame you."

She hugs her midsection tight. "Rewind the tape, Theo. Plenty of people are blaming me already."

"I know the truth. They don't."

Her breathing grows shallower as the cloud of panic slowly filters over her. I try to step closer, but she backs away.

"If I surrendered, would all of this stop?"

"Harlow. Don't go there."

"You read those letters he sent. I'm what Pastor Michaels wants. If he gets me back, the killings will stop."

"I don't give a fuck what that psychopath wants! We're going to find him and put an end to all of this."

She slams her hands over her ears, scrunching her eyes shut to block me out. I grip her shoulders and pull her into my arms, burying my nose in her sweet-scented hair.

"You're going to be okay," I whisper against her covered ear. "We will fix this, I promise. It'll be over soon."

"I never should've left that basement."

"Come on. Don't let her get in your head."

Thick, shining tears roll down her cheeks. "Everyone that's died… all the pain and suffering… it's my fault."

"Beautiful, please. Don't think like that."

"What if I killed myself? Would he be sated then?"

Her words slip out in a dark, anguished whisper. So quietly spoken, for a moment I think I've imagined it. Her eyes open, and the limitless lake of blue is cracked with guilt.

"You don't mean that."

"I can't watch anyone else die," she pleads. "My life isn't worth more than whoever he kills next."

The ringing in my head grows louder and louder, until it feels like I'm trapped beneath a frozen lake, battering my fists against the frosted, crème brûlée surface, trying to break free.

She's in my arms. I can feel her. Smell her. Touch her. Yet, our hands are being ripped apart at the same time. Fate is threatening to tear us apart, and I don't know if I can stop it.

If I don't hold on tighter, she's going to drown. I can already see it happening. Defeat has infected her, and it's spreading. Someone has to pull her back to the surface.

"Look at me." I pry her hands from her ears. "You listen carefully."

More tears pour down her red-stained cheeks as I trap her against my chest. She's biting back another pained sob.

"Your death will not stop this bastard from killing again. It won't. He's trying to manipulate you. Don't let him."

Her knees give way all at once. I'm dragged down with her, and we end up collapsing in a tangle.

"Breathe for me, beautiful."

Her chest contracts with each shuddered breath. I'm thrown back into the past—back to a time when there was an ocean of secrets between us, and I offered her Laura's bone to say goodbye to. It worked to bring her back from the edge.

I can fix this.

She needs to feel safe.

Banding my arms around her, I use my feet to shuffle backwards across the rough carpet. The solid wood of my desk looms above us. Dodging computer cables and bundled wires, I slip beneath it, taking Harlow with me.

Curling up in the tight, cramped space, I hold her spooned in my lap like she's a newborn baby. Her back rests on my chest, glueing us together as two halves of the same whole.

I don't say anything.

Words don't matter.

They mean absolutely nothing when you're staring into the abyss and searching for a reason not to take that short walk to oblivion. All I can do is hold her through it.

"Theo," she hiccups after several minutes.

"Yeah, beautiful?"

Her fingers search my flannel shirt, crawling up my throat until her palm rests on my cheek. I place my hand over hers, our fingers fitting together.

"Thank you for being here. You should hate me for all the trouble I've caused."

"I could never hate you," I reply softly.

Her adrenaline finally crashes, leaving her breathing to even out. It's uncomfortable hiding under here, but I don't care. We'll stay until the end of time if that's what she needs.

"Living keeps getting harder," she admits.

I smooth her hair in slow, rhythmic strokes. "Surviving doesn't make you guilty. Even if you feel like it does."

"Then what does it make me?"

Taking a moment to think over my response, I dare to drop a kiss on the top of her head. She feels so good in my arms.

"Lucky."

CHAPTER 5
HARLOW

PUT IT ON ME - MATT MAESON

LEIGHTON DEPOSITS a bowl of sweetened popcorn in my lap, collapsing next to me on the sectional with a huff. He curls his legs up to his chest and drops his headful of messy, brown hair on my shoulder.

"Ready for this?"

I rest my head against his. "Yep."

"My number one movie. It's been a long time coming."

"The suspense is killing me."

My joke falls flat. I can't hide the exhaustion from my voice. My sleep last night was riddled with dreams of Kiera, her dead, empty eyes watching me as they carved the limbs from her torso.

Her sister's words were the soundtrack.

Why did she live?

What makes her so special?

Why won't she speak up?

"Goldilocks."

Snapping his fingers in front of my face, Leighton's watching me with concerned green eyes. The scent of lemons and tropical fruit clinging to his hair drags me back to the present.

"Yeah?"

"Where did you go?"

I avoid his gaze. "Nowhere. What were you saying?"

Leighton is the youngest of the group at twenty-four. He wears his youth with casual unkemptness. His hair covers his ears, in need of a good cut, while his jeans and revolving door of frayed nineties band t-shirts are always crumpled.

He hesitates, biting his bottom lip. "You can talk to me if you want to. I'm a pretty good listener."

Snatching a handful of popcorn, I shove it in my mouth to avoid answering.

"Is this about your dad?" he guesses.

"It's nothing. Let's watch the movie."

When the hospital called a couple of hours ago to say that my father was a lot more awake this week and beginning to respond to treatment, I didn't know how to feel.

Relieved. Confused.

But mostly, angry with the world.

After finding a donor match, his surgery has been confirmed for next week. It's the first progress we've had in over a month, but I still feel sick thinking about it.

I know it's only a matter of time before he'll want to speak to me. Sitting in a hospital room with a groggy shade of the man I can't remember is one thing. Facing the past head on is entirely different. I'm not sure if I can handle it yet.

Leighton's eyes are still lasered on me, awaiting an answer.

"Look, I appreciate you… but I don't want to talk. Can we pretend everything is normal? Just for one night?"

His face softens into a grin. "Heck yeah, we can."

"Great."

"But I'm warning you, this movie might make your brain hurt a bit. Be prepared to have your mind blown."

Loading the movie, he slides lower on the sofa and positions his head in my lap instead. I automatically tangle my fingers in his hair, sifting the citrus-scented strands as he munches on handfuls of popcorn.

"What delight am I suffering through tonight?"

Leighton chuckles from my lap. "This is *The Matrix*. Ultimate nineties sci-fi classic. Awesome."

"I had to watch a video to explain the last sci-fi movie we watched together."

"*Interstellar*? How could you possibly be confused by that movie? Wormholes, time travel. Very straightforward stuff."

"I know for a fact you were searching for explainer articles afterwards, and it's not even the first time you've watched it."

"I am a big believer in learning something new every time you watch a movie. Besides, you loved it. We both know you cried your eyes out at the end."

I steal some popcorn from his hand. "As did you."

"I'm fully in touch with my emotions."

"And your tear ducts, apparently."

"Don't tell anyone, please?" He makes big, pleading puppy eyes up at me. "I have a reputation as a hardened criminal to maintain, after all."

"Your secret's safe with me."

Relaxing into the velvet cushions, I let the movie take me to a bleak, faraway land, where our problems pale into insignificance. Leighton has well and truly instilled his love of movies in me.

There's nothing quite like the transformative power of stories to put everything you're worried about into context. My life seems almost normal in comparison, and that's the best feeling. More than anything, I crave normality.

"Hang on, I'm confused."

Leighton peers up at me. "What's up, princess?"

"He was living in an alternate reality for this entire time?"

"Erm. Pretty much."

"Well, who the hell would choose to go to the real world? I'd definitely take the blue pill and go back to the fantasy."

His lips twist in a rueful smile. "Not everyone is a pessimist like you. What if the truth sets you free? Isn't it worth the risk? I'd take the red pill."

"I'm not a pessimist," I grumble back. "Sometimes the truth isn't the blessing people think it is."

"What if I had a pill that would give you all of your missing memories back? Would you take it?"

My hand freezes, buried in his hair.

"I… don't know."

Leighton's fingers wrap around my ankle. "I get it. If I could take a pill to forget my time in prison, I don't know if I'd do it."

"Why?" I ask curiously.

"Well, that shit makes or breaks you. I spent three years inside, and I want it to count for something."

His thumb traces the sliver of bare skin exposed by my yoga pants riding up. I shiver at his light, teasing touch.

"Sorry, Goldilocks," he apologises. "I promised you a normal night. Ignore me thinking about this deep shit."

"Deep shit." I laugh as his hand sneaks higher. "You really do have a way with words sometimes, Leigh."

"Just call me a motherfucking poet."

The hand dancing its way up my leg has landed on my thigh. It's a good distraction. Tingles are zipping over my skin with each touch. I have to fight the urge to squeeze my legs together.

Ditching the bowl of popcorn on the floor, Leighton rolls over until he's facing away from the TV and is able to stare straight at me. The movie is abandoned.

Sliding a hand underneath my loose t-shirt, his fingertips stroke a path over my stomach, reaching the underside of my breasts. His eyes widen when he discovers my lack of a bra.

I flush pink. "Leigh."

"Problem?" he teases. "Since when did you stop wearing bras? I'm not complaining, by the way."

"We're having a movie night. I took it off."

His eyes glint with mischief. "Naughty, naughty."

Dragging his thumb over the peak of my nipple, I can't hold back a low moan of pleasure. Leighton gently pinches the bud before palming my breast in his hand.

"I've made a point of keeping my hands off you, but keep making noises like that, and I can't promise I'll behave."

"You… have?"

"Obviously," he quips back. "Things were pretty fucked up after Northumberland. I figured you needed time."

"Time for what?"

"To figure out what you want."

Gently squeezing my breast, he moves to the next nipple, tweaking it until it hardens into a point. I'm turned on and panicking at the same time. I have no idea what I want.

"Well?" he prompts.

"Did you speak to the other two?"

Leighton smiles lazily. "What if I have?"

His thumb doesn't stop teasing me. Warmth is gathering between my thighs as he continues to play with my nipple.

"Did they tell you to speak to me?"

"Nope," he answers easily.

"But what do you think of our… erm, situation?"

"Is that what we're calling it now?"

"Stop playing around."

"Oh! You mean that you've fooled around with my brother and his best friend, kissed the hell out of me and wrapped Theo around your finger without even touching him?"

I agree with a strangled squeak.

Leighton's smile turns dark. "Well, Goldilocks, my opinion of our *situation* is that it's a mess. You're fucking trouble."

"Trouble?" I breathe.

"The best kind."

Tugging my face closer, he plants a kiss against my mouth. "But I don't mind playing dirty to get what I want. Those assholes better bring their A game if they think they're gonna win this fight."

Dancing lower, his fingers reappear and brush over the seam of my yoga pants, right over my pussy. I'm on the verge of begging him to touch me down there.

"Why does it have to be a fight?"

Leighton hesitates. "Because I've been second best for my entire life. Hunter has taken every accomplishment away from me. He doesn't get you too."

He suddenly sits up and pushes me backwards. I flop across the sectional in a breathless tangle. Leighton swaps positions, pouncing on me in one smooth move.

"Gotcha," he declares.

I'm trapped beneath his grinding hips. He holds my hands over my head, leaving me powerless and at the mercy of his body pinning me to the sofa.

"Is that what you want, baby?" he croons. "You want us to fight over who gets to fuck your sweet cunt first?"

I squirm under him. "I d-don't want anyone to fight."

"You've chosen already?"

"No!"

Lips peppering open-mouthed kisses at the base of my throat, his tongue flicks across my pulse point next.

"Choose me then," he commands.

My hips rise automatically, seeking more friction. Every inch of his stocky, muscled frame is pressing into me.

"I'll walk into HQ and break my brother's legs, if that's what it takes."

"Leigh!" I gasp.

"What? I'm being serious."

The tantalising hardness between his legs pushes into me, right where I want it. My body's instincts have taken over. I'm desperate to feel him everywhere. I need his touch.

He feels huge and powerful on top of me. With the lack of air between us, and so much electricity humming beneath my sensitised skin, I feel alive for the first time since we found that damned chapel and my entire life changed.

"I don't know if you're ready to play this game with me."

"What game?" I stutter.

Tugging the t-shirt over my head, Leighton drops it on the floor next to the bowl of popcorn. His smouldering eyes sweep over every inch of twisted, scarred skin on display.

"I want to fuck that pretty mouth of yours, princess, and watch you choke on my cock. That kind of game."

Lips feathering over the swell of my breasts, he takes a nipple back into his mouth. The light graze of his teeth sends sparks through my whole body as he gently bites down.

"Oh God, Leigh."

"I love it when you say my name," he praises, his tongue flicking across my bud. "I don't want to hold back anymore."

All my inhibitions disappear.

"Then don't."

His forehead collides with my chest. "I also don't want you to get hurt. You know I'd never actually make you choose."

Burying my hands back in his hair, I yank his head up. "Maybe I want to get hurt. Maybe I want to feel something."

Darkness crosses his sweet, rounded features as he slips a hand into my hair. Alarm bells sound when his fingertips coast over the ache of my expanding bald patch.

"Isn't this enough pain for you?"

His question leaves me breathless.

"I don't know what you mean," I divert.

"Don't lie to my face. We all know what's going on here. It's gotten worse since Northumberland."

"I'm f-fine."

"Are you? Really? No bullshit."

Every fibre of my being is screaming at me to run far away from him. I'm so confused. My core is throbbing with need while my mind is desperate to hide the truth from him.

That I can't sleep.

Can't eat.

The pulling is worse than ever.

Guilt is eating me alive every single day, and I don't know how to claw myself out of this hole. Not even Richards can help. This is a living hell of my own making.

"I'm not here to lecture you about how you're choosing to cope, even if I don't like it. We all have secrets, Goldilocks. I have no right to judge yours."

A flicker of hope sears my chest.

"What secrets do you have?"

"Wouldn't you like to know," he replies with a smirk. "Everyone has something to hide. Some more than others."

"What if we agreed to a trade?"

"Trading what?"

I tease his lips with mine. "Secrets."

He deepens the kiss, causing my core to tense. His lips are hard against mine, demanding every breath. Each rock of his hips increases the haze of lust contaminating my mind.

Despite my fear, I want to feel him inside me. I want to be needed. Loved. Devoured. Even if we're all doomed to heartbreak and this mess will never amount to anything good. Right now, I couldn't care less.

"Tell me about your secret," Leighton murmurs. "Why are you hurting yourself?"

"It started by accident," I admit between stolen kisses. "The pain is all I can control right now. It feels good."

"Better than this?" he asks, his cock rubbing against the heat burning between my thighs.

Mouth descending over the slope of my belly, Leighton seizes the waistband of my yoga pants. He pulls them down, exposing the pink lace of my panties and more gnarly scarring across my hips.

"Answer the fucking question."

"No," I moan loudly.

Removing each leg, he chucks them over his shoulder. Warm air kisses my skin, setting off fireworks of excitement. I'm left in nothing but lace and gooseflesh.

"Keep talking," he orders sternly.

When his thumbs hook underneath my panties and ease them off to expose the patch of dark hair over my pussy, I see stars. Months of anticipation are sending me into overdrive.

"Harlow. Words."

"God," I curse as his unshaved stubble teases my inner thighs. "I have to punish myself. It's all I've ever known."

"That's what this is? Punishment?"

My spine arches. "Yes."

Leighton clasps my damp panties in his hand, an eyebrow raised. "You're wet, baby. Maybe you chose me after all."

My cheeks flame hotter than I thought possible. The lacy scrap of cotton lands on top of my discarded yoga pants, leaving me completely naked. There's nowhere to hide.

I'm burning under the weight of his green eyes, searching every exposed, vulnerable inch of me. When he glides the tip of his finger over my mound, I shift my hips up to meet him.

"Please," I whimper.

"Please what? I'm not a mind reader."

My teeth pierce my bottom lip. "Please… touch me."

"Where do you want me to touch you?"

His fingertip vanishes, and a wicked grin slashes across his face. He's loving every second of this torment. My secrets aren't enough for him. Leighton wants my complete and utter submission.

"Here?" He pinches my nipple. "Or here?" His other hand cups my aching pussy, his thumb swirling over my clit.

A groan tears from my lips as he pushes his finger between my folds, coating it in slick moisture. Everywhere he touches erupts into unholy flames.

"Beg me, Harlow."

The circling finger pushes against my slit, breaching the tight opening without entering me fully. I try to move and force him inside me, but I still can't.

"Beg me to touch your pussy and I'll give you exactly what your body is screaming out for. I want to hear it first."

My patience fizzles out.

"Jesus, Leigh."

"Not quite. I said beg."

"Please… stop torturing me."

"Why should I?" He crooks an eyebrow. "How do you think it felt to hear that my brother had his hands on you first? You've been torturing me for months."

"I didn't mean to."

His thumb swipes over my clit again, sending bolts of pleasure up my spine. I bite back a moan that would give him too much satisfaction, but he doesn't let me off that easily.

His finger suddenly thrusts inside me, stretching my pussy. He works the wet digit in and out until he steals the moan from my lips.

"Such a good girl," he whispers. "You're going to beg me to let you come."

I cry out when he pushes another finger deep inside me. The sense of fullness is overwhelming. Hunter and Enzo have touched me like this, but Leighton's filthy mouth and need for control add a whole other layer of excitement.

On the verge of exploding into spectacular pieces, Leighton quickly pulls his hand from between my thighs. The building release that was on the cusp of taking over fizzles out.

"I told you to beg," he growls.

Hanging over me, his shaggy hair falling across his forest-green eyes, he looks like Lucifer himself in human flesh. Leighton could be a fallen angel, swooping down to earth to claim the unsuspecting souls of sinners.

I'd like to be sacrificed.

I'll beg at his altar.

Anything to be adored by him.

"Please let me come, Leigh," I plead through the choking hand of embarrassment.

"My name sounds so good on your tongue." His eyes darken. "I'm going to fuck your pretty mouth next."

Sliding back inside me, he thrusts his fingers in a fast-paced rhythm, guiding me back to the edge of an orgasm. I fist his t-shirt as my release finally crests.

"Let go. Show me how well you fall apart."

It hits me hard and fast. One more swipe of my clit, and he's stolen the keys that unlock something buried deep inside. Hips bucking, I let the wave of sensation wash over me.

"Perfect," Leighton praises.

Floating in the aftermath, the clink of his unfastened belt startles me back into the room. Peeking through my lashes, I watch as he reaches into his jeans and pulls out his thick shaft.

It's the first time I've seen a man like this. I haven't even touched Hunter or Enzo. He will be the first. But I want to explore. I'm no longer afraid, not now that they've taken the time to build my trust.

Leighton grips his length, pulling it from his boxers. "It's your turn now, baby. I'm all yours."

I lick my lips. "Tell me what to do."

Settling back on the sofa while the movie still plays in the background, Leighton pushes his jeans down his hips. I study his erection—long, veined and glinting with something round and silver through the velvety tip.

"Ever seen a pierced cock before?"

I can barely form words.

"Um, I didn't know you could do that."

Leighton laughs under his breath. "It was a drunken impulse when I got out of prison."

"Did it hurt?"

"It didn't tickle, princess. Come here."

I take a deep breath for courage and crawl closer on my hands and knees. I'm still naked, but we're alone in the house and he's already seen me. I don't need to hide anything.

Opening his legs, Leighton gives me space to settle between them. My fingers tremble as I reach out to touch his shaft. It feels strange in my hands, like a warm length of steel. Pumping his length, I love the way his eyes flutter shut.

His head hits the overstuffed cushion behind him as air hisses out from between his teeth. Gently squeezing again, I stroke my hand up and down, getting the hang of it.

"What should I do next?"

"Suck my cock. I'm going to ride your perfect mouth."

His demands make me wet all over again. I feel excited just touching him like this, wielding power I never imagined being able to possess. He's at my mercy for once.

"Then tell me your secrets," I order him. "We agreed, fair and square. You need to keep your end of the bargain."

"What do you want to know?"

"Tell me how you ended up in prison."

With a breath for courage, I duck down and take his cock into my mouth. He groans under his breath, fisting a hand in my long mane of hair to hold it out of my face.

"I hurt somebody," he grinds out. "It was one stupid, angry mistake that ruined my whole life. I'll regret it forever."

His shaft slides against my tongue, nudging the back of my throat. It takes some getting used to. The coldness of his metal piercing feels weird at first, but as I circle my tongue around it, Leighton groans in delight.

"Fucking hell," he curses. "I was dating someone for several years. It was going well. We were serious. I even thought about… you know, proposing."

Encouraging him to keep going, I tighten my lips, bobbing up and down while wrapping my hand around the base of his length.

"Something didn't sit right, though I couldn't figure out what. Then, I came home one night and found them together. My best friend was fucking my girl."

Feeling braver as Leighton bares his soul, I slide a hand down his ropey, muscled thigh, reaching around to cup the softness of his balls. He makes a guttural sound when I give them a gentle, curious squeeze.

"Jesus, princess. You're killing me here."

I stop for a breath. "Finish the story."

His grip on my hair tightens as his hand balls into a fist. "I lost it. Got into a fight with the bastard. I'd been drinking, which didn't help, and things got out of control."

Wrapping my lips back around his cock, I move a little faster, teasing the truth from him. Part of me doesn't want to believe that my sweet, lighthearted Leighton could hurt someone. I need to know what he's hiding from me.

"I was punching him, over and over," he says around a moan. "I couldn't think straight. We'd been friends since we were five years old, and he betrayed me."

His hips thrust upwards to feed his dick into my mouth. The tip nudges my throat. It takes a moment for me to adjust, then I suck deeper, loving the intensity of it.

"I smashed him into the wall at the wrong angle," Leighton grunts out. "He broke three vertebrae. Wheelchair-bound for the rest of his damn life, and it's my fault."

There it is. The twisted secret that I've seen festering inside of him. Leighton's original wound. It makes sense now; the broken state he was in after what happened with Diablo. His actions got someone else hurt.

We're not so different.

He knows what guilt tastes like.

"Keep going and I'm going to come in your mouth."

I pause for another breath. "You can do that?"

"Sometimes, I can't take how fucking innocent you are. Keep going if you want to see."

Nodding, I retake his sheath in my mouth and tilt my head to suck him deeper. My eyes burn with the pressure of each upwards thrust from his hips. I kinda like it though.

This is exhilarating, exploring something I've always associated with darkness and sin. Each jerk of his cock in my mouth feels like its own liberation. I'm flying free from my shackles and retaking my sexuality on my own terms. It's a sick thought to have, but a twisted part of me wishes Pastor Michaels could see what's become of his prisoner.

"So perfect," Leighton purrs as he strokes my hair. "Not so innocent now, are you?"

His muscles are tensing beneath my touch. The movement of his hips increases in time to my sucking, causing stray moisture to slip from the corners of my eyes. His pierced hardness is on the verge of making me gag, but I hold it in.

I love how rough he's being with me. I'm just a normal girl, experiencing a first. It's everything I've been looking for since I escaped. I've craved the tantalising glimmer of another life.

"I'm coming. Move if you want."

Gripping the base of his dick, I stay put. I'm too curious for my own good. He bellows loudly, his length spasming against my tongue. I gasp as hot fluid shoots into my mouth.

Leighton pours himself into me, his come bursting with an odd, salty flavour that I can't describe. I hold my position until his hips still, and his seed slides down my throat.

Releasing him to wipe off my mouth, I look up into his eyes and swallow every drop. He watches the show with wild eyes.

"Fuck me, Harlow. That was…"

"Bad?" I worry aloud.

His knuckles stroke against my cheek. "I was going to say hot. You didn't have to swallow, baby."

I shrug with a satisfied smile. "I was curious."

"I can see that. You're full of surprises."

Sitting back on folded legs, I watch him tuck his cock into his boxers and pull his jeans into place. I suddenly feel bare, my body still quaking with aftershocks and nerves.

"Can you pass my t-shirt?"

Leighton grabs it from off the floor. "Here."

"Thanks."

Quickly pulling it on to cover my chest, I fumble around for my panties. A cold voice lashes us both before I can slide them back on to cover my naked bottom half.

"Did I miss the party?"

We both freeze. I can't bear to look over my shoulder. I know who it is. Hunter's presence would startle even a blind man. He's the electric buzz in the air as a thunderstorm sweeps in.

Leighton doesn't bat an eye. "Sorry, bro. Wasn't expecting you until later on."

"No doubt," Hunter thunders. "For the record, this isn't the worst thing I've walked in on you doing. I didn't expect to find you fooling around with my girl, though."

The entire humiliating debacle falls away as my world narrows to those two unfathomable words.

My.

Girl.

I wish it didn't give me an ill-timed thrill to hear the violent note of possession in Hunter's voice, even while I'm semi-naked and straddling his younger sibling. Not to mention the come still staining my throat.

"*Our* girl didn't last long then," Leighton accuses.

"You lost the right to call her that when your stupidity almost cost Harlow her life."

"You never had any intention of letting the rest of us have a chance with her," he argues back. "You're a selfish dick."

"Do you want to join Diablo's dismembered corpse at the bottom of the river? Because that can totally be arranged."

Praying for the ground to swallow me up, I clamber off Leighton while doing my best to pull the t-shirt down to cover my bare behind. By accident, I briefly meet Hunter's eyes. The hurt I find there leaves me gutted.

Anger is twisting his features into a familiar mask that I thought I'd seen the last of. But beneath that, there's something else—the green-eyed monster rearing its ugly head. He's actually jealous.

I shove my legs through my panties as fast as possible, snatching up my yoga pants in another breath. When I attempt to dart past Hunter to escape the embarrassment, he clamps down on my arm.

"Been busy, sweetheart?" he asks throatily.

"Um, no. Just hanging out."

"I warned you before about lying to me. If you want a war, I'll happily give you one. Don't think I won't burn this house down to walk away with you."

A terrified chill settles over me.

"You don't mean that."

Hunter licks his parted lips. "Don't I?"

Yanking my arm from his bruising grasp, I take a big step backwards. His jaw sets into a hard line as he folds his arms, biceps straining against his white dress shirt. Dark, intricate tattoos bleed through the material, begging to be licked and explored.

I'm losing my mind. They're pushing me over the edge and waiting to see which way I'll fall. I need to get out of here.

Still clutching my remaining clothing, I flee upstairs as fast as my legs will carry me. I can hear their voices bickering with each ashamed step I take.

Bedroom door slammed shut behind me, I collapse on the bed in a boneless, flustered slump. I'm picking up my phone and tapping out a desperate text message in a heartbeat.

> Harlow: Hey, Brooke. You around? I could use a place to stay for a few days.

Her response comes fast.

> Brooklyn: I've got you. These twats are driving me insane too. Pick you up in ten minutes.

My head hits the soft pillow.

Now, I have to convince Hunter to let me leave.

CHAPTER 6
HARLOW

NO MORE HIDING – GINA BROOKLYN

"HARLOW."

Someone is roughly shaking me awake, their fingertips digging into my arms. I grunt and pull the blanket closer to my chest. I'm comfortable. It isn't time to wake up yet.

"Wake up. He's coming."

"No," I complain sleepily. "Leave… alone."

"You need to get up."

Suddenly, the scents of blood and mould seep into my lungs. My comfort vanishes. I'm freezing cold. Wet. Aching. The basement steals every ounce of warmth from my body as my eyes fling open in a rush of fear.

"You have to kneel. Come on."

Kiera's whispered voice filters through my half-awake brain. I startle upright in the dark, and a smooth object in my hand hits the floor. Light cuts the suffocating darkness of the room as my phone screen illuminates.

I take an unsteady breath.

This isn't the basement.

There's nobody else here.

I'm surrounded by two huge brown-leather sofas framing a massive television. Clutter is scattered around the room, and the walls are filled with framed photographs of someone else's family.

Brooklyn's house.

I'm still here.

Shining my phone around the room, I search for the person who startled me awake. Kiera's gone. Slinked back to her grave, festering at the back of my mind. I'm alone here.

The quilt and pillow that Brooklyn gave me to sleep on the sofa with are damp with sweat. Scrubbing my hands over my face, I make myself take a deep breath.

This is getting ridiculous now. My sleep schedule is so messed up. I need to learn how to sleep alone, without one of the guys there to hold my hand like I'm a child.

The guys.

I miss them so much.

Pain spears me in the chest. I've been staying here for a few days, spending time with Brooklyn and her family while hiding from my problems. The break came at the perfect time as I was on the verge of going insane back there.

The sound of glass shattering from somewhere else in the two-story townhouse causes shards of fear to slice into me. I'm not convinced it isn't in my head like everything else.

"Breathe," I tell myself. "You're in control."

He's a monster, Harlow.

I always knew there was evil in him.

Her voice returns, whispering through my consciousness. I still have one hand in the dream-world. Kiera's playground. She comes to me in fragments—choppy memories, broken flashes, the slow patter of drip-fed information.

You're going to be okay now.

I have a plan to get us out.

One of many failed plans. Kiera was the first to offer me that hopeless promise as a lifeline. However she knew Pastor Michaels, it didn't stop him from terrifying her. In that basement, she unmasked the evil that she'd suspected.

And he killed her for it.

Blow after skull-crushing blow.

Grabbing the woolly pink sweater that I left balled up on the carpet, I throw it over Leighton's t-shirt and my grey sweats. The house is silent around me as I stand up and quietly creep from the room.

Brooklyn shares this generous-sized home with five loud, boisterous men, but it doesn't feel cramped. The house rivals Hunter's in size. It has a smaller garden and kitchen, but an extra bedroom upstairs to accommodate everyone.

Unlike the clean lines, steel accents and polished floorboards of Hunter's modernised, Victorian-style mansion, this is comfortably informal.

The walls are clustered with hilarious photographs from Brooklyn and her family's European adventures, and the personality of each inhabitant is reflected in the little touches dotted throughout every room.

Hudson has a very impressive whiskey collection. Kade leaves discarded silk ties everywhere. Brooklyn has a stack of vinyl records, gifted from an old friend. Those brightly coloured discs I'm particularly jealous of.

Eli has a tiny library tucked under the spiral staircase, brimming with enough books to rival Theo's collection. On another shelf, Phoenix's vast array of video games are safely stored. Even their stuff is close together, like them.

Finally, Jude has a quiet office, tucked away from them all at the back of the house. He disappears in there a lot when his eyes cloud over and his face darkens. Sometimes for hours at a time. The others don't seem to mind though.

Following the sound of cursing and glass being swept up, I find the door to Jude's office cracked open. He's kneeling on the patterned rug, cleaning up the remains of a photo frame.

I hesitate, deciding to turn back and give him some privacy, but his caramel eyes land on me through the open door. He has scarily sharp hearing.

"I… heard a noise," I say lamely.

He pushes the door open further. "You're allowed to walk around, Harlow. I heard you wake up anyway."

"Your hearing is kinda scary."

Jude picks glass from his rug. "So I've heard."

"Are you okay?"

He freezes, his intelligent eyes downturned to avoid mine. With a closely cropped headful of brown hair, a thin but even nose and strong, prominent features, Jude is handsome in a wholesome way that contrasts the person I know lies within.

When you take a closer look, that illusion dissipates. His whole body, while toned from an obsessive exercise regimen, is littered with scars. We have that in common. Some are nastier than others, mottling his skin into a macabre sight.

As he picks up the last shards of broken glass, the stump where his right hand belongs is propping him up. It doesn't seem to hurt him. The skin is smooth and taut, healed with the passing of time.

"Jude?" I ask again.

His gaze snaps up to me. "Sorry, zoned out. I'm okay, just couldn't sleep. You know how it is."

I slip inside his office, hugging myself tight. "Yeah, I know. Do you want to talk about it?"

"You don't need to be there for me, as much as I appreciate the offer. You've got enough on your plate."

"You were there for me before."

Jude waves it off. "You needed a friend."

In the weeks after our close encounter with Pastor Michaels' brutality, I struggled to anchor myself to the present. Richards says that my episodes of dissociation are a defence mechanism. The frantic paddle of a mind drowning, overwhelmed by a frightening world.

Jude came around to introduce himself soon after. He seemed to know about the war inside my head without me having to explain. His reassurance that the world would come back when it was ready was enough to calm me.

Sure enough, the numb prison I was stuck in for countless blurred days slowly released its grip on my sanity. I came back to myself, bit by bit. It just took some time to remember that I was safe and free. Unlike the remains of Laura's corpse.

"I'd like to be a friend for you too," I offer him. "Or just tell me to go away, if you'd rather talk to someone else."

"I don't like worrying them."

"Brooklyn and the others?"

He nods. "They've spent the best part of a decade worrying about me. Especially Brooke."

"It bothers me that the guys have to worry so much about me too. They tell me off for not talking to them."

"But it's easier not to," he supplies.

"Exactly. Simpler for everyone."

Jude scrubs a hand over his drawn face. "Don't make my mistake. Keeping everything inside isn't healthy."

"You should take your own advice, doc."

Chuckling, he dumps the smashed glass into the small bin under his desk. "I guess I deserve that."

"Richards would be disappointed. He still talks about you as his star patient."

"Great. I love everyone knowing my business."

"He didn't tell me anything else," I rush to explain. "It's just that we've been through similar stuff, I think."

His caramel eyes fix on me, studying the goosebumps across my arms. "You're shaking. What happened?"

"Nothing."

Sighing, Jude climbs to his feet. "Do you like ice cream?"

"Uh, what?"

His mouth hooks up. "I know where Eli keeps his secret stash. He thinks we don't know about it."

Leading the way, Jude pads towards the kitchen with bare feet. I quickly glance around and spot the photo torn from the broken frame he tossed in the bin.

My heart stops.

I know that person.

A pretty, smiling face stares back at me from his desk. It's Alyssa. She's standing next to a younger-looking Jude in a graduation cap and gown. The contrast to the version of him I know is stark. I had no idea he knew her.

"Harlow," he beckons.

"I'm coming."

Closing the door behind me, I follow Jude into the kitchen. He keeps the overhead lights off, and I don't mind. Like me, he's accustomed to darkness. Jude steps into it like he's arriving home, svelte and at ease in the familiarity of shadows.

I take a seat at the huge glass table. This is where they gather each night. Unlike Hunter and the others, Brooklyn's family prides being together above all else.

They love each other with such ferocity, even as they throw food or threaten death for stealing the last slice of garlic bread. I've loved being here for that reason.

Taking a seat, I accept the spoon Jude hands me, a tub of ice cream tucked under his arm. We sit next to each other, and he lets me take the first bite before I pass the tub back. Salted caramel gooeyness melts on my tongue.

"This is good ice cream."

"That's why Eli hides it," he answers as he licks the spoon. "Since he was promoted to head lecturer at King's College, he has to mark all these papers. Hence the need for ice cream."

"Doesn't he enjoy teaching?"

"I'd imagine teaching a roomful of know-it-alls can't be much fun. Eli loves to learn, but dealing with people on a daily basis? Not so much."

"He's a quiet person," I observe.

"But a hell of a lot chattier than he used to be. Trust me."

Passing the ice cream back to me, I take another spoonful. Like Eli, Jude is a confusingly complex person to be around. While he's calm and soothing in a way that only someone who has experienced trauma can be, there's darkness festering in him.

If you look closely, you can see it. Hidden in the tiniest glimpses. His sharp hearing. Fast reflexes. Flashes of bad temper. It's the same darkness that sparkles in Brooklyn's silver-grey eyes.

When I look in the mirror, I see it staring back at me in my reflection too. We're all walking around with madness in our veins—a sickness that, unlike most, is entirely incurable.

Instead, we have to live with the pain that was inflicted by a force beyond our control. Being broken by someone else is fixable with enough time and care. The self-destruction that follows when you miss the familiarity of that pain is far harder to treat.

"What was it this time?" Jude asks quietly.

I swallow my mouthful. "I'm fine."

"You really don't need to bullshit me like you do everyone else. I've been in the game long enough. Nothing you say will go any further. Not even to Hunter or his team."

Placing the ice cream down, I let myself droop. "It's her again. She finds me every single night."

"Kiera?" he guesses.

"Yeah. I'm taking those pills that Richards prescribed me. It hasn't helped. I still wake up screaming."

"Medication doesn't get rid of the shit in our heads." He places his spoon down, now licked clean. "It isn't that easy."

"Clearly not."

"What does Kiera say to you?"

"Mostly, she's warning me. There are bits of memories coming back. We're in the basement, and she's trying to protect me from him."

"Do you remember anything else about her?" he quizzes.

"Not really. Only flashes. I've gone over the memories a thousand times with Richards, but we've hit a brick wall."

"Perhaps you could try a different way."

I send him a puzzled look. "Like what?"

Smoothing the t-shirt he's wearing over loose-fitting sweats, Jude stands back up. "I'll show you what worked for me."

I follow him back to his office, our midnight snack returned to Eli's hiding place in the freezer. Jude flicks the lamp on, lighting the sparse, obsessively organised space.

It almost resembles a prison cell, but with a luxurious rug and a set of blue armchairs. Part of me thinks that's deliberate. Material possessions mean nothing to Jude. Like me, he's lived with nothing for long enough to lose that desire.

Clicking the door shut, he gestures for me to take a seat in an armchair. I sink into the comfortable cushion.

"When I first went into treatment with Richards, I could only remember snippets of who I was before what happened to me. Flashes, here and there."

I know a little of the group's colourful past. Enough to understand why their bond is so unique and indestructible.

"Can I ask you a personal question?"

"Sure," he obliges.

"How long were you held prisoner for?"

Jude leans against the desk. "Seven years, give or take. But it wasn't me who was held captive and tortured. My mind locked the real me away. That's how I survived."

Unlocking a drawer in his dark-wood desk, he begins to pull out a stack of slim, leather-bound journals. Stacking them up one by one, there's seven in total. Jude gestures to them.

"One for each year that I was held. Afterwards, I spent three years at an inpatient facility, piecing myself back together with Richards' help."

"And it worked?"

"Mostly," he answers with a thin smile. "I spent years working through the fragments. Writing everything down helped me to document my life. It's how I regained control."

Reaching back into the desk drawer, he pulls out another journal. This one isn't bent and worn, bound in supple, dark-red leather. I hesitate as he offers it to me.

"For you."

Tentatively accepting the gift, I turn it over in my hands. Jude packs his journals away and locks the drawer again.

"Kiera can't give you the answers you're looking for," he says while cleaning up. "She isn't real."

Stupid tears rise to my eyes. "I know."

"Only you can find your own truth. It's up here." He taps his temple. "Waiting for you to find your way back."

Thumbing through the blank journal, I wrestle with my fear. For months, I've wanted nothing more than to uncover my past and use it to forge a new future.

But Leighton was right when he called me a pessimist. I'm afraid of what I'll find when I start digging, looking for answers. Or more accurately, *who* I'll find.

"Thank you." I hold the journal to my chest. "It helps just knowing that someone else has been through this too."

"Of course. Any friend of Brooklyn's is a friend of mine." His eyes flick back to the broken frame in his bin. "We have to look out for each other."

I bite my lip. "How did you know her?"

"Hmm?" he replies absently.

"Alyssa."

Her name startles Jude, and his head slumps, falling into his single hand. "She was my sister."

"Wait, really?"

"We were separated for years and… well, I forgot about her. By the time we reunited, it was too late. The damage was done. She died before I could fix things."

"I had no idea."

"Nobody talks about her much."

Fiddling with my sweater sleeve, I battle a wave of curiosity. Jude could give me every last detail about the mysterious woman who came before me. I've been desperate to know more since the beginning, but too afraid to ask.

"They were dating her? Hunter, Enzo and Theo?"

His eyes flick over me. "Yeah, the four of them were in a relationship for a long time."

"Like you guys are with Brooklyn? How does it work?"

Jude smothers a smile. "I'm probably not the best person to ask about how this stuff works. I was a latecomer."

Feeling embarrassed, I glance out of the small window to study the dark night. Jude clears his throat.

"If it helps, I found it hard."

"The sharing?"

He shrugs it off. "We made it work eventually."

"Did you ask her to choose?"

"None of us were willing to lose her."

It seems so perfect—a family of choice with no one left out. I know that's what Enzo wants for us, even if Hunter is adamant that it will never happen. I don't know where that leaves me.

I'm not good enough for all of them. They deserve more than me, especially after losing Alyssa. I want them to be happy, and I'll never be able to give them that.

Footsteps pad down the staircase above us, interrupting our conversation. We fall silent until the office door creaks open. A mop of messy raven hair, numerous black facial piercings and arctic-blue eyes peek around the door.

"Thought I heard voices," Hudson greets.

I wave from the armchair. "Sorry. Only us."

"It's two o'clock in the morning."

"Come and join the sleepless club," Jude jokes.

Yawning loudly, Hudson slinks into the room. I watch, slightly fascinated, as he swoops down and smacks his lips against Jude's mouth while gripping the back of his neck.

Quickly looking away, I give them a private moment as they share a kiss. I'm not attracted to them or anything. I just find their dynamic fascinating as a whole group.

Hudson straightens. "Sorry, Harlow."

"No w-worries," I stammer.

He tangles Jude's hand in his. "Come back to bed. It's Eli and Phoenix's night with Brooklyn, so my room is empty."

"I came down because I couldn't sleep," Jude explains hastily. "You go back up. We're fine here."

Hudson glances between us. "Since we're all awake… let's have some fun. I'm off work tomorrow, so no early start."

I'm not entirely sure how we end up spreadeagled across the thick carpet of the den, a pack of cards and a bowl of leftover Christmas sweets laid out between us.

"You got the rules?" Hudson asks me.

Filtering through my hand of cards, I begin to arrange the numbers. "I think so. Can I watch you guys play first?"

"No problem."

Jude lowers his voice. "Watch him, Harlow. He likes to cheat and will lie his ass off to pretend otherwise."

"Hey, dick." Hudson throws a handful of wrapped toffee pennies at his head. "It's not my fault that you lost the last game we played and had to pay the bar tab."

"This is exactly why we need Brooklyn to come as a chaperone on our date nights."

"We do not need a chaperone."

"I disagree. You're too competitive for your own good."

"Am not," Hudson disputes.

Picking up their sets of cards, they play the first round of Rummy. It's hard to wrap my head around the rules at first, but it soon starts to make sense. The winner has to match two groups of four and three cards, either consecutive or across the different suits.

"Too slow," Jude boasts as he lays his cards down. "Give it up."

"Goddammit. How do you do that?"

"By not being a moron."

Hudson tosses his cards. "Motherfucker."

"Alright, Harlow. You're up. Stakes?"

Taking a chocolate finger and a toffee penny, I place them down in the middle. "Here's mine."

Jude reciprocates and awkwardly shuffles the cards with his good hand before dealing them back out. Still grumbling about losing, Hudson accepts them and adds his own sweets to the pile in the middle.

"I'm going to win this time," he announces.

Jude snorts. "Good luck with that."

"Shut up and play."

We take it in turns to pick up a card and swap it out for another, looking for the magical combination. Hudson curses with each new card that he selects. His hand isn't going well.

I can see the combinations surprisingly easily. The numbers click into place in my head as I rearrange the cards I have into a pattern. My trick is to imagine the numbers as I used to when measuring time in the confines of my cage.

One bowl of food.

Two lashes of the whip.

Three punches.

Four broken ribs.

"Got it," I declare, laying down my cards.

Both men blink at me.

"One, Two, Three and Four of Hearts."

Hudson's mouth clicks open. "Huh?"

"Are you just going to stare at me?" I raise an eyebrow.

Jude recovers the quickest. "That was like, thirty seconds into the round. I can't believe it."

"Beginner's luck." Hudson narrows his eyes.

After collecting my sugary winnings, I watch him shuffle the cards and deal them out again. My hand isn't so good this time. We begin taking it in turns to pick up and drop a card, going several rotations with no breakthrough.

"You need an Ace of Spades."

All three of us startle at the new voice. Standing behind the sofa, an ice cream tub in hand, Eli studies Hudson's cards over his shoulder. His brown curls are wild and pointing in all directions, framing vivid green eyes and a contrite smile.

"Thanks for ruining my strategy," Hudson snarls as he tosses the cards down. "You did that on purpose."

Eli snickers. "Maybe. It was fun though."

A heaping of ice cream disappears into his mouth as he collapses onto the nearest sofa. He grins at me before offering the tub.

"Midnight snack?"

I decline with a head shake. "We already stole some."

Eli glowers at Jude. "Do I seriously have to find a new hiding spot? You ate all of my Ben and Jerry's last week."

"It was an emergency," he defends. "What are you doing up anyway?"

He shrugs while eating. "Phoenix is snoring his head off and Brooklyn stole all of the covers again."

"We bought that pillow for him," Hudson complains. "The whole goddamn house vibrates with his snoring."

"It's in his room, not hers."

"That's helpful."

"Not really." Eli snorts. "But that's Phoenix for you. I decided to leave them to it and come downstairs instead."

Going for a fresh round, we quickly reach a stalemate. I abandon my strategy and switch up the suits, aiming for another matching pair. Eli is watching us as he munches.

The next card I pick up is a Seven of Clubs. Perfect. I can see my plan forming. Five beatings, six shattered noses and seven hours of screaming. All I need is an eight.

"Stupid game," Hudson says under his breath.

"You really don't like losing, do you?" I laugh.

"I lived with Kade after I was adopted by his folks. Imagine competing with that asshole."

"I'll pass on that fun," Jude comments.

"Not like there was much competition," Hudson continues with a scoff. "Even now, he's still pissed I found this house first and closed the deal before he could."

"The house he wanted was twice this size," Eli adds.

"Are you complaining about my purchase?"

He licks the last smears of ice cream from his spoon. "You think I give a shit about that? This place is too big as it is."

"Some of us like space and don't sleep on top of Phoenix every night like some kind of sloth." Jude lays down his cards with a grin. "Game's up. I win."

"Fuck!" Hudson bellows.

Jude smacks him around the head, telling him to be quiet. He really hates losing. Agreeing to a truce, they seal the peace agreement with another kiss.

"What should we play now?" I ask around a yawn.

Eli sets his spoon down. "I've got a game."

Surrendering the cards to him, Jude shuffles so Eli can take a seat next to us on the floor. He stops by the adjacent sofa, grabbing the knitted blanket from the back and wrapping it around my shoulders without a word.

My chest burns. "Thanks, Eli."

"No problem," he replies. "It's cold in here. Kade's in charge of the thermostat, and he's a hot bod."

"Someone really needs to steal that remote from him," Jude suggests. "I'd rather be too hot than too cold."

"Leave it with me." Hudson grins evilly. "I'll get it back."

"You promised Brooke that you'd stop winding Kade up," Eli responds. "Especially after you hid his car keys for a month."

"Well, now I'll hide the remote for a month instead." Hudson rubs his hands together. "Problem solved."

Several rounds into the next game, things have gotten serious. Turns out, Eli is a whole league above us and consistently beats all three of us at every game that Hudson suggests. I reckon his brain could rival Theo's any day.

While they shuffle cards and argue about the last result, I excuse myself to grab some water from the kitchen and check my phone in private since I heard it buzzing.

It's nearly four o'clock in the morning, but there's a series of text messages waiting in my group chat with the guys that we recently set up. Nobody is asleep right now.

Leigh: I miss you, Goldilocks.

Enzo: Your fault she left, dickhead.

Leigh: Aren't you supposed to be getting your beauty sleep?

Enzo: I'm not fucking Cinderella.

Hunter: Shut up, the pair of you. Harlow, please come home. Let's talk.

Theo: Some of us are still in the office working. Give it a bloody rest, will you?

Pain wrings every last drop of annoyance from my heart. It's only been a few days, but I hate the distance between us.

Harlow: Miss you guys too. I just needed a break.

It doesn't take long for the responses to come.

Enzo: Why are you awake? What's wrong?

Hunter: Are you okay?

Harlow: Same reason you're all up.

Leigh: I'm sorry, princess.

Hunter: We're here when you're ready to talk.

Enzo: Say the word and I'll pick you up.

My phone vibrates with a separate text message from Theo in our own private chat. We usually only talk about books, but lately, things have felt different between us.

Theo: Ignore them. Take the time you need.

Harlow: Still sure you don't hate me?

Theo: Not a chance. Sleep tight, beautiful.

I crash my forehead against the fridge. My blossoming feelings for Theo only complicate this mess further. He's become a good friend, and sometimes, I catch myself wanting more. I can't keep up with my own emotions.

We keep going around in circles and it's exhausting. The guys are determined to protect me from the world. I love and appreciate their care, but they don't seem to realise I also need protection from them.

CHAPTER 7
ENZO

FOOL & THE THIEF – THE HARA

MY FOREHEAD COLLIDES with the office wall. I pray that when I open my eyes, I'll be back at home and curled up in bed with Harlow, her sweet body tucked into the crook of my arm.

Instead, I'm stuck in this hellhole. We're running on two hours of sleep, and I am on the verge of losing my shit. Hunter is in another board meeting with the superintendent, getting a thorough spanking for our lack of results.

We're losing steam.

This case is beating us.

"Knock some sense into yourself?" Theo laughs.

"Do you ever wish you could pack up your entire life, jump on a plane and disappear to some foreign island?"

His eyes are glued to a screen full of complex computer code. "Only five thousand times a day. Usually when Hunter is chewing my ear off."

With a sigh, I stomp back over to the black-leather sofa in the corner of his untidy office. Unlike our semi-neurotic overlord, who demands tidiness in every corner of his office, Theo thrives on disorganisation.

How his super-powered brain functions in such a mess, I'll never know. He lives in a perpetual state of chaos, and it doesn't seem to bother him one bit.

Pulling out my phone, I log in to Sabre's secure server and pull up our bespoke tracking program. Harlow doesn't know it, but we added her phone to our list of tracked individuals the day she unwrapped it.

I have no doubt that she'd hate the fact we have constant surveillance of her, twenty-four hours a day. None of us even batted an eye about invading her privacy in such a way.

"She's still with Brooklyn." I toss my phone aside. "We agreed to a few nights. What the hell is she still doing there?"

"Painting Brooke's toenails?" Theo suggests absently. "Having pillow fights in their frilly underwear? Having afternoon tea and discussing eligible bachelors for courting?"

Grabbing the nearest book laying discarded, I curve it through the air, watching with satisfaction as it hits the back of his head. Theo yelps, spinning in his chair to glare at me.

"You've been watching too much *Bridgerton*."

Theo snorts in derision. "Like I have the time. I spend every second of the day on this investigation while you two sit around worrying about Harlow."

I stretch my legs out. "She asked for a break. Hunter gave it to her. That was a week ago. I can't focus knowing she isn't safe at home, protected by an army of agents."

Theo flashes through several programs on his laptop. "Harlow's an adult. She can make her own decisions."

"Her safety isn't a decision. It's non-negotiable."

He rolls his eyes. "She's hanging out with Hudson, the man who salivates over removing people's tongues. He makes you look like a fluffy teddy bear."

"I am not a fluffy fucking teddy bear."

"My point is that she's safe. Focus, we have work to do tonight."

Dragging my sore body upright, I contemplate the huge stacks of paperwork on his mug-clustered coffee table. Since Reagan's interview, we've followed up on the names she was able to provide.

Two members of the church's congregation are refusing to be interviewed. They were cagey and extremely evasive over the phone and reserved their right to remain silent.

No explanation given.

More good news for us.

I think not.

On the plus side, Frederick Houghton, the village busybody, was more than willing to be interviewed. At the ripe old age of eighty-five, he's too frail to travel down to London. Hunter and I will drive to Newcastle next week to take his statement.

During difficult cases, I sometimes get this feeling. My blood boils and I can't focus on anything but chasing down that lead until it reveals its secrets.

Some might call it a gut instinct, honed after years in this messy business. I see it more as a bleak belief that humans will always fulfil your worst expectation of them.

We're circling something big.

I can taste it in the air.

"You get anything on Rosetta Stone from that contact of yours?" I flick through paperwork half-heartedly.

"I'm waiting for him to do a search. All government records are gone, but sometimes hard copies were kept in storage. They could have missed some."

"Sounds like a long shot."

He takes several gulps of coffee. "All we have are long shots. It only takes one to make a difference though. We need to know more about that children's home."

"Mrs Michaels is dead. Why does it matter?"

Theo pauses, and I know he's up to no good. Hunter likes to think that he's the pioneer of this operation, but Sabre runs off a high-powered steam engine that works quietly behind the scenes. Namely, Theo's obnoxiously large brain.

"I have a theory," he says hesitantly.

Dumping the paperwork, I crack my neck. "Go on then. Entertain me, Sherlock."

"What if Rosetta met Pastor Michaels there?"

My head snaps back up so I can stare at him. He's turned in his office chair, a lukewarm coffee clasped in his hands.

"What makes you think that?"

"Why not?" he counters.

"Well, there's no evidence."

"So what?" Theo cocks an eyebrow. "They had to meet somewhere. Rosetta disappeared for a reason."

"Because she lived in an abusive shitshow?"

"And vanished into thin air," he finishes. "Pastor Michaels is a ghost. We've got nothing on either of them. What if his files were erased along with Rosetta's during the cleanup?"

My mind whirrs with possibilities. We've been banging our heads against the wall for too long. Perhaps this is why. The trail we need to follow has been conveniently wiped.

"What motivates a killer to kill?"

Theo stares at me. "You want me to sit and list the reasons? We'll be here all day."

"Humour me. We've been working on the assumption that Pastor Michaels is a religious fanatic, punishing sex workers for what he categorises as a sin."

"He's an unhinged religious extremist," he points out.

"Yes, who butchers innocent women for pleasure."

"We already know this, Enz."

"But why? Where did this impulse come from?"

Theo rubs a spot between his brows. "I'm too fucking sleep deprived for this conversation."

"This was your theory, dumbass. All this time, we've been looking at the victims, searching for a connection. We never stopped to consider whether Pastor Michaels had family."

"Or… whether he started killing because of them."

"If Rosetta came from this place, maybe her future phoney husband did too. He learnt his violence from somewhere."

He nods in agreement. "We need proof."

"You reckon your contact will find anything?"

"I think we need a back-up plan. The government has gotten good at covering its tracks over the years."

"Don't we know it," I mutter.

Falling silent, we wrack our brains. All we need is a smoking gun. These children's homes were a dirty secret for a very long time.

They took public funding and used it to exploit the charges under their care. When the truth was exposed, the government took every precaution to bury it.

"Hunter and Leighton's dad," Theo exclaims.

"You want to call Ben in?"

"He ran the local police department for twenty-five years. If anyone knows where to start with this, it's him."

My heart sinks. "You know that breaks Hunter's rules. We agreed never to involve our families. It's too risky."

"Fuck the rules."

"He'll crucify us both."

Theo shoots me an impatient look. "This business *is* our family, Enz. We have to do whatever it takes to end this."

Pacing his littered floorspace, I wrestle with our options. Locating Rosetta's lost identity was a strike of luck that fell into our laps when we needed it most.

It's given us a much-needed step up to bring this tower of lies tumbling down. We owe it to Harlow to see this through and squeeze every bit of information out of the lead.

"All we're asking for is some information," Theo justifies. "We aren't involving Ben with anything else."

"That's still involving him."

"Maybe he has an old buddy who knows something, or he can point us in the right direction. Just think about it."

I massage my temples. "Fine, I'll make the call."

"Good." Theo nods. "This is the right decision."

"We're keeping this between us, alright? Hunter's enough of a dickhead these days as it is. He doesn't need to know."

"You got it, boss."

Retrieving my phone again, I unlock the screen and prepare to fire off a text message to Ben Rodriguez. He's a decent bloke, despite being headstrong and strict as hell after years spent serving in the police force.

My phone unlocks on the tracking program, and I frown down at the screen. Harlow's on the move, along with the little purple dot that signifies Brooklyn's tracker.

What the fuck?

Constant monitoring is a condition of employment when you join Sabre. That's why the entire Cobra team is also being monitored. Hudson's marker hasn't moved from their home a few miles away from ours. He isn't with them.

Harlow and Brooklyn are heading into Central London, coasting along the main road and heading for the bright lights of Soho. Unbelievable.

"You've got to be kidding me."

Theo perks up. "What is it?"

"Brooklyn is taking Harlow into the city. Are they seriously going drinking right now? Is she out of her mind?"

"That can't be right. Brooklyn isn't that stupid."

I meet his puzzled gaze. "Wanna bet?"

"Well," he admits after a beat. "If Hunter forbade her from taking Harlow out, you can bet your ass that Brooke's doing exactly that just to spite him."

He's fucking right.

Son of a bitch!

"I'm going to kill that woman, once and for all." I sling my leather jacket over my t-shirt and gun holster. "Send their location to my car. I'm going to drag them home."

Theo offers me a salute. "Want me to send backup?"

"Call Hudson and find out why the fuck he let them go out alone. I'll deal with him myself. He doesn't need his arms attached to work for this company."

Swooping from the office before Theo can point out what a terrible idea dismembering our best agent is, I bypass the elevator and skip each step down to the parking garage.

With my car ruined and stuck in the shop for the past few weeks, I've been driving one of our spare company SUVs around. Peeling out of the building, Theo programs the tracker's location into the built-in computer within seconds.

They have arrived in a popular drinking district, right outside a well-known bar I've scouted out on a previous case. I watch Harlow's and Brooklyn's trackers move inside.

They're going clubbing.

Oh, heads are going to roll.

It takes me over an hour to cut through the bustling traffic of London on a Friday night. Despite the frigid February temperature, the streets are lined with tottering heels, alcohol-tinged smiles and hopeful expectations.

I'm ready to flatten the three cars in front of me for holding the queue. The row of taxis releases their inebriated passengers into the throng of clubbers outside several popular venues. There are people everywhere.

Pulling up on the curb, I park—very much illegally—and slam the door shut so hard, it rocks the stupid car. Fuck the inevitable parking ticket. We won't be staying long.

There's a shivering queue of punters outside the bar I'm heading for. I cut past them and pull a stack of notes from my wallet, palming them to the bouncer without a word.

"Mr Montpellier," he greets.

I've done enough undercover work in Soho for every staff member working this street to know who I represent. Funnily enough, the dangerous and disturbed criminals who pay Sabre's salaries often frequent Soho's array of seedy bars.

"Evening, Zayne."

"You looking for anyone in particular tonight?"

"Two female suspects. First one is five foot four, brunette, probably being strong-armed by a tall, blonde-haired chick with a big mouth."

The corner of his mouth lifts. "She's got a mighty gob on her, that one."

"Sounds like my target."

"Even threatened to castrate me if I didn't let them inside to get out of the cold. She paid good as well."

Brooklyn motherfucking West!

"Yeah, she would," I grumble.

Slipping inside the dark, smoky space, the thump of loud bass music pounds into my head. I'm too goddamn tired for this shit. Writhing bodies pack the nightclub to the rafters. The queue for the bar alone is several people deep.

When a hand lands on my shoulder, I react on instinct and yank the perpetrator forwards. A tattooed mass slams into my shoulder, breaking my hold with a level of precision that only I could have taught.

"Jesus, Enz."

"Hudson?! Fuck."

He plants his feet. "Theo called while you were driving."

I grab him by the scruff of his black t-shirt. "Why did you let them leave? Are you seriously that thick?"

He shoves me backwards, unkempt hair hanging over his hardened blue eyes. Hudson Knight is the kind of man that inspires fear in the hearts of his enemies without uttering a single word.

"I was asleep, dammit."

"Asleep?" I repeat incredulously.

"Yes, asshole! Your sadistic best friend has had me working overtime for a month. I had no idea they snuck out."

"Hunter told you to keep Harlow safe! That was the sole reason he allowed her out to spend time with Brooklyn."

"Allowed her out?" Hudson's pierced eyebrow lifts. "Do you hear yourself? Harlow isn't your fucking pet. She's allowed to have a life as well."

I am going to pulverise his face.

He's really fucked me off now.

"If a serial killer was stalking Brooklyn, plotting to imprison and torture her, would you let her out of the house?"

His mouth snaps shut.

"Yeah, I didn't think so."

"Brooklyn has a gun," he offers.

"Oh, awesome. Brooklyn West and a deadly weapon in a nightclub full of grabby hands. What could possibly go wrong with that?"

Dismissing him before I commit a very public murder, I begin to filter through the melee of people. Hudson follows hot on my heels as we part the sea of people with nothing but sheer intimidation and scowls.

Clearing the dance floor, we scan through the crowd and eliminate several writhing couples trying to subtly snort cocaine off each other's hands. Definitely not our girls.

Hudson lifts his chin towards the back of the club, where the emergency exit signs point towards the smoking area. Stepping outside together, we gulp down fresh air.

If you want to enter an introvert's version of hell, go nightclubbing in London after pay day. This place is a cesspit of revelry and cheap hook-ups. Not my kind of scene.

"There."

I follow Hudson's stare. Bingo.

"You wanna deal with Brooklyn?" he asks.

"She's your problem, Hud."

"Since when?"

"You're marrying the lunatic, not me."

Hudson groans loudly. "Fuck, don't remind me."

Smoking a cigarette with her feet propped up on a bench, Brooklyn watches us approach with palpable exasperation. She wears her shoulder-length, blonde hair loose, but her usual jeans and band t-shirt have been replaced by a tight, black-leather dress and Doc Martens.

"Here come the party poopers!"

"Fancy seeing you two here," I snarl at them.

"Seriously, guys. That was barely an hour."

Marching up to his fiancée with a thunderous expression, Hudson takes the cigarette from her fingertips and crushes it.

"I'd expect this from you, blackbird. But bringing Harlow out unprotected? What were you thinking?"

Brooklyn wears a smarmy grin. "Harlow has been cooped up for months. She needs to live a little."

"It isn't safe, and you know it."

"I can keep her safe!" she argues.

Ignoring the smart-mouthed hellion, I step in front of Harlow to gain her attention. She's staring at the ground, her shoulders slumped and aquamarine eyes averted.

At least she's wearing more than Brooklyn. Her tight blue jeans and a loose, floaty blouse show off her naturally pale complexion and defined collarbones.

"Little one?"

Her eyes don't lift to mine.

Things have been strained between us lately. I'll admit that I have been an overprotective douchebag. I've felt shitty about how we left things after our argument, too shitty to crawl between her sheets and take her into my arms.

But I wasn't wrong.

Her safety will always be a priority.

"I'm sorry," she murmurs quietly.

"I know, angel."

"I just wanted to do something normal."

Sending Brooklyn an accusing look, she winks at me and lifts her chin in defiance. Fucking smartass.

"Told you," she mouths.

"Take her home," I order Hudson.

Brooklyn shakes her head. "I'm fine here."

I jab a finger at her. "We'll be discussing this tomorrow, wildfire. Get out of my face."

"Or what?" Brooklyn fires back.

"You don't want to find out."

"Wake up, Enz! You need to stop wrapping her up in cotton wool, or you'll lose her for good."

"Brooke," Harlow whispers. "Please don't."

"He needs to know how you're feeling."

"Got it," I shout before lowering my voice. "Seriously, Brooke. Go home and be thankful you're a woman, otherwise I would've beaten the shit out of you by now."

"Take a shot, big guy. My fucking gender has nothing to do with it. I'll still win in a fight against you."

"Go!" I roar, my patience fizzling out.

Still scowling, Brooklyn shoves Hudson aside when he tries to grab hold of her. She leans closer to whisper in Harlow's ear before giving her a tight squeeze and sashaying away.

"Sorry," Hudson offers.

"Just take her home and fucking keep her there."

With a nod, he disappears. Once they've gone, I take a seat next to Harlow on the bench. It groans beneath my weight, threatening to collapse into dust. The frozen statue next to me releases a tiny laugh.

"Shut up," I tease, trying to cut the tension.

"Please don't break it."

Nudging her shoulder, I rest a hand on her thigh. "If you want to go drinking, I could take you somewhere way better than this shithole."

"Really?" Harlow says hopefully.

"You should see Hunter dance. It's a sight to behold."

"I can't imagine that."

"After enough tequila and lime, nothing can stop him. I'm not sure it qualifies as dancing, though. More like a crime against humanity."

"That bad, huh?"

Harlow finally looks up and meets my eyes. I'm stabbed in the chest by the bleak, bottomless pit of loneliness looking back at me. It's the same empty stare I used to see in the mirror. That was before she came into my life.

"I'm sorry," we say at the same time.

Her cheeks flame. "That was my line."

"Mine too."

I reach for her hand and take it in mine. Her bones are so delicate and bird-like, I feel like with one wrong move I could snap her entire body without batting an eye.

She's all wrong for me.

Fragile. Broken.

Vulnerable.

But I'm falling for her even more with each day that passes. Curiosity has melted into mindless infatuation. I need her. She's the air in my lungs and the choking hand at my throat all at once. That's the power she holds.

"You didn't swap one prison for another."

"Didn't I?" She scoffs.

I stroke her knuckles. "All I want is to keep you safe, little one. But I know that sometimes I get carried away."

"You're right, though. Coming here was stupid."

"I get it."

She gives me a side look. "You do?"

"Yeah." I slide our fingers together. "We're not the easiest people to live with, and you've been cooped up for too long."

"It isn't you. I needed to do this for myself."

"Well, there are better ways to cool off than by running away with Brooklyn as your sidekick."

"Seemed like a good idea at the time," she offers with a sigh. "I needed to get away from Hunter and Leighton."

Hunter was tight-lipped about why Harlow decided to go on an impromptu overnight visit that turned into hiding from us at Brooklyn's for the rest of the week.

"What happened last week?"

She anxiously fiddles with her hair. "The inevitable. I know you think we can make this work, but it isn't going to happen."

I slide a finger along her jawline, tilting her brilliant blue eyes back up to mine. Staring at her is like escaping a burning building by jumping into the sea, no matter the very real risk of drowning.

I know the risk.

I'll still take it.

Whatever she's willing to give me is enough. We're under fire, and a storm of acid rain is threatening to hammer down on us. I'll fill my lungs and let my own skin slough off to keep her dry, if that's what it takes.

"Why not?" I breathe.

"Because I'm going to hurt you. All of you."

"You don't know that."

She bites her lip, her eyes sparkling with emotion. "I'm not like Pastor Michaels. I can't hurt the people I'm supposed to… to…"

Drawn to one another by an invisible string lacing our two hearts together, I let my lips brush hers in a tender caress.

"Finish that sentence."

She shudders. "I can't."

My self-control snaps. I won't let her slip away again. We've already been down this road before. I seal my mouth on hers, needing to taste her sweet essence.

Harlow doesn't see herself like I do. She's everything that's good and pure in this world. Everything that I'm not but hope to be. Around her, I can feel the darkness inside me melting.

I want to shackle her inside the protective depths of my soul, safe and secure, where no motherfucker can bruise her skin again. The world is full of people trying to break us. It's my job not to let them.

Her lips part on a blissful sigh as she melts into the kiss. A natural, silent symphony guides our colliding mouths. My hand slides up to bury in her thick, flowing tresses.

She breaks the kiss. "Enzo, don't."

But it's too late.

My fingertips are already sifting through her hair, following the grooves of her skull. When velvety softness is replaced by scabbed, raw skin that feels hot to the touch, I pull away.

"Is that—"

Her face crumples. "Please don't look."

Leighton told me her hair pulling has gotten worse since Northumberland. Amidst the chaos, we've let our surveillance slip. She's careful not to do it when we're eating together or watching TV in the den.

I grip the back of her neck. "It's okay. You don't need to be afraid. I need to see, or I can't help you."

"But I don't need help."

"Harlow," I say gruffly. "I swore an oath to keep you safe, no matter what. You can trust me with this."

Her eyes shut as she nods. "Okay."

Lifting her mousy-brown hair to expose what used to be a small-sized bald patch, violent armies of rage filter my vision into shades of red.

Beneath a thin layer of untouched hair to hide the truth from the world, almost the whole left half of her head is bleeding and scabbed over with bright patches of soreness.

She must be in agony.

This is months' worth of pulling.

I can't begin to fathom the determination it must have taken to tear all of this hair out by hand. Strand by strand. Pluck by pluck. I want to roar in fury just thinking about it.

"That." She cracks an eye open to study me. "That look right there is exactly why I didn't want you to see it."

I let her hair drop and carefully smooth it over. Tears are racing down her cheeks in thick rivulets. Pressing my lips to the side of her head, I kiss above the secret she's kept from us all.

"We need to get you some more support."

"Richards already knows," she whispers.

"And? What does he think?"

Harlow shrugs. "He gave me a bunch of coping techniques. It's just hard to use them when everything's so… loud."

Fuck. This is bad. Even worse than I thought.

"You need to try," I attempt to encourage.

"Yeah, I know."

I trace a finger over her lips. "You're not in this alone, even when you feel like it. It will get easier with time."

"And if it doesn't?"

My lips meet hers in a breath-stealing kiss. Salty tears are burning my skin. I can feel her pain taking on a life of its own and crawling inside me. It's sending my protective instincts into overdrive.

"I will not let you give up," I murmur into her mouth. "Not in a million years."

"You can't fight all my battles for me."

"But I can hold your hand while you fight for yourself. I'll do everything in my power to make this easier for you."

Harlow lets me tuck her into my side, her face burying in the crook of my neck. We sit there, curled around each other, in the smoky darkness of the biting London air.

"I didn't mean what I said the other week," she says in a timid voice. "About wanting to leave. I was feeling overwhelmed, and I needed some space to breathe."

"You don't need to apologise."

"But I shouldn't have said that to you."

"We both said things we didn't mean in the heat of the moment." I sigh against her head. "I could communicate better instead of threatening you with house arrest."

"Probably, yeah."

We both laugh, the last drops of tension dissipating. I take her hand and tug her onto her feet. Right now, I want to hold her close and never let go. That's step one to begin fixing this.

"Let's go home. The other idiots are on strict orders to behave or find somewhere else to live."

Harlow winces. "You didn't have to do that."

"Nobody upsets you on my watch and gets away with it. Hunter's lucky I love him, or he'd be dead and buried by now. Don't get me started on his asshole brother."

"Thought you were going to stop threatening?"

"Threatening *you*," I correct her. "I can't commit to not beating the living daylights out of my teammates on a semi-regular basis. Especially when they behave like jealous teenagers."

Harlow summons a weak smile.

"Guess I can't complain about that."

CHAPTER 8
HARLOW

ME AND MY BRAIN – AIRWAYS

WITH A RED-PLAID BLANKET wrapped around my shoulders, I take my steaming cup of tea and click my tongue for Lucky to follow. She zips to my side, preening as I rub her ears.

Having her with me calms the itching static of anxiety humming through my body as I wait for my phone to ring. My stomach cramps aren't helping me feel any better.

"Good girl." I stroke a finger over her crown. "Why hasn't the doctor called yet? It's been hours."

Her pleading eyes stare up at me.

"What if his operation went wrong?"

The steady, reassuring love in her animal eyes answers me without the need for words. I have to be patient. My father's operation commenced at eleven o'clock this morning.

I'm afraid.

Even if I don't know why.

I didn't think it was possible to care about someone that you don't know, but the past few hours of waiting have proven that I do care. Perhaps more than I should. He's still my father, even though we don't know each other.

Lucky trots by my side as I approach Hunter's office, tucked behind the wide staircase leading upstairs. He left early this morning with Enzo to begin the long drive up to Newcastle.

They're both trying to be more open. It's a new development after my stint with Brooklyn and my later heart-to-heart with Enzo. True to his word, he spoke to Hunter and the others about the new status quo.

We're starting fresh.

Hunter revealed last night that they're interviewing an elderly pastor for the case. This man worked at the church Kiera attended. We're hoping to understand more about her life, and why Pastor Michaels decided that it had to end.

Like Jude said, the answers are there.

I just have to find them.

Despite spending hours spilling the inky darkness of my soul onto lined paper, my memories are still disjointed. I can only remember flashes. Whispered promises and pleas.

It's going to be okay, Harlow.

I won't let him hurt you again.

She should have been afraid. Pastor Michaels slaughtered her with a lascivious smile on his face. Her empty carcass was torn apart, limb for limb. Now, she's trapped.

Kiera has joined the faces that I wish I could go back to not remembering, all pointing their accusing fingers at me. Every breath I take is an insult to them.

You lived.

You lived.

You lived.

My hand spasms with the urge to grab a tantalising handful of hair and rip it clean out. I need a distraction. Enzo wrote down a few things, along with the password to Hunter's desktop computer in his office before he left.

I've got a few hours before I'm due to meet Richards for a session. He moved up the appointment—another one of Enzo's ideas, along with the additional security that's been posted at the front gate while they're gone.

With the thump of Leighton's terrible music pounding through the floor, I slide into Hunter's office. The residue of his spicy aftershave seeps over me. I take a breath, running my fingers over a discarded checked scarf on the sofa.

He has an impressive selection of books, but unlike Theo's insatiable thirst for classics and science fiction, Hunter seems to enjoy memoirs and tear-inducingly boring business books.

Yikes.

Glossy black shelving fills an entire wall, casting shadows over a brown sofa, overhanging lamp and sheepskin rug that covers the floorboards. Taking a seat at his desk, I wiggle the mouse and input his password.

The screen opens on a background that makes my heart twinge. Hunter and Leighton both look younger, their faces softened and pulled taut in bright, almost identical smiles that advertise their shared genes.

On either side of them, two older people are smiling at the camera. The resemblance is stark. Della, their mum, is short and grey-haired, with an understanding smile and hazel eyes softened by wrinkles.

Their father, Ben, wears a sharp haircut, and he's in good shape despite his older age. With an unwavering brown stare, I can see where Hunter gets his intense air of authority.

Sometimes, I forget that Hunter and Leighton are family. They weren't always imprisoned in this fractured phase. Hunter is ready to murder his younger brother most days, and Leighton is determined to put him in a premature grave.

Lucky harrumphs as she settles beneath the huge desk, her fur brushing against my feet. Reaching underneath to rub her ears, I bring up the browser and head for the online education website that Enzo suggested.

They're adamant that getting a job is out of the question, but the idea of going back to school gave me food for thought. I don't remember ever attending school.

I love reading and learning new things about the world. This could be a way for me to escape the constant feeling of oppression that comes with my current situation.

"Goldilocks?" Leighton calls out.

"In the office."

He thumps up the staircase from the basement gym. "You hungry? I'm just going to take a quick shower."

"I'm fine, thanks."

Engrossed in a course catalogue, the choices available are endless. Half of the subjects are unrecognisable to me. I'm going to be learning with children laughing and pointing at the idiot adult. I feel sick at the thought.

There's so much I don't understand about this world. I'll never recapture the normalcy that was stolen from me. It will forever be a far-off dream. Crap, this was a mistake.

The door creaks as Leighton pokes his sweaty head around it. "Harlow? You want tea?"

I gesture to my cup. "Beat you to it."

"Just trying to look after you." He hesitates before leaving. "You should eat something. I make a mean grilled cheese."

"You're fussing again."

He slips inside the room, revealing his loose workout shorts and bare chest, glistening with droplets of sweat that define the slopes of his tightly packed muscles. My throat tightens.

Raising his hands, he mimes clawing the air. "Grrr, grrr. Little Harlow. Must. Eat."

"What on earth is that?" I frown at him.

"Are you not impressed by my best Enzo impression? Should I growl more? Did I not threaten enough?"

"Erm, he usually follows up his fussing with action."

I yelp when the office chair spins. Leighton grins down at me with amusement dancing in his eyes. He boxes me in with a hand on each side of the leather chair.

"You want action? I'm more than happy to give it."

"Knock it off, Leigh. I'm trying to look through this stupid catalogue. Stop distracting me."

He flashes two gorgeous dimples. "What is this, anyway? Are you seriously going back to school?"

"Maybe. Why not?"

"Most people can't wait to leave it."

"I'm not most people." I glance back at the computer. "All I want is to experience what other people take for granted. I had none of that."

Leighton leaves me to flop across the leather sofa, propping his bare feet up on the armrest. Lucky launches herself across the office and barks until he starts rubbing her belly.

"So, what is this then? Online classes?"

I glance over another course description. "Richards recommended it to me. You can attend online in your own time, no pressure."

"Sounds good, Goldilocks."

"I guess so."

"Why the long face?"

Struggling to understand another paragraph of information, I exit the website and turn in the chair to face Leighton.

"Do you think I'm stupid?"

"What?" He chuckles.

I try to shrug off my embarrassment. "None of it is making any sense to me. How am I supposed to catch up?"

"Hell, it doesn't make sense to me either."

"Not funny. You went to school and can understand basic things like maths and science. I feel like an idiot."

"I flunked both of those subjects," he reveals.

"Seriously?"

"School was not my strong suit. I liked sports and drinking beer at the back of the football pitch. That's about it."

"No wonder you flunked out if you spent all day drinking beer and kicking a ball around."

"Ouch, princess."

Leighton flashes across the room, banding his corded arms around me. I squeal as I'm lifted out of the office chair.

"Hey! Put me down!"

"Not a chance," Leighton replies.

My legs automatically wrap around his waist. He holds me against his bare chest and pins me. When his nose buries in my hair, he takes a deep, indulgent inhale.

"Are you sniffing me?"

"You smell incredible," he whispers back. "For the record, I don't think that you're stupid. If you want to go back to school, then we can all help you catch up."

"Thank you," I hush. "That means a lot."

"Always, Goldilocks. Lunch?"

"I'm not really hungry."

Leighton looks me in the eye. "What's really going on?"

Busted. He knows me far too well.

"The hospital still hasn't called." I bite down on my sore bottom lip. "He's been in surgery for hours now."

"Give it time. Doctor Bannon will call."

That doesn't ease my anxiety. He reads it on my face, stroking his thumb along my cheek.

"I can practically hear your brain churning." Leighton kisses the tip of my nose. "What else is bothering you?"

"I don't know what happens if the surgery is a success."

"Well, Jude and Phoenix have found a bed in the rehab centre they work at. They will take care of your dad there."

I don't realise I'm twirling a long strand of hair between my fingers, tugging roughly with each rotation. Leighton's eyes narrow on the movement, and he catches my hand.

"Stop," he murmurs.

"I'm sorry."

"You don't need to do that. I'm here."

I blow out an unsteady breath. "What if he doesn't pull through? I haven't even spoken to him."

"Do you want to now that he's responsive?"

"Maybe. I think I have questions."

His eyebrows pull together. "What about talking to Giana instead?"

Nose wrinkled, I suppress a full-body shudder.

"She calls every week," he adds. "Hunter stopped passing the messages along to you after Northumberland."

At the mention of my estranged mother, my already aching stomach twists painfully. It's been in knots all morning.

"Maybe I'll feel better if I talk to her again," I concede with a sigh. "We left things in a pretty bad way."

"You don't have to if you don't want to."

"I think some closure might help. If she can tell me what she knows about my childhood, the memories might return."

Leighton pecks my cheek. "She's due to come into HQ for a second interview in a couple of weeks. You could see her then, rather than travelling back to Devon."

"Yeah, I don't want to go back there."

"Then it's settled. Come on, let's go make some lunch. I'm withering away here. I'll shower after."

"Withering away? Hardly."

He narrows his eyes. "What are you saying?"

"You're making Enzo look small with all the working out you're doing at the moment."

Grin darkening with deliciously malevolent intentions, he flexes for my benefit, his growing biceps rippling.

"I warned you. This is a fight I intend to win. Trust me, I look even better naked."

"Christ, Leigh."

"Wanna see the rest of me?" he proposes.

"Keep your pants on and make me a sandwich instead."

Leighton links our fingers together and drags me away from the office. In the kitchen, he grabs my hips and lifts me onto the marble breakfast bar.

I cross my legs at the ankle and watch him pull a teetering tower of sandwich ingredients from the fridge. He sets up a chopping board, bread and two plates before constructing our sandwiches. I steal bites of cheese while waiting.

"Patience, young Jedi."

"Don't Yoda me." I grab a slice of tomato before he can smack my hand away. "You're the last one to be patient when food is involved."

Leighton squeezes mayo into my sandwich. "Point taken. I'm not a good example to follow, as we've established."

"I learned that a while ago."

He slices off the crusts on my sandwich without being told and cuts it into neat, bite-sized mouthfuls. My heart skitters with appreciation. Large portions of food are intimidating.

"Get that in you." He hands me the plate. "Then, we're going to go back to that course catalogue together."

Chest burning, I touch my lips to his stubbly cheek. "Thank you for being amazing."

"I know, I'm fucking awesome. Eat up. I'm gonna go take that shower."

"You're not eating with me?"

"Harlow, I stink."

With a mouthful of sandwich, I sniff the air. "You really do smell bad."

"Don't be mean now. I fed you, didn't I?"

Depositing a kiss on my head, he crams his sandwich into his mouth and disappears. Left alone, I munch through another bite-sized chunk before my stomach twists again.

With Leighton gone, I push my plate away. The stomach cramps are making me feel nauseous. A dull, throbbing pain pulses through my abdomen and lower back.

When I stand up to make another cup of tea, hoping to ease my nausea, a strange warmth soaks into the fabric of my jeans. Oh my God. It's coming from between my legs.

Biting my lip, I run out of the kitchen, making a beeline upstairs for the privacy of my bedroom. The door is barely shut before more warmth rushes out with a spike of pain.

This can't be what I think it is.

Not after all this time.

I didn't think it was even possible. The doctors said it might never happen after years of malnourishment. Hands shaking, I unfasten my jeans and slowly push them over my hips. My heartbeat is roaring in my ears.

With denim swamping my knees, I blanch at the bright-red stain on the fabric. Blood. I'm bleeding. Kicking the jeans aside with a cry working up my throat, I look down at the soaked material of my panties.

Blood is smeared on both of my thighs, painting my skin with swirls of dark crimson. It's definitely coming out of me. Panic sets in as the past takes over, and I'm too freaked out to stop myself from spiralling.

The bedroom melts away.

Darkness slinks back in.

The sound of crying shreds my grasp on sanity. It was grief, tinged with the paradox of twisted relief, that fuelled her screams as the blood poured out of her.

"Adelaide," I sob.

I can feel her, invisible and wrapping her arms around me when my knees buckle. Crumpled on the bedroom floor, I hug my midsection as the memories overwhelm me.

The swell of her belly.

Every syllable of her anguished lament.

The thump of fists on flesh.

Bruises blossoming like oil paint.

Covering my ears, I try to block it out. Her petrified cursing. Pastor Michaels' hissed promise of retribution as she stole the unborn life from him that he intended to puppeteer.

A mother, protecting her kin.

Even by means of death.

No matter how hard I clamp down on my ears, it gets louder. She lives inside me, surrounded by ranks of tortured souls, all waiting for their own turn to tear a slice off me.

"Harlow?"

Leighton's voice slips through my closed bedroom door. I should scrub my tears and attempt to hide the mess I've found myself in, but I can't move a muscle. I'm tucked in the corner of my cage, cowering out of sight.

If I move, Pastor Michaels will remember me. He'll abandon the other cage and return to mine. Unlock the door. Prowl inside. Beat, whip and break his way to domination.

You'll always be a sinner.

It's my job to teach you.

One day, you'll thank me.

Two strong hands grip my shoulders and peel me off the plush, grey carpet. I'm too scared to open my eyes. He's here. Pastor Michaels blamed me for that baby's death.

When Adelaide died, his rage exploded out of him. He stomped my bones into broken dust while the scent of her blood poisoned the basement around us.

"Harlow," the voice snaps.

I recognise it. That isn't Pastor Michaels. He wouldn't be stroking my back or whispering reassurances.

"Talk to me. Where are you hurt?"

"Leigh," I gasp.

"It's me. I've got you."

"I c-c-can't breathe…"

Cradled in his arms, my cheek is pressed against the hot skin of his pectorals. I suck in a stuttered breath and focus on the rise and fall of his chest, using it to anchor myself.

"That's it, princess."

Dragging my eyelids open, I find Leighton staring down at me, searching for answers. Shame colours my cheeks.

"What happened? Where are your clothes?"

"I f-freaked out when I saw the blood."

"What blood?"

"I'm so sorry, Leigh."

He cups my cheek. "Why are you bleeding? Did you fall or something?"

"Oh my God." I attempt to scramble off his lap as his arms tighten. "Let me go. I'm going to get it all over you."

Six feet of toned muscle and tanned skin holds me prisoner. He's only wearing a pair of tight blue boxers, leaving nothing to the imagination. I fight harder to escape.

"I'm going to lose my shit in a sec. What is it?"

I bury my face in his chest to hide. "I d-didn't think I was ever going to get it. The doctors warned me."

There's a beat of hesitation.

"Oh," Leighton breathes. "*Oh.*"

"Yeah," I deadpan.

"That. Okay."

"Let me up. This is gross as hell."

His hand moves to my back to hold me in place. "Don't be ridiculous. It's just a bit of blood. I'm not bothered."

"Well, I am bothered."

Leighton ignores my squirming and lifts me up. I'm carried into my en-suite, where he finally drops me back on my feet before turning on the walk-in shower.

"Get cleaned up. I'll sort out some supplies."

"Supplies?" I repeat.

"You know, girly shit. Tampons and things." He mock-shudders with a wink. "We don't keep that stuff around the house."

"Ground, please swallow me up," I mutter.

He ruffles my hair. "No can do. Are you… erm, gonna get in? I'll find you some clean clothes to wear."

My sweater is loose enough to cover my body and upper thighs, but I'm standing in nothing but stained panties from the waist down. My legs are crossed tight to hide the mess from him.

"If you breathe a word of this to anyone, you're dead meat," I threaten him. "Promise?"

Leighton laughs as he leaves the bathroom. No answer. Humiliated, I slam the door and pull my sweater over my head, dropping it in a heap on the tiled floor with my bra.

My sodden panties go next. Stepping into the thick steam pouring from the shower, the hot water beats down on me, soothing the last spasms of anxiety. Water makes me happy.

She's still here.

Adelaide.

Lingering in the outermost frontier of my mind, like the others, she's biding her time. I watch the pink swirls escaping down the drain and fight to silence her screaming.

"I'm coming in," Leighton warns.

The bathroom door creaks open as I'm sloughing jasmine-scented shower gel off my legs.

"Leigh!"

"My eyes are covered. Got you some comfy clothes. I'll be downstairs."

"Wait," I rush out.

He freezes before escaping, a hand clamped over his eyes. Breath held, I crack open the shower door. Leighton lifts his hand to peer at me.

"Climb in."

"You sure?" he double-checks.

"I don't want to be alone. I might freak out again."

Closing the door, he shrugs. "I should warn you that you'll find me irresistible when you see me naked."

"Just get in here before I change my mind."

Reaching for the shampoo, I hear Leighton approaching as he finishes stripping down. The shower door closes, and hard planes of muscle meet my back.

Leighton reaches around my waist to take the shampoo from my hands. He lathers the fragranced liquid and begins to work it into my hair, taking care to avoid the stretch of sores running across my scalp.

"Harlow?"

"Mmm," I moan back.

"What scared you so badly about getting your first period?"

Hands braced on the tiled wall, I let my head slump. "I had a flashback to Adelaide's death. The blood triggered me."

"You weren't expecting it?"

"I didn't think I'd ever get my period."

"You've been eating better and putting on some weight." He gently massages the safe side of my head. "I guess your body is starting to catch up with where it's supposed to be."

"I guess so."

"That's a good thing. Trust me."

Leighton guides my head back under the spray of water to wash the shampoo out. He's moved closer, and I can feel his erection pushing against my behind.

My breath catches. "Leigh—"

"Sorry," he says quickly. "Can't help it."

Reaching for the conditioner, he begins to lather it into my hair. His hard length brushes against my ass again, causing my pulse to spike.

I can't help shifting against his crotch, my breath held. The friction is a delicious tease, distracting me from the remnants of ghosts still haunting my mind.

"Princess," he warns. "I didn't get in here to take advantage while you're still upset."

"You're not taking advantage."

"Potato, patata. It's taking advantage in my books, no matter how you slice it."

He begins to rinse the conditioner out, and I glance down at the shower basin. The bleeding has stopped for now. I swivel around to face him.

"All clean," he announces.

My eyes flick down. "Want me to—"

"No," he says firmly. "I'm not the kind of guy that asks his girl to get him off just because she's on the blob."

"On the blob?" I laugh.

"You've never heard that before?"

"Nope, never."

"Ah, man. I'm going to have so much fun with this."

Smacking his water-laden chest, I slip out of the shower and wrap myself in the towel he put on the rack to get warm for me. He turns off the shower and disappears to get dressed.

On the bed, my favourite pair of sweats have been laid out with clean panties and fluffy bed socks. I pack my panties with some tissues as a temporary measure.

My phone is vibrating where I left it next to the bed this morning. The group chat has been going crazy for the last half an hour I've spent in the shower.

Leigh: Theo, can you swing by the pharmacy on your way over? Harlow needs something.

Theo: Erm, sure. Everything okay?

Enzo: What the hell happened?

Hunter: Answer my fucking phone call, Leigh. Why does she need something from the pharmacy?

Enzo: If she's hurt, I'll personally skin you alive and sell your hide for profit on the dark web. Answer the phone.

"Bloody hell." I flush hot with even more humiliation as I read the next instalment.

Leigh: Calm down, assholes. She needs some of those tampon thingies and whatever else girls use.

Enzo: It came?

Leigh: Good inference, genius.

Theo: I have no idea what girls use.

Hunter: Ask the pharmacist.

The next message comes fifteen minutes later. It's a picture of a brightly coloured aisle, overflowing with different brands and types of neon packaging.

Theo: A little help here? Why are there a million different kinds of tampons? And what the fuck are extra-large wings?

Enzo: Google that shit.

Theo: Tried that, not helpful. Now I'm even more confused.

Collapsing on the bed, I tap out a response.

Harlow: Oh my God. I'm never speaking to any of you ever again. This is humiliating.

Leigh: Sorry, Goldilocks. I needed to enlist help.

That asshole is in serious trouble. I can actually hear him laughing all the way from his own bedroom right now.

Harlow: Stay out of my room, Leigh. I do not want to speak to you.

Enzo: You upset her, shithead. Prepare to be skinned.

Leigh: Princess! Help me.

I shake my head with a snort.

Harlow: Not a chance.

Hunter: Can we save the first-degree murder for later? I'm trying to concentrate here. Some of us have a case to solve.

Theo: On my way over with ice cream.

Harlow: Theodore, you're allowed in my room.

Theo: Uh, thanks?

Leigh: Dammit.

Storming back into my bedroom, Leighton's weight bounces on the bed next to me. I've ditched my phone and buried my face in my pillow to hide from the world.

"What's up, buttercup?" he singsongs.

"I officially hate you."

"Hey, I'm the one getting skinned alive."

"You deserve it. I'm never speaking to you ever again. You promised not to tell anyone."

He yanks the pillow off my head and begins tickling my ribcage, forcing me to roll over and gasp for air.

"I'm sorry." His eyes are twinkling. "I didn't want to leave you here alone. Theo is coming over later anyway."

"They were debating different tampon brands!"

"I mean, you want the best, right?"

Stealing my pillow back, I smash him around the head with it. Leighton slumps on the mattress with a cackle, dodging the swinging feathers clasped in my hands.

"Okay, okay," he says between laughter. "I'm sorry. Can I bribe your forgiveness with pizza and a movie?"

"Fine, but I'm choosing both."

"You drive a hard bargain."

Offering me a hand, Leighton pushes me towards the door. He stops to grab my pillows and duvet, hefting them over his shoulder to carry downstairs.

We end up snuggled together under the duvet, sprawled out on the sectional sofa. Leighton is passing me handfuls of my favourite chocolate-covered pretzels as I scroll through the pizza menu on his phone.

"Hey," Theo shouts as the front door opens. "Your delivery man has arrived."

I let my head hit the sofa cushions. "We are so not doing this. I've been humiliated enough for one day."

Strolling into the room with a huge brown paper bag in his hands, Theo offers me a sweet smile in greeting.

"You okay?"

"Peachy," I drone. "Good day at work?"

"It was alright. Did you guys eat already?"

"We're ordering pizza." Leighton takes the phone back from my hands. "Want your usual?"

"With extra olives, please." Theo drops the paper bag in my lap. "For you. Hope it's okay."

"Thank you for getting the stuff."

He peels off his denim jacket and tosses it on the other sofa. "No worries. I was about to come over anyway."

"Here. Sit down."

Vacating my spot for him to take, I clutch the paper bag to my chest and run from the room before their chuckling can catch up to me.

In the bathroom, I open the bag and my mouth drops. Theo has brought enough stuff for an army of hormonal women. At least five different brands of tampons and pads, all varying in sizes and thickness.

Panic creeps back in. I have no idea what to use or where to even begin. Tears burn my eyes as my emotions swell back up to the surface. This is so stupid.

Sliding my phone from my back pocket, I ignore the still-pinging group chat and pull up Brooklyn's contact. It takes a few seconds for her to answer the video call.

"Hey," she greets with a lit cigarette dangling from her mouth. "Is everything okay?"

"Brooke, thank God," I whisper under my breath. "Wait, are you smoking?"

"Wedding planning is fucking stressful, alright?"

"Noted. I need your help. Are you alone?"

Flicking the cigarette aside, she walks away from the hum of another two voices behind her. I can make out the tinted-glass structure of HQ in the background.

"Am now. Who do I need to kill this time?"

"I got my period, and I have no idea what to do."

Her playful smile softens. "Take a breath. Need me to go to the shop?"

"Theo already went."

"Bloody hell, Theo buying sanitary pads. I would've paid to see that. Okay, let's see what we're working with."

I tip out the entire contents of the bag and flip the camera to show her. She whistles under her breath.

"Damn, Theo went to town."

"There's so much!" I hiccup.

"I don't know if this is cute or crazy."

"What should I do?"

Snickering, she pulls a pair of headphones from her pocket and plugs them in so nobody can overhear our conversation.

"Start with the pink pack. I'll talk you through it."

CHAPTER 9
HUNTER

2008 – CLEOPATRICK

KNOCKING BACK a handful of headache pills, I wash them down with a swig of tea from my thermos. Enzo is draining his own coffee as he drives us through the village streets.

We set off for Newcastle early this morning, leaving Harlow still curled up in bed with her thumb buried in her mouth. It was my turn to sleep in her bed last night, but Enzo soon found his way in to sandwich her between us.

He's stubbornly clinging to the idea that we can somehow share her, even after he had to rescue her from some dingy London nightclub. We drove her away with our fighting and he still won't let it go.

I have zero interest in dividing Harlow's attention between us. I want her eyes on me, and me only. We fooled ourselves into thinking we could all have what we wanted before, and it resulted in death.

I won't watch Harlow die.

Not for us fools.

"Ten more minutes."

I drain the last of my tea. "Good. What do we know about this guy?"

"Theo printed his records off." He jerks a finger over his shoulder. "He ran a full background check too. Seems trustworthy enough."

Straining to reach the briefcase in the backseat, I manage to unclip the lock and pull out a sheath of paperwork in a manilla folder. Theo has compiled a full and detailed profile.

Frederick Houghton is a wizened, shrunken slip of a man at eighty-five years old. He's lived at the same address since 1975 and was married for almost sixty years before his wife passed away from bowel cancer.

He has paid his taxes, mortgage and bills, all while serving the local parish and running St Peter's church for his whole career. On the surface, he seems to be a normal, law-abiding Christian. And potentially, our golden fucking ticket.

This could be our big break.

It's come at last.

"Kiera knew Pastor Michaels," Enzo reiterates. "If we can identify him from the congregation, we're in business."

"You think Michaels would risk everything by killing a fellow church member and potentially blowing his cover?"

He shrugs. "Harlow made it clear that Kiera's death was some kind of punishment. I'm betting that Michaels is the one she fell out with."

It feels a little too good to be true. We know that serial killers tend to live in plain sight, often leading normal lives under the alias of their alter-egos. We could be on to him.

"We need to wrap this up fast. I'm not comfortable being this far from Harlow while her father is under the knife."

"Agreed," Enzo mutters.

"She's far too worried about that son of a bitch."

"Theo's there now with the stuff from the pharmacy." He watches the traffic lights change. "He's going to look at that schooling programme with her later."

Pulling my compact black handgun from the glove box, I check it over before slotting it into my holster. Old age pensioner or not, I'm not taking any risks.

The case is too widely known for people not to recognise us. Every single day, the newspapers and airwaves are dripping with criticism. The country is reaching a boiling point. Disgusting hate speech against Harlow and the company is whipping everyone into a frenzied mob.

"You think she'll apply?"

"I have no idea," he replies. "Richards thinks it will be good for her to have some routine. I think it's a great idea."

"And safer, doing it online."

"Exactly."

My phone rings in the pocket of my navy quilted jacket. I clock Giana Kensington's name before answering with a sigh. She'll only keep calling until I do.

"Giana," I answer stiffly.

"Mr Rodriguez. Thanks for taking my call."

"This isn't a good time."

"I've been informed that my ex-husband's surgery was successful," she states. "I'm still registered as his next of kin along with Let—uh, Harlow."

"I'm glad to hear it."

Her voice chills. "Under no circumstances must that man be allowed anywhere near my daughter. Do you understand? No circumstances."

"Giana, with all due respect, Harlow is an adult. She's entitled to make her own decisions about whether or not she wants to see him."

"She won't even return my phone calls," Giana accuses. "She's my daughter, not his. I won't sit here and allow that monster to poison her against me. I want to see her."

"I'm afraid that's up to Harlow."

"Then you will have to convince her."

"No, I won't do that. I cannot force her to speak to you. She's still coming to terms with all that she's been through."

"It's been months. I cannot go on like this!"

Holding the phone away from my ear, I wince as her voice reaches a hysterical whine. My hearing aid buzzes in protest. Enzo is silently laughing, able to hear her ranting.

Returning to the phone call, Giana is breathing heavily, but silent. I clear my throat as Enzo parks up on the curb outside a small cottage, draped in glossy green ivy and winter moss.

"I'll speak to Harlow," I offer her.

"You will? When?"

"No promises. Goodbye."

Ending the call, I tuck my phone away with an annoyed growl. I still don't trust her story. I'll tolerate her for as long as I need to, but that doesn't mean I have to be polite.

The moment Harlow says the damn word, I'll cut Giana from her life like the cancerous tumour she is and ensure that she never bothers her again.

"Having fun?" Enzo snickers.

"She's off her rocker, that woman."

"Oh, she's clinical for sure."

"I don't care what crap is going on between Harlow's parents. They need to keep it away from her."

"Seconded. She doesn't need that stress."

"Apparently, Oliver's operation went well." I straighten my knotted tie and check my reflection. "I'll call Jude on the way back and see when he can be moved to the centre."

"How do you think Harlow will react?"

"Well, he isn't dead. That has to offer her some relief."

Enzo shakes his head. "I don't understand why she wants to hear the scumbag out in the first place. He was an abusive piece of crap who landed himself in prison."

Grabbing my briefcase and voice recorder for the interview, I climb out of Enzo's new Audi and crack my neck. He follows, stretching his trunk-like arms above his head.

"There are two sides to every story, and Harlow's figuring out who to believe." I slam the door shut. "I, for one, want to know what Oliver has to say about Harlow's disappearance."

We crunch up the gravel path that leads to the cottage. Enzo thumps on the door before stepping behind me. If I saw his two hundred pounds of pure muscle hammering on my front door, I'd sure as hell run away.

We don't want to scare the elderly pastor before the interview has even begun. When the door creaks open, it reveals a short, young woman dressed in pressed medical scrubs.

"We're here for the interview," Enzo snaps.

I stifle an eye roll at his bad manners. "Good afternoon. I believe Mr Houghton is expecting us?"

She ushers us inside with a tight smile. "Sure. I'm just taking Mr Houghton's blood pressure. Come through."

The low-ceilinged living room is lit by crackling flames from the open fireplace. The nearby high-backed armchair is occupied. Frederick Houghton waves us in, an open copy of the Bible on his leg.

"Mr Houghton," I greet.

"Gentlemen. Please, sit down."

I stick a hand out for him to shake. "My name is Hunter Rodriguez. You spoke to my colleague, Theodore, on the phone. This is Mr Montpellier."

"Please, call me Frederick," he gushes, pumping my hand. "Helen, bring us some tea and biscuits, will you?"

"We're fine," Enzo interrupts with a forced smile. "If you'll excuse our bluntness, we're on a tight schedule."

He snaps the Bible shut with wrinkled, pale hands. "Well, that's quite alright. How may I help you? I understand you're investigating these dreadful murders."

Opening my briefcase, I pull out a full-page photograph of Kiera. It was taken on her last birthday before her future was ripped away from her. I hand it to the retired pastor.

"Kiera is one of almost twenty victims we're investigating at this time. Do you remember her? We've been informed she attended your church services regularly."

He squints at the photograph. "Such a pity. Kiera was a wonderful woman, so devoted to her faith."

"Did you know her well?"

"Oh, I did. She attended my services for a number of years. The church mourned her loss deeply."

"What do you remember about her disappearance?" Enzo starts the slim recorder to capture our conversation.

"I was interviewed by a couple of detectives at the time."

"We're conducting our own investigation." I sit down in the nearby armchair. "If you wouldn't mind going back over it for our benefit."

He nods, fingering his gold-paged Bible. "Kiera was very active in the church. She helped with a lot of our charitable work. When she disappeared, it was out of character."

"Did you raise your concerns with the police department?" Enzo asks.

"I'm afraid to say the police weren't particularly interested. It was suggested that Kiera was romantically involved with someone, and that she took off without informing anyone."

"And that didn't strike you as suspicious?" I shake my head, disbelieving. "What did the church do to find her?"

"Hunt," Enzo mutters.

Taking a deep breath, I scrape a hand over my slicked-back ponytail. "My apologies, Mr Houghton."

"That's alright." He touches the golden crucifix resting on his clavicle. "A concerned member of the church organised a search party that turned up no results."

Enzo nods, a small notepad in hand. "Do you have a name for this individual? We'd like to interview them."

"Oh, Lee moved away several years ago with his wife."

"Do you have a contact number?"

He shakes his head. "I'm afraid not."

"Going back to Kiera," Enzo redirects the old man. "We've been informed that she had a disagreement with a member of the church. Do you recall this?"

Clearing his throat, Frederick looks uncomfortable. "I wouldn't want to speak out of turn."

"Mr Houghton." I plaster on a fake smile. "All we want is to give Kiera's family some closure. Help us to do that."

"Well, I wouldn't want this *sensitive* information getting into the wrong hands. We're a traditional bunch around here."

It's taking all my self-control not to ram his stupid Bible up his ass. We don't have time for this.

"Sensitive?" Enzo prompts.

He sighs, his brows knitted. "There was a rumour going around that Kiera had been involved with a married man."

That doesn't sound right.

"A member of the church?" I ask him.

"Indeed. This led to a bit of a heated moment between Kiera and the gentleman's wife. If I remember correctly, Kiera was most upset by the accusation."

He's looking back down at his Bible again, his eyes clouded over with the confusion of time. Enzo coughs deliberately, attempting to startle him back.

"Who knows what took place back then," he concludes. "Like I said, I wouldn't want to sully Kiera's name."

I sit on the edge of my seat. "Who did this accusation involve?"

"Lee was distraught when she vanished. He organised the search to find her. I'm sure he felt guilty for the rumour, which Kiera always maintained was false."

Stricken silence ensues.

He… organised the search?

Exchanging loaded glances with Enzo, we both grip our notepads a little tighter. "You're telling me the man accused of infidelity with Kiera, a claim she denied, also organised the search party to find her?"

Frederick nods emphatically. "They moved away from the village not long after Kiera's body was found."

"I need full names and addresses." Enzo flips to a clean page in his notebook. "Everything you can tell me."

Frederick looks taken aback but calls for Helen to return and fetch his address book. I pause for a moment to take a breather and gather my thoughts.

We've worked in this industry for long enough to understand the sickest of minds. Serial killers are depraved, calculating creatures, driven by the most heinous of desires.

Most people don't realise they are also entirely fallible and, ultimately, human. They have to revel in their crimes. It's like oxygen to them. The attention feeds their addiction.

Sometimes, they will insert themselves into criminal investigations, even flaunt their facades in front of law enforcement to seek a twisted thrill.

It's clear that Kiera was devastated by the accusation levelled against her. We know she had no romantic relationships, and I doubt she became embroiled in an affair.

So, what happened?

Was this man involved?

What if it wasn't consensual?

If Pastor Michaels was hiding behind a false identity, he could have hurt Kiera, even imprisoned and tortured her, all while directing a neighbourhood-wide search to locate her. His old base of operations isn't far from here.

Stepping into the corridor, I dial Theo's number. He takes a moment to answer, and I can hear the rumble of the TV in the background.

"Hold on," he whispers.

My heart pounds when I hear Harlow's voice, sweet and sleepy, asking where he's going. Theo mutters something about grabbing a drink before returning to the line.

"Hunt. What is it?"

"How is she?" I ask urgently.

His sigh rattles through the receiver. "The hospital called. She's still worried, but we're trying to keep her mind off it."

"Good. Listen, I need you to send the intelligence department some information. We need an urgent confirmation."

"You've found something?"

"Maybe. I want a full background check on Mr Lee Heston and his wife, Natasha. I'm texting you their old addresses now. They moved away around five years ago."

The tapping of his fingers on his phone echoes down the line as he begins texting the team.

"Do you have a photo?" Theo asks.

"Of what?"

"This man," he clarifies. "You think he's Michaels, right? If we have a photo, we can show Harlow. She'll confirm it."

"We can't do that to her."

"She wants to help, Hunt."

"This won't help her though."

"Actually, I think it will. I'm not sure how much longer she can go on like this, powerless and afraid. It's killing her."

"How is involving her in this bloodbath going to help?"

Theo hesitates. "She needs to be back in control of her own life. I can't watch her sit there, tearing her own goddamn hair out, for a second longer. Let her help."

Eyes screwed shut, I battle the impending migraine that's causing my stomach to revolt. Uncertainty isn't something I've dealt with in recent years. I've always known the right path to take.

Every step is planned, timed and organised to the finest fucking degree of detail. The guys laugh at Kade and his obsessive, control-freak ways, but he's a disorganised toddler compared to the life I lead.

That is, until Harlow.

She invaded my world, set the entire ocean alight and left me on a sinking life raft with no land in sight. I wasn't prepared to lose every ounce of control I've spent years perfecting. It all fell to ruin in the path of her blue eyes and staggeringly sad smiles.

"I'll see what I can do. If it is this asshole, she's going to be triggered. Stay with her until we get home. Understood?"

"Understood," he complies.

"Keep your phone on."

Hanging up the call, I slip back into the musty living room. Enzo's head snaps up as I approach them both, my phone clutched in a white-knuckled grip.

"Mr Houghton, I don't suppose you have a photograph of Lee Heston and his wife?"

Frederick taps his lips with a papery finger. "If I do, it will be in one of the old Parish booklets we distributed at Christmas time. Helen! Come here, dearie."

The weary care worker slinks back into the room. I spare her an apologetic look. She deserves to be paid a hell of a lot more than I'm sure this old bastard is giving her.

Bringing his Zimmer frame in front of the armchair, she helps Frederick stand up on spindly legs. They walk over to the tall, mahogany dresser at the back of the room beneath a pair of ugly net curtains.

Frederick grumbles under his breath as he searches through the drawers, pulling out odd trinkets and scraps of clipped newspapers along the way.

"Maybe I didn't save one, after all." He frowns at a stack of news articles. "My wife used to collect obituaries before she passed on."

"Charming," Enzo comments.

"You'll be old one day too, young man. Appreciate your youth and family while you have it. My wife left me for the Lord's grace far too early for my liking."

Enzo shoots me a desperate look. On a good day, his patience is a shoestring verging on disaster. Perhaps he was the wrong person to enrol for this particular assignment.

"Oh look, my winning scratch card." Frederick hands it to him with a smile. "I won three pounds in 1987. It was quite the excitement at the time."

I watch Enzo faceplant and mouth a pained *fuck my life.* I have to swallow my laughter.

"Ah! There's the ticket."

Flourishing a crinkled, palm-sized booklet, Frederick flicks through the pages with his lips parted. When his expression lights up as he taps a page, I know we've struck gold.

"Here he is," he declares. "This was taken seven or so years ago. Oh, Kiera is in this photo too. How precious."

Enzo snatches the booklet from his hands and scans over it. Lips pursed, he passes it to me and watches as I snap a picture for Theo. I hate doing this when I'm not there to hold Harlow's hand at what could be a pivotal moment.

Lee Heston looked to be in his early fifties, wearing an unassuming, cheap suit and sparkling gold crucifix over his white shirt. His wife, Natasha, wore a demure, flowery dress and a thin smile that didn't reach her eyes.

"Why are you sending it to him?" Enzo asks quietly.

I pull him aside for some privacy. "Harlow's going to check if she recognises him."

"What the fuck? Why?" he exclaims.

"Because she needs to. If not for the investigation, then her own sanity."

"You should have waited. What if she needs us, huh? We're five damn hours away."

"And if Michaels has another girl in a cage right now? Raping, beating and brutalising the poor sod? Can she wait?"

His mouth clicks shut as my phone vibrates with a text message. We both stare down at the two words.

Six letters. Nineteen murders. One living victim… and one chance to finally nail this motherfucker.

Theodore: It's him.

CHAPTER 10
HARLOW

DO IT FOR ME - ROSENFELD

EXCRUCIATING *pain flares through my entire body, twisting and writhing in an inferno of agony. I try to pull my arm from Pastor Michaels' grip, but his knee is pinning my elbow to the stained, blood-slick concrete as he attaches the pliers to my next fingernail.*

"I told you to pray, filthy demon spawn," he hisses, hot spittle hitting me in the face. "Why do you defy me? Don't you love your daddy?"

"No! You killed my friend!" I scream hoarsely.

In the adjacent cage, Tia's dirty, bloodstained face is gone. There's nothing left. Just a pummelled, oozing meat salad where her pretty features once resided. Beaten to a crimson paste by Pastor Michaels' ring-laden fist.

On his sneering face, a small cut is spilling blood down his stubble-peppered cheek. Tia's feistier than the other girls… or rather, she was. When he pinned her naked body against the bars and shoved a hand between her legs, she fought back, managing to get in a blow of her own.

It only enraged him more.

I no longer recognise her demolished corpse.

"Please," I beg, my face slick with sweat.

"I have to hurt you." He traces his lips against my dirty cheek. "It's the only way for you to learn, daughter of mine. The Lord spared you, unlike this sinful whore. You're Daddy's special girl."

Tugging the pliers away from my finger in one brutal move, he rips the other fingernail out with a snarl. My voice cracks and the endless screams erupting from my throat fall silent. My face is slick with a waterfall of tears.

"When I bring the next girl down here, what are you going to do?"

The stench of his breath stops me from succumbing to unconsciousness.

"P-P-Pray harder," I wheeze out.

"Good. Now, let's hear those prayers. From the top."

He moves the pliers to my final fingernail, primed and ready for the taking. Blood is seeping across my palm from the other tender, torn-out wounds. The pain is almost numbing, it's so overwhelming.

"Harlow," he warns, tugging on the nail.

"Our F-Father." I choke down a bubble of vomit. "Who art in H-Heaven..."

My head falls to the side, dizzy from pain, and I stare at the place where Tia's eyes used to be. Squelchy, red-slick sockets stare back at me. In my semi-conscious daze, I swear her visible jawbone moves, shifting to mouth an accusation.

"Your fault."

Sliding out of the sweaty bedsheets and almost falling to my knees, I battle to remain upright. Hunter groans in his sleep, snuggling closer to my vacated pillow.

He takes a deep inhale of the fabric where my head rested and relaxes with the comfort of my familiar scent sending him back to sleep.

Clamping a hand over my mouth, I stumble as fast as possible for the en-suite bathroom. The door has barely clicked shut behind me before I'm crouched over the toilet, throwing up over and over again.

It's only stomach acid coming out. I haven't eaten anything since yesterday's breakfast. My stomach revolts again, forcing more acid up my aching throat.

When the onslaught finally stops, I curl up on the cold, tiled floor, my entire body slick with sweat and limbs trembling. Nineteen women are screaming inside my head in a deafening chorus.

Your fault.

Your fault.

Your fault.

"Please stop," I whisper to the invisible ghosts. "He k-killed you, not me. I t-tried to stop him... I really did."

Your fault.

Your fault.

Your fault.

"Stop it! Stop!"

Scrambling to my feet, I hoist myself up and make it over to the sink basin. Running the tap as quietly as possible, I splash my face and scrub hard enough for my skin to ache.

I need to get Pastor Michaels' poison out of my pores. It's infecting me from the inside out. Hands braced on the sink, I try to catch the breath that's determined to escape my lungs.

I can't suck it in before it disappears through my fingertips like sand. My head is spinning so fast, I'm on the verge of passing out.

A strange, deep gurgle emanates from the plug hole. The water that just washed down begins to rise back up the pipe, bubbling and spitting, but it's no longer clear.

Crimson-soaked droplets fill the sink basin in a bloodied tidal wave, growing higher and higher. Taking a step back, I cover my mouth in horror as blood begins to spill over the edges, pooling on the tiles.

It's everywhere.

Covering everything.

Red trails leak down the walls, adding to the macabre scene of death. Every corner of the bathroom is stained with the dark tinge of blood.

"Hunter!" I scream.

My back hits the wall as I scratch at my own throat, physically trying to grapple the air and shove it into my lungs. The blood has started to gather into a huge, dramatic crest.

"Sweetheart? Where are you?"

The bathroom door cracks against the wall with such force, the glass pane shatters and collapses into jagged pieces. Bare-chested and frantic, Hunter hops over the mess, his hair sticking up in every direction.

"Harlow?"

I'm scratching so deep into my neck, blood and skin are gathering beneath my nails. The same fingers that Pastor Michaels attached his pliers to, threatening with each sharp rip.

"H-Help me," I stutter.

"What is it? Did you have a bad dream?"

Gesturing towards the sticky trails of blood pouring from every corner of the room, I launch myself towards him before I'm swallowed whole by the devil.

Hunter grunts when I smack into him so hard, we both stumble and hit the towel rack. He narrowly avoids landing in a pile of smashed glass.

"Woah." He runs his hands over my back. "Harlow, I need you to breathe. You're going to pass out if you don't."

"The b-blood!"

He grips my chin tight and drags my eyes up to meet his. "What blood? Where?"

"Everywhere! Can't y-you see it?!"

Heartbreak sizzles across his expression.

"Baby… there's nothing here. No blood."

Tilting my head to the side, he encourages me to look. With tears still stinging my cheeks, I take a tiny, terrified glance around the bathroom. The entire scene has changed.

It's spotless.

Completely, irrefutably spotless.

My chest rises and falls in a bruising rhythm, causing my heart to slam against my ribcage. It's all gone. Not a single speck of blood. Where did it go? Am I losing my mind here? Everything has changed before my very eyes.

"Harlow," he murmurs. "Breathe for me. Come on, like Enzo showed you. There's a good girl."

Easily lifting me up, Hunter exits the bathroom. I'm met by softness as he deposits me on the edge of the bed and kneels in front of me.

His face is laced with uncertainty. It hurts me to see him so afraid, far from the lion-hearted dictator who swept into my hospital room months ago to lay the law down.

I did this to him.

I'm breaking them all.

"Tell me what you need," he pleads, his thumbs circling my bare legs. "Want me to call Enzo? He's at the office with Theo. I can get them both here."

I shake my head. "The b-blood and Pastor Michaels… he killed her. It was my fault… all my fault."

"What are you talking about? Come on, sweetheart. We've talked about this."

"It's m-my fault!" I sob harder.

"Harlow, you did nothing wrong. Watching isn't the same as perpetrating. You couldn't have saved them from him."

I raise a trembling hand and grab a handful of loose hair hanging over my shoulder. Hunter curses as I yank hard, pulling several strands out at once.

The faint *pop* of snapped hair follicles causes pain to race over my sore scalp in a blissful release. More. More. More.

I have to hurt.

Just like they did.

Taking more strands of hair, I dodge his hand clamping around my wrist and pull again—harder, faster, ripping a handful out. When Hunter captures my hand and slips a finger beneath my mane of hair, his skin comes away wet with fresh blood.

"Jesus Christ," he swears in a panic. "Please, tell me what you need. I'll do anything. Just stop hurting yourself."

"No, I need to hurt. He hurt them… I have to hurt as well. Let go of me!"

"I won't," he yells back. "Don't expect me to sit here and watch you tear yourself apart."

More frantic sobs gnaw at my chest, demanding an outlet. His drawn face hardens into a mask of determination.

"You need to hurt?"

"Yes," I choke out. "It's the only thing that works."

"Fine. I'll fucking hurt you."

Standing up, Hunter roughly yanks me to my feet. I almost fall over from dizziness, but he refuses to let me fall. I'm still wearing Leighton's t-shirt, stolen from his wardrobe as he fell asleep on the sofa downstairs.

Beneath it, I'm only wearing plain panties. My period left several days ago, as abruptly as it arrived.

"Arms up," he orders in a harsh voice.

"What?"

Hunter grabs the hem of my shirt and yanks it over my head. He tosses it over his shoulder without a second glance. I stand beneath his towering, muscled height, my breasts bare and torso scarred with the carving of the Holy Trinity.

"Hunter," I whimper.

He drags a hand down my arm, moving to the curve of my hip. "Do you trust me?"

Hesitating, I muster a timid nod.

"Then let me take care of you. We can deal with this together, without you hurting yourself. I have another idea."

Still gripping my hip, he ducks down and places a gentle kiss against the slope of my stomach. I let my eyes flutter shut as his lips lower, tracing the line of my plain white panties.

Hunter hooks a finger underneath the elastic and pulls them down inch by torturous inch. His warm hand wraps around my ankle, and he guides them off.

"You won't be needing these," he says with heavy-lidded eyes peering up at me.

When he rises back to his full height, I'm completely naked and feeling more than a little vulnerable. Everything is on display. There's nowhere to hide from his fearsome gaze.

"What are you g-going to do to me?"

His mouth hooks up. "Turn around, sweetheart. Hands on the bed."

When I don't move, he wraps his fingers around one of my stiffened nipples and tugs. I gasp at the sudden burst of pain.

"Turn around. Now."

With chills sweeping over my skin, I follow orders and face the bed. His fingertip touches the top of my spine and dances downwards over gooseflesh and vertebrae, leaving a burning trail of heat that pools between my thighs.

"Bend over, little Harlow," he breathes in my ear. "I'm going to give you the pain you're looking for."

My entire body is screaming out for a release, awash with building tension. I want to tear every last hair from my head and bathe in my own blood as penance. Hunter can't save me, no matter what he thinks.

It's too late.

I'm already broken.

Placing my hands on the rumpled sheets, I arch my back, pushing my behind outwards. It feels wrong to expose myself like this, without a single scrap of fabric covering my body.

But instead of fear, anticipation is thrumming through my veins. I can't help my curiosity. Hunter promised pain. Relief. A punishment of sorts. He's toyed with me for months, offering only the barest flickers of affection.

Even if I don't deserve it, I want more. I'm dying to be consumed by him. Controlled. Silenced by a hand other than my own. It's the only light at the end of a very dark tunnel.

I bite back a moan as Hunter's palm strokes my left butt cheek in a slow, tender caress. "Such a beautiful girl."

I'm just relaxing into the soothing contact when his hand slams against my ass in a punishing spank. Pain lances up my spine, setting off exploding fireworks.

Stroking my sensitised skin, I can't hold back a gasp when Hunter hits me again. Harder, against the same cheek, causing thunder to crackle across my entire frame this time.

"Does that hurt, sweetheart?"

"Yes," I pant.

"Do you want more?"

Arching my back more, I push my ass against the hardness tenting his sweatpants. "Yes. Please, more."

He soothes the sting across my skin with another reverent stroke. "Please what, Harlow?"

"Please hit me," I say in a strangled whisper.

"Why, baby?"

"Because… I need it. I need the pain to survive."

He smooths a calloused palm over my other butt cheek. Tingles from his last spank race through my system. When he hits me this time, it toes the line between pain and pleasure. Each aching blow makes my core clench tight.

"I could get used to the sound of you begging," he teases, still stroking me. "Do you want it harder this time?"

"Yes."

"Ask me properly then."

It should be humiliating to be bossed around by him. I don't think I'd let any other man control me with such blatant lust for my submission. But with him? It comes down to trust.

I want to please him and satisfy the demanding creature beneath his human skin. His whispered praise is the tonic to Pastor Michaels' cruel poison. I can't get enough of it.

"Hit me harder, Hunter." I smack a frustrated hand on the mattress. "Stop being gentle with me."

"You're not triggered?" he checks in.

"No. Keep going."

My pulse spikes as his hand snakes around the curve of my hip to dip between my legs. His bare foot nudges between mine, pushing my thighs open. When he cups my mound, I realise how wet I am for him.

"Such a good girl, aren't you?" he purrs in my ear. "You're so wet for me, sweetheart, and I've barely touched you."

Another moan escapes as he slips a skilled finger through my folds. Circling my entrance, sparks of pain race over my earlobe with the light bite of Hunter's teeth.

I gasp loudly when he pushes a thick finger deep inside my slit. His delicious hardness is pressing up against my tingling ass cheeks, separated by the friction of his sweatpants.

"Goddammit, love," Hunter grumbles. "I want to bury my cock in you so badly. Tell me to stop."

I'm panting with need as he slips another finger inside me. The pressure intensifies. Both digits move in a steady, teasing rhythm. His thumb circles my nub with each rotation, adding to the flames of desire.

"I want… I…"

"What do you want?" he coos.

"Everything. I want it all."

His tongue flicks against my ear. "I want to fuck you so bad, Harlow. But I won't do it. Not until you choose me."

"Choose?" I moan.

With his fingers teasing the tender spot that sends sparks across my skin, a traitorous part of me wants to submit. I'm so tired of the fighting. But I can't. I won't do it. Not like this.

Before I burst, Hunter's hand disappears from between my thighs. I cry out, my eyes burning with unshed tears. I'm so overwhelmed. All of these twisted feelings need to escape my body before my sanity finally snaps.

He raises his glistening fingers to my mouth and pushes them inside. "Suck. Taste yourself."

My throat clenches as his fingers glide against my tongue, spreading the salty tang of my own come. I lick over his digits before Hunter pulls them back out.

His hand disappears, ghosting back down the length of my spine. I'm still bent over the bed, trapped and powerless to his divine will. He could do anything to me right now, and I wouldn't give a damn.

"You want me to prove myself? I can make you feel even better than that, sweetheart. Just wait."

My legs tremble as his moistened fingers stroke over my pussy from behind, daring to skate higher. He isn't going to… is he? I try to lift myself, and his hand pushes against my lower back to shove me down again.

"Trust me," he says simply.

Letting the tension drain out of me, I hold my breath as he pushes between my cheeks. The intrusion is nerve-wracking. My instincts are still yelling at me to run as his wet fingertip circles the tight ring of muscle at my back entrance.

"Pleasure can take many forms," Hunter whispers. "I want to know what makes my baby feel good."

"Oh God, Hunt!"

His finger pushes deep inside me, using the coating of saliva to ease the ride. It's a burning intrusion at first. Unwelcome. But when the first flash of anxiety dissipates, the pleasure comes barrelling through me.

"Can you take both?" he wonders.

Rotating his hand, Hunter pushes another finger back into my pussy. With both holes filled, I grip the sheets tighter. It's too much. My entire body is spasming with waves of pleasure.

"Ready to let go?"

"Yes," I mewl.

"Then come for me, baby. Scream my name."

It keeps coming—stronger than the time he teased my orgasm with his lips, or when Enzo tasted me in the kitchen. Even more intense than Leighton toying with me on the sofa.

The tip of his covered cock is pushing against me, feeling like it's going to burst free from its fabric prison. I can imagine how it will feel, sliding deep inside me for the first time.

He drives right to the edge and leaves me to freefall as my orgasm takes over. I writhe and moan, my whole world shattering with the spasms wracking over me. Hunter buries his face in my hair, savouring the power he holds.

"Perfect," he praises.

Carefully turning me over, I'm spread across the bed on my back. His smile is crooked as he adjusts the tight material banded across his erection.

When I try to reach for him, intent on putting the lesson Leighton taught me to use, he brushes my hand aside.

"I don't want anything from you," he says with a smouldering look. "This was about proving a point."

I summon the remaining wisps of my voice.

"You want me to choose you."

His eyes refuse to leave mine. "Yes."

"Just you."

"Yes," he repeats.

An invisible hand chokes my windpipe. "You know I can't do that, Hunt."

His smile drops. "I won't share you. I'm a selfish fucking bastard, and I want you to myself or not at all."

"Not at all?"

"You heard me," he confirms.

Covering my bare breasts with my arms, I pull myself up, needing some space to think. Hunter's expression shuts down into familiar coldness as I inch backwards on the mattress.

"I… need them too," I whisper. "You can't ask me to stop caring about the others. I can't just turn my feelings off."

His feet drag backwards, widening the distance between us. "And what about my feelings, Harlow?"

My hand flashes to my hair and back down again, wracked by indecision. He looks ready to lock me in a brand-new cage. This time, it's one of his construction, shiny and deceptive, where the other pieces of my heart can't reach me.

"I can't let them go," I answer around my rising tears. "I just can't."

"Even if I've fallen in love with you?"

I feel like I've been slapped across the face with a brick. Hunter's eyebrows are drawn together in an accusing frown, and the space keeping us apart feels like an endless ocean.

I suddenly wish Leighton would wake up and come rescue me. Violence clings to Hunter like a second skin, and though I know he'd never hurt me, his words cut just as deeply.

"You're… in love with me?" I repeat.

"I've spent the last five years living the life of a ghost. I didn't know I was capable of feeling such things again."

I have no idea what to say.

He knows it too.

Hunter turns his back and tries to escape. Leaping up from the bed, I snake my arms around his naked, tattooed torso from behind and hold him in place. He'll have to drag me.

"Please don't leave," I whimper against his skin. "I'm so confused, but I know I can't do this without you."

"You don't mean that."

"Hunter." I dive in front of him. "It's true. You have saved my life, over and over again. Nobody has ever cared about me the way you do."

Insecurity flashes through the molten depths of his irises. I draw his lips down to mine and kiss him, unable to find the words to express what I need to say. My wordless desperation is all I have to offer him.

"I'm falling in love with you too," I whisper against his lips. "Don't close yourself off from me again. Please."

His forehead leans against mine. "Fuck, Harlow. All we're going to do is hurt each other in the end."

"I don't care. I'll get hurt if that's what it takes. I need you to stay, but please, don't ask me to choose. You know I can't."

It feels like the entire house is burning to ashes around me as I wait for his answer. I'm silently pleading with an uncaring God to give me this one tiny thing—their patience.

I'll find a way out of this mess because I have to. It's a matter of life and death. Light and dark. Salvation and destruction. Living with them… or dying without them. I can't see any other alternative.

"I know." He sighs, his two hands landing on my shoulders. "Get back into bed. You need to rest."

My eyes dart over to the tangled sheets. "I'm s-scared to sleep. The dreams… they feel so real."

"I can get Leighton instead."

"No!" I raise my voice and cling on tighter. "I don't want him to hold me. I want you."

I don't need to look up to see his smile. I can feel it. He lifts me into his arms and walks over to the bed. We crawl between the sheets together, and I'm settled in the crook of his arm, so he's spooned behind me.

His face buries in my neck. "Sleep, Harlow."

"You'll protect me?" I murmur.

"No one is going to hurt you while I'm here. Not even the nightmares. I'll always keep you safe."

My eyes fall shut, commanded by the authority in his voice. The blood-slick nightmares don't return. Not with Hunter's promise still ringing in my ears.

CHAPTER 11
LEIGHTON

MY HAND/LAWLESS DREAM – MATT MAESON

THE LARGE CONFERENCE room in Sabre HQ is bustling with bleak conversation, cracked-open energy drinks and the splash of fresh coffee being poured. It's a bleak morning.

Everyone is here at Hunter's urgent command. Last night, we received word from Derby's police department that a young sex worker has vanished without a trace.

Candace Bernard was reported missing by two friends when she didn't return from a job. They saw her leave with a customer around midnight and called the police the next morning after searching for her.

What they found terrified them.

That's when we were called in.

Her skimpy, sequinned dress was found in a nearby alleyway, covered in fresh blood. A note was tucked into the pocket with a written message and a hand-drawn calling card—the Holy Trinity, etched in fresh ink.

Surrender, Harlow Michaels.
Or the next death is on you.

Harlow has barely spoken since we broke the news. There wasn't even a glimmer of satisfaction when Enzo agreed she could attend this emergency meeting. He's determined to do right by her and fix his mistakes by keeping her in the loop.

The Anaconda and Cobra teams have gathered, plus the whole intelligence department. Everyone involved in the case so far has been put on high alert by this violent development.

"I don't think I can do this."

Harlow's voice is cracked with fear.

"We can go in together," I offer.

She lingers behind me, bouncing on the balls of her feet, which are cloaked in thick-soled leather boots to protect against the February chill. Her usual skinny jeans and sweater seem rumpled, like she got dressed without paying attention.

I tug her closer until she collides with my chest. Harlow buries her face in my grey t-shirt, her breathing unsteady.

"Hunter, Enzo and Theo are all in there with the teams. It's safe. We're going to deal with this together."

Her head shakes. "Every single one of them is thinking the same thing; the longer I hide, the more death there will be."

"You know that isn't true."

"Isn't it?" she scoffs.

"Nobody here is going to let you fall for this sicko's trap. This is part of his game. We can't play into it."

Catching her wrist as her fingers attempt to tangle in her long mane of hair, I push them aside before she can begin pulling. Harlow glances up at me, her shining blue eyes filled with embarrassment.

"I have just the thing." I press a soft kiss to the corner of her mouth. "Let me try something."

Pushing back my coat sleeve, I reveal the collection of elastic hair ties I've been wearing around my wrist on a daily basis. Her eyes widen as I take one and gesture for her to turn around.

"How long have you been carrying those around for?"

Taking three big bunches of her hair, I begin braiding. "A few weeks."

I work fast as the plait begins to grow in length, stretching down her back in a corded rope of hair. Tying it off with the elastic, I drop a kiss on top of her lowered head.

"I figured that if it's out of your way, you won't be tempted to pull without realising."

Harlow turns around to stare up at me, her eyes brimming with sparkling tears. One dares to leak down her cheek, and I use my thumb to gently brush it aside.

"What did I do to deserve you?"

"Plenty," I reply easily. "If you need to take a breather or it gets too much, poke me and we can step outside. Deal?"

She summons a smile. "Deal."

Taking Harlow's hand, I tuck her into my side. We enter the room together and approach the table where Enzo and Theo are talking in low, urgent whispers. They both fall silent and look up at us.

"Good morning," I say cheerfully.

"What are you so chipper about?" Enzo stares at me.

"Just trying to lighten the mood. I had a great sleep last night, snuggled up with Harlow. You should work late more often, Enz."

His glower deepens. "Hilarious."

He looks like he wants to obliterate me with his stare alone. Since their little excursion to Newcastle earlier this month, Enzo's been working most nights alongside Kade and Theo to gather information on Michaels' false identity.

Pulling out the chair next to Theo, I guide Harlow into it before she can have second thoughts and bolt from the room.

She shoots Enzo a strained smile and wraps Theo in a quick, tight hug. To my surprise, he hugs her back, his eyes closing briefly. Enzo watches on with his own smile.

"You okay?" she asks Theo.

"Been better. We worked through the night."

"You need to sleep." Harlow glances at Enzo too. "And you. The pair of you look ready to keel over."

"We're fine, little one," Enzo offers as he knocks back more coffee. "Sleep can wait for when we find this girl."

"I'm sorry I wasn't there when Hunter told you last night," Theo apologises. "I couldn't get away."

Harlow shrugs it off. "I understand."

"Things have been crazy for the last few weeks, and now all this shit too. We must have a stack of books to discuss."

She helps herself to a mug of tea. "More like a whole bookcase. I've been reading lots."

Avoiding the empty seat next to Enzo, I take the other end of the table, where he can't beat my ass for rubbing last night's cuddle session in his face.

He really does look like shit. The dark circles beneath his eyes are full-blown thunder clouds, while his untidy mop of jet-black hair is getting unruly as it awaits a needed haircut.

"Did you complete the registration for online school?" Enzo asks her.

Harlow takes another sip and nods. "Theo helped me do it while you were away last week. Basic Maths and English for now. I want to catch up on what I missed."

"You'll do fine," I reassure her.

"We'll see about that."

Silenced by a flash of bright-blonde hair and two scarred arms circling her neck from behind, Brooklyn draws her into a bear hug, squeezing before quickly releasing.

"I didn't know you were coming," she greets. "Are you doing okay with the news?"

"Peachy," Harlow replies. "How are you? Aside from the case. I feel like that's all I've thought about."

Helping herself to our cafetière of coffee, Brooklyn rolls her eyes. "Oh, you know. Planning a wedding to five dickheads is a challenge. Hudson wants to hold it in a graveyard."

"You're kidding?" Enzo chuckles.

"He thinks it'll be ironic." Brooklyn gestures towards the table where Hudson and Kade are conspiring. "I'm seriously outgunned as the only female."

"Do you want some help?" Harlow asks uncertainly.

Brooklyn's face lights up. "You'd do that?"

"I know absolutely nothing about weddings, let alone planning one. I'm happy to give it a go though."

The squeal she makes is so unlike Brooklyn, I clamp my hands over my ears. This woman has slaughtered whole rooms full of people without blinking an eye, yet here she is getting excited about choosing wedding flowers.

"Blackbird!" Hudson bellows.

The Anaconda team and intelligence department fall silent as they watch her turn, a hand propped on her hip. Becket pauses halfway through showing Rayna and Fox something.

"Yes, Hud?" Brooklyn beams.

"Mind keeping the screaming down? You, Phoenix and Eli fucking like rabbits kept me awake last night."

Rather than blushing like a sane human being, Brooklyn's grin widens. "Hey, we invited you and Jude to join in."

"That is not the mental image I need this early in the morning," Enzo grumbles under his breath. "Brooke, go deal with your fiancé before I throw up."

Winking at us both, Brooklyn thumps away in her tightly laced, patent leather Doc Martens. Ethan, Becket's second-in-command, wolf whistles as she passes.

"That's my future wife you're checking out." Hudson shoots him a death glare. "I'd shut up if I were you."

His smile drops. "Oh, uh. Sure."

"That's what I thought."

Breaking their standoff, the door to the conference room slams shut. Hunter storms in, flanked by our PR agent, Lucas. Both are dressed in pristine suits and wearing identical grim expressions.

"Sorry we're late."

"Everything okay?" Enzo frowns at him.

Hunter pulls off his jacket and gun holster. "We're moving the building to level three security with immediate effect."

He stiffens, reaching for his own weapon. "What happened? Are we secure?"

Lucas pours himself a coffee. "There was a leak from Derby's police department."

Enzo's head thumps on the table. "Fuck."

"Every newspaper in the country has a copy of Pastor Michaels' note printed across its front page this morning."

"With Harlow's name included?" Theo asks.

Hunter nods, his jaw clenched.

"There's also a protest being staged outside." Lucas drains his coffee with a wince. "The media has turned up to film it and a crowd's gathering already."

"P-Protest?" Harlow stammers.

Hunter clears his throat. "We're facing increasing pressure to capture the killer… or give him what he wants. Pastor Michaels has a number of supporters."

Her face turns white. "Me."

"That's not fucking happening," Enzo barks. "They'll have to tear the building down to get their hands on Harlow."

"Nobody is suggesting we do that," Hunter placates him. "These lunatics are exactly that. Lunatics. We ignore them."

Mumblings of agreement sweep over the room. Humans disgust me sometimes. Giving Michaels what he wants won't stop the killings, no matter what the media prints.

He will continue to slaughter and terrorise the country, even with Harlow back in his possession. Rule number one in prison? You never give a bully what he wants because they will keep taking until you've got nothing left.

Harlow sacrificing herself won't keep people safe. She would lose her freedom, and her life, for nothing. Our biggest job is convincing her of that fact, not the public.

"We've tripled security. The protest is contained," Hunter explains. "Let's move on to the case. Where are we at?"

Enzo shuffles through the paperwork. "We know Michaels cleaned house in his previous kill site and left Rosetta's corpse behind. He must be holding this victim in a new bolt hole."

"Why speak up now?" Kade questions.

"It was only a matter of time," Hudson finishes for him. "He killed Rosetta Stone to cover his tracks, and an accomplice is an unnecessary risk. Her death didn't sate him."

"No, that's not right," Harlow disagrees.

She catches herself and flushes red, her lips pursed. Rather than scold her as she seems to be expecting, Hunter smiles and gestures for her to continue.

"Well, he relied on her for everything." Harlow fiddles with her nails. "Mrs Michaels did all the dirty work. Killing her didn't make his life easier. She was his biggest asset."

"Then why do it?" I ask the room.

Raising a hand, Rayna waits for Hunter's nod of approval before speaking. Her purple hair is loose today, spilling over her oversized sweatshirt and tight leggings.

"He didn't just kill Rosetta," she explains nervously. "It was a message. He didn't even take her wedding ring with him. It's like… he wanted Harlow to find her."

"For what purpose?" Hudson growls.

Twirling the end of her braid in a trembling hand, Harlow looks at me. I raise a single brow, asking if she wants to leave. Taking a deep breath, she shakes her head.

"Did he want us to identify Rosetta?" Brooklyn suggests. "We're missing something. He wants us to know whatever that is."

"Or whoever she is," Theo finishes. "Rosetta is the key to his past. He's taunting us."

"To what end?" Hunter sighs.

"Well, we have a theory. My contact in government was useless, so I… uh, went in search of answers elsewhere."

He stares at Theo. "What did you do?"

"I might have hacked the High Court's criminal database and looked through some sealed case files."

"Might have?" Hunter exclaims.

"It was… an accident?" Theo offers.

"Jesus Christ. You are costing me a fortune in legal bills. The High bloody Court, Theo. This is serious!"

"I know this is serious," he answers evenly. "That is exactly why I did it. We need answers that no one can give us."

"There are only so many times I can stop your stupid ass from being thrown in prison on computer misuse charges."

"I was careful," Theo defends. "Nobody even knows that I infiltrated their system. Easy peasy, lemon squeezy."

"No, it's not. You're a loose cannon!"

"Hunt," Enzo says calmly. "Hear us out."

"You were in on this too?" Hunter accuses.

"We needed to test if our theory was right," he replies before glancing at his accomplice. "Fill them in."

Smoothing his blue flannel shirt and tight, faded-grey jeans, Theo connects one of his laptops to the projector. A series of images are painted across the empty back wall.

Four old, peeling cardboard boxes of paperwork have been emptied out to be manually scanned. The array of evidence is vast, all sealed by the court's authority.

"An estimated eight hundred children's homes were operational between the fifties and nineties," Theo explains. "This was before the government cracked down, facing lawsuits and allegations of severe neglect."

He moves to the first image. It's a black-and-white shot of a four-story manor house. Dark vines of ivy creep over the antiquated bricks, and the sinister structure is surrounded by a thicket of towering trees.

"Genesis Home for Wayward Children."

"This was the place?" Hunter clarifies.

"Rosetta spent four years here. It was a Catholic-run orphanage that has been implicated in countless cases of child abuse and sexual violence."

"Why haven't we heard of this scandal?" Ethan speaks up as he studies the images. "If government funding was involved, we should've heard of the fallout."

"None of this is public knowledge," Theo responds. "The victims reached a settlement and the clean-up initiative buried everything, including this court case."

"Any prosecutions?" Kade asks next.

"The home was managed by a string of well-paid Catholic churches."

Theo checks his notes. "Several priests were liable for prosecution, but they bought off the defendants."

I study the images. "Do we have a list of the victims?"

"Negative. It's safe to assume that Rosetta Stone was not among them. She left custody and shed her identity to avoid being dragged back there."

One hand stroking his beard, Hunter listens while sparing Harlow glances every few seconds. He seems desperate to keep his eyes on her at all times.

She's also studying the projected photograph of the children's home with creased eyebrows, as if the grainy pixels will reveal the secrets of the universe if she stares for long enough.

I shuffle closer to her. "What is it?"

"The answers are all in that place." She shakes her head. "What is he trying to tell me? Why leave Rosetta behind?"

"I don't know, princess."

"It's just another dead end, isn't it?""

"That's not exactly true," Theo intervenes. "We may have found someone who worked on the original investigation in the eighties."

"What? How?" Hunter urges.

"We did some digging around with a police contact," Enzo answers for him. "A retired constable got back to us, but he's unwilling to go on record."

"Even the superintendent refused to touch this place." Hunter eyes them both. "Who on earth did you speak to?"

Neither answers him.

"Does this have anything to do with the missed calls from my father?" he continues in a lower voice.

"We did what we had to." Enzo clears his throat. "Whether this guy goes on record or not, he has information about that place. I'll get it out of him."

Hunter's eyes narrow. "You involved my father."

"All we asked for was a contact."

"That's fucking involving him!"

"It was a calculated risk," Enzo defends.

Turning his back to take a breath, Hunter mutters a colourful curse. I sure as hell am not getting involved in anything to do with our parents. Fuck that.

When Hunter turns around, I can see he's buried his annoyance for a private bollocking later. Theo gulps hard. He's going to get shafted for breaking the rules.

"We have a lead on Michaels' false identity," he redirects. "What information have we uncovered about Lee Heston?"

"Not a lot," Theo admits. "No birth certificate. There's a record of his marriage to Natasha in 1983. Their address was half a mile from the church that Mr Houghton ran."

"Nothing else?" he pushes.

"No registered employment. The house was rented from a private landlord who was part of the parish. They were quiet, unassuming. No reason for anyone to suspect their lives were a sham."

"Do you think he would go back there to hide out?" Becket asks from his table. "Given the chapel has been uncovered."

"Unlikely," Hunter dismisses. "Let's send a team to Newcastle to search the property regardless." He looks at Hudson and Kade. "Take forensics with you."

Kade quickly nods. "We'll leave today."

"I'm sorry, but how is murdering nineteen women quiet and unassuming?" Brooklyn interrupts angrily. "Someone should've caught this guy years ago."

"Brooke." Kade rests a hand on her shoulder. "We have no control over what the police did back then."

"So what? We can't be angry? He was living a happy fucking life while Harlow was locked in a basement."

"That's enough," Hunter scolds.

"No, it's not. How was he allowed to get away with this for so long? Now another woman is about to lose her life."

"I said enough!" he shouts at her. "Harlow is here, and she doesn't need to hear this right now."

"Don't tell me what to fucking do!"

Brooklyn storms out of the room. Kade hesitates for a second before chasing after her, leaving Hudson to shrug.

"She's pissed about the news report."

"What news report?" Harlow speaks up.

Everyone looks uneasy. I know that the Cobra team is protective about their past. Sabre is a pretty accepting place, but even here, people talk. They prefer to keep it private.

"A few newspapers are running some old stories about us." Hudson stares at his clenched hands. "I tried to stop her from reading them, but you know what she's like."

"Motherfuckers," Enzo curses. "The minute they see our name in the press, the vultures come circling."

"They'll move on soon enough."

Brooklyn's outburst makes more sense. She can't protect her family from the cruel bullshit that the newspapers print. Just like she couldn't protect Harlow from this sick bastard.

Where people she cares about are concerned, her temper runs incredibly hot. Brooklyn loves deeply, and it comes out as rage. That's how she shows her devotion, through violent, territorial friendship that would scare most people.

Theo touches Harlow's hand and recoils when she shudders at the contact. She's closing in on herself, hugging her stomach tight and staring down at the table.

"Someone should have stopped him," she agrees hoarsely. "If not the police, then me. All I did was watch."

Hunter turns away again, looking on the verge of a furious meltdown. He's really struggling to be professional today.

"I don't know how we can convince you that none of this is your fault." Enzo sighs. "You weren't responsible."

It's the same crap that my mum shoved down my throat before she knew what I did to Thomas Green. I didn't believe her. This is different, but the same thing applies.

"It doesn't matter what we think, does it?" I try instead.

Harlow looks up at me, her eyes wide.

"What matters is how you feel about it, not us."

She nods in acknowledgement. Enzo slumps in his chair, defeated. For a smart guy, he can be a hard-headed idiot when it comes to Harlow and her emotions.

"I know I could have done more," she admits. "Regardless of what you think. Every single person protesting out there is thinking the same thing."

"What do you need to let this go?" I propose.

The whole room is watching our exchange with bated breath, including Hunter from the corner of his eye. Even Enzo is waiting for her answer.

"Justice," Harlow decides.

Hunter's phone rings at the worst possible moment. He answers the call, listens, and swiftly hangs up.

"Giana is here for her second interview. I forgot to cancel it last night." He looks at Harlow apprehensively. "You don't have to speak to her with all this going on. We can postpone."

"No, I need to see her. The rehab unit keeps calling. I can't speak to my father until I hear Giana out first."

"Harlow," Enzo warns. "I don't think—"

"I'll be fine," she cuts him off.

He bites back whatever macho bullshit he was about to suffocate her with. I think the gruff idiot is finally learning.

"I can come with you," Theo offers.

She doesn't flinch this time when he takes her hand. I first noticed their blossoming friendship when he ate pizza with us. It's the first time I've seen Theo initiate contact with anyone.

"Let's get it over and done with." She tightens her grip on Theo's hand. "Will you interview her after?"

Hunter nods. "Yeah. Go first."

Smoothing her sweater, Harlow bends down to press a kiss to my lips in front of the entire damn room. My chest burns with pride as both Hunter and Enzo glare daggers at me.

"Wait for me?" she whispers.

"Like I'd go anywhere without you. Good luck with Giana. Be strong."

"I'll try my best."

Before she can follow Theo out, Enzo thuds around the table to reach Harlow. She squeaks as he bundles her into a back-breaking hug, her head barely reaching his ribcage.

"Remember, you don't owe her anything." He smooths her braided hair. "Just shout if you need us."

"I will, Enz."

"I mean it."

She crosses her finger over her chest in a silent promise. Enzo gives her a secret smile before kissing her forehead.

"I won't hesitate to toss her outside by her hair if she upsets you. With fucking pleasure."

"I know," she murmurs back.

When Enzo releases her, Hunter completes the ridiculous show we're giving the whole room by sweeping her into a bear hug. God knows what everyone will think now.

"Enzo's right." Hunter kisses her temple. "Get what you need, but don't let her make you uncomfortable."

"Guys." Harlow struggles to break his suffocating embrace. "I'll be fine. I just want to ask her a few questions."

"Hug her any tighter and I'll need to call an ambulance," Hudson heckles them. "Run while you can, Harlow."

Grinning, she pecks Hunter's fuzz-covered cheek and slips out from between his muscled arms. Theo offers her his hand again and the pair exit the room together.

Enzo rounds on me. "What the fuck were you doing in her bed last night? While she was upset, no less."

"What were you doing in it last week?" I counter, checking no one is listening. "Or Hunter over the weekend?"

Hunter scrubs his face. "This is ridiculous."

"She isn't going to choose," Enzo hisses at his partner. "Get on board, or let us move ahead without you."

"I am not having this conversation here," he fires back. "We have work to do. Candace's friends are waiting to be interviewed."

Hunter walks over to the Cobra team as Brooklyn and Kade return from the corridor. Her expression is hard and pissed as hell, but she looks a little calmer.

"You think he'll come around?" Enzo sighs.

I glance up at him. "Hunter? Doubt it."

"If we don't compromise, this is only going to end one way. I won't let Hunter fuck up our chance with Harlow."

"Enz, I can't pretend to understand a single thing that goes on inside my brother's head. We can only hope."

"I don't believe in hope."

"Real optimistic of you."

"I'm going to win him over," he vows.

Slapping his shoulder, I help myself to another coffee. "You better start plotting. Good luck. You're going to need it."

Enzo harrumphs. "Fucking watch me."

CHAPTER 12
HARLOW

PRAY – READY THE PRINCE

SITTING on the overstuffed brown sofa, I attempt to focus on the task at hand rather than the fact that another innocent woman is being stripped, beaten and tortured right now.

Candace Bernard.

Another name across my heart.

The clock hanging on the wall in the interview room is ticking loudly, worsening the anxiety gripping my throat. Every second is another slice against her skin, another bruise, another rape.

Pastor Michaels is laughing at us.

We're losing this endless fight.

Hearing voices down the corridor, I scrub my face and take a deep breath. I haven't seen or spoken to my estranged mother, Giana, since the incident in Devon last year.

Being reunited with her and confronted by the picture-perfect family she's created was traumatising. I've had zero desire to repeat the experience, but with my father back in the picture, I can't hide from the past for much longer.

I need to know her side of the story before I can consider giving my father a second of my time. He's done nothing to earn it. My relationship with Giana may be rocky, but I owe it to her to hear her out. That's only fair.

The door beeps with a security pass being scanned. I force myself to take a deep breath as it swings open and Theo's headful of blonde ringlets enters the room.

He shoots me a look and mouths, *"Breathe."* All I can do is nod, unable to speak. Following behind him, Giana's green eyes immediately land on me.

Bouncy brown hair hanging loose over her shoulders, she's wearing a smart cream blouse and pressed trousers, paired with shining court heels. She's even wearing lipstick.

"Harlow," she gushes, dropping her handbag. "I saw the news last night. I've been calling and calling—"

"I know," I interrupt her. "I wasn't ready to talk."

She tries to mask the hurt on her powdered face. "I understand. Last time we spoke, things didn't end well."

"That's one way to put it," Theo mutters as he takes a seat in the corner. "I'll be right over here if you need me, Harlow."

I cast him a grateful smile. "Okay."

Giana narrows her eyes on him with a look of displeasure that bothers me. So much of the bad feeling she sparks within me is silent. It defies explanation, but something about her doesn't sit right. I wish I could remember why.

Yet, I was the first one at my father's bedside. I've forgotten him too, but my instincts guided me there. I know I'm missing something important in this tale. The truth is right there, and it's up to me to solve the riddle.

"Sit." I gesture towards the chair opposite.

She takes a seat, crossing her legs at the ankle as she sweeps her perceptive eyes over me again. I'm sure I look different. I've put on a few more pounds, and my arm is healed now. The way she studies every single detail makes my skin crawl.

"How have you been?" she asks nervously. "That poor girl, and those people out there… you must be feeling so…"

"I'm fine," I deadpan.

"Well, we should talk about what happened."

"I don't want to talk about Devon. That's not why I asked to speak to you."

"I wanted to apologise," she continues in a rush. "I'm sorry you were overwhelmed. That's the last thing I wanted. I know you've been through a lot."

"A lot?" I repeat.

"Well… yes."

"I want to know about the man who turned up half-dead at our front gate. You said my father was gone forever."

Giana twists her fingers together. "He's been missing since he was released from prison. Frankly, I was happy for him to stay that way."

"How could you say that?"

She looks startled by my tone. I'm not the same person she met, trembling and afraid in her kitchen. I've donned a new mask today, one I've spent months perfecting.

"He's still my father," I reason.

"That man is nothing," she spits. "He has no right to hold that title. I raised you myself, not him."

"Why?"

"He was abusive, physically and emotionally. You were too young to remember most of it."

Looking away from her, I stare at the potted plant in the corner of the room. It's drooping, shrivelled, gasping for a single drop of sustenance.

Theo's pretending to be immersed in his laptop, but I can tell he's listening to every word. His eyes briefly connect with mine, but he doesn't smile. It's a silent show of support.

"Abusive how?" I ask carefully.

"I'd rather not go into specifics."

"Then why did you come here?"

Her bottom lip begins to wobble. "What has gotten into you? I thought you'd be happy to see me."

Swallowing the nausea crawling up my throat, I try to lift my mouth in a smile to appease her, but it doesn't come. Imprinted over her face is another. The only mother I can remember. She's stolen that title and won't give it back.

Mrs Michaels.

Only, my memories have warped and changed. Gone is the caustic lash of her voice, the hammer of her fists, my bones crunching beneath her boot.

Now, I see a scared girl, abandoned in a children's home and left to flee from a violent man with a Bible. I've been that girl too. I hate how this bloodied cord now binds us.

Rosetta.

That's her name. In death, she's earned herself something. The confusing paradox of my pity. But that can't be right. Monsters don't deserve our pity.

Do they?

Her wedding ring still rests beneath my mattress, protected from harm. I get it out daily and spin it around my pinkie, remembering the glimmers of goodness coming back to me now.

Hunks of bread.

A cup of milk.

Once, a meagre bar of soap.

"Harlow!"

I nearly leap from my chair. Giana has leaned forward, a hand resting on my jittery leg.

"You zoned out," she says with a frown.

"I'm sorry, got distracted."

"It's like you couldn't hear me. What happened?"

I can't help but reach for the flyaway strand of hair that's escaped my braid. When she looks away to adjust her blouse, I quickly tear it out and brush it aside.

"It happens sometimes."

Her frown deepens. "Are you still seeing that therapist?"

"How do you know about him?"

"I'm your mother. It's my job to know these things."

That tastes like a lie. I don't know why, but I don't trust her intentions. This so-called concern doesn't ring true.

"Going back to Dad," I deflect.

Head lowering, she rubs her temples. "The truth is, I was planning to leave him before you were taken from us. He was a heavy drug user. Heroin mostly."

My throat closes up.

That's what he overdosed on.

"Why didn't you?" I ask more gently.

Giana flicks invisible lint off her leg. "You were so young, and we didn't have any money. I was trapped."

In the corner of the room, Theo's phone buzzes with an incoming phone call. He mutters an apology and slips outside to answer it, leaving us alone.

"What happened after I was taken?"

"Your father spiralled out of control in his grief." She sniffles. "He began forging identities to buy more drugs. The abuse got a lot worse until he was arrested."

I'm not sure what drives me to reach across the coffee table and take Giana's hand in mine. She looks up, surprised, but flourishes a smile of appreciation.

"When the authorities caught up to him, it was a relief. He was convicted, and I tried to rebuild what was left of my life."

Her fingers are gripping mine, and I note the sparkling diamond band wrapped around her ring finger. The reminder is a sharp slap around the face.

She rebuilt.

Her life continued.

My anger comes racing back, justified or not. I can't see past it. I suddenly regret initiating contact with her.

"You made yourself a new family."

"I never stopped searching for you," she insists. "We didn't just forget about you."

"I've seen my gravestone, Giana."

Her face falls at the formal name.

"You buried me after the police closed my case. Life continued, and you let everyone forget I ever existed."

Her hand tightens around mine. Sharp nails bite into my wrist. At first, I think it's an accident.

"How old is your son? Does he know that he has a half-sister?" I blink away tears. "Does he care?"

"Ulrich is just a child."

"So was I."

Giana's emerald eyes narrow on me. "It's my job to protect him. He's too young to understand all this."

"Protect him?" I laugh weakly. "Like you protected me?"

"I am not the bad guy here, Letty."

My wrist is searing with pain. Her nails are cutting into me so deeply, I can feel blood welling up. Still, she doesn't move to release me. It's on purpose.

"Stay away from your father," Giana orders me. "Do not visit him. Do not speak to him. No contact. Understood?"

Teeth gritted, I wrench my arm backwards. Her nails slice across my skin with the move, but I manage to separate us, rubbing my sore wrist. Crescent-shaped marks are left behind.

"It's a little late to start protecting me from monsters, isn't it?" I say in an empty voice. "Thirteen years too late."

"You need to listen to me."

"I don't need to do anything for anyone, including you. I'm sorry, this was a mistake. I'll leave you to your interview."

"Please! Don't go."

Tears are sliding down her cheeks, matching the sparkle of her diamond wedding ring.

"I'm begging you for a second chance," she pleads. "I want to fix our relationship."

"You can't."

She tries to grab me again. Standing up, I dance backwards, running from the flames of her deceit before I'm burned again.

A better person might forgive her. Maybe they'd even admit that she was put in a shitty situation. Giana simply made the best of the rest of her life.

I'm not a better person.

I don't believe those things.

While I can't control the decisions she has made, I can control one thing—who I choose to forgive, and how. Right now, I'm not ready to reconcile with her. That's my choice.

"That's it?" She stands up and tries to follow me. "Months of silence, and that's all you have to say to me?"

When I look over my shoulder, she's watching me with soaked cheeks, her hands clenched into fists.

"I'm sorry that I'm not the person you hoped for. I know that must be hard for you. But more than that, I'm sorry Leticia didn't come home."

Escaping before she can answer, I quickly close the door behind me and slump against the frosted glass. The tears spill over as my facade finally crumbles.

I'll never be her daughter.

She'll never be my mother.

There's too much water under that bridge for us to cross it now. I'm not willing to risk drowning in the current as I attempt to swim back into her perfectly ordered life.

Glancing up and down the thickly carpeted corridor, I spot Theo in front of the tinted, floor-length window adjacent to the elevators. He's staring outside, his phone forgotten.

Approaching him, I rest a hand on his flannel-covered shoulder. He startles, his blue eyes colliding with mine. The palpable fear and anxiety there makes my stomach churn.

"What's wrong?"

He glances outside. "This is bad."

The roar of shouting and rhythmic chanting penetrates through the tinted, bulletproof glass protecting us from sight. We're on the tenth floor, closer to the ground than where I've spent most of my time here.

Outside, what Hunter described as a small protest is in fact a furious mob.

Countless people are being held back by temporary metal railings and the brute force of Sabre's security team.

Placards are waving in the air, accompanied by frenzied chanting, even some scattered prayers as they call up to the heavens in desperation. Fanatics and protestors blur together.

"End the slaughter!"

"Who is funding this investigation? The taxpayer!"

"Hand her over! Save our streets!"

"Oh my God," I breathe out.

Theo's hand takes mine. "We're safe up here. They can't breach the perimeter."

"I don't understand why they're doing this."

"People are afraid. They're grasping at straws." He pushes his glasses back up his nose. "The media is a powerful force."

One man is screaming at an agent who attempts to push him back. In his hands, the placard shows a wide-angled shot of a pretty, young woman with curling red hair.

My heart somersaults behind my rib cage. I recognise the woman from the police report that Hunter showed me on his phone last night. Candace Bernard. Our missing girl.

"I did this," I whisper to myself.

"This wasn't you," Theo combats. "It was the devil."

"Are we so sure the devil isn't in me too?"

He gently turns my shoulders, tearing my gaze from the army demanding my head on a stake. Behind his glasses, crystalline blue eyes are cracked with unease.

"We will never let them take you."

"Wouldn't me disappearing solve all of your problems?"

Hesitating, his hand slides higher. "No."

He holds the back of my neck, drawing me even closer until I'm pressed against the flannel of his shirt. I can taste the thick tension sizzling between us.

"It wouldn't," he finishes.

Closer still, the scent of antique books and peppermint rolls off him in an enchanting wave. I'm drawn into the warmth of his embrace as my arms wrap around his narrow waist.

Theo stops breathing, his eyes darting from side to side. I wait for his anxiety to pass. I know he can't control his reaction.

He gradually relaxes against me. His lips are close enough to taste, but I can't cross the chasm between us. Not yet.

"Do you want to get out of here?"

"What?" I laugh awkwardly.

"Let's just leave. Me and you."

"But… it isn't safe."

My mouth falls open when he lifts the flap of his shirt, wearing a smirk that looks foreign on his face. He's wearing a loaded gun holster attached to his belt.

"I may be a techie, but I can still keep you safe." Theo lets his shirt fall back down. "Let's get out of here."

Anticipation travels down my spine.

"And go where?"

His thumb slides along my jaw, featherlight and exploring. He lifts my chin so that my lips are exposed to him and leans closer. Our mouths are almost touching.

"I'll go anywhere with you. Anywhere but here. We can leave the death and destruction behind for one night."

My eyes fall shut as his lips brush against mine in the most excruciatingly light touch. It's almost imperceptible.

"What about the case?"

"I'm not the only person working for Hunter," he replies in a whisper. "They can find someone else to boss around and treat like shit. I'd rather be with you."

His thumb is still stroking my cheek, even as his lips retreat. Pain rips through me at the loss of contact. I want more. So much more.

"What have you got to lose?" he challenges.

My eyes stay shut with implicit trust.

"Nothing. Let's go."

CHAPTER 13
THEO

FANTASTIC – BLAME MY YOUTH

"ARE WE SAFE?" Harlow asks again.

"Nobody saw us sneak out of the back entrance. They were too busy protesting in front of the media's cameras."

She worries her bottom lip with her teeth. "I don't know about this. The entire world knows my face."

Reaching out, I tug the beanie lower on her head. Between hiding her face and the darkness of night, her identity is well concealed.

Unlike Hunter and Enzo, nobody knows what I look like. My seclusion from the world is strategic, beyond my social anxiety. I don't want to be known or seen. I'm much happier working in the background.

"Not much further," I console.

Harlow's beginning to drag her feet after walking for a couple of hours in the phosphorescent glow of London at night. We pass red phone boxes, double-decker buses and the roar of drunken students exiting packed pubs.

I'm sure Hunter has the entire intelligence department looking for us by now. He won't get anywhere. I built that team myself, and I know their pitfalls by heart.

When I joined Sabre, I took great care to make sure I could leave undetected if needed. For many years, I didn't trust Hunter or his motives in recruiting me.

He swooped in and saved my life when I was staring down the barrel of a fifteen-year prison sentence. To me, that was far too good to be true. That's why my phone and laptop run off invisible redundancy systems that I coded myself.

They're impenetrable.

Not even Rayna, whose coding skills rival mine, could hope to infiltrate the systems I've installed to protect my privacy.

"Where are we going?" she questions.

"I want to show you something."

Harlow's arm links with mine. "We're going to get thrown in the back of a dark van at any moment."

"Hunter won't find us." I let her snuggle closer. "I might have sent the team a false location ping on the other side of the city. That should keep them busy for a while."

She looks up at me beneath her cute purple beanie. "You sent them on a wild goose chase, didn't you?"

I shrug it off with a smile. "Hunter should know that you're safe with me. We're both adults, and I think we've earned ourselves a break."

"Yeah, he's going to kill you."

"He's certainly welcome to try." I direct her across a quiet street, slick with rain. "I could hack into his car's control system and blow it up from across the world."

"You could?" she squeaks.

"Probably with my eyes shut."

Checking up and down the road, I spot the deserted, age-spotted building I'm looking for. It screams of abandonment, but I'm not afraid to approach the derelict structure.

"People with real power don't talk about it," I explain. "We leave that to the Hunters of the world. Everyone knows his face. Nobody knows mine."

"That's exactly how you like it, right?"

My chest burns with a strangely warm feeling. It feels weird to be seen by someone, and not fading into the background, unnoticed and forgotten. I'm stunned that I like it so much.

"Right. I like to be invisible."

"Doesn't it get lonely?" Harlow queries.

We pause on the pavement, trapped in a bubble amidst the hustle and bustle of England's capital. Nobody can find us here, lost in the darkness and steady patter of falling rain.

Her sparkling blue eyes stare up at me, wide with curiosity. She isn't repulsed by my awkward social skills or inability to function like a regular human being.

Harlow sees… me.

Unfiltered and unafraid.

That's what has drawn me in from the beginning and strengthened my determination to serve her justice. What began as a professional endeavour has grown into a full-blown, unhealthy obsession to know every inch of her mind.

"Yes," I reply honestly. "It gets lonely, and for a long time, I was perfectly fine with that. I wanted to be alone."

"And now?"

I startle from staring at her lips and meet her eyes again. She's looking at me like she can peel my skin away from my bones, unveil the darkest depths of my soul and drag out the entrails for her own examination.

"Now what?" I respond.

Her mouth quirks in a smile. "Do you want to be alone now, Theodore?"

Fucking Christ, the way my body tingles when she uses my full name. I want to kiss her right here in the middle of the damn street.

"I don't know anymore. Not right now, I don't."

Harlow nods. "Me neither."

Taking a leap of faith, I take her hand from my arm and let our cold fingers tangle together. Her smile bulldozes any misgivings I have about being vulnerable.

"Then it's a good thing we have each other."

"I guess so," she agrees.

I don't need to be scared of her. Harlow understands me in a way that few people do. She sees beneath the veneer I've painted on, and she isn't running away screaming.

"Where are we?" She looks up at the building. "This looks like a quiet spot for a murder. Did we have to walk all this way for you just to kill me?"

I reach for the heavy padlock bolting the metal door shut. "You're not getting out of this that easily."

"Well, there goes my plan for an easy exit."

Inputting the code into the rusted dials, the padlock unlocks and falls into my hands. I tuck it in my pocket and check the street before wrenching the iron door open.

"Need a hand?"

"I've got it." I gesture for her to step into the darkness. "After you."

Harlow tentatively peeks inside at the cloying shadows and heady scent of damp. "Um, are you sure?"

"Just trust me. You're safe."

Taking a deep breath, she nods and sinks into the impenetrable darkness. I heave the door shut behind us and lock it from the inside, checking the three locks I installed to the interior. Nobody's getting in.

"Theo?"

Harlow's voice is high with fear.

"Hold on, beautiful."

Activating my phone light, I illuminate the narrow, brick-lined alleyway. Harlow zips to my side and burrows close to me, her breathing a little unsteady.

For someone who grew up in darkness, she's developed an incredible fear for her natural habitat, despite a part of her seeing it as home. I guess that's the same for all humans.

We like to shed our skins and pretend like we've moved on from the past, even as it burrows beneath our bones, ready to emerge again when we least expect it.

There's no avoiding the inevitable realisation that we're all just a little too broken to forget. No matter how hard we try.

"What is this place?" she whispers.

Leading her down the corridor, the whistling wind grows louder. Bare lit bulbs hang from wires attached to the ceiling, left behind when construction work ceased two decades ago.

"When I joined Sabre, I was on the verge of being convicted for computer hacking," I reveal with a wince. "This was eight or so years ago. I was nineteen at the time."

"Wait, who did you hack?"

My cheeks flush in the dim light.

"I worked for the cybersecurity department in the Ministry of Defence. During a routine check, I came across a hidden partition in the server, full of classified information."

"What happened?"

"Turns out the department head was selling privileged information on the black market to the highest bidder."

Her hand tightens in mine.

"He was getting paid to protect a cartel moving illegal weaponry through London. Probably earned a small fortune while others were killed with those same guns."

At the end of the gloomy alleyway, we reach a metal grate protected by a keypad. I lean close to punch in the ten-digit code and heft it aside, revealing a steep set of concrete stairs.

"After you," I invite with a wave. "Anyway, I needed to prove what I suspected before taking it any further. If he was dirty, who knew if anyone else was involved, right?"

Harlow takes the first few steps, gripping the rusted handrail. I drag my eyes from her tight ass waving in my face with each step, sculpted through her skinny blue jeans.

"Let me guess, it went further than that?"

"And some." I follow her up, my chest tightening. "I hacked into his hard drive and compiled years' worth of evidence. Fraud, corruption, taking bribes. He'd done it all."

We emerge into a cavernous space, our voices echoing off the cold bricks. Harlow is rooted to the spot as I locate the nearest industrial switch and reboot the generator.

"When I took it to his superior, I was arrested and thrown into a prison cell. Senior management was in on the whole thing. I'd stumbled into a criminal conspiracy by accident."

The abandoned, half-constructed London Underground platform is lit by dim, yellow light as the power comes on. It stretches out all around us. The tunnel was sealed long before I came across this place on a dark web auction.

Down the platform, clusters of glimmering lights reveal the remains of a rusted carriage, forever frozen in time. Inside, the destruction gives way to a miniature home.

"Do you live here?" Harlow gasps as she looks around. "This is insane."

"I don't live anywhere. Sometimes, I need to get away from the world. I bought this place years ago. According to public records, it doesn't exist."

Her unease forgotten, Harlow steps inside the furnished carriage. I installed strip lights along the ceiling, framing the small kitchenette and a sagging, mustard-yellow sofa.

"You sleep here?" she asks, aghast.

"There's a bedroom on the other end, behind the partition door. Bathroom too. Mr Talahan in the gym above us knows me. I'm hooked up to his electric and water."

"You're stealing from him?"

Dropping my backpack and plugging the portable space heater into a socket, I laugh off her snap judgement.

"More like I hacked his competitor and fucked with their payment system. They closed down and went into retail instead. Mr Talahan kept all of their customers."

"Theo!"

She sounds horrified, but when I glance up, Harlow is grinning from ear to ear. Hell, she looks fucking impressed.

"You really don't care, do you?"

"About what?" I ask with a shrug.

"The law. I didn't believe Enzo when he told me that. You seem so… uh, normal. Law-abiding."

Setting the heat to high, I wrench the carriage doors shut to block out the wind's current. It'll warm up in here soon.

"It took years of court battles and looking over my shoulder for my name to be cleared and the conspiracy dismantled," I answer her. "Hunter and Enzo saved my life. Not the law."

Tugging off her purple beanie, Harlow pulls her braid over her shoulder. She begins to poke around the space, and I feel like I'm lying on a shrink's sofa, under examination.

She's inspecting the most private corners of my life in here. Nobody knows I own this place. It's the last bit of respite I have in a loud, overwhelming world full of people that trigger my social anxiety.

Dragging her fingers over the spines of books I have stored on a shelf fitted to the low ceiling, she studies the different titles. Fuck, I should've hidden the comic books.

"You wanna eat?" I ask, hoping to distract her.

She's engrossed as I pull the two ham and cheese subs from my backpack that we picked up en route. Setting them down on the cluttered table, I shift on the balls of my feet.

She still isn't speaking.

Have I blown this shit?

What am I even doing?

This wasn't some elaborate plan to lure her down here, away from the others. She was in pain, and I wanted to fix it. This is the only way I know how. Hiding until it stops hurting.

"What are the odds of the others finding us?" She breaks the silence with an old, dusty book in hand.

"Zero."

"That's the point, right?"

"Pretty much." I chuckle.

Harlow turns around to face me across the carriage. "Why are you showing me this, Theo?"

Spasming with nerves, I inch closer. She stands stock still as I ease the book from her hands and place it down. There's only a scant breath between us.

Her sweater is brushing against my flannel shirt. She's biting her lip again. I can't maintain a safe friendzone when she looks at me like that.

"Because I want you to know me," I answer in a low rasp. "The real me. Not many people do these days."

She brushes her fingers over my chest, still staring up at me with wide eyes. "Then tell me who the real Theo is."

I awkwardly gesture around the space—comic books, old cereal boxes, second-hand coding manuals and a thick coating of dust, wrapped in a coffin of loneliness.

"I am, this is him."

"A closeted comic book nerd, who eats stale cereal, hacks people for a living and hangs out in an abandoned train station on his own?"

I can't help but grin at her.

"Pretty much, yeah."

Her fingers are tangled in the material of my shirt. Unable to help myself, I pick up her braid and stroke my thumb over the plait. Her hair is so soft, and it smells amazing, like jasmine shampoo and fresh blossoms in springtime.

"How do I know you're not wearing a mask?" Her eyes search over me. "Just like the rest of us?"

I let my hand travel to the back of her neck, tilting her head upwards. "We can't always live in our masks. Every now and then, we have to take them off to breathe."

"And this is where you do that," she answers for me.

"Precisely. If you want… it's where you can do the same."

Her eyes narrow. "You think I'm wearing a mask?"

Closer still, I let our noses brush. "I think you've been wearing one since the day we found you. I think you're wearing one right now. I think… you don't know how to live without it."

"You're wrong. I'm not hiding."

But she is. I'm the only one that knows it.

"I know about what you did to Enzo's car," I blurt out.

Ah, fuck. That was a secret I had no intention of bringing up. I really need to stop interacting with other humans.

"The c-car?" she stammers. "What are you talking about?"

"It was you. Or at least, a version of you."

Her blue eyes are blown wide with a heavy dose of fear. "I have no idea what you're talking about."

"You're the one who trashed it."

Whether she believes me or not, a part of her knows. I can see the truth dancing in her eyes. Her dissociated mind just locked those memories away, along with everything else.

"But it was those people."

"What people, Harlow?"

"The people!" Her voice rises, bordering on hysterical. "The ones that worship Pastor Michaels… his fan club. Enzo told me about them sending emails and stuff."

"A couple of anonymous troublemakers sending shitty emails because they have nothing better to do?"

"Yes, them!" she insists.

"It wasn't them. Believe me."

Harlow sinks down on the small sofa and buries her face in her hands. Every inch of her is trembling like a leaf. This is where the mask meets reality, and it's never a pleasant sight.

I crouch in front of her and rest my hands on her knees to gain her attention. Her cheeks are wet with tears, and she touches them in confusion. Even her body knows what's happening.

"I've torn the hospital's CCTV systems apart," I spell out. "After leaving physiotherapy on the ninth floor, you snuck away and headed downstairs alone."

She shakes her head again. "Stop."

"There was maintenance work taking place in the reception." I ignore her. "Nobody noticed you swiping a small can of red paint that they were using to freshen up the place."

"I didn't do this… I would know."

"From there, you took the elevator downstairs and ducked beneath the single CCTV camera. You don't reappear for almost ten minutes, sweating and without the paint can."

"Theo, stop it! I don't believe you."

"From there, you take the elevator back up to see your father, stopping at a bathroom to wash up on the way. When Enzo caught up to you, he was none the wiser."

She's having a full-blown panic attack now. *Shit. Great job, Theo. Awesome work.* I reach up to cup her cheeks, my thumbs stroking beneath her screwed-shut eyes.

"Breathe, Harlow. You're not in trouble. I just wanted to know if you remembered or not. The others don't know what I found when I checked the surveillance."

"W-Wasn't me," she falters.

"I'm not wrong, beautiful. It was all there. But I know that it wasn't you who did those things."

"Then who w-was it?"

"Your mask," I say simply.

Tears stream thick and fast down her pink cheeks as she shakes her head from side to side. I should've known this wouldn't be an easy pill to swallow. That's why I kept her secret. She didn't need the guys obsessing over this.

There's nothing worse than realising that no matter your best efforts, you are not in control of your life. Mental health is too fucking cruel for that to be true.

We're all victims of its violent tide, rising and falling to an unchanging rhythm, no matter how loud we scream for it to stop. That Godless infliction doesn't listen.

"You can't remember when you escaped from the chapel, right?" I point out.

"N-No."

"Or chunks of time inside the cage?"

She peeks a bloodshot eye open. "No."

Her tears soak into my skin, stinging with the harsh lash of grief. I can feel her pain slipping beneath my skin, poisoning what's left of my nonchalance. I hold her even tighter, hard enough to creak bones.

"Why can't I remember these things?" she keens.

"Because it's too much. Your mask is keeping you safe. Like it did for all those years in the cage that you can't remember."

"You mean… d-dissociating?"

I nod. "Yeah. Richards talked to you about this?"

"A little. I can't control it."

"I know, it's okay. We can figure this out. But first, I need to ask you something else."

She looks afraid, peering up at me. "What is it?"

"Do you remember telling me that you killed Laura?"

Face draining, Harlow shoves my hands away. If I wasn't blocking the carriage, she'd be running at full speed to escape above ground.

"It's okay," I quickly placate. "We can talk about this."

"No," she weeps. "H-How? I didn't… I…"

"You told us on the way home from Northumberland. None of us have wanted to bring it up since."

Chest rising and falling with each panicked breath, she shakes her head. "No… no… I didn't say anything!"

"Just breathe. You were pretty out of it at the time."

I feel awful for ripping the rug out from under her feet, but we're already down the rabbit hole. Her periods of dissociation are dangerous. Ignoring it won't help us.

"You told me that you killed her. Why do you think that?"

Her oceanic eyes meet mine. "I did."

"It was Pastor Michaels. We all know that."

"After he performed the ritual… she was bleeding out," Harlow says in a choked whisper. "She was in so much pain. I didn't want to, but she begged me to make it fast."

The realisation connects all the dots that have been bothering me for some time. Suddenly, so much of her destructive, guilt-ridden behaviour makes sense.

Hunter was wrong.

She did it. I believe her.

"You're telling the truth?" I double-check.

Harlow manages a nod. "It's true."

My mouth clicks open and shut. I thought she was rambling on the plane. None of us thought she ended Laura's life. I feel sick at the thought that she's been struggling with this alone for months.

Laura's life was already earmarked for death. That's not the same thing as killing. Harlow isn't the guilty one. She's spent all this time blaming herself for someone else's brutality. Her actions were merciful.

"Why didn't you tell us this before?"

"I… I didn't want you to know that I k-killed her," Harlow sobs. "I wrapped my h-hands around her throat and squeezed until she s-stopped breathing. It w-was me."

"She was already dying. You gave her peace."

"So? I still ended her life!"

Leaning in, I rest our foreheads together. I want her closer, beneath the protective sarcophagus of my skeleton, where she can't hurt herself any longer. This is exactly why I kept my distance. Already, it's too late to turn back.

After losing Alyssa, I vowed to never again allow myself to care about someone. I stayed away from Harlow to stop that from happening, but I can't watch her go through this alone. Regardless of the fear screaming at me not to get involved.

"You did not kill her," I say emphatically. "Pastor Michaels did. You saved her from something far worse."

"I n-never wanted you guys to know."

"I promise you that I'm not judging you. Don't worry about that. Worry about forgiving yourself first."

"Forgiving myself?" She laughs weakly. "I deserved to be the one left rotting in a cell, not Laura. She should've gotten out instead of me."

"That's complete crap."

"You can't tell the others," she urges. "Please."

"They need to know. We can help you get through this. And frankly, they've probably already figured it out."

Harlow cusses, her eyes scrunched shut.

"Let me help," I plead again.

"The only way you can help is if you tell me that you hate me," she demands. "Tell me this is all my fault. I need to hear it."

"That's never going to happen because it isn't true."

"Then why am I here? What do you want from me?"

I carefully pull her up, banding an arm around her back so she doesn't topple over. She's pinned against me, and I can feel every stuttered intake of her struggling lungs.

"Because I care about you, and I won't watch this world break you any more than it already has."

Her lips part on a cry. "I'm not yours to protect, Theo. You need someone who can make you whole."

"Who are you to say that you're not that person?" I reason with her. "That's my decision to make. Not yours."

Before she can run, I finally take the risk I've spent months wrestling over and let all of my fears melt away. I've spent the best part of six years running from the possibility of grief and allowing that same loss to dictate my future.

I'm tired.

I'm alone.

I'm fucking done.

"Can I kiss you?" I ask awkwardly.

Harlow's bottomless eyes widen, flecked with surprise.

"You d-don't have to ask," she stutters back.

My lips seek hers out, securing our mouths together in a frenzied panic. I feel like she's slipping through my fingers, even as I grip her arms tight and let our mouths collide.

Harlow tastes exactly as I imagined she would—the sweet, terrifying taste of hope, dawning on a shadowed sky. That light reveals all of the damage inflicted in the dark, but with it comes the chance to begin again.

She's kissing me back.

Over and over again.

Running my hands over her body, I touch the curves I've longed to explore for the last six months. The times I've imagined doing exactly this don't bear thinking about. I never thought it would actually happen.

With more confidence than I expected, Harlow pushes me backwards. My legs collide with the nearby sofa. I slump on it, and she follows, placing a leg on either side of my waist.

Her arms wind around my neck, drawing us back together. When her lips land on mine again, the heat has grown unbearable. Our tongues touch, hesitant at first, before tangling together in a pleasured waltz.

She must be able to feel how fucking hard I am for her right now. I can't remember the last time I even slept with a woman. There were only a handful of hook-ups after Alyssa.

I stopped pretending to be even remotely human a long time ago and quit one-night stands in favour of complete isolation from the human race.

Breaking the kiss to gasp for air, Harlow's mouth is bee-stung and swollen. I run a thumb over her bottom lip, feeling my cheeks and neck burn with a fierce blush.

"I wasn't expecting that."

"I'm sorry," she rushes to apologise.

I stroke her jawline. "Don't be. I've been thinking about doing that for a long time. It's a good thing you did it before I could chicken out again."

Smiling sweetly, she rests her head against my collarbone. I tuck her closer to my chest and cuddle her tight, drinking in the reassurance of her weight on top of me. She isn't leaving. The world didn't end because we finally kissed.

I can't lose her.

Not now, not ever.

I was wrong, for all this time. Pretending like keeping my distance could protect me from heartache, even as I stock-piled evidence to fight her case and obsessed about her from afar. It was all a delusion.

She was under my skin long before I started playing this futile game. All I've done is hurt us both by avoiding the chance of something good, something pure, in favour of letting fear rule my life.

No more.

"Harlow," I murmur against her hair. "I know you've got shit going on with the others too, but I need you to know that I really care about you."

"You do?" she whispers.

"I don't just want to be your friend. I'm not sure where that leaves us, but I thought you should know."

Her head doesn't lift. "I'm tearing your family apart, Theo. You can't care about me. I'm going to ruin your lives."

I force her to look up at me. The tears are back, helpless and afraid. I brush them aside, the salty proof of her anguish soaking into my thumb pads.

"I want you to ruin my life," I tell her.

"What?"

"Please ruin this miserable, lonely life that's slowly choking me to death. Please. I'm begging you to hurt me."

Her lips twitch in the tiniest of smiles.

"This is going to end in disaster," she predicts.

I kiss her again with so much certainty, it unnerves me.

"I really fucking hope so."

CHAPTER 14
HARLOW

HARD TO BE ALONE – BARNS COURTNEY

"HARLOW? CAN YOU GIVE ME A HAND?"

Enzo's voice carries through the open front door, where cold, rain-laced air is leaking into the warmth of the house. He's already brought in three bags of food, alcohol and ice.

Apparently, there's more.

"Coming," I shout back.

Putting the last bottles of flavoured vodka on the packed countertop, I tighten Leighton's lemon-scented hoodie around me and head back outside into the falling rain.

Enzo is smiling today, his mood improved by the newly repaired SUV parked in the driveway. It came out of the shop last week, much to his delight.

"How many people are coming to this party?" I cringe at the mere thought.

He grabs another two bags from the car. "All of us, Brooklyn and her lot and Hunter's folks. We're a big bunch."

"Hunter's parents are coming?" I squeak.

His amber eyes pin me to the spot. "Well, it is their son's thirty-fifth birthday. I couldn't not invite them."

"Does Leighton know about this?"

That's when his smile drops.

"Well, the surprise is for both of them."

I pinch the bridge of my nose. "Hunter's going to kill you for throwing him a surprise birthday party. Now, you're saying Leighton has no clue they're coming either?"

"He has to see his parents sometime," Enzo rationalises as he closes the boot. "It would've happened at Christmas if shit didn't go down. He can't put this off forever."

"I don't think you've thought this through."

Balancing several more armfuls of alcohol, Enzo nudges me to head inside. "Like you didn't think through running off with Theo two weeks ago and giving me a heart attack?"

"I thought I already apologised for that."

Slipping off my Chucks, I pad back into the messy kitchen. Hunter would have a heart attack of his own if he saw the chaos in here in preparation for tonight's family reunion.

Leighton is on his way home from meeting his parole officer, and Theo's in charge of delaying Hunter at work until everyone arrives. This whole thing was Enzo's idea. It's been hard to carve out family time amidst the recent chaos.

I had no clue it was even Hunter's birthday. I feel crappy about that. Things have been rough since the latest girl was snatched, and Pastor Michaels is being suspiciously quiet about it, beyond his initial note.

We're all on edge. The guys are working overtime to hunt down any potential clues before it's too late, not to mention working on the false identity lead. Hunter's birthday didn't even scratch the top ten of things I'm worried about.

Unpacking the whole bag dedicated to crisps and dips, I accidentally drop a tub of hummus. It explodes across the tiled floor, and Enzo immediately bursts into laughter.

"Shit," I curse. "I'm so sorry."

"Language, little one. We're going to start a swear jar for you soon."

"Bite me, Enzo. I'm nervous, alright?"

Dodging the mess, his intimidating height towers over me. He backs me against the marble breakfast bar, his wide hips pinning my back to it as his huge, calloused hands circle my wrists.

"Is that an invitation?" he purrs. "I don't mind biting."

My breath catches. "Maybe."

"We're home alone." Enzo trails a fingertip down the uneven slope of my nose. "The party doesn't start until later. What trouble can we get up to in that time?"

"Brooklyn's coming around to help me get ready." I writhe to escape as he pins my wrists to the marble surface. "We need to clean up before then."

"Fuck the mess. I know what I'd rather be doing." His fire-lit eyes search my face. "Tell me, how was it?"

"H-How was what?" I stutter.

"Your kiss with Theo the other week."

I feel myself turn beetroot red. Enzo reads the truth on my face without me having to say a traitorous word.

"So, it did happen," he concludes smugly. "Thanks for the confirmation. I was wondering what his intentions were when he smuggled you away from us."

"I d-don't know what you're talking about."

"No need to get all shy and squirmy. You know I'm in favour of us pursuing a shared relationship. Kiss him all you want."

I buck and pull, attempting to break his hold, but I'm completely stuck. Enzo chuckles as he stares down at me.

"You want to share me," I point out. "Hunter wants to murder you all, and Leighton wants to steal me away. Theo is the only one acting like a sane adult about this."

"Sane?" Enzo lifts a thick eyebrow.

"Yes! Unlike you testosterone-fuelled idiots, bickering over whose turn it is to do what. That's why I left with Theo."

Nose nudging mine, Enzo takes a sharp inhale. "So, you've chosen him? Is that what you're saying?"

"I haven't chosen anyone, and I'm not going to do that to your family. Besides, I didn't think you wanted me to."

"I don't," he fires back. "Hunter thinks he's the one keeping this family together right now, but he's wrong."

I gasp quietly as his leg slides between mine, nudging them open until the denim of his jeans is pressed up against me. I'm tingling from the slightest of touches at the moment.

"In fact, he couldn't be more wrong," Enzo murmurs, his lips meeting my ear. "You're the one keeping us all together."

"That isn't true."

"But it is. I'm scared that if you choose…"

"It will all fall apart," I rasp.

"That's what Hunter doesn't get. He has never been more wrong about anything in his life. The sooner we make him see that we all belong together, the better."

"And what about what I want?"

Eyes darkening with desire, Enzo's lips crash against mine in a heart-pounding kiss that scrambles my thoughts. When he releases me, I feel a tingling warmth gather down low.

"I know exactly what you want," he utters. "Say the word, little one, and I'll bend you over this breakfast bar and fuck you so hard, all of London will hear."

My legs turn to jelly, until his solid weight is the only thing holding me up. Every inch of honed muscle that builds his powerful frame is pressed against me in a cruel taunt.

"I want to bury my cock so deep inside of you, not even Hunter could argue that we don't belong together."

"And then?" I practically pant.

Enzo's teeth sink into my earlobe as he kisses his way around to the slope of my exposed throat.

"Then I'll own every inch of you. Those three knuckleheads can watch as you're dripping in my come, head to fucking toe."

The hard press of his erection is rocking against me, driving my pleasure higher and higher. The anticipation is torturous. I want everything he's said and more.

On the verge of agreeing to an impromptu fuck amongst the dips and melting ice, the security system buzzes with an alert as the front door clicks open. Enzo doesn't move an inch, even when Brooklyn steps inside.

She's shaking rain from her choppy blonde hair and leather jacket. Bellowing our names, she peeks into the kitchen and freezes.

"Am I interrupting?"

"No," I retort.

"Yes," Enzo cuts me off.

Grinning, Brooklyn kicks off her usual Doc Martens and hitches the backpack she's wearing higher on her shoulders.

"I'll be upstairs setting up," she says with a wink. "Don't keep her for too long, Enz. We have hair and makeup to do. Phoenix and Eli are coming soon with the speaker system."

"Bloody party," he grumbles.

"Your idea," I remind him.

With an eye roll, Enzo releases me and takes a step back. "Brooke, didn't we discuss you being a cockblock before? I don't need Hunter's permission to fire you."

She's already halfway upstairs. "You know the company would crumble without me!"

"But it would be a damn sight quieter," he adds. "Go on then. I'll sort this shit out and wait for the others to arrive."

Standing on my tiptoes, I peck his stubble-strewn cheek. "Don't forget to clean up the hummus."

His annoyed cursing follows me upstairs. Closing my bedroom door, I find Brooklyn rifling through my wardrobe, her belongings haphazardly deposited everywhere.

"I know that you hate doing hair and makeup." I sit down on the end of the bed. "So, why the ruse?"

She scrutinises my clothing with a frown. "You were about to be mauled by Enzo. I was doing you a favour, trust me."

"How so?"

Turning around, her smile is devious.

"Would you take your driver's test in a monster truck?"

"Excuse me?" I splutter.

"Your first time is always a bit awkward. I'd advise choosing a smaller, *ahem*, model. Hell, Hunter is probably gentler in bed than Enzo's caveman ass."

"Brooke! Oh my God."

"What?" She cackles. "This is what friends are for, right? I figured we'd have this talk soon, though I'm surprised they've behaved for this long."

Grabbing one of my pillows, I flop backwards and cover my head with it. Every inch of me is on fire. The bed bounces with Brooklyn's weight falling next to me.

"Hey." She pulls the pillow from my head. "Trust me, now's the time to ask questions. Once they know you're fair game, things are going to move very fast."

"We are so not talking about this."

Her playful expression grows serious. "If anyone has pressured you, I will personally hospitalise them with a baseball bat. Just say the word."

"It's not like that. No baseball bats."

Brooklyn turns onto her back. "Fuck, there go my plans for this evening's entertainment. What's stressing you then?"

Twirling a strand of hair between my fingers, I fight the urge to pull it out. "Whoever I choose to sleep with first, it's going to send a message to the others that I've chosen."

"And you don't want to do that?"

"Of course not."

"Just checking," she snickers.

"No matter what, I'll end up hurting someone. I'd rather be alone than put any of them through that kind of pain."

"Pain happens, whether you think you're in control or not," she says seriously.

"That isn't comforting."

Her smile is bittersweet. "You want my advice?"

"Always."

Grabbing my hand, Brooklyn squeezes tight. "Take exactly what you want and never let go, because this world will tear you apart. It's your job not to let it."

"What if I want… all of them?"

She smiles again, and the devil rears its threatening head within her. Confidence gleams in the silver flecks of her eyes, unapologetic and ready to dance in the dark.

"Trust me, they're yours," she whispers conspiratorially. "I think they were from the moment you met."

The strength of sheer determination in her voice steels my spine. I nod back, feeling my own demonic smile rise. Brooklyn squeezes my hand again before releasing.

"Come on, we need to sort that mess out on your head." She gestures to my rain-mussed hair. "Now, I have no fucking clue what I'm doing, so bear with me."

"You can't be any worse than me."

"Wanna bet?"

She bounces off the bed and begins setting up various appliances, glaring at each one as she attempts to figure out a game plan. The nerves set in fast.

I don't like people touching my hair, but more than that… I don't want her to see the damage. I'm sure she knows. They all do by now. But knowing and seeing are different things.

"I think I'll be fine," I blurt out. "Let's just leave it, yeah? Everyone's attention will be on Hunter anyway."

With a curling tong in hand, Brooklyn shoots me an unreadable look. "Harlow, I am the absolute last person you have to worry about judging you."

"It's not that."

"Then what?" she quizzes.

Trapped, I rub the pain in my chest. "I… um, I… fuck."

She arches an eyebrow. "Yes?"

"Fine, you're right. I'm worried about you judging me."

Pulling out the armchair tucked into the corner of my room, that Hunter once insisted on sleeping in, Brooklyn pats the cushion with a weirdly patient smile.

"You're safe with me," she reassures. "I'm better qualified than most to understand this shit. I'll be gentle and avoid the bad areas. We don't even have to talk about it."

"Promise?"

"Always," she throws back at me.

With a breath for courage, I take a seat and stare straight ahead at the wall, avoiding my reflection. She picks up a hairbrush and begins to comb through the snarled knots.

"Yell at me if I pull too hard."

"Got it," I grit out.

Working her way around my head, she's surprisingly gentle, holding the long length at the root to avoid tugging. I force myself to breathe, focusing on each painful inhale.

"You got an invite too, huh?"

"What?" I reply in a daze.

Her finger appears over my shoulder to point towards my desk in the corner of the room. The memorial invitation rests on top of my journal, tucked back inside its envelope, hand addressed to me.

"Kade told me about it on the phone last night. He's on his way back from up north with Hudson. Forensics are tearing the Michaels' old house apart now."

"They haven't found anything?" I check.

"Not yet. Some other family's been living there for the past five years. They're going to do a thorough search though."

"It will be another dead end."

"You don't know that yet," Brooklyn disputes. "So, are you going to go? The memorial's next month."

"Laura's brother asked for me specifically. He wants me to give a eulogy or something. It was on the invite."

"Well, it's going to be a pretty private event, now he's got the whole… you know, body back."

"Why would he even invite me to come?"

The curling tong beeps as it heats to full temperature, and she begins sifting through the layers of hair on my head.

"You were the last person to see her alive," she guesses. "He probably wants to meet you for that reason."

The pain in my chest intensifies.

"You were on the plane with me on the way home at Christmas, weren't you?"

"I was," she answers neutrally.

"So, you heard… what I did."

"That you killed her? You said something about it."

I recoil like I've been whipped. Since hearing how much my broken mind has been hiding from me, I've been feeling sick to my core. I can't trust myself at all.

"You believed me?"

Brooklyn sighs as she fiddles with a curl. "I've hurt enough people I care about to know what it feels like. I looked in your eyes. I knew you were telling the truth."

"Is it sick I'm glad you believed I was capable of doing that?" I ask honestly. "Sorry. I'm just struggling to know what to believe at the moment."

"We're all sick," Brooklyn says with a laugh. "If that makes you feel better, then sure. I believed it."

Somehow, it does.

She's never underestimated me.

"But I'm not here to judge anyone for how they think or feel," she remarks. "Especially not my friends."

Looking straight into the mirror I've been avoiding, I find her eyes boring into me, the curler forgotten. I didn't want them to know, but on some level, I'm glad.

The mask has slipped.

My control has frayed.

The secrets that've been eating me up inside are out there now, and I can finally confront them. I know Brooklyn won't let me do it alone. She's a good friend like that.

"Then how do I face Laura's brother?" I croak. "I'm the reason he no longer has a sister. How do I stand up and read a eulogy like it wasn't my fault?"

Placing the curler down, she moves around the armchair and kneels in front of me. Her hands grip my knees, and I'm held prisoner in the ferocious emotion of her gaze.

"You stand up there knowing that you granted Laura the last shred of control she had left," Brooklyn says fiercely. "You gave her what she wanted when everything else had been ripped away from her. That's how."

"But… what if you're wrong?"

"About what?"

"What if I killed her because I'm a monster, just like him?"

She reaches up to brush a tear off my cheek. "You're human, Harlow. All humans are monstrous. Some of us just hide it better than others."

"Including you?"

"Especially me," she replies flatly. "I've done some fucked-up shit. Trust me when I tell you, there isn't a bad bone in your body. I'd know if there was."

"You seem confident." I laugh nervously.

"I sure am. Shall we finish this hair then?"

With a shuddered breath, I nod. “Let’s do it and crack open the vodka downstairs before everyone arrives.”

“You got it.”

Before she can stand up, I grab her hand. “Brooke?”

“Yeah?”

“Thanks for not running away screaming from the crap inside my head. I’m glad you’re in my life.”

Her smile is lopsided. “Not much scares me, so you’re in luck. I’ll always have your back.”

CHAPTER 15
HARLOW

VILLAIN – MISSIO

"THERE IS no way I'm drinking that."

Kade eyes the pint glass surrounded by playing cards with a look of distaste. It's swirling with a mixture of different drinks, blended together to form a disgusting, grainy cocktail.

Brooklyn said this card game was a bad idea. Every time someone selected one of the kings, they had to add some of their drink into the glass. It's full now as the game nears its conclusion.

"You know the rules for Ring of Fire." Hudson nudges the drink towards him with a wink. "You picked up the last king. Now, you have to drink."

"This game is fucking stupid," Kade complains.

Leaning over Hudson, Phoenix claps him on his shirt-clad shoulder. "Don't puke either. No one wants to see that."

"Wouldn't be the first time," Jude comments, glued to something on his phone. "Clearly, you've forgotten Mardi Gras in Paris. Red wine everywhere."

"That was Eli's fault." Kade narrows his eyes at the silent, green-eyed suspect in question. "We drank to make him feel more comfortable around all those people."

Eli shifts on the carpet, avoiding eye contact. "Didn't help. That festival was hell."

With a headshake, Kade picks up the pint glass and swears as he begins to down it. The entire room starts clapping and cheering, causing Lucky to yip with excitement from the rug.

I nudge Leighton's shoulder with mine. "This is your fault for suggesting this game. Where did you learn it?"

He takes a pull from his beer. "I used to hang out with the university crowd a lot. England's full of drunk students playing this game and throwing up their guts."

"For what possible reason?"

His eyes meet mine. "Fun. You want a sip too?"

"Not a chance. I'm not falling for that."

Snickering, Leighton wraps an arm around my shoulders and pulls me close for a side hug. "We'll make a party animal out of you yet, Goldilocks."

"You'll be waiting for a long time."

His lips tease the shell of my ear. "What can I say, I'm a patient guy. I'll wait forever if that's what it takes. Remember that."

Flushing red, I wriggle out of his embrace. Enzo is watching us with such piercing interest from his perch behind the sofa, his amber eyes seem all animal tonight, leaving no glimpse of humanity behind.

I half expect him to tear Leighton limb from limb, no matter what he preaches about sharing me. Clearly, the poised Bengal tiger biding its time beneath his tanned skin didn't get that memo.

The alarm on the front gate's security system cuts through the cheering as Kade finishes downing the pint of death. He looks almost green. Brooklyn leans in to give him a congratulatory kiss.

"Motherfucker," Phoenix swears.

He's forced to surrender a ten-pound note to Hudson, having lost his cruel bet that Kade wouldn't finish the pint.

"Who's at the gate?" Leighton asks.

Straightening from his perch, Enzo runs a hand over his hair. "I'll go and see."

I want to bury my face in my hands and hide from the incoming car crash. Enzo shoots me a loaded look before he disappears from the room.

Ignoring my instincts, I stay put. Leighton's going to need me. He was in prison for three years, and in the seven months we've both been home, he's refused to see his parents.

That's about to change.

A couple of tense minutes pass before the front door buzzes open and shut again. Lucky barks loudly, and she races out of the room to greet our guests, her golden tail wagging.

From their seats in front of us on the woven rug, Brooklyn and Hudson have a perfect view behind us. Her eyes bulge when she spots whoever has walked in.

The tinkle of a female voice sneaks into the room over the ruckus of drunken laughter and conversation. I feel Leighton tense beside me as his back goes ramrod straight.

"Did we make it in enough time? You know how slow Ben drives in the city."

"You'd rather get here safely, wouldn't you?" a man responds in a grumpy bark. "Damn traffic."

"You've got to be fucking kidding me," Leighton whispers to himself. "Is that my parents?"

I grab his hand before he can run. "Leigh, breathe."

He looks up at me. "Did you know about this?"

"Well, I…"

"You did," he concludes. "Fucking hell, Harlow. You know why I don't want to see them!"

I grab his stubble-covered chin, gripping tight. "I didn't want any of you to see that chapel, or my scars or my bloody hair."

"That's not—"

"Don't think about telling me it's not the same thing. I didn't get a choice either. Grow up and go see your mum."

Mouth hanging open like he's witnessed a brutal murder, Leighton gapes at me. I refuse to back down, channelling the dominance that Hunter wears like a protective shield. I can be that person too. I'm learning.

"Go," I repeat firmly.

Fear crackles across his expression.

"Come with me?" he pleads.

Standing up, I keep our fingers entwined. "Of course."

Following Enzo's path out of the crowded room, Leighton's grip on my hand tightens to a bone-crunching vice. Enzo leads our two newcomers into the kitchen, giving us a second to prepare before entering behind them.

"Fuck." Leighton suddenly stops. "I can't do this."

I rest my hand over the erratic beat of his heart. "You're not alone, Leigh. All of your family is here with you."

"That's exactly the problem. My family."

"Could they be any worse than mine?" I joke.

He chuckles under his breath. "Point taken. I just haven't seen them since I was sentenced. Fuck, I'm nervous."

"All the more reason to go in there. You've got nothing to be ashamed of."

"Haven't I?" he mutters.

I brush a kiss against his cheek. "No. You haven't."

He shudders a breath. "I'm scared of what they'll think, princess. I let them down. I let everyone down."

"You're their son," I remind him quietly. "That's all that will matter to them. Come on."

With a nervous breath, Leighton smooths his plain black jeans and button-down shirt, the collar casually gaping open.

"Alright. Let's get it over with."

In the kitchen, Enzo is fixing two glasses of red wine. His eyes meet mine and he smiles reassuringly as we approach. Our two guests are facing away from us, depositing bags of presents on the breakfast bar.

Leighton stops inside the kitchen, still crunching the bones in my hand with his grip. He clears his throat, and his father is the first one to turn around.

"Dad," Leighton forces out.

"Well, I'll be damned."

With short, buzzed silver hair, formidable features and tension lines afforded by a lifetime of service to his country, Benjamin Rodriguez is an intimidating presence.

He steps closer, his dark-blue jeans neat, matching an unbuttoned white shirt that shows off his still-toned physique. His eyes perfectly match his son's, but seem colder.

"Let's get a look at you." His fuzz-covered jaw clenches tight. "You look well."

Leighton coughs awkwardly. "I am."

With her pink trench coat removed, his mum turns around next. Her deep hazel eyes are already shining with tears, highlighting smile lines and a sweet, hopeful smile.

"Oh, Leigh." Her delicate, wrinkled hands move to cover her mouth. "I can't believe it's really you."

"Hi, Mum."

Rushing across the kitchen, she bundles him into a back-breaking hug so fast, Leighton almost falls over. His mum is a full head shorter than him, but clearly, very strong.

"Get over here and hug your son," she orders her husband.

Ben unveils a small, strained smile and joins their hug. Leighton is caught between them, his shock of chaotic brown hair peeking out between their sealed chests.

Inching around them, I dart to Enzo's side and let him tuck an arm around my waist. He's watching the reunion with a pleased smile on his face.

"Nice job," I whisper to him.

"Someone had to push Leighton." He shrugs while grinning down at me. "He needed to get over himself."

"You did good, Enz."

"Thanks, little one."

With the hug disbanded, Leighton subtly wipes under his red eyes when he thinks we're not looking. His mum is trying hard not to sob as she blows into a tissue pulled from her designer purse.

"Let me introduce you." Enzo puts a hand on my lower back to guide me forwards. "Della, this is Harlow. She moved in with us last year."

Tissue pocketed, Della steps closer with a bright smile. "Of course! Harlow, we've heard so much about you."

I briefly panic, thinking she's going to try to hug me as well, but she keeps a respectful distance.

"Hello," I say nervously.

"This is my husband, Ben. We're so happy to finally meet you. Hunter has kept us updated on your case."

Hunter's eagle-eyed father is studying me in an authoritative way, like he can see all of my darkest secrets.

"Nice to meet you," he offers.

"You too, sir."

"Drinks," Leighton declares, breaking the awkward introduction. "Harlow, want a beer?"

I nod, thankful. "Please."

He disappears inside the fridge and returns with two beers. Della and Ben both take seats at the formal dining table in front of the French doors.

"Come and sit down, son." Ben pulls out the chair next to him. "We've got a lot to catch up on."

Yanking the cap off his drink, Leighton takes several gulps for courage and heads over to sit opposite his parents. They're both staring at him like he's an exotic animal.

"How's retirement?" he begins.

Ben takes a sip of red wine. "Quiet. Your mother had me join a walking club last year."

She swats his arm with a laugh. "Don't sound so affronted. You needed to get out after your fall."

"You had a fall?" Leighton replies.

"He toppled over in June and broke his collarbone!"

"Jesus, Dad. Why didn't you tell me?"

"How? By telepathy?" Ben frowns at his son.

I watch Leighton's face crumple. He rubs the back of his neck, polishing off his beer in one long gulp. I want nothing more than to wrap my arms around him, but he needs to do this alone.

"I needed some time," he offers them both. "It took a lot of adjusting when I came out of prison."

"We wanted to help you." Della brushes a tear from her powdered skin. "Three years, Leigh. No visits, no calls. Not even a letter."

"We tried to visit," Ben adds. "You refused every request."

"Yeah… I know," he hushes.

"Eventually, we stopped trying." Della's tears intensify. "It was like you had died. We mourned you every single day."

"Mum," Leighton mumbles. "Don't say that."

"It's the truth. I felt so powerless."

Glancing away, Leighton swipes under his eyes again. I'm desperate to protect him from their disappointment, but they're not wrong. He chose to block out his family and old life to survive behind bars.

Unlike them, I can't blame him. Captivity, whether legally sanctioned or not, forces the new, embattled version of yourself to tear free from the carcass of who you used to be.

Loneliness kept Leighton alive.

His family would've made it worse.

"I don't have a good enough reason for what I've done," he explains thickly. "But I needed to do this alone. All I can hope is that you'll forgive me."

Reaching across the table, Della takes Leighton's clenched hand in hers. She brushes her thumb over the scarring across his knuckles, evidencing years of violence to survive a world behind bars that most will never understand.

"There's nothing to forgive, Leigh."

His head snaps up. "But, you said…"

"You may have hurt us with your choices, but I know for a fact that it hurt you far more than it did us. You were all alone."

Leighton shrugs. "I lived."

"And you did your time," she confirms with a tearful smile. "All we ever wanted was for you to come home again."

"Even after what I did?" He shakes his head.

Della looks to her silent husband for help. Ben is staring at his folded hands, still frowning. He looks so much like Hunter when he does that. They're clearly cut from the same cloth.

"You're still my son," he finally cuts in. "Regardless of the mistakes you've made. Nothing will ever change that fact."

Della nods. "We love you so much."

Releasing a breath that's poisoned him for three long years, Leighton looks between his parents with tears in his eyes. Everything about him seems lighter, relieved, unburdened by the constant fear of rejection.

"I'm sorry I shut you out."

She seizes his hand and kisses it. "You're here, and that's all I care about. We can be a family again."

"You're getting back on your feet," Ben agrees with a chuckle. "I hear you've been driving your brother up the wall too."

Deeming it safe to approach, Enzo claps Leighton on the shoulder. "He's keeping us all on our toes."

"Someone has to," he comments.

"We'll make an adult out of you yet, Leigh."

The front door buzzes as it clicks open again, followed by loud cursing as the beat of heavy rain travels through the air.

"Here we go," Enzo announces.

I slip out of the kitchen to meet them first. Shaking his long, wet ponytail out, Hunter peels off his navy peacoat and holds the door open for Theo to sneak in behind him.

"Hey, guys."

"Sweetheart." Hunter's eyes eat me up as he drags a tie over his head next. "Wow. You're looking different."

Smoothing my purple skater-style dress, paired with thick tights and a black cable knit cardigan, I try not to blush. Hunter stalks towards me, his warm gaze lit with interest, but he's halted by a roar of voices.

"Surprise!"

"Happy Birthday!"

Brooklyn and her guys have swarmed out of the den and surrounded us, clapping and smacking Hunter on the back. He spares me an eye roll before Hudson wrestles him into a man hug.

Leighton and Enzo appear in the doorway next, with Ben and Della behind them. Hunter does a comical double take when he sees his parents still cuddled up to Leighton.

"Mum, Dad," he wheezes. "You're here."

"We couldn't miss your birthday," Della explains, her arm around Leighton's waist. "The family is all together again."

I feel someone approaching me before warmth circles my waist. The scent of books and peppermint drapes over my skin in a comforting mist. It's fast becoming my favourite scent. Theo cuddles me from behind, kissing my temple.

"Hi, beautiful."

"Hello, Theodore," I answer breathily.

"You look stunning. Purple is your colour."

"I can't take the credit. Brooklyn helped."

"I'll have to thank her."

Enzo takes charge, directing everyone into the kitchen to start attacking the mountain of food we've laid out on the table. Hanging back to let everyone pass us both, Hunter blocks the doorway with a muscled arm.

Stopping in front of him, I strain onto my tiptoes to land a featherlight kiss against his bearded cheek.

"Happy Birthday, Hunt."

His hand grips my hip as he catches my lips in a fast, passionate kiss. Even with the boom of voices, cutlery scraping and beers being popped inside the kitchen, it feels like we're alone in the world.

Hunter's bottomless brown eyes trained on me always have that effect. Since the moment we met, I've felt the pressure of the pedestal he puts me on, even though he fought against it at first. He was so ready to give everything to me.

That's exactly why Brooklyn is right about our current situation. It's up to me to fix what I've broken. I want them, and I finally realise that doing nothing will only make this worse. I have to be the one to win Hunter around.

"Let's go on a date," I blurt against his lips.

His eyebrows knit. "A date?"

"It will be fun. We can celebrate your birthday."

His chocolatey eyes blow wide with surprise, and it takes a moment for the corner of his mouth to hook up in a pleased smirk. He looks like the cat that got the cream.

"Just us?" he clarifies.

I push my mouth against his again. "Just us."

With a low growl, his hand cups the back of my head, and he deepens the kiss. His lips work like the magnetic pull of steel train tracks, luring me closer into the depths of his tempting embrace.

I can taste his excitement, feel it running through every sinewy muscle pressed against me beneath his dress shirt. Regardless of our surroundings, he quickly flips us around and pushes me up against the wall.

"I would love to go on a date with you," he says between kisses. "But why now?"

"Because I want to do something fun with you. We can act like a normal couple for once."

The tiniest flash of insecurity sneaks across his expression. For a nanosecond, I can see Leighton in him, putting on a front to avoid rejection. It's soon smoothed over into Hunter's mask of self-assuredness.

"What about the others?" he asks pointedly.

I stroke a fingertip over his brows. "One date, Hunt. No fighting, no jealousy. Give me one single night of normalcy with you alone."

Hunter deliberates before answering. "We can talk after," he eventually submits. "I want to do something normal too, without worrying about what it means for us all."

"Then it's settled."

"I'll plan something nice." He strokes a hand over my curled hair. "Leave it with me, sweetheart."

"Nothing fancy," I warn him.

"We'll see about that."

Someone shouts our names from inside the kitchen, bursting the bubble of privacy that's protecting our intimate moment. Hunter strokes his hands down my shoulders.

"We should go back in. I can't believe my parents are here. How did Leighton take it?"

"He'll be okay, I think. It went well."

"Enzo must be a miracle worker."

"For his family?" I shrug. "I think he might be."

Tangling our fingers together, Hunter pecks my lips a final time and lingers for a teasing second before dragging me back into the kitchen. The buffet of food looks like it's been ravaged by a pack of hungry wolves.

Phoenix is neck deep in three plates full of food, rivalling even Leighton's impressive tower of snacks. In the corner, Eli and Jude are both drinking beers and talking, neither eating.

They both dislike big crowds, even when it's family. Their trust is hard won, and it took me a while to break down their defences. They offer me smiles from across the room.

Hudson, Kade and Brooklyn are gathered in the corner of the kitchen with Della. The wedding talk must be boring Hudson—his darting eyes and silent plea for a distraction are obvious even from here.

I wink at him as I pass. He mouths the word *"traitor"* when I don't offer to intervene as Brooklyn's official co-wedding planner. He's clearly having such a good time. I wouldn't want to ruin it for him.

We join Enzo and Theo at the table, and Hunter pulls the chair out for me to slip in next to our awkward techie wearing his usual flannel shirt, faded-blue jeans and slightly crooked glasses.

"Did you get your class schedule?" he asks quietly.

I eat a curly fry from his plate. "It came through yesterday to start next week. Two hours a day for three months."

"That's good, right?"

"I guess so."

"I've set up one of our work laptops for you to use. It's in my backpack. You can attend the classes online that way."

"You did that for me?" I ask in surprise. "I was just going to use Hunter's computer in his office."

"I know that you hate using it. Now, you don't have to."

My chest burns with gratitude. The tips of Theo's ears turn pink when I quickly kiss his clean-shaven cheek before retreating. I can feel Ben's attention on us both.

"Thank you," I whisper to him.

"Don't mention it. Oh, and those books you asked for are in there too. Help yourself."

"*The War of the Worlds*? I've been dying to read that after finishing *The Time Machine* last week. Early-era science fiction is my new obsession."

"It's the best," Theo agrees happily. "I'm wondering if my reading tastes are rubbing off on you."

"I think they might be."

"Feel free to ignore me and read more Jane Austen shit, no judgement."

"Hard pass. I'll stick with alien invasions and time travel."

His smile widens. "That I can help you with."

Sitting down next to Ben with his several servings of food demolished, Enzo ducks his head low and begins a rapid-fire conversation in conspiratorial whispers.

With Theo engaged in conversation, I'm free to eavesdrop. I subtly move my chair under the pretence of grabbing a cocktail sausage and catch a few words.

"NDA agreement… off the record."

My heart rate triples.

"Time for cake!" Della shouts above the noise.

Startled back to the room, Enzo offers Ben a solemn nod, and the pair disband. I sit back in my seat, attempting to slow the racing organ in my chest. Doubt and fear have slipped back in while my defences are lowered.

We're all sitting here, drinking and eating, while Candace could be taking her dying breath. She feels so out of reach. I can't save her, no matter what I do. I'm just as powerless now as I was then.

The team has been working tirelessly, attempting to gather any information on Genesis Home in the hope it will lead us to Pastor Michaels.

It's like searching for a needle in a haystack. These government-endorsed children's homes used to be littered all over England. Rosetta was one horrifying case among many tragedies.

It doesn't change the fact that Pastor Michaels wanted us to find her. She wasn't left as a boast of divinely ordained power, not like the others. He was whispering into my ear with a hidden message.

I don't know what it is yet. Our one lead is Lee Heston and his past, left behind like rotting breadcrumbs. Until the house search is complete, we won't know if it's just another dead end.

This normal, happy family life will always be hollow until then. I'm surrounded by loved ones. We're safe and secure. My guys are okay. But it doesn't stop the pain creeping back in and ruining every good moment.

"Harlow. You okay?"

Theo's voice cuts through the fog that's descended over me. Everyone is gathered around the table, and the gleam of flickering candles lights the space doused in darkness.

"Fine," I choke out.

Everyone starts to sing. The chorus of "Happy Birthday" rings hollow around me. I brush Theo's concerned hands off and mouth along, plastering my perfected mask back into place.

Smile. Sing.

Breathe. Blink.

I'm a living mannequin, hiding the festering cancer inside me that no one can see. I never celebrated my birthday. Candace may never do that again.

As Hunter blows out the number thirty-five with another eye roll, everyone starts clapping. I follow suit, stuffing my emotions back down before someone catches on. I promised myself that I'd try to enjoy every last moment of freedom.

If they can't find Pastor Michaels before it's too late, then this will be the last birthday I spend with the family that found me in that hospital. I'm planning for a future part of me believes I'll never see.

Hunter's eyes meet mine from across the table. His lips move with a silent message. Words only meant for me. No one's allowed to know what he whispers in the dark, exposing the bare violin strings of his heart. Three words that make my heart hammer and body hum with butterflies.

I love you.

I wish I could say it back. All I can do is smile and hope that God forgives me enough to grant me the luxury of living to see his next birthday. Maybe I can say it then.

In perfect sync, all four of the guys' phones begin to blare with loud alarms. Adding to the chaos, the security system in the hallway screams for attention, cutting off our festivities.

"What the hell is that?" Ben exclaims.

"Front gate emergency alert." Theo stares at his phone as it falls quiet. "Looks like the system is malfunctioning."

Hunter curses at his phone. "The gate is opening. I think we've got company."

Opening the glass door to the wine fridge behind him, Enzo pulls out a hidden silver handgun from between the bottles and checks the barrel. Della's frightened squeak does little to deter him.

"You all armed?" he barks.

Kade lifts the flap of his usual suit jacket to reveal a gun holster. Hudson and Brooklyn nod with their own assent, both pushing an unarmed Eli and Phoenix behind them.

"Alright, on me." Enzo sends the rest of us a sharp look. "Stay here. We'll check it out."

"Enz," Hunter begins.

"I've got it. Stay with Harlow."

Rising from his perch in the corner, Jude zips past everyone and grabs

Brooklyn's arm. He's snatched the hunting knife from her grasp before she can block his theft.

"Don't fucking move," he snarls at her.

"Give me the knife back. I'm going out there."

"Sit your ass down, Eight! I mean it!"

The entire room stills at the strange word that's escaped his mouth. Kade and Hudson both gape at him with matching looks of concern.

"Brooklyn," Jude corrects. "I meant Brooklyn. Fuck, wait here. Don't move."

Face paling, she slumps backwards into Eli's open arms. Jude storms from the kitchen ahead of Enzo, Hudson and Kade, his shoulders pulled back.

Everyone stills as the sound of raised voices filters inside when they open the front door. I can hear someone shouting, over and over. A repeated, choreographed taunt. It sounds desperate. Frantic, even.

"Who is it?" I ask through my panic.

"We lost visual, but it looked like a male intruder." Theo's fingers dance across his phone screen as he attempts to reboot the security program. "He appeared to be armed."

Stepping in front of his wife, Ben touches Hunter's arm. "You got more guns stashed in this kitchen of yours, son?"

"There are seventeen hidden across the house," he replies.

"Good. You remembered your training."

"You drilled it into me enough, Pops."

Straining to reach underneath the dining table still full of plates and drinks, Hunter reappears with a gun and checks the safety is on before tossing it through the air to his father.

Ben catches it with ease, clicking off the safety and holding it steady in his expert grip. He prowls across the room to step in front of me, pushing me backwards into the safe zone.

"They're not taking you anywhere," he snarls protectively. "Alright, out the back. Both of you."

"Outside?" Della repeats.

Ben jerks his head. "We'll keep whoever it is occupied."

She snakes an arm around my waist, murmuring reassurances, but a fierce shriek halts us both.

"Letty! I'm here!"

That's when the penny drops.

The name I've heard being called, over and over again, isn't mine. It's *hers*. The broken, damaged girl curled up in the depths of my fragmented mind, never to be seen again.

"Letty! Let—hey, get off me!"

"Wait!" I escape Della's clutches. "That's my father. What is he doing here?"

"We'll deal with him," Hunter interjects while stepping in front of me. "He's supposed to be in rehab."

"Move! He might be in trouble."

"For breaking my front gate?" he accuses. "He sure as fuck is in trouble."

The sound of a scuffle echoes from outside. I throw myself at Hunter, desperate to get past him. I won't allow Enzo to hurt my father in the name of protecting me.

He's sick and needs our help. Whatever drove him here on a freezing cold, dark night, leaving the safety of his spot in a rehab unit behind—it must be important.

Staring up at Hunter, I meet his steely eyes. "Please. I need to see if he's okay."

"It isn't safe. I won't say it again."

"I'm not a fucking child!"

"Then don't act like one!" he yells at me.

With a huff, I pull my arm from his grip and reluctantly slump back into my empty chair. Brooklyn gently touches my leg underneath the table in a show of solidarity.

"Breathe," she murmurs.

"This is ridiculous."

"I know. Just hang on for an opening and make a run for it." She checks Hunter isn't listening. "I'll cover you."

"You'd do that?"

"Obviously. On my mark, alright?"

It's another five minutes before footsteps enter the house. I shoot back onto my feet. Hudson and Kade return first, both muttering under their breaths.

Enzo's unmistakable footsteps announce his presence next. I gasp when I see who's trapped in his huge arms, two hands restrained behind him.

My father looks different from the time that I haven't seen him. There's colour back in the sickly pallor of his skin, and his dark-blonde hair is washed, clean even.

The biggest difference is his crystal-clear blue eyes. They're open and alert, pinned on me as he struggles against his captor. Jude follows behind them, an unfamiliar gun being inspected in his hands.

Enzo shoves my father against the wall. "Alright, we agreed on ten seconds. Better start talking before I lose my patience and shoot you in the skull."

"Letty," he gasps in pain.

"Enzo, let him go!" I yell. "He isn't here to hurt me."

"I just want to talk to my daughter," Dad groans.

"Then do things the right way," Enzo growls back. "Don't break into our home, armed with an illegal gun, and act surprised when we don't trust your intentions."

"I didn't have time! It isn't safe!"

"What isn't safe?" I stare at my father.

"She isn't on your side, Letty! I came to warn you." His eyes are bugged out with fear. "You have to believe me."

"More family crap?" Enzo tugs his arm higher, causing my father to yelp loudly. "You and Giana need to keep away from Harlow."

"Giana is lying to you," he shouts louder.

"Alright, that's enough," Hunter announces as his short patience expires. "Enz, get him out of here."

"No, stop!" I implore them. "I want to hear him out."

"Not like this." Hunter gestures towards my gasping father. "He can set a meeting and follow protocol. He's lucky I'm not having him arrested for breaking and entering."

"I had no choice." My father moans in pain, losing steam. "She isn't safe here. I came to warn you all."

Enzo pulls him back and smashes him into the wall again, even harder this time. My father screams in pain, and the sound lances through my skull like a bayonet.

"Time's up, asshole," Enzo snarls in his face. "Be thankful Harlow's here, or else your brains would be splattered across the driveway right now."

"You h-have to b-believe me… Giana's behind it all."

"Take him away," Hunter orders before meeting my father's eyes. "If you leave rehab again, I'll have you thrown back in prison instead."

Enzo begins to strong arm him away, and I catch Brooklyn's eyes. She steps in front of Ben and his gun, allowing me to dart around the table.

Before I can get far, Hunter catches me and pins me against his firm chest. "Not so fast, sweetheart."

I batter his back with my fists, screaming at the top of my lungs for him to let me go.

"You have to run, Letty! Get away from her!"

"Let him go," I shout helplessly.

Following Brooklyn's lead, Leighton steps in front of his brother and shoves his shoulder, helping to break me free. I land back on my own feet with a grunt.

"This isn't right, Hunt," he argues. "Harlow can make her own choices. You can't do this."

"That lunatic broke in here with a gun," Hunter hisses back. "He's unhinged and dangerous!"

Ignoring their arguing, I take Leighton's distraction and make it outside as Enzo's wrenching his car boot open. He easily plucks my thin father off his feet and tosses him in the back, despite his continued yelling.

Something drops.

"Letty," he screams. "Take it!"

A sizable, tightly bound package has landed on the paved driveway, fallen from my father's grip. Enzo is too busy to notice. Darting outside, I snatch it from behind him before he can steal it away too.

"Take her back inside," Enzo orders as he climbs into the driver's seat. "I'll deal with this one."

Suddenly, two steely iron bands ending with a single hand wrap around my waist from behind. Jude captures me this time. I'm dragged like a sack of potatoes back into the house, staring down at the package clutched in my hands.

It's a bound collection of sealed letters. I quickly shove it inside my cable knit cardigan to conceal it. I have no doubt they'll confiscate this too, in the name of bloody safety.

"I'm sorry, Harlow." Jude finally releases me inside. "It's for your own protection. He could be violent."

With my feet back on the floor, I see red. Violence spikes through my veins as my fist draws back and slams straight into Jude's face. He falls and hits the wall, seeming more surprised than hurt.

"You, of all people, should know better than to do that to me." I clutch my aching fist. "Screw you."

His face falls. "I'm sorry."

Ignoring his useless apology, I turn to include the others in the sentiment. "Screw you all."

Theo abandons his perch against the wall, fiddling with the security system. He attempts to approach me, his hands raised. I take several large steps back.

"Don't touch me! Any of you."

He freezes, his face paling. "I'm sorry, Harlow."

"Sweetheart," Hunter begins from inside the doorway. "We had to ensure your safety. He could be dangerous."

"How many times will you use that excuse?"

Stumped for an answer, he's silent.

"That's what I thought," I finish.

Turning on my heel, leaving them all gaping after me, I flee upstairs with the package held against my chest. None of them dare to follow.

This time, they've gone one step too far. I'm not their prisoner, and I won't be treated like one. Never again.

CHAPTER 16
HARLOW

INTO IT – CHASE ATLANTIC

"PLEASE SIT DOWN."

Pacing in the spacious therapy room, I turn the handwritten letter over in my hands. It's one of almost three hundred, spanning several years. I only managed to read the beginning before the tears and grief took over.

I know you're still out there, Letty. I'll never stop looking for you. No matter what the world thinks.

I put it back in its envelope and counted them all instead, over and over again, attempting to calm down last night. Not even the knocks on the locked bathroom door or Hunter's pleading convinced me to open up. I cried myself to sleep on the tiled floor, surrounded by letters and torn out hair.

"Harlow," Richards urges.

"He wrote to me, year after year, while the rest of the world presumed me dead. He kept writing. It's all here."

"Sit down and talk to me."

"I don't want to talk!"

"Well, I want to help you," he pleads.

"Then tell me what my father meant about Giana. Is he trying to manipulate me?"

Richards watches me, his spectacles balanced on his nose. "We can work through this, but you need to calm down first."

"How can you possibly fix this?"

"I understand that you're angry," he tries again. "You experienced a scare last night."

"A scare? I'm not scared of my father. I'm scared of the people I'm living with."

"Sabre is contractually obligated to maintain your security," he points out. "I understand that your father was armed when he broke in."

"He's sick and afraid. He needs our help!"

Richards clears his throat. "Harlow… I'm sorry, but look at yourself. In their eyes, you are exactly the same. This is their way of helping you."

I freeze on the carpet. His words punch into me like needlepoints, slashing deep with the bitter pill of truth.

"You think I'm sick?" I repeat. "I should've known that you'd be on their side. You don't want to help me."

"That isn't true at all," Richards argues softly. "You're self-harming again." He nods towards the hair I've torn out during our session. "This isn't a healthy way to cope."

"Who are you to tell me how to cope?"

"I'm your therapist, but I also care about you. We've come so far since our first session last year. Don't throw all that progress away now."

Tossing the letter back on his desk with the rest of the pile, I scrub my hands over my face, smearing hot tears. I haven't felt this out of control for a while. I'd forgotten how terrifying it is.

Nothing is working to stop the barrage of untamed emotions and anger from flooding through me and distorting everything. Not even the pain that's led me here.

"Your coping techniques don't help." I shake my head. "You expect me to sit here and meditate while Candace is being held captive, my father is sick and my entire life is falling apart?"

Richards tidies the bundle of scattered letters on his desk. He neatly ties the package and places it back inside my discarded handbag.

"I understand you're at a breaking point. It's up to you whether you continue down this path or accept my help."

"What is your help, exactly?" I ask him. "Another seven months in this room, doing nothing to fix my problems?"

Richards hesitates, his smile tight. "I'd like for you to agree to an inpatient stay at the local hospital."

His words almost knock me over. I have to grip the back of my empty chair for balance.

"Wait, what?"

"Hear me out," he says quickly. "It's nothing to be afraid of. You can take some time out, away from all of this."

My feet begin to backtrack. "You want to lock me up. Just like you did to Brooklyn and Jude."

"They weren't locked up," Richards placates. "You need time and space to heal. You're in a dark place right now. Let me help."

"What if I say no?" I challenge.

"Then I can't force you. But if you continue down this path and I think your life is at risk, we may be having a different conversation."

The walls are closing in. Another prison. Another cell. He wants to lock me up, steal my freedom, my life, my future. I'm staring down the barrel of an inevitable gunshot to the head.

"I won't be put in another cage." I walk towards the door. "Not now, not ever. I can't go back to living like that."

"Nobody is putting you in a cage. I want to give you the space to heal and get help in a safe environment."

"No! I don't want to go. I'm done talking."

Picking up my handbag, I leave Richards staring after me with sadness in his clear eyes. The door slams shut behind me as I escape into the silent corridor in Sabre's HQ. Down the stretch of dark carpet, Leighton's sprawled out in an armchair, scrolling on his phone.

He's the only one of the guys I allowed near me after last night's debacle. At least he attempted to reason with Hunter and allowed me the chance to chase after my father.

He drove me here today for my regular session, respecting my need for silence and distance. The others have all been notably absent and unable to face me.

"Leigh," I gasp through tears.

He sits up, abandoning his phone. "Harlow? You've still got half an hour to go."

"I'm done talking to him."

"Why? What happened in there?"

I hug my handbag. "I want to get out of here."

Tucking his phone into his jeans pocket, he twirls a set of car keys on his finger. "You sure?"

Nodding, I bounce on my feet. "Let's go."

"Well, I have good news. Hunter has his tail between his legs, so we're off the hook for the day."

"What do you mean?"

Leighton flourishes a shiny black card from his pocket. "I have his credit card and free rein to turn your frown upside down. Let's get into some trouble."

"Hunter's trying to make this better by throwing money around? Seriously?"

"Well." He plasters on his best holier-than-thou expression, complete with an invisible halo. "He told me to take you to buy school supplies. Technically, that's free rein."

I manage a tiny grin. "What's the plan then?"

"We should check into a crazy expensive hotel, eat everything on the menu and leave those dickheads to come to their senses. Maybe even some online shopping."

That sounds too good to be true.

"I want his bank account to hurt," he adds.

"Can we do all that? Is it safe with the protests going on outside and Candace still missing?"

"Fuck everyone and the protests. We can take security." He sticks his hand out for me to take. "Come on. I'll text the others and tell them to give us some space."

I squash my fear and tentatively take his hand. The pressure of his long fingers gripping mine grounds me back in the present. I'm not locked in the back of a faceless van, being driven to Richards' fancy prison disguised as a hospital.

"Hey," Leighton murmurs. "What is it?"

"I f-feel like everything is spiralling out of control."

His green eyes soften beneath shaggy chestnut hair, and Leighton tugs me closer. I wrap my arms around his waist and bury my nose in his citrus-scented t-shirt.

"I'm here, princess," he whispers against my lowered head. "I know things feel bleak right now, but I swear to you, we're doing our best to make this right."

"You saw what they did to my father last night. How can I ever trust them?"

"Because the one thing that Hunter and Enzo agree on right now is their love for you," he replies easily.

Love.

There's that word again.

"Sometimes it makes them behave like wankers." He laughs under his breath. "But they care about you."

"Enough to hurt someone I care about?"

"In the name of keeping you safe? Yes. They didn't blink an eye last night, and I'm sure they'd do it all over again."

I release his waist. "Maybe that's the problem."

Leighton strokes a hand over my messy, uneven hair. There's no point even attempting to hide it. The right side is thinning so severely, it's enough to be noticeable now. I can tell it's bothering him.

"Harlow," he begins. "You have to know how much we all fucking adore you. I can't imagine my life without you in it. It's killing me to watch you go through this."

"I'm sorry."

"Don't be." He tucks a strand of hair behind my ear. "Tell me what you want me to do, and I'll do it. Shall we stain all of Hunter's clothes pink? Set Enzo's car keys in jelly?"

"I was thinking something bigger than your usual pranks."

Leighton waves the credit card. "In that case, I think we'll head for the best hotel in the city. Come on, milady. Hunter's inevitable bankruptcy is calling."

Linking my arm in his, Leighton escorts me down to the car parked in the garage and we head out into the busy city traffic. The blacked-out windows of security tailing us in their expensive SUV threaten to derail my mood, but I block them out, pretending we're alone.

Half an hour of terrible singing along to the radio later, Leighton pulls up on the curb beneath the towering shadow of a glitzy, multi-story hotel rising above us. I feel my mouth drop open.

Turning off the engine, he hops out of the car and surrenders his keys to the beaming man in a fine suit that appears. I take an unsteady breath before Leighton opens my door and offers me a hand.

"Shall we?" He waggles his eyebrows.

"Sure about this?"

"Hell yeah. Come on."

We're steered inside the bustling reception of the five-star hotel, tailed by two plain-faced agents pretending to be invisible. With thick, red carpets, high ceilings and gilded chandeliers casting sparkling light across the polished mahogany furniture, I feel a little out of place in here.

"Damn," Leighton mutters. "This is fancy as fuck."

"What are we doing here?"

"Being fancy," he teases.

At the front desk, Leighton charms the concierge with the promise of his brother's limitless credit card. She accepts it with a bright smile, racking up a two-thousand-pound bill in less than ten seconds.

"You're lucky the master suite is available," she chatters animatedly. "It comes with its own butler service and valet parking. The three on-site restaurants are at your disposal."

"Perfect." Leighton grins as he curls his arm around my waist. "My wife has very expensive tastes."

I choke on air. "Um."

"Isn't that right, honey?" He winks at me. "She insisted on visiting London on the way to our honeymoon. I'll be needing a new credit card before much longer."

"You are such a beautiful couple!"

"She's my little honey bear. Aren't you, pumpkin?"

"Mmm," I respond, internally dying. "That's me."

Leighton plants a big, sloppy kiss on my cheek. "Do you want anything else, my sugar pea? Perhaps a massage?"

"No… *darling*."

"Oh, that's right. I'll be doing all the massaging later."

I smack his chest, on the verge of a giggling fit.

"Tell you what, I'll throw in a complimentary bottle of champagne," the concierge offers. "Congratulations on your wedding. I hope you have a lovely stay!"

Leighton is doing his best to hold in a laugh. "That's kind of you. I'm sure we will. Come on, darling wife."

He tows me away before I fall into a fit of laughter. Following a well-dressed busboy in his perfectly tailored suit, we ride the gleaming elevator up to the sixteenth floor.

"Don't laugh," he whispers to himself.

I'm biting my tongue to hold my own in. Plush carpets swallow our footsteps down to the hotel room. Leighton lets me in before closing the door in the faces of our security and finally bursting into hysterics.

"You are insane," I break down.

"The look on your face was priceless."

"I can't believe you pulled that off."

Leighton chucks his coat aside. "I am a master."

Inside the suite, I take a moment to look around. It's huge, spanning across two giant rooms. Rich brocade wallpaper meets polished accents in the sitting area, showcasing velvet sofas, a huge flat-screen television and a fully stocked bar.

In the bedroom, through gleaming sliding doors, the world's biggest bed is covered in decorative pillows and sheets. There's an attached bathroom, glistening with flashes of crystal, marble and shining glass.

Leaving Leighton to inspect the mini bar, I peek out of the floor-to-ceiling curtains held back by silk ties and gasp at the panoramic view of Canary Wharf.

It's pulsating with light and lunchtime activity. Business drinks, first dates and the reunion of friends meeting in the city all add to the menagerie of life unfolding beneath us.

"The city is beautiful."

Leighton sidles up to me. "You think?"

"I'm not sure I could ever live here, but I love watching the people. There's so much energy everywhere."

Leaving me to approach the massive bed, Leighton flops on the crisp, gold-accented linens. His t-shirt rides up to flash a sliver of abdominals and soft, black hair trailing into his fitted blue jeans.

He picks up the leather-bound menu from the bedside table and the nearby telephone to begin reciting his order—dish after dish, until there's nothing left that he hasn't charged to Hunter's credit card.

"Food's coming. Hope you're hungry."

"Your brother is going to flip out."

"He makes this kind of money every thirty seconds. Consider it a lesson for next time he decides to be a colossal controlling asshat."

Pulling off my parka and boots, I take two steps and collapse on the bed, narrowly avoiding crushing Leighton with my body. He rolls onto his side, propping his chin on his hand to study me with a crooked grin.

"You likey?"

I relax into the butter-soft mattress with a sigh. "It's away from home and HQ. That's good enough for me."

"Wanna get naked and watch a movie?"

"What?" I laugh.

His eyes are twinkling with mirth. "Watching TV while naked is one of the best perks of being an adult."

"Is that a fact?"

"Well, along with taking a pizza into the bathtub or eating your whole advent calendar on December first."

Staring up at the chandelier, I clutch my belly, which hurts from laughing so hard. He's certifiably insane.

"I'm not sure you've quite grasped the concept of adulthood," I wheeze out. "But for the record, I prefer your definition. It sounds a lot more fun."

Leighton fist pumps the air. "I knew it. I'm totally winning at adulting here. So, how about it? Shall I run us a hot bubble bath?"

"Did you order pizza as well?"

"Obviously," he quips back. "You know it's one of my five a day."

"Then I guess it would be rude not to."

Depositing a kiss on the corner of my mouth, Leighton bounds into the attached en-suite with the excitement of Lucky when I take her for a sunset walk.

By the time the food arrives, the cloth-covered trolley checked by our overzealous security, Leighton's half naked and the bath is full of steaming water.

He pushes the trolley into the room and dismisses the waiter, already cramming several delicate, miniature cakes into his mouth and spilling crumbs on his bare chest.

I stare at his hamster cheeks. "You're an animal."

"What?" he replies around his mouthful. "I'm hungry. These cakes are so small, you have to eat three at a time."

"Have to?"

"Obviously."

Pulling the complimentary bottle of champagne from its ice bucket, he sets to work removing the cork. With the bottle popped, I watch as he disappears into the bathroom with it.

"Bring the pizzas," he yells over his shoulder.

"Plural?"

"I ordered six, plus sides. Everyone knows these fancy restaurants serve tiny portions and charge twice as much."

Lifting the lids on various serving platters, I gape at the ridiculous amount of food he's ordered. I have no idea how eating in the bath will work. I grab two pizzas to start with.

In the en-suite bathroom, a headful of shaggy hair pokes out from an avalanche of honey-scented bubbles. Leighton is naked in record time, drinking champagne from the bottle.

"I have no words to describe how crazy you look right now." I bark a laugh. "You don't want a glass?"

He sits up, letting slick bubbles cascade over his defined pectorals. "Do I look that sophisticated?"

"Not right now, no."

Leighton looks at the platter in my hands. "You gonna get your clothes off and climb in with that?"

Flushed, I bounce on my feet. "Shut your eyes."

"Princess, I've seen you naked before. Stop being a pussy and come feed me before I get hangry."

"I'm being a pussy? Really?"

His defiant gaze doesn't waver. "Yup."

"Well then."

Balancing the platter on the edge of the clawfoot bathtub, it's big enough to fit at least four people. Leighton's searing eyes are locked on me, and I feel a burst of confidence. He's seen every inch of me, good and bad. There's nothing to be afraid of.

I kick off my jeans and toss my long-sleeved t-shirt next. He doesn't look away once, even as he begins stuffing pizza in his mouth using a soapy hand.

Moving fast, I whip off my bra and drop my panties, leaping into the bath. The water sloshes loudly as I slide into the welcoming heat.

"Not even a twirl for me?" he pouts.

"That wasn't a striptease, Leigh."

"Rude. No pizza for you."

Parting the cloud of fragranced bubbles, I move closer and ease the slick bottle from his hands. Leighton watches with amusement as I take a gulp of the gross, fizzy alcohol.

"This is so disgusting."

"Champagne always is."

"Then why drink it?" I chuckle.

"I reckon the rich-as-fuck assholes who drink it are pretending to be fancy and secretly necking rum and Cokes when no one's looking."

Ditching the bottle on the tiled bathroom floor, I snag a slice of cheese-covered goodness, narrowly avoiding covering it in a carpet of bubbles.

"Eating pizza in the bathtub is impractical."

"But fun." Leighton inhales a slice. "You'd rather eat downstairs in one of those stuffy, pompous restaurants?"

"I'll pass."

He grins widely. "Knew it."

When I go in for another slice, Leighton shifts his huge leg to knock me off balance. I fall forwards in the warm water, sloshing and landing straight in his lap.

His arms wrap around my torso, pulling me up against his chest. My legs move without being told to slip around his waist, until we're pressed together in the steam and bubbles.

"Whoops," he singsongs.

"You did that on purpose!"

Leighton drops a kiss on my shoulder, his lips leaving a path of static electricity up to the curve of my neck. Teeth playfully nipping against my throat, he plants a gentle kiss.

"I could get used to you naked and wet in my bathtub."

I moan as his hips shift to grind into me. The solid press of his dick brushes right against the heat gathering between my thighs. There's nothing between us.

Leighton's mouth caresses mine. His lips move in a perfect, merciless attack formation, nipping and teasing until his tongue touches mine.

I hold his shoulders, my entire body quaking with the sudden rush of desire that obliterates my previous shyness. Every wet, glistening inch of his muscles is on display.

When his hand cups my bare breast and squeezes gently, I gasp against his swollen lips. The darkness metastasising in my mind is overtaken by one single thought.

I want him inside me.

Right now.

I'm done playing it safe.

"Leigh," I gasp as his lips wrap around my stiffened nipple. "Please…"

"Hmm?" he replies, teeth tugging on my hardened peak before he sucks my breast into his mouth.

Grabbing a handful of his dripping brown hair, I yank his head back up. Leighton gasps in pain, but his eyes are lit with excitement.

"I need you," I plead breathlessly.

Reaching into the depths of the water, his hand begins to skate down my stomach to slip between my legs. I'm still holding his hair tight, and I tug again to regain his attention.

"No. Not like that."

His brows furrow. "I don't understand."

I channel my best inner Brooklyn and lean close to capture his mouth in a searing, confident kiss. She's been coaching me for this ever since I admitted that I'm ready.

I stop for a breath to speak. "I need you inside me, and I'm not talking about your fingers."

He searches my face. "You want to…"

"Yes."

Leighton hesitates. "Harlow, I know I've been joking around about this, but seriously, there's no pressure."

"You've given me time and respected my boundaries. I love you for doing that, but I'm ready now. I trust you."

"But… last night. You're still upset and—"

Frustrated, I sink a hand beneath the bubbles and find the promising steel of his pierced cock in the water. Leighton cuts off mid-sentence. I stroke his shaft, showing him my intentions.

"Stop talking and take me to the bed."

"Fuck, princess. Are you sure?"

"Ask me one more time and I'll walk out of this hotel and find one of the others to do this with."

His lust-filled eyes harden. "You wouldn't dare. I'll never hear the end of it if Hunter or Enzo fuck you first."

"This isn't a competition."

"It sure as fuck is, and I'm gonna win."

Water cascades off his toned body as Leighton steps out of the bath and grabs a towel. I lift my arms up and let him pluck me out. Wrapping me in laundered cotton, I'm cradled in his arms.

Leighton walks back into the bedroom, scattering water across the expensive carpet. He kisses along the exposed skin of my neck, his teeth nipping and lips sucking.

I'm deposited on the end of the bed with a thump. Unwrapping the towel, he exposes my naked body. Standing in front of me, every inch of his long, thick length is on display, a glint of silver piercing the velvet tip. I swallow hard.

"We need to get a few things straight."

I shiver under his watchful stare. "Like what?"

Resting a hand on my shoulder, he pushes me backwards. I land on the mattress, my bare legs hanging over the edge.

"Are you going to be a good girl?" he asks.

"M-Me?"

"Do you see anyone else here? Answer the question."

"Yes," I recite softly.

"And you'll do as you're told?"

A quiver of desire sparks deep inside me. I press my thighs together, gasping at the ache between my legs.

"Yes."

"You'll say if I make you uncomfortable or if you want me to stop?"

Leighton didn't bother with a towel. He's hanging over me, stark naked. Fisting his erection, he begins to pump it with lazy strokes. It's so big. How will it fit in me? I'm suddenly nervous while watching him.

"Harlow," he snaps. "Words."

"Yes, I'm sorry. I'll tell you."

Scanning the hotel room, he heads for his discarded jeans on the floor and searches in the pocket for his wallet. I wait, shivering with need and splayed out for his perusal.

"What are you looking for?"

"As much as I'd love to watch my come drip down your thighs, we're in too much shit to have a kid right now. Unless you want to, that is."

"Huh?" I squeak in shock.

Leighton snorts as he walks back over, a foil packet in his hand. "It's a condom, Goldilocks. I was only joking."

"That was a terrible joke. I'd be a crap mother."

He returns to his position of power looming over me. I watch with fascination as he rolls a length of plastic over his erection, checking that it's securely in place.

"I'd be a shitty father, hence the rubber. Hunter would hospitalise me if I knocked you up."

Despite my nerves, I burst out in inappropriate laughter. Leighton snorts as his cheeks flush pink in the most adorable way. He always knows how to set me at ease.

"Last chance. You sure about this?"

Rather than answer again, I hook my foot around his powerful thigh and tug him forwards. Leighton lands above me with a huff, his arms holding him upright.

I squirm on the bed, my thighs rubbing against each other. I'm so flustered and desperate for a release. We've been dancing around this moment for months and I'm done.

"Poor little princess," he teases with a sly look. "If it hurts so bad, why don't you touch yourself?"

"Touch… myself?"

Leighton bites down on my earlobe. "Make yourself ready for me. I want to see your fingers covered in juices."

His mouth should be illegal. It adds fuel to the fire burning me up inside, and I don't feel my usual shyness or embarrassment. Leighton builds me up. He makes me feel powerful and confident in a way no one else does.

Biting down on my lower lip, I move my hand over my body to dip it between my legs. I'm quivering all over.

"Legs open wider," he instructs.

I follow orders, spreading them apart.

"Perfect. Let me see you touch your pussy."

It feels like there's no air to breathe in the room. It takes all of my bravery to hold my legs open so he can scrape his eyes over every inch of my exposed body.

My fingers travel over the now-neat patch of hair above my mound. I spent some time taming it after a thoroughly embarrassing conversation with Brooklyn about girl stuff.

"Lower," Leighton orders. "Don't be shy."

Finding the furnace between my folds, I slip a finger downstairs and stroke over my clit. It feels good, but nowhere near as pleasurable as when the others do it.

Biting back a moan, I gather the slick promise of moisture across my fingers before circling my tight entrance. I've touched myself a couple of times, mostly in exploration.

This is something different.

Leighton's simmering emerald eyes are locked on me with a look of pure fascination. He's enraptured by my every move. There's no hiding from him.

With a sharp inhale, I push my index finger inside myself and groan out loud. It feels so good to swirl it in a slow rotation, my thumb swiping over my bundle of nerves.

"That's it, princess," Leighton encourages in a raspy voice. "Let me see you fuck yourself."

I slide another finger inside, and my lower stomach clenches with pleasure. The pressure of his gaze locked on me is what makes this so hot. I'm performing for him.

"Faster," he orders. "You need to be nice and wet for what comes next, Goldilocks."

Copying the moves I've watched the guys use several times, I begin to move my fingers in and out. They stroke deep inside me, reaching for an invisible chord that sets off fireworks.

It's not quite the same, but when Leighton hovers over my spreadeagled body and sucks my nipple into his mouth, the pleasure intensifies. His mouth is so hot and teasing.

"Look at these perfect tits."

"Leigh," I gasp.

"That's it, baby. Keep going."

Thumbing my clit as the pressure begins to build, I let him guide my legs even further open with his spare hand. I've got a foot propped up on either side of him.

He releases my nipple to lean back and study me, inch by inch, leaving no part of my naked skin untouched by his eyes. When his hand slides between my legs, I writhe on the bed.

Placing his hand over mine, he takes over and pushes my own fingers deeper. The pressure is reaching a breaking point as I hit that strange spot of ecstasy.

"Does it feel good?" he teases me. "I want to see you come before I even think about touching you."

"I can't… do it myself."

"Sure you can. Let me help."

With his guidance, my fingers thrust faster inside me. The feeling begins to peak into an approaching wave. I'm working my own nervous system into a frenzy.

"Your cunt is so wet." Leighton leans closer to bite down on my bottom lip. "Make yourself come, baby girl."

He disappears from above me as I crawl closer to my breaking point. Leighton takes a step back, giving him a perfect view between my thighs.

I thrust my fingers deep into myself, pausing to swipe a thumb over my nub every second or so. It feels so good to be on display, trapped in this sexy, vulnerable state of objectification.

"That's a fine fucking sight," he comments.

Grabbing my left breast with my other hand, I tweak my nipple, needing some inexplicable push to cross that final line. I'm so close, pinching my nipple again, but harder.

The sharp burst of pain shatters the expanding bubble of anticipation. I cry out in pleasure. My back arches off the bed as warmth sweeps over my fingers, still buried deep in my slit.

Leighton's fisting his hard cock, watching every last detail. Heat sweeps over me, and I let my legs go limp, easing my fingers back out of myself as I come down from my high.

"Did I say you were finished?" he scolds.

The fire in his eyes is mesmerising.

He captures my glistening hand mid-air. "Give me your fingers so I can clean up your mess."

I'm tensed up with desire and excitement from the filth that escapes his mouth alone. Bringing my fingers to his lips, I hold his eye contact as he licks my wet, salty digits.

"See how wet you are for me? You're such a good girl, coming all over yourself like that."

Crawling back on top of me, he rests his weight on an elbow and grips my wrist tight. I watch my fingers disappear into his mouth again and his tongue glides over my skin.

"You taste heavenly," he groans. "Dammit, Harlow. The things I want to do to you."

My legs begin to quiver with nervousness. I'm trembling all over and wetter than I've ever been before. That little show was just a warmup. Leighton's tongue runs along my jawbone before he kisses my throat, his breath a teasing whisper.

"I'm going to fuck you now, and you're going to scream my name for the whole hotel to hear. Understood?"

I see stars as he grabs my nipple and twists.

"I understand. Please…"

"Please what? I can't hear you."

His hips brush against mine as he settles between my splayed legs, two hands resting on the bed to hold himself up.

"Please… fuck me," I mewl.

"That's what I wanted to hear—the sound of you begging. Fuck, how I've dreamt about this moment."

My legs are pinned open as he positions himself, and his eyes refuse to grant me a sliver of privacy. Leighton's staring deep into the unreachable wilderness within my psyche.

Lungs seizing with anticipation, I forget how to draw in a breath. The hard press of his sheath is pushed up against my entrance, on the verge of entering me fully. I'm ready to scream in frustration when he stops at the last moment.

"Are you okay?" he checks again. "Tell me to stop if you want. It's not too late to change your mind."

I draw his lips in for a kiss of confirmation. His mouth slants against mine in a perfect, God-given fit. We were always meant to be. This moment feels more right than anything.

He starts to push inside me, and I'm overcome by sharp, shooting pains. Leighton moves slowly, watching me closely for any glimpses of hesitation.

"Still okay?" he worries.

"It h-hurts, but it's fine."

He kisses me again. "Want me to stop?"

"No. Keep going."

"It'll start to feel good soon."

The bonfire crisping my skeleton from the inside out intensifies with each inch of steel sliding into me. I've never felt such intensity before.

The moment it's all in, Leighton's eyes roll back with a satisfied sigh. I can just feel the cool kiss of his piercing through the protective rubber.

"You feel so good around me," he whispers, gripping my hip. "I'm going to start slow, okay?"

I gasp as he retracts before pushing back into me. It burns at first, the pain threatening to unlatch a box full of dark memories, but Leighton won't let me drown in the past.

With each tender thrust, the sense of pressure eases. A new feeling takes over. Pain melts into the first wisps of sweet, welcome relief, before blossoming into euphoria.

"Does that feel good, baby?"

"Fuck… uh-huh."

He pushes even deeper into my pussy. I grab his hard biceps and dig my nails in, a moan tearing out of my parted lips. My nerves are on fire. It's all too much.

"You like my cock buried deep inside your cunt?"

"God, yes."

Leighton moves a little faster, broadening his strokes to slide into my slit. He nudges that mysterious place hidden away that feels so good. I cry out, louder this time.

My mind and body are both overwhelmed. Not even Pastor Michaels or the bottomless pit of traumatic memories can steal my attention from this single, perfect moment.

Leighton is the only thing that exists in my world right now. His tongue darting out to lick his lips. The verdant depths of his eyes, pinned on me with awe. His tanned skin, with lean muscles carved like hewed beams of steel.

"Shit, Harlow. I can't hold on for long."

I have no idea what he means, but I think I know what's coming. I'm tensing up without realising, the edges of my mind beginning to fray with sensory overload.

He's moving at a steady pace, pushing into me with each pump. The pain is completely gone. It feels incredible, so far from the depraved torture I've associated sex with for so long.

Leighton pulls out with a grunt, and I growl at the sudden loss. His cock is standing proud, glistening with moisture and a smear of blood as he waits at the end of the bed. Wrapping his hands around my ankles, I'm yanked down to stand up too.

"Turn over," he grunts.

Too boneless to move, I let Leighton lift my sweat-slick body with a chuckle. My hands land on the sheets and he places me on my tiptoes, raising my backside into the air.

The fierce heat of his body presses against my legs from behind. Unable to see him, I wiggle and moan, silently praying for his length to slide back inside me.

"Look at this gorgeous ass."

His hand smacks against my right cheek, sending warm tingles across my skin. He spanks me again, harder, the sizzling pain blurring into waves of agonising bliss.

"I love seeing my palm print on your skin."

"Leigh," I whine. "Please."

"Sorry, princess. Did I leave you hanging?"

Arching my back, I push against him, loving the tantalising promise of his cock nudging against my ass. He clasps my hips and drives back into me, eliciting a high squeak. From this angle, every sensation is intensified.

Deeper.

Faster.

Harder.

His caution disappears from sight as our bodies collide, his cock slamming back into me in a feverish tempo. Leighton isn't holding back anymore, and it's mind-blowing.

"Goddammit, baby."

My hands are twisted in the sheets as another release begins to reach its apex. This rush of ecstasy feels bigger. More threatening. I'm on the verge of being swept up by the tide, adrift and lost in the sea of intoxication.

"Let go," Leighton growls out. "Let's come together, princess. Fall apart for me."

His barked command is all it takes to knock me over the edge. I fall into a destructive meltdown as sensation explodes through me.

Screaming out his name in a voice that doesn't sound like my own, I hold on for dear life as Leighton chases his own release. His hips are crashing into me with each punishing thrust until he roars in my ear.

"Fuck!"

I've never had an orgasm like it. My entire body feels like it's burnt to a crisp, and I can't move a muscle. Leighton's breathing is ragged as he slumps on the bed, pulling me into the welcoming cradle of his arms.

Burying a hand in my hair, he pulls our lips together. I let him consume me. Over and over. Kiss after kiss. I'm his and he is mine in a way that not even God could dispute.

Our kiss is slower, more tender, silently reassuring the other after taking that inexorable step together. I can hardly keep my eyes open. Exhaustion has slipped over me as the aftershocks of my release fade.

"Jesus Christ," Leighton says after a minute. "Are you okay? Did I hurt you? I didn't mean to get carried away."

"I'm good. Better than good."

Cursing, he pulls the condom from himself and ties it off to be tossed out. I protest when he peels himself from me to disappear into the bathroom. He returns with a damp washcloth and gestures for me to open my legs again.

I hesitate. "Um, I'm fine."

"You seriously can't still be shy? After that?"

"Well, a little bit."

"You are too fucking adorable for me to handle."

Stifling a nervous giggle, I spread my legs, still shuddering with the final whispers of pleasure. Leighton holds my eyes as he dips the warm washcloth between my thighs, gently cleaning me up before tossing it on the floor with my towel.

"Thank you for trusting me, Goldilocks."

When he lies back down, I tangle our legs together and rest my head above his heartbeat. "How couldn't I?"

"I dunno. I'm far from perfect."

"You've been the most incredible friend to me, Leigh."

"Friend, huh?"

"At first." I squash my fear down. "But I think I've loved you since the first day we met, when you made popcorn and forced me to watch *Friends*. You cared so much."

The word slips out before I can stop myself. I'm not sure when I stopped seeing him as my best friend and started referring to him in my head in a different way. I don't like him. I don't even care about him. I love him—fully and irrevocably.

His hand brushes my cheek, allowing his thumb to stroke beneath my eye. I savour each circle of his skin on mine. His malachite irises are muddled with emotion.

Shock. Hope. Relief. Fear. A kaleidoscope of humanity at its best and worst. His broken pieces are calling out to mine. He's pieced me back together, one shattered shard at a time.

"You love me?" he hushes.

I bring our faces closer so our noses brush. It's an intimate embrace, with every single part of our bodies touching somewhere, until we're breathing the same air.

"Yes," I admit. "I love you."

His mouth warps into a painfully wide grin. It's so big and comical, I worry his lips will actually split with happiness.

"I love you," he echoes without hesitating. "I have for so long. All I want in this world is you."

I curl up against him, letting his arms swallow me in safety and protection. His heart is still working overtime. The steady thump is the best sound I've ever heard.

"You have me, Leigh. Forever."

CHAPTER 17
ENZO

VIA – VOICES FROM THE FUSELAGE

SITTING NEXT to Theo in his office, we're both leaning forward in our chairs. On his array of monitors, Giana's perfectly choreographed sadness plays out in real time.

She dabs at her reddened eyes with a tissue, looking anywhere but at Hunter. Every time she sniffles, unease twists in my gut. I don't buy it. Not for a second.

"You see, we have a slight problem."

"What kind of problem?" she snips back.

Hunter watches her from across the table. "Your ex-husband disputes your version of events relating to Harlow's disappearance."

"He's a liar! I warned you."

It's hard to decide who is telling the truth in this cesspit of complicated family dynamics and falsehoods. Our conversations with Oliver Kensington have been very interesting, to say the least.

We paid him a visit in the rehab centre to warn him against invading our property again, and he sang like a fucking songbird when given the opportunity to comment.

He shredded Giana's version of events, throwing everything we thought we knew into dispute. Everything Giana has offered us now has to be re-evaluated and torn apart.

"Oliver insists that Harlow must be protected from you," Hunter continues. "He claims that you orchestrated her disappearance before arranging his own incarceration."

With the bomb dropped, Giana turns a bright shade of purple beneath her perfectly curled hair. She looks up at the camera recording the interview, scolding us both with her eyes alone.

"Do you see what kind of monster he is now? You never should have listened to him. He's full of shit."

"Oliver is still Harlow's father," Hunter defends.

"Who would make up such a twisted lie? This is exactly why I wanted Letty to stay away from him."

"Because she didn't want him to tell Harlow what she doesn't remember," Theo supplies next to me.

"You reckon Oliver's telling the truth?" I wonder.

"That Giana was an abusive witch who hated her own family? It's plausible. Maybe she wanted them both gone."

"We don't know that for sure."

"Not yet," he agrees. "But something's off here."

"What happened the day that Harlow was taken?" Hunter redirects, drawing our attention back to the interview.

"We've been over this!" Giana protests.

"I want to hear it again."

She shakes her head in disgruntlement. "I was dealing with an emergency at work. Letty was told to stay inside the school until I arrived to pick her up. Instead, she decided to walk home alone."

"Oliver claims that she would never leave school grounds of her own accord. You've said that she decided to disobey your instructions, leading to her abduction."

"I do not wish to blame her; she was a child." Giana's eyes flit around the interview room. "But Letty was known to be rebellious and… difficult. She's a lot like her father."

"We've interviewed Oliver extensively this week," Hunter combats. "He also rejects your accusations of domestic abuse and claims that it was you who was abusive towards him and your daughter. Violence, both mental and physical."

"That son of a bitch. I can't believe it. You know this is the drugs talking, don't you? He's an unstable addict."

"We know that he's had a drug problem for many years. Oliver says that it was worsened by the severe domestic violence he endured."

"That's nonsense!"

"It was rather convenient when he was arrested, wasn't it?"

Giana splutters. "Excuse me?"

"The authorities were spoon-fed all the evidence they needed to convict him. You were left with full access to the court settlement. That's a lot of money. All yours."

Chair scraping back, she launches to her feet. "I don't have to sit here and listen to this."

"Sit back down, Giana."

"No, I don't think I will. If you have any further questions, please direct them to my legal counsel."

"Lawyering up already?" Hunter chuckles.

"I don't appreciate this spiteful character assassination," she hisses at him. "I had nothing to do with Letty's disappearance. I lost my daughter. My whole life."

"But you still tried to silence your ex-husband." Hunter stacks his paperwork and stands. "If you're innocent, the question is why. What does he have on you?"

She jabs an accusing finger in his face. "Tell my daughter that I want to speak to her immediately. I will not allow that animal to turn her against me with these lies."

"Harlow doesn't want to speak to anyone right now." Hunter squares his shoulders. "I suggest you think carefully about what you say next. All I want is the truth."

Fucking hell. The tension is practically leaking through the screen. I almost miss the soft vibrating of my phone, enraptured by the drama. Fishing it from my pocket, I punch the icon below Hudson's name.

"Yeah?"

"We just got to HQ," he rushes out. "We heard back from Forensics in Newcastle. Where the hell are you?"

"Theo's office. Come down."

"Be there in five."

Hudson hangs up with the sound of raised voices blurring in the background. I leap up, my spine crackling with impatience. We've been anticipating this report. Forensics accessed the family-owned property where Pastor Michaels once lived and performed a thorough search.

"What is it?" Theo asks from his desk.

"Update from Newcastle."

"About time."

Pulling up Hunter's contact, I drop him a quick text message. He'll want to hear this. On Theo's computer screen, Hunter checks his phone and stiffens. Giana continues to rant and rave as he quickly wraps up the interview.

"You'll be hearing from my solicitor," she threatens. "Whatever you're trying to pin on me, it won't stick. I'll see you in court."

Hunter shoves her out the door at lightning speed, paying zero attention to her idle threats. We both wait impatiently until the door to Theo's office slams open and he strides in, short of breath, and tosses his suit jacket on the nearby sofa.

"Having fun?" I tease him.

Hunter narrows his eyes. "Oh, I'm living the life. That woman is a fucking loose cannon. I have a headache."

"You and me both."

"What's the update?" he barks.

"Hudson called. They're coming now."

He scrapes a hand over his loose ponytail. "Giana's being escorted off the premises. Apparently, she's going to sue me for defamation of character."

"She loves a court case," Theo comments.

"Franky, I'd enjoy the chance to drag her over the coals in court. She needs taking down a peg or two."

I approach Hunter. "Why did you push her so much? She's going to shut down completely now. We've shown our hand."

"She was never going to deviate from the narrative she's been pushing for months," he returns with a shrug. "I wanted to catch her off guard. Her defensiveness is telling."

Despite his risky tactics, I reluctantly agree with him. Innocent people don't threaten investigators with legal action for no reason. We're supposed to be on the same side.

If she had nothing to hide, she wouldn't be fighting us at every turn and attempting to control Harlow's life from afar. I didn't trust her from day one. She knows more than she's letting on.

We wait in fraught silence until the office door reopens, admitting Hudson and Kade inside. Both look pale and worn out after several days spent on the ground in Derby, interviewing locals and tracing Candace's steps.

"Where's Brooklyn?" I ask first.

"She's at home with Harlow," Kade answers, out of breath. "They're writing the eulogy for Friday's memorial."

"Good. Tell us what you've got."

Hudson braces his hands on his knees, gulping down air. He really needs to stop smoking before he hacks up a whole lung.

"They found something big."

Hunter leans forward. "What is it?"

"You know the property is owned by a new family," Kade explains. "This delayed the search. Forensics were packing up to leave when they noticed a notch in the floorboard behind a bookcase."

My stomach bottoms out. I don't like where this is going.

"It leads to an old crawl space from the original property, before it was renovated in recent years," Hudson interjects. "It was sealed years ago, but they managed to get inside."

"And?" I urge them.

"They did a cursory search and called me immediately. We need to send major reinforcements right now."

Motherfuck.

For once, it's silent.

None of us want to know what's coming, even if we've been scrambling for any tiny clues for months now. People don't have hidden crawl spaces for no reason.

"What did they find?" Theo asks uneasily.

It takes a lot to make Hudson Knight look queasy. I wasn't sure that it was even possible, but right now, he looks ready to throw up his guts in front of us.

"The skeletal remains of multiple corpses."

"Multiple?" Hunter repeats in disbelief.

"They were all hidden under the family's home. Undisturbed for years now. It's a mass grave."

I have to sit back down before I fall on my stupid, clueless ass. Hunter's mouth is open, but no words are coming out. Theo hasn't moved an inch as he processes the news.

"Are we sure it's him?" he muses.

"Forensics found the bodies buried with a copy of the Bible and a hard-carved crucifix. A specific page was marked."

Pulling out his phone, Kade passes it around for us to see. There's a Bible passage marked with a gold filigree bookmark, inscribed with the symbol of the Holy Trinity.

God himself will kill tens of thousands if it pleases him. Samuel 6:19.

The silence resumes.

Sick, suffocating silence.

It takes a lot to stun us into submission. We've dealt with the outermost fringes of humanity's sickest souls. This has accelerated far beyond our worst nightmares.

Michaels has already killed nineteen women. Nineteen innocent lives brutalised and stolen. That number is about to be pushed a hell of a lot higher with this discovery.

"Fuck," Theo swears, his head in his hands. "*Fuck.* If this gets out, we can kiss the remaining public support we have goodbye."

"We'll be crucified for missing this." Hunter's mouth is pinched tight. "We're in serious shit now."

"But we didn't miss anything!" Hudson argues. "It's the police and their shitty investigations. Why are we taking the heat for them?"

"Because the case is ours now," Hunter replies grimly. "And this family has been living on top of a crime scene for years. The public won't care whose fault that is."

"Their anger will hit us all regardless," I agree.

"Some good news. This evidence ties Lee Heston to multiple counts of murder." Kade crosses his arms, contemplating. "We can use this."

Hudson perks up. "Let's put out a nationwide call for information leading to his arrest."

"Any number of people have lived at that address over the years." Theo hits his forehead with the heel of his palm. "We can't assume Lee is responsible yet."

"You're kidding me?" he seethes.

"We'll be dragged in front of an ethics board within the hour if we do. There's no connection without proof."

"For fuck's sake!" I snap at them. "This is ridiculous. We know that motherfucker is really Pastor Michaels. We have his picture. Let's release it and end this bullshit right now."

Hunter's hand lands on my shoulder. "Theo is right, Enz. We can't do that. The superintendent will shut us down."

"I don't care. We need to find him! Screw her money. We don't need it. Let her punish us."

"Think this through," he urges. "If the case is taken away from us, Harlow's security will be reassigned."

"We'll lose her," Theo deadpans.

That stops me.

Fuck, he's right.

Seeing red across my vision, I stomp over to Theo's overflowing bookshelf and roar in frustration. It topples easily beneath my rage. Books, trinkets and folders of paperwork fly across the room. I'm left standing amidst the carnage, Theo's office semi-destroyed as he watches on without a word.

"You're telling me that our best shot at finding this asshole will take Harlow away from us."

Hunter's jaw clenches. "If the SCU resumes control of the case, she'll be moved into their witness protection program instead of ours. We'll never see her again."

Nope. Not a chance.

They won't protect her.

"Then how the fuck do we fix this?" I ask frantically.

"We need to tie the bodies to Lee Heston," Theo answers. "When we have probable cause, we can issue a warrant for his arrest and use that to smoke Michaels out."

Kade grabs his phone and turns to leave. "We have Michaels' DNA from the basement in Northumberland. All we need is a match to any DNA found in that mass grave."

"You think he'd be that sloppy?" I clench my fists tight. "He's never left evidence before. All the other victims were spotless."

"It only takes one slip-up. We could be lucky."

"Wouldn't that make a change," Theo mutters.

"Call Forensics," Hunter snaps at Kade. "If there's any DNA to be found in that grave, I want it. We'll send another team and pull every bit of evidence we can."

Kade nods in agreement and leaves to make the call. Scrubbing his tired face, Hunter pulls the scar bisecting his eyebrow taut.

I still remember the day he got it, way back in Sabre's long and colourful history. It was an early security job gone wrong. That seems like so long ago now. We were so naïve, clueless as to the dark and twisty path this business would take us on.

"We have to hold a press conference," he says with a sigh. "Appeal for any information from locals in the area. We need to identify when these murders took place."

"And Lee Heston?" I supply.

"If we get the evidence that we need to name him, we'll release his photograph to the press later on. If anyone's seen Michaels recently, they'll make the connection."

It's another stupid, bureaucratic delay, but we have to play by these ridiculous rules. I won't allow Harlow's safety to be jeopardised by letting the SCU take her from us now.

If it means playing ball until we have the evidence we need, I'll have to suck it the hell up. No fucker on this planet will take my girl from me. Not without a fight.

"We'll announce the update today and start appealing for information,"

Hunter decides. "That buys us some time while we sort Heston and make the connection."

We all nod in agreement.

Hunter steps aside to make the call to Lucas. He'll have a shit fit when he hears this fiasco. I drag my phone back out and bring up Leighton's name. He's with Harlow and Brooklyn, keeping an eye on them.

Enzo: Make sure Harlow doesn't watch the news and stays away from the internet.

His response comes quickly.

Leigh: What happened?

Enzo: We've got more bodies. Under wraps for now, but it will hit the media soon. We should be the ones to tell her.

Leigh: Fuck my mouth. Alright, I'll handle it.

Enzo: We'll be home when we can. Sit tight.

"Leighton's gonna keep Harlow occupied until we can get home and update her ourselves."

Theo nods as he begins picking up stray books and stacking them haphazardly. I should offer to help given I just fucked his entire library, but I'm too mad to see straight.

Finishing his phone call, Hunter returns to our group. Hudson is texting rapidly from the corner, updating his own family that we're going to be working very late tonight.

"Lucas is organising a press conference," Hunter fills us in. "We won't disclose Frederick Houghton as our source on Heston or what led us to the property."

"When they ask how we found this place?"

"We tell them jack shit," he says tiredly. "The less they know, the better. We need to protect an active investigation."

"Are we sure this is the right approach at all?" Hudson questions, his phone discarded. "We've never played ball with the media before."

Hunter strokes a hand over his beard. "Our best shot is facing this head on. If we leave them to find out for themselves, we'll be buried alive. We're on our last life as it is."

"I don't like it either," I offer him. "But we're short on time and this is the quickest way to get information."

Hudson nods in defeat. "I hate this."

"Ditto." I clap his shoulder. "But let's get it done."

But if we leave this, we'll be facing a full-blown shitstorm when the story leaks. Which it inevitably will. This way, we're cutting out the middleman and getting out in front of this.

"Fucking hell," I curse, my eyes gritty from exhaustion. "This is going to hit Harlow hard. We need to go home."

I leave out the fact that she isn't even speaking to us right now. Not after the way we dealt with her nut-job father at Hunter's birthday. My apologies have fallen flat ever since.

This chaos is spiralling.

The situation is already a hair's breadth from imploding in a spectacular manner, and I have a very bad feeling this update might just be the final straw for all of us.

CHAPTER 18
HARLOW

TOO FAR GONE – THE PLOT IN YOU

HUNTER'S HAND lands on my rapidly bouncing leg, wrapped in a thick pair of black tights beneath my simple, black shift dress. I snatch his hand up, too nervous to fight him off.

Our falling out feels insignificant in light of the recent discovery. I can't think about it, let alone say it out loud. We're still waiting on a final body count from Forensics.

More victims.

More death.

More despair.

There has to come a point when everything stops. The world falls off its axis. Gravity ceases to function. Pain reaches a level of saturation that reality can no longer contain.

I'm close.

Too fucking close.

"Just breathe," Hunter advises. "Say the word and we'll turn this car around and go home. You don't have to do this."

Looking out of the car window at the first glimmers of spring emerging from the chrysalis of cold and rain, I shake my head.

"I have to, Hunt."

"Why? You owe Laura nothing, sweetheart."

"This is my chance to say goodbye."

He nods in understanding. "What about the eulogy? If it's too much—"

"I'll be fine," I interrupt.

His hand releases mine and skates higher, brushing over my inner thigh. The warmth of his body heat curls around my cold sarcophagus. I've been chilled since the news came in.

Staring straight ahead at the back of Enzo's head in the driver's seat, he's silent and wearing a hardened grimace. I let him back into my bed last night. We were both too tired and emotionally raw to sleep apart.

Hunter's lips touch my ear. "You don't have to lie to me. None of us are fine. We won't survive this if we don't talk to each other."

"Talking won't help the families of those people."

"We're doing everything we can to identify the victims. I know it's hard, but I need your patience right now."

"I'm sorry, Hunt. I have no patience left. It's only a matter of time before we find Candace's body next."

"You don't know that," he returns.

"Don't I? Just leave it. I told you that I don't want to talk."

"How about we discuss your impromptu hotel visit with my little brother instead? Either way, you're going to talk to me. I won't let you shut me out."

Jaw clenched, I turn in the backseat to look up at Hunter's handsome features. His hair is slicked back in a severe bun, highlighting his tired, cocoa-coloured eyes and the slim black hearing aid fitted to his left ear.

He looks good enough to eat in an expensive Armani suit, complete with a black shirt, silky tie and the bulge of a concealed weapon strapped to his body. I swallow the bubble of fear in my throat.

"You hurt me," I whisper to him.

"Harlow…"

"No matter your intentions, you took my choice away from me. I had every right to speak to my own father."

"I was trying to protect you from him," he grits out.

"And who's protecting me from you?"

He recoils like I've slapped him. "You don't need protecting from me. Hate me if you want, but I'll always stand between you and danger. That's my job."

"Why?" I raise my voice. "I don't need you to."

"Because I love you too goddamn much to watch you die like everyone else." His eyes burn bright with determined fire. "That's why."

I catch Enzo watching our exchange in the rearview mirror. The same fear and anxiety stares back at me in his amber eyes. I'm caught between both of them.

Their terror of losing me has infiltrated the air in my lungs. I'm choking on it. We all are. The fear is contagious.

"That's what you're supposed to do for someone you love." Hunter's hand grips mine. "And I know it's real love, because I don't give a fuck that you slept with my brother last week."

Busted. I try to summon a response and fail.

"I've spent months trying to keep you all to myself," he adds in a rasp. "But it doesn't matter anymore, does it?"

"Why not?" I force out.

"All I care about is keeping you safe from the world. I need you to be okay. We're in too much danger to bicker amongst ourselves right now. No more fighting."

Enzo stares at him instead of the winding country lane that we're driving down. I never thought I'd hear Hunter change his tune. We've been battling this problem for months.

It's over.

We won.

All it took was for Pastor Michaels to exceed our worst expectations. His inhuman depravity has finally tipped the scales in Enzo's favour. I gave Leighton my virginity, but they're all still here, demanding a slice of my heart.

The intimate confines of the blacked-out car are interrupted by the roar of distant voices. We turn a corner, approaching the quaint village chapel buried amongst pine trees in the distance.

My heart explodes with fear. We're not alone out here in the peaceful countryside, far from London's smog and traffic.

"Oh shit," Hunter curses.

Outside the chapel where Laura's final goodbye is being held, a swarm of news vans, reporters and screaming protestors are shattering the morning's fragile peace.

Camera crews record the cluster of people waving placards and yelling at the top of their lungs. I have no idea how they found out about today's service, but the usual suspects from outside HQ are all here. An unruly, furious mob.

"How the fuck did they find out?" Enzo barks as he hits the brakes. "We told them to back off and let us do our jobs in that damned press conference."

"The media must've leaked the memorial's location. They're desperate for a glimpse of us."

"Dammit! This is a disaster." Enzo scowls ahead.

I scan the crowd and my stomach somersaults. Something has changed. Amongst the calls for justice, several new faces have infiltrated the angry horde. It takes me a moment to realise what they're doing.

"Praying," I surmise flatly.

Hunter leans between the seats to look. "What the hell?"

Where others are here to torment Sabre and release their own anxieties about the crawl space full of corpses, a new faction has decided to pile on to the madness.

Pastor Michaels' fans.

I can see the gleam of crucifixes around their necks as they fervently pray. One middle-aged woman is leading the group, dressed in a demure frock that screams of Mrs Michaels and her cold-hearted ways.

Rolling down my window a crack, I listen in on their calls to the heavens. The frenetic whisper of prayers is an awful, familiar taunt that tosses me back into the throes of the past.

"Oh, Lord Almighty," she calls out. "Protect our saviour on his quest to save the souls of those cursed with damnation."

"The emails," I whisper to myself. "This is them."

Enzo punches the steering wheel. "They're seriously picketing the funeral of one of his victims. Who does that?"

"You'd be surprised." Hunter wrinkles his nose. "That's it, turn the car around. It isn't safe here. We're going home."

"No!" I shout in a rush. "I have to do this."

"Harlow, this is a volatile situation. I won't put your safety at risk while these fanatics are on the loose."

"Laura's brother invited me himself. I can't let him down now, not after… what I did to her." My voice catches. "Please, Hunt. I need this closure."

His eyes soften. "You owe him nothing."

"Maybe not, but I have to do this. Not just for him, but for myself."

That breaks his resolve.

"Fuck. Don't make me regret this." He points towards the back of the stone chapel. "Enz, take the rear entrance. I'll call the others and redirect them."

"Tell Theo to call the police," Enzo instructs as he reverses away from the mob. "They need to be here to contain this shit. It isn't right."

Barking off rapid orders down the phone, Hunter instructs the rest of our convoy to park around the back of the chapel. Theo, Leighton, Hudson and Brooklyn are following behind us with a back-up security car.

Killing the engine after parking, Enzo hops out with a thud and opens the door for me. He's dressed in his usual armour, an all-black ensemble, adding to his threatening presence as he checks his gun is in place.

I grab my handbag, a hand-written eulogy inside, and let him lift me out of the backseat. I'm crushed into his side. He feels like a furnace, his black t-shirt saturated with the woodsy scent of forests and bonfires.

"Stick with me." He buries his face in my hair and inhales. "I don't like this one bit."

Allowing myself to relax a fraction, I fist his leather jacket and hug him tight. Things have been difficult recently, but right now, I need him. Enzo is my stable foundation.

When I raise my head, his lips are on mine before I can react. Enzo's kiss is an agitated plea for the world to cut us some slack. I can taste his trepidation. He's petrified of losing me again.

When the kiss breaks, his forehead meets mine. "Sorry."

"Hey, it's okay," I whisper back. "I'm sorry for being a pain in the ass recently."

"Don't even think about apologising. I should be saying sorry. We're gonna get through this. I know we will."

The squeal of tyres approaching interrupts our moment, and we separate. Theo's still on the phone with the police as he climbs out of the matching SUV, closely flanked by Leighton and Hudson in their own all-black clothing.

Brooklyn hops down from the driver's seat, a lit cigarette caught between her red-painted lips. When her eyes meet mine, she offers a tight, reassuring smile. All I can do is shake my head in dismay.

"Goldilocks!"

Zipping to my side, Leighton drags me into a lung-squeezing cuddle before kissing my temple.

"You okay? This shit is crazy."

"I'm fine, Leigh."

"Stick close to us, yeah?"

He sandwiches me between himself and Enzo as the last of our security detail arrives. Several burly agents offer me emotionless nods. Sabre's finest are here to defend us.

"Police are aware of the protest," Theo informs us all. "Until it's a case of public disorder, they aren't getting involved. They don't want any more bad press."

"Public disorder?" Brooklyn laughs. "People are praying for the victim's fucking murderer at her bloody memorial!"

Hudson drops a hand on her shoulder. "Keep your voice down. We don't want them to spot us."

"I ought to go around there and beat the shit out of every single twisted fuck chanting their stupid heads off!"

"Brooke," Enzo interrupts her rant. "We're trying to keep a low profile here. Shut up."

She flicks her cigarette butt at him. "Eat shit, dickhead."

"Love you too, wildfire. Come on, let's move."

Trapped in a protective nest of muscled shoulders, loaded holsters and fierce scowls, I'm escorted into the rear of the chapel.

It's an older building, carved from slick stones and brightly coloured stained glass. The smell of old Bibles and damp meets my nostrils with sickening familiarity.

I clutch my handbag tighter and remind myself to breathe. This isn't the basement. I can walk out of here. I'm safe. Memories are bubbling up, attempting to overwhelm me.

Low conversation emanates from the chapel as we cut through the outdated kitchen, and that's when my anxiety decides to punch me in the face. I grab a handful of Theo's dark-wash flannel shirt in front of me and tug.

He looks over his shoulder. "You good?"

"I can't d-do this… I c-can't…"

Turning on the spot, he parts the sea of security and people surrounding us to take me into his wiry arms.

"Shhh, beautiful. You can do this."

"I can't!"

"We're all here with you."

"What if… what if he hates me? I killed his sister. It's all my fault that she's gone."

Theo grabs my face and traps me between his warm, dry hands. I latch on to the scent of old books and minty freshness clinging to his denim jacket. It's just him. My Theodore. Nobody else.

"He invited you to speak about his sister and honour her memory," he reminds me. "That kid doesn't hate you."

"He's alone because of me."

"Because of Pastor Michaels," Theo adds meaningfully. "Hold my hand, Harlow. I've got you."

Forcing myself to take a stuttered breath, I let our fingers entwine. Theo doesn't even flinch anymore. He's allowed his sky-high barriers to melt around me.

"Promise you won't let go?" I whisper.

Even with the press of people around us invading our bubble of privacy, he comes close to feather a kiss against my lips.

"I won't let go. I promise."

He squeezes my hand to reiterate his vow. We separate and I let him guide me forwards, following the mammoth set of Enzo's shoulders ducking through arched doorways.

The chapel falls silent as we enter, extinguishing the low murmur of conversation from the small group of guests. Rising from his front-row seat, a slim, auburn-haired teenager watches us approach with slightly widened eyes.

I don't need an introduction to recognise Laura's brother, Carlos Whitcomb. He's barely eighteen years old and far too young to be dealing with all of this alone. Laura was the only family he had left.

With agony constricting my heart, I clutch Theo's hand even tighter and approach the inevitable confrontation. Hunter directs everyone to take seats in the second row, leaving me to stop in front of Laura's brother.

"Harlow?"

"Hi, Carlos."

"You look different from the photos I've seen on the news." A dusting of pink colours his freckled cheeks. "Thanks for coming. I wasn't sure if you'd turn up."

"I wanted to be here. Laura was my friend." I watch the sheen of tears rise in his eyes. "More than that. She was my ray of hope in a very dark time."

Carlos nods with a heartbroken smile. "I'm sure she'd say the same thing for you."

The guilt is choking me alive. Every inch of my mind is flooded with shame and resentment. I wasn't Laura's ray of hope. In the end, all I was to her was an escape route.

The perfect executioner.

He lowers his voice as the tears spill over. "Thank you for bringing her back to me."

The backs of my eyes burn as the devil's claws wrap around my throat. I try to release Theo's hand, but he holds on.

"It was nothing," I answer stiffly.

"It meant a lot to me, so thanks."

Shivering from head to toe, I manage a final nod and escape to my seat. Hunter, Enzo and Leighton are already sandwiched in down the aisle, leaving me to take the outer seat, with Brooklyn and Hudson behind me.

The tinkle of the organ suffuses the air, calling the service to order. I'm surprised that Carlos chose to hold the memorial here of all places, although the grey-haired chaplain notably doesn't hold a Bible. That's a relief.

"We're gathered here today to honour the life of Laura Whitcomb. Beloved sister, co-worker, and friend, she is greatly missed by all who knew and loved her."

Fire ants are itching at my skin, whispering their mindless taunts. I can feel every single hair on my head—heavy, suffocating, begging to be torn free. The pain is so tempting.

As I stare ahead, ignoring the hum of gossip behind us from the small gathering of people, the chaplain's voice is accompanied by shouting from outside.

Theo's thumb draws circles against the skin of my inner wrist. Each rotation tugs my escaping lucidity back down to earth, forcing me to remain strong.

He's got me. I'm okay. This will all be over soon. The words should be calming, but instead, my own inside voice begins to morph into a familiar, cold taunt.

You fucking whore!

Thwack. Thwack. Thwack.

Watch your friend, Harlow.

Thwack. Thwack. Thwack.

Watch her bleed out for her insolence.

I tried my best to cower and make myself small as Laura was raped and carved into blood-slick ribbons. I tried to block my ears. I tried to pray for her. None of it worked.

She screamed so loud.

All while I was fatally silent.

Carlos takes his place at the front of the chapel, a scrap of paper caught in his shaking hands. He looks over us all, his eyes briefly landing on me. Nausea engulfs me.

He can see the guilt written across my face. I know it. Everyone can. The words of his short, grief-stricken speech don't penetrate my cotton-wool brain. All I can hear is her endless, excruciated screaming.

When he steps down from the pulpit, turning to glance at the printed photograph of a smiling Laura displayed for the whole chapel to see, Carlos blows his sister a final kiss.

I watch his lips move.

Goodbye. I love you.

Theo gently nudges me when I don't move. He's pulled the speech from my handbag and slips it into my hands. I can feel the others all staring at me, searching for any warning signs of a breakdown.

Falling back on years of practiced silence, I plaster a blank mask into place. I don't need them inside my head. It's loud enough in here as it is.

The long walk to the front of the room is the loneliest I've felt in months. I smooth out the folded piece of paper, avoiding looking up at the eyes locked on me.

I stare down. Blink. Gulp air. Plead for courage. The entire chapel is waiting for me to speak, but nothing's coming out. In the silence, the outside sneaks back in.

Shouting.

Chanting.

Praying.

"Laura was a bright, beautiful soul," I begin with downturned eyes. "The day we met, she made me a promise. One that she fought until her last breath to keep."

My words are drowned out by the protest and steady sobbing of a woman a few seats behind Carlos. I recognise her face from Sabre's case files. She worked with Laura.

"Laura protected me. She kept me alive with her stories, her laughter, the promises she made to get us both out alive."

My voice breaks on the final syllable as horror takes over. When I dare to glance up, the chapel has melted away. Shadows, cobwebs and soulless darkness infect the aisle, framing the steady footsteps of a skeletal ghost.

Laura doesn't resemble her beautiful, hopeful photograph displayed to my right. In my imagination, she's skin and bone, blood and flesh, all hashed together in a crimson-soaked patchwork quilt.

I watch her approach. Closer, closer, the entire chapel ambivalent to her movements. They can't see her. She's dead and gone, but her ghost lives on in the fibrous connections between my nerve cells.

"I w-wanted to save you," I rasp through painful breaths. "Please, Laura. You gave me no choice."

The low murmurings of the audience don't halt her steps. Paper scrunching in my hands, I feel my chest catch on fire. Searing hot tears flood down my cheeks.

Before Laura's ghost can lay her bloodstained hands on me, I turn and flee the room at full speed, leaving my speech scattered across the floor.

Shouts of my name chase after me. I can hear Enzo and Hunter, both trapped in the aisle and bellowing at mourners to move out of the way.

Without looking over my shoulder, I know that she's following, invisible to all but me. The girl who died at my hands. Now, we're tethered together, body and soul.

Caught in the grasp of a panic attack, I shove the rear exit door open and spill outside into the spring air. That's when terror spikes through me. Our ruse has been uncovered.

"Harlow Michaels!"

"Over here. Give us a statement!"

"Harlow! Smile for us!"

Blood-thirsty reporters have clustered around the back of the chapel, battling with the three burly security officers who we brought with us. They're overwhelmed by people.

The protestors have followed them in earnest, bringing their anger and hatred with them as they crowd the back entrance. It's a confusing mixture of political anger and frantic shouts of Bible verses, prayers and insults.

They're here.

The devil's brood.

Clutching my aching chest, I attempt to dodge the nearest microphone being shoved in my face. Hyland, our biggest agent, grabs the reporter by the scruff of his neck and tosses him down to the cracked concrete.

It's an explosion of chaos and opposing sides, all battling for one thing—me. For their exclusive, for the killings to stop, for a sacrificial lamb to offer their careless overlord.

It doesn't matter.

They all want me.

Common sense abandons my sputtering mind. All I want to do is run. Full speed, without direction, as far away from these snakes as possible. When I stumble down the set of stone steps, I'm bombarded by the protestors first.

"He's killing because of you," someone screams in my face. "End the slaughter! Surrender yourself."

The chants grow more extreme. Placards are waved with malice, all depicting familiar faces. Girls who I outlived and failed to protect. Now, these people want justice for them.

"I'm sorry," I try to shout above the riot of noise. "I never w-wanted any of this to happen."

"The Lord is just and merciful! We must protect his servant and pray for our salvation!"

These chants overwhelm the tangle of angry people. Pastor Michaels' deranged fan club, clutching their own crucifixes and Bibles, intermingle with the protestors.

The two sides collide in a riot of anger. I scream and duck as one woman attacks another, wrapping her hands around her throat to cease the mindless barrage of Bible talk.

"How can you support that monster?"

"God bless his divine work. Those sluts deserved to die!"

"They were people!"

When the first punches fly, I know I'm in trouble. I can hear the guys screaming and shouting my name after catching up, but I'm stuck amidst the fighting.

"Take that back! You're as bad as that piece of shit!"

"He will rejoice in our salvation and save our souls from damnation."

Thuds of fists meeting flesh accompany the wail of punched faces. Bibles are thrown as nails scrape down cheeks, drawing blood and screams.

I can see Enzo wrestling with a fearless reporter, attempting to shove her aside and get closer to me. Theo is back on his phone, yelling at the police for backup.

Ducking and weaving in a blur of determination, Hunter abandons Leighton and Hudson, trying to restrain various protestors. He's the closest, leaving Brooklyn to fight behind him to move a single inch.

His fearful brown eyes bug out, and my heart freezes dead in my chest. I can't hear the shouts pouring from his open mouth, frantic and afraid. We're both watching the same horror show in slow motion.

Death.

Its claws are unfurling.

Behind a fight blurring with fists and battered knuckles, one of the protestors has inched closer. His cheeks are tear stained. Resolution fills his gaunt face. I know who he is immediately.

Candace's older brother.

He was interviewed a few weeks ago by Hudson and Kade. I heard about his heartbreak second-hand in one of Hunter's very sparse updates about the case.

That heartbreak has changed now. Morphed. Grown into a new branch of rage. Pastor Michaels demanded my surrender in exchange for Candace's life, and I'm still here.

His sister is going to die.

That's on me.

And he knows it.

The gun clutched in his wavering hands registers too late. It glints in the sunlight, a deadly weapon that holds no fear for me. If I die right here, right now, the slaughter will end.

I want him to pull the trigger. My feet refuse to move. I won't run. I won't fight. If my path is set to end here, I will go with the knowledge that my death ensures the safety of countless more women.

"Harlow!" Hunter screams my name.

I ignore him.

Candace's brother draws closer, fingering the trigger. He's at almost point-blank range. Still, the panic doesn't set in. Numbness is all I can summon in the face of my end.

Seconds pass in fragments. Disjointed. Individual cuts of a wider movie scene that are haphazardly stuck together. The crowd parts. Hunter's fingers touch my arm. The gun nears.

BANG.

I'm not sure what happens first. The piercing gunshot, the spray of blood across my face or Hunter throwing his entire body in front of me at the last moment. It's all a blur.

Candace's brother is barrelled over by Hyland, bellowing for his two fellow agents to follow suit. The gun hits the ground, but it doesn't make a sound. Nothing does.

Silence.

It's all around me.

Floating above my body, I watch my eyes tilt downwards, expecting a flow of blood to pour from the bullet wound in my chest. Instead, my dress is untouched. Pristine.

A river of blood coats the cobblestones of the car park instead. But it isn't mine. Is it? I can't feel any pain. Only the petrified hammering of my heart. The organ knows what's happened here before I do.

A body is tangled at my feet. Collapsed and limp. No signs of life. Blood pours from his head, growing into a rapidly expanding puddle. His ear is a ragged hole.

That's when reality kicks me in the teeth, and I scream at the very top of my lungs.

"HUNTER!"

CHAPTER 19
LEIGHTON

THE WAY THAT YOU WERE – SLEEP TOKEN

FOR MY ENTIRE LIFE, I've withered in my brother's impressive shadow. As kids, we'd bicker and fight. He wanted to help me. Push me. Inspire my success. All I cared about was seeing him fail.

I wanted our parents' love, and for him to know how it felt to be the odd one out. The family screw-up. Not smart enough. Hard working enough. Handsome enough.

Hunter's all of that.

I wanted to take it from him.

Standing at the bottom of an occupied hospital bed, accompanied by the hum of a heart monitor and ventilator, I'd do anything to take it all back. I've been so selfish.

He can have our parents' love.

Success. Money.

The dream house.

A glittering career.

Fuck, he can even have the girl he wants. I'll surrender Harlow to him and kill the last shreds of hope left inside me. I'll cut my own heart out and squash it beneath my shoe if it will bring him back.

I need my brother to live.

Hunter cannot fucking die.

Someone touches my shoulder, but I don't move. If I tear my eyes from the rise and fall of his chest, I know it'll stop. He'll slip away. I have to stand here and keep guard so the devil doesn't end his life when no one's looking.

"Leigh," Enzo says quietly. "You should go home and get some rest."

I shrug him off. "I'm fine here."

"You've been camped out in this room for days. Go eat and shower, at least."

I'm not sure how it's only been two sleepless days since the gut-wrenching moment that I almost lost my sibling. He still isn't out of the woods after being placed in a medically induced coma while the swelling on his brain eases.

The gunshot was so close, it tore through his left ear and fractured his skull in the process. He's got to be the luckiest son of a bitch alive that the shot was shitty at best and his brains weren't painted across that car park.

"Where's Harlow?" I summon the energy to ask. "She was gone when I woke up."

"Asleep in the waiting area. Theo took her home yesterday, but she didn't stay long. Maybe you can convince her to go home with you tonight."

"I'm going nowhere."

Sighing with a level of exhaustion most can't even imagine, Enzo collapses in the creaky chair next to Hunter's bedside. The circles under his eyes are a vivid purple, much like mine. We've been camped out here since our lives changed in a split second with that single bullet.

"Your mum's making a few phone calls in the corridor," he reveals in a flat voice. "And Ben's lecturing the security outside for bad posture."

I brace my hands on the bed's railing. "They don't know what else to do but fuss while Hunter's sedated."

"You heard what the doctors said. The swelling on his brain is severe. It needs time to go down before he'll be safe to regain consciousness."

Glancing up at Enzo, his huge frame is blurred by a sheen of tears. I can't remember the last time I properly cried, not counting the few stray tears that escaped when I reunited with my parents. Hell, I didn't even cry as they read my sentencing and I was shipped off to prison for three years.

"I never thanked him."

Enzo's eyebrows knit together. "For what?"

"For saving my life when I left prison. He gave me a home, money, a job. Everything. All I've ever given him is grief."

With a heartbroken nod, Enzo's head falls into his hands. I know he doesn't want me to see him cry, but the rhythmic shake of his shoulders betrays his despair.

"Hunter never wanted your gratitude," Enzo says into his hands. "All he ever wanted was to see you happy again. That was enough for him."

I grab the clipboard hanging on the end of the hospital bed and throw it so hard, it hits the wall and breaks in half. Enzo's head shoots up as he glares at me.

"Leigh, what the fuck?!"

"Stop using past tense!" I bark at him. "Hunter is lying right there in front of you. He's still alive."

His face falls back into misery. "Hunter's in a coma with a fractured skull. We came too fucking close this time."

I'm so tempted to lay him out across the linoleum with a broken nose. Hunter doesn't quit. Not once. His whole life has been an exercise in conviction. This is no different.

"Go home," Enzo says again.

"I can't leave him here."

"I'll stay and watch him."

I want to protest, but I haven't showered in days. I smell like absolute death incarnate. My head is dizzy from lack of sleep, and my muscles are steadily burning. I need to lie down before I end up in here myself.

"Swear to keep your eyes on him at all times?"

Enzo crosses his heart with a half-hearted smile. "I won't leave him alone in here, Leigh. He's my brother too."

"Alright. I'll take Harlow with me."

"Richards had some more sleeping tablets delivered. Stick some in her tea if she refuses to lie down again."

"Jesus, Enz. I'm not drugging her."

"She hasn't spoken! Not a single goddamn word in days. All she does is cry and stare. Drug her if you have to and make sure she gets some bloody sleep. That's final."

Shaking my fuzzy head in disbelief, I leave him to his guard post. His shoulders are still trembling with silent tears that he won't let anyone else see. Enzo's hope has gone already.

He's expecting the worst. I can see it on his face. Losing his parents, then his baby sister, really fucked him up. Add Alyssa passing away on top of that, and he's far too used to the people he loves being ripped away.

Hunter's death would break him.

Irreparably so.

I offer my father a terse nod as I pass him in the corridor. He's taken the phone from my mum and leans against the wall, pinching the bridge of his nose as he quietly speaks.

"Leigh," Mum exclaims.

Flinching, I dodge her rumpled embrace. "You okay?"

She looks as rough as the rest of us, her clothes worn and sweat stained. "Yes, darling. Are you leaving?"

"I'm going home," I say robotically. "Enzo's going to take this shift. I'll be back in the morning."

She strokes a hand over my hair. "Need a hand with Harlow? She's just making another cup of coffee."

"I'll convince her to come with me. Stay with Enzo." My throat seizes with emotion. "He needs looking after too."

"I left a message for Hayley and asked her to call me back," Mum reveals. "We'll fill her in when she does."

"Good idea." I watch my father begin to pace the corridor. "Who is he speaking to?"

Mum's eyes glance over to her frustrated husband. "The Chief Constable. Hunter's attacker has been charged with attempted murder."

Murder.

He came so close to death.

"What about the protestors?"

"We're slapping them all with criminal charges," she says defiantly. "Public disorder and abusive behaviour offences for every single one of them who incited the violence."

"That's something."

Burying my face in her wrinkled neck, I allow myself a sliver of weakness. I can crumble with my mother's arms around me. She won't tell the world that I'm not the strong one. That has always been Hunter's job.

He's the glue who holds this dysfunctional family together. We've taken him for granted all this time, ignoring the fact that he's the one keeping us all alive and well. We owe him our lives. Now, he's fighting to keep his.

"Your brother needs you to step up, Leigh. If he pulls through… he's going to be in for a long recovery."

I swipe my damp cheeks. "Yeah, I know. I'll speak to Enzo. We'll figure something out about the company."

Mum smiles weakly. "Be the man I know you're meant to be. If not for yourself, then for your brother."

Her words add weight to the growing pressure of responsibility piling on my shoulders. With each day that Hunter has remained unconscious, my resolve has grown.

Now, I have to step up.

It's time to be a fucking adult.

We still have a violent serial killer to catch, decomposed bodies to identify and teams to run. We can't afford to let the darkness win. Hunter deserves more from us than that.

Pressing a soft kiss to my mother's cheek, I leave her to wrangle my father. He spares me a blank nod as I pass, heading for the waiting area where we've been camped out.

I emerge into the quiet, yellow-painted room and wince at the sound of loud banging. It hasn't woken Theo up yet. He's still passed out and snoring, his head covered by a magazine.

In the corner of the room, a disgruntled Harlow is beating the shit out of a vending machine. Her mousy-brown hair is matted, emphasising the visible bald patch beneath the thin layer of protection. She's been ripping it out nonstop.

"Kicking the machine won't make the coffee any better," I try to joke, but it falls flat. "What's up?"

She braces her hands on the cheap hunk of metal. "It swallowed my coins."

Those are the first words I've heard her speak. All we've exchanged is a constant stream of anguished tears and exhausted half-hugs.

"Well, that's a good reason to go home. I need to shower and eat some real food."

Harlow waves absently. "Go."

"No. You're coming with me."

Her head is lowered with defeat as she ignores me. I crouch down next to her and peer underneath her braced arms, attempting to catch her line of sight.

"Harlow," I repeat. "Home. Now."

She shakes her head, sending stray tears flying.

"That wasn't a request. We both need to get some decent rest and a hot meal. We're no good to Hunter like this."

"I'm not leaving here until he does," she says, barely above a whisper.

I tuck her curtain of dark, curling hair over her shoulder. It reveals the swollen slits where her eyes should be. She's cried herself to the point of being sick in past days. I've heard her throwing up between sobbing gasps and lamentations.

"When Hunter wakes up, he's going to need us," I remind her. "Come home and clean up, at least."

"I can't sleep, Leigh. Every time I shut my eyes, I see him lying at my feet, bleeding across the ground."

Moving slowly, I ease my arms around her and hold her against my heaving chest. Harlow struggles at first, but she's too exhausted to put up much of a fight. Her head collapses on my slumped shoulder.

"You don't have to sleep," I murmur into her ragged hair. "Just come home and eat something. Please? For me?"

"I don't want to eat."

"Bloody hell, Harlow. Enough!"

She recoils at my raised voice.

I grab her chin tight to implore her. "My brother is in a fucking coma. I can't worry about you keeling over as well. You're coming home. Now."

Her usually clear blue eyes are fogged over and uncertain, staring into mine with such intense guilt, it physically burns me. Fucking hell. How on earth did we get here?

"Okay," she says in a tiny voice.

"Okay," I repeat.

"What about Theo?"

"Let's go wake him up and drag him home too. He'll appreciate sleeping in a proper bed."

I tow her back over to the cluster of empty seats to grab her parka and handbag. Theo yelps loudly and shoots upright when I tug on his left leg.

"How's that bed working out for you?" I pull again, causing him to fall on the floor. "Get up, sleeping beauty."

His jaw cracks with a yawn. "What time is it?"

"Just after midnight."

"Fuck, I need to go to the office."

"Now? It's the middle of the night."

"Forensics are moving the unidentified bodies to HQ's morgue in a few hours. I need to be there to sign off."

"You're coming home to sleep and eat first. None of us are travelling alone right now."

"Leigh—"

"No fucking arguments," I cut him off. "Get downstairs and in the car before I have Enzo escort you out instead."

His mouth pops open before snapping shut again. Without another word, he grabs his heavy backpack and laptop before taking Harlow's trembling hand.

The pair trail towards the exit, exchanging low murmurs. Harlow's leaning heavily on him, almost limping with exhaustion. My mother offers them both a tearful smile of farewell as they head for the elevator.

"Mr Rodriguez?"

I turn to find Hunter's main doctor approaching with a steaming coffee balanced along with her thick notepad.

"Yeah?"

"Can I have a moment?" Doctor Lane takes a sip of coffee. "I was just on my way to speak to your parents."

"They're dealing with the police investigation right now. What is it? Is there an update?"

Glancing around the empty waiting room, she gestures for me to take a seat. I wave off my mother before she can approach, gesturing for her to stay with Dad for now.

"We've got the results back from your brother's CT scan." Her grey eyes soften with sympathy. "We've ruled out any permanent brain damage at this time."

The air whooshes from my lungs.

"Thank God."

"The skull fracture is significant, but the surgery was successful, and it will heal with time. There are no signs of internal bleeding. He's lucky to survive a direct hit like that."

"And the ear?" I ask next.

That's when her smile droops.

"Our cosmetic surgeon has done her best to salvage Hunter's left ear. She performed a partial reconstruction, but the scarring will be extensive."

"He's alive. Scars are a small price to pay."

Doctor Lane nods. "We'll keep him in intensive care until the swelling reduces before easing him off sedation. Only time will tell how he responds from there."

Slapping my knees, I stand up and straighten my creased t-shirt. "I'm taking my family home. We'll be back tomorrow."

"Mr Rodriguez, before you go, I want to discuss something else with you. It's a little sensitive."

My burst of hopeful optimism fades.

"What is it?"

She looks down, her mouth twisted unhappily. "Your brother is already partially deaf. The ear that was affected in the attack is the one that retained some functioning."

"Yes, there was an accident several years ago. His left ear still works with a permanent hearing aid."

"I'm aware of his medical history," she inserts with that damned pitiful smile again. "This gives me some concern, given the localised nature of the bullet wound."

My tired brain doesn't compute what she's saying. I blink with gritty eyes, the pounding of a headache causing the low-lit room to tilt on its axis.

"What are you saying?" I sigh tiredly.

"His head injury and the damage to his ear are extensive," she clarifies. "We have reason to believe this may impact his current level of hearing, given the pre-existing damage."

Jesus Christ.

Is she saying what I think she is?

Authoritative footsteps slap against the cheap hospital linoleum to join us. I know it's my father from the beat of his feet. He halts beside me, resting a hand on my shoulder.

"Dad," I begin.

His hand squeezes hard. "I overheard. Be straight with us, doc. How much damage can we expect there to be?"

"Difficult to say," Doctor Lane offers. "But his hearing was minimal to begin with. I'm expecting there to be a reduction in line with the severity of his injuries."

A lead brick settles in the pit of my stomach. I reach up to grab Dad's hand, resting mine on top as our fingers entangle. I need someone to comfort me right now.

"How bad could it be?"

The doctor's grimace seals my dread.

"We're looking at total hearing loss."

CHAPTER 20
HARLOW

TWO WEEKS – FKA TWIGS

STANDING in the freezing cold bowels of HQ, the usual hum of chatter and activity is absent. I'm deep underground, far from the staff and their sympathetic glances.

On the other side of the two-way mirror, post-mortem examinations are taking place. Three skeletal, decomposed bodies are being picked over by Sabre's on-site pathologists.

They found five bodies in total.

Five more lives turned to dust.

Sitting next to me, Theo's fingers are hammering against his keyboard as he takes notes. With his black-framed glasses holding his blonde ringlets back from his face, I can see every tired line and eye bag on display.

It's been a long week.

None of us have stopped.

We've been attempting to identify the bodies with a series of post-mortems. Sabre's morgue is overflowing. Using dental records, two families have been brought in for interviews with the Cobra team. The other relatives have yet to be located.

With Hunter still in intensive care and the outside world deemed unsafe for us to enter without protection, we've all holed up at HQ, mucking in to push the case forward.

"This is the last round of post-mortems," Theo comments. "Then we're done. You don't have to be here for this."

"What else do I have to do?"

"Studying?" he suggests.

My tongue is heavy with the bitter taste of disappointment. I've had to make some hard calls this week.

"Richards spoke to my school tutor. They've deferred me to the next cohort. So, I have nothing else to do."

Theo halts. "You did that?"

"I can't focus on school right now. Not with the case going on and Hunter in the hospital. It was the right decision."

He nods thoughtfully. "Then I'm proud of you for making that call. You're prioritising your mental health."

"And failing again."

"Beautiful, it's not a failure."

"After attending two classes? Not a failure?" I laugh without humour. "It doesn't matter anyway."

"You can still change your mind."

"Hunter is more important than school right now."

Turning my back on the endless stainless-steel tables of blackened bones and decomposed bodily matter, I rest my aching head against the white wall.

"Where's Enzo?"

"Upstairs speaking to one of the families," Theo answers from his laptop. "I've got the intelligence department building case files on the new victims for the next press briefing."

"Any leads?" I hold my breath.

"Nothing yet."

Pastor Michaels is out there somewhere, enjoying the chaos that he's created from miles away. He has the entire company in a tailspin. We're desperately trying to keep up with the constant onslaught of death and violence.

"Same MO, it's definitely him," Theo confirms. "All five victims were sex workers and off the radar. The bodies are being dated at roughly seven years old."

"He had me in the cage then," I finish for him.

"Yeah. The timeline checks out."

"So what? Maybe he just didn't think to bring these victims down there to kill them. That formality came later."

Theo cocks his head. "Perhaps these were practice kills. The ritual wasn't right, so he didn't display them for the police to find."

"And he stuffed them under the floorboards instead." I rub my temples, feeling sick to my stomach. "They were there all along. Buried and forgotten."

"I'm sorry, Harlow. I know this is hard."

When his phone vibrates with an incoming phone call, Theo offers me an apologetic look and accepts. He mutters a strained *okay* before hanging up.

"You're wanted in Hunter's office."

"Something wrong? Is it Hunter?"

Theo avoids my eyes. "To do with the case. Enzo and the Cobra team are waiting. I'll finish up here."

Seized by anxiety, I quickly press a kiss to his lips. "Will you meet us at the hospital?"

"I'll be there later on."

"Okay. Be safe."

He catches me in another kiss. "You too."

Leaving the underground morgue, it's a long elevator ride up to the office levels back amongst the living. I've spent a lot of time here this past week, more than ever before.

None of us are able to face being at home with Hunter's discarded ties, the growing pile of unread newspapers and boxes of English tea. Without him, it's a house. Not a home.

I was more than happy to throw myself into the case and help the others wherever possible. It's given us reason to keep going rather than drowning in the uncertainty that's currently wrecking our lives.

Reaching Hunter's carpet-lined office, I take a breath for courage before letting myself inside. Expecting everyone to be waiting for me, I'm surprised to find Enzo alone, his burly shoulders hunched over.

He's staring at the collection of framed photographs behind the desk. The precious memories of his family are one of Hunter's most prized possessions. Several more frames have been added in recent months, and I've only just noticed.

"Enz? You wanted to see me?"

He waves me forward. "Yeah."

I click the door shut and approach. Enzo's tanned, sinewy form slumps when my arms wrap around his waist from behind. I can barely get my arms around his muscular body.

Burying my nose in his back, I breathe in deeply. The scents of moss, pine trees and bonfire embers still cling to his usual black t-shirt, despite the days camped out in this office.

"What is it?" I ask fearfully.

"Michaels has made contact."

His voice is hard, clipped.

"Is Candace… alive?" I gulp hard.

"Fuck, Harlow. I want to protect you so badly, but I can't keep you safe from this. We're fighting a losing battle."

"I know. You don't have to."

"Looking after you is the only thing that matters to me, but we're taking fire on all sides. I don't know what else to do."

Slipping around his mountainous torso, I slide into his arms and force him to hug me back. Enzo has to bend in half to cuddle me close, and his chin rests on my head.

"Feel me," I say into his abdomen.

He shudders with an unsteady breath.

"I'm here, Enz. Safe. Protected. We're good. You're going to make yourself sick with worry at this rate."

"I almost watched my best friend die last week," he answers gruffly. "I have no idea if he will ever come back to us. I'm allowed to worry."

"Not when I'm in your arms. That's when you hold me close and tell me everything's going to be okay. That's when you believe it yourself too."

His chuckle smooths over me, soft and broken. "Jesus, little one. I have no clue how you're still standing after everything that's happened these past few months."

"You're holding me up, dummy."

He kisses the top of my head. "I'll always be here to do that. No matter what happens. Nothing will tear this family apart while I'm still alive and kicking."

We cuddle for several silent minutes, our breathing aligned and heartbeats hammering together. When Enzo sighs and pushes me away, I know reality has come knocking.

"He contacted Channel Ten News," Enzo reveals.

"Pastor Michaels did?"

"Yeah. Our old friend, Sally Moore, broke the news an hour ago."

Great. I bet she loved that.

"How bad is it?" I wince.

"He sent a grainy photograph of Candace and a warning. She looked to be badly beaten and shackled in some kind of abandoned property. No cage this time."

My meagre breakfast of dry toast and tea threatens to resurface. Enzo's hands gripping my shoulders are the only thing preventing me from crumpling to my knees.

"What was the warning?"

He shakes his head. "You don't need to read it."

"Yeah, Enz. I do. Show me."

"No."

"You asked me to trust you again," I remind him. "Don't break that trust now. I need to know what we're dealing with."

Cursing, he stares deep into my eyes for a moment, seeing my resolve. We're past him wrapping me in cotton wool now. I steel myself as he reaches for the iPad on the desk and pulls up a breaking news report.

The bright-red letters blur on the screen as I fight to remain calm. It's the longest message he's sent us in several months. My monster is still alive and kicking in the darkness.

Harlow,

I know you've found my playthings in their shallow grave. I've saved them for all these years. It's brought me happiness to know they rotted alone in the dark. The devil's spawn deserves no less.

Say hello to Candace.

She's running out of time.

Have you found out our little secret yet? I'm sure you'll

want to talk when you do. I'll be waiting with answers. My offer still stands.

A life for a life.

With love,

Your father.

"He sent this to the national press. Why?"

Enzo studies the note with narrowed eyes. "Showmanship. The more pressure he applies, the quicker he thinks we'll break and surrender you back to him."

I read the warning again, more confused than ever. There's something here, whispered between the written lines. He's luring me closer with his lies and I can feel the inevitable pull, but I'm powerless to stop myself from being hooked like bait.

"Do you think he's telling the truth?" I bite my lip.

"About what? The man's a fucking lunatic."

"I mean… does he know something I don't? About my past? I feel like I'm missing something huge. I just can't remember what. It's driving me crazy."

Taking the iPad away from me, Enzo switches it off. "No. I think he's unhinged and desperate to get you back. This is another tactic, nothing more."

Enzo believes what he wants to. I know that now. He can't bear the thought of another twist in the road, not while we're on the back foot and battling to remain afloat.

"Are my parents still trying to contact me?"

"Daily," he answers. "Giana's called five times since the article dropped alone. Your father keeps calling too."

"I was going to go and see him when the news hit about the bodies, but then we had the memorial, then… Hunter."

He bumps my shoulder. "Don't beat yourself up. Our lives are a fucking disaster zone right now. He can wait his turn."

Staring at the photographs that first occupied his attention, I try to hold the swell of burning hot tears back. Hunter selected these new memories to add to his collection.

Various crappy selfies taken over the span of the last year, our tongues flopping out and lips stretched wide. Decorating the Christmas tree. Family dinners. Walks with Lucky.

It's our life. Together.

He treasured every moment.

To the world, he's brash, unemotional, cruel even. Hunter has spent the last eight months battling his urges to both control and cherish me. He's threatened the very foundation of his life, determined to have me to himself.

But in private?

This right here is the truth about Hunter Rodriguez. He is absolutely nothing without the people he cares about. That survival instinct I recognise so clearly within him is a fearsome drive to protect the one thing he loves most in the world. His fucking family.

"We need to go back to the hospital to see Hunter's consultant this afternoon." Enzo's heat meets my back as we face the photos together. "They're easing the sedation."

"You think he'll wake up?"

"The doctors seem to think so. His scans are looking better, and the swelling has gone down. We have to give it a go."

He doesn't need to say what we're all thinking. We all want Hunter back in fighting form, but today could change his entire life. Forever. All of our lives.

None of us know how much of his hearing has survived the accident. He'll be recovering from his injuries for months to come as it is, but once he's awake, they can perform the relevant tests to answer that terrifying question.

"I don't know if I can be there when he wakes up," I make myself admit. "He should be with his family, not… me."

Enzo turns me around. "You are his family."

"He's lying in that hospital bed because of my stupidity." I feel the tears spill over. "That bullet was meant for me."

"You should know by now that Hunter will always throw himself in harm's way if it keeps the people he loves safe."

"Maybe he shouldn't," I murmur back. "I wish that bullet had hit me. Enz… I wanted it to. I actually wanted it to."

Stroking a roughened thumb over my wet cheek, the pain in Enzo's expression makes me regret my confession. It's no secret that I'm lurching from one breakdown to another.

The accident has tipped me over the edge into a very dark place. Not even the case has kept the whisper of ghosts from my mind, their daily taunts increasing. More than once, I've considered leaving and returning to Pastor Michaels.

When Hunter does wake up, he should have his family and loved ones around him. Not the baggage he got lumped with from the case that's ruined his life and career. That's all I am now. A threat. A burden. The girl who almost got him killed.

"Whatever you're thinking, stop," Enzo scolds. "This wasn't your fault. Hunter would say the same thing."

"Because none of you will admit the truth."

Teeth gritted, his defeat dissipates into red-hot anger. The emotion swirls in his golden eyes, spreading agony and indignation with each furious breath he sucks in.

"You want the truth?" Enzo entreats.

I try to back away from him and end up colliding with Hunter's nearby desk. The solid press of wood meets my tailbone, and Enzo steps into the space between us.

I'm caught between two obstacles, pinned and out of escape routes. His hands stroke down my arms to encircle my wrists like handcuffs. He's grinding my bones together.

"The truth is that our family would've fallen apart long ago if you weren't here," he says fiercely. "You are the only thing holding us all together."

I try to wriggle free and fail.

"Enz, I'm the one tearing you apart."

"No," he disagrees. "You're wrong, and I'm so fucking glad that you are. You will never know just how much you've changed our lives for the better."

Bending to press his plump lips to my cheek, he plants a soft kiss, his stubble scratching against my skin. I pull again at my wrists, but it's no use. I can't run from him.

"Enzo…"

"Shut up and let me kiss you."

When his mouth crashes onto mine, I'm too tired to fight it. The inevitable road to disaster is careening towards us, right on target. Enzo has always wanted to own me—inside out, from the moment we met. He stamped me with his seal of possession the day we bonded over unlaced Chucks.

I saw then what I see now.

Possession. Hunger.

But more than that, the security and certainty that comes with imprisoning those you love most. For months, I've thought that he wanted to entrap me. Control me. Force me to live in the shadows while they risk their lives.

No. I was wrong.

He wants me to be his equal.

Releasing one wrist, he grabs my jean-covered hip and lifts me up. I fall backwards onto the desk, scattering pencil pots and stacks of paperwork across the carpet.

"We can't do this here," I gasp loudly.

"I need to feel you, little one."

"Enz—"

"Please. I need to know that we're okay."

My legs part without being told, letting him pin me against the polished wood. His mouth is hot on mine, demanding, seeking, torturing the answers from me that he needs to hear.

I'm on fire. Pins and needles spread everywhere as his hand pushes my shoulder, forcing me to lie down on the wide desk. Every carved muscle pressed against me adds to the sense of spiralling. I'm falling in a rapid, dizzying corkscrew.

Maybe he'll catch me.

Maybe he'll follow me to hell.

Lifting the hem of my blue sweater, his calloused hand leaves a searing path against my stomach. Everywhere he touches erupts into flames. This is wrong. We can't be doing this right now, but I do not give a fuck.

We're in Hunter's office while our entire world crumbles around us with each passing day. I shouldn't be wet and writhing in my desperation to taste him, but I am. I can't live with this tension suffocating me for a second longer.

Enzo growls under his breath as he tugs my sweater over my head. His hands are everywhere, unbuttoning my jeans, pushing my bra cups aside, rolling my nipples between his roughened fingers.

"You're so beautiful," he grunts into my lips. "Fuck, Harlow. I've wanted to touch you so bad these past few months."

"Why didn't you?"

"Because I'm an idiot. I'll make up for that now."

"Enzo, we can't do this here," I repeat.

"Nobody can get in without the code."

I want to protest more, but his hand shoves inside my jeans and finds the delicate lace of my panties. Unlike the gentle exploration of our previous collisions, he's almost delirious with need this time. There's no slow build up.

We're both on the verge of ruin.

I need him to make everything better.

"Do you want me to stop?"

His fingers are a short walk from heaven. I'm desperate to feel his touch between my thighs, relieving the burning ache that nothing else will fix. My pussy is his to own.

"No," I moan. "Don't stop."

When his thick finger parts my folds, swirling moisture and desire, I see stars. My moans grow louder as he drives a digit deep inside me.

"So tight, little one."

Each thrust of his finger threatens to unhinge my grip on the world. This is so inappropriate, and it's turning me on even more. I'm soaking wet, more than ever before.

"Can you take another finger?"

"Yes," I plead.

"That's right. I heard you've been fooling around with our Leigh. Why did that asshole get to fuck you first?"

When I don't answer him, Enzo pumps the two fingers in and out of my slit with a smirk lighting his face. He's packed inside me, moving fast and hard to force me into submission.

"Answer the damn question."

"It… just happened," I mewl.

Enzo snickers with a dark grin. "I'm going to fuck you so hard, you'll forget all about the other men battling for a taste of you. My name is the only one allowed on your tongue now."

His other hand moves to clasp my throat. It's a loose necklace at first, but his grip gradually tightens until I can't breathe properly. The promise of danger only adds to my anticipation. He literally owns the air in my lungs.

"I'm your God now, Harlow."

I release a strangled gasp.

"You want to breathe, baby?"

My head bobs.

"Just a quick one. That's all you're allowed."

Loosening his grip long enough for me to suck a breath deep into my lungs, his fingers tighten again.

"Do you understand how this works now?" Enzo asks with inky darkness in his eyes.

I blink, silent and complacent.

"You belong to me, angel. That means you breathe when I say so. Spread your legs when I order. Show me your gorgeous fucking tits if I want them in my face."

If he keeps going like this, I'm going to come from his words alone. Old Harlow would've been terrified by this demanding beast. I'm glad we waited, because I'm ready for him now.

Ready to surrender.

I'll worship at his feet.

When his hand releases, allowing me to suck in a glorious mouthful of air, his fingertips move to let his teeth pierce my skin. He sucks so hard, I can feel the bruise forming for the entire world to see.

"I'm going to leave my marks all over your perfect skin," Enzo announces. "When the others want to fuck you, they'll have to plead on their knees for my permission."

"P-Permission?" I rasp.

"I'm willing to share you with my brothers, but not without conditions. They'll have to beg me for a taste of your cunt."

His path of destruction sweeps over my skin. Everything feels overly sensitive and swollen beneath his lips. I'm putty in his hands, my nipples reacting with the coldness of the room outside of my bra cups.

Touching the harsh zigzag of scars cutting deep into my pale skin, Enzo's eyes search my body. I hate how inadequate I feel beneath his gaze. He could do so much better.

"Stop," he warns as I squirm to escape. "You are forbidden from hiding or being ashamed. Fucking *forbidden*."

Sucking my breast into his mouth, Enzo tortures my tingling skin, leaving another dark bruise to form. I feel like I'm covered in his scent and marks of possession.

"All mine," he declares. "Say it, Harlow."

When I don't immediately respond, his hand crashes against my bare breast in a painful slap.

"Argh," I cry out.

"I said say it."

"I'm yours. I always have been."

"Good little angel," he praises.

Hand pressed against my lower belly, he traps me on my back. The desk is hard beneath my spine, but the delicious pressure of his cock brushing my panties is all I can think about. It's so close to being inside me.

Enzo tugs off my jeans, one leg at a time, and tosses them over his shoulder. If someone were to walk in right now, they'd see every scrap of my scarred skin on display outside my remaining bra and panties.

The sound of tearing fabric is the final straw. He does not give a fuck right now. Enzo holds my ruined panties in his hand like a trophy, an eyebrow cocked in amusement.

"You won't be needing these."

A shiver rolls down my spine.

"I want to see every inch of you," he adds.

The human facade that conceals Enzo's monster from the world has fallen away. I'm staring at a crouched tiger, preparing to pounce on its prey. He's going to consume me.

Left hand returning to clasp my throat, he smashes our lips back together. His tongue steals any remaining doubt from my mind, battling with mine to claim ultimate ownership.

I allow myself to be dominated by him. His touch. His tongue. Hips grinding against mine. Hands roaming my goosebump-covered skin. Chest rumbling with a contented purr.

"Turn over," he orders into my lips.

"Now?"

Amber eyes burning, Enzo grabs my hip and tugs until I'm forced to flip over. My arms stretch across Hunter's desk as my breasts and body meet the cool surface of the wood.

My feet barely touch Hunter's office carpet. Enzo pulls me into a position that leaves nothing to the imagination. My butt is raised high, laying bare the wet heat of my slit for him to see from behind.

"Look at this perfect ass just begging for my handprint," he comments hoarsely.

"Enz," I whine.

"Yes, little one?"

The ache inside me is so intense, it steals my breath. I feel like one stroke of his hand will make me explode. Months of anticipation and tension are swirling inside me.

"Please. I just… want to forget, for a moment. Help me."

The buckle on his black jeans clicks open and causes my pulse to spike. I recognise the rustle of foil being ripped as his body heat shifts behind me. My exposed pussy lips feel every small movement.

"We can forget together," he replies as his palm stokes my ass cheek. "The world can wait."

When his hand draws back and collides with my skin in a hard spank, the sizzle of pain causes my self-control to snap. I cry out, unable to swallow the sound in case anyone can hear us. I don't care who knows what we're doing in here.

Huge hands engulfing my hips, Enzo pulls my behind even higher, at the perfect angle for the tip of his length to tease my soaked opening. He's so close to crossing that final line.

"Last chance," Enzo advises.

I'm so sick of them treading carefully around me. Hands gripping the edge of Hunter's desk, I use the position to push myself backwards so that Enzo's cock slips inside.

"Fuck, Harlow!"

The sheer size of him causes a satisfying burn. Shifting my hips, he pulls out and pushes back inside me at a deeper angle, making me swallow more of his huge length.

"We're gonna start slow. I don't want to hurt you."

I can't answer beyond tiny, frenzied pants. Every time he surges back into me, I feel myself stretching around him. This feels easier than my first time, and the tingle of pain soon melts into pleasure.

Every inch of me is screaming with satisfaction. I want more. All of it. With him filling me, the overwhelming darkness in my head falls silent for the first time in days. He leaves no space for the devil or his machinations.

"Take my cock, baby. Take it all."

"More," I groan.

"Such a greedy little slut, aren't you?"

His hand cracks against my ass again, harder this time. It sends spikes of sizzling electricity through my body. My legs are trembling with each thrust, his speed slowly increasing.

Pots of fountain pens and stray paperclips rattle. More papers fall, and the desk lamp crashes loudly on the floor. We're causing mayhem as the desk threatens to collapse beneath his weight slamming into me.

Enzo doesn't hesitate for a second. It's the surest he's ever been around me. His grip on my hips turns bruising, but I don't care. Let him break me. I want the punishment. I deserve to be disciplined for what I've done to them all.

He's finally letting himself go with me. His control is fraying, falling apart, leaving us adrift in no man's land. I gasp and moan with each pump of his hips.

Enzo slips free from my pussy and quickly flips me back over. I squeak in surprise, sitting on the very edge of the desk. He roughly shoves my legs open and steps between them.

"I want your beautiful eyes on me. Do you understand?"

My legs sneak around his waist. "I understand."

"Say *I understand, sir.*"

Thighs clenched, I fight back a groan. I never expected the formal title that the company uses to refer to him to be so hot.

"I understand… sir."

"Good, angel."

I place my hands on the wide, threatening set of his shoulders. At some point, he discarded his t-shirt. The corded muscles and exquisitely carved V of his hips are hard to look away from. He's a deliciously toned boulder of masculinity.

When he pushes back inside me from this angle, I cry out again. The pressure is reaching a boiling point. He's almost completely buried inside me now; it's too much for my control to take.

Digging my nails deep into his bronzed skin, I feel the warmth of his blood against my fingertips. Each second of sweet torture is setting off fireworks beneath my skin.

"That's it," he purrs. "Let me see my pretty girl come. Are you gonna scream my name, angel?"

"Yes," I submit.

"Then let's see it."

His hips move like steel engines. Faster. Harder. Coaxing my obedience with each pump. I scream out his name just as the desk groans ominously, on the verge of collapsing.

Enzo gasps and picks me up right before one of the legs breaks. The slabs of solid wood crumple with a loud bang, semi-destroying Hunter's office in the process.

I'm holding on to Enzo's huge body, a tiny limpet clinging to his chest in comparison. He buries his face in my neck as he walks across the office and slams me against the wall instead.

"Again," he demands, his teeth cutting into my neck. "I want to hear that gorgeous scream of yours again."

It's a good thing he's holding me against the wall, else I'd be tangled in a boneless puddle at his feet. My limbs have turned to jelly with my first mind-melting orgasm.

"Come." Enzo slams into me with a loud thump. "For." His mouth is hot on mine. "Me." He licks my pulse point. "Again."

That's all it takes.

"Arghh!" I cry out.

The room fades into blackness as the most intense release I've ever had shatters my consciousness. I'm all light and sensation, floating untethered in space.

Enzo's face hides in the rapid rise and fall of my breasts as he bellows through his own intense climax. We're both gasping dramatically for air and struggling to remain upright.

"Jesus," he curses. "Are you okay? Did I hurt you?"

I struggle to form a sentence.

"Harlow! Answer me."

"No… I'm okay. That was crazy."

When he has the willpower to move, Enzo lets me slide down his frame. His eyes are ducked low as he pulls the condom from himself and tosses it into Hunter's bin.

That's when he gets a good look at the war zone we've created. The office is a complete wreck. It looks like a bomb exploded in here.

"Well, shit."

"Uh-huh," I echo.

"If he saw this, he'd kill us both."

That sobers me up.

The carefree haze draped over me slinks away without warning, leaving me cold and ashamed. Hunter's lying in intensive care while I'm hooking up with his best friend.

"Hey." Enzo clasps my jaw firmly. "Let's get dressed and we'll go straight to the hospital to see Hunter."

"How did you know I was thinking about him?"

"I can tell." He shrugs. "You love him."

"You got all that from a look?"

"I can read you easily enough. Please don't feel guilty about this. You've done nothing wrong, alright?"

I blow out a breath. "Then why does being with all of you feel so wrong and yet so right at the same time?"

His smile softens. "Because the world wants us to stay in our tidy little boxes. We're just choosing not to."

"So, what are we choosing instead?"

"Love," he answers without missing a beat.

CHAPTER 21
HARLOW

DRIFTING – NF

THE INTENSIVE CARE unit's dreary waiting area is packed. Hunter's whole family is here—us, his parents, the Cobra team and several steely-eyed agents glowering at anyone not with us.

We've been here for a few hours, tense and silent, awaiting any news as they attempt to ease Hunter off sedation. Leighton has stepped outside to smoke with Hudson and Brooklyn, needing an escape.

We're all on edge.

You could hear a pin drop.

When the click of Hunter's hospital room door opening draws all our heads up, my heart leaps into my throat. Doctor Lane, accompanied by two nurses and an anaesthetist, steps outside.

Ben is the first one on his feet, even faster than his wife. The doctor gestures for Hunter's parents to follow them into the quiet family room down the corridor to talk in private.

"This is bad," I mutter to myself. "Why are they speaking to them alone?"

Next to me, Richards is half-heartedly reading an article in a psychiatry magazine he pulled from his briefcase. He spares me a small, tense smile.

"Standard procedure. They have to update Hunter's next of kin first."

Pulling the hair tie wrapped around my wrist, I snap the band against my skin several times. It's one of the techniques Richards advised upon seeing the mess I'd made of myself. It sears, but the pain is nowhere near enough.

Anxiety is eating me alive.

I can't pull and rave like I want to with everyone's eyes primed for any movement. I'm sure that's why they arranged for Richards to be here. That decision has Enzo written all over it.

"Shall we take a walk?" Richards suggests. "Some fresh air might be good."

"I don't want to miss anything."

"I'm sure they'll call if you do."

"No. I'm staying," I insist.

Avoiding looking up at his perceptive eyes, I can feel him studying me behind polished spectacles and bushy grey eyebrows. My trust in Richards is hanging on by a shoestring.

He hasn't mentioned the inpatient idea since our last session, but I can still see it in his eyes. I'm not so sure he isn't a threat. Inching my chair further away, I fold my hands in my lap.

At least I can fool the others and hide the guilt shredding me apart until it's physically painful to breathe. Richards isn't so easily fooled. He sees too much after months of exploring the deepest depths of my brain.

Someone nudges my shoulder, and a steaming styrofoam cup appears in front of me. I look up at Eli's pursed lips and bright-green eyes, softened with concern.

"Uh, thanks, Eli." I take the cup of tea and place it at my feet to cool down.

"You got it. Want something to eat?"

He's always so sweet and thoughtful.

"No, I'm okay," I decline. "But thanks."

He looks uncertain for a moment before clasping my shoulders and dragging me into a quick hug. I'm stunned for a second before cuddling him back.

He's comfortable around me now, but physical contact is usually a no-go. His narrow frame and bird-like bones feel delicate in my arms as we embrace tightly.

"I won't bother saying that everything is going to be okay," Eli whispers in my ear. "I know that means fuck all right now. But we're all here with you. Remember that."

A lump gathers in my throat.

"Thank you for being here."

"Of course," he murmurs. "If you change your mind about food, let me know. I'll locate ice cream."

"Okay." I laugh through tears. "Thanks."

"Don't mention it."

Returning to the nearby drinks machine, Eli works his way around the rest of the room, ensuring everyone has a hot drink clasped in their hands.

Phoenix takes his black coffee and pulls Eli into his lap after he's finished his rounds. The pair cling to each other, neither saying a word yet somehow conversing through little glances and smiles. It's rare to see them apart.

They're a package deal outside of their relationship with Brooklyn. But in a different way to how I've caught Hudson and Jude locking lips. They love to hate each other.

Leighton, Brooklyn and Hudson return, retaking their seats with the rest of the Cobra team. Enzo paces up and down the linoleum. Richards pretends to read his magazine.

Tick, tock.

Tick, tock.

I want to smash that clock.

Tick, tock.

Tick, tock.

I'm losing my mind here.

Tick, tock.

Tick, tock.

When the sound of crying emanates from the family room after a while, I lose patience. I'm about to storm into Hunter's hospital room when the doctors finally reappear.

Enzo halts, wound tighter than a coiled spring. "Well? Can we see him now?"

Doctor Lane dismisses her colleagues. "Hunter regained consciousness a little while ago. His parents are going in to spend some time with him."

"And?" he urges. "What's the verdict?"

"I'm sorry, Mr Montpellier. I can't disclose anything without Hunter's consent. You'll have to wait."

"Enough waiting! We're his family!"

Stopping beside him, Leighton clasps his bicep. "Enz, calm down. Mum and Dad will fill us in soon."

"I want to see him right now."

"That isn't how this works." Doctor Lane offers a placating smile. "Excuse me."

She disappears to guide Della and Ben into their son's hospital room. Hunter's mum is leaning on her husband for support, and she doesn't look up at us as she dabs her red eyes. I have a very bad feeling about this.

We all sit back down, even more on edge than before. Enzo cracks his knuckles with menace, glowering down the corridor, while Leighton taps out a text message.

I send a silent prayer up to the heavens.

Please, God.

Don't punish him for my mistakes.

"Where the fuck is Theo?" Enzo growls under his breath. "He was supposed to be here an hour ago."

Leighton shrugs, his eyes glued to his phone. "The post-mortems are done. I don't know why he's held up."

"Fuck." Enzo rakes a hand over his unshaven face. "I'll go and call him. We shouldn't be separated right now; it isn't safe. The damn press is camped outside the hospital."

"It's their fault that Hunter's here," Leighton agrees angrily. "This is a clusterfuck. Nowhere is safe."

Enzo stands to stride from the intensive care ward, but a newcomer stops him by entering the waiting area. She's short and round, her jet-black hair brushing her jaw in dense curls.

The duo of agents immediately crowd her, demanding identification and answers. She disappears behind their towering physiques and visible weaponry.

"Stop," Enzo shouts, heading for the foray. "Stand down. She's not a threat."

Grumbling to themselves, the two agents dip their heads in respect and backtrack. The woman is left to dust herself off, her olive complexion flushed a light shade of pink.

"What are you doing here?"

She opens her arms for Enzo to step into. "I heard today was the day, so I'm here. There are a lot of reporters and angry people outside."

"I know. Did they recognise you?"

"Not a chance. I snuck around the back."

The pair embrace tightly, exchanging hugs and kisses. She barely reaches Enzo's shoulder, not much taller than me. The moment I see them entangled, I spot the resemblance.

Studying the beautiful, middle-aged woman hanging off him, it's clear to see the relation between them. She shares the same strong Spanish heritage as her sister, Enzo's mum.

"That's Hayley," Leighton whispers in my ear. "Enzo's aunt. My mum's kept her posted on Hunter's condition."

Smoothing my rumpled blue jeans and sweater tucked in at the waist, I blow out a nervous breath. Enzo hugs his aunt close and directs her over to us.

"Leigh," she gasps with tear-filled eyes. "You've grown up so much. It's been years since I last saw you."

"Hey, Hayley." He doesn't move, keeping a reassuring arm around my waist. "Thanks for coming."

"Of course. I wanted to be here."

I stammer a timid hello before I'm yanked from Leighton's arms and bundled into a tight hug. Hayley's hair tickles my face, thick and glossy, as she whispers my name.

She smells like rose-scented perfume and freshly baked bread, wafting off her plain blouse and flared black jeans. I can't help but panic a little when she doesn't let go.

"Oh, Harlow." Her lips press against my head. "I'm so sorry it took this long for us to finally meet. Are you okay?"

"Um." I try to peel her off, but she clings on even tighter. "I'm f-fine. You're… uh, Hayley?"

"Hay," Enzo says. "Let her bloody breathe."

"Gosh, I'm sorry," she apologises again. "I've just heard a lot about you from my nephew. All good, I swear."

Swiping a painted fingernail under her sparkling gold eyes, Hayley smiles sweetly. I plaster what feels like a grimace on my mouth and attempt to smile back.

"Hayley is my aunt," Enzo grumbles. "And absolutely terrible at respecting boundaries."

"Excuse me," Hayley complains with a playful scowl. "I'm a hugger. That is not a bad thing."

After pinching her nephew's cheeks, Hayley works her way around the room for hugs. She seems to know everyone and gasps when she spots the black-diamond engagement ring on Brooklyn's finger.

"Those bastards finally decided to make it official, eh?" She winks at Hudson and Kade, both grinning themselves.

Brooklyn kisses her cheek. "Well, you threatened all five of them with a beating enough times if they didn't."

"She's scarier than you are, Brooke," Hudson agrees with a wince. "Nice to see you again."

Hayley messes up his hair. "Good job on the ring, hot shot. Nice touch with the black diamond."

"I had some help." Hudson chuckles. "The colour choice was all Eli's and Phoenix's doing."

Still snuggled on Phoenix's lap, next to where Jude is answering emails on his work phone, Eli shrugs off the compliment.

"When's the wedding?" Hayley enquires.

Brooklyn smiles. "September."

"Not long to go now!"

"We still have a shitload to do, but we'll get there."

All settling back in our seats, we wait together and converse in low whispers. The tension has eased with Hayley's arrival. She's a light, easy presence, doling out physical affection without blinking an eye. I like her already.

"What's the latest?" Hayley asks.

Enzo resumes cracking his knuckles. "Della and Ben are in there now. He's awake."

She touches his hands to make him stop. "Patience, *querido*. It's going to be okay."

"Did you close the bakery to come over here?"

Hayley waves him off. "Gordon is closing up shop for me this evening."

"I hate that douchebag," Enzo complains. "Why are you still dating him? Is he still driving that shitty car?"

"Because he's a nice man and you aren't in charge of my dating life, as I've said a million times before." She clips him around the ear. "His car choice is none of your business."

"We'll see about that," Enzo mutters.

"Is he this much of a pain in the ass to you too, Harlow?"

I choke on a mouthful of lukewarm tea. "Uh."

"That's a yes," she concludes.

Enzo narrows his eyes at me. "Traitor."

Leighton is trying his best not to laugh as he hides behind his phone. Glowering at his aunt, Enzo makes a point of laying a possessive hand on my thigh.

"I am not a pain in the ass," he defends.

My skin tingles where he touches me. I had to deal with Brooklyn's smug, knowing grin when I semi-limped into the waiting area earlier. I'm sore after our earlier activities.

"Yeah, right," Hayley continues with a snort. "Enz, we've discussed this. You'll scare poor Harlow off if you keep acting like a caveman for all your life."

"I am not a caveman," Enzo protests.

"That's debatable." Hudson coughs to conceal his words. "No one has ever defined the word caveman more than you do, Enz."

When Enzo shoots him a death glare, he grins wide. I think Hudson's the only one who isn't afraid of our less-than-cuddly resident enforcer. Enzo trained him too well to feel such fear. I wouldn't want to watch them fight.

The tentative banter ceases when Hunter's father emerges from the hospital room. Ben doesn't even cast us a look, striding out of the ward without a second glance.

Leighton watches him go with unease. "I should go after him. He looked upset."

I gently nudge him. "Go."

"You'll be okay?"

"I'm fine, Leigh. Your family needs you."

Nodding, he grabs me by the chin to plant a heavy kiss against my lips. I linger for a second before his mouth is torn from mine and he chases after his father's hurried footsteps.

The pressure of Hayley's eyes burning a hole in my head causes me to blush. I get the impression that nothing escapes her attention. While I have no idea what Enzo's told her, she doesn't seem surprised by them all touching me.

Della's splotchy, tear-stained face appears around the hospital door next, and we all stand up at the same time. Her smile is appreciative, but strained.

"Harlow," she rasps.

I clutch Enzo's arm tight. "Yeah?"

"Can you come here, please?"

When the ever-present shadow at my side steps forward, Della shakes her head, causing Enzo to freeze.

"Just Harlow for now."

He looks crestfallen, but nods as he sits back down. Releasing his arm, I catch sight of Hayley's reassuring smile. I must look as terrified as I feel right now.

Passing Richards and his discarded magazine, I leave the waiting room and meet Della in the corridor. She's been sobbing. Her face and greying hair are a stressed-out mess.

I freeze outside the door. "Yes?"

"You can come in," she encourages, offering me a withered hand. "Come and say hello."

Reluctantly accepting her offer, I'm ushered into the shadows of the hospital room. The plain-white blinds are drawn against the dreary, cloud-covered day.

The moment I set eyes on the bandaged, wire-wrapped figure in the bed, I know this is going to hurt. Buried amongst the medical paraphernalia, Hunter is hardly recognisable.

"He's awake?"

Della squeezes my hand. "He woke up a few hours ago from the coma. They've just been running some tests."

"Is he okay?"

She pushes me forwards. "He needs you right now. I'll give you two some privacy."

I wait for the door to click shut behind me before taking another breath. I'm petrified of the contents of that bed. The person I'm staring at isn't Hunter, but the consequences of my cowardice.

I practically begged that bullet to pierce my chest and end it all. With the cruel, malicious irony of a God that has forsaken me, it almost took Hunter's life instead.

He should've died.

His survival is a miracle.

Trembling all over, I stop an inch from his bedside. Hunter's head is partially swathed in bandages. His scruff-covered face and two open eyes peek out through the cotton, the only sign that he isn't a mummified corpse.

The endless, intelligent brown depths are locked on me for a brief second before he returns to staring up at the pocked hospital ceiling. Not a single word of greeting.

"Hunt," I whimper. "It's me."

Hunter blinks but still doesn't acknowledge me. Throat seizing, I dodge several tangled IV lines and stroke my fingertips over his forearm. No response.

He could be dead.

There's no light left in him.

"I know you don't want to talk to me right now, and that's okay. But I need you to know that I love you."

Nothing.

Watching his pale, gaunt face for any glimmer of recognition, I choke up when a solitary tear escapes down his cheek. It's soaked up by the rough scruff of his beard.

"Please don't cry," I say through my own tears. "You're going to get back on your feet. We're all here to help you."

He still isn't looking at me or saying anything. My worst fears are confirmed. Hunter hates me. I'm the reason he's confined to this bed, unable to walk or feed himself.

Driven by wild desperation, I duck down to brush my lips against his cheek. There isn't much skin on display amongst the bandages protecting his butchered ear and fractured skull. They performed surgery to staple everything back together. He resembles the infamous monster created by Frankenstein that I've read so much about.

When I begin to retreat, his eyes finally slide over to me. I'm caught in a storm of horrific pain staring back at me. My breath catches. I feel like I'm drowning in his palpable misery. It's crawling up my nose and throat.

"It's g-g-gone," he stammers.

"What's gone? What is it?"

It takes great exertion for his pinkie finger to lift and capture mine. Linked together, he squeezes ever so softly before releasing. The brief moment of contact doesn't comfort me. This feels like a goodbye.

"I can't…"

His voice is garbled and sounds off.

I lean closer. "Can't what? Tell me what you need. Please, Hunt. I'll do anything to make this right."

More tears soak into his sunken cheeks, highlighting his weight loss while trapped in this hospital. My own cheeks are dripping wet. I reach out to brush the moisture aside.

"Hunt," I croak. "Please talk to me."

Our eyes collide again. He's always been my strength. My certainty. My protector. The irrevocable storm that sweeps all into its tide, powered by the promise of justice beyond the horizon.

That strength is gone.

I'm staring back at myself. The familiar prison of terror is reflected in his irises now too. His pinkie squeezes mine again. A silent apology. A plea. I can't give him what he wants.

I already know what pain-stricken words are struggling to leave his tongue. Even if I don't want to hear them.

"Can't h-hear you," he finishes with a silent sob. "Can't hear a-a-anything."

"Your hearing aid? Where is it?"

Hunter blinks twice and I recognise the message. He's saying no. There's a couple of hearing aids on the bedside table, but they've been dismissed. Deemed useless.

His next stuttered word slams the final nail in the coffin of my guilt. My head falls and his pinkie releases mine.

"D-Deaf."

CHAPTER 22
THEO

KIJO – MEMORIST

"AFTER THE TRAGIC accident earlier this month, we understand that Sabre's director, Hunter Rodriguez, remains under medical supervision."

Propped against the cold brick wall of the basement gym, I tug my hood up to cover my blonde curls while listening to the news report through my headphones.

Enzo asked me to flick the heating on before he comes down to train, but it's still fucking freezing sitting on the floor in the corner of the well-equipped gym.

April has arrived with the first sprigs of fresh grass, constant random rainfall and chirp of birds, but we're too busy being held prisoner in our own home to enjoy it.

"What about their appeal for information?"

Sally Moore rolls her eyes as she gestures towards the familiar, Victorian-style mansion behind her, the curtains drawn to conceal the inside occupants. It's a livestream.

"Clinging at straws, Clive. Since uncovering the mass grave, we've been given a vague timeframe for the killings and Sabre has asked for any witnesses to come forward."

"So, no connection to our killer?"

"Not yet," she responds with a smile. "We'll keep our viewers informed of any developments as this story continues. Now, let's go back to the studio for the weather."

Exiting the trashy news channel's website, I crash the heel of my palm against my forehead. These gossiping sell-outs are filling the airwaves with the stupidest of speculations.

The case is complex and difficult enough to manage without them adding fuel to the fire of furious public opinion. With cases like this, it's guaranteed that the world will turn on you somewhere down the line.

We've become the bad guys.

The scapegoats.

Even the enemies.

I just never thought that it would lead to abject violence. Some, perhaps. But nothing on this scale. We're confined to the house while reporters and protestors crowd the front gate.

It was only a matter of time until our home address was leaked online. The added security threat comes at the worst possible time, with Hunter still in the hospital, out of action.

We have a full team of agents posted outside, armed and very much prepared to use force if needed. Nobody leaves the house alone and without the protection of an armed convoy.

"I am not going down there."

Harlow's stubborn complaint echoes down the concrete staircase from the floor above me.

"You agreed to learn some self-defence after what happened," Enzo reminds her. "Move it."

"Yeah, but not in the basement!"

"Would you prefer to train outside under the glare of the media's helicopters? Be my guest. I couldn't care less."

"You're an asshole."

"*Your* asshole," he snips back.

"Stop trying to butter me up."

The sound of annoyed footsteps stomps down the staircase. I quickly minimise the pages of countryside house listings I was trawling through while watching the news.

It's official.

We're moving.

Enzo made the decision that we need to leave London behind, in light of recent events. I don't blame him. If the world knows where we live, then so does Pastor Michaels. It isn't safe here anymore.

"Theo?" Harlow exclaims.

Pausing on the threshold of the cold room, she anxiously peeks around the well-lit space. Her shoulders are drawn tightly together with anxiety.

I offer her a wave. "Hey."

"What are you doing down here?"

"Leighton was singing in the shower again. I couldn't concentrate in the office upstairs. His voice carries."

"He's auditioning for a new career, apparently." Harlow places a tentative foot inside. "Something about running away to Hollywood and leaving this madness behind."

"Somehow, I doubt Hollywood is holding its breath for Leighton and his terrible rendition of *Mamma Mia*."

Sneaking up behind her, which is a seriously impressive feat at his size, Enzo swoops Harlow off her feet. She screams in shock before beginning to yell her head off.

"It's a gym," he scolds, his palm cracking across her behind. "It won't bite. Stop being a wimp."

"You know why I haven't been down here," she shouts while hammering his back. "Let me down, now."

All of the screaming attracts Lucky's attention as she comes bounding down the staircase next. After declaring the room safe with a loud sniff, she curls up next to me, her nose buried in my faded-blue jeans. Bloody hypervigilant dog.

"Good girl." I pet her ears.

Enzo deposits Harlow in the middle of the spongy workout mat surrounded by state-of-the-art machines, weights and equipment. Don't ask me what any of this stuff does.

I keep in decent enough shape by running around like a lunatic after Hunter and his constant list of demands, not working out. Physical exercise is really not my thing.

Shaking my head to clear the automatic stab of worry, I refocus on my laptop screen. Enzo's keeping Harlow busy as he orders her around, watching with interested eyes when she stretches in front of him in a pastel workout set.

"I'm going to take you through some basic self-defence." He rolls his broad shoulders. "We'll train for two hours a day until I'm satisfied you can defend yourself."

"Two hours?" Harlow groans.

Folding his arms, Enzo huffs. "Hunter's been working in the field for over a decade, and he got shot in the fucking head. Don't argue with me on this. You need to learn fast."

Gulping hard, Harlow ducks her eyes to the workout mat. I shoot Enzo an exasperated glare. He doesn't need to guilt trip her into doing this. She's beating herself up enough.

"Let's start with your form. You're gonna have to come closer, little one."

Sneaking forward with her chin tucked down, Harlow stands opposite him, her arms loose at her sides. I watch over my laptop screen as Enzo holds her by the hips to correct her posture.

"Eyes up and alert," he scolds her. "Shoulders back, feet planted, hands raised to block an attack. You never know when one might come."

With her body correctly positioned, Enzo scans over Harlow with an expertly trained eye. I sure as hell hope he's not going to teach her in the same way he taught his other recruits. That won't go down well with anyone.

Hudson spent months walking around with black eyes and split lips throughout his induction to Sabre. I'm convinced Enzo beat the shit out of him on a daily basis, purely for his own entertainment. He's a sadistic fuck at times.

"You're small and light." He pushes her shoulder in demonstration, almost causing her to fall.

"I feel like I should be offended by that."

"Quite the opposite," Enzo compliments. "Use it to your advantage. Speed is your best friend in a combat situation. How did you escape Diablo before?"

Harlow's face drains of colour. She clears her throat, looking uncomfortable.

"I bit him," she admits quietly. "Then I ran for my life."

Enzo actually looks impressed. "That's so hot."

"Enz! Christ."

"Thinking outside of the box. I like it. Ideally, you don't want your attacker close enough to bite. Basic evasive manoeuvres can help you there."

Without warning, he flashes across the mat and wrenches her up into the air. Harlow squeals in shock, her body restrained by the vice-like suffocation of Enzo's arms trapping her in place.

"Your first instinct is to panic," he breathes in her ear. "You want to beg and plead for me to let you go, right?"

She attempts to stomp on his foot and snarls when he doesn't react by bellowing in pain.

"The trick is to detach yourself." His hands roam down her arms, crossing a multitude of professional boundaries. "Allow your breathing to slow, and your movements to halt."

I feel kinda weird watching this private moment. He sure as fuck didn't semi-molest Hudson like this while kicking his ass. Harlow's eyes flutter shut as she takes a measured breath.

"There you go," Enzo purrs. "Let them think you're compliant. Play into their judgement. They aren't worried about a little slip like you."

"I am not a little slip," she seethes.

He tilts his head to brush his lips against her temple from behind. "When their guard is down, that's your chance to show them exactly that. No one expects you to fight back."

Harlow's eyes meet mine with half-lidded curiosity. I hastily look back down at my laptop again, caught red-handed. I need to pretend to be immersed in something until it's safe for me to resume watching them.

"Twist your wrists outwards, like this." Enzo pulls her arms into the correct form. "You're going to feint to the left and tug hard. Slip beneath my arm when the hold breaks."

Teeth gritted together, Harlow relaxes against his towering height. Enzo's enjoying this far too much. Leighton will kill him when he finds out what he missed by working out first, then showering.

With his guard down, Harlow decides to strike out. She twists her arms and moves fast, lurching forward to slip through his heavily muscled prison. Enzo lets her escape without much of a fight.

"I did it!" she says excitedly.

His smile is broad. "See? Simple but effective."

Dancing backwards on the mat, she pumps the air in a very un-Harlow like manner. Hell, she's too darn cute. I'd happily pin her to the ground and kiss the life out of her right now.

My cock twitches just watching her small, inviting curves straining against the tight material of her Lycra leggings and t-shirt. These workout clothes should be illegal for her to tease me with.

"Again," Enzo commands with a grin. "We're going to practise until you can do this with your eyes shut. No hesitation. Understood?"

More enthused now that she's had her first win, Harlow nods and jumps back into his arms. He tightens his grip and they run through the manoeuvre again.

Refocusing on my laptop to distract myself from the blood rushing to my dick, I flick back through the houses I've narrowed down. Enzo's criteria is obsessively detailed.

There are several viable options outside of London, but still close enough to commute. The city is too risky for us to consider, even though we have a range of different safe houses scattered throughout. Too many prying eyes.

When my laptop dings with an email on our secure server, I check again to make sure Harlow's absorbed in her training. She's ducking from fake punches now as Enzo chases her around the room, laughing his head off.

Logging in with a scan of my thumbprint in the top corner of my keyboard, I open the password-protected report from the team. My eyes race over the complicated jargon.

Forensics would've been my second career choice if I didn't fall into tech and programming. It offers similar insight into a world that most are content to let pass them by.

For me, I want to understand the complex systems and invisible rules that dictate our reality. The more we know, the easier it is to control. Techies can do more damage within half an hour at a terminal than the president in his Oval Office.

"Enz," I summon.

He glances over at me, pulling his blow short at the last minute before he would've struck Harlow in the gut. She's already ducked sideways to avoid the collision.

"Yeah?" he snaps.

I wave him over. "You need to see this."

Sighing, he plants a kiss on Harlow's braided hair. "Keep practising for a minute."

She swats him away. "Like hell. What's happening?"

Scanning back over the results, I feel giddy. It's unnerving. These conversations usually begin with disappointment, but this time, I'm staring at the biggest breakthrough we've had in months. About fucking time.

"Forensics found hair fibres on one of the bodies," I quickly recite. "We have a positive DNA match with the samples taken from Northumberland. It's him."

"Pastor Michaels?" Harlow squeaks.

"We have evidence tying the two crime scenes. One perp. This proves that Lee Heston and Pastor Michaels are the same person."

"Fuck." Enzo crouches to look over my shoulder. "Fuck! This is enough to go public. We can issue an arrest warrant and flush this son of a bitch out."

"How?" Harlow frowns at him. "We still have no idea where he's hiding. What difference will this make?"

"The photograph from Frederick Houghton," I remind her. "We can release it to the press. Someone's seen him in the last six months. We spread this far and wide."

Enzo rises to his feet. "What about the landlord?"

"In Newcastle?" I clarify.

"Yeah. I want him arrested and brought in for questioning. He rented that damn place to Michaels five years ago and allowed another family to live above a crime scene."

"You think he knew?"

"Doubtful, but I don't want any loose ends. We need to send someone to monitor Frederick Houghton's residence too. Michaels knows we've linked his two identities. He may decide to retaliate."

"Seems risky."

"I wouldn't put it past him though," Enzo argues.

His phone rings, and Enzo sighs as he notes the caller ID. Hunter's mum. She's at the hospital with the Cobra team, keeping an eye on things while we're trapped by the madness going on outside.

"Take it." I shrug without looking up from my email reiterating his instructions. "I'll tell Becket and the Anaconda team to hit the road. They can track down the landlord."

Enzo nods and heads upstairs for some privacy. Lucky bounds after him, yipping for attention, leaving Harlow to sink down next to me on the floor. Her expression is conflicted.

"What's up?" I ask while typing furiously. "This is good news. We're getting closer to Michaels. All it takes is one tip-off to expose his current location."

She worries her bottom lip. "It's nothing."

Setting my laptop aside once finished, I tentatively reach out and stroke my fingers against her clenched hand. She's staring at her folded legs, doing her best to ignore my touch.

"Beautiful," I murmur.

"I just… it's selfish of me, but I know that when we catch him, it will all be over. Everything will change."

"What do you mean? Us?"

"Yeah. I'll have to leave, and you'll all go back to your lives without me."

Is she being serious right now? I will never understand how her brilliant mind can be so fucking naïve at times.

"Don't look at me like that."

"Um, hard not to." I tug her hand into mine. "Do you actually think that Michaels is the only reason we're all here? Nothing else?"

Harlow shrugs. "I don't know."

The anger comes rushing back.

We've sacrificed everything to get to this point—a DNA match and solid lead that could bring the entire house of cards crashing down. We're getting close.

"Like I said, it's stupid and selfish." She winces at her own words. "I sound like a spoiled brat, complaining about this while Hunter's lying in a hospital bed."

"I understand how you're feeling," I admit.

Her iridescent blue eyes lock onto me. "You do?"

"Yeah. Ever since you came into our lives… I feel like I've started to get my family back." I pick at a loose thread in my jeans. "I'm scared of losing them all over again when this is over. In a fucked-up way, the case has brought us together."

"You know that won't happen though."

"Won't it?" I point out.

"The only reason they're getting hurt is because of me. Look at Hunter. Look what I did to him. You'd all be better off with me far away."

"You still don't get it, do you? None of this matters without you. Literally none of it."

She tries to shy away from me, and my patience fizzles out. I pull her hand and hook an arm underneath her slim legs. Harlow lands in my lap, sprawled out with her head tipped up towards me.

Our mouths gravitate together. I'm not in control of it, and neither is she. Something greater ties us together now. Something that can't be undone, no matter how much she worries it will all fall apart the minute Michaels is caught.

Harlow tastes like everything bright and good in the world. Her lips are velvety, moving against mine in a nervous waltz. We're too alike for our own good, but I feel stronger around her.

More capable.

Confident.

Whole.

It's a feeling I only ever experienced around one other person. I know that Harlow matters to me, on a level that cannot be described, because I no longer dream about Alyssa. She's been absent for a while now.

My nights are haunted by another face. Sweetheart-shaped and innocent, framed by inquisitive blue eyes that excite the people pleaser within me. I want to please her. Protect her. Love her. All of it.

Harlow has snuck into my system and planted her exploit. Now, my code is failing, and I cannot safely reboot as the malware corrupts my hard drive. She has become my new master. Everything I am, I want to give to her.

"With or without that son of a bitch in custody, we all belong to you," I whisper into her mouth. "None of us have the power to walk away. In our world, family is forever."

"Forever," she echoes. "You don't mean that."

Her fingers knot in my t-shirt and tug, betraying her uncertainty. She still doesn't believe me. It's infuriating.

"I fell in love with you before we even met, beautiful. For months, you existed in the printed ink of case files and witness statements. I didn't need to see you to know that you were something special."

"I'm nobody," she hushes out.

"Respectfully, Harlow, shut the fuck up."

Bursting into anguished laughter, her eyes flutter shut. "I don't want to wake up from this dream. When we find Pastor Michaels… everything will shatter. I feel like the worst person on the planet for admitting that out loud."

Nudging her nose with mine, I force her eyes to reopen. There she is. The kind-hearted, curious angel that stole my attention from the pages of police reports and crime scene photographs. She's far better than any book I've ever loved.

"That's when our lives will really begin," I reply. "We'll be free to live without fear. I cannot bloody wait to see what you do with that freedom."

A tentative smile blooms on her pink lips, and it's the most breathtaking sight I've ever seen. I know she still feels guilty as hell, but that tiny hint of positivity is enough for me.

"What *we* will do with it," Harlow corrects.

"What *we* will do with it," I repeat. "Together."

"I don't want to do this alone."

"And you'll never have to. That I can promise."

We kiss again, and the gym melts away around us. Enzo's and Leighton's voices talking upstairs become background noise. All that exists is the pressure of Harlow's sweet body cradled in my lap.

Clasping her chin, I deepen the kiss, needing more than her lips can give me. I want an eternal vow, signed in blood across the tender flesh of her soul, that she'll never abandon us.

Alyssa's death demanded its own solemn oath from me—the promise that I'd never let myself love again. Not for the toll it eventually extracts when that love is stolen away. Yet here I am, head over heels. I have no idea how it happened.

Her hand slips beneath my plain t-shirt and strokes over my ribcage. Every touch sends my heart into palpitations. I've wanted to taste every damned inch of her since that night we spent in the underground station.

"We need to go upstairs and deal with this fiasco," I gasp.

"No." Harlow yanks my lips back to hers when I pull away. "I need… I need something else from you first."

She shifts on my lap and moves to straddle me instead. My throat seizes with the weight of her rocking against my hard dick. Fuck. She has no idea how much she turns me on.

"And what's that, beautiful?"

Harlow's lips brush my clavicle. "Your trust."

"You already have it."

"Prove it then. No more hiding."

She shimmies backwards and lets her mouth travel down my body. When her hands move to the waistband of my jeans, I flinch with surprise. The guys are mere metres above us. They could return at any moment.

"Harlow—"

The button pops as she eases a hand inside the denim folds, cutting my complaint off. I hardly recognise the sexy confidence of the angel cupping my cock. Eyes rolling back, I let the protests die on my tongue.

"You'll need to be quiet," she instructs, easing my length out of my boxers. "I don't want them to interrupt us."

Wrapping a hand around the base of my shaft, Harlow sneaks a look up at me through her thick lashes. I stroke my hand over her hair, feeling like my heart is ready to burst.

"Is this okay?" she checks.

"As long as you're okay with it."

Grinning to herself, I watch her mouth descend on my erection. The minute it enters the warm, welcome prison, I have to swallow a grunt of pleasure. Her lips feel incredible tightening around me.

"Fuck, beautiful."

The light graze of her teeth against my shaft is a silent warning. Neither of us wants an audience for this, no matter the times I've shared with Hunter and Enzo in the past. I want her to myself for now. The sharing will come later.

Carefully holding her two thick braids to avoid triggering her, I lean back against the brick wall. Her mouth is tentative at first before she begins to take me deeper into her throat.

Her head rotates with each suck, determined to squeeze every last drop of pleasure from me. After the longest period of celibacy, I won't last long, riding her mouth like this.

Enzo's voice sneaks into my awareness as his footsteps begin to descend the stairs. Harlow doesn't seem to notice, too absorbed by her task. I try to pull her head back, but she holds firm.

A hot wave of awkwardness washes over me as Enzo's headful of sweaty black hair pokes around the corner. He freezes in the doorway the moment he spots me, pinned and gasping, while Harlow lets me fuck her mouth.

Enzo grins ear-to-ear and shoots me a pleased thumbs up. *Oh Lord, kill me now.* Flipping him the bird, I wave him away while trying not to burst into humiliated flames.

Biting down on his lip to suppress a laugh, he spreads his hands in surrender and ducks back upstairs. Perfect timing, as I'm about to finish in Harlow's mouth if she doesn't stop.

"Beautiful," I warn her.

She takes my warning as encouragement and sneaks a hand downwards to take a handful of my balls. *Jesus H Christ.* Someone taught her this shit. My money is on Leighton, the sneaky little asshole.

With a gentle squeeze of my balls, I'm driven to the edge. My hand fists in her braids as my release explodes out of me. Her lips tighten, milking my cock with a final suck.

I don't know why I'm stunned to silence that she swallows, glancing up at me with glistening lips. This dirty, gorgeous angel is a different creature entirely to the Harlow I know and love.

I'm not complaining.

That was incredible.

"Who taught you that?" I ask suspiciously.

Her lips contort in a rueful grin. "I had some help. Was it good?"

"You're asking me if I enjoyed you giving me a blow job?"

"Well… yeah."

Now I know exactly what Enzo means when he talks about loving her innocence. I didn't quite get it until now. It's so goddamn hot.

I stroke the pad of my thumb along her lips, stealing the droplets of come that have slipped out. Her luminescent eyes widen when I lick the remnants of my own release up.

She has no idea of the things I could show her. I've only held back for so long because I was confused about my feelings, and frankly, a little nervous about the kind of relationship I would need with her.

Alyssa understood me perfectly. She respected my need to be dominated and controlled in the bedroom. It was her domain. That's why I was more than happy for Harlow to take control of this moment. I need her to lead.

"Is it safe to come down?" Leighton bellows from upstairs.

Sitting back on her heels, Harlow watches me straighten my clothing back into place. There's a healthy dose of intrigue in her hot and heavy gaze. I'll happily be her guinea pig again for anything else she learns.

"It's safe," I call back.

"Could've lied," she mumbles. "Now he's gonna come and sing *Mamma Mia* down here too."

CHAPTER 23
HARLOW

SAD MONEY – CALL ME KARIZMA

PULLING Leighton's baseball cap lower to cover my face, I tug the collar of my coat upwards for extra protection. With my long hair down, I'm hoping to blend into the buzz of people exploring Hyde Park in the sunshine.

Families hum around me, pushing prams or carrying picnic baskets. Kids squeal and race through the ancient bodies of oak trees. This undisturbed green space is a bizarre contrast to the city, a slice of nature in the heart of London.

"There's a bench up ahead opposite the lake," Enzo's voice whispers into my ear. "Sit down there. We have a perfect line of sight."

I adjust my headphones. "I don't need a team of agents watching my every move. He isn't going to hurt me."

"The last we saw of your father, he broke into our house with a weapon. I'm not taking any chances. If I had my way, you wouldn't be meeting that wanker at all."

"He's out of rehab," I justify under my breath. "That's something. I have to give him a chance to explain himself."

"Doesn't make him any less of a security risk," he cuts back. "Stay alert and keep it short. If you need anything, you know the signal. Our agents will come running."

"Got it."

"Good luck, little one. I'll give you some privacy."

He ends the call, and I tuck my headphones away in my pocket. The peeling varnish on the bench is cool beneath my butt as I take a seat. In front of me, a glimmering lake wraps around the intimidating presence of trees far older than London's industrialisation.

The request came in a few days ago as we were leaving the hospital. It was another painfully silent visit, with Hunter staring into space, unresponsive. He refuses to interact with anyone, and I can't look at him without sobbing my eyes out.

I broke him.

And I'm scared that it's permanent.

When Enzo showed me the email from my father, I finally cracked and agreed to meet him. I can't fix Hunter's agony right now, but I can offer my father the chance to explain himself. That's still within my control, if nothing else.

Leg jiggling with nerves, I watch the ducks bob across the lake water. It feels good to be out in the fresh spring air after being cooped up inside all week, only leaving the house for therapy or to visit the hospital.

"Harlow?"

I recognise his voice without looking up. Shuffling up to me in jeans, a dark zip-up jumper and an oversized raincoat, my father halts a few feet away. He looks like a completely different person to the gaunt, inebriated ghost who first re-entered my life.

"You know my name."

His narrow lips hook upwards in a smile. "I wish I could take the credit, but your security team threatened some pretty horrific stuff if I called you Letty again."

Huh. Sounds about right.

Swiping a hand over his clean, dark-blonde hair, freshly trimmed and hanging over sharp blue eyes that match my own, he gestures towards the space next to me.

"Mind if I sit?"

I shuffle over to make room. "Sure."

Sinking down next to me, Dad spares me a fast, searching glance. I try not to squirm as he studies my features. Even if it's subconscious, I trust him for reasons I can't fathom. My racing heart recognises him even if my brain doesn't.

"You're so grown up," he croaks. "I wasn't sure if I'd recognise you when we met again. I spent so many years picturing what you'd look like now."

"When?" I repeat in surprise. "Not if?"

He wrings his hands together. "I never stopped believing that you were still alive. Did you… read my letters?"

My chest constricts with grief. "A couple with my therapist. You wrote to me a lot. I've kept them safe."

"Not much else to do in prison. I needed to find a way to keep you alive in my head. It helped me."

Staring ahead as a couple strolls past us, their limbs entwined while flirting, I clear my throat. The stark difference from Giana and her actions is indisputable. Dad never gave up on me. She did. That's something.

"How did you find me?" I ask tightly. "You tracked me down months ago."

"The answer to that question is a little complicated."

"Then uncomplicate it." I look up and meet his uncertain eyes. "I've taken a huge risk to meet you. I need to know what happened thirteen years ago."

Sighing heavily, he nods and looks ahead at the lake. I watch him from the corner of my eye. Everything about him is familiar—from the smile lines etched around his mouth, to the sparkle of his eyes and the wide set of his shoulders.

I know him.

We had a life together.

Distant fragments of a memory crash over me. Those same shoulders held my child-sized weight as we bounded across a quiet beach. He splashed into the water and threatened to throw me in before swooping me upwards and planting a kiss on my cheek.

More often than that, I dream about that beach. It featured in so much of my childhood. The pieces of it that I can remember, at least. Grandma Sylvie took me there. It was a place of happiness, before that was ripped away forever.

His voice drags me back to the present.

"Whatever Giana's told you… it isn't the truth. She's been playing an elaborate game for all these years."

My skin breaks out in gooseflesh.

"What kind of game?"

"Two truths and a lie," he answers flatly. "I'm no saint. I've always owned up to that. But she choreographed the whole thing, and even I couldn't stop her plan from working."

I pull the elastic band wrapped around my wrist and repeatedly snap it against my skin. If I didn't know that Enzo and his army spooks are watching our meeting, I'd be tearing whole chunks of hair out.

"You know about the drugs." He crosses his arms. "I'm not proud of it. She was so temperamental to live with, especially after you were born. Her mood swings were unpredictable."

My thoughts go back to the day she grabbed me during our meeting at HQ. I can still feel her nails cutting into my wrist.

"I'm not sure when things got out of control," Dad admits. "I owed people money, a lot of it. Work was fine, but it didn't cover the cash I was snorting on a daily basis."

"What did you do?"

He looks uncomfortable. "I worked for the Home Office at the time. Anti-fraud division, if you can believe it. That's where I got the idea to start forging identities."

Another family settles on the bench next to us. They're sitting close enough to overhear our conversation. Rising to my feet, I gesture for him to come with me.

"Come on. Let's walk."

"I don't want to piss off your protection any more than I already have," he frets.

Glancing around, I can feel the weight of invisible eyes. "Don't worry. They will follow us, I'm sure."

Nodding, Dad falls into step next to me as we set off down the winding path through the park. He's a lot steadier on his feet than the unstable wreck who recklessly broke in before.

"I swore to myself that once my debts were paid, I'd stop," he says in a low voice. "But Giana was getting worse. It wasn't her violence towards me that I cared about; I was used to it."

I startle as his hand brushes my arm before releasing. The brief touch causes my heart to stutter.

"When I came home from work one night, you were doing your homework with a black eye." His voice chills. "She scared you into silence, but we both knew who did it."

"I don't remember that," I admit.

"It wasn't the first time it happened either."

Tiny sparks are firing in the back of my mind. The memories are there, swelling and growing in size. His words resonate, even if I don't want them to.

"She started to behave strangely," he continues. "I was convinced that she was having an affair, but when I caught her with a Bible one night, I knew it was something else."

"Wait, a Bible?"

Dad rolls his shoulders back. "She was carving scripture into her arm with a kitchen knife. I tried to get her to stop, but she came for me instead."

Pulling the collar of his zip-up hoodie to the side, he flashes a stretch of skin. The deep, uneven scar twists beneath his collarbone. I've got enough knife marks of my own to recognise one.

"She was never religious." He pulls his clothes back into place. "Things got worse. She was obsessive, borderline manic. Convinced the rapture was coming and we all needed to repent."

Dread slips down my spine. I should be disturbed by his story, but it all sounds sickeningly familiar. I've had the same fanatical nonsense crammed down my throat before, accompanied by the beat of fists on flesh.

"That's when I decided to keep forging identities. I was saving the money from every single job, ready for us to start a new life. We were ready to go. Passports, flights, the lot."

Halting on the pavement, I frown up at him. "You were going to run away with me?"

"I had no other choice," he pleads with widened eyes. "You weren't safe with her. She was getting out of control."

"Like how?"

"She'd plastered the house in printed-out hymns and scripture about Hell. I caught her yelling at people in the street, getting violent when I challenged her. It scared me to death."

I blink back tears. It's hard not to wonder how my life might have turned out if we did run away together.

"And then, you were gone."

He suddenly stops, looking up at the heavens while taking a breath. I fidget on the spot. I'm torn between wrapping him into a hug and running in the opposite direction. I don't know who to believe.

"She played it so well," Dad chokes out. "Her alibi was solid. Giana convinced the world that she was a hysterical, heartbroken mother trapped in an abusive marriage."

"They said I decided to walk home from school that day," I add through my own rising nausea. "Giana was running late from work, apparently."

"You didn't decide to walk." Dad gives me a grief-laden look. "I usually took you, but I was too out of it that day. She'd broken my rib, and I was in agony. Regardless, I made you swear long before then that you'd never walk alone."

"Then why would she say that?" I ask in confusion.

"Because it was all planned, Harlow. She told you exactly where to go. The kidnapping was a setup."

"W-What?" I stammer.

He tries to reach for me, grimacing when I take a protective step backwards.

"I could never prove it, no matter how hard I tried." Tears leak down his face. "I kept pushing for months, searching for any clues. Giana knew I was on to her and got me arrested."

"This can't be right."

"She testified that I was an abusive addict, and she was the victim. It all fit together like a lock and key."

"No…" I moan.

"The perfect lie. I was quickly convicted, and your case was left to rot. Giana skipped off into the sunset."

I want to scream and run for my life. This is another flight of fantasy, a horror-filled fiction being sold to gain my loyalty. He wants to destroy my mother. I know that. I'm being used.

"You're lying," I say as my courage fails. "She isn't perfect, but Giana isn't a monster. She would never do that to me."

"Harlow, please. I'm telling the truth. You've been lied to… she isn't the person you think she is."

"Neither are you."

"I'm still your dad, petal."

"No. You're not. I haven't had a father for thirteen years… and I don't need one now."

I turn to leave, and he grabs my arm. Immediately, I spot movement from the treeline ahead of us. Two black-clothed agents are already racing towards us to contain the threat.

"Let go of me."

"You aren't safe here," Dad urges. "That's how I tracked you down. I still have connections in the Home Office. Say the word, and I'll have us on a flight to Mexico with brand-new identities by tomorrow."

"You seriously think I'd run away with you?"

"Giana knows her days are numbered." His voice raises as panic takes over. "She's been threatening me for months. I don't know what she'll do to keep her secret intact."

"I'll take my chances."

"No! You're in danger here."

"The only danger to me right now is you," I reply sternly. "I heard you out. Now, we're done. I'd like you to leave me alone."

His grip on my coat tightens. "Please, Harlow. You have to listen to me. I won't lose you a second time."

Security is almost upon us. They'll batter him senseless if he doesn't let go, and no matter how messed up this whole charade is, I don't want to see that happen to him.

"I'd like both of you to leave me alone and settle your fight without involving me. I have enough going on as it is."

Peeling his fingertips from my coat, I shove his hand back towards him. The hurt written across Dad's face is a punch in the gut, but I clamp down on my emotions. He and Giana are cut from the same cloth.

"I'm so sorry," he hushes, tears glittering in his blue eyes. "I should've protected you from her. It was my job, and I failed. I understand why you hate me."

"That's the thing." I step backwards, needing space to breathe. "I don't hate you… or Giana, for that matter. Even though I should."

Dad nods with an unhappy smile. "I won't make the same mistakes again. You know where to find me when you're ready. Don't forget my offer."

Before he can be beaten to within an inch of life at Enzo's command, Dad turns on his heel and walks away. The two agents are about to blur past me to chase after him when I shout for them to stop.

Hyland halts at my side, searching for any injuries. "Are you okay? Did he hurt you?"

"I'm fine. Let him go."

"But—"

"Forget it. I want to go home now."

Looking conflicted, Hyland nods. I'm sandwiched between the two agents and ushered towards the park's exit where Enzo is waiting in a blacked-out SUV, hidden from the world and cameras constantly tailing us.

At the last second, I look over my shoulder. Dad has stopped at the edge of the clustered oak trees, watching us leave. Anguish is written across his entire shivering frame.

He lifts a single hand and waves.

I don't wave back.

CHAPTER 24
HUNTER

TAURUS – MACHINE GUN KELLY & NAOMI WILD

PROPPED upright in the raised hospital bed, I half-heartedly read the closed captions on the TV screen. I'm like the rest of the world now. Deafened by silence and desperate for unreachable answers.

The statement from Sabre has been signed off with Lucas's name, on behalf of management. Not Hunter Rodriguez. He doesn't exist anymore. My authority has vanished along with my hearing.

Officials are appealing for any information relating to Mr Lee Heston, also known by the alias Pastor Michaels. DNA evidence has tied this individual to the discovery of a mass grave in Newcastle.

It feels poetic that it's Sally Moore delivering the news on my screen. We finally have our killer pinned down by real, tangible evidence. It's the single biggest breakthrough in the whole case, and I'm not there to see it.

Her bright-red lips move with each sentence, but her words are lost in translation. I can't hear her sharp, irritating voice. Nor the dramatic channel's music associated with a breaking news story. The busy hospital ward around me is lifeless too.

There's nothing.

Endless, empty nothingness.

This man is the prime suspect in Sabre's ongoing serial killer investigation. The public is being urged to contact law enforcement and not approach this extremely dangerous individual if seen.

Pastor Michaels stares back at me from the screen. The single photograph that Frederick Houghton provided has been joined by many others from over the years. People are discovering that this bastard has been living right under their noses and coming forward to testify.

Years of aliases and bolt holes.

He's been hidden in plain sight.

The screen fades to black as the remote is deposited on the table over my bed. Her usual forced smile in place, Mum begins chatting like everything is normal as she arrives for her daily visit. I can see her lips moving, but nothing comes out.

She's been doing this for the past couple of weeks. I treat her the same as the others who've rotated through this room, bringing with them pitiful smiles and tears that turn my stomach. I tune them out.

After the explosion six years ago, I had a glimpse of the hellish reality waiting for me down the road. Partially losing my hearing back then was the scariest experience of my life.

Far more terrifying than assassinations, car chases, espionage and landing in war zones. Nothing compared. Nor did I think it ever would.

I was wrong.

That terror pales into insignificance compared to the moment my consultant explained the situation with a whiteboard and pen. The damage to my left eardrum is so severe, the limited hearing I had left has been permanently obliterated.

I've lost my last lifeline.

It's gone, forever.

Mum's hand touches mine, and I flinch in surprise. She appeared next to me without warning. Lips moving in an apology for catching me off guard, she automatically moves to brush my hair aside, but it's gone.

My head was shaved before the surgery performed to pin my broken skull. I haven't looked at myself yet. I don't need to see how closely I resemble a monster. Feeling the lumps and bumps of my bald head was horrifying enough.

"Doctor's buying a farm," she mouths.

I squint at her lips. "Wait, what?"

Mum speaks more slowly. "Doctor… thawing… pram."

"I have no clue what you're saying to me!"

Eyes softening, she sits on the edge of the bed and spells out a word at a time until it finally clicks into place in my head.

"Doctor… drawing up… discharge plan."

"Oh."

"Home soon… tough weeks… on the mend."

"No," I quickly blurt.

She frowns at me. "No?"

It's disconcerting to speak without hearing my own voice echoing inside my head. Another grim reminder. I've barely spoken to avoid the pain it causes to lance through my chest.

"I don't want them caring for me."

Mum shakes her head, appearing dumbfounded at me. She speaks so fast, I can only distinguish bits and pieces of her words. She's pissed at me now. Great.

"Your family!" Her lips carve out the words. "Love you."

"No, they don't," I repeat. "I'm a burden."

Eyes narrowed, she grabs me by the chin like I'm an insolent child.

Leighton was regularly on the receiving end of her lectures. I was more obedient than him as a kid. Apparently, we've reversed. I fucking hate irony.

"Harlow." The word filters through as I follow her lips. "Guilty… enough… home."

The rest of her response is shattered into confusing fragments. I can only ever pick up odd words here and there.

"This isn't Harlow's fault," I insist.

"Tell… yourself," Mum mouths angrily. "*Home.*"

She slaps something hard into my hand. I look down at the slim metal of my phone. The soft vibrating is almost thrilling now in a world of black and white, silence and numbness.

Harlow's name is on the screen. She texted me dozens of times this morning alone. Throat burning, I scroll through the increasingly upset messages. I never respond to them.

> Harlow: I'll come after my therapy session to see you. Do you need anything?

> Harlow: Please stop ignoring me, Hunt.

> Harlow: If you don't want me there… just say.

> Harlow: I dropped by. You were asleep. Coming back later.

Now, it's my turn to feel guilty. I was only pretending to be asleep earlier. She stayed for almost an hour, staring at the wall while clasping my limp hand in hers. All she did was cry, and it killed me inside to see.

I couldn't bring myself to butcher a conversation in mouthed words and scraps of paper. The quicker they realise the person they know is gone and never coming back, the easier this drawn-out goodbye will be.

The other texts vary in tone.

I'm sent regular updates from the team as Sabre continues to tick over in my absence. Leighton makes the most effort to keep me in the loop, weirdly enough. He's been helping out more and supporting Enzo at a senior management level.

> Enzo: The press release went well. Tips are pouring in. We're close.

> Leigh: Turn on the news. We're gonna catch this motherfucker.

> Enzo: Harlow called me crying. Text her back.

Theo: I've found an auditory specialist in the States. Emailing you the details now.

Mum gently shakes my arm again to guide my eyes back up to her mouth. The fucking tears are back. When she cries and looks at me like that, I wish the bullet actually had killed me.

"They love you," she repeats. "We all do."

And that's the problem.

Their love. It will drag them to the pits of this miserable existence with me. I've had a lot of time to think while holed up in here, and I won't do that to them. It's no life.

I don't need an audience for the slow death that lies ahead. Will I ever be able to work again? Live a normal life? I got used to the idea of living with partial hearing.

That was hard enough.

But I was grateful for that glimmer of hope, and I treasured it for years. Now, I'll never hear Harlow's laugh again. High-pitched and laced with such zest for life, it's impossible not to smile in her incandescent presence.

It's gone forever. I'll never hear that bright spark of hope ever again. Nor my parents' voices. Leighton's shitty attitude. Enzo's gruff complaints. Theo's sarcastic quips. Hell, my kids' first cries. Endless unrealised possibilities.

Gone. Gone. Gone.

It's all been stolen.

I squeeze my eyes shut and ignore the pressure of Mum's hand attempting to regain my attention. Eventually, she gives up. When I dare to peek an eye open again, she's left me in peace. Probably gone to cry in private this time.

The nurses helped me to stand and walk around last week. I've been moving more with each day. Without them here, it's difficult to wrench my legs into position, but I manage to stand up alone.

Disconnecting my IV port from the line attached to a bag of painkillers, I grab the nearest piece of clothing—a discarded hoodie. Leighton must've left it here. It covers my sweats and loose, black t-shirt.

I need out of this room. This hospital. This world. Nobody can look at me. Not even the doctors and specialists. I know what they're all thinking. *Oh, the tragedy.* It makes me fucking sick that I've become the gossip of tea breaks.

I'm not a charity case dependent on their pity to figure out what the fuck I'm going to do now. The last month has proven that I'm not needed. Sabre is safe. My family is fine without me. The case is being wrapped up.

I'm dead weight.

It's time for me to go.

Leaning against the wall, I pull on a pair of shoes and stumble over to the door to peek out at the male ward I was moved to not long after I woke up. The usual afternoon nurse is dozing, her chin propped on her hand.

Pulling the hood up to cover my bald, stapled head, I slip out and hope I'm moving as silently as the world is to me now. The ward passes in a soundless blur. It's easy to limp through the barely organised chaos of the hospital without being seen.

With no direction, I begin walking. My steps are slow and awkward, with regular pauses to regain my balance. London continues to thrive around me. I'm the silent ghost, locked out from its sensual whispers.

Afternoon fades into night. Office blocks become billboards for advertising, while coffee shops transition into packed bars for after-work drinks. To the world, I could be another jogger, taking a stroll.

They don't need to know the truth—that I'm a failed case study, the millionaire businessman brought to his knees by a single motherfucking bullet. In that instant, years of hard-won success vanished. My legacy died an early death.

Without my phone on me, I have no idea what time it is. The darkness is a cold prison that I walk into willingly. I don't want to be found this time.

I cross the Millennium Bridge, and wind whips around me. The twisted metal structure offers me a wordless welcome as cold air lashes against my face. From here, I can see the bright lights of St Paul's Cathedral, all lit up at night.

God is my witness here.

I won't take another step.

Stopping halfway, my elbows propped on the handrail, I study the domed structure of the cathedral. Warm strobe lights break the suffocation of shadows. Perhaps they're singing inside. What I wouldn't give to hear it.

Leaning forward on the railings, I look down at the black water of the River Thames beneath me. It's choppy, lashing against the bank. I can imagine the sound of crashing waves.

This entire city used to mean something to me. It represented a land of opportunity, the tempting luxury that success and fame afforded my family for our hard work. London is my home.

Like everything else, it's lost.

Just like me.

I'm not sure how long I stand there for, shivering in the frigid night. A storm is approaching. I can taste the electricity in the air. I'm left undisturbed as pedestrians rush to take cover before the heavens open.

I don't want to live anymore. This is no life. Don't get me wrong, I know that deaf people can function. Scrape by. Make do. Relearn their whole existence. I don't want to do any of that. I refuse, and that's my fucking choice.

I'll jump.

Quick and painless.

Hooking one leg on the railing, I take a step up. It's a big drop down to the river. Glancing around me, there's no one in sight. Not a single soul to stop me from doing this. I'm thankful.

This wasn't the plan. My life isn't supposed to end this way. I'd rather die doing what I do best than take the coward's way out, but I'm backed into a corner.

I don't want this life.

I should be back at Sabre, fighting for justice and battling corruption in the most sinister corners of the world. Protecting those who can't do it themselves. That's who I am.

Who I was.

Who I'll never be again.

Taking another step up, I teeter in the air. Fear takes hold, no matter how hard I try to crush it down. Don't blink. Don't hesitate. Don't even think about it.

If I do, I'll stop.

On the verge of taking the final step, the tension in the air breaks. Clouds release the first specks of rain. Sweet droplets kiss my skin in the most excruciating way, entrapping me on the verge of oblivion.

It's raining. Heavier and heavier. Water soaks into my skin and brings sharp sensations. The pleasure is so intense, like each individual feeling has been dialled to ten without my hearing.

Gasping for a breath, I tilt my head upwards. Fuck. It feels so good. Like I'm breathing for the first time in weeks. Air bursts in my lungs as I swallow the lash of rain on my tongue.

It's sweet.

Almost metallic.

I could cry in relief. Part of me thought I'd never feel again. Numbness had become my new normal in the hospital, but that smothering tomb is breaking wide open.

Swinging my other leg over the railing, I sit down on the edge of a dangerous drop. The metal beneath my backside is the only thing holding me in this world.

I'm soaked to the bone. The heavens are pouring down on me. Near hypothermic, I almost don't notice when someone taps my shoulder. It startles me back to the real world, where normal people don't sob in the middle of a violent rainstorm.

Phone pressed to his ear, Leighton sweeps his viridescent eyes over me, checking for injury. I watch his lips move in the angry vortex of the storm encapsulating us.

"Found him," he recites.

His hand snags on my stolen hoodie. Unpeeling his fingers, I push him backwards. "Leave me alone."

Shaking his head, he tries to reply, but I turn my head to silence his words. London has vanished in the blur of falling water, obscured from sight. The temptation of darkness still lashes below me, but the whisper in my head has quietened for a second.

Clarity comes, and I panic.

I can't do this with him here.

Slapping his hands on the railing, Leighton boosts himself up and hooks his stocky legs over the metal poles. He sits down next to me, holding on for dear life.

Waving his hand to get my attention, he sticks his phone beneath my nose. I look down at the text message he's typed out for me to read.

What the hell are you doing up here? Why did you leave the hospital without telling anyone?

"I want to be alone, Leigh. You can go."

His thumbs batter his phone screen as he types a response.

That's not going to happen. Please come down. Whatever this is… you don't need to do it.

"Just go. We're not discussing this."

Come home with me then. No talking required.

"Home?" I scoff back. "So you can all sit around, staring at me? Feeling fucking sorry for me? I'll pass."

He wavers in the air for a second when there's a powerful gust of wind. I move on instinct, grabbing hold of his sleeve so he doesn't fall. Leighton rights himself and types a reply.

Give me a chance to help you, Hunt. Just like you did for me. I know you're hurting, but this isn't the answer.

"I don't need anyone's help."

But we need yours. I need you. Harlow needs you.

I shove his phone away. "Nobody needs the help of a deaf man. You're better off without me dragging you down."

He sticks it back under my nose.

Deaf or not, you're our leader. We don't give a shit about your hearing. You're still you. So get the fuck up and lead.

Leighton tucks his phone back into his pocket, abandoning our stunted conversation when I scowl in defiance. He slings his legs back over the other side of the railing and lands on his feet.

When I think he's going to leave me in peace, he grabs my arm and tugs hard. I teeter for a breathless second, a millimetre from falling to my death, before gravity takes hold.

I fall backwards and hit the hard floor of the bridge with a gasp. The impact is absorbed by my shoulder as pain burns through the smacked limb. Leighton hovers over me, poised to block my path back up onto the railing.

"What the fuck?" I yell at him.

His lips move, but I can't make out what he's shouting back at me. The rain is falling thick and fast as I attempt to stand up. The burst of energy that led me here is gone. I'm cold and exhausted, in every way possible.

He won't move.

Leighton stands between me and the promise of death. I bat his phone aside when he shoves it back in my face, but he grips my hoodie tight and makes me read the message.

If you jump, then I will too.

"No!" I shout in a rush.

Leighton cocks an eyebrow. The challenge is clear. We're facing off on opposite sides of an impasse, neither one of us willing to back down or compromise.

"Please." I break down. "I can't do this anymore."

Kneeling down next to me, Leighton holds my shoulder tight as I decipher his words. "You can."

I'm bundled into his arms before I can fight him off. Leighton hugs me so tight against his chest, we could melt into each other. It's the first time my brother has hugged me in years.

I try to push him backwards to escape. His grip only strengthens, no matter how hard I shove him away. He clings on tighter and tighter, swallowing every punch I throw at him. Blow after blow. Insult after insult. He takes it all.

It's no use.

He won't fight back.

My body turns against me. I can't battle the fatigue anymore. I slump into his embrace and my head falls. Shoulders slump. Throat tightens. Eyes burn. Gripping my shoulders, he forces me to try to read his lips.

"Brother… will not leave… bridge. Staying… so am I. In… together."

Angry wind freezes the stray tears on my cheeks that have dared to escape my control. His cheeks look wet too, beyond the lash of rain. We're a pair of sobbing idiots, both trying to keep the other alive.

"I'm fucking scared," I admit.

Leighton's forehead wrinkles as he stares into my eyes.

"Me too," he mouths back. "Why… don't do… alone."

His hand claps my forearm and squeezes.

"I can't go back to that hospital, Leigh."

"Home."

The word clings to his lips in a tempting poison. More than anything, I want to be with my family. This isn't my choice. This pain. This dark, desperate walk, looking for an easy escape. Leighton's offering a different way out.

"I can't face them," I stumble. "None of you can bear to look at me. Especially not Harlow. She's disgusted."

He punches me in the shoulder so hard, it reignites the forming bruise from where I was pulled off the bridge's edge.

"Harlow… guilty," he spells out.

"She feels guilty?"

Leighton nods. "Really… bad."

Nausea curls in the pit of my stomach. I let her sit there today, sobbing her goddamn eyes out. Maybe she wasn't crying for me, but for herself. The sins she feels guilty for. I'm such an idiot for not spotting it sooner.

This wasn't her fault. I chose to jump in front of that bullet. That was my decision and, given another chance, I'd do exactly the same thing. It was worth it to save her life.

I can't leave her like this.

Not while she's blaming herself.

Reaching out a hand, I let Leighton drag me back onto my feet. His arm encircles my shoulders. Both of us are violently trembling from the freezing cold rain.

"Home," I whisper back.

We walk back down the Millennium Bridge, fighting to stay upright in the worsening weather. Leighton nudges his phone back into my hand with another message.

Can you have a mental breakdown somewhere warm and dry next time? I think I have hypothermia now.

He's fucking grinning at me, even though this is a complete shitshow. I came out here to throw myself off the damn bridge, and yet, I break into semi-neurotic laughter.

"I'll consider it."

Leighton claps my shoulder. "You pepper."

"Pepper?"

He rolls his eyes. "Better."

It takes all of my remaining brain power to decipher his next words, even when he talks deliberately slowly.

"Want… take home… compromised."

"Compromised? What?" I demand.

"Moving… safer location."

"Why? What happened?"

His lips move fast as I fight to keep up.

"Whole world… address… no choice."

Shitting hell. I've spent too long staring at hospital walls while they've been firefighting a growing disaster. I can feel his eyes on the flash of my bald head.

Tugging the hood further up to cover the gnarly staples pinning my skin back together, I pretend not to notice the concern on his face, even as it kills me inside.

Inside the warmth of my parked convertible down a side street, I discover my hospital bag already packed and thrown in the back seat. Leighton slides behind the wheel and passes my phone over.

I raise an eyebrow.

He shrugs. "Coming… bust out… anyway."

Shaking my head, I quickly bring up my text messages. The dark, depressive fog that's clouded my mind is still there, but I can think clearly enough to see the pain I've caused. I need to make this right before it's too late.

Hunter: I'm sorry. Still owe you that date.

It doesn't take long for her reply to come. She must've been clutching her phone, waiting for an update from Leighton's trek across London to fetch me.

Harlow: I'll hold you to it. Come home.

CHAPTER 25
HARLOW

ROOM TO BREATHE - YOU ME AT SIX

CURLED up in the back of Hudson's throaty Mustang GT, the tap of Theo's fingers abusing his laptop blurs with the latest pop song blaring from the radio.

Lucky is crammed between us, snoring her head off. She's been clingy all day. I think she's missed us despite staying with Enzo's aunt while we've been caught up at HQ and the hospital.

Our empty home disappears into the distance. I can't help but feel a twinge of grief. When Enzo revealed that we were moving, I understood the decision. This was my first real home in a very long time, though, and I'm sad to see it go.

Behind the steering wheel, Hudson is fighting off a yawn, his pierced face tired after a late night of packing bags. Only the Cobra team is being trusted with our new location.

I'm exhausted too, but for a different reason. Since speaking to my father, sleep has become an elusive luxury. My nightmares have gotten worse, and with the guys working all hours at Sabre, I've been sleeping alone most nights.

I scrub my sore eyes. "How far away is the house?"

"About an hour." Theo scans over another anonymous tip with pinched eyebrows. "I swear, people have nothing better to do than email us fake information. It's pathetic."

I glance over his shoulder to read the email sent to Sabre's tip line. This moron actually thinks their teacher is Pastor Michaels. Their *female* teacher. Another childish prank and, unfortunately, one of many received. Time wasters.

"You hear from Enzo?"

Theo nods while opening the next batch of emails to be checked over. "He's loading the last boxes up. It was a good call moving the big furniture last night. The press saw nothing and haven't caught on yet."

"Leighton and Hunter?" I worry. "They're safe?"

"Waiting for us at the new house."

Fear wraps around my spinal cord. "How is he?"

Theo glances at me over the black-framed glasses balanced on his nose. "He's… Hunter."

"And you're very Theodore. What's your point?"

He snorts in derision. "I don't know what else to say, beautiful. Leighton talked some sense into him for now. He's in a dark place. We need to help him get through it."

"Did you tell him about the auditory specialist you found in the States? That might help him."

Theo's lips purse. "He didn't respond."

"Crap. We can talk to him tonight."

"Worth a shot, I guess."

I stroke a hand over Lucky's head in my lap beside the red-leather journal I was jotting in. I don't own much, but the pages of dreams and secrets matter to me as much as the gold ring tucked into my bra for safekeeping.

Writing has kept me sane. There are months of entries here, documenting the fascinating world around me. Jude told me to take back control, and I've filled these pages in an attempt to piece my past back together.

As Sabre swims through a barrage of information, inching ever closer to the end of this chaotic case, I'm far behind, drowning in a sea of secrets.

I now know this is a battle that I have to fight alone. The priority is catching Pastor Michaels, and we're closer than ever. I can't distract the guys now with my mental anguish, especially not with Hunter still in a fragile mental state. We're both balancing on a knife's edge. He's the priority.

Over an hour later, we arrive at the red-bricked streets of a quiet Midlands town. It's close enough to the motorway for the guys to commute into London, but removed from the risk of cameras tracking us down again.

"How did you find this place so quickly?" I stare out of the window at billowing cherry trees, bright-pink blossoms and middle-class families walking their pampered pets.

"We're cash buyers," Theo replies. "Made the owners an offer they couldn't refuse, and here we are. There's still paperwork to do, but they were happy for us to move in."

At the end of a winding cul-de-sac, Hudson parks up on the curb and shuts off the purring engine. He flicks the remains of his half-smoked cigarette out of the open window.

"Time to pay up," he declares. "This taxi ain't free."

Theo shuts his laptop. "Do you accept takeout as payment?"

"I could be persuaded," Hudson submits. "The moving vans should already be here."

Sliding out of the car, Theo stretches his arms high above his head. My mouth turns into the Sahara Desert as his t-shirt rides up, exposing his firm stomach, narrow waist and the flash of blonde hair trailing into his jeans.

He flashes me a smile. "Let's take a look inside."

"Okay."

With a bone-tired sigh, I stuff the journal back into my bag. Lucky hops over me to escape the car, already yipping and wagging her tail as she drinks in the fresh, blossom-scented air. She hates travelling in cars.

"You like it here, girl?"

She barks loudly, and I follow her up the steep, brick-lined driveway surrounded by flowering trees that cast shade against the warmth of sparkling sunshine.

Two moving vans are parked up next to Hunter's cherry-red convertible that Leighton has been using to get around. Two heads poke out of the vans, bickering between wrapped furniture and boxes.

"I'm just here to supervise," Phoenix protests, tucking lime-green hair behind his ear. "You're the one with the brains, Eli."

"You don't need brains to lift boxes." Eli grimaces as he hefts a box over his shoulder. "Stop being a lazy son of a bitch."

"It's my day off work!"

"You think I give a shit?"

I watch Lucky launch herself into the back of the first van. She rugby-tackles Phoenix, and he ends up on his ass beneath her huge limbs and overexcited tongue.

"Fucking dog!" he bellows. "Argh."

Eli shoots me a thumbs up as he hops down, a box in hand. He offers Theo a nod of greeting before heading for the two-story house tucked amongst billowing greenery.

It's beautiful, adorned with white hatched windows, a wraparound porch and cute balcony swing. It's smaller and cosier than our old home, perfectly matching the quiet farmer's fields surrounding the small town.

An arm winds around my waist and squeezes.

"You like it?" Theo asks.

"It's beautiful. I love it."

"Good." He beams at me. "I know this situation is less than ideal, but I wanted to find somewhere that would make you happy. Silver linings and all that."

I'm distracted as Phoenix saunters past us, carrying two boxes labelled with Theo's name in permanent marker.

"Are you moving back in?" I ask hopefully.

Theo releases my waist with a shrug. "Figured it's about time. We need to pull together now more than ever."

My stomach flips. I can't help but ask.

"Is that the only reason?"

His lips stroke against my cheek in a breathless kiss. "You might have something to do with it. I don't want to live in my office anymore. I want to be with you every day."

Burying my fingers in the perfect blonde curls hanging over pale-blue eyes, I pull his lips to mine. He kisses me back with the biggest smile I've ever seen on his usually shy face.

"Does this mean we can make our own shared library in the house?"

Theo rests his nose against mine. "That sounds like the best idea I've heard all day. Go and take a look around, I'll help these two."

"I'll see you inside."

Shifting my bag higher on my shoulder, I run after Phoenix. Inside the house, multicoloured tiles meet polished, light-brown bannisters on the staircase leading upstairs. To the left, an archway leads into a decent-sized living room with an open-plan kitchen attached.

Complete with an original fireplace and stripped flooring, I spot the gleam of cupboards and checked tiles around the corner. The kitchen is a decent size, with a space at the back for a family-sized table.

Compared to the sleek modernity of Hunter's London mansion, this place is a welcome departure. I love the traditionalism and quirky sense of character.

"Leigh?" I call out.

Shooting upright from his perch inspecting TV brackets, Leighton curses as he smacks his head on the solid oak beam built above the fireplace's chimney.

"Shit!" he curses.

I wince as he rubs the sore spot on his head.

"Did you knock your brains out?"

"According to my idiot brother, I haven't got any for agreeing to buy this place," he complains. "Was the journey okay?"

"Bit cramped in Hudson's car with Lucky as well, but it was fine. Does Hunter hate it that badly?"

"You know he hates anything that isn't made of stainless steel."

He strides across the room with determination. Hands landing on my shoulders, Leighton backs me up against the papered wall and peppers kisses along my jawline.

"Fancy christening the place? The others can unload the boxes."

"Leigh," I gasp as his hips grind into mine. "Get off me, you lunatic. We have a houseful of people."

"I feel like I haven't seen you in days," he purrs throatily. "Don't take this the wrong way, but you look like shit. Are you not sleeping again?"

"Thanks for the insult. I'm fine."

"I'm sorry. How can I redeem myself, princess?"

"Stop being a fucking sleazeball and come help," Hudson's loud voice heckles from the hall. "Want me to punch him for you, Harlow?"

Utilising one of the new techniques Enzo taught me, I bend my knees and push my elbow out. It connects with Leighton's stomach, and he stumbles backwards from the sharp blow.

"She can punch him herself if needed," I retort.

Leighton groans as he rubs his stomach. "I'm never leaving you with Enzo again. He'll have you jumping out of helicopters in no time."

"I'm not sure secret-agent school is my kinda thing."

"I'm not sure co-running the company is my calling either," he admits.

"Honestly, I've been making it up as I go along and pretending like I know what I'm talking about."

I nuzzle his bristled cheek. "You're doing a great job. I'm sure Hunter appreciates you stepping up to cover for him."

His eyes cloud over. "He's out back. You should go say hi."

"Has he spoken?"

"Not much since I dragged him off that bridge."

Patting his shoulder, I sneak past him and head for the glass door leading to the back garden. Eli is in the spacious, slightly dated kitchen, unloading utensils and plates. He waves at me with a spoon as I pass.

"Good luck with that chatterbox."

Coming from someone like Eli, that's more than a little worrying. He's hardly the biggest talker around. Hunter must be stealing all his introverted awards from him now.

"Thanks," I mumble back.

Outside, the first hints of impending summer are beginning to reveal themselves as May approaches. The garden is bathed in shades of lush green ivy and sprouting wildflowers. It's overgrown and chaotic with weeds, but I love the untamed feeling of the shrubbery.

Far down the lawn, a long tangle of limbs and wiry muscles is sitting cross-legged amongst blooming daisies. Hunter is staring up at the cloudless sky, tearing out handfuls of grass while lost in thought.

My lungs seize up.

I have no idea what to say to him.

The baseball cap on his head almost hides the devastation underneath. The edges of a white bandage peek out the back, but I won't tell him that. This veneer of normality is the only thing keeping him semi-sane.

Sinking down on the soft pad of grass, Hunter's eyes follow me. He's dressed in his grey sweatpants and a loose, black t-shirt that conceals the weight that's dropped from his frame in the past month or so.

"You okay?"

He shrugs, his lips pursed.

I gesture to the house behind us. "Good?"

"Can we not do this?"

His defeated words strike me across the face, and I try to conceal my hurt.

"Do what?"

Hunter's eyes flit back to his bare feet. "You don't have to sit out here and babysit me. I didn't come home from the hospital for that."

If he wasn't recovering from a near-death experience, I'd throttle him myself. Instead, I snatch his hand and lace our fingers together. Hunter relents and glances back up at me.

"Do you have any idea how much I missed you?"

His eyes narrow. "Huh?"

"I missed you," I emphasise.

"You want… fruit tea?"

I bury my face in his broad shoulder. This is impossible. When I look back up, Hunter's eyes are drenched in sadness, and I feel awful for letting my frustration win out.

"I'm sorry. Still working on my lip reading."

"No, no. I'm so sorry," I try to enunciate. "We should learn sign language."

Hunter shrugs. "I know a little bit. Enzo learned some when I first lost my hearing."

Leaning close, I rest my hand over his cheek and stroke the softness of his beard. "Missed you."

A brief smile touches his lips. "Gotcha. Yeah, me too."

"Hungry? Theo's going to order takeout."

Hunter frowns in confusion. "Cake?"

I blink back the rising tears that want to spill over. I'm too tired to control my emotions, but he really doesn't need my pity right now. We'll get used to communicating like this soon. I need to be strong for him. We all do.

Hand dipping into his sweats pocket, Hunter pulls out his phone and drops it in my hands. I look down at the notes app open on the screen.

"Type," he explains.

With a nod, I tap out my previous question.

"Oh," he echoes. "Yeah, I could eat."

Standing up, I offer him a hand. Our fingers interlink as we walk back up the lawn together. In the kitchen, Eli has finished unboxing and now sits on the counter with a beer in hand.

He's watching Phoenix heft the dining table into place with Hudson, the pair sweating and cursing repeatedly. Leighton's in the living room, shoving our sectional sofa into place before wiping off his gleaming forehead.

"We're never moving again," he huffs. "Too much work. Where the fuck are the other three?"

"Jude's working late," Phoenix answers.

Theo appears in the doorway. "Brooklyn and Kade are keeping the press occupied while Enzo moves the last of the stuff. She already soaked Sally Moore while driving past on live TV."

"Please tell me that's gonna make the six o'clock news," Leighton hoots gleefully. "I will pay to see that shit."

"I'm sure the other channels will show it."

"Score." He celebrates with a fist pump.

Right on time, the front door slams shut. Everyone stiffens until the shadow of Enzo's intimidating frame enters our new kitchen. He's carrying several plastic bags of groceries and wearing a tired grimace.

"We are never, ever moving again," he grunts.

"That's exactly what I just said!" Leighton grins and helps himself to the multipack of beers in one of the bags. "Fuck the rest of the boxes. Let's drink and order food."

"Amen," Enzo praises. "I am shattered."

Everyone gravitates towards the living room, helping themselves to beers and seats. Tucking himself into the corner where no one can engage him in conversation, Hunter sits on the floor and begins to drink alone.

It causes intense pain to flare through my heart again. He looks as broken as I feel inside. This move hasn't patched over the wounds that are still threatening to break us for good.

"Angel?"

Enzo wraps his arms around me from behind and rests his chin on the top of my head. I relax into his embrace, letting my forced brave face fall off. We're alone in the kitchen.

"This place is really nice. Looks like you might get that quiet, countryside life after all."

"I'm glad you like it," he rumbles. "I'd go back to the city in a heartbeat if we could, but it isn't safe anymore."

"Why? You hate London."

"Because Hunter hates hiding," Enzo replies. "I'd suck it up for him. He said anything?"

"Not much. Communicating is a bit tricky. I didn't know that you could speak sign language."

He cuddles me tighter. "Only the basics. We started learning years ago, but when the hearing in Hunter's left ear stabilised, we stopped."

"Can you teach me?" I request.

My heart rate triples when his hand smacks my ass. He's fully obsessed with spanking me at this point.

"You want a lesson, little one?"

Gripping the countertop, I push backwards against his crotch. Enzo grunts under his breath, a meaty palm moving to clasp my hip.

"Depends on how good of a teacher you are," I return.

"Why don't I bend you over this counter and eat your cunt to prove myself? Feel free to rate my performance then."

My core quivers at his filthy words. The mental image alone is enough to make me wet. He's become an insatiable animal since we slept together for the first time.

"Somehow, I think the others might have a problem with you doing that in front of Hudson, Phoenix and Eli."

"I've seen their pasty asses sprawled out after fucking enough times. Brooklyn loves an audience."

"Thanks for that mental image."

Enzo snorts. "You're so welcome."

"Hey, guys," Theo calls from the living room. "Come and choose what you want. We found a decent Mexican restaurant a few miles away."

Leaning over my shoulder to graze my ear with his teeth, Enzo mutters a curse word that makes me blush. I disentangle myself from his arms and head for the living room, leaving him to adjust his snug jeans.

"I'll have anything." I snag Leighton's beer from his hand. "The spicier, the better."

Theo wrinkles his nose. "I can't believe they corrupted you into liking spicy food."

"Don't be a pussy, Theodore." Phoenix snickers, his head pooled in Eli's lap on the sofa. "We'll win you over to the dark side one of these days."

"Not gonna happen."

With my stolen beer in hand, I plonk down next to Hunter. He's frowning at the spider-like cracks in the bricks around the fireplace. Amidst the bickering and insults, his silence has already been forgotten.

He's becoming a ghost.

No. I won't allow that.

I won't let him fade away. Even if he wants us to let him do exactly that. We vowed to face this as a family, and that's what we're going to do. Leighton dragged him home for a reason.

Tapping his leg, I point towards Leighton's phone. "Food?"

Hunter shrugs. "Sure."

Ditching my beer, I curl up on the hardwood floor and use his shoulder as a pillow. My eyes are so heavy, even the hard floorboards don't bother me. Hunter hesitates before his arm wraps around my torso to pull me closer.

His heart is pounding fast, panicked even. Something isn't right. Sliding the phone from his pocket, I manoeuvre his thumb to unlock the screen and bring the notes app back up.

What's wrong?

He hesitates before whispering back. "Nothing."

I can feel your heart going crazy.

"I'm fine."

I subtly point a finger around the room, indicating to the others still arguing over food choices. No one is listening to our conversation. I feel Hunter's chest vibrate with a sigh.

"I hate this," he murmurs, barely audible. "I can't hear a word of what anyone's saying, and it's freaking me out. I feel like I don't exist."

My breath catches as I tap out a response.

I know how that feels. It's terrifying, but you didn't let me go through it alone.

"That was different. I need to get a fucking grip."

You're allowed to struggle. That doesn't make you weak.

"Doesn't it?" he sighs back.

Before I can jab him in the ribs, Leighton's loud voice interrupts our conversation. He's managed to turn on the TV, though it's still resting haphazardly against the fireplace. The six o'clock news is playing a report from outside our old house in London.

"Brooklyn West, former resident of the infamous Blackwood Institute, has never been one to play well with media requests."

Phoenix laughs at the reporter's sarcastic tone. "That's one word for it."

"She'll love that," Eli concurs.

A clip is shown of Brooklyn reversing out of the driveway in a company car, the window rolled down as she lights a cigarette caught between her teeth. Reporters are screaming questions about us and the case at her.

It's raining heavily in London. She takes full advantage of the torrential downpour, yelling while hitting a huge puddle next to the nearest news crew. It sprays outwards with the impact.

"Fuck you, goddamn vampires!"

Sally Moore emerges from the dirty tidal wave of water, soaking wet with mascara trailing down her cheeks. She walks up to the camera and forcibly shoves it away to stop filming her embarrassment.

"Oh my God." Leighton clutches his belly as he falls into hysterics. "That's the best thing I've ever seen. I'm gonna print her face off and frame it."

Even Hunter is smirking as he drinks his beer, watching Phoenix replay the clip several times. I bet the rival news station thanked their lucky stars they captured this footage. It plays very badly for Sally's channel and her reputation.

"Serves her right," Enzo remarks.

Theo nods in agreement. "I hope she gets sacked."

"Or goes viral looking like a soaking wet clown."

Flicking over to a movie, Leighton bounces from the room to retrieve more beers. I gesture for Enzo to pass me the remote and quickly flick the subtitles on so Hunter can read them.

He drops a kiss on my forehead. "Thanks."

"Welcome," I mouth back.

Snuggling closer to him, I let my aching eyes glide shut. Hunter's head slumps as he nestles his face in my hair. With his arms around me, I try to lock the plague of bad thoughts into a little box. Numbness is approaching.

I'm so tired.

Five minutes won't hurt.

CHAPTER 26
HARLOW

HOTEL – MONTELL FISH

THE VIBRATING *engine of a car hums beneath me. Details come in flashes—the swinging dice hanging from the mirror, a radio playing, morning mist leaking across the road.*

I'm... scared.

"Get your dirty feet off the dashboard, Letty," a cold voice lashes.

With fear straightening my spine, I watch the mud-caked leather of my school shoes lower from the dashboard. Someone's clicking their tongue in the seat next to me.

"Why are you taking me to school?"

"Your father is passed out drunk." Mummy's voice is thick with disgust. "After school, you will walk home by yourself. Understood?"

I'm frozen by confusion.

"Why, Mummy?"

"Because," she snaps. "Walk through the field with the blackberry bushes. You'll be fine."

"I'm not supposed to walk home alone. Daddy said so."

"I'm telling you, Letty. Not him. Do as you're told."

"What if I get scared?"

"I don't give a shit! You will walk home."

Grabbing my wrist, she twists until tears burn in my eyes. The ink splotches of dark bruises beneath her grip peek out from underneath my uniform. It still throbs from the other night.

I tried to ease the Bible from her hands—she was asleep with it on the sofa again. Mummy attacked me instead, smashing the worn leather into my body over and over as she wrenched me around the room.

"You never do as you're told. The devil's in your blood, Letty. I'm trying to save you from him."

"The d-devil?"

Her bloodshot eyes meet mine, lit with a manic gleam. "This will be our redemption. We have to atone before the rapture comes."

"I d-don't understand."

The scream of brakes accompanies my body being thrown forwards against the seatbelt. Mummy slams her hands on the wheel and her cheeks soak with tears as she screams abuse at me.

Her palm slaps my cheek so hard, I bite down on my tongue. Blood floods into my mouth, hot and coppery. Holding my aching cheek, I look through my tears up at her.

"Please, Lord," she mumbles to herself. "Show me the righteous path away from my sins. Forgive me for what I must do."

I tug on her shirt sleeve, bracing myself for another slap.

"Mummy? Are you okay?"

Wiping her tears aside, she spares me a frenzied look. "This is for your own good. You're a sinner, just like me."

"But, Mummy—"

"Enough! He's going to save us both, Letty. Everything will be okay now. The Lord is going to forgive us. I just have to pay the price first."

"P-Price?" I stammer.

She strokes my tears aside with a sick grin.

"That's you."

Someone roughly shaking me awake cuts through the hazy dream. I shoot upright in a state of panic. The darkness of the room is cut by moonlight soaking through the window.

I'm lying on tangled, sweaty sheets. Gasping for air, my lungs feel like they're on fire. I can still feel the car vibrating beneath my butt and the rush of blood to my sore, swollen cheek as my mother struck me over and over again. Her anger knew no bounds, even then.

The real world settles around me, but the widened torment of my mother's eyes is superimposed over the room. Her voice clings. Echoing. Sinking deep into the depths of my brain and dissolving into bloodied shimmers.

"Harlow! Snap out of it."

I scoot backwards to get away from the giant in front of me. He's kneeling upright in the bed, sandwiching me in with another lump of muscle on the other side. Their faces settle into focus.

Hunter. Enzo.

Both look wide-eyed with terror.

"Where am I?" I whimper.

"Your new bedroom," Enzo explains in a rush.

"But we were… the dinner, then… I can't remember…"

"That was earlier on. We came upstairs hours ago," he explains calmly. "You've been thrashing and crying out for a while, but we couldn't wake you up."

His explanation redoubles my anxiety. It happened again. I've lost time. It's been a while since I last fell into one of dissociation's bottomless pits. I can't remember a thing after falling asleep on Hunter's shoulder. It's a complete blur.

"She knew," I pant, fisting the sheets. "She knew!"

"Harlow, breathe. You're not making any sense."

"Giana knew!"

"Knew what?" Enzo demands.

"She did it… it was all her…"

His fear-laden eyes widen further. "What do you mean?"

Unable to answer him, I fall back into hyperventilating. Another pair of arms bands around me, and I'm pulled against Hunter's bare, tattooed chest. His lips meet my ear as he squeezes tight, and the burst of pain is welcome.

"Take a breath," he advises. "In for four, out for four."

"No… no… she knew. I don't understand."

"Calm down," Enzo urges. "What did Giana know?"

"No! Please, don't let him take me!"

Throwing out a fist, it catches Enzo right in the jaw. He barely flinches, grabbing my wrist instead to prevent another blow. In an instant, he vanishes. My mother is bruising my skin all over again, slashing into my veins with her hatred.

"Get away from me! No!"

He lets go like I've burned him.

"Please, Harlow. It's me."

Shoving Hunter away next, I fall from the bed and cower in the furthest corner from them both. I can't do this. It was staring me in the face all along. The harrowing truth.

Right there, reality was taunting me with the future that was stolen through blood and violence. She took it. Her. The one person in the world whose job it was to keep me safe.

I didn't believe it.

Dad tried to warn me.

I threw it all back in his face and refused to believe the truth. That scenario was too disturbing to contemplate. I should've known by now that nothing is ever too evil. Humans hold the depraved ability to exceed all expectations.

"Please," Hunter begs from the bed.

"Say something," Enzo implores.

Shaking my head, I grab handfuls of my hair instead. Enzo lunges for me too late. I tear at the fragile strands, ignoring the sharp sting and light trickle of blood on my scalp.

"Harlow! Stop!"

"Leave me alone!" I shout back.

Waving at Enzo to back off, Hunter kneels on the bare floor of my new bedroom and knee-walks towards me. I watch him approach through the hot blur of tears.

Without his baseball cap on as armour, he looks worse than me now. We're both sporting balding heads and visible anguish. How the tables have turned.

"Sweetheart." He raises his hands. "It's just me."

"Too much… too much…"

"Can I hold you? Is that okay?"

Rubbing my face with trembling hands, I manage a timid nod. Hunter nods back and his hands curl around my forearms. I'm gently eased into his lap, and the moment his arms pull me close, I let myself implode.

"Shhh, I've got you," he hushes. "You're not alone, remember? That's what you said to me. The same goes for you."

Burying my face in the warmth of his neck, he smells the same as he did a few months short of a whole year ago, holding me in the darkness of the hospital as we hid from the media's first show of depravity.

We've always kept each other safe, but he can't protect me from the past. Not this time. It's rushing up to meet me.

A calloused hand strokes down my spine, and I feel the brush of Enzo's head against mine. He boxes me in from behind until I'm enveloped in both of them.

I'm safe.

My guys are here.

The monster isn't waiting for me amongst the blackberry bushes. They hold me in silence until I can draw a ragged breath. We're sitting on the floor in darkness, shivering from the cool air while the rest of the house sleeps.

"Alright, let's move to the bed," Enzo implores. "It's cold on the floor. I don't want you to get sick."

Too tired to lift my head, I let him pull me from Hunter's lap. My legs band around his midsection as I cuddle closer to his warmth. I'm so cold and tired. More than physically. Every single part of me is done with this world.

I want this all to be over, but it won't end when Pastor Michaels is rotting behind bars. It won't even end when I figure out why the memories of my mother haunt my nightly dreams.

The damage is done.

It'll always be there—festering, digging deeper, nesting into the pits of my brain. I need to dig it out. Tear it fibre by fibre if necessary. I can't keep living like this.

"No, stop that." Enzo traps my hand as I begin to pull again. "Please, baby. We're here."

"I can't escape what he did to me, no matter where I go," I choke out. "It's always going to be there, isn't it?"

"Maybe," he admits uncertainly.

A sob tears from my chest.

"But you're so much more than what he did to you. Don't let him win now. We've come too far for that."

The bed dips as Hunter slides back in, his anxious eyes darting over us. Blinking through my tears, I catch Enzo's hands moving fast. Hunter replies with several waves. I think they're speaking sign language.

"What are you saying?"

Enzo halts, kissing my temple. "Hunter's suggesting that we jump on a plane and leave the country tomorrow."

"For real?"

Hunter bobs his head. "I'm done. You are too."

Sucking in a breath, my cheeks sting with tears. "It's my fault, isn't it? I've done this to you all."

"Harlow, no."

"The media rampage, Sabre falling apart, Hunter's accident, the move… everything. I've ruined your lives."

"Don't you dare," Enzo scolds again.

The cruel lash of his voice causes me to flinch. Engulfing my face in his huge hands, he forces me to meet his fiery amber eyes. Determination still burns bright.

"You are the best thing that's ever happened to us, Harlow Michaels. I won't hear you talk about yourself like that. We've been dealt a shitty hand, but that is not your fault."

Hunter's hand snakes out and takes mine. It's the first contact he's initiated for a long time. I meet his widened cocoa eyes, the irises spiked with defeat.

"I love you," he says simply.

Enzo's thumbs stroke across my cheeks. "I love you."

My eyes flutter shut in pain. The truth tears itself free. I'm being selfish, but I can't let them go. Not now. They're the only thing keeping me alive and fighting.

"I love you," I reply to them both. "Too much."

"No such thing as too much," Enzo murmurs.

Leaning close to press a kiss on my nose, he hesitates, battling with himself. Despite Hunter's gaze trained on us both, I break his indecision and slant my mouth against his.

Enzo's hesitant at first, then his mouth melts into mine and we collapse into each other. The tip of his tongue brushes mine, asking a silent question. I reply by letting my lips part, inviting him to deepen the kiss.

A hand lands on my thigh, teasing bare skin as the oversized t-shirt I'm wearing rides up to my waist. But Enzo's hands are still on my face. It's Hunter drawing slow circles against the sensitive flesh of my upper thigh.

With both of them touching me, a spark is lit deep inside my core. The suffocation of pain and fear gives way to a low burn of desire. I can't hold back the darkness in my head alone. I'm going to drown if they don't offer me a lifeline.

"We need to stop," Enzo says against my mouth. "I don't wanna take advantage."

Feeling emboldened by the intimacy of midnight darkness, I nudge him aside and drag Hunter closer instead. Unlike Enzo, his lips greedily meet mine. I can see the same gaping chasm in his eyes. We both need this right now.

Dragging a hand down the sharp blades of his clavicles, I trace the dark swirls of tattoos that paint the violent thunderstorm on Hunter's skin. Muscles tightening, I stroke down his firm abdominals next.

Every inch of him is a canvas to be explored, from the curling smoke of his tattoos to the healing stitches that traverse the entire length of his skull. Hunter is a patchwork quilt of his stubborn will to survive, no matter what.

"You're giving him all the attention now?" Enzo growls out. "I don't mind sharing, but I'm gonna need to see more of your gorgeous body first."

"Thought you didn't want to take advantage?"

"Fuck it," he decides.

"Such a gentleman," I quip back.

"I'll show you a fucking gentleman."

He lifts the hem of my t-shirt, and I'm forced to break the kiss with Hunter so it can be tugged over my head. Beneath it, I'm wearing a pair of bright-pink girl boxers and nothing else. Goosebumps race over my skin.

"On your back, brother," Enzo orders.

Hunter must've read that on his lips. He eases backwards on the bed, stretching his long legs out. I'm left dangling over him as Enzo holds me by the hips, raising my behind into the air like I'm his puppet.

"Remember what I said in the kitchen?" Enzo's lips tease the edge of my panties. "I'm gonna eat your cunt while Hunter watches now. Would you like that, angel?"

I gasp as he tugs my panties down, exposing the wet heat between my thighs. The cool air kisses my pussy lips in the most excruciating way. I'm left completely naked and at his mercy from behind.

"Answer me," Enzo demands.

"Yes, please."

He smacks my ass, sending spikes of electricity up my spine. "What did I tell you to call me?"

"Sorry… sir."

"Good girl. I want to see you looking after my brother too."

Pressing my lips against Hunter's pectorals, I drag my lips downwards. "What should I do, sir?"

Pain spikes through me as Enzo's palm cracks against my ass cheek again. "Suck his cock. If you do a good job, I'll let him fuck you next. He's waited for a very long time."

Breath held, I meet Hunter's gaze before dipping a hand inside his sweatpants. *Ah, hell.* He hasn't bothered to put any boxers on. The generous sheath of steel trapped inside is hard and eager to see me.

"Fuck," he moans.

I wrap a hand around the base of his dick. Feeling emboldened by their gazes fixed solely on me, the whispers in my head die down to a low murmuring. All of my attention is on the task at hand as I drop a kiss against Hunter's length.

His hips raise, silently seeking more. Trailing my lips to the head of his dick, I spare him a quick glance beneath my eyelashes before taking it deep into my mouth. His eyes roll back in his head with another moan.

My confidence has grown so much when it comes to being physically intimate. I'm no longer terrified of someone else's touch, and seeing the power I hold over them is so empowering.

They make me feel beautiful and wanted. With my mouth driving them to the edge of falling apart, I become their deity. They worship me and fall victim to whatever I desire.

It's heady. I'm more than the timid shell of a person they rescued from the hospital, broken and alone in the world. I can bring these men to their knees.

"So perfect," Enzo praises, stroking my tingling skin. "Don't stop."

Keeping a gentle grip on Hunter's length as I bob my head up and down, my focus is derailed by the warmth of Enzo's breath on my entrance. His lips are planting open-mouthed kisses against my quivering pussy.

"Focus," I hear him whisper as I pause to moan.

Taking Hunter's cock back into my mouth, it hits against the back of my throat. I want to gag but swallow it down, loving the intensity of taking him deeper. He's huge, as I expected.

Enzo's tongue slides between my folds as he dives into his meal. It's a challenge to maintain my focus. When Hunter's hand reaches down to clench around my neck, I feel the first flickers of a release building.

I'm overstimulated, set to fall apart fast with both of them demanding my attention. The pressure of a finger easing inside my entrance is another shove towards that inevitable explosion. Enzo thrusts it inside me, curling his digit at the perfect angle to brush the tender spot I can't find myself.

"You're soaked, angel." Enzo's stubble scratches against my clit in a painful taunt. "I'm dying to fuck this perfect pussy, but I think Hunter's waited long enough. Don't you?"

I gasp as his lips are torn away. Enzo smacks my ass again with a chuckle. He seriously loves marking up my skin. The sharp burst of pain blurs with the desire swelling in my veins. It feels so good when he punishes me with a firm spank.

Releasing Hunter's cock, glistening with moisture and the first beads of pre-come, I sit up. The hand that was wrapped around my throat moves to my arm as Hunter tugs me closer so that I fall on top of him.

"Hunt," I gasp in shock.

I'm terrified of hurting him.

"I'm okay," he assures me.

This isn't quite what I imagined for our first time, but we almost lost him, and I hated myself in that moment for never showing him how much he means to me. Time is precious.

Raising a hand, Hunter catches the foil packet that's thrown over my shoulder. I hear the shuffle of Enzo dropping his sweats back on the floor before he settles behind me again.

Hunter's eyes don't leave mine as he rolls the condom on to his long, thick length. When he crooks a finger, inviting me closer, I move to straddle his waist. It feels weirdly good to be on top for once.

"I don't want to hurt you," I mouth.

"Go slow," he whispers back, running a finger over my skipping pulse. "You look like a fucking queen on top."

Positioning myself, I push the remaining flickers of insecurity aside and slowly sink down on his cock. Hunter's head slumps against the pillows as he groans loudly. He breaches me, and the pressure is exquisite.

I love watching his reactions. The others were more controlling in the bedroom, but this is on my terms. Hunter is trapped beneath me. Circling my hips, I adjust to his length before taking it all inside.

"Fuck, sweetheart," he cusses.

Hunter is big, but not as intimidating as Enzo's monstrous sheath. That was a bruising, blissful experience. Holding Hunter's biceps for balance, I begin to grind on him, being careful not to disturb his injuries.

His hips rise to meet me, but without the frantic urgency of the others. He's surprisingly loving and tender. His fingertips stroke every inch of my skin as he stares up at me with adoration.

One hand gripping my hip, his thumb finds my clit and begins torturously circling. I roll my hips and take him deeper, chasing my own explosions of painful pleasure. I've imagined this moment so many times.

The giant running a teasing fingertip up and down my spine never featured in these daydreams, but I love knowing that Enzo's watching every thrust. He's giving me permission, just like he said.

"Good job, angel," he encourages.

We're being choreographed while he watches us both from his throne, never once taking his eyes off our tangle of limbs. Every gasping pump of our hips is under his control. We're his puppets, performing on demand.

"You're not allowed to come until he does," Enzo says darkly. "Disobey my command and you'll be getting punished. I want you to hold it in."

Hunter chooses that moment to surge up into me, his hands now holding my hips to deepen his thrusts. Every slam of his cock into me sets my nervous system alight.

"Please," I whimper. "I can't hold it."

"I won't lay a finger on you if you finish now," Enzo warns. "Make my brother come first. That's an order."

He is turning out to be a strict master in the bedroom. I love how rough and unfiltered he is with his temperament. It's a glimpse of the man that the rest of the world sees. Around me, he melts. In the bedroom, he becomes a monster again, long enough to choke submission from my lungs.

Biting back a moan, I splay my hands across Hunter's chest and ride him as fast as my protesting legs will allow. He tweaks my nipple, sending sparks flying across my chest. His palm kneads my breast as he worships me with his eyes.

"You're so damn beautiful," he rumbles.

I'm so close. All it would take is a little nudge over the edge of the cliff, and I'll be falling into bliss. It takes all of my control to walk the tightrope until Hunter's nails are digging into my skin.

The biting lash of pain threatens to unseal the box of demons seething in my head, but I focus on Hunter's eyes trained on me. He's got me. Nothing can hurt me while I'm in his arms. Not even the invisible monsters that like to play in my head.

He grunts and smashes his eyes shut, still gripping me tightly as his release peaks. Being able to watch him come feels intimate. No one else sees this side of him, defenceless and vulnerable. I'm one of a privileged few.

Watching his implosion finishes me off. I did that. With a mewl, I feel my core clench tight. It hits me in an overwhelming influx of tingles, racing over my skin and driving me to cry out his name.

When his eyes flutter open, they're dark, almost black with the rapid expansion of his pupils. Slumping on his chest, I press a fervid kiss to his lips. His breath tangles with mine as we rest for a moment.

"Christ," Hunter gasps.

I tap his forehead. "You okay?"

He nods, his throat bobbing. "Yeah."

"Was it weird, not being able to hear me?"

His eyebrows knit for a moment. I repeat myself and he eventually catches on.

"It was different. Intense. I could almost feel more in the silence."

When I've caught my breath, Enzo's voice pops our bubble.

"Time's up, Rodriguez. Hand her back."

My cheeks flame. "I'm not some toy to be passed back and forth."

Enzo's hand snakes around my torso and takes a handful of my breast, squeezing tight. My nipples are hard as studs.

"Aren't you?" he snickers in my ear. "How disappointing. I thought my beautiful little slut didn't mind a bit of sharing."

Flushed, I kiss Hunter's lips in full view of Enzo and his snide attitude. Only I dictate when I'm done. Not him.

"And if I want to fuck Hunter again just to make you mad?" I challenge him without fear. "You'll have to play nice and wait your turn."

"Play nice?" Enzo repeats, teeth bared. "I'm not sure I know how."

"Better learn, Enz."

Pecking Hunter's mouth again, I stretch to my full height and twist to face Enzo's frown. He's perched behind me, a thick eyebrow raised beneath his shock of raven hair.

"Careful," I warn.

"How so, angel?"

"You're dangerously close to getting everything you wanted. Don't mess it up now by getting cocky."

"I'm just enjoying my victory. Don't pretend like you aren't too. You're fucking loving being shared. Admit it."

"I'll admit no such thing."

I attempt to climb off the bed to aggravate him further, but he darts up and blocks my exit. Stark naked, I put my hands on my hips and raise an eyebrow right back at him.

"Problem?" I sigh.

"You think you're done here?"

"You told me to look after your brother. Last I checked, he's more than satisfied."

Skulking towards me with palpable menace, Enzo backs me up until my legs hit the bed. His fingers wrap around my nipple and tug so hard, it causes my breath to catch.

"What about you?" Enzo smirks down at me. "Are you satisfied, little one? You only came once."

My knees knock together as he ducks down, taking a hardened nipple into his mouth. I was right. He really is the devil in disguise.

"Poor little angel," he breathes against my flushed chest. "Bend over for me. Hell, Hunter can even watch."

My pulse skitters at the thought. I offer him an innocent smile and rotate. With my hands fisting the bed sheets, facing Hunter and his interested eyes, I bend over the end of the bed.

"Damn." Enzo's voice is accompanied by the tearing of a condom wrapper. "Now that's a fine sight. All that dripping wet pussy laid out for me to see."

His mouth is going to be the death of me. I groan as his hardness brushes against me, one tiny move from surging inside my entrance. I'm still soaked from being with Hunter.

If this is what sharing will be like, then I could get used to it very quickly. I feel like a completely different person splayed out between them, begging to be touched and owned.

"You can't look away from him," Enzo grumbles in my ear. "I want him to see every single moan that leaves your lips. I want him to know that you're mine, first and foremost."

"You're cruel."

"Nope. This is me being fucking fair, my love."

Taking a handful of my long hair, Enzo pulls until my head rises up. I meet Hunter's gaze again. There's still heat there, even as he ties off the condom, full of his release. He looks ready to fuck me all over again.

"That's it," Enzo encourages. "Show him who owns every inch of your gorgeous body. Let him see it all."

The bed shakes as he shifts behind me. I gasp out in surprise when he thrusts inside my slit, quickly burying himself to the hilt since I'm already warmed up. I moan so loud, it's certain to wake up even the snoring Leighton from his dead sleep.

Enzo pulls back before surging into me again, taking long, punishing strides. He fucks like he rules—without mercy or restraint. We're all pawns to be manoeuvred in his eyes.

"My girl's still so tight," he grunts.

Eyes locked on Hunter's while Enzo fucks me from behind, he refuses to look away from the show we're putting on. This should be humiliating, but I find myself even more turned on.

This whole thing is a performance drenched in desire. If I wasn't a sinner before, I'm dancing with the devil now.

Slamming into me with each pump, Enzo batters his ownership over every inch of my mind. I can't think straight. My senses are overwhelmed by the sheer intensity of being trapped between two greedy men, both determined to devour me.

"You can come now, angel," Enzo obliges through ragged breaths. "Let him see you scream my name."

Twisting the sheets in my hands, I release a strangled pant for air. It's too much. My consciousness is splintering apart. I'm overwhelmed by sensations and the lick of flames burning through me.

Taking a scrap of control back, Hunter sits forward and claps my chin between two fingers. His mouth crashes against mine, and his tongue plunges between my lips. It tangles with mine in a sensual tango that causes my release to peak.

Crying out through the dizzying rush of my orgasm, Hunter swallows every last syllable. It's Enzo's victory, but his best friend won't let him have it. He still wants the final say.

I feel Enzo's movements grow stilted. He pounds into me with a final grunt and his grip on my hair slackens. The roar of him coming apart will probably wake up our neighbours.

"Harlow," he breathes unsteadily.

When he pulls out of me, I slump on the bed. Enzo collapses next to me in a heap, fighting for air. I don't think I can move a muscle. My limbs have turned into spaghetti.

I poke Enzo's side. "You alive?"

He groans under his breath. "Just about."

Shifting with a wince, I wriggle to ease the burn between my legs. Having them both inside me was an experience. My mind can't help but wonder if anyone else would be up for it.

"If we're sharing her, this better be a regular occurrence," Hunter supplies.

"I've never had a problem with him watching me have sex," Enzo whispers to me. "Want to know a secret?"

"Always."

"Hunter loves it too. He's a total voyeur."

I smother a laugh. "You can't tell me his secrets just because he can't hear us. That's mean."

Enzo smirks. "It seemed to me like you quite enjoyed an audience too, based on that little performance."

I bury my face in the sheets to shield my embarrassment, even though the growing bonfire of curiosity inside me wholeheartedly agrees. I did secretly love it, and I want more.

I can imagine Leighton and Theo being a good team.

Now that's one hell of a thought.

CHAPTER 27
THEO

DEAD – 228K

"JESUS, Enz. I really don't wanna die in this car."

"Quit whining."

Careening down the motorway at breakneck speed, Enzo pisses off a right-lane hogger driving a dated estate car. At this rate, we'll arrive at HQ in road-splattered pieces.

"Ben said to come quickly," he justifies while undercutting another driver. "This guy's refused to go on record for months. He could back out if we leave him waiting."

Glancing down at my laptop, I look over the case file again. Rosetta Stone is an important piece of the puzzle, but she's fallen to the wayside as we've assigned the full might of Sabre to narrowing down Michaels' current location.

That was before Ben's police contact finally broke and agreed to meet late last night. We had been sitting tight since he rejected our interview request. It was another dead end. Now, we have a second chance to nail this lead down.

All we need is an eyewitness to confirm our children's home theory and we have a solid connection between Michaels and Rosetta Stone. Our case against the sick bastard is getting stronger by the day.

The end is coming.

I can fucking feel it.

I look over my shoulder into the backseat. Harlow's curled up against the door, headphones tucked in her ears as she furiously scribbles in her leather journal. Something's been eating at her all weekend.

She hasn't been herself while slowly unpacking and settling in. Everyone has noticed it. Harlow refuses to discuss her violent nightmares any further, retreating into herself instead.

"She said anything else about Giana?" I ask quietly.

Enzo checks the mirror before answering. "Not a word after the other night. She says it was a bad dream, that's all."

"You believe that?"

"Not a chance in hell, but I can't force her to talk to us."

"Maybe she'll talk to Richards in her session today. He'll fill us in if we should be worried about something."

"I warned Hunter about this happening the minute he gave Giana Kensington the attention she wanted. Harlow's parents are screwing with her head for their own benefit."

"Isn't that what parents do best?"

He gives me a side look. "I wouldn't know. Mine are dead, remember?"

"Better dead than heartless assholes," I snip back. "At least you had parents."

Enzo winces, running a hand over his messy hair. "Didn't think. I'm knackered."

"Forget it. We're all wrecked at the moment."

"Ain't that the truth."

Looking out of the tinted-black window, I study the blur of greenery morphing into cinder-block buildings and drooping train wires. The team knows better than to broach the subject of parents with me. Usually, it's an off-limits topic.

Enzo may have lost everyone apart from his aunt, but he had something to lose in the first place. They will always be with him. My parents abandoned me before I could walk, and England's fucked-up foster care system became my family instead.

The team has always blamed me for walking away first after Alyssa's death tore our lives apart. There's a reason why. Truthfully, I abandoned them, just like I'd been taught to do before I could speak for myself.

That was my default reaction, regardless of the pain it caused them. It's one of many regrets I have about the last six years. I'm trying to fix that now.

"You get an update from Kade on that potential sighting?" Enzo asks.

Bringing up the file, I squint over the lines of information. "The tip came in from a bus driver in Exeter. Reckons he spotted Michaels leaving a church last week."

"Is it legit?"

"Hard to say. The whole country thinks Michaels is their next-door neighbour based on the bullshit sightings we've had coming through. Hudson's driving to Exeter to scout it out with Brooklyn."

Enzo nods as London's outskirts come into view. "We have to be thorough. If this bastard slips through our fingers now, I'll never forgive myself. We're too close."

I know his tormented thoughts are on our silent passenger in the back seat. I pack my laptop away and clear my throat.

"We'll get him, Enz. It's just a matter of time."

"Time." Enzo scoffs. "We've wasted enough of that."

"Nothing's wasted if it guarantees Harlow's future," I correct him. "This is her life we're talking about. Her justice. We promised to get that for her."

He scrubs his face and sighs. "Fuck off, Theodore. I'm all too aware of that fact."

"Then bloody remember it."

We fall silent as London's outskirts melt into busy city streets and mid-morning traffic. The blacked-out windows of his car hide us from any onlookers as we approach HQ's glittering height on the horizon.

After we've parked in the relative safety of the garage, we hop out and prepare to head inside the building. Harlow's tucked her journal into the bag hooked under her arm, but she leaves her headphones in, discouraging any conversation.

Her eyes are sagging with painfully obvious exhaustion. She's woken the whole house up with blood-curdling screaming for the past few nights. Even Hunter wakes up, deaf as a damn bat. It's like he can sense her distress.

I approach her and ease an arm around her shoulders. She offers me a weak smile as I tug a headphone out and peck my lips against her cheek before dropping my voice low.

"Come and find me after your session with Richards. Enzo's interviewing the witness. I'll be in my office watching the livestream."

"Sure," she replies. "You'll fill me in?"

"Of course, beautiful."

"Thanks, Theo. I appreciate you."

My chest warms. "Anytime."

ID badges scanned and stray employees greeted, we bundle into the elevators together. Enzo smashes his lips against Harlow's when the doors slide open on the tenth floor.

She's without an escort today—Leighton is taking Hunter to the hospital for a checkup with the audiologist. The whole team seems to be scattered across the country.

"You'll be okay on your own?" Enzo worries.

Harlow steps out into the foyer. "Richards is just down the hall. I'll see you guys later."

Her tentative smile is plastered on as we mutter our goodbyes before the doors slam shut. Enzo shifts impatiently on his feet, eyeing the floor numbers ticking upwards.

"Stop fidgeting. Whatever's going on, Richards will get it out of her. We need to worry about this perp first."

"Yeah," he grunts.

Enzo storms out of the elevator without another word as he reaches the interrogation floor. *Chatty son of a bitch.* I continue upwards until my office is in sight.

Despite settling into the blank walls and bare carpets of my new bedroom, this place still feels like home. I've missed its book-lined corners and warm light dappled across old case files.

The live feed from the room holding our tight-lipped ex-police officer fills my screens as I make a coffee to perk myself up. By the time I sit down, Enzo's slid into his seat opposite the silver-haired, elderly man in his cheap blue suit.

"Mr Prescott," Enzo greets. "Thanks for coming in."

Ben didn't go into great detail about how he tracked this dinosaur down using his old law enforcement contacts. We know this constable was on the lead investigating team that dismantled Genesis Home and three of its sister branches.

Like many others back then, Mr Prescott was silenced with a healthy pension and a promise that the government would punish the powers that be behind our string of children's homes.

Complete crap, of course.

We now know that the wealthy Catholic churches running our less-than-legal homes escaped punishment, buying off their victims instead. History was erased with crumpled cash and pursed lips, as it often is.

"No problem," he answers stiffly.

"May I begin by asking why you changed your mind? Last we spoke, you were very reluctant to engage with our investigation."

Mr Prescott straightens his striped tie. "We all signed non-disclosure agreements when we exited the force. I'm putting my neck on the line by being here today."

Enzo cocks his head. "Interesting. Is this standard procedure for a retiring officer of your rank?"

"Depending on their division. I worked for the major crimes unit up in Sunderland. Certain aspects of my career have been made classified."

This guy has clearly been around the block. It's rare that police investigations are hidden from public record, but it's not unheard of. Some information is deemed too sensitive.

"I understand you spent many years investigating a string of child abuse cases involving private children's homes in the area."

"That's correct."

Enzo leans forward on the table. "I'm interested in Genesis Home, in particular."

Mr Prescott swallows hard. "My partner and I spent many years building a case on that particular location. We visited on numerous occasions between the late seventies and mid-eighties."

"It has since been demolished."

"I'm aware," he confirms.

"We have reason to believe a person of interest to our current case resided at the property within this time period."

Nodding again, he twists the wedding band strangling his wrinkled finger. "We developed a relationship with the owners. Both devout Catholics and church members."

I sit back in my chair. In our line of work, we call out red flags like winning numbers on a bingo card. This entire timeline has been screaming of suspicion since we uncovered Rosetta's real identity. There's far more to the story.

"Did you find any instances of abuse?" Enzo asks brusquely.

"Numerous cases. We kept tabs on a number of minors as we built a case for prosecution. Excuse my bluntness, but I've seen a lot of battered children. The kids in this case were next-level messed up."

Enzo doesn't waste time taking notes. My fingers are blurring across my keyboard instead, and I know the rest of the intelligence department is watching in their own offices.

"I've seen the photographs you released on the news," Mr Prescott interjects. "That's why I changed my mind."

"The photographs of our suspect?" Enzo clarifies.

"He's been using a false name. Sickos like this always do. My partner and I knew him by another alias back then."

I lean closer, locked on the movement of his lips. Our hair-brained theory from months ago is on the verge of validation or destruction.

"You recognised him from recent photographs?"

Mr Prescott nods. "He was sixteen at the time, but the resemblance is there. I followed the cases of two children before they absconded from custody together."

"Rosetta Stone," Enzo guesses.

He does a double take. "You know her?"

Enzo waves for him to continue. "We do."

"Well, Rosetta was a person of interest in our investigation. She was in a relationship with a fellow resident that came to our attention for his… frankly, worrying behaviour."

"Worrying?"

"Another resident reported him, several months into the case." Mr Prescott's expression hardens. "He was accused of sexually assaulting a female. Rosetta, in fact."

My blood chills.

What the fuck?

"Rosetta? I thought you said they were romantically involved?" Enzo asks, confused. "Why would he rape her?"

"Rosetta maintained that story, but the witness was certain of what she saw occur between them. We performed a follow-up interview and the story changed."

"Changed how?"

"Our witness was sitting there with two black eyes and a crucifix-shaped bruise on her damn cheek. She refused to say another word."

Holy. Shit.

Pastor Michaels didn't just know his bloody accomplice from childhood. They attended the same abusive hellhole, and he already had a proclivity for rape as a sixteen-year-old child. She was his first fucking victim… that we know of.

Gotcha.

We were right.

"You're suggesting that management, *ahem*, intervened?" Enzo narrows his eyes. "I assume Rosetta refused to press charges?"

He shrugs it off. "She never spoke to us again. We returned to Genesis Home several more times. A matter of months later, she'd run off in cahoots with her supposed abuser."

Fists clenched on the table, Enzo shakes his head. "And none of this was deemed valuable for the public record? These sickos got off without prosecution. Not even a slap on the wrists."

"You think I wanted that?" Mr Prescott argues back. "Watch your tone, son. We tried our best to close that place down. I was just one man against a whole corrupt system."

Taking a moment to restrain himself, Enzo pushes his hair back and refocuses. We know better than most that money talks in this world, and it takes a whole army to dismantle something this insidious.

"I kept tabs in the years before I retired. Neither of them ever showed up again. They disappeared into thin air and left us with nothing but questions and no answers."

"I want a name," Enzo presses.

The suspense shatters into spectacular pieces as our entire case changes with two words.

"Michael Abaddon."

My hands are flying before Enzo's even caught a breath. I'm across all the systems that we're granted access to and some I've hacked myself—prison records, bank accounts, prosecution files—and there isn't a single shred of evidence after 1978.

Another ghost.

But our killer finally has a name.

"Michael Abaddon," I repeat to myself. "Pastor… Michaels. Fucker."

From the evidence I pulled when I hacked the High Court's sealed case files, I have a list of the children allocated to Genesis Home. Three rows down, there the bastard is.

Michael Abaddon.

It seems so innocuous, the typed letters of a child's name, lost to the gradual erosion of history and its sins. No one knew this kid would become a vicious killing machine decades down the line.

"Strange boy." Mr Prescott frowns to himself. "It was clear that Rosetta was being abused by him. Even at sixteen, Abaddon was a master manipulator. He scared the crap out of my partner."

Part of me wonders what Harlow would think of this. To her account, Mrs Michaels was a perpetrator herself. Not a victim of the same monster that imprisoned our girl.

"Are you aware of the suspect having any family?" Enzo questions.

"Not that I ever saw. Genesis Home didn't attract many kids with families. I was glad to see it demolished in the nineties."

Turning away from the interview, I trawl back through the scanned documents on my screen but find no more information on Michael Abaddon. By the time the case went to trial in 1994, he'd been gone for over two decades.

A perfect monster, born from the hottest depths of Hell. No prizes for guessing where Pastor Michaels got his extreme religious beliefs and love of violence from. This place practically birthed him.

The creator of evil incarnate.

My concentration is shattered by the scream of our emergency alarm erupting. The lighting shifts to a deep red as I startle, fumbling to reach for my laptop and open the secure server.

With a few clicks, I've narrowed the triggered alarm down to the third floor. Relief comes fast before dissipating again. It's not Harlow's floor, but she could still be in danger.

Tripping over myself, I tear from the room, swiping my gun from my under-desk safe along the way. My hands shake as I quickly fire off a text message to Enzo, telling him to meet me downstairs.

With my gun cocked and ready, the elevator feels like it's moving at a snail's pace. My ears are aching from the deafening alarm still screaming for attention.

The doors *ding* open on a floor now unrecognisable, doused in shadows and the neon tinge of emergency lighting. When the door to the adjacent staircase slams open, admitting a red-faced Enzo and several armed agents, I wave him forward.

This area is dedicated to staff—an expansive break room, showers and a cafeteria serving freshly cooked meals twenty-four hours a day. All are in chaos as people flood out, disgruntled and covering their ears.

"Fan out!" Enzo barks loudly. "If we have an intruder, I want them found."

"I'm gonna go check on Harlow," I shout above the noise. "She's probably freaking out."

He shoves two of his men towards me. "Take backup and make sure she's secure. This might be Michaels."

Flanked by the two agents, we return to the elevator and climb out on Harlow's floor. It's empty compared to the madness downstairs. Not many people come here as it's reserved for more informal meetings or appointments.

With an invisible hand strangling my windpipe, we clear the whole floor, heading for the final therapy room on the right. The door is slightly ajar, and my terror triples.

Stepping in front of me with a wordless conversation in hand signals, the two agents storm into the room. It's a matter of seconds before they shout back for me to enter.

Every step seals my dread. The room is empty apart from two still-warm, half-drank cups of tea on the low table and Richards' discarded binder of notes. They were here.

As I'm ordering the agents to sweep the whole floor again, I check my phone and notice an incoming message from fifteen minutes ago.

Harlow: I'm sorry. I have to find the truth on my own. It's the only way to save me from myself.

"Fuck!" I scream at the screen.

This can't be happening.

She wouldn't be that stupid.

Logging in to our tracking software, I search for the small dot that represents Harlow's live location. It's in the same fucking building as me.

When I call, a soft vibrating fills the therapy room. Tucked down the side of the high-backed armchair, I find Harlow's phone stashed inside the pages of her leather journal.

Her stuff is here, but she isn't. The pages of her journal blur with a hot, heady wave of sheer panic. Her phone was tucked in at the most recent entry, leaving it open for me to find.

Control is an illusion.

Control is an illusion.

Control is an illusion.

Ice spikes through my veins. The frenzied scrawl continues across three pages. The same four words, over and over again. This is bad; she's spiralling worse than we thought.

Enzo's contact flashes up on my phone and I stick him on loudspeaker while flicking back through her journal, searching for any clues.

"Yeah?"

"Tenth floor is secure," he growls down the line. "I've got Richards down here. He was locked outside in the staff garden and set off the alarm. His security pass is gone."

"Where the fuck is Harlow?"

"He brought her down here for some fresh air when she was triggered. She lost her shit and attacked him. Sounds like he was out cold for a while."

"Goddammit!" I slam a hand on the table, rattling a vase. "She must've set off the alarm herself as a distraction to escape. This was planned."

"What is she thinking?"

The journal is a crushing weight in my hands.

Control is an illusion.

"I think she's going for Michaels," I suggest.

We were so busy worrying about the threat that Michaels poses to Harlow, we forgot about the more destructive enemy lapping at her heels.

Herself.

"Motherfuck! She can't have gotten far." Enzo's gravelly voice is spiked with fear. "Not unless she had help."

We are in so much shit if she did. This wasn't a mere accident. It was choreographed and planned to take full advantage of the opening in her security.

"I'll mobilise all units and alert the local police departments to set up traffic blocks. We don't have much time."

"What is her plan here?" he asks, mostly to himself. "We're supposed to be in this together. I don't understand."

Pain practically spills from the journal's pages. I know what Harlow wants. The biggest thing that's been taken from her.

"She's looking for something."

"What?" Enzo snarls at me.

"Control."

CHAPTER 28
HARLOW

MAKE THIS GO ON FOREVER – HAHLWEG

SILVERY BULLETS of rain slam into the ground like machine-gun fire. God's violent wrath is punishing the earth for daring to challenge his almighty rule.

I watch with fascination from my resting place against the school's painted railings. The swollen storm clouds in the sky scream with the same rage keeping me upright.

It was impossible to sleep on the road while knowing what chaos and heartbreak I've left behind. I batter the life out of that thought before it takes over and I change my mind.

I don't have time to feel.

Not until this is done.

Beneath the brim of a baseball cap and oversized hoodie concealing my face, I wear a pair of sunglasses to hide from the world. Parents are running in all directions, dropping off children in their hurry to get to work.

It isn't long before a familiar headful of brown hair joins the crowd of disgruntled parents running from the morning rain. Her green eyes are downturned, hidden by a navy-blue raincoat.

Clutching his mother's hand tight, my half-brother, Ulrich, squeals in excitement as he splashes into a muddy rain puddle. Giana shouts at him to stop and drags him along, her annoyance clear.

Ulrich doesn't look much like her, aside from his hair. We all have the same mousy shade of brown on our heads. They disappear inside the bustling school, and that's when I move.

My feet splash through excess rainwater in a rhythmic thump. Each footstep mirrors my calm heartbeat. A cloud of determination has slipped beneath my skin and silenced my fear.

I've waited long enough.

The truth won't find itself.

When Giana emerges from dropping her kid off, I fall into step behind her. She's cowering beneath an umbrella to protect her from the stormy weather for the walk home.

The small coastal village of Croyde passes us by as we leave the school behind. I never thought I'd be back here again, but this time, I'm not running away from my demons.

This is a head-on collision.

My face is still tucked low, and I maintain a safe distance, ensuring she can't hear my footsteps. Giana walks all the way home in the rain from her son's local school.

The irony isn't lost on me. We've found ourselves back at the beginning, walking home from school together on a day that will change the course of our lives. I'm rewriting my own history.

When the bright-red door of her home appears, I falter. There's no telling what she's capable of. I've sacrificed my safety in the name of sanity, but this is a risk I had to take.

"Why did you do it?" I call out.

She freezes halfway through the picket-fence gate. Turning to find me standing a few short metres away, Giana's mouth falls open in shock.

"Letty? What are you doing here?"

I inch closer. "Did he pay you? Was that it?"

"What are you talking about? Where is your security team?"

"Or perhaps it wasn't for the money," I continue, removing my sunglasses to reveal my bloodshot eyes.

"Money?" she repeats. "What is this? Are you… having another episode? Do you know where you are?"

"I know where I am, Giana. Nobody else will be joining us. This is between me and you."

She hesitates, clutching her phone tight. I make a point of pulling out my coat pockets, showing that I'm unarmed with no secret phone or weapon stashed.

"It's just us," I assure her.

Giana bites her lip. "Why did you come here alone?"

"I thought you wanted to see me."

"I… I do," she stumbles, glancing behind her at the house. "Foster is at work. You should come inside."

With a quick look up and down the street, I nod and approach her. Giana's hands shake as she fights to unlock the front door, her eyes darting from side to side.

I take the house keys from her hands and unlock the door myself, gesturing for her to head inside. Her bag-lined eyes are locked on me. It's there again.

That look.

Fear-fuelled mania.

With a gulp, she enters her home and removes layers of clothing. I take a deep breath and follow suit. The last time I was in this house, it ended in disaster.

"Take a seat," she invites, opting for the cramped, carpeted living room on the left. "You want tea?"

"I don't have a lot of time."

Giana nods and perches on the sofa opposite. "I heard about the accident. How is Hunter?"

"He's alive."

"I'm sorry, Letty. You must've been terrified."

Even her apologies are tainted with lies. I can see it now. Everything became crystal clear as soon as I made the decision to retake control. Arms folded, I stare straight into her eyes.

"I remember," I deadpan.

She flinches. "Excuse me?"

"Let's cut the small talk. We've done enough of that. I'd like to have an honest conversation for once."

"I should call someone," Giana worries as she eyes me. "You're not well, darling. Let me call for some help."

"I'm finally thinking clearly for the first time ever. Put the phone down. You owe me the truth… for Ulrich's sake."

The blood drains from Giana's face. "What?"

"Nice school. Good to see you walking your kid to class now. Learned your lesson, did you?"

Her hands clench in her lap. I can see the blueish lightning strike of veins popping against her pale skin.

"You followed me?" Giana accuses. "What is this? Some kind of game? I won't have you threatening my son."

"I'm not you," I fight back. "I'd never threaten a child. But frankly, I think the safest place for him is far away from you. That can be arranged."

Her pink-painted nails are digging into her palms. She's slowly turning bright red, accompanying the rising hysteria gathering in her gaze.

The wolf has been backed into a corner, its sheep's clothing stripped off. We don't need to pretend to be strangers anymore. This charade has gone on for long enough.

"Walk through the field with the blackberry bushes." I brace my elbows on my knees. "You sent me to him, wrapped like a Christmas present."

"I d-don't know what you m-mean," Giana splutters.

"He was supposed to save us from the rapture, right? I remember that much. Why did you believe his lies?"

"Letty, please…"

"I won't say it again. My name is Harlow. You should know, it's the name *he* gave to me. Was that planned too?"

She looks ready to bolt from the room and call the police herself. The obnoxiously loud tick of her grandfather clock is the only sound above the downpour of angry rain outside.

I never considered Giana to be my mother, not in the real sense. Still, it's a painful stab in the heart to see the slow realisation spread across her face as she realises I'm not kidding around.

"I know everything," I repeat again. "So, drop the pretence and tell me the truth."

Her mouth snaps open and shut as the tears pool in her eyes. Panic and hysteria reign chaos across her face.

"Your father is lying. He's tricked you! I warned you to stay away from him for this reason."

"He is the only person that has never lied to me. I was just too stupid to believe what was right in front of me."

"Please," Giana begs. "You don't understand. He was always so controlling. You're being used by him."

There's that word again. Control. The invisible thread that undercuts our lives, whether we acknowledge it or not. I've been grasping in the dark for that elusive power long enough.

"I have never been in control of my own life," I admit, looking around her comfy family home. "All these months, I've been pretending. Acting like I'm the one in control."

Giana's poised on the edge of her seat, ready to run. "I don't know what he's told you…"

"Enough! Shut up and listen."

Fury jolts through me as I stand up, on the verge of wrapping my hands around her throat. The anger I've been suppressing for months on end is making it hard to see straight.

"You hurt me," I force out. "Not him. That morning, you were the one who told me where to go. For my own good, right? That's what you said to me."

She gulps hard. "This isn't what you think it is."

"I was scared. It was getting dark, but I had no choice. You warned me what would happen if I disobeyed you again. I was already limping and covered in bruises."

"Please—"

"Pastor Michaels was there, waiting for me." I let the tears splash across my cheeks. "He seemed… so nice. All I wanted was for someone to take care of me for once."

"I can't… I don't…"

"Don't what, huh? You don't remember agreeing to sell me to a mass murderer? You can't believe how unlucky you are that it didn't work, and I escaped? What?"

"I did not sell you!" she snaps, rising to her feet. "He… he told me that it was the only way. I had to repent, Letty. He was going to save us all from damnation."

"No!" I jab an accusing finger in her face. "He didn't save me, Giana. That monster stole everything from me, and the women he murdered in God's name. That isn't salvation."

She breaks down, crumpling until her knees hit the carpet. "I d-didn't know what h-he'd become… I thought I was doing the right thing by tracking him down."

I freeze mid-rant. "Tracking him down?"

Her hands cover her face. "Sylvie told me not to look for him when my mother passed away, but I had to know. I wanted so badly to have a real family."

"Grandma S-Sylvie wasn't your real mum?"

"I was adopted," Giana hiccups. "My real mother was a s-sex worker. She abandoned me. Just l-like she did to him."

The sound of rainfall is drowned out by the ringing in my head. I stumble into the sofa and almost fall over, struck by a wave of fearsome dizziness.

"Pastor Michaels… he's…"

"My half-brother," she finishes with a sob. "Your uncle."

I feel like the whole house is shaking as my world falls apart. We're trapped in the same earthquake, neither able to save ourselves from the inevitable destruction in the road ahead.

"When we reunited, I was so happy," she continues, her head lowered. "I finally h-had a real family. But Michael… he was so angry with our mother."

"M-Michael?"

"His real first name. Our mother abandoned him too, but he wasn't adopted like me. S-Something was broken in him. He got in my head and… and… twisted everything."

The puzzle pieces click into place with Dad's words and scraps of memories. Her frantic, terrified praying. Pouring over Bibles late at night. The obsession, the fear. Lashing out in waves of uncontrolled violence.

That wasn't Giana.

It was all him.

Planting a poisonous seedling and fanning the flames until it grew into a semi-psychotic, unhinged obsession. The same obsession he distilled into Mrs Michaels and those fanatics.

"I did everything he told me to." Giana weeps into her hands. "But the d-demons, they still whispered to me. I was losing my m-mind, and he told me that he could make it all stop… if I let him take you."

With vomit burning my throat, I kneel down in front of her. Giana's head lifts when I slide a finger under her chin.

"You gave me to him," I whisper in horror.

Her mouth contorts into a pleading smile. "The things I was seeing, Letty… the voices, everything. He convinced me the rapture was coming, and I had to repent."

"You just… sacrificed me?"

"I tried to forget." Her tears flood faster. "Afterwards, I realised what I'd done. I wanted to fix it, but it was too late. Michael was gone. You were gone."

"You got Dad arrested instead when he began to figure it out," I fill in the gaps. "And you found yourself a perfect new family to cover up the mistakes of the past."

"I'm sorry, Letty. I never meant for any of this to happen! It all spiralled out of control so quickly."

"Out of control? You fed me to the wolves!"

She screams as I launch myself at her, our bodies colliding and rolling across the carpet. I latch my hands around her throat and begin to choke with all my God-given strength.

"You ruined my life!"

Giana's nails scratch against my hands. Pinned beneath me, her limbs writhe and buck. All I can see is red—anger, hatred, the stain of Laura's blood on my hands, Kiera's body being sliced into easily disposable pieces.

Spit bubbles slip from Giana's lips as she gasps for air, the tear of her nails slowly losing steam. I want her to lose everything. She needs to know how it feels to be unmade.

With her eyes on the verge of falling shut forever, Brooklyn's voice cuts through the haze that's fallen over me. She could be in the room, I hear it so clearly.

Trust me when I tell you, there isn't a bad bone in your body.

My hands fall from Giana's neck as I scream out my rage. She splutters, grappling at her throat. I hang over her, my own chest on fire as an ugly sob escapes my mouth. I can't do it. She hurts people—not me. I'm not like them.

"You're going to admit to everything," I choke through tears. "You will never see Ulrich again. He deserves to be loved, and you're not capable of it."

Staring up at me with every heaving breath she sucks in, Giana's eyes widen at something over my shoulder. The sound of creeping footsteps registers too late for me to react.

"You shouldn't have come back," she whispers.

Something heavy smashes against my head, followed by the sound of ceramic shattering. Pain. It overcomes me.

I slump over her body, feeling the gush of hot, sticky blood spreading across my scalp, littered with shards of a broken vase. With the room swaying, a dark shadow approaches.

"I knew you'd find your way home." Pastor Michaels grins down at me, his silver crucifix glinting. "All lost lambs do in the end."

His laced boot hovers over my face, obscuring the insidious grin stretching his mouth wide open. It slams down with an audible crunch that blackens my vision.

Darkness swallows me whole.

I'm welcomed back into its arms.

CHAPTER 29
HARLOW

HOLD YOUR BREATH – ASTYRIA

THE RUGGED COASTLINE *stretches out in front of me. Waves lap at the shore, and the tang of salt rests on my tongue. The summer sunshine casts a brilliant glow that I welcome with open arms.*

Digging my toes into the wet sand, I let my eyes slide shut.

I'm home. Safe.

This is paradise.

I can't remember a time I ever felt content. Even my happiest moments have been tinged with darkness. But here, in this beautiful, windswept place, all I feel is peace at last.

"Hey, Harlow!"

Running down the beach, Laura's platinum-blonde hair streams over her shoulders in a glistening curtain. With a huge smile on her face, she races towards me, the floral fabric of her dress trailing behind her.

We meet in the middle, and she tackles me to the golden sand. Falling over in peals of laughter, we scream when the tide rolls back in. Water soaks into our clothes and I shove Laura off me with a squeal.

"I'm soaked!"

"What kind of idiot stands next to the sea if they don't wanna get wet?" she teases, wringing out her dress.

Clambering to my feet, I offer her a helping hand up. She curls her arm around my waist, and we walk along the shore, both barefoot and laughing in the glow of sunshine.

"What are you doing here?"

"I'm here to see you," she answers like it's obvious. "Figured you could use a friend right about now."

I glance around the empty beach. "But… where are we?"

She offers me a knowing grin and taps her temple.

My smile falters. "You're not real."

"Hey, I'm no more real than you are. Why should that matter? Imaginary friends are still friends."

We walk in companionable silence, our steps swallowed by the swill of water and chirping seagulls flying above us. There isn't another soul in sight. We're alone in our own personal utopia.

"I wish you were still alive," I blurt.

"You've been blaming yourself for my death for too long." Laura squeezes my waist. "I know you're hurting right now. That's why I'm here."

We stop and wait for the sea water to return. It races back up the sand in a twinkling wave, hitting us with a rush of warmth that laps at our ankles. Laura turns to face me, her smile understanding.

"Only you can forgive yourself for what happened."

I shake my head. "I think it's too late for that. I'm dead."

"Dead? Oh, no. Not yet. You are in danger, though, and I need you to wake up. You can't let him win again. Not when he's taken so much from us both."

The wind picks up as storm clouds roll in. Our pocket of happiness is swept away with the rising winds, leaving us both shivering and doused in shadows.

"What do I do?"

Laura presses a kiss to my cheek. "You fight, Harlow Michaels. Fight like hell for all of us. We'll be here watching."

Her eyes flick over to the sandbank high above us, wrapped in swaying patches of grass. Their faces stare back at me—too many to count now. The girls that filled my childhood, intermixed with the new victims.

Some don't have faces, their mottled skin smoothed over in an eyeless, mouthless blur. Five souls extinguished without anyone knowing, butchered and buried out of sight. I'll never know their names.

At the forefront, two faces stand out. One dead. One alive. Candace's fiery auburn hair stirs in the wind. She's small, petite, her body covered by a dress that hides the assortment of vicious bruises from sight. I recognise her from my dreams.

She nods once.

Breath held, I nod back.

Next to her, Kiera has found her final resting place. Her purpose has been fulfilled now. She blows me a kiss, slinking backwards to join the other girls. They all turn and begin to walk away, hand in hand.

With a loud crack of thunder, the shadows stretch outwards, swallowing the whole beach. Laura's hand brushes against my cheek, tracing the path of her kiss.

"Forgive yourself," she repeats.

It's the last words to leave her lips. She vanishes into the blackness that takes over, wrapping around me in ice-cold tendrils. The beach disappears from sight and the real world rushes up to meet me.

All-consuming pain is the first sensation that reality brings. Fierce, pounding pain, like someone peeled the skin from my skull and started smashing it to death with a hammer.

I groan while battling to open my heavy eyes. It's hard to breathe.

Everything feels stuffy, and the sharp, coppery taste of blood is clogging up my throat.

"Hey," someone hisses.

Blinking to settle my vision, I lift a shaking hand to my face and search my blood-crusted nose. It's bent out of shape and pulsating.

"Hey!"

Darkness surrounds me on all sides. The scent of unwashed filth, sweat and urine welcomes me home. This is more familiar than the luxury I've spent so long living in.

"Are you awake? Say something!"

"I'm awake," I garble.

Trapped in a litter-strewn room, the bare walls are coated in damp and rotting cream wallpaper that sags from the exposed bricks. Ancient, bare floorboards dig into my spine.

When I attempt to roll over, something metal clanks, and I gasp in pain. A pair of handcuffs are cutting deep into my left wrist, securing me to the wall.

"Are you Harlow?"

Across the room, her skin is painted in nasty shades of black, blue and green. Blood streaks cover her face and naked body, blending with weeks of layered dirt.

Her auburn hair tips me off. This isn't a dream. I haven't wound back the clock and returned to my imprisonment in Pastor Michaels' basement. This is a new iteration of hell.

"Candace," I gasp. "You're alive."

Her laugh is choked. "I'm not sure I'd call it that. You've been out for hours. I thought you were dead."

The numbness shatters. This is it. He's got me again. As terror sets in, I scream out, tugging sharply on the handcuff pinning me in place. Candace watches with a tired look.

"No use. You don't think I tried that?"

"Where is he? Pastor Michaels?"

She recoils, staring down at her bare legs. She has one hand free, the other cuffed high above her at a painful angle. She won't look at me now that I've named the elephant in the room.

"Candace," I say more gently. "I know you're afraid, but I won't let him hurt you again. You aren't alone."

"He's been waiting for you. At first, I believed him when he said you'd come, and I could go home."

"He… said that?"

Candace winces as she pulls her legs up to her chest, exposing raw, oozing ulcers eating into her skin. Jesus. They look infected. It's a miracle she's still here.

"That woman carried you in here earlier and just left me here. They'll never let me go home, will they?"

My stomach lurches, and I strain against the handcuff, a hot burst of vomit surging up my throat. Tears sear the backs of my eyes with each heave.

She was helping him all along.

"Woman?" I cough out. "Giana?"

"Never told me her name. Some miserable-looking, brown-haired bitch. Loves to throw a punch or two. She feeds me whenever she remembers to."

Throwing up again, I splutter and sob until there's nothing left inside me but resentment. The pit of darkness keeps burrowing deeper. I won't make it out alive this time.

"*He* comes for prayers every night."

I know what that means. If there was anything left in me, I'd be sick again. All these weeks, I've slept in a warm bed, had a bellyful of food and the love of an incredible family.

All while Candace was being beaten, starved and raped on a daily basis. My freedom has cost her an unfathomable price. One she will never be able to take back.

"Does he sleep here?"

Candace shudders. "No. It's just me."

Searching around the room, I look for any clues as to our location. There's nothing beyond piles of energy bar wrappers, squashed water bottles and an array of mice droppings.

This wasn't part of the plan. I had it all laid out. Exposing Giana's lies was all I wanted. I didn't know her deceit would lead to a rabbit hole of evil, landing me straight back in Pastor Michaels' grasp.

"What do you remember?" I urge her. "Where are we?"

"There's nothing here," she mumbles back. "I screamed and screamed, but no one has ever heard me. Only him."

Shit, this is bad. We know from the taunting image he sent that Candace has been held captive in some kind of abandoned building. We could be anywhere in England.

But if Giana's involved, that narrows down the search radius. We must be reasonably close to Croyde for her to be feeding Candace on a semi-regular basis.

"Don't worry," I whisper into the dark. "They'll come for us soon. I'm going to get you out of here."

"Don't make promises you can't keep, Harlow."

Her words lash against me in a painful whip. I did the same thing for Laura—promised her salvation as our pinkies linked between rusted cage bars. I failed her.

It won't happen again.

This is my chance to fix the past.

We lapse into silence as the sound of heavy rain continues to patter in the dark night, lashing against the grimy window high above us.

Hours pass, and the sun rises, illuminating the dank room. In the cold light of day, Candace's condition is further revealed. If we have to fight our way out of here, she will be in trouble.

Her entire body is beaten and slashed while her face is misshapen from too many blows. She's in bad shape, nursing infected wounds and probably severe dehydration.

"Are you in pain?"

She shrugs, cursing when it jolts her handcuffed arm. "I don't really feel it anymore. How's the nose?"

"I'm okay. It's not the first time."

"Jesus. How long did he… you know, have you?"

"Thirteen years."

Candace gapes at me. "All that time? How did you survive? I feel like I'm going insane in here on my own."

"I don't remember a lot of it," I admit. "After a while, you learn to switch off. It was years before he brought the first girl to torture and kill."

"So, you were alone for all that time." She shakes her head as tears streak down her dirty face. "I'd rather die. I don't know how much more of this I can take."

"That's not happening. We're getting out of here together or not at all."

She stares back down at her toes. "How long have I been here? Did anyone even look for me?"

"I think it's been eight weeks or so. The whole country has been looking for you. There's been huge protests about the case. Your brother was looking, too."

"My brother?" She laughs weakly. "That can't be right. I haven't spoken to him in years. Why would he care?"

Biting my tongue, I hold back that he's staring down the barrel of a lengthy prison sentence for attempted murder. She needs hope right now, not more heartbreak.

"He was devastated," I say vaguely.

"Huh. I wasn't expecting that."

"I guess people can surprise you. Stuff like this either brings out the best or worst in them."

We lapse back into silence until she breaks it.

"I don't get it," she mumbles. "How has he gotten away with this for so long? Why did no one care before?"

"Pastor Michaels has spent years picking off the invisibles." I wince, attempting to get comfortable. "That's what allowed him to remain hidden."

Candace sniffles as she cries even harder.

"But that's changing now," I add.

"Nothing's changed, Harlow."

"No, it has. People are finally waking up. Violence against women isn't okay, no matter who they are or what they do."

She manages a thin smile. "Things have always been different for people like me. To the world, we're whores up for a cheap fuck. Not people."

"You're a person," I assure her. "You matter. The people out there who love you have fought for you since day one."

"Who? My waste-of-space brother who disowned me the day he found out how I was paying the bills?"

"Well, it was your friends who alerted the police."

"They did?" She perks up.

"You were reported missing by the next morning."

"Holy shit."

"They came all the way to London to be interviewed by Sabre and help with the investigation. Do you believe me now?"

Candace's tears are still flowing, but her smile widens. She nods, wiping her face off with her free hand.

"What about you? Who's looking for you?"

My heart aches behind my ribcage, broken into jagged pieces that slice against the fragile remains of my hope. I wouldn't blame the guys if they didn't look for me.

I did this to myself. One day, they will get sick of constantly worrying about me, and that'll be it. The end of the road. This could very well be it this time.

Before I can choke out an answer, the creak of footsteps sounds out from the floor below us. A door slams, followed by the murmurings of two voices.

"Is that help?" Candace asks, but her hope dies quickly. "Shit. It's him. I recognise his voice."

Wrestling myself as upright as possible, I stretch my limbs and attempt to move into a prepared position. I need every defence I can get if we're going to survive this.

"Be quiet and let me handle him," I order her. "Don't get involved. He'll leave you alone as long as you do that."

"Wait," she rushes out. "I won't sit here and watch him… hurt…"

"Don't worry." I plaster on a smile, even if it feels alien on my lips. "I'm the one he wants. You're safe."

"No! Harlow, please."

"Be quiet!"

Heavy, aggressive steps preclude the devil's arrival, cutting off her frantic pleas. My heart is pounding so fast, I can feel it throbbing throughout my body.

Fear is my automatic response, bred into me after years of violence and death. It quickly fades into newfound determination. Pastor Michaels won't lay another finger on her.

Even if I have to take every cut and punch he needs to inflict, I'll keep her safe. I have to keep him occupied long enough for backup to track us down.

At the last second, I fall back on old habits and send a silent, desperate plea up to the heavens.

Please, Lord.

Give me the strength to survive.

I don't want to die here.

The door slams open and cracks against the wall. Broad shoulders are cloaked in thick, perfectly pressed robes. The twinkle of a crucifix resting on his chest sets my pulse alight.

No more running.

Pastor Michaels looks as I remember him, albeit wearier, his grey-streaked hair a little overgrown and his beard scraggly. Sunken cheeks sit below piercing green eyes that steal my breath.

Oh my God.

I never realised it before now, but his eyes are identical to Giana's bright shade of green, down to the tiny flecks of brown blurring with emerald irises.

Pastor Michaels steps into the room and sweeps his gaze over us both, a slimy grin slashed across his face. When his eyes land on me, trapped and bloodied, that grin triples.

"Let us be thankful, and so worship God with reverence and awe, for our God is a consuming fire."

I lift my chin and, for the first time ever, meet his gaze head on. I'm no longer afraid to stare into the depths of pure, unadulterated evil. Cowering never protected me.

"Hebrews, 12:28."

"You remember your scripture," he praises as he touches his crucifix. "I'm impressed."

"You made me recite it enough."

Scanning over my dirty, ripped clothing, matted hair and blood-slick face, he chuckles darkly.

"You look different. It's been a long time, Harlow. But you're home now, with me. Exactly where you belong."

I swallow the lump in my throat. "I was never yours, Uncle. That was just one of your lies."

His bushy eyebrows raise. "I see you've stumbled across our family secret. Took you long enough. Let's dispense with the formalities then, shall we?"

"Please do."

Kicking aside a crushed water bottle, Pastor Michaels crouches down in front of me, his wrinkled hands braced on his robe-covered knees.

He still smells the same. Blood, sweat and fresh tears. I wonder how much of it is my imagination, blurring with countless excruciating memories from the past.

"Your mother is downstairs," he reveals gleefully. "Say the word, and I'll slit her throat for you. Call it a welcome home present."

I flinch. "You would kill your own sister?"

"You think she matters to me?" He cracks his knuckles. "That whore is no better than the poisonous slut who birthed us. Giana's the reason we ran away together."

"You kidnapped me," I snarl back.

"No, I wanted to save you from her."

"Save me? Really?"

"You had the chance to repent. The women in this family are cursed with the devil's blood."

He is genuinely insane. More than I remember.

"I saved you from her corrupted ways and raised you in the Lord's light. That was your repentance, Harlow."

His delusions stare back at me in the insidious depths of his eyes. He truly believes every twisted word. Seized by fury, I gather saliva in my mouth and spit right in his face.

"You took everything from me," I shout at him. "I hope you both rot for what you've done to us all."

His hand strikes out, and my head snaps to the side, fire racing across my cheek. Punching me again, his ring slices into my top lip. I savour the warm splash of blood.

As long as it hurts, I'm still alive. He hasn't won. I'll swallow whatever self-obsessed, psychotic bullshit he wants to throw at me as long as it keeps him distracted.

"Filthy sinner," he screams in my face. "I see you've forgotten all the lessons I taught you. I'm disappointed, but not surprised. This world is full of temptations."

"The only thing you taught me was hatred! You aren't the Lord's saviour. God is disgusted by you."

His meagre patience expires.

"Silence, demon!"

Hitting me harder, I feel the blood begin to pour from my broken nose again. The pain barely registers. This is child's play compared to what he's done to me before.

"I know who you really are." I cough up blood-flecked saliva at his feet. "Why did you kill Rosetta? Another failed experiment?"

He flinches, his knuckles stained red. "Mrs Michaels outlived her usefulness."

"Is that why you left her body for me to find?"

"I killed her for you!" he bellows. "Now, you can take her place at my side. We will face the rapture together."

My near-hysterical laughter echoes around us, over and over. With each wheezing chuckle, his rage metastasises, leaching into every limb. I watch the cloud of sickness descend over his face.

"I would rather hang like her than help you kill more innocent women. You'd be better off killing me now."

The tip of his steel-capped boot slams into my stomach. I double over, heaving and sobbing in pain.

"You dare to defy me? After all I've done for you?" Pastor Michaels howls. "You will take your rightful place at my side."

"Fuck you! I'll die instead."

Another sharp kick. The air is torn from my lungs with each strike. I try to curl inwards and protect my ribs.

"Those men have deceived you," he screeches. "Look what they've made you into! A sinful whore, just like the rest of them."

With another laugh, I drop the killer blow.

"I'd rather be their whore than your prisoner."

Pastor Michaels freezes. "You dare speak such words."

"They love me more than you ever could."

His glare is enraged. "I can still save you. It isn't too late. Only I can lead you back to the path of the righteous."

"No," I wheeze out. "You will always be alone, unloved and unwanted. I won't join you. Not now, not ever."

"Disobedient bitch! You will surrender to me!"

My eyes squeeze shut as I take another furious blow, retching up the blood that runs down my throat. He's sweating now, his eyes wild with untamed madness.

"Rosetta was a puppet under your control. You victimised her too. How does it feel, knowing you killed the only person who was ever loyal to you?"

Pastor Michaels snarls as he looms over me, hand raised for another punch. "Enough of this. We're leaving."

"You indoctrinated Giana next, twisted her mind and convinced her to surrender me to you," I stall further.

"Giana needed saving! I gave her the second chance she wanted. You were the price for her redemption."

"She was just another woman for you to control. That way, we can't abandon you like your mother did, can we?"

That stops him dead in his tracks.

"No," he falters. "That whore has nothing to do with this. Stop these lies before I cut your filthy tongue out."

"You told me to call you Daddy," I continue defiantly. "And tortured me until I spouted the same ugly lie. It didn't work, though, did it? You had to keep on killing."

"I saved you from a sinner's life," he spits out. "I am your God, Harlow. Your salvation. You're nothing without me."

"No, that's where you're wrong. My God doesn't hate the world and everyone in it. My God doesn't preach violence and evil."

"Enough!"

"My God isn't you," I finish. "You're an animal, and you'll get what you deserve for killing those women. I'll see to it."

When he boots me in the side of my tender rib cage, I slump against the rotten floorboards. Blinding pain is tearing through every inch of me.

Candace's eyes connect with mine across the room. She looks utterly terrified of Pastor Michaels, frozen in horror while watching our power struggle.

I try to shake my head, warning her off speaking. I can take it. He's losing control and unravelling fast. The sooner his madness consumes him, the quicker this will end.

"You could've had it all, my child. A seat in the kingdom of paradise while the rapture razes this world to ash."

My eyes flutter shut for a brief, exhausted moment of reprieve. I'm so tired. Adrenaline and pain have sapped my strength to its last reserves.

"Instead, you have forsaken me. Your own flesh and blood! Lucifer was thrown from Heaven for less."

He slams my head against the wall with each hateful word, reigniting the sore, swollen egg on the top of my skull. I scream myself hoarse, unable to hold it in.

"We'll have to start again," he decides with a nod. "From the beginning. Let God decide your fate now that you've been tainted by temptation and sin."

Opening the flap of his ceremonial robes, the glint of the ornate ritual knife catches my eye. Pastor Michaels slides it free, inspecting the sharp blade with an excited smile.

"You survived the ritual once before. Let's see if the Lord will forgive your sins twice. I will abide by his will."

"No!" Candace wails. "Stop! Leave her alone!"

Reaching above me, Pastor Michaels ignores her shouts and unlocks my handcuff. My arm screams in protest as it falls down into my lap, limp and completely numb.

He hovers over me. "Beg the Lord for forgiveness. Pray for his divine mercy. You have much to atone for."

I blink through my tears. "Never."

"I said fucking pray!"

With the sharp blade poised to slice through my clothing, the sound of voices causes him to halt. Giana's shouting at someone downstairs, her voice high with fright.

I sag in relief. "Time's up."

Pastor Michaels' lip curls. "What did you do?"

"Did you think I wouldn't bring backup?"

Footsteps thud up the staircase before two shadows cross into the room. A blood-slick knife pressed against her exposed throat, Giana's escorted inside by her captor.

It's a family reunion.

Dad looks around the room as he holds his ex-wife's life in his hands. He's wearing the same rumpled clothing as yesterday when we travelled to Croyde together.

I knew that I couldn't escape Sabre's protection alone. Knocking Richards out and stealing his security pass was merely the first step. We came to find the truth.

Father and daughter.

Retaking our stolen lives, together.

It took his masterminding and experience to evade capture long enough for me to confront Giana myself. This was a road that needed to be travelled alone.

But I knew it was a risk to leave the security of Sabre's protective custody and the four men determined to keep me there, even as I died more inside with each passing day.

That's why I left my father with strict instructions—if anything went wrong, his job was to raise the alert. If he's here, that means the guys can't be far behind him.

"Step away from my daughter," he shouts. "Or the bitch dies. You're done, Michaels. The game is over."

Poised over me, Pastor Michaels' eyes shut for a second. The ceremonial blade is primed and ready to sink deep into my flesh. My life is hanging on a literal knife's edge.

"Oliver," he greets with an air of exasperation. "How nice of you to join us. This truly is a family affair now."

"Knife down!" Dad barks at him.

"Do what you please with Giana."

"Don't test me! I'll do it."

"In fact, if you plan to slit her throat, I would be quite happy to watch the show myself. Go right ahead."

Giana sobs even harder, a thick stream of blood staining her neck and soaking into the collar of her blouse. She blinks at me, pleading as the knife slices ever closer.

"She's your sister, isn't she? You both kept that secret very quiet. My own wife… related to a fucking serial killer."

Pastor Michaels shrugs. "She's from the demon seed of my mother. That's all that binds us. Kill her and end her pitiful existence, once and for all."

My father's face twists, and I can see the indecision in his agitated blue eyes. The temptation. One slip of the hand and the woman who ruined his life will be dead.

"Dad," I wheeze. "Don't do it."

He looks over to me, his eyes shining with unshed tears. We found our truth, and it's an ugly sight to behold. I wipe blood from the corner of my mouth and try to sit up.

"Please. Killing her won't bring anyone justice. She needs to be punished for what she's done. If you do this, you're no better than she is."

"Goddammit," he curses. "She did this to us, Harlow! It was all part of her plan. She gave you to this bastard."

"And I want to see her punished for it. Death would be too kind for the pain she's inflicted."

The tears spill from his eyes and begin to pour in thick, defeated trails of sadness. His determination broken, Dad lowers the knife from her throat.

Giana moves before I can scream his name, taking advantage of the opening rather than collapsing in relief as I thought she would.

Reaching inside her coat pocket, her hand reappears clutching a gun. She's fumbling with inexperience, but Dad's movements are too slow to escape even her terrible aim.

"No!" I shriek.

It's too little, too late.

Blood sprays across the floor as the bullet pierces Dad's left thigh. He flops backwards with a bellow of agony, leaving Giana to crumple, staring at the gun in her hands.

Her lips move on a remorseful whisper. "I'm sorry. I have no other choice."

"Well," Pastor Michaels singsongs. "I didn't think you'd have it in you. Well done, sister. Perhaps you aren't so useless after all."

Dad's hand is pressed over his bleeding thigh as he writhes in pain on the dirty floor. He lashes out when Giana attempts to approach, her face overcome with regret.

"Should've shot me in the head if you wanted to stop me," he threatens. "You're going to pay for what you did to our family."

"Shut up, Oliver," she blusters. "Take some damn responsibility. Harlow had two parents who failed her."

Pastor Michaels locates my handcuffs and kicks them across the room to her. "Secure him while I finish this."

When Giana pauses, his voice raises.

"Remember our deal. I have no problem taking another child from you if you start disobeying me now."

Her face turning ash white, Giana bows her head, following his orders without further question. That's when it all clicks into place. She's being blackmailed with Ulrich's life.

Dad is handcuffed across the room, his wrist secured to a rusted pipe. With the task done, Giana breaks down. She collapses and curls into a tight, sobbing ball.

"Now, where were we?" Pastor Michaels crouches over me, pressing the knife to my sternum. "Let's make this quick. I don't have time for any more delays."

Cutting my sweater, he exposes the twisted, silvery scars crisscrossing my torso from the last time we played this game. I look away from Dad's tear-filled eyes as he shouts his head off with each knife flick.

"This is for your own good," Pastor Michaels whispers as he works. "You've been led astray. We must pray to God for mercy. If you live, we will escape together."

"Do whatever you want to me," I fire back. "You will never own me ever again. I'm free now. I'm alive."

"Feeling brave? Perhaps this will change your tune." The knife slices through my bra strap. "Time to pray, sinner. You know the words."

As my bra slumps, the sound of something metallic bouncing against the floor halts his movements. Mrs Michaels' shining gold wedding ring has fallen from its hiding place.

Pastor Michaels wavers. I know he recognises it. The strangest of looks crosses his face. A glimmer of… regret.

"She's dead because of you," I accuse.

"Rosetta had to die," he justifies with a bobbing throat. "Her sins were too great. I couldn't help her anymore."

"Help her? That's what you were doing? She helped you butcher my friends! She was a fucking monster!"

Infuriated, he disregards the wedding ring and slashes the knife with an enraged roar. When the first cut parts the skin of my rapidly bruising rib cage, Candace's sobs ricochet throughout the room. She's curled into herself to hide from the inevitable.

Dad's panicked yelling mingles with her cries, echoing into a maelstrom that does little to distract Pastor Michaels from his task. The feeding frenzy has set in.

"Why do none of you obey me?" he screeches.

I hold back a sob as the knife digs into my stomach and begins circling, cutting over old scars to lay new, oozing wounds. He digs deeper, mixing fresh blood with slashed flesh, parting skin and cutting muscle fibres.

"I said fucking *pray*!" His spittle hits my face. "Beg the Lord for his divine retribution, heathen child."

Teeth locked together, it takes all my mental strength to hold back the screams. I won't give him what he wants. Not now, not ever. His complacent songbird is long gone.

When the knife moves up to slice the first line of the Holy Trinity, his concentration breaks. Pastor Michaels' head cocks to the side, listening intently.

Wind.

Beating rotors.

Someone's coming. The sound of an approaching helicopter rattles the bricks of the abandoned house. I almost choke on a sob of relief.

"No," he mutters to himself. "I'm not done!"

"They're coming for you."

Face hardening, he glances over my sliced, blood-slick frame, cuts and scars melding into a grotesque portrait. The ritual isn't complete. With a low curse, he straightens to his full height.

"It's too late to run," I warn him.

His feet are already retreating. The rotors of the helicopter still sound a way off. Pressing a hand to the deep slashes in my stomach to stem the bleeding, I grab the edge of his robes.

"Scared now? How does it feel?"

"Let go, whore!"

Pastor Michaels kicks me in the face, his dark eyes flitting around the room. I'm slammed backwards, agony ripping through my mouth. A tooth is pulled loose, and I spit it out.

"No," I garble. "Never."

He tries to retreat again, intent on running. It takes all of my energy to stumble after him, woozy and weak. I'll follow him for as long as it takes. Pain be damned.

The throaty growl of an approaching car engine causes his movements to halt again. The brief flicker of hope in my chest is extinguished by his pleased smile.

"You think I didn't bring backup too?" He leers at me. "There are plenty of people who believe in my mission."

I grapple with his robes, trying to hold on to something. "No! I won't let you get away. Not this time."

"Don't worry, child. I'll be seeing you again. We won't stop until every sinner has been exposed to God's wrath."

The car's horn blares. I stumble while gripping his robes, driven by desperation. Pastor Michaels wrestles with me as I attempt to scratch my nails down his face in a last-ditch effort.

I'm smashed so hard into the wall, the air is knocked from my lungs. Blackness is eating at my vision as I fight to remain conscious, even though my body wants to shut down.

I sway on my feet, verging on collapse. "Is that all you've got? God's mightiest servant is running like a scared child."

Pastor Michaels holds the knife high above him, prepared to inflict one final stab that will silence my taunts forever. His eyes narrow into slits as he contemplates me.

"I gave everything to you. I'm the one that saved you from damnation. You've thrown it all away, and for what?"

I bare my blood-stained teeth. "Freedom."

"That is pathetic."

"How would you know? I love, and I am loved. That's something you'll never understand."

He lowers the knife with a cackle. "You're right. But what fun I'm going to have, ripping those you love away from you, one by one. I want you to live to heed my words."

Pivoting on his heel, he launches towards the door. I throw myself across the room and wrap a hand around his ankle with my absolute last glimmer of strength.

Pastor Michaels kicks me in the stomach again, throwing me onto my back. With the knife in his hand, he catches me off guard by going for Candace instead.

"Aha," he taunts.

"Leave her alone!"

"Let's play one last game. Keep following me and let her die if that's what you want more. Your choice."

Candace screams at the top of her lungs as Pastor Michaels lifts her up by the throat. In one brutal slash, he cuts deep into both of her wrists, unleashing the arterial spray of veins.

A crimson waterfall splashes across the sagging wall, and she hits the floor with a thud, her eyes blown wide and breathing laboured. Blood is pouring out of her in a petrifying river.

"Your choice," he repeats.

I watch Pastor Michaels bounce from the room with a final, deranged laugh. Doubt holds me prisoner. The helicopter is close. If I delay him, they'll be able to track the escaping car.

"Go, Harlow," Candace murmurs, turning a ghostly shade of translucent white. "Stop h-him. I'm f-fine."

Every fibre inside me is screaming so loud, I can't think straight. I have to chase after him. It's the only way to end this, once and for all. He's going to escape again.

Candace's head smacks against the floorboards as the last of her consciousness dissipates. Blood is pooling in a copper-tinged puddle, framing her auburn hair in a halo.

No.

I can't do it.

Not again.

Revenge isn't worth more than her life. I couldn't give Laura the freedom she wanted, but I can give Candace a fighting chance at survival. Only if I stay.

Hauling myself past Dad's slumped, bleeding form, I swim through warm blood and gather Candace into my arms. She's too weak to protest, her eyes fighting to remain open.

Clasping her slashed wrists, I apply as much pressure as my weakened state will allow. She's losing too much blood. Flashes overtake my vision with awful déjà vu.

Bright-red spit bubbles sliding from Laura's parted lips. Her pained gasps as I squeezed her throat, choking the final wisps of life from her veins. The echoing rattle of my sobs around the basement.

"You're not allowed to die," I say fiercely.

Her head is limp, lifeless.

"Please. I have a promise to keep. We're getting out of here together, remember?"

The inherited strength of countless stolen lives keeps my eyes open, even as unconsciousness threatens to overwhelm me. Candace will live. The ghosts in my head demand it so.

"Harlow."

A shaking hand touches my shoulder. Dad protests weakly, but Giana ignores him as she shuffles closer to me.

"Here, use this."

Her swollen, bloodshot eyes lock on mine. She pulls off her cardigan and presses the fabric against Candace's gaping wounds.

"I'm sorry," she offers with finality. "All I wanted was to protect my child. Everything I've done has been for him."

Blood quickly soaks through the cardigan. Giana cuddles up to me, shaking as hard as I am and silently crying into my hair.

I let myself sag against her. "You kept him safe. It's done now. I can't control what happens next. You hurt people."

"I know, darling. For what it's worth, I'm sorry for all of it. I'll take my punishment. Just promise me one thing."

My eyes fall shut as the helicopter roars directly above us. The rotors are slowing down. It's preparing to land.

"What is it?" I mumble.

"Please tell Ulrich that I love him."

Unconsciousness is pulling me into her warm, newly protective embrace. Barked orders and frantic voices echo from outside the building. Our saviours have arrived.

"Please, Harlow," she begs. "Promise me."

My name leaving her lips seals my defeat.

"I promise, Mum."

EPILOGUE

WE ARE NOT OKAY - NIKKITA

ENZO

STARING into the depths of my empty suitcase, I glower at the lack of clothing. Leighton had one fucking job while we cleaned out our desks at Sabre—pack the damn suitcases in time for our early morning flight.

My mind is too weary to fight with him about it. Turns out, Hunter was right about one thing. We're done. All of us. This case has broken our family; left, right and centre.

My phone vibrates with another phone call. It must be Lucas calling with more shitty news. Press coverage of Pastor Michaels' daring escape has been absolutely brutal.

I accept the call with an exhausted sigh. "If this is another depressing update, you can thoroughly fuck off."

"Mr Montpellier."

Shitting fuck!

"Superintendent." I clear my throat. "My apologies. It's been a trying few days, to say the least."

She sniffs in derision. "I've been notified that your team is leaving the country. Care to explain yourself?"

Tucking the phone under my chin, I start tossing clothes at random into the case. No idea where the fuck we're headed. Out of England and hopefully, far away.

"Our staff will continue the investigation while we take a short break," I reply tiredly. "I'm taking my family somewhere safe. Not even you can begrudge me that."

Her own sigh rattles down the line. "I understand that you've all been through a great ordeal, but we still have a serial killer to catch, and his new accomplices."

"We have reason to believe that the suspect is being aided by his… *ahem*, fan group. Sabre is following up with our current leads. He won't get far."

"I need results, Mr Montpellier. You are not the only one with superiors to answer to. The Prime Minister is very concerned about recent events."

Abandoning my haphazard packing, I glance outside at the wild, overgrown garden stretching behind our new home. The sun is setting in a blazing, fiery riot.

In her usual place, Harlow sits on the lawn, a hand buried in Lucky's fur as they watch the sinking horizon together. The hospital discharged her this morning, to our collective relief.

She's silent and still, her battered face hidden from sight. Finding her unconscious and bathing in a pool of blood almost stopped my heart for the last time.

Our family is broken.

Exhausted.

Beaten and bruised.

We have to leave and heal these wounds, or I fear we'll never recover from the chaos of the past few months.

"Mr Montpellier," the superintendent repeats. "Are you listening to me? I'm not paying you to skip off on bloody holiday when the country is in crisis!"

"With all due respect, I will hand back your money and leave with my family regardless. We have sacrificed everything for this case. Enough is enough."

She hesitates, muttering to someone in the background to wait their turn to speak. I slam my bedroom door shut and head downstairs, almost too tired to walk.

"Candace Bernard's rescue will sate the Prime Minster for the time being," she submits. "When you return, we will be having a full and frank conversation about your actions."

"Can't wait. Please contact Hudson or Kade Knight if you have any further concerns during our absence. They will be acting as interim directors."

"Is that appropriate, given their history?" she scoffs.

Annoyance prickles across my scalp. Too weary to act like I give a fuck about her fancy title, I prepare to end the call.

"They are fine agents, and if you wish to receive our continued support with this investigation, you'll treat them with some fucking respect."

My thumb jabs against the red button. Head colliding with the wall, I allow myself a sliver of satisfaction. I've been wanting to stick her stupid cheques and bad attitude up her ass for well over a year now.

"Enz?" Theo calls from the kitchen.

Tucking my phone away, I sidle into the room. He's cleaning out the fridge, throwing away anything perishable that will turn to sludge while we're abroad.

"Yeah?"

He spares me a glance. "Um, did you just hang up on the superintendent? You know she pays our wages, right?"

"Fuck her and the damn money. She won't pull our contract. We all know the police can't handle this case."

"Can we handle it?" Leighton interrupts.

He's sitting at the family table, crouched over a laptop. Next to him, the printed plane tickets sit with five passports.

"Right now?" I reply flatly. "No, we can't handle it. That's precisely why I'm calling time. We need this break."

"Not arguing with you, bro." Leighton takes a slurp from his beer. "The case can survive a few weeks without us."

Slapping his shoulder, I peer out through the glass door leading to the garden. Harlow hasn't moved an inch in hours. The sun has almost vanished entirely now.

"She spoken to any of you?"

"A little," Theo answers as he pours milk down the drain. "The doctor signed her off for air travel."

"Candace Bernard is still in the ICU," Leighton chimes in. "Two transfusions and sixteen stitches later, she's alive. Bloody miracle."

"That's great news."

"Hudson's gonna do the debrief and take her full statement once she's stabilised. I've arranged a security team for her protection until Michaels is apprehended."

I nod. "Good work, Leigh."

"Um, thanks," he stumbles.

The doorbell rings, and Theo darts out of the room to answer it. In the living room, sprawled out on the sectional sofa, Hunter's glaring at the newspaper while slurping his millionth cup of tea.

The exact details of what happened have been kept under wraps. As far as the public is concerned, Candace is alive, and Pastor Michaels escaped with an unnamed accomplice.

We were lucky to find them, following Oliver Kensington's emergency call from the middle of fucking nowhere, several miles into the Devonshire countryside.

I'm not sure if any of us are ready to forgive Harlow for skipping out and deliberately putting herself in harm's way. She knows that. It's exactly why she's hiding from us.

But I get it.

Very begrudgingly.

This clusterfuck is enough to scramble anyone's mind, and she's done a hell of a good job keeping it together for this long. Now, at least, she has her truth. She can finally begin to heal from the past.

Theo returns with company in tow. Limping and favouring his right leg, Oliver's dressed in casual jeans and a loose t-shirt. He offers us all cool nods of greeting.

"What are you doing here?"

"Came to say goodbye," he says gruffly. "Heard you're leaving for a while. I wanted to check on Harlow."

"She'd be fine if it wasn't for you," Leighton grumbles darkly. "Dickhead."

Ignoring him, I shake Oliver's outstretched hand. Leighton is right. He's lucky we didn't murder him. Just about. If he wasn't her last decent relative, he'd be dead and buried.

"How's the leg?"

"No permanent damage." He runs a hand over his dirty-blonde hair. "Doctor says I'm gonna be just fine."

Theo wipes off his hands on a tea towel. "I heard Giana's been transferred to Bronzefield Prison while awaiting trial."

Oliver nods. "She's facing a minimum of fifteen years and they're still adding charges. The trial's been set for December."

"Does Harlow know?" I ask with a frown.

"I called to let her know last night," he answers. "She was relieved, I think. Hard to tell. She didn't say much else."

We all exchange worried glances. None of us can truly understand what happened between Harlow and her mother, but we know it's left her gutted. Even if she hated the bitch.

"Where are you guys going?" Oliver takes a seat at the table. "Harlow mentioned something about a trip."

We all turn to Leighton.

"Costa Rica," he declares proudly.

"You're serious?" Theo gapes at him.

"You guys told me to go wild, so I did. Blue waters, sandy beaches, floating cocktail bars. I know, I'm the best."

"Costa Rica? It's the other side of the world," I complain. "What if we need to come home? It's so far away."

"Wasn't that the whole point?" Theo pipes up. "We need total removal from reality for a bit. I think it's a great idea."

Leighton punches the air in triumph. "Knew it. Fuck me, I'm too good. Maybe I should work as a travel agent."

"The further away from me, the better." I level him with a glare. "You almost broke the company managing it for one bloody month. You know, I saw the credit card statement."

He winces, caught red-handed. "Wasn't that supposed to be used for, uh, business expenses?"

"How is a year-long pizza subscription and a Christian Bale cardboard cut-out a business expense?"

Theo doubles over, laughing hard. "For fuck's sake."

"Don't start on the Batman bullshit with me again," Leighton defends. "I have experience now. I'm basically an assassin. I can kick your ass for insulting my man, Christian."

"Assassin." Theo snorts. "The country would implode if you were its replacement for James Bond."

"Watch it, four eyes. I can soon lose your plane ticket to Costa Rica. No more topless waitresses for you."

"You hired a topless waitress?!"

Leighton smirks over his beer. "Kidding."

Gaze bouncing between all three of us, Oliver's smiling to himself. We may have threatened to break his neck if he steals our girl again, but I think we got the old man's approval.

Leaving the sofa, Hunter walks straight up to the bin and tosses the newspaper in it. He spins around, catching us all staring at him, and flicks us the bird instead.

"You know it pisses him off when you stare." Leighton slides the paperwork to his brother. "He punched me the other day for touching his stitches."

"Why the hell did you touch them?" I exclaim.

He shrugs. "Curious. Wanted to see if the doctors managed to staple his brain back in there or if I'm the smart brother now."

Theo buries his face in his hands. "I don't think that I can survive an international trip with you."

"Zip it, Theodore. You're gonna love it."

Picking up the collection of papers, Hunter leans against the wall and runs his eyes over them. He checks the plane tickets and I nearly fall over when he… smiles? Weird.

"We have a private beach?" he asks.

Leighton nods. "And a villa."

"Huh? What filler?"

"*VILLA*," he shouts loudly.

"Great plan." I facepalm. "Shout louder so the deaf man can hear you. Clearly, you're not the smart brother."

Hunter's hand collides with the back of my head. His eyes are narrowed as he smacks me hard enough to rattle my teeth.

"I can read your lips," he warns. "I've been out of action, but I'm still your damn boss, Montpellier. Tread carefully."

Unable to suppress a grin, I bundle Hunter into a tight hug. He squeezes back with that weird, smiley thing still twisting his lips. It's starting to freak me out a bit.

"Well, I should go." Oliver moves to stand up. "Got a meeting at the rehab centre tonight. Jude's a stickler for punctuality."

"We're shocked," Leighton says under his breath.

"Mind if I say hey to Harlow before I go?"

I gesture for him to go ahead. "Be my guest. Try to run away with her again, though, and I'll shoot you in the head."

"Yeah, I got the message the last two hundred times you threatened to do that. Loud and clear, sarge."

With a mock salute, Oliver slips outside into the garden. I watch him go, keeping a watchful eye. It's not that I don't trust Harlow… but I don't fucking trust her. Not right now.

This shit is still a red-hot mess and she's got a lot to come to terms with. We need some time to figure out how to move past what happened, and how she chose to go about it.

"I like him," Theo announces.

Leighton laughs him off. "He's the douchebag who put Harlow in danger. You're not allowed to like him."

"He's got some skills." I shrug casually. "Sabre could use a new forger. We can keep an eye on him that way."

"You want to offer him a job?" Leighton looks gobsmacked. "He's an ex-junkie criminal who broke into our house. Don't get me started on the last forty-eight hours, too."

"We've hired worse. Look at the Cobra team and their rapsheet. Besides, that's a good resume in my mind."

We bicker amongst ourselves until Oliver returns, his smile strained. He offers us a short goodbye before leaving, requesting we keep in contact.

Harlow is still sat outside, even as night descends. I send Theo and Leighton out to pick up some takeout, giving us some privacy. The pair arm wrestle for who gets to drive Hunter's convertible.

"I win!" Leighton declares.

Theo curses in displeasure. "How are you so strong?"

"Come on, Clark Kent. We can discuss my admittedly fantastic biceps on the way out."

"Fucking kill me now," he complains.

With the arguing idiots gone, Hunter follows me into the garden. It's warm enough now to sit outside even without the sun. Lucky barks loudly as we approach, her tail wagging. She chases the ball that Harlow throws half-heartedly.

We take a seat on either side of her. She's staring down at the flower-laced grass, her technicolour face shielded by a curtain of uneven hair. I reach out to tuck the thinning strands aside.

"Talk to us, little one."

Harlow doesn't stir.

Meeting my eyes over her lowered head, Hunter's fingers spell out a simple command. *You yelled at her. Fix this.*

"Hey," I try again, kissing her temple. "I was rough on you at the hospital. We need to talk about this."

"You were right," she replies in a small voice. "I know that I betrayed your trust."

"I was so afraid when we realised that you were gone," I admit. "That fear turned into anger when we got you back. I shouldn't have taken it out on you."

"You were right to. I scared you all."

Sliding a finger underneath her chin, I raise her bottomless blue eyes to mine. Her broken nose is strapped into place over the bloom of devastating, pitch-black bruises.

I've seen her in worse states, but this shit never gets easier. The thought of that asshole daring to hurt what's mine makes my vision dim with rage. When I find him, he's fucking dead.

I channelled my anger in the wrong direction. I've grown enough to see the tendency I have to do that. Harlow knows she fucked up. She had her reasons for taking that risk, and harrowing injuries and near-death experiences aside, she got what she was looking for.

The truth.

Now, she has to live with it.

We all do.

"I'm so sorry, Enz," she whispers tearfully. "I couldn't take the not knowing any longer. I did what I had to."

I stroke her tears aside with my thumbs. "I know, angel. Sometimes, we're backed into a corner and forced to make a shitty decision. You played your last move."

She nods timidly. "Yeah."

"Just wish you'd talked to us."

"Would you have let me go alone?"

"Not a chance in hell."

Harlow lifts an eyebrow. "Case in point."

"Alright, don't get sassy. I'll still spank your ass raw even if you look like you've gone three rounds with Mike Tyson."

"Who on earth is that?"

Chuckling, I lean in and lock our lips together. We can figure out an appropriate punishment for her as soon as we're in the air, leaving England and its chaos behind.

I doubt Hunter will mind if I tie Harlow to the bed and fuck her senseless while he rides her smart mouth. Then she can lecture us about being overprotective.

"What's the plan?" She leans against Hunter's shoulder, looking between us both. "We're really going?"

Hunter kisses her temple after deciphering her words. "I told you that I'd show you the world one day."

She looks up so that he can clearly read her lips.

"Pastor Michaels is still out there. The work isn't done."

"The work can wait," he replies sternly. "We were attacked. I lost my hearing. You got tortured by a serial killer. We're taking a motherfucking holiday."

"Amen to that," I chime in.

Snuggling between us, Harlow accepts the slobber-covered ball caught between Lucky's fangs. She strokes over her ears with a low coo of appreciation.

"I'm gonna miss you, girl."

"Brooklyn's on babysitting duty while we're gone," I say, watching Lucky skip after the ball. "She's very excited to be a dog mum again after losing their pup last year."

"How long will we be gone for?"

Hunter meets my eyes with a frown. I quickly reiterate her question in sign language. We're picking it up fast, thanks to some helpful YouTube tutorials.

He brushes his lips against Harlow's ear, his teeth briefly sinking into her lobe. A shudder runs over her body.

"As long as it takes," he whispers.

Harlow lets out a long-held breath. "What if Pastor Michaels hurts someone else? We have to find him."

"We have our best agents on it," I remind her. "But none of us can pour from an empty cup. We're going, no arguments."

Lips pursed, Harlow's head falls on Hunter's shoulder as her eyes slide shut. We sit on the grass, wrapped around each other and playing fetch with Lucky, until the other two return.

"I come bearing pizza!" Leighton calls from inside. "Courtesy of my brand-spanking-new subscription. Thank you, Sabre Security."

"Little asshole," I mutter.

Harlow snorts. "Heard that."

"You don't pay the credit card bill. Have a word with your boyfriend about his Batman obsession too. It's unhealthy."

She stills, her aquamarine eyes coasting up to meet mine. "Boyfriend, huh?"

I brush our noses together. "That's what we are to you, aren't we?"

"All of you?" she clarifies.

"Well, why not?"

"I didn't realise we were finally doing labels. You guys were still sizing each other up last time we discussed this."

With an eye roll, I yell for Theo and Leighton to join us outside. A blush overtakes Harlow's cheeks, but it's too late. She's admitted it's bothering her. I'm gonna settle this, once and for all.

All seated in a circle, several pizza boxes laid across the grass between us, I clear my throat. Leighton freezes, a huge slice of pepperoni pizza halfway down his throat.

"Harlow has a very serious question for us."

She covers her face with her hands. "I really don't."

"What is it?" Theo asks anxiously.

"Nope, nothing."

He's glancing between all of us in a panic. I stifle a laugh while relaying the situation to Hunter in sign language. He grins evilly, elbowing Harlow in the waist.

"Come on," I goad her. "Put Anxious Nelly over here out of his misery before he explodes."

"Screw you, Enz," Theo cusses. "Harlow, what is it?"

She's flaming a bright tomato red. Even the tips of her ears are pink. It's so damn cute, my dick is actually hard.

"Please," Leighton pleads around a mouthful. "Pinkie swear, we won't laugh if it's embarrassing."

"Why would it be embarrassing?" Theo frowns to himself. "It's not… about periods, is it? Because Leighton's next on the rotation to buy tampons. I did my duty."

"No!" Harlow squeals. "You guys are such idiots."

I ruffle her hair. "Your idiots?"

Still blushing hard, she glances between all four of us. Her face is turned towards Hunter for his benefit, but her words are for everyone.

"Well… I was just asking if… you know, erm. If we're… or you're… well. *Ahem.* The thing is, ah—"

"Fuck me gently," I interrupt her rambling. "Harlow wants to know if we're *all* her boyfriends."

Leighton chokes on his pizza and Theo has to hammer him so hard on the back, a chunk of pineapple shoots out of his nose. Hunter curses up a storm as it lands in his lap.

"Leigh! Jesus!"

"Sorry!" Leighton splutters, his eyes streaming. "That was fucking cool. Reckon I can do it again?"

When he's done coughing a lung up, Leighton offers Harlow a bright smile.

"I've been yours since day one, Goldilocks. If they don't want you, I'll happily steal you away."

"Watch it, fucker," I warn in a low voice. "That's the kind of talk that gets you buried at the bottom of a lake."

"Forget we ever had this conversation," Harlow begs.

I tuck her into my side and inhale her fresh, sweet scent. If I died with her in my arms, blushing like a maniac and being cute as hell, I think I'd be okay with that.

"I'm all in too," I whisper to her.

She smiles to herself, glancing up at Hunter next. He's been tracking the whole conversation and takes her hand into his. Harlow shivers as his lips graze her knuckles.

"I miss the sound of your voice," he murmurs. "But I can live without it as long as I have you by my side for the rest of my life. Hearing or not."

"You're… okay with sharing?"

He nods, deadly serious. "We've all lost enough. I'm ready to risk it all to feel a bit of happiness again."

They kiss passionately, his fingers sliding through her hair. I catch Leighton watching as intently as I am, and we exchange knowing smirks. Looks like the younger Rodriguez doesn't mind a bit of voyeurism either.

Theo's the last one to answer. He's been flagging behind the group since the first time Harlow blew into our lives, and the descent of chaos began. His grief never quite left him.

Straightening his crooked glasses, he bites his bottom lip and looks up at Harlow. She's holding her breath.

"I am in love with you," he finally answers. "I don't give a fuck if I have to share, as long as you're in my life."

With a grin blossoming, Harlow launches herself over the pizza boxes and ends up tackling Theo back onto the grass. She grunts in pain, yet it doesn't seem to slow her down.

After kissing Theo until he's sporting a similarly red face, Harlow comes up for air. We're all hanging on for her reaction. She takes the time to look between us all.

"Let's get the first plane out of here."

To be concluded in...
Hollow Veins (Sabre Security #3)

BONUS SCENE

HARLOW

Walking up the aeroplane steps, I wave off Hunter's silent offer of help. I'm used to taking a beating from Pastor Michaels, and his last one was no less savage. Every inch of me hurts fiercely.

I was discharged from the hospital and came home to find our lives being packed up, ready to flee the country. We're taking a trip to Costa Rica to escape and heal after all we've endured these past few months.

"Harlow?"

Hunter's voice is an uncertain rasp. I look up into his eyes, finding a question there. He's suffered more than all of us and now faces a lengthy recovery from his injuries. Just looking at him hurts me.

"You ready for this?" he asks.

I nod back. More than anything.

"Good."

Taking his hand, I let him lead me onto the private aeroplane. It's as plush and luxurious as I remember, the cream-coloured leather seats, flat screen TVs and fully stocked bar adding to the opulence.

Taking my place, I watch as Enzo follows me, carrying my bag full of books and toiletries for the long flight. He stashes it overhead and gives me a weak, exhausted smile.

"Everything okay?"

"Fine," I reply, getting comfortable.

"Are you in any pain?"

"I'm okay, Enz. Stop worrying."

"Still my job to worry, little one."

"Well, take a break. I'm good."

Throat bobbing, he nods tightly and moves to help Theo with his stuff. He's bringing bags full of computer equipment with him, unable to fully let go of the reins despite our impromptu trip abroad.

Hunter takes the seat opposite me and rests his head against the window, his bag-lined eyes sliding shut. I study pale pallor of his face, drained of all life. He looks wrung-out.

"Princess?" Leighton stops beside my seat.

"If you're going to ask if I'm okay, save it."

He flashes me a dimpled smile. "I wasn't going to."

"Then what's up?"

Handing me a plastic bag, he watches hopefully as I open it and find it full of my favourite snacks. I stare up at him in surprise.

"It's a long flight." He shrugs.

"Thanks, Leigh."

"Don't mention it."

Dropping a kiss on top of my head, he moves to the back of the aeroplane to take his seat. I stash the snacks beneath my seat, my chest burning with warmth. He's so sweet and thoughtful.

Settling back into my seat, I let my eyes close as the rest of our stuff is loaded, and pre-flight checks take place. The aeroplane hums with vibrations as it takes off smoothly into the air, taking us far from England and its troubles.

"Holiday time!" Leighton hoots.

Enzo glowers at him. "This is hardly a celebration."

"Screw you, Enz. I'm excited for white sand beaches and cocktails."

"I could drink a cocktail or two," I offer.

Leighton winks at me. "That can be arranged."

Behind his laptop, Theo glances at me beneath his glasses. I catch him staring and smile back. The corners of his mouth tilt upwards just for me, making my toes curl.

Pulling a book from my bag, I lose myself to a tale of distant cities, fantasy and magic, letting the others talk in low whispers around me. Hunter is lightly snoring as he rests opposite me, fast asleep.

When the air hostess delivers a round of drinks, he wakes up long enough to knock back a cup of tea with his pain meds before promptly passing back out. Enzo watches him closely.

"He's doing okay, Enz."

"Is he?" Enzo sighs.

"You really need to stop worrying about all of us so much."

"Someone has to."

"That someone doesn't always have to be you."

Shaking his head, he stares down at the black coffee in his hands. I want to take him into my arms and tell him that everything is going to be okay, but I can't do that. Not anymore.

Pastor Michaels escaped, and he's still out there, plotting his next move. We're fresh out of leads, beaten and scarred. This case has broken all of us in so many ways. Hope is in short supply right now.

Chest tight, I unclip my belt buckle and head for the bathroom. The moment the door clicks shut behind me, I slump against it and fight to control my shallow breathing.

The mirror on the wall taunts me with a harrowing glimpse of my reflection. My face is swollen and heavily bruised, marked in a technicoloured painting of vivid colours. I look horrific.

Falling into a panic attack as the memories of being beaten wash over me, the minutes pass by, painful and terrifying. I can't seem to pull myself out of it this time. All I can see is the blood pouring from Candace's wounds.

"Harlow?" A fist knocks on the door.

I startle, scrubbing the tears from my bruised face. "Yeah?"

"You okay in there?" Enzo checks.

"I'm f-f-fine, Enz."

"You've been in there for a while. Open up."

Bracing my hands on the sink, I suck in through my gritted teeth, trying to find some semblance of control. I don't want him to see me like this. He'll only worry even more.

"Harlow," he repeats. "I'll break this door down if I have to."

Knowing he fully will, I quickly unlock the door and step back to let Enzo slide into the bathroom. His head brushes the aeroplane ceiling, but the both of us fit inside the private space.

Enzo takes one look at my tear-stained face and his expression shifts into cold, hard anger. His huge paw lifts to cup my cheek and he ever so gently strokes the moisture aside, teasing my bruised skin.

"Baby," he pleads.

"I'm okay, Enz. Just having a m-moment."

"Talk to me. Tell me what's going on."

I gulp hard. "All I can see is what he did to her."

"Candace?"

"Yes. The memories are just too much. It's all I can think about."

Hand raising to smooth my hair, his face softens back into the tender, loving Enzo I know. He looks defeated, his mouth turned down at the corners, and utterly powerless to fix the mess I've made of myself.

"He isn't here," he says gently. "You're safe."

"My brain is struggling to believe that right now."

"You're with me," he tries again. "Does your brain feel safe with me?"

I take a moment to consider. "Yes."

"Then hold on to me for as long as you need to. I'll always keep you safe. I promised that, didn't I?"

Fingers fisting in his black t-shirt, I bury my face in his chest, breathing in the familiar, earthy scent of all things Enzo. He's right. I'm always safe with him. Ever since the moment we met, he's kept that promise.

"He will come for me again."

"Let him try," Enzo threatens.

Rhythmically stroking my hair, he moves lower, his coarse fingertips gliding over my neck and shoulders. I breathe him in, a slow, treacle-like river of warmth pulsing through my veins and heating my core.

"Enz," I moan.

Massaging my skin, his touch stills, trapped by uncertainty.

"You're hurt, little one."

"Please." I look up to plead with my eyes. "I just want to feel something good. I want to feel *you.* The thoughts are so loud."

Cursing under his breath, Enzo tilts a finger beneath my chin so our eyes meet. "You sure about this?"

"I'm safe with you, aren't I?" I throw his words back.

"Always, baby."

"Then yes. Please make me feel good again."

With the aeroplane roaring around us, he backs me up against the sink and his lips land on mine. Mouths devouring each other, we kiss like we're not thirty thousand feet up in the air, and nothing else matters.

Enzo's lips move against mine in a torrent of need, and his hands lower to cup my butt. I'm pinned against his hard frame, the pressure of his cock pushing into my belly.

Lifting me up, he deposits me on the edge of the sink, his teeth sinking into my bottom lip. I gasp into his mouth, my entire body alight and trembling with need.

"Fuck, Harlow. I want you so badly. But we can't do this here."

I reach for his belt buckle. "Like hell we can't."

Unbuttoning his plain black jeans, I slip a hand inside to free his length. It's hot and pulsing in my hand, begging to be sucked. I hop down from the sink and fall to my knees in the private bathroom.

"Harlow—"

"Shut up, Enz."

He braces a hand against the wall as I take his cock into my mouth and suck. His other hand moves to grip my hair tight, creating a delicious sense of pressure that makes me even wetter.

With the tip of his cock nudging my throat, my eyes burn, but I don't relent. I want him powerless and begging for more. It's the only way to retake what's been stolen from me.

"Shit," Enzo curses.

He quickly pulls out before he can finish in my mouth. I blink up at him through my lashes, fighting a grin. I love seeing him panting and wild-eyed.

"I'm going to bury my cock in your tight little cunt," he rasps with a savage smile. "Stand up and bend over, little one."

"Yes, sir."

"Good girl."

Following his order, I turn my back to him and grasp the edges of the sink, tilting my ass until it's bent outwards at the perfect angle. I feel the spank coming before my ass cheek tingles from the rush of heat.

"You better be quiet," he murmurs, soothing the hit with a stroke. "I don't want any of the others to hear us through these thin walls."

Peeling my leggings over my hips, he pushes them down my legs with my panties. I gasp as his palm grips my ass before moving to dip between my legs.

"Let me feel how wet this pretty cunt is for me."

Dipping a finger through my folds, he slides through the wet warmth to push into my entrance. I can't help groaning out loud at the sense of fullness his thick finger provides.

"So wet," he marvels. "Is getting fucked on a moving aeroplane some secret kink I didn't know about?"

Gripping the sink tight, I move against his finger, seeking to increase the friction. He pushes in and out of me in quick succession, his thumb swiping over my bundle of nerves until I'm seeing stars.

"Maybe," I gasp out.

"Then I'll bend you over this sink and fuck you like the good girl you are, little one. How does that sound?"

Pushing a second finger into my slit, he stretches me wider, pumping into my pussy with rapid movements. I'm left on the cusp of falling apart when he suddenly removes his hand.

"Not yet. I want you coming all over my cock."

With a palm on my lower back, he bends me further and I feel his hardness nudging against me. I have enough time to suck in a breath before he pushes into me in one fast surge.

"Enz!"

Holding my hips tight, he slides back out and pushes in, finding a deeper, excruciatingly perfect angle. I cry out again, unable to hold it in, as Enzo spanks me another time.

He soothes the smack with a gentle caress across my skin. Despite the bruises and lacerations between us, I'm glad he's fucking me like he always has —with rough, yet also surprisingly gentle handling.

"Goddamnit, Harlow. You're so fucking perfect."

Slamming back into me, he trails a hand beneath my oversized t-shirt to find my breast. Enzo groans when he finds me braless for the long flight. Cupping my mound, he softly squeezes before tweaking my nipple.

Hips pushing into me, his cock worships me, over and over. Pumping. Thrusting. Slamming. The bathroom hides our secret tryst as Enzo roughly fucks me. I can feel the cusp of my orgasm beginning to rise.

"Come for me, baby," he begs.

Vision hazy, I let the whispers build, louder and louder until it feels like my body is screaming out for a release. When he thrusts into me again, the tension snaps, and I scream out his name.

Head hanging, I pant through the aftershocks. Enzo gives me a moment before pulling out and spinning me around so he can lift me to sit on the edge of the sink again.

Pushing my legs open, he settles between them, sealing his lips back on mine. I wrap my legs around his waist and let him slip back inside me, his length filling me to the brim.

"That's it," Enzo growls into my mouth. "Take every inch of my cock."

My nails dig into his biceps, holding on as he slows down, moving at a tender, careful pace, taking long strokes into me. His eyes lock on mine, searching for all of my secrets.

Gripping my chin, he holds on tight as his tongue slips between my lips to tangle with mine. We both battle for ownership of the other, fighting for dominance in an impossible contest.

"I fucking love you," he gasps.

Kissing him again, I echo his words back.

"I fucking love you."

Forehead meeting mine, he moans a warning before pouring himself into me. The warmth of his hot seed filling me up sets off another orgasm, and I lose myself to the rising tides of bliss threatening to drown me.

The sensations hit again—over and over. Battering pleasure and relief into my skin, far deeper than any bruise already marking my body. The ecstasy takes over everything and leaves me breathless.

We slump together and Enzo has to hold me upright against him so I don't fall. I fight for breath while hiding my face in the rapid rise and fall of his chest.

"Are you okay?" he asks urgently.

I nod into his t-shirt. "Mmm."

"Words, little one."

"I'm good. I can't move."

Enzo chuckles. "I've got you."

Flicking on the tap behind me, he soaks a paper towel in water and dips it between my legs to clean me up. I let him wash me, feeling my cheeks burn. His attentiveness never fails to satisfy me.

With my clothes pulled back into place, Enzo lifts me into his arms so he can carry me back out onto the main floor of the aeroplane. My blush only intensifies at the interested look Leighton gives us.

"Could you make me any more jealous?" He pouts.

"I can certainly try," Enzo quips back.

Sitting back down in his seat, Enzo drops me in his lap. I snuggle close to him and wink at Leighton across the carpeted aisle, watching us both with an annoyed glower.

"Snooze you lose, Leigh."

"Meanies," he complains.

"You get dibs next time."

Fist pumping, he settles back in his seat. "Damn right, I do."

Enzo snorts beneath me, his chest rumbling. "This isn't fucked up at all. Arguing over who gets the next turn with you."

Peering up at him, I can't help but smile. "I think we're the best kind of fucked up."

"Yeah?" He grins down at me.

"Definitely."

Enzo ducks down to peck my lips. "Good, because you're stuck with us now."

"I wouldn't have it any other way."

PLAYLIST

BIT.LY/SKELETALHEARTS

Black Water – The People's Thieves
Empty – Letdown
All I Have – NF
The Kid I Used To Know – Arrested Youth
Put It On Me – Matt Maeson
No More Hiding – Gina Brooklyn
Fool & The Thief – THE HARA
Me and My Brain – Airways
2008 – cleopatrick
Do It For Me – Rosenfeld
My Hand/Lawless Dream – Matt Maeson
Pray – Ready the Prince
Fantastic – Blame My Youth
Hard To Be Alone – Barns Courtney
Villain – MISSIO
Into It – Chase Atlantic
Via – Voices From The Fuselage
Too Far Gone – The Plot In You
The Way That You Were – Sleep Token
Two Weeks – FKA Twigs
DRIFTING – NF
Kijo – Memorist
Sad Money – Call Me Karizma
Taurus – Machine Gun Kelly & Naomi Wild
Room To Breathe – You Me At Six
Hotel – Montell Fish
Dead – 228k

Make This Go On Forever – Hahlweg
Hold Your Breath – Astyria
We Are Not Okay – NIKKITA

HOLLOW VEINS

SABRE SECURITY #3

TRIGGER WARNING

Hollow Veins is a contemporary reverse harem romance, so the main character will have multiple love interests that she will not have to choose between.

This book is very dark and contains scenes that may be triggering for some readers. This includes physical and psychological abuse, torture, sexual assault and abuse, imprisonment, graphic violence, serial murder, PTSD, Trichotillomania, mass suicide and cult-worship.

If you are triggered by any of this content, please do not read this book.

Additionally, British Sign Language (BSL) is used throughout and is distinguished through the use of italicisation.

Settle in and enjoy the final chapter of Harlow's story!

"Better to reign in Hell than serve in Heaven."

- John Milton

PROLOGUE

GOD SAVE ME – GENOSKY & PROMOTING SOUNDS

MICHAEL ABADDON

With my knees pressed against the floor of the bedroom, I stare up at the hewed wood of the crucifix nailed into the wall. My hands are tightly clasped together, the gold-edged Bible laying open in front of me.

"Lord Almighty. Forgive me, for I have sinned. My flesh is weak. I have wrestled with sin and failed. Grant me your holy forgiveness, Lord."

I roll up the sleeve of my simple shift shirt that has the scent of cheap soap clinging to the fabric. Then I lift the knife that rests beside my Bible. The blade is curved into a wicked arc, the hilt glinting with rich engravings.

As steel meets flesh, the flow of hot, cleansing blood seeps from the deep wounds I inflict upon my inner forearm. Over and over. Slash after slash. Cut. Slice. Bleed. Repent.

"Forgive me, Heavenly Father. I did not mean to hurt her."

Yes. You did.

For as long as I can remember, there's been this dark, murmured voice in the back of my mind. On occasion, it escapes the shackles I've forged from fire and brimstone to keep it imprisoned in the safety of my imagination.

When it does come out, my scripture fails. The Lord's light disappears from my inner landscape, overshadowed by the cloying shadows of the devil's soldiers, preparing to invade.

Slicing deep into my arm, I repeat the words bruised and beaten into me throughout the years we spent at Genesis Home, despite the decades that have passed. The twisted symphony has accompanied my darkest hours ever since.

You are a sinful demon, Michael.

Pain cleanses us of all our sins.

Remember your scripture.

Placing the bloodstained knife down with a shaking hand, I take a strip of clean cotton from inside the hand-carved wooden box that houses my equipment. The pure-white fabric is soon soaked through with dark, sinister crimson.

It doesn't stop the memories of her voice screaming for mercy. I didn't mean to hurt her. All I wanted was to talk. The short walk home from the chapel that hosts evening prayers snakes through the depths of the city. It's impossible to ignore the walking sacks of flesh and sin.

They heckle as you pass, tempting demons in with their disgusting offers and bare legs. One shouted that she'd suck my cock for little more than the price of a newspaper. Filthy fucking whore.

I'm not sure how it happened. The world flashed in and out in shades of red, and before I knew it, her face was pummelled into a paste beneath my swollen fists. I ran before the authorities could be alerted.

Rosetta and I move regularly, adopting new names and identities. It has become second nature to us now, after we were forced to flee our previous home when a similar *incident* occurred. For that, I can only blame the devil.

"M-Michael?"

While my head stays lowered, my hands curl into fists.

"What have I told you about interrupting me while I'm praying?"

"I'm s-sorry," Rosetta stutters. "I just wanted to remind you about your meeting. The train leaves in half an hour. You're going to be late."

Seething, I push the box back underneath our plain double bed and stand. She still dares to speak to me, even through her split lips and the dark clouds of bruises that ring her eyes.

I should've broken her fucking jaw. That would keep her quiet. She's lucky to even be breathing. The Lord only punishes those who deserve it. Those who are corrupted enough to draw his wrath.

There's a reason why Rosetta lost our child—she's a sinner, like the rest of them. After years of attempting to fill her barren womb, we were finally rewarded, only for her to screw everything up. Again.

"Have you done your afternoon prayers?" I ask curtly.

Her eyes duck in fear. "Daphne called. I was on the phone."

"But you thought interrupting mine was appropriate?"

"I w-was only trying to help."

"Silence. I don't want to hear any more of your lies."

She swallows a cry of pain as my fist connects with her cheek. A spray of dark blood hits the wall and leaves a smeared imprint like one of those Rorschach inkblot tests that doctors used to make me do.

I still don't know what they were looking for. The demons within me aren't so easily discerned. They speak in shadows and the silent pauses between breaths. No one can cure my God-given right to rule.

"You're going to kneel on the floor. Now."

With tears soaking into the weathered flesh of her cheeks, Rosetta nods and follows my command. Her blue dress is tucked beneath her legs as she assumes the position beneath the watchful gaze of the crucifix.

"And you're going to pray," I spit at her. "Pray for God's forgiveness. That child's death is on your head."

"Please," she whimpers. "I didn't mean to lose our baby. I had a miscarriage."

"You think I care what you meant? This is your punishment for allowing sinful thoughts to enter your mind. Now you have to pay the price for your lustful ways."

Rosetta screams when I grab a handful of her brown hair and use it to smash her face into the wall. The quiet *crunch* of her already crooked nose colliding with the flat surface sends spikes of violence through my veins.

More.

She deserves more.

They all do.

"I'm going to go deal with this situation." I stroke a hand over her head. "God grants his hardest battles to his most dedicated soldiers. It seems I am being tested today."

She doesn't respond, her gaze focused on her laced fingers. I can see the movement of her lips forming the words I've whipped, beaten and bruised into her soul.

Rosetta must repent, like every other woman who dares to lead me astray. They must all earn God's mercy to receive it. He sees their lies and bad intentions, no matter what mockery they preach.

I leave her crying on the floorboards and head for the train station. We're currently based out of Wolverhampton, eighteen months into our latest identity. There's no telling how long this one will last.

The people who once pursued us have long since lost interest or have passed on. This was supposed to be our fresh start, along with the life God granted us.

Instead, I have a useless whore of a wife, and the demonic slut who abandoned me as a baby has dealt me another blow. Her death allowed my half-sister, Giana, to track me down.

I wasn't expecting to find a sibling when I attended to my mother's meagre affairs. Michael Abaddon's life was abandoned years ago, much like she did to me as a child, but I still kept tabs.

The train ride to the quiet countryside is a painful three hours. Leaving the stifling heat of strangers packed together like sardines, I summon a taxi then rattle off the address written on my palm.

After a short drive through the countryside, a small, cramped house nestled amidst a bad neighbourhood greets me. There's a battered, centuries-old truck parked outside the family home.

My knuckles rap against the door in a reluctant lament. The reasons for allowing this interaction are selfless. I'm trying to save Giana. Our mother was a godless cunt wrapped in the skin of a whoring demon.

My so-called sister has that bitch's blood in her veins, so she is cursed. Our whole family is. That's why the devil is buried deep in my bones and comes to me in murderous whispers. I've been cursed too.

I have to help her.

I have to save her.

When the door opens, the first thing I notice is the smattering of toys across my sister's threadbare carpet. She's short and thin, her blonde hair untidy and framing uncertain green eyes that match my own.

"Michael. You came."

"I did." Stepping inside, I peer around the messy porch. "I don't have long. I've left my wife at home."

"How is she? And the baby?"

Anger curdles in my gut. I offered Giana a smattering of details at my mother's unmarked graveside. In the handful of weeks that have passed since then, the cruel lash of fate has cut my luck short.

"Fine," I lie stiffly. "Healthy."

Giana smiles. "That's good. Those first few months are so crucial."

"Indeed, they are. Is your husband home?"

She guides me through the house towards the kitchen. "He's at work. I thought it might be best if we talked first, before I introduce you to anyone."

More lies. I can sense it. She's hiding something about her life and the people she lives with. There's no love in her voice, no pride.

"You didn't tell them about her, did you?" I guess.

Giana's gaze ducks. "You can't even say *her* name?"

"No. I refuse."

She sighs. "I left my old life behind when I was adopted as a child. After marrying Oliver and having Letty, I didn't feel the need to share my birth mother's story with them."

The children's toys were a dead giveaway, but the moment I hear her name, darkness rears its head inside of me. Glossy black wings unfurl, and hell's fires begin to burn beneath my skin.

"How old is Letty, exactly?"

"She turned eight-years-old a couple of weeks ago."

"Precious." I take a seat at her round, cloth-covered table. "Children are a blessing from God."

"Oh, well, I suppose they are." Giana hesitates, seeming doubtful. "Are you excited to become a father yourself?"

Acid slips over my tongue. "Oh, yes. We are thrilled. We've been trying unsuccessfully for many years."

"I didn't expect to have Letty. We had only been married for a couple of months when I got pregnant."

If I'm not mistaken, there's a hint of displeasure in my sister's voice. Just a whisper. The smallest grain of resentment.

"She was unplanned?" I poke further.

Her eyes lower. "Very much so."

"You should be thankful for such a blessing."

The crease between her furrowed brows deepens. I remain silent as she fills a chipped teapot and hands me a similarly damaged mug. Clearly, they don't entertain much.

"Do you go to church?"

"Church?" she repeats. "No. We aren't religious. My adoptive mother was an atheist."

Blasphemous bitch.

"The Lord grants all his children mercy, if they will only ask for it," I inform her. "You should think about that."

"Uh, well... Like I said, we're not religious."

"When the time for judgement comes, it won't matter who believes in the Lord's divine work and who does not. The sinners will be judged regardless."

Her eyes slide over to me before quickly darting away. The awkward silence is broken as she sits down and pours the tea.

"Are there moments in your life that you regret?" I question softly. "Things you wish that you could take back? Mistakes? Sins?"

"Of course," she admits.

"Are you happy, Giana?"

"I … *ahem*. Well, I am."

"There's nothing in your life that you'd change?"

"Why are you asking me these things?" she snaps, becoming flustered.

I lean forward to bring our eyes level. "I know that you have a feeling deep inside of you. A sense that something is broken, somehow."

Her lips fall open on an unsteady breath. "I… I…"

"It's always been there. No matter where you go or what you do, the voice still whispers."

Her green eyes sparkle like pine trees draped in morning dew, and her bottom lip wobbles. There it is. The lie. The story she tells the world. I can see the deceit buried in her irises.

"How old were you when she left you?" I ask, barely above a whisper.

"Seven," Giana chokes out. "I was seven."

"So young to be left alone in the world, isn't it? I didn't make it that long. Our mother squeezed me out then abandoned me at the first children's home she could find."

"I'm sorry, Michael. She hurt us both. You know that."

"Do I? Seems to me that you had seven years of knowing one of your parents. You were cared for, however briefly. Maybe you were even loved."

"She gave me up for adoption. That isn't love."

"It's a damn sight better than being abandoned in an abusive prison."

Her chair scrapes back as she stands in an attempt to regain some futile sense of power.

"I have to pick Letty up from school," Giana blurts. "Perhaps we should talk another time."

Drawing to my feet, I reach inside my coat pocket and pull out the slim, leather-bound book I tucked inside earlier. It's a smaller version of my own Bible and well-worn from use.

Placing it down on the kitchen table, I offer my half-sister a knowing grin. The deep grooves of her frown have evaporated into a look of discomfort and almost… fear.

She looks just like that disgusting slut did last night as I prowled closer, my fists raised and ready to beat the Lord's sermon into her.

"For you." I push the book towards her. "God is willing to accept all strays, Giana. No matter how lost. Perhaps it's time for you to come home."

Turning my back on her startled facial expression, I let myself out of her home. Giana doesn't follow. When I look over my shoulder before closing the door, she's clasping the Bible in her hands and has begun to thumb through the pages.

Hook, line and sinker.

Her heathen soul is ripe for the taking.

But if my dearest sister wants me to save her from a loveless marriage and a child she never wanted, she will have to pay for her ticket into the Lord's light. No redemption is free of charge. A debt must be paid.

Rosetta will never give me a child.

I'll have to steal one for myself.

CHAPTER 1
HARLOW

WHO ARE YOU FIGHTING FOR? – GINA BROOKLYN

"CATCH THE FUCKING BALL!"

The sound of a football whooshing over me disturbs my swelteringly hot afternoon study session. I peer down the stretch of sandy beach in time to see it collide with Leighton's lowered head.

"Ouch!" he bellows. "You asshole."

On the other side of our private beach, Enzo's golden, sun-kissed skin glows in the afternoon warmth. His shoulders look like carved trunks of oak that are painted a flawless shade of caramel.

"I warned you. What the hell are you looking at?"

"My damn mosquito bite," Leighton shouts back. "Look at the size of my leg! It looks like it's gonna fall off or something."

"Want me to amputate it for you? Free of charge."

"You'd like that, wouldn't you?"

Enzo chuckles. "Very much so."

With an eye roll, I refocus on the notebook in front of me. Normally, Theo helps me with the algebraic formulas we're currently learning in my online maths course.

Every single day for the last two months, I've woken up to the same bubble of peace and tranquillity. They are two words I never thought I'd use to describe my life, but we've somehow found it, even if only temporarily.

I landed on these shores broken and bruised, but our break from reality has healed wounds I didn't even know existed until they were gone. Our two-week holiday soon stretched into a two-month sabbatical.

With a dramatic huff, Leighton collapses on the sand-covered beach towel next to me. Flopping onto his back, he throws a lazy hand over his face that's framed by salt-mussed brown locks.

"Who won?" I ask absently.

His warm, emerald eyes flick over to me. "Who do you think? That man needs to learn how to lose. It'll be good for his ego."

"Thought you were just letting him win?"

"Well, obviously. I'm nothing if not a gentleman."

Placing my pen down, I roll sideways on my towel to snuggle up against his bare torso. With Leighton dressed in only a tight pair of blue swim shorts, every sculpted line of his stocky build is exposed to my kisses.

My lips travel up his sand-dusted skin then over blemishes and adorable freckles brought out by the constant sunshine, until his button nose is brushing mine.

His features are handsome and symmetrical, much like his brother's model-perfect looks. Leighton's face is softer, though, clearly younger and always lit with a gleam of mischief.

"That's a very skimpy bikini you're wearing today," he murmurs appreciatively. "Looks good, Goldilocks."

"It would look even better on your bedroom floor."

Leighton's lips part. "Fuck yeah, it would. You offering?"

"My classes are done for the day."

Before our mouths can meet, the sand we're lying on almost shudders with the weight of Enzo thumping his mountainous body down on my other side, the football now abandoned.

That man could shake heaven and Earth, if he felt so inclined, without breaking a sweat. I don't think I've seen him wear a single shirt in the eight weeks we've spent in Costa Rica.

"I won," Enzo declares triumphantly.

"So I heard."

Two paw-like hands wrap around my waist from behind and drag me backwards, away from Leighton, until the press of firm abdominals meets my spine.

"Mine," Enzo growls out. "What's my prize, little one?"

"Thief," Leighton mutters.

"Shut up, little shit. She's mine to steal."

Stifling a giggle, I twist in Enzo's embrace until I'm on my back, staring up into the vivid amber depths of his irises. They're almost covered by jet-black hair so overgrown, it brushes his earlobes.

The sharp planes and strong angles of his face have been brought out by the almost glowing quality of his tan. In the Costa Rican sunshine, he's darkened to a gorgeous, bronzed colour.

Enzo's looks are too harsh to be classified as traditionally handsome, but he could rival a Viking warrior. Every ridge of muscle that carves his Herculean frame screams intimidation.

"What would you like?"

His full lips twist into a smirk. "I can think of a few things."

Trailing a thick finger over the strap of my red, halter-neck bikini, he ever so softly pushes it off my shoulder. It took me almost a month to work up the courage to wear my scarred skin so freely.

"Whoops." Enzo's smile darkens. "My bad."

"This is my favourite bikini," I protest. "Please don't wreck it like you did the last one."

"You wrecked her bikini?" Leighton repeats, sounding almost jealous. "That's it. Hand her back, you fucking caveman."

"Why don't you come and get her?" Enzo challenges. "Spoiler alert, you'll lose. Again."

"I let you win!"

"Bullshit. I declare a rematch."

"Winner gets to sleep in Harlow's bed tonight?" Leighton suggests. "Alone this time. I'm sick of you hogging the whole mattress."

"Hey! Don't I get a say in this? It's my bed."

But neither of them answers me, too busy shaking hands over my head. The idiots abandon me to resume their game, now kicking the football even more violently than before.

Left alone with my laptop, notebook and a dog-eared textbook that barely survived the international postage from England, I give up the pretence of studying. It's almost lunchtime anyway.

Thanks to Theo's daily tutoring, I was able to begin my deferred classes online and settle in with relative ease. Lounging in the sunshine quickly grew boring after the first couple of weeks.

Once I healed up and my technicoloured face was fit for live videos two hours a day, I decided to take a leap of faith. Turns out, it was the best decision I could've made.

It wasn't even that hard to catch up. After the first few classes, I surprised myself with how much knowledge I've retained, despite the almost fourteen years since I last attended a school class.

"You are such a fucking dick!" Leighton shouts as he chases after the football, now floating out to sea.

Enzo folds his arms, smirking to himself. "I'm calling it. You lost, Leigh. Loser has to go fetch the ball."

Still cursing, Leighton throws himself into the crystal-clear water lapping at the edges of our private, white-sand beach. His head disappears beneath the waves, chasing after the ball.

"That should keep him occupied." Enzo lopes towards me, full of swagger. "Finished for the morning?"

"I'm all done. Just have a pop quiz to prep for tomorrow."

"Fuck that," he declares. "Let's go out. Theo's gonna be stuck in his briefing with the intelligence department for hours yet."

Stretching, I crack my stiff neck. "He really can't bear to take a single day off, can he?"

"He lasted about a week longer than I expected without opening his laptop." He offers me a hand up. "Hunter and I placed bets."

Enzo tugs me to my bare feet. With July merging into early August, it's a pleasantly hot day on the shoreline. After never once leaving England, adjusting to this climate took some time.

"Is Hunter asleep?"

"Knocked out cold," he confirms. "Another migraine. Leighton convinced him to take one of those pills the specialist prescribed."

"Shit. It must be a bad one for him to cave."

"Not quite as bad as last week, I don't think. Hard to tell. You know how weird he is about admitting when he's in pain."

Rolling up my beach towel, I protest when Enzo steals it from me, along with my belongings, insisting on carrying them himself. His spare arm circles my shoulders to pin me against his side.

Our private villa stretches out behind the beach that we get all to ourselves. The nearest town, Quepos, is a twenty-minute drive through luscious rainforest and winding, dusty roads.

The villa is carved from glowing, stained beams of wood with thick floorboards and floor-to-ceiling windows covered in flowing, white curtains. It was an excellent call on Leighton's part.

With five individual bedrooms, a sprawling open-plan kitchen and complete isolation from other human beings, we've lived out the last couple of months in blissful peace and quiet.

"What do you want to do?" Enzo asks, holding open the billowing curtain for me.

I step inside the coolness of the villa. "How about another dirt bike lesson?"

"Keep it up and you won't be needing many more lessons from me. We'll have to get you a bike of your own at home."

The first day Enzo unveiled the slightly rusted, off-road bike he rented from a local, I was too terrified to even lay a finger on it. That soon changed after I had my first few lessons, though.

There's no feeling quite like racing along the winding, helter-skelter roads of rural Costa Rica with the warm wind in my hair and Enzo's strong arms strangling my waist as he hoots in approval.

"Go put some clothes on," he orders. "We can grab a drink in town after. I need to check the post office for a package anyway."

"Anything important?"

"Just some paperwork that Kade needs us to sign for the company. Nothing crazy important."

I circle my fingertips over my exposed sternum. The mention of home causes my heart to ache. As much as I've loved our time here, this isn't where we belong. We can't hide forever.

After snagging a pale-yellow sundress and pair of Chucks from my bedroom, I make a beeline for the small office at the back of the villa. The chatter of voices emanates through the ajar door.

I can see Theo rubbing his temples while glowering at his laptop. The black frames of his glasses are pushed up to hold his white-blonde ringlets out of his face. On the screen, his team is bickering amongst themselves.

"We've run our facial recognition software on every camera in the fucking country," Fox argues defensively. "It didn't work."

"We're doing the best we can to find him," Rayna adds.

"I don't give a fuck about what you think you're doing." Theo puts his glasses back on. "Nobody disappears off the face of the planet. Run the damn software again."

"But—"

"That wasn't a request. Call me when it's done."

Slamming his laptop shut, Theo lets loose a groan as his forehead collides with the desk. I sneak into the room on silent feet then bury my face in his head full of curls.

"I had no idea that you were so bossy," I breathe into his hair. "Poor Rayna and Fox."

His head doesn't lift. "I designed that software myself. Nothing gets around it. I'll break every last security law in the country if that's what it takes to get a lead."

Winding my arms around his neck, I pull him back against my chest and snuggle him tight. Theo relaxes into me, taking a calming breath to settle his impatience.

"He's been silent for two months," I point out. "No more victims, no messages. Not even a sighting. You're being too hard on yourself for coming up empty-handed."

"Don't mistake his silence for defeat, beautiful. This isn't over. Not by a long shot."

Savouring his scent, a tantalising blend of fresh mint and the pages of the books we both hold so dear, I ponder his words. He's right. Silence doesn't equal defeat.

We all know that Pastor Michaels—or Michael Abaddon as we now know him—is still out there, lurking in the shadows and biding his time. He's evaded capture for far longer than any of us anticipated.

Hudson and Kade have continued the manhunt in our absence, providing us with regular updates. We've theorised that my monster has found himself allies. I think it's the only reason he hasn't been caught.

"Got any homework you need help with?"

I release Theo with a sigh. "Nope. Enzo's taking me out on the dirt bike. We're gonna go pick something up then get a drink."

"Sounds good. I've got some more work to finish up here. Will you two be okay?"

"Yes, Theodore." I plant a kiss on his cheek. "Don't worry so much. This is supposed to be a holiday, you know."

Grabbing my wrist before I can leave, Theo tugs me backwards. I topple onto his lap, almost falling over before his slim arms catch me and two pale-blue eyes stare down at my face.

The hesitant kisses he once offered have long since dissolved into hungry, bruising collisions. He's no longer afraid of breaking me, and I love it.

We've fooled around a few times but have never taken that final step. Each time, we inch a little closer to the end goal, and I'm desperate for that day to come.

My lips automatically part, allowing his tongue to slide into my mouth and tangle with mine. He tastes like the half-finished cup of coffee on the desk, mingled with something entirely Theodore.

When we break apart at the sound of Enzo shouting my name, his nose nudges mine. My legs are trembling as warmth begins to pool in my lower belly, demanding more of his attention.

"Be careful," he whispers throatily.

"Always am."

"Doesn't stop me from worrying about you. All it takes is one mistake."

"Hey." I grip his chin so our eyes meet. "Stop waiting for this to be taken away from you, because it isn't going to happen. I'm staying right here, where I belong."

The thin slice of darker blue, almost black around his irises, expands, leaking fear and apprehension. I can read him like a book after all the time we've spent together.

"I can't help it. Everyone I've ever loved has left me, and I can't lose you too, Harlow. I won't."

I press our foreheads together. "You never have to."

"Promise?"

"I fucking promise."

He smirks. "Potty mouth."

"You love it."

Slanting my mouth against his again, I brush a stray ringlet from his face before getting up from his lap and grabbing my Chucks. As I retreat from the room, his mobile phone is already ringing again.

With a final blown kiss, I head for the third bedroom down the bamboo-lined corridor. Inside, the curtains are drawn tightly shut, plunging the king-sized bed into complete darkness. There's a lump under the duvet.

I watch for the rise and fall of Hunter's sleeping form. Where his long, chestnut waves would've once spilled over the pillows, his hair is kept very short now, neatly shaved to show the grisly scar from his surgery.

It's been a trying couple of months for Hunter. Well, for the whole family. We've all been learning British Sign Language to help with communication, but it's an imperfect process, and everyone's patience has been tested.

There are some days when he doesn't leave his room or utter a single word —signed or spoken. Others, there's a glimmer of the person he used to be before the world broke him. There's no predicting which mood he will wake up in.

My fingers itch with the urge to approach him and curl up in the warm shell of his body. I want to keep Hunter safe, like he's done for me since the moment we met.

But I can't protect him from this.

Nobody can.

"Harlow! You coming?"

Closing the door, I follow the sound of Enzo's voice. He cocks an eyebrow as I slip the sundress over my bikini while walking. He's ready to go with two helmets and a shirt thrown on to cover his broad chest.

"He's still asleep." I slip on my shoes. "Maybe we should call his doctor. These headaches are so debilitating for him."

"The specialist said they're to be expected."

Enzo lifts my long hair then begins to twist it into a braid. His fingers deftly weave through the strands, lacing them together into a tight plait.

Every time he strokes the sensitive slopes of my scalp, I have to bite back a sigh of pleasure. My hair is still a no-go for almost everyone, apart from the guys and their reverent touches.

"He can't live like this forever."

"And we can't fix everything for him," he says curtly. "Hunter has to figure out some things for himself, including how to live with his injuries."

Removing the ever-present elastic from his wrist when the braid is complete, Enzo ties it off and nods to himself. Leighton has trained them all to carry elastics around when I need an intervention to stop from pulling my hair again.

Enzo positions the helmet to cover my head. I pout at him as he fastens the strap tight under my chin and declares the job done.

"He's in pain, Enz."

"I know, angel. Trust me, if I could take his pain away and have it myself, I'd do it in a heartbeat. But I can't do that."

Holding my breath to stop the frustrated tears from rising against my will, I make myself nod instead. Enzo drops a kiss on the tip of my nose and tangles our fingers together.

"Come on, let's go. Drive all the way into town without stalling the bike, and I'll throw dinner on top of those drinks."

I squeeze his calloused hand.

"You've got yourself a deal."

CHAPTER 2
LEIGHTON

STRANGERS – BRING ME THE HORIZON

POKING the strips of sizzling chicken in the pan, I slide the chopping board and knife over to Hunter. His eyes connect with mine before he tackles the pile of fresh veggies and begins to neatly slice them.

Spread out across the three-foot dining table that dominates the open-plan kitchen, Harlow is frowning down at her notebook as she works through some complicated maths problem with Theo's help.

Sliding my phone from my pocket, I shoot her a message and watch as she picks her phone up to read it with a tiny grin.

Leighton: Aren't you bored?

Harlow: To death.

I smother a laugh. Knew it. Theo's tutoring is exhausting to watch, let alone participate in.

Leighton: How haven't you murdered him yet?

Harlow: I finished my period yesterday. Feeling less stabby.

Leighton: Damn. I was hoping for more period sex.

Harlow: I can still do the latter ;)

Leighton: It's a date, princess.

"You need to carry the three over," he instructs from behind his laptop.

"Like this. Then you can circle back and divide the sum by four to find the overall fraction."

The palm of her hand crashes against her forehead. "When on earth am I ever going to need to use fractions? I thought these skills were meant to be important."

"You'll never need to use fractions," I chime in. "They're just one of the many bullshit hoops the education system makes you jump through. Complete waste of time."

"That isn't true." Theo casts me a glare. "Fractions are helpful."

I point towards him with a spatula. "Name one example."

"You walk in with three pizzas, and there are five of us waiting to eat. How do we divide them up?"

"We don't, obviously. I eat all three. Fuck the lot of you. Get your own damn pizza, or starve to death. It's not my problem."

Laughing to herself, Harlow smothers her grin. "Charming."

Glowering at me, Theo's eyes narrow in annoyance. This is precisely why he's her tutor for this pointless schooling mission she's on and not me.

I did offer, though.

She laughed in my face.

"Food ready yet?" Enzo emerges from his bedroom, his black hair wet from the shower. "I'm fucking starving after that run."

He has taken to signing his words as he speaks to help Hunter's comprehension. We're trying our best to be thoughtful and inclusive, but my shit-for-brains attention span is making learning a new bloody language difficult.

"Ten minutes," Hunter mutters.

Glancing over at him, I notice he's slicing the veggies wrong. I tap his shoulder to gain his attention then freeze up, uncertain of what to say next.

"Uh, what's the sign for *dicing*? Anyone?"

"There isn't a sign for it," Theo responds like it's obvious. "You'll have to fingerspell. There aren't words in BSL for everything. The same as there aren't full sentences, just words."

"How the hell do I fingerspell?" I growl out. "And what's the point of inventing a language if you don't have all the words?"

"I didn't invent it, Leigh. Take it up with someone else."

"I intend to."

"You need to use a combination of sign language, fingerspelling, lip-reading and body language."

"All four fucking things?" I snarl in frustration.

"Yes!"

Hunter takes a swig from his beer, watching me with a grin tugging at his lips. I'm glad he's finding this situation funny. In his position, I don't know that I'd find our inability to communicate properly so amusing.

"You need to start studying more." Enzo tosses me an unimpressed look. "His hearing isn't coming back. You can't write text messages to him instead of speaking forever."

"Thanks, idiot. Like I didn't know that."

"You're the one being an idiot, Leigh. We're all making an effort to learn a new way to communicate, except for you."

"It's hard, alright?"

"Harder than what he's going through right now?"

"Guys." Harlow snaps her notebook shut to cut us off. "You're both acting like assholes, and it ends now. We're in this together."

"But, Harlow—"

"Enough, Enz. Leighton is trying his best. Back off."

Enzo mutters an apology under his breath then drops it. I cast Harlow a grateful look. She winks back at me, tidying up her school stuff before clearing the table for dinner.

Sliding behind the floating kitchen island, she cuddles up to Hunter's back. With her arms around his waist, Harlow takes hold of the knife and demonstrates dicing the veggies instead.

"All he had to do was tell me if he wanted them diced," Hunter complains, retaking the knife. "I'm not a mind reader."

Feeling like a total dickhead, I glare at the chicken while pushing it around the frying pan. It's not my fault they've all picked up sign language like it's easy. I'm trying my best here.

We're all struggling in our own ways. This whole situation is challenging, but we're doing our best to muddle through and help Hunter get back on his feet, one day at a time.

With all the food ready, we kick Theo's work-from-home setup off the dinner table then spread out everything we've made. Enzo locates a pack of cold beers from the fridge and doles out the brown-coloured bottles.

He attacks the food first, piling his plate high with chicken, salad, veggies and fresh bread from the local bakery. Hunter sticks to his second beer, gingerly poking some lettuce around his plate.

"I was thinking about taking a hike tomorrow," I announce, breaking the tense silence. "We haven't been to the national park since our first week here."

Enzo nods, chewing his mouthful. "I wouldn't mind doing some sightseeing. Why don't we all go? Together?"

Everyone's eyes automatically slide over to Hunter's slumped shoulders. I know he despises the fact that our day-to-day schedule depends on his health now.

His severe migraines and occasional dizzy spells are aftereffects of his head injury. Even months later, it's still healing, and he requires regular check-ups with his consultant to monitor his progress.

"*Hiking? Tomorrow?*" Enzo signs.

Hunter shrugs. "You guys can go."

Wiggling her fingers to gain his attention, Harlow's brows arch as she replies, "*Come.*"

My brother's chocolate-brown eyes slide back down to his plate. The scar that slashes through his eyebrow is joined by several new patches of tight, pink skin that span from his reconstructed ear.

"You don't have to include me." Hunter takes another swig from his beer. "I'm fine alone here. It doesn't matter."

"We don't have to exclude you either," I snap back, even if he can't hear me. "Someone tell him what I'm saying. This is ridiculous."

"Leigh," Harlow warns.

"He's the one pushing us away!"

"And it's your job not to let him," she argues, reaching out to touch Hunter's tattooed arm. "*Come.*"

Shrugging once more, he pushes her hand aside. His chair loudly scrapes backwards. He takes his beer to his bedroom without a word. The sound of the door slamming shut reverberates around us.

I wish I could say this was a one-off, but his intense mood swings have become normal. My brother has always been a grumpy bastard, and now he has a legitimate reason to lose his shit.

Theo spears a slice of cucumber. "That went well."

I slam my fork down. "Look, I'm trying my best here. He's not exactly making it easy to help him. That wasn't all my fault."

"It's no one's fault," Harlow corrects. "Just give him some space. He made it out of bed today, so that's an improvement."

We lapse back into tense silence until Enzo breaks it.

"He needs to go home. All this moping around isn't good for him. We should get him back to work. He needs to feel like himself again."

"How do you know what he needs?" I accuse.

"I'm trying a lot harder than you are to help him. You did what, one sign language class? Months ago?"

"Not this again." Harlow shakes her head in despair. "The pair of you need to grow up, and fast. We don't have time for this."

Pushing her plate aside, she stands then disappears through the floating curtains that lead to the back porch overlooking the shoreline.

The sun slants through the translucent material, lighting the beach beyond. My stomach twists with shame. None of us are handling this situation well, apart from Harlow.

Her patience is seemingly unlimited. I wish she could lend some of it to the rest of us. It feels like we're careening towards a cliff's edge right now, and I don't know how to stop it.

"She's right," Theo concurs. "We're supposed to be supporting each other, not bickering. Hunter doesn't need that."

Taking a deep inhale, I meet Enzo's eyes. "Look, I'm sorry. I know you're only trying to do what's best for Hunter."

"I'm sorry too," he offers. "There are no rules on how this works. We're just figuring it out. I know you're doing your best to learn."

"I should go check on her."

Enzo rises, his food abandoned. "I've got Hunter."

We both leave Theo sitting at the table alone, his gaze bouncing between us. "I'll just eat all the food, then."

As my feet sink into the cool sand, the warmth of the fading sunbathes me in burnt-orange hues. It's a beautiful evening, perfectly still and hot, the faint chirping of birds echoing with the waves.

At the edge of the ocean, Harlow stands immersed in water, her gaze fixed on the fiery ball of light sinking below the horizon. I stop beside her, letting the bathtub-like water lap at my toes.

"I'm sorry, Goldilocks."

She doesn't respond, her luminous, blue orbs locked on that sunset. I can almost see the golden flames reflected in her eyes. The light sparkles off her skin, gleaming with a healthy glow.

This trip has done her so much good. She's put on at least half a stone of weight, filling out her body with gorgeous, inviting curves that keep me up at night. Her butt and breasts have grown to healthy proportions too.

The biggest change is the thick tufts of shiny brown hair slowly reducing the bald patches that once marred her scalp. It'll take time for the hair to grow back fully, but the damage has stopped spreading now that her relapses are few and far between.

She's healing.

Growing.

Emerging from her chrysalis.

I won't lie. It was the single most harrowing moment of my life when we got the call that she'd disappeared from HQ, taking our broken hearts with her. My entire world ceased to turn.

But the longer we spend here in our private bubble, hidden from the relentless cruelty of the world, I can see that it was necessary. That baptism of fire allowed her to rise again, beaten but unbroken.

"Can you believe this is the same sun we see rise and fall in England?" Harlow murmurs. "It looks different out here."

"Maybe you're different here, not the sun."

"Maybe, but I think I like who I am here."

Tentatively, I steal her hand. "I like who you are here too. But for the record, I love every goddamn version of you."

Her head falls to rest on my shoulder. "If we can't make our relationship work here without fighting, how on earth do we do it back home?"

"We'll do it together, princess. Like we always have."

Extricating herself from my arms, Harlow steps farther into the ocean. She's wearing one of her light linen dresses, but it's quickly pulled off her body and discarded in the water.

"Uh, Goldilocks?"

"I want to swim," she calls back while wading deeper into the water in her underwear. "It's still warm."

Tearing my t-shirt over my head, I toss it back onto the beach then follow her into the waves. It feels like the world's largest bathtub, glinting with the final rays of sunshine.

Above us, the pearlescent half-circle of the moon is visible, peppered with stars growing brighter as darkness falls. Soon, we'll be under nothing but moonlight and God's all-seeing eyes.

When a soaking-wet, cotton bra floats past me, I realise that Harlow is stripping naked. Her panties bob on the surface of the water next. Fuck me. All I can see are her creamy skin and wet hair sinking into the water.

Dumping her wet clothes on the sand along with my boxer shorts, I dive beneath the water then swim fast to catch up. The sea is shallow enough for us to stand, despite being far from the shore.

Water laps at Harlow's clavicles, almost covering her shoulders. When she swims closer to me, her short legs find my waist and wrap around it to bring us flush against each other.

"If we drown out here, Enzo will kill us both."

"I don't care." She clings to me, bringing her rounded, glistening breasts to my chest. "Forget everyone else for a second."

I hold her against me, letting her feel the brush of my hardening cock pushing into her belly. "Happy to."

Her mouth clashes with mine, magnetised together beneath the enigmatic pull of the moon controlling the tide. We're equally as powerless, caught by an invisible force that ties us together.

With her lips caressing mine in languorous strokes, Harlow tastes so sweet. I can't get enough. I want more. Need more. Her touch keeps me alive amongst the chaos.

Our teeth clash as our kiss deepens, each vying for control of the other. I hold her upright in the water. We're alone with nothing but waves and silence intensifying the moment.

Even out here, at the mercy of Mother Nature, Harlow still belongs to me. Mind, body and soul. I'd take her beneath the water and drown us both before letting anyone ever take her away from me again.

When her hand disappears and slender fingers wrap around the steel of my cock, I groan into her lips. We're both completely bare and covered by nothing but the ocean surrounding us.

I grab a handful of her breast, palming the now generous swell. Her nipples are stiffened into peaks beneath the water, begging to be tasted. I break the kiss to suck one into my mouth before biting down.

"Leigh," she whimpers.

Her body is writhing against mine, undulating with each calm wave washing over us. I grasp her hips, controlling her movements to find the exact spot I want to be buried in.

"I'm so fucking glad you went on birth control," I moan into her lips. "Now there's nothing stopping me from doing this."

Harlow cries out as my cock surges inside of her at the perfect angle. Her pussy clenches around me, so damn tight it's almost painful. We fit together like lock and key.

She wasn't expecting that so soon, but I couldn't wait a second longer. Around her, my control is non-existent. She drives me wild without having to utter a single word.

"What if … someone sees?" Harlow gasps.

"Look around." I bite down on her plump bottom lip. "There isn't a soul in sight. I can fuck you wherever I want, baby. Remember that."

She slips her arms around my neck to hold on tight as I thrust into her slit, pushing my hips upwards. Water sloshes around us with each pump, easing the glide of my dick slamming into her.

Her tits are shoved in my face, and water clings to the buds of her hardened nipples. It should be illegal to look this gorgeous. How can I be expected to control myself?

"Do you like it when my cock stretches your sweet little cunt, princess?" I goad her.

"Oh God, Leigh. Yes."

The last sparks of sunlight vanish, bathing us in evening shadows. Darkness encroaches across the water, turning vivid aqua into dark and deadly blackness, broken by the moon's strobe lights.

Out here, it's hard to believe that the rest of the world still exists. This paradise feels like a self-contained universe all on its own. I'd hand my soul to the devil if it meant we could stay here forever.

Legs cinching my waist, Harlow uses momentum to draw her hips upwards and push down on me just as I thrust up into her. We meet in the middle, stroke for stroke, both gasping for air.

"That's it, princess." I palm her ass cheeks. "I wanna see you come for me in the ocean. Now there's a story."

Her breaths escape in adorable little mewls, and her voice is saturated with pleasure. Each time she bounces on my pierced cock, I feel my balls tighten, begging to spill deep inside her cunt.

I love that I can fill her up now. That little white pill she takes each morning is my new best friend. The sight of my come running down her thighs on my birthday two weeks ago was the best present ever.

"I'm gonna come inside you," I say gruffly. "Then I'll take you back inside and fuck you again, bent over the kitchen table."

"You can't do that," she squeals. "Not in front of the others."

"Can't? You really want to use that word?"

Cut off mid-moan, she yelps in surprise when I pull myself out of her. Before she can yell at me for snatching her orgasm away, I lift her from the water and throw her over my shoulder in a fireman's carry.

"Clearly, I need to prove a point." I swat my hand against her dripping ass cheek. "You should never doubt me."

"Leigh! Wait!"

"Shut it, gorgeous."

Walking straight past our sopping wet clothes, I emerge from the sea then heft her higher on my shoulder. Harlow protests the whole way up the beach until we step back inside the villa, then she stops.

Theo is still sitting at the table, his laptop now relocated in front of him as he nurses a second beer. The moment we step inside, he nearly drops the damn thing. His eyebrows shoot upwards.

We're both completely naked and leaving a trail of saltwater across the flooring. Poor Theo has no idea what's coming if this stuns him to silence.

"Leighton," Harlow scolds again. "Put me down this instant."

"Oh, I'll put you down."

Pulling her back over my shoulder, I shove discarded plates and cutlery aside, clearing a spot on the table right next to where Theo is sitting in a state of disbelief.

Harlow squeals as she lands on top of the table, her spine pressed against the wood. Grabbing her wrists, I pin them down, ensuring she can't attempt to escape the situation.

Her eyes are locked on Theo. He hasn't moved away from her sprawled out body, every naked inch glistening with drips of seawater and enticing him in.

"I'm proving a point." I yank her body closer to me. "This is what you're missing out on, Theodore."

Harlow's eyes don't tear from his as I settle back between her thighs, now at the perfect height. She's entirely at my mercy. Theo sits frozen, but he can't seem to find the willpower to leave.

I know they haven't slept together yet. He's taken months to even get this far, but their relationship is progressing, however slowly. He just needs some encouragement to take that leap.

"Looks like we have a witness to me proving my point," I tease. "You gonna show him how good my name sounds on your tongue, Goldilocks?"

Harlow swallows her complaints as I dip a hand between her legs, finding the molten heat at her core. My finger pushes inside her entrance, swirling moisture up to her swollen clit.

Strumming her bundle of nerves, I savour the high-pitched gasp that tears free from her throat. She's desperately trying to hold it in to save embarrassing Theo, but I know exactly how to please my girl.

Pushing a finger back inside her, I pump it in and out, adding a second digit to stretch her wider. She writhes on the table, her hips rising to grind against the heel of my palm.

"So wet, baby. Does Theo watching turn you on?"

"Screw you, Leigh," she groans.

"Soon, princess."

Pinching her bundle of nerves again, I remove my fingers from her pussy. She flames bright-red when I offer the glistening digits to Theo with a confident smirk.

"Want a taste?" I lift an eyebrow. "She's fucking soaked just knowing that you're sitting there, unable to move a muscle."

His lips are pursed, but the bob of his Adam's apple working overtime answers my question. If he wanted to leave, he would. Instead, he's fascinated by the sight of me finger-fucking Harlow.

"Let's give him a real show, shall we, Goldilocks?"

Grasping her narrow hips, I line myself up with her entrance then push back inside her. Harlow grips the edges of the table, crying out so loud, I wonder if we'll have even more company soon.

She still feels heavenly around me. All I can see is her luscious brown hair, spilled out around her head in a halo that complements her blue eyes.

My gorgeous girl.

All. Fucking. Mine.

Holding her hips in a bruising grip, I thrust into her with insatiable hunger. I'll tease the submission free from her throat until it spills out in a scream of pleasure just for Theo's benefit.

The table shakes with our movements, rattling plates and cutlery, all while Theo is held prisoner by his own curiosity. If this doesn't cause his resolve to break, nothing will.

"How incredible does she look right now?" I goad him between thrusts. "Sure you don't want a taste, Theodore?"

His mouth opens and shuts. "Uh."

"Leigh," Harlow mewls. "Stop it."

"Not a chance." I pump into her pussy, loving the way her walls clench tightly. "I wanna see my baby fall apart first."

Her hand slaps across her mouth, holding back a loud moan that would undoubtedly draw Enzo back out here. With a snarl, I recapture her wrist then pin it down to the table.

Her gasps break free in a whispered torment, high-pitched and so fucking adorable, it pains me. The innocent, blue-eyed slip of a girl I first met has blossomed into an incredible woman.

But deep down, past all the layers that she plasters on to fit into the world around her, Harlow's still just a lost soul looking for her home. Like us all. That's why we work… Together or not at all.

As her slick cunt tightens around me, our bodies smashing together in a frenzy of need, I feel my own release approaching. I never thought I'd have Theo as a captive audience, but a sick part of me loves it.

He's allowed to watch her juices spill over my cock, but I'm the one buried deep inside of her right now. She belongs to me and me alone for these brief, blissful moments.

When we're done, I'll surrender the rest of her heart again, but not a second sooner. When I'm fucking Harlow into a boneless puddle, she belongs to only me.

"I'm so close," Harlow whines.

"Come for me, princess. Show Theo what he's missing."

With a roar, I pound into her for a final time and feel myself explode. Harlow's clenched tight around me, and the drawn-out cry that bursts free from her mouth is music to my ears.

Watching her come will never lose its novelty. I never understood the fascination people have for admiring stupid shit like expensive artwork or a rare bottle of wine.

I get it now… the obsession.

She's mine.

I'd kneel at her feet and watch the rise and fall of her chest all day long without stopping for air. She's my addiction… my hedonistic, unjustifiably indulgent expense.

I am endlessly fascinated by this woman and everything about her. The last twenty-five years of my life cease to exist now that I know what life looks like with Harlow in it. I wasn't alive until I met her.

"That's it, baby. Louder."

"Fuck, Leigh!" she screams.

Spilling into her, I love the way her legs tighten around my waist, ensuring I fill every inch of her pussy with my seed. There's nothing like the feeling of complete and utter surrender.

Slumping between her legs, I bury my face in her neck, gasping for air. Harlow barely lets me catch a breath before she tugs my hair and guides her lips to mine.

"I can't believe you just did that," she murmurs.

"I'm not gonna apologise for taking what's mine."

"Did you have to do it in front of him?"

I hesitate for a second. "Yeah. I did."

Groaning under her breath, Harlow hides her face in my chest. She's still painfully shy at times, even when her bodily instincts take over and demand to be satisfied.

I doubt many people would ever bring themselves to even consider the possibility of vulnerability after enduring what she has. This beautiful creature is the one percent.

The survivor.

Our blessing in disguise.

Once I've caught my breath, I look back over to the silent, stammering man caught amongst our chaos. Theo's cheeks are flushed the most violent shade of red, even if his fascination is clear to see.

"I should … g-go," he stutters.

With a nod, he abruptly stands. The bulge tenting his usual faded blue jeans is painfully obvious. I bite back a remark that would only make him blush harder. Harlow might actually kill me in that case.

He disappears into his bedroom so fast, I'm surprised he doesn't leave a trail of smoke behind him. The moment he's vanished from sight, Harlow smacks my chest, blushing beetroot-red herself.

"You two really belong together." I trail a finger over her flaming-hot cheek. "Can't even have a bit of harmless voyeurism without turning into a tomato."

"I am not a tomato."

"You should look in the mirror."

"Well, it's your fault," she complains. "You jumped on me like some kind of wild animal."

"Well, I didn't see you complaining." I push sticky hair from her forehead. "Especially not at the end there."

Before she can shove me off, the door to Hunter's bedroom slams shut, and a looming shadow emerges. Enzo takes one look around the room—plates dislodged, Harlow's bare tits, my ass on display—before halting.

"What the fuck did I miss?"

CHAPTER 3
HARLOW

LET THE RIGHT ONE IN – BOSTON MANOR

"I'M IN MY CAGE, listening to the falling rain. If I concentrate hard enough, it covers the sound of her dying whimpers. I've always loved water and the cleansing power it holds. Even over death."

On the laptop screen, Doctor Richards listens to me, tapping a fountain pen against his closed lips. I set the journal down and breathe through the revulsion reading my own memories brings.

"Which victim was this referring to?" he questions.

"It was Tia. There was a rainstorm the night she died."

Jotting something down, he looks thoughtful. "You don't speak about her a lot. Why was this memory significant to write about?"

"We were close. It's still hard to think about her." I glance at the open door where sea air is leaking inside. "She loved the beach. I've thought about her a lot more since we got here."

"It's important not to erase her existence from your mind simply because it's painful," Richards advises. "You're doing well to write about her in a safe, controlled way."

"Thank you."

I still feel weird being complimented by Richards, especially after what I did to him. I never wanted to hurt him, not even when he threatened me with detainment in a mental health ward.

But after an awkward apology, we fell back into our regular weekly schedule, holding sessions over video call instead. For the first time since starting therapy, I feel like it's helping me.

"How many journals have you filled now?" Richards asks.

"This is my third. Jude supplies me with new ones." I laugh to myself. "He's particular about his stationary, and it's rubbed off on me. I can't write in anything else."

Richards shakes his head. "I have never met anyone more particular than

Jude. I'm glad the writing is working out. You've come a long way in the past few weeks."

"I guess."

"You have. It's a great achievement."

Looking back down at the journal that I've spent countless hours spilling my darkest, innermost thoughts into, I allow myself a sliver of satisfaction. Just a tiny bit.

I'm working hard on myself right now, and it's paying off. I still struggle with the compulsion to pull when things get overwhelming—you can't break a deeply ingrained habit in a couple of months.

But I've now trained myself to stop, breathe and find a pen instead of falling into the familiar comfort of hurting myself. Instead, I batter the pages with ink and determination to get the pain out.

My writing isn't always chronological, nor is it exclusively memories I've pieced back together. These pages are my life. Messy, imperfect, chaotic life in all its varying extremes of good and bad.

"I had an idea I wanted to discuss with you."

His words startle me back to the video call.

"Oh?"

"You've overcome so many obstacles." Richards rests his chin on his laced fingers. "There are a lot of people out there who would benefit from hearing your story. You could do so much good with it."

"I don't understand. My story?"

"Have you considered turning these journals into something more? Perhaps a memoir?"

I frown at the screen. "You think I should write a book?"

"Something to think about," he suggests. "Words are our last unlimited resource. If nothing else, humans will always hold the ability to inspire hope with them."

Clutching the journal a little tighter, I battle a wave of anxiety. It's been the biggest challenge of my life to relive the contents of these pages, word by word, to reconstruct my past.

I don't want someone picking apart my story and writing a callous hit piece for the local newspaper to earn some measly commission. My heart couldn't take that level of rejection, even from a stranger.

"What are you thinking?" he prompts.

"It's just … being vulnerable." I gulp down the lump in my throat. "It's hard for me. This would be putting my entire life out there for the world to read and judge."

"I appreciate that it's a big step. You don't have to do it if you're not comfortable. You've been through so much. Helping others can be its own form of healing, though."

Amidst the panic, a glimmer of something lights my chest. I don't know what this feeling is, but my fingers are twitching with the urge to put pen to paper again. He's lit a tiny spark deep within me.

"That's the end of our session. Same time next week?"

"Sure. Thank you for listening," I offer sincerely. "I appreciate all the help you've given me."

His smile pulls taut the wrinkle lines beneath his spectacles. "I am so incredibly proud of how far you've come since we first met, Harlow. You should be proud too."

Throat tightening, I offer a quick wave then leave the call before I burst into tears. Richards's pride isn't something I thought I needed, but fuck if it doesn't feel good.

Stretching my arms above my head, I quickly return the journal and laptop to my bedroom. The guys are all outside, giving me some privacy. We're due to head into town for some groceries this afternoon.

Sticking my head out through the curtains, I spot them on the back veranda, sprawled out across several sun loungers. Theo's nose is buried in a well-loved copy of *Animal Farm*, lost in its crinkled pages.

On the lounger next to him, Hunter is stretched out, a pair of aviators resting on the tip of his nose as he lightly snores. He doesn't stir when Leighton squirts sun cream on his chest and begins drawing with his finger.

"Hey!" I shout.

His head snaps upwards. "What's up?"

"Stop drawing a dick on your brother. You know that'll burn onto him in this heat."

"Well, duh. That was the plan, Goldilocks."

Heading outside, I nudge Hunter's leg to startle him awake. He catches Leighton red-handed and looks down at the crooked drawing of a lopsided cock on his chest in layers of sun cream.

"Sometimes, I wish I'd been an only child," he says, wiping it away. "Try it again and you won't have a finger to draw with."

Leighton pouts at him. "Spoilsport."

"You did what?" he repeats, confused.

"Fuck, I don't know the sign for that."

"Spell it out," Theo advises. "Like I showed you yesterday."

Brows furrowed, Leighton stares down at his fingers then begins to clumsily spell out the word. It only takes a second for Hunter to catch on. He flips him the bird before stretching his limbs, now wide awake.

"Hey, Theo." Leighton holds his fingers ready to sign. "You're a *N E R D*. You know what that spells?"

"It spells *you're an awesome friend and a brilliant teacher*," he quips back. "Aw, thanks, Leigh."

"Do you just make up half the shit you're teaching us?"

"Don't like it? Find another teacher. I won't complain."

"We need groceries," I interject before they try to throttle each other. "Let's go into town."

When a massive pair of arms circle my waist to wrench me off my feet, I scream loudly. Enzo snuck up behind me," and I'm twirled in a huge circle. His breath is hot against my earlobe.

"You wanna drive, little one?"

"Not sure we can get groceries on a dirt bike," I wheeze out.

"We're going in the car. You need to start practising."

"She doesn't have her provisional licence yet." Theo sighs, folding the corner of the book page.

"Who's gonna care out here?" Enzo combats. "We're living in a damn jungle."

Theo's reply is cut off by an outstretched hand whacking him around the head. Hunter points at the folded page he just damaged to mark his place in the book.

"That is sacrilege, Theodore."

He rolls his blue eyes and signs back, "*Mine.*"

"Do it again and I'll be taking that book into custody for its own protection."

Hunter wears an unexpected grin, and when he glances at me, he removes his sunglasses to wink. A miasma of butterflies explodes in my belly. I'd forgotten how much I love his smile.

Leaving Enzo to herd the troublemakers to the car, I slip inside to gather my stuff. We meet outside the villa where a dirt-streaked Jeep has been haphazardly parked in front of the palm trees.

"What kind of parking do you call that?" Enzo booms.

Leighton claps his shoulder. "You like it? I tried really hard."

"A fucking blind man could park better than that! Jesus Christ."

"You know I'm the looks and he's the brains." He jabs a finger towards Hunter. "You want better parking, get Hunter to do it."

Strolling past his brother, Hunter nabs the keys from Enzo's hands. He's behind the wheel in a heartbeat. Enzo blinks, poised to protest. I grab his hand and haul him towards the Jeep.

"If he wants to drive, let him," I encourage. "It's a miracle he's leaving his bed."

Hopping in the back seat, I scoot over Theo to slide between him and Leighton. Enzo takes the passenger seat and keeps a wary eye on his best friend, ready to intervene if needed.

Hunter peels off in a spray of gravel before we careen down the winding roads. Glossy, billowing trees, sparkling sunshine and the chirp of tropical birds accompany the music blasting from the radio.

With his sunglasses on and a tattooed arm slung outside the car, Hunter looks like his old self for the first time in weeks. That tiny smile still pulls at the corners of his mouth.

It's the best thing I've ever seen.

The old Hunter is still in there.

We return to civilisation in record time. Quepos is a bustling coastal town, humming with tourists, local business owners selling their wares and backpackers passing through.

Shopfronts are painted in vivid shades of yellow, green and red, while the nearby cruise port is filled with intimidatingly large ships docked for the day in brilliant-turquoise waters.

Arriving intact and without incident, Enzo's hunched shoulders relax as we all exit the car. While I'm relieved his overprotective attention has moved on from me, I'm not sure Hunter appreciates it.

"Let's get food," Leighton pleads, his eyes on a nearby restaurant.

"You literally ate breakfast two hours ago," Theo replies.

"Exactly. How have I not withered away already?"

"I could eat," Enzo chips in. "We can hit the market afterwards. Where's that fish place you guys tried last week?"

I point towards the boardwalk, littered with bars and cafes overhanging the pearly-white beach. "Down there."

He takes off with renewed purpose, his nose upturned like a bloodhound. I watch Leighton follow, his spirits buoyed by the prospect of food. Catching up to Hunter, I capture his hand.

"*Are you okay?*" I sign.

He nods. "Yeah."

I tap my temple and furrow my brows in question.

"No headache today," he replies. "We're good."

With a smile, I reach onto my tiptoes to press a kiss against his parted lips. His hand cups the back of my neck to trap our mouths together, dancing a symphony in front of the whole street.

"Stop worrying," he whispers. "I'm okay."

Stroking my hands over his closely cropped hair, I kiss him firmly, communicating everything I can't say. He's spent the last year worrying about me. It's my turn to look after him now.

Tucking me into his side, Hunter holds me close and leads the way into the nearby restaurant. It's busy, given the sweltering hot weather in peak tourist season.

I came here with Leighton last week when we visited the bigger, public beach for an afternoon. We're bustled over to the best table in sight, courtesy of the over-friendly waiter who recognises Leighton.

There's a perfect view of the beach, packed with sunbathers and young couples enjoying cocktails in the blazing sunshine. I love this place. It's like paradise on earth.

"I am going to order the whole menu this time," Leighton declares excitedly. "What were those weird things we ate last time, princess?"

"Mussels," I supply.

"They were so fucking good. I want a double portion."

"You can foot the bill, in that case," Enzo grumbles.

"I'll have to ask my boss for a pay raise if we stay here for much longer." Leighton sighs. "I'm all in favour of us permanently relocating. Fuck going home."

"We have to go back sometime," Theo says while studying the menu. "I'm stunned that Hudson and Kade haven't burned HQ down yet."

"Or that Brooklyn hasn't killed them." Enzo waves over the waiter. "She did not appreciate us giving them full authority in our absence."

With food and drinks ordered, we settle into a round of ice-cold beers and fresh bread dipped in oil. Hunter slings his arm over the back of my chair, lazily drawing circles against my shoulder.

In public spaces, he tends to zone out. I suppose it's his way of coping with not knowing what anyone around him is saying. He's found his own ways of dealing with the world.

After stuffing ourselves with fresh seafood and a few too many beers, Enzo disappears with Theo to visit the nearby market. I rattle off my list of requests then head for the beach with the brothers in tow.

The pearlescent grains of sand feel like velvet beneath my bare feet. Slipping and sliding over sand so white, it almost looks like snow, my toes dip into the water's edge. It's a balmy afternoon.

"Incoming!"

Leighton's yell precedes a blur of bronzed skin racing past me. He throws himself into the water headfirst, his unbuttoned blue shirt discarded. I watch him disappear beneath the water.

Stopping at my side, Hunter's eyes are fixed on the horizon. With afternoon succumbing to the tempting embrace of evening, the sun highlights his skin in rich, warm beams of light.

All I want is to curl against his chest and have one last normal conversation with no fear of upsetting him or making him feel alienated. The ability to talk and be heard is a precious commodity that we take for granted.

His arm bands around my waist, and he pulls me close for a cuddle. Even in the silence of our new reality, he still finds a way to understand the darkest, innermost corners of my psyche.

"Don't be sad," he murmurs. "Enjoy the moment."

God, how I want to.

Even as my heart shatters.

Tapping his arm, I guide his eyes down to me. One of the first signs I learned was *I love you.* His eyes crinkle with a satisfied smile as I cover my heart with both of my hands before pointing up at him.

"I love you," Hunter echoes.

"*Promise?*" I sign back.

His head dips down to secure our lips together in a soft, lingering kiss that curls my toes. "How could I not?"

Mouths locked together, the beach melts into the background. I willingly step into Hunter's lonely silence and let his darkness shroud me in shadows. We don't need anything but this moment.

His scent is different here. Gone is the spicy, peppery fragrance of designer aftershave worth more than a one-bedroom apartment. Instead, he smells like saltwater and linen sheets.

Our lips break apart when the mumblings of discontented sunbathers shatter our peace. Leighton is still causing havoc in the water, now playing volleyball with a young kid.

But his antics haven't disrupted this oasis. It's the click of a camera lens and several hurried shouts calling for attention. Up the sandy bank, a gaggle of people are inching towards us, weighed down by gear.

A lead weight drops in my stomach. Reporters. I can spot them a mile off. Their usual casual business wear and corporate smiles have been replaced with equipment bags and sunglasses.

It's the cameras clasped in their hands that betray them, poised at the ready. I tug on Hunter's shirt sleeve and point over my shoulder. His easy smile dissolves into a horrified stare.

In two whole months of hiding out here, we haven't seen a single reporter. Our location is a very well-guarded secret. Not even Sabre's staff know where their bosses are on sabbatical.

"Maybe they're not here for us?" he guesses.

"Hunter Rodriguez! Can we get a statement?"

Fuck!

Quickly replacing his sunglasses, Hunter tightens his arm around my shoulder to hide me. I shout Leighton's name, waving like crazy to draw him out of the water. We need to haul ass right now.

"Harlow! Can you tell us what happened with Candace Bernard? Why did the killer escape? Where is he right now?"

The barrage of ridiculous questions reaches a fever pitch. All around us, interested tourists have turned their attention to us. Some are even filming on their smartphones.

"Leave us alone!" I yell at them.

"Tell us what happened." A reporter shoves a portable microphone towards me. "Why are you hiding? What about the investigation?"

"We will not be answering any questions." Hunter's grip on me reaches a bruising intensity. "Don't say a word, Harlow."

Their crazed eyes fix on him, along with the glint of recording lenses. Leighton splashes out of the sea and runs towards us as fast as he can move, but Hunter's quickly surrounded by vampires.

"Mr Rodriguez, will you apologise for allowing the suspect to escape? Is your company going to step up their search efforts for Michael Abaddon?"

The colour has drained from Hunter's face. I can feel his entire frame trembling as he holds me in a protective vice. It's all he can do to attempt to shield me and conceal his own fear.

He can't hear a word they're screaming at him right now, and it's too much. His façade is on the verge of crumbling in front of live cameras and Sabre's harshest critics.

"Get away from us," I plead, trying to drag him backwards to escape. "We won't be answering your questions."

"The public deserves to know the truth," a female reporter snarks. "You've hidden behind Sabre for almost a year now. Why won't you speak up?"

Recoiling like I've been slapped, anger spikes through me, and I snatch the camera straight from her hands. She squeals in protest as I throw it into the sea.

"I don't owe anyone an explanation," I spit in their faces. "You have no right to invade our privacy like this."

Leighton passes the bitch chasing after her expensive camera. I'm soon sandwiched between them and being hauled back up the beach, letting the cameras chase behind us.

"Where the fuck did they come from?" Leighton snarls.

"I have no idea. How did they track us down?"

"Someone must have recognised us last week and contacted the media." His voice is hard as nails. "The whole circus will be here by tomorrow."

We run towards the car, dodging more startled holidaymakers watching the fiasco with open mouths. Leighton hits speed dial then shoves me in the back to escape the onslaught of more questions.

Behind the wheel, Hunter waits impatiently, his eyes on the rearview mirror positioned on the market's swinging doors. His hands clench the steering wheel so tight, the vinyl creaks.

"We have to leave," he announces. "Tonight."

CHAPTER 4
ENZO

THE ONE YOU LOVED - THE PLOT IN YOU

ENGLAND IS FUCKING COLD.

Even in August.

The pitiful summer temperatures don't compare to the tropical paradise we've grown accustomed to. Stepping off the private plane, cold air smacks me in the face and shouts *welcome home, idiots.*

Yeah, home.

Somewhere I would've been happy to never see again, until our secure location was leaked to the world's media. News travels fast amongst soulless newscasters and their overpaid drones.

We had half of Costa Rica's journalists and a crew of international assholes camped outside the villa within three hours. They even filmed us hurling our suitcases into the Jeep and getting the fuck out of there.

This isn't the ceremonious welcome I had anticipated upon returning home—Hudson's scowling mug smoking a cigarette while the Anaconda team guards our airstrip. Some welcoming committee.

"Enz." Hudson clasps my hand tight. "Good flight?"

"Long and uncomfortable."

"Private jet not to your liking?"

Leighton offers him a wave as he throws bags into the awaiting car. "Preferred the private beach, thanks. Where's the Mustang?"

"Phoenix spray painted the alloys bright pink." Hudson's frown is thunderous. "He's paying for it to be fixed. And I beat his ass."

"How bad was it?" I wince.

"He's fine. Got off easy, in my opinion."

Joining us on the tarmac, Theo and Harlow both offer the team tired smiles in greeting. Hudson clasps her in a quick hug before starting to load up the company SUV with our luggage.

Last to leave the aeroplane, Hunter pauses at the bottom of the metal steps. I can read the hesitation carving his features into unyielding lines from here. His shitty attempts to seem emotionless don't work on me.

He's nervous.

It's an odd sight.

Welcoming their boss with handshakes, Becket and Ethan follow the email guidance we distributed weeks ago and greet him in sign language. The narrowing of Hunter's eyes is his only response.

"All ready to go?" Hudson slams the car boot shut. "We should get moving. Got a lot to catch you up on."

Inside the blacked-out car, it's a snug fit. We follow behind Becket and his team, exiting the airport with no interference. Our passports were checked on board, courtesy of a discreet fee.

I'd rather the press doesn't know the moment we land back in the country. Clearly, two months wasn't long enough for the media feeding frenzy to move on to its next victim.

Harlow lies down across the seats, settling her head in Theo's lap. She quickly falls asleep, her arms curled inwards for protection. With her eyes shut and Hunter relegated to the back, I lower my voice.

"Any more developments?"

"We haven't had a single sighting," Hudson replies, his eyes on the road. "He's clearly gone deep undercover somewhere, aided by accomplices. We've scoured the whole country."

"Have you alerted the local parishes? I still reckon he's using their church networks to remain undercover. Those religious nutjobs think he's the goddamn saviour."

"Not everyone is a nutjob," Hudson points out.

"But you can bet your ass that the ones aiding Abaddon are."

Refocusing on the road, Hudson takes the first exit and bears down on the accelerator. We overtake the Anaconda team and tear off up the motorway, heading east.

"What about the familial connection?" I check to make sure Harlow is still asleep. "We know Abaddon is Harlow's maternal uncle. That's a direct link."

"She doesn't have any other family who could be harbouring him," Theo chimes in. "I did a thorough search in case there was a third abandoned child. Michael and Giana were the only ones."

"Speaking of, her trial has been moved up to early December," Hudson informs us. "She entered a not guilty plea at the hearing last week to charges of false imprisonment and kidnapping."

"Shit," I curse. "Harlow won't take that well."

"Yeah, Candace Bernard didn't either. She's planning to testify against Giana." Hudson gives me the side-eye. "Harlow will have to do the same."

"I want to keep her well away from that madness."

"The prosecution has to build a case against Giana," he reasons. "Establish a pattern of behaviour. Getting both Harlow and Oliver on board will ensure she rots behind bars."

"We have no choice, Enz," Theo agrees with him. "Harlow has to testify against her."

Already, a killer headache is pounding behind my eyes. We've only been back in the country for ten minutes. I was right to get us the hell out of here in the first place. Perhaps we should've stayed away.

The journey passes in tense silence until we're pulling into the familiar, quiet cul-de-sac of our new home, safely outside London's smog-covered madness.

The house is dark and draped in evening shadows. It's still weird to think of this place as home. We left before ever truly settling in. I'm not sure any of us knows what life we're returning to.

"I'll let you guys settle in and unpack." Hudson parks behind Hunter's covered convertible. "Let's debrief tomorrow. I'll bring the dog back."

"Thanks for the ride."

"Anytime. It's good to have you back."

Leaving Hunter and Leighton to unload our luggage, I pop open Theo's door. He's pinned beneath Harlow, her eyes stuck shut and lips slightly parted.

She barely stirs as I lift her from his lap and cradle her to my chest. Despite putting on some much-needed weight, she's still tiny and featherlight in my tree trunk arms.

The house is pitch-black and musty, the scent of dust thick in the air. Hunter steps inside and begins to flick on lights. It's exactly how we left it—semi-decorated, messy and impersonal.

"I'll run out for some milk," Hunter offers.

I cock my head in a silent question.

"For tea."

With that simple explanation, he snags the keys to his convertible from the dresser and vanishes back into the night. I pretend not to notice the tremble of his hands as he slams the front door shut behind him.

I'm sure that in the long run, returning to his usual routine will help to drag him out of the mental hole he's dug for himself. Before that can happen, he has to let go of the paranoia eating him up.

None of us are judging or pitying him. All we want is to help make this transition as smooth as can be. That's a little hard to do when he's constantly isolating himself and pushing us away.

"Did you instruct all the staff to learn sign language?" Leighton asks, carrying a suitcase. "The Anaconda team used it."

"It was my idea," Theo explains. "We emailed a couple of weeks ago. They've only learned the basics."

"I thought it would help ease his transition back into work."

Leighton shakes his head. "He looked pretty offended by it."

"He can be offended all he wants." I toe off my thick-soled boots. "Ignoring everyone isn't going to protect him. He needs to learn to communicate like we're all doing."

Thumping up the staircase, I leave them to continue lifting luggage inside.

Harlow snuggles against me, her fingers curled in my T-shirt. Her features are slack, the grip of sleep still holding her captive.

It was a long twelve-hour flight across several time zones. We're all exhausted and jet lagged. Nudging her bedroom door open with my shoulder, I step into the welcoming darkness.

All I want right now is to collapse on her unmade double bed and hold her close for a few hours of undisturbed sleep, but the problems we left this country to avoid haven't gone away.

They just festered and grew, awaiting our return to reality. We couldn't avoid our responsibilities forever. Still, I don't regret our two-month sabbatical.

It didn't fix all the wounds this past year has inflicted. Nothing ever could. Yet I feel more confident that we can face the impending chaos now as a united front. We've rebuilt those burned bridges.

"What time is it?" Harlow mumbles sleepily.

"Almost ten o'clock at night." I ease her onto the bed, brushing hair from her face. "We're home, little one. Do you want to shower first or just get some sleep?"

"Shower. I feel so gross."

She manages to peel her lids open, revealing bloodshot eyes in the lightest shade of blue. Even half-awake and rumpled, she's still the most stunning creature I've ever seen.

I tuck tangled hair behind her ear. "Come and wash."

"Can't … move."

With an eye roll, I scoop her back up. Her face buries in the crook of my neck, lips brushing against my throat. In the darkness of the room, I can almost fool myself that we're back in our warm, cosy villa.

"Lucky?" she whispers.

"Coming home tomorrow, baby."

"I missed her."

Inside the bathroom, I place her down on the counter next to the sink basin. "I'm sure she's missed you more."

Harlow's en-suite is the nicest in the house but still a little cramped and dated. Plain cream tiles meet frosted glass, encasing the old-style, combined shower and bathtub.

The whole house needs a bit of a refresh. We bought the place practically unseen in our rush to get the hell out of London. It needs some investment and TLC to make it feel like a home.

"We seriously need to redecorate."

"It's fine, Enz."

"This place is a dump compared to home."

Harlow stretches her arms over her head. "This is home now, remember?"

"Don't remind me."

Pressing a gentle kiss against her temple, I turn my back to heat the shower. The shuffle of Harlow pulling off wrinkled clothing causes my pulse to spike, despite being as exhausted as she is.

With steam filling the room, a flash of bare skin slips past me. Harlow's small curves and soft, sloping hips step inside the shower. Her nipples are two hard points, beckoning me in.

"You coming?" she asks over her shoulder.

"I should help the others get settled."

"They're big boys. Climb in and wash my back."

"Demanding much?" I scoff.

Her eyes burn bright with challenge. "You bet."

I fucking love it when she gets all stroppy and confident. This stronger, cheekier side of Harlow has been showing itself more often. I couldn't be prouder of her.

Stripping off my plain, black t-shirt and jeans, I flick the lock on the door then climb in behind her. It's a tight squeeze, but she shuffles farther under the spray of water so I can press up against her spine.

Arms wrapped around her waist, I plant a delicate kiss on her shoulder. The beat of hot water slips between us, melding our skin together. I love the small curves that have filled out her frame.

"Are you glad to be home?" Harlow asks.

Reaching for a bottle of shower gel, I lather the jasmine-scented liquid across my hands then begin to massage it into her skin. Her head tips back, lips parted on a sigh.

"Yes and no," I admit.

"We had to return sometime."

"I would've preferred if it was on our own terms. Now we're back on the radar, and all the bullshit will start over again."

After washing the shower gel from her skin, I take the shampoo and work it through her long, tumbling hair. Almost all the bald patches are covered in a short fuzz of hair now.

She leans back into me, her eyes semi-closed. I massage her scalp next, taking time to memorise each ridge of bone carving her skull. When her eyes reopen, she peers up at me.

"Can I run something past you?"

"Sure, angel."

"Richards had an idea," she says uncertainly. "He thinks I should write a memoir and set the story straight. I've got enough filled journals to make a whole book at this point."

Damn nosy doc.

"I don't think that's a good idea, little one."

Her face falls. "Why not?"

"We've tried to work with the media before," I try to explain. "It never goes as planned. They have their own agendas and will always find a way to fuck us over, no matter what they promise."

"This wouldn't be working with the media, though. I could publish the book with a company or even by myself. It's not like I'm giving them a direct statement or interview."

"But they'll still host round-the-clock debate sessions and analysis segments ripping apart every word you print. This book would spread like wildfire. That I can guarantee."

Washing out the bubbles from her hair, I lean over her shoulder to peck the soft slope of her throat, hoping she doesn't hate me.

I'd love nothing more than to see Harlow take control of her own life, but this would be a monumental step at a very bad time. Her story will set the world on fire and burn us all to death.

We can't track down Michael Abaddon and put an end to his reign of terror if we're too busy fighting fires on all sides to keep Harlow safe from the world's morbid curiosity.

"Maybe it was a stupid idea," she backtracks.

"No." I turn her around under the spray of water. "It's a good idea but the wrong time. We're in a sticky situation right now, and I don't want to make it worse."

Her eyes are downturned, hiding the tinge of disappointment. I slide a finger underneath her chin to raise them back up. She looks inexplicably sad. It stabs me right in my foolish fucking heart.

"Let me catch this motherfucker and break his spine first." I stare deep into her cerulean eyes. "Then you can publish whatever you want. I'll be first to cheer you on."

She summons a tiny smile. "You will?"

"Damn straight, I will."

The sharp edges of her smile slump. "But writing… Enz, it's giving me control back for the first time in my life."

"I'm not saying you have to stop writing. Write your little heart out if it helps. All I'm concerned about is keeping you safe until we can see this case through."

Nodding, Harlow stretches to kiss my lips. "I guess I can understand that. Thank you for always looking out for me."

"You don't need to thank me. It's my job."

"Your job? Still?"

"I didn't mean it like that." I shut down her presumption. "My job as your boyfriend, or whatever the fuck you call me."

"Boyfriend, huh?" she teases. "That title suits you."

"Well, I'm that first and foremost. Always will be."

"Oh, Enz."

Hitching her leg on my hip, she twines her arms around my neck and draws us together. The swell of her breasts meets my chest, causing my cock to twinge with excitement.

Grabbing her pert ass cheeks, I press my hardening erection into her, biting back a groan. I can't fucking think straight around this sexy, little vixen.

"Are you still tired?"

"A little," she admits.

"I'm gonna make you feel good, then you can sleep. My perfect angel deserves an orgasm first."

Cheeks flushed, her lips part on a sigh as I kiss my way over her neck, throat and clavicles. My tongue drags between her tits, tracing the curve of her sternum before continuing down her torso.

Lowering to my knees, I crouch down in the shower, surrendering myself to her in the most vulnerable way possible. There isn't another creature on this planet I'd kneel for—only her. My goddess.

Wrapping a hand around her ankle, I encourage her leg to rise and prop itself on my shoulder. She obeys without complaint. Her trust in me is dizzying, even after all this time.

"Let me see that perfect pussy. Are you wet for me, angel?"

"Yes," she moans.

With her leg raised and spine pressed against the tiled wall, I'm eye height with her dripping cunt. There's nowhere to hide. It's all on display, glistening and begging to be tasted.

Pressing a kiss against her mound, I drag my lips downwards, over the swollen swell of her clit. Harlow's hips buck, pushing her pussy into my face. I swirl my tongue over her bundle of nerves.

"Oh God, Enz."

Gently flicking the bud, I let my mouth traverse even lower so my tongue slides through her wet folds. She's soaked to the core, and her sweet juices burst across my tastebuds, making my cock stiffen even more.

Her innocence coats my tongue, and I lap at her core, sucking and licking in a punishing rhythm. I fucking love the way she tastes. I'd be quite content to suffocate in the slick warmth between her thighs.

Shifting her hips, she rocks against my face, encouraging me to eat her sweet cunt. I spear her slit with my tongue, lifting my thumb to rub her clit in slow, teasing circles.

"Please," she begs. "More."

Running a thick finger between her folds, I coat it in stickiness and push it inside her pussy. The moment I enter her warmth, Harlow cries out, her moans swallowed by the beat of the hot water.

"Still so tight, little one." I strum her clit again before thrusting my finger in even deeper. "Your cunt was made for me to devour."

Grinding against the heel of my palm, she moves her hips in time to the pump of my finger working in and out of her entrance. When I add a second digit, her moans reach a fever pitch.

Still buried inside her, I return my mouth to her clit, sucking the bud between my lips. The light graze of my teeth elicits the most enticing mewl of pleasure from her throat.

As much as I want to drive my cock deep into her cunt right now, this isn't about me. Harlow needs to know that she will always be my priority, regardless of anything else.

I live and die by the continued beat of her heart. The moment she takes her last breath, I'll cease to exist in this world, because I refuse to take a single step without Harlow by my side.

"I'm going to come," she whines.

I stop for a breath. "Spread those juices all over my face, baby. I want to be dripping in your come."

Driving my fingers into her in a relentless beat, I coax her to the edge then flick her clit one last time. It's enough to throw her into the darkness of ecstasy. Quivers overtake every limb.

Her hips still as she falls apart, crying my name so loud, I doubt the others will neglect to hear it downstairs. Her sweetness rushes across my tongue and stains my mouth.

Still kneeling at her mercy, I look up at her haze-filled gaze and make sure she's watching as I lick the fluid from my lips. Harlow's breath hitches, her blue eyes locked on me.

There's something primal and satisfying about knowing I'm swallowing her essence. She can never escape my orbit if I own a precious piece of her and keep it locked up, safe in the cradle of my inner self.

Rising to my full height, I slide a finger underneath her chin and seize her lips in a possessive kiss. Our teeth clash and tongues tangle, the salty burst of her come being exchanged between us.

"Enzo," she gasps into my mouth. "I need you to know that no matter what happens, I love you."

I rest our foreheads together. "I love you, Harlow, and I'll always keep you safe, even if I have to let the entire world burn to do that."

"And what happens if the only way to beat Michael is to give him what he wants?" She hesitates, uncertain. "My … death?"

Fingers digging deep into her skin, I ensure she's hanging on to my every word. "Then I'll stand back and watch him slaughter to his heart's content. I don't give a fuck about anyone but you."

"No." Harlow looks horrified. "I'm not worth all of this. I know you love me, but we have a job to do. You can't protect me at the expense of everyone else."

"Like hell I can't."

"Enz—"

"End of discussion."

"No, it's not. We're not going back to our old patterns."

Harlow turns off the shower and sneaks past me to escape. Sighing hard, I step out and grab the towel before she can, wrapping it around her body. She really is infuriating in all the best ways.

"That's not what I'm trying to do," I reason.

"Yes, it is. I can look after myself. I'm not going to spend the rest of my life living in fear to satisfy your need to wrap me in cotton wool. We're past that now. Catch up or move on."

Tucking a towel around my hips, I hug her from behind, stopping her from running away into the bedroom.

"I've lost everyone I ever cared about. My sister. My parents. Alyssa. Friends, co-workers. The lot. All dead and gone."

Spinning her around in my arms, I pin her against my bare chest, ensuring she can see the fire simmering inside of me.

"I refuse to add your name to that list. And I'm sorry, but I don't give a fuck if that makes you feel guilty. I'm in love with you, and I won't apologise for prioritising you above all else."

She shakes her head in annoyance. "Didn't I warn you months back about being possessive now that you officially have the *boyfriend* title?"

"You did, and I paid absolutely zero attention. Just imagine how possessive I'll be when I have the *husband* title."

Harlow halts, her mouth open. "Huh?"

"You don't think I'll marry you one day?" I cock an eyebrow. "Like I'd let any other bastard call you his wife and not me. You're mine. Get used to it."

Her anger melts into a shy, timid smile that reminds me of the broken girl I found in that hospital bed last year. She's still in there, however deep her damaged soul has been buried.

"You'd marry me? How would that even work?"

Unlocking the bathroom door, I follow her into the bedroom. "We'll see when Brooklyn marries those five oafs, I guess. If they can make it work, anyone can."

Harlow drops her towel then crawls into the unmade bed, completely naked. A lump sticks in my throat. Not even a fucking t-shirt. Now sleep is the last thing on my mind.

"She's asked me to be her bridesmaid," Harlow mumbles beneath the sheets. "I have no idea what I'm supposed to do. What if I let her down?"

Following her example, I leave my clothes off and climb into the bed. Her tiny frame immediately snuggles up to me, and her limbs curl against my side like garden vines.

"You could never let her down. All you have to do is turn up and look absolutely fucking beautiful. That shouldn't be hard at all for you."

Harlow scoffs. "Flirt."

"Complaining?"

"Not in the slightest."

She's out like a light and falls asleep with her ear resting above my heartbeat. In the darkness of the room, I let my terror escape its man-made prison. I finally have her, safe and sound.

We've survived so much.

If we were to lose her now, after a year of fighting tooth and nail for any scrap of hope, I can safely say that it would fucking devastate us. Irreparably so. My family would be done for.

I will do anything to prevent that from happening—even bloody my hands and risk becoming the monster myself. She's worth that risk.

The first name on my list?

Michael fucking Abaddon.

CHAPTER 5
HARLOW

1X1 – BRING ME THE HORIZON (FT. NOVA TWINS)

WITH THE BACK patio doors open, balmy summer air leaks into the house. It still smells a little musty after being sealed for two long months, though I've been airing it out every day since we returned.

Spread out all around me, paint samples litter the worn floorboards. I'm trying to decide which colour to paint the accent wall that runs along the whole side of the house, joining the living room and kitchen together.

"Harlow Michaels has yet to make a single public statement," a voice emanates from the TV. "When will she speak up?"

The news is playing in the background with a hum of impassioned voices. I'm only half-heartedly listening. They've been playing the awful clips from the beach in Costa Rica non-stop.

Their speculation has yet to dissipate. I'm the focus of a whole bloodthirsty industry, and the pressure is starting to take its toll. I've found myself flicking on the news more and more often.

I want to know what they're saying. The whole world has an image of me that couldn't be further from the truth. Part of me is willing to disregard everyone's advice just to set that record straight.

"Tea or coffee?" Leighton breaks my thoughts.

Frowning at a paint sample, I hold it up against the wall. "Tea, please. Do you think this orange is too dark?"

"I'm not sure Hunter would approve of an orange wall, princess. So I think you should paint the whole damn house orange instead."

Snorting under my breath, I swap out the sample for a different strip. It's more of a burnt, homey orange colour, reminiscent of baked clay rather than a lurid neon.

Galloping in from chasing her ball outside, Lucky wraps her huge body around my legs, almost knocking me over. Her tongue laps at my right hand, demanding ear scratches.

"We're not leaving again," I whisper to her. "Don't worry, girl. I know you missed us."

Burying my fingers in her velvet fur that's coloured the lightest shade of golden blonde, she yaps happily. Ever since Hudson and Kade brought her home, she's been glued to my side.

Returning with two steaming mugs, Leighton boosts himself up to sit on the dining table. He takes one look at the TV screen then reaches for the remote to switch it off.

"Wait!" I exclaim. "I'm listening to that."

"They're just saying the same shit over and over again," he objects. "Why are you even watching this nonsense?"

"Because I want to know what they're saying about me. I refuse to bury my head in the sand any longer. It isn't healthy."

"Goldilocks, as proud as I am for you facing this head-on, listening to their constant stream of bullshit isn't helping anyone."

"Just leave it on. Please."

Deflated, he hits the mute button but leaves the TV on for my benefit. We return to studying the array of paint samples spread out all around us, denoting a million different shades of orange and grey.

"This one," he decides, tapping an orange square. "It's warm enough to make the room more inviting, but it's not too intense. It will work well with that light grey we already chose."

"You're right. It also matches the wood finishings in the kitchen, right? Nice and rustic."

"Rustic," Leighton echoes, smirking to himself. "Look at you, Little Miss Homemaker."

I smack a hand against his bicep. "You'll be the one painting, not me."

"I hate painting. Besides, I'm supposed to be clearing out the basement today to install the home gym later this week."

"Please? I can't do this alone."

He sighs dramatically. "Fine. You better make it worth my time."

"You know I will."

Dancing away from his grabby hands, I retrieve the furniture catalogue to show him the new rug and light fittings that I've narrowed down.

Hunter left us with his credit card and strict instructions to make this house a home. While we brought furniture with us, everything feels disjointed and out of place right now.

"I've picked out the other bits we need."

Leighton steals the catalogue to look at. "Nice cabinets. I like these new doorknobs too."

"Those ugly brass ones have got to go."

"We can take a trip out this afternoon." He drops the catalogue on the table. "We have to fix this place up before Mum comes over. She'll take one look and run away screaming otherwise."

"If you guys had let me call her, she could've fixed it up for us. Who chooses their own furniture when their mum is a literal interior designer?"

He pins me with a knowing look. "Because we don't want her input. This is your home, Goldilocks. You have to decorate it exactly how you want it. We all agreed on that."

I duck my gaze, feeling myself flush pink. I'm not quite sure when things shifted. Maybe it was the moment we were reunited among blood and death in that abandoned house.

The guys have treated me differently since then, not like I'm a china doll on the verge of shattering as I'd been dreading. Enzo's overbearing protective instincts aside, I feel like they see me as an equal now. A rightful member of their team.

I've finally earned their unconditional trust, and all it took was breaking the flimsy facsimile of what we kidded ourselves was enough before.

"Okay, then." I grin at him. "But if it looks terrible, I'm totally blaming you."

He playfully bops my nose. "I'll take it. I'm used to Hunter kicking my ass."

"There's no doubt about that."

The doorbell rings before the front door swings open. Theo has ordered a brand new, state-of-the-art security system, but it's yet to arrive. Until then, we're remaining armed and vigilant.

Leighton hops down from the table, and his easy smile vanishes. He starts to reach underneath the dining table where Hunter strapped a gun into place before a voice stops him.

"Only me!"

His shoulders slump. "Brooke."

The loud thump of her Doc Martens clatters down the wood-lined hallway. Platinum-blonde hair pulled up in a ponytail, her grey eyes sweep over the room then land on us.

"Hey, guys. Room for one more?"

Tall and muscled, her wiry limbs are wrapped in a pair of ripped black jeans and a faded band tee tucked in at the waist. She looks the same as always. Edgy. Dangerous. Aloof.

Ditching the samples, I race over to bundle her into a tight, breath-stealing hug. Brooklyn quickly reciprocates.

"I missed you." I squeeze her tight. "You're looking good."

"Hot as always, I know," she teases. "Costa Rica clearly agreed with you. Look at these fucking tits! Where did they come from?"

The tips of my ears burn hot at her compliment. I can hear Leighton chuckling to himself. My time abroad and a lot of calories have given me a newfound lease of confidence.

Releasing me, Brooklyn scans me up and down with a broad grin. "You look amazing."

"Stop it," I mutter. "I look the same."

"Fuck off! I'm so jealous of this tan you've got going on."

Ducking past me to ruffle Leighton's scruffy hair, she peels off her leather jacket then flops on the nearby sofa. I study her out of the corner of my eye while Leighton brews another cup of tea.

She's looking a little peaky. Although her skin is naturally fair, she's paler than usual, and her eyes are lined with dark circles. Even her frame appears slimmer than it was two months ago.

"What have we missed?" I ask pointedly.

Her eyes dart away. "Nothing really."

Warning bells sound in my head. We've been gone for a long time. Whenever we've spoken over the phone, Brooklyn couldn't wait for me to come home again. Now she can barely look at me.

"How's the last-minute wedding prep?"

"We're all on track." She shrugs, still not looking up. "Hudson and Kade have been pretty busy at HQ, so I've done most of it myself. Oh, Phoenix got the shit beaten out of him."

"So we heard." Leighton reappears and hands her a mug. "He should know better than to mess with Hudson's precious baby."

Brooklyn stares into her mug. "Eli still hasn't forgiven Hudson for almost breaking Phoenix's jaw in the fight. It was messy. Jude had to intervene to get them to speak to each other again."

"They better make up fast." I take a sip of hot tea. "You're getting married in six weeks."

She's still not looking at us. While I may not be the most socially experienced human, I can spot Brooklyn's red flags well enough.

The first thing to go is her eye contact. She's pathologically incapable of looking you in the eye when there's something eating away at her. It's like she doesn't trust us not to read it on her face.

"Leigh, do you want to go grab that paint?" I narrow my eyes on him. "We can get a head start before the guys get home from work."

"Now?" he asks in surprise.

"Yeah. We will get the woodwork all taped up."

"I'm not supposed to leave you home alone."

"Brooklyn's here now. I'm well-protected."

He seems to catch on when I raise my brows in a pointed look. His eyes dart over to Brooklyn and back to me, reading my silent order. Even he can sense that she's off.

"Alright, then. Don't burn the house down while I'm gone."

Brooklyn doesn't even acknowledge his bad joke, her attention fixed on the dark brown liquid in her mug. With a mouthed command to call if I need him, Leighton grabs the paint samples and ducks out.

When the front door closes, I take a seat on the sofa next to Brooklyn. She stares at the place where my fingers grasp her forearm in an attempt to drag her back to the present.

"What's going on, Brooke?"

"I'm fine," she rasps.

"How many times have you called bullshit on me? I'm about to do the same to you."

Shaking her head again, she worries her bottom lip with her teeth. I'm surprised to see that tears are pooling in her eyes, the shining trails streaking down her cheeks in threads of silver.

"What is it? Did one of the guys upset you?"

"No, no." She scrubs the tears from her face. "It's nothing. Leave it."

"The wedding? Did something go wrong?"

"Please, Harlow. I really don't want to talk about this."

But she does, otherwise, she wouldn't be here in the middle of the day. Her trust issues just don't allow her to blurt it out. I'll have to tease the truth free in order to get what I want from her pursed lips.

Tugging her hand into mine, I clasp her fingers. "I'm sorry that I haven't been around."

"You don't need to apologise to me. I understand why you guys left."

"Well, I am apologising. We packed up and left without properly explaining ourselves. I think we all needed some time away to repair what was broken, you know?"

Brooklyn exhales. "Yeah, I know."

"But I'm here now. Please talk to me. What's going on?"

Tears flowing faster than she can mop them up, Brooklyn finally looks up at me. I'm almost stunned to silence by the look of palpable fear wrapped around her silver irises.

"I think… I m-may be pregnant."

Mouth hanging open, I have no clue how to respond. Not a single word comes to mind. She takes one look at my speechless expression and bursts into even louder fits of tears.

"I don't understand." I pull her into a hug. "How? When?"

"My period is three weeks late," she hiccups. "I came off birth control last year when I started having side effects. We've been so careful since… but we had a drunken night last month."

"With whom?"

"All of them."

Ah, hell. I did not need the mental image of the six of them having an orgy in my head right now. Despite the part of me that's burning with curiosity at the sheer logistics of managing such an … um, endeavour.

"Did you do a test?" I ask next.

She shakes her head. "I'm too scared."

"Of what? The guys all love the shit out of you. They'd never leave you."

"It's not that." Her eyes clench shut. "I don't want kids. My parents fucked me up, and I can't risk doing that to another kid."

I cup her wet cheek. "You're not like your parents, Brooke."

"Aren't I?" she scoffs. "You know my condition can be hereditary. My whole family is dead because of the sickness in our blood."

Hesitantly, I stroke her tears aside with my thumb. I know that she was diagnosed with Schizophrenia as a teenager, earning herself a one-way ticket to the institute where she met the guys.

These days, she's medicated, and her condition is well-managed, aside from the odd slip-up. I can't think of a single person stronger than Brooklyn West.

She's been to hell and back, but she's lived to tell the tale. I'm not sure I could've pulled through the last year without her unwavering friendship and support.

"If you didn't have this diagnosis, would you want children?"

Eyes fluttering open, she shrugs. "I … don't know. How could I be a good parent? I'm barely capable of looking after myself. I'd be a disaster—"

"Now that's blatantly untrue," I interrupt. "You have survived shit that most people wouldn't dream of in their worst nightmares. You look after five idiots like a pro, and you're an amazing friend to us all."

"Harlow. Come on."

"No, I won't hear it." I grab her hand again. "I am in awe of your strength, and I don't know how I would've survived the past year without you. Give yourself some credit."

She laughs under her breath. "You're starting to sound like your damn therapist."

"Maybe you should listen to me, then. You can get from me what you'd pay Richards a hundred quid an hour to hear."

When her laughing subsides, she's sobbing again. I snuggle up to her side and hold her head against my chest. The tears flow until she has nothing left to offer and settles for a pained hiccup.

"I don't even know if the guys want kids," she admits. "It just never came up. We didn't exactly plan any of this. What if I want to … you know, get rid of it? And they don't?"

"Then you talk to them. How can you know what they're thinking if you haven't told them what's happening?"

She barks a bitter laugh. "Is this coming from you? The person who spent the last year bottling everything up and refusing everyone's help?"

I pinch her leg through her ripped jeans. "I'm gonna let that slide because you're a hot mess right now, otherwise, I'd be chewing your ear off. I've learned from my mistakes. You should too."

"You're right." Brooklyn sighs. "I'm sorry, that was mean."

"I'll let you off. We need to go buy some pregnancy tests."

Her head snaps up. "No."

"I won't let you do this alone. We're going to buy the tests and do them together. No matter the result, I'll support you and whatever you want to do. Deal?"

Bottom lip trembling, she summons a shaky nod. I stand up then pull her to her feet, but screaming red letters on the muted TV catch the corner of my eye.

Brooklyn freezes at my side as I grab the remote to unmute it. The same headlines they've been running for days have vanished, replaced by one far worse than I could've imagined.

"Local media discovered Harlow Michaels and her security team in rural

Costa Rica. It is now believed they have re-entered the country, and for the first time in months, the suspect has resurfaced."

A blanket of ice slams into me, painful and petrifying. Brooklyn snatches my hand and holds on for dear life, ensuring I don't fall over with the weight of terror awash inside of me.

A helicopter shot shows an aerial view of a familiar beach. The feed is sweeping over the scene, crawling with flashing blue lights and authorities rushing to hide the awful sight from cameras.

"We warn our viewers, the following images are disturbing."

Emotion drains from my body, an unrelenting geyser draining me of all sense and care. I must be trapped in another lifelike dream. This cannot be real life.

"Fucking Christ," Brooklyn curses.

Vomit sears the back of my throat. The beach that features in my rare, happy dreams, usually walking hand-in-hand with the grandmother I'll never be reunited with, is painted across the screen.

But that isn't all.

There are bodies.

Countless dead bodies.

CHAPTER 6
HUNTER

LIVING IN COLOUR - TROPIC GOLD

MY USUALLY EMPTY office is packed to the rafters with agents and various panic-stricken faces watching on in disbelief. The TV on the back wall holds everyone's attention, and the report is dubbed with subtitles.

You don't have to see the uncensored version to understand this message. The unmistakable shape of lifeless bodies has been arranged in meticulous detail.

Their limbs are positioned to spell a single word, ensuring the message meets its target without a crack of doubt.

REPENT.

I can't even count how many there are. One after another, the sand stained crimson-red. There must be at least ten to form the letters in sufficient detail. All lined up and left like a damn Christmas present.

Even if I can't hear the hum of voices all around me, the sharp snap of jaws moving and lips screaming out silent questions are enough to understand the hell that's just been unleashed.

At the back of the office, Theo is surrounded by his team, all ghostly white and a little green at the gills. Fox looks ready to hurl his guts up, and Rayna is clutching his arm tight.

Hudson and Kade are both flanking Enzo, the three exchanging what looks like urgent orders. I step between them to halt their conversation.

"We need boots on the ground. Forensics, security, the lot. We're going to have every reporter in Europe on that beach by tonight."

"*Need … go,*" Enzo signs back.

"Wheels up in half an hour. Call Lucas to start damage control. I want both security teams on the next helicopter out of here."

Kade asks Enzo a question, gesturing towards me. He translates his words in rapid, jerky sign language that I have to decipher.

"*Move … body?*"

Abaddon can't have pulled this off alone. The sheer strength it would have taken to lift and position so many corpses is unimaginable, let alone in a public place.

This must have been completed overnight. We know that he has supporters—the timely appearance of an accomplice allowed him to escape our clutches two months ago.

It's plausible that he had help this time around to pull off this stunt. If that's the case, then we're facing an even graver threat than before.

"He wasn't alone," I say grimly.

Pressing his phone to his ear, Hudson backs out of the room to make some calls. We've left Harlow at home with Leighton and a healthy fund to redecorate.

If she's seen the news, she'll be racing over here. That's the last thing we need right now. I tap Enzo's arm to regain his attention.

"Tell Harlow to stay away."

He signs a response. "*Bad idea.*"

"This isn't about us sheltering her. It's for our benefit. We need to move fast and secure the scene. I can't afford to lose agents to keep her safe from the cameras right now."

With a terse nod, he follows in Hudson's footsteps to make a phone call. Theo leaves his team to get packed up and ready to move, coming to stop at my side instead.

His gaze is hard behind glasses framing fearful blue eyes. I'm sure the same apprehension is reflected in mine. He pulls his phone from his pocket to tap a text message to me so we can speak in full sentences.

If he managed to pull this off, there's no telling what he'll do next. Things are going to escalate.

"Yeah," I respond flatly. "That's exactly what I'm afraid of."

The coastal breeze is chilly, despite the August sun beating down on us. Silent waves spread across the shoreline where one hundred of our finest men and women are battling against the elements.

Behind a yellow-taped cordon, local police have joined our best efforts to hold back a swarm of cameras, reporters, angry residents and fascinated onlookers.

With the collar of my light jacket turned up, I stand at the foot of a sloping sand bank. Metres in front of me, the first body is being sealed in a bag by our suit-covered forensics team.

Enzo is caught in an animated conversation with our head pathologist, Doctor Wheelan, discussing the thirteen bodies that were left for us to find when the sun rose.

The word *REPENT* is disappearing with each victim that's removed. You don't need a degree in forensic pathology to determine what happened here.

Every last deep, violent slash carved into each victims' wrists tells a harrowing tale. They all died still holding their bloodstained blades.

Thirteen identical suicides.

This is their repentance.

Back when I was in school as a kid, history was one of my favourite subjects. I always loved the stark, black-and-white certainty of facts that can't be changed by the present moment.

History is already bagged and buried. Controllable. Set. Even now, I remember writing a paper on Charles Manson for a module we'd taken on religious cults.

Everyone thought it was awesome, learning about that sick fuck. They were fascinated by the power he wielded, enough to turn his supporters into murderers, all in the name of some bullshit religious fanaticism.

Part of me wonders what those now-adult classmates are thinking while watching this unfold with the news playing on repeat. Bet they don't think it's so cool when there are thirteen corpses laying dead with slashed wrists.

My phone vibrates with another text message. I know it's her before I even look. She's been freaking out in the four hours it's taken for us to board an urgent flight to Devon to set up a cordon.

Harlow: What's happening? Did he kill them?

My protective instincts are screaming for attention right now, but I won't make the same mistakes that tore us apart already. She isn't a child. We're all in this together as equals.

Hunter: Looks like a mass suicide to me. We'll check for DNA.

Harlow: It has to be him. He brainwashed them into doing it.

Hunter: I think so too.

Harlow: He used to say that when the time came, the holy ones would have to prove themselves to earn passage to heaven.

Hunter: Earn passage?

Harlow: A payment. This is their sacrifice.

I tuck my phone away, feeling sick to my stomach. If he's working underground to inspire mass hysteria before his so-called rapture arrives, we're looking at a nationwide bloodbath coming straight for us.

Enzo dismisses the pathologists to continue their examination then walks over to me, his expression grim. I turn my back on the growing frenzy of onlookers to shield our private conversation.

"Well? What did they say?"

He scrubs a hand over his face. "*Suicide.*"

"You reckon he orchestrated it?"

Pulling his phone out as Theo did to communicate, he passes it over to me so I can read the message.

I think they walked down here, took their places and slit their own wrists on his command. Bled out within minutes. He arranged their bodies then left.

I've been thinking the same thing since we arrived, but if that's true, we're up against an even more formidable foe than we thought. That's a lot of power to wield over a whole group of people.

"We need IDs on all these people." I gesture to the bodies. "There has to be a connection between them. If we can find out where they came from, it could lead us back to Abaddon."

Enzo nods. "*Time.*"

"We don't have fucking time."

He pins me with an exasperated look.

"Enz, I want this son of a bitch rotting in a prison cell before anyone else gets hurt. He won't stop until he has an army of people like this, and then we won't be able to stop him."

Enzo glances back over at the madness threatening to overpower our barricade. The case has grown far beyond what we ever imagined. The whole world is watching us now.

He taps a reply into his phone and shows me.

What if we can't beat him?

"That isn't an option. We made a promise the day we met Harlow, and I'll die before I break it. She deserves to live in peace, and we won't rest until we get that for her."

Becket waves Enzo over, shouting something I can't discern. Letting him sidle away, I catch sight of a familiar face wading through the nearby crowd.

The agent holding Lucas back stands down when I shout his name. Appearing frazzled, Lucas straightens his shirt and meets me at the edge of the crime scene.

He begins talking, distracted by the scene, before he realises I can't hear a word coming out of his mouth.

"Sorry," he mouths.

I wave him off. "It's fine. What's the latest?"

He holds up a finger and fishes his phone from his pocket. Humiliation burns in my gut as he's forced to tap out an update in the notes app on his phone. This is fucking ridiculous.

No one would ever admit it, but I see the way they all look at me now. Equal parts pity and confusion as to why the hell I'm even here. Enzo's running the show in their minds.

Lucas sticks his phone under my nose. I'm getting really sick of having to communicate through text messages and hastily written notes.

We need to hold a press conference and release an official statement. I want to get Harlow in front of a camera.

"What? No."

He quickly types out a response.

A direct plea to the suspect and his supporters for their surrender will appease the media. If anyone can convince him to stop, it's her. She can appeal to them all for the violence to end.

I slap his phone against his chest. "Not happening. I won't say it again."

Lucas tries to stop me from storming off, but I brush straight past him and head for the shoreline. Being deaf has some benefits. Amidst all this chaos, I'm calm and collected in my silent bubble.

Starting out at the murky waters, lit by the beam of weak sunshine, I close my eyes. The tang of salt dances across my tongue, intermingled with the smell of death.

We have to catch this motherfucker.

I won't play his games again.

We've faced some monsters in our time. Real top-level, evil scumbags, the worst that humanity has to offer. I thought we'd peaked the day we saw Blackwood Institute lock its wrought-iron gates.

Then came this case.

It's taken everything from us. None of us have emerged unscathed, and we still have nothing to show for it. More bodies. Victims. Broken-hearted families. Exhaustion. Despair. A reputation in tatters.

What's worse is I wouldn't go back and stop myself from taking the case even if I could. This disastrous case has brought us the one thing that's given me the strength to keep fighting.

Our Harlow.

That's why we will see this through to the bitter end. Even if it bankrupts our firm and leaves us with nothing to return to when all is said and done. I couldn't give a fuck. I'll watch my legacy burn.

All for her.

And our future.

I'm not sure how long I stand there in total silence and darkness. My eyes don't reopen until someone taps my arm. Theo looks pensive as he gesticulates with his hands, spelling out a plea.

"*Listen. Harlow … camera.*"

"Not you as well. This is a terrible idea."

His brows knit together, signalling his disagreement.

"You know full well this sicko can't be reasoned with."

"*Try*," he signs.

Pinching the bridge of my nose, I grapple with the tell-tale twinges of an oncoming migraine. I can't even blame the healing head injury for this one. Coming back to England was a shitty idea.

It's not about protecting Harlow. She isn't the timid, damaged wreck we found curled up in a hospital bed. The past year has allowed her to grow into a strong woman who's capable of handling herself.

But fighting this out in the public sphere won't be a clean battle. Centuries of torrid investigations into serial killers have proven that much. Public appeals are powerful, but monsters cannot be bargained with.

The last time I made decisions on her behalf, Harlow bypassed my authority and took matters into her own hands. I know she'd do it again in a heartbeat if there were even the smallest chance it would stop the violence.

She will have to decide.

This is her risk to take.

"This has to be her choice," I submit. "Harlow gets the final say."

Theo nods in agreement.

"Fine. Then let's make it happen."

CHAPTER 7
HARLOW

THE DAY THAT I RUINED YOUR LIFE - BOSTON MANOR

I NEVER THOUGHT I'd be back in the bowels of HQ witnessing another post-mortem take place. A stupid, optimistic part of me believed that I was ending this saga the day I ran from this very building.

On the other side of the tinted glass, the pathologists are picking over two bodies. After testing for any DNA evidence, they've snapped photographs of the gaping wrists and noted down their findings.

"Harlow?"

A hand lands on my shoulder, startling me. Theo's dressed in a green flannel shirt and faded blue jeans, looking even scruffier than usual after sleeping in his office the past few days.

"Hey."

"You okay?" He frowns.

"Are you?" I gesture towards the sliced open corpses. "This is the third post-mortem today. How are we back here?"

"I don't know, beautiful." Theo scrubs his weary face with the hem of his shirt. "I've never seen anything like this in all my time at Sabre."

"These people … they were innocent. It's not their fault that Michael manipulated them into taking their own lives. They deserve better than this."

He rests a hand on my shoulder. "We're doing the best we can for them. It takes time to identify so many bodies."

"What about the connection between them?"

"So far, we've identified three individuals belonging to the same church parish. We're sending the Anaconda team to investigate."

My skin is itching with nervous energy. I want to grab handfuls of my loose hair and rip it clean out. It's not just this press conference... I feel like we're sitting on a ticking time bomb. This wasn't a parting gift—it's a warning shot.

Michael is ready to come out to play, and when he does, the streets will run red with blood. He has no qualms about butchering innocent people to achieve his goals. In his mind, God is on his side.

"We can still call the press conference off," Theo offers, taking the elastic from his wrist and giving it to me. "You're upset, and I don't want to make this any harder for you."

"No. I need to do this."

After quickly tying my hair up in a smooth ponytail, I try to scrub the nervous sweat from my palms. Even my breathing is shallow.

"Sure?" he double-checks.

"I'm not going to sit at home and wait for the next pile of bodies to turn up. The world needs to know what we're up against."

Snatching my wrist, he drags me into a tight hug that steals my breath away. "You're doing the right thing."

"I'm doing the bare minimum, that's all," I force out. "Listen, have you seen Brooklyn? Or heard from her?"

"Uh, no." He takes a step back. "Why?"

Shit. I can't betray her trust, even if she is avoiding my phone calls and text messages.

"Never mind. Let's go."

Taking Theo's hand, I let him guide me from the basement, then we ride the elevator to the ground floor. Tucked behind the reception, Sabre has a dedicated room for live conferences.

People are out there right now, being exploited and manipulated by my sadistic uncle. I know firsthand the sheer strength of psychological power he can wield.

Those victims were exactly that. Victims. He might as well have slit their wrists for them. That's why I have to do something before another drop of blood is spilled. Too many lives have been lost.

The hum of raised voices escapes the conference room, and I freeze in the middle of the foyer amidst a crowd of people. A wave of terror nearly knocks me off my feet.

"Shit," I curse.

Theo halts in front of me, inching a finger beneath my chin to tilt my eyes up to meet his. The certainty staring back at me leaves no room for the panic threatening to take over.

"You don't have to do this."

I blow out a nervous breath. "Yeah, I do."

"Seriously, Harlow. If it's too much, just say, and we'll call the whole thing off. I don't want you to be triggered by this."

"I can handle it."

His gaze softens. "I'm proud of you, beautiful."

"You are?"

"Of course, I am. This takes guts, and I'm going to be right there for every step of the way. You're not facing the world alone."

Tiny, electrified butterflies explode in my belly. I grab his shirt collar and yank him close, locking our lips together, despite Sabre's staff humming all around us.

Theo isn't like the others.

His care and affection aren't so freely given, but they're always there, however invisible they may seem to the outside world. He shows love through the pages of second-hand books and quiet gestures, not mere words alone.

Kissing me back with fervour, he forgoes the doubtful uncertainty that kept him from touching me for months on end. Now his true colours are unfurling, and his hunger sets me on fire.

Someone clears their throat. "Harlow?"

Breaking apart, we're both embarrassed to realise several members of the staff are giving us the side-eye. Standing close by, a spotlessly dressed stranger waits for us to separate.

No, he's not a stranger.

I almost didn't recognise him.

With his dirty blonde hair trimmed and gelled back, a pressed white shirt covering his filled-out frame and tucked into smart work trousers, my father looks like a brand new person.

"Oh," I squeak.

He chuckles under his breath. "Only me."

Theo releases me. "Oliver."

The guys told me a few weeks back that they intended to hire my father after he successfully helped me escape from Sabre's custody.

Who knew that my reckless self-destruction would be a successful job interview for his skills? Either way, I'm glad he was recruited and can now rebuild his life.

"Dad. What are you doing here?"

"Mandatory training," he answers with an easy smile. "I started my new job last week. Enzo's got me doing drills all afternoon."

"Are you settling in okay?"

"Well enough. It's been a long time since I had a proper job."

Dad still manages to look awkward, unable to close the distance between us. The last time I saw him, I was violently bruised, battered and broken after our shared close encounter with death.

He promised me that he'd do whatever it took to rebuild our relationship when I was ready to come home again. I wasn't able to answer him then, but staring at him now, my heart is set to burst.

"Can I … hug you?" I blurt.

His crystalline blue eyes widen. "Of course, love."

Stepping closer, I slowly wind my arms around him. It's like embracing a statue at first, frozen solid into stone, until the shock wears off and he bundles me into the tightest hug I've ever received.

With his face buried in my hair, we stand there for a moment, neither of us needing to say a word. The chatter of impatient journalists isn't enough to hurry this reunion.

"Did your break help?" he murmurs.

I blink back tears. "Yeah, it helped. I needed some time."

"I know. You're looking good."

"Thanks, Dad. You too."

Reluctantly releasing me, his eyes scan me up and down. While my injuries have healed into even more scars that mark my mottled skin, he still looks pleased to see me doing well.

"I missed you, kid."

My throat constricts. "I wanted to call you, but I didn't know what to say after everything that happened."

He shakes his head. "You don't need to apologise for taking the time you needed to get better. I'm here when you're ready."

Theo's voice interrupts us. "I'm sorry, but we should get in there before Enzo throws the lot of them out by their hair. You know how impatient he is."

That prompts a laugh from my father. It's low and barked, sounding foreign to me, but at the same time, I recognise the sound. It causes happiness to surge through my veins.

"I have to say, I wasn't sure what to expect when I accepted your job offer." He shakes his head. "Having my daughter's boyfriend take such pleasure in beating the hell out of me wasn't my first thought."

"I'll tell him to lay off." I look over him again, searching for bruises. "Enzo's got a reputation for being hard on new recruits, from what I've heard."

"No need. The challenge is good for me." Dad hesitates, his brows drawn together. "I want more time with you, Harlow."

"More … time?"

"To get to know each other again," he clarifies. "I'm renting an apartment just outside of the city, now that I can afford it. Perhaps we could have dinner there one night?"

Dinner. It sounds so unassuming, but I haven't eaten a meal with my father in well over a decade. My ever-present anxiety dissipates into a strangely welcome sense of … excitement.

"I'd like that."

His smile broadens. "You would?"

"You have my number, right?"

"I do." His hand brushes my arm. "Thank you. I know you don't have to give me a second chance. I've done nothing to deserve it."

I have to blink aside tears to stop them from spilling over. "Everyone deserves a second chance."

"I want to be a real father to you. We lost so much time, and I refuse to waste another second. I hope you're okay with that."

Feet backtracking towards the hum of awaiting reporters, I summon a small, hopeful smile. "I am. I have to go."

"Good luck in there. Stick to your guns, and don't take any crap."

"Thanks, Dad."

Accepting Theo's hand again, I leave my father's grin to face the music.

His words still ring in my head, warming the empty space in my heart left by every second of parental love I've missed out on.

Perhaps I can forgive him.

Perhaps I can forgive myself too.

The closer we get to the conference room, the louder the ruckus of conversing voices becomes. I take deep, even breaths, keeping the blank mask I perfected in the bathroom mirror in place.

"Got your statement ready?" Theo asks.

I pat the folded papers in my pocket. "It's here."

"Remember, they're going to throw all sorts of questions at you. We'll intervene if there's anything you shouldn't be answering that could compromise the investigation."

"You'll be there the whole time?"

"Of course. If you need me to get you out of there, just give me a nod." Theo tucks loose hair behind my ear. "I'll be watching."

Nodding, I pause on the threshold of the room for a final breath before stepping inside. Immediately, the chatter dies down into anticipatory silence.

The conference room is packed to the rafters with people. On a brightly lit, raised platform at the front of the room, a polished black table with built-in microphones faces the sea of faces and flashing cameras.

Sitting behind a name plate, Enzo's amber eyes lock on to me. He's already grimacing and looks on the verge of smashing the room to pieces just to get some peace and quiet.

"Smile," I mouth at him.

His glower deepens.

Well, I tried.

Kade and Becket sit on his right, both representing their teams and wearing equally grim expressions. I know it was a tough call, but Enzo decided it would be best for Hunter to sit this one out.

Giving my hand one last encouraging squeeze, Theo surrenders me. I walk alone up to my spot on Enzo's left side. Low murmurings follow every step I take.

Enzo pulls the chair out for me then settles a meaty paw on my shoulder as I sit down. His lips touch my ear to whisper low enough that the mic won't pick up his words.

"You've got this, little one."

"Thanks," I whisper back.

Pulling the handwritten statement from my pocket, I chance a look up at my audience. There must be at least fifty reporters in here, all poised and ready to tear my story to shreds.

The dead eyes of their cameras follow me. Even with a room full of strangers, I can feel his presence at the edges of my mind. Michael Abaddon. Pastor Michaels. Father. Uncle.

His many names are irrelevant. I won't let fear rule my life anymore. Clearing my throat, I tug the microphone closer.

"My name is Harlow Michaels. The world once knew me as Leticia

Kensington, before I was kidnapped by the man this country has come to fear as much as I do."

Snap. Scribble. Mutter. Cough. The weight of countless eyes bore into me, broken by snippets of sounds, threatening to break my concentration. I clutch my statement a little tighter.

"I spent thirteen years in captivity, being beaten and tortured by someone who called himself my father. I have witnessed first-hand the atrocities that he has committed."

Memories threaten to overwhelm me. I pause, taking a sip from the glass of water next to my microphone.

"But I'm not here today to rehash what you already know. This week's discovery has proven that this monster is far from done with us yet."

Theo's anxious eyes connect with mine from his perch in the doorway. He nods in encouragement, his lips pursed into a flat line.

"I'm here to speak directly to Michael Abaddon." I flatten the paper clutched in my shaking hands. "I am begging for you to stop the bloodshed. You don't have to hurt anyone else."

A hand touches my leg beneath the table, squeezing my thigh. The warmth of Enzo's furnace-like skin is of little reassurance as the pace of snapped photographs picks up.

"You're killing in the name of God. He preaches mercy and love, not violence and hate," I continue unsteadily. "You can still stop this before it's too late. No one else has to die."

"You're the one who let them die!" a voice heckles.

My throat seizes up, the invisible hand of grief clamping down on the flow of air fuelling my words. One of the reporters—a young, scowling man—has risen from his chair.

"Take a seat, or you will be escorted from the premises," Enzo threatens. "That's your first and final warning."

When the cocky reporter refuses to back down, two of the silent, black-clad agents circling the perimeter of the room march towards him. I swallow down the nausea silencing my response.

"No, wait!" I shout.

Both agents halt.

"None of you know what happened to me during those years." I meet the reporter's gaze. "I've never spoken publicly before, and I know many have equated my silence to guilt."

"Harlow, why are you the only one who survived?" someone else interrupts.

"I didn't survive," I answer honestly. "I went into a cage as a scared, eight-year-old child, and I came out as a different person, thirteen years later."

"You're alive," she rebuffs. "Unlike others."

"That wasn't survival. There are parts of me that I can never rebuild. I'm not looking for sympathy, but I need the world to know that I tried my best to save the women held captive with me."

"No one else escaped the killer's clutches," an older female reporter speaks up. "What makes you so special compared to the other lives that were taken?"

"She isn't."

The harsh snap of Kade's voice startles me. His usual matter-of-fact demeanour and calm control aren't present today. A red blush of anger is creeping up his throat as he faces the room.

"Harlow is one of countless victims. If you all spent more time worrying about what Michael Abaddon is planning next rather than picking faults in our investigation, you'd know that."

"Kade," Enzo mutters. "Enough."

Sitting back in his chair, Kade ducks his gaze. Becket has rested a warning hand on his shoulder, cutting off another rant. The reporter sinks back in her chair, appearing chastised.

"He's right," I add with a shrug. "There is nothing special about me. I spent years watching the brutality of Michael Abaddon's warped ideology. I don't want to see anyone else get hurt."

Enzo leans forward towards his mic. "There are people out there who know where he is. Our suspect is being aided and abetted by a group of loyal followers."

"We are appealing directly to them to reconsider," Becket chimes in. "You are in control of what happens next."

Lifting the black remote control next to his nameplate, Enzo clicks the button that illuminates the projector screen behind us. I don't look back, knowing the scores of faces I'll find there.

Every single victim who has died at Michael's hands is being splashed across the wall. Countless lives. Bright smiles. Hopeful expressions. Family photographs, graduation pictures, the lot.

Their lives are right there, indisputable and forever lost. The old me would've allowed the thought of their deaths to tear my will to live apart, but now… I know that self-destruction isn't the answer.

I don't have to die for them.

I *have* to live in their memory.

"Is this a man you want to protect?" Enzo addresses those not in the room. "Think about what you are doing by helping him. He will continue to slaughter innocent people because of you."

"Can you confirm if the recent crime scene has been linked to Michael Abaddon?" another reporter questions.

Enzo nods. "While we haven't found any DNA evidence, we are confident in our theory that Michael has begun a campaign of mass suicides using brainwashing techniques."

"Should the public be concerned?"

"We are urging the public to remain calm—"

Before Enzo can continue the perfectly phrased reply that Lucas has scripted for him, I jump in with God's honest truth.

"Yes," I cut him off. "They should be very concerned. No one is safe from Michael's violence. No one."

A bubble of hysteria sweeps over the room as all of the reporters begin to talk over each other, shouting questions and vying for my attention. Theo's face has paled as he stares at me.

"This is what he does," I shout over the noise. "Michael manipulates and abuses. He beats and he kills. Those helping him should be afraid too. Once their usefulness expires, they'll be next."

Grabbing my arm, Enzo yanks me back from the microphone to silence me. I peel his fingers from my blazer and push him away.

"We will never stop hunting you, Uncle." I ignore the flash of cameras. "You're going to pay for every single person you've hurt."

"Harlow, stop," Enzo hisses in my ear.

"I won't stop until your judgement day comes." I ignore him. "You will repent and be punished for all the lives you've taken."

Letting my chair scrape back, I shove past Enzo and leave the platform. Kade and Becket watch me slip around the back of the table to reach the exit at the rear.

"Harlow! Harlow!"

An agent opens the door for me then follows me out. When the sheet of metal slams shut behind me, I slump against it, a burst of defiant rage draining from my extremities.

I've escaped into a quiet corridor, where more agents maintain a tight perimeter for security. A familiar figure is leaning against the wall, fiddling with the shorter length of his dark beard.

When an agent taps his shoulder, Hunter's head snaps up, his chocolate-brown eyes wide with worry. The moment he sees me, his shoulders slump with visible relief.

I step straight into his arms, needing to feel the thud of his heartbeat against my ear. His chin lands on top of my head.

"I've got you," he hums.

That might have been the stupidest thing I've ever done or the bravest moment of my life. Either way, we have fired the next shot.

I have no doubt that Michael will fire back, and that's exactly what I want. We're going to find him before his rapture burns us all to ash.

I'm the only one who can do it.

His capture will be my reward.

CHAPTER 8
HARLOW

HALF-LIFE - ESSENGER

POKING plain porridge around my bowl, I ditch my spoon and opt for a swig of tea instead. Next to me on the table, my phone rests. It's still open on my text message conversation with Brooklyn.

Harlow: I'm worried about you.

Harlow: Have you told them about the baby? What's happening?

Harlow: You don't have to do this alone.

She hasn't responded since we did those pregnancy tests together. The guys were at an urgent briefing with the Cobra team when all five pee sticks lit up with the same glaring answer. Positive.

Frustrated, I tap out another text message.

Harlow: I've been on house arrest since the press conference. Please come and break me out. Let's talk.

The sound of footsteps thudding down the staircase breaks my solitude, and I quickly lock my phone to hide the messages. No one else knows about Brooklyn's situation. I won't betray her trust in me.

Eyes half-open, Theo stumbles into the kitchen while slotting his black-framed glasses into place. His blonde curls are sticking up in a million directions. He looks far too cute for his own good.

"Morning."

He halts, yawning loudly. "You're up early."

"Couldn't sleep. What time did you get home last night?"

"More like this morning. I managed a few hours of sleep."

I frown at the pronounced circles beneath his half-open eyes. "You should go back to bed."

Stumbling towards the coffee machine, he locates a mug. "I have too much to do. The country is in meltdown after that press conference. We had over one hundred interview requests yesterday."

With his hot black coffee poured, Theo turns and spots the look on my face. I try to conceal my guilt, but seeing his frazzled state and knowing it's my fault is tough.

"I'm not blaming you," he explains.

"I blame myself, but I still don't regret it. I said what I had to. The world needed to know what he's capable of. Everyone should be worried, and lying to them won't help."

He sinks into the chair next to me. "I agree with you, but a head's up would have been good. Everyone wants to speak to you now."

"Enzo may regret telling me not to write that book."

Theo looks thoughtful, slurping on his drink. "For the record, I thought it was a great idea."

"You did?"

"People will always talk, whether you remain silent or not. The last year has proven that. I think you should seize the opportunity to take control of the narrative. Give them something real to talk about."

Staring up at him, I'm lost for words. "Huh."

"What?" He smirks at me. "It's your life, Harlow. You should live it however the fuck you want. Don't let Enzo or any of us stop you from doing that. We will support you, no matter what."

"I don't get it. Why?"

"Why? You're still asking us that?" Theo repeats, incredulous. "Fuck, Harlow. We all love the bones of you. That's why."

I feel my cheeks flush. "Maybe I just wanted to hear you say it."

He shakes his head. "You're such a fucking troublemaker."

Chest burning with emotion, the kitchen falls away until it's just Theo and his big blue eyes, staring at me like I'm his entire world. The months I spent waiting for him to admit that are insignificant.

He's mine.

In every damn sense of the word.

A wild energy takes over me, and I climb up on the table to knee-walk over to him. Pushing mugs, discarded newspapers and cutlery aside, I grab his plaid pyjama shirt and yank him towards me.

His eyes are wide with shock, but it doesn't stop his plump, inviting lips from slamming against mine. Positioned above him, I grip his shirt tightly and take control of our kiss.

The taste of coffee clings to his lips. When a groan rumbles from his throat, his mouth moves against mine, and I feel the brush of his tongue silently pleading for more.

That's the thing about Theo... He thrives on surrendering control to others. Our souls are so alike, and yet we still fit together in a perfect harmony, like night and day battling for control of dusk.

Scrambling off the table, I land on his lap then slip a leg on either side of his waist. Two hands grip my hips, balancing me as I writhe against the growing hardness pushing into my core.

"Harlow," he murmurs into my lips. "Should we…"

I moan in agreement while rocking against the firm press of his erection, now painfully stiff beneath me. Months of pressure are blurring my vision with an intense wave of need.

"Bedroom?"

"Right now," I agree.

Curling my arms around his neck, I cling to his body like a limpet as he rises to his bare feet. My lips suckle against the soft skin of his throat, covered in an almost invisible smattering of blonde hair.

He's lean and trim compared to the toned muscles of the others, but the ridges of carved iron beneath his skin are still well-honed. Theo lifts me and carries me up the staircase towards his bedroom.

Peppering kisses along his neck, jawline and lips, I begin to unfasten the buttons on his pyjamas. Theo pushes open his bedroom door and clicks it shut before setting me back on my feet.

"Harlow." He grabs my wrists, halting me. "We should talk before we do this. There's something you need to know about me."

"What is it?"

His eyes flick down, a frosting of pink dusting his cheeks. "I don't like the same things as the others … in the bedroom. That's why I've moved so slow with you."

Walking backwards, I settle at the foot of his double bed. "Then what do you like?"

Rubbing the back of his neck, he looks everywhere but at me. His room is still sparse and barely furnished, but there are wobbling stacks of books scattered across the floorboards, waiting to be organised.

A cluster of wires and computer equipment crowds the plain pine desk tucked into the corner of the room, and his curtains are a dark navy blue, blotting out the rising sun.

"I like to be dominated," he admits.

My breathing halts. "Dominated?"

"You know … controlled. I'm submissive."

The internet is a wonderful thing. I've trawled the depths of Google for answers about all the things I don't understand in the world. Before I lost my virginity, I even did research.

"Do you go to clubs and stuff?" I rack my brain for what I've read online. "Do … people tie you up and things like that? I've read a few books that had BDSM in them."

"Wait, you read dirty books?"

I quirk an eyebrow. "Sometimes. You told me to buy a Kindle."

"Hey, you burned through my whole paperback collection in less than a year. I had no choice."

"It's your fault for getting me hooked on books."

Stretching out my hand, I curl my fingers to beckon him closer. Theo steps between my splayed-out legs and runs a hand over my hair. I love the way his undivided attention makes me feel.

"Why didn't you tell me sooner?"

He bites his bottom lip. "I thought it might freak you out and ruin everything. Most men aren't submissive. I figured you wouldn't want me once you knew what I like."

"I would never judge you, Theo. And I sure as hell wouldn't walk away because you like something different from the others."

"It doesn't weird you out?" he worries.

"Of course not."

My heart is hammering hard with intrigue. I have no idea how to be what he needs, but I'm nothing if not resilient. I can figure it out for him. It may even be hot.

"You're going to have to talk me through this, though."

"It's fine," he rushes out. "You don't have to do this for me."

"But I want to."

He's studying me with such intensity, it's like he's pulling out the fleshy depths of my brain to inspect the neurons under a microscope.

"I could take you…" Theo finally says. "To a club."

My pulse skips a beat. "You'd do that?"

"We wouldn't have to participate or anything; we could just watch. It may help you to understand. But only if you want to."

Grabbing his wrist, I drag him closer until he collapses next to me on the mattress. Theo quickly pivots so that I can position myself above him, a hand on either side of his head.

"I'd love to."

"You would?" he laughs.

"I want to be a part of your world, Theo. If you'll have me."

He grabs my chin, clasping tight. "Just seeing you pinned beneath Leighton in Costa Rica had me hard. I wanted to fuck you there and then."

Treacle-like warmth pulses through my veins. Hearing the low rasp of Theo's usually soft voice is doing things to me. I'm convinced there's a dirty-mouthed devil in there somewhere.

"So why didn't you?" I purr back.

"Believe me, I wanted to. The sharing doesn't scare me, but I wanted to talk to you about this first."

"You are the sweetest person I know."

Straddling him, our mouths find each other again. This time, I push my tongue past his lips, demanding more of the fascinating gentleness that suffuses everything about him.

Clasping my hips, he rocks into me, the tantalising press of his hardness throbbing between my thighs. I now know what he needs. Submission. Control. All of the things I give to the others.

For Theo, I have to be someone else. The one in control of his desires and needs. Even thinking about it gives me a thrill I wasn't expecting to feel. He trusted me with this secret.

"I want you to take me to this club and introduce me to your world," I demand, our lips entangled. "Show me what you need."

"Fuck, Harlow." He peppers open-mouthed kisses down to the slope of my throat. "You never cease to amaze me."

Just as I'm about to tear the pyjamas from his body, the sound of the front door slamming downstairs, followed by loud shouting, causes us to jump apart.

"What was that?" I freeze.

Theo curses, lunging for his phone next to the bed. "Everyone else is still asleep. No alert on the security system."

"Brooklyn!" someone yells. "Are you here?"

I slump, clutching my chest. "That sounds like Jude."

We leave the bedroom and find Enzo racing downstairs ahead of us. He's the world's lightest sleeper, unlike Leighton who wouldn't wake up even if a nuclear bomb dropped.

We chase him down the staircase and emerge in the kitchen where two disgruntled men are searching the room like they're possessed.

Jude and Hudson work in tandem, checking every last corner. They both look equally rumpled, wearing sweats and T-shirts with matching bird's nest hair.

"What the fuck?" Enzo shouts at them. "Why are you shouting your heads off in my goddamn house? That key is for emergencies."

"This is an emergency," Hudson yells back. "Brooklyn didn't come home last night."

"What?"

"She's turned her phone off so we can't track her location either." Jude's gaze is lit with frenzy. "Have any of you seen her?"

"Not since our daily debrief yesterday morning." Enzo pushes rumpled hair from his eyes. "What happened?"

"We assumed she was in with Phoenix and Eli when we all got home late from work, but she wasn't there this morning."

Terror wraps around my heart, its razor-sharp nails digging deep into my ventricles and cutting off the flow of blood. She's missing. I knew something didn't feel right.

"Did you guys have a fight?" Theo quizzes.

Hudson fists his hair. "No! She's been quiet, but we just assumed it's the case and stuff. We're all stressed as fuck right now."

"If you hadn't beaten the crap out of Phoenix, she wouldn't be upset with us," Jude snarls at him. "This is all your fault."

"My fault?" Hudson snaps. "Fuck you."

"Don't like the truth, Hud?"

"Get off my fucking back!"

"Guys." Enzo steps between them. "Blame each other later once we've found Brooklyn and made sure she's alright."

They take a step away from each other, though Hudson still looks ready to cave Jude's head in. Enzo stands firm in the middle.

Grabbing my phone from the dining table, I check the slew of unanswered text messages again. Nothing. She could be in trouble.

"Guys." I interrupt their scowling match. "We have to find her. She's … well, I don't know… she needs you. More than ever."

"What are you talking about?" Jude glances at me. "Do you know something that we don't?"

Not even Leighton, semi-asleep and stumbling into the kitchen, breaks the pressure mounting on my shoulders. They clearly don't know what's going on.

"Harlow?" Enzo urges. "What is it?"

"I promised her that I wouldn't tell," I whisper dejectedly.

"Tell us what?" Hudson demands.

Wringing my hands together, I crack under the weight of their terrified eyes. I've never seen Jude look so scared. He's usually the solid pillar at the heart of their family, alongside Kade.

"The thing is, Brooklyn found out that she's pregnant a few days ago." I wince, feeling awful. "The tests we did were all positive."

Hudson's mouth hangs open while Jude blinks several times, as if he's expecting himself to wake up from one of those scarily realistic dreams. I shuffle my feet, feeling like the worst friend in the world.

"Pregnant," Hudson deadpans.

I manage a terse nod.

"With … our baby," Jude finishes.

They look like they've just witnessed Santa Claus leaving presents under their fucking Christmas tree. That would probably be less shocking than hearing this news.

"That's typically how it works," Enzo mutters. "Did you two skip sex ed in school or something?"

Baring his teeth, Jude rests a hand against the wall to hold himself upright. "We're having a baby. An actual … child."

"She's really pregnant?" Hudson repeats.

"Yeah. One hundred percent."

"Fuck," he curses. "Fuck! We're gonna be fathers."

Jude's mouth flaps open. "Holy shit."

When the shock wears off, the pair throw themselves at each other to kiss and embrace. Tears well up in my eyes just watching them.

Enzo's grinning from ear-to-ear, and Leighton's managed to wake up enough to join the bear hug with a cheer. Even Theo's cracked a grin.

"We still need to find her," I point out.

All sobering up, their joy is short-lived. Hudson and Jude look even more worried than before, their arms still wrapped around each other for support.

"Where would she go to hide?" Theo wonders.

"More importantly, why the hell is she hiding?" Hudson retrieves his phone and glowers at it. "She should've just told us."

"Brooklyn was scared of how you'd react," I answer his question. "She doesn't know if you even want kids, and she's worried about passing on her diagnosis. I've been trying to help her through it."

"Why the fuck didn't you tell us, then?" he barks.

"Hey," Jude interrupts. "Back off, Hud."

"We deserved to know!"

"Harlow's trying to help. It isn't her fault that Brooklyn didn't feel able to come to us. That's on us and us alone. We need to make this right."

Hands trembling, Hudson turns his back to collect himself. "Sorry, Harlow. I didn't mean to take it out on you."

"It's okay. I'm sorry that it's come to this."

Wrapping his arm around my shoulders, Enzo pins me to his side. I don't think he even realises that he's doing it, his attention captured by the phone in his hand. I can hardly move.

"Enz," I whisper under my breath. "I'm right here. Safe. It's Brooklyn we should be worried about."

"I just need to hold you for a second." His grip on me tightens painfully. "I can't fucking lose her too. Why didn't she call me?"

"I don't think she's thinking straight right now. We should all split up and start searching for her."

Enzo exhales deeply and releases me from his arms. "Go and wake Hunter up. I have a few ideas."

CHAPTER 9
THEO

BAD DECISIONS – BAD OMENS

ARCHED SLABS of moss-covered limestone topped with turrets mark the entrance to the City of London Cemetery. The air is heavy with thick humidity and the beginning wisps of a thunderstorm.

I haven't set foot through these gates in a very long time. For the first few months after we lost Alyssa, I'd visit her on a weekly basis, bringing flowers and an endless supply of tears.

Then I stopped.

It became too hard to live with the constant reminder of her absence. The hours I'd spend at her graveside were the darkest, loneliest moments of my life, and I had no choice but to stop visiting.

"She isn't going to be here," Hunter mumbles.

He's behind the wheel, driving us to the half-empty car park that precedes the thousands of graves. His grip on the wheel has tightened with every metre we've inched closer to Alyssa's final resting place.

We've split up into groups of two, scouring a list of spots across London where Brooklyn could be hiding. From her favourite restaurants and bars all the way back to our dark, shared past.

"She could have travelled up north to visit her mum's grave."

"*Scotland?*" I sign.

He watches me from the corner of his eye. "She can handle herself. I think she's hiding out somewhere. We'll find her."

I wonder if he has to believe that. We've lost friends and loved ones along the way, more than most people will experience in their lives. If we lost Brooklyn too, none of us would know what to do.

With the engine turned off, we both hop out of the car. The sun has disappeared, obscured by bubbling clouds. We're a minute away from being drenched in rain.

Checking that my weapon is secured, we take off down the stone pathway.

Neither of us wants to be here right now. Hunter never even visited Alyssa's grave. Not once. He couldn't bear it.

Only a small handful of mourners are braving the volatile weather, ducking beneath willow trees and overgrown ferns to reach their lost relatives. It's a short minute walk to the top corner of the graveyard.

"Come on," I say to myself. "Please be here."

Banking right, I creep past dirt-streaked stones and overgrown tufts of parched grass. There's an ominous rumble above us, but the swelling clouds don't release their moisture yet.

Jude chose the position of the grave, tucked beneath a cherry blossom tree that blooms with beautiful pink flowers in the spring. Her gravestone is clean, unlike the others, and adorned with old flowers.

Hunter stops beside me. "She's not here. Let's go."

I hold up a hand to halt him.

"I'm not going any closer," he insists.

"*Why?*" I spell out with my hands.

"For the same reason you stopped visiting her years ago. Come on, we still have other places to check off our list."

With a huff, I leave him behind and creep closer. I know Brooklyn and Jude visit here together. While Alyssa was her best friend, Jude lost his sister. He can't stop acknowledging the fact that she existed like we did.

After checking that the coast is clear, I crouch down in front of the letters that are still scored on my heart. I can admit that I love Harlow now, but part of me will always belong to Alyssa.

I know Harlow understands that. It's part of the reason I love her so much. She has enough space in her heart to accept our flaws and imperfections without letting them change her feelings for us.

I miss Alyssa, but the moments when I'm with Harlow are the closest I've felt to feeling alive in years. She's defibrillated my long dead heart and given me a second chance at life.

That's worth risking everything for.

Even at the risk of heartbreak.

"Hey, Lys." I stare at the clusters of decomposing roses. "It's been a while since I last came and saw you."

It isn't enough. She's laid here all alone, abandoned by the people who swore to keep her safe. I owe Alyssa's ghost more than that.

"I'm sorry I left you all alone. It was too much."

The silent stone grave doesn't answer me. We have other places to be, but the carved letters of Alyssa's name demand the truth.

"I met someone," I admit. "You'd like her. She's sweet but fiery when she wants to be. In many ways, she's the total opposite of you. Her vulnerability is her strength, and she isn't afraid to use it."

The crunch of footsteps approaches. Hunter settles by my side, his lips pursed together. When the first drops of rain begin to fall, neither of us moves. We sit side by side, united in our grief.

"Do you think she'd be happy for us?" Hunter asks thickly. "For finding Harlow?"

After a beat, I nod back.

"Yeah. I think she would too."

We sit for several silent minutes, the rain slowly picking up speed and drenching us in warmth. When Hunter stands, he offers me a hand up. I accept with a sigh and meet his reddened eyes.

"I'm sorry," he blurts.

I frown at him in confusion.

"I spent years punishing you for what happened to Alyssa. Sabre took over, and I left you to struggle alone. I hate myself for it. I'm so sorry."

Pulling him into a hug, I slap him on the back and gulp down a rush of emotion. I never thought I'd hear him say those words, and I didn't know I even needed them until now.

Somehow, somewhere, I hope that Alyssa is content while watching down on us, knowing that we made it.

Holding him at arm's length, I pray he can read my lips. "You kept … us safe. Let us … help you … now."

His smile droops. "I don't need your help."

"You don't have to do this alone."

He frowns at my mouth, and I know my words have gotten lost in translation. I sign them out instead, watching Hunter sigh as he pieces the sentence together.

"I don't recognise my own life right now." He looks back at Alyssa's gravestone. "I haven't felt this lost since she died."

"*Help*," I sign back. "*Your … family.*"

"You can't fix this, Theo. No one can. I need to figure out how to live with this on my own."

I can almost feel Alyssa's sharp-eyed glare cutting into the side of my head, like she's sat atop her own grave and watching me fail to punch through Hunter's shields.

Nearby rustling drags me back to the rising storm around us. I blink through the rain to find a soaked figure traipsing between the gravestones. *Fuck!* It's her.

"Brooklyn!" I shout.

Hunter follows my line of sight. She doesn't respond to our shouts of her name, wandering up and down the lines of graves without stopping to look at any of them.

Racing through the grass, we catch up to Brooklyn, and Hunter seizes her hand. She's wrenched to a halt, but her glazed-over eyes remain fixed on the clouds.

"Brooke." I cup her wet cheek. "It's me. Theodore."

Two shiny, silver-grey eyes slide down to me. "I can't find him."

"Find who?"

She shakes her head, like she's blowing the cobwebs free. "Logan. He told me to meet him here. I can't find him."

"Logan?" Hunter reads her lips. "Did she just say Logan?"

I wave him off. "Brooke, we need to get out of this rain. Come and get dry in the car for a moment."

"No," she protests. "I need to find Logan. He's expecting me."

Jerking my head, I gesture for Hunter to grab her other arm. We capture her between us, towing her rain-soaked body through the graveyard.

Her protests are feeble at best, another blaring warning sign. Brooklyn doesn't do anything against her will. She should be punching us in the dicks and threatening death if we don't let her go.

"You're okay." I stroke a hand over her goose-pimpled skin. "The car's just over here. A few more steps."

Resting Brooklyn against the bonnet, we check her for injuries. Her clothes are dirty and soaking wet, but she's unscathed.

We can't fit three people in the convertible. Hunter's texting fast, updating the others and sending the nearest team our location.

"They're coming."

I approach Brooklyn with caution. Her hands are clasped over her flat belly as if she's envisaging the life growing deep inside of her.

"Brooke? You with me?"

"Logan," she murmurs. "He'd know what to do. Is he here yet? Did you see him?"

Right now, I'm glad Hunter can't hear Brooklyn begging to see her brother. He's been dead for over two decades. God knows what she's seeing that we can't.

"Where did you see him?" I ask gently.

Tears slick down her pale cheeks. "Last night. He told me to meet him here. I need him to tell me what to do."

My heart splinters in my chest. I hold her close and rub circles on her back. She shudders from the rain coupled with her rising sobs, and every stuttered breath pains me to hear.

"I can't have a baby," she hiccups.

"Shh. It's going to be okay."

"No, it's not. I can't be a mum. I'm going to fuck this kid up like I've fucked up everything else in my life."

Tightening my grip on her, I watch Hunter begin to pace up and down the car park, his agitation growing. Every glance he takes in Brooklyn's direction increases his restlessness.

While he may not always show it, he's the reason Brooklyn and her men are still alive. Hunter gave them all a chance when no one else would, and he loves each of them to death.

"What's going on?" he snaps.

Tucking Brooklyn's head under my chin, I free up my hands to fingerspell. "*Logan.*"

"Goddammit. She hasn't had an episode in years."

Keeping her trapped against me where she can't run off, we wait for backup to arrive. It doesn't take long for the throaty purr of Hudson's Mustang to break through the torrential rain.

With a squeal of tyres, it comes screeching around the corner, breaking several speed restrictions. Brooklyn snuggles closer to me, subconsciously seeking reassurance.

"Is it Logan?"

I stroke a hand over her hair. "No, Brooke. We're all here with you, though. You don't need to be scared."

The car lurches to a halt next to the convertible, then three pairs of legs climb out. Hudson, Phoenix and Eli are all frantic, their clothes creased from hours spent driving around.

"Brooke," Eli yells louder than I've ever heard him speak before. "You found her."

He and Phoenix approach together to ease her from my arms. She collapses in the middle of them, and her cries echo throughout the rain-slick car park.

"Firecracker." Phoenix runs his hands all over her, needing assurance that she's intact. "You scared the living fuck out of me."

"Nix," she breathes. "You're here."

Pressing himself into her spine, Eli buries his face in Brooklyn's drenched, blonde hair. He's shaking like a leaf with nerves.

"You promised to never run away from us," he accuses. "We deal with things together, not apart."

That's when she breaks, and all of the terror spills out. Brooklyn sobs into Phoenix's t-shirt, and the pair of them have to hold her upright.

"Where was she?" Hudson walks over to us, each step laden with exhaustion. "We've been driving around the city for hours."

"She was just walking around the graveyard." I gesture towards the gravestones behind us. "Not far from Alyssa."

"The others are on their way. Has she said anything to you?"

"She's been asking for Logan."

"Logan? You're sure?" he repeats.

"She's seeing him again."

With a curt nod, Hudson approaches Brooklyn to embrace her. Eli and Phoenix surrender her to him, both hanging within touching distance for their own sanity.

"Blackbird." Hudson tugs her into his arms. "I'm gonna scream at you later for doing this. Just let me hold you first."

I watch the four of them cling to each other like the storm will tear them apart. Relief crashes over me in tumultuous waves. Our fucked up family isn't intact without them in it.

"Thank God." Hunter stops at my side. "That was a close call."

"I'm going to take her home," Hudson announces. "We need to deal with this together. Can you ask Richards to make a home visit?"

I nod back. "I'll give him a call."

"Thanks, Theo."

Letting them bundle Brooklyn into the Mustang to get warmed up, Hudson hands Phoenix his car keys so that he can drive them home. He climbs in the back with Brooklyn instead.

We're in serious shit if Phoenix can't even crack a smile at being given the privilege of driving the Mustang. He still looks shaken up, even with Eli holding his hand tight.

Pulling out my phone, I hit Richards's name on speed dial. He answers within seconds, his rich baritone laced with worry.

"Theo? Do you have an update?"

"We've got her. Who called you?"

"Enzo." He sighs in relief. "He put me on standby hours ago. I returned to Clearview in case she somehow found her way there."

"Graveyard," I rush to explain. "They're heading home now, and you're needed. She's had a relapse. A bad one."

Richards doesn't often swear, but his muttered curse is all too appropriate in this situation.

"Tell them I'll be there in an hour."

"Thanks, doc."

He disconnects the call without a goodbye as the low growl of another engine joins us in the car park. Enzo's beast of an SUV tears into the space next to us in record time.

"Theo! Hunter!"

Harlow flies out of the back door, almost tripping and faceplanting in her haste to get to us. She's been distraught all morning.

"What happened? Is Brooklyn alright?"

"It's okay, beautiful. She's fine."

Enzo climbs out of the car, his expression steely. "I thought we'd find her at that weird record shop she likes. Good work, guys."

Still flustered, Harlow slips her hand into Hunter's and sags into his side. I know she feels shitty about spilling Brooklyn's secret. I can see the guilt overpowering her relief.

"Should we go over to theirs?" she suggests.

"They want to be alone."

Her shoulders slump. "This is all my fault. I should have raised the alert when Brooklyn stopped replying to me days ago."

"You couldn't have known," Enzo comforts. "She's an adult. All we can do is our best to look out for each other when things get bad."

His eyes flit over to Hunter, standing slightly back from the group and locked in his own world. I watch Enzo swallow hard.

Harlow shakes her head. "I'm worried about how the guys will react. Brooklyn may need someone there to have her back."

"They love her to death," Enzo disagrees. "None of them would ever leave her, even if she killed a fucking puppy."

"I guess you're right."

"Come on." He tugs her hand into his. "Leighton's waiting at home for us. You can choose what takeout we order tonight."

"A high honour indeed," she snorts. "Leighton may have something to say about that. You know how weird he is about food."

"And I'm tired of eating pizza like it's going out of fashion. Let's get out of this place. We have work to do."

After untangling herself from Enzo's possessive hold, Harlow approaches me and drops a kiss on my cheek. Her lips tease the shell of my ear so she can whisper without being overheard.

"So… about this morning."

I wind an arm around her waist. "What about it?"

"Can we pick up where we left off?"

Letting the other two climb back into their cars, I back her up against the polished metal before pecking her lips. She feels so fucking good clasped in my arms.

I have no idea how I survived so long without touching her, but that time is long gone. After this morning, I want to finish what we started. We've wasted enough time.

"Date night this weekend?" I suggest in a low voice. "I'll take you to a club in London."

"Really?" she asks excitedly.

"If that's what you want. I have somewhere in mind."

"Then it's a date."

CHAPTER 10
HARLOW

WHO DO YOU WANT – EX HABIT

CHECKING my reflection for the fifth time, I anxiously smooth the loose, glossy brown curls that hang over my shoulders. I spent an hour applying my makeup, something I've never bothered to do before.

I'm wearing full war paint tonight—thick, glamorous lashes and deep-red lipstick that highlight my blue eyes. Brooklyn even gifted me one of her little black dresses for good luck, sending it over with Hudson while she remains at home recuperating.

The short, flowing chiffon fabric teases my upper thighs, covering my matching pink lace bra and panties. I've shaved every inch of myself in preparation for my first date with Theo tonight.

"Princess?"

Bedroom door creaking open, Leighton's headful of hair pokes inside. He looks me up and down with a low whistle of appreciation.

"Shit. I am so jealous of that four-eyed fucker right now."

I slip my ID and phone into my handbag. "Thanks, Leigh."

"Seriously, you look incredible." He bites his bottom lip. "Sure I can't convince you to stay at home with me instead?"

"I'm sure you'll survive one night without me."

After striding into the room, he steals my handbag and throws it on my unmade bed. I'm scooped into his arms, my breasts straining against the square neckline of the dress as he smashes me into his chest.

"You know where he's taking you, right?" he murmurs.

"I do."

"Enzo's furious. I think he's ready to lock Theo in his car boot instead of letting him take you to some kinky sex club for a first date."

I click my tongue. "You make it sound so seedy."

Leighton chuckles. "Oh boy. You're really in for a shock tonight. Do you have any idea what happens in these kinds of places?"

"Well, no. But I'm going in with an open mind."

Sliding a chunk of hair behind my ear, his lips tease mine. "Just the idea of him fucking you in front of an audience makes me stabby."

"An audience?" I choke out.

A grin lights up his face. "Precisely my point. Just take it slow. Things can get crazy in these clubs, and you need to be careful."

Pecking his lips, I try to sound more confident than I feel. Leighton doesn't need to know how nervous I am about this date.

"I'm not going to be doing anything in front of anybody. Stop worrying. You know Theo will look after me, no matter what."

"True." His lips trail along my jawline, planting soft kisses. "Watch yourself, and call me if you need us to come rescue you, alright?"

"Deal."

His hands sneak beneath the hemline of my dress, and he groans as his fingertips stroke the edges of my panties. My stomach somersaults at his light touch.

"You better leave before I bend you over this bed, and trust me, Theo won't be able to tear you away from me if that happens."

Placed back on my feet, I kiss him again, slower and with all of my appreciation. If it wasn't for Leighton, I doubt I'd even have the confidence to consider going to a place like this.

He was the first one to build me up and give me power over my own life. While the others thrive on protecting me, all Leighton wants is to cherish every inch of my soul, and I love him for it.

After grabbing my handbag and heels, I tangle my fingers with Leighton's and follow him downstairs. The hum of the TV playing accompanies pots and pans being loudly bashed together.

In the kitchen, Hunter is knee-deep in ingredients and cooking some complicated dinner. Enzo sits at the breakfast bar, a pile of folders and paperwork spread out in front of him with a beer.

He swivels on his barstool, his mouth falling open. Following Enzo's line of sight, Hunter freezes mid-chopping with a knife in hand.

"Fuck," Enzo curses. "I'm gonna murder that bastard."

"I called dibs." Leighton skips to the fridge to retrieve a beer. "Form an orderly queue behind me for your turn."

With an eye roll, I walk into Hunter's arms, careful of the knife still clasped in his hand. His chin lands on top of my head.

"You look beautiful, sweetheart," he rasps. "I know I still owe you a date. I should be the one taking you out tonight."

I look up into his espresso eyes and mouth, "I love you."

I'm rewarded with the thing I wanted most: his smile. They're few and far between still, so I've made it my personal mission to score one every single day.

"Becket and Tara will meet you both there." His eyebrows knit together. "They'll give you some privacy, but don't go anywhere without them."

I know better than to argue with Hunter. This was their one condition for letting us go into the city despite the investigation and current risks. Two of Sabre's best agents are going to be tailing us the whole time.

He squeezes me tight then plants a kiss where his brother's lips claimed mine. I'm handed off to Enzo, his paperwork forgotten.

"I don't like this." Enzo picks me up in a hug. "Keep your phone on you at all times. The tracker is activated. Watch your back too."

"This is supposed to be a bit of fun. You're making it sound like we're heading into a war zone."

"You are," he growls. "The entire country is freaking out over those suicides and the press conference. If anyone recognises you, Becket and Tara are under strict instructions to haul ass."

"We'll be fine, Enz."

Gripping my chin, his eyes scour my face. "Promise me you'll be careful, little one. Don't make me regret approving this date."

I doubt he gives a shit how controlling that sounds, but the reality is, we're all beholden to Enzo's approval these days. Nothing is safe.

"I promise," I assure him.

He ducks down to whisper in my ear. "I'm fighting the urge to rip off this stupid little dress and fuck you right here on the breakfast bar for both of them to see."

"Hands off the goods. This dress isn't mine."

"You think I give a rat's ass whose it is?"

Teeth sinking into my earlobe, the violent growl of his voice causes warmth to flood between my thighs. The worst part is, I wouldn't even complain.

The staircase creaks as Theo heads down to join us, and Enzo begrudgingly puts me down with a scowl. My heartbeat stops the moment my date arrives.

"Oh," I squeak.

Who the hell is this guy?

His timid, unassuming disguise thrown to the flames, the Theodore I know has been replaced by a smouldering stranger. Any coherent thought flies straight out of my head.

From the tight black dress shirt highlighting his wiry lines of usually concealed muscle to the fitted seam of his trousers and open leather jacket, Theo has abandoned his chrysalis.

Even his black-framed glasses have been replaced by contacts. His blonde ringlets are slicked back, showing off his sharp angles, cut-glass cheekbones and a freshly shaven face.

"Here, let me get that for you."

I feel Enzo's finger beneath my chin as he clicks my mouth shut. I'm surprised there isn't a puddle of drool gathering at my feet.

"Why doesn't she react like that when I walk into a room?" Leighton pouts.

I expected perhaps a fresh flannel shirt, maybe a pair of jeans without holes in them. Not this sexy Greek god who wouldn't look amiss on the pages of a glossy magazine.

"You ready?" Theo asks awkwardly.

"I'm gonna need a minute."

His cheeks darken. "Isn't that my line? You look phenomenal."

"Alright," Enzo mutters. "That's enough flirting for my ears. Get the fuck out of here before I lock the pair of you up."

Theo grabs my coat then opens his arms for me to step into it. I let him assist me, my belly awash with those damned nervous butterflies again.

He kisses my temple and intertwines his fingers with mine. All three sets of jealous eyes in the room are narrowed on us both.

"Head's up."

Hunter tosses a pair of car keys through the air, leaving Theo to catch them. I recognise the Costa Rican keyring I bought him as a joke—a bright pink tortoise.

"*Sure?*" Theo signs.

Resuming his methodical chopping, Hunter nods. "Crash it and there'll be hell to pay."

"Alright, then." Theo tucks the convertible's keys into his pocket. "Ready to go, beautiful?"

"As I'll ever be."

The moment I slide out of the cherry-red convertible, leaving my handbag safely stowed inside, I'm hit by a column of heat. London feels boiling hot tonight.

Shadows drape the quiet street, and the hum of music emanates from behind locked doors. We've parked in a tight space that's surrounded by expensive sports cars.

"Just how exclusive is this place?"

Theo clicks the car door shut. "Members only. I haven't been here in a long time, but it's the best around and costs a small fortune."

"And you can afford somewhere like this?"

"I own a portfolio of stocks that outweighs Sabre's entire net worth. Who do you think bought the house?"

I gape at him. "Um, Hunter?"

Theo shakes his head.

"Wait, it was you?"

"I covered it," he reveals shyly. "Sabre isn't my only source of income. I just don't like to flaunt it like other people."

His eyes stray over to Becket and Tara, both dressed down in matching black outfits, idling in their car down the street.

"Let's go inside."

Clinging to his arm, I follow him towards the sound of music. There's a discreet door in the red-brick building, tucked beneath an overhang and marked by roped barriers.

After ringing the buzzer, the door swings open to unveil a heavily-built security guard. Theo pulls out his wallet then hands over a gold card that has an engraving in the matte material.

TARTARUS.

"Mr Young," the man booms. "It's been a long time."

"It has," Theo says stiffly.

"Donatella will be glad to see you."

His hand clenches mine tighter. "I'm paying for discretion, Kaleb. Remember that."

"Right you are." He clears his throat. "She's hosting a private show in the Indigo room. I'd avoid going there tonight."

With a terse nod, Theo steers me inside, and I'm engulfed in darkness. Thick, blood-red carpets swallow the click of my heels while black and gold brocade wallpaper muffles all sound from outside.

The throaty purr of violins and a crooning voice beckons us farther into the low-lit shadows. My nails dig into Theo's hand.

"Who is Donatella?"

"Someone best left in the past," he answers.

"Could've warned me that we'd be bumping into your ex-girlfriend."

"She never made it that far." He holds open a lacquered black door for me. "I'm here with you, Harlow. No one else."

With a breath for courage, I step into the unknown. Music meets my ears, soft and sensual, breaking the silence of the welcoming bar.

Velvet chairs surround flickering candles, offering intimacy to the darkness. Behind the well-stocked bar, a gilded mirror gives a snapshot of the luxury on all sides.

The handful of guests wear smart business attire and dresses, sipping on their crystal glasses of liquor. No one looks up at our arrival, all content to mind their own business.

"Drink?" Theo asks.

"Sure. It's quiet here."

"For now. It's still early."

Escorting me to the bar, Theo orders two glasses of wine, sliding a stack of cash from his wallet. I bite my lip, curiously studying him as the barman pops the cork and locates two glasses.

"I can feel you looking at me." Theo accepts the wine. "Look, I didn't know she'd still be here."

"It's not that. I don't care about her. She's in the past, right?"

"Right."

"Then she isn't my problem."

He clinks our glasses together. "What is it, then?"

I hesitate. "You're different here."

Placing a hand on the small of my back, he guides me into an empty corner where a loveseat is quietly tucked away from sight. I slide in, taking a sip of wine.

"Is that a bad thing?" he asks nervously.

"No." I rest a palm on his leg. "I just haven't seen you … well, comfortable in your own skin."

Theo inclines his body, blocking out the rest of the bar. His hand scrapes through his gelled curls and messes them up. I lean closer so our thighs brush under the table.

"How did you end up coming to clubs like this?"

He shrugs. "I grew up in foster care. You see some sick stuff in those places. A friend introduced me to the scene when I was sixteen, and it offered me an escape."

"What happened to your parents?"

"Your guess is as good as mine. I have no memory of them. My records said I was abandoned before I even spoke my first words."

Pain lances across my chest. "I had no idea."

"It's fine," he consoles. "I don't like to talk about them. Family didn't matter to me until I met Hunter and Enzo."

I take another small sip. "So you came to places like this to get away from it all?"

"I thought I had no control over my life. When I watched someone be dominated for the first time, I realised that control is meant to be surrendered. That's where power lies."

His hand runs up and down my arm in a slow, agonising rhythm, following the melody of violins in the background. If it wasn't for the music, I'd forget we're still inhabiting the real world at all.

I can't see beyond his quirked lips and the oceanic shimmer of his eyes. He's observing every last tell, reading my mind for any signs of judgement.

"You're waiting for me to run," I guess.

"Do you want to?"

I place my hand on top of his, covering my thigh. "Nope. I want you to tell me what you like. Show me your world."

"Sure that's what you want?"

Pushing his hand higher, I spread my legs, forcing him to feel the damp lace covering my pussy beneath my dress. His eyes blow wide.

"Show me, Theo."

His nail skates over my covered clit, sending pulses straight to my core. He barely has to touch me, and I'm already panting with need.

"Follow me. Remember, we can leave at any time."

After letting him pull me to my feet, I tug the hem of my dress down to hide my state of arousal. We knock back our wine then link hands again, winding through the darkened bar.

Bearing left, there's another door leading deeper into the club. We have to pass a second security guard, the flame-haired woman checking Theo's card again.

"Only certain membership tiers are allowed beyond this point," he explains under his breath.

Tucked into his side, the thump of the doors closing behind us sets my pulse skittering. A pair of curtains is drawn back to admit us into the next level of the club, and the entire scene changes.

"This is Tartarus," Theo explains.

The huge room is split into sections: observing and participating. On curved, raised stages, satin-covered beds are dotted about. Perfectly aligned rows of chairs offer seating to the audience.

Half of the beds are full, occupied by onlookers. To my right, a plump woman in emerald

is bent over a bed, her bright-red ass cheeks being swatted with a paddle.

Each time the bare-chested man at her rear strikes her, the crowd seems to lean closer, drawn into the punishment. The crack of the leather paddle smacking her flesh elicits loud moaning.

"Come on." Theo's arm circles my waist. "I want to show you something."

We merge into the buzz of people, their eyes too distracted by debauchery to clock our identities. Another stage holds a couple—the man restrained with leather cuffs and pinned to the bed.

I gulp as his back arches, exposing his asshole to the lube spread over it. The naked woman held above him flourishes a long, black-coloured instrument, trailing it down his spine.

I've googled enough to know what a dildo is. Brooklyn even suggested I should buy one a few months back during one of our embarrassing conversations.

"Is she going to put that inside him?" I ask in a hush.

"She's going to wear it," Theo whispers back.

That's when I notice the belt attached to the base of the dildo. It's pulled around the woman's waist and fastened, positioning the shaft over her crotch.

I can't tear my eyes from the show. Her fingers are buried in her partner's ass, stretching him wide to receive the dildo's swell. He strains against the cuffs when she eases inside his rear.

"Oh my God," I breathe.

Theo stands behind me, his body pressing into my back. I can't help grinding against his hardening dick while watching the pair beginning to fuck for everyone to see.

"He seems to be enjoying it. I didn't know women could do that."

His breath is hot on my neck. "You'd be surprised. It's a pretty common fantasy, but no one talks about it for some reason."

"Have you ever done it?"

His silence answers me. Holy shit. I really don't know my blue-eyed book geek at all. That only increases my determination to understand the real Theo.

Thighs pressing together to ease the ache, I undulate against his cock rocking into my butt. The man is grunting loudly on stage, the cuffs keeping him pinned as he's fucked from behind.

A distant part of me wonders if I should be triggered by this, but the consenting agreement of these two adults is nothing like the depravity I watched. I can separate the two.

"Does watching them fuck turn you on?"

"Yes," I admit. "Am I … supposed to do that to you?"

Theo's laugh is warm like molten caramel, oozing over my heightened senses.

"Easy, angel. Let's learn to walk before we run."

Tugging on my hand, Theo makes me tear my gaze from the show. They've amassed quite the crowd. I want to watch what happens next, but the adjacent stage catches my eye.

Instead of a bed, there's a single chair placed in the middle. Ankles and wrists bound with thick ties, a brown-haired man is tightly restrained. It's the ball between his lips that shocks me.

"What is that?"

"A gag," Theo supplies.

"Doesn't it hurt?"

"No. It's a little uncomfortable."

He's being circled by a seasoned predator, inching ever closer to her kill. The woman's angelic, blonde hair brushes her lower back in a tumbling wave. It offers the only coverage for her naked body.

But it's the confident sway of her hips that fascinates me. She's lording herself over him, her gagged partner unable to utter a single word, though I doubt he'd protest.

When she unveils a silk tie, I watch her wind it around his head. He's tied, gagged and blindfolded. There is no greater state of surrender than the trust he's placing in her.

"You okay?" Theo checks.

I absently nod back. All I can think about is how much power she has right now. This man's life is held in the palm of her hand. I can see every ounce of confidence that power is imbuing her with.

"We can sit down if you want," he offers.

I'm steered over towards the nearest chair. Theo takes a seat then tugs me onto his lap. The welcome pressure of his cock returns.

"She's so stunning," I whisper in awe.

He sweeps hair over my shoulder. "Not a scratch on you, though."

We both watch as the woman kneels in front of her captive and takes his length deep into her mouth. She sucks his dick, bobbing up and down until it's glistening with saliva.

"How does she know if he's enjoying it?"

"There are rules." His arms squeeze my waist. "He can tap out at any time if it gets too much. There's an agreed upon signal."

Gorgeous curves rising, the woman spreads her legs on either side of his waist, holding her entrance above his erection. Her hand clenches around his throat before she sinks down on him.

"I know it looks scary, but this is what he needs. Total submission. And she needs that potent sense of power just as much."

Riding her partner's cock with bouncing strokes, her head is thrown back, and hair tumbles down her back in a glistening curtain.

She looks like one of God's precious angels, twirling in the devil's arms with a smile on her face. Liberation is her reward for embracing that sin.

"I want to be that formidable." I shift, relishing the thickening shaft beneath me. "No one could ever hurt someone as powerful as her."

Theo tugs my dress strap aside to kiss my shoulder. "I want to give you that power, beautiful. All of it and more."

His hand sneaks beneath my dress to cup my mound. I moan under my breath, glancing from side to side to check that no one is looking at us. We're all caught under the same spell.

Theo squeezes, his thumb circling my clit through the wet lace. I grind on his hardness, wanting a relief to all the excruciating tension that's built between us.

Pushing my panties slightly to the side, his finger eases between my folds to find my entrance. I have to bite my tongue to hold in a moan as he drives a digit deep inside my pussy.

"That's it, angel," he encourages. "Ride my fingers. No one is watching us, trust me."

I should be finding a quiet corner to die of embarrassment in, but the feeling never comes. All I want is to emanate the beauty in front of me, taking the pleasure she wants with zero apologies.

She's her own god.

I want to steal her confidence for myself and let it burrow beneath my skin. It's all there for the taking—power, control, confidence. There are no bars holding me captive now.

Lifting my hips, I gasp as Theo pushes a second finger into my slit. I'm so wet and wildly turned on, I can almost feel my pulse thrumming against the shell of my skin.

Every time his fingers thrust back into me, I move on his lap, deepening the intrusion. It feels so forbidden to be chasing an orgasm in front of strangers, but their eyes don't touch us.

Just as the woman I'm copying halts and screams out her own release, an orgasm barrels into me, hard and fast. The wave overwhelms me without warning.

I sink down on Theo's fingers and slap a hand over my mouth to silence the moan begging to escape. My entire body is tingling, but still, I want even more from him.

"Fuck, Harlow. You are the most stunning creature I've ever seen," he purrs underneath me. "Did my angel come?"

"Yes." I sigh happily.

"You're not done, are you?"

He slides his fingers out from beneath my dress then lifts them to his mouth before greedily sucking them clean. Holy hell.

"I've dreamed of tasting your juices for months," he rasps. "You're as sweet as promised."

"Theo," I pant. "Do we have a room or something?"

"I've booked one for the night."

"Take me there right now."

Standing on trembling legs, I lean heavily on him as we leave the show behind. The flashes of bare skin and a cacophony of moaning melt into insignificance. His hand in mine is all I can feel.

Through another set of doors, a long, carpet-lined corridor offers reprieve from the people. Door after door stretches down the hallway, all numbered.

Struck by desire so intense it blurs my vision, I seize a handful of Theo's shirt and slam him into the wall. My mouth attacks his with such violence, I hardly recognise myself.

Tongue breaking past his lips, I steal the breath from his lungs with each crazed second. Something has been ignited deep within me, kindling flames that promise to devour us both.

Hitching my dress up to my waist, Theo grabs my ass and lifts me up. I wrap my legs around his waist and let him carry me down the corridor, too busy sucking on his bottom lip.

Room twelve.

The snick of the lock turning cuts through my hunger, and I offer him a second to breathe. We're in our own private room, where another satin-covered bed fills the space.

On the panelled walls, two racks of equipment await my perusal. Everything is available—cuffs, ties, gags, whips … too many toys to count. I don't recognise half of it.

"Woah."

"Everything is cleaned by the staff." Theo places me back on my feet. "It's part of the membership, so it's safe to use."

On him, my inner-demon finishes.

Seizing hold of that tiny voice that's vying for ownership, I let its darkness shroud me. There's no one watching now. I can risk dipping a toe into Theo's world.

Walking to the first rack, I drag my fingers over a red leather riding crop. "How many women have you brought here?"

He doesn't immediately answer.

Stroking a long purple dildo, I round on him. "Answer the question, Theodore, or this is going to end very quickly."

"Just Alyssa," he submits.

"And how many times have you visited here alone?"

"I used to come once a week before I met Alyssa. But never since her death."

Lifting a pair of thick leather cuffs from the wall, I test the weight in my hands. "You should have told me about this long ago."

He swallows hard. "Yes."

"So why didn't you?"

His eyes follow me over to the bed, the light blue depths almost entirely covered by the expanded black expanse of his pupils. I drop the cuffs on the bed and return to the rack.

"Theodore," I prompt.

"I … was afraid of losing you. Before we'd even met, I felt like I knew you." He hesitates, his voice cracking. "The day I handed you Laura's bone, I realised I loved you too."

And there it is.

The thing I've been waiting for.

Heart squeezing with emotion, I fight the urge to wrap myself around him. I've died a thousand deaths while waiting for those words to leave his mouth.

I didn't think a human heart could hold so much love until I met the guys and realised I could love four people equally, with enough left over to learn to love myself as well.

"Harlow?" he asks uncertainly. "Everything alright?"

"Yeah. Good."

Too curious for my own good, I select a ball gag next. It's smaller than the one the woman was using and a little less intimidating. It gets thrown on the bed.

I turn back to him. "Take your clothes off."

Theo obliges without hesitation, unbuttoning his shirt then sliding it off his sinewy shoulders. His trousers go next with his shoes, revealing the tented material of his black boxer shorts, where he stops.

"Didn't you hear me?" I snap, loving the thrill of being so demanding. "Everything off."

His mouth quirks with a smile. "Sorry."

Stepping out of his boxers, Theo stands completely naked. His cock is generous, smaller than Enzo and Hunter's terrifying lengths, but still a real handful.

Sliding the dress straps off my shoulders, I drag the flowy fabric down, exposing my lace underwear. He hums in appreciation but remains frozen in place.

"Lay on the bed," I instruct.

Theo's head dips in a nod. "Yes."

Positioning himself on the satin sheet, his eyes eat me up, noting every last angle on display. Attempting to embrace my newfound courage, I saunter over to him.

"How does this work? What do I do?"

"Whatever you want," he explains.

"The consent is implied?"

"If I need you to stop, I'll shake my head from side to side three times. Happy with that?"

My chest warms. "I'm happy."

Climbing onto the bed, I knee-walk to him, unclasping my bra in the process. My breasts fall free, and Theo licks his bottom lip.

"You're fucking perfect, Harlow."

Picking up the gag, I climb onto his lap to straddle him. "Quiet. I'm the only one allowed to talk now."

It feels foreign in my hands, but Theo's mouth opens, and he accepts the ball between his lips. I fasten the buckle at the back of his head then quickly mess up his hair.

"I hate this gel," I complain. "You look so handsome, but I prefer your curls all messy and wild."

He blinks in response.

Stroking a hand down his chiselled abdominals, I palm his cock then gently squeeze. His Adam's apple bobs tellingly.

"Do you want me to suck it?"

He blinks again.

"I can't hear you, so I guess it's my choice."

I swear, Theo smiles around the gag.

Pushing his shoulder, I lay him down then kneel between his legs. Uncertainty threatens to break my veneer of self-assuredness, but I quickly crush the feeling.

Tonight, I'm not Harlow Michaels.

I'm just … Harlow.

Whoever the fuck I want that to be.

His velvet shaft pushes past my lips to nudge the back of my throat. I suck my way down to his balls and cup the softness in one hand. Theo's hips buck upwards.

"No." I halt, licking my wet lips. "Still."

When he's stopped moving, I return to his length, taking it even deeper into my mouth. It's heady, the sense of empowerment I get from him obeying my commands.

Mouth popping off his dick, I pump his shaft and spread the stickiness of my salvia. All I can think about is finally feeling his cock filling me up, ending months of waiting.

"You made me wait." I sigh dramatically. "It's only fair that I do the same to you, don't you think?"

I have no idea what his blinking means this time, but I'm pretty sure he's acquiescing. Standing up, I hook my fingers into my panties then slowly drag them over my hips.

"Touch yourself, Theodore."

His hand dips between his legs to fist his cock. I watch him work his shaft for a moment. Tiny tremors quake across my skin at the sight.

When I bring my fingers to my pussy, I find slick warmth waiting. I'm still humming from the orgasm he teased out of me, and I easily slide two digits inside my entrance.

Theo's eyes are trained on me, watching every flick of my bud, thrust of my fingers and moan tearing free from my mouth.

The weight of his gaze is so sensual, I don't even need to feel his skin on mine. We're connected at this moment. The air between us is charged with our mutual longing.

Moving back to the bed, I pick up the leather cuffs, inspecting the supple material. They're thick and strong. Unbreakable. A lump gathers in my throat, but I swallow it down.

No fear.

I'm in control.

As I kneel next to him, Theo doesn't have to be told what to do. He offers me his wrists, holding them out to me like a peace offering. It feels eerie to be cuffing him.

I have to pause for a second, struggling with the brush of anxiety that brings. Theo touches my arm, his thumb circling in a silent soothe. He can read my hesitation from a mile off.

"I'm in control," I say aloud, needing the certainty to quash the memories. "I'm in control."

His stroking continues, reiterating my words. With the nerves dissipating, I tug his wrists into the cuffs then lift his arms above his head to the bed's metal railings.

After attaching the cuffs to the bed, I inspect my work. He's fully restrained, every line of supple, hair-dusted muscle exposed. Not a single word can escape his mouth.

"You pushed me away for so long," I scold. "All I wanted was to be yours, Theodore. In any way that you'd have me."

His legs spread as I settle above him to straddle his waist. I drag my nails down his torso, tracing the tantalising 'V' marking my target.

"I fell in love with you long before I allowed myself to admit it. The distance between us didn't matter to me."

Guiding the head of his cock to my entrance, I circle the tight slit, almost groaning at the exquisite torture. The relief is so close.

"It didn't matter because I love you too." I meet his gaze. "I'm tired of taking this slow. You complete me."

Taking his full length inside my cunt, I watch his eyes roll back in his head with pleasure. Fireworks explode inside me, revelling in the moment of pure satisfaction.

He's mine.

And I am his.

Lifting my hips, I push down on him, stealing every proud inch of his length. He stretches my walls, filling me to the brim with the perfect amount of pressure.

Cupping my breast, I tweak my nipple, loving the bite of pain. My hips rise and fall, finding a steady pace that strokes the wild, untamed animal inside of me that's beginning to find her voice.

I wish I could hear him, but the intensity reaches a boiling point without that line of communication. All I have are his upward thrusts, sliding deep into my pussy.

This is his surrender. His torn-out heart is being offered to me on a platter. He doesn't care what I do with it as long as I keep his trust safe, tucked safely inside where it can't be broken.

"I need more," I whine.

Riding him a little faster, each pump chases that elusive dose of ecstasy I can feel at the edges of my mind. It's on the cusp.

The increased pace intensifies the sense of fullness, his length surging into me at a bruising pace. More. More. There's no space left for doubt or hesitation in our relationship.

It's just us.

Forever.

Not even God can change that now.

With my climax nearing, Theo grants me control of every step closer to the edge we're both longing to dive off. I set the pace, the speed, the battering of our bodies.

All while his eyes stare up at me, filled with longing and the inevitability of his soul tangling with mine. I'm being worshipped and claimed in the same fell swoop.

Grabbing the gag's buckle, I quickly unfasten it then throw the ball aside. Trails of saliva spill from Theo's lips, but his ragged breaths don't last long before my lips seal on his.

Our mouths clash—silent, deadly, determined to paint the other in promises only our souls can keep. There's no taking this mutual branding back now.

"Are you close?" he growls into my mouth.

"Yes," I moan back. "I want you to fill me up."

Rutting into me, Theo steals the tiniest bit of power back and delivers the final, punishing blow. My orgasm hits me again, stronger this time, like a bulldozer demolishing any remaining lucidity.

I cry out his name, stilling to feel the rush of warmth that follows his seed spilling into me. He jerks beneath me, grunting through gritted teeth as his climax follows mine.

When my body feels too heavy to hold up, I slump onto his chest, my face hiding in the crook of his neck. Even without clothes on, his scent is still the same, like the pages of books are baked into him.

"Harlow," Theo heaves. "Fuck, angel."

Body humming with an incandescent sense of bliss, all I can do is groan a wordless response. I've gone boneless on top of him.

"Why didn't we do this six months ago?" he laughs.

Managing to lift my head, I grin back at him. "No idea. We wasted a hell of a lot of time reading books and trading theories."

"When we could have been fucking between the chapters?"

"Something like that."

Lifting myself off his chest, I unfasten the cuffs to release his wrists. Theo winces as he brings his arms down, working the blood back into his limbs.

"Are you okay?"

"I'm perfect." He cups my cheek, running a thumb over my bottom lip. "You're perfect. That was perfect."

And just like that, I'm a blushing fool all over again. I can't quite hold the strong, sexy persona in place, but she's still there. Biding her time beneath the surface.

"What I said earlier… I meant it. No more hiding. I love you, Harlow. And I'm all in. No matter what."

I'm not sure my body can hold the doubling of my heart. It's fit to burst with so much happiness, and I don't know what to do with it.

"I love you," I murmur back.

"Swear on it?"

Curling up on his chest, I kiss the throbbing vein at his neck, evidencing the organ that now beats solely for me.

"Yes. I fucking swear on it."

CHAPTER 11
HARLOW

HEARTLESS – YOU ME AT SIX

DOCTOR RICHARDS'S attention is glued to the heavily laden pages of the notebook I surrendered to him almost an hour ago. He's barely come up for air, allowing his cup of tea to go cold.

"Harlow, this is really excellent stuff." He glances up. "When did you write all this?"

I fiddle with a loose thread in my cardigan. "After we found those bodies on the beach a couple of weeks ago. I didn't know how to deal with it, so I started writing instead."

"I'm glad that you found a healthy way to cope with how it made you feel. It must have brought up a lot of emotions."

"Yes, it did, but it also helped to get it all out."

"This is written as if to an audience. I wonder if you've given our last conversation some more thought?"

I anxiously twist my fingers together. "I'm not sure when I stopped writing for myself and started writing for someone else."

Richards nods. "Tell me why you wrote these words."

"I want the world to know that I'm not him," I say slowly. "We share the same blood, but we couldn't be more different."

"For a long time, you couldn't see that difference." He smiles broadly. "How does it feel to acknowledge it now? To release guilt that doesn't belong to you?"

"It feels … free."

He runs a finger over the indents in the paper where my handwriting grew manic. I wrote until my hand screamed in pain.

It's like this elemental energy took over, and all I could think about was spilling my guts on the page. With every word, I was chasing that freedom, determined to keep it in sight.

"So what now?"

"Enzo's warned me off publishing anything." I shrug, trying not to let my disappointment show. "Especially after that press conference."

"Is that so?"

"He thinks it's the wrong time, and it'll cause more harm than good."

"Enzo is allowed to have his opinions," Richards dismisses. "But he isn't my patient. I want to know what you think."

"I think I want to do it. The whole world is against us. How could telling my truth make things any worse than they already are?"

Placing the notebook down, Richards crosses his ankles. "Have you heard of the Chinese proverb that says break the kettles and sink the boats?"

"Uh, I don't think so."

"Soldiers going into battle burned all their supplies and escape routes, leaving no choice but to advance into enemy territory. In doing so, they won the war."

I retake the notebook and hug it to my chest. "I'm not sure I understand."

"Sometimes, we need risk in order to succeed. You're standing at that same crossroads right now. To burn or not to burn."

His words give me pause. Enzo suggested the exact same thing. The power of destruction is within my grasp if I want it.

"Set the world on fire," I whisper to myself. "That's what he said my story would do. You think I should do it anyway?"

Richards chuckles. "I'm your therapist, Harlow."

"So?"

"I can't tell you what to do, but I think you have the power to change the world with your words. You get to decide what to do with that power."

This risk could backfire and destroy what remains of our life here. People don't always want the truth—especially not if it's ugly. But if I don't tell it, I know I'll always live with regret.

To burn or not to burn.

The choice is mine.

A sharp rap on the door to our meeting room interrupts the session. The door slams open, and Brooklyn walks into the room. She stops still when she sees me.

"Oh, crap."

"Brooke!"

Throwing myself at her, it takes her a moment to break free from her automatic urge to recoil and finally hug me back.

"Hi."

"I've been calling and texting all week."

She releases me, her smile contrite. "I needed some time to get my head screwed back on after what happened."

"Are you feeling better?" I ask, searching her face.

"A little bit. I'm still off work for now."

Clearing his throat, Richards rises from his chair. "You're early, Brooke. I never thought I'd see that day come."

"Sorry, doc. I didn't mean to interrupt."

"No bother. Shall I give you two a moment?"

I nod, prompting him to slip outside. With the door clicked shut, tears fill her silvery eyes and quickly spill over.

"I'm so sorry, Harlow. I didn't mean to scare you. When I have a relapse, I don't know that what I'm seeing and hearing isn't real."

"It's okay. We were just worried about you. I'm so sorry for breaking your trust. I didn't mean—"

"Hey," she cuts me off. "You're a good friend. I needed help, but I wasn't ready to admit that. I'm glad you guys tracked me down."

I'm so relieved, I hug her again. She laughs it off and lets me deposit her in my vacated chair. I crouch down next to her then rest a hand on her leg.

"What happened?"

"I told the guys everything," she explains. "We talked it through together as a family. With the wedding in three weeks, I guess everything got to me."

I swipe the moisture from her cheek. "Did you figure out what you're going to do?"

"I think so." A tentative smile blooms despite her tears. "We want to keep the baby."

Unable to stop myself, I squeal in excitement. I promised myself that I'd keep a straight face and support her no matter what, but it just slips out.

Brooklyn looks terrified still, but her smile is so darn wide. She seems like herself for the first time since we returned to England.

"You're going to be a mum." My own eyes burn with tears. "Oh my God. I'm going to be an auntie!"

"Hell yeah, you are. I'm not doing this shit without you."

"I can't believe it."

We embrace again, both choking on happy tears. Among all the pain and anguish, this is a glimmer of hope that our family needs.

"I have no idea what the fuck I'm doing."

"We'll figure it out." I squeeze her leg reassuringly. "Parenting can't be that hard, right? I'm sure there are books and crap on it."

"Trust me, Kade's already ordered them all. We've had boxes full of stuff arriving for days."

"You're kidding me?" I scoff.

"I wish. Kade was already a controlling asshole, but now he's monitoring my vitamin levels and meal planning."

I'm not even surprised. If she gets to the end of her pregnancy without murdering all of them, I'll take that as proof God does indeed grant miracles.

"Eli was the hardest to convince." She rubs her temples. "He's freaking the fuck out about being a parent. Neither of us had good examples to follow, more so than the others."

"Is he okay?"

"Not really, but we're working on it." Her hands move to cup her flat midsection. "We have to make this work, for the baby's sake."

A twinge of pain cuts across my chest. The whispered voice of a ghost sneaks in before I can halt its progress, like Richards has trained me to do.

I want my baby to live.

But not in this place.

I won't let him win.

Excitement wasn't a word I ever had cause to use in the basement, but watching Adelaide's belly grow with each passing day inspired hope in my soul for the first time in years.

That twisted hope only grew when she bled to death. When she died, I was given a glimpse of a way out from all the bloodshed.

It was the first time Michael had the doors of heaven slam shut in his face, no matter how loudly he screamed and begged for her baby to live so he could steal it for himself.

"Are you okay?" Brooklyn prods.

Snapping out of it, I force a smile. "Yeah. I should leave you to your session. I'm sure you have a lot to get your head around."

"Wait. You don't need to plaster a smile on for my sake, Harlow. Finding those bodies was seriously fucked up."

"Yeah," I deadpan.

"You want to talk about it?"

"I think I'm done talking." My grip on the notebook tightens. "It's time for me to do something about this. People need hope."

She rests a hand on top of mine. "I'm proud of you. I wish I was bringing my kid into a better world. You actually have the chance to make that difference."

"I think you're all overestimating me."

Brooklyn rolls her eyes. "Trust me, I don't overestimate anyone. People let you down less that way. You survived something truly harrowing. The world needs to know that hope is out there."

Patting her leg, I stand up before tucking my notebook back into my handbag. Richards waits outside the meeting room, but his back is turned to me.

"She's ready for you."

He doesn't respond, too busy staring down at the phone clasped in his hands. His shoulders are carved with tension.

I stop next to him. "Same time next week?"

Fear spikes through me at the pale pallor of his skin. It's like the life has been drained from his veins and overcome by shock instead.

"Is everything okay?"

My voice seems to startle him from his daze, and he slams the phone against his chest to hide the screen from me.

"Doctor Richards? What is it?"

"Harlow." His voice is a panicked wheeze, eyes darting from side to side. "I … uh. *Ahem.* Same time, that's fine."

"What were you looking at?"

"I … well, nothing."

The lie is painted all over his face.

"What is it?" I push him. "Is someone hurt?'

"It's just…"

With his mouth hanging open on another excuse, I snatch the phone from his hands. I can hear Brooklyn joining us, but I can't see beyond the live newsfeed in front of me.

"Harlow," Richards warns. "Don't look at that."

"What is this?" I whisper in terror.

The news is playing a video that's been sent to them. It's almost black, but the weak light of an underground room illuminates the haggard, bearded face staring back at me.

Even through a screen, his sick smile drips with evil. Michael looks thinner than the last time I found myself bloodied at his hand.

His grey hair is unwashed and limp, but his usual robes appear to be clean. There's something different about him, though.

"Hey." Brooklyn tries to grab the phone from me. "Come on, give me the phone. Let me check it first."

"No. It's him."

The malevolence behind Michael's smile isn't laced with his usual unholy intent. He looks smug. Confident, even. His eyes are gleaming bright, full of familiar, maniacal fire.

"Did she fool you all with her little act?" he cackles. "Poor, innocent Harlow, playing the victim for the whole world to see."

The video crackles, overtaken by a grey-scale clip of my now-infamous press conference, superimposed over his face. My voice is tinny over his laughter, the clips intermingling.

I won't stop until your judgement day comes.

You will repent and be punished.

"Will I?" Michael mocks. "I wonder, darling niece, what the world would think about your sob story if they knew the real truth."

I fight the urge to smash Richards's phone against the wall, over and over until that voice disappears from my consciousness. Worse still, I know this is being broadcast around the world.

Michael has broken cover.

We're being fed to the wolves.

"Sabre has been keeping a secret from you all," he continues gleefully. "I am not the one you should be worried about. They're protecting a cold-blooded killer."

"Okay, enough," Richards interrupts. "I think you should stop watching. He's trying to get in your head—"

"No," I interrupt.

"She has branded me a monster for enacting the Lord's mercy." Michael tuts under his breath. "The only killer here is you, Harlow. You're the only one with blood on your hands."

I feel like the floor falls out from beneath my feet, leaving me to plummet to my death. Richards's hand grabs my forearm to stop me from slumping. I'm unable to tear my eyes from the screen.

He's gone.

Another video plays.

Even from the strange angle, offering a bird's eye view of the basement, I recognise the cage where I spent so many years of my life. Shadows stretch across the walls and floor, but two figures are clear.

"No," I moan. "No, no, no."

Laura lies still in an expanding puddle of blood while a thinner, dirtier version of myself strains to reach between the rusted iron bars to strangle the life from her lungs.

Wringing.

Twisting.

Squeezing.

I choked her until her jerking limbs stilled. On the phone screen, I watch myself flinch away from my friend's corpse, curling into a tight, sobbing ball on the floor.

The phone falls from my hands, hitting the thick carpet with a thud. That moment is permanently charred on my mind, haunting every breath I've taken since I murdered Laura.

"We all know who the killer is here." His voice echoes from the dropped phone. "Behold, the real Harlow Michaels."

The worst part is he's right. This is the real me. The bare, stripped-back, animalistic version of myself he made me into.

"Is this a person you want to protect?" Michael taunts. "Will you believe the lies she tells about me? She is a cold-blooded killer."

"Where the hell did he get that video?" Brooklyn snarls.

I swallow the acid searing my vocal cords. "He must've been filming in the basement. I had no clue."

"You wanted to fight me," the voice continues. "I will bring a war to your doorstep. Nothing will stop me from completing my mission. You've been warned."

The buzz of reporters reacting to the footage melts into the background. I'm trembling with rage. I won't accept his guilt. Never again. He's the evil one here.

"Harlow." Brooklyn strokes a hand down my arm. "You need to stay calm. We can fix this."

I brush her aside. "I am calm."

Richards eyes me apprehensively. "You are?"

Ignoring both of their stares, I pick up the fallen phone and offer it to Richards. He gingerly takes it, preoccupied by studying me.

"If Michael wants a war, then that's exactly what he'll get. I refuse to spend another moment of my life feeling guilty for his crimes."

Richards tucks the phone into his pocket. "What are you going to do?"

"Give the people what they want." I tap the notebook tucked in my handbag. “He will have no supporters left by the time I’m done telling the truth. This is a fight I’m going to win.”

Darkness fills Brooklyn’s gaze. “He’s going to come for us all. This won’t be a pretty fight. Are you ready for that?”

Courage steels my spine.

“Bring it on.”

CHAPTER 12
LEIGHTON

PIRATE SONG – MEHRO

MY PUNCH CONNECTS with Harlow's ribcage, and she hisses out in pain. Drawing back, I dance around her on light feet. Her hands are curled into fists and waiting for an opening to clock me.

"Again!" Enzo shouts.

"I'm trying!" she yells back. "He's too fast."

Ducking low, I snake an arm around her waist and use it to flip her over. She smacks into the workout mat, and the air is knocked from her lungs with a grunt.

"Or you're just too slow." I loom over her. "You're not concentrating, Goldilocks. Focus your mind."

"I am fucking focused."

"No. You're still thinking about that video. Focus!"

Straying too close while lecturing her, I'm late to dodge her hand that snaps out to catch my ankle. She wrenches me off balance, using her weight to send us both tumbling across the mat.

"Focus *your* mind," Harlow growls back. "I'm concentrating just fine."

Manoeuvring herself on top of me, her fist draws back for the perfect strike. She halts the killer punch at the last second, and her knuckles scrape my nose.

"You can't pull your punches in real life."

"Do you want me to break your nose?" she smarts. "And ruin such a pretty view?"

"Aw. You think I'm pretty?"

Pacing the edges of the room, Enzo glowers at us both. "Stop fucking flirting, and beat his ass. I'm not training you to have morals."

With a grin lighting her lips, Harlow draws back her fist then clips me in the face. It's a tamer blow than the one she pulled, but it still makes my teeth rattle together.

"Better." Enzo crouches down to eye us both. "Again."

After scrambling to our feet, we resume our dangerous dance, circling one another like predators on the hunt. She's been training with Enzo for months, and his hard work has paid off.

Our little Harlow isn't a timid, broken wallflower anymore. She's managed to hold her own for forty-five minutes of fighting, and I haven't gone easy on her.

"Getting tired, Goldilocks?" I taunt her.

She wipes sweat from her forehead. "Hell no."

Lashing out, my kick connects with her torso. She grunts in pain, folding over to cushion the blow. Enzo threatened death if I wasted his time, so I've got to at least act like I want to hit her.

Although I can't lie … the look on her face when she punched me so hard I spat blood turned me on so fucking much.

"Come on. You gonna wimp out on me? I expected better."

"Fuck you, Leigh," she hisses.

"Not until you finish the job, princess."

Harlow lunges towards me and moves so fast, I can't stop her from jabbing her fist into my throat. She rises to her full height then pulls her fists back up to go again.

"Good! Advance," Enzo orders.

There's no time to retreat before she's on me—strike after strike, her knee smashing into my stomach, an elbow in my ribs. I collide with the weight bench and almost trip over it.

Her teeth are bared in a grimace, but her attack doesn't let up. She leaps on top of me, her legs trapping my waist in a vice. When her knuckles crack into my cheek, I spit more blood on the floor.

"Do you relent?" she gasps.

Grasping her ponytail, I yank hard and force her head to tilt up to me. She grits her teeth against the pain, letting me capture her lips in a furious kiss before I release her hair.

"Do you?" I mimic.

"Never."

With a huff, I heave her from my lap and flip us around so her back meets the smooth leather of the weight bench.

"So be it."

Settling between her splayed legs, my hips rock into hers, mere millimetres of sweaty fabric keeping me from fucking her senseless while Enzo watches the show.

I'm not particularly shy, and if it pisses him off, then even better. I'll fill his precious girl with my come and make him watch as she swallows a mouthful of my cock.

"Surrender. I win."

"You son of a bitch," she spits.

Each shift of her gorgeous curves hardens my dick. I'm pressed right up against her heat, desperate to slide into her wet cunt. Cheeks coloured pink, she looks sexy as hell right now.

"This wasn't part of the training," Enzo complains from across the room. "Take your hands off *my* woman before I remove them with a blunt knife."

"Why don't you go find that knife while I make Harlow come a few times?" I retort. "Then you can do whatever you want."

"Do I not get a say in this?" Harlow sighs.

With an eyebrow quirked, I grab the mound of her hot, soaked pussy through her leggings. She can't help but react and digs her nails into my biceps.

"You don't want me to bend you over this bench and slide my cock inside your tight little pussy?" I sneer in her face.

"No," she whines.

"I don't believe you."

Something tells me I could make her come just by whispering filth in her ear. I will die without a single complaint as long as I'm buried between her thighs, making her body sing.

Enzo crouches down on Harlow's other side, scraping his eyes over her tight clothing and the obvious pebbling of her nipples that poke through her pink sports bra.

"She looks fucking good, doesn't she?" he muses.

Still cupping her cunt, I squeeze gently. "She'd look even better without these stupid clothes on. You got a preference, Enz? Front or back?"

"I've wanted to fuck her tight backside for months." Enzo runs a fingertip over her chest, circling both nipples. "What do you think, little one?"

"I-I've never d-done that," she stammers.

"We can help you," I purr, shifting my crotch against her core. "It takes some preparation, but I can just imagine your perfect tits bouncing while we fuck both of your holes."

"Amen to that," Enzo agrees.

Grabbing her leggings, I tug them down her legs then toss them over my shoulder. She's wearing a scrap of drenched cotton, the fabric white against her slim, tanned legs.

"Were you this wet when you fucked Theo?" I wonder.

"Leigh!" she exclaims. "I am not answering that."

"I want to hear all the details. What did you do to him, huh? Was it some freaky shit?"

"We are not discussing this!"

Enzo takes over to slide her panties down. With the scrap of fabric bunched in his fist, he brings it to his nose and inhales deeply.

"I can smell just how much you want it," he comments with a smirk. "A few dirty words and you're soaked for us."

Harlow blushes red. "I can't help it. I'm sorry."

I deliver a sharp slap to her now bare cunt. Her back arches as her mouth falls open on a gasp.

"Never apologise for that," I berate.

Enzo nods in agreement. "Not unless you want us to punish you."

"P-Punish me?" she gasps.

A dark smile in place, Enzo looks up at me. "Shall we?"

"Be my guest, man."

While I haven't shared with Enzo before, I'm not going to turn down the opportunity. Even if it entails seeing his bare backside and dick. It's nothing I didn't see in prison. I can deal.

Gripping her sports bra, Enzo yanks it over Harlow's head, allowing her tits to spill out. He kisses across her chest, sucking a nipple between his teeth.

"Enz," she moans. "Fuck."

Enzo traces her lip, pushing his thumb into her mouth. "I want to push your boundaries, little one. Mind if I play a little rough?"

"Please do."

I step back to give him some room. Enzo studies the wall of supplies in our basement gym, and when he pulls the long, rubber length of a skipping rope from a hook, my interest piques.

Harlow looks equal parts fascinated and nervous, but she doesn't freak out. Not even when he tugs her to stand up from her splayed-out position on the bench, her entire frame bare.

"Do you trust us?" Enzo demands. "I'm not doing this if there's even a crack of doubt, so tell me straight."

She licks her lip. "I trust you both with my life."

"Give me your wrists, then."

Surrendering to him, Enzo loops the skipping rope around her wrists in a perfect sliding knot. He drops a kiss on her shoulder before holding her hips to boost her up into the air.

The rest of the rope is wound around the high, metal frame of the workout equipment. Tied in another knot, Harlow is left suspended, her arms above her head and tiptoes brushing the floor.

Enzo steps back to admire his handiwork. "That's a hell of a sight. What do you think, Leigh?"

"Fucking perfect."

"She's all ours."

"You want to go first?" he invites.

"Go ahead. I want to see her writhe while you fuck her senseless."

Enzo snickers. "That can be arranged."

Harlow hangs helplessly while we talk, barely able to hold herself up. The entire length of her scar-laden body is exposed to us both. She can't even attempt to cover herself.

The old slashes that carve the Holy Trinity into her torso are more faded than her newer scars, including the bright-pink, taut lines where that asshole Abaddon started to carve her up.

Even covered in more scar tissue than skin, she's the single most beautiful sight in the whole goddamn world. Every mark is evidence of her sheer resilience and determination to survive.

Harlow Michaels is a lioness.

Our fucking lioness.

"Guys," Theo shouts from upstairs, his voice breaking the moment. "You need to come and see this."

"We'll be right there," Enzo calls back.

But he doesn't move. He's far too busy circling Harlow's prone form, devouring every part of her with his eyes. When he smacks her ass, she vaults in the air.

"Oh God!"

"You can't hide from us like this," he teases. "We can do whatever we want to you now. This is your punishment."

"More," she pleads.

"You want me to spank you again, baby girl?"

Harlow nods, biting her lip in earnest. "Yes."

"What did I tell you before?"

"Yes, sir," she recites.

Fuck. Me.

That's so hot.

She cries out again when he slaps her ass. My cock twitches with need at the sight.

"Good girls get spanked when they ask nicely," Enzo taunts. "But if you want me to let you come, you'll have to beg."

"Please," she immediately begs.

"Not yet, baby. Be patient."

His hand strikes her left breast, and blood rushes to the area, leaving a mark on her skin. She whimpers, the sound sending heat rushing straight to my painfully hard cock.

"I want you to ride my face."

"What?" Harlow breathes.

Growling to himself, he lifts her legs then encourages them to wrap around his neck. She's suspended at the best height for his mouth to access the folds of her cunt.

Gripping her ass cheeks, Enzo buries his face between her thighs. I slip a hand inside my shorts to find my shaft. This is hot as fuck to watch. Even if he's the one eating her sweet pussy instead of me.

"Didn't you hear him?" I recapture her attention. "Ride his face, princess. Move your hips, and let his tongue fuck your hole."

Fingers curling around the rope at her wrists, Harlow lifts herself, using her legs around his neck for balance. She pushes her pussy into him and slowly begins to gyrate.

Her eyes find mine. "Like … this?"

"Perfect," I praise.

Enzo laps at her centre, his mouth attacking her heat like he's a starving man gifted his first meal in months. I can hear how turned on she is by the wet smack of his lips devouring her.

"Enzo," she cries out.

He pauses for a breath. "Come on, beautiful girl. I want you to squirt your juices all over my face."

Diving back into his meal, he attacks her with the kind of ravenous need that only Harlow can inspire. Everything about her innocent, untouchable demeanour makes her irresistible.

She's gorgeous without even realising it, and there is nothing more attractive than that. I've been with my fair share of women, and none of them compared to the goddess caught between us four idiots.

Still grinding herself against his mouth, Harlow finds her rhythm. Her hips move faster, and Enzo can't get enough, holding her ass tight as he sucks on her clit.

I fist my cock and stroke, base to tip, imagining Harlow's pert pink lips wrapped around me instead. I'll wait for my turn. The sight of her riding Enzo's face is worth my patience.

Pushing a thick finger inside her slit, Enzo works her cunt into a drenched furnace. Every time he circles her nub, she throws her head back, and a guttural noise erupts from her mouth.

"I'm almost there."

"Good girl," Enzo approves.

I have no doubt that Theo can hear her falling apart as he works in the kitchen above us. Let him listen. This incredible creature is ours to toy with as we please.

Shuddering through the waves of her climax, Harlow's legs tighten around his neck. She guides herself to a peak and screams out his name.

When she's still, Enzo lifts his head and gulps down air. There's moisture scored across his mouth and cheeks, evidencing her orgasm. He dives in for a lip-smacking kiss so she can taste herself.

Harlow doesn't bat an eye, stealing her own come back with each stroke of their tongues colliding. She kisses over his lips and cheeks, her tongue flicking out to cleanse him.

"That's my perfect girl." Enzo nuzzles her neck. "You did good."

I love watching Harlow when she's feeling embarrassed. It's hilarious. The way she wraps herself in innocence to disguise the curious demon rearing its head within her is so hot.

"Guys!" Theo yells again. "This is urgent. You can screw each other later. Get up here."

Still fisting my dick, I consider putting a bullet between Theo's eyes. As we discovered in Costa Rica, the little shit has an uncanny ability to act as a cockblock at the worst possible moments.

"Move," I snap.

Pushing past Enzo, I'm still pumping my shaft. Harlow's widened blue eyes watch me approach, and she wiggles in the air when I stop in front of her.

"Leigh," she whispers.

"I know, Goldilocks. I want to fuck you right now, but Captain Cockblock calls, so we're gonna have to pick this up another time."

Seizing her hip, I shove my face in the swell of her tits. Her high-pitched groan when I bite down on her rosy bud finishes me off. I can't hold it in for a second longer.

Squeezing my length, I explode all over her belly and legs. Harlow holds steady, letting me paint her in my seed.

"Oh my God."

Stifling a laugh, I hold her up to relieve the pressure on her wrists. "Sorry. I couldn't stop myself."

Running my finger over the slope of her stomach, I collect a sample of come then lift it to her lips. She doesn't even fucking hesitate before accepting the gift and licking my finger clean.

This girl.

This motherfucking *queen*.

Pulling off my T-shirt, I use it to wipe the stickiness from her body then loosen the rope from her wrists. Harlow slumps in my arms, her body still trembling as I place her on her feet.

"You good, baby?"

"Uh-huh," she hums back.

Her eyes flick over to Enzo. Even I can see the strain against his black workout shorts. He's struggling to contain himself.

"Go on." I push her towards him. "I'll go upstairs and keep Theo occupied until you're done. Make it quick, though."

"I can do quick," Enzo affirms.

Harlow nods. "Me too."

Leaving my ruined T-shirt on the floor, I swipe the hair from my face and head for the stairs. A glance over my shoulder reveals Harlow bent over the workout bench as Enzo settles at her rear.

I can't resist watching for a few seconds—my cock is getting hard again already. Harlow slaps a hand over her mouth to remain quiet as Enzo pushes into her slit from behind.

"Hold on," he warns.

Pinning her against the bench, his huge hands cup her breasts while spearing her cunt. He's like a fucking wild animal. That bench is going to break in half if he moves any faster.

Jesus Christ.

What I wouldn't give to pin her sexy body in a sandwich between us. I wouldn't mind rubbing dicks with Enzo if it means I can fill every available hole she has to offer.

Repositioning my dick, I emerge upstairs. In the kitchen, Theo and Hunter are sitting at the dining table. I can hardly see them through the stacks of case files.

They're working on the connection between each of the thirteen suicides. Four are from the same church parish, while the others were based in nearby cities and towns.

"Only me. They're just finishing up."

Theo snorts. "So I can hear."

"You were listening?"

"Kinda hard not to."

Grabbing a bottle of water from the fridge, I take a second to admire Harlow's hard work in the past few weeks. This place looks brand new.

The whole open-plan kitchen and living room has been refreshed, courtesy of several long days spent decorating. Her clean white lines, black accents and burnt orange paint really did the trick.

"Leigh," Theo calls. "Come look at this."

"What is it?"

"I've got something."

"You managed to trace the origin of that video?" I guess.

"He was sloppy this time," he confirms. "I've decrypted the metadata and triangulated a location for the source. It correlates with four of the connected suicide victims."

Blood roaring in my ears, I race over to the table to look over his shoulder. Hunter's sitting to his left, his eyes racing over the laptop screen.

Even Lucky has perked up from her snoozing under the table. She's still attached to us at every available opportunity and demanding cuddles whenever we have a spare second.

"We've got him this time," Hunter declares.

"*Maybe*," Theo replies with sign language. "*Fake*?"

He shrugs. "Only one way to find out if it's authentic."

The intricate, black-and-white map on Theo's laptop is reminiscent of something from a movie. Major cities, busy motorways and the red spots of surveillance feeds are laid out.

Theo highlights the coordinates he's located, magnifying the location embedded in the data behind the video. By retaliating to Harlow's threat, Abaddon has shown his hand.

"Tregaron?" I read off the screen. "That can't be right."

Theo rubs his eyes behind his glasses. "It's a quiet market town. Perfect place to hide. That video looked like it was shot in a basement or crypt."

Finger tapping the search area, Hunter narrows his eyes. "There. Is that a church?"

Nodding, Theo is preoccupied by pulling up the government's curated list of church parishes. If this piece of shit is hiding anywhere, it'll be there. The rural location is a great disguise.

"We need to dispatch a team immediately." Hunter pulls his phone out to fire off text messages. "Who knows how long he's planning to remain there?"

I grab his wrist to still him and mouth, "Already gone?"

"Thong?"

"*GONE*," I enunciate.

"What if Michael is already gone?"

I nod in confirmation.

"Well, then at least we can pick up his tail easier," he muses. "This is still a solid lead."

How he still has the strength to be so damn optimistic, I'll never know. I can't stand to think about how long we've wasted on Michael Abaddon and this endless wild goose chase.

In less than five minutes, Theo pulls together a bare bones profile on Tregaron's church. Registered clergy, public finances, affiliated members, the works.

"Jesus, Theo. You should do this for a living."

"Hilarious," he says dryly.

"How do you dig this information up?"

"I could tell you the colour of the royal family's underpants if I had enough time. This is a piece of cake."

"People would pay good money for that information."

"Huh. Maybe a career change is in order."

"You hate the royal family."

He snorts. "People can't afford to put clothes on their kids' backs. We don't need a throne made of gold."

Theodore Young—closeted anarchist and the voice of reason in this backwards fucking country. We really must be in the end times if he's talking politics.

Harlow's red-tinged face appears from the gym first, walking with an ever so slight limp. Her ponytail has fallen out, spilling curling hair over her shoulders, the flyaways stuck to her forehead.

"What is this, the walk of shame?" Hunter chuckles.

Closing the door to the basement, Enzo pins him with a glare. It only makes him laugh even harder. They couldn't be more obvious.

Harlow glows an even brighter shade of violent-red. "Can we move on? Theo, what have you found?"

"We've got a possible location."

Theo tilts the laptop screen so she can study the small search radius. Hunter's poised to intervene if she shows even a crack of panic.

None of us expect her to be eerily calm and devoid of emotion when she looks up from the laptop and finally responds.

"Let's go get this son of a bitch."

CHAPTER 13
HARLOW

HOPE – NF

THE HUM of the helicopter drowns out the sound of my erratic heartbeat. Even with headphones in place to protect my ears, I can feel each frantic flap of the rotors taking us over the Welsh border.

In the seat next to me, Hunter's cocoa eyes are lit with anticipation. He's clinging to the edge of his seat, his palpable excitement held back by nothing but his belt.

I tap his shoulder then sign, "*Are you okay?*"

His mouth stretches in a smile. "I can feel it."

"*What?*"

"The helicopter." He rests a palm against the door. "I can feel the rotors beating. It's almost like I can hear again."

I'd forgotten how handsome he is when smiling from ear-to- ear. I love every version of Hunter, but this is the person who stole my heart. Pieces of him are coming back to life.

Dressed in a pressed, white shirt, his favourite leather holster and a suit jacket rolled up to show off his tattooed forearms, Hunter looks every inch the heartless businessman who found me in the hospital.

But this time he wears a bulletproof vest on top. Enzo threatened extreme violence if Hunter refused to wear it. He's taking no more risks with his best friend's safety.

"It's like I can taste it," he says in wonderment. "The vibrations are running through me, but I can't hear the sound. My other senses are piecing it together."

He can hear it then.

Only in his own, unique way.

I lean close and speak slowly so he can read my lips. "Sounds like?"

The look he offers me is pure magic.

"The best fucking thing I've ever heard."

An invisible hand clenched around my throat, I grab his shoulder and slant my mouth against his. I want to swallow his happiness and lock it in a strong box, where he can't dismiss it again.

This is living.

He's still capable of it.

After lifting the case at his feet, Hunter scans his thumbprint on the concealed pad and clicks it open. Inside, nestled in black foam, is a compact handgun that's far fancier than the one I've trained with.

"For you," he says simply.

I frown at him.

"You've been training hard for months." Hunter lifts the gun. "This is your graduation present."

"*Really?*" I sign.

"Just don't shoot me. I'm full of holes as it is."

Fingers spasming with excitement, I eagerly accept the gun. It feels perfect in my hands—not too heavy, the grip melded to my palm.

I check the magazine to ensure the safety is clicked on before aiming it at the helicopter's metal wall, finding the perfect aim that's been drilled into me.

"You look good with it," he compliments.

I kiss him deeply, despite the pilot sitting metres in front of us. We're minutes from touchdown to meet the others, but I don't care. Every second with Hunter is precious after almost losing him.

Tapping my fingers to my chin, I push them forward, signing *thank you.* His lips curve in another heart-stopping smile, all lit up for me.

"You're welcome," he whispers back.

The pilot's voice buzzes through my headset, warning of impending touchdown. I settle in my seat and let Hunter strap a sleek leather leg holster to my cargo-covered thigh.

"You're all set, sweetheart."

Slotting the gun into place, he drops a kiss at my temple. I'm kitted out just like one of them, mirroring Enzo in my all-black ensemble and matching bulletproof vest.

"Nervous?" Hunter murmurs.

I shake my head.

"It's okay if you are. This is your first active operation. I was shit scared during my first raid."

Holding his hand in mine, I draw circles on his palm, realising just how calm I feel. After so much torment, it's like my mind has finally decided that enough is enough.

Descending through the cover of night, the darkness of Wales's rolling hills greets us. We cruise above shadowed farmland and countryside, all concealed by the lack of city lights.

From our research, we know the picture-perfect town of Tregaron is nestled amongst steep hills and white-painted cottages. It's a quiet market town, unassuming and quaint.

The perfect hideout.

This better be it.

"There." Hunter leans over my shoulder to point. "Church."

The two glossy black helicopters embossed with Sabre's logo descend ahead of us, circling the arched turrets of an old, medium-sized church. The structure is lit by flashing blue lights.

Theo used his terrifyingly fast computer skills to locate the council's clerk and contact him, granting us permission to land in a farmer's field at the edge of the village.

The town's local police force is awaiting our arrival. A cordon has already been established, ensuring that no one enters or escapes. If there are people inside that church, they're trapped.

After touching down, we step out into the swaying crops to join the others. Becket and Enzo disembark from the left helicopter, leaving Hudson, Kade and two other agents to jump from the last.

"Harlow."

Hunter taps my shoulder, his palm outstretched. I take the tiny, nude-coloured earpiece then slot it into place. He checks it before pulling my ponytail over my shoulder.

"You're my ears tonight."

"No pressure," I mutter to myself.

"Hmm? I didn't catch that."

Plastering a weak smile into place, I nod instead. "I said *okay*."

"No, you didn't. Don't lie." Leighton's disembodied voice speaks into my ear. "You read me, princess?"

"Copy that. We've arrived safely."

Another familiar voice joins him and whispers straight into my brain. It's like I'm carrying them around with me.

"Be careful," Theo cautions. "We're keeping surveillance from above. No heat signatures or signs of life."

"Michael isn't here?"

"He could still be underground."

The hum of a drone passing above us marks his words. Theo's eyes and ears are everywhere, even from his office two hundred miles away. He doesn't need to be here to be deadly.

"I see you," he offers.

I wave up at the drone. "Hi."

"You look good, beautiful. Nice holster."

Playfully wiggling my leg for the drone to spot, I blow him a kiss. "Thanks. Little graduation present."

"Suits you."

Enzo races to my side, searching over me with a tension that only I can read on his schooled expression. He notes the gun strapped to my thigh and nods to assure himself.

"You like it?"

I tap the holster. "Love it."

"We chose it especially for you. There's a sensor in the grip. It's coded to scan your fingerprints, so only you can fire it."

"Seriously? That's awesome."

"You're welcome," Theo speaks into my ear. "I designed the tech myself. Consider it a precaution."

"Thanks, Theo. Very thoughtful."

"Fuck roses and chocolates, right?" he chuckles. "Women want martial arts lessons and guns to shoot us idiots with."

"You're right there."

"Police have a cordon up, the place is surrounded," Leighton cuts in. "No way in or out. If Abaddon's in there, he's ours."

I study the flash of blue lights, with numerous urgent voices wafting through the night from the crime scene up ahead. Judgement day has arrived for my uncle.

The prospect of coming face-to-face with Michael again should put the fear of God in me. Instead, I'm almost salivating with the need to see him cuffed and humiliated.

Before I can take off, Enzo snatches my arm. "Not so fast. The only reason you're not grounded with Brooklyn is the fact that I've trained you myself. Watch your six, and be careful."

"Brooklyn's pregnant," I lash back. "You trained her yourself too."

"Want me to stick a fucking baby in you? I'll do it right here. At least then I'll have a reason to lock your ass down, safe at home."

"So romantic."

"It could be," he combats.

"We can hear everything you're saying," Theo hisses into our earpieces. "Threaten to impregnate Harlow again and I'll be forced to crash a ten-thousand-pound drone into your head."

"And be thankful my brother is deaf, or you wouldn't live long enough to put a bullet in our target," Leighton adds cheerfully.

"No impregnations today, then," I surmise.

Shrugging off Enzo's grip, I shake the hand that Becket offers to me. He claps my shoulder, also noting the weapon on my thigh with a pleased grin.

"You're looking well, Harlow."

"Thank you. Where are Ethan and the others?"

He slots his earpiece into place. "Mexico. We're running a sting on a human trafficking ring with connections to big players in London and the States."

"Mexico?" I whistle. "That's far out."

"Ethan's boyfriend introduced us to a victim living in a town not far from here called Briar Valley. She's helping our investigation bring down the assholes trafficking kids on our fucking doorstep."

"Sounds like a hell of a woman."

"She really is." He smiles. "You'd like her. I'll introduce you guys sometime."

"Alright," Enzo barks. "Let's move out."

After clambering through the stalks of corn, we emerge on the nearby road, moving across in a tight formation. Several police cars are parked outside the church with flashlights marking the perimeter.

Enzo walks ahead to shake the nearest outstretched hand. Dressed in an ill-fitting suit that barely contains his potbelly, the grey-haired man who greets him scans over us all.

"Mr Montpellier, I presume?"

"Detective," Enzo answers. "Any trouble?"

"Not a peep. We spoke to Father Yule. Evening prayers finished at six o'clock, and he left an hour after. Door's unlocked."

"Is the scene secure?"

"No one's entered or left."

When Enzo moves to walk past him, the detective shoots out an arm, preventing him from passing.

"We've seen that video circulating in the news." His eyes stray over to me. "Seems to me like the person you should be investigating is standing right there."

"We don't have time for this." Enzo scowls at him. "Unless you'd like to explain to the Prime Minister himself why you allowed our suspect to escape, I suggest you step aside."

"You can't barge into my jurisdiction and—"

With a snarl, Hunter flashes past us both and seizes the detective by his shirt. He hauls him so close their noses brush, and the frosty bite of his voice sets my teeth on edge.

"This is our crime scene," he hisses. "Step aside before I do something I won't regret in front of all your men."

"Just who do you think you are?"

Hunter's very limited patience snaps, despite not being able to hear the asshole's remark. Enzo yells at him to stop just as he clocks the detective in the face.

"Motherfucker!" the detective howls.

"I did warn you," Hunter drones. "We're in charge now."

Taking my hand into his, he yanks me past the stunned faces of several police officers. I've seen Hunter in action before, but he's well and truly done with bullshit now.

God help us all.

"What happened?" Leighton asks urgently.

"Your brother punched a detective."

"Jesus Christ. Keep an eye on him."

"Copy that."

With agents flanking us on both sides, we duck beneath the cordon and approach the church. Enzo and Hunter both have their guns raised, leaving Hudson and Kade to watch their backs.

Keeping my weapon in place, I straighten my spine and lead the group. With the sheer weight of highly-trained muscle behind me, I can put one foot in front of the other without fear.

"Careful, Harlow." Enzo checks the entrance before gesturing for me to go ahead. "Stay sharp. Don't forget your training."

"Do you want to go first?"

"No. You've got this."

Fuck, if that doesn't feel good to hear. The lazy smile he offers me seals the deal. I need a repeat of our sexy gym session after this.

Breath held, I twist the ornate knob to creak open the church's arched door. Pitch-black darkness and the dampness of stone floors awaits, laden with the scent of burned candles.

"Flashlights," Enzo instructs.

Bright beams of light cut through the suffocating darkness. Stepping into the devil's lair, I glance around. It's a fairly small church, with a few dozen carved pews presided over by an altar.

The air is deathly still. Too still. No signs of life break the shadows draped over the furniture and gleaming crucifixes. Fanning out, the guys scour the place in less than a minute.

"Clear," Hudson shouts.

"Nothing here," I relay into my earpiece. "You guys see anything?"

"Negative," Theo replies. "Check the crypt. You'll lose us underground, but we're keeping watch from above."

"Be careful," Leighton adds.

"We will, Leigh."

"You fucking better, Goldilocks."

Enzo points to the iron gate holding the stairs leading beneath the church. With a nod, Hunter ducks in front of him to lead. The gate creaks as it's wrenched open, unveiling our next stop.

Most churches have crypts beneath them, especially the old ones. The basement where I spent my childhood was thankfully empty of gravestones or ancient corpses. Only fresh ones graced its halls.

I snatch Hunter's arm to stop him. "Wait."

He glances at my mouth, confused.

"I hear something."

His brows furrow. "You what?"

Stopping beside us, Enzo's head is cocked. "I hear it as well."

There's a tinny sound echoing up the steps leading into the inky-black depths. I quickly sign a warning to Hunter. He cocks his gun, nodding and taking a tentative step into the unknown.

Step.

Step.

Step.

We inch farther into the belly of the beast. The sound morphs from a distant whisper to the scratching melody of a gospel song being played. Terror inches up my spine.

Those awful songs were the soundtrack to many clean-up sessions. Mrs Michaels loved a soundtrack to accompany her work. It was the only time I ever saw a phone.

"He's playing music."

Enzo's big hand lands on my shoulder. "I'm right behind you, baby. He won't get a chance to hurt you again."

"Swear it?" I ask, feeling insecure.

"On my damn life. You won't let him."

His implicit trust in my new skill set propels my feet forward. I can confront the devil with Enzo propping me up every step of the way. He won't let me fall, but if I do, I know he'll follow me.

With flashlights illuminating the thick dust of the crypt, the bodies behind us fan out, ready to fire off a shot at any moment. My heart leaps into my throat when light sweeps over the back corner.

The phone is resting on top of a large, rusted, blue barrel, surrounded by several others. Voices intermingle, reaching a harmony and ending the song on a high note.

The Lord has heard my plea.

The Lord accepts my prayer.

Humble yourselves under the mighty hand of God.

In my mind, the unknown voices meld into one that's deep and booming. I can hear him in my head, his sadistic laugh echoing on a loop. He has to be here. We can't have lost him again.

"Fan out," Enzo orders.

In less than a minute, the crypt is declared clear. No trace of our demon. But when the song crackles, its symphony interrupted by the lash of laughter, my hackles raise.

"Did you really think it would be that easy?" Michael cackles through the speaker. "I'm disappointed. I thought taking down the almighty Sabre Security would at least be hard."

"Hiding again, Uncle?" I shout back.

"Not at all, dearest niece."

"Come and face me yourself, then."

"I'm too busy for your childish attempts to derail the Lord's plans for us all. There's work to be done before judgement day comes."

"So what? Where does it all end?"

"With a world purged of all its evil sins," he says simply, like it's the most logical thing in the world. "I'll consecrate this new earth with the blood of those who must die first."

"Killing more innocent people isn't the answer," I try to reason. "Tell me what you really want. Why did you release that video?"

"Because you needed a reminder," he sneers back. "I am the one in control, Niece. I gave you the chance to rule with me. You refused."

"You won't stop me from showing the world who you really are. Video or not. Your downfall is coming."

"My downfall?" He laughs hysterically. "Oh, precious, little Letty. You were supposed to rule by my side. I didn't want it to end like this."

"Guys," Hudson murmurs.

He gingerly inches closer to pick up the phone. We're connected to a live voice call, but the phone is plugged into something else.

"Hud?" Kade prompts.

"Hang on."

He traces the wire from the phone's port to a small, black fuse box tucked between the barrels. A single red light blinks on the dashboard.

"Is that…?" Hunter's voice catches.

"For everyone will be salted with fire," Michael taunts. "Do you remember your scripture? You've heard that one before."

All pairs of uncertain eyes lock on me. I gulp down the bubble of nausea threatening to choke my words.

"Mark, 9:49."

"Very good," he compliments. "You could have ruled by my side. The kingdom of God was right there for the taking, and instead, you chose a life of sin."

Kade joins his brother then, and with difficulty, they manage to crack open the lid of one barrel. The eye-watering scent of fuel infiltrates the crypt.

"Your rapture has come early," Michael declares through the phone. "I won't allow you to interfere with my work any longer."

"It's a fucking bomb." Kade drags his brother backwards. "The phone… That's the detonator. We need to get out of here!"

Michael's voice almost sounds sad. "I will finish the work we started alone. Goodbye, Harlow."

"Wait!" I scream.

"Ten, nine, eight…"

"Move!" Enzo roars, almost yanking me off my feet. "Everyone outside!"

My vision flashes in and out, the seconds slowing into an agonising crawl. It feels like God himself has hit slow motion on his remote and sits back, enjoying the show from the comfort of his crumbling throne.

Enzo half-drags me back upstairs, and I have enough sense to grab Hunter's hand to pull him along with us. I will not lose them. Not like this.

We emerge back in the church, all stumbling and racing at full speed to clear the blast zone. Theo and Leighton's voices return, both shouting for an update.

"Bomb!" I yell back.

Several police officers startle and shout as we burst outside, screaming our heads off. None of them move at first, too confused to understand us.

I've barely set foot on the cobblestone path snaking through the graveyard when there's an ungodly rumble behind us. The sound obliterates everything, blotting out the rest of the world.

The gates of hell open underneath us, rumbling and shaking the very earth that supports our feet. Searing heat sets my back alight before the blanket of night is ripped wide open by fire.

"Harlow!" someone screeches.

We're all propelled forward, tumbling through nothingness with the force of the explosion at our backs. Stained glass shatters, voices wail in pain, and God laughs at our stupidity.

Foolish fucking humans, being swiped away with a flick of his thumb. Perhaps Michael was right... His God doesn't care after all.

Colliding with something hard and jagged, my head explodes in a riot of blistering pain. I peer through the layer of hot, gushing blood that soaks into my face.

But I can't see anything apart from smoke and flames. Gloom has ravaged the night and obliterated any specks of light that previously guided our steps. Smoke burns my eyeballs and poisons my throat.

"Goldilocks!"

I'm dreaming.

Someone's speaking.

"Fuck, please talk to me!"

Who is that?

"Please, baby. Answer me. I'm begging you. Please be alive."

It takes a moment for reality to sink in, my mind wading through the waves threatening to drown it. The earpiece is still intact in my ear. Leighton's begging for a response.

Coughing so hard I retch, it takes several panicked seconds of chest clutching and moaning in pain before I manage to draw a breath.

"Harlow! Stay with us."

Clutching my throbbing forehead, my hand comes away slick with blood. I have no idea how I'm still conscious, but the acrid stench of fumes pierces my grogginess.

"I'm bleeding," I wheeze out.

"Harlow!" Leighton shouts in my ear. "Jesus Christ. You're alive! Help is on its way. I need you to hold on."

Hunter. Enzo.

Kade. Hudson.

It's impossible to see even an inch in front of my face. The air is choked with ash and thick black smoke, making breathing almost impossible.

I wipe blood from my eyes again, battling another wave of dizziness. It's taking all of my willpower to remain conscious.

"F-Find … them…"

"No!" Theo shouts frantically. "Don't move."

"Find … H-Hunter and Enzo. F-Find th-them."

Ignoring their disembodied protests in my ear, I grab handfuls of dirt as I try to pull myself upright. The whole world is tilted on its axis, a breath away from falling into an abyss.

With bloodstained hands cupped around my mouth, I scream at the top of my lungs.

"Enzo!"

Nothing.

No answer.

Vision clearing, I can see smoke rising from the smouldering, semi-destroyed ruins of the church on the left of me. Flames climb so high, they seem to lick the black night sky.

"Enzo!"

The muffled groans of someone responding guide my steps. I fall to my knees and have to drag myself back up several times, feeling the hot wash of blood leaking down my neck.

My feet connect with a boulder, spreadeagled on the dirt. Fuck. It's him. Letting my legs collapse, I fall on top of Enzo's body. He's coated in a layer of ash, streaked with blood and dirt.

"Enzo," I whimper, shaking his arm. "Please wake up."

After several desperate shakes, a tiny moan escapes his lips. Pain-filled amber eyes slowly open and land on me through the haze.

"H-H-H…"

"Shh." I check him for injuries, finding blood everywhere. "Don't talk. Help is coming."

"H-Hunter," he gasps.

Holding back a sob, I pull my earpiece out then slot it into his ear, shouting at the others to keep him awake. Enzo's hand is limp as I drop it back at his side.

Sheer desperation drives me forward, tripping over rubble and debris. Destruction surrounds me on all sides. We've been abandoned, left to die out here in fire and brimstone.

Even though he can't hear me, I scream Hunter's name until my dying voice shrivels up. The sound of shouting is intensifying, and the falling ash eases enough to reveal the flash of emergency lights.

Please, I beg the silent observer to our agony. I'll die right here, right now, as long as Hunter and Enzo can walk free. My life is worthless without them.

On the verge of passing out, my foot catches on something. I stumble to the ground, warmth smacking into me as a tangle of broken limbs breaks my fall.

Sobbing frantically, I search for a face with the last wisps of my strength. They're twisted at all the wrong angles, shards of bone slashed through skin and drenched in crimson.

My fingers connect with an arm, searching higher to find the torso. I want to throw up when I realise that it isn't attached to the nearby body, the limb torn clean-off by the explosion.

With the bellows of help growing louder, I drag myself closer to the dead body, a heartbroken plea on my lips. Pieces of bone and disconnected flesh are scattered all around me.

Please, Lord.

Don't punish them for my sins.

Let them live.

But this Lord is not the merciful, benevolent God who graces the pages of Bibles replicated millions of times across the globe.

If people would only dig a little deeper, they'd find God's far darker truth in those pages.

Nobody is spared his wrath. Not even the good ones who don't deserve it.

We're all victims at the whim of an indifferent being. The trick is to realise that no amount of faith can prevent the inevitable punishment.

"Please don't be dead."

But it's too late.

Becket's eyes are empty.

Lifeless. Gone.

CHAPTER 14
ENZO

WHO I AM – PARKER JACK & CHYDE

PROPPED up by Leighton's arm curled around my chest, he guides me over to the nearby sofa with tentative steps. Each movement causes the stitched wound on my side to burn.

"Almost there," he grunts. "Fuck me. You're heavy."

"Didn't ask for your help."

"We almost lost you. Let me do this." Leighton carefully guides me onto the sofa, his usual smirk nowhere in sight. "Do you need anything?"

"My gun," I growl back. "So I can put a fucking bullet in that sick son of a bitch's brain once and for all."

He rolls his eyes humourlessly. "Painkillers and a cup of tea it is."

"I'm not Hunter. Make that a whiskey instead."

Leighton offers me a salute then heads into the kitchen where Theo's on the phone with the superintendent, getting his ear chewed off. His forehead rests on the breakfast bar.

I didn't bother to offer to take the call. I'd tell her to fuck her own ignorant asshole with a goddamn breadknife right about now.

"With all due respect—"

He's interrupted again.

"Yes, ma'am. I understand that."

His ability to remain calm and rational is exactly why Theo is handling the avalanche of shit raining down on us and not me. Though he has kept a keen eye on me since I walked in, as if he thinks I'll vanish at any moment.

We had a close call.

It's shaken us all.

The explosion sent shrapnel tearing through my abdomen, narrowly missing my left kidney. After undergoing minor surgery and being held overnight, I discharged myself from the hospital.

"Harlow!" Hunter calls out.

Limping into the room, she ignores him attempting to tow her back to bed. He escaped the blast relatively unscathed, with only bad bruising and a few deep scratches.

"Enzo," she gasps. "You're home."

Harlow limps over as quickly as her bruised body will allow, throwing her arms around my neck and showering me in tearful, relieved kisses.

"I was so worried about you."

"I'm here," I reassure. "Nothing a few stitches couldn't fix."

"You were in surgery when they discharged me. I've been waiting all night to hear from you."

"I'm sorry, little one. Doctor said I'll have a nice grisly scar, though."

"Sexy," she jokes.

"Now we're even."

"Not quite. I'm still winning in the scar department."

Curling up next to me on the sofa, her legs pull up to her chest for comfort. Lucky immediately appears and jumps up to stretch across our laps. She licks my hand for attention.

I stroke her golden ears. "It's okay, girl. I'm here."

"She's been like this since we got home." Harlow rubs her underbelly. "I think she can sense when someone's hurt. I haven't been able to shake her all day."

"Dogs are intelligent. She's worried about us."

"About *you*," Harlow corrects.

My heart fucking twinges, barely held together by imaginary scraps of bandages and duct tape. While I laid there, choking on ash and blood, all I could think about was Harlow.

Losing her.

Losing our future together.

And what I'll sacrifice to stop that from happening.

"Are you in pain?"

"No," she whispers. "They gave me some painkillers. It looks a lot worse than it is. Mild concussion and seven stitches."

The nasty gash is on her forehead, stapled and bandaged to hide the flash of bone. She'll have a hell of a scar to boast about her survival.

"Did you discharge yourself?" Harlow asks.

"Yeah. Pointless place."

"You had to have surgery." Her eyes narrow on me. "Leaving the hospital against medical advice is stupid."

"They fished the shrapnel out and stitched me back together. I'm fine."

We're lucky that no one else was seriously injured, including Hudson and Kade. But we still sustained one casualty. That's one too many.

"I can't believe he's dead." I cover my face with my hands. "Becket was a good agent. Loyal to the bone."

She takes my hand and squeezes. "I'm so sorry, Enz. Did you train him yourself?"

"I trained the whole Anaconda team." With a sigh, I look into her tearful eyes. "He'd been with us for almost a decade."

"Christ. How's the team?"

"Ethan's broken the news to Tara and Warner. The whole team is fucking devastated. They're going to fly home tonight."

The two brothers reappear with drinks in tow. I'm handed a crystal tumbler of whiskey while Harlow accepts an herbal tea from Leighton.

"Thanks."

"You're due to take some more painkillers."

"I'm good, Leigh."

"Nuh-uh." He waggles a finger in her face. "Enzo's out of action, so I'm on overbearing asshole duty. I'll get your meds."

I flip him the bird, and he blows a mocking kiss at me. Even in the midst of a full-scale crisis, we can still count on Leighton to be a jackass, though I can see the strain behind his smile.

"How's he coping?" I whisper.

Harlow winces as she swallows a mouthful of tea. "As well as we can expect. Both him and Theo were shaken up when we got home."

"What about Hunter?"

"Not a word. He's in shock."

"Shit."

Sitting cross-legged on the floor with his usual steaming cup of tea in hand, Hunter is paying us no attention as he stares at the violent red letters blasting us on the TV's news channel.

Prolific killer strikes again.

Huge blast destroys local village church.

Sabre Security confirms one casualty.

"I've kept an eye on him," Harlow adds. "The doctors ran some tests on him at the hospital before we were declared fit to leave."

"And?" I wince.

"He should count his lucky stars that the blast didn't worsen his condition."

Lucky. That word doesn't really feel applicable at the moment.

"Did you hear from your aunt?" Harlow sighs tiredly.

"She's been calling all day. I can't face her yet."

Hayley's protective as hell, and her fussing isn't needed right now. All I want is to take a machine gun to the streets and kill every last sympathiser that Abaddon has out there.

"Oh my God," Harlow curses.

Following her line of sight, I look up at the TV again. There's a live shot of Sabre HQ in the background, but it's surrounded by swarms of furious people waving placards.

Countless enraged faces scream at the top of their lungs, hurling abuse at our security team, who are attempting to hold them back from crossing the strict perimeter.

"Is that blood?" Leighton reappears with a pill bottle. "Holy shit."

Someone in the mob has thrown a water bottle of gloopy, red liquid through the air. It hits one of our agents, Franklin, square in the face, leaving him covered in what I hope is fake blood.

"Please tell me this isn't live." Harlow covers her mouth. "Is that a photo of me?"

Sure enough, some asshole has pasted a snippet of that godforsaken video on their placard. Harlow's naked, emaciated body strangling Laura to death is being touted for everyone to see.

"Enough. Leigh, turn it off."

Before he can oblige, the video shifts back to the studio where *BREAKING NEWS* is flashing across the screen. I watch Hunter's face darken as Sally Moore takes over the coverage.

"We can confirm that responsibility for the blast has been claimed by none other than serial killer, Michael Abaddon. The following message was anonymously published online minutes ago."

Rather than Michael's familiar, ugly mug swimming into sight, three hooded figures wear masks that cover their faces. Painted in bright-red on the black material of each is a Holy Trinity.

"The blast was just the beginning," an eerie voice warns. "A season of violence has commenced. Now is the time to rise up and join the Lord's holy army."

A person steps into the forefront, their shoulders hunched. "Together, we will cleanse the world of all its sinners."

"The rapture is almost upon us," the other adds. "We have much work left to do. Take to the streets, and reclaim this world in God's name."

A third figure raises their hands in a call to prayer. "We are the Angels of the Abyss. This will be your only warning."

Leighton turns off the TV, his face paler than fresh snow. "Fucking hell."

Stepping into the room with his laptop in hand, Theo rests against the wall. "I've got the intelligence department working on tracing that video. It isn't looking good, though."

"Angels of the Abyss?" I repeat.

"We did some research a couple months ago." Theo checks the case file on his laptop. "Michael's surname is actually interesting. The definition of the word *Abaddon* is a bottomless pit in the depths of hell."

"What does that have to do with these people?"

"In mythology, Abaddon is an Angel of the Abyss and servant to chaos. It seems he's formalising his following into an official cult."

"Even his fucking name is evil?" Leighton scoffs. "What is with this guy?"

"It's what he was born to do," Harlow replies flatly. "The devil marked his soul from the moment he was born. He's pure evil, walking in human skin."

Slumping next to Hunter on the floor, Theo drops his head into his hands. I'm shocked when Hunter slides an arm around Theo's shoulders and tries to offer some comfort.

Huh. That's new.

"What's going on?" Hunter asks.

Theo types an answer on his phone as he speaks. "The blast has been designated an act of terrorism. The superintendent has handed the investigation over to the Counter Terrorism Division."

"What?" I demand. "It was Abaddon and his supporters. That's our case."

"Apparently, the decision has been made."

"Well, tell her to fucking unmake it!"

"You think I didn't try that?" Theo hisses at me. "Go and call her yourself if you think you can do any better."

I back down, gutted by the image of Becket's broken corpse sprawled across the ground. I woke up long enough to see him.

"Clearly, I can't do any better." I ignore their gazes. "Becket was a good man and an even better agent. His death is on me."

"Enz—" Harlow begins.

"No. I was running that operation, and now I have to call his family to tell them he why he isn't home. He had a wife and three kids."

Letting my head fall against the sofa cushions, I stare up at the freshly painted ceiling. We've arranged our fair share of funerals over the years. It doesn't get any easier.

I feel sick to my stomach that I'm still alive to feel relieved and sitting in this room, a little broken but unbeaten. So many lives have been lost on my watch. Yet I still live.

"We can't let him win," Harlow declares. "Terrorising people to get their compliance is what Michael does. If we let this beat us, he'll strike again, and harder."

Draining his tea, Hunter runs a hand over the shaved expanse of his head before interjecting. "We need to send a team to go door-to-door in Tregaron."

"*Why?*" Leighton signs.

"He knew exactly when to strike, and four of those suicide victims were from the same region. His followers are there. They will know where he's going next."

Dread slips into my veins and metastasises until it feels like the blood has frozen inside of me. We were so stupid, too eager to end this case to consider the risk.

The attack was orchestrated, planned to perfection. He baited us with the video, drew us in then went for the jugular. It's sheer chance and a dose of luck that we escaped with our lives.

"We can't send the Cobra team back there." Theo pins me with a glare. "You should have seen Brooklyn at the hospital with them."

"How bad was it?" I sigh.

"She was a nervous wreck."

"That reminds me… I'm tripling the security at the wedding next weekend." I knock back a mouthful of liquor. "That bastard won't get another chance to hurt the people I care about."

"You think she'll go ahead with it, given all the crap going on right now?" Leighton wonders. "Is it too late to cancel?"

"There's no chance I'm letting her cancel." I shift into a comfier position. "That bastard doesn't get to take anything else from us."

Theo's phone chirps again to demand his attention. He answers with a lacklustre grunt that betrays his exhaustion.

"Hey, Rayna. What is it?"

A second later, he sits ramrod straight.

"She's on the line now?"

His eyes have lasered in on Harlow at my side, nursing her herbal tea. She lifts her head, limbs stiffening at his facial expression.

"What is it?" Harlow asks.

He holds a hand over the phone. "Incoming call to the Sabre line from Bronzefield Prison. It's your mother. She's asking for you."

Harlow almost drops the cup of tea until I snatch it from her, narrowly avoiding the slosh of boiling hot liquid.

"Why is she calling me now? After all this time?"

Theo grimaces. "Sounds like she heard about the explosion on the news. She's asking to speak to you."

"Not a chance," I cut in. "You don't owe that evil bitch a second more of your time. Let her sit and fester."

Harlow shakes her head. "Theo, hand me the phone. I'm not afraid of her."

He lifts his hand from the mic. "Rayna, patch us through. Keep the call monitored in case we need it for court evidence."

"Harlow," I mutter under my breath. "You don't need to do this. She's only reaching out to try to stop you from testifying against her."

"I know that," she whispers back. "But I'm not going to live my life in the shadow of her crimes. I've wasted enough time feeling scared."

She takes the phone from Theo, pausing for a deep inhale before hitting speakerphone. We all lean a little closer.

"Harlow?" Giana's voice is a tearful whine. "Are you there?"

"I'm here," she responds coolly.

"Oh, thank God. I saw a news report about the explosion, but they wouldn't let me call until this afternoon."

"Why did you call?"

She sniffles. "I didn't know if you were alive. The news said there was a casualty. I've been sick with worry, thinking it was you."

Elbows braced on her knees, Harlow's eyes screw shut. "I'm fine. Minor injuries. Goodbye, Giana."

"No, wait—"

"We have nothing further to discuss."

"Harlow, please," Giana begs. "I've left you alone since that night, but we need to talk. I've added you to my visitation list."

She scoffs. "I'm not coming to see you."

"There's still so much that you don't know. I've done some terrible things, but I'm trying to put it right. Let me explain."

In the corner, Theo is transcribing all of Giana's words into a text message on Hunter's phone for him to read so he isn't left hanging. We're all silent, allowing Harlow to make the final decision.

"I spent so long wondering what I did to deserve all the pain your brother put me through," Harlow says thickly. "But it wasn't my fault, was it?"

"No, darling," Giana concedes, sounding unlike herself. "It was entirely my fault, and I know that now. Please hear me out."

Hesitating, Harlow looks around the room, meeting each of our eyes. Hunter and Theo both shake their heads, but Leighton nods, encouraging her to do it.

She looks at me last. I have to cage my protective instincts in an unbreakable prison in the furthermost corner of my mind.

Sliding my thumb along her jaw, I gently stroke her cheek. "It's your call. I'll support you, no matter what."

Harlow nods tightly. "Fine."

"You'll come?" Giana gushes.

"If this is an attempt to stop me from testifying at your trial, then don't bother."

"I know," she submits. "It's not about that. I have information about Michael that I think you should know."

This manipulative shit-stain has been dodging the authorities' questions for months. I've kept up with her case over its slow progress.

She's facing serious charges for the false imprisonment and torture of Candace Bernard alone. This trial is for those charges, and Harlow will be called as a witness.

If she decides to proceed with prosecuting her mother for the kidnapping, Giana could be facing another messy legal battle and a life sentence.

"Was there something else?" Harlow sighs.

"Just... please be careful." Giana chokes up again. "You know what he's capable of."

"I'm well-protected."

"Not from him. Nobody is. I know you don't want to hear it, but I love you. I've lost Ulrich, and I can't lose you too."

That's when the tears break free from Harlow's eyes, slipping down her cheeks in a sparkling waterfall that boils my blood.

"That's the thing, Mum. You already lost me."

She hangs up the call, unclenching her white-knuckled fist and handing it back to Theo. Before any of us can say a word, Harlow swoops from the room, and we're left gaping after her.

"Shit," Leighton curses. "Should we have intervened?"

I finish the rest of my whiskey. "She needed to do that herself. We can't fight her battles for her anymore. That time has passed."

"Harlow was already devastated about that damn video leak before the explosion," he highlights. "I'm worried about her."

"She's stronger than you think."

"Speaking of," Theo intervenes. "Harlow asked me to find some publishing houses that would be interested in her memoir. We've got floods of offers coming in already, especially after the video."

"Theo! You know this is a bad idea."

"Do I?" he snaps back. "Abaddon is making a mockery of us with these taunts. This is an opportunity to regain the public's confidence."

"By sacrificing Harlow to their judgement?"

"Yes," Hunter speaks up, his eyes on our mouths. "Until she knows the world forgives her for what she did to Laura, she can't let go of her guilt. This is how she heals."

"We have to support that," Leighton agrees.

"And if they don't forgive her?" I challenge. "You saw those placards. What happens when this backfires? This could destroy the progress she's made."

"Then we're here to catch her," Theo answers. "Fuck everyone else. But she will never get that closure if she doesn't try."

I can't argue when all three of them gang up on me. I want Harlow to heal and move on more than anything, but the thought of her getting hurt because of this stupid book is unbearable.

"Fine." I struggle to my feet, intending to refill my glass. "You better get her a good deal. She deserves to be paid a small fortune for this memoir."

Theo offers me a crooked grin. "Like I'd settle for anything less for our girl."

"Too fucking right," I growl.

Returning to the kitchen to pour another glass of whiskey, I flinch when a pounding fist almost smashes through the glass of the front door. The cavalry has arrived.

"Leigh!" I bark. "Your parents are here."

"Let them in, then."

Grumbling to myself, I disable the brand-new security system then unlock the door, only to be barrelled over by all five feet of a dishevelled Della in designer sweats.

"Enzo Montpellier!" she yells at me. "Your aunt has been trying to get hold of you all day. Answer your bloody phone!"

"Della," I wheeze, concealing the pain her tight hug brings. "I'm not long home from the hospital."

"Then you should have called in the car on the way home," she scolds. "She raised you better than that, young man."

Letting her ball of frantic energy pass me, I accept the firm handshake that Ben, Hunter and Leighton's father, gifts me.

His smile is nonexistent, replaced with a worried frown beneath his ice-cold, brown eyes and quiff of styled silver hair.

"What the hell have you got yourselves into?" he hisses quietly. "I've heard from my contacts in the force that the blast has been labelled a terror attack."

"It was him." I clap his shoulder. "Targeted attack, not terror. It's a ploy to remove our jurisdiction. We've pissed off some powerful people."

"I taught you to know when to cut your losses. This is a zero-sum game. Maybe it's time to relinquish control."

"With all due respect, Ben, you didn't teach either of us to quit in the face of evil. If we don't win this war, no one ever will."

His intelligent eyes soften. "You're living for all the people you've lost, son. Remember that. Don't waste what God's given you."

Letting Ben pass me, I ignore the sound of emotional reunions in the living room and drain my second glass of whiskey. It boils in the pit of my belly.

My entire family may be dead, but that doesn't mean I can't risk my life doing whatever the fuck I love. If I die fighting evil, then I can be proud of the work I've done.

Snaking back into the living room, I watch Della fuss over her oldest son. She's more overbearing than ever, smothering Hunter in kisses and attempting to speak in bungled sign language.

Ben is more reserved. He's a good man, no doubt about that. But the approach he's taken to his son's deafness would infuriate most.

It's prompted him to retreat, and I know Hunter sees that as shame, even if it's just Ben's emotionally-stunted way of dealing with trauma. He hates being powerless to help his son.

"What about Harlow?" Della traps Leighton in a hug. "Was she hurt?"

"Pretty bad head injury, but thankfully, no permanent damage," Theo replies. "We got lucky."

"Becket didn't," I interject.

All eyes in the room turn on me. Recoiling, I start to back away on instinct. I don't need their half-assed platitudes. It was my call to send Becket in on active duty.

Mine.

And mine alone.

Fleeing upstairs, I check each room in turn until I arrive at my own bedroom. A lump beneath the sheets, Harlow has slipped one of my loose, oversized hoodies on.

She lies curled up, her hand working overtime as she writes furiously in her newest journal—I've lost count of which number this is. She burns through so many.

"Little one?"

Her head doesn't lift.

"All he does is kill. Kill, kill and kill some more." Harlow sniffs, her tears flowing. "That's why I have to write this book, Enz."

"I know, baby." I slip into the room then click the door shut. "You aren't him."

"But does everyone else see that? The entire world has probably watched that video. They've all seen me kill Laura."

"Fear brings out the worst in people. You survived when no one else did. That makes you an easy scapegoat."

"I want nothing to do with him." She scrubs the tears on her cheeks. "The moment anyone hears my name, they think of him."

Thumping over to the bed, I move slowly to avoid pulling my wound and climb in next to her. Harlow snuggles into my chest, her tears staining my loose, black t-shirt.

"What if you changed it?" I suggest.

"What do you mean?"

"Your name. It's a simple legal process; our lawyers could take care of it overnight."

"I don't understand."

"You could remove all traces of Leticia Kensington and Harlow Michaels. Become someone entirely new if that's what you want."

Eyebrows screwed together, she looks torn. "But… I am Harlow. She's the person I became to survive, and I'm proud of that."

"Well, what about getting rid of the Michaels part that Abaddon gave you? It isn't really your name. You don't need to keep it."

That makes her pause.

"Whose surname would I take?"

"You've got three available for the taking," I point out with a grin. "Harlow Montpellier has a nice ring to it."

Her breath catches. "Is this… are you proposing to me?"

"No! That's not what this is."

The disappointment that infiltrates her blue eyes makes me feel like the stupidest bastard on the planet. I cup her cheeks.

"I didn't mean it like that. You know how I feel about you. When I do propose, I want it to be special. This is more of a solution."

"It's not exactly romantic," she murmurs.

"Just think about it. If doing this will give you some peace, I know any one of us would happily give you our surname to use instead."

She leans into my touch, wearing a tiny grin. "Thanks, Enz. I'll think it over. You don't need to do this for me, though."

"You think it'll be a hardship? Seeing my name after yours, marking your gorgeous little ass for the whole world to see?"

"Well, maybe."

I drop a kiss on her nose. "Think again. I'd tattoo it on your forehead if I could. Don't tempt me."

"You have some serious control issues."

"Stating the obvious, huh?"

She buries her face in my neck. "Can we just hide here forever? I don't want to face the world anymore. I'm tired of everything."

Clamping my arms around her, I hold her so tight, I can feel the expansion of her lungs with each breath. I came so close to losing her all over again.

Each time we face death, I wonder if this will be the final crushing blow that finishes us off. I'm not a God-fearing man, but part of me wonders how we've survived so much, if not for divine intervention.

"Harlow," I whisper brokenly. "I love you too fucking much to lose you. Promise me that you'll walk away if things go south."

"Walk away? From whom?"

"From us. We have no choice but to fix the mess we've made of this investigation, but I won't put you in danger again."

She looks up, her eyes burning with indignation. "Fuck you. I won't let you fight this war alone."

"Harlow, please."

"No!" She shoves my chest to move away from me. "We're a family. That means we live and die together, no matter what."

"Our family means fuck all if we're dead."

"Then I'll follow your infuriating, over-controlling, possessive fucking backside to the afterlife and haunt you there instead."

"Now you're sounding like one of us." I wrap a strand of hair around my finger then gently tug. "I love you to death, Harlow."

"You once told me that's exactly what it would take to tear us apart." Her smile slices my chest open and takes my heart into her bare hands. "But not even that could keep me from loving you."

Our lips seal the promise—meeting, parting, exchanging a lifelong vow in the whispers of our stolen breaths. From the moment I saw her in that hospital bed, I knew she would be my salvation.

All we have to do is beat the devil.

Then perhaps we'll get our happy ending.

CHAPTER 15
HARLOW

FOXGLOVE – BOSTON MANOR

"ALRIGHT." Brooklyn claps her hands together. "Listen up, dickheads. The wedding is in less than twenty-four hours, and we have a lot to get done."

Spread throughout their kitchen, our entire family is sipping on extra-strong doses of coffee and attempting to keep up with her pacing the length of the room.

"Phoenix! Wake up!"

Startled out of his semi-awake daze on their sofa, Phoenix offers her a contrite smile in apology. Eli's head is pooled on his lap, the pair lazily curled together like sleeping cats.

"Sorry, firecracker."

"Your grandma is arriving in two hours." She glowers at him. "I'm trusting you to keep her the fuck away from Kade's sister and her boyfriend."

"Still can't believe she's coming," Phoenix mutters.

Kade glowers at him. "None of us can."

I lean closer to Jude. "What's the deal?"

"Phoenix's nana used to be … well, I guess you could say she was a gang leader. She retired a few years back, but before then, she supplied half the drug trade in London."

"My sister's been dating Ajax for six years," Kade adds, his still-bruised face drawn into a grimace. "He was the best friend of Pearl's old runner, Zeke. He died of an overdose years ago."

"She killed him?" I gasp.

"Her drugs killed him. Though she tried to murder his fiancée before that. Real pleasant woman."

"You're the one who told me to invite her!" Phoenix objects.

"Yeah, because I didn't think she'd actually come."

"Hey!" Brooklyn snaps at them. "Didn't I say shut up and listen?"

"Yes," Kade submits.

Phoenix hangs his head. "Sorry."

"We have guests to pick up and keep from killing each other. The flower lady has the flu. Teegan's car has broken down, and I'm pregnant, so my dress doesn't fit! I don't need you two fighting as well."

"But your tits look amazing," Hudson hoots.

"You assholes knocked me up three months before my wedding. Be glad we're still getting married at all, bigger boobs or not."

Moving stiffly, Enzo intervenes. "Alright. Sit your pregnant backside down, wildfire. I need to run through security measures."

I pat the empty barstool next to me. "Come finish your coffee, Brooke."

"Is it decaf?" Kade's head lifts. "No caffeine allowed during pregnancy. I bought more of that lactose free milk too."

"Kade motherfucking Knight," Brooklyn seethes. "You won't live to make it down the aisle if you lecture me about my diet one more time. Sit down, and shut up."

He spreads his hands and backs off. Brooklyn cuts him a final stern look before retaking her seat at my side to finish her coffee.

"We're all driving to the venue in convoys of three." Enzo folds his arms and scowls. "No one moves a fucking muscle without an armed escort. Keep your security trackers on you at all times."

"Isn't this overkill?" Phoenix sighs.

Enzo rounds on him. "If you get killed by some cult-worshipping fuckhead, you can dig your own grave and pay for the funeral too."

"That won't be necessary." Eli burrows closer into Phoenix. "He'll be on his best behaviour. Won't you, Nix?"

"Always am," he replies cheekily.

"Was the pair of you fucking in my office with the door open being on your best behaviour?" Jude drawls. "You messed up my filing system."

"Like you haven't done that with Hudson," Phoenix combats. "You shouldn't have left it unlocked if you didn't want us to use it."

"Enough," Enzo bellows. "Jesus H. Christ. Pay attention, or there isn't gonna be a wedding tomorrow."

Brooklyn wasn't kidding when she said they were all antsy and getting rowdier the closer the wedding has gotten.

"There are going to be fifty agents guarding the ceremony and reception," Enzo continues. "Everyone needs to follow protocol and be prepared for anything."

Leaning back, I feel a column of warmth against my spine. Hunter is standing behind me, gazing out of the window at the rain clouds while nursing his cup of tea.

I tap his shoulder.

"Hmm?" he startles.

"Okay?" I mouth.

Hunter nods. "Looks like it's going to rain."

Leaning over me to look at the rain clouds, Brooklyn grumbles under her breath. "It wouldn't dare."

After running through the safety measures—four times, to be precise—Enzo reluctantly dismisses the group with a final barked command to remain armed at all times.

Three cars are heading to the train station to collect guests while Kade is off to pick up his sister and mother from the airport. Both are flying in from the States.

The only ones without family attending are Eli and Jude. Neither has any family left, and even though Hudson is also an orphan, he still has his adoptive family to support him.

"Harlow, are you well enough to pick up our dresses?" Brooklyn shoves her hair up into a ponytail. "I need to sort out this flower disaster."

"Of course." I instinctively touch the dressing smoothed across my forehead. "I'm feeling fine. Leighton and Hunter are coming into the city with me."

Enzo opens his mouth to complain, and I wave him off.

"We will have security with us."

"Take the SUV," he orders. "It's armoured."

Hunter's chin lands on my shoulder. "Is he fretting?"

I lift my fist to mime a knocking motion, spelling out *yes* in sign language.

"I'm more than capable of taking care of them, Enz," Hunter smarts. "I don't need my hearing to kneecap anyone who threatens Harlow's safety."

Enzo backs off, signing a quick apology. After the explosion, he's been hanging over us both like a fucking rash. It's only worsened as the daily protests outside HQ and beyond have continued.

Everyone grabs suitcases and strewn-about luggage, piling out of the house in formation. There are seven cars in total, and we'll all congregate again tonight at the hotel near the venue in outer London.

"Ready?" Leighton kisses my temple.

"Let's go. Can I drive?"

"If you're feeling up to it? Did you take any painkillers today? I don't want you falling asleep at the wheel."

"For the last time, I am fine. My head doesn't even hurt anymore. I've got a job to do, so let's go."

He chucks me the keys. "I'll put the learner plates on. Hyland and Ethan will follow a few cars back."

"The Anaconda team's back at work?"

Theo appears in the doorway from his silent perch at the back of the room. "They insisted. The funeral isn't until next week."

"Which straw did you draw?" I step into his arms.

"I'm giving Brooklyn's maid of honour a ride. You haven't met Teegan yet, have you?"

"Not yet. Is she nice?"

"She's quirky as hell, but you'll like her."

An insecure part of me wants to feel threatened by Brooklyn's best friend coming to town, but I'm happy she's going to have all of her loved ones there. No one deserves this more than her.

The company SUV is parked behind Hudson's Mustang, overflowing with boxes of liquor to be transported. We throw our luggage into the boot.

"You remember that lesson I gave you a couple of weeks ago?" Leighton asks. "This isn't a cheap dirt bike."

"I think so."

"Try not to get us killed on the road." He winks at me. "I've got a hot date tomorrow with a sexy bridesmaid."

"Oh? Who would that be?"

"Not sure yet. I'll have to use my charm and magical pickup abilities to score. Any thoughts on how I should wear my hair?"

"How about stuck down a fucking toilet?" Hudson shouts from the Mustang.

Leighton shoots him the bird. "Shut it, Romeo. You want a black eye at your wedding?"

"I'd like to see you try, Leigh. It's been a while since I broke anyone's legs."

"Guys," I moan. "Literally drowning in testosterone here. Get in the bloody car, and give it a rest before I get a migraine."

After piling into the SUV, Hunter takes the seat directly behind me and drops a kiss on my head. Leighton attaches the learner plates then climbs into the passenger seat.

"Okay then, like we practised. It's an automatic, so just ease down on the accelerator. Don't do what you did last time."

"You didn't warn me it would shoot off the tarmac," I complain.

"I'm supportive of you being a petrol head." Leighton cranks the volume on the radio. "Just pass your driver's test first, alright?"

I start the engine, slot it into gear and gently press down on the pedal to back out of the drive. Enzo watches me reverse before he gives me a thumb's up and disappears.

With the blare of Leighton's music in the background, I pull a stolen pair of Hunter's aviators on and merge into traffic. Ethan follows closely behind in another blacked-out SUV.

Driving an automatic is a hell of a lot easier than navigating a temperamental dirt bike. Learning to drive was on my list of things to do, along with the school classes I'm still taking.

"The dress shop is in Shoreditch." Hunter leans between the seats. "Keep an eye out for idiot drivers. London is full of them."

"Ladies and gentlemen, my brother." Leighton scoffs. "The king of the idiot drivers in his stupid red convertible."

I indicate left and turn. "You love that thing."

"Only because I don't have a car of my own."

"I wondered about that. You never wanted to buy one?"

Leighton's jaw clenches. "When we met, I was fresh out of prison. The past year has been for me to acclimatise to the world again too."

Reaching over the console, I rest a hand on his thigh. "I'm sorry, Leigh. I didn't mean it like that."

"No, it's fine. It's just..." his eyes dart to the mirror to check that Hunter isn't watching. "I've taken handouts from everyone since I was a kid. I want to stand on my own two feet now."

The traffic begins to pick up, so I stick to the left-hand lane, following the navigation deeper into the East End.

"What do you want to do?"

He shrugs. "I'd like to start my own marketing agency. I just don't want to accept family money to do it. If I can find an investor, then great."

"Leigh… I had no idea. Why haven't you talked to us about this? I think you'd be great at that."

"For the same reason I don't want Hunter to know," he answers easily. "I don't want to be helped. I fucked up my life, and I'm going to get it back on track."

My heart swells for him. Leighton is the most underestimated member of our family. But when shit hit the fan, he was the first one to step up and take control of Sabre.

"I know that whatever you decide to do, you'll be amazing at it. I'm so proud of you, Leigh."

He turns his megawatt smile on me. "Thanks, Goldilocks."

"When you figure it all out, let me know. I'll be the first one there to cut the ribbon and pop the champagne."

"You hate champagne."

I stifle a laugh. "Yeah, I do."

The glare of red lights alerts us to halting traffic. I carefully brake and draw us to a stop, craning my neck to figure out what the holdup is. Everyone's jammed into a tight, winding London street.

"What is it now?" Leighton grunts. "Fucking traffic."

"Is it an accident?"

"Let me hop out and look."

Boosting himself up in the open door, he peers over the lines of parked cars. Hunter slides a hand between the seats, and it reappears holding … a bloody gun.

"Hunt!" I wave my hands in his face.

He checks the chamber and shrugs. "You can never be too careful. I don't trust London anymore, and neither should you."

Leighton hops back down and shuts the door. "We need to get out of here. Right now."

"What is it?"

"Some kind of demonstration."

"Protest?" Hunter checks.

Leighton shakes his head.

Before I can fire off another question, the buzz of coalescing voices breaks through the blaring car horns. It's an odd humming sound, raising high then dipping low in a haunting harmony.

"Is that … praying?" I ask in disbelief.

Slamming the car door, Leighton hits the locks. "It's chanting. They're coming. Let's move."

"I can't! We're boxed in."

Cars have gathered behind us, sandwiching us between impatient drivers and the belch of their exhausts. Ethan and Hyland are trapped several cars behind us.

"Thank God for tinted windows," he mutters. "Keep your fucking head down, and stay away from the window."

Heads bob through the crowd of cars, and that's when I begin to panic. Hands are raised high into the sky, palms up to receive the Lord's light with each lament.

The crowd of people are crying out in prayer, filtering between parked cars and causing havoc. Glinting crucifixes circle their throats, blessing them in holiness.

But it's their faces that are truly terrifying. All have mirrored the lunatics that appeared on our TV screen—scrawling Holy Trinities across their cheeks in bright-red ink.

"The team found nothing when they went door-to-door in Tregaron." I watch the flow of people. "Not even the priest knew what was in his crypt. Where did all these people come from?"

"I think it's safe to assume Abaddon has supporters across the country," Leighton says grimly. "They're coming out of the woodwork for his sick cult."

Hidden behind the tinted glass, we sink lower in our seats and watch the parade filter past. My heart is bruising itself against my ribcage with fear that we'll be spotted.

"I think I prefer the protests over this," I whisper from my ducked position. "Why are they doing this in public? Everyone thinks Michael is a terrorist."

"Hasn't stopped his message from spreading like wildfire," Leighton replies. "These nutbags still support him."

"Support what? Butchering people?"

The crack of a window rolling down startles us both. Hunter has inched his open enough for their prayers to float inside the car.

"What are they saying?" he asks.

Lord above, hear our prayers. We cleanse ourselves before you. Grant the Angels of the Abyss your mercy. We are your faithful servants on this earth.

"This is fucking twisted," Leighton hushes.

I fingerspell the word *prayer* to Hunter, and he quickly rolls the window back up. Floods of people are passing us now. There must be dozens of them joining the show.

In front of us, a car door slams, emitting a tall, middle-aged man in a slick business suit. He begins screaming at the people, jabbing his finger towards the blocked road.

"Ah, hell. This is going to get messy."

I glance behind us. "We're still stuck."

"Should we make a run for the dress shop?"

"We can't just leave the car here."

"Screw the fucking car!" Leighton exclaims.

Shouting erupts, then a man from the praying masses steps forward to placate the angry motorist. Their noses almost touching, they scream at each other, a breath apart.

When the first punch flies, the man with the Holy Trinity painted on his face lunges aside to duck the blow. This only infuriates his opponent more, and the pair begin to grapple.

"We need to run." Hunter tucks his gun into the waistband of his fitted black jeans. "This is about to escalate."

Sure enough, the shouting reaches a fever pitch. Prayers turn into furious barbs. More drivers exit their cars and begin screaming, their collective aggression spiralling.

"You crazy psychopaths!" someone screams at the praying herd. "Get out of the road, and go see a doctor!"

"Sinner!" another shouts back. "You will burn in the Lord's almighty fire. Now is the time for repentance."

The glint of a small knife being pulled catches my eye. It slashes through the air, warning the motorist off his furious attack.

When the pair collide, the knife caught between them, they fall backwards and hit my window. The car shudders from the impact, but Enzo's bulletproof glass holds strong.

Michael's indoctrinated drone looks like a demon brought to life, his eyes swirling with divine rage as he lashes out with the knife. It catches his opponent in the arm, and blood sprays across our car.

"That's it!" Hunter yells. "Let's move."

He leaps out, and we follow suit. Hunter rushes to grab me before I get lost in the tangle of people and half-throws me over the bonnet where I land in Leighton's strong arms.

"Gotcha," he huffs.

Fighting echoes all around us. With a glance back, I catch the next strike of the blade. Nursing an arm injury, the poor guy has slumped to his knees, the knife cutting a jagged slash into his face.

"Repent!" the fanatic bellows.

Blood sprays through the air, intensifying the bubble of panic and rage. Hunter takes a running jump and glides across the car's bonnet on his ass, landing on the other side with us.

"There!" He points towards a side street leading away from the road. "Ethan and Hyland will find us on the GPS."

Leighton snags my hand and drags me along. I can't move fast, my head spinning with vertigo from each jolt causing spikes of pain to tear through my healing head injury.

"Leigh," I puff. "Slow … down."

When my legs are swept out from underneath me, I slump against Hunter's chest. He's scooped me up in a fireman's carry after catching up to my stunted running.

I snake my arms around his neck and take the gun from his waistband. Violence is breaking out all around us as tensions boil over. I can't run, but I can shoot anyone who chases us.

We almost run headfirst into a gaggle of Michael's newest fans, standing slightly back and watching the others with stunned faces. None look ready to partake in the fighting.

"Go!" I shout at them. "You don't have to be a part of this."

The blare of approaching police sirens causes them to scramble, bailing before the handcuffs are pulled out. I curl closer to Hunter to conceal the gun from the authorities as we run.

"Here!" Leighton shouts, pointing to get his brother's attention. "Inside."

We're across the street and close to escaping when two bodies step into our path. Their faces are stained with the painted marks, separating them from the melee of drivers swarming in a panic.

Leighton skids to a halt. "Get out of our way."

The taller woman, her silvery-black hair pulled back in a severe bun, sneers at him. She looks like she's just discovered the holy grail.

"You know who she is?"

"More importantly, do you know who we are?" Leighton lashes back. "Move before I make you."

"No can do." Her friend steps forward. "I can't believe my eyes. Harlow Michaels, in the flesh."

"Sweetheart," Hunter whispers, barely audible. "Take the gun back out, and point it at them. We're too exposed here."

I gape at him.

"Do it," he demands. "I don't give a shit what the law says."

Before I can raise the gun, Leighton launches himself at the pair. His fists blur, smashing into their unwitting faces and drawing blood.

I've never seen Leighton move so fast, stepping out of his skin and becoming a person we haven't seen before. A deeper, darker version of himself, left behind bars.

"I warned you." He boots the man in the ribs. "Feel free to pass the message along to your friends. We won't be intimidated."

With a terse nod, he gestures for us to walk past the groaning pair. Neither say a word, too busy moaning in pain.

We run past them and down the street, bursting into a tiny antique bookshop. It's deserted, but I can hear the whimpering of someone hiding behind their counter.

Taking shelter behind a stack of books, Hunter crouches down but still holds me in his lap. His gaze is fixed out of the window at the flash of bright-blue lights arriving.

Leighton struggles to catch his breath. "What kind of prayer circle carries knives? Like, what the hell?"

"This is what Michael wants," I wheeze. "Mass slaughter of those he deems unworthy."

"Those assholes recognised you straight away. I don't like this. It feels like a witch hunt."

"I can see Ethan," Hunter rumbles beneath me. "I think he's bleeding. They're coming this way."

Remaining crouched behind the book stacks, we all flinch when the door to the shop is thrown open. Hyland's shoulders brush against the frame before he ducks inside, followed by Ethan.

"You alright?" Hyland approaches us.

Leighton waves him off. "We're fine."

Seeming slightly unsteady, Ethan slumps against the closed door. Blood is trickling from the corner of his mouth and nostrils. Someone's given him a damn good punching.

"This crazy son of a bitch clocked me when I told him to move," he struggles out. "Some of them were even armed."

"It isn't a demonstration," I supply. "This is an armed mob."

And something tells me this is just the first of many. Fear is a formidable contagion, and there's no quarantining this sickness.

He promised, after all.

Our world will burn.

CHAPTER 16
HARLOW

AURA (REIMAGINED) – THE BRAVE

I'VE NEVER ATTENDED a wedding before. The only marriage I had to observe as a child was the sham perpetuated by Pastor and Mrs Michaels. A partnership forged in darkness.

My parents' marriage was equally flawed and toxic. Part of me is glad that I suppressed those memories and portions of that time are still fragmented, never to be pieced back together.

Sliding into the deep-purple silk slip that we managed to rescue from the dress shop after our ordeal yesterday, I slide the spaghetti straps up my shoulders to hold it in place.

"Okay," I reassure myself. "We're all in."

The silky material is butter-soft and whispers over my scarred skin, covering the worst of the marks while leaving my clavicles and a sensual hint of cleavage on display.

It's a beautiful, gothic shade, reminiscent of amethyst but dipped in a stunning hue of darkness. Brooklyn wanted me to be comfortable and checked that I liked the cut beforehand.

I'm wearing my long hair loose in lightly tousled waves to conceal the bandage still on my forehead. The stitches are due to be removed next week, so coverage was a last resort.

I turned down the offer of professional makeup. The thought of a stranger breathing all over me wasn't appealing. I've kept it simple—thick lashes, glossed lips and light eyeliner.

"Harlow?" Theo knocks on my door.

"Come in."

Stepping into my hotel room, his appearance takes my breath away. Theo cleans up seriously well. His blonde curls are slicked back while his contact lenses are in place, and his blue eyes shine with excitement.

The suit he wears is perfectly fitted and highlights every single lean inch of muscle that builds his frame, topped off with a dark-purple bowtie that matches my dress.

"Holy shit," he curses.

"That bad?"

He takes my hand, spinning me in a circle so he can inspect me. "Of course not. You look phenomenal."

My neck burns with a blush. "Thank you, Theodore. You don't look so bad yourself. Nice bowtie."

"Brooklyn insisted."

"Of that I have no doubt."

Planting a heavy kiss on my lips, he lingers for a moment, his tongue stroking mine in a seductive beat that scatters my thoughts.

Even his kisses taste like home—warm, familiar, comforting. Like stepping into a room with a roaring fire while it's raining outside and curling up with your favourite book.

His hands slip down the curve of my body to cup my ass through the dress's clingy material. I gasp into his lips, rocking against his crotch and the hardening press of steel.

"I have bridesmaid duty to do."

"Screw the wedding," he purrs. "Let's hide up here together instead."

With great self-control, I push him back. "No can do, I'm afraid. You don't want to see what happens when Pregnant Brooke meets Bridezilla Brooke. It's not pretty."

Theo groans. "I really don't want to see that."

Grabbing my clutch bag and phone, I kiss his freshly-shaven cheek then escape before we miss the wedding entirely. We're staying in a nice hotel that's a couple of streets behind the venue.

"I need to go check on Brooklyn." My short high heels sink into the hotel's carpet. "Who's our ride to the venue?"

"Enzo. He refused to let anyone else do it."

"Figures. See you down the aisle?"

Theo's smile lights up his face. "I'll keep an eye out for you, beautiful girl. You're going to smash it."

"I'm going to trip up and embarrass myself."

"But you'll look gorgeous doing it," he jokes. "Go on. I've got to give Kade's sister and boyfriend a ride."

After blowing him a kiss, I slip down the corridor to Brooklyn's room and knock on the door. It opens to reveal a stranger grinning at the sight of me.

"Harlow?" she guesses.

"Um, hi."

I'm bundled into a patchouli-scented hug. The girl's a few inches taller than me, her short, styled, black pixie cut revealing rows of ear piercings that contrast her pale, rice-powdered skin.

She's a quintessential goth, decked out in layers of silver jewellery, dark tattoos and raccoon eyeliner, but her smile is wide and genuine.

"Teegan, I'm guessing?" I laugh.

"Tee!" Brooklyn's voice calls. "Let her breathe."

"Oh God, I'm sorry." She lets me go. "Yep, I'm Teegan. I promise, I'm not a total weirdo. Brooklyn's just told me a lot about you."

"It's nice to finally meet you."

"Likewise."

She's dressed in a matching dress to mine, the purple silk showing off the ink on her arms and chest. I love her already. Warmth exudes from her in a way I wasn't expecting from an old friend of Brooklyn.

Led inside the bedroom, there's another woman inside. She's pushing sixty but wears her age with refined elegance. Her silvery hair is twisted in a classy up-do, contrasting her light blue dress and heels.

"This is Janet," Teegan introduces. "Kade's mum."

I tentatively accept her handshake. "Hello."

She beams, stretching deep smile lines. "Oh, Harlow. I hope my boys have made you feel welcome in London."

"Your Hudson's adoptive mother, right?"

"Yes. My daughter and I have been looking forward to meeting you. Cece is a defence lawyer in New York. She's kept an eye on your case."

"Thanks. That means a lot."

"Harlow! Get your ass over here."

Sitting at the dressing table in the corner of the bridal suite, the sight of Brooklyn causes me to freeze. She's kept her dress choice a closely-guarded secret until this moment.

"Oh, Brooke," I gush.

She looks over her shoulder. "Too much?"

"It's perfect."

Her flawless, ash-blonde curls lay in stark comparison to her stunning midnight black dress. She stands, lifting the full, A-line chiffon skirt to fan out in a cloud of inky blackness.

The fitted bodice is peppered with tiny sapphires, setting sparkles off against her skin. A thin thigh split offers a flash of her long, toned leg.

"Teegan said I look like the Corpse Bride."

"Hey," she protests. "That was a compliment. The guys are going to fucking lap it up."

"You are getting married in an abandoned church," I point out. "It doesn't even have a roof."

"Like I'd ever step foot in a real one. It was this or a graveyard. I had to make an executive decision."

Lifting the split in her dress, she pulls a black lace garter higher up her thigh. Tucked inside, the flash of a small blade catches my eye.

"Is that a penknife?"

Brooklyn strokes a finger over the blade. "It belongs to Eli. Personal joke."

Fussing over her, Janet smooths the back of Brooklyn's dress and straightens the black-diamond crusted piece in her hair. She declares the job done with a nod.

"Darling, before we leave… I have something for you."

Janet opens her purse then slips out a tiny silver coin. Eyes shining with tears, Brooklyn covers her mouth.

"Something old." She winks. "It's good luck to put a sixpence in your shoe. Call me old-fashioned."

"I think I like old-fashioned. Thank you, Janet."

"How many times have I told you? It's Mum."

Even I'm choking up. I accept the arm Teegan wraps around me for moral support. Watching them together is so beautiful.

"Mum," Brooklyn echoes shyly. "Thank you for being here on my wedding day. It… It means a lot that I'm not alone."

Her eyes move over to us. We crowd them both until the four of us are hugging and laughing through our tears.

"You've got all of us," Teegan reassures.

"Forever," I add.

Janet breaks the hug to rest a hand on Brooklyn's still-flat belly. She's smiling like her whole life has culminated in this single moment.

"Let's get you married, then. My sons are waiting with those other three handsome men. You're going to give them all heart attacks."

Brooklyn blows out a breath. "That's the plan."

London is full of quirky surprises. This one may be even better than Theo's abandoned underground carriage, tucked out of sight in a bustling neighbourhood.

On the outskirts of the city, the destroyed ruins of a mid-eighteenth-century church have been left undisturbed. Crumbled limestone slabs and smashed stained glass litter the grounds.

With the sun hanging low in the sky, the state of desolation is lit with tiny glowing lights strung to every piece of rubble and the beams exposed by the collapsed roof. The effect is mesmerising.

It's a carcass, dressed in light.

I've never seen such imperfect beauty.

Enzo pulls up outside the venue then kills the car's engine. He's quiet today, his posture carved with obvious emotion. This is a big day for him too. His little sister is getting married.

"Can you guys give us a sec?" he asks thickly.

"Of course." I step out, holding the door for Janet and Teegan. "We'll be here when you're ready."

Remaining inside the car, I watch Enzo turn to speak to Brooklyn. His words for her are private. She laughs and has to wipe even more tears aside. The pair hug tight before joining us.

"I think I've cried all my makeup off." Brooklyn smooths a hand over her dress. "I'm not sure I can do this."

I tuck a loose curl behind her ear. "We're going to be with you every single step of the way. Your boys are waiting in there for you."

She takes an uneven breath. "I'm about to be a wife … and a mum soon too. I never thought I'd see either of those things happen."

"You deserve this, B," Teegan says. "The girl I met in Blackwood didn't want to mean anything to anyone. But look at this beautiful family you have instead."

"I'm damn lucky, aren't I?"

Enzo joins us on the pavement. "You sure as fuck are."

He looks good enough to eat in black trousers and a matching pressed shirt, gaping open at the neck with no tie in sight. His amber eyes are almost glowing, and his smile is incandescent.

Janet snaps a quick photo on her phone before tucking it away. "I am so proud of you, Brooke. I'll see you inside."

Letting her head inside to join the other guests, Enzo checks in with security, who maintain a water-tight perimeter. After our close call in Shoreditch, he arranged an additional twenty agents for security.

Satisfied that we're secure, he takes his place at Brooklyn's side, though his apprehension is still clear. The police arrested dozens of people last night, but many fled too fast.

"Ready?"

She nods. "I am. Please don't let me fall over."

"I wouldn't dare, wildfire."

The roar of guitars and thumping rock music invites us inside. Teegan stands next to me, linking our arms before handing me a black-rose bouquet to carry.

"Is that *Bring Me The Horizon*?" she laughs.

Brooklyn accepts Enzo's arm to hold. "Like I'd walk down the aisle to anything else. Eli chose the song, though."

"Of course, he did."

Stepping inside the ruins, the flicker of hundreds of red-wicked candles on the stone floor light the early evening shadows. I hold on to Teegan as we walk to the heavy beat of music.

There aren't many guests, only family and friends. I spot the guys first, their heads all straining to catch sight of me. Leighton and Hunter stand shoulder-to-shoulder with Theo behind.

But nothing compares to the five stunned faces at the head of the church, their mouths all hanging open as they spot their bride for the first time.

Brooklyn's men are dressed in matching, all-black suits and dark-red bowties. They've all cleaned up—even Phoenix has styled his currently lime-green hair into a semi-tidy state.

When he thinks no one is looking, Jude brushes a stray tear from his cheek. Kade notices and punches him in the arm as Hudson kisses him, fighting his own smile.

After completing our walk, we hug each of the guys then take our places on the left-hand side.

"Thank you," Jude says to us. "You both look amazing."

"Purple suits you both," Hudson agrees.

Teegan sticks her tongue out at him. "Eyes on the prize, Hud."

He looks back at the incoming spectacle, his mouth slack. Brooklyn and Enzo walk down the aisle with all eyes trained on them. I've never seen Enzo look so bloody proud before.

Brooklyn's fighting another wave of tears as he kisses her cheeks and hugs her so tight, it must creak her bones, before handing her off to Kade. Theo makes room for Enzo next to him.

The guys take turns greeting their bride, exchanging kisses and secret whispers. Watching them together is mesmerising. For all their sharp barbs, their love is incomparable.

Kade turns to face everyone. "Thanks for coming, everyone. This isn't a normal wedding. Nor is it a legal one. We wanted to do this our way with all of our loved ones here to watch."

Standing opposite them, Brooklyn lets Kade take her hands first. He ducks to kiss her knuckles and gives her a boyish smile.

"The day we met, I thought you were the most beautiful thing I'd ever seen. Even when you shut me down. I'm so glad I didn't take no for an answer."

She sniffles. "Me too. You saved my life, Kade."

"I'll spend the rest of our lives keeping the promise I made to you all those years ago." He looks down at her midsection. "I love you and our baby. Thank you for being mine."

Teegan steps forward to hand Brooklyn the white-gold ring, engraved with a secret message inside that none of us have seen. She shakily slides it onto Kade's finger then kisses him.

"I love you."

"Ditto, love."

After another kiss, Kade steps back to let his brother move forward. In typical Hudson style, he sweeps Brooklyn backwards until she's bent over in his arms to accept the smack of his lips.

"Words have never been my strong suit," he says with a short laugh. "I'm not sure I ever deserved your love or forgiveness, but I will never take either for granted. You're my whole fucking world."

Stepping forward, I pull the next ring from my dress's built-in pocket and hand it over. Brooklyn slots it into place on his finger.

"Can't get rid of me now," Hudson smarts.

"Looks like it. We're stuck together for life."

"I've wanted that since we were sixteen years old." He smiles down at the wedding ring. "Always and forever, blackbird."

Sealing the deal with a kiss, he's reluctant to release her so Phoenix and Eli can step forward together. Like they'd ever dare to do anything apart. These two are a package deal.

They take one of Brooklyn's hands each, their bodies so in tune, they move like shadows of each other. Phoenix keeps one arm wrapped around Eli's waist, but he lets him go first.

"Baby girl," Eli rasps just loud enough for us to hear. "I wanted to thank you for giving me a voice again. For making me strong and for showing me what it means to be loved."

Teegan hands Brooklyn the next ring, and she hesitates, lifting her dress to reveal the penknife stuck inside the black lace garter.

"Donec mors nos separaverit," Brooklyn murmurs. "Until death do us part, Elijah. Nothing will ever change that."

With the sweetest smile bringing out the emerald green of his eyes, Eli accepts his ring then captures her in a whirlwind kiss that communicates all they don't want to say aloud.

"I'm still terrified of being a dad, though," Eli admits with a tiny laugh. "Like, petrified."

"If this baby has half of the beautiful soul inside you, we're on to a winner," she says into his lips. "Trust me."

"Always," he echoes.

Phoenix steps into the mix and kisses Eli first, burying a hand in his dark crop of curls. Brooklyn's mouth surrenders to him next, tying the three of them together.

"What he said," Phoenix jokes. "I'm not sure how any of us ever survived without you in our lives. Good thing we'll never have to find out."

"Don't speak too soon." Brooklyn accepts the next ring from me. "I may trade you in for a younger model yet, Nix."

"Good luck getting rid of me. I'm notoriously difficult to remove once I've latched on."

"Don't we know it," Eli comments.

Brooklyn wiggles the ring onto Phoenix's finger, then the three of them crash together, kissing and hugging. I swear, I catch the shimmer of a tear running down Eli's cheek.

His smile is the biggest I've seen so far. He's always carried his sadness around with him, even in his happiest moments. But right now, joy is flowing off him in waves.

When they eventually part, there's just one person remaining. Most of the occupants of the abandoned church are in tears—including Kade's mum and his sister, Cece, in the front row with her boyfriend, Ajax.

None of us knew what to expect for this ceremony beyond the unconventional. There's no scripture or bullshit, semi-sexist vows in sight. Just love, respect and honesty in their purest forms.

Sat a few seats behind them, Leighton has an arm slung around his brother's shoulders. Theo's doing his best to relay their vows in rapid sign language with Hunter's smile showing his appreciation.

"Jude," Brooklyn calls. "Come here."

Lingering at the edge of the group, Jude appears the most nervous of them all, at total odds with his usual veneer of self-assuredness. Flashes of his tortured alter ego still filter through at times.

Teegan hands the last ring over to be slotted into place, and Brooklyn takes his right hand instead. The smooth stump of his missing left hand is tucked into his pocket.

"Saving the best until last?" Jude laughs.

Her lips crinkle in a smile. "I knew you'd be the most nervous. I just wanted to make you wait."

"Sadistic much?"

"Only for you, Sev."

Holding his hand tight, she gently slides the ring into place. "You kept me alive when nothing else in the world could've convinced me to take another breath."

Jude nods, not trusting himself to speak.

"I vow to spend the rest of my life repaying you for holding my hand through the darkest of times."

Stepping back into the mix, Hudson pulls a ring box from the pocket of his suit jacket. He offers it to Jude. Nestled amongst blood-red velvet is the most stunning ring I've ever seen.

The gold band is embedded with tiny, dark green emeralds, perfectly contrasting the black-diamond of Brooklyn's engagement ring. It's totally unique and one of a kind.

"We chose it together," Kade reveals.

Taking the ring from the box, Jude carefully slides it onto her finger. "Will you take us to be your fucked up, over-controlling, somewhat mentally unstable husbands?"

She throws her arms around his neck. "I fucking do."

The ruins of the church erupt in raucous applause. Everyone is on their feet, clapping and shouting in celebration. It's a deafening roar that bounces off the crumbling structure.

Brooklyn kisses each of her men again, then they all turn to face the crowd as a united front, their hands linked together. I can barely see through my streaming tears.

"Let's go party!" Phoenix yells.

The applause intensifies, and they lead the way through the broken church to the courtyard outside that's lit with more clusters of red candles. I hang back.

Theo is the first one to catch up to me. "You did well, beautiful."

I hide my face in his neck, letting people slip past us to enjoy the last glimmers of sunshine. The warmth of bodies presses around me as the others join us for a group hug.

With all of their hands touching my body, hope swells deep inside the coldest pits of my heart. If Brooklyn and her men can make it work against the odds, so can we.

"Drinks?" Leighton suggests hopefully.

I swipe beneath my eyes to clean the trails of mascara. "Make mine a double."

CHAPTER 17
HUNTER

HOMEMADE DYNAMITE – LORDE

SITTING AT OUR CORNER TABLE, the flicker of hundreds of candles lights the night air. Tiny lanterns are strung between willow trees and huge branches, adding to the romantic glow.

I wish I could hear the music everyone sways to on the paved area that's turned into a makeshift dance floor. Instead, all I have is my own silent breathing.

It's enough.

Nothing can ruin this moment for me. Not even the gaping loneliness that's been clawing at my chest for months. We don't get much cause to celebrate in our lives.

But tonight?

We're fucking *alive.*

Knocking back my glass of red wine, I stand to head for the dance floor. My parents are locked in a waltz, having arrived a little late but keen to celebrate the family's day.

Behind them, Brooklyn is caught in a gentle sway between Phoenix and Eli, looking so goddamn content it hurts my soul. Not everyone we rescue makes it, but she has.

We can be proud of that.

Searching through the dancing throng, I spot Harlow's shimmering, purple dress in the back corner. She's drinking wine with Kade and his sister, the three of them laughing about something.

As if she can sense my attention, her eyes search through the crowd then land on me. The smile that tugs at her lips is breathtaking.

I crook a finger, beckoning her over. Making a swift exit, she finishes her drink and ditches it to approach me. I extend a hand, silently inviting her to dance.

I don't need to hear the stupid music. The sheen of happiness glowing in her eyes will be my melody. It speaks loudly enough.

Her lips move on a word. "France?"

I frown at her.

She shakes her head with another laugh. "Dance?"

"Oh." I take her hand and draw her close. "I happen to be an excellent dancer. But only for special occasions."

Harlow's hand moves to cup the back of my neck, then she presses against my chest, flashing delectable cleavage that beckons my eyes down. I think my heart stopped the moment I saw her earlier.

My lips touch her ear. "Have I told you how beautiful you look tonight?"

With a smile, her mouth trails up my throat, planting feverish kisses until her lips meet mine. She replies with touch alone. It speaks far better than words now.

I twirl her around, moving in a slow, languid rhythm to the chasm of utter silence. She steers our turns, guiding me by the sounds I can no longer recognise.

In my head, I can remember all the sound fragments I cherish more than anything. The high, timid tinkle of her voice when we first met. The hammering of her heartbeat. Her contagious laugh.

The sounds are still there.

Locked up safe.

That doesn't stop grief from strangling my throat like spikes of barbed wire, though. I would give anything in the entire fucking world to hear her laugh one more time. Anything. Even my life.

She was the one strobe of light in my dreary, black-and-white world after Alyssa's death. Everything and nothing have changed since then. Harlow is still my compass, guiding me through the night.

With one hand, she points to me and draws an invisible circle in the air to sign her question. It's easier now to piece the words together in sign language.

"*Are you okay?*"

I swallow the burning lump in my throat. "I really wish you'd stop asking me that."

Her gaze doesn't waver, still seeking an answer.

"Fine. I want to experience this like everyone else is."

Sadness invades her blue eyes.

"No," I blurt. "I don't need you to feel sorry for me, sweetheart. I'm having a good time. It's just … not all there."

Gaze hardening with conviction, she takes my hand and steers me past dancing guests. At the front of the courtyard, a DJ is playing songs behind a professional setup of decks.

There's a full-sized speaker blasting music to the wedding party, almost as tall as me. Harlow guides me over to it then stops.

"*Listen,*" she signs.

I stifle a laugh. "I can't fucking hear, remember?"

With an eye roll, she lifts my hand and places it on top of the hole-spotted casing of the speaker. Immediately, all of my other senses are drowned out by the sensation.

Vibrations pulse through my palm, exploding across my skin until I'm tingling all over. Each time the bass in the track plays, it thumps through the speaker and my hand.

I can feel it.

Hear it.

Breathe it.

Ignoring the fact that I must look like a lunatic, I wrap an arm around the speaker and press my ear to it. The effect is so intense, I could cry from the sheer sense of relief.

The vibrations are rattling through my bones. Head to toe. Beat after beat. The hum of the music slips beneath my skin and surges its way up my spinal cord to be composed by my mind.

Harlow's fingers move in a semi-circle. "*Music.*"

I'm glad the only light comes from the lanterns and candles. No one can see the tears I have to blink away. Months of numbness are forgotten in a single moment of bliss.

Grabbing Harlow's waist, I hold her close, and we sway to the music. She's listening with her ears while I listen with my soul. Together, the soundtrack is complete.

The need to show her how much this means to me is so strong, I have to fight the urge to tear the silk from her body and bend her over in front of the entire crowd.

She's like a drug to me—potent and life-destroying in all its addictive power. I'd tear down civilisations and slaughter whole armies to get my next fix.

"Sweetheart," I growl.

Harlow glances up at me. Her features are softened by alcohol, the oceanic depths of her eyes glassy with slight inebriation. I can feel the wine humming in my veins too.

Her lips move on a word I can recognise. "Yes?"

"I'm done dancing."

Clutching the lapels of my shirt, she searches around, her gaze landing on Enzo. He's talking to Phoenix's grandma, Pearl, and avoiding the cigarette smoke she blows in his face.

Harlow jerks her head. "Okay."

Letting her tow me this time, we stop at Enzo's table. He's resolutely refused to drink, preferring to check in with our agents at their posts every half hour instead to ease his paranoia.

I watch Harlow take a seat in his lap and plant a kiss on his stubble-covered cheek. Pearl laughs behind her large serving of whiskey and offers me a nod. She knows I'm far from her biggest fan.

Enzo quickly ditches her then casts one last look around the remaining guests. At his post, Ethan nods to him, confirming he'll keep an eye on things so we can bail.

"*Hotel?*" Enzo signs to me.

I nod, accepting Harlow back into my arms. It's taking all of my self-control not to grab the pert, rounded cheeks of her ass that her silk dress is accentuating in all the right places.

Making a hasty exit, we leave Leighton and Theo to their increasingly messy drinking game with Hudson and Jude. I'm too busy pressing Harlow between us in our haste to escape.

Locating Enzo's SUV, I take the passenger seat, yanking Harlow's arm so she falls onto my lap. Her dress pools at her waist, legs planting on either side of my thighs.

"You look so gorgeous today." I grab a handful of her hair and pull to seize her lips. "My cock has been hard for hours."

Her mouth falls victim to my savagery, teeth and tongue bruising and nipping. The alcohol fuels our collision until she's kissing me back just as hard to stake her own claim on me.

Enzo climbs behind the wheel and floors it, clearly desperate to join our gasping tangle. I slide my hands beneath her dress and groan. She's literally torturing me.

"Where are your bloody panties?"

Harlow shrugs, wearing an innocent smile.

"If I'd known your pussy was bare beneath this dress all day, I would've fucked you in front of the whole church hours ago."

Her mouth returns to mine, fierce and demanding. I sneak a hand between her thighs to find the heat at her core. With a mere few touches, she's wetter than a nun with her damn crucifix.

"Fuck, sweetheart. This pretty little cunt of yours is so wet."

Thumb circling her clit, I have to grab her hip as the car swerves to prevent her from falling off my lap. Enzo's driving at breakneck speed to pass the two streets between the church and our hotel.

Her mouth falls open on a silent moan as I push two fingers into her slit, curling them slightly to hit that inner sweet spot that I know she loves. Harlow lifts from my lap then moves to ride my fingers.

"That's it, baby," I praise. "Enz, hurry up, or I'm going to fuck her in this car for the world to see."

I'm not able to decipher the movement of his lips, but he's probably cussing me out. I won't get her to myself tonight, but that's okay.

The car judders to a halt, and he shoots out, the slam of his door rocking the structure. Harlow's still grinding on my lap, greedily taking the slow thrust of my fingers into her cunt.

When the door is ripped open to reveal Enzo, wild-eyed and baring his teeth, I realise we're in for a rough night. I pull my hand from between her legs and let him take her.

The security guard on the reception desk gives us a very strange look as we race past—Harlow tossed over Enzo's shoulder with her silk-covered rear being spanked by him.

When the elevator seals us in privacy, the hunt is back on. Enzo lowers

Harlow from his shoulder then slams her spine into my chest. By some miracle, I'm able to string together the words his lips spell out.

"*Fuck you … raw … tonight.*"

Grabbing Harlow's wrists, I pin them to her sides so Enzo can do what he pleases to her. She's imprisoned at my mercy, a tiny slip in comparison to his intimidating height above her.

Harlow's head tips back to release a moan as he skates his teeth down her neck, one hand cupping the generous mound threatening to spill from her neckline. I can see her hard nipples from here.

He releases her when the doors open, and Harlow lets me escort her to our bedroom, my steely grip on her wrists not easing. Once Enzo's unlocked the door, all bets are off.

He lifts her body and holds her against his waist to walk over to one of the two double beds. I follow, stripping off my suit one layer at a time, fumbling over the buttons in my haste.

Harlow is tossed on the bed in a flustered heap. Ripping the shirt over his head, Enzo quickly steps out of his suit trousers. His boxers go flying next. He's wasting no time.

Plunging my hand into my tight boxer shorts, I push them down then fist my shaft. Enzo lazily prowls towards Harlow's splayed-out body. He grabs her dress, pulling it off to reveal her scarred frame.

With the scrap of silk discarded on the floor, Enzo kisses his way up her legs to reach between her thighs. She's fisting the bedsheets already. Our angel is so sensitive to touch. It's hot as hell.

Moving closer, I pump my cock, standing off to the side so I have a perfect view of Enzo lifting Harlow's legs and pushing them open to dive into her sweet cunt.

Ducking down, I seize Harlow's lips and swallow her moans. She's writhing on the bed, her thighs clamped around Enzo's head as he eats her out with the enthusiasm of a fucking food critic.

"I'm going to fuck that pretty mouth of yours while Enzo eats your cunt." I spread her lips with my thumb. "Open wide, sweetheart."

Kneeling on the bed next to her, I turn Harlow's head then feed the length of my dick into her mouth. The minute her pink lips wrap around the head, I'm done for.

"Christ, Harlow."

She greedily takes my length deep into the prison of her throat, lips cinching around the shaft to create the most delicious sense of pressure. I pump my hips and roughly fuck her mouth.

I know the minute Enzo pushes his thick fingers inside of her. Harlow's mouth tightens even more and almost finishes me off. I'm cutting her moans off with my cock.

Stopping for a breath, Enzo drops a mouthful of spit directly on the quivering lips of her cunt. I watch with interest as he slathers it across her clit and entrance before lining himself up.

His lips carve out a readable sentence. "Going to … split … gorgeous pussy … in half."

Harlow's teeth graze against my length when he surges inside in one smooth, brutal pump. It takes all of my self-control not to shoot my load down her throat.

Every time he thrusts inside of her, she milks my cock even harder, fighting to remain attached. Enzo's fucking her as roughly as promised, and it's one hell of an amazing view.

On the verge of losing it, I grab her chin and pull myself out. Trails of saliva and pre-come are leaking from her lips, and I can't stop myself from dragging my tongue over the seam of her mouth to clean it up.

"My turn," I purr. "Enzo needs to learn how to share. Let's teach him a lesson."

Holding up a hand to halt his thrusts, I crawl behind Harlow on the bed and pull her upright. Following my pointed finger, Enzo takes her place, lying down opposite us on the mattress.

She kneels on her hands and knees, curving her spine at the perfect angle as I move her into a doggy position. Harlow takes a handful of Enzo's cock then accepts it into her mouth instead.

Settling behind her, I have a perfect, undisturbed view of her dripping folds and tight asshole. Harlow holds Enzo by the hips and lets him abuse her mouth as brutally as he pleases.

But I still have control.

They're both my victims tonight.

Dragging two fingers through the slick juices of her cunt, I spread the moisture upwards to cover her back entrance. Harlow's entire frame shudders. This hole is still unexplored.

"You have such a tight little asshole." I run my thumb over the ring of muscle. "It's just begging for my cock to fill it up."

God, I'd love to hear her whines right now. Her attention is still fixed on the grunting lump beneath her as she sucks his dick.

Finger drenched in her come, I gently push against her hole, easing it inside the vice-like warmth.

"We need to start getting this hole ready to be fucked. I want to watch you fall apart with both of us buried inside of you."

The tiny earthquakes wracking her body betray how much she's enjoying being caged between us. I can see how wet her pussy is from the glistening moisture covering it.

With Enzo fucking her throat and my finger pushing in and out of her ass, her senses must be on overdrive. Spreading moisture over another finger, I push her further and slide it into her cunt.

With a digit in each hole, I begin to thoroughly fuck my girl in time with the upwards thrust of Enzo's hips. We're filling every available inch of her right now.

When Harlow's walls tighten around my finger, I know an orgasm is sweeping over her. Enzo takes advantage and increases his strokes until the widened 'O' of his lips communicates his own climax.

Harlow swallows every last drop, even as her release holds her captive. Head hitting the mattress, Enzo pants for air, allowing her to look up and lick the drops of escaping come from her lips.

I don't give her even a second to recover. I've waited long enough. Holding her hips, I position myself against the curve of her ass then spear her cunt in one fell swoop.

God-fucking-dammit.

Without my hearing, every other sense is dialled to ten. I can feel every single curvature of her sweet pussy, clenching tight around my cock and daring me to fill it up.

I move hard and fast, making eye contact with Enzo as he catches his breath beneath Harlow. He can deny it all he likes—voyeurism is as much his kink as it is mine.

When I push a finger into her backside, Harlow's head throws back. I can imagine her overwhelmed howling. That sweet, innocent-as-fuck voice contorted with agonising pleasure.

All those painful months we wasted will always prey on my mind. Our lives aren't guaranteed. I've learned that we can lose everything we ever held dear in a single fucking heartbeat.

There's no time to live safely. We have to walk on our tiptoes along the edge of a cliff and pray the wind doesn't knock us off our feet into the clutches of an early death.

That's the exhilaration. Living every single moment like it could be our last and not taking a single breath for granted. Harlow is my reason for living now. She's my redemption.

Cracking a hand against her ass, I savour the pink print that tarnishes her skin. I'm close to exploding. She's hugging my cock in all the right places.

With a final pump, I bellow and spill my seed deep into her. I can feel her orgasming again. Her pussy is clenched tight around me, and every limb trembles with the aftershocks.

Enzo grabs a handful of Harlow's hair and kisses her to silence the screams I cannot hear. Slumping behind her, my lungs are on fire. The haze of alcohol has dissipated after our frenzied fucking.

She doesn't protest as I find the willpower to scoop her up, loving the shine of my come streaming down her thighs. Where it fucking should be.

"Let's get you cleaned up."

In the attached en suite to the hotel room, I turn on the walk-in shower then set her down beneath the hot spray. Harlow moves to make space for me to join her.

It takes a couple of minutes for Enzo to catch up. The shower is big enough to fit all three of us with multiple shower heads exuding steam-laced heat. We all huddle together.

Lathering her hands in hotel shower gel, Harlow begins to massage it into my chest, taking the care to clean each ridge. I tip her head up so our eyes meet.

"Thank you."

Her eyebrows crease.

"For never giving up on me."

"Never," she mouths. "Love… you."

"Even when I drive you crazy?"

Harlow laughs and nods back.

"Well, same. Even when you drive me crazy too."

I thought I had unconditional love before. I'm not so sure now. I loved Alyssa… but the way I feel about Harlow defies such easy categorisation. She's everything.

The air in my lungs.

The pump of my heart.

My world begins and ends with her.

I stroke my thumb over her cheekbone. "One day… that's going to be us up there."

Her head tilts in a question.

"Branding our names on your fucking soul for the rest of eternity." I look up at Enzo's grin to include him in the sentiment. "I want forever with you."

Enzo leans close to kiss her wet shoulder, the curve of his lips reiterating my vow. We've talked about our intentions. I know he feels the same way.

I'd marry her tomorrow if I didn't think the idea would scare her. But one day… that dream will be a reality. I won't let life tear the chance of happiness away from my family again.

I'll keep fighting for that.

For her.

For the rest of our lives.

CHAPTER 18
HARLOW

MISERY BUSINESS – PARAMORE

ADJUSTING my ponytail for the millionth time, I stare into the window in the corner of my laptop at the shiny pink scar on my forehead. It's relatively neat now that the switches have been removed.

Who thought it was a good idea to add that distraction to online video calls? I'm freaking out with every second I have to stare at my own reflection while waiting.

This meeting has been scheduled for the last couple of weeks, and I've grown even more apprehensive as it has drawn closer. I wouldn't even be here if Theo didn't sort everything for me.

With Brooklyn on the third week of her six-week honeymoon and Sabre fighting fires on all sides, I've kept busy with preparing for exams this week, marking the end of my online classes.

"Just breathe," Theo advises.

"Easy for you to say."

"Everything's going to be okay. I'm here with you."

We're hidden in the quiet sanctuary of his office in HQ. I opted to tag along with the others into London, needing moral support for this call.

"What if they don't want to publish my book?" I bite my lip. "I know nothing about writing. It's just a bunch of messy journals."

Theo reaches across the desk to take my hand. "It's far more than that, and you know it. Just hear what they have to offer."

"What did their email say?"

"Not much," he reveals. "We got a lot of interest in the proposal I put together for you. This publishing house was the most reputable."

"What if they laugh at me? This could be some sick prank. The entire world hates my guts for what I did in that video."

Theo squeezes my fingers. "Have a little faith, beautiful. There are people out there who still want the truth. They're just being drowned out by fear and suspicion."

Taking another measured breath, I smooth my plain white blouse and watch the clock tick down to the hour. Faith is in short supply around here, especially with the mob still protesting outside.

There's a beep before the meeting starts, and Theo sits up a little straighter next to me. I refused to do this meeting without him.

"Hello, Harlow."

On the screen, a brown-haired woman with friendly almond eyes and an easy smile appears in her smart business wear. I give her a little wave.

"Hi. Thank you for meeting with me."

"Good morning," Theo chimes in.

"My name is Abigail. I'm the executive editor here at Hawkstone Publishing. One of my agents passed your information along to me."

"We were expecting to meet with William." Theo stacks the sheaths of paperwork in his hands. "I've been communicating with him regarding Harlow's submission to your press."

"Of course," Abigail begins. "But given the pseudo-celebrity status of Harlow and Sabre Security, I thought it best to handle this myself."

Anxiety floods my system. This woman is the top dog. This could go one of two ways, and I'm terrified of the potential rejection.

"There is a lot of interest in your story, Harlow." She smiles kindly. "I'm sure you are apprehensive about publishing your story."

"It's a little nerve-racking," I admit. "But I think I could do a lot of good with this memoir. I want to help other people like me."

Abigail spins her fountain pen in hand. "And that is exactly what I wanted to hear. Tell me more about your motives."

"I'm not sure she—"

I rest a hand on Theo's leg beneath the desk. "No, it's fine. I know many people think I'm doing this for fortune or fame. My intentions relate to neither of those things."

She nods enthusiastically. "So what do you want?"

"To show the world that it's possible to survive and rebuild your life. I lived without hope for so long. I want to give the world what I needed as a scared child who thought she'd never escape."

Scribbling notes, Abigail's eyes are lit with a gleam of excitement that punches through my overwhelming fear.

"This is a very competitive market that you're breaking into," she advises. "But something tells me your book will be in very high demand. I'd be honoured to publish it."

"You … would?"

Abigail's smile softens. "I think it's time the world heard from the girl who lived, rather than the monster who silenced her. I want to give you that voice, Harlow."

A confusing concoction of relief and appreciation causes my eyes to sear with tears. That was the one thing I lived without for thirteen years of my life: a voice.

That's what this whole journey has been about. Rediscovering my own strength and using it to build a life beyond my trauma. This feels like the end of a very long and tumultuous road.

"I'm sure you're fighting off our rivals' attention, so I'd like to make you an offer. We're anticipating a great deal of demand for this memoir, and I hope you'll find the terms favourable."

Theo's phone pings with an incoming email. He quickly opens it and scans over the lines of text in the attached documents. I watch his mouth fall open on a silent curse.

"That's … reasonable," he rasps.

"I'm glad you think so," Abigail chuckles. "I wouldn't want to lose this opportunity to our competition. Feel free to consult your legal counsel, and let me know as soon as possible."

I can't fully read the blur of numbers over his shoulder, but the rows of zeros scrawl across his phone screen.

"Harlow?"

My eyes snap back to the laptop. "Yes?"

"I wanted to say that I think what you're doing is incredibly brave," Abigail offers. "Not many people would have the conviction to share their demons with the world."

I gulp down the lump in my throat. "Thank you."

"We want to honour you and your story in the most authentic way possible. I hope that you'll think about my offer."

"I will."

"Good. Well, then. I'll await your call." She flashes teeth in a bright smile. "Thanks for your time."

Theo signs off the call for me then shuts the laptop. "That was interesting."

"What the hell just happened?"

"You got yourself a publishing deal." He kisses my cheek. "And half a million pounds in advance."

My heart stops. "Half... What?"

"You fucking did it!"

Theo crushes me to his chest so tight, I struggle to breathe. My head is spinning from the last ten minutes. None of this feels real.

When he releases me, Theo's grinning from ear to ear. I cup his jaw and drag him into a heart-pounding kiss that brings me back to reality.

"None of this would've happened without you," I murmur into his lips. "I didn't do this. You did."

"Not a chance. Don't do yourself a disservice. They want to publish your book because of *you*, angel. No one else."

A tentative knock on his office door forces us apart. Theo calls for them to come in, then my father appears in the doorway, his dirty blonde hair matted with sweat from another training session.

"And?" he asks excitedly.

"I … got offered a deal."

"Oh my God! That's amazing!"

He rushes into the room and nearly yanks me off my feet with the strength of his bear hug. With my dad's arms around me, the tears finally break free.

"I'm so proud of you," he whispers into my hair. "I know this can't be easy, but you're doing something incredible."

"Thanks, Dad."

"He isn't going to win, love. This is your fight, and we're all here to support you every step of the way."

My heart explodes with love as he kisses my temple. I had no idea what having my father around would be like, but I want him in my life. Regardless of the past.

"I need to get washed up." Dad releases me. "Shall we celebrate tonight?"

"I'd like that. Want to come over to ours?"

"Sure. I'll bring the food."

"Leighton eats for three," Theo chips in. "He suffers from hollow bone syndrome, apparently. That was his latest excuse."

Dad snorts. "Got it. Lots of food, then."

He disappears, leaving us to pour over the complicated contracts and legal jargon attached to the publisher's email. Theo forwards it to Sabre's legal team, seeming satisfied with the content.

"What happens now?"

"Once we get the all-clear from legal, we'll contact Abigail and take it from there. They will handle everything."

"This is really happening, isn't it?"

Theo runs a hand down my arm. "It sure is. Your dad's right. This is an amazing achievement. You should be proud of yourself."

Before I can respond, his ringing phone cuts me off. Theo quickly answers then listens to the roar of Enzo's voice down the line.

"Woah. Slow down, Enz."

As he listens, his eyes widen in a look I've become sickeningly acquainted with. Horror. It's never far from our lives of late.

"We're coming up."

Ending the call, Theo glances up at me with pupils split wide open. Darkness and death stare back at me in familiar shades.

"Reports of bodies are coming in from local police. The team's waiting upstairs for us to do an emergency debrief."

"Bodies?" I repeat. "Plural?"

All he can offer is a terse nod.

Leaning heavily on him for support, we race upstairs to Hunter's office. Theo fumbles the code several times in his nervousness. The door wrenches open before we can unlock it.

Leighton's face is pale as he spots us. "Quick. Come in."

Entering the evidence-lined walls of Hunter's office, the remaining members of the Anaconda team sit at the long conference table opposite Enzo and Hunter.

All eyes are focused on the TV screen relaying a live feed from a body cam. No one dares to speak a word. Not even a greeting as we hastily take our seats.

"What's happening?" Theo asks.

Ethan spares us a glance. "Reports started coming in half an hour ago. One location at first. Then two others were confirmed in different cities by local departments."

"Is it him?"

"The markings are all there."

I reach for Leighton and curl my arm around his, needing a tether. Since the violence that broke out before the wedding, tensions have been escalating daily, but Michael has remained silent.

It's almost like he doesn't need to speak anymore. This country is a tinderbox sitting next to a raging inferno. The spark he lit was enough to achieve his aim. Widespread terror.

"Three l-locations?" I stammer.

"That's three separate murders at the same time in totally different corners of the country," Enzo confirms grimly. "Copycat kills."

"So it wasn't Michael?"

"He could have coordinated the attacks with help." Leighton blows out a breath. "Unless this is some asshole looking for a cheap thrill."

"Local police just sent us this footage," Enzo adds.

On the screen, we're guided into the depths of a sunlit forest. The trees are all burnished in autumnal colours as October arrives. Each crunch of the police officer's footsteps strikes me in the chest.

But the awaiting sight defies expectations. I know the depths of my uncle's depravity. This senseless violence is branded with his trademark.

Swinging in the trees, three bodies drip with congealed trails of blood. Their flayed skin is on display, bare without clothing. It exposes the vicious slashes of the Holy Trinity disfiguring their chests.

Roughly tied nooses hold the victims by their necks, faces blue and skin waxy as they gently sway. Slashed and displayed like hung meat.

"Fuck me," Hunter mutters.

The remaining members of the Anaconda team—Tara, Warner and Ethan—sit together in horrified silence.

"Three deceased," the officer reports. "All marked and hung from nooses. No signs of life. They've been here for a few hours, at least."

"I need you on the ground immediately." Enzo points at Ethan and Tara. "I don't want this leaking to the press until we have the scene secured."

He nods solemnly. "We'll take the helicopter to Grantham."

"There are reports of another crime scene fifty miles east in Wisbech." He turns to Warner. "Establish a perimeter and report back. Take Hyland with you."

Following a round of agreement, all three of them disappear. Enzo slumps and bangs his head on the table as soon as they've gone.

"Fucking copycats. This can't be real."

"It was inevitable," Theo consoles. "I'm surprised this didn't happen sooner. Abaddon may not even be involved."

"It's worse if he isn't. We don't need more psychotic killers terrorising the country when we can't even catch the first one."

Still silent, Hunter is watching the recorded police feed, his lips pressed into a tight line. Officers are roping the scene off with blue tape and going about their formalities.

I wish I didn't recognise the look on his face. Hell, I wish I wasn't feeling the exact same thing. Defeat. We've barely come up for air, and another wave is crashing down on us.

"Michael has formed a whole underground network," I croak. "This has gone beyond a few crazed supporters."

"He's escalating," Enzo agrees. "Abaddon organised those suicides. Hid undetected in Tregaron. Blew up the church. Now this."

Theo nods thoughtfully. "No one causes all this chaos alone. We aren't fighting him anymore. We're fighting a whole fucking army."

"So how do we beat them?"

No one jumps to answer my question. With hysteria crawling up my throat, the brief sense of empowerment I felt coming out of that meeting is blown to pieces. I can never win.

Not while he's still out there.

Hunting and killing.

"Giana," I blurt. "She claimed to have new information about Michael. I've delayed visiting her for weeks now."

"No," Leighton says flatly. "She's bluffing."

"Probably."

"Then don't waste another moment of your time on that woman. We all know she doesn't have shit on Abaddon. She's just desperate."

I don't need to say aloud what we're all thinking—*so are we*. Michael has driven us to the point of desperation and beyond.

"What other leads do we have?" I point out. "The suicide victims have turned up nothing but a flimsy connection. Tregaron was a dead end. Any evidence in that crypt died with Becket."

"We're about to have a morgue full of bodies," Theo supplies. "If Abaddon's training copycats, they'll be sloppy. We may have a lead."

"Can we wait that long? What if he goes out tomorrow and orders the deaths of a dozen more people? What then?"

Enzo slams a hand down on the table. "It won't get that far. Go and see Giana. Get any information you can."

I nod, deflating.

He looks to Theo. "Call the superintendent, and set a meeting. I want every fucking police officer in the country on the streets going door-to-door. It's time to kick things up a notch."

Relaying his words to Hunter in sign language, Theo looks solemn. Even among the clouds at the top of Sabre's skyscraper, the screaming and shouting on the street below us filters through.

Violence has become widespread, with more and more public demonstrations breaking out into scuffles between those driven hysterical by Michaels's warning and everyone remaining sane.

"We need to request some kind of nationwide curfew. The entire country is on fire. Abaddon is using that chaos to his advantage."

"Once you make that call, we can't take it back," Theo argues. "We'll be playing into public fear by locking people down."

"I don't give a flying fuck," Enzo spits back. "We're going to flush this bastard out by force. Someone knows where his base is."

With the decision made, Theo drops a kiss on the top of my head then disappears to make the call. If anyone can convince the superintendent to launch such a huge operation, it's him.

Standing up to follow in his wake, I fish my phone out of the pocket of my parka.

"I'll request visitation with Giana in Bronzefield. She's already added me to her list. I can go after my exam finishes tomorrow."

"I'll take you there." Leighton sighs. "You're going to need backup. It'll be like a trip down memory lane."

"You were in Bronzefield?"

"The one and only."

Hunter pauses the video and opens another email, a new file attached. "I need to review these before we make any official statements."

"*Lucas*?" Enzo fingerspells to him.

"Make the call. It won't be long before the vampires are hammering on our front door. He needs to handle the fallout."

Hesitating on his way out of the room, Enzo turns to face me. "Fuck, Harlow. I forgot about your meeting."

"Oh. It doesn't matter now."

His brows pinch together. "Like hell it doesn't. What happened?"

All three of them are waiting for my answer. Flushing under the spotlight, I wrestle with my guilt for still feeling excited, despite the fresh wave of violence.

"I've been offered a contract and … *ahem*, half a million pounds in advance. They're going to publish my book."

Shooting out of his seat, Leighton rugby-tackles me in a hug that almost knocks me off my feet.

"Jesus fucking Christ, princess!"

Spun in a circle, he sets me down on my feet again, only for Enzo to swoop in next. He flattens me against his chest, and his lips bruise mine in a celebratory kiss.

"I am so proud of you."

"I haven't done anything," I laugh into his mouth.

"This is all you. Own it, angel."

When he kisses me again, all of the anguish dissipates. The blood. The bodies. The threats and violence. In Enzo's arms, he is my single point of existence.

I never would've survived the past year if I didn't have them by my side, but Enzo was the one who tossed all reservations aside, putting his love and devotion into a total stranger.

He gave me a life.

A future.

A brand-new family.

This moment isn't mine. I don't own even a fraction of it. All that I am is a result of their faith in the broken, damaged girl they rescued from that hospital.

When Enzo finally sets me back down, there's one more set of eyes burning a path across my skin. Hunter has abandoned his urgent emails in favour of joining us.

"You got it?" he asks.

I nod back.

"I knew you had it in you." He shakes his head in mirth. "Come here, sweetheart."

Stepping into his arms is easier than drawing in one breath after another. My body recognises his on an instinctual level, our souls imprinted with the same lifelong brand.

"When we first met, I knew that you were something special," he whispers into my hair. "It has been an absolute fucking honour watching you blossom into the person I always knew you were."

My tears soak into the pressed fabric of his dress shirt, revealing the dark swirls of ink underneath. That is Hunter's power—the ability to make me feel like I'm the only person in his entire world.

Fuck the investigation. Fuck Michael Abaddon. Fuck everything and everyone but us. Our family. None of this means anything if I don't have them … forever.

Even if our love is relegated to the afterlife. For the first time, I can see the end in sight. It's coming up on the horizon. But we won't reach it without a final sacrifice.

They've done enough.

I won't let the devil take them too.

CHAPTER 19
HARLOW

LOST IN THE MOMENT – NF & ANDREAS MOSS

BOUNCING on the balls of his feet beside me, Leighton is palpably nervous. Enough that he didn't crack a single joke during the two-hour car ride it took to reach the prison.

We both stare up at the imposing, barbed wire topped gates of Bronzefield Prison. It's a dreary, grey-scale structure, uniform and utterly devoid of any personality.

Pain and sadness seem to ooze from the cinder blocks, baked in between layers of cement and security alarms. This place is high security and notorious for its violent offenders.

"Never thought I'd be back here."

I glance up at Leighton's grimace. "Only this time, you're not entering as the same person you were all those years ago. Don't forget that, Leigh."

"You have too much faith in me," he mutters.

"Someone has to."

"And I love you for it, Goldilocks. Let's get this over and done with. We're needed back at HQ for a debrief in three hours, and we still need to celebrate you passing those exams."

"I'm really not in the mood to celebrate."

He locks Hunter's red convertible. "I'm not having any of that. You've been working towards this for months. We're celebrating."

"We'll see."

Taking his hand, Leighton leads me up the long, paved walkway towards the prison. Each step causes my anxiety to spiral.

There are tall guard towers on both sides, boasting the beady eyes of surveillance cameras and posted prison guards. No one gets in or out of this place without it being monitored.

The closer we get to the unscalable, high walls of this utilitarian nightmare, the tighter Leighton's white-knuckled grip on my hand becomes. I'm almost holding him upright.

We're stopped in the entrance and accosted by a circle of security officers, preventing us from travelling any farther. After checking their paperwork, I'm led to the side and have to surrender my handbag to be searched.

"Christ alive," an officer exclaims. "Rodriguez."

Leighton removes his belt and drops it in a tray to be scanned. "Dean. Bet you didn't expect to see my face here again, did you?"

Dressed in a neat uniform, Dean chuckles. "To be honest, we placed bets on how long you'd survive the outside world. I lost a hundred quid because of you."

"You bet against me? Seriously?"

"Sorry, kid. Thought it was a safe bet."

With another grumble, Leighton lifts his arms to be scanned over with a wand, searching for any contraband. We're both declared clear and given back our valuables.

"Who are you here for?" a female officer drones behind Perspex glass.

"Giana Kensington. She's expecting us."

Peering at her computer screen, she pops a dramatic bubble of gum. "She's been on suicide watch for the past month. No visitors allowed."

"Wait, what? Suicide watch?" I exclaim.

"We booked an appointment with the warden." Leighton pulls his wallet out then slides a professional-looking ID badge across. "Sabre Security."

Dean whistles under his breath. "Fuck me sideways. You're working for big bro now?"

Leighton resolutely ignores him and waits for his ID to be slid back. Our female officer disappears to make a quick call, clearly annoyed that we've forced her to get off her ass.

When she returns, a pot-bellied man in a blue suit follows her. His eyes are sharp and unimpressed, landing on us both with a look of disgruntlement.

"You're here for Giana Kensington?"

I straighten my spine. "We are."

"We don't normally allow visitation for high-risk inmates, but I've been instructed to make an allowance." His voice is dripping with displeasure. "I don't take kindly to being told what to do with my damn inmates."

"Look," Leighton cuts in. "We're here on official business with clearance from well above your pay grade. Giana is being questioned as part of an official investigation."

"I'm quite aware of her charges. We don't usually take inmates pre-trial. She's an exception to that rule."

"Then this isn't a normal visitation request, is it?"

The warden's shoulders slump. "I suppose not."

"So take us to the inmate, and stay out of our way, or I'll happily make a call to your superior and inform them of this delay to our investigation."

Knowing he's beaten, the warden waves for us to follow him into the depths of the prison. We're sandwiched between Dean and another security officer, giving me a second to grab Leighton's arm.

"Where did you get that ID badge from?" I whisper.

"Like it?" He smirks at me. "Perks of taking over while Hunter was laid up. Pretty sure I'm the first recruit Enzo hasn't had the pleasure of torturing for weeks on end."

We fall silent as the layers of air-locked security doors and barred grates are unlocked in turn, each with a loud screech. My head is thumping with a headache already.

Our escorts guide us past ajar office doors and the odd inmate being supervised while carrying out chores. The signs take us down three flights of stairs, into the lower levels of the prison.

"You remember this floor?" Dean goads. "I enjoyed slinging your ass in solitary confinement enough times for getting into the stupidest of fights."

Leighton winces, avoiding my eyes. "I remember."

"Who would've thought you'd be on the other side of these doors, huh?"

"Look," I snap at him. "We didn't come to reminisce. Leighton is here in an official capacity as my security detail. You're not permitted to speak to him."

Chastised, his mouth flops open comically before he wrenches it shut. The dumbfounded look on his face is priceless, but Leighton's grateful smile is even better.

At the front of the solitary wing, its wiped-clean floors dripping with the scent of industrial bleach, a tiny interview room sits behind the guard's station. We're directed inside.

"You have fifteen minutes," the warden informs us curtly. "Make it count."

"We'll take as long as we need," Leighton drones. "Now go."

His face slowly turning purple, the warden makes a hasty exit. We take our seats in the two metal-framed chairs on one side of a rickety table, then I curl my hands into fists underneath it.

"You're sounding more and more like your brother with every day that passes," I mutter.

Leighton snorts. "That's a terrifying thought. How are you holding up?"

"I … really don't know. I thought I'd be more nervous, but now I'm sitting here, all I feel is anger."

"Talk to me," he entreats.

"It's just that it didn't have to be this way."

"I know, princess. But Giana made her choice."

He's right. She chose this. But that doesn't change the fact that in the hazy state of relief that followed Michael's escape, I was able to say that one word aloud.

Mum.

But she isn't my mother. Giana hasn't earned the privilege of that title. She knew what her half-brother did to me, and still, she led me straight back into his clutches.

"We'll find out what we need to know then split," Leighton decides. "I have zero interest in staying in this hellhole for a second longer than we have to."

I look around the plain, mouldy room. "How many times were you put in solitary for fighting?"

He shrugs. "Lost count."

"I can't imagine you being that … angry."

"Trust me, I can be angry when I need to be. You don't survive prison without demanding other people's respect. That's earned in blood, not happy sentiments."

I study his hands, clasped together on top of the table. The thick layers of scar tissue that mar his knuckles told me of the violence he'd seen the moment we met.

Yet still, I can't fathom how my Leighton—sweet, affectionate and caring—could hurt someone enough to earn himself a ticket to this circle of hell. He doesn't have a bad bone in his body.

"Sometimes I catch myself missing this place," he admits.

"Why?"

"It's hard to explain. I didn't have to live up to anyone else's expectations here, only my own. I was free to be as violent and self-destructive as I wanted to be."

My heart twinges. "Leigh."

"I know. It wasn't healthy, and I don't really miss it. But sometimes my brain does subconsciously."

"I'm glad you're not still in here," I say quietly. "We never would've met otherwise, and I couldn't have survived the last year without you."

Leighton's eyes soften, his smile blossoming. "Me too, Goldilocks. You saved me in more ways than I can explain."

I grasp his hand. "We saved each other."

"And we always will."

"Always," I echo.

The slap of footsteps approaching interrupts our conversation, and we both smooth on blank expressions. When the door swings open again, a stranger is emitted into the room.

Hair lank with grease and sallow cheeks framing haze-filled eyes, Giana Kensington is far from the put together housewife that offered me tea and biscuits at her dinner table.

She's cuffed at the wrists and ankles, the pointy bones of her slimmed-down body concealed in a baggy, grey jumpsuit. The moment she sees me, her lips part on a relieved whine.

"Harlow."

She remembers my name now, at least.

"Giana," I say stiffly. "Sit down."

Shoved into the chair opposite by the unknown guard escorting her, Giana winces slightly at the rough treatment. He retreats to the corner of the room to keep a wary eye on her.

"You came," she breathes out. "I'd given up hope when you didn't show after our phone call."

"Some things came up."

She cuts her escort a wary glance. "I'm not given much access to the outside world. They stopped giving me updates on the case when I was put in solitary confinement."

"The warden said that you're on suicide watch," Leighton chips in. "Didn't fancy making it to your own trial, huh?"

Her head sinks. "It's not like that."

"You deserve your day in court for all the deaths you've enabled by protecting that sick son of a bitch. Killing yourself won't stop justice from finding you."

"Leigh," I interject. "Enough."

He sinks back in his chair, starts the voice recorder on his phone and places it on the table. Giana's tears are falling in silent trails down her cheeks.

"I never meant for things to turn out like this," she says in a distraught voice. "I'm sorry for so many things, Harlow. But I'm not sorry for bringing you into this world. I'm proud of the woman you've become."

Looking away from her, I strangle my own emotions to keep them at bay. I can't be fooled by her again.

"I'm not here to talk about us, Giana. Tell me about Michael."

She looks crestfallen but nods in defeat. "I had no idea what I was getting myself into when I first met Michael."

"We know about your mother. Did you meet him after she died?"

Giana nods. "I tried to build a relationship with Michael, but I didn't know the truth. He was living with his wife a couple of hours away under a false identity at the time."

"What happened between you?"

"He came to visit me. You were very young at the time, and … there was something about him. This strange, dark power that clung to him like a shadow."

"Seriously?" Leighton scoffs.

"He was very manipulative," she hits back. "You didn't know that you were under his spell until it was too late. I was lost, and … and … I hated my life."

"You had me and Dad."

She wipes her eyes with her cuffed wrist. "Your father is no saint, Harlow. He had demons of his own. I couldn't cope with being a parent alone. Things were hard for us."

"So what did Michael have on you that made you so blind to the truth?" I lean forward in my seat. "We've spoken to witnesses from his past, and we know he abused Rosetta."

"She was his victim too," Giana agrees. "I didn't see it until it was too late. He told me that the baby was fine… I didn't know that she'd lost it."

My breathing halts. "What baby?"

"Their baby. Rosetta was pregnant when I met Michael. She lost the baby a few months before … he took you."

"Who told you this?" Leighton snaps.

"Rosetta did." Giana sniffles. "She tried to warn me about him, but I was so blinded by the crap he stuffed my head full of. I couldn't see past the madness he sparked inside me."

"You met her?" I ask next.

"Only once. She came on his last visit to our house. Michael convinced me that if I didn't surrender you to him, my soul would be damned. I was so afraid of him."

The thought of Rosetta trying to warn Giana off her plan to sacrifice me, concocted in the manic state of insanity she fell into, sparks a feeling deep in my chest.

Rosetta had been under his almighty control for years by then—beaten, brutalised, her mind broken and moulded into an inhuman mockery of her former self. But she still tried to stop him.

How did that final spark of light get snuffed out, birthing the hateful, bitter woman I later came to know? The Mrs Michaels who spent a decade torturing me was not the same person Giana met.

"How did she lose the baby?" Leighton's question drags me back.

"I don't know. She wouldn't say, but it was obvious that he was beating her. She was black and blue. I think he brought her there as a warning to stop me from backing out of the plan."

"A warning," I repeat. "Because you didn't have even a crack of doubt about sacrificing your only child to the devil himself, right?"

"Please, Harlow," she begs. "It wasn't that simple. He spent months terrorising me. I was already a wreck, and he used that to his advantage to break me down."

I want to throw up on the scratched metal surface of the table. I'd almost forgotten how flimsy her excuses are when spoken out loud.

"That's why he wanted me, isn't it?" I slam my hands on the table. "Rosetta lost his child, and he wanted a replacement. I was his newest pet project."

Giana breaks down. "Yes. I believe so."

With the floodgates open, every last repulsive detail makes sense. He spent months torturing and assaulting the women he brought down into the basement. It was a vicious cycle.

Only when he grew bored of their screams would he enact the final stages of the ritual and take their lives. After they'd proven themselves worthless … by failing to produce him another child.

Holy shit.

"That's why he hurt all those women," I rush out. "He chose sex workers like his mother … and tried to impregnate them to recreate his own childhood. To rewrite his own history."

"This is sick," Leighton curses. "That's his mission? To kill off all the unworthy in his stupid fucking rapture and repopulate the earth with his rape babies instead? Seriously?"

I can't answer him. All I can see in my mind's eye is the look of unadulterated rage on Michael's face as Adelaide bled out—stealing yet another potential life from his grasp.

She survived far longer than any of the other girls, even as he continued to inflict his twisted desires on her. All because of the miracle she carried.

"I need your help." Giana's voice is high with desperation.

"My help?" I laugh.

"Please. You know he won't stop until he completes this godforsaken mission. I need you to keep Ulrich safe for me, Harlow. Don't let Michael hurt him too."

"That's why you called me? To bribe me into protecting the kid you replaced me with?"

"No," she blurts. "Of course not. I needed to see you and make you understand. I'd do anything to take back what I did to you, but I can't. I'm paying the price for my sins now."

Leighton clenches my hand, encouraging me to end the conversation. I let go of him and push his touch aside.

"I could press charges against you for my kidnapping and have you sentenced to life inside this prison. Give me one good reason why I shouldn't do exactly that."

"I can't give you that," Giana admits. "I deserve to die in this place. I've made my peace with that fact. But I'm begging you… Don't let Michael punish my son. He's innocent in all of this—"

"Ulrich is safe," Leighton interrupts. "I know Enzo has had someone checking on him ever since you were arrested. Call your damn husband, and speak to him instead."

"Foster has been refusing my calls for months." She chokes back another sob. "He won't even let me speak to Ulrich. I know Michael will come for him to punish me."

If Enzo has Ulrich under surveillance, then he's safe as can be. I know that Enzo wouldn't let anything happen to an innocent child.

"You promised me information," I snarl impatiently. "Tell me what you dragged us here for, and I'll see what I can do about your family. No promises."

"You'll protect him? Ulrich?"

"I'll speak to Foster and tell him to return your calls. The rest isn't up to me."

Her nod is jerky. "I'll take anything. I just need to hear my son's voice."

"Then give us your information. Last chance."

I watch the defeat settle over her in an invisible cloud of volcanic ash. It saps the last of her strength, and she folds, barely able to lift her head.

"There's another one of us."

"What do you mean? Another what?"

Her tears drip into her lap. "Another sibling. Our mother had a third child. If anyone knows where Michael is right now … it's Daphne."

CHAPTER 20
THEO
OVERGROWN – MOUNTAINS OF THE MOON

SPREAD across the living room floor, old cartons of last night's Chinese food and empty beer bottles litter the space between our stacks of files. *The Office* is on in the background, courtesy of Harlow and Leighton.

It's almost dusk on our second day of research. We've been scouring the depths of the internet and public records for information about our target in an attempt to build a profile.

Daphne Portcastle.

She's the twist in this tale that none of us anticipated. Giana kept the existence of her half-sister secret for all these years. She hasn't even seen or heard from her in well over a decade.

"My eyes feel like they're on fire." Leighton lays spreadeagled on the floor amidst the leftover food. "Is there more coffee?"

"Just brewed a fresh pot," Enzo rumbles from behind a stack of printed sheets. "What was the name of Daphne's husband again?"

"Christopher Lang," I recite tiredly.

"I've tracked down a marriage certificate," he confirms. "Christopher was declared dead seven years ago, and Daphne sold their house two years after that."

"Where?"

Enzo peers down at the records. "Fuck me. Fifteen miles outside of Newcastle."

Shooting upright from her position in the corner of the room, Harlow startles Lucky's sleeping form spread across her legs.

"Did you just say Newcastle?"

Checking the paperwork again, Enzo nods. "Affirmative."

"And what years were Abaddon and Rosetta living in Newcastle? Before Kiera's death?"

I scour through the case files on my laptop, tracing a messy, winding path through the last fourteen years. It's all here. The final puzzle pieces that need to come together to catch our killer.

"Lee and Natasha Heston, aka Abaddon and Rosetta, moved away from Newcastle after Kiera's body was discovered." I scan the complex timeline. "They were in the area at the same time."

"Son of a bitch," Enzo curses.

Leighton reappears in the room with a steaming mug of coffee. "Michael was hiding out near Daphne's hometown after he kidnapped Harlow. That can't be a coincidence."

"And when Kiera's body rocked up, Michael and Rosetta ran to escape suspicion," Enzo adds. "Assuming brand-new identities elsewhere in the country."

"At the same time Daphne's husband miraculously dies and leaves her an expensive home to sell," I finish for them. "This all fucking stinks, doesn't it?"

"We need to track her down." Harlow strokes a hand over Lucky's golden fur. "She has to know something."

Compiling all the information into a secure message to the intelligence team, I send it off, marked as an urgent action. We've got all of Sabre's might driving this investigation to its close.

Now that we've successfully tracked down Daphne's identity, we can begin running my facial recognition software. The moment she surfaces, we'll have a location to follow up.

With much persuasion, the superintendent obliged our request to order a nationwide crackdown. Every police force in the country is out on the streets, breaking up the hysteria and scouring for intel.

We'll rain down the power of the whole fucking country and its rage on Daphne's head, if that's what it takes for her to give up Michael.

"Any update on those post-mortems?" Enzo checks.

"Nine bodies across three different crime scenes have been transported to HQ for processing. All adults, most middle-aged, found carved up and hanging from nooses."

Leighton slurps his coffee. "Suicides?"

"The nooses were tied all wrong. They were hung by someone. Almost like—"

"Rosetta's body," Harlow finishes.

I close my laptop. "Exactly."

"He's taunting us. Michael wants us to know that he's behind these copycat kills, even from afar."

"We need profiles on all of them." Enzo glances over to me. "See if there's any correlation with the previous victims from the beach."

"Already got Rayna on it. She's working overtime with her new intern, so we should have some more information soon."

"That intern's gonna run away screaming from the company after this fiasco." Leighton chuckles. "Way to scare them off."

"We're running a company here," Enzo complains. "If they don't like it, they can go work in a bloody tea room instead."

"That's great for staff retention, Enz."

"I really don't give a shit."

The creak of Hunter moving around upstairs abruptly silences them. He's been unresponsive since taking a large dose of migraine medication.

"How long was he out?" Harlow sighs.

"Only a couple of hours." Enzo scrubs a hand over his face. "I've told him to talk to his specialist about these headaches at his checkup next month."

"Like he'd do that willingly," I comment.

"Maybe they can offer something else that will help." He turns to Harlow. "Will you go with him? He's refusing to let me come."

"Enz…" she begins.

"You know Hunter won't ask for our help, even when he needs it. He should have someone there with him for moral support."

"What makes you think he'll listen to me?"

Leighton waggles his eyebrows. "You could always persuade him."

"Classy. I'm not going to sleep with your brother to blackmail him into taking me to his appointment."

"Who said anything about blackmail?" Leighton snickers. "That asshole will do anything for you, and you know it. Don't underestimate the power you have over him."

"He's right," Enzo agrees. "Talk to him."

"Alright, alright. I'll give it a shot."

Clambering to her feet, Harlow dislodges Lucky then disappears upstairs to track Hunter down. I hope she'll be able to talk some sense into him. The rest of us don't have any hope.

He's had several regular checkups since his accident and has forbidden any of us from attending outside of driving him there. Hunter the control freak is out in full swing.

"He won't do it." I take a swig of long-cold coffee. "You know how terrified of weakness he is."

"Leaning on his family's support isn't a weakness," Enzo argues. "We're supposed to look out for each other."

"I'm not disagreeing with you. But he doesn't see it that way, no matter what we do. This is a road he wants to walk alone."

"Like everything else," Leighton mutters. "How the hell did we end up here? Mum calls me fishing for information on Hunter. Me!"

"Regardless of the shit going on with Hunter, you should be proud of how far you've come." Enzo looks at him meaningfully. "He's lucky to have you as his brother."

Gaze ducking, Leighton smothers his grin with another sip of coffee. "I guess so."

"Sorry to break the moment," I interrupt. "But what are we going to do about Giana? We've got eyes on her husband and son. They're both secure."

"Is she still on suicide watch?" Enzo studies another sheet of paper.

"It sounds like that'll be the case until her trial begins." I stretch my arms above my head. "The warden told me what happened. Giana made some threats to the prison counsellor and was found cutting herself."

I wish I didn't feel any empathy for that batshit crazy woman, but part of me empathises with her. In Giana's own way, she was also a victim of Abaddon and his depravity.

That doesn't negate her own crimes, though. She still made the choice to support a murderer and lie to us all. For that alone, she can never be forgiven in my mind.

"What exactly does she want Harlow to do?"

"Giana wants her to meet the husband and convince him to allow visitation for the kid," Leighton answers. "He hasn't taken any of Giana's calls for months and cut off all contact."

Enzo scoffs. "They're better off without her."

Two pairs of footsteps thump down the stairs. Bare-chested and wearing low slung pyjama bottoms, Hunter pads into the room, escorted by Harlow.

"Look who's up," she says cheerfully. "Make some room."

Sweeping paperwork and several manilla files off the sofa, Enzo clears space for Hunter to sit down. He looks barely awake and a little disorientated.

I point to my forehead then tap.

He collapses on the sofa. "Still pounding."

Leighton disappears, returning with a glass of water to wash down the handful of brightly coloured pills in his palm. For once, Hunter doesn't protest and accepts the medication.

"What's the latest?" he grumbles.

Passing over the marriage certificate for him to inspect, Enzo quickly fills him in on our findings. No one drops off the radar entirely. Not even Abaddon managed to do that. We might have picked up his trail through our newest suspect.

The strange sound of scuffling from outside the front window causes Enzo to freeze, hands raised mid-sentence. "Is the pizza here?"

Leighton bounces on the spot. "He's probably lost again. I'll get it."

Stealing Enzo's wallet full of cash, he sprints for the front door to fetch our food. I'm convinced he has a tapeworm. He eats like he's been starved his entire life.

"Little shit," Enzo curses. "Can't he use his own money?"

"He prefers yours," I joke.

Hunter studies the marriage certificate. "We need to pull on the superintendent's resources and have the police looking for Daphne too."

Enzo shakes his head. "If we spook her, she'll run."

"Or it may do the opposite and flush her out," I argue.

"She may not even be in the country. Harlow doesn't remember her. It's possible she's got nothing to do with this case at all."

"Guys," Hunter snaps. "Still here. I asked the fucking question in the first place."

I apologise in sign language then quickly translate our conversation. If

Daphne's been aiding Abaddon from the shadows all along, she may be our smoking gun.

"There's no one here!" Leighton calls through the house.

BANG.

A sudden explosion of shattering glass drowns out the sound of his voice. The front window explodes, sending sharpened shards tearing through the curtains.

Shouting follows the blast. Several bricks crash through the remaining broken windowpanes, adding to the confusion and noise as the security alarm blares.

Enzo bolts upright and slides a hand beneath the coffee table. It reappears wrapped around a compact, black handgun.

"Get down!"

That's when the first flames appear. Clinging to the curtains, the fire catches at the bottom then begins to spread fast. A burning bottle hurtles through the window.

It's a Molotov cocktail.

They're flying through the gap in the destroyed window, spreading the potent stench of fuel across the room. Roaring flames reply in turn.

"Fire!" Harlow screeches.

Launching across the wooden floor, I tackle her, and we hit the teal-coloured rug with a thump, my body absorbing the impact and bite of glass.

When another bottle is launched through the now-destroyed window, it almost sails straight into us until Hunter bats it aside.

"Move!" he roars.

Harlow yanks me up. "Where is Lucky?"

Faintly, we can hear her panicked yipping from the dog bed in the kitchen. We bolt from the burning room then chase after Enzo to find safety from the fire.

Enzo's biceps bulge against his T-shirt as he lifts Lucky's huge, muscled body into his arms. We break outside together, the growing flames illuminating the scene.

"Leighton!" Harlow screams.

Through the smoke pouring from our house, we can see the cause of all the commotion. Figures dart between the parked cars in the driveway to join the group gathered in front of the garage.

Curled into himself to absorb the blows raining down, Leighton's trapped between four of the dark-clothed men. All of them are kicking and punching, giving him no time to fight back.

"One more move and I'll blow your goddamn brains out." Enzo trains the gun on their group. "Step back. All of you."

Three of them reluctantly raise their hands, but one of the guys boots his foot straight into Leighton's face. It causes Hunter to break out in a run, spurring on the others to do the same.

"Someone stop Hunter!" Enzo shouts.

He's already thrown himself into the melee to protect his brother. Fighting breaks out as the group of attackers swells in size, even with the gun aimed at them.

I have to grab hold of Harlow to stop her from chasing after Enzo. He's determined to balance the scales. We're outnumbered, and the house is exploding into ravenous flames behind us.

"Let go of me. Theo!"

Pinning her back against my chest, I hold her in a vice. "I'm sorry. I have to protect you."

"No! I need to help them!"

All we can do is watch as Enzo tucks the gun into his jeans then unleashes hell, his fists moving in a ruthless blur to cut down the sheer muscle and numbers stacked against him.

Hunter strikes one of the attackers in the stomach and breaks his nose with a punch to the face. He moves to trip up the guy's friend, knocking him unconscious with a brutal blow.

Moving in a blur, Lucky launches herself at the closest figure and takes him down with all of her weight. She begins to tear into the skin on show through his dark clothing—biting, grinding and ripping him to shreds.

"Lucky!" Harlow calls.

"She's fine," I try to soothe. "Enzo trained her well."

"I don't want her to get hurt!"

But Lucky moves just as she's been trained to, zipping between Enzo and Hunter, tearing at any available body parts.

They cut down the group with deadly ease, overpowering the hotheads and betraying their lack of preparation. Enzo halts before getting the last standing asshole in a headlock.

"Enough. Who are you?"

With his backup now bleeding and collapsed across our driveway, the man lifts his head to reveal his identity. A lead weight settles in the pit of my stomach.

"Fuck you, Enzo," he spits.

"Matthew? Seriously?"

I ease my grip on Harlow. "Becket's brother."

She breaks free from my hold and races over to Leighton. He's conscious but grunting in pain from being challenged four-to-one.

With Hunter's help, the pair of them get Leighton sitting upright, his face already swollen with multiple bruises and a split lip. Enzo strangles Matthew a little harder for good measure.

"Why are you here?" he demands. "This location is classified information. How'd you find us?"

"From the person you got killed." Matthew coughs out -bloodstained spit. "Becket is dead, and there's no accountability."

"He was on active duty," Enzo snarls. "Burning my fucking house down isn't going to bring your brother back!"

"We had to bury him in pieces!"

"Becket knew exactly what he was getting into when he joined Sabre." He drags Matthew to his feet. "You're going to pay for this. I don't care whose brother you are."

"You didn't even attend his damn funeral!" Matthew yells back.

If Becket wasn't already dead and buried, Enzo would kill him for spilling classified information to his brother. He's hospitalised ex-employees for less. Our safe location is now burnt.

"Are you okay?" Harlow fusses over Leighton.

"Fucking peachy," he replies nasally.

"You're bleeding!"

"It's alright. Bit more concerned about our house."

Her attention turns to Matthew, pinned and unable to run away with his thugs. Harlow crouches down in front of him, her features obscured by thick plumes of smoke.

"Be thankful I understand what losing someone you love feels like, otherwise, I'd be letting Enzo snap your neck for hurting one of our own."

Stretching to her full height, she turns to return to Leighton's side, but a sneer from Matthew halts her steps.

"My brother is dead because of you."

"Watch your mouth." Enzo tightens his headlock. "Or this won't end well for you."

"I've seen the video." Matthew coughs through the smoke. "You're a murderous little whore, aren't you?"

The nerve in Harlow's jaw tics. She's halted on the pavement, the reflection of flames flickering deep within her eyes.

"My brother died protecting you! And from what? You're no better than that sick monster."

"One more word and I'll end you myself," Enzo threatens. "No one talks to her like that."

The scream of an approaching police siren and multiple fire engines punctuates his words. Behind us, glass explodes and smoke billows out of our house. The flames are only getting bigger.

Our lives are burning to ashes, and there's nothing we can do about it. Case files. Clothing. Framed photographs. We're well versed in loss, but this still fucking hurts.

"Don't get me started on him," Matthew spits at Hunter. "Am I supposed to feel sorry for him? He's the worst of them all. That bullet should've killed him."

Spinning on her heel, Harlow marches right up to him and gets in his face. She's almost unrecognisable beneath the growing cloud of fury that's consuming the person I know.

"Your brother was a good man," she hisses. "He died doing what he loved. That's his legacy."

"Is that what you tell yourself so you can sleep at night?"

"It's what I know."

Before Enzo can choke him to unconsciousness, Matthew hacks another mouthful of spit and launches it straight into Harlow's face. The bright-red mixture of saliva trickles down her cheek.

"I hope the killer finds you and finishes what he started. We've leaked this address to the media. Good luck hiding now."

Right on cue, the hum of an approaching helicopter slices through the sound of our home burning. He wasn't lying. The cameras will be flashing very soon.

Her anger replaced by cold calculation, Harlow looks up into the narrowed slits of Enzo's eyes. He lifts a brow, silently seeking her permission to dole out a punishment.

"He hurt him," she states in a cold, calm voice. "Nobody hurts *my* Leigh."

The tiny nod of approval she gives him makes me so hard, I'd let her fuck me in the splattered blood stains covering our driveway.

"What the lady wants, the lady gets." Enzo smirks with pleasure. "See you in court, motherfucker."

His scarred fist smacks into Matthew's face so hard, I can hear the crack of his bones breaking. He's forced to spit out a bloodied tooth at Enzo's feet, but he refuses to back down.

"If my brother could see you now…"

"He'd be the one breaking your spine for being fucking stupid instead of me," Enzo returns.

Punching him over and over until his face resembles a swollen, meaty pulp, Harlow watches the whole thing. She doesn't flinch once, even as blood splatters across the driveway.

When Enzo grabs his arm and pulls at such a sharp angle that it elicits a disgusting *crack* of bones shattering, Matthew finally screams. The sound causes my stomach to roll.

This isn't us.

We don't hurt innocent people.

I approach Harlow and rest a hand on her shoulder. "Enough. He's an idiot, but he isn't our enemy."

"Look at Leighton," she replies emotionlessly. "They started this."

"And we have to end it. But not like this."

Thwack. Thwack. Thwack.

The blows rain down. All of Matthew's remaining conscious friends have taken several steps back from Enzo in preparation to run away. His face is dripping in splattered blood.

"Stop," Harlow commands.

Enzo freezes with his fist drawn back, a second from delivering another killer punch. He glances back at his commander.

"Let the police have what's left of him," she instructs.

"Sure I can't just kill him?"

Harlow looks around at the now-terrified onlookers. "They've got the message."

With a curse, Enzo cracks Matthew's skull against the pavement. Blood streams down his beaten face as he falls unconscious, though he's still breathing, which is a miracle in itself.

Harlow glowers at the slumped, bleeding body at her feet. The darkness that crept over her is receding like waves washing back out to sea, bringing her back to herself.

"Thanks," she mumbles.

Enzo flashes his teeth. "Don't mention it."

"Our location is blown."

With Leighton's arm slung around his neck to carry him, Hunter helps his brother hobble despite his pained wincing.

"We need to go," Hunter declares. "Let the police haul these assholes away."

Enzo nods, the flash of blue lights illuminating his grimace. "If the world knows where we are, then Abaddon and his psychopaths do too."

CHAPTER 21
HARLOW

DEVIL IN HER EYES – BRYCE SAVAGE

BEING SMUGGLED into HQ like a fugitive is a new experience. Even in the dead of night, it hums with activity and teams still immersed in their workday. The company never sleeps.

Hunter leads the charge, taking us through an empty service floor that has access to the emergency staircase. We wind higher through the building—limping, ash-streaked and exhausted.

"Where are we going?"

Theo adjusts Leighton's weight leaning on him. "Remember those apartments we told you about? They're kept for emergencies. We need somewhere to lay low."

I clutch the dog lead in my hand. "We should've stayed and faced the cameras. Those people attacked us."

"You really think the world will have much sympathy?" he says bitterly. "They'd pour more fuel on the flames if given the opportunity."

Down a thickly carpeted corridor, we reach the apartments. It's quieter up here with just the hum of the building accompanying our hurried footsteps. Hunter uses his swipe card to unlock the door.

Inside the welcoming darkness, he begins to flick on light switches. It reveals a huge, luxurious apartment with polished floors and full-length, tinted windows offering a panoramic view of London.

I unclip Lucky's lead. "In you go, girl."

She chases after Hunter, her ears still pricked up and muscles tensed. For a dog, she's remarkably in-tune with our emotions. I think she'll bite the heads off the next people to fuck us over.

The kitchen and living room are all open-plan, lit by a chandelier hanging from the ceiling that stretches up into the heavens. All the furniture is made from glass, polished steel and butter-soft leather.

Lingering by the door, Enzo's unable to take another step. He's still covered in dried blood, despite cleaning up in the frantic, high-speed car ride over here to escape the media.

I stop in front of him. "What are you thinking?"

His raw amber orbs peer down at me. "They attacked us in our own fucking home."

"I know, Enz."

"If I can't keep my family safe there, where can I?"

"This isn't your fault. You can't blame yourself."

With a roar, his fist crashes into the wall. Plaster cracks in rapidly spreading spider webs, and he barely bats an eye. Not even when blood trickles across his busted knuckles.

"Please, Enz," I beg. "Talk to me."

"I'm tired of this life," he snaps. "We've spent our careers fighting for justice for people who can't do it themselves, and it means nothing. Nobody has our backs."

"You've helped so many people. Don't let this convince you otherwise. What happened to Becket isn't on you."

"Yeah, it is," he deadpans. "I'm done."

"What does that mean?"

"It means that I'm done fighting. We built this business, and we can tear it all down just as easily."

I try to catch his arm, but he pulls it free then stalks off down the corridor towards the elevator. It takes all of my self-control not to follow him and attempt to patch all his mental wounds.

"Harlow!" Theo calls. "Come inside. He'll be fine."

I reluctantly close the door. "I'm worried about him."

"Let him beat the shit out of some punching bags for a few hours, and he'll come back."

A feral part of me is itching to join him. The overwhelming anger I experienced in that moment was more intense than anything I've ever felt before.

I couldn't handle the sight of Leighton on the ground. Gone is the girl who could watch the people she loves get hurt without doing something about it. Now I have the freedom to *be* fucking angry.

"Goldilocks," Leighton croaks. "Come here."

My feet are rooted to the spot.

Hunter checks the freezer and wraps a handful of ice cubes up to give to his brother. Accepting it, Leighton's demanding stare doesn't stray from me, even as Lucky yips for his attention.

"Now," he adds.

"Is Becket's brother going to be okay?"

Theo fishes out his phone. "I'll check in with the police department to get an update. The fire should be out by now."

Stepping through the balcony doors that lead outside, he leaves me with the two brothers and all of our pent-up emotions.

Hunter scavenges the minibar tucked into the corner of the room and settles on the sofa, clicking his tongue for Lucky to join him. He checks her paws for any injuries then rubs her belly.

"You did good, girl," he coos.

She licks his face, happily snuggling up for a celebratory cuddle. Hunter tucks into a bottle of rum and leaves me to face Leighton.

"Come on, Harlow. You're safe now."

"Safe?" I scoff. "I'm not worried about my safety. I told Enzo to beat the shit out of Matthew back there. Me. I'm the reason he feels like crap."

Leighton moves the ice to his other cheek. "The son of a bitch deserved it."

"That doesn't excuse my behaviour. I don't hurt people. That isn't me." I wince as blood dribbles down his chin. "But I couldn't just let him get away with hurting you."

Leighton ditches the handful of ice and throws his arms open. "I can't move, so you're gonna have to come to me to hug this out."

"Hug it out? We're not kids."

"And that wasn't a fucking invitation. Get over here."

Reluctantly crossing the room, I step between his open legs and bury my face in the stained material of his shirt. He smells like blood and smoke, but he's still my Leigh beneath the acrid scents.

"You're exactly who you are meant to be." He strokes a hand over my ashy hair. "Never doubt that. I love you for who you are."

"Even when I scare myself?"

"Especially then."

With a sigh, I take his hand in mine. "Let's get you cleaned up. Do we have a first aid kit? You've got some nasty cuts."

"We should check the bathroom."

Leaving Hunter to nurse his bottle of rum, we inch through the darkened apartment. Three bedrooms branch off from the hallway, the beds unmade and air thick with dust.

"People don't stay here much?"

"Don't think so." Leighton hisses in pain. "How the fuck did we end up here? Running for our lives? We're supposed to be the ones in control."

"I don't have a good enough answer for you."

"Well, someone owes me a bloody good answer for trashing my pretty face. I'm going to look like a bruised piece of fruit by morning."

Despite everything, I choke on a laugh. "You're still beautiful to me, Princess Leigh. Bruised fruit and all."

"Better be," he snarks.

In the bathroom, I sit him down on the closed toilet lid then peel his stained t-shirt off, leaving his sweats still in place. There's a first aid kit tucked underneath the sink with some other toiletries.

Soaking a washcloth in warm water, I tilt his chin up then begin gently wiping the blood away. The swelling is pretty bad, but he's a tough cookie and doesn't complain as I poke the mottled skin.

"What's the verdict?"

I narrow my eyes on him. "No more fighting for you."

"Can't cage a wild animal, Goldilocks."

"Watch me. I don't give a shit if it hurts your ego. Next time a group of people come for you, run in the other direction."

"I thought I could take them all."

"Maybe we need to check you for a brain injury too. You were outnumbered and didn't stand a chance."

"Ouch. You're mean."

"No. I'm just done watching the people I love get hurt."

After cleansing the cuts across his forehead and lip, I declare the job done. He doesn't need stitches, just more ice and a damn good talking to for picking a fight with an army of fully grown men.

With my task complete, the darkness crawling across my mind comes rushing back. I busy myself, cleaning up the first aid kit so Leighton can't see how badly my hands are shaking.

I'm still angry.

Fucking furious.

No matter how hard we try, the world is constantly pushing us ten steps back for every inch we claw ourselves forward. God is laughing in our faces and destroying everything with a swooped hand.

"Harlow? Want to come and choose a bedroom?"

"I … need a minute. You go."

"But—"

"Go, Leigh!" I shout.

In too much pain to argue, Leighton slips from the bathroom. I'm left with my hands braced on the sink as I stare deep into the pits of my black pupils. I don't recognise who stares back at me.

Giana. Michael. All the women living in the shell of my heart, forcing me to put one foot in front of the other for them.

I've spent months trying to figure out exactly who the real Harlow is, beyond the people who have dictated my life for so many years. But the idea of that angry, violent person being me is horrifying.

Before I realise what I'm doing, my hand lifts to tangle in my long mane of smoky hair. I twirl a strand around my finger then halt on the verge of tearing it clean out.

"No," I whisper to myself.

But the voice is still there—rising from the depths and making its presence known. I doubt it ever left. More like it hibernated.

Flicking the walk-in shower on, I'm about to strip off and step inside when it hits me again. Begging. Pleading. Demanding pain and control in the only way my broken self knows.

I'm not sure what drives me to call Theo's name. It tears from my throat without being told. I hold myself on the verge of relapsing as his hurried footsteps approach from the other room.

"Harlow? Where are you?"

"Bathroom!"

The door crashes open, and when Theo spots me, the tears threatening to spill down my cheeks and a hand tangled in my hair, he blanches.

"What's going on?"

Eyes closing, I feel the tears escape. "I'm so fucking scared of being the person the world thinks I am."

"Oh, beautiful."

It has to be him. Theo knows me better than I know myself, even the corners of my soul that will never see the light of day. He conquered them long before I even knew his name.

"You're in shock," he murmurs, his arms wrapping around my waist. "Can you let go of your hair and talk to me, please?"

My grip on the strands tightens. "We're spiralling out of control. Even Enzo is ready to walk away. The case has beaten us all."

"Bullshit. I promised you that we'd end this, and that's exactly what we're going to do. You have a book to publish when we're on the other side of this fight."

"And who will I be on the other side?" I throw back. "Am I battling to see this through just to lose myself all over again?"

Clasping my hips, he flips me around then shoves my back into the ceramic sink. Theo doesn't peel my hand from my hair. Instead, his mouth slams onto mine with the strength of a fatal collision.

His ferocity steals my breath and locks it in a bomb-proof box in the deepest, darkest pits of his heart where I can't take it back.

"You listen to me," he whispers fiercely. "I don't care who you are on the other side of this because I know the woman I love."

"What if she isn't me?"

"Then I'll love whatever version of you remains when all is said and done. There's nothing you can do to stop me from wanting to spend every single moment of my life by your side."

"Theo," I sob into his lips.

"I won't hear it. You need control?" He releases my mouth and grabs my wrist. "I'll give it to you with pleasure."

Theo moves my hand to clasp his throat, encouraging my nails to slice deep into his skin. I can feel the pounding of his heartbeat beneath my fingertips.

"I wouldn't give myself to you if I didn't trust the person I know you are," he says throatily. "And believe me, angel, you own every inch of my mind, body and soul."

When he kisses me again, it's softer, coaxing, whispering to me in dulcet tones. He's torn his heart out and now offers it to me, blood-slick and still beating, on a platter.

I want it.

I want him.

I want *us*.

Pushing his chest, I shove him backwards into the still-running shower. We meet beneath the hot spray, the water soaking into our clothing and melding us together.

I don't care. All I want is for him to pick up the shattered shards of my heart and glue them back together. I can't do it myself right now.

Theo's mouth devours mine, submitting to the beat of my tongue lashing his. He grabs the hem of my t-shirt then pauses to yank it over my head, exposing my bare breasts.

Still wearing blackened pyjama bottoms, I shove them over my hips then kick them out of the shower. "Strip."

"Yes, angel."

Peeling off his soaking-wet flannel shirt, jeans and boxers, he throws them out to join my pyjamas. With all his bare, chiselled body on display, I let myself return to the confidence I found in Tartarus.

I remove his glasses and yank sharply on his curly hair, encouraging him to sink to his knees in the shower. Theo obliges without a single ounce of protest.

"Take my panties off," I order.

His thumbs hook into my panties to pull them down, exposing my pussy to his awaiting mouth. He plants kisses on my pubic bone, skating down until his tongue flicks across my clit.

I fist his hair tighter. "More, Theo."

His tongue slides between my folds and licks up the length of my slit. When his finger circles my bundle of nerves before pushing inside me, I have to brace a hand on the tiled wall.

"My beautiful girl has such a pretty cunt," he purrs against my pussy lips. "Tell me what you want me to do."

Head thrown back, I savour the thrust of his finger gliding into me. My legs are already trembling from the slow tease.

"I want you to make me come with your tongue."

Sucking my clit between his teeth, he chuckles against my folds. "You're the boss, beautiful."

Pushing a second finger into my core, his mouth attacks me in a frenzy of licking and sucking, mirroring the stroke of his digits entering me.

With my emotions still running haywire, it doesn't take long for the pressure to begin to build. Each time he slides back inside, his thumb circles my clit.

"So sweet. You're perfect."

I can hardly see him through the steam billowing inside the shower. His grip on my hips and the torture of his tongue against my folds cuts through the temporary blindness.

When my lower belly tightens, I feel my walls clench around his fingers. A loud moan escapes my lips as my release quickly overwhelms me. I come all over Theo's face buried between my thighs.

Still quaking with aftershocks, I don't need a second to breathe. The darkness will only come flooding back. I yank Theo to his feet then wrap a hand around his proud length.

"I want you to fuck me until I can't think of anything but your cock worshipping me," I command. "You got that?"

He parts the steam to kiss my lips. "Anything for you."

Following my instincts, I keep a firm grip on his shaft and tug him along. He follows me out of the shower, letting me gently pull him as we return to the bedroom.

Pushing aside pillows, I flop onto the bed, spreading my legs wide open. Theo's eyes eagerly eat me up, his hand stroking over his length.

Movement over his shoulder causes me to sit up. Leighton has tracked us down and saunters into the room, still managing to look like a prowling tiger beneath his mottled, purple bruises.

"You kicked me out to replace me with Theo, huh?"

I gulp hard. "It wasn't like that."

Stopping behind Theo, he rests a hand on his bare shoulder. "You're hogging all of my girl's attention, Theodore."

His throat works up and down. "You want me to apologise or something?"

"Actions speak louder than words. I want to join this sexy little game of yours. Think I've earned myself an invitation."

"I'm not in charge, man."

Leighton winks at me. "Harlow?"

I wave him forward. "You can join us."

Dropping his hand, he pushes Theo forward until he's crawling across the unmade bed on his knees. Leighton stands over us both in a position of supreme power.

Settling himself between my thighs, Theo peppers kisses across my breasts, taking a hardened nipple between his lips. I can feel his length nudging my leg close to where I want it.

"Please," I mewl.

"Did you hear her?" Leighton growls. "She needs you to fill her up. Look at that perfect, pink cunt just begging to be touched."

Spurred on, Theo lines himself up. "That I can do."

With a slick thrust, he slides deep inside of me. Seeing his wide blue eyes above me as he groans in pleasure feels strange after the intensity of our first time.

He may be on top, but with Leighton dictating our movements, Theo's still surrendering. His hips draw back, then he pushes back into me as Leighton watches on.

"You can do better than that," he goads. "I thought you liked following orders, Theodore? I told you to fuck her. Hard."

With a secret smile that only I can see, Theo picks up the pace until he's hammering into me. With both of their eyes watching my every move, I feel like I'm under a spotlight.

"Better," Leighton praises.

Sneaking around the bed, he runs his fingers through Theo's wet curls before stroking a hand across the sheets. My heart seizes when he kneels on my right side, pushing his sweats and boxers down.

"While Theo's doing such a good job of pummelling your sweet pussy, I want to ride that gorgeous mouth of yours."

I tilt my head to the side, my lips parting to greedily accept his length. Leighton pushes his cock into my mouth until I'm filled with both of them and trapped in torturous submission.

With Theo still thrusting into me, determined to steal another climax, Leighton begins to fuck my mouth as roughly as promised. I'm overwhelmed by the sense of fullness.

"Doesn't she look good being fucked by us both?"

"Too right," Theo hums back.

Tongue sliding against Leighton's shaft, he nudges the back of my throat with each pump of his hips. Moisture sears the corners of my eyes, but I don't care. I love his playful roughness.

Between them both, I'm a gasping, shaking mess in minutes. There's no escaping the onslaught, but rather than being triggered by the vulnerability, I'm revelling in it.

"Stop," Leighton orders.

Leighton pulls out of my mouth before he can finish, his breathing ragged. He forces Theo to halt with another barked command.

"On the bed. I want her on top of you now."

I cry out when Theo follows his orders and pulls out, leaving me on the cusp of another orgasm. He lies down on the mattress next to me and lets me climb on top of him.

"I want you to ride Theo's cock like the good little princess you are," Leighton instructs smugly. "Then we'll let you come."

Biting my lip, I line up his dick then eagerly sink down on it. From this position, it reaches an even deeper angle, setting off tiny fireworks beneath my skin.

When I feel Leighton's weight dipping on the bed behind me, I lift my hips and begin to find the rhythm that worked for me before. Knowing he's watching the show only makes me more eager to please.

"Is our girl doing a good job?" Leighton asks.

Beneath me, Theo's nails cut into my hips. "Fuck yes, she is."

"Perhaps I should reward her with another cock, then. What do you think, Goldilocks?"

His fingers skate down the length of my spine, curving around my ass before delivering a hard spank. I can't help yelling a curse, the burst of pain heightening my state of arousal.

Leighton finds the ring of my asshole then glides a moistened finger over it. I cry out again when he eases it inside, the intrusion feeling almost normal after the last few times he's experimented.

"You need to be nice and relaxed for what I have planned," he whispers behind me. "So that means I need you to come again."

With Theo rutting up into me to meet my strokes, I can feel the crest of my release approaching. Between both of them, it's impossible not to feel spoiled, drowning in their love and attention.

Leighton spanks me again, harder this time, jolting Theo's length still buried inside my core. With his finger pumping in and out of my back entrance, I can't hold it in any longer.

"Oh God!" I scream out.

His mouth falling open, Theo finishes at the same second, his length jolting from deep within me. I can feel the rush of warmth as his seed fills me up, our releases feeding each other.

He slumps on the bed, still clasping my hips and staring up at me with those bottomless, light-blue eyes that are filled with lazy satisfaction.

Leighton's chin drops on my shoulder. "Good show, guys. But I have an even better one planned."

Lifting my ass so that Theo slips out of me, Leighton's hand dips between my legs. My face feels like a furnace when I realise what he's doing with the warmth leaking out of me.

"Jesus, Leigh," Theo curses.

"You had your turn. Now it's mine."

He's spreading Theo's hot come all over his own length, lubricating it up without an ounce of shame for swapping fluids like they're neighbours borrowing baking powder.

I feel his fingers back at my aching core, soaking them in my come to move to my asshole. I'm a dripping, sticky mess, but that doesn't slow Leighton down.

"You still trust me?" he asks gruffly.

Hands splayed on Theo's chest for balance, I wrestle with my nerves. "I do, but I'm not sure about this."

"I'll look after you, princess. I'm not going to hurt you. If you want me to stop, I'll stop. Okay?"

"Okay."

"Keep your eyes on Theodore. I want him to see just how much you love my cock in your asshole."

Beneath me, Theo tightens his grip on my hips. "I've got you, angel."

I'm not sure I can blush any harder. There's no room to hide. I haven't got a single ounce of privacy as Leighton blows past the limits of my experience in the bedroom.

Pushing his finger back into my ring of muscle, he spreads the lubrication farther to moisten everything up. I'm as relaxed as possible after being awarded two orgasms already.

"I'm going to go nice and slow," he murmurs.

Then I feel the tip of his length pressing at my rear. He holds it there for a moment, gently nudging against me and letting me get used to the strange sensation.

"Easy, baby."

"It's okay," I moan.

"Reckon you can take some more?"

"Yes… More."

Theo chuckles beneath me. He has a front-row seat to Leighton's performance, trapped by the weight of my body. But I don't see him even attempting to escape.

Moving slowly, Leighton ever so gently pushes another inch inside. I gasp loudly, too overwhelmed to know how to feel.

The sense of pressure is greater than when he's fucked me with his fingers back there, and while it's uncomfortable at first, the pleasure quickly follows as my body adjusts.

"Fuck, Harlow," he grunts in my ear. "I've wanted to do this since I fucked you in that hotel. Now I own all of your firsts."

"Don't get too cocky," I groan back.

"Try and stop me. I want everyone to know that fact. You were mine before any of these idiots even had a chance."

Theo's hands move to cup my breasts, massaging them and tweaking my stiff nipples. The extra stimulation makes me dizzy with the tides of ecstasy threatening to consume me.

Drawing back out, Leighton pushes into me again, still moving slow so I can adjust to the burning sensation of his cock stretching me. The initial spikes of pain melt into mind-numbing pleasure.

"Does it feel good, baby?"

"Y-Yes."

"Do you like it when I fuck your tight asshole?"

He pushes deeper inside me, stretching me even further. My eyes scrunch shut as another mountainous wave of bliss crashes over me.

"Oh, fuck. Yes. I like it."

"I always knew you were a dirty girl," he teases, hitting my ass cheek again. "Look at your precious angel now, Theodore."

"She looks damn good to me," he returns.

Leighton keeps inching in, testing the boundaries of my sanity and shattering them beyond comprehension. The idea of doing this scared me before, but I trust him with my life.

The waves of strange, paralysing pleasure are too strong to contain. My limbs are shaking as moans fall from my lips.

There's a throat clear from elsewhere in the room that has us all freezing up. I wrench my eyes open to look over my shoulder.

Kill me now.

Enzo and Hunter are watching our tangle of sweaty limbs with matching surprised expressions. Neither looks like they expected to walk into this particular scenario.

"Well..." Hunter leans against the wall. "Don't stop on our account."

"We'll just patiently wait our turn," Enzo adds, his bare chest slick with sweat from the workout he's returned from.

"Our turn?" I squeak.

Leighton spanks me again, jolting his dick inside of me. "Focus, princess. I said eyes on Theo. Not them."

When I don't immediately look back down, his hand dips around my waist to find my bundle of nerves. He flicks it before slapping his hand directly on my cunt.

"Fuck!" I cry out.

"I said *focus.*"

With Theo still fondling my breasts and Leighton beginning to move at a gentle pace, I can hardly hold myself upright.

The weight of four pairs of eyes is searing my flesh and melting it down to the bone. Every single inch of me is theirs to peruse.

Leighton grabs a handful of my hair then tugs to pull my head back. His teeth graze my earlobe before biting down.

"Want two of us inside you at once?"

"What?" I manage to gasp.

Chuckling, he releases my hair. "Mind shifting up a bit, Theodore? I want to see how my girl handles two of us fucking her."

Theo wiggles out from underneath me, using the space Leighton creates by lifting my hips without exiting me. I can't see who he waves over, but the pad of footsteps joins us.

Standing behind Hunter, Enzo nudges him forward, giving him first dibs. Both of them can't tear their eyes from me.

"Now this I want to see," Enzo says with a filthy grin. "You're caught in a Rodriguez sandwich, little one."

Taking Theo's place on the bed, Hunter's already stripped off his ash-stained clothing. Leighton lowers me back down onto him, his cock still sliding in and out of my rear with increasing strokes.

Sandwiched between both brothers, all I can do is hold on for dear life as Hunter sheaths himself inside my pussy. He drives into me slowly, letting me release a strangled, inhuman sound.

"Jesus Christ," he swears, sliding out and back in again even deeper. "Fuck, sweetheart."

I feel like I've been dipped in fuel and set alight. They're both inside me, breezing past every mental barrier and setting up shop. My body is no longer my own.

It belongs to them.

I think it always has.

My mind is being bulldozed and scattered in ashes by the rhythm of them both fucking me. I don't even have enough mental strength to question the ethics of their cocks rubbing up inside me.

"Shit," Leighton hisses over my shoulder. "I'm going to come. You're too tight. I can't hold it."

"Come, Leigh," I mewl.

When he roars behind me, I feel his release mix with the stickiness of Theo still covering me. The silent man in question is sitting at the head of the bed, watching everything with fascination.

Leighton slumps on my back, holding his weight off me as he catches his breath. He's slipped out of me, and his come is spilling down the backs of my thighs.

I hold on to Hunter's shoulder for balance when he clambers off the bed. Leighton stumbles and lands next to Theo, still panting. The pair are sitting there like cinemagoers. All that's missing is the popcorn.

"Harlow," Hunter growls. "Look at me, baby. Not them. Let me see those beautiful eyes."

Refocusing on him, I let his hand sneak up my body and wrap around my throat to ensure I can't look away again. Without sound, he's reliant on sight alone to experience this moment.

"I've come close to losing you too many times," he says darkly. "I fucking hate that you're not safe with us."

Resting my hand on top of his, I encourage him to squeeze my throat harder, giving him the sense of total control he needs. None of us are okay right now, or we wouldn't be doing this.

Hunter's hand forms a tightening necklace that cinches around my neck, restricting the flow of air. But there's no panic. No fear. I'm safe in his hands, and that's exactly what he needs to see.

"Yours," I mouth clearly.

His brown gaze is almost pitch-black. "Mine."

Hips bucking at a brutal pace, far faster than the others and their tentative efforts to ease me in, he sprints towards the finish line.

My chest begins to burn from the restriction of air, but it only makes things more intense. Each feeling is tripled, increased by my mind grasping for anything to hold on to.

When Hunter dives off the edge into his own climax, he finally finishes. The timing is excruciating. Air races down my windpipe to inflate my lungs, on the verge of screaming for relief.

Gasping, I slump onto his chest, feeling his release mingle with the mess that's staining every inch of me. All of them mix and become one deep inside of me.

Kneeling on the bed beside me, Enzo grasps my jaw and tilts my lips to meet his. He smells sweaty from whatever he disappeared to beat to take care of his aggression.

"You tired, baby?"

"Hmm," I hum unintelligibly.

His lips tease mine. "I think you're done."

Eyes flinging open, I grab his wrist before he can retreat. "No, I'm not done. I want you too."

Enzo chuckles. "I'll carry you to the shower. How about that?"

I narrow my eyes. "Don't you want to fuck me, Enz? The rest of your family has."

Challenged levied, I watch his pupils expand, devouring the floating embers that light his amber eyes. I haven't come this far to leave him unsatisfied now.

With the others still watching, Enzo lifts me from Hunter's lap. He disregards the slick mess we've created for ourselves and positions me on his waist, like I weigh little more than air.

"You're so fucking bad," he says under his breath. "I was going to be all gentle and shit, but not when you tease me like that."

"I never asked for you to be gentle."

Sneaking a hand between us, I nudge down the waistband of his grey sweatpants. Those tight things should be illegal anyway.

"Greedy tonight, aren't you?"

My hand sneaks inside his boxers to find the promise of his hard length. "Just enjoying what's rightfully mine."

"All at once, huh?"

I look over at Leighton's pleased grin. "Leigh interrupted. I take no responsibility for this mess."

"Aren't you sore after all three of them?"

"A bit," I admit, feeling the ache between my thighs. "But I still want you."

"I'll try to be gentle, baby girl, but I need you so fucking bad."

Pinning my back against the bedroom wall, Enzo shoves his sweatpants and boxers down low enough to free his cock. His hips pin me in place before his hands return to my ass cheeks.

"I don't need you to be gentle with me," I goad.

His grin widens. "Well, it's their turn to watch you take my cock. You just saved the best until last."

When he surges into me, I hold on to his neck to take the rough thrust of his hips. I have a perfect view of the other three lounging on the bed like purring lions, full of their latest meal.

"Are they watching?" Enzo asks.

"Yes," I moan.

"Yes, what?"

He stills, holding back his next thrust.

"Yes, sir."

"Good girl. They may have had you first, but I'll be the one finishing the job."

When he slams back into me, I scream out his name for all of them to hear. Enzo's intensity is on a whole different level.

Battering his seal of possession into the very fabric of my being, he adopts the quickest pace of them all. His gentleness never arrives, and I'm so thankful for that. I want him to be rough with me.

I feel tiny in his arms, caught between the hard wall and his rippling, mountainous muscles. He ducks his head to bury it in between the rise and fall of my breasts.

His teeth nip each swell, sucking my skin into his mouth to leave a dark trail of bruises for the world to see. None of us would be here, together right now, in this room, if it wasn't for him.

He spent months keeping us all together as life tried to rip us apart at the seams. For that, I owe Enzo. My life. My soul. My vulnerability. Everything I have left to give.

Taking every beat of his cock slamming into me, he reignites my core through the fog of exhaustion. I didn't think I could possibly orgasm again, but the pangs are already starting.

"Come," he coaxes, slamming home each word with a thrust. "I know my perfect little whore has another one in her."

"You are the only man on this planet I'd allow to call me that," I pant. "Be honoured."

"You bet I am."

With my eyes locked on Hunter, Leighton and Theo, I relinquish my last scrap of control. It starts slow—building, expanding, taking over every last sense.

Enzo follows me into oblivion and surrenders at the same time, roaring through his own climax. We're both panting and tangled, our bodies slumped against the wall as we ride our releases.

I tuck my head into the crook of his neck, too tired to hold it up for a second longer. My entire body is quivering with the after-burn of another shattering orgasm.

"You okay?" Enzo huffs.

"I don't think I can walk right now."

His body vibrates with a laugh. "Good thing I've got you, then."

Tucking his arm underneath my legs, he pulls me into a cradle position so I'm tucked into his chest. My eyes fall shut, a warm hum of satisfaction pulsing through my veins.

Returning to the bathroom, Enzo yells at the others to get the bed made up then closes the door. He props me on the bathroom sink then turns to flick the shower on.

"Where did you go?" I ask sleepily.

His shoulders tense. "Downstairs to the gym. Needed to punch something."

"You didn't do enough of that tonight?"

"Clearly not." He finally turns to me, his gaze shadowed. "I meant what I said, Harlow. I don't know if I can do this job anymore."

Catching his hand, I tug him closer and press a kiss right above his sternum. "You don't have to. All I want is for you to be happy."

"If we don't do this, who will?"

"Anyone. I don't care, Enz. You're more than the people you save. After all you've been through, you deserve some peace too."

Eyes lowered, Adam's apple bobs. "I swore to you that I'd wipe out every last trace of Abaddon, and I intend to keep my word."

"And when the work is done?" I prompt.

"Then … I'll do what I should have done a long time ago and walk away. No one else is going to live my life for me. I have to do it."

Letting him lift me into the shower, I curl up against his body beneath the spray. "Where will you go?"

"Where will *we* go?" he corrects. "Our family is all that matters to me now. We can choose our next steps together."

"Sabre is Hunter's whole life. Do you think he'd walk away just like that?"

"I doubt he would have returned from Costa Rica if we didn't make him. Everyone has their limits, little one. We've reached ours."

Lifting onto my tiptoes, I strain to capture his lips. "Then we run. Together. I'll follow you four to the ends of the earth."

"Then it's a deal."

Lathering his hands in shower gel fished out from underneath the sink, I let Enzo wash every inch of me, cleansing all evidence of what just occurred in the bedroom.

He dips a hand between my legs to wash me, taking care to be gentle and checking that I'm comfortable, even after that sex-pile. His attention is still focused entirely on my needs.

"I'm so tired."

Stepping out, Enzo grabs a towel then wraps me in it. "You can rest now, baby. We're safe here for tonight."

"What about tomorrow?"

Tucking a towel around his hips, he lifts me back into his arms and carries me into the bedroom.

"That's tomorrow's problem."

Another bare mattress has mysteriously appeared on the carpeted floor next to the bed. Theo and Leighton are already collapsed on it, leaving space for us to join Hunter on the bed.

Enzo dries me off and passes me into Hunter's arms. I'm tucked beneath a sheet and spooned in the curvature of his frame. The bed dips with Enzo's solid weight joining us.

In the darkness of the room, I whisper that I love them. We may have lost everything we own tonight, but we still have each other.

Nothing can take that away.

Not now. Not ever.

CHAPTER 22
HARLOW

SAD DAY – FKA TWIGS

HOLDING Enzo's hand in a deathly tight grip, I stare past the layers of armed security at the madness swarming HQ's entrance. This is the biggest crowd that we've seen by far.

It's impossible to avoid the hysteria sweeping over the entire country now that we're holed up in the apartment above us. Anger has transformed into something far more worrying in the past week.

Madness.

Terror.

Sheer fucking delirium.

Gaggles of people form prayer circles, calling up to the heavens for protection when the approaching rapture arrives. Their hands are marked with symbols—identical Holy Trinities.

"How has Michael caused so much damage in such little time?"

Enzo shrugs in dismay. "Fear spreads far quicker than any disease. People genuinely believe the shit he's drilling into his followers."

"It feels like the world is ending."

"I suppose in their minds, it is."

It's clear that they all believe it too. Michael and his Angels of the Abyss have spread their insane message far and wide. Many people now believe that some kind of rapture is approaching.

"The sooner we get a hit on Theo's software for Daphne, the sooner we can end this." I blow out a breath. "I don't want to see where this is going."

"Me neither," he says grimly.

"Are Ethan and his team back from scouting out Grantham?"

"Arrived home last night. They're travelling to Wisbech tomorrow to investigate the other pool of victims and their families."

"And? Any leads?"

"The three victims all attended the same Bible study class," Enzo explains.

"He interviewed the other attendees, but they didn't see anything out of the ordinary."

"How did Michael get his hands on them, then?"

His expression is haunted. "By speaking in whispers. That's why people are so afraid. Anyone could be next, and there's nothing they can do to keep themselves safe."

"This is ridiculous. He isn't the devil. Michael is just a man."

"Could just a man do all this?" Enzo gestures outside. "I'm not so sure anymore."

I want more than anything to be able to disagree with him. But after all the death and destruction I've seen my uncle inflict, I'm lying to myself by pretending like Lucifer himself doesn't dwell beneath his skin.

No mere mortal could commit so many atrocities and still have the strength to rain chaos on a whole nation. Still, it isn't enough. He wants more... More pain. More blood. More atonement.

Michael isn't human.

He's a spawn of Satan.

"When's your call with the publisher?"

I try to blink the grit from my eyes. Compiling my journals into something semi-resembling a manuscript has taken countless hours of painstaking work. Thankfully, I stored them in Theo's office and avoided losing them in the fire.

"This afternoon."

"You signed the contract?" he asks.

"Yesterday. I'm turning over my work, and then it'll go into editing. Abigail wants me to be involved every step of the way to make sure they don't lose my voice."

"That's good, little one. It sounds like they're looking out for you." He drops a kiss on top of my head. "I'm so fucking proud already."

"I haven't published anything yet."

"But you will. I'm glad you didn't listen to me." Enzo gestures outside. "This is exactly why you need to speak up for yourself."

"Well, I think it's safe to say I can't make the situation any worse."

"Unfortunately, that's true."

Hyland appears and waves at us from across the reception where a tall, dark-haired man wearing thick black glasses over his eyes awaits. Foster. He's arrived.

"Here we go," I mutter.

"Still don't think you should be doing this."

"A deal's a deal, Enz. I'm not a liar. Giana gave us the information we needed, so I need to keep my end of the bargain."

"You're far too much of a good person for this world."

"Says you."

"Me?" Enzo scoffs. "I've never been called a good person before. An angry, oversized wanker with a penchant for violence? Sure."

I squeeze his hand then release it. "Well, that too. Particularly the violence part, but we love you for it."

"Ha. Thanks, baby."

Forcing myself to ignore the shouts of frenzied prayers that still manage to leak through Sabre's tinted glass entrance, we approach Foster together. That's when I spot him.

I've only ever seen my half-brother once, the day I stalked his school, hunting Giana down after I ran from Sabre. He must be eight or nine years old. His cute face is rounded with youthful innocence beneath lightly curling hair that matches mine.

Foster's eyes connect with mine from across the room. His reluctance is clear. Neither of us wants to be doing this. Unfortunately, Giana has fucked us both over.

I let Enzo stretch out a hand for him to shake first. "Thanks for coming in. I hope the protests didn't make things too difficult."

"We were brought in through the loading bay," Foster returns in a deep voice. "Quite the scene you've got outside."

Enzo gently pushes me forward. I take Foster's hand with the same enthusiasm I'd have for hugging a venomous snake.

"Harlow," he says.

"Hello."

"It's been a while. Mind telling me what you invited us here for before we go any further?"

I anxiously wring my hands together. "I thought it was time we talked." My eyes stray to the boy at his side. "All of us."

Looking over me with interest, Ulrich's mousy brown hair lays on his head in an untidy pile. We don't look much alike, despite our half-shared DNA.

Foster clears his throat. "This is my son, Ulrich." He tugs on his hand. "Ulrich, this is Harlow. She's..."

He trails off, unable to finish.

"I'm a friend of your mum," I quickly add. "It's nice to meet you. I'm sorry about all the noise outside."

"It's okay," he replies softly.

"No school today?"

He looks up at his father. "Dad said we were visiting London. I want to go to the Natural History Museum to see the dinosaurs."

A lump sticking in my throat, I crouch down on one knee to reach his height. "Do you like dinosaurs?"

Ulrich watches me suspiciously. "Yes."

I can't explain the tangled ball of emotion tightening my chest. There are too many warring sides to categorise. I'm ashamed to admit that a broken, bitter part of me wants to hate this kid.

He got a life.

A childhood.

The family I never had.

But a greater part of me feels a strange, unexpected sense of kinship. We have the same coloured hair. Giana's DNA flows in both of us—and therefore, Michael's DNA too.

He's like me.

An anomaly.

Hope born from darkness.

"I wanted to have a chat with your dad for a bit." I smile apologetically. "Is that alright? If you're hungry, my friend here can take you to the canteen to get some food."

Enzo lifts an intimidating paw to wave. "It's burger day. We even have milkshakes to go with them."

"Can I go, Dad?"

Foster unlatches his clenched jaw. "I don't know."

"The building is secure," Enzo reassures. "No one's getting in or out. You can come find us when you're done talking."

Taking a moment to deliberate, Foster eventually nods. He makes Ulrich take Enzo's hand, despite his wariness of the giant boulder that stands several feet over him.

"Meeting room on the tenth floor is all yours."

"Look after him," I instruct.

Enzo flashes me a toothy grin. "I'll have made a Sabre agent out of him by the time you get back. Don't you worry."

At the look of horror on Foster's face, Enzo guides Ulrich away. I can't help but watch the kid go, and at the last moment, he glances over his shoulder to frown at me again.

"He seems pretty switched on."

Foster laughs weakly. "You could say that. He's smarter than me already. No idea how such a bright spark came from us."

Eyes meeting again, his smile quickly fades. I let Hyland take the lead to guide us to the elevator, falling back into an awkward silence that doesn't break until we reach the meeting room.

"I'll be just outside." Hyland holds the door open for us. "Shout if you need me."

"Thanks."

The look he flashes Foster must put the fear of God in him. I gesture for him to take a seat and sit down opposite.

"Sorry. He's being paid a small fortune to keep me safe. It makes him pretty standoffish at the best of times."

"I noticed." Foster braves a chuckle before growing serious. "Why am I here, Harlow?"

I take a breath. "I've been to see Giana in prison. She asked me to reach out to you in return for information on Michael Abaddon."

His face pales. "I've not answered her calls for a reason. You could've spared me the trip. I'm not discussing Giana."

"She's still your wife, and Ulrich's mother." I sigh tiredly. "She's still *my* mother. We at least need to talk about this."

"There's nothing to say. That woman spent our entire marriage lying to my face. As far as I'm concerned, Ulrich has one parent."

"As do I. See? We're on the same page."

"Then why are you delivering her damn messages?" he snaps, his patience fading. "Look what she did to you."

"Because I am nothing like her," I fire back. "Nor my uncle. I take promises very seriously. Talking to you was her price."

That knocks the fight out of him. He scrubs his face, appearing far older than his years. Giana has well and truly broken him.

"You're right. I'm sorry."

I shrug off his apology. "I get it. If I could pretend like she never even existed, my life would be a lot easier. But that's not how family works."

"I've tried to keep all of this from Ulrich, but he's far from stupid," he replies defeatedly. "Her face was splashed all over the news for weeks. I never answer his questions."

"If it makes you feel any better, I don't have the answers to my own questions. I'm just trying to survive this and live to tell the tale."

Nodding, Foster sits back in his chair. "Go on, then. What does she want from me?"

"Contact with Ulrich."

"That isn't going to happen."

"Then tell her that yourself," I reason. "She's on suicide watch until the trial. At least put her out of her misery."

"Doesn't she deserve to be miserable?"

Hesitating, I stare up at the ceiling. "Giana and Michael became who they are through hatred. If we live our lives in the same way, we're only continuing their legacy."

Foster remains silent.

"I refuse to breed more evil from my suffering," I finish with a half-smile. "All I want is to have a normal life."

"You don't want revenge? Not even a little bit?"

"All that would create is more heartache and pain."

"Christ, Harlow," he curses. "How can you sit there and say that after all they put you through? Aren't you angry?"

"I'm angrier than people realise. But I have four men hell-bent on destroying Michael. One of us has to be thinking about the future too."

"You deserve that," Foster says honestly. "A happy future. No one deserves that more than you do. And I really hope you get it."

Sharing a moment, we both take a pause to gather ourselves. He smooths his polo shirt then offers me a nod.

"I'll speak to Giana. I'm not promising anything more than that."

"Thank you."

"I've been asked to testify at her trial. Her defence lawyer wants me to fuck up the prosecution's entire case."

"What are you going to do?"

"Tell the truth, I guess. The person who traded you off to that monster isn't the woman I married. At least I didn't think she was."

When I don't immediately respond, he braces his elbow on his knees to lean closer to me.

"The prosecution is calling you as a witness?"

"Yeah," I say flatly. "I don't want to dig up the past and have my trauma picked apart by a jury. But I have no choice."

"Getting her prosecuted is the right thing to do. You're not the only person she hurt."

"I know… It's just going to be hard seeing her up there."

"You really care about her?" he asks.

"I wish I didn't care at all, but I know what Michael did to her. She didn't stand a chance. Neither did his wife."

"I'm not sure I can ever forgive Giana for lying to me." His hands clench into fists. "But I can make this right for Ulrich's sake."

"Forgiveness isn't as black-and-white as people think." I spare him a sad smile. "You can hate someone with every fibre of your being and still forgive them for breaking you. The two can coexist."

"Do you forgive him? The killer?"

I don't answer at first.

"Shit," Foster swears. "I'm sorry, Harlow. You don't have to answer that. I have zero right to be digging around in your head."

"No, it's fine." I swallow to clear my suddenly dry throat. "I can't forgive him for what he did to my friends, but I can understand the reason his evil came to be."

"Is that enough?" He stares openly at me.

It takes a moment for the right answer to come.

"It's enough for me," I reply thickly. "I can't live my life otherwise, and honestly, all I want is to live. More than anything."

Looking into each other's eyes, I feel like we've found common ground for the first time. We've both been betrayed by the people we love. But that doesn't mean we can't choose to let go of that hurt.

"We should go and rescue Ulrich before Enzo gets him running drills with the new recruits."

"I promised him a trip to the museum for coming with me." He shakes his head. "That kid is obsessed with dinosaurs."

Holding the door open for him, I'm shocked to silence as he bundles me into a fast, tight hug that ends as quickly as it began.

"I know this means absolutely nothing to you, and I'm just some stranger, but I'm happy that you've found a home here."

"Thank you," I croak. "That actually means a lot. Even coming from you."

He flashes me a grin. "I guess I'll see you at the trial next. Save me a spot in the shitshow?"

"You bet."

We return downstairs then track down Enzo in the canteen. As promised, he's elbow deep in a tray stacked high with greasy cheeseburgers and loaded fries.

Ulrich is slurping on a strawberry milkshake and dipping his fries into the thick, pink liquid with enthusiasm. We join them in the quiet dining area where only a handful of others are eating.

"Hey, bud." Foster takes a seat next to his son. "What the heck are you doing to those fries?"

"Enzo taught me to dip them into my milkshake," he replies matter-of-factly. "I thought it was gross until I tried it."

Curious, Foster steals a fry and dips it in. His nose is scrunched up in distaste at first before he changes his tune.

"That's actually not bad."

I steal a bite of Enzo's burger. "Where did you learn that?"

"Leighton." He shrugs, his cheeks packed like a hamster. "He made us all try it out."

"Knew it. Only Leighton would think to do such a thing."

When Ulrich's done devouring his milkshake and fries, he shyly studies me from out of the corner of his eye. His dad stands and gestures for him to follow.

"We should get going." Foster glances at me. "I'll see you soon, Harlow. Keep in touch."

Enzo's eyebrows shoot up into his crop of wild black hair. It's amazing what sharing mutual trauma can do for a relationship.

"I will. Be safe."

Taking his father's hand, Ulrich politely thanks Enzo for the food, and the pair are escorted away by Hyland to leave the building. But at the last second, Ulrich breaks away and comes running back.

"Um, Harlow?"

I stand up. "Yeah?"

"I heard Dad shouting on the phone when Mum got taken away by the police. Are you really my sister?"

Heart squeezing, I kneel on the floor to reach his height again. "We have different dads, but yes, I am your half-sister."

"I always wanted a sister to play with." He frowns to himself. "Mum bought me a dog instead."

"Ulrich!" Foster calls.

"You should go with your dad."

But he stays rooted to the spot.

"Can I see you again? I miss my mum. It's quiet at home without her. I… I'd like a friend."

It takes all of my strength to hold the rush of tears at bay. Unleashing a smile instead, I rest a hand on his shoulder.

"We can be friends if you want. I'd like that too. I've never had a brother before."

"If you want to come to the museum with us, you can. It has a Titanosaur that's twelve metres long."

"It's a bit hard for me to go outside right now," I let him down gently. "But next time we'll go to the museum together."

"You promise?" he challenges.

Drawing an invisible cross over my heart, I release his shoulder. "I promise, little man. Your dad has my number if you want to call and talk to me."

"Okay." Ulrich begins to backtrack. "Bye, then."

Watching them leave, bundled away by security to slip outside discreetly, I feel the first blooms of hope in a very long time. The roots unfurl around the broken mess of my heart and begin to bud.

That's exactly why I can't hold on to my anger and hatred. No matter the pain. No matter the damaged voices in my head, screaming for their own taste of vengeance.

We still have hope, and I won't ever let that be stolen away from me again. Even if Michael wins and this has all been for nothing.

"We have incoming," Enzo warns.

Looking up, I spot them before Brooklyn shrieks my name at the top of her lungs. She's flanked by Hudson and Kade.

"Brooke!"

The handful of staff in the canteen watches us rush across the room to throw ourselves at each other like a pair of lunatics. She cinches me into a lung-squeezing hug.

"Miss me?"

"You're back." I release her then gawp down at the swell of her belly. "And looking pregnant all of a sudden."

"I'm almost nineteen weeks."

Hudson and Kade bundle me into hugs next, the former messing up my hair with a playful snort. I shove him away then inspect their matching golden tans.

"How was Bali?"

"Hot," Kade complains.

"It was beautiful." Brooklyn swats his arm. "We got home last night."

His meal discarded, Enzo sweeps her off her feet in a bear hug. "I missed your annoying backside around here, wildfire."

"Same here." Her smile fades. "We heard there has been some trouble while we were gone. What the hell is going on outside?"

"Michael's new friends." I wave off her frown. "I want to hear all about your honeymoon before we talk about this crap."

"Kade has some great stories to share." Hudson laughs. "You want to tell them about your drunken antics, or should I?"

"You promised," he accuses. "What happened in Bali, stays in Bali. I was celebrating."

"I'll totally tell you everything later," Brooklyn whispers to me. "He was in a state after a few too many strong cocktails."

"Brooke," he whines.

"Sorry, sorry!"

Unable to stop myself, I yank her back into another hug. "I missed you guys so much."

CHAPTER 23
ENZO

EVERYTHING ONCE - HOTEL MIRA

PACING UP and down Hunter's office, the countless printed photographs covering every inch of the walls around me are a constant taunt. The list of victims has only grown.

We've added the nine bodies from last month's copycat killer to the melee of destruction. With no DNA evidence or witnesses, their fates still remain unknown.

"The news has broken about Harlow signing a publishing contract." Lucas's voice rattles through the speaker of my phone. "Surprisingly, the response hasn't been awful."

"Come again? Did you say *not* awful?"

"Sabre has its critics, but the public seems genuinely interested in hearing her story. They want to know what really happened to all those women."

Propping an arm against the floor-length window, I rest on it. "Well, that's an unexpected turn of events."

"We're working with the company's marketing team to ensure that Sabre is represented in the best light. My team is handling it."

"This is her story. It isn't about us or the company. Harlow should be able to tell it however she wants."

"I'm just doing my job, Enz. There's not much else I can do to help these days. Let me keep what remains of your reputation intact."

I resist the urge to pull the trigger and give him free rein to destroy the remnants of the company we've built from scratch. Since talking to Harlow, all I can think about is leaving.

Running.

Hiding.

Fucking anything.

I just want out. The years of trauma and emotional exhaustion are finally catching up to me after being buried in the irretrievable pits of my psyche. We're all burnt out and at our wits' end.

"I have to go, Lucas. Got a briefing with the superintendent in half an hour, and I need to practise my nice face."

"You have one?" He snorts.

"Apparently not, hence the practising."

"Well, good luck with that. Tell Harlow to check her emails later. I need a few quotes to go in our press release about the book."

Ending the call, I toss my phone on Hunter's cluttered desk. He's at the hospital with Harlow, attending his monthly checkup.

The stack of paperwork that Sabre's legal team had delivered sits discarded next to my phone. I took the liberty of getting the necessary forms together for Harlow.

I wish I could say that it doesn't bother me whose surname she chooses. This isn't about us. It's her way of reclaiming her identity.

That doesn't stop me from itching with a caveman-like need to fill out the paperwork myself and stamp my surname on there, regardless of what anyone else thinks.

My phone vibrates with a text, and I snatch it back up.

Harlow: Arrived at the hospital safe. Just waiting to go in.

Enzo: Good. How is he?

Harlow: Nervous, I think. I'll keep you posted.

Enzo: Stay with Ethan, and be safe.

Harlow: Always x

The door to the office creaks open, emitting a bleary-eyed Theo back in his usual flannel shirt and tight grey jeans.

"You got a minute?"

I wave him in. "Sure."

He lumbers over to the conference table then perches on the edge. "Two of Matthew's friends have been released on bail."

"What the fuck?"

"They've been told to steer clear of us or risk being thrown back in prison if they violate the rules."

I bury my face in my hands. "Jesus fucking Christ. They burned down our goddamn house, and no one gives a shit?"

"They were charged, Enz. Matthew and the others couldn't afford the bond and are still locked up. That's something."

"What did the fire department say?"

"It's still a disaster zone," he confirms. "Massive structural damage caused by the fire. The property has been condemned."

"Awesome. That's just what I wanted to hear. So we're now homeless on top of being totally fucked, right?"

"I'd hardly call being forced to live in a multi-million-pound skyscraper homeless, but if you insist on being dramatic, sure."

"I really don't want to hear your optimism right now." I sigh.

Hopping off the table, Theo trails closer to rest a palm on my shoulder. "We made it out safely."

"This time. What about the next time our family is in danger? We never should've taken this case in the first place."

"But then we wouldn't have Harlow," he reasons.

And the thought of living a single goddamn moment without Harlow makes me want to jump off a fucking cliff.

Theo moves to the desk, picking up the stack of legal papers. "Harlow's going ahead with the name change, then?"

"She wants to get it sorted before things progress with the book. That bloody surname has haunted her for too long."

"Not sure one of ours is much better. The entire world knows and hates us all by now."

I look back out of the window at the early November mist clinging to London's skyline. It's a wet, dreary day as winter arrives, replacing golden leaves with rain and misery.

"Where would you go?"

"Hmm?" Theo hums distractedly.

"If you could leave the city. Hell, this whole country. Anywhere in the world to start a brand-new life, where no one knows our names."

Dropping the paperwork, he moves to my side. "Honestly? I have no clue. This life is all I've ever known."

"Maybe that's the problem. We've spent so long running from one fight to the next, we forgot to stop and actually live for ourselves."

"I'd be open to a change."

"You would?" I repeat in surprise.

Theo shrugs, his eyes on the gloomy sky. "Hacking began as a way for me to survive. I've been lucky to make a career out of it. That doesn't mean I want this forever."

"I don't think I've ever seen you without your laptop in hand." I gesture towards the device left on the table. "Who's this new Theodore Young?"

He fights off a laugh. "He grew up."

"Speaking of… You still haven't told Harlow that it was your birthday last week, have you?"

Ducking his head, he stares down at his Chucks, battered and mud-streaked from overuse.

"I don't celebrate. You know that."

"She'd kill us both if she knew."

"Which is exactly why I've kept it a secret," he retorts. "I've never celebrated my birthday, and I'm not starting now."

I clip him around the back of his head. "You're still a mystery to me, even after all these years."

"I'm going to take that as a compliment."

"Yeah, it really wasn't one."

Theo pushes his glasses up to rest in his blonde curls so he can scrub his face. "You know I grew up without a family. Birthdays just weren't a thing. It isn't a big deal."

"Do you ever think about finding your family?"

He spares me an uncertain look. "Where is all this coming from today? You're starting to freak me out a bit."

"Just thinking about stuff. That's all."

Replacing his glasses, he wipes a non-existent speck from the window. "I used to. Sometimes, I dream about them, but I can never see their faces."

"Maybe they had a good reason for leaving you in foster care all those years ago. You don't want to find out?"

"I don't fucking know, Enz." He sighs unhappily. "I have my family right here. That's all that matters to me now."

The blare of a screeching alarm emanating from his phone interrupts us. Cursing, Theo grabs it and peers down at the screen.

"No way."

"What is it?" I ask urgently.

"We've had a hit on the facial recognition software we've been running on public CCTV feeds. Daphne's emerged."

"Fuck!"

Racing over to his laptop, Theo loads his complex, hand-coded surveillance program. It's taken years of perfection and first helped us when Harlow went missing in Croyde.

Fingers flying across the keyboard in a frantic blur, Theo locates the hit then loads the feed for us to check. It appears to be a camera outside a tiny village shop and petrol station.

I scan the grainy feed, unable to suck in a breath. Theo's frozen in place next to me, waiting for our target to come into sight.

"Please," he begs.

When a short, rounded woman walks into shot as she heads for the cash machine, I feel my heart explode. Her head tilts up, clocking the camera before quickly hiding her face and leaving with her cash.

I search through the stacks of files scattered across the table and locate the sparse profile we've gathered on Daphne. We managed to find an old driver's licence photo in government records.

"Is it her?" I hold the piece of paper next to his laptop screen. "She left as soon as she spotted that camera."

Theo rewinds the footage. "Maybe."

Setting it to slow motion, we both glance between the two images. It's all there. The sharpened hook of her nose, round chin and wide-set features beneath floss-like, silvery hair.

"Fuck," I repeat in awe. "Fuck! That's her."

He double-checks the location. "Holcombe. Christ, that's close to where those bodies were found on the beach."

"When was this?"

"Couple of hours ago. It takes time for the software to process through millions of CCTV feeds across the country."

I grip the edges of the table, taking a moment to focus myself. We've been waiting for this news ever since Giana spilled her guts about her secret half-sister. It's been agonising.

"Call Rayna. We need to speak to the owner of that petrol station and get a trace on the bank card she used to withdraw the cash."

Theo's already on the secure channel we use to communicate. His fingers quake with each movement across his keyboard.

"This is it," he says excitedly. "If she's helping Abaddon, she will lead us straight back to where he's been laying low."

I clap his shoulder. "Nice work, Theo. You just broke this case wide open."

"We still need to find the damn woman."

"Just take the compliment for once in your life."

He snorts. "Thanks."

"Alright, enough of that. Get an ID on that bank card, and see if she owns any property in Holcombe. I'll call the others."

"Leighton's at lunch with his parents," Theo replies. "He's going to pick Hunter, Harlow and Ethan up from the hospital."

Stepping out of the office, I try Leighton's phone first and get no answer. The same for Hunter and Harlow. Ethan picks up on the first ring with a barked greeting.

"Enzo."

"We've got something here. I need you to bring them straight back from the hospital when Hunter's done with his checkup."

"Got a bit of a situation here too. Hunter had a meltdown after his appointment. I think Harlow's with him now."

"What?" I snap. "You're there to keep them both safe, goddammit. You need to find them right now."

"Copy that."

"Call me when it's done."

With the call disconnected, I look around the office again. The faces staring back at me suddenly feel alive—their eyes lit with defiance and demanding my attention.

I can't let this be my legacy. If we're going to leave Sabre to serve the next generation, we have to finish this. Our chance to bring Abaddon down has finally arrived.

"Fox is speaking to the owner now." Theo sits at the table, facing his laptop. "We'll hack into her banking records to get an address."

"Good. Ethan's tracking down Hunter and Harlow to bring them both back here. Sounds like the appointment didn't go well."

"Are they okay?"

"I don't know yet. He's going to check back in."

Firing off a text message to Hudson, I take a seat and wait. It doesn't take long for him, Brooklyn and Kade to bound into the room, leaving their late breakfast in the canteen behind.

"You found Daphne?" Kade exclaims.

"Almost." Theo pulls out the chair next to him. "I could use your help overriding these security protocols."

Kade takes a seat as Brooklyn nears to circle an arm around my neck. She's on light-duty after insisting on still working despite her pregnancy. None of the guys were happy about it.

"You okay?" she murmurs.

"I just need this to be it."

"I know, big guy." She moves a hand to her belly. "We're going to finish this together."

"There's no *we* in it. You're grounded. No exceptions this time."

"Hey!" she protests. "This is my case too. I want to see it through just as much as you do."

"That's final, Brooke. I'm not risking anyone else. We've lost too much already, and I won't fucking lose you too."

With a sour look, she reluctantly backs down. I don't give a shit if it hurts her precious feelings. Becket already paid the price for my decisions, and that won't happen ever again.

"Fox?" Theo picks up his ringing phone. "Tell me you have something."

He listens and curses under his breath. Kade hands him a piece of paper so he can write the information down that Fox is relaying.

"Good work." Hanging up, Theo looks around at us all. "We've got a name. She's been living under a false identity."

Springing into action, Kade takes the information and begins to input it into the laptop he brought with him.

"Do we really think she's spent the last decade helping this asshole without anyone knowing?" Hudson wonders.

"Why else would she leave her entire life behind and adopt a new identity?" Brooklyn replies. "She has to be with him."

"You said that Harlow has no memories of her," he reasons. "She can't have been there."

I crack my knuckles impatiently. "Harlow would also be the first to admit that her memory isn't the most reliable thing."

When Kade yells at his laptop, hazel eyes blown wide and darting between us, my anticipation peaks. I've never felt so nervous before.

Taking a look, Theo breaks out in a smile. "We've fucking got her."

CHAPTER 24
HARLOW

I RUN TO YOU - MISSIO

SITTING in the hospital waiting room, I watch Hunter's leg jiggle. He's wound tighter than a coiled spring and refuses to speak to me, despite allowing me to come along today.

Dropping a hand on his shaking leg, I squeeze to get his attention then lift an eyebrow in a silent question.

It's weird to see him dressed in a plain T-shirt and fitted, designer jeans, forgoing smart attire. He's wearing his hair shaved still, the scar across his skull shining in the light.

"I'm fine," he grumbles.

I don't need to use sign language for him to see my disbelief.

"It's just a checkup. You didn't need to come."

His lying is so obvious. I know Hunter better than he thinks. This stubborn, macho display only solidifies my belief that he's actually crying out for help.

The hair on the back of my neck stands on end. Breath held, I glance around the quiet waiting room. It's empty aside from two women sitting opposite and whispering to each other.

Nudging Hunter, I glance over at the women, indicating for him to look. His thick brows are drawn together as he studies them, his leg still shaking up and down to an anxious beat.

"Ignore them," he murmurs.

The scowl on the older woman's face deepens. Neither of them looks happy to be trapped opposite us, even in a hospital waiting room.

I'm surprised by how much it hurts to be hated by total strangers, but having Ethan standing on guard makes me feel better.

"Mr Rodriguez?" a voice calls.

Gently touching his arm, I point towards the audiologist peeking his head out of the office door. Hunter grabs my hand so fast, I almost jump out from my seat.

He squeezes my fingers in a death grip but refuses to move. I mouth a question, asking him what's wrong.

"Nothing," he blurts.

I raise a brow. I'm not blind.

"Just… I don't want to go in."

Offering him a hand, I mouth back. "*Here.*"

Even if he thinks that he doesn't need me, I know he does. Trying to cope with this alone is killing him inside. I'll follow him until he's sick of the sight of me if that penetrates his shields.

He must read it on my face—the sheer desperation I feel to carry some of this burden for him. His expression breaks, offering a peek of the torment beneath his façade.

"Please don't leave me," he whispers, unable to hold it in for a second longer.

The last piece of my heart shatters.

"*Never*," I sign back.

Inside the doctor's office, we take seats opposite a paper-strewn desk. Doctor Vorderman took over from the intensive care team when Hunter was discharged and has monitored his recovery in the many months since then.

She accompanies her words with sign language. "*How are you?*"

"Fine," he grinds out.

I have to bite my tongue to prevent myself from answering for him. The stress of the investigation and being forced to flee our second home in less than six months is far from *fine*.

"I've looked over the results from your recent set of scans." She writes on a whiteboard to communicate the longer sentences. "You're seven months into your recovery."

"And?" Hunter prompts.

"There has been no improvement in your right eardrum's functioning. This is likely to be the final result now."

Hunter turns to look out of the window, offering a view across London's many glittering skyscrapers. He doesn't respond to her attempts to recapture his attention with waved hands.

We didn't expect his hearing to ever come back on its own. The other doctors confirmed that the accident permanently damaged the remaining functionality of Hunter's hearing.

But I think a part of him was still holding out hope, no matter how remote. We can't help but wish for the unattainable in life. Hope is simultaneously our biggest flaw and greatest asset.

"I'm sorry," I rush to apologise. "He's having a difficult time right now."

"Understandable," the doctor hums. "I'm sure this isn't the news he was wanting to hear after all these months of recovery."

"What are our options?"

"Now that we have a better understanding of his situation, we're willing to consider a surgically fitted cochlear implant."

"Surgery?"

"Yes," she confirms. "But I must stress, it isn't a guaranteed fix. Hunter has sustained severe damage to both of his eardrums, and there's no fix for that."

I turn to the frozen statue of tension next to me. Hunter has completely zoned out, his gaze unfocused and hands curled into white-knuckled fists. He's done engaging.

Poking his side, I make him look at me. "*Listen.*"

He dismisses me with a shrug.

I grab his shoulder. "*Surgery.*"

I want to smack him hard enough to knock some sense back into his stubborn backside. Avoiding reality isn't going to make this any easier.

"Here." Doctor Vorderman slides a brochure over. "This details the pros and cons. He needs to think over this carefully."

Hunter reluctantly accepts the paperwork and scans over it, his eyes slowly widening as he reads through the complex procedure.

"Will it work?" I ask.

"Not necessarily. There are risks involved with this operation. The implant bypasses the internal damage to stimulate the auditory nerve directly. It doesn't cure his deafness."

"So he still won't be able to hear?"

"At best, it will offer a representation of the environment that will allow Hunter to comprehend and piece together certain sounds."

"Like a puzzle."

"Precisely," she answers.

Hunter watches our exchange, his eyes tracing our lip movements and following the doctor's written communication on the whiteboard.

"How soon can we do it?" he demands.

She taps the list of potential complications and risks outlined in the brochure. Hunter ignores her completely, his mind already made up.

"I want to do it as soon as possible."

"*Think,*" she signs.

"I don't need to think about it. I've made my decision. I want to do the surgery. You said that I'm ready, so let's do it."

He flinches when I try to take his hand in mine. I halt, my chest stinging from the rejection. His shields are slamming back down.

"I'm doing this. That's my choice."

Reluctantly, Doctor Vorderman nods. "*Okay.*"

With a throat clear, Hunter abruptly stands up and storms from the room, the brochure still clutched in his hands like a precious diamond. The office door slams shut behind him.

"I'm so sorry."

"Please don't apologise," she consoles. "Sudden loss of hearing is a deeply traumatic event."

"He's been struggling for a while now. His headaches are so debilitating. Is there anything we can do?"

"Unfortunately not. They may ease over time, but this is an aftereffect of his head injury that we anticipated."

I bite my lip, wrestling with the truth. "I'm worried about his mental health too. We thought returning to England would help, but he still won't let us in."

"Do you know if Hunter has been accessing any psychological support? Perhaps talking to a professional will be beneficial."

"We tried to convince him to speak to a therapist, but he refused. He isn't exactly the talking type."

"Of that, I'm convinced." She laughs. "I can recommend several local charities and services that work with the deaf community that may be useful. He should talk to someone."

Once she's scribbled down some websites and contact numbers, I accept the sheet of paper with a weary sigh.

"I'll talk to him."

"If he's going to do this surgery, he needs to be in the best frame of mind. It will be a long recovery, and Hunter will have to relearn how to communicate if the implant is successful."

I already know that none of us will be able to talk Hunter out of this, no matter the risks involved. He'd risk a deadly infection or making his condition worse if it meant he may hear again.

"There is support available for you as well," she adds meaningfully. "You're all adjusting to a new way of living, and that's tough."

"We have each other for that."

"It's something to bear in mind."

Muttering my thanks, I take the papers and stuff them into my handbag. "What happens now?"

"We will schedule an appointment with the surgical team to discuss the procedure and make the necessary arrangements."

"Good. We'll wait to hear from you."

"Thanks for coming in, Harlow."

Taking my handbag, I rush to leave and head back into the now-deserted waiting area. Hunter is nowhere to be seen, but Ethan is still propped up in the corner of the room.

"He went for some fresh air."

"Please can you bring the car around?" I sigh. "I'll track him down and meet you downstairs."

"Sure you don't need help?"

"No, I've got this."

Exiting into the adjacent concrete stairwell leading deeper into the hospital, I search around for Hunter's broad shoulders and shaved head. It doesn't take me long to track him down.

Knees pulled up to his chest and face hidden from sight, he's sitting on the top step, his shoulders shaking. It breaks my heart to see him so lost and alone.

"Hunt," I croak.

None of us can truly penetrate the lonely bubble that's suffocating him, using sign language or not. It's just a sticking plaster.

Sitting on the step next to him, I lean my head on his shoulder. His breaths are coming in sharp, pained inhales, and his head droops to rest against mine, too heavy to hold up.

"I can't live like this anymore," he says in a thick voice. "It's killing me inside. I've lost everything—my hearing, my work, my whole life."

Lifting my head, I slide a finger under his scruff-covered chin to bring his dark eyes back to mine. The espresso-coloured depths shine with angry tears.

"You haven't lost me," I enunciate slowly so he can read my lips.

He tries to shake his head, but I grip his chin tighter.

"You will never lose our family."

When he can't interpret what I'm saying, I repeat the words slower, signing out the words to accompany my lip movements.

"It's so fucking hard just to have a normal conversation," he rasps. "Look at us. I wish I could hear what you're saying to me."

Pecking the corner of his mouth, I kiss along his cheekbones, up to the socket of his left eye. Tears soak into my lips, allowing his grief to pierce deep into my heart.

"I've given you my heart, and I won't take it back, no matter how much you're breaking it by pushing me away."

"You want me to do what to you?"

Hunter is completely confused now and fighting to hold in a strangled laugh. Sometimes, even I forget he can't hear me.

"*Lip-read*," I spell out with my hands instead. "*Practice*."

"Or maybe I just hear what I want to now," he jokes, wiping his cheeks. "The world is more tolerable that way."

Sliding his hand into the mass of my hair, he tilts my head up to crash his lips into mine. I squeak in shock, caught in the hungry storm of his teeth and tongue.

His other hand roams down my body to squeeze the swell of my breast through my T-shirt. I don't have a bra on. With the madness of the past couple of weeks, we haven't done laundry yet.

Hunter's finger teases the hardening pebble of my nipple, sensitised by the cotton covering my chest. Fire sweeps over me until all I can think about is climbing inside his skin to meld us into one.

"Come on." He takes my hand. "I want to feel your pretty cunt hugging my cock, and I don't give a fuck who hears us."

Half-carrying me down the stairs, we burst onto the floor beneath the auditory clinic. It's a quiet treatment centre, but the reception desk is deserted, and there's no one in sight.

Two powerful arms latch around my waist, and I swallow a squeal as Hunter hoists me up. I'm pinned over his shoulder, and the hospital blurs around me.

He sneaks into an empty booth then drags the medical curtain across to hide us. When his palm cracks against my ass, I yelp in shock.

"Hunt—"

Dropping me to the linoleum, Hunter shoves me against the wall. His hips pin me with no space to flee, allowing his mouth to pepper kisses against my throat.

Teeth cutting into my skin, he sucks on my neck to leave a mark, his cock pushing into my core. This angry brand of hunger is new, but it turns me on far more than I'd ever expect.

Gripping the waistband of my jeans, Hunter shoves them over my hips and peels them off. I grab his shoulders as he lowers himself to the floor, kissing my quivering pussy through my panties.

"I want to taste your come on my tongue," he says darkly.

"We can't do this here."

But his eyes aren't watching for my response. He's preoccupied by yanking the panties down my thighs and securing his mouth to my bare mound. I arch my back, unable to hold in a groan.

Swiping his thumb over my clit, his tongue slips between my wet folds to lap at the heat gathering inside of me. When he spears my entrance with his tongue, my thighs close around his head.

With desire-flecked eyes flicking up to watch me, he sucks my clit into his mouth. The attention of his lips on my bundle of nerves sends bolts of sizzling electricity up my spine.

I don't care where we are anymore. All I can feel is him—kissing, sucking and licking every inch of me with so much enthusiasm, I'm on the verge of bursting already.

"That's it," he purrs. "Let me taste those sweet juices."

Hips bucking, my vision explodes when he pushes a finger deep inside my slit. He barely has to touch me. I'm already gone, the pent-up backlog of sensation washing over every inch of me.

"So soon?" he teases. "You're such a fucking good girl. Let me clean that up for you."

Hunter's tongue laps up the warmth trickling over my cunt, cleaning up the mess he's made for himself. I blink to clear my vision, my legs trembling from the powerful aftershocks.

Drawing to his full height, there's a wicked gleam in his eyes. Holding my hips, he quickly spins me around and steers me over to the unmade hospital bed in the corner.

"Bend over, sweetheart. Spread those legs for me."

Wrapping my fingers around the metal bars of the bed frame, I push backwards against his erection. Fuck, he feels so big and hard against my entrance, even through his jeans.

The clink of his belt causes my pulse to spike. I pant and writhe, bent over the bed until the softness of his tip is pushing up against my slit. He's an inch from heaven. I need him to fill me up right now.

Hunter's cock inches just inside of me. "You're so goddamn tight."

The bed rattles as he pushes deep in one thrust. I scream out, gripping the bars tighter. Stars explode behind my eyelids, and Hunter curses before pulling out to slam straight back in.

With only a scrap of curtain protecting us from anyone who may walk in, I'm so wildly turned on that I don't even care why Hunter's doing this. If he'd rather fuck than talk, then I'll take his rage.

Hand snaking around me, his fingertips crawl upwards to press against my lips. I accept the digits and swirl my tongue around them.

"Perfect, baby," he praises.

With his fingers soaked in my saliva, I have no idea what to expect until I feel them reappear between my spread ass cheeks. Moving higher, Hunter circles the tight ring of my back entrance.

"Being inside you with the others was so hot," he admits. "I've thought of nothing else since. I can't wait to share you again."

Head thrown back, I bite out another loud moan as his index finger pushes inside me.

He moves so slow; it's a torturous tease, feeling his finger easing into me while I'm still full of his huge length.

"My tight girl. Does that feel good?"

I find the sense to nod.

"Let me fuck both holes now, then."

Easing his finger out, his breath is hot against my ear as he pushes it back in at the same time his cock surges into my slit. His timing is perfect.

Swivelling his hips, a hand pushes against my tailbone to bend me even farther over. I'm splayed across the cheap hospital mattress, the cool plastic making my nipples sing.

With his length battering into me, thrust after thrust, the pressure inside my core grows again. The bed is rattling with each movement, but the echo of voices snaps me out of the haze.

"First appointment is in thirty minutes. Can we get the booths all prepped and ready?"

"Of course, Doctor Malik."

Startled, I push myself upright and grab Hunter's wrist to force him to stop. My nails bite into his skin, and his hips halt behind me. Looking over my shoulder, I mouth through my panic.

"People."

"Shit," Hunter curses.

Pulling out, he allows me to stand and turn around. Before he can pull his jeans back into place, I grab a handful of his white t-shirt.

"No," I enunciate.

"What do you want?"

Warmth is soaking into my thighs from my first release. He's transformed me into this needy, wanton animal, and I refuse to leave this booth without getting exactly what I want.

"You."

Brows raised in surprise, his hands seize my hips and lift me up. My legs automatically wrap around his waist until I'm clinging to the hard, chiselled lines of his chest.

"I want to come again," I mewl desperately.

He reads the plea on my lips. "Better be quiet then, if you don't want to get caught."

The hum of conversing voices picks up, adding weight to his words. I battle to hold in a strangled cry when he slides back into me, taking advantage of the position to seek an even deeper angle.

Kneading my ass to lift me with each pump, Hunter controls the frenzied tangle of our bodies like a merciless puppet master with no morals. All he wants is the promise of my release seeping into him.

"Check booth thirteen for swab packs, will you?"

"On my way," a voice acquiesces.

I smack his chest to mouth a warning. "*Coming*!"

With a wickedly devilish grin, he slaps a hand over my mouth and ducks behind the screen separating the two beds in the booth. We just fit behind it, our bodies barely covered by the plain fabric.

I scream into Hunter's hand when his cock surges back into me, despite the shadowed figure that draws back the booth's other curtain and enters to check the supply cupboard.

They're only a couple of metres away, but the voice counting supplies doesn't stop Hunter from trapping me against the wall and resuming his cruel, battering pace.

He leans close to whisper in my ear. "Come all over my cock, sweetheart."

Driving into me, he takes me to the edge of oblivion and gleefully shoves me off into the abyss. I throw my head back, my loud moan silenced by his palm.

The threat of getting caught adds power to the waves lapping at my insides. They're encroaching higher, forcing my release to rise into a threatening tsunami.

If he wasn't holding me up, I'd melt into a satisfied puddle at his feet. I'm nothing more than putty in his hands, being moulded into a shape of his choosing, and it feels so good to be owned.

"Fuck," he pants.

The nearby shadow suddenly halts. "Is someone there?"

Heart leaping into my throat, I slap my hand over Hunter's mouth. We're both shuddering and fighting to breathe evenly, but the rush of panic only heightens my surging adrenaline.

Letting the silence drag for a moment, the footsteps eventually move away, leaving the booth. The need to giggle inappropriately rises up my windpipe, but I hold back.

This is not a position I want to be caught in by a complete stranger—butt naked with Hunter's come running down my legs.

Releasing my clamp on his mouth, I let his forehead connect with mine. We suck in each other's air for a moment, neither willing to move despite the people moving around us.

"I'm sorry," he blurts, his nose nudging mine. "I've pushed you all away. It doesn't mean that I don't want to be with you."

I stroke a hand over his neat beard, silently forgiving him.

"Thank you for sticking with me," he continues gruffly. "Not many people would. You've saved my whole family, Harlow."

I'd give anything in the world to be able to whisper how I feel and for this awful barrier keeping us apart to crumble. But there's nothing that would ever convince me to abandon this man.

He saved me once.

I'll happily spend the rest of my life, long or short, repaying that debt a thousand times over. If nothing else, I can die knowing that I have loved, and I am loved, so very deeply.

Sliding my arm around his chest, I use the tip of my finger to carefully trace a reply on his back. His eyes narrow as he attempts to decipher each imaginary letter drawn on his t-shirt.

I LOVE YOU.

His mouth crinkles in a satisfied smile. "Yeah. Ditto."

As we rush to replace our clothing and find a way to sneak out of the clinic without being spotted, I feel my phone vibrating in my jeans pocket.

"Shit," I curse to myself.

There are four missed calls from Ethan and a dozen more from Enzo. The additional text messages from Theo force my heart to leap into my throat.

Theo: We've got a location for Daphne. This is it.

Hunter peers over my shoulder and blanches. "They've found her?"

I nod back.

His hand slides into mine. "You're not happy?"

Chest tight, I try to categorise what I'm feeling. The relief I was expecting never comes. Instead, I manage a shrug.

"I'm scared."

His eyes are fixed on my lips. "Scared?"

I nod in confirmation.

"Of what?"

Confused tears begin to roll down my cheeks. Hunter takes the time to kiss them away, one by one, his thumbs stroking my skin.

"The end," I mouth back.

It takes him a second to compute my words before he smiles in that toe-curling, forbidden way that first entranced me, despite how utterly petrified I was of him back when we first met.

"This isn't the end, sweetheart. It's the start of our forever."

CHAPTER 25
HARLOW

ALONE MADE OF ICE - MALDITO

CROUCHED in the back of the insulation-lined van, I let Enzo adjust the straps on my bulletproof vest. He's been hard-faced and deep in concentration since we landed at the private airfield a few hours ago.

"Is that tight enough?" he asks.

"I can barely breathe."

He loosens one of the straps to release the pressure on my lungs. "Better?"

"Yeah, thanks."

Checking over my body armour one more time, he nods to himself. "You're ready to go."

I grab his hand before he can pull away. "Please talk to me."

Blowing out a breath, Enzo sits back on his haunches. He's had to crouch low to fit inside the support van that's accompanying our convoy of vehicles, carrying weapons, supplies and surveillance tech.

"You've already made up your mind about coming on this raid. I can't stop you."

"You trained me yourself," I remind him.

"That didn't stop us from getting blown to hell in Wales. We can handle this. I don't know why you're taking the risk."

"Because if Michael is in there, I want to be the one who puts an end to this. If you don't get why that's important to me, then I can't help you."

When I try to dodge past him to slip out of the van and join the others, Enzo bands an arm in front of the door to block me.

I'm trapped and pulled backwards until I fall onto his lap. Two terrified amber eyes peer down at me, shadowed by the scruff of his raven hair falling over his face.

"Little one," he rasps.

"Just let me go."

"No, listen. We haven't come this far for me to lose you now. I promised you his head on a platter, and I will deliver."

"I don't need you to deliver," I snark back. "This is my fight as much as it is yours. We do this together or not at all."

His chest vibrates with a sigh. "You're getting as stubborn as Brooklyn. Do you know that?"

I can't help but laugh. "Someone has to keep your ego in check. We're a team. Let's end this as a team."

Lips finding mine, he kisses me passionately, communicating all of the fears that we could spend hours arguing about.

We're both fucking scared, but that isn't going to stop me from doing this. I've earned the right to be on this team.

"I love you," Enzo murmurs into my lips. "Whatever happens to us when this case is over, I need you to remember that."

"And I need you to know that the only reason I've made it this far is knowing that after this, I get to keep all of you. Forever."

"Forever," he echoes.

Swinging the door open, he helps me climb out into the cool lash of winter air. The memory of Costa Rica's warm sandy beaches from the summer feels like a distant dream now.

"Can I start a petition for us to go back to our private villa afterwards?" I joke. "I've decided this country is too cold."

Enzo kisses my temple. "Works for me. I miss our daily dirt bike rides. We still need to get you a bike for this country."

"Let's add it to the after list."

"The after list?"

"I'm keeping one for when this is all over."

Linking hands, we head for the gathering of teams outside Theo's blacked-out surveillance van. We're set up in a remote field, surrounded by abandoned barns that our police contact cleared.

Suited up and ready to go, Leighton is handing out earpieces to the rest of our raiding party—Hunter, Hudson, Ethan and Hyland.

Theo and his team are on comms, with Brooklyn monitoring from the safety of HQ, much to her displeasure. Her husbands refused to compromise on this occasion.

"Here." Leighton hands me an earpiece. "Never thought I'd say this, but you look hot in bulletproof armour."

I slot it into place. "I'll take the compliment. Are you sure about joining us on this raid?"

"No way am I sitting behind a damn computer screen and listening to shit go south again. I'm sticking to you like glue."

"Sounds hot."

"It could be." He waggles his eyebrows. "Maybe I'll get to take that armour off you later when all this is done."

"If you like it so much, don't you want to see me in the armour and nothing else?"

His tongue flops out like an overexcited puppy. "Now you're speaking my language, Goldilocks."

"Alright, listen up." Enzo claps his hands at the front of the group. "The target's house is half a mile from here. We don't have a police cordon in place to avoid spooking her."

Everyone's loading up with weapons and gear, listening to his instructions. I unlock the case that carries my gun then strap it in the holster fastened around my thigh.

"We have reason to believe that Michael Abaddon may be holed up with the target. It's crucial that we capture this bastard alive."

Enzo looks pointedly at Hudson, who flips him off.

"You always ruin my fun."

"That goes for all of you." Enzo looks around the group. "Use force only if necessary. I want this to be a clean extraction."

Poking his head out of the nearby van, Theo is geared up in his headset. "I'll be keeping surveillance with the team."

I catch his eyes and force a smile on my face. His reassuring stare gives me the boost of strength I need to do this.

"Don't forget about me." Brooklyn's voice buzzes in our earpieces. "Enzo, bring my husbands back alive, or there will be hell to pay."

"You got it, wildfire. Let's move out."

We split into three groups, taking a darkened van each to blend into the early evening shadows. The rural rolling hills of Holcombe pass by in a blur with Hunter driving our van.

"Did you fill out that paperwork last night?" Leighton asks from the passenger seat.

"No, Leigh."

"Why not?"

I pull my earpiece out. "For starters, we were prepping for this last-minute raid. But I also still don't know which surname to take."

He removes his earpiece as well to give us a moment of privacy. "It's a big decision, especially with the book coming out next year."

"I thought you were about to convince me to publish it under Harlow Rodriguez."

"As much as I'd fucking love that, I don't think you should choose our surname."

"You don't?" I ask in surprise.

Leighton looks over his shoulder to face me. "There's still us with that name. My parents. Enzo has his aunt. We've got a family."

"So?"

"We have other people."

I quickly catch on. "And Theo doesn't have anyone."

"Exactly. Young isn't even his real surname. It's just what he was assigned when his parents abandoned him as a child."

"You don't think it would upset the others?"

"Why?" Leighton challenges. "Theo is our brother. You're ours. So it doesn't matter whose name you choose."

I want to melt into a relieved puddle at his feet. "Thanks, Leigh. I needed to hear that."

"I've got you, princess."

Hunter pulls into a small residential area, the thatched roof cottages all painted in mottled shades of white.

We pass the tiny shop and petrol station that captured Daphne's face and replace our earpieces to get ready for the final approach.

"This place is tiny."

"Perfect for hiding in plain sight," Leighton agrees.

Theo's voice whispers into my ear. "There's an old farmhouse on the edge of town registered under her false identity. Lots of land."

I don't need him to fill in the blanks. Michael's running his base of operations from somewhere. This is the ideal hideout.

We all congregate in an empty car park, surrounded by fields of corn and the distant spires of a local church. I climb out, following the two brothers.

"The house is over the back of this field." Enzo gestures into the distance. "We're going to approach as three teams to cover the perimeter and request their surrender."

"Request?" Hudson scoffs incredulously.

"We don't know who is in there. Could even be innocent lives. I'm not having anyone caught in the crossfire this time around."

Chastised, Hudson checks the various close-hand combat knives he keeps strapped to his gear and nods in submission.

"Look out."

Theo's voice follows the quiet hum of his drone zipping above us, offering a bird's eye view of the cornfield that reaches beyond our line of sight.

"If anyone makes a run for it, I'll call them out. We've got the whole team running surveillance. No one makes it out of our sight."

All prepared, we move in single file and dive into the deserted cornfield. The stalks have long since been stripped and cut down, leaving empty husks behind for the winter.

I follow Hunter and Hudson with Enzo at my back, keeping me sandwiched between walls of muscle. We move at a slow pace, approaching the shadow of a three-story house on the horizon.

"It's big," I whisper.

"Grade II listed property purchased five years ago," Brooklyn answers in my ear. "I've got the deeds up. She was a cash buyer."

"How did Daphne afford it?"

"Don't forget the husband," Theo reminds. "He left her a handsome sum, plus the property to be sold. Very convenient."

There isn't a single part of me that wants to meet this woman. Even if she is technically another relative. The signs are all pointing towards her being a soulless psychopath like her brother.

"Focus up," Enzo growls. "Fan out, and get the place surrounded."

Emerging into the clearing that surrounds the wooden frame and wide, peeling porch of the farmhouse, there's a faint light emanating from inside.

Before we can take another step, the front door opens with an ominous creak. A shadowed figure emerges, her short, curved body lit by the light leaking out from inside.

"Don't move!" Enzo bellows. "The place is surrounded. We just want to talk to Daphne Portcastle."

Everyone has their weapons trained on the person, taking tentative steps against Enzo's command. I keep my weapon stashed and move forward an inch.

"Who are you?"

Creeping down the porch steps, her wrinkled face is revealed. "Don't recognise your own flesh and blood, girl?"

She's small, her back slightly hunched beneath the weight of the world. Her eyes are sharp and perceptive, scanning over the numerous weapons threatening to split open her skull.

"Took you long enough," she rasps, her voice low and grating. "I gave it twenty-four hours before you broke down my door."

Enzo keeps his gun raised. "You baited us?"

"Thought someone with a reputation such as yours would be smarter, Mr Montpellier. I've kept my face hidden for a reason."

Impatient and unable to read her lips, Hunter cocks his gun in warning. "Come out with your hands raised. We're not here to chat."

"This one can't even hear me," she snickers. "Why do you keep him around? For entertainment?"

"Enough," I shout. "Where is Michael?"

"Why don't you come inside and find out, Harlow?"

"Like hell." Kade steps in front of me in a protective stance. "She's going nowhere."

"Tell me..." Daphne smooths her plain shift dress, the golden crucifix at her neck front and centre. "Did you enjoy your visit with Giana?"

I swallow hard. "How do you know about that?"

"She's kept me a dirty little secret for all these years. I figured she'd cash in her last bargaining chip soon enough."

Something about this woman is causing my brain to stutter, overwhelmed by the scream of mental alarm bells. I've never seen her in my life, but somehow, the hiss of her voice is familiar.

"Come on," Daphne goads. "You really don't remember, do you? Michael always wanted an empty vessel for his will."

"I am not an empty vessel!"

"Did you really think he could come up with all of this alone? My brother is a smart man, but not even he could bring down an empire of sin without help."

Months of terror, violence and rampant destruction burn bright in the flickering embers of her eyes. She's proud. Fucking giddy with satisfaction. He did have help, after all.

From her.

His puppeteer.

"Our sister never quite understood the work we are doing here." Daphne touches her crucifix. "She cowered away from getting her hands dirty. The Lord doesn't condone such disloyalty."

Dread is slamming into me, over and over. Thick, cloying, suffocating waves of dread. We're missing something.

"If you hurry, you may still be able to say goodbye," she taunts. "He isn't quite done yet."

"What are you talking about?"

She cackles. "Stupid child."

"I've heard enough." Enzo advances with his gun. "Get down on your fucking knees before I put a bullet in you."

Hands raised, she follows his instructions with a maniacal grin on her face. The moment he slaps a pair of handcuffs on her, I take off in a run.

"Harlow!" Leighton yells.

But my feet are already thumping up the porch steps that lead into the farmhouse. I can hear the others following as I duck inside the living room, warmth emanating from a lit fire.

Empty.

Moving deeper into the house, darkness welcomes me home. The furniture is all antique and probably older than me. Wooden crucifixes hang from the walls, nailed into place over ugly wallpaper.

"Archived blueprints show a root cellar beneath the first floor," Brooklyn recites quickly. "There's access in the kitchen."

"Harlow." Hudson stops me. "Please let me go down first. I'm not letting that bastard touch you again."

I gesture for him to go ahead, and he nods, taking the lead into the kitchen. Dingy cabinets and peeling linoleum match the rest of the strange, antiquated house.

Beneath the adjacent staircase, there's a triangle-shaped door leading down. Weak light spills up from whatever lies beneath us.

"Theo," I say into the earpiece. "We're going into the cellar."

"Be careful," he responds.

As we begin to descend, off-key humming is the first sound that warns me we're entering the devil's lair. I recognise it without needing to see my uncle's dead eyes and leering grin.

The whisper in my head steals the relief I should feel, knowing we're about to end a whole year of emotional anguish. He's here. It's over, and yet the victory rings hollow.

It's too easy.

There's no way they could have known about my visit to see Giana. Not unless they had inside knowledge or it came from her.

Yet the dread persists. Spreading. Infecting. Metastasising into a terminal cancer that rots the flesh from my bones.

"Holy shit." Hudson's voice echoes up the staircase. "Harlow, stay the fuck upstairs!"

But it's already too late. I'm chasing after him and running straight into the arms of cold-hearted inevitability. The time has come.

Thudding down the last few steps, I'm slapped in the face by a familiar scent from my past. Blood. Litres of it. Copper perfuses the thick, dusty air inside the root cellar.

Hudson stands a few inches from the base of the staircase, his gun raised and trained on a figure perched in the corner of the dank room. The first thing I see is his mouth stretched in a smile.

"I was wondering when you'd show up," Michael says casually, as if greeting an old friend. "I'm afraid you're too late for the show."

His usual pressed robes are stained, the fabric covered in dark, sticky splotches. Red splatters mark the dog collar peeking out at his neck, the droplets congealing on his crucifix.

"The family … all together again." Michael swoops a hand around the cellar. "Reunited at last."

The useless lump of organ that lives behind my ribcage stops, stutters then explodes into shards. I can't move. Blink. Breathe. My feet are glued to the floor as I take in the awaiting sight.

"Giana?" I whimper.

It can't be her. She's hundreds of miles away, locked in a high-security prison with twenty-four-hour supervision for her own protection.

And yet I'm staring into the dead, glassy eyes of my mother. Her mousy-brown hair is sticky with blood and clumped together. Mouth slack. Limbs stiff. Body naked.

The symbols that carve a violent path of scars into my own body are mirrored perfectly, slashing her twisted, limp body and adding to the congealed puddle of blood staining the floor.

"She didn't last long." Michael chuckles. "Your record remains unchallenged, darling niece. I was curious."

When I screw my eyes shut and shove them back open, the view hasn't changed. This isn't a dream. It isn't even a nightmare.

She's dead.

Butchered.

Gone.

Reality blurs as everyone moves around me—apprehending Michael, cuffing his hands behind his back and beginning to beat the ever-loving shit out of him.

None of it matters. Not their relief. Nor his satisfaction. All I can feel is the widening pit of nothingness in my chest as I stare down at my dead mother.

A soft pair of hands lands on my arms and pulls me back into someone's chest. They're stroking me. Whispering. Shaking. It doesn't break the numb mist that's taken over everything.

"She was a filthy fucking whore!" Michael screams, his veneer of calmness dissipating. "May she rot in hell with my useless wife."

His voice cuts through my shock, and I find myself shrugging the pair of hands off, landing next to Giana in a puddle of her blood.

"No," I choke out a sob.

She's cold. Waxy. Lifeless. The only colour on her skin is from the shocking slashes of crimson sliced into her with unimaginable rage.

"Harlow," the voice in my ear coaxes. "Medical help is on its way. I need you to talk to me, beautiful."

"She's d-dead!"

"Who is dead? What happened, angel?"

Taking Giana's hand in mine, I can hardly see through the ribbons of tears soaking into my face. All I can hear is what she said to me in the prison. I couldn't find it in myself to even give her a response.

I'm sorry for so many things, Harlow. But I'm not sorry for bringing you into this world. I'm proud of the woman you've become.

I left in tears then, unable to fathom the entirely foreign need I'd felt to throw my arms around her and share a single moment of love with the woman who gave birth to me.

"Harlow!" Theo shouts down the line.

"It's my m-mum. He killed her."

CHAPTER 26
LEIGHTON

QUEEN – PERFUME GENIUS

STANDING at the back of the press conference room, I watch Enzo and Hunter artfully perform for the sea of reporters. My brother has even dug up an old smile to offer the room as the BSL interpreter translates their questions for his benefit.

Sitting on their left, the well-dressed, pompous hide of the superintendent herself, Natalie Hart, has made a rare appearance. Her perfect blonde hair is slicked back in a severe bun.

"I would like to take this opportunity to publicly thank Sabre Security for their hard work and determination."

Even I can see that Enzo's working his ass off to hold back a sarcastic remark. He was ready to lynch her not too long ago.

"Thanks to them, the most heinous, violent serial killer this country has ever seen will now face his day in court."

To my dismay, the room breaks out in a round of enthusiastic applause. The journalists that have spent the last year making our lives a living hell are now singing our fucking praise.

No.

I'm done.

Turning to leave the room, Enzo's response makes my feet halt.

"We still have a long way to go in this investigation. Michael Abaddon was aided by a co-conspirator and still has many supporters at large who need to be apprehended."

That's when the sea of questions begins. None of them knew about Daphne's involvement before now. Abaddon had a mastermind all along, operating in the shadows.

"Can you account for the presence of an inmate from a high-security prison being found dead at the scene?"

I have to glance back and relish the embarrassed look on Natalie's face.

That particular failing has nothing to do with us.

"We are actively looking into how Giana Kensington was able to escape from Bronzefield," she answers curtly. "I have commissioned a full investigation into their security measures."

As the roar of questions begins again to vie for their attention, I sneak out of the room. I don't need the events rehashing. The memory is burned on my mind well enough.

We won.

But it cost … everything.

Outside the entrance to Sabre's HQ, there is relative peace for the first time in months. No one can quite believe the silence.

Accusatory placards and screamed curses vanished overnight, leaving only a gaggle of praying lunatics behind as they beg the Lord for his protection.

The moment the first headline was published to reveal Abaddon's capture, the world stopped caring. Their fear was the only thing causing them to give a shit.

We don't think about the suffering of others until our own lives are caught in the crosshairs. It's easier to move on. Forget. Give up. That's more convenient for everyone.

Until that threat reaches our shores and we pretend to have a moral compass for those five minutes of fame. Those people never wanted justice for Abaddon's victims.

We did.

Now we have it.

But that victory is far from the sweet release we were promised. Instead of relief and jubilation, all we have are handfuls of the still-burning embers of our lives, sacrificed to reach this moment.

Back upstairs, I return to our temporary apartment. There's been talk of going home to our abandoned London house that's sat empty since we left, but we haven't had the time to organise the move yet.

"Harlow?" I step inside.

"Shh." Theo's voice hisses from the living room. "I've just got her to sleep."

On the L-shaped sofa that dominates the airy space, he's working on his laptop with one hand, the other stroking Harlow's tangled hair.

She's curled up in a ball next to him, her eyes closed, and a brand-new journal gifted from Jude trapped in her arms.

"Did she take one of those tablets Richards gave her?"

Theo nods. "Took some convincing."

"She hasn't slept since we got back from Holcombe." I look around the messy room. "This will do her good."

Abandoning the email he was attempting to type with one hand, Theo glances up at me. "How's the press conference?"

"As you predicted. The reporters are kissing our asses now that we have Abaddon in custody. That bitch Natalie is loving it."

He scoffs bitterly. "She'll be lapping this up for months and claiming it as her victory."

"You bet."

Sitting down on Harlow's other side, I run a hand over her curled spine. She's in the foetal position, cuddling her journal for any semblance of comfort while unconscious.

I get better than most why Giana's sudden death has ripped the carpet out from under her feet. Loss isn't something that follows any man-made rules.

We can mourn things that we didn't even know we needed. Including the idea of a person. I grieved for months behind bars for the privileged life I'd so carelessly tossed aside.

She didn't love Giana.

Not in a normal sense.

But that didn't mean she wasn't still her mum. Without even a shitty, imprisoned bitch of a person to fill that void, it's just another empty reminder of everything Harlow will never have.

"Fuck, Theo. How do we fix this for her? It's killing me to watch her go through this."

"I don't know that we can," he admits quietly. "She's still in shock. We just need to be there for her until she comes back."

"And what if she doesn't come back?"

Looking down at Harlow, he nods with a strange sense of certainty. "She will. I've never met anyone stronger than our girl."

Wincing in her sleep, she shifts and almost wakes up. Theo hushes her, stroking the hair from her face until she relaxes again.

"Even now she's fighting back," he jokes. "Can't even make her sleep when she doesn't want to."

"I blame Brooklyn. She's a bad influence."

"Speaking of, she brought over two trays of lasagne for us. Extra burnt. I think we're being punished or something."

"God, I am not eating that shit."

Chuckling, he returns to looking at his laptop screen. I peer over Harlow's lightly snoring body to look at the live video feed he's studying intensely.

"Has Abaddon moved at all?"

"Nope." Theo sighs. "Been in the same position praying for the last three hours. His sister too."

The live feed of the detention cell holding Abaddon is crystal clear, allowing for no misinterpretation. The psycho is sitting cross-legged on the floor and happily praying in his cell.

"He's still refusing to speak to anyone." Theo catches himself. "Well, anyone but Harlow. It's the only thing he's asked for."

"Enzo still hasn't told her?"

"Not yet. She's fragile right now, and letting this bastard rub his latest kill in her face will only make it worse."

The no-more-sane sister, Daphne, is sitting in an almost identical position as she follows the same routine in a completely different cell. Their actions are identical.

"What about Daphne?"

Theo shakes his head. "Nothing."

"Goddammit. We need to know who is still out there doing their dirty work. This isn't over yet."

"We're trying, Leigh."

"Clearly not hard enough!"

My slightly-raised voice causes Harlow to stir again, and this time, her eyes flutter open. The usually crystal clear, aquamarine depths are muddied with exhaustion and bloodshot from crying.

"Sorry, princess. Go back to sleep."

"Leigh? You're back."

"Nice work," Theo mutters.

Cutting him a glare, I take hold of Harlow's elbow and gently pull her onto my lap. She snuggles into me, her lips brushing my throat.

"You need to sleep, baby."

"I'm fine," she whispers. "Is the press conference over?"

"Not yet. Hunter and Enzo are holding down the fort. They've even got a BSL interpreter in so he can take questions."

I can hear the smile in her voice.

"I'm sure he's loving that."

"Quite the opposite. Hunter looked bored to death and like he wanted to get the fuck out of there. His days of playing boss are long gone."

She points over towards the kitchen. "A letter from the hospital came. Hunter told me to open it while he's gone. His surgery has been scheduled for six weeks' time, right after Christmas."

Anxiety spikes through me. "Shit. So soon? That isn't great timing with all this crap still going on."

"It's a relatively simple procedure, so it shouldn't be an issue," Theo explains. "The recovery time is about a month before they activate the device to see if it worked."

"And what? He can hear again?" I question.

"No," he answers.

"I don't understand."

"The device receives sound from the environment and sends electrical signals to the auditory nerve for the brain to then recognise and process."

"What's that in English?" I sigh.

"It isn't normal hearing." Harlow cuddles closer to me. "He'll need months of speech therapy to learn how to interpret the sounds."

I'm sure my brother considered none of this when he made the decision to get the surgery. Even after all this time, he's still looking for some damned miracle cure that doesn't exist.

I rub circles on Harlow's back. "Did you speak to Foster this morning?"

"No, I haven't called him back yet. I can't face him."

"You have to speak to him sometime, Goldilocks. Talking to him may actually help."

"Help what?" she snaps. "Nothing about this can ever be fixed. Talking or not. Giana is still dead."

"Maybe he wants to talk to you about a funeral," Theo chimes in. "Do you want to say goodbye?"

She sniffles on my chest. "I don't know what I want anymore. Losing her was never supposed to hurt like this."

"When do our hearts ever do what they're supposed to?" I reply gently. "You're allowed to hurt and mourn her."

"Like she mourned me?"

Pulling free from my embrace, Harlow struggles to climb to her feet. She hasn't changed out of a borrowed pair of my sweats and Hunter's t-shirt that we wrestled her into upon returning.

Beginning to pace the living room, she ignores our favourite show, *Friends*, softly playing in the background. Angry tears are leaking from her eyes. Theo stops me before I stand up and intervene.

"I thought I'd be happy once Michael was behind bars, but instead, I feel empty. It won't bring anyone we've lost back."

"But it will stop anyone else from getting hurt," Theo points out.

She slows, offering a nod. "I guess so. What's going to happen now that we have him in custody?"

"He's been charged with twenty counts of first-degree murder, including Giana's death, and for kidnapping Candace. That's potentially twenty life sentences."

"Twenty?" I frown at Theo. "Weren't there more?"

"They aren't willing to discuss charges for the mass suicide or copycat kills until he talks or we have evidence. There's no proof."

"That's complete crap!"

"I don't make the rules."

"Then we need him to talk." Harlow turns to face us both. "Those people deserve justice too. It's not their fault he used them."

Exchanging a silent conversation with Theo, I wave towards her, encouraging him to spill the beans. She doesn't need our protection.

"What?" Harlow demands.

He clears his throat. "Abaddon has said that the only person he'll speak to is you. He's been silent ever since."

Wringing her hands together, she resumes pacing on the silver-threaded rug but remains weirdly calm.

"You don't have to do this," Theo reasons. "We have interrogators who are trained to get information out of people. Let them handle it."

"No. It has to be me."

"Beautiful—"

"I'm the only one who understands how his mind works. I can get him to admit what he did. We need those charges to be added."

"He's going to be behind bars until the day he dies no matter what happens," I supply. "Why does it matter?"

"Because," she cuts in. "They were his victims too. Their families need closure."

Realising she's got me beat, I back down. I don't give a shit what we have to do. If she needs this to feel better, we'll damn well do it.

"Okay. Then talk to him."

Harlow gapes at me. "You're seriously on board with this?"

"If you want to do this, then I think you should. Only you can know your own mind. All I care about is your feelings."

"I want to do it. No, I *need* to do it."

"Then we'll make it happen," Theo agrees. "We all want closure, angel. For you and everyone else."

Knuckles rapping on our front door breaks the moment, and I get up to answer, squeezing Harlow's arm on my way past. Pale-faced and antsy, Oliver waits on the other side.

"Is Harlow here?"

I hook a thumb over my shoulder. "She's okay. Nobody else got hurt during the raid."

"I need to see her."

"Dad?" her voice calls.

Stepping aside, I let him bounce past me in his haste to reach her. Harlow doesn't even flinch when he almost tackles her, and she's swooped off the floor in an emotional reunion.

"I was so worried about you," he rushes out. "We weren't told about the raid until it was all over, and the news broke."

"It happened so fast. We didn't want to worry you."

"I'm your father, Harlow!" He sets her back down. "I'll worry about you until the day I die, and you need to understand that."

When he realises what he's said, Oliver blanches. She takes his hand and pulls him back into another hug.

"I'm sorry, Dad."

He deflates. "Me too, love. When I heard what happened… I didn't know what to think or feel."

"She's dead. He killed her."

"Did … did she suffer?" he dares to ask.

When Harlow can't even fathom a response, Oliver breaks down. He looks as confused by his feelings as Harlow does. They hold each other through the tears and shaking.

"I know she hurt both of us so much, but no one deserves to die like that," Oliver croaks. "Not even her."

Finding the strength to separate themselves, Harlow guides him over to the armchair next to the sofa. The life drains out of him as he slumps into it.

"I spoke to her husband," he admits.

We all tense up.

"You did?" Harlow exclaims.

"He reached out to me a few hours ago. Seems like a decent bloke. He had the consideration to call me himself."

Harlow perches on the armrest. "Foster is a good man. I know he'll see to it that she's laid to rest properly."

"What about the kid? Ulrich, is it?"

"I can't imagine what he's thinking right now." Her hands move to cover her face. "I saw him a few weeks ago. He said that he misses his mum."

Sensing that this conversation needs alcohol, I retrieve the emergency bottle of whiskey that Brooklyn also delivered with her terrible food offerings.

Harlow and Theo each accept a glass while Oliver declines. He looks in better need of a good night's sleep than hard liquor.

"I think you should call the kid," Oliver suggests.

"Why? I can't offer him any comfort."

"You can," he encourages, squeezing Harlow's knee. "Just the sound of your voice will let him know that he's not alone."

Harlow's head falls. "All he wanted was his mum back. Regardless of what everyone else said she'd done."

Reaching over to take hold of her hand, I let our fingers curl together. "That's why he needs you. No one else can understand what that feels like."

With a final sigh, she submits. "I'll call Foster back and ask to speak to Ulrich."

Disappearing to make the phone call, she's still holed up in her bedroom when Enzo and Hunter return from the press conference. Enzo takes one look at us then pours himself a glass of liquor.

"That woman is an insufferable piece of shit," he grumbles. "I never want to work with her again."

"That good, huh?" I snort.

"Natalie is still down there taking credit for the entire investigation and acting like this is some grand victory for us all."

Crouching down next to the glass fireplace, Hunter hides his face in his hands. None of us have slept much in the whirlwind since the raid.

"Harlow wants to go into the interview with Abaddon," Theo interjects. "She's agreed to get him to talk."

"What?" Enzo explodes.

I hush him with a waved hand. "This is her call. She wants answers, and keeping this shit from her is pointless."

"I wasn't going to keep it from her forever." He deflates, knocking back a mouthful of whiskey. "I don't want her anywhere near him."

"What's the worst he could do?" Theo challenges. "Not like he can butcher or hurt anyone else. We're in control now."

Somehow, that sentiment doesn't ring true. None of us believe it, even if we're not willing to admit that. Abaddon handed himself to us on a gold fucking platter, and I don't trust it.

Several drinks in, and with Brooklyn's terrifying lasagne warming in the oven, Harlow rejoins us from her bedroom, eyes swollen from more crying.

"Did you speak to him?" Oliver asks.

She bites her lip. "Yeah, he answered. Giana's body is going to be cremated next week. Nothing fancy."

Walking into Enzo's arms, she brushes her lips against his and crawls closer to snuggle up.

"Are you going to go?"

"I think so," she answers me. "Someone should be there."

"We'll all go," Enzo decides.

"You don't have to do that."

"Trust me, it's not for her." He pecks the top of her head. "We're going to be there for you, little one. No one else."

We all chime in our agreement, even Oliver. I personally think the world is a far better place without Giana's sick brand of evil in it, but if Harlow needs us, our feelings are irrelevant.

Leaving Enzo's embrace, Harlow retrieves the open hospital letter from the table and brings it to Hunter. His throat bobs.

"What did it say?"

Rather than answer, Harlow encourages him to take it himself. Hunter sighs and slides the letter out of the ripped envelope to read.

His gaze scans over the printed text, and the smile that blooms on his lips is so fucking happy, it actually hurts to see that part of my brother reappearing.

"Six weeks," he recites. "This is it."

Despite everything—the pain and bloodshed still boiling at our feet—we all toast to that. If hope is what he needs, then we're not going to take that precious commodity from him.

"There's something else I wanted to talk to you guys about," Harlow begins nervously. "Changing my surname."

Everyone sits a little straighter.

She glances over to Theo. "I wanted it to be yours before all this happened. Please don't hate me, but I think I need to be Harlow Kensington now."

"You know, pulling out your earpiece doesn't stop me from being able to hear you," Theo replies with a wink. "Doesn't work that way."

"Leigh!" she chastises.

I spread my hands in surrender. "You're the one who started the conversation. I didn't think he was listening."

Her cheeks flush pink. "You're not upset?"

"Of course not," Theo offers. "Leighton said it himself... You're ours, regardless of what a piece of paper says."

"But why Kensington?" Enzo questions.

She fiddles with the hem of Hunter's oversized t-shirt that she stole to wear. Wearing our clothes comforts her.

"I thought that I wanted a new identity, but I was wrong. I want to honour the girl who survived that cage."

When he thinks no one is looking, Oliver subtly swipes under his reddened eyes. Harlow takes one look at him and chokes up.

"This is the start of my future," she says assertively. "Leticia Kensington lost everything."

"And now?" Oliver asks.

"Now Harlow Kensington is going to give it back to her."

CHAPTER 27
HARLOW

CHOKEHOLD – SLEEP TOKEN

SHAKING OUT MY HANDS, I stand frozen on the other side of the interview room. It's one of the secure, soundproof rooms on the same floor as the detention cells, complete with metal walls and floor.

On the other side of that steel sheet is the man who kidnapped and tortured me. Raped and murdered my friends. Brutalised countless victims. Tore the country apart and … killed my mother.

No pressure.

"Are you ready for this?" Theo checks in.

He's sitting on the other side of the two-way mirror with Hunter and Kade. All three of them are poised to watch the interview, with Enzo opting to accompany me for security.

"Yeah." I smooth down my blue sweater and plain skinny jeans. "Let's do this."

"Don't let him get into your head," Kade advises, his hand poised to take notes. "You're the one in control. Not him."

"I've got this."

Theo looks over the different feeds on his laptop. "Hudson's next door interviewing Giana's assigned guard from the night she escaped."

"You hauled them all in?" I ask.

"All five who were on duty that night, plus Bronzefield's head of security and the warden. We're interviewing them all."

"Doing the superintendent's dirty work for her again," Enzo grumbles. "Come on, Harlow. Let's get this over with."

Hunter smiles reassuringly. "Go get him."

With a deep breath, I pass Enzo, who scans his badge to unlock the door before setting foot in the lion's den. The room is cold—bitingly so. It leaches all the life and sustenance from my veins in a second.

Seated on the other side of a steel table, his hands cuffed to the centre bar that separates the two sides, sits my uncle. He wears a grey jumpsuit, and for the first time ever, no visible crucifix.

"Harlow," he rasps.

"Michael."

"First name basis now, huh?"

"We are family, after all."

I take a seat in one of the chairs, and Enzo settles next to me. The gun strapped to a holster on his hip is very much visible but remains safely out of Michael's reach.

In stark comparison to the last time I saw him, my uncle looks on the verge of collapsing. His skin is tarnished with purple and green bruises, swelling his beaten face to almost twice its size.

Hudson and Enzo did a real number on him when they first slapped those handcuffs on. I don't remember a lot of it, just the unhinged cackle that Michael unleashed as they beat him.

"How's dear old Mum?"

I restrain myself from flinching. "You know full well how she is."

"I thought you'd be happy, darling niece. She deserved to be punished for what she did to you. Are you not pleased?"

"I never asked for this."

"You didn't have to." His smile widens. "The Lord tasked me with cleaning the earth of all its sinners. I am only fulfilling his will."

"Killing countless innocent people, butchering vulnerable women and murdering anyone you come into contact with isn't God's will."

Settling back in his chair, he strains against the handcuffs. "You're weak, Harlow. It's such a disappointment. I raised you to be better than that."

"Raised her?" Enzo spits.

Michael's darkened green eyes slide over to him. "Ah, he speaks! What are you here for, Mr Montpellier? Her guard dog?"

"I'm here to finish what I started if you try any clever shit with us. I'll happily pulverise the rest of your face. You can even choose which bones I break first."

"Charming." Michael snorts in derision. "You've aligned yourself with such *wonderfully* sadistic people, Harlow. I'm proud."

"Cut the crap. You asked to see me." I gesture around the room. "I'm here. So let's talk."

Trailing his cold eyes over me, Michael takes time to catalogue every last change. It's like he's seeing me for the very first time. I don't move, refusing to flinch under his gaze.

"When you survived the little present I left for you in Wales, I realised that the Lord has greater plans for your suffering."

"Give me a fucking break," Enzo mutters, staring up at the ceiling.

"Death was not enough to punish you for deserting me," he continues, ignoring him. "That would be far too quick."

"Is that what this is?" I hiss angrily. "Punishment?"

"This is the result of your selfishness. You never should have left your cage. This wouldn't have happened if you did as you were told."

"Enough," Enzo snaps. "Tell us about your co-conspirators. Where are they? Who is the copycat killer?"

"Harlow." Michael sighs dramatically. "Please muzzle your attack dog. I'm growing tired of his disobedience."

Rising to his feet, Enzo's on the verge of grabbing his jumpsuit and strangling Michael to death until I rest a hand on his thigh.

"Go stand in the corner. I've got this."

"No. He isn't to be trusted."

"I'm not telling you to leave us alone. But I can't do anything with you on the verge of killing him for the whole interview."

Cursing colourfully, Enzo smashes his chair backwards and escapes to the corner of the room, resting a hand on his gun.

"You really do have them wrapped around your finger, don't you?" Michael chuckles. "How did I raise such a filthy little whore?"

"You didn't raise me. Period."

His amused gaze hardens. "I saved you from a life of sin. I gave you the Lord's light! And this blasphemy is how you repay me?"

I lean closer across the table. "You tried to break me. Surviving you is the greatest thing I'll ever accomplish. I saved myself."

"You ungrateful slut. All those years… wasted!"

"Because you failed. That will be your legacy. Failure to complete your mission. Do you think God will forgive that?"

He moves so fast, I don't have time to lean back out of the danger zone. His forehead smashes into my face with a resounding crack, and pain explodes across the bridge of my nose.

"Demon whore!"

Flashing across the room as fast as his muscled weight will allow, Enzo has the barrel of his gun shoved against Michael's throat before I can swallow the blood pooling in my mouth.

"You dare to hurt her!" he thunders in a terrifying voice. "I'll cut your goddamn hands off and make you choke on them for touching her."

"Do it!" Michael yells. "Kill me!"

The door to the interview room blows open as Enzo shoves his gun between Michael's open lips, intending to penetrate his throat with it. Kade and Hunter bound into the room.

"Enzo! Stop it!"

"She's bleeding," he snarls animalistically. "This motherfucker made my girl bleed, and I'm going to bury him for it."

It takes both of their strength to wrestle Enzo away before he can fulfil his promise and cover us all in Michael's splattered brains.

Enzo manages to knock the wind out of Hunter with a well-placed elbow and breaks free from Kade's grip.

"Enzo," I entreat.

That's when he stops.

"Go. We need him alive."

"Harlow—"

"I have this under control! Go."

Head bowed, he submits to my command and grumpily storms from the room. Hunter spares me an eye roll, gesturing for Kade to follow after him.

He disappears then returns a minute later with a handful of tissues. I accept them and banish Hunter to the corner of the room, holding the tissues against my bleeding nose.

"Interesting." Michael watches the whole thing. "Do you keep them on their leashes at night too?"

"You're on very thin ice," I say nasally. "I'll forgive that if you tell me what I want to know. Who is the copycat killer?"

"Me."

"You couldn't have been in three places at once. Give us the names, and then we can discuss what happens to you next."

He rattles his handcuffs again. "Listen to me, you stupid child. I am everywhere. The Lord has granted me a devoted army of believers, and my will inhabits them all."

"You're insane."

"And you even speak like the devil now," he spits back. "You'll rue the day that you dared to venture from the path I gave you."

"Was murdering your wife part of that path? Or brutalising your sister? Torturing your niece? Trying to impregnate innocent women before killing them? The only devil here is you."

Absorbing the verbal blows, Michael slumps in his chair. His eyes turn down, and his mouth presses into a tight line.

"My bloodline is cursed, Harlow. From the moment that nameless whore birthed me to Rosetta losing our God-given child. I took you from Giana to prevent the same thing from happening."

"You wanted to raise me as your own. But then why kidnap, rape and butcher all the other women? Why end their lives?"

"Because someone had to protect the innocent from their poisoned blood!" His spittle hits the table. "All of those sluts deserved to die. They failed in their one purpose. I was protecting the world from their sinful ways."

The worst part is, he actually believes what he's saying. The lunacy is written into his DNA and perfuses every part of him with divine certainty.

He can't feel empathy. Regret. Guilt. The cycle of violence has repeated over and over, across the decades, fuelled by his own ingrained hysteria that no amount of begging could dig out.

"I never stood a chance, did I?"

He looks up at me. "What?"

"All this time… I've hated myself for being unable to protect those women. I've blamed myself. But I didn't stand a chance of stopping you."

"I enacted God's will!"

But I've already tuned him out as something fundamental clicks inside of me, and the whole world shifts. Even after everything, I still carried that survivor's guilt with me.

I don't need to anymore.

It … wasn't my fault.

None of it was.

Pulling the tissues from my nose, I ball up the blood-soaked material then breathe in the most incredible sense of vindication for the first time since I escaped his hellhole.

"I can forgive myself," I whisper beneath my breath. "It wasn't my fault. It was all his."

"Stop it." Michael convulses in his chair, desperate to escape. "Don't you remember Laura? The world knows what you did."

"I saved her life," I reply softly.

"You killed her!"

"No. I saved her from a slow, painful death. I gave her dignity in her final moments. I'm done taking responsibility for your guilt."

Standing up, I take one last look at him and walk away. He will never divulge his secrets. The more air we give him to breathe, the longer he will continue to spout his hateful lies.

"Harlow!" he screams for attention. "This isn't over. You only caught me because I wanted you to."

I look over my shoulder. "You think we don't know that? Look around you. There's nothing you can do from here."

His smile is dripping with vicious delight. "Wait and see. I warned you about defying me. Your punishment will be my final act."

The farther I walk away, the louder his soulless screaming becomes. It bounces off the walls and attempts to pierce my skin, but I refuse to give it power.

His reign is over.

We're in control now.

Hunter follows me out, his hand circling my wrist. "Are you okay? We need to take a look at that nose."

I brush him aside with a shake of my head. The door to the interview room slams shut, finally silencing Michael's madness. Enzo, Kade and Theo are watching with matching proud expressions.

"What?" I stare at them.

Leaving his laptop, Theo takes two strides then smashes me against his chest. "You are the most incredible human being I've ever had the pleasure of meeting."

"Um, thanks?"

His lips seek mine out, and we share a fast kiss. My head is spinning from the events of the last ten minutes, and their behaviour is freaking me out even more.

"Way to go, Harlow." Kade gives me a high five. "That was fucking brilliant, watching you tear him down."

"I didn't do anything."

"Yes. You did." Enzo steals me and kisses my forehead. "Only you can get beneath his skin. He's coming apart at the seams."

"But we didn't get a name."

"We will," Theo reassures.

Bursting into our area kept separate from the interview space, Hudson is wild-eyed with triumph. He grins at us all.

"I've got him. Two of the guards have admitted to slipping Giana a dose of sleeping pills with her evening meal and breaking her out."

"They drugged her?" Enzo repeats.

He nods. "Both of them were paid well by a third party. Sounds like one of Abaddon's foot soldiers."

"Probably acting on behalf of Daphne," I fill in. "She's the one funding this entire thing and planning it all."

"The brains to the brawn." Kade laughs without humour. "How the hell did we miss her all along?"

"We overestimated Abaddon," Enzo answers grimly. "He's mad as a box of twats, but even a deadly weapon needs guiding."

Despite the thick tension in the room, everyone bursts out laughing. Theo has to wipe stray tears from beneath his glasses.

"Mad as a box of twats?"

Enzo frowns at him. "You haven't heard that before?"

"I can't breathe," Hudson splutters.

Flipping us all off, Enzo mutters something about getting a coffee then escapes the room to cool off. We're still laughing when he's gone.

"I want to talk to Daphne."

Everyone quickly sobers up, and their attention fixes on me. Repeating my words for Hunter to decipher, his eyebrows knit together.

"Why?"

I tap my forehead.

"Because you don't remember her," he guesses.

"*No,*" I sign back.

"You've done enough, sweetheart."

"He's right," Theo agrees. "She's a spiteful old cow. You don't need to put yourself through that as well."

"I want answers. When I have them, I can finally close this chapter of my life."

With a sigh, Hudson holds the door open for me. "I'll take you. Pre-warning… She's just as crazy as her whack job brother."

"It's a wonder I ended up even half-sane."

"Fucking miracle."

With Hunter trailing after us, we move to the next room down the silent corridor. This floor is kept off-limits to only those with the highest security clearance in the building.

Hudson scans his badge to let us both inside. Warner and Tara are manning the observation side of the room while Ethan attempts to interview a silent Daphne behind the tinted glass.

"Harlow?" Warner looks up at me. "Jesus. You're covered in blood."

I wave his concern off. "Just a misunderstanding. I'm fine."

"She's gonna have a crack at Daphne," Hudson explains. "We've got the two guards admitting involvement in Giana's escape on record."

"In that case, be my guest. This one won't say a damn word."

After Hudson opens the door for me, we filter into the room. Ethan backs away at Hunter's command and allows us to step into the walled-off interview area.

"I wondered when you'd grace me with your presence." Daphne snickers to herself. "Good to see you again, Harlow."

With her silvery hair pulled back in a no-nonsense ponytail, she looks significantly better than her beaten-up brother, though their grey jumpsuits match.

"I see you've spoken to my brother." Her eyes catalogue the blood on my sweater. "You should know better than to provoke him."

I take one of the seats. "Let's keep this brief. You're going to prison for a very long time. This is your last chance to save yourself."

"Save myself?" She laughs.

"We know you both had help. Give us the information we're looking for, and it will work in your favour."

"I don't need any favours from you, little girl."

"How did he do it?" I ask with narrowed eyes. "I understand about Giana. She couldn't protect herself. But how did he break you too?"

"I didn't need breaking," she snarls at me. "The Lord chose me. When I found Michael, I was lost. We saved each other."

"By killing innocent people?"

"By doing God's bidding! That useless wife of his certainly wasn't strong enough to do it. Look at you. She failed to keep you tamed."

"No, she spent a decade making every second Michael wasn't beating me a living nightmare. But I know now it wasn't her fault. She only did what he wanted her to do."

Daphne breaks down in hysterical laughter. "You really don't remember me, do you? Who do you think kept Rosetta in line?"

I can feel Hunter lingering behind me, keeping close enough to prevent any further attacks. His warmth at my back injects strength into me.

"I was there every step of the way," Daphne explains with a satisfied glint in her eyes. "The truth was staring you in the face all along. You're just too stupid to see it."

Our gazes locked, that awful, rushing sense of realisation filters over me again. It's in her eyes. Those sinister green orbs. The flash of them glowering at me through cage bars penetrates my mind.

"You're lying."

"So forgetful," she taunts.

"I won't let you manipulate me."

"What purpose do I have to lie? My work on this earth is done. I want you to know how much of a failure you are."

"Michael worked alone!"

"He found me long before our mother passed on. The Lord brought us together to enact his will."

The more she speaks, the more that sense of disjointed realisation increases. I can feel the truth in her words on an intrinsic level.

Her smile takes a dangerous edge. "He wanted to keep you at home. It was my idea to put you in that cage. Pain is the only way to cleanse a heathen's soul."

"You were there."

"For every single beating," she confirms. "Who do you think stopped him from killing you when Adelaide bled to death?"

This time, I can't suppress a shudder. I thought I was going to die that night. He was seconds from crumbling my bones to dust as punishment for his own failings.

The rush of returning memories stings like needlepoints slicing into my skull. I can still see Michael beating me limp and useless while his body was covered in hot, slick blood.

"There it is," she goads.

Her voice was there that night in my semi-conscious haze. Interrupting his violent assault and warning him that the work was not yet done. He wasn't allowed to kill me.

"I've been the voice in the back of your mind all this time." Daphne sneers. "You'll never dig me out. Never."

"I … remember." I gulp down a bubble of vomit. "You're the one who started it all. You killed Kiera."

"He needed a push." She shrugs it off. "Didn't she scream so beautifully, though? Full of such desperate, delicious fear."

"She was my friend," I choke out.

"Kiera was a demonic whore. She got exactly what she deserved. But still, you didn't learn. We had to bring more girls in to teach you."

The flashes come thick and fast. I watch the memories play out on a mental movie screen—Michael carrying in unconscious women, one after another, imprisoning them in the cage next to me. All while Daphne watched on.

My mind forgot her.

Locked her out.

The greatest monster of all.

"And it was you who saved him from the house where you held Candace before help arrived. You helped Michael escape again."

Daphne sits back, satisfied by the horror painted across my face. "There she is. Still a scared little pup, locked in her cage."

I scrape my chair back, unhinged by the explosive realisations rocking every inch of me. I'm done. She doesn't get to hurt me again.

I'm not going to be her victim for a second longer. She's admitted to every charge we needed, and her sick pride will be her undoing.

"That's where you're wrong. I was scared then. But I will never be afraid of you again."

"We'll see about that."

"You're going to die behind bars. That's your reward for all you've done. Enjoy living the rest of your life in a cage."

"Your threats mean nothing," she combats. "The rapture will reward me. While you burn to death, I shall rejoice in my salvation."

Turning my back on the monstrous darkness that's preyed upon me since I left my cage, I let the mental walls slam down on every drop of sickness she indoctrinated me with.

A scared little girl was thrown into the cage she created. But a strong, powerful, unbroken woman is walking away from her now.

She failed.

And I fucking won.

CHAPTER 28
HARLOW

DROWNED IN EMOTION – CASKETS

IT FEELS FITTING to breathe the same air that began this journey for me as I say goodbye to my mother. The fresh, salty coldness swirls in my lungs and keeps the grip of grief at bay.

Croyde is beautiful in the late November sunshine—cool and crisp, with the silence broken by squawking seagulls flying overhead.

"We have a team of agents holding the media at bay." Enzo rests against the side of the SUV. "They won't get close."

"Are there many?"

"All the usual suspects. Everyone wants a glimpse of the funeral, but they aren't getting one. We'll protect your privacy."

Looking away from the sea, I peer up into his amber eyes. He's cleaned up for today, taming his long black hair and squeezing into a well-fitted, charcoal suit and black shirt.

"Shall we go in?"

I bite my lip. "I don't know if I can do this."

He takes my hand and squeezes. "We're all here with you, baby. Every single one of us. We will get through this together."

"You didn't have to come. I know how all of you feel about Giana and what she did."

"That doesn't matter to me," he interjects. "All I care about is you. Fuck my feelings. Fuck all of our feelings. Yours are all that matters."

Reaching up, I cup his scruff-covered chin. "I love you so much. You've saved my life every single day just by being you."

His eyes crinkle at the corners as he offers me the same gentle, understanding smile that first calmed me in the hospital when we met.

"I think I loved you the moment I laid eyes on you, screaming your damn head off. I knew you were a fighter. You've shocked the shit out of me ever since."

"Well, I do my best," I joke.

"And I fucking love that about you."

Our foreheads meeting, I breathe in his ever-present woodsy scent. I'm not sure how I lived two decades of my life without his constant, unshakeable support at my side.

I'll spend the rest of my life being thankful that I never have to find out. I doubt I could tear Enzo from his permanent role as my protector, even if I wanted to.

"The others are waiting inside the crematorium. We can stay out here for as long as you want, though."

Pressing a final kiss to his lips, I release him then step back. "Let's just go in. The sooner this is done, the sooner we can go home."

"I'm so ready to get back to our actual house." He smooths a hand over my loose, curly hair. "I've missed it."

"Not as much as Lucky has, I'm sure. I never thought we'd see it again for a moment there."

"We still own the other house if we need to get out of London again," he adds. "It needs some serious repair work first."

"Do you still want to stay in the country?" I ask nervously.

Enzo wraps a strong arm around my shoulders. "I want to go wherever you'd prefer. But if I'm being honest, there's nothing left for me here."

"What about your family?"

"There are such things as telephone calls and aeroplanes, little one. It's not like it would be goodbye forever. We'll see them at our wedding."

"Our what?" I splutter.

He holds back a laugh. "Got you. Although it's gonna happen, sooner rather than later if I have anything to say about it."

Unsure of how to respond, I gape at him. "I think you're losing it."

"I'm fully sane, angel. And if you think I'm not going to put a ring on your finger and a baby in your belly when you're ready, then we need to have a serious talk."

With a single finger slid under my chin, he closes my mouth that's flopped wide open.

"Move it. People are waiting."

I clear my throat. "Right. People."

We leave the parked SUV with the other vehicles, taking the winding cobbled path along the country lane. The crematorium is set outside of the town on a quiet, grassy hilltop overlooking the sea.

"What about Sabre?"

"What about it?" Enzo claps back.

"You've spent years of your life building it from the ground up. Are you willing to just walk away from it and never look back?"

"In a heartbeat." He sucks in the ocean air like he's taking his very first breath. "I don't want fame and fortune. I don't even want a career. I just want a happy fucking future."

My throat catches. "Me too, Enz."

"Then that's exactly what I'm going to give you. Dirt bike rides, white sand beaches and endlessly happy fucking futures."

Before we enter the crematorium, I pause to kiss his stubbled cheek. "It's a deal."

Enzo's arm around me is the grounding force I need to step inside. The crematorium is a small, plain building with cream walls and dark wood pews lining the carpet. The simple coffin resting at the front of the room is on a platform, surrounded by open velvet curtains.

The guys offered to act as pallbearers, purely for my benefit, when we realised there was no one else to do it. We opted for simplicity instead. This entire service is a mere practicality.

On the left side, Sabre has turned out to support me. The entire Cobra and Anaconda teams are present, along with the rest of Brooklyn's husbands —Eli, Phoenix and Jude.

Hunter, Theo and Leighton stand in their places in front of them, deliberately putting themselves in my direct line of sight.

The other side features only three people in the unlikeliest of collaborations. My father, Foster and Ulrich. I'm sure Giana would have a meltdown at seeing them together in the flesh.

Wiggling out from underneath Enzo's arm, I give everyone a grateful smile and take the space next to my father. He immediately pulls me into a tight hug.

"Hey, love."

"Hi, Dad. You okay?"

His breathing is unsteady against my head. "I'm fine. You sure about this?"

"I want to be here. But you don't have to stay."

He kisses my temple before releasing me. "I need some closure too. You're not doing this alone."

Looking down the aisle, I briefly catch Ulrich's eyes, but he quickly looks away. His cheeks are stained with freshly fallen tears that punch me straight in the chest.

Foster manages a small, tense nod. "Harlow."

"Hi. Thank you for arranging everything."

"Of course."

At the front of the room, a grey-haired officiant takes his place. The service is simple and to the point. No emotional speech or words of comfort. When he's done, he opens the floor to us.

"Ulrich?" Foster prompts. "Do you want to say anything?"

My brother stares resolutely at his well-shined shoes, unable to lift his head. The tears silently drip down on the thick carpet. When his dad touches his shoulder, he flinches and bolts from the pew.

"Ulrich!"

Ignoring the shouts of his name, he runs back down the aisle between the pews and breaks out of the back door. Foster murmurs his apologies then chases after his son.

The slam of the door closing breaks the heavy, awkward silence. No one knows what to say. When my dad nudges me in the side, I look up at my mother's coffin, and resolution settles in my gut.

"Someone has to say something for her."

The weight of the entire room watching me doesn't sway my decision. I take the vacated spot at the front and face everyone, my hands scrunched into tight fists.

"I … wasn't planning to do this. Frankly, I wasn't sure I'd be able to attend at all. But even someone as flawed as Giana deserves better."

Hunter meets my gaze and holds it. He refuses to look away or leave me up here alone.

"She was my mum. But not in any of the ways that mattered. Instead, she was responsible for the darkest days of my life."

I force a breath into my lungs. The tears I expected never come. Emotion is gathering in my throat instead—thick and cloying.

"I'm not going to stand here and pretend like she was perfect or even a good person. But Giana was human. Flawed, messy and so very imperfect. For that, I'm willing to forgive her."

Turning away from them all, I approach the coffin. It bears an inscribed plaque but no flowers or finishing touches. My palm strokes the smooth wooden surface before I trace the letters of her name.

"I forgive you, Mum. What happened to you wasn't your fault. You're forgiven, and I want you to find peace with Grandma Sylvie."

Glancing back at my dad, I find him breaking down in tears. Theo gives me a nod then goes to his side to support him in my place.

"We're ready," I tell the officiant.

With silence encapsulating us, a button is pressed and the curtains surrounding the coffin close. The last remaining pieces of Giana Kensington vanish from sight.

Still, the tears don't come. All I feel is a weirdly light sense of relief. In my mind, I can see her, green eyes narrowed and lips pinched in one of her grimaces.

That changes as she stares back at me on a mental plane. Instead, a smile emerges. Soft and accepting. The version of her I always imagined overtakes the truth.

She's at peace.

Forgiven and free.

Maybe I can be the same. All of us can walk away from this battlefield, bleeding and scarred, but we're still alive to tell the tale. Perhaps we'll even find a shred of hope in it to warm our souls for the road ahead.

Stepping down from the platform, I walk straight into Hunter's open, tattooed arms. He tucks my head beneath his chin and rubs circles into my back.

"That was perfect, sweetheart."

The warmth of two more bodies at my back crowds me. I recognise Theo's scent—peppermint and well-loved book pages—and the hum of Leighton's voice.

"We're proud of you, Goldilocks."

"Your words were beautiful," Theo adds. "Just like you."

When they release me, I'm pulled into another hug from Brooklyn. She kisses my cheek and doesn't let go until Enzo laughs at her.

"You can't rush hugs," she snaps at him.

"Come on, wildfire. Let my girl go. We have places to be."

"She was my girl first, Enz. Hoes belong far, far before bros."

I gently push her away. "Enough, the pair of you. Let's get out of here."

Filtering out of the crematorium, we return to the lash of salty sea air. I look around for any signs of Foster or Ulrich but come up empty.

From here, I can see the cluster of camera vans and baying reporters being held back by our security detail in the distance.

"Where's Foster? Can anyone see him?"

Leighton stops at my side. "He's probably giving Ulrich some space. Want us to have a look around for them?"

"Please. I don't want to leave without saying goodbye."

He disappears with Theo and Enzo to search around, leaving me with Brooklyn and her men while Hunter and my father frown at the crowd of reporters.

Phoenix is halfway through a rant about choosing his latest hair colour when Leighton shouts my name, silencing us all.

"Over here! Quick!"

Legs pumping, the windswept landscape around me becomes a blur. The thud of several people at my heels accompanies the sudden roaring of my heartbeat.

Tucked behind a service building at the back of the crematorium, Leighton is waving us down. We reach him then race behind it to find Theo crouching down in the gravel.

"Oh God!" I screech.

Crumpled and unconscious, Foster's bleeding steadily onto the ground from a nasty gash on his forehead. His mouth hangs open as his eyelids refuse to lift.

"He's breathing." Theo lifts him into his arms. "We need an ambulance. He's got a bad head wound."

My eyes trace the droplets of blood to a nearby brick, lifted from a pile discarded at the back of the building. It's been tossed aside, still covered in slick blood.

"Someone hit him." My heart explodes into horrified butterflies that make my chest ache. "Where is Ulrich?"

"He wasn't here when we found him," Leighton replies.

"Shit! Did he do this?" Enzo exclaims.

"No," I cut him off. "He wouldn't do this to his dad. That kid's already lost one parent. Someone must have taken him."

Leaping into action, Enzo grabs his phone and calls down to the security team protecting the funeral, demanding they begin searching.

"Split up," Ethan barks at his team. "They can't have gone far. We were only inside for ten minutes."

Clutching my impossibly tight chest, I battle to remain calm, but I want to scream and rave at the top of my lungs. Ulrich is innocent in all of this. If he's hurt… I don't know what I'll do.

"Harlow," Brooklyn murmurs. "Take a breath for me. We're going to find him."

"Who would take him? Why?"

That's when reality hits.

I can hear him whispering straight into the depths of my mind, even from his secure cell hundreds of miles away in Sabre HQ.

This isn't over.

Your punishment will be my final act.

"It's him!" I scream hysterically. "Michael has him."

Theo pulls me into his chest. "Calm down, angel. He's locked in a cell with twenty-four-hour surveillance. Ulrich isn't with him."

"No. This is his people. His army. They're still doing his bidding, even without a master. You know Michael wanted us to catch him."

Looking down at me, his eyes are flecked with fear that vindicates my panicked rant. I know I'm right. The game is still on, and this is just his next move on the chessboard.

Well, checkmate.

He doesn't get to win.

Not while I'm still breathing.

CHAPTER 29
HUNTER

VACCINE – HOMETOWN & YOUNG

IT'S funny how the silence can sound so much louder than the world itself. Even amidst a chaotic scene that plays out like I've sitting on the mute button, I can feel every last frenzied shout and scream.

Harlow's loudest of them all. She's pacing up and down in the police station, tearing at her hair and demanding updates every second. This destructive behaviour hasn't stopped since we arrived several long hours ago.

Up. Down.

Back. Forth.

Step. Step.

The sounds are still there, even if I can't hear them. That's the strangest thing of all. Their existence isn't conditional on my hearing. The world turns on its own just fine without me.

But I won't allow it to.

I want to exist.

Our worst fears were confirmed when Theo located traffic cam footage of a green estate car careening away from the funeral at breakneck speed. They quickly stopped to swap cars with two others and derailed our tail.

They took advantage of our security detail being overwhelmed by shouting journalists. Enzo fired the agents that allowed Ulrich to slip past on the spot. Too fucking right.

After taking over the small village police station, Theo and Kade traced the paths of three identical vehicles. All using fake registrations and heading in totally different directions.

That's where things went wrong. With a well-oiled system of matching green estate cars working in harmony, we followed the wrong vehicle and lost our targets in a decoy chase.

Licence plates were changed, and the trail went cold. We're now searching for a needle in a haystack as Harlow and Foster become increasingly worried about Ulrich.

Enzo stops at my side, his entire frame carved with the same building tension we're all feeling. I nudge his shoulder and lift an eyebrow.

"*Nothing*," he signs back.

"What about traffic cams? CCTV? We've got the most advanced facial recognition software in the whole fucking country."

With a head shake, he dismisses our best assets. All the fancy tech and money in the world still can't plug the inevitable gaps that people with enough determination can exploit.

The wound on his head stitched and bandaged by paramedics, Foster is looming over Theo and Kade, watching their every move. His face is a mask of raw terror.

Harlow was right.

This was all part of the plan.

We know that Abaddon still has an underground network of supporters—the Angels of the Abyss—across the country that he's painstakingly built over the last few months.

Daphne was the tip of the iceberg, and her location was given to us wrapped in a red fucking bow. We've been playing by his rules all along, facing setbacks at every turn.

But it can't end like this.

We won't allow it.

Regardless of my feelings towards Giana and her scum of the earth relatives, Ulrich is an innocent child. I'm not prepared to sacrifice him to another one of Abaddon's sick games.

Enzo gestures toward the other side of the room, asking for me to take over with Harlow while he picks up an urgent phone call. I unlatch my tightly-folded arms and approach the hurricane of emotion.

She fists handfuls of her hair then tugs sharply, falling back into old patterns that haven't emerged since before we fled the country in a broken mess.

Approaching slowly, I take hold of her wrists then tug until she releases her hair. Harlow's anger-filled blue eyes look up at me, demanding answers that I'm powerless to give her.

"You don't need to do that," I murmur. "I've got you, sweetheart. We're going to find Ulrich."

Her lips move too fast, spilling out a rush of panicked words that I can't keep up with. Cupping her cheeks, I encourage her to slow down and recognise the two words she hisses out.

"My fault."

"No. This is on us. They shouldn't have had the chance to get anywhere near him."

Her lips quirk in a pained smile as she mouths back, "Can't … keep … all safe."

"I can fucking well try. If Abaddon dies, then his army dies with him. He's too dangerous to be kept alive."

Harlow's hand presses against my chest. "No."

"What prison can ever hold someone as powerful as that? He's far more than just a man now. He's become an idea, and we need to kill that idea to end this."

Gaze hardening, she shakes her head and frees up her hands to sign. "*Prison.*"

"You think that'll stop him from doing this again?" I scoff.

When she tries to escape my arms and walk away, I tighten my grip, cradling her against my chest. She can hate me all she wants. Not all of us have the luxury of a moral compass.

This is the last time he will be allowed to fuck with my family. I have no regard for what the right thing to do is. Killing Michael Abaddon will be my final act as Sabre's director.

More hours pass, and the tension in the room reaches a breaking point. Theo's scoured traffic cams covering every main road out of Croyde and identified our perps, all wearing ski masks.

There are no identities to even attempt to trace. These assholes are ghosts, enacting the will of a madman from afar. Not even we can counteract such mindless delirium.

On another laptop screen, the live video feed of a camera is strapped to Ethan's bulletproof vest. He's stepping through darkened rooms, searching the empty space with his flashlight and gun.

He took one of the SUVs a couple of hours ago to drive from Croyde to Holcombe, intending to check if there's any activity at Daphne's abandoned farmhouse.

Each room is declared empty one after another, killing our latest theory. Not a soul in sight. The rest of his team has taken a police helicopter to Tregaron in case our targets have returned there.

Nothing.

Not a damn lead.

As the dawn light rises, we've progressed to the cracked vinyl sofa in the corner of the police station break room. Harlow finally passed out, head pooled in her father's lap as he strokes her hair.

"Coffee?" I ask him.

Oliver shakes his head.

"Stay with her. She needs to sleep for a few more hours. I don't like how pale she is."

Even in the middle of this growing disaster, he can't help but roll his eyes at me. It's not every in-law relationship that the boyfriend can boss his girlfriend's parent around, or even be more protective than them.

Back in the main office, Theo miraculously holds his eyes open and scours the depths of the internet for any mention of Abaddon.

Our perp is a hot topic in online traffic, so there's a small chance we may find his supporters conspiring from the anonymity of the internet.

Brewing myself a cup of tea strong enough for the spoon to stand up in, I take Theo a black coffee and pat his shoulder. Again, he signs back that goddamn word that I want blacklisted from the English language.

"*Nothing*."

"There has to be something," I insist. "We can't go another day like this. Harlow's on the verge of losing her mind in there, and Foster isn't much better."

The man in question is pacing up and down just outside the window, his headful of dark hair and glasses bobbing past every second or so while he smokes a cigarette.

"Keep looking. All we need is one strike of luck."

Scribbling on his notepad, Theo tilts the page for me to read.

We need to speak to Abaddon. He knows where they're hiding.

"Absolutely not. We cannot trust that monster."

What else do you suggest? They're already a step ahead of us. We need to play this smart.

Pinching the bridge of my nose, I attempt to battle the rising migraine threatening to take me out of action. Stress always triggers them to return.

"There has to be something. We've got all this evidence and not a single scrap of it correlates. That can't be possible."

Theo grimaces as he writes back to me.

He's perfected the art of making people disappear without a trace over the last decade. We will never find Ulrich alone.

If I still had hair to fist, I'd be following in Harlow's footsteps and ripping the whole lot out in frustration.

"Just keep looking."

He doesn't watch me storm away, unable to disobey my directive. The intelligence team is working hard back at HQ following the same steps, and for hours now, there's been nothing.

This isn't working.

But working with Abaddon is exactly what he wanted all along. He's trying to leverage us, using Ulrich's life as the bargaining chip. We don't negotiate with serial killers.

Sliding my phone from my pocket, I pull up the conversation with Brooklyn, safely tucked away in London for her own protection.

Hunter: What's Abaddon doing?

It only takes her a second to reply.

Brooklyn: Been sat in the middle of his cell praying since Ulrich vanished. Hasn't eaten or slept. It's like he's waiting for something.

Dammit. He's waiting for us to cave and give in to his no doubt psychotic demands. We should've seen this coming.

Hunter: He's baiting us. Be careful. Don't go anywhere near him.

Brooklyn: Phoenix, Eli and Jude are here. Call when you have news. Look after Harlow.

Hunter: I will.

Enzo grabbing my shoulder startles me back to the busy room. Exhaustion and weariness have been replaced by alarm. He quickly signs an explanation.

"*Message.*"

"From whom?" I demand.

"*Army,*" he signs back.

We run back to the crowded table full of maps, laptops and documents. Theo is connecting his screen to a projector, offering us a wide-screen view of the video that's been uploaded to the internet.

Harlow races into the room, bleary-eyed and rumpled. Capturing her mid-stride, Enzo traps her between us so we can keep her calm.

With the Cobra team joining us, the room becomes crowded. Foster returns, stinking of cigarette smoke, and Theo hits play. His laptop automatically generates subtitles.

In the video, four figures are dressed in identical robes to the ones that Abaddon once wore. Their faces are concealed behind smooth black masks, adorned with Holy Trinities painted on.

"We are the Angels of the Abyss. You have taken our messiah, and we won't stop until he is safely returned to us."

Hudson's teeth are bared in a snarl, his fist banging on the table. Beside me, Enzo stiffens and clutches Harlow even tighter.

"The child has been born of cursed, demon blood. We will sacrifice his life to honour our Lord unless you submit to our demands."

The camera pans to the left, skipping over cracked, mould-covered brickwork to find a set of rusted iron bars. Behind them, a shivering, curled-up ball rests on the damp floor.

Ulrich.

Harlow writhes between us, desperate to throw a fist into the screen and release her frustration. I pin her in place by her arms.

"Our messiah knows where to find us. Searching is futile. You have twelve hours before the ritual will commence."

The message ends, and even I can tell that it leaves deathly silence in the room. Foster is turning a very dark shade of purple as he stares at the wall where the image of his son was projected.

Twelve hours. We can waste it searching for the ghosts who have slipped through our fingers or align ourselves with a vicious murderer in order to save an innocent life.

This is it.

The rapture has arrived.

Slipping free from our embrace, Harlow begins to shout and rave, demanding immediate action. I know instinctively what she wants.

Her brother, alive. Regardless of the price. It's taken us years to track Abaddon down, and now that we've got him, he's playing his final hand to escape his sentence.

"We cannot surrender Abaddon," I announce. "He will butcher more innocent lives, and that will be our fault."

She rounds on me and signs, "*My brother.*"

"There has to be another way."

"*No,*" Enzo speaks and signs.

Staring at him, defeat burns in the pits of his hopeless eyes. I simmer with anger.

"We can make that sick son of a bitch bleed and beg for death until he reveals their location. I'm not playing his games. Not like this."

Even saying it aloud, I know it won't work. That man doesn't feel pain or regret. He's as empty as his false idols.

Grabbing a handful of my shirt, Harlow gets close to my face so I can't mistake her words, laced with desperation.

"*Can't ... lose ... too.*"

"We can't give Abaddon what he wants. Do you want more women to die like your friends?"

Her distraught expression fractures further. "*No ... choice.*"

Everyone in the room is on her side, waiting for me to crack. Even Enzo nods in reluctant acceptance. I know what he's thinking. We follow Abaddon to these lunatics then blow them all to hell.

If it goes wrong, we could lose them all. We'd be breaking every remaining rule in the book by taking Abaddon from our custody and using him in a prisoner swap.

This will end our careers. There's no coming back from this. Stomach twisting, I crumple beneath the weight of the world. At least we'll go out with a bang.

"Fine." I sigh, feeling an inappropriate smile rise. "Fuck the rules. Let's go find the kid."

CHAPTER 30
HARLOW

BURN DOWN MY HOUSE – ARCHITECTS

MOONLIGHT ILLUMINATES THE SUFFOCATING DARKNESS, offering glimpses of light. Midnight strikes, and the dawn of a new day doesn't relieve the pressure sitting on my chest, determined to strangle me.

Theo's hand is slowly turning white as I grip it hard in my lap. It's taking all of my strength to sit in the helicopter without moving. I want to throw myself from it to escape the man sitting opposite me.

Michael doesn't need a headset to communicate. Ankles and wrists handcuffed with a chain between them, his wide smile drips with anticipation, and his eyes refuse to stray from mine.

"Bearing east," Enzo announces from the cockpit. "The coordinates are taking us to a remote village on the Scottish border."

He's flying one of the three helicopters taking us to our destination, following the instructions that Michael was more than happy to give once we submitted to his plan.

This won't be a simple trade that allows him to disappear into the night. I know that Hunter will put a bullet through Michael's skull long before he allows him to escape and hurt anyone else.

"Stick to the plan," Theo advises from his seat next to me. "The Cobra and Anaconda teams will move first to circle around. Then we'll bring Abaddon in with Hunter and Enzo."

Sat on my right side, Leighton is adjusting the straps on his bulletproof armour. "Don't leave my damn sight, Harlow."

"We're walking into a trap," I point out.

"A trap isn't a trap if we know it's coming."

"Then what is this, Leigh?"

His dark brown eyes meet mine. "This is a showdown."

Even though being in Michael's presence should reduce me to a sobbing, terrified wreck, I take each of my guys' hands and stare straight ahead without an inch of fear.

He stares back.

Lip curled.

Eyes hard.

No matter what happens next, Michael won't get to take another innocent life. Ulrich doesn't belong in the middle of this mess. Giana already died for her so-called sins, and I won't let her son do the same.

As the miles tick by, the atmosphere in the helicopter thickens. Anxiety dances in the air, and we clutch each other a little harder. We have no idea what we're walking into.

"I'm flying a drone over the area ahead of us," Theo says into his headset. "Detecting a huge heat signature."

I look over at the tablet in his lap, relaying the data. "What does that mean? People?"

He shakes his head. "Not necessarily."

Opposite me, Michael starts laughing. Deep, belly-vibrating laughter that bounces around us despite the roar of the helicopter.

Leighton tenses in his seat, holding himself back from pummelling his face into an unrecognisable paste that won't get us anything in return.

"I think…" Theo hesitates, frowning at the screen. "It's fire."

My heart freezes into a lump of ice in my chest. With Michael staring at me without saying a word, his voice still manages to slither through my mind. I vocalise the words he used to repeat out loud.

"In flaming fire, we will inflict vengeance on those who do not know God and those who do not obey the gospel of our Lord."

Michael watches my mouth move with satisfaction, his silent nod a recognition of his agreement. We're not walking into a hostage situation.

No.

This is a war zone.

As the helicopter begins to descend with the other two accompanying us, darkness fades, but it doesn't lift entirely. Instead, a warm, orange glow overtakes the night sky, belching ash and smoke.

"We're going to need the fire brigade," I whisper into the headset's microphone.

"Already alerted them," Theo responds. "But we're descending into thick woodland. It's going to take time for them to arrive."

"Holy fucking shit," Leighton curses. "Look."

Leaning over his black-clad shoulder, I gape at the awaiting sight. Thick, impenetrable trees smother any hint of life. But instead of luscious greenery, there's a canopy of flames.

The woods are on fire. Burning, razing, almighty fire, spreading in all directions. The flames reach so high, they kiss the atmosphere and engulf us in smoke. Blackness swallows our line of sight.

"Fuck!" Enzo curses.

Careening through the ash clouding the air, we swoop low and all strain against our belts, preventing us from falling out of the sky. A column of heat rises and causes the temperature to spike.

Into the darkness we go.

Down. Down. Down.

Emerging in the mouth of hell, there's a tiny break in the flames and thick woodland. Enzo aims for it, guiding the rest of the convoy to relative safety.

We touch down in an adjacent field with an inelegant thud, barely making it without crashing into something while lost in the smoke. Enzo rips off his headset and takes a breath.

"Everyone out. We're here."

Packing up our stuff, I hop out of the helicopter into the acrid air, trying hard not to cough. Hudson and Kade appear to help Enzo remove our prisoner safely, leaving me to locate Hunter.

Beneath his bulletproof vest, all-black combat gear and multiple layers of weapons, he's hardly recognisable as the gentle, sweatpants-wearing man I've come to know beneath his harsh exterior.

We all look like soldiers going into war, unsure if we'll make it out alive. Michael has driven us to the point of no return and left us with nothing but insane choices.

"Not a goddamn word," Hudson barks as he wrestles Michael out in handcuffs. "Play by our rules, and you may live to see tomorrow."

All he can do is laugh hysterically. Michael's mind has fractured, and beneath the still-visible bruises that mar his face, his madness is palpable. He's waited years for this very moment.

"Alright, listen up." Enzo gathers the teams together. "You all know the plan. Nobody makes it out, including this son of a bitch."

With a snarl, Hudson slams Michael back into the side of the helicopter again, attempting to knock the laughter from his lungs.

"We will find them and locate the kid," Enzo continues. "As soon as we have a visual, the Cobra and Anaconda teams will advance from the west to close the perimeter."

Kade nods, a hand resting on his semi-automatic gun. "Affirmative."

"We'll do the exchange, and that's when we make our move. I want them all apprehended. Dead or alive. They cannot be allowed to escape with the suspect."

"Great plan," Michael chokes out between laughs. "Can't even honour your word. The Lord will punish your deceit."

"You don't need a tongue to be exchanged," Hudson hisses in his ear. "Shut up, or I'll cut it out to keep as a fucking trophy."

"Keep each other safe." Enzo raises his voice above them. "Remember your training. Stay focused. Every single one of us walking in there is coming out alive. Understood?"

Everyone chimes in their agreement with varying degrees of optimism and apprehension. Even Ethan and his hardened team look afraid of the unknown facing us.

"We see this through, and the first round of beers is on me tonight." Enzo summons a weak smile. "Move out."

Whispering goodbyes and clasping hands, Hudson, Kade and Brooklyn's replacement, Hyland, take off first. Ethan and his team follow, leaving us to approach head-on with Michael.

Hunter takes over, grabbing his shoulder and shoving him forward. "Where are we going?"

Michael gestures ahead towards the north. Right into the path of the raging fire. "This way."

"One wrong step and I'll blow your brains out without hesitation," Hunter threatens. "Start walking."

Keeping in a tight formation that leaves no one exposed, we creep forward into the burning midnight hour. Michael leads a path through the smoke, grinning the entire time.

We should be thankful that his supporters don't seem to give a shit about Daphne. Like every other woman who's come in touch with Michael, she's outlived her usefulness and been discarded.

The closer we get to the forest fire, the hotter it burns. Heat lashes against my face, stinging and searing until my eyes stream with tears.

Michael bears left, skirting around the flames and leading us farther from safety. Keeping their guns up, Leighton and Enzo press into my sides, leaving nothing exposed.

"There's some activity ahead." Theo checks the tablet in his hands, connected to the drone overhead. "Signs of life."

"How many?" Enzo barks.

"I can't tell. The fire's messing with the drone's surveillance program. All I can tell is there's something going on."

Terrifying, unknown something. Scruffy jaw tightening, Enzo nods and crashes the back of his gun into Michael's skull.

"What are you planning?"

"My people understand the concept of loyalty," he snarls back. "They're earning their passage to the heavens while the rest of you will be left to burn."

"I'm sure God appreciates you setting his bloody forest on fire." Leighton laughs bitterly. "Makes total sense."

Michael throws him a vicious look. "This earth must burn before it can be reborn. I will be here to lead a new generation of humanity."

"He's even more unhinged than before," Enzo mutters. "We're going to take great pleasure in executing every last one of your people in front of you."

Unbothered by the threat, Michael continues with stilted steps, his ankles still imprisoned by the cuffs connecting to his wrists.

"We're in position." Kade's voice hums through our earpieces. "There're some abandoned buildings along the west side."

"Copy that," Enzo answers. "Ethan?"

"Approaching now," he replies with a crackle. "Nothing here. Just fire and ash. This thing is getting out of control."

"The authorities have been informed." Theo tucks the tablet under his arm. "Backup is on its way."

When the outline of a crumbling building rises on the horizon of a large clearing, our hackles rise. The nearest town is miles away, leaving ruins to fall into disrepair amidst the thick trees and shrubbery.

"Grant me your strength, Lord above," Michael calls out. "I am your loyal servant, and here lies my offering to you."

"Eyes sharp," Enzo orders.

When the first figures emerge, cutting through smoke with their painted masks in place, all guns rise to meet them. My horror intensifies as even more appear.

One after another.

Dozens of them.

We're surrounded on all sides by even more people than we anticipated, all dressed in their matching black robes and homemade masks. The sight of them makes me sick. He's indoctrinated them all.

"My angels," Michael calls out gleefully. "Your messiah has returned to reward your efforts."

Enzo butts him with his gun again, creating a gash that oozes fresh blood. "Silence. I have no qualms with gunning them all down."

"Save me!" Michael screams regardless.

Inching forward, the crowd of people shows no fear of the countless weapons trained on them. They're protected by their beliefs. This is their holy war, and we're their lambs to slaughter.

In the light of the rising fires from the forest, we meet on opposing sides of the battleground. Us, drenched in darkness, and their matching outfits lit by the glow of orange light.

That's when I spot it.

The towering pile of wood.

Sickness rises up my throat and threatens to erupt. Leighton curses, and Theo almost runs into the back of me. Hunter and Enzo are the only ones remaining even remotely calm.

Behind his trained puppets, Michael's ultimate revenge lies in wait. He's determined to wipe the last speck of his bloodline from this earth. Not even Giana's death sated him.

"I warned you," he says over his shoulder. "You had the chance to join me. This is your punishment for throwing God's grace aside."

Secured to a tall wooden post around which branches and logs are gathered, Ulrich is secured to it with tightly bound rope. Tied. Gagged. Tear-stained and petrified.

Oh my God.

He's going to be burned at the stake in front of us. It takes Leighton's arm barred across my chest to stop me from attacking Michael, even if it would provoke his people to do the same.

He isn't locked in a cell, awaiting to be exchanged. I'm staring at my brother on the verge of a public execution. They're planning to burn an innocent child alive for their messiah.

"Stop there," a voice calls as one steps forward. "Surrender, and we will let the boy go as promised."

"That isn't how this is going to work," Enzo shouts back. "Release the child now, and we won't kill your leader in front of you."

Michael breaks out in loud laughter. "You think I am afraid of death, sinner? Do as you please. My legacy will outlive me."

Enzo bares his teeth, desperate to sink a bullet into him. "I'll kill you in front of them if need be. This ends tonight."

"Then do it!" Michael shrieks.

Realisation of his plan settles in my mind. To him, this is the end of his mission. The culmination of all his hard work. The world is burning, and his angels are in place.

He can die safe in the knowledge that they will continue slaughtering on his behalf, even as he walks into the sunset to join his twisted false god in the burning heat of hell.

"Enzo, no!" I grab his shoulder. "Kill him and they set that bonfire alight. We have to follow their rules."

Silently communicating with my eyes, I urge him to remember the reason we came. We can still pull this off. Our teams are in place and ready to strike. None of them are making it out of here.

"Why don't you take your masks off and face us yourselves?" I yell at the crowd. "Only cowards hide their faces."

Grasping their masks, glowing with the symbol that adorns my body, one by one, they begin to pull them off. My breath catches, and the guys curse colourfully around me.

They're just normal people. Average men, women and even a couple of teenagers. Michael has captured them all. Bent their minds. Beaten. Manipulated. Warped and broken.

The ultimate cult.

Hidden in plain sight.

"Whatever he's told you is a lie," I try to reason. "You can still walk away from this. You don't have to follow his orders."

"The messiah has saved us from a life of sin," a young woman drones in a lifeless voice. "We have cleansed ourselves before God."

Enzo cocks his gun. "This is your last chance to walk away. All we want is the boy. I don't want to kill you all, but I will."

"And we would happily die for the cause." A man steps closer, drawing a knife from his robes. "Give us what we want."

I duck my head to whisper to the others listening on the line. "Be ready. This is going to get ugly."

"We're in position," Kade responds.

"Now!" the man roars angrily, his face contorted with devilish rage. "Give him to us, or we light that bonfire up."

"Enzo," I beg desperately. "Just do it. Give him to them."

With a sigh, Enzo unlocks Michael's handcuffs. The moment he's free, he takes a big, deep inhale, stretching his arms above his head.

He turns to face me. "I warned you this would end in blood, Harlow. The rapture is here, and your time is at an end."

"Give us Ulrich," I demand.

"That child is the last of my cursed bloodline. He must die like the rest of you." Michael turns away. "Arise, my angels!"

Moving in a flash, more masked figures emerge from the smoke rising on all sides, tearing through the flames like demons escaping the mouth of hell. We didn't clock any of them.

"Incoming!" Hunter screams.

All hell breaks loose. Enzo takes aim and guns down two of the approaching shadows at the same moment Michael launches himself into Leighton to tackle him aside.

The pair collide and tumble, punching and screaming at each other. I pull the gun from my thigh holster and almost unload a round into Michael's head when a robed-blur smashes into me.

"Advance," I hear Kade scream in my ear. "Get the fucking kid!"

A pair of hands wrap around my throat, grappling to choke me to death. I lose grip of my gun in the melee and fall back on my training, bucking to shake off the masked attacker.

When the blast of a gun being fired cracks through the night, warmth washes over me, hot and sticky. Hunter stands above me, splattered with gore as he offers me a hand up.

He snatches my gun from the ground then hands it back. "Get to your brother!"

With the fire inching closer throughout the woodland surrounding us, the battleground is bathed in hellish light. Robed fanatics descend from all directions, colliding with the teams appearing from the west.

Scanning past Enzo and Leighton caught in their own fistfights, I catch sight of Ulrich at the centre of the unlit bonfire. Someone stands at the edge, a burning branch in hand.

"Ulrich!" I scream.

His gaze finds me amidst the madness.

"I'm coming!"

That's when the bonfire erupts into flames. The stench of burning fuel permeates the smoky air, and I can see him screaming around the gag in his mouth.

Breaking out into a run, I duck past whizzing bullets and flying fists, my attention focused on one point. Someone tries to tackle me, but Hudson appears, easily cutting them down with a knife.

"Go," he shouts at me. "I'll cover you!"

Without hesitating, I continue to duck and weave with him on my tail, slicing apart more obstacles. Michael's unhinged angels have the advantage of numbers, but they're sloppy and untrained.

In front of me, Kade is locked in a bloody fistfight, his gun lost in the chaos. Fists flying and flesh slapping with the landed blows, he hammers his opponent into the ground.

Passing him, I screech to a halt at the edge of the bonfire, surrounded by violence. Smoke fills my lungs and silences my screams of Ulrich's name. He's lost inside.

I can't see past the thick black ash and smoke. On the verge of throwing myself in to try to reach him, a figure emerges from the darkness, and his strong arms wrap around my waist to pull me back.

"Not so fast." His hot breath lashes against my ear. "I want you to watch him burn before I feed you to the flames as well."

I buck against Michael, his wrinkled but muscled arms trapping me in a vice. No one responds to my wails for help. He's snuck through the smoke to hold me back from Ulrich.

"Stop this!" I scream at the top of my lungs. "You can have me, but he doesn't have to die!"

"Everyone must die, my darling niece. We will begin again with a clean slate and no more filthy sinners poisoning this world."

"Ulrich! Ulrich!"

"He's going to burn in hell with his whore of a mother," he spits in my ear. "Just like you will once I've butchered every last person you love while you watch."

Keeping his iron grip on my body, Michael spins us around so I have an undisturbed view of the violence devouring us all. My men are lost in the war zone of bullets and blood.

I can't see anything. The fires have created a burning hot prison all around us, and smoke muddies my line of sight. The wails and screams are the only indication of life amidst the haze.

"Watch them die for their sins," Michael taunts. "I tried to warn you. I tried to *save* you. This is all your doing."

A flash of steel slicing through the smoky air catches my eye, eliciting a pained bellow. Nearby, Leighton's face is blood-stained, his mouth hanging open on the agonised syllable.

The knife is buried deep into his shoulder, forcing him to halt his attack on the man trapped beneath him. I howl his name, but it's silenced by the roar of noise drowning everything else out.

"If only you'd stayed safe in your cage." Michael drags his tongue down my cheek. "My perfect little girl. It pains me to do this, but you've left me no choice."

"Pain," I gasp through my tears. "You don't know the meaning of the word. No one has ever truly loved you. You're alone, Uncle!"

"Alone." He chuckles. "But victorious."

"Not yet."

Losing all sense of control, I buck and fight against him, throwing myself around in an attempt to escape. Michael evades every last attempted punch, his iron-clad grip refusing to relent.

I have to watch as blood is spilt, and flames reach the point of no return.

We're trapped on all sides, and the bonfire is raging behind us. I can't see if Ulrich's alive.

My spirit breaks. Shatters. Implodes. Violent rage slips into my bloodstream and expands, dissolving all intentions I had of granting my murdered friends the legal justice they deserved.

They will have justice.

God's justice.

Fire and fucking brimstone.

Managing to sneak a hand underneath my armoured vest, I feel for the small blade I stashed inside. It slots into my hand, and Michael howls when I bury it deep in his side.

We fall together, and I'm crushed beneath his weight, blood seeping over me. He wrenches the knife from his side and howls like a crazed animal at the sight of red.

"You fucking whore!"

The knife comes curving towards me, intent on slamming into my chest to pierce my heart. I manage to lunge at the last second, dodging the blow and rolling across the ash-laden grass.

Michael follows, slicing and stabbing, seeking a single blow to stop me from sliding away from him. We tangle together, and my fist connects with his face.

Taking advantage of the brief second of distraction, I pull the blade from his fist and redirect it up into his chest. The knife slips into his breastbone, and he screeches like a banshee.

"You took everything from me!" I pull it out and stab again, harder this time. "I won't let you take them too."

Bleeding everywhere, Michael pushes through the pain and launches another frantic attack. His forehead crashes into mine, causing stars to burst behind my eyes and blur my vision.

"Enough!" he shouts.

Punching me in the jaw hard enough to rattle my teeth, he prises the knife from my hand then takes aim. The slash of the blade parting flesh in my arm barely registers, though he leers in satisfaction.

The pain is inconsequential to the terror twisting my heart into a knot. I can't see any of my men. Michael has got me trapped, and the knife is firmly grasped in his bloody hand.

"You're an ungrateful slut," he lashes, slicing my arm with a long stab. "I should have killed you the moment I saw you."

"Yes!" I scream back. "You should have! I won't let you hurt anyone else!"

Jabbing my fist into his throat, he falls back, the air knocked out of him. I desperately search around, but the hazy air carries only grunts of pain and the sound of fists hitting flesh.

The bonfire behind me is a blazing inferno. I can see the huge wooden structure at the centre burning. Ulrich's body is just visible, still untouched by flames, but quickly running out of time.

"Ulrich!" I yell. "Hold your breath!"

Michael finds his feet then attempts to throw himself at me again when the glow of piercing, bright lights illuminate the disaster around us. He freezes, peering up into the sky.

It's as if the heavens have opened, and God's light is pouring down on us all. Michael's face is a mask of open adoration, his hands raising in a frenzied prayer.

"I'm here, Lord! Your servant!"

When the hum of spinning rotors accompanies the bright light, his smile fades into a stunned glower. Four helicopters break through the haze, their powerful lights smothering us all.

I spot the letters on the side.

SCU.

Ladders fall from the side of the first helicopter, allowing multiple bodies to descend into the battle. The flash of bright green hair is the first thing I see as Phoenix makes an appearance.

A familiar voice shouts through my earpiece. "I told you motherfuckers not to leave me at home!"

In the cockpit with a pilot lowering them to land in the clearing, Brooklyn leans out of the window, searching for us. She releases a spray of bullets from her gun and shouts our names.

All four helicopters have reinforcements climbing down from them. Phoenix lands on his feet in the clearing, with a furious-eyed Jude jumping down from the ladder a second later.

He takes one look at me, bleeding and semi-collapsed, before making a beeline straight towards me. Michael screams in anger, his body failing him as he slips and slides on the blood-slick grass.

"Get away from her!" Jude bellows, deftly weaving through the night with deadly ease.

Running straight at Michael, he throws his arms at his waist, then the pair goes sailing through the smoke. Jude slams him back into the ground, and they both roll, grappling for control.

"Jude!" I shout in a panic.

Clutching my screaming arm, I find my knife then battle to stand back up to help him. Phoenix appears at my side and hangs the gun from his arm to offer me a hand.

"He's fine!" he shouts. "Where are the others?"

"I don't know!"

"Shit!"

Shoving past him, I run towards the bonfire, begging for another sight of my brother. Phoenix follows, attempting to stop me from approaching the stench of fuel and flames.

"Harlow, wait!"

I ignore him.

Ulrich needs me.

Bolting around the back of the structure, I spot an opening where the wood has collapsed so the flames are lower. Phoenix roars but can't stop me from taking a running jump into the fire.

The world vanishes.

Only the fire exists.

Swimming through the devil's flames, searing pain licks at my skin, cooking my hands. Pain doesn't stop me. Not even as I feel my skin pop and sizzle.

I push onwards, clambering over fire-slick piles of wood. Numbness spreads over me, and my lungs scream in protest against the onslaught of smoke stealing all of the oxygen.

"Ulrich," I choke on a sob.

His head lolling forward, Ulrich is unconscious in a cloud of acrid smoke. Every second is pure torture, the few inches between us protected by an ocean of fire that I have to wade through.

Move, Harlow.

Fucking move.

With the voices in my head roaring to life, I dig deep to find the courage to take a jump. Piles of burning branches crack beneath my feet, almost dropping me into the pits of the bonfire.

When I lay my hand on the rope holding my brother prisoner, I position the knife in my shaking hand and begin slashing. It's barely working, my nerves exposed by melted skin.

Slash. Stab. Saw.

Tears burn my sizzling cheeks. When the rope finally breaks, Ulrich's small body slumps straight into my arms. I almost drop him as I fight to remain balanced on a blackened plank of wood.

"Ulrich! Please ...wake up."

His heavy lids twitch and he moans. "Harlow."

"Hold on."

With the last vestiges of my strength, I throw us both back through the flames rising ever higher. Michael's rapture consumes us both, and we tumble through acid and pure agony.

Falling.

Falling.

Falling.

My shoulder impacts with something hard. We roll in a tangle of limbs, hitting the ground with Ulrich still cradled in my arms. The moment we're out of the fire, I feel someone grab my ankle and pull.

"Harlow! Breathe!"

But I can't do it. Not alone. My lungs aren't responding to me, and the air is clogged in my ash-filled throat. Eyes glued shut, I hold on to Ulrich in my arms and let the world fade.

I did it.

Ulrich will live.

Nothing else matters. If I was only meant to leave that cage in order to save his life, then I've prevented another lost childhood. More pain. Suffering. The endless cycle of violence.

My vision darkens. The world begins to wink out of existence, but at the last possible moment, I hear something. A shout. Bellowing my name in sharp tones of panic.

Lungs on fire, someone blows clean, pure oxygen straight into my mouth. Over and over. Pumping. Squeezing. Inflating. The purest essence of life fills me up and escapes my gasping mouth.

Eyes opening despite the endless stream of tears, I roll onto my side and cough until there's nothing left in me to give. Someone is braced over my body, trying to pull Ulrich from my arms.

Blue eyes.

Dirty blonde hair.

Familiar smile lines.

"I'm here, love." Dad holds the oxygen mask against my face. "I'm not leaving you. I need you to breathe."

My father is here.

Saving me.

I'm safe.

With the mask pressed back on my face, I gulp down the air, letting someone else take Ulrich from me. It's all I can do to suck in each agonising breath and hold it in my searing lungs.

More bodies in uniform stream from the helicopters, and when another face swims into my line of sight, I question whether I'm dead already. He's disturbingly familiar.

"I've got him," Sanderson barks, a medical kit slung over his shoulder. "Evac is five minutes out."

He looks at me, and our eyes connect for the first time since the hospital bed I woke up in last year. His smile is tight but filled with awe, unlike the obnoxious lash of his voice tormenting me before.

"You're going to be okay, kid," he tries to comfort. "We're here with backup. Try not to move too much."

"The g-guys," I splutter.

"Harlow—" Dad begins.

"S-See them…"

"They're okay, love."

Sliding an arm around my shoulders, he lifts me enough to have a look at the carnage around us. The clearing is littered with bodies, some writhing in pain and others still as the SCU takes control.

Bright lights flash, and uniformed figures tackle the blaze. God's fury fights back, lashing them with heat. The fire can't spread farther as it's pelted with water cannons.

The last few fights are being broken up—armed agents pulling apart robed madmen and their vicious clawing. I watch as Ethan is rescued by an SCU operative, his face covered in blood.

"Harlow!" a voice yells.

Broad shoulders are running towards me faster than a freight train. Enzo. He's followed by Theo and Leighton, both limping badly and supporting each other. Leighton's clutching his bleeding shoulder.

Enzo skids to a stop then falls to his knees on the grass next to me. I've been dragged several metres away from the still-raging bonfire to a place of relative safety.

His eyes race over me, taking in the burned skin of my hands and neck, which were unprotected by thick fabric. I know it's bad. I can't feel my extremities, and the pain has vanished into numbness.

"Fuck," he spills out in a panic. "You're .... fuck! We need an ambulance."

"Three minutes out," Sanderson retorts. "Good thing you called, Montpellier. You owe me for saving your backside."

Enzo spares him a glance. "Took you long enough."

"You're welcome."

"You c-called the SCU?" I choke out.

His face softens in a worried smile. "Always good to have a backup plan, just in case. Even if it is this asshole."

"Pleasure working with you too," Sanderson mutters, stepping aside so Phoenix can get a look at me.

"Next time you're planning to run headfirst into a blazing fire, give me a bit of warning," Phoenix tries to joke, even though his terror is obvious.

"I'm sorry, N-Nix."

"You're okay, Harlow. Just breathe. Help's coming."

Beneath me, Dad is trying to offer comfort in any way he can. He's struggling to find an unburned place to touch me. The areas that weren't covered by my protective gear are all crisped.

Enzo pulls a wedge of bandages from a laid out medical kit and applies pressure to where the blade slashed through an opening in my armoured clothing.

"Where the hell is that ambulance?" he shouts.

"One minute out." Sanderson drops another medical bag at his side. "I'll bring them in. Don't move."

"D-Dad."

"I'm here, Harlow." He smooths a hand over my charred hair. "You're doing good. Keep breathing."

At my side, Ulrich suddenly wakes up with a pained splutter, pushing the oxygen mask away from his face. He wrenches his eyes open and looks over at me.

"Hey," I sob through my mask. "Got you, little man."

His bloodshot eyes fill with tears. "H-Harlow."

Phoenix hovers over him, taking over Sanderson's position. "Put this mask on for me, kiddo. Nice deep breaths."

Surrendering to the mask placed back on his face, Ulrich returns to lying on his back. His hand reaches out to clasp my wrist. If I could feel my hands, I'd hold him too.

Rotors spinning above us, the fourth and final helicopter lands. Brooklyn and Eli climb out together, both appearing petrified of what they'll find on the ground.

Through the light of the bonfire, I can see her reunite with her husbands. Everyone is converging around us. Jude and Kade run straight for them, and the four collide in a tangle.

"Where is Hudson?" Brooklyn yells.

"H-Hunter," I rasp.

"Shh," Enzo hushes. "They're coming."

With a group of firefighters appearing to tackle the bonfire behind us, three outlines stumble past them through the smoke. Michael's slumped frame is trapped between two lumps of muscle.

He's still alive.

Barely clinging on, his entire body soaked in blood from our fight. He can't walk alone, too weak to even hold his own head up. But Hunter and Hudson refuse to let him get away that easily.

"I caught him about to blow his own brains out!" Hudson shouts. "Does that mean I get a medal or some shit?"

The pair throw Michael on the grass a few metres from us. His hard green eyes are glazed over, like he's been hollowed out at the core by a swoop of God's hand.

Empty.

Defeated.

Gone.

His angels are dead while his mission floats in the destroyed embers that settle around us. Michael failed. The slump of his body carries that defeat with each unwanted breath he takes.

Hunter delivers a swift kick to his ribcage before he turns to face us. The moment his eyes land on me, his face changes. Euphoria flicks to horror in a split second.

"Harlow!"

The darkest shade of rage filters over him. Hudson breaks his reunion with Brooklyn and the others to guide them over to us, until everyone is settled around us.

"It's … over?" I grit out.

Brooklyn falls at my side, her belly protruding from her clothes. "It's over, Harlow. Christ. What did you do?"

Almost hacking up a lung in a coughing fit, I stare up at her. "I c-couldn't let … s-someone else die."

Cheeks wet with flowing tears, she strokes my hair from my face, her face lit by steadily increasing blue lights. An army of people are arriving as the fires rage on around us.

Metres away, Michael groans in the most exquisite sound of pain. "N-Not over… W-Won't stop."

Face twisted in an animal-like snarl that matches Hunter's predatory expression, Enzo ducks low to brush a kiss on my forehead, above the oxygen mask keeping my lungs going.

"I'll kill him for this."

"No," I wheeze out.

"Look what he's done to us all. He deserves to die in agony."

Leaving me in my father's lap, Enzo rises to join his best friend. The pair of them stare down at our enemy—defeated and alone, abandoned by God and the drones he created.

"This is for every life that you've ruined." Enzo takes the knife that Hunter offers him. "You'll never hurt my fucking girl again."

Before he can sink the knife into Michael's black heart, I scream as loud as my damaged lungs will allow. He freezes at the last second, restraining himself long enough to look back at me.

"Living is h-his … punishment." I wrestle the mask aside with my good hand. "Death is too m-merciful."

Enzo's eyes briefly sink shut. "Please, Harlow. You know what he's done."

"I-I know."

"Then let me fucking do this!"

"I r-remember." I take a shuddered breath. "M-Make sure he does t-too."

When Enzo fails to move, held prisoner by indecision, Hunter kneels down next to him and prises the knife from his grip. It has to be him. Our leader. Our protector. The man who kept us together.

His gaze is fixed on me, but it's filled with the knowledge of all we've sacrificed for this defeat. All of us. In so many ways. There isn't a single member of our family emerging unscathed from this.

"You're sure?" Hunter checks.

With a final burst of energy, I nod back.

"Then I'll give him a nice little reminder instead."

Straddling Michael's crumpled body, Hunter hovers the knife over his face. The tip of the blade circles his eye socket in a slow, cruel tease, eliciting a thin stream of blood.

"I hope you live a very long, healthy life and look in the mirror every day. I want you to remember this moment."

Phoenix covers Ulrich's eyes to make sure he can't watch as Hunter sinks the knife deep into Michael's cheek. His screams ricochet around us in a beautiful, perfect harmony.

Hunter holds him beneath his weight, carving with slow precision. There's no emotion on his face. No pleasure. This is the final task on his list to be ticked off before we find our freedom.

"You're going to look in the mirror every single day for the rest of your life and remember this. You. Fucking. *Lost.*"

We all watch the expert curve of the blade, slashing the triangle across the entire length of his face, from ear to ear. Michael's shrieking reaches a fever pitch as Hunter begins to cut the external circle in.

The Holy Trinity.

Father, Son and Holy Spirit.

"Your God has abandoned you," Hunter spits into his butchered face.

"Failure will be your legacy. You couldn't complete your mission, and you never, ever will."

My own scars burn, knowing the pain that their inception brings. Only this time, that symbol will be etched on Michael's face forever, unable to be hidden or removed.

A constant, infallible reminder. For every woman he raped and carved up, he will see that same symbol scarred onto his flesh.

"Your ritual is complete." Hunter finishes his work with a flourish, parting flesh and muscle, skin and blood.

Bright blood is seeping through the deep wounds, flashing sickening flaps of skin and gaping soft tissues that will never be pieced back together. Now we match.

In life.

In death.

Into the forever.

The wails of my barely conscious uncle mourning his destroyed face are the last thing I hear. My eyes sink shut, safe in the knowledge that my friends have the justice they died for.

CHAPTER 31
LEIGHTON

MORE THAN LIFE - MACHINE GUN KELLY & GLAIVE

"I'D LIKE to petition to bulldoze this waiting room."

Sitting next to me, his laptop unopened and coffee discarded, Theo stares up at the ceiling. His blonde curls are ruffled from sleeping across the plastic seating all afternoon.

"Seconded," he mutters.

"Really?"

"I'm sick of the sight of it too. You know, there's a scene in this book I just read—"

"Theo," I cut him off. "If you're going to talk about books, I'm going to leave you in here while I knock it down."

He glowers at me. "It wouldn't hurt you to pick one up and expand upon your three single brain cells."

"I didn't see you complaining about the pizza I ordered you last week. Only a genius would think to combine anchovies and olives."

"Or a psychopath."

"Well, let's ask Richards. He'll make that judgement."

Sitting on the other side of the hospital waiting room with Brooklyn asleep on his shoulder, Richards is staring at the magazine in his hands. He insisted on coming down when Enzo called him.

"I can tell you the answer right now." Theo picks up his cold coffee then drains it with a wince. "Certifiably insane."

"Ouch. No more pizza for you."

"Thank God for that. I'm surprised we haven't gotten food poisoning already."

Both emerging from freshening up in the bathroom, Enzo and Hunter retake their creaky plastic seats opposite us. I try to reach for my water bottle and hiss in pain as it pulls my bandaged shoulder.

"Idiot," Hunter curses. "Just ask for help."

I gape at him as he passes me the water bottle. "He really doesn't get the irony of that after the last eight months, does he?"

"Don't start a fight now," Enzo grumbles, folding his arms. "At least give it twenty-four hours since our last firefight."

Lapsing back into silence, we all anxiously watch the doors that lead to the intensive care ward. At this point, we might as well move in here instead of returning to our empty London home.

Harlow and Ulrich were airlifted here after being stabilised in a hospital near Carlisle in the early hours of this morning. We've been waiting for an update since then.

The doors to the waiting room open, emitting Oliver and Foster with hot drinks in their hands. Weirdly enough, the pair have stuck close together, supporting each other in their fear.

"Anything?" Oliver asks worriedly.

"Not yet," Enzo grunts. "What's taking them so fucking long?"

"They're looking after her, Enz," Theo tries to comfort him. "She's in good hands."

"The only hands I want her in are ours. I don't trust anyone else as far as I could throw them."

"We aren't doctors." I roll my eyes. "Sit your oversized ass down, and be bloody patient for once in your life."

With a curse, he sinks back down into his seat, haggard and exhausted. None of us have slept, although my parents dropped off clean clothing after taking Lucky for us.

The past twelve hours have been a whirlwind of hospitals, helicopters and cordoned off smoking wreckages. None of it feels real. We've got a lot of shit to process.

"She's going to be okay," Oliver says, mostly to himself. "I cannot lose her again."

Foster clasps his shoulder. "Harlow's tough as nails. She's going to pull through."

"I just got her back. We haven't had enough time together."

"You're going to get all the time in the world," Theo reassures him. "The burns were localised to her hands and neck."

Oliver's face pales further.

"Good work," I whisper. "You freaked him out even more."

"Why is it my job to make people feel better?" Theo replies quietly. "You're the damn people person. Not me."

The doctors come to retrieve Foster first. Ulrich is stabilised and awake. He sustained minor burns on his arms and a nasty case of smoke inhalation, but he will make a full recovery.

My parents make a reappearance as evening settles, bringing food for everyone and setting up camp with Richards and Brooklyn in the corner.

Hudson and Kade are held up at HQ, managing the fallout along with our unexpected allies at the SCU, but Phoenix, Eli and Jude soon arrive with updates and more food.

"Abaddon has been detained in Belmarsh along with Daphne." Phoenix pauses to kiss his wife. "After surgery, that is."

"They did what?" Brooklyn snarls, a hand on her burgeoning belly. "I'll go and fuck his face up again myself."

"Let me rephrase that," he adds to appease her. "Surgery to make sure the son of a bitch has to see that mangled mess until the day he dies. He's under medical supervision but stable."

Satisfaction fills me. As much as I would've liked to see him dead and buried, Harlow was right. This victory is far sweeter. His one purpose in life has been taken away from him forever.

He will serve the rest of his life behind bars, tormented by the knowledge that he did not complete his mission. God has forsaken him, and he will forever bear the marks of that failure.

That gives me the smallest smidgen of comfort, though I fucking hate what it's taken to get us here. We all fought for our lives, but Harlow was the one who sacrificed everything to save her brother.

She won that fight.

For all of us.

"Belmarsh, huh?" Enzo chuckles happily. "Neither of them will ever get out of that place. It's literally hell on earth."

"Fitting, then," Oliver chimes in with a smile. "They're both where they belong."

"Anyone need coffee?" Eli asks, taking a group order to hydrate us all. "Be right back."

"I'll come," Phoenix says.

The pair disappear to fetch everyone's drinks, and Jude takes the vacated seat next to Brooklyn, ducking down to kiss her belly first.

"The country's on fire with everything that happened, but it's contained," he reveals. "Kade and Hudson are managing it."

Face thoughtful, Enzo stares down at his hands in his lap. The knuckles are swollen and scabbed over, much like the rest of us. No one escaped without at least minor injuries.

By some miracle, we suffered no casualties on our side. Both teams emerged bloodied and broken, but still in possession of their lives. Perhaps God is watching out for us.

"How many of Abaddon's people were arrested?" Theo asks.

"Twenty-eight. Another nine are dead. The ones who were captured are giving up more names in a bid to save themselves."

"Not so loyal, after all." He snorts.

"More like rats fleeing a sinking ship," Jude agrees. "Hudson is coordinating the arrests with Ethan and some dick called Sanderson. The superintendent's managing the media like she does best."

"Taking all the credit?" Enzo supplies.

Jude shrugs. "Surprisingly not. That scene was a literal bloodbath. There's a lot of unanswered questions, and she's taking the brunt of it for the time being."

That's a change. We're usually the first ones to be thrown to the wolves. After all of this, it seems we've earned her allegiance. Even if it is temporary at best.

"Just got an email from Harlow's publisher." Theo sits straighter, eyeing his phone. "Apparently, pre-orders of her book have quadrupled in the last twelve hours."

"Jesus Christ," Oliver swears. "She's lying in a hospital bed right now."

"And becoming a millionaire," Theo answers. "Everyone's calling her a hero for what she did. The world wants to read her book."

That woman has given every single scrap of herself to this fight, trauma be damned, and she's going to be rewarded for her bravery. If that isn't hope in action, then I don't know what is.

"What happens now?" Hunter asks aloud.

We all look at each other, none of us knowing how to respond. Sabre may connect our family, but Harlow is the glue that allowed us to find each other again.

"I'm done," Enzo says flatly.

Hunter nods, reading his mouth. "Me too."

Looking between them both, Theo's face is impassive. "Sabre represents the last thirteen years of your lives. You'd walk away? Just like that?"

Enzo nods without hesitating. "Yes."

"And do what?"

"Anything. We've done our duty. It's time to pass Sabre on to the next generation to take forward. I can think of the perfect people."

"Who?" I frown at him.

Enzo's eyes stray over to the corner of the room where Brooklyn's accepting a steaming cup of tea from Eli and kissing him firmly on the mouth. He gives her a secret smile, ruffling her ashy blonde hair.

His one hand clutching his phone, Jude is keeping up with the developing situation and exchanging whispers with Phoenix. Despite leaving Sabre, both are well-versed in managing disasters.

"The Cobra team has proved themselves time and time again." Enzo's voice thickens with emotion. "I can't think of anyone better to take Sabre from us."

He's actually serious. I can tell by the look on my brother's face that they've already had this conversation. The pair of them are united in their sheer exhaustion.

"Hudson and Kade will burn the place down within a week." I laugh under my breath. "But I'm totally on board."

Arms folded, Theo considers it for a moment. "We could go anywhere. Do anything. Whatever the hell Harlow wants."

I cross my fingers and pout. "Please let it involve that awesome seafood restaurant in Costa Rica. My stomach is begging you."

Enzo jabs a thumb at me. "We can leave this one here and go find a hot, sandy beach to bake ourselves on."

"Hey!"

"Obviously, Sabre would crumble without you." He winks at me. "Seeing as you work *so* hard for us, Leigh."

"I happen to have a great work ethic."

"It's truly next level."

I glare at him. "I'm glad you agree."

Hunter clears his throat. "We need to stay here for my surgery and recovery, but after that, I'm happy to go basically anywhere."

Enzo squeezes his forearm then signs back, "*Of course.*"

"While you're all busy making plans..." Brooklyn's voice interrupts us. "I'm going to be squeezing a baby out in a few months. You ain't leaving me here alone with these bastards."

"Your husbands?" Enzo laughs.

"Yes. They'll drive me insane." She points a finger at him. "You have babysitting duty too, Uncle Enz. No excuses."

"Ah, hell."

"Harlow's going to be busy with the press tour for her book," Theo interjects. "And Hunter will need months of speech therapy after his surgery to relearn how to communicate."

Enzo groans. "Looks like we're here for a while, then. But I want a holiday, and we're not moving back to London. I want out of the city."

Ending our conversation, the female doctor who took Harlow into the ward exits through the sealed doors. We all fall silent as she scans over the waiting room, packed to bursting with people.

"There certainly are a lot of you here." She chuckles in amusement. "Harlow is a lucky girl to have such a big family."

Enzo shoots to his feet. "What's happening?"

"She's stable and awake," the doctor confirms. "We intend to perform surgery to attach a skin graft to her right hand. She has severe third-degree burns there, but the left hand is only second-degree."

My gut twists with worry. "What about her neck?"

"Also second-degree. She will have some scarring. The team has done their best to treat the wounds. Overall, this is a good outcome."

Everyone breathes a sigh of relief and slumps, hugging each other for moral support. Theo quickly translates the update to Hunter in a text message as all four of us gather in front of her.

"She's a little groggy from sedation," the doctor warns. "Don't keep her up for long. We need to hold her for a few days to monitor her lungs after the smoke inhalation and for any signs of infection."

"Wait," Hunter says. "Oliver should go first. She'll want to see her dad."

Enzo slumps in disappointment but reluctantly agrees. With a muttered thanks, Oliver follows the doctor into the ward. It's another nail-biting half an hour before he reappears.

His eyes are misted with tears. "She wants to see you guys."

Clapping his shoulder, Hunter passes him first and leads us into the intensive care ward. Harlow's room is the last door on the right. We pass Ulrich's room, where he's quietly murmuring to his dad inside.

Stopping outside Harlow's room, we all freeze in the cold clutches of fear. It was hard enough seeing Harlow get hurt before. This is going to be far worse.

"Come on," Hunter orders sharply. "Our girl needs us. Grow some goddamn balls."

Nice to see my brother has made a very miraculous reappearance in time for our collective near-death experience. And here I was thinking he'd finally mellowed.

Filtering into the calm, low-lit room, the beep of a heart monitor accompanies the drip of fluids and drugs being fed into the bandaged angel in the bed.

Harlow's eyes are closed, her lips parted and breathing steadily. Thick, bright white bandages wrap around her throat while her hands are gauzed and immovable at her sides.

"Princess?" I murmur.

Eyes flicking open, two devastating blue jewels land on all four of us. Beneath the burns, bruises and scratches, she summons the same hopeful smile that first ensnared my heart and refused to surrender it.

"Hi."

That's all it takes. The distance between us vanishes as we all crowd her, fighting the urge to scoop her into our arms. Multiple needles and IV lines feed into her arms and body.

"You're awake," Enzo rasps, overcome with emotion. "Fuck, little one. I thought we'd lost you for a moment there."

"Like hell," Harlow says in a wispy voice. "It'll take more than that to get rid of me."

Bowing his head, he hides his face in the crisp white sheets of the hospital bed. The shake of his shoulders tells us enough. Hunter rests a hand on his best friend's shoulder to comfort him.

"You did so fucking good, sweetheart," he whispers in awe.

Harlow's mouth twitches in a grin. "I love you."

He can read those words well enough.

"I love you," Hunter echoes. "Never do that to us again."

When her glassy eyes flicker over to me and Theo, she whispers for us to come closer. Theo moves first, his days of being able to maintain a safe distance relegated to the past.

"Are you in any pain?" he asks gently.

"I'm okay. Can't really feel anything at all." Her throat catches. "Where is Ulrich? Is he okay?"

"He's fine, angel. Just down the corridor."

Lips pinched together, she can't stop the fat tears from rolling down her cheeks. "I thought he was dead. I thought—"

"Enough," Theo hushes her. "You saved his life."

"Then … nothing else matters. It was worth it."

With the three of them crowding her, Harlow looks up at me last.

Somehow, I can't cross the final space holding us apart. I'm terrified that if I blink, she'll be unconscious and bloody in that field again.

"Leigh," she croaks.

Still, I can't move.

"Come here."

"You could have died," I force out.

"But I didn't," she combats in a barely audible whisper. "Please, Leigh. I need you too."

Staring at the woman who went from being a stranger to a friend to my entire fucking universe all in one goddamn year, the final wall around my heart collapses.

One that I didn't realise I still held in place after going to prison and losing everything. She's dissolved all the defences I built up in myself to survive and showed me a better way to live.

My feet pull me over to the bed where I bury my face in her stomach, amidst wires and dripping tubes. A finger sticking out of her gauze-covered hand strokes over my earlobe.

"Your shoulder?" she murmurs.

"Fuck my shoulder." I look up at her, my own face wet with the stupidest of tears. "I'll take a knife for you any day, Goldilocks."

"R-Romantic."

A pained gasp slips past her lips, and we all flinch, shifting backwards. She squeezes her eyes shut and shakes her head.

"Don't leave me here alone. I can't… I don't want to be alone."

Enzo smooths her hair back to softly kiss her forehead. "Never, little one. Let me get the doctor to come check your meds."

He slips out of the room, leaving us to hold her close. Harlow can't stop now that the tears have started to flow, her hiccups fading as Hunter strokes her hair and whispers in her ear.

"Where is h-he?" she stammers.

Theo draws circles into the unburned skin of her arm. "Prison."

"He's alive?"

"Yes."

Her tear-filled eyes reopen. "Good."

When the door to the hospital room opens again, we expect to see Enzo running back in with a harassed nurse or doctor. Instead, Ulrich's nervous smile comes through the door.

"Harlow?" he asks in a scratchy voice.

The tears stream down her cheeks even faster. "Ulrich."

He limps into the room in his small hospital gown. I move out of the way so he can take my spot at Harlow's side. Ulrich reaches onto his tiptoes to plant a very gentle kiss on her cheek.

"Hi, little man," she rasps.

"You're okay." His bottom lip wobbles. "I thought… I didn't know if you were okay. Dad told me to leave you alone to rest."

"You don't need to do that. Ever."

Ulrich sniffs, trying to maintain composure but struggling. "This is all my fault. I shouldn't have run away. You're hurt."

"Stop." Harlow winces as she tries to move too much. "None of this is your fault. All that matters to me is that you're here. Safe."

"Because of you."

Wiggling her only two unburned fingers, she encourages him to link up with his little digits, connecting the pair without causing her any pain.

"What are big sisters for?" she whispers.

Resting his head on her chest, Ulrich holds on tight and slams his eyes shut, afraid that, at any moment, she may disappear on us. I think we're all feeling the same way.

If I could take a photo of this moment and ship it to those two sickos rotting in Belmarsh for the countless life sentences they must now serve out, I would.

Instead of violence and death, this right here is their everlasting legacy. A brother and sister, united not in death, but in life.

Love has prevailed in the end.

That's our mission complete.

CHAPTER 32
HARLOW

OUTRO – M83

"LEIGH! I can open my own presents."

Sitting cross-legged next to me on the floor, he shakes the wrapped present in his hands and frowns, deep in contemplation. I poke him in the ribs with my scab-covered left hand.

"I think it's a book," he muses.

"Leighton Rodriguez! Stop it!"

He laughs, passing it over then hunting for more presents beneath the Christmas tree. Hunter went overboard this year, even more so than he did last year.

The moment we moved home almost three weeks ago, he was out furniture shopping with Enzo to furnish our old home in time for the quickly approaching holiday season.

The giant fir-scented beast is a monstrosity that had to be cut to fit under the high ceiling. It looks like Christmas threw up on it with ornaments, tinsel, lights and all manner of festive crap.

Leighton was like a kid on a sugar rush as he overloaded the branches with decorations and made us suffer through *Home Alone* for the second year running.

"Leigh," Theo snaps as he strides in with a steaming coffee. "Stop winding her up."

He shoots me an innocent smile. "Sorry, Goldilocks."

"You're a shitty liar."

"Guilty as charged."

Taking the present with my good hand, I try to unpeel the Sellotape with my bandaged right hand pinned against my chest in a sling. My fingers fumble and fail.

After the surgery to attach a skin graft a little over two weeks ago, I've begun the slow recovery process. It promises to be a long road, but we're not unfamiliar with having to persevere.

I was relieved to finally be released from hospital after a week in intensive care following the fire fight, though the surgery and several rounds of antibiotics knocked the life out of me.

Coming home to the familiar, welcoming warmth of our abandoned house in outer London was worth those sleepless nights in a hospital bed. Lucky and her over-excited tongue definitely agreed.

"I can help," Theo offers.

"Thank you. I can't get into it."

"This is from me anyway," he admits shyly.

Making space for him next to me on the thick carpet, he lends me a hand and tugs the paper until it rips down the side. Pulling the rest off, the most stunning set of books is revealed.

"Ooh," I coo.

The covers are made of plush, gold-embossed leather in a luxurious shade of red. Engraved letters lined with filigree carve out the titles of the matching set, all with illustrated spines.

"The complete works of H.G. Wells." Theo's cheeks are covered in a dusting of pink. "First editions. I know you love early sci-fi."

"You're kidding," I breathe.

"Found them earlier this year in this tiny antique bookstore on the street behind the underground station."

"And you kept them all this time?"

He shrugs it off. "I was waiting for the right opportunity."

Moving slowly, I curl an arm around his neck and pull his lips to mine. He kisses me back passionately, his tongue sliding between my lips to touch mine in a teasing whisper.

"Alright." Enzo's voice barks. "No live sex shows on Christmas Day, thanks. We have guests on the way."

Striding into the room with Hunter and Lucky hot on his heels, Enzo distributes breakfast sandwiches. It's still early, the sun barely risen in the sky, but Leighton woke us all up like a big kid.

"Thank you," I whisper onto Theo's lips. "I love it and you."

He pecks the tip of my nose. "Always, angel."

With everyone settling around the Christmas tree, I eat my sandwich with one hand and watch the two brothers exchange gifts. Leighton gets Hunter an air horn, joking that he can use it after his surgery.

The prank doesn't go down well, and Hunter gets him in a headlock, intent on strangling his younger brother until Enzo breaks the pair apart with his wrapped gifts.

"What the hell are these?" Theo eyes a pair of socks with tiny pink crabs on them. "Seriously, crabs?"

Enzo barks a laugh. "Just thought you'd like a reminder of getting food poisoning in Costa Rica and puking your pretty little guts up."

"You are such an asshole."

"I've been called worse. I'll take the compliment."

Enzo unwraps his gifts, unimpressed by the bright green gardening gloves that Leighton dedicates to his upcoming retirement from Sabre. He's going to get a sandwich thrown at his head any moment now.

When Theo picks up the thin, wrapped rectangle beneath the tree with his name on it, Hunter and Enzo both tense up.

"Um, Theo." Enzo stops him from opening it. "That's from all of us, but Hunter was the one who made it happen."

Theo looks at Hunter questioningly.

He rubs the back of his neck. "Consider it an apology for the way I've treated you over the last six years. I hope it answers any questions you have."

"Questions? About what?"

"Just open it," Enzo demands.

Biting his lip, Theo tears into the present and pulls out a thin manilla folder. As he flicks it open and scans over the paperwork inside, his face drains of colour, mouth falling open without a word.

"What is th-this?" he stammers.

"Your family," Enzo supplies. "We know that you grew up without any answers, and Hunter wanted to give them to you."

Shuffling forward, I look over Theo's shoulder at the paperwork. It looks like Hunter hired a specialist private investigator to look into Theo's childhood and how he ended up abandoned in foster care.

"My parents were missionaries in Rwanda," he reads aloud. "It looks like I was sent here as a refugee in the early '90s. That's why I had no identity on record."

I cover my mouth with my good hand. "Shit, Theo. What happened to them?"

He swallows hard. "Looks like my mother was killed during a riot. Someone must have taken me and gotten me out of there."

Hunter clutches his cup of tea close. "Our investigator has been compiling information for almost six months."

"We think that we've found your father," Enzo adds hopefully. "He was caught up in the civil war and had no idea what happened."

Eyes red behind his glasses, Theo looks up. "You found him?"

Enzo nods. "He's still living in Rwanda. Teaches at a local school and works for a foreign aid charity. He stayed, hoping he'd find you."

"This … can't be real. I have a family?"

When they nod again, Theo removes his glasses to hide his face in his hands. I rub his shoulder in a silent, comforting circle.

"I have a family," he repeats.

When he looks up again, his dismay has disappeared, and hope rises to the surface. The biggest smile breaks out on his face.

"I wasn't abandoned, was I?"

Enzo grins back. "No."

Overwhelmed by emotion, he throws himself at Hunter. The pair crash into a tight, emotional hug, and I meet Hunter's eyes as his chin lands on Theo's shoulder.

I raise an eyebrow.

He smirks. "I still have some tricks up my sleeve."

Breaking apart, Theo returns to studying the paperwork. I can see his energy rising from here—eyes jumping from side to side, fumbling through the documents with his trembling hands.

"Does he know about me?"

"No," Enzo admits. "But our investigator found his address and contact information. We thought we'd leave the rest to you."

"I'm gonna need a minute."

Giving them both grateful smiles, Theo leaves the folder on the coffee table then slips outside into the falling snow for some air. Hunter watches him go apprehensively.

"Did I fuck up? Was it too much?"

I tap his arm to gain his attention. "*Perfect.*"

It's a tense ten minutes before Theo returns, looking a lot calmer. He sits down and takes a gulp of his coffee, his eyes still on the file.

Leighton claps his hands together. "Shall we show Harlow her present? I'm dying over here."

"Wait, my present?" I repeat.

Four identical, excited stares land on me.

"Oh, Christ. What the hell did you guys do?"

Enzo offers me a paw. "Let us show you."

Taking his roughened palm, I let him gently guide me up. His arm circles my shoulders, careful not to disturb the light bandages still covering the healing, second-degree burns on my neck.

The other three follow us through the house that feels a little alien after all our months apart. I still remember the day I set foot in here, trembling and afraid, feeling completely out of place.

Back then, I had no idea that this house would quickly become my home, and the strangers who brought me here would be my family.

I wish I could go back eighteen months and tell that terrified girl she would become a strong, independent woman, strengthened by the love and support of men who would sacrifice it all for her.

We made it.

Scarred but alive.

Toeing on my Chucks, Enzo makes me laugh by kneeling down to lace them for me so I don't need to move or hurt myself.

"I can lace my own shoes, Enz. You did teach me."

"If I had my way, you'd never lift a finger again for the rest of your life. Be glad I'm letting you walk at all."

Holding my laughter in, I snuggle into his side and follow him out into the steadily falling snow. The driveway outside our modern Victorian mansion is covered in a thick carpet of white.

There's another vehicle parked in front of the high security gate, covered beneath a huge white sheet and adorned with the world's biggest purple bow across the bonnet.

"Um... Whose is that?"

"Yours," Theo whispers in my ear.

"I can't drive!"

"We're going to continue your lessons once you're healed up," Leighton says with a wink. "You were doing really well before."

Skipping ahead of us, Hunter grabs hold of the sheet and tugs. It's pulled off to reveal a dark-red, armoured SUV with beautiful black rimmed wheels, tinted windows and matte accents.

"Is it a fucking tank?" I can't help but blurt.

"Well, the glass is bulletproof," Enzo reveals. "You know, just in case. There's something else you should see on the back."

Following him over, I pitch my voice low. "Do I need bulletproof glass to drive around rural London?"

Leighton bumps my shoulder. "He'd put you in a bulletproof glass house if he could. This is a fair compromise."

Gathering at the back of the car, there's a black frame stretching across the rear with a tow bar. A shining, silver dirt bike is fixed to it.

I freeze on the spot. "No way."

Enzo crouches down to study it. "Bought it myself from an old friend in Oxford. It's a custom bike just for you."

Gaze skipping between them, the car and the bike, I'm lost for words. This must have cost a small fortune. All for me.

"This… Guys, it's too much!"

Leighton's arm finds my waist as he kisses my temple. "Nothing is too much for you. We're gonna spoil you like the motherfucking queen you are."

"Smooth," Theo mutters.

"Smoother than you, four-eyes."

Slipping past them, I approach the car to peer through the window. The inside is full of luxurious black leather and sleek control panels with a dark tortoise finish.

I feel Enzo at my back, crowding me.

"Do you like it?"

"Like it? Enz, I love it, but you shouldn't have spent all this money on me."

He slowly turns me so my back is pressed against the car door then smacks his lips on mine, careful not to disturb my healing wounds.

"This is just the beginning of us spoiling the hell out of you. Better get used to it. You've got the rest of your life to spend like this."

Then his lips are on mine again—attacking, demanding, nipping and biting. All I can do is let myself be consumed by the indomitable force that is Enzo freaking Montpellier.

When the security gate beeps and begins to slide open, he very reluctantly releases me. Hudson's Mustang purrs as it manoeuvres past us.

"Let her go, you animal!" Brooklyn shouts from the window.

Flipping her off, Enzo lets them drive past and kisses me again. Slower this time, with silent tenderness, whispering secrets to me through the gentle stroke of his lips.

"I promised you the world, Harlow," he murmurs into my mouth. "Now I'm going to give it to you."

"What if I don't want the world? What if I only want you four and nothing else?"

The corner of his mouth hooks up. "You already have us, come hell or high water. This is our happy fucking forever, baby."

I press my forehead against his.

"Fucking forever."

With the Christmas dinner spread out across the table, we somehow manage to cram our houseful of guests into the space. It's a tight squeeze with some creative organisation.

Della and Ben are at the head of the table with Enzo's aunt, Hayley, and my father completing the set of parents. Brooklyn and her husbands take the entire right side of the table.

Enzo orders me to sit down, refusing to let me carry a tray of golden roasted potatoes even in my good hand. When he swats my butt with a pair of oven gloves, I relent.

"Harlow!" Hayley pats the empty space between her and Brooklyn. "Come sit here, darling."

I slink over, wrapping my arms around Jude's neck from behind and pecking his cheek on the way. He gifted me a whole set of matching, personalised journals for Christmas.

When I take a seat, Hayley pulls me into a cuddle, being careful not to hurt me. Her thick, glossy black hair tickles my jawline.

"How are you feeling, *querida*?"

"Tired," I answer honestly.

"You're still on pain medication?"

"Here and there. Some days are easier than others. But I'm slowly getting there, a step at a time."

She brushes her thumb over my cheek. "I'm so glad. The thought of these boys almost losing you breaks my heart."

"That's not going to happen," Brooklyn chips in. "I'm not dealing with this lot alone."

I cuddle into her side next. "I still can't believe you're having a little boy. What happened to female solidarity?"

"Technically, the male is responsible for the part of the DNA that decides the baby's sex." She scoffs. "So blame them."

Phoenix fists bumps the air, his hair dyed bright red in honour of the festive season. "You know it, firecracker."

"I wouldn't have minded either way," Kade says while stabbing a roasted parsnip. "Maybe we'll have a girl next time."

Choking on her mouthful of non-alcoholic wine, I have to hammer Brooklyn on the back so she can suck in a breath.

"I'm sorry, next time?"

Kade glances at her with a crooked smile. "Yeah?"

"There's going to be a next time? We're not even done with *this* time yet, and it was a fucking accident!"

"Language," Hudson scolds. "There are parents present."

"I happen to be on Brooklyn's side here," Della says. "She's the one who has to give birth. You lot have it easy in comparison."

"Thank you, Della!"

Surprisingly, neither Ben nor my father disagree. Both simply look at the guys next to Brooklyn and nod in confirmation.

"See," Della says smugly.

"Turkey time!" Enzo calls over the ruckus. "Stop debating, and shut up for the toast. That includes you, Leighton."

"Ah shit," he curses from the stereo, where he was fiddling with the Christmas music. "Fine, I'll turn it down."

With everyone gathered in their places and taking seats, Enzo steers Hunter to his seat at the head of the table then sits down on his left side.

Still standing, Hunter clears his throat. "I just wanted to say that I'm glad we're all here together to celebrate Christmas as a family."

Smiling up at his son, Ben raises his glass in a toast. Everyone follows, their eyes still on Hunter, who picks up his filled wine glass.

"We've been to hell and back this year," he continues. "All of us. But we've still lived to tell the tale. For that, I'm thankful. I love you all."

Leighton makes a fake throwing up noise. "Spare us."

Grabbing his fork, Enzo jabs it into Leighton's hand until he's yelling in pain. He retracts the fork and pins him with a glower.

"Listen to your fucking brother before I serve your severed head instead of the damn turkey."

Hunter lifts his glass with an eye roll. "Merry bloody Christmas, folks."

We all clink our glasses together in unison.

"Merry bloody Christmas!"

Dinner is a messy affair of veiled barbs, arguing over Christmas cracker jokes and Hudson arm-wrestling Leighton for the last turkey leg. The former wins, almost breaking Leighton's arm in the process.

When Brooklyn raids our cupboards and returns with a jar of pickles, everyone gapes at her. Enzo locates the peanut butter she was looking for and smiles as she dips the pickles in it to satisfy her craving.

"S'good," she moans.

"I think I'm going to throw up," Phoenix announces.

Smacking him upside the head, Eli smiles encouragingly at his wife. "Eat whatever you want, baby girl. I'll go buy more if you want."

"Suck up," Hudson mutters.

Brooklyn points a pickle at him. "You should be taking notes, Hud. Eli wins husband of the week. Congrats."

Green eyes twinkling with mirth, Eli grins at her. "Does this make me top of the leaderboard, then?"

"Not so fast," Kade jumps in. "I'm still ahead with five points. Gotta work harder than that, Elijah."

With all of the food devoured, everyone moves to the living room to watch Hunter's favourite Christmas movie. I catch Theo slipping outside again and quietly creep after him with Lucky at my side.

The door clicks shut and we're both immersed in the falling snow. It's coming thicker now, coating everything in a crisp winter wonderland. I follow Theo's footprints to the middle of the lawn.

"Theo?"

He startles, a slip of paper in hand. "Oh. Sorry, I just needed some breathing room. It's loud in there."

"Want me to leave you in peace?"

"No. Come here."

Stepping into his arms, we both watch Lucky zipping up and down the garden, attempting to catch the snowflakes melting on her tongue. Theo chuckles when she flops on her back in frustration.

"What's on the paper?"

"That investigator got a phone number for my father," he mutters, holding it tight. "It was in the file."

"So what are you thinking?"

"I don't know, beautiful. I've spent my entire life thinking that I was abandoned and left alone with no family. But it was all a lie."

Snuggling closer to his slim frame, I cradle my head in the crook of his neck. "I'm so sorry, Theo. You didn't deserve that."

"It's no one's fault. I'm just struggling to wrap my head around the idea of having a real family."

"You know… I struggled when I found out about Giana and my father," I admit, shivering in the cold. "It didn't feel real."

"How did you cope?"

"You guys helped me. I wasn't alone in it, and neither are you. Whatever you choose, I'll be here every step of the way."

His breathing is short. "I want to know him so badly, but I'm terrified of opening my heart, only to be disappointed."

"If you don't try, you'll never know. Can you live with the knowledge that he's out there without contacting him?"

"I … don't think I can."

"Then call him," I encourage. "You've got nothing to lose and everything to gain."

"Stay with me?" Theo pleads.

"I'm not going anywhere."

Standing in the swirling snow, I hold his shivering torso tight as he dials the number. Theo hesitates, taking a breath for courage before hitting the call button and putting it on speakerphone.

It takes a moment for the line to connect for an international call, then the ringing begins. Over and over. My heart rate rockets higher with each second until the line cuts off without an answer.

"Fuck it," Theo growls out. "What am I doing? I don't need him in my life. I shouldn't even be calling."

"Hey, slow down. It's an international call. He's in a different time zone too. Just try one more time, and then we can go inside."

Reluctantly, he repeats the process again. The ringing starts, and I hold my breathing, silently pleading to God for a Christmas miracle.

The line clicks.

"*Muraho.*"

"Uh," Theo splutters, panicked. "Hello?"

"Who is this?" The voice switches to English.

"I'm … uh, looking for Horatio."

"This is him. Who might I be speaking to? You're ringing up a hell of a bill calling me from a British number."

I squeeze him tighter, silently willing him to be strong. Theo sucks in another laboured breath then clears his throat.

"My n-name is Theo. Well, Theodore Young."

"Hello, Theodore Young. Listen, I'm running a busy school here. I don't have time for cold-callers. Whatever you're selling—"

"Dad?" Theo croaks.

Horatio stops, the line going deadly silent. For every wordless second that passes, Theo's shaking increases. I hold on tighter.

"Who… Who is this?" Horatio repeats.

"I think my name used to be Noah. Before … everything. That's what the paperwork says, at least."

Come on, I internally beg.

"Noah?" His voice breaks. "Is that… Oh God. Is that really you?"

"Yeah," Theo rasps. "I'm here."

"Son," Horatio begins to sob. "You're alive. I've been looking for you for over twenty years… I thought…"

"I was dead," he fills in.

"What are you doing in England? You're not in Rwanda?"

"I haven't been since I was a toddler. It's a bit complicated. I just found out that I have a family."

Horatio sucks in a shocked breath. "It must have been… Christ, twenty-five years since I last saw you."

"Yeah," Theo confirms. "I'm twenty-nine now."

"My boy. You're still alive."

"I'm here, Dad."

Breaking down, his father openly cries, and it doesn't take long for Theo to join him. I press a kiss to his cheek then step away, giving him some privacy as I slip back inside.

Hunter is waiting in the doorway, his nose almost pressed against the glass. He's freaking out over his present. I pull him into my arms and hold him close to silence his worries.

"I just wanted to give him something to show how much I care," he admits roughly. "I've treated him like shit since Alyssa died."

Leaning back, I move my lips slowly for him. "She would be proud."

"Mad?" he guesses.

I bite back a laugh. "*PROUD*."

"Ah." Hunter's face softens in a smile. "I hope so."

Raising my left hand, I sign out a question. "*Surgery? Ready?*"

He shrugs, but I can see the excitement humming beneath his tattooed skin, covered in his usual delicious, pressed white shirt. I've missed his smart outfits, even if I love his sweatpants far too much.

"As I'll ever be. I need to go in for the pre-op in a couple of days. Should be home by New Year's, though."

Sliding the phone from his back pocket, I unlock it then pull up the notes app to tap out a longer message.

No matter what happens, your family will be here for you. Successful surgery or not. Deaf or not. We're here, and we aren't going anywhere.

Kissing my lips, he rests our noses together. "You saved us all, Harlow. I'm not sure how I can ever repay you for that."

Hand lifting to his back, I trace out the only words I'll ever be able to respond with. I didn't save them. We saved each other, night after nightmare-filled night, through thick and thin.

Hunter chuckles in my ear.

"Yeah, sweetheart. I love you too."

EPILOGUE

DOG DAYS ARE OVER - FLORENCE & THE MACHINE

HARLOW - 2 YEARS LATER

STARING INTO MY CLEAR-BLUE EYES, I take advantage of the final seconds of silence. My shoulders are squared. Determined. Lips stretched in a smile of anticipation. Stomach flipping with nerves.

The person looking back at me would be unrecognisable to the old Harlow. She's the result of turmoil and bloodshed, a scar-laden phoenix who found the strength to rise from the flames and rebuild.

She's a person I can be proud of.

After all these years, I finally love myself.

It took the dismantlement of my uncle's underground empire to find peace. Watching him and Daphne being found guilty on multiple murder charges set me free from the final bit of their control still buried in my mind. They're both serving life sentences and will never see the light of day again.

The thud of Enzo's footsteps is unmistakable. I'd recognise his authoritative thud even with my eyes shut. Slipping into the small dressing room, he ducks beneath the door frame then straightens.

"Little one?"

I turn away from the mirror. "Enz."

His crisp charcoal suit is form-fitted and brings out the glow of his tanned skin, complemented by his fire-lit, amber eyes. The Australian sunshine we've spent the past eighteen months living in agrees with him.

"Fuck, baby," he curses. "You look incredible."

"It isn't too much?"

"You're kidding, right?"

Stepping farther into my dressing room, his eyes scan over my floor-length gown, the deep purple silk hugging my curves in all the right places. Brooklyn helped me choose it.

My now short, mousy brown hair brushes my shoulders in perfect curls, revealing the twisted scar tissue that marks my neck and throat. I don't care. Let the world see my scars.

They've gotten me here, to this exact moment. Minutes away from stepping on a stage in front of hundreds of people and flashing cameras. I'm walking in there as myself—on show and unapologetic.

Enzo's hand finds my lower back, running a thick finger up the length of my spine. "I want to take you back to our hotel room and tear this flimsy piece of silk from your body."

"I could get on board with that."

"Pretty sure you have something important to do first. We didn't fly ten thousand miles to hide beneath the covers. I miss the ocean breeze already."

Leaning back into his warmth, I savour the final seconds of silence. "Enjoy the moment, Enz."

"Trust me, I intend to. Leighton's taking advantage of time off from building his company and getting wasted out there."

"So he should. He's been working day and night on the marketing firm. I still can't believe we're in New York. None of this feels real."

Enzo's chuckle is throaty as he spins me around to find my lips. "You're the one who's brought us here, baby. I am so fucking proud of you."

"I know, Enz."

"We're all out there waiting for you at the front. I can't come on stage with you, though."

"It's okay." I kiss him again. "I can do this alone."

His gaze burns bright with pride. "Of that, I have absolutely no doubt."

With a final kiss, he leaves the dressing room, then I face myself one more time. Around my neck lies a thin gold chain, holding Giana's wedding ring at my clavicle.

I briefly touch it and whisper up to the heavens. "I hope you're watching up there, Mum. We made it."

Before I can start crying and ruin my makeup, I take a final breath and make myself leave the safety of my dressing room. There's an assistant waiting in the corridor to direct me.

When the hum of voices reaches my ears, I have to steel myself. I've faced far more terrifying things than this. Journalists. Television interviews. Conferences. Public speeches.

But this is a culmination of everything. All the hard work and hours I've poured in to the last two years of my life in the wake of leaving Sabre and England behind.

"Ready, Miss Kensington?"

I steel my spine. "I'm ready."

Standing at the back of the stage, I overlook the packed ballroom. Hundreds of faces fill the round tables, dressed in their fineries and awaiting my arrival. I can see the guys from here.

Hunter and Leighton are bickering like usual, gripping their champagne flutes. Enzo appears, stopping to kiss the top of Brooklyn's head before taking his seat next to Theo.

Brooklyn's eagerly watching the stage, bouncing not-so-little baby Logan on her lap. He's grown so much since his first birthday several months ago, taking after his mountain-like fathers all seated around him.

"Dad," I hum to myself. "Where are you?"

My anxiety builds until I spot him at another table with Della, Ben, Hayley, Foster and Ulrich. They're all here. My entire family has flown to the States to watch this huge moment.

Tapping the microphone at the front of the stage, the silver-haired president of Columbia University calls the room to attention.

"When I first read our next prize winner's book, *From the Ashes*, I was moved to tears. I can assure you all here tonight that this is no easy feat after the years I've spent doing this job."

There's a rumble of laughter.

"I was moved by the candour of the author and the magnetism of her raw, unfiltered honesty, even in the darkest of narratives. But more so, I was left with something far more precious... Hope."

Della's already sobbing her eyes out. My father has to pull her into a hug while Ben searches for the tissues stashed in her purse.

"It gives me the utmost pleasure to introduce the winner of this year's Pulitzer Prize for non-fiction, Harlow Kensington."

Everyone is on their feet, applauding and beaming up at me. I focus on my feet—one step in front of the other, like every other day of my life. Pushing forward. Breathing. Living. Even in the hardest of times.

When I do manage to look up, they're all there. The purest of souls at the very front table, all four of them wolf-whistling, even if it is inappropriate in front of this crowd. They couldn't care less.

Having an out-of-body moment, I accept the president's outstretched hand and shake. He hands me the certificate that never once entered my mind when I published my book late last year.

My name is there, etched in fine, curling calligraphy. The person I was made into, and the surname I left behind. Both versions of me melded into one, emerging from the chrysalis I hid in for so long.

Hugging the framed certificate, I hold it at my side and face the room. Tears burn my eyes just seeing my father's incandescent smile, filled with so much pride, I don't know how he's holding it all inside.

"Good evening, everyone," I speak into the microphone. "I want to thank Columbia University for this incredible honour. This means more to me than I'll ever be able to express."

As the applause dies down, everyone takes their seats, all eyes on me. The flash of cameras still bothers me, but I've trained myself to get used to the sense of vulnerability.

"*From the Ashes* was never meant to be published," I admit with a laugh. "These journals were written for one person. Me. I needed to make sense of a lot of things that happened to me while in captivity."

Meeting my eyes, Hunter nods for me to keep going. The huge smile on his face has to hurt, framed by long hair that he's regrown.

"I published this book not for fame nor publicity. My aunt and uncle's trials last summer brought me enough of that. I needed something good to come out of all the pain they put into this world."

Looking down at the certificate, my throat clogs. I take a moment to find my voice again.

"For a very long time, I thought I was alone in a cruel, uncaring world. That I wasn't loved, and I couldn't survive the abuse and bloodshed. That broken person desperately needed hope."

Passing Logan off to Eli for a cuddle, Brooklyn wipes the tears from her face, holding my gaze as she mouths her encouragement.

"I found it in the love, care and affection of the family I never thought I needed and had no intention of finding. They gave me the strength to rebuild my life, each painful step at a time."

His eyes shining bright, Leighton pouts his lips then blows me a kiss from across the room. Uncaring, I reach up a hand to capture it for everyone to see. The cameras go wild.

"I hope this book gives those who read it the truth they're looking for. That survival is possible. Hell, finding the courage within yourself to actually live is possible. There's always hope for a new beginning."

Touching the necklace around my neck again, I feel the first tear spill down my cheek.

"This prize doesn't belong to me. I would like to dedicate it to the eighteen women who died at my side and the countless others who perished in the fight that followed."

One by one, I list their names. Every single last one. All those who lost their lives and will never get to tell their stories. I will spend eternity speaking for them and honouring their memory.

"Their voices were silenced by hatred and evil. My message is simple... In their honour, we must live with love in our hearts, forgiveness within our reach and hope in all that we do. Thank you."

To another roar of applause, I pick up the certificate and head for the set of steps leading off the stage. Hunter rushes forward to meet me at the bottom, sweeping me off my feet.

I hide my face in his neck. "Did I do okay?"

"You did perfect, sweetheart. I heard every beautiful word."

Placing me back on my feet, the circular metal disk attached to the implant in his head is visible in his hairline. He doesn't always catch everything, but I know he was determined to hear my speech.

Guiding me back to our table, I'm overrun by people. Of course, Brooklyn's the first to lay her hands on me. I'm smothered into one of her lung-squeezing hugs as her tears soak into my face.

"Fuck, Harlow. I told you not to make me cry."

"Sorry." I smile into her neck. "Couldn't help myself."

Releasing me, she hands me off to Theo and Leighton. The pair trap me in a sandwich of muscle and aftershave that makes me want to do things definitely not appropriate for the public.

"Good job, angel," Theo whispers in my ear.

Leighton kisses my scarred neck. "Fucking perfect, princess."

Their sandwich doesn't last long. Enzo snatches me from between them and boosts me into the air, even as I squeal in front of the entire room. He spins me in a circle before dropping me back down.

"You are the most beautiful thing I've ever seen," he says gruffly. "And I'm really done sharing you with hundreds of people."

"Come on." I laugh. "Let's get out of here."

I shouldn't be surprised that Hunter took the liberty of hiring an entire restaurant for our brood to descend upon. We take over the whole place, popping champagne and exchanging hugs.

My father summons the attention of the room with a tap on his glass, silencing our family. We all turn to look at him.

"I just want to thank everyone for being here to watch this moment." He turns to me. "Harlow, I am so incredibly proud of the person standing in front of me. You blow me away every day."

"Dad," I croak.

"Don't *Dad* me," he corrects with a grin. "I know the last two years haven't been easy for you, but you've made it through. This moment is a monumental accomplishment."

With champagne flutes clinking together, everyone toasts his words. Brooklyn has to scold Phoenix to stop him from feeding champagne to baby Logan. Eli smacks him for extra good measure.

"I believe there's something else we should be toasting tonight," Dad says innocently. "And with that, I'll hand this over."

"Hand it over to whom?" I laugh.

There's a tap on my shoulder, and I spin around, every single part of my body freezing in sheer, utter shock. While everyone was focused on my father, the four guys snuck behind me.

"Oh my God."

Every single one of them is resting on the carpet with one knee bent. The rest of the room disappears as I gape at their faces.

"Um, guys?"

Leighton beckons me over first, taking hold of my hand. "Harlow, we've been waiting for the right moment to do this."

"And arguing over it a lot," Hunter adds.

"But we've decided that it's time." Theo smiles up at me. "And what better moment than this, in front of our whole family."

"I voted for the beach in Brisbane," Enzo grumbles.

Silencing him with a glower, Leighton strokes his fingers over the twisted, mottled skin of my hand. He's smiling like a complete fool.

"We want forever with you," he says simply. "And even that won't be enough, but it's a start."

My breathing stops. "Leigh."

"Will you marry me?"

Vision blurred with tears, I nod numbly. "Yes. I will."

After he's pulled me into a hug, Hunter takes my hand from his. I'm pulled along the line before I can take a breath.

"I spent a year in speech therapy to hear those damn words for myself," he reveals. "Will you marry me, Harlow?"

"Yes. Of course, yes!"

Pulled into his chest, his mouth finds mine. I can feel his brother at my back, trapping me between both of them and their lips. Enzo breaks us apart with a deliberate cough.

I'm passed off to him, his huge height bringing us to eye level even with one knee pressed into the carpeted floor.

"You are my heart and soul, little one. I promised you forever, and this right here is it. Will you marry me?"

"God, Enz. Don't you know the bloody answer?"

"I'm a selfish bastard, and I want my own yes."

Kissing his mouth, I whisper into his lips. "Then yes."

He manages to keep the kiss to a parent-appropriate display of affection, but I can see the fire burning in his eyes. I lean close to whisper under my breath.

"I meant *yes, sir.*"

"You'll be saying it again later around a mouthful of my cock," he replies quietly enough to disguise his words.

Choking on a breath, I face the final person. Our entire story has been a beautiful case of better late than never. Theo was the last piece of my heart to slot into place, but he's the one who completed me.

"Beautiful girl, I didn't know I was lost until I found you." His smile is wry. "Turns out, I wasn't alive at all. Not until the moment you entered my life."

Reaching into the pocket of his smart trousers, he pulls out a velvet ring box. Theo pops it open to reveal a stunning, heart-shaped diamond, encased in smaller diamonds on a white gold band.

"Will you marry all of us?" he asks.

I fall to my knees so we're nose to nose, cupping his cheeks. "I will, Theodore. A thousand times yes."

He slides the ring into place then steals the last kiss. It feels so right on my finger, a physical representation of the bond that's tied us all together since day one of this wild journey.

Our relationship has been tested at every turn. Even after Hunter's successful surgery, surrendering Sabre to the Cobra team and leaving to start our lives abroad in the bright lights of Brisbane.

But while everything changed, the very fabric of our lives warping and transforming into something new, one thing remained the same.

Us.

It's always been us.

Our family.

From Leighton setting up his marketing business and Hunter taking a sabbatical from all paid work to recover properly, to Theo landing a contract working for the Australian government in cybersecurity.

Even Enzo got what he wanted after years of longing, finally setting up a chop shop. The tiny, family-run business is right on the Gold Coast. My father helps him during his regular visits every few months.

With the ring in place, our family engulfs us. I'm showered in hugs and kisses, tears and sobs. Hayley is a happy wreck as she reaches onto her tiptoes to kiss her red-faced nephew.

When my father pops the next bottle of champagne and begins to shake the hands of his future sons-in-law, I take a step back from them all to watch my family celebrate as one.

In the back of my mind, Harlow Michaels still lives. Watching her crazy, beautiful, wonderful life unfold from within her rusted cage. Awaiting the day she'll find the strength to break free and run.

"We did it," I tell her. "We survived."

And what a beautiful fucking life we're living.

THE END

BONUS SCENE

THEO

Hands clenched on the steering wheel, I stare straight ahead at the packed motorway leading to Heathrow Airport. In my chest, my heart hammers to a silent, erratic beat of pure panic.

"Theo."

Harlow's hand touches my arm, trembling from the force of my grip on the wheel. I startle, keeping my eyes locked on the road to avoid her gaze.

"Stop freaking out. It's going to be okay."

"Easy for you to say," I point out.

Blowing out a shaky breath, I indicate to turn off the busy road and onto the route leading to the airport. The clock is ticking down. My father's flight should be landing in London in half an hour.

I haven't spoken to him since our phone call on Christmas Day, aside from confirming the flight details. The moment he learned I was still alive, he planned an immediate trip to England.

"I haven't seen him in over two decades," I point out nervously. "I have no idea what to expect."

"Your dad is going to be so happy to be reunited with you."

"What if he isn't? We don't really know each other."

"That won't matter. You're his son."

I wish I believed her, but that niggling voice of doubt is still there. My father stayed in Rwanda for all of this time, maintaining the flimsiest shred of hope, even if deep down he thought I was dead like my mother.

I need that hope right now.

Winding through traffic, we park the car and I switch off the engine. "Shit. Why am I so nervous?"

Harlow leans across the console to peck my cheek. "I'm here."

Grabbing her hand, I hold her close. "Thank you for coming."

"Always. Shall we go wait inside?"

"I just… need a minute."

"Take as long as you need."

Taking several deep breaths, I watch the passing cars, trying to steady my heartbeat. I have no idea how I'll react when I see Horatio. Part of me just wants to run away from this whole situation.

But a bigger part of me wants to meet this man and see what I've missed out on. I've never known what it's like to have real blood family before. Only the adoptive one I found by pure chance.

"I just don't know what I want from him," I admit.

Harlow watches me closely. "Do you want a relationship?"

"Maybe. But I don't know what that would even look like."

"It can be whatever you need it to be, Theo. Your dad will respect whatever you want. He just wants to get to know you."

"And what if he doesn't like what he finds?"

"Impossible." She scoffs. "Nobody could ever hate you. I won't hear it. You're one of the good ones."

Throat tight, I take another breath. "I don't know about this. Maybe we should call it off."

Holding out her good hand, palm up, she wriggles her fingers, flashing me a reassuring smile. "We're walking in there together. You're not alone."

Hesitating, I make myself place my hand in hers. "Don't leave me."

"I wouldn't dare."

Sharing a tender kiss, her lips move against mine in a slow waltz. I slide a hand into her hair, careful to avoid her bandaged neck, prolonging the kiss until it feels like there's no air left between us.

"Come on," she whispers onto my lips. "We should go in."

"Sure we can't find a hotel or something instead?"

Harlow rolls her eyes. "Rain check."

"Damn. Rejection."

"You'll get over it," she jokes.

Climbing out of the car, I tuck her into my side and we head towards the packed airport together. It's crammed full of people, bustling towards their departing flights with heavy luggage in tow.

We head for the arrivals lounge, and I shield Harlow from prying eyes looking at her burns with interest. She's still heavily bandaged and only just beginning her long road to recovery.

"Ignore them," I mutter.

She shrugs. "I'm not ashamed."

Pausing, I kiss the side of her head. "I'm glad."

The smile she flashes me is appreciative. Wrapped up in each other, we stand amidst reuniting families and waiting drivers, locked in our own personal bubble of privacy.

"I love you," she murmurs.

"I love you too, Harlow."

"You can do this."

Keeping my arm slung around her shoulders, we turn to face the doorway where arrivals are flooding out. I know who I'm looking for after seeing photos of my father gathered by Hunter's private investigator.

Pushing a trolley loaded down with luggage, he rounds the corner, his head on a swivel as he searches around for any familiar faces. He looks just like his photos, with slicked back, silvery hair and bright-blue eyes that match mine.

Dressed in casual jeans and a white t-shirt that stretches over his small potbelly, he looks in decent shape, if a little weary from his long flight. When our eyes meet across the room, I know he recognises me.

"He's coming this way," I whisper anxiously.

"Breathe, Theo."

Clutching her tight, I use the warmth of Harlow's body to steady myself. She's here. I'm not alone. We will face this as we've done every other challenge that's come our way—together.

Stopping several metres away, Horatio parks up the trolley and steps around it to face me. We stare off, neither able to say a word or close the distance between us, caught by shock instead.

"Noah?" he calls.

I swallow the lump in my throat. "It's Theo now."

Horatio nods in apology. "Son."

My heart squeezes, cinched into a tightening noose. "Dad."

Like lightning cracking through the suffocating darkness of night, the moment breaks. Shatters. Implodes. Every single inch of air between us constricts until we're magnetised together. Closer, and closer still.

Then I'm in his arms.

His tight, strong embrace.

My father pulls me into his chest and traps me there, holding me so fiercely, I can't suck in a breath. I don't mind. All that matters is the feeling of being held with such force, I know he won't disappear again.

"Dad," I repeat in a choked rasp.

"I can't believe it's you," he replies nasally. "You're here."

Clasping my shoulders, he pulls back to look me over, head to toe. His eyes slip beneath my skin and search out all the years that have kept us apart, demanding to know everything about me.

"You're so big." His light-blue, oceanic eyes sparkle with unshed tears. "You could barely walk last I saw you. Now… you're a man."

I choke on a laugh. "I guess so."

That's when the tears spill over, leaking down his weathered cheeks covered in five o'clock shadow.

"We've lost so much time, son."

My voice fails as I feel my own cheeks grow wet. "I know."

"All these years… I thought you were lost forever. I didn't know what happened to you. And your mother…"

He trails off, unable to continue.

"None of that matters now. We're together."

Mustering a smile, Horatio nods again. "We are."

Footsteps approach as Harlow joins us, sliding an arm around my waist. Horatio's eyes bounce between us, and a grin blossoms.

"Hi. You must be…"

"Harlow," she supplies easily.

"Theo mentioned you on the phone. Nice to meet you, Harlow."

"Likewise. How was your flight?"

"Long and tiring, but worth it." He looks back at me and beams.

"You're coming home with us," she insists.

"I can get a hotel."

"No," Harlow cuts in. "We have space."

"If you're sure?" Horatio ends the question on a high note, studying me again.

"Of course," I rush out.

"Okay, then. Thank you."

Keeping his arm around my shoulders, he steers his trolley towards the exit with one hand. Harlow walks ahead of us, casting me little looks over her shoulder as she tries to figure out what I'm thinking.

All I can do is smile.

My father is real.

I have a family.

Accepting a round of handshakes from Enzo and Leighton, Horatio falls into easy conversation with them. The whole family was waiting in the doorway when we pulled up in the drive.

"You two look alike." Enzo looks between us.

Horatio claps a hand on my shoulder. "He's got my eyes, but his mother's looks."

I feel my cheeks flush. "Dad."

"Sorry, sorry. Embarrassing you already, am I?"

Snorting, Enzo lets him pass into the house, all decked out for New Year's Eve celebrations. After the chaos of Christmas, we've opted for something more low key for tonight, knowing Horatio would be here.

Meeting the whole Sabre brood at once would be overwhelming for anyone, let alone after reuniting with his long-lost son. We didn't want to put him through that madness quite yet.

Waving for Harlow to head inside, I follow after her, moving slowly to gather my thoughts. The car ride was a little awkward—neither of us knew what to say to each other after so long apart.

"You good?" Leighton asks me.

I shrug. "Not sure."

"He seems nice."

"He is. Things just aren't that easy."

"They never are," he replies, nudging me with his elbow. "But he came, didn't he? That's a start."

"I guess you're right."

"This is your chance to have a relationship with your dad. Don't waste it."

Nodding, I squeeze past him, following the others into the kitchen where Enzo's doling out measures of whiskey. Harlow's slipped upstairs to check on Hunter, in bed after his surgery a couple of days ago.

Leighton passes me a glass. "Drink up."

"Thanks."

Horatio takes his glass, an eyebrow cocked. "You boys live here together with Harlow and Theo?"

Choking on his mouthful, Enzo has to be hammered on the back before he coughs up a lung. I didn't have the chance to explain our unique relationship to my dad during our brief phone call.

"Something like that." Enzo has a twinkle in his eyes. "Harlow's ours."

My father falters. "Yours?"

"All of ours," I supply.

He glances between us for a moment, uncertain. "I see."

Just when anxiety is beginning to curl back up my throat, he breaks out in another bright smile that flashes his pearly whites.

"Are you happy, son?"

I nod back. "Very."

"Then that's good enough for me."

Lifting his glass, Enzo holds it up in a toast. "I'll drink to that."

We all clink our glasses together and drink the fiery, amber-coloured liquid to celebrate. It slips down and warms my belly, but it doesn't compare to the warmth in my over-full heart right now.

I didn't think I needed my father's approval.

But fuck, does it feel good to get it.

Footsteps on the staircase precede the others' arrival. Hunter walks heavily into the room, his eyes bleary and bloodshot, but with a smile still plastered into place. He leans on Harlow for support.

The moment he spots my father, his smile widens. If it wasn't for Hunter, this moment never would've been possible. He made this happen for me, and I couldn't be more grateful for that second chance right now.

"This is Hunter," Enzo explains.

Horatio sticks out a hand for him to shake. "Pleasure to meet you."

Reading his lips, Hunter accepts the handshake. "You'll have to excuse me, I'm recovering from surgery. It's good to meet you too."

Harlow tugs on his elbow to steer him over to the sofa. She fluffs up the cushions before positioning him on them and fusses over the gauze on the side of his head, covering his new cochlear implant.

"Harlow," Hunter drones. "I'm fine."

She pins him with a glare.

He's a terrible patient.

"Hunter's your deaf friend?" Horatio lowers his voice.

"Yes. His surgery was to fit an implant to hopefully improve his hearing once it's switched on."

"That's good. I hope it works out."

"We do too."

Looking around our home, Horatio seems thoughtful, his eyebrows pinched together. He studies everything from the framed photographs to the bowl of car keys, taking in the little personal details that reveal our life together.

The other two filter into the living room to join Harlow and Hunter, giving us a moment of privacy in the kitchen. My father finishes the last of his whiskey and turns the glass over in his hands.

"You have a real life here, Theo. It's so good to see."

"Thanks, Dad."

"And a family too… one that cares about you. I was so worried that you'd be all alone after what happened. All those years—"

"Don't matter," I interrupt. "I made it through with the help of my family. They kept me alive. We look after each other."

His eyes shine with tears again. "I'm glad you have them."

"Me too. Even when they're driving me nuts."

"What else is family for, eh?"

Looking down at his shoes, he bites his lip. I rest a hand on his shoulder, surprising myself. Horatio looks back up so our eyes meet again.

"There's space for you in my life," I tell him. "If you want to be."

"I do," he rushes out. "More than anything."

"I'd like that as well. I want a relationship with you, in whatever form that takes."

Placing his hand on top of mine, he squeezes. "All I ever wanted was to find you and have another chance to be the father you deserve. We're lucky to have found each other again."

"Then let's not waste it."

Horatio shakes his head. "I wouldn't dream of it."

Placing our glasses down, we pull each other into another tight embrace. I hide my face in his t-shirt to conceal my tears, overflowing with relief and pure fucking happiness at the luck that brought him back to me.

When I look up, Harlow's watching us from the sofa, her own cheeks wet as she watches on. I meet her eyes, and she grins through her tears.

"I love you," I mouth.

Wiping her face, she blows me a kiss.

"I love you."

And that will always be enough for me.

Her… and our fucking forever.

PLAYLIST

BIT.LY/HOLLOWVEINS

God Save Me – Genosky & Promoting Sounds
Who Are You Fighting For? – Gina Brooklyn
Let The Right One In – Boston Manor
THE ONE YOU LOVED – The Plot In You
1x1 – Bring Me The Horizon (ft. Nova Twins)
Living In Colour – Tropic Gold
The Day That I Ruined Your Life - Boston Manor
Half-Life – Essenger
Bad decisions – Bad Omens
Who Do You Want – Ex Habit
heartLESS – You Me At Six
Pirate song – mehro
HOPE – NF
WHO I AM – Parker Jack & Chyde
Foxglove – Boston Manor
Aura (Reimagined) – The Brave
Homemade Dynamite – Lorde
Misery Business – Paramore
Lost In The Moment – NF & Andreas Moss
Overgrown – Mountains of the Moon
Devil in Her Eyes – Bryce Savage
Sad Day – FKA Twigs
Everything Once – Hotel Mira
I Run To You – Missio
Alone Made Of Ice – Maldito
Queen – Perfume Genius
Chokehold – Sleep Token
Drowned In Emotion – Caskets

Vaccine – hometown & young
burn down my house – Architects
more than life – Machine Gun Kelly & glaive
Outro – M83
Dog Days Are Over – Florence & The Machine

WANT MORE FROM THIS SHARED UNIVERSE?

If you loved Brooklyn and her merry band of psychopaths, check out their completed stories in the Blackwood Institute trilogy—a dark, why choose romance set in an experimental psychiatric institute where monsters walk among us and nothing is quite what it seems.

https://mybook.to/twistedheathens
https://mybook.to/sacrificialsinners
https://mybook.to/desecratedsaints

Follow Willow's story as she flees an abusive marriage and takes refuge in the small mountain town of Briar Valley, assisted in her hunt for justice by Sabre Security.

https://mybook.to/WBWF
https://mybook.to/WWTF

ACKNOWLEDGMENTS

Wow. I'm struggling to believe that I'm actually writing these words. The end. Harlow's story is done and dusted after a whirlwind year of living in the Sabre Security world.

Harlow's character came from a very well-concealed, vulnerable part of myself that needed to be heard. A victim, broken and bruised, but also capable of rebuilding herself into someone she can be proud of. I've grown with her character, and I hope that you have too.

If you've experienced trauma, know that you are loved, seen and able to live the life that you want. Your pain isn't you. Take those wounds and use them to strengthen yourself.

You're a warrior.

Cherish that fact.

Let's dive into my usual list of amazing people who made this book and whole series a reality. The list continues to grow.

To Eddie, my love and soulmate. There's nothing else to be said. I love you with all that I am, and I always will.

To my girls – Lola, Kristen and Lilith. All three of you are my rocks and provide me with so much love every single day. You deal with my anxiety, tears and self-doubt, even when I can't do it myself. I love you guys.

And a massive thank you to everyone on my dedicated street and ARC teams for being there to support me. I appreciate every single one of you.

Finally, I want to thank you – the reader. You've stuck with this story through thick and thin, witnessing Harlow become a badass and finding her inner strength. Thanks for your trust and support. It means so much to me.

Over and out.

Stay wild,

J Rose xx

ACKNOWLEDGMENTS

NEWSLETTER

Want more madness? Sign up to J Rose's newsletter for monthly announcements, exclusive content, sneak peeks, giveaways and more!

Sign up now:
www.jroseauthor.com/newsletter

ABOUT THE AUTHOR

J Rose is an independent dark romance author from the United Kingdom. She writes challenging, plot-driven stories packed full of angst, heartbreak and broken characters fighting for their happily ever afters.

She's an introverted bookworm at heart, with a caffeine addiction, penchant for cursing and an unhealthy attachment to fictional characters.

Feel free to reach out on social media, J Rose loves talking to her readers!

For exclusive insights, updates and general mayhem, join J Rose's Bleeding Thorns on Facebook.

Business enquiries: j_roseauthor@yahoo.com

Come join the chaos. Stalk J Rose here…

www.jroseauthor.com/socials

ALSO BY J ROSE

Buy Here:

www.jroseauthor.com/books

Recommended Reading Order:

www.jroseauthor.com/readingorder

Blackwood Institute

Twisted Heathens

Sacrificial Sinners

Desecrated Saints

Sabre Security

Corpse Roads

Skeletal Hearts

Hollow Veins

Briar Valley

Where Broken Wings Fly

Where Wild Things Grow

Standalones

Forever Ago

Drown in You

Writing as Jessalyn Thorn

Departed Whispers

If You Break

www.ingramcontent.com/pod-product-compliance
Lightning Source LLC
LaVergne TN
LVHW012322120225

803630LV00035B/725

* 9 7 8 1 9 1 5 9 8 7 1 7 4 *